The Newford Stories

Also by Charles de Lint

The
Newford
Stories

Dreams Underfoot
The Ivory and the Horn
Moonlight and Vines

CHARLES DE LINT

DREAMS UNDERFOOT Copyright © 1993 by Charles
de Lint
    Publishing History: Tor hardcover, April 1993; Tor
paperback, July 1994

THE IVORY AND THE HORN Copyright © 1995 by
Charles de Lint
    Publishing History: Tor hardcover, April 1995; Tor
paperback, March 1996

MOONLIGHT AND VINES Copyright © 1999 by
Charles de Lint
    Publishing History: Tor hardcover, January 1999

First SFBC Fantasy Printing: April 1999

Published by arrangement with:
Tor Books
Tom Doherty Associates
175 Fifth Avenue
New York, NY 10010

Visit the SFBC online at *http://www.sfbc.com*
Visit Tor's website at *http://www.tor.com*
Visit Charles de Lint's website at: *http://www.cyberus.ca/~cdl/*

ISBN # 0-7394-0261-7

CONTENTS

Dreams Underfoot

ACKNOWLEDGMENTS

Creative endeavors require inspiration and nurturing, and these stories are no exception. I'd like to take this opportunity to thank a few people who were important to the existence of this collection:

First and foremost, my wife MaryAnn, not only for her indefatigable work as first reader and editor, but also for her part in the genesis of many of the individual stories;

Terri Windling, for her ongoing support, both professionally and personally, especially with this cycle of stories, and for providing the collection's title, which was also the title of her 1992 one-woman art show at the Book Arts Gallery in Tucson, Arizona;

Kris Rusch and Dean Smith of Axolotl Press/Pulphouse Publishing, who were always asking for more stories and provided the first home for many of these;

And for all those other editors who gave me the opportunity to take a holiday from longer work to explore Newford's streets: Bruce Barber, Ellen Datlow, Gardner Dozois, Robert T. Garcia, Ed Gorman, Martin H. Greenberg, Cara Inks, Paul F. Olson, Jan and George O'Nale, Byron Preiss and David B. Silva.

Contents

Tread softly because you tread on my dreams.

—W. B. Yeats, from "He Wishes
for the Cloths of Heaven"

INTRODUCTION

The book you hold is neither a novel nor a simple gathering of short stories. Rather, it is a cycle of urban myths and dreams, of passions and sorrows, romance and farce woven together to create a tapestry of interconnected dramas, interconnected lives—the kind of magic to be found at the heart of any city, among any tightly knit community of friends. If the imaginary city of Newford is more mythic, more mysterious than the cities you have known, that may be only because you've not seen them through Charles de Lint's eyes, through the twilight dreams he weaves out of language and music. Here he spreads these dreams before us and bids us, in the words of Yeats's poem, to *tread softly,* for urban magic is fleeting and shy . . . and its touch is a transformation.

Joseph Campbell, Carl Jung, James Hillman, Louise-Marie von Franz and others have written eloquently and extensively about the importance of myth in our modern society, the need for tales rich in archetypal images to give coherence to fragmented modern lives. "Using archetypes and symbolic language," writes folklore scholar and author Jane Yolen, "[fantasy tales] externalize for the listener conflicts and situations that cannot be spoken of or explained or as yet analyzed. They give substance to dreams . . . [and] lead us to the understanding of the deepest longings and most daring visions of humankind. The images from the ancients speak to us in modern tongue though we may not always grasp the "meanings' consciously. Like dreams, the mean-ings slip away, leaving us shaken into new awarenesses. We are moved by them, even when—or perhaps *because*—we do not understand them on a conscious level. They are penumbral, partially lit, and it is the dark side that has the most power. So when the modern mythmaker, the writer of literary fairy tales, dares to touch the old magic and try to make it work in new ways, it must be done with the surest of touches."

De Lint is one of those writers who mine this vein with a deft, sure touch. Readers new to his distinctive brand of "urban fantasy" might find his mix of ancient folklore motifs and contemporary urban characters somewhat startling—for ours is a society that loves to separate and classify, putting "fantasy" fiction on a shelf far away from books of "realistic" or "mainstream" fiction (despite the fact that the mainstream shelves include works of modern fantasy by foreign authors such as Calvino, Allende and Garcia Marquez). While American book distributors and critics continue to build up genre walls, writers like de Lint are quietly laboring to take them down again, brick by brick, story by story. Forget the labels. Forget the assumptions you make when you think of *fantasy,* or even *short story collections.* And then you will be able to fully enter the enchanted streets de Lint has created.

We enter Newford via the more familiar streets of Los Angeles, via the tales of Newford author Christy Riddell; and then de Lint leads us on to Newford itself, a North American city that might exist anywhere or nowhere, thousands of miles away or just past the next exit on the Interstate. Like any city, Newford has its posh districts, its slums, its day-life and night-life and the twilight between; but most of all it's the street people, the downtown people, that de Lint wants us to meet: the buskers and artists, punkers and gypsies, street walkers and wizards and runaway kids, people for whom magic is not just a supernatural visitation but a manifestation of the soul's deepest longings and a bright spark of hope lodged within a desperate heart. The greatest magic on the streets of Newford is the magic of community, of friendship and love, support and compassion—for these are the larger themes de Lint uses the bright symbols of folklore to address.

In Newford, *creation* is the supreme act of magic, whether that creation be a painting, a fiddle tune or a poem, an AIDS clinic or battered children's shelter, or one's own family and a harmonious way of life. By these acts we create magic in our own lives; by these acts, large and small, we reinvent the world. For de Lint, these acts are transformed into stories to nurture the growth of his Tree of Tales, which contains the collective stories of the world:

"The Tree of Tales," says de Lint's Conjure Man, "is an act of magic, an act of faith. Its existence becomes an affirmation of the power that the human spirit can have over its own destiny. The stories are just stories—they entertain, they make one laugh or cry—but if they have any worth they carry with them a deeper resonance that remains long after the final page is turned. . . ."

The interconnected stories of the Newford cycle are a particularly lovely new limb on that ancient tree, and one that shall grow and flower beyond the pages of this single book as de Lint continues to explore Newford's myriad streets.

In his own city of Ottawa, in Canada, Charles de Lint is a novelist, a poet, a fiddler, a flute-player, a painter, a critic and folklore scholar; but most of all he is a magician: the kind who makes magic with his multi-disciplined creativity, with the tools of myth, folklore and fantasy. "I think those of us who write fantasy," said fellow author Susan Cooper in her Newbery Award acceptance speech, "are dedicated to making impossible things seem likely, making dreams seem real. We are somewhere between the Abstract and Impressionist painters. Our writing is haunted by those parts of our experience which we do not understand, or even consciously remember. And if you, child or adult, are drawn to our work, your response comes from that same shadowy land. . . . I have been attempting definitions, but I am never really comfortable when writing about 'fantasy.' The label is so limiting. It seems to me that every work of art is a fantasy, every book or play, painting or piece of music, everything that is made, by craft and talent, out of somebody's imagination. We have all dreamed, and recorded our dreams as best we could."

In these pages, de Lint has recorded dreams: Jilly Coppercorn's and Geordie's, Sophie's and Christy's, Tallulah's and the dreams of Newford itself. There are dreams underfoot here, some fragile as spiders' webs, others solid as asphalt and brick-cobbled streets. As you walk into the heart of the city of Newford, remember: tread warily. Tread softly.

—Terri Windling
(Co-editor of "The Year's Best
Fantasy" annual collection)
Weaver's Cottage, Devon, 1992

Uncle Dobbin's
Parrot Fair

1

She would see them in the twilight when the wind was right, roly-poly shapes propelled by ocean breezes, turning end-over-end along the beach or down the alley behind her house like errant beach balls granted a moment's freedom. Sometimes they would get caught up against a building or stuck on a curb and then spindly little arms and legs would unfold from their fat bodies until they could push themselves free and go rolling with the wind again. Like flotsam in a river, like tumbleweeds, only brightly colored in primary reds and yellows and blues.

They seemed very solid until the wind died down. Then she would watch them come apart the way morning mist will when the sun burns it away, the bright colors turning to ragged ribbons that tattered smoke-like until they were completely gone.

Those were special nights, the evenings that the Balloon Men came.

In the late sixties in Haight-Ashbury, she talked about them once. Incense lay thick in the air—two cones of jasmine burning on a battered windowsill. There was an old iron bed in the room, up on the third floor of a house that no one lived in except for runaways and street people. The mattress had rust-colored stains on it. The incense covered the room's musty smell. She'd lived in a form of self-imposed poverty back then, but it was all a part of the Summer of Love.

"I know what you mean, man," Greg Longman told her. "I've seen them."

He was wearing a dirty white T-shirt with a simple peace symbol on it and scuffed plastic thongs. Sticking up from the waist of his bell-bottomed jeans at a forty-five degree angle was a descant recorder. His long blonde hair was tied back with an elastic. His features were thin—an ascetic-looking face, thin and drawn-out from too much time on the streets with too little to eat, or from too much dope.

"They're like . . ." His hands moved as he spoke, trying to convey what he didn't feel words alone could say—a whole other language, she often thought, watching the long slender fingers weave through the air between them. ". . . they're just too much."

"You've really seen them?" she asked.

"Oh, yeah. Except not on the streets. They're floating high up in the air, y'know, like fat little kites."

It was such a relief to know that they were real.

" 'Course," Greg added, "I gotta do a lot of dope to clue in on 'em, man."

Ellen Brady laid her book aside. Leaning back, she flicked off the light behind her and stared out into the night. The memory had come back to her, so clear, so sharp, she could almost smell the incense, see Greg's hands move between them, little colored afterimage traces following each movement until he had more arms than Kali.

She wondered what had ever happened to the Balloon Men.

Long light-brown hair hung like a cape to her waist. Her parents were Irish—Munster O'Healys on her mother's side, and Bradys from Derry on her father's. There was a touch of Spanish blood in her mother's side of the family, which gave her skin its warm dark cast. The Bradys were pure Irish and it was from them that she got her big-boned frame. And something else. Her eyes were a clear grey—twilight eyes, her father had liked to tease her, eyes that could see beyond the here and now into somewhere else.

She hadn't needed drugs to see the Balloon Men.

Shifting in her wicker chair, she looked up and down the beach, but it was late and the wind wasn't coming in from the ocean. The book on her lap was a comforting weight and had, considering her present state of mind, an even more appropriate title. *How to Make the Wind Blow.* If only it *was* a tutor, she thought, instead of just a collection of odd stories.

The author's name was Christy Riddell, a reed-thin Scot with a head full of sudden fancies. His hair was like an unruly hedgerow nest and he was half a head shorter than she, but she could recall dancing with him in a garden one night and she hadn't had a more suitable partner since. She'd met him while visiting friends in a house out east that was as odd as any flight of his imagination. Long rambling halls connected a bewildering series of rooms, each more fascinating than the next. And the libraries. She'd lived in its libraries.

"When the wind is right," began the title story, the first story in the book, "the wise man isn't half so trusted as the fool."

Ellen could remember when it was still a story that was told without the benefit of pen and paper. A story that changed each time the words traveled from mouth to ear:

There was a gnome, or a gnomish sort of a man, named Long who lived under the pier at the end of Main Street. He had skin brown as dirt, eyes blue as a clear summer sky. He was thin, with a fat tummy and a long crooked nose, and he wore raggedy clothes that he found discarded on the beach and wore until they were threadbare. Sometimes he bundled his tangled hair up under a bright yellow cap. Other times he wove it into many braids festooned with colored beads and the discarded tabs from beer cans that he polished on his sleeve until they were bright and shiny.

Though he'd seem more odd than magical to anyone who happened to spy him out wandering the streets or along the beach, he did have two enchantments.

One was a pig that could see the wind and follow it anywhere. She was pink and fastidiously clean, big enough to ride to market—which Long sometimes did—and she could talk. Not pig-talk, or even pig-Latin, but plain English that anyone could understand if they took the time to listen. Her name changed from telling to telling, but by the time Long's story appeared in the book either she or Christy had settled on Brigwin.

Long's other enchantment was a piece of plain string with four complicated elf-knots tied in it—one to call up a wind from each of the four quarters. North and south. East and west. When he untied a knot, that wind would rise up and he'd ride Brigwin in its wake, sifting through the debris and pickings left behind for treasures or charms, though what Long considered a treasure, another might throw out, and what he might consider a charm, another might see as only an old button or a bit of tangled wool. He had a good business trading his findings to woodwives and witches and the like that he met at the market when midnight was past and gone, ordinary folk were in bed, and the beach towns belonged to those who hid by day, but walked the streets by night.

Ellen carried a piece of string in her pocket, with four complicated knots tied into it, but no matter how often she undid one, she still had to wait for her winds like anyone else. She knew that strings to catch and call up the wind were only real in stories, but she liked thinking that maybe, just once, a bit of magic could tiptoe out of a tale and step into the real world. Until that happened, she had to be content with what writers like Christy put to paper.

He called them mythistories, those odd little tales of his. They were the ghosts of fancies that he would track down from time to time and trap on paper. Oddities. Some charming, some grotesque. All of them enchanting. Foolishness, he liked to say, offered from one fool to others.

Ellen smiled. Oh, yes. But when the wind is right . . .

She'd never talked to Christy about the Balloon Men, but she didn't doubt that he knew them.

Leaning over the rail of the balcony, two stories above the walkway that ran the length of the beach, Christy's book held tight in one hand, she wished very hard to see those roly-poly figures one more time. The ocean beat its rhythm against the sand. A light breeze caught at her hair and twisted it into her face.

When the wind is right.

Something fluttered inside her, like wings unfolding, readying for flight. Rising from her chair, she set the book down on its wicker arm and went inside. Down the stairs and out the front door. She could feel a thrumming between her ears that had to be excitement moving blood more quickly through her veins, though it could have been the echo of a half-lost memory—a singing of small deep voices, rising up from diaphragms nestled in fat little bellies.

Perhaps the wind *was* right, she thought as she stepped out onto the walkway. A quarter moon peeked at her from above the oil rigs far out from the shore. She put her hand in the pocket of her cotton pants and wound the knotted string she found there around one finger. It was late, late for the Balloon Men to be rolling, but she didn't doubt that there was something waiting to greet her out on the street. Perhaps only memories. Perhaps a fancy that Christy hadn't trapped on a page yet.

There was only one way to find out.

2

Peregrin Laurie was as sharp-faced as a weasel—a narrow-shouldered thin whip of a teenager in jeans and a torn T-shirt. He sat in a doorway, knees up by his chin, a mane of spiked multi-colored hair standing straight up from his head in a two-inch Mohawk swath that ran down to the nape of his neck like a lizard's crest fringes. Wrapping his arms around bruised ribs, he held back tears as each breath he took made his chest burn.

Goddamn beach bums. The bastards had just about killed him and he had no one to blame but himself. Scuffing through a parking lot, he should have taken off when the car pulled up. But no. He had to be the poseur and hold his ground, giving them a long cool look as they came piling drunkenly out of the car. By the time he realized just how many of them there were and what they had planned for him, it was too late to run. He'd had to stand there then, heart hammering in his chest, and hope bravado'd see him through, because there was no way he could handle them all.

They didn't stop to chat. They just laid into him. He got a few licks in, but he knew it was hopeless. By the time he hit the pavement, all he could do was curl up into a tight ball and take their drunken kicks, cursing them with each fiery gasp of air he dragged into his lungs.

The booger waited until he was down and hurting before making its appearance. It came out from under the pier that ran by the parking lot, black and greasy, with hot eyes and a mouthful of barracuda teeth. If it hadn't hurt so much just to breathe, he would have laughed at the way his attackers backed away from the creature, eyes bulging as they rushed to their car. They took off, tires squealing, but not before the booger took a chunk of metal out of the rear fender with one swipe of a paw.

It came back to look at him—black nightmare head snuffling at him as he lifted his head and wiped the blood from his face, then moving away as he reached out a hand towards it. It smelled like a sewer and looked worse, a squat creature that had to have been scraped out of some monstrous nose, with eyes like hot coals in a smear of a face and a slick wet look to its skin. A booger, plain and simple. Only it was alive, clawed and toothed. Following him around ever since he'd run away. . . .

His parents were both burnouts from the sixties. They lived in West Hollywood and got more embarrassing the older he became. Take his name. Laurie was bad enough, but Peregrin . . . Lifted straight out of that *Lord of the Rings* book. An okay read, sure, but you don't use it to name your kid. Maybe he should just be thankful he didn't get stuck with Frodo or Bilbo. By the time he was old enough to start thinking for himself, he'd picked out his own name and wouldn't answer to anything but Reece. He'd gotten it out of some book, too, but at least it sounded cool. You needed all the cool you could get with parents like his.

His old man still had hair down to his ass. He wore wire-framed glasses and listened to shit on the stereo that sounded as burned-out as he looked. The old lady wasn't much better. Putting on weight like a whale, hair a frizzy brown, as long as the old man's, but usually hanging in a braid. Coming home late some nights, the whole house'd have the sweet smell of weed mixed with incense and they'd give him these goofy looks and talk about getting in touch with the cosmos and other spacey shit. When anybody came down on him for the way he looked, or for dropping out of school, all they said was let him do his own thing.

His own thing. Jesus. Give me a break. With that kind of crap to look forward to at home, who wouldn't take off first chance they got? Though wouldn't you know it, no sooner did he get free of them than the booger latched onto him, following him around, skulking in the shadows.

At first, Reece never got much of a look at the thing—just glimpses out of the corner of his eyes—and that was more than enough. But sleeping on the beaches and in parks, some nights he'd wake with that sewer smell in his nostrils and catch something slipping out of sight, a dark wet shadow moving close to the ground. After a few weeks, it started to get bolder, sitting on its haunches a half-dozen yards from wherever he was bedding down, the hot coal eyes fixed on him.

Reece didn't know what it was or what it wanted. Was it looking out for him, or saving him up for its supper? Sometimes he thought, what with all the drugs his parents had done back in the sixties—good times for them, shit for him because he'd been born and that was when his troubles had started—he was sure that all those chemicals had fucked up his genes. Twisted something in his head so that he imagined he had this two-foot high, walking, grunting booger following him around.

Like the old man'd say. Bummer.

Sucker sure seemed real, though.

Reece held his hurt to himself, ignoring Ellen as she approached. When she stopped in front of him, he gave her a scowl.

"Are you okay?" she asked, leaning closer to look at him.

He gave her a withering glance. The long hair and jeans, flowered blouse. Just what he needed. Another sixties burnout.

"Why don't you just fuck off and die?" he said.

But Ellen looked past the tough pose to see the blood on his shirt, the bruising on his face that the shadows half-hid, the hurt he was trying so hard to pretend wasn't there.

"Where do you live?" she asked.

"What's it to you?"

Ignoring his scowl, she bent down and started to help him to his feet.

"Aw, fuck—" Reece began, but it was easier on his ribs to stand up than to fight her.

"Let's get you cleaned up," she said.

"Florence fucking Nightingale," he muttered, but she merely led him back the way she'd come.

From under the pier a wet shadow stirred at their departure. Reece's booger drew back lips that had the rubbery texture of an octopus' skin. Row on row of pointed teeth reflected back the light from the streetlights. Hate-hot eyes glimmered red. On silent leathery paws, the creature followed the slow-moving pair, grunting softly to itself, claws clicking on the pavement.

3

Bramley Dapple was the wizard in "A Week of Saturdays," the third story in Christy Riddell's *How to Make the Wind Blow.* He was a small wizened old man, spry as a kitten, thin as a reed, with features lined and brown as a dried fig. He wore a pair of wire-rimmed spectacles without prescription lenses that he polished incessantly, and he loved to talk.

"It doesn't matter what they believe," he was saying to his guest, "so much as what *you* believe."

He paused as the brown-skinned goblin who looked after his house came in with a tray of biscuits and tea. His name was Goon, a tallish creature at three-foot-four who wore the garb of an organ-grinder's monkey: striped black and yellow trousers, a red jacket with yellow trim, small black slippers, and a little green and yellow cap that pushed down an unruly mop of thin dark curly hair. Gangly limbs with a protruding tummy, puffed cheeks, a wide nose, and tiny black eyes added to his monkey-like appearance.

The wizard's guest observed Goon's entrance with a startled look, which pleased Bramley to no end.

"There," he said. "Goon proves my point."

"I beg your pardon?"

"We live in a consensual reality where things exist because we want them to exist. I believe in Goon, Goon believes in Goon, and you, presented with his undeniable presence, tea tray in hand, believe in Goon as well. Yet, if you were to listen to the world at large, Goon is nothing more than a figment of some fevered writer's imagination—a literary construct, an artistic representation of something that can't possibly exist in the world as we know it."

Goon gave Bramley a sour look, but the wizard's guest leaned forward, hand outstretched, and brushed the goblin's shoulder with a feather-light touch. Slowly she leaned back into the big armchair, cushions so comfortable they seemed to embrace her as she settled against them.

"So . . . anything we can imagine can exist?" she asked finally.

Goon turned his sour look on her now.

She was a student at the university where the wizard taught; third year, majoring in fine arts, and she had the look of an artist about her. There were old paint stains on her jeans and under her fingernails. Her hair was a thick tangle of brown hair, more unruly than Goon's curls. She had a smudge of a nose and thin puckering lips, workman's boots that stood by the door with a history of scuffs and stains written into their leather, thick woolen socks with a hole in the left heel, and one shirttail that had escaped the waist of her jeans. But her eyes were a pale, pale blue, clear and alert, for all the casualness of her attire.

Her name was Jilly Coppercorn.

Bramley shook his head. "It's not imagining. It's knowing that it exists—without one smidgen of doubt."

"Yes, but someone had to think him up for him to . . ." She hesitated as Goon's scowl deepened. "That is . . ."

Bramley continued to shake his head. "There is some semblance of order to things," he admitted, "for if the world was simply everyone's different conceptual universe mixed up together, we'd have nothing but chaos. It all relies on will, you see—to observe the changes, at any rate. Or the differences. The anomalies. Like Goon—oh, do stop scowling," he added to the goblin.

"The world as we have it," he went on to Jilly, "is here mostly because of habit. We've all agreed that certain things exist—we're taught as impressionable infants that this is a table and this is what it looks like, that's a tree out the window there, a dog looks and sounds just so. At the same time we're informed that Goon and his like don't exist, so we don't—or can't—see them."

"They're not made up?" Jilly asked.

This was too much for Goon. He set the tray down and gave her leg a pinch. Jilly jumped away from him, trying to back deeper into the chair as the goblin grinned, revealing two rows of decidedly nasty-looking teeth.

"Rather impolite," Bramley said, "but I suppose you do get the point?"

Jilly nodded quickly. Still grinning, Goon set about pouring their teas.

"So," Jilly asked, "how can someone . . . how can I see things as they really are?"

"Well, it's not that simple," the wizard told her. "First you have to know what it is that you're looking for—before you can find it, you see."

Ellen closed the book and leaned back in her own chair, thinking about that, about Balloon Men, about the young man lying in her bed. To know what you were looking for. Was that why when she went out hoping to find Balloon Men, she'd come home with Reece?

She got up and went to the bedroom door to look in at him. After much protesting, he'd finally let her clean his hurts and put him to bed. Claiming to be not the least bit hungry, he'd polished off a whole tin of soup and the better part of the loaf of sourdough bread that she had just bought that afternoon. Then, of course, he wasn't tired at all and promptly fell asleep the moment his head touched the pillow.

She shook her head, looking at him now. His rainbow Mohawk made it look as though she'd brought some hybrid creature into her home—part rooster, part boy, it lay in her bed snoring softly, hardly real. But definitely not a Balloon Man, she thought, looking at his thin torso under the sheets.

About to turn away, something at the window caught her eye. Frozen in place, she saw a dog-like face peering back at her from the other side of the pane—which was patently impossible since the bedroom was on the second floor and there was nothing to stand on outside that window. But impossible or not, that dog-like face with its coal-red eyes and a fierce grin of glimmering teeth was there all the same.

She stared at it, feeling sick as the moments ticked by. Hunger burned in those eyes. Anger. Unbridled hate. She couldn't move, not until it finally disappeared—sliding from sight, physically escaping rather than vanishing the way a hallucination should.

She leaned weakly against the doorjamb, a faint buzzing in her head. Not until she'd caught her breath did she go to the window, but of course there was nothing there. Consensual reality, Christy's wizard had called it. Things that exist because we want them to exist. But she knew that not even in a nightmare would she consider giving life to that monstrous head she'd seen staring back in at her from the night beyond her window.

Her gaze went to the sleeping boy in her bed. All that anger burning up inside him. Had she caught a glimpse of something that *he'd* given life to?

Ellen, she told herself as she backed out of the room, you're making entirely too much out of nothing. Except something had certainly seemed to be there. There was absolutely no question in her mind that *something* had been out there.

In the living room she looked down at Christy's book. Bramley Dapple's words skittered through her mind, chased by a feeling of . . . of strangeness that she couldn't shake. The wind, the night, finding Reece in that doorway. And now that thing in the window.

She went and poured herself a brandy before making her bed on the sofa, studiously avoiding looking at the windows. She knew she was being silly—she had to have imagined it—but there was a feeling in the air tonight, a sense of being on the edge of something vast and grey. One false step, and she'd plunge down into it. A void. A nightmare.

It took a second brandy before she fell asleep.

Outside, Reece's booger snuffled around the walls of the house, crawling up the side of the building from time to time to peer into this or that window. Something kept it from entering—some disturbance in the air that was like a wind, but not a wind at the same time. When it finally retreated, it was with the knowledge in what passed for its mind that time itself was the key. Hours and minutes would unlock whatever kept it presently at bay.

Barracuda teeth gleamed as the creature grinned. It could wait. Not long, but it could wait.

4

Ellen woke the next morning, stiff from a night spent on the sofa, and wondered what in God's name had possessed her to bring Reece home. Though on reflection, she realized, the whole night had proceeded with a certain surreal quality of which Reece had only been a small part. Rereading Christy's book. That horrific face at the window. And the Balloon Men—she hadn't thought of them in years.

Swinging her feet to the floor, she went out onto her balcony. There was a light fog hazing the air. Boogie-boarders were riding the waves close by the pier—only a handful of them now, but in an hour or so their numbers would have multiplied beyond count. Raking machines were cleaning the beach, their dull roar vying with the pounding of the tide. Men with metal detectors were patiently sifting through the debris the machines left behind before the trucks came to haul it away. Near the tide's edge a man was jogging backwards across the sand, sharply silhouetted against the ocean.

Nothing out of the ordinary. But returning inside she couldn't shake the feeling that there was someone in her head, something flying dark-winged across her inner terrain like a crow. When she went to wash up, she found its crow eyes staring back at her from the mirror. Wild eyes.

Shivering, she finished up quickly. By the time Reece woke she was sitting outside on the balcony in a sweatshirt and shorts, nursing a mug of coffee. The odd feeling of being possessed had mostly gone away and the night just past took on the fading quality of half-remembered dreams.

She looked up at his appearance, smiling at the way a night's sleep had rearranged the lizard crest fringes of his Mohawk. Some of it was pressed flat against his skull. Elsewhere, multi-colored tufts stood up at bizarre angles. His mouth was a sullen slash in a field of short beard stubble, but his eyes still had a sleepy look to them, softening his features.

"You do this a lot?" he asked, slouching into the other wicker chair on the balcony.

"What? Drink coffee in the morning?"

"Pick up strays."

"You looked like you needed help."

Reece nodded. "Right. We're all brothers and sisters on starship earth. I kinda figured you for a bleeding heart."

His harsh tone soured Ellen's humour. She felt the something that had watched her from the bathroom mirror flutter inside her and her thoughts returned to the previous night. Christy's wizard talking. *Things exist because we want them to exist.*

"After you fell asleep," she said, "I thought I saw something peering in through the bedroom window. . . ."

Her voice trailed off when she realized that she didn't quite know where she was going with that line of thought. But Reece sat up from his slouch, suddenly alert.

"What kind of something?" he asked.

Ellen tried to laugh it off. "A monster," she said with a smile. "Red-eyed and all teeth." She shrugged. "I was just having one of those nights."

"You *saw* it?" Reece demanded sharply enough to make Ellen sit up straighter as well.

"Well, I thought I saw something, but it was patently impossible so . . ." Again her voice trailed off. Reece had sunk back into his chair and was staring off towards the ocean. "What . . . what was it?" Ellen asked.

"I call it a booger," he replied. "I don't know what the hell it is, but it's been following me ever since I took off from my parents' place. . . ."

The stories in Christy's book weren't all charming. There was one near the end called "Raw Eggs" about a man who had a *Ghostbusters*-like creature living in his fridge that fed on raw eggs. It pierced the shells with a needle-fine tooth, then sucked out the contents, leaving rows of empty eggshells behind. When the man got tired of replacing his eggs, the creature crawled out of the fridge one night, driven forth by hunger, and fed on the eyes of the man's family.

The man had always had a fear of going blind. He died at the end of the story, and the creature moved on to another household, more hungry than ever. . . .

Reece laid aside Christy Riddell's book and went looking for Ellen. He found her sitting on the beach, a big, loose T-shirt covering her bikini, her bare legs tucked under her. She was staring out to sea, past the waves breaking on the shore, past the swimmers, body-surfers and kids riding their boogie-boards, past the oil rigs to the horizon hidden in a haze in the far-off distance. He got a lot of weird stares as he scuffed his way across the sand to finally sit down beside her.

"They're just stories in that book, right?" he said finally.

"You tell me."

"Look. The booger it's—Christ, I don't know what it is. But it can't be real."

Ellen shrugged. "I was up getting some milk at John's earlier," she said, "and I overheard a couple of kids talking about some friends of theirs. Seems they were having some fun in the parking lot last night with a punker when something came at them from under the pier and tore off part of their bumper."

"Yeah, but—"

Ellen turned from the distant view to look at him. Her eyes held endless vistas in them and she felt the flutter of wings in her mind.

"I want to know how you did it," she said. "How you brought it to life."

"Look, lady. I don't—"

"It doesn't have to be a horror," she said fiercely. "It can be something good, too." She thought of the gnome that lived under the pier in Christy's story and her own Balloon Men. "I want to be able to see them again."

Their gazes locked. Reece saw a darkness behind Ellen's clear grey eyes, some wildness that reminded him of his booger in its intensity.

"I'd tell you if I knew," he said finally.

Ellen continued to study him, then slowly turned to look back across the waves. "Will it come to you tonight?" she asked.

"I don't kn—" Reece began, but Ellen turned to him again. At the look in her eyes, he nodded. "Yeah," he said then. "I guess it will."

"I want to be there when it does," she said.

Because if it was real, then it could all be real. If she could see the booger, if she could understand what animated it, if she could learn to really *see* and, as Christy's wizard had taught Jilly Coppercorn, *know* what she was looking for herself, then she could bring her own touch of wonder into the world. Her own magic.

She gripped Reece's arm. "Promise me you won't take off until I've had a chance to see it."

She had to be weirded-out, Reece thought. She didn't have the same kind of screws loose that his parents did, but she was gone all the same. Only, that book she'd had him read . . . it made a weird kind of sense. If you were going to accept that kind of shit as being possible, it might just work the way that book said it did. Weird, yeah. But when he thought of the booger itself . . .

"Promise me," she repeated.

He disengaged her fingers from his arm. "Sure," he said. "I got nowhere to go anyway."

5

They ate at The Green Pepper that night, a Mexican restaurant on Main Street. Reece studied his companion across the table, re-evaluating his earlier impressions of her. Her hair was up in a loose bun now and she wore a silky cream-colored blouse above a slim dark skirt. Mentally she was definitely a bit weird, but not a burnout like his parents. She looked like the kind of customer who shopped in the trendy galleries and boutiques on Melrose Avenue where his old lady worked, back home in West Hollywood. Half the people in the restaurant were probably wondering what the hell she was doing sitting here with a scuzz like him.

Ellen looked up and caught his gaze. A smile touched her lips. "The cook must be in a good mood," she said.

"What do you mean?"

"Well, I've heard that the worse mood he's in, the hotter he makes his sauces."

Reece tried to give her back a smile, but his heart wasn't in it. He wanted a beer, but they wouldn't serve him here because he was underage. He found himself wishing Ellen wasn't so much older than him, that he didn't look like such a freak sitting here with her. For the first time since he'd done his hair, he was embarrassed about the way he looked. He wanted to enjoy just sitting here with her instead of knowing that everyone was looking at him like he was some kind of geek.

"You okay?" Ellen asked.

"Yeah. Sure. Great food."

He pushed the remainder of his rice around on the plate with his fork. Yeah, he had no problems. Just no place to go, no place to fit in. Body aching from last night's beating. Woman sitting there across from him, looking tasty, but she was too old for him and there was something in her eyes that scared him a little. Not to mention a nightmare booger dogging his footsteps. Sure. Things were just rocking, mama.

He stole another glance at her, but she was looking away, out to the darkening street, wine glass raised to her mouth.

"That book your friend wrote," he said.

Her gaze shifted to his face and she put her glass down.

"It doesn't have anything like my booger in it," Reece continued. "I mean it's got some ugly stuff, but nothing just like the booger."

"No," Ellen replied. "But it's got to work the same way. We can see it because we believe it's there."

"So was it always there and we're just aware of it now? Or does it exist *because* we believe in it? Is it something that came out of us—out of me?"

"Like Uncle Dobbin's birds, you mean?"

Reece nodded, unaware of the flutter of dark wings that Ellen felt stir inside her.

"I don't know," she said softly.

"Uncle Dobbin's Parrot Fair" was the last story in Christy Riddell's book, the title coming from the name of the pet shop that Timothy James Dobbin owned in Santa Ana. It was a gathering place for every kind of bird, tame as well as wild. There were finches in cages and parrots with the run of the shop, not to mention everything from sparrows to crows and gulls crowding around outside.

In the story, T. J. Dobbin was a retired sailor with an interest in nineteenth-century poets, an old bearded tar with grizzled red hair and beetling brows who wore baggy blue cotton trousers and a white T-shirt as he worked in his store, cleaning the bird cages, feeding the parakeets, teaching the parrots words. Everybody called him Uncle Dobbin.

He had a sixteen-year-old assistant named Nori Wert who helped out on weekends. She had short blonde hair and a deep tan that she started working on as soon as school was out. To set it off she invariably wore white shorts and a tanktop. The only thing she liked better than the beach was the birds in Uncle Dobbin's shop, and that was because she knew their secret.

She didn't find out about them right away. It took a year or so of coming in and hanging around the shop and then another three weekends of working there before she finally approached Uncle Dobbin with what had been bothering her.

"I've been wondering," she said as she sat down on the edge of his cluttered desk at the back of the store. She fingered the world globe beside the blotter and gave it a desultory spin.

Uncle Dobbin raised his brow questioningly and continued to fill his pipe.

"It's the birds," she said. "We never sell any—at least not since I've started working here. People come in and they look around, but no one asks the price of anything, no one ever buys anything. I guess you could do most of your business during the week, but then why did you hire me?"

Uncle Dobbin looked down into the bowl of his pipe to make sure the tobacco was tamped properly. "Because you like birds," he said before he lit a match. Smoke wreathed up towards the ceiling. A bright green parrot gave a squawk from where it was roosting nearby and turned its back on them.

"But you don't sell any of them, do you?" Being curious, she'd poked through his file cabinet to look at invoices and sales receipts to find that all he ever bought was birdfood and cages and the like, and he never sold a thing. At least no sales were recorded.

"Can't sell them."

"Why not?"

"They're not mine to sell."

Nori sighed. "Then whose are they?"

"Better you should ask what are they."

"Okay," Nori said, giving him an odd look. "I'll bite. What are they?"

"Magic."

Nori studied him for a moment and he returned her gaze steadily, giving no indication that he was teasing her. He puffed on his pipe, a serious look in his eyes, then took the pipe stem from his mouth. Setting the pipe carefully on the desk so that it wouldn't tip over, he leaned forward in his chair.

"People have magic," he said, "but most of them don't want it, or don't believe in it, or did once, but then forgot. So I take that magic and make it into birds until they want it back, or someone else can use it."

"Magic."

"That's right."

"Not birds."

Uncle Dobbin nodded.

"That's crazy," Nori said.

"Is it?"

He got up stiffly from his chair and stood in front of her with his hands outstretched towards her chest. Nori shrank back from him, figuring he'd flaked out and was going to cop a quick feel, but his hands paused just a few inches from her breasts. She felt a sudden pain inside—like a stitch in her side from running too hard, only it was deep in her chest. Right in her lungs. She looked down, eyes widening as a beak appeared poking out of her chest, followed by a parrot's head, its body and wings.

It was like one of the holograms at the Haunted House in Disneyland, for she could see right through it, then it grew solid once it was fully emerged. The pain stopped as the bird fluttered free, but she felt an empty aching inside. Uncle Dobbin caught the bird, and soothed it with a practiced touch, before letting it fly free. Numbly, Nori watched it wing across the store and settle down near the front window where it began to preen its feathers. The sense of loss inside grew stronger.

"That . . . it was in me . . . I . . ."

Uncle Dobbin made his way back to his chair and sat down, picking up his pipe once more.

"Magic," he said before he lit it.

"My . . . my magic . . . ?"

Uncle Dobbin nodded. "But not anymore. You didn't believe."

"But I didn't know!" she wailed.

"You got to earn it back now," Uncle Dobbin told her. "The side cages need cleaning."

Nori pressed her hands against her chest, then wrapped her arms around herself in a tight hug as though that would somehow ease the empty feeling inside her.

"E-earn it?" she said in a small voice, her gaze going from his face to the parrot that had come out of her chest and was now sitting by the front window. "By . . . by working here?"

Uncle Dobbin shook his head. "You already work here and I pay you for that, don't I?"

"But then how . . . ?"

"You've got to earn its trust. You've got to learn to believe in it again."

Ellen shook her head softly. Learn to believe, she thought. I've always believed. But maybe never hard enough. She glanced at her companion, then out to the street. It was almost completely dark now.

"Let's go walk on the beach," she said.

Reece nodded, following her outside after she'd paid the bill. The lemony smell of eucalyptus trees was strong in the air for a moment, then the stronger scent of the ocean winds stole it away.

6

They had the beach to themselves, though the pier was busy with strollers and people fishing. At the beach end of the long wooden structure, kids were hanging out, fooling around with bikes and skateboards. The soft boom of the tide drowned out the music of their ghetto blasters. The wind was cool with a salt tang as it came in from over the waves. In the distance, the oil rigs were lit up like Christmas trees.

Ellen took off her shoes. Carrying them in her tote bag, she walked in the wet sand by the water's edge. A raised lip of the beach hid the shorefront houses from their view as they walked south to the rocky spit that marked the beginning of the Naval Weapons Station.

"It's nice out here," Reece said finally. They hadn't spoken since leaving the restaurant.

Ellen nodded. "A lot different from L.A."

"Two different worlds."

Ellen gave him a considering glance. Ever since this afternoon, the sullen tone had left his voice. She listened now as he spoke of his parents and how he couldn't find a place for himself either in their world, nor that of his peers.

"You're pretty down on the sixties," she said when he was done.

Reece shrugged. He was barefoot now, too, the waves coming up to lick the bottom of his jeans where the two of them stood at the water's edge.

"They had some good ideas—people like my parents," he said, "but the way they want things to go . . . that only works if everyone agrees to live that way."

"That doesn't invalidate the things they believe in."

"No. But what we've got to deal with is the real world and you've got to take what you need if you want to survive in it."

Ellen sighed. "I suppose."

She looked back across the beach, but they were still alone. No one else out for a late walk across the sand. No booger. No Balloon Men. But something fluttered inside her, dark-winged. A longing as plain as what she heard in Reece's voice, though she was looking for magic and he was just looking for a way to fit in.

Hefting her tote bag, she tossed it onto the sand, out of the waves' reach. Reece gave her a curious look, then averted his gaze as she stepped out of her skirt.

"It's okay," she said, amused at his sudden sense of propriety. "I'm wearing my swimsuit."

By the time he turned back, her blouse and skirt had joined her tote bag on the beach and she was shaking loose her hair.

"Coming in?" she asked.

Reece simply stood and watched the sway of her hips as she headed for the water. Her swimsuit was white. In the poor light it was as though she wasn't wearing anything—the swimsuit looked like untanned skin. She dove cleanly into a wave, head bobbing up pale in the dark water when she surfaced.

"C'mon!" she called to him. "The water's fine, once you get in."

Reece hesitated. He'd wanted to go in this afternoon, but hadn't had the nerve to bare his white skinny limbs in front of a beach full of serious tanners. Well, there was no one to see him now, he thought as he stripped down to his underwear.

The water hit him like a cold fist when he dove in after her and he came up gasping with shock. His body tingled, every pore stung alert. Ellen drifted further out, riding the waves easily. As he waded out to join her, a swell rose up and tumbled him back to shore in a spill of floundering arms and legs that scraped him against the sand.

"Either go under or over them," Ellen advised him as he started back out.

He wasn't much of a swimmer, but the water wasn't too deep except when a big wave came. He went under the next one and came up spluttering, but pleased with himself for not getting thrown up against the beach again.

"I love swimming at night," Ellen said as they drifted together.

Reece nodded. The water was surprisingly warm, too, once you were in it. You could lose all sense of time out here, just floating with the swells.

"You do this a lot?" he asked.

Ellen shook her head. "It's not that good an idea to do this alone. If the undertow got you, it'd pull you right out and no one would know."

Reece laid his head back in the water and looked up at the sky. Though they were less than an hour by the freeway out of downtown L.A., the sky was completely different here. It didn't have that glow from God-knows-how-many millions of lights. The stars seemed closer, too, or maybe it was that the sky seemed deeper.

He glanced over at Ellen. Their reason for being out here was forgotten. He wished he had the nerve to just sort of sidle up to her and put his arms around her, hold her close. She'd feel all slippery, but she'd feel good.

He paddled a little bit towards her, riding a swell up and then down again. The wave turned him slightly away from her. When he glanced back, he saw her staring wide-eyed at the shore. His gaze followed hers and then that cold he'd felt when he first entered the water returned in a numbing rush.

The booger was here.

It came snuffling over a rise in the beach, a squat dark shadow in the sand, greasy and slick as it beelined for their clothing. When it reached Ellen's tote bag, it buried its face in her skirt and blouse, then proceeded to rip them to shreds. Ellen's fingers caught his arm in a frightened grip. A wave came up, lifting his feet from the bottom. He kicked out frantically, afraid he was going to drown with her holding on to him like that, but the wave tossed them both in towards the shore.

The booger looked up, baring its barracuda teeth. The red coals of its eyes burned right into them both, pinning them there on the wet sand where the wave had left them. Leaving the ruin of Ellen's belongings in torn shreds, it moved slowly towards them.

"Re-Reece," Ellen said. She was pressed close to him, shivering.

Reece didn't have the time to appreciate the contact of her skin against his. He wanted to say, this is what you were looking for, lady, but things weren't so cut and dried now. Ellen wasn't some nameless cipher anymore—just a part of a crowd that he could sneer at—and she wasn't just something he had the hots for either. She was a person, just like him. An individual. Someone he could actually relate to.

"Can—can't you stop it?" Ellen cried.

The booger was getting close now. Its sewer reek was strong enough to drown out the salty tang of the ocean. It was like something had died there on the beach and was now getting up and coming for them.

Stop it? Reece thought. Maybe the thing had been created out of his frustrated anger, the way Ellen's friend made out it could happen in that book of his, but Reece knew as sure as shit that he didn't control the booger.

Another wave came down upon them and Reece pushed at the sand so that it pulled them partway out from the shore on its way back out. Getting to his knees in the rimy water, he got in front of Ellen so that he was between her and the booger. Could the sucker swim?

The booger hesitated at the water's edge. It lifted its paws fastidiously from the wet sand like a cat crossing a damp lawn and relief went through Reece. When another wave came in, the booger backstepped quickly out of its reach.

Ellen was leaning against him, face near his as she peered over his shoulder.

"It can't handle the water," Reece said. He turned his face to hers when she didn't say anything. Her clear eyes were open wide, gaze fixed on the booger. "Ellen . . . ?" he began.

"I can't believe that it's really there," she said finally in a small voice.

"But you're the one—you said . . ." He drew a little away from her so that he could see her better.

"I know what I said," Ellen replied. She hugged herself, trembling at the stir of dark wings inside her. "It's just . . . I *wanted* to believe, but . . . wanting to and having it be real . . ." There was a pressure in the center of her chest now, like something inside pushing to get out. "I . . ."

The pain lanced sharp and sudden. She heard Reece gasp. Looking down, she saw what he had seen, a bird's head poking gossamer from between her breasts. It was a dark smudge against the white of her swimsuit, not one of Uncle Dobbin's parrots, but a crow's head, with eyes like the pair she'd seen looking back at her from the mirror. Her own magic, leaving her because she didn't believe. Because she couldn't believe, but—

It didn't make sense. She'd always believed. And now, with Reece's booger standing there on the shore, how could she help *but* believe?

The booger howled then, as though to underscore her thoughts. She looked to the shore and saw it stepping into the waves, crying out at the pain of the salt water on its flesh, but determined to get at them. To get at her. Reece's magic, given life. While her own magic . . . She pressed at the half-formed crow coming from her chest, trying to force it back in.

"I believe, I believe," she muttered through clenched teeth. But just like Uncle Dobbin's assistant in Christy's story, she could feel that swelling ache of loss rise up in her. She turned despairing eyes to Reece.

She didn't need a light to see the horror in his eyes—horror at the booger's approach, at the crow's head sticking out of her chest. But he didn't draw away from her. Instead, he reached out and caught hold of her shoulders.

"Stop fighting it!" he cried.

"But—"

He shot a glance shoreward. They were bracing themselves against the waves, but a large swell had just caught the booger and sent it howling back to shore in a tumble of limbs.

"It was your needing proof," he said. "Your needing to see the booger, to know that it's real—that's what's making you lose it. Stop trying so hard."

"I . . ."

But she knew he was right. She pulled free of him and looked towards the shore where the booger was struggling to its feet. The creature made rattling sounds deep in its throat as it started out for them again. It was hard, hard to do, but she let her hands fall free. The pain in her chest was a fire, the aching loss building to a crescendo. But she closed herself to it, closed her eyes, willed herself to stand relaxed.

Instead of fighting, she remembered. Balloon Men spinning down the beach. Christy's gnome, riding his pig along the pier. Bramley Dapple's advice. Goon pinching Jilly Coppercorn's leg. The thing that fed on eggs and eyeballs and, yes, Reece's booger too. Uncle Dobbin and his parrots and Nori Wert watching her magic fly free. And always the Balloon Men, tumbling end-over-end, across the beach, or down the alley-way behind her house. . . .

And the pain eased. The ache loosened, faded.

"Jesus," she heard Reece say softly.

She opened her eyes and looked to where he was looking. The booger had turned from the sea and was fleeing as a crowd of Balloon Men came bouncing down the shore, great round roly-poly shapes, turning end-over-end, laughing and giggling, a chorus of small deep voices. There was salt in her eyes and it wasn't from the ocean's brine. Her tears ran down her cheeks and she felt herself grinning like a fool.

The Balloon Men chased Reece's booger up one end of the beach and then back the other way until the creature finally made a stand. Howling, it waited for them to come, but before the first bouncing round shape reached it, the booger began to fade away.

Ellen turned to Reece and knew he had tears in his own eyes, but the good feeling was too strong for him to do anything but grin right back at her. The booger had died with the last of his anger. She reached out a hand to him and he took it in one of his own. Joined so, they made their way to the shore where they were surrounded by riotous Balloon Men until the bouncing shapes finally faded and then there were just the two of them standing there.

Ellen's heart beat fast. When Reece let go her hand, she touched her chest and felt a stir of dark wings inside her, only they were settling in now, no longer striving to fly free. The wind came in from the ocean still, but it wasn't the same wind that the Balloon Men rode.

"I guess it's not all bullshit," Reece said softly.

Ellen glanced at him.

He smiled as he explained. "Helping each other—getting along instead of fighting. Feels kind of good, you know?"

Ellen nodded. Her hand fell from her chest as the dark wings finally stilled.

"Your friend's story didn't say anything about crows," Reece said.

"Maybe we've all got different birds inside—different magics." She looked out across the waves to where the oil rigs lit the horizon.

"There's a flock of wild parrots up around Santa Ana," Reece said.

"I've heard there's one up around San Pedro, too."

"Do you think . . . ?" Reece began, but he let his words trail off. The waves came in and wet their feet.

"I don't know," Ellen said. She looked over at her shredded clothes. "Come on. Let's get back to my place and warm up."

Reece laid his jacket over her shoulders. He put on his T-shirt and jeans, then helped her gather up what was left of her belongings.

"I didn't mean for this to happen," he said, bundling up the torn blouse and skirt. He looked up to where she was standing over him. "But I couldn't control the booger."

"Maybe we're not supposed to."

"But something like the booger . . ."

She gave his Mohawk a friendly ruffle. "I think it just means that we've got to be careful about what kind of vibes we put out."

Reece grimaced at her use of the word, but he nodded.

"It's either that," Ellen added, "or we let the magic fly free."

The same feathery stirring of wings that she felt moved in Reece. They both knew that that was something neither of them was likely to give up.

In Uncle Dobbin's Parrot Fair, Nori Wert turned away from the pair of cages that she'd been making ready.

"I guess we won't be needing these," she said.

Uncle Dobbin looked up from a slim collection of Victorian poetry and nodded. "You're learning fast," he said. He stuck the stem of his pipe in his mouth and fished about in his pocket for a match. "Maybe there's hope for you yet."

Nori felt her own magic stir inside her, back where it should be, but she didn't say anything to him in case she had to go away, now that the lesson was learned. She was too happy here. Next to catching some rays, there wasn't anywhere she'd rather be.

The Stone Drum

There is no question that there is an unseen world. The problem
is how far is it from midtown and how late is it open?
—attributed to Woody Allen

It was Jilly Coppercorn who found the stone drum, late one afternoon.

She brought it around to Professor Dapple's rambling Tudor-styled house in the old quarter of Lower Crowsea that same evening, wrapped up in folds of brown paper and tied with twine. She rapped sharply on the Professor's door with the little brass lion's head knocker that always seemed to stare too intently at her, then stepped back as Olaf Goonasekara, Dapple's odd little housekeeper, flung the door open and glowered out at where she stood on the rickety porch.

"You," he grumbled.

"Me," she agreed, amicably. "Is Bramley in?"

"I'll see," he replied and shut the door.

Jilly sighed and sat down on one of the two worn rattan chairs that stood to the left of the door, her package bundled on her knee. A black and orange cat regarded her incuriously from the seat of the other chair, then turned to watch the progress of a woman walking her dachshund down the street.

Professor Dapple still taught a few classes at Butler U., but he wasn't nearly as involved with the curriculum as he had been when Jilly attended the university. There'd been some kind of a scandal—something about a Bishop, some old coins and the daughter of a Tarot reader—but Jilly had never quite got the story straight. The Professor was a jolly fellow—wizened like an old apple, but more active than many who were only half his apparent sixty years of age. He could talk and joke all night, incessantly polishing his wire-rimmed spectacles.

What he was doing with someone like Olaf Goonasekara as a housekeeper Jilly didn't know. It was true that Goon looked comical enough, what with his protruding stomach and puffed cheeks, the halo of unruly hair and his thin little arms and legs, reminding her of nothing so much as a pumpkin with twig limbs, or a monkey. His usual striped trousers, organ grinder's jacket and the little green and yellow cap he liked to wear, didn't help. Nor did the fact that he was barely four feet tall and that the Professor claimed he was a goblin and just called him Goon.

It didn't seem to allow Goon much dignity and Jilly would have understood his grumpiness, if she didn't know that he himself insisted on being called Goon and his wardrobe was entirely of his own choosing. Bramley hated Goon's sense of fashion—or rather, his lack thereof.

The door was flung open again and Jilly stood up to find Goon glowering at her once more.

"He's in," he said.

Jilly smiled. As if he'd actually had to go in and check.

They both stood there, Jilly on the porch and he in the doorway, until Jilly finally asked, "Can he see me?"

Giving an exaggerated sigh, Goon stepped aside to let her in.

"I suppose you'll want something to drink?" he asked as he followed her to the door of the Professor's study.

"Tea would be lovely."

"Hrumph."

Jilly watched him stalk off, then tapped a knuckle on the study's door and stepped into the room. Bramley lifted his gaze from a desk littered with tottering stacks of books and papers and grinned at her from between a gap in the towers of paper.

"I've been doing some research since you called," he said. He poked a finger at a book that Jilly couldn't see, then began to clean his glasses. "Fascinating stuff."

"And hello to you, too," Jilly said.

"Yes, of course. Did you know that the Kickaha had legends of a little people long before the Europeans ever settled this area?"

Jilly could never quite get used to Bramley's habit of starting conversations in the middle. She removed some magazines from a club chair and perched on the edge of its seat, her package clutched to her chest.

"What's that got to do with anything?" she asked.

Bramley looked surprised. "Why everything. We *are* still looking into the origins of this artifact of yours, aren't we?"

Jilly nodded. From her new position of vantage she could make out the book he'd been reading. *Underhill and Deeper Still,* a short story collection by Christy Riddell. Riddell made a living of retelling the odd stories that lie just under the skin of any large city. This particular one was a collection of urban legends of Old City and other subterranean fancies—not exactly the factual reference source she'd been hoping for.

Old City was real enough; that was where she'd found the drum this afternoon. But as for the rest of it—albino crocodile subway conductors, schools of dog-sized intelligent goldfish in the sewers, mutant rat debating societies and the like . . .

Old City was the original heart of Newford. It lay deep underneath the subway tunnels—dropped there in the late eighteen hundreds during the Great Quake. The present city, including its sewers and underground transportation tunnels, had been built above the ruins of the old one. There'd been talk in the early seventies of renovating the ruins as a tourist attraction—as had been done in Seattle—but Old City lay too far underground for easy access. After numerous studies on the project, the city council had decided that it simply wouldn't be cost efficient.

With that decision, Old City had rapidly gone from a potential tourist attraction to a home for skells—winos, bag ladies and the other homeless. Not to mention, if one was to believe Bramley and Riddell, bands of ill-mannered goblin-like creatures that Riddell called skookin—a word he'd stolen from old Scots which meant, variously, ugly, furtive and sullen.

Which, Jilly realized once when she thought about it, made it entirely appropriate that Bramley should claim Goon was related to them.

"You're not going to tell me it's a skookin artifact, are you?" she asked Bramley now.

"Too soon to say," he replied. He nodded at her parcel. "Can I see it?"

Jilly got up and brought it over to the desk, where Bramley made a great show of cutting the twine and unwrapping the paper. Jilly couldn't decide if he was pretending it was the unveiling of a new piece at the museum or his birthday. But then the drum was sitting on the desk, the mica and quartz veins in its stone catching the light from Bramley's desk lamp in a magical glitter, and she was swallowed up in the wonder of it again.

It was tube-shaped, standing about a foot high, with a seven-inch diameter at the top and five inches at the bottom. The top was smooth as the skin head of a drum. On the sides were what appeared to be the remnants of a bewildering flurry of designs. But what was most marvelous about it was that the stone was hollow. It weighed about the same as a fat hardcover book.

"Listen," Jilly said and gave the top of the drum a rap-a-tap-tap.

The stone responded with a quiet rhythm that resonated eerily in the study. Unfortunately, Goon chose that moment to arrive in the doorway with a tray laden with tea mugs, tea pot and a platter of his homemade biscuits. At the sound of the drum, the tray fell from his hands. It hit the floor with a crash, spraying tea, milk, sugar, biscuits and bits of crockery every which way.

Jilly turned, her heartbeat double-timing in her chest, just in time to see an indescribable look cross over Goon's features. It might have been surprise, it might have been laughter, but it was gone too quickly for her to properly note. He merely stood in the doorway now, his usual glowering look on his face, and all Jilly was left with was a feeling of unaccountable guilt.

"I didn't mean . . ." Jilly began, but her voice trailed off.

"Bit of a mess," Bramley said.

"I'll get right to it," Goon said.

His small dark eyes centered their gaze on Jilly for too long a moment, then he turned away to fetch a broom and dustpan. When Jilly turned back to the desk, she found Bramley rubbing his hands together, face pressed close to the stone drum. He looked up at her over his glasses, grinning.

"Did you see?" he said. "Goon recognized it for what it is, straight off. It has to be a skookin artifact. Didn't like you meddling around with it either."

That was hardly the conclusion that Jilly would have come to on her own. It was the sudden and unexpected sound that had more than likely startled Goon—as it might have startled anyone who wasn't expecting it. That was the reasonable explanation, but she knew well enough that reasonable didn't necessarily always mean right. When she thought of that look that had passed over Goon's features, like a trough of surprise or mocking humor between two cresting glowers, she didn't know what to think, so she let herself get taken away by the Professor's enthusiasm, because . . . well, just what if . . . ?

By all of Christy Riddell's accounts, there wasn't a better candidate for skookindom than Bramley's housekeeper.

"What does it mean?" she asked.

Bramley shrugged and began to polish his glasses. Jilly was about to nudge him into making at least the pretense of a theory, but then she realized that the Professor had simply fallen silent because Goon was back to clean up the mess. She waited until Goon had made his retreat with the promise of putting on another pot of tea, before she leaned over Bramley's desk.

"Well?" she asked.

"Found it in Old City, did you?" he replied.

Jilly nodded.

"You know what they say about skookin treasure . . . ?"

They meaning he and Christy, Jilly thought, but she obligingly tried to remember that particular story from *Underhill and Deeper Still.* She had it after a moment. It was the one called "The Man with the Monkey" and had something to do with a stolen apple that was withered and moldy in Old City but became solid gold when it was brought above ground. At the end of the story, the man who'd stolen it from the skookin was found in little pieces scattered all over Fitzhenry Park. . . .

Jilly shivered.

"Now I remember why I don't like to read Christy's stuff," she said. "He can be so sweet on one page, and then on the next he's taking you on a tour through an abattoir."

"Just like life," Bramley said.

"Wonderful. So what are you saying?"

"They'll be wanting it back," Bramley said.

Jilly woke some time after midnight with the Professor's words ringing in her ears.

They'll be wanting it back.

She glanced at the stone drum where it sat on a crate by the window of her Yoors Street loft in Foxville. From where she lay on her Murphy bed, the streetlights coming in the window wove a haloing effect around the stone artifact. The drum glimmered with magic—or at least with a potential for magic. And there was something else in the air. A humming sound, like barely audible strains of music. The notes seemed disconnected, drifting randomly through the melody like dust motes dancing in a beam of sunlight, but there was still a melody present.

She sat up slowly. Pushing the quilt aside, she padded barefoot across the room. When she reached the drum, the change in perspective made the streetlight halo slide away; the drum's magic fled. It was just an odd stone artifact once more. She ran her finger along the smoothed indentations that covered the sides of the artifact, but didn't touch the top. It was still marvelous enough—a hollow stone, a mystery, a puzzle. But . . .

She remembered the odd almost-but-not-quite music she'd heard when she first woke, and cocked her ear, listening for it.

Nothing.

Outside, a light drizzle had wet the pavement, making Yoors Street glisten and sparkle with its sheen. She knelt down by the windowsill and leaned forward, looking out, feeling lonely. It'd be nice if Geordie were here, even if his brother did write those books that had the Professor so enamoured, but Geordie was out of town this week. Maybe she should get a cat or a dog—just something to keep her company when she got into one of these odd funks—but the problem with pets was that they tied you down. No more gallivanting about whenever and wherever you pleased. Not when the cat needed to be fed. Or the dog had to be walked.

Sighing, she started to turn from the window, then paused. A flicker of uneasiness stole up her spine as she looked more closely at what had caught her attention—there, across the street. Time dissolved into a pattern as random as that faint music she'd heard when she woke earlier. Minutes and seconds marched sideways; the hands of the old Coors clock on her wall stood still.

A figure leaned against the wall, there, just to one side of the display window of the Chinese groceteria across the street, a figure as much a patchwork as the disarray in the shop's window. Pumpkin head under a wide-brimmed hat. A larger pumpkin for the body with what looked like straw spilling out from between the buttons of its too-small jacket. Arms and legs as thin as broom handles. A wide slit for a mouth; eyes like the sharp yellow slits of a jack-o'-lantern with a candle burning inside.

A Halloween creature. And not alone.

There was another, there, in the mouth of that alleyway. A third clinging to the wall of the brownstone beside the groceteria. Four more on the rooftop directly across the street—pumpkinheads lined up along the parapet, all in a row.

Skookin, Jilly thought and she shivered with fear, remembering Christy Riddell's story.

Damn Christy for tracking the story down, and damn the Professor for reminding her of it. And damn the job that had sent her down into Old City in the first place to take photos for the background of the painting she was currently working on.

Because there shouldn't be any such thing as skookin. Because . . .

She blinked, then rubbed her eyes. Her gaze darted left and right, up and down, raking the street and the faces of buildings across the way.

Nothing.

No pumpkin goblins watching her loft.

The sound of her clock ticking the seconds away was suddenly loud in her ears. A taxi went by on the street below, spraying a fine sheet of water from its wheels. She waited for it to pass, then studied the street again.

There were no skookin.

Of course there wouldn't be, she told herself, trying to laugh at how she'd let her imagination run away with itself, but she couldn't muster up even the first hint of a smile. She looked at the drum, reached a hand towards it, then let her hand fall to her lap, the drum untouched. She turned her attention back to the street, watching it for long moments before she finally had to accept that there was nothing out there, that she had only peopled it with her own night fears.

Pushing herself up from the sill, she returned to bed and lay down again. The palm of her right hand itched a little, right where she'd managed to poke herself on a small nail or wood sliver while she was down in Old City. She scratched her hand and stared up at the ceiling, trying to go to sleep, but not expecting to have much luck. Surprisingly, she drifted off in moments.

And dreamed.

Of Bramley's study. Except the Professor wasn't ensconced behind his desk as usual. Instead, he was setting out a serving of tea for her and Goon, who had taken the Professor's place behind the tottering stacks of papers and books on the desk.

"Skookin," Goon said, when the Professor had finished serving them their tea and left the room. "They've never existed, of course."

Jilly nodded in agreement.

"Though in some ways," Goon went on, "they've always existed. In here—" He tapped his temple with a gnarly, very skookin-like finger. "In our imaginations."

"But—" Jilly began, wanting to tell him how she'd *seen* skookin, right out there on her very own street tonight, but Goon wasn't finished.

"And that's what makes them real," he said.

His head suddenly looked very much like a pumpkin. He leaned forward, eyes glittering as though a candle was burning there inside his head, flickering in the wind.

"And if they're real," he said.

His voice wound down alarmingly, as though it came from the spiraling groove of a spoken-word album that someone had slowed by dragging their finger along on the vinyl.

"Then. You're. In. A. Lot. Of—"

Jilly awoke with a start to find herself backed up against the frame of the head of her bed, her hands worrying and tangling her quilt into knots.

Just a dream. Cast off thoughts, tossed up by her subconscious. Nothing to worry about. Except . . .

She could finish the dream-Goon's statement.

If they were real . . .

Never mind being in trouble. If they were real, then she was doomed.

She didn't get any more sleep that night, and first thing the next morning, she went looking for help.

"Skookin," Meran said, trying hard not to laugh.

"Oh, I know what it sounds like," Jilly said, "but what can you do? Christy's books are Bramley's pet blind spot and if you listen to him long enough, he'll have you believing anything."

"But skookin," Meran repeated and this time she did giggle.

Jilly couldn't help but laugh with her.

Everything felt very different in the morning light—especially when she had someone to talk it over with whose head wasn't filled with Christy's stories.

They were sitting in Kathryn's Cafe—an hour or so after Jilly had found Meran Kelledy down by the Lake, sitting on the Pier and watching the early morning joggers run across the sand: yuppies from downtown, health-conscious gentry from the Beaches.

It was a short walk up Battersfield Road to where Kathryn's was nestled in the heart of Lower Crowsea. Like the area itself, with its narrow streets and old stone buildings, the cafe had an old world feel about it—from the dark wood paneling and hand-carved chair backs to the small round tables, with checkered tablecloths, fat glass condiment containers and straw-wrapped wine bottles used as candleholders. The music piped in over the house sound system was mostly along the lines of Telemann and

Vivaldi, Kitaro and old Bob James albums. The waitresses wore cream-colored pina-fores over flowerprint dresses.

But if the atmosphere was old world, the clientele were definitely contemporary. Situated so close to Butler U., Kathryn's had been a favorite haunt of the university's students since it first opened its doors in the mid-sixties as a coffee house. Though much had changed from those early days, there was still music played on its small stage on Friday and Saturday nights, as well as poetry recitations on Wednesdays and Sunday morning storytelling sessions.

Jilly and Meran sat by a window, coffee and homemade banana muffins set out on the table in front of them.

"Whatever were you *doing* down there anyway?" Meran asked. "It's not exactly the safest place to be wandering about."

Jilly nodded. The skells in Old City weren't all thin and wasted. Some were big and mean-looking, capable of anything—not really the sort of people Jilly should be around, because if something went wrong . . . well, she was the kind of woman for whom the word petite had been coined. She was small and slender—her tiny size only accentuated by the oversized clothing she tended to wear. Her brown hair was a thick tangle, her eyes the electric blue of sapphires.

She was too pretty and too small to be wandering about in places like Old City on her own.

"You know the band, No Nuns Here?" Jilly asked.

Meran nodded.

"I'm doing the cover painting for their first album," Jilly explained. "They wanted something moody for the background—sort of like the Tombs, but darker and grim-mer—and I thought Old City would be the perfect place to get some reference shots."

"But to go there on your own . . ."

Jilly just shrugged. She was known to wander anywhere and everywhere, at any time of the night or day, camera or sketchbook in hand, often both.

Meran shook her head. Like most of Jilly's friends, she'd long since given up trying to point out the dangers of carrying on the way Jilly did.

"So you found this drum," she said.

Jilly nodded. She looked down at the little scab on the palm of her hand. It itched like crazy, but she was determined not to open it again by scratching it.

"And now you want to . . . ?"

Jilly looked up. "Take it back. Only I'm scared to go there on my own. I thought maybe Cerin would come with me—for moral support, you know?"

"He's out of town," Meran said.

Meran and her husband made up the two halves of the Kelledys, a local traditional music duo that played coffee houses, festivals and colleges from one coast to the other. For years now, however, Newford had been their home base.

"He's teaching another of those harp workshops," Meran added.

Jilly did her best to hide her disappointment.

What she'd told Meran about "moral support" was only partly the reason she'd wanted their help because, more so than either Riddell's stories or Bramley's askew theories, the Kelledys were the closest thing to real magic that she could think of in Newford. There was an otherworldly air about the two of them that went beyond the glamour that seemed to always gather around people who became successful in their creative endeavors.

It wasn't something Jilly could put her finger on. It wasn't as though they went on and on about this sort of thing at the drop of a hat the way that Bramley did. Nor that they were responsible for anything more mysterious than the enchantment they awoke on stage when they were playing their instruments. It was just there. Something that gave the impression that they were aware of what lay beyond the here and now. That they could see things others couldn't; knew things that remained secret to anyone else.

Nobody even knew where they had come from; they'd just arrived in Newford a few years ago, speaking with accents that had rapidly vanished, and here they'd pretty well stayed ever since. Jilly had always privately supposed that if there was a place called Faerie, then that was from where they'd come, so when she woke up this morning, deciding she needed magical help, she'd gone looking for one or the other and found Meran. But now . . .

"Oh," she said.

Meran smiled.

"But that doesn't mean I can't try to help," she said.

Jilly sighed. Help with what? she had to ask herself. The more she thought about it, the sillier it all seemed. Skookin. Right. Maybe they held debating contests with Riddell's mutant rats.

"I think maybe I'm nuts," she said finally. "I mean, goblins living under the city . . . ?"

"I believe in the little people," Meran said. "We called them bodachs where I come from."

Jilly just looked at her.

"But you laughed when I talked about them," she said finally.

"I know—and I shouldn't have. It's just that whenever I hear that name that Christy's given them, I can't help myself. It's so silly."

"What I saw last night didn't feel silly," Jilly said.

If she'd actually seen anything. By this point—even with Meran's apparent belief—she wasn't sure what to think anymore.

"No," Meran said. "I suppose not. But—you're taking the drum back, so why are you so nervous?"

"The man in Christy's story returned the apple he stole," Jilly said, "and you know what happened to him. . . ."

"That's true," Meran said, frowning.

"I thought maybe Cerin could . . ." Jilly's voice trailed off.

A small smile touched Meran's lips. "Could do what?"

"Well, this is going to sound even sillier," Jilly admitted, "but I've always pictured him as sort of a wizard type."

Meran laughed. "He'd love to hear that. And what about me? Have I acquired wizardly status as well?"

"Not exactly. You always struck me as being an earth spirit—like you stepped out of an oak tree or something." Jilly blushed, feeling as though she was making even more of a fool of herself than ever, but now that she'd started, she felt she had to finish. "It's sort of like he learned magic, while you just are magic."

She glanced at her companion, looking for laughter, but Meran was regarding her gravely. And she did look like a dryad, Jilly thought, what with the green streaks in the long, nut-brown ringlets of her hair and her fey sort of Pre-Raphaelite beauty. Her eyes seemed to provide their own light, rather than take it in.

"Maybe I did step out of a tree one day," Meran said.

Jilly could feel her mouth forming a surprised "O," but then Meran laughed again.

"But probably I didn't," she said. Before Jilly could ask her about that "probably," Meran went on: "We'll need some sort of protection against them."

Jilly made her mind shift gears, from Meran's origins to the problem at hand.

"Like holy water or a cross?" she asked.

Her head filled with the plots of a hundred bad horror films, each of them clamoring for attention.

"No," Meran said. "Religious artifacts and trappings require faith—a belief in their potency that the skookin undoubtedly don't have. The only thing I know for certain that they can't abide is the truth."

"The truth?"

Meran nodded. "Tell them the truth—even it's only historical facts and trivia—and they'll shun you as though you were carrying a plague."

"But what about after?" Jilly said. "After we've delivered the drum and they come looking for me? Do I have to walk around carrying a cassette machine spouting dates and facts for the rest of my life?"

"I hope not."

"But—"

"Patience," Meran replied. "Let me think about it for awhile."

Jilly sighed. She regarded her companion curiously as Meran took a sip of her coffee.

"You really believe in this stuff, don't you?" she said finally.

"Don't you?"

Jilly had to think about that for a moment.

"Last night I was scared," she said, "and I'm returning the drum because I'd rather be safe than sorry, but I'm still not sure."

Meran nodded understandingly, but, "Your coffee's getting cold," was all she had to say.

Meran let Jilly stay with her that night in the rambling old house where she and Cerin lived. Straddling the border between Lower Crowsea and Chinatown, it was a tall, gabled building surrounded by giant oak trees. There was a rounded tower in the front to the right of a long screen-enclosed porch, stables around the back, and a garden along the west side of the house that seemed to have been plucked straight from a postcard of the English countryside.

Jilly loved this area. The Kelledys' house was the easternmost of the stately estates that stood, row on row, along McKennitt Street, between Lee and Yoors. Whenever Jilly walked along this part of McKennitt, late at night when the streetcars were tucked away in their downtown station and there was next to no other traffic, she found it easy to imagine that the years had wound back to a bygone age when time moved at a different pace, when Newford's streets were cobblestoned and the vehicles that traversed them were horse-drawn, rather than horse-powered.

"You'll wear a hole in the glass if you keep staring through it so intently."

Jilly started. She turned long enough to acknowledge her hostess's presence, then her gaze was dragged back to the window, to the shadows cast by the oaks as twilight stretched them across the lawn, to the long low wall that bordered the lawn, to the street beyond.

Still no skookin. Did that mean they didn't exist, or that they hadn't come out yet? Or maybe they just hadn't tracked her here to the Kelledys' house.

She started again as Meran laid a hand on her shoulder and gently turned her from the window.

"Who knows what you'll call to us, staring so," Meran said.

Her voice held the same light tone as it had when she'd made her earlier comment, but this time a certain sense of caution lay behind the words.

"If they come, I want to see them," Jilly said.

Meran nodded. "I understand. But remember this: the night's a magical time. The moon rules her hours, not the sun."

"What does that mean?"

"The moon likes secrets," Meran said. "And secret things. She lets mysteries bleed into her shadows and leaves us to ask whether they originated from otherworlds, or from our own imaginations."

"You're beginning to sound like Bramley," Jilly said. "Or Christy."

"Remember your Shakespeare," Meran said. " 'This fellow's wise enough to play the fool.' Did you ever think that perhaps their studied eccentricity protects them from sharper ridicule?"

"You mean all those things Christy writes about are *true*?"

"I didn't say that."

Jilly shook her head. "No. But you're talking in riddles just like a wizard out of some fairy tale. I never understood why they couldn't talk plainly."

"That's because some things can only be approached from the side. Secretively. Peripherally."

Whatever Jilly was about to say next, died stillborn. She pointed out the window to where the lawn was almost swallowed by shadows.

"Do . . ." She swallowed thickly, then tried again. "Do you see them?"

They were out there, flitting between the wall that bordered the Kelledys' property and those tall oaks that stood closer to the house. Shadow shapes. Fat, pumpkin-bodied and twig-limbed. There were more of them than there'd been last night. And they were bolder. Creeping right up towards the house. Threats burning in their candle-flicker eyes. Wide mouths open in jack-o'-lantern grins, revealing rows of pointed teeth.

One came sidling right up to the window, its face monstrous at such close proximity. Jilly couldn't move, couldn't even breathe. She remembered what Meran had said earlier—

they can't abide the truth

—but she couldn't frame a sentence, never mind a word, and her mind was filled with only a wild unreasoning panic. The creature reached out a hand towards the glass, clawed fingers extended. Jilly could feel a scream building up, deep inside her. In a moment that hand would come crashing through the window, shattering glass, clawing at her throat. And she couldn't move. All she could do was stare, stare as the claws reached for the glass, stare as it drew back to—

Something fell between the creature and the house—a swooping, shapeless thing. The creature danced back, saw that it was only the bough of one of the oak trees and was about to begin its approach once more, but the cries of its companions distracted it. Not until it turned its horrible gaze from her, did Jilly feel able to lift her own head.

She stared at the oaks. A sudden wind had sprung up, lashing the boughs about so that the tall trees appeared to be giants, flailing about their many-limbed arms like monstrous, agitated octopi. The creatures in the yard scattered and in moments they were gone—each and every one of them. The wind died down; the animated giants became just oak trees once more.

Jilly turned slowly from the window to find Meran pressed close beside her.

"Ugly, furtive and sullen," Meran said. "Perhaps Christy wasn't so far off in naming them."

"They . . . they're real, aren't they?" Jilly asked in a small voice.

Meran nodded. "And not at all like the bodachs of my homeland. Bodachs are mischievous and prone to trouble, but not like this. Those creatures were weaned on malevolence."

Jilly leaned weakly against the windowsill.

"What are we going to *do*?" she asked.

She scratched at her palm—the itch was worse than ever. Meran caught her hand, pulled it away. There was an unhappy look in her eyes when she lifted her gaze from the mark on Jilly's palm.

"Where did you get that?" she asked.

Jilly looked down at her palm. The scab was gone, but the skin was all dark around the puncture wound now—an ugly black discoloration that was twice the size of the original scab.

"I scratched myself," she said. "Down in Old City."

Meran shook her head. "No," she said. "They've marked you."

Jilly suddenly felt weak. Skookin were real. Mysterious winds rose to animate trees. And now she was marked?

She wasn't even sure what that meant, but she didn't like the sound of it. Not for a moment.

Her gaze went to the stone drum where it stood on Meran's mantel. She didn't think she'd ever hated an inanimate object so much before.

"Marked . . . me . . . ?" she asked.

"I've heard of this before," Meran said, her voice apologetic. She touched the mark on Jilly's palm. "This is like a . . . bounty."

"They really want to kill me, don't they?"

Jilly was surprised that her voice sounded as calm as it did. Inside she felt as though she was crumbling to little bits all over the place.

"Skookin are real," she went on, "and they're going to tear me up into little pieces—just like they did to the man in Christy's stupid story."

Meran gave her a sympathetic look.

"We have to go now," she said. "We have to go and confront them now, before . . ."

"Before what?"

Jilly's control over her voice was slipping. Her last word went shrieking up in pitch.

"Before they send something worse," Meran said.

Oh great, Jilly thought as she waited for Meran to change into clothing more suitable for the underground trek to Old City. Not only were skookin real, but there were worse things than those pumpkinhead creatures living down there under the city.

She slouched in one of the chairs by the mantelpiece, her back to the stone drum, and pretended that her nerves weren't all scraped raw, that she was just over visiting a friend for the evening and everything was just peachy, thank you. Surprisingly, by the time Meran returned, wearing jeans, sturdy walking shoes and a thick woolen shirt under a denim jacket, she did feel better.

"The bit with the trees," she asked as she rose from her chair. "Did you do that?"

Meran shook her head.

"But the wind likes me," she said. "Maybe it's because I play the flute."

And maybe it's because you're a dryad, Jilly thought, and the wind's got a thing about oak trees, but she let the thought go unspoken.

Meran fetched the long, narrow bag that held her flute and slung it over her shoulder.

"Ready?" she asked.

"No," Jilly said.

But she went and took the drum from the mantelpiece and joined Meran by the front door. Meran stuck a flashlight in the pocket of her jacket and handed another to Jilly, who thrust it into the pocket of the coat Meran was lending her. It was at least two sizes too big for her, which suited Jilly just fine.

Naturally, just to make the night complete, it started to rain before they got halfway down the walkway to McKennitt Street.

For safety's sake, city work crews had sealed up all the entrances to Old City in the mid-seventies—all the entrances of which the city was aware, at any rate. The street people of Newford's back lanes and alleys knew of anywhere from a half-dozen to twenty others that could still be used, the number depending only on who was doing the bragging. The entrance to which Jilly led Meran was the most commonly known and used—a steel maintenance door that was situated two hundred yards or so down the east tracks of the Grasso Street subway station.

The door led into the city's sewer maintenance tunnels, but had long since been abandoned. Skells had broken the locking mechanism and the door stood continually ajar. Inside, time and weathering had worn down a connecting wall between the maintenance tunnels and what had once been the top floor of one of Old City's proud skyscrapers—an office complex that had towered some four stories above the city's streets before the quake dropped it into its present subterranean setting.

It was a good fifteen minute walk from the Kelledys' house to the Grasso Street station and Jilly plodded miserably through the rain at Meran's side for every block of it. Her sneakers were soaked and her hair plastered against her scalp. She carried the stone drum tucked under one arm and was very tempted to simply pitch it in front of a bus.

"This is crazy," Jilly said. "We're just giving ourselves up to them."

Meran shook her head. "No. We're confronting them of our own free will—there's a difference."

"That's just semantics. There won't be a difference in the results."

"That's where you're wrong."

They both turned at the sound of a new voice to find Goon standing in the doorway of a closed antique shop. His eyes glittered oddly in the poor light, reminding Jilly all too much of the skookin, and he didn't seem to be the least bit wet.

"What are *you* doing here?" Jilly demanded.

"You must always confront your fears," Goon said as though she hadn't spoken. "Then skulking monsters become merely unfamiliar shadows, thrown by a tree bough. Whispering voices are just the wind. The wild flare of panic is merely a burst of emotion, not a terror spell cast by some evil witch."

Meran nodded. "That's what Cerin would say. And that's what I mean to do. Confront them with a truth so bright that they won't dare come near us again."

Jilly held up her hand. The discoloration was spreading. It had grown from its pinprick inception, first to the size of a dime, now to that of a silver dollar.

"What about this?" she asked.

"There's always a price for meddling," Goon agreed. "Sometimes it's the simple curse of knowledge."

"There's always a price," Meran agreed.

Everybody always seemed to know more than she did these days, Jilly thought unhappily.

"You still haven't told me what you're doing here," she told Goon. "Skulking about and following us."

Goon smiled. "It seems to me, that you came upon me."

"You know what I mean."

"I have my own business in Old City tonight," he said. "And since we all have the same destination in mind, I thought perhaps you would appreciate the company."

Everything was wrong about this, Jilly thought. Goon was never nice to her. Goon was never nice to anyone.

"Yeah, well, you can just—" she began.

Meran laid a hand on Jilly's arm. "It's bad luck to turn away help when it's freely offered."

"But you don't know what he's like," Jilly said.

"Olaf and I have met before," Meran said.

Jilly caught the grimace on Goon's face at the use of his given name. It made him seem more himself, which, while not exactly comforting, was at least familiar. Then she looked at Meran. She thought of the wind outside the musician's house, driving away the skookin, the mystery that cloaked her which ran even deeper, perhaps, than that which Goon wore so easily. . . .

"Sometimes you just have to trust in people," Meran said, as though reading Jilly's mind.

Jilly sighed. She rubbed her itchy palm against her thigh, shifted the drum into a more comfortable position.

"Okay," she said. "So what're we waiting for?"

The few times Jilly had come down to Old City, she'd been cautious, perhaps even a little nervous, but never frightened. Tonight was different. It was always dark in Old City, but the darkness had never seemed so . . . so watchful before. There were always odd little sounds, but they had never seemed so furtive. Even with her companions—

maybe because of them, she thought, thinking mostly of Goon—she felt very much alone in the eerie darkness.

Goon didn't appear to need the wobbly light of their flashlights to see his way and though he seemed content enough to simply follow them, Jilly couldn't shake the feeling that he was actually leading the way. They were soon in a part of the subterranean city that she'd never seen before.

There was less dust and dirt here. No litter, nor the remains of the skells' fires. No broken bottles, nor the piles of newspapers and ratty blanketing that served the skells as bedding. The buildings seemed in better repair. The air had a clean, dry smell to it, rather than the close, musty reek of refuse and human wastes that it carried closer to the entrance.

And there were no people.

From when they'd first stepped through the steel door in Grasso Street Station's east tunnel, she hadn't seen a bag lady or wino or any kind of skell, and that in itself was odd because they were always down here. But there was something sharing the darkness with them. Something watched them, marked their progress, followed with a barely discernible pad of sly footsteps in their wake and on either side.

The drum seemed warm against the skin of her hand. The blemish on her other palm prickled with itchiness. Her shoulder muscles were stiff with tension.

"Not far now," Goon said softly and Jilly suddenly understood what it meant to jump out of one's skin.

The beam of her flashlight made a wild arc across the faces of the buildings on either side of her as she started. Her heartbeat jumped into second gear.

"What do you see?" Meran asked, her voice calm.

The beam of her flashlight turned towards Goon and he pointed ahead.

"Turn off your flashlights," he said.

Oh sure, Jilly thought. Easy for you to say.

But she did so a moment after Meran had. The sudden darkness was so abrupt that Jilly thought she'd gone blind. But then she realized that it wasn't as black as it should be. Looking ahead to where Goon had pointed, she could see a faint glow seeping onto the street ahead of them. It was a little less than a half block away, the source of the light hidden behind the squatting bulk of a half-tumbled-down building.

"What could it . . . ?" Jilly started to say, but then the sounds began, and the rest of her words dried up in her throat.

It was supposed to be music, she realized after a few moments, but there was no discernible rhythm and while the sounds were blown or rasped or plucked from instruments, they searched in vain for a melody.

"It begins," Goon said.

He took the lead, hurrying them up to the corner of the street.

"What does?" Jilly wanted to know.

"The king appears—as he must once a moon. It's that or lose his throne."

Jilly wanted to know what he was talking about—better yet, *how* he knew what he was talking about—but she didn't have a chance. The discordant not-music scraped and squealed to a kind of crescendo. Suddenly they were surrounded by the capering forms of dozens of skookin that bumped them, thin long fingers tugging at their clothing. Jilly shrieked at the first touch. One of them tried to snatch the drum from her grip. She regained control of her nerves at the same time as she pulled the artifact free from the grasping fingers.

"1789," she said. "That's when the Bastille was stormed and the French Revolution began. Uh, 1807, slave trade was abolished in the British Empire. 1776, the Declaration of Independence was signed."

The skookin backed away from her, as did the others, hissing and spitting. The not-music continued, but its tones were softened.

"Let me see," Jilly went on. "Uh, 1981, the Argentines invade—I can't keep this up, Meran—the Falklands. 1715 . . . that was the year of the first Jacobite uprising."

She'd always been good with historical trivia—having a head for dates—but the more she concentrated on them right now, the further they seemed to slip away. The skookin were regarding her with malevolence, just waiting for her to falter.

"1978," she said. "Sandy Denny died, falling down some stairs. . . ."

She'd got that one from Geordie. The skookin took another step back and she stepped towards them, into the light, her eyes widening with shock. There was a small park there, vegetation dead, trees leafless and skeletal, shadows dancing from the light cast by a fire at either end of the open space. And it was teeming with skookin.

There seemed to be hundreds of the creatures. She could see some of the musicians who were making that awful din—holding their instruments as though they'd never played them before. They were gathered in a semi-circle around a dais made from slabs of pavement and building rubble. Standing on it was the weirdest looking skookin she'd seen yet. He was kind of withered and stood stiffly. His eyes flashed with a kind of dead, cold light. He had the grimmest look about him that she'd seen on any of them yet.

There was no way her little bits of history were going to be enough to keep back this crew. She turned to look at her companions. She couldn't see Goon, but Meran was tugging her flute free from its carrying bag.

What good was that going to do? Jilly wondered.

"It's another kind of truth," Meran said as she brought the instrument up to her lips.

The flute's clear tones echoed breathily along the street, cutting through the jangle of not-music like a glass knife through muddy water. Jilly held her breath. The music was so beautiful. The skookin cowered where they stood. Their cacophonic noise-making faltered, then fell silent.

No one moved.

For long moments, there was just the clear sound of Meran's flute, breathing a slow plaintive air that echoed and sang down the street, winding from one end of the park to the other.

Another kind of truth, Jilly remembered Meran saying just before she began to play. That's exactly what this music was, she realized. A kind of truth.

The flute-playing finally came to an achingly sweet finale and a hush fell in Old City. And then there was movement. Goon stepped from behind Jilly and walked through the still crowd of skookin to the dais where their king stood. He clambered up over the rubble until he was beside the king. He pulled a large clasp knife from the pocket of his coat. As he opened the blade, the skookin king made a jerky motion to get away, but Goon's knife hand moved too quickly.

He slashed and cut.

Now he's bloody done it, Jilly thought as the skookin king tumbled to the stones. But then she realized that Goon hadn't cut the king. He'd cut the air above the king. He'd cut the—her sudden realization only confused her more—strings holding him?

"What . . . ?" she said.

"Come," Meran said.

She tucked her flute under her arm and led Jilly towards the dais.

"This is your king," Goon was saying.

He reached down and pulled the limp form up by the fine-webbed strings that were attached to the king's arms and shoulders. The king dangled loosely under his strong grip—a broken marionette. A murmur rose from the crowd of skookin—part ugly, part wondering.

"The king is dead," Goon said. "He's been dead for moons. I wondered why Old City was closed to me this past half year, and now I know."

There was movement at the far end of the park—a fleeing figure. It had been the king's councilor, Goon told Jilly and Meran later. Some of the skookin made to chase him, but Goon called them back.

"Let him go," he said. "He won't return. We have other business at hand."

Meran had drawn Jilly right up to the foot of the dais and was gently pushing her forward.

"Go on," she said.

"Is he the king now?" Jilly asked.

Meran smiled and gave her another gentle push.

Jilly looked up. Goon seemed just like he always did when she saw him at Bramley's—grumpy and out of sorts. Maybe it's just his face, she told herself, trying to give herself courage. There were people who look grumpy no matter how happy they are. But the thought didn't help contain her shaking much as she slowly made her way up to where Goon stood.

"You have something of ours," Goon said.

His voice was grim. Christy's story lay all too clearly in Jilly's head. She swallowed dryly.

"Uh, I never meant . . ." she began, then simply handed over the drum.

Goon took it reverently, then snatched her other hand before she could draw away. Her palm flared with sharp pain—all the skin, from the base of her hand to the ends of her fingers was black.

The curse, she thought. It's going to make my hand fall right off. I'm never going to paint again. . . .

Goon spat on her palm and the pain died as though it had never been. With wondering eyes, Jilly watched the blackness dry up and begin to flake away. Goon gave her hand a shake and the blemish scattered to fall to the ground. Her hand was completely unmarked.

"But . . . the curse," she said. "The bounty on my head. What about Christy's story . . . ?"

"Your curse is knowledge," Goon said.

"But . . . ?"

He turned away to face the crowd, drum in hand. As Jilly made her careful descent back to where Meran was waiting for her, Goon tapped his fingers against the head of the drum. An eerie rhythm started up—a real rhythm. When the skookin musicians began to play, they held their instruments properly and called up a sweet stately music to march across the back of the rhythm. It was a rich tapestry of sound, as different from Meran's solo flute as sunlight is from twilight, but it held its own power. Its own magic.

Goon led the playing with the rhythm he called up from the stone drum, led the music as though he'd always led it.

"He's really the king, isn't he?" Jilly whispered to her companion.

Meran nodded.

"So then what was he doing working for Bramley?"

"I don't know," Meran replied. "I suppose a king—or a king's son—can do pretty well what he wants just so long as he comes back here once a moon to fulfill his obligation as ruler."

"Do you think he'll go back to work for Bramley?"

"I know he will," Meran replied.

Jilly looked out at the crowd of skookin. They didn't seem at all threatening anymore. They just looked like little men—comical, with their tubby bodies and round heads and their little broomstick limbs—but men all the same. She listened to the music, felt its trueness and had to ask Meran why it didn't hurt them.

"Because it's their truth," Meran replied.

"But truth's just truth," Jilly protested. "Something's either true or it's not."

Meran just put her arm around Jilly's shoulder. A touch of a smile came to the corners of her mouth.

"It's time we went home," she said.

"I got off pretty lightly, didn't I?" Jilly said as they started back the way they'd come. "I mean, with the curse and all."

"Knowledge can be a terrible burden," Meran replied. "It's what some believe cast Adam and Eve from Eden."

"But that was a good thing, wasn't it?"

Meran nodded. "I think so. But it brought pain with it—pain we still feel to this day."

"I suppose."

"Come on," Meran said, as Jilly lagged a little to look back at the park.

Jilly quickened her step, but she carried the scene away with her. Goon and the stone drum. The crowd of skookin. The flickering light of their fires as it cast shadows over the Old City buildings.

And the music played on.

Professor Dapple had listened patiently to the story he'd been told, managing to keep from interrupting through at least half of the telling. Leaning back in his chair when it was done, he took off his glasses and began to needlessly polish them.

"It's going to be very good," he said finally.

Christy Riddell grinned from the club chair where he was sitting.

"But Jilly's not going to like it," Bramley went on. "You know how she feels about your stories."

"But she's the one who told me this one," Christy said.

Bramley rearranged his features to give the impression that he'd known this all along.

"Doesn't seem like much of a curse," he said, changing tack.

Christy raised his eyebrows. "What? To know that it's all real? To have to seriously consider every time she hears about some seemingly preposterous thing, that it might very well be true? To have to keep on guard with what she says so that people won't think she's gone off the deep end?"

"Is that how people look at us?" Bramley asked.

"What do you think?" Christy replied with a laugh.

Bramley hrumphed. He fidgeted with the papers on his desk, making more of a mess of them, rather than less.

"But Goon," he said, finally coming to the heart of what bothered him with what he'd been told. "It's like some retelling of " 'The King of the Cats,' isn't it? Are you really going to put that bit in?"

Christy nodded. "It's part of the story."

"I can't see Goon as a king of anything," Bramley said. "And if he *is* a king, then what's he doing still working for me?"

"Which do you think would be better," Christy asked. "To be a king below, or a man above?"

Bramley didn't have an answer for that.

Timeskip

Every time it rains a ghost comes walking.

He goes up by the stately old houses that line Stanton Street, down Henratty Lane to where it leads into the narrow streets and crowded backalleys of Crowsea, and then back up Stanton again in an unvarying routine.

He wears a worn tweed suit—mostly browns and greys with a faint rosy touch of heather. A shapeless cap presses down his brown curls. His features give no true indication of his age, while his eyes are both innocent and wise. His face gleams in the rain, slick and wet as that of a living person. When he reaches the streetlamp in front of the old Hamill estate, he wipes his eyes with a brown hand. Then he fades away.

Samantha Rey knew it was true because she'd seen him.

More than once.

She saw him every time it rained.

"So, have you asked her out yet?" Jilly wanted to know.

We were sitting on a park bench, feeding pigeons the leftover crusts from our lunches. Jilly had worked with me at the post office, that Christmas they hired outside staff instead of letting the regular employees work the overtime, and we'd been friends ever since. These days she worked three nights a week as a waitress, while I made what I could busking on the Market with my father's old Czech fiddle.

Jilly was slender, with a thick tangle of brown hair and pale blue eyes, electric as sapphires. She had a penchant for loose clothing and fingerless gloves when she wasn't waitressing. There were times, when I met her on the streets in the evening, that I mistook her for a bag lady: skulking in an alleyway, gaze alternating between the sketchbook held in one hand and the faces of the people on the streets as they walked by. She had more sketches of me playing my fiddle than had any right to exist.

"She's never going to know how you feel until you talk to her about it," Jilly went on when I didn't answer.

"I know."

I'll make no bones about it: I was putting the make on Sam Rey and had been ever since she'd started to work at Gypsy Records half a year ago. I never much went in for the blonde California beach girl type, but Sam had a look all her own. She had some indefinable quality that went beyond her basic cheerleader appearance. Right. I can hear you already. Rationalizations of the North American libido. But it was true. I didn't just want Sam in my bed; I wanted to know we were going to have a future together. I wanted to grow old with her. I wanted to build up a lifetime of shared memories.

About the most Sam knew about all this was that I hung around and talked to her a lot at the record store.

"Look," Jilly said. "Just because she's pretty, doesn't mean she's having a perfect life or anything. Most guys look at someone like her and they won't even approach her because they're sure she's got men coming out of her ears. Well, it doesn't always work that way. For instance—" she touched her breastbone with a narrow hand and smiled "—consider yours truly."

I looked at her long fingers. Paint had dried under her nails.

"You've started a new canvas," I said.

"And you're changing the subject," she replied. "Come on, Geordie. What's the big deal? The most she can say is no."

"Well, yeah. But . . ."

"She intimidates you, doesn't she?"

I shook my head. "I talk to her all the time."

"Right. And that's why I've got to listen to your constant mooning over her." She gave me a sudden considering look, then grinned. "I'll tell you what, Geordie, me lad. Here's the bottom line: I'll give you twenty-four hours to ask her out. If you haven't got it together by then, I'll talk to her myself."

"Don't even joke about it."

"Twenty-four hours," Jilly said firmly. She looked at the chocolate-chip cookie in my hand. "Are you eating that?" she added in that certain tone of voice of hers that plainly said, all previous topics of conversation have been dealt with and completed. We are now changing topics.

So we did. But all the while we talked, I thought about going into the record store and asking Sam out, because if I didn't, Jilly would do it for me. Whatever else she might be, Jilly wasn't shy. Having her go in to plead my case would be as bad as having my mother do it for me. I'd never be able to show my face in there again.

Gypsy Records is on Williamson Street, one of the city's main arteries. It begins as Highway 14 outside the city, lined with a sprawl of fast food outlets, malls and warehouses. On its way downtown, it begins to replace the commercial properties with ever-increasing handfuls of residential blocks until it reaches the downtown core where shops and low-rise apartments mingle in gossiping crowds.

The store gets its name from John Butler, a short round-bellied man without a smidgen of Romany blood, who began his business out of the back of a hand-drawn cart that gypsied its way through the city's streets for years, always keeping just one step ahead of the municipal licensing board's agents. While it carries the usual best-sellers, the lifeblood of its sales are more obscure titles—imports and albums published by independent record labels. Albums, singles and compact discs of punk, traditional folk, jazz, heavy metal and alternative music line its shelves. Barring Sam, most of those who work there would look just as at home in the fashion pages of the most current British alternative fashion magazines.

Sam was wearing a blue cotton dress today, embroidered with silver threads. Her blonde hair was cut in a short shag on the top, hanging down past her shoulders at the back and sides. She was dealing with a defect when I came in. I don't know if the record in question worked or not, but the man returning it was definitely defective.

"It sounds like there's a radio broadcast right in the middle of the song," he was saying as he tapped the cover of the Pink Floyd album on the counter between them.

"It's supposed to be there," Sam explained. "It's *part* of the song." The tone of her voice told me that this conversation was going into its twelfth round or so.

"Well, I don't like it," the man told her. "When I buy an album of music, I expect to get just music on it."

"You still can't return it."

I worked in a record shop one Christmas—two years before the post office job. The best defect I got was from someone returning an in-concert album by Marcel Marceau. Each side had thirty minutes of silence, with applause at the end—I kid you not.

I browsed through the Celtic records while I waited for Sam to finish with her customer. I couldn't afford any of them, but I liked to see what was new. Blasting out of the store's speakers was the new Beastie Boys album. It sounded like a cross between heavy metal and bad rap and was about as appealing as being hit by a car. You couldn't deny its energy, though.

By the time Sam was free I'd located five records I would have bought in more flush times. Leaving them in the bin, I drifted over to the front cash just as the Beastie Boys' last cut ended. Sam replaced them with a tape of New Age piano music.

"What's the new Oyster Band like?" I asked.

Sam smiled. "It's terrific. My favorite cut's " 'The Old Dance.' It's sort of an allegory based on Adam and Eve and the serpent that's got a great hook in the chorus. Telfer's fiddling just sort of skips ahead, pulling the rest of the song along."

That's what I like about alternative record stores like Gypsy's—the people working in them actually know something about what they're selling.

"Have you got an open copy?" I asked.

She nodded and turned to the bin of opened records behind her to find it. With her back to me, I couldn't get lost in those deep blue eyes of hers. I seized my opportunity and plunged ahead.

"Areyouworkingtonight — wouldyouliketogooutwithmesomewhere?"

I'd meant to be cool about it, except the words all blurred together as they left my throat. I could feel the flush start up the back of my neck as she turned and looked back at me with those baby blues.

"Say what?" she asked.

Before my throat closed up on me completely, I tried again, keeping it short. "Do you want to go out with me tonight?"

Standing there with the Oyster Band album in her hand, I thought she'd never looked better. Especially when she said, "I thought you'd never ask."

I put in a couple of hours of busking that afternoon, down in Crowsea's Market, the fiddle humming under my chin to the jingling rhythm of the coins that passersby threw into the case lying open in front of me. I came away with twenty-six dollars and change—not the best of days, but enough to buy a halfway decent dinner and a few beers.

I picked up Sam after she finished work and we ate at The Monkey Woman's Nest, a Mexican restaurant on Williamson just a couple of blocks down from Gypsy's. I still don't know how the place got its name. Ernestina Verdad, the Mexican woman who owns the place, looks like a showgirl and not one of her waitresses is even vaguely simian in appearance.

It started to rain as we were finishing our second beer, turning Williamson Street slick with neon reflections. Sam got a funny look on her face as she watched the rain through the window. Then she turned to me.

"Do you believe in ghosts?" she asked.

The serious look in her eyes stopped the half-assed joke that two beers brewed in the carbonated swirl of my mind. I never could hold my alcohol. I wasn't drunk, but I had a buzz on.

"I don't think so," I said carefully. "At least I've never seriously stopped to think about it."

"Come on," she said, getting up from the table. "I want to show you something."

I let her lead me out into the rain, though I didn't let her pay anything towards the meal. Tonight was my treat. Next time I'd be happy to let her do the honors.

"Every time it rains," she said, "a ghost comes walking down my street. . . ."

She told me the story as we walked down into Crowsea. The rain was light and I was enjoying it, swinging my fiddle case in my right hand, Sam hanging onto my left as though she'd always walked there. I felt like I was on top of the world, listening to her talk, feeling the pressure of her arm, the bump of her hip against mine.

She had an apartment on the third floor of an old brick and frame building on Stanton Street. It had a front porch that ran the length of the house, dormer windows—two in the front and back, one on each side—and a sloped mansard roof. We stood on the porch, out of the rain, which was coming down harder now. An orange and white tom was sleeping on the cushion of a white wicker chair by the door. He twitched a torn ear as we shared his shelter, but didn't bother to open his eyes. I could smell the mint that was growing up alongside the porch steps, sharp in the wet air.

Sam pointed down the street to where the yellow glare of a streetlamp glistened on the rain-slicked cobblestone walk that led to the Hamill estate. The Hamill house itself was separated from the street by a low wall and a dark expanse of lawn, bordered by the spreading boughs of huge oak trees.

"Watch the street," she said. "Just under the streetlight."

I looked, but I didn't see anything. The wind gusted suddenly, driving the rain in hard sheets along Stanton Street, and for a moment we lost all visibility. When it cleared, he was standing there, Sam's ghost, just like she'd told me. As he started down the street, Sam gave my arm a tug. I stowed my fiddle case under the tom's wicker chair, and we followed the ghost down Henratty Lane.

By the time he returned to the streetlight in front of the Hamill estate, I was ready to argue that Sam was mistaken. There was nothing in the least bit ghostly about the man we were following. When he returned up Henratty Lane, we had to duck into a doorway to let him pass. He never looked at us, but I could see the rain hitting him. I could hear the sound of his shoes on the pavement. He had to have come out of the walk that led up to the estate's house, at the same time as that sudden gust of wind-driven rain. It had been a simple coincidence, nothing more. But when he returned to the streetlight, he lifted a hand to wipe his face, and then he was gone. He just winked out of existence. There was no wind. No gust of rain. No place he could have gone. A ghost.

"Jesus," I said softly as I walked over to the pool of light cast by the streetlamp. There was nothing to see. But there had been a man there. I was sure of that much.

"We're soaked," Sam said. "Come on up to my place and I'll make us some coffee."

The coffee was great and the company was better. Sam had a small clothes drier in her kitchen. I sat in the living room in an oversized housecoat while my clothes tumbled and turned, the machine creating a vibration in the floorboards that I'm sure Sam's downstairs neighbors must have just loved. Sam had changed into a dark blue sweatsuit—she looked best in blue, I decided—and dried her hair while she was making the coffee. I'd prowled around her living room while she did, admiring her books, her huge record collection, her sound system, and the mantel above a working fireplace that was crammed with knickknacks.

All her furniture was the kind made for comfort—they crouched like sleeping animals about the room. Fat sofa in front of the fireplace, an old pair of matching easy chairs by the window. The bookcases, record cabinet, side tables and trim were all natural wood, polished to a shine with furniture oil.

We talked about a lot of things, sitting on the sofa, drinking our coffees, but mostly we talked about the ghost.

"Have you ever approached him?" I asked at one point.

Sam shook her head. "No. I just watch him walk. I've never even talked about him to anybody else." That made me feel good. "You know, I can't help but feel that he's waiting for something, or someone. Isn't that the way it usually works in ghost stories?"

"This isn't a ghost story," I said.

"But we didn't imagine it, did we? Not both of us at the same time?"

"I don't know."

But I knew someone who probably did. Jilly. She was into every sort of strange happening, taking all kinds of odd things seriously. I could remember her telling me that Bramley Dapple—one of her professors at Butler U. and a friend of my brother's—was really a wizard who had a brown-skinned goblin for a valet, but the best thing I remembered about her was her talking about that scene in Disney's *101 Dalmatians*, where the dogs are all howling to send a message across town, one dog sending it out, another picking it up and passing it along, all the way across town and out into the country.

"That's how they do it," she'd said. "Just like that."

And if you walked with her at night and a dog started to howl—if no other dog picked it up, then she'd pass it on. She could mimic any dog's bark or howl so perfectly it was uncanny. It could also be embarrassing, because she didn't care who was around or what kinds of looks she got. It was the message that had to be passed on that was important.

When I told Sam about Jilly, she smiled, but there wasn't any mockery in her smile. Emboldened, I related the ultimatum that Jilly had given me this afternoon.

Sam laughed aloud. "Jilly sounds like my kind of person," she said. "I'd like to meet her."

When it started to get late, I collected my clothes and changed in the bathroom. I didn't want to start anything, not yet, not this soon, and I knew that Sam felt the same way, though neither of us had spoken of it. She kissed me at the door, a long warm kiss that had me buzzing again.

"Come see me tomorrow?" she asked. "At the store?"

"Just try and keep me away," I replied.

I gave the old tom on the porch a pat and whistled all the way home to my own place on the other side of Crowsea.

Jilly's studio was its usual organized mess. It was an open loft-like affair that occupied half of the second floor of a four-story brown brick building on Yoors Street where Foxville's low rentals mingle with Crowsea's shops and older houses. One half of the studio was taken up with a Murphy bed that was never folded back into the wall, a pair of battered sofas, a small kitchenette, storage cabinets and a tiny box-like bathroom obviously designed with dwarves in mind.

Her easel stood in the other half of the studio, by the window where it could catch the morning sun. All around it were stacks of sketchbooks, newspapers, unused canvases and art books. Finished canvases leaned face front, five to ten deep, against the back wall. Tubes of paint covered the tops of old wooden orange crates—the new ones lying in neat piles like logs by a fireplace, the used ones in a haphazard scatter, closer to hand. Brushes sat waiting to be used in mason jars. Others were in liquid waiting to be cleaned. Still more, their brushes stiff with dried paint, lay here and there on the floor like discarded pick-up-sticks.

The room smelled of oil paint and turpentine. In the corner furthest from the window was a life-sized fabric mâché sculpture of an artist at work that bore an uncanny likeness to Jilly herself, complete with Walkman, one paintbrush in hand, another sticking out of its mouth. When I got there that morning, Jilly was at her new canvas, face scrunched up as she concentrated. There was already paint in her hair. On the windowsill behind her a small ghetto blaster was playing a Bach fugue, the piano notes spilling across the room like a light rain. Jilly looked up as I came in, a frown changing liquidly into a smile as she took in the foolish look on my face.

"I should have thought of this weeks ago," she said. "You look like the cat who finally caught the mouse. Did you have a good time?"

"The best."

Leaving my fiddle by the door, I moved around behind her so that I could see what she was working on. Sketched out on the white canvas was a Crowsea street scene. I recognized the corner—McKennitt and Lee. I'd played there from time to time, mostly in the spring. Lately a rockabilly band called the Broken Hearts had taken over the spot.

"Well?" Jilly prompted.

"Well what?"

"Aren't you going to give me all the lovely sordid details?"

I nodded at the painting. She'd already started to work in the background with oils.

"Are you putting in the Hearts?" I asked.

Jilly jabbed at me with her paintbrush, leaving a smudge the color of a Crowsea red brick tenement on my jean jacket.

"I'll thump you if you don't spill it all, Geordie, me lad. Just watch if I don't."

She was liable to do just that, so I sat down on the ledge behind her and talked while she painted. We shared a pot of her cowboy coffee, which was what Jilly called the foul brew she made from used coffee grounds. I took two spoons of sugar to my usual one, just to cut back on the bitter taste it left in my throat. Still, beggars couldn't be choosers. That morning I didn't even have used coffee grounds at my own place.

"I like ghost stories," she said when I was finished telling her about my evening. She'd finished roughing out the buildings by now and bent closer to the canvas to start working on some of the finer details before she lost the last of the morning light.

"Was it real?" I asked.

"That depends. Bramley says—"

"I know, I know," I said, breaking in.

If it wasn't Jilly telling me some weird story about him, it was my brother. What Jilly liked best about him was his theory of consensual reality, the idea that things exist *because* we agree that they exist.

"But think about it," Jilly went on. "Sam sees a ghost—maybe because she expects to see one—and you see the same ghost because you care about her, so you're willing to agree that there's one there where she says it will be."

"Say it's not that, then what could it be?"

"Any number of things. A timeslip—a bit of the past slipping into the present. It could be a restless spirit with unfinished business. From what you say Sam's told you, though, I'd guess that it's a case of a timeskip."

She turned to grin at me, which let me know that the word was one of her own coining. I gave her a dutifully admiring look, then asked, "A what?"

"A timeskip. It's like a broken record, you know? It just keeps playing the same bit over and over again, only unlike the record it needs something specific to cue it in."

"Like rain."

"Exactly." She gave me a sudden sharp look. "This isn't for one of your brother's stories, is it?"

My brother Christy collects odd tales just like Jilly does, only he writes them down. I've heard some grand arguments between the two of them comparing the superior qualities of the oral versus written traditions.

"I haven't seen Christy in weeks," I said.

"All right, then."

"So how do you go about handling this sort of thing?" I asked. "Sam thinks he's waiting for something."

Jilly nodded. "For someone to lift the tone arm of time." At the pained look on my face, she added, "Well, have you got a better analogy?"

I admitted that I didn't. "But how do you do that? Do you just go over and talk to him, or grab him, or what?"

"Any and all might work. But you have to be careful about that kind of thing."

"How so?"

"Well," Jilly said, turning from the canvas to give me a serious look, "sometimes a ghost like that can drag you back to whenever it is that he's from and you'll be trapped in his time. Or you might end up taking his place in the timeskip."

"Lovely."

"Isn't it?" She went back to the painting. "What color's that sign Duffy has over his shop on McKennitt?" she asked.

I closed my eyes, trying to picture it, but all I could see was the face of last night's ghost, wet with rain.

It didn't rain again for a couple of weeks. They were good weeks. Sam and I spent the evenings and weekends together. We went out a few times, twice with Jilly, once with a couple of Sam's friends. Jilly and Sam got along just as well as I'd thought they would—and why shouldn't they? They were both special people. I should know.

The morning it did rain it was Sam's day off from Gypsy's. The previous night was the first I'd stayed over all night. The first we made love. Waking up in the morning with her warm beside me was everything I thought it would be. She was sleepy-eyed and smiling, more than willing to nestle deep under the comforter while I saw about getting some coffee together.

When the rain started, we took our mugs into the living room and watched the street in front of the Hamill estate. A woman came by walking one of those fat white bull terriers that look like they're more pig than dog. The terrier didn't seem to mind the rain but the woman at the other end of the leash was less than pleased. She alternated between frowning at the clouds and tugging him along. About five minutes after the pair had rounded the corner, our ghost showed up, just winking into existence out of nowhere. Or out of a slip in time. One of Jilly's timeskips.

We watched him go through his routine. When he reached the streetlight and vanished again, Sam leaned her head against my shoulder. We were cozied up together in one of the big comfy chairs, feet on the windowsill.

"We should do something for him," she said.

"Remember what Jilly said," I reminded her.

Sam nodded. "But I don't think that he's out to hurt anybody. It's not like he's calling out to us or anything. He's just there, going through the same moves, time after time. The next time it rains . . . ."

"What're we going to do?"

Sam shrugged. "Talk to him, maybe?"

I didn't see how that could cause any harm. Truth to tell, I was feeling sorry for the poor bugger myself.

"Why not?" I said.

About then Sam's hands got busy and I quickly lost interest in the ghost. I started to get up, but Sam held me down in the chair.

"Where are you going?" she asked.

"Well, I thought the bed would be more . . ."

"We've never done it in a chair before."

"There's a lot of places we haven't done it yet," I said.

Those deep blue eyes of hers, about five inches from my own, just about swallowed me.

"We've got all the time in the world," she said.

It's funny how you remember things like that later.

The next time it rained, Jilly was with us. The three of us were walking home from Your Second Home, a sleazy bar on the other side of Foxville where the band of a friend of Sam's was playing. None of us looked quite right for the bar when we walked in. Sam was still the perennial California beach girl, all blonde and curves in a pair of tight jeans and a white T-shirt, with a faded jean-jacket overtop. Jilly and I looked like the scruffs we were.

The bar was a place for serious drinking during the day, serving mostly unemployed blue-collar workers spending their welfare checks on a few hours of forgetfulness. By the time the band started around nine, though, the clientele underwent a drastic transformation. Scattered here and there through the crowd was the odd individual who still dressed for volume—all the colors turned up loud—but mostly we were outnumbered thirty-to-one by spike-haired punks in their black leathers and blue jeans. It was like being on the inside of a bruise.

The band was called the Wang Boys and ended up being pretty good—especially on their original numbers—if a bit loud. My ears were ringing when we finally left the place sometime after midnight. We were having a good time on the walk home. Jilly was in rare form, half-dancing on the street around us, singing the band's closing number, making up the words, turning the piece into a punk gospel number. She kept bouncing around in front of us, skipping backwards as she tried to get us to sing along.

The rain started as a thin drizzle as were making our way through Crowsea's narrow streets. Sam's fingers tightened on my arm and Jilly stopped fooling around as we stepped into Henratty Lane, the rain coming down in earnest now. The ghost was just turning in the far end of the lane.

"Geordie," Sam said, her fingers tightening more.

I nodded. We brushed by Jilly and stepped up our pace, aiming to connect with the ghost before he made his turn and started back towards Stanton Street.

"This is not a good idea," Jilly warned us, hurrying to catch up. But by then it was too late.

We were right in front of the ghost. I could tell he didn't see Sam or me and I wanted to get out of his way before he walked right through us—I didn't relish the thought of having a ghost or a timeskip or whatever he was going through me. But Sam wouldn't move. She put out her hand, and as her fingers brushed the wet tweed of his jacket, everything changed.

The sense of vertigo was strong. Henratty Lane blurred. I had the feeling of time flipping by like the pages of a calendar in an old movie, except each page was a year, not a day. The sounds of the city around us—sounds we weren't normally aware of—were noticeable by their sudden absence. The ghost jumped at Sam's touch. There was a bewildered look in his eyes and he backed away. That sensation of vertigo and blurring returned until Sam caught him by the arm and everything settled down again. Quiet, except for the rain and a far-off voice that seemed to be calling my name.

"Don't be frightened," Sam said, keeping her grip on the ghost's arm. "We want to help you."

"You should not be here," he replied. His voice was stiff and a little formal. "You were only a dream—nothing more. Dreams are to be savoured and remembered, not walking the streets."

Underlying their voices I could still hear the faint sound of my own name being called. I tried to ignore it, concentrating on the ghost and our surroundings. The lane was clearer than I remembered it—no trash littered against the walls, no graffiti scrawled across the bricks. It seemed darker, too. It was almost possible to believe that we'd been pulled back into the past by the touch of the ghost.

I started to get nervous then, remembering what Jilly had told us. Into the past. What if we *were* in the past and we couldn't get out again? What if we got trapped in the same timeskip as the ghost and were doomed to follow his routine each time it rained?

Sam and the ghost were still talking but I could hardly hear what they were saying. I was thinking of Jilly. We'd brushed by her to reach the ghost, but she'd been right behind us. Yet when I looked back, there was no one there. I remembered that sound of my name, calling faintly across some great distance. I listened now, but heard only a vague unrecognizable sound. It took me long moments to realize that it was a dog barking.

I turned to Sam, tried to concentrate on what she was saying to the ghost. She was starting to pull away from him, but now it was his hand that held her arm. As I reached forward to pull her loose, the barking suddenly grew in volume—not one dog's voice, but those of hundreds, echoing across the years that separated us from our own time. Each year caught and sent on its own dog's voice, the sound building into a cacophonous chorus of yelps and barks and howls.

The ghost gave Sam's arm a sharp tug and I lost my grip on her, stumbling as the vertigo hit me again. I fell through the sound of all those barking dogs, through the blurring years, until I dropped to my knees on the wet cobblestones, my hands reaching for Sam. But Sam wasn't there.

"Geordie?"

It was Jilly, kneeling by my side, hand on my shoulder. She took my chin and turned my face to hers, but I pulled free.

"Sam!" I cried.

A gust of wind drove rain into my face, blinding me, but not before I saw that the lane was truly empty except for Jilly and me. Jilly, who'd mimicked the barking of dogs to draw us back through time. But only I'd returned. Sam and the ghost were both gone.

"Oh, Geordie," Jilly murmured as she held me close. "I'm so sorry."

I don't know if the ghost was ever seen again, but I saw Sam one more time after that night. I was with Jilly in Moore's Antiques in Lower Crowsea, flipping through a stack of old sepia-toned photographs, when a group shot of a family on their front porch stopped me cold. There, among the somber faces, was Sam. She looked different. Her hair was drawn back in a tight bun and she wore a plain unbecoming dark dress, but it was Sam all right. I turned the photograph over and read the photographer's date on the back. 1912.

Something of what I was feeling must have shown on my face, for Jilly came over from a basket of old earrings that she was looking through.

"What's the matter, Geordie, me lad?" she asked.

Then she saw the photograph in my hand. She had no trouble recognizing Sam either. I didn't have any money that day, but Jilly bought the picture and gave it to me. I keep it in my fiddle case.

I grow older each year, building up a lifetime of memories, only I've no Sam to share them with. But often when it rains, I go down to Stanton Street and stand under the streetlight in front of the old Hamill estate. One day I know she'll be waiting there for me.

Freewheeling

There is apparently nothing that cannot happen.
—attributed to Mark Twain

There are three kinds of people: those who make things happen, those who watch things happen, and those who wonder, "What happened?"
—message found inside a Christmas cracker

1

He stood on the rain-slick street, a pale fire burning behind his eyes. Nerve ends tingling, he watched them go—a slow parade of riderless bicycles.

Ten-speeds and mountain bikes. Domesticated, urban. So inbred that all they were was spoked wheels and emaciated frames, mere skeletons of what their genetic ancestors had been. They had never known freedom, never known joy; only the weight of serious riders in slick, leather-seated shorts, pedaling determinedly with their cycling shoes strapped to the pedals, heads encased in crash helmets, fingerless gloves on the hands gripping the handles tightly.

He smiled and watched them go. Down the wet street, wheels throwing up arcs of fine spray, metal frames glistening in the streetlights, reflector lights winking red.

The rain had plastered his hair slick against his head, his clothes were sodden, but he paid no attention to personal discomfort. He thought instead of that fat-wheeled aboriginal one-speed that led them now. The maverick who'd come from who knows where to pilot his domesticated brothers and sisters away.

For a night's freedom. Perhaps for always.

The last of them were rounding the corner now. He lifted his right hand to wave goodbye. His left hand hung down by his leg, still holding the heavy-duty wire cutters by one handle, the black rubber grip making a ribbed pattern on the palm of his hand. By fences and on porches, up and down the street, locks had been cut, chains lay discarded, bicycles ran free.

He heard a siren approaching. Lifting his head, he licked the rain drops from his lips. Water got in his eyes, gathering in their corners. He squinted, enamored by the kaleidoscoping spray of lights this caused to appear behind his eyelids. There were omens in lights, he knew. And in the night sky, with its scattershot sweep of stars. So many lights . . . There were secrets waiting to unfold there, mysteries that required a voice to be freed.

Like the bicycles were freed by their maverick brother.

He could be that voice, if he only knew what to sing.

He was still watching the sky for signs when the police finally arrived.

"Let me go, boys, let me go. . . ."

The new Pogues album *If I Should Fall From Grace With God* was on the turntable. The title cut leaked from the sound system's speakers, one of which sat on a crate crowded with half-used paint tubes and tins of turpentine, the other perched on the windowsill, commanding a view of rainswept Yoors Street one floor below. The song was jauntier than one might expect from its subject matter while Shane MacGowan's voice was as rough as ever, chewing the words and spitting them out, rather than singing them.

It was an angry voice, Jilly decided as she hummed softly along with the chorus. Even when it sang a tender song. But what could you expect from a group that had originally named itself Pogue Mahone—Irish Gaelic for "Kiss my ass"?

Angry and brash and vulgar. The band was all of that. But they were honest, too—painfully so, at times—and that was what brought Jilly back to their music, time and again. Because sometimes things just had to be said.

"I don't get this stuff," Sue remarked.

She'd been frowning over the lyrics that were printed on the album's inner sleeve. Leaning her head against the patched backrest of one of Jilly's two old sofas, she set the sleeve aside.

"I mean, music's supposed to make you feel good, isn't it?" she went on.

Jilly shook her head. "It's supposed to make you feel *something*—happy, sad, angry, whatever—just so long as it doesn't leave you brain-dead the way most Top Forty does. For me, music needs meaning to be worth my time—preferably something more than 'I want your body, babe,' if you know what I mean."

"You're beginning to develop a snooty attitude, Jilly."

"*Me?* To laugh, dahling."

Susan Ashworth was Jilly's uptown friend, as urbane as Jilly was scruffy. Sue's blonde hair was straight, hanging to just below her shoulders, where Jilly's was a riot of brown curls, made manageable tonight only by a clip that drew it all up to the top of her head before letting it fall free in the shape of something that resembled nothing so much as a disenchanted Mohawk. They were both in their twenties, slender and blue-eyed—the latter expected in a blonde; the electric blue of Jilly's eyes gave her, with her darker skin, a look of continual startlement. Where Sue wore just the right amount of makeup, Jilly could usually be counted on having a smudge of charcoal somewhere on her face and dried oil paint under her nails.

Sue worked for the city as an architect; she lived uptown and her parents were from the Beaches, where it seemed you needed a permit just to be out on the sidewalks after eight in the evening—or at least that was the impression that the police patrols left when they stopped strangers to check their ID. She always had that upscale look of one who was just about to step out to a restaurant for cocktails and dinner.

Jilly's first love was art of a freer style than designing municipal necessities, but she usually paid her rent by waitressing and other odd jobs. She tended to wear baggy clothes—like the oversized white T-shirt and blue poplin lace-front pants she had on tonight—and always had a sketchbook close at hand.

Tonight it was on her lap as she sat propped up on her Murphy bed, toes in their ballet slippers tapping against one another in time to the music. The Pogues were playing an instrumental now—"Metropolis"—which sounded like a cross between a Celtic fiddle tune and the old "Dragnet" theme.

"They're really not for me," Sue went on. "I mean if the guy could sing, maybe, but—"

"It's the feeling that he puts into his voice that's important," Jilly said. "But this is an instrumental. He's not even—"

"Supposed to be singing. I know. Only—"

"If you'd just—"

The jangling of the phone sliced through their discussion. Because she was closer—and knew that Jilly would claim some old war wound or any excuse not to get up, now that she was lying down—Sue answered it. She listened for a long moment, an odd expression on her face, then slowly cradled the receiver.

"Wrong number?"

Sue shook her head. "No. It was someone named . . . uh, Zinc? He said that he's been captured by two Elvis Presleys disguised as police officers and would you please come and explain to them that he wasn't stealing bikes, he was just setting them free. Then he hung up."

"Oh, shit!" Jilly stuffed her sketchbook into her shoulderbag and got up.

"This makes sense to you?"

"Zinc's one of the street kids."

Sue rolled her eyes, but she got up as well. "Want me to bring my checkbook?"

"What for?"

"Bail. It's what you have to put up to spring somebody from jail. Don't you *ever* watch TV?"

Jilly shook her head. "What? And let the aliens monitor my brainwaves?"

"What scares me," Sue muttered as they left the loft and started down the stairs, "is that sometimes I don't think you're kidding."

"Who says I am?" Jilly said.

Sue shook her head. "I'm going to pretend I didn't hear that."

Jilly knew people from all over the city, in all walks of life. Socialites and bag ladies. Street kids and university profs. Nobody was too poor, or conversely, too rich for her to strike up a conversation with, no matter where they happened to meet, or under what circumstances. She'd met Detective Lou Fucceri, now of the Crowsea Precinct's General Investigations squad, when he was still a patrolman, walking the Stanton Street Combat Zone beat. He was the reason she'd survived the streets to become an artist instead of just one more statistic to add to all those others who hadn't been so lucky.

"Is it true?" Sue wanted to know as soon as the desk sergeant showed them into

Lou's office. "The way you guys met?" Jilly had told her that she'd tried to take his picture one night and he'd arrested her for soliciting.

"You mean UFO-spotting in Butler U. Park?" he replied.

Sue sighed. "I should've known. I must be the only person who's maintained her sanity after meeting Jilly."

She sat down on one of the two wooden chairs that faced Lou's desk in the small cubicle that passed for his office. There was room for a bookcase behind him, crowded with law books and file folders, and a brass coat rack from which hung a lightweight sports jacket. Lou sat at the desk, white shirt sleeves rolled halfway up to his elbows, top collar undone, black tie hanging loose.

His Italian heritage was very much present in the Mediterranean cast to his complexion, his dark brooding eyes and darker hair. As Jilly sat down in the chair Sue had left for her, he shook a cigarette free from a crumpled pack that he dug out from under the litter of files on his desk. He offered the cigarettes around, tossing the pack back down on the desk and lighting his own when there were no takers.

Jilly pulled her chair closer to the desk. "What did he do, Lou? Sue took the call, but I don't know if she got the message right."

"I *can* take a message," Sue began, but Jilly waved a hand in her direction. She wasn't in the mood for banter just now.

Lou blew a stream of blue-grey smoke towards the ceiling. "We've been having a lot of trouble with a bicycle theft ring operating in the city," he said. "They've hit the Beaches, which was bad enough, though with all the Mercedes and BMWs out there, I doubt they're going to miss their bikes a lot. But rich people like to complain, and now the gang's moved their operations into Crowsea."

Jilly nodded. "Where for a lot of people, a bicycle's the only way they *can* get around."

"You got it."

"So what does that have to do with Zinc?"

"The patrol car that picked him up found him standing in the middle of the street with a pair of heavy-duty wire cutters in his hand. The street'd been cleaned right out, Jilly. There wasn't a bike left on the block—just the cut locks and chains left behind."

"So where are the bikes?"

Lou shrugged. "Who knows. Probably in a Foxville chopshop having their serial numbers changed. Jilly, you've got to get Zinc to tell us who he was working with. Christ, they took off, leaving him to hold the bag. He doesn't owe them a thing now."

Jilly shook her head slowly. "This doesn't make any sense. Zinc's not the criminal kind."

"I'll tell you what doesn't make any sense," Lou said. "The kid himself. He's heading straight for the loonie bin with all his talk about Elvis clones and Venusian thought machines and feral fuck—" He glanced at Sue and covered up the profanity with a cough. "Feral bicycles leading the domesticated ones away."

"He said that?"

Lou nodded. "That's why he was clipping the locks—to set the bikes free so that they could follow their, and I quote, 'spiritual leader, home to the place of mystery.' "

"That's a new one," Jilly said.

"You're having me on—right?" Lou said. "That's all you can say? It's a new one?

The Elvis clones are old hat now? Christ on a comet. Would you give me a break? Just get the kid to roll over and I'll make sure things go easy for him."

"Christ on a comet?" Sue repeated softly.

"C'mon, Lou," Jilly said. "How can I make Zinc tell you something he doesn't know? Maybe he found those wire cutters on the street—just before the patrol car came. For all we know he could—"

"He *said* he cut the locks."

The air went out of Jilly. "Right," she said. She slouched in her chair. "I forgot you'd said that."

"Maybe the bikes really did just go off on their own," Sue said.

Lou gave her a weary look, but Jilly sat up straighter. "I wonder," she began.

"Oh, for God's sake," Sue said. "I was only joking."

"I know you were," Jilly said. "But I've seen enough odd things in this world that I won't say anything's impossible anymore."

"The police department doesn't see things quite the same way," Lou told Jilly. The dryness of his tone wasn't lost on her.

"I know."

"I want these bike thieves, Jilly."

"Are you arresting Zinc?"

Lou shook his head. "I've got nothing to hold him on except for circumstantial evidence."

"I thought you said he admitted to cutting the locks," Sue said.

Jilly shot her a quick fierce look that plainly said, Don't make waves when he's giving us what we came for.

Lou nodded. "Yeah. He admitted to that. He also admitted to knowing a hobo who was really a spy from Pluto and asked why the patrolmen had traded in their white Vegas suits for uniforms. He wanted to hear them sing 'Heartbreak Hotel.' For next of kin he put down Bigfoot."

"*Gigantopithecus blacki,*" Jilly said.

Lou looked at her. "What?"

"Some guy at Washington State University's given Bigfoot a Latin name now. *Giganto—*"

Lou cut her off. "That's what I thought you said." He turned back to Sue. "So you see, his admitting to cutting the locks isn't really going to amount to much. Not when a lawyer with half a brain can get him off without even having to work up a sweat."

"Does that mean he's free to go then?" Jilly asked.

Lou nodded. "Yeah. He can go. But keep him out of trouble, Jilly. He's in here again, and I'm sending him straight to the Zeb for psychiatric testing. And try to convince him to come clean on this—okay? It's not just for me, it's for him too. We break this case and find out he's involved, nobody's going to go easy on him. We don't give out rain checks."

"Not even for dinner?" Jilly asked brightly, happy now that she knew Zinc was getting out.

"What do you mean?"

Jilly grabbed a pencil and paper from his desk and scrawled "Jilly Coppercorn owes Hotshot Lou one dinner, restaurant of her choice," and passed it over to him.

"I think they call this a bribe," he said.

"I call it keeping in touch with your friends," Jilly replied and gave him a big grin.

Lou glanced at Sue and rolled his eyes.

"Don't look at me like that," she said. "I'm the sane one here."

"You wish," Jilly told her.

Lou heaved himself to his feet with exaggerated weariness. "C'mon, let's get your friend out of here before he decides to sue us because we don't have our coffee flown in from the Twilight Zone," he said as he led the way down to the holding cells.

Zinc had the look of a street kid about two days away from a good meal. His jeans, T-shirt, and cotton jacket were ragged, but clean; his hair was a badly mown lawn, with tufts standing up here and there like exclamation points. The pupils of his dark brown eyes seemed too large for someone who never did drugs. He was seventeen, but acted half his age.

The only home he had was a squat in Upper Foxville that he shared with a couple of performance artists, so that was where Jilly and Sue took him in Sue's Mazda. The living space he shared with the artists was on the upper story of a deserted tenement where someone had put together a makeshift loft by the simple method of removing all the walls, leaving a large empty area cluttered only by support pillars and the squatters' belongings.

Lucia and Ursula were there when they arrived, practicing one of their pieces to the accompaniment of a ghetto blaster pumping out a mixture of electronic music and the sound of breaking glass at a barely audible volume. Lucia was wrapped in plastic and lying on the floor, her black hair spread out in an arc around her head. Every few moments one of her limbs would twitch, the plastic wrap stretching tight against her skin with the movement. Ursula crouched beside the blaster, chanting a poem that consisted only of the line, "There are no patterns." She'd shaved her head since the last time Jilly had seen her.

"What am I doing here?" Sue asked softly. She made no effort to keep the look of astonishment from her features.

"Seeing how the other half lives," Jilly said as she led the way across the loft to where Zinc's junkyard of belongings took up a good third of the available space.

"But just look at this stuff," Sue said. "And how did he get that in here?"

She pointed to a Volkswagen bug that was sitting up on blocks, missing only its wheels and front hood. Scattered all around it was a hodgepodge of metal scraps, old furniture, boxes filled with wiring and God only knew what.

"Piece by piece," Jilly told her.

"And then he reassembled it here?"

Jilly nodded.

"Okay. I'll bite. Why?"

"Why don't you ask him?"

Jilly grinned as Sue quickly shook her head. During the entire trip from the precinct station, Zinc had carefully explained his theory of the world to her, how the planet Earth was actually an asylum for insane aliens, and that was why nothing made sense.

Zinc followed the pair of them across the room, stopping only long enough to greet his squat-mates. "Hi, Luce. Hi, Urse."

Lucia never looked at him.

"There are no patterns," Ursula said.

Zinc nodded thoughtfully.

"Maybe there's a pattern in that," Sue offered.

"Don't start," Jilly said. She turned to Zinc. "Are you going to be all right?"

"You should've seen them go, Jill," Zinc said. "All shiny and wet, just whizzing down the street, heading for the hills."

"I'm sure it was really something, but you've got to promise me to stay off the streets for awhile. Will you do that, Zinc? At least until they catch this gang of bike thieves?"

"But there weren't any thieves. It's like I told Elvis Two, they left on their own."

Sue gave him an odd look. "Elvis too?"

"Don't ask," Jilly said. She touched Zinc's arm. "Just stay in for awhile—okay? Let the bikes take off on their own."

"But I like to watch them go."

"Do it as a favor to me, would you?"

"I'll try."

Jilly gave him a quick smile. "Thanks. Is there anything you need? Do you need money for some food?"

Zinc shook his head. Jilly gave him a quick kiss on the cheek and tousled the exclamation point hair tufts sticking up from his head.

"I'll drop by to see you tomorrow, then—okay?" At his nod, Jilly started back across the room. "C'mon, Sue," she said when her companion paused beside the tape machine where Ursula was still chanting.

"So what about this stock market stuff?" she asked the poet.

"There are no patterns," Ursula said.

"That's what I thought," Sue said, but then Jilly was tugging her arm.

"Couldn't resist, could you?" Jilly said.

Sue just grinned.

"Why do you humor him?" Sue asked when she pulled up in front of Jilly's loft.

"What makes you think I am?"

"I'm being serious, Jilly."

"So am I. He believes in what he's talking about. That's good enough for me."

"But all this stuff he goes on about . . . Elvis clones and insane aliens—"

"Don't forget animated bicycles."

Sue gave Jilly a pained look. "I'm not. That's just what I mean—it's all so crazy."

"What if it's not?"

Sue shook her head. "I can't buy it."

"It's not hurting anybody." Jilly leaned over and gave Sue a quick kiss on the cheek. "Gotta run. Thanks for everything."

"Maybe it's hurting him," Sue said as Jilly opened the door to get out. "Maybe it's closing the door on any chance he has of living a normal life. You know—opportunity comes knocking, but there's nobody home? He's not just eccentric, Jilly. He's crazy."

Jilly sighed. "His mother was a hooker, Sue. The reason he's a little flaky is her pimp threw him down two flights of stairs when he was six years old—not because

Zinc did anything, or because his mother didn't trick enough johns that night, but just because the creep felt like doing it. That's what normal was for Zinc. He's happy now—a lot happier than when Social Services tried to put him in a foster home where they only wanted him for the support check they got once a month for taking him in. And a lot happier than he'd be in the Zeb, all doped up or sitting around in a padded cell whenever he tried to tell people about the things he sees.

"He's got his own life now. It's not much—not by your standards, maybe not even by mine, but it's his and I don't want anybody to take it away from him."

"But—"

"I know you mean well," Jilly said, "but things don't always work out the way we'd like them to. Nobody's got time for a kid like Zinc in Social Services. There he's just a statistic that they shuffle around with all the rest of their files and red tape. Out here on the street, we've got a system that works. We take care of our own. It's that simple. Doesn't matter if it's the Cat Lady, sleeping in an alleyway with a half dozen mangy toms, or Rude Ruthie, haranguing the commuters on the subway, we take care of each other."

"Utopia," Sue said.

A corner of Jilly's mouth twitched with the shadow of a humorless smile. "Yeah. I know. We've got a high asshole quotient, but what can you do? You try to get by— that's all. You just try to get by."

"I wish I could understand it better," Sue said.

"Don't worry about it. You're good people, but this just isn't your world. You can visit, but you wouldn't want to live in it, Sue."

"I guess."

Jilly started to add something more, but then just smiled encouragingly and got out of the car.

"See you Friday?" she asked, leaning in the door.

Sue nodded.

Jilly stood on the pavement and watched the Mazda until it turned the corner and its rear lights were lost from view, then she went upstairs to her apartment. The big room seemed too quiet and she felt too wound up to sleep, so she put a cassette in the tape player—Lynn Harrell playing a Schumann concerto—and started to prepare a new canvas to work on in the morning when the light would be better.

2

It was raining again, a soft drizzle that put a glistening sheen on the streets and lamp-posts, on porch handrails and street signs. Zinc stood in the shadows that had gathered in the mouth of an alleyway, his new pair of wire cutters a comfortable weight in his hand. His eyes sparked with reflected lights. His hair was damp against his scalp. He licked his lips, tasting mountains heights and distant forests within the drizzle's slightly metallic tang.

Jilly knew a lot about things that were, he thought, and things that might be, and she always meant well, but there was one thing she just couldn't get right. You didn't make art by capturing an image on paper, or canvas, or in stone. You didn't make it by writing down stories and poems. Music and dance came closest to what real art was—but only so long as you didn't try to record or film it. Musical notation was only so much dead ink on paper. Choreography was planning, not art.

You could only make art by setting it free. Anything else was just a memory, no matter how you stored it. On film or paper, sculpted or recorded.

Everything that existed, existed in a captured state. Animate or inanimate, everything wanted to be free.

That's what the lights said; that was their secret. Wild lights in the night skies, and domesticated lights, right here on the street, they all told the same tale. It was so plain to see when you knew *how* to look. Didn't neon and streetlights yearn to be starlight?

To be free.

He bent down and picked up a stone, smiling at the satisfying crack it made when it broke the glass protection of the streetlight, his grin widening as the light inside flickered, then died.

It was part of the secret now, part of the voices that spoke in the night sky.

Free.

Still smiling, he set out across the street to where a bicycle was chained to the railing of a porch.

"Let me tell you about art," he said to it as he mounted the stairs.

Psycho Puppies were playing at the YoMan on Gracie Street near the corner of Landis Avenue that Friday night. They weren't anywhere near as punkish as their name implied. If they had been, Jilly would never have been able to get Sue out to see them.

"I don't care if they damage themselves," she'd told Jilly the one and only time she'd gone out to one of the punk clubs further west on Gracie, "but I refuse to pay good money just to have someone spit at me and do their best to rupture my eardrums."

The Puppies were positively tame compared to how that punk band had been. Their music was loud, but melodic, and while there was an undercurrent of social conscience to their lyrics, you could dance to them as well. Jilly couldn't help but smile to see Sue stepping it up to a chorus of, "You can take my job, but you can't take me, ain't nobody gonna steal my dignity."

The crowd was an even mix of slumming uptowners, Crowsea artistes and the neighborhood kids from surrounding Foxville. Jilly and Sue danced with each other, not from lack of offers, but because they didn't want to feel obligated to any guy that night. Too many men felt that one dance entitled them to ownership—for the night, at least, if not forever—and neither of them felt like going through the ritual repartee that the whole business required.

Sue was on the right side of a bad relationship at the moment, while Jilly was simply eschewing relationships on general principle these days. Relationships required changes, and she wasn't ready for changes in her life just now. And besides, all the men she'd ever cared for were already taken and she didn't think it likely that she'd run into her own particular Prince Charming in a Foxville night club.

"I like this band," Sue confided to her when they took a break to finish the beers they'd ordered at the beginning of the set.

Jilly nodded, but she didn't have anything to say. A glance across the room caught a glimpse of a head with hair enough like Zinc's badly-mown lawn scalp to remind her that he hadn't been home when she'd dropped by his place on the way to the club tonight.

Don't be out setting bicycles free, Zinc, she thought.

"Hey, Tomas. Check this out."

There were two of them, one Anglo, one Hispanic, neither of them much more than a year or so older than Zinc. They both wore leather jackets and jeans, dark hair greased back in ducktails. The drizzle put a sheen on their jackets and hair. The Hispanic moved closer to see what his companion was pointing out.

Zinc had melted into the shadows at their approach. The streetlights that he had yet to free whispered, *careful, careful,* as they wrapped him in darkness, their electric light illuminating the pair on the street.

"Well, shit," the Hispanic said. "Somebody's doing our work for us."

As he picked up the lock that Zinc had just snipped, the chain holding the bike to the railing fell to the pavement with a clatter. Both teenagers froze, one checking out one end of the street, his companion the other.

" 'Scool," the Anglo said. "Nobody here but you, me and your cooties."

"Chew on a big one."

"I don't do myself, *puto.*"

"That's 'cos it's too small to find."

The pair of them laughed—a quick nervous sound that belied their bravado—then the Anglo wheeled the bike away from the railing.

"Hey, Bobby-o," the Hispanic said. "Got another one over here."

"Well, what're you waiting for, man? Wheel her down to the van."

They were setting bicycles free, Zinc realized—just like he was. He'd gotten almost all the way down the block, painstakingly snipping the shackle of each lock, before the pair had arrived.

Careful, careful, the streetlights were still whispering, but Zinc was already moving out of the shadows.

"Hi, guys," he said.

The teenagers froze, then the Anglo's gaze took in the wire cutters in Zinc's hand.

"Well, well," he said. "What've we got here? What're you doing on the night side of the street, kid?"

Before Zinc could reply, the sound of a siren cut the air. A lone siren, approaching fast.

The Chinese waitress looked great in her leather miniskirt and fishnet stockings. She wore a blood-red camisole tucked into the waist of the skirt which made her pale skin seem even paler. Her hair was the black of polished jet, pulled up in a loose bun that spilled stray strands across her neck and shoulders. Blue-black eye shadow made her dark eyes darker. Her lips were the same red as her camisole.

"How come she looks so good," Sue wanted to know, "when I'd just look like a tart if I dressed like that?"

"She's inscrutable," Jilly replied. "You're just obvious."

"How sweet of you to point that out," Sue said with a grin. She stood up from their table. "C'mon. Let's dance."

Jilly shook her head. "You go ahead. I'll sit this one out."

"Uh-uh. I'm not going out there alone."

"There's LaDonna," Jilly said, pointing out a girl they both knew. "Dance with her."

"Are you feeling all right, Jilly?"

"I'm fine—just a little pooped. Give me a chance to catch my breath."

But she wasn't all right, she thought as Sue crossed over to where LaDonna da Costa and her brother Pipo were sitting. Not when she had Zinc to worry about. If he was out there, cutting off the locks of more bicycles . . .

You're not his mother, she told herself. Except—

Out here on the streets we take care of our own.

That's what she'd told Sue. And maybe it wasn't true for a lot of people who hit the skids—the winos and the losers and the bag people who were just too screwed up to take care of themselves, little say look after anyone else—but it was true for her.

Someone like Zinc—he was an in-betweener. Most days he could take care of himself just fine, but there was a fey streak in him so that sometimes he carried a touch of the magic that ran wild in the streets, the magic that was loose late at night when the straights were in bed and the city belonged to the night people. That magic took up lodgings in people like Zinc. For a week. A day. An hour. Didn't matter if it was real or not, if it couldn't be measured or catalogued, it was real to them. It existed all the same.

Did that make it true?

Jilly shook her head. It wasn't her kind of question and it didn't matter anyway. Real or not, it could still be driving Zinc into breaking corporeal laws—the kind that'd have Lou breathing down his neck, real fast. The kind that'd put him in jail with a whole different kind of loser.

Zinc wouldn't last out a week inside.

Jilly got up from the table and headed across the dance floor to where Sue and LaDonna were jitterbugging to a tune that sounded as though Buddy Holly could have penned the melody, if not the words.

"Fuck this, man!" the Anglo said.

He threw down the bike and took off at a run, his companion right on his heels, scattering puddles with the impact of their boots. Zinc watched them go. There was a buzzing in the back of his head. The streetlights were telling him to run too, but he saw the bike lying there on the pavement like a wounded animal, one wheel spinning forlornly, and he couldn't just take off.

Bikes were like turtles. Turn 'em on their backs—or a bike on its side—and they couldn't get up on their own again.

He tossed down the wire cutters and ran to the bike. Just as he was leaning it up against the railing from which the Anglo had taken it, a police cruiser came around the corner, skidding on the wet pavement, cherry light gyrating—screaming, *Run, run!* in its urgent high-pitched voice—headlights pinning Zinc where he stood.

Almost before the cruiser came to a halt, the passenger door popped open and a uniformed officer had stepped out. He drew his gun. Using the cruiser as a shield, he aimed across its roof at where Zinc was standing.

"Hold it right there, kid!" he shouted. "Don't even blink."

Zinc was privy to secrets. He could hear voices in lights. He knew that there was more to be seen in the world if you watched it from the corner of your eye than head on. It was a simple truth that every policeman he ever saw looked just like Elvis. But he hadn't survived all his years on the streets without protection.

He had a lucky charm. A little tin monkey pendant that had originally lived in a box of Crackerjacks—back when Crackerjacks had real prizes in them. Lucia had given it to him. He'd forgotten to bring it out with him the other night when the Elvises had taken him in. But he wasn't stupid. He'd remembered it tonight.

He reached into his pocket to get it out and wake its magic.

"You're just being silly," Sue said as they collected their jackets from their chairs.

"So humor me," Jilly asked.

"I'm coming, aren't I?"

Jilly nodded. She could hear the voice of Zinc's roommate Ursula in the back of her head—

There are no patterns.

—but she could feel one right now, growing tight as a drawn bowstring, humming with its urgency to be loosed.

"C'mon," she said, almost running from the club.

Police officer Mario Hidalgo was still a rookie—tonight was only the beginning of his third month of active duty—and while he'd drawn his sidearm before, he had yet to fire it in the line of duty. He had the makings of a good cop. He was steady, he was conscientious. The street hadn't had a chance to harden him yet, though it had already thrown him more than a couple of serious uglies in his first eight weeks of active duty.

But steady though he'd proved himself to be so far, when he saw the kid reaching into his pocket of his baggy jacket, Hidalgo had a single moment of unreasoning panic.

The kid's got a gun, that panic told him. The kid's going for a weapon.

One moment was all it took.

His finger was already tightening on the trigger of his regulation .38 as the kid's hand came out of his pocket. Hidalgo wanted to stop the pressure he was putting on the gun's trigger, but it was like there was a broken circuit between his brain and his hand.

The gun went off with a deafening roar.

Got it, Zinc thought as his fingers closed on the little tin monkey charm. Got my luck.

He started to take it out of his pocket, but then something hit him straight in the chest. It lifted him off his feet and threw him against the wall behind him with enough force to knock all the wind out of his lungs. There was a raw pain firing every one of his nerve ends. His hands opened and closed spastically, the charm falling out of his grip to hit the ground moments before his body slid down the wall to join it on the wet pavement.

Goodbye, goodbye, sweet friend, the streetlights cried.

He could sense the spin of the stars as they wheeled high above the city streets, their voices joining the electric voices of the streetlights.

My turn to go free, he thought as a white tunnel opened in his mind. He could feel it draw him in, and then he was falling, falling, falling. . . .

"Goodbye. . . ." he said, thought he said, but no words came forth from between his lips.

Just a trickle of blood that mingled with the rain that now began to fall in earnest, as though it, too, was saying its own farewell.

All Jilly had to see was the red spinning cherries of the police cruisers to know where the pattern she'd felt in the club was taking her. There were a lot of cars here—cruisers and unmarked vehicles, an ambulance—all on official business, their presence coinciding with her business. She didn't see Lou approach until he laid his hand on her shoulder.

"You don't want to see," he told her.

Jilly never even looked at him. One moment he was holding her shoulder, the next she'd shrugged herself free of his grip and just kept on walking.

"Is it . . . is it Zinc?" Sue asked the detective.

Jilly didn't have to ask. She knew. Without being told. Without having to see the body.

An officer stepped in front of her to stop her, but Lou waved him aside. In her peripheral vision she saw another officer sitting inside a cruiser, weeping, but it didn't really register.

"I thought he had a gun," the policeman was saying as she went by. "Oh, Jesus. I thought the kid was going for a gun. . . ."

And then she was standing over Zinc's body, looking down at his slender frame, limbs flung awkwardly like those of a rag doll that had been tossed into a corner and forgotten. She knelt down at Zinc's side. Something glinted on the wet pavement. A small tin monkey charm. She picked it up, closed it tightly in her fist before anyone could see what she'd done.

"C'mon, Jilly," Lou said as he came up behind her. He helped her to her feet.

It didn't seem possible that anyone as vibrant—as *alive*—as Zinc had been could have any relation whatsoever with that empty shell of a body that lay there on the pavement.

As Lou led her away from the body, Jilly's tears finally came, welling up from her eyes to salt the rain on her cheek.

"He . . . he wasn't . . . stealing bikes, Lou. . . ." she said.

"It doesn't look good," Lou said.

Often when she'd been with Zinc, Jilly had had a sense of that magic that touched him. A feeling that even if she couldn't see the marvels he told her about, they still existed just beyond the reach of her sight.

That feeling should be gone now, she thought.

"He was just . . . setting them free," she said.

The magic should have died, when he died. But she felt, if she just looked hard enough, that she'd see him, riding a maverick bike at the head of a pack of riderless bicycles—metal frames glistening, reflector lights glinting red, wheels throwing up arcs of fine spray, as they went off down the wet street.

Around the corner and out of sight.

"Nice friends the kid had," a plainclothes detective who was standing near them said to the uniformed officer beside him. "Took off with just about every bike on the street and left him holding the bag."

Jilly didn't think so. Not this time.

This time they'd gone free.

That Explains Poland

1

Maybe that explains Poland.

Lori's mother used to say that. In the fullness of her Stalinism, the great hamster (as Lori called her) was convinced that every radical twitch to come from Poland and Solidarity was in fact inspired by the CIA, drug addicts, M&Ms, reruns of "The Honeymooners" ("To the moon, Alice!") . . . in fact, just about everything except the possibility of real dissension among the Polish people with their less than democratic regime. It got to the point where she was forever saying "That explains Poland!", regardless of how absurd or incomprehensible the connection.

It became a family joke—*a proposito* to any and all situations and shared by sundry and all, in and about the Snelling clan. You still don't get it?

Maybe you just had to be there.

2

"Listen to this: `bigfoot spied in upper foxville`," Lori read from the Friday edition of *The Daily Journal*. "Bigfoot. Can you believe it? I mean, can you *believe* it?"

Ruth and I feigned indifference. We were used to Lori's outbursts by now and even though half the *clientela* in The Monkey Woman's Nest lifted their heads from whatever had been occupying them to look our way, we merely sipped our beer and looked out onto Williamson Street, watching the commuters hustle down into the subways or jockeying for position at the bus stop.

Lori was an eventful sort of a person. You could always count on something happening around her, with a ninety-nine percent chance that she'd been the catalyst. On a Friday afternoon, with the week's work behind us and two glorious days off ahead, we didn't need an event. Just a quiet moment and a few beers in *la Hora Frontera* before the streets woke up and the clubs opened their doors.

"Who's playing at Your Second Home this weekend?" Ruth asked.

I wasn't sure, but I had other plans anyway. "I was thinking of taking in that new Rob Lowe movie if it's still playing."

Ruth got a gleam in her eye. "He is *so* dreamy. Every time I see him I just want to take him home and—"

"Don't be such a pair of old poops," Lori interrupted. "This is important. It's history in the making. Just listen to what it says." She gave the paper a snap to keep our attention, which set off another round of lifting heads throughout the restaurant, and started to read.

"The recent sighting of a large, hairy, human-like creature in the back alleys of Upper Foxville has prompted Councilman Cohen to renew his demands for increased police patrols in that section of the city. Eyewitness Barry Jack spotted the huge beast about 1 am last night. He estimated it stood between seven and eight feet tall and weighed about 300 to 400 pounds."

"Lori . . ."

"Let me finish.

" 'While I doubt that the creature seen by Mr. Jack—that a Bigfoot—exists,' Cohen is quoted as saying, 'it does emphasize the increased proliferation of transients and the homeless in this area of the city, a problem that the City Council is doing very little about, despite continual requests by residents and this Council member.'*

"Right." Lori gave us a quick grin. "Well, *that's* stretching a point way beyond *my* credibility."

"Lori, what are you talking about?" I asked.

"The way Cohen's dragging in this business of police patrols." She went back to the article.

"Could such a creature exist? According to archaeology professor Helmet Goddin of Butler University, 'Not in the city. Sightings of Bigfoot or the Sasquatch are usually relegated to wilderness areas, a description that doesn't apply to Upper Foxville, regardless of its resemblance to an archaeological dig.'

"Which is just his way of saying the place is a disaster area," Lori added. "No surprises there."

She held up a hand before either Ruth or I could speak and plunged on.

"Goddin says that the Sasquatch possibly resulted from some division in the homonid line, which evolved separately from humans. He speculates that they are 'more intelligent than apes . . . and apes can be very intelligent. If it does exist, then it is a very, very important biological and anthropological discovery.'"

Lori laid the paper down and sipped some of her beer. "So," she said as she set the glass back down precisely in its ring of condensation on the table. "What do you think?"

"Think about what?" Ruth asked.

Lori tapped the newspaper. "Of this." At our blank looks, she added, "It's something we can do this weekend. We can go hunting for Bigfoot in Upper Foxville."

I could tell from Ruth's expression that the idea had about as much appeal for her as it did for me. Spend the weekend crawling about the rubble of Upper Foxville and risk getting jumped by some junkie or hobo? No thanks.

Lori's studied Shotokan karate and could probably have held her own against Bruce Lee, but Ruth and I were just a couple of Crowsea punkettes, about as useful in a confrontation as a handful of wet noodles. And going into Upper Foxville to chase down some big *muchacho* who'd been mistaken for a Sasquatch was not my idea of fun. I'm way too young for suicide.

"Hunting?" I said. "With what?"

Lori pulled a small Instamatic from her purse. "With this, LaDonna. What else?"

I lifted my brows and looked to Ruth for help, but she was too busy laughing at the look on my face.

Right, I thought. Goodbye, Rob Lowe—it could've been *mucho primo*. Instead I'm going on a *gaza de grillos* with Crowsea's resident madwomen. Who said a weekend had to be boring?

3

I do a lot of thinking about decisions—not so much trying to make up my mind about something as just wondering, *¿que si?* Like if I hadn't decided to skip school that day with my brother Pipo and taken El Sub to the Pier, then I'd never have met Ruth. Ruth introduced me to Lori and Lori introduced me to more trouble than I could ever have gotten into on my own.

Not that I was a Little Miss Innocent before I met Lori. I looked like the kind of *muchacha* that your mother warned you not to hang around with. I liked my black jeans tight and my leather skirt short, but I wasn't a *puta* or anything. It was just for fun. The kind of trouble I got into was for staying out too late, or skipping school, or getting caught having a cigarette with the other girls behind the gym, or coming home with the smell of beer on my breath.

Little troubles. Ordinary ones.

The kind of trouble I got into with Lori was always *mucho* weird. Like the time we went looking for pirate treasure in the storm sewers under the Beaches—the ritzy area where Lori's parents lived before they got divorced. We were down there for hours, all dressed up in her father's spelunking gear, and just about drowned when it started to rain and the sewers filled up. Needless to say, her *papa* was *not* pleased at the mess we made of his gear.

And then there was the time that we hid in the washrooms at the Watley's Department Store downtown and spent the whole night trying on dresses, rearranging the mannequins, eating chocolates from the candy department. . . . If it had been just me on my own—coming from the barrios and all—I'd've ended up in jail. But being with Lori, her *papa* bailed us out and paid for the chocolates and one broken mannequin. We didn't do much for the rest of that summer except for gardening and odd jobs until we'd worked off what we owed him.

¿No muy loco? Verdad, we were only thirteen, and it was just the start. But that's all in the past. I'm grown up now—just turned twenty-one last week. Been on my own for four years, working steady. But I still wonder sometimes.

About decisions.

How different everything might have been if I hadn't done this, or if I *had* done that.

I've never been to Poland. I wonder what it's like.

4

"We'll set it up like a scavenger hunt," Lori said. She paused as the waitress brought another round—Heinekin for Lori, Miller Lites for Ruth and I—then leaned forward, elbows on the table, the palms of her hands cupping her chin. "With a prize and everything."

"What kind of a prize?" Ruth wanted to know.

"Losers take the winner out for dinner to the restaurant of her choice."

"Hold everything," I said. "Are you saying we each go out by ourselves to try to snap a shot of this thing?"

I had visions of the three of us in Upper Foxville, each of us wandering along our own street, the deserted tenements on all sides, the only company being the bums, junkies and *cabrones* that hung out there.

"I don't want to end up as just another statistic," I said.

"Oh, come on. We're around there all the time, hitting the clubs. When's the last time you heard of any trouble?"

"Give me the paper and I'll tell you," I said, reaching for the *Journal.*

"You want to go at *night*?" Ruth asked.

"We go whenever we choose," Lori replied. "The first one with a genuine picture wins."

"I can just see the three of us disappearing in there," I said. " 'The lost women of Foxville flats.' "

"Beats being remembered as loose women," Lori said.

"We'd be just another urban legend."

Ruth nodded. "Like in one of Christy Riddell's stories."

I shook my head. "No thanks. He makes the unreal too real. Anyway, I was thinking more of that Brunvand guy with his choking Doberman and Mexican pets."

"Those are all just stories," Lori said, trying to sound like Christopher Lee. She came off like a bad Elvira. "This could be real."

"Do you *really* believe that?" I asked.

"No. But I think it'll be a bit of fun. Are you scared?"

"I'm sane, aren't I? Of course I'm scared."

"Oh, poop."

"That doesn't mean I'm not up for it."

I wondered if it wasn't too late to have my head examined. Did the hospital handle that kind of thing in their emergency ward?

"Good for you, LaDonna," Lori was saying. "What about you, Ruth?"

"Not at night."

"We'll get the jump on you."

"Not at night," she repeated.

"Not at night," I agreed.

Lori's eyes had that mad little gleam in them that let me know that we'd been had again. She'd never planned on going at night either.

"A toast," she said, raising her beer. "May the best woman win."

We clinked our mugs against each other's and made plans for the night while we finished our beer. I don't think anyone in the restaurant was sorry to see us go when we finally left. First up was the early show at the Oxford (you didn't really think I'd stand you up, did you, Rob?), then the last couple of sets at the Zorb, where the Fat Man Blues Band was playing, because Ruth was crazy about their bass player and Lori and I liked to egg her on.

5

By now you're probably thinking that we're just a bunch of airheads, out for laughs and not concerned with anything important. Well, it isn't true. I think about things all the time. Like how hanging around with Anglos so much has got me to the point where half the time I sound like one myself. I can hardly speak to my grandmother these days. I don't even think in Spanish anymore and it bothers me.

It's only in the barrio that I still speak it, but I don't go there much—just to visit the family on birthdays and holidays. I worked hard to get out, but sometimes when I'm in my apartment on Lee Street in Crowsea, sitting in the windowseat and looking out at the park, I wonder why. I've got a nice place there, a decent job, some good friends. But I don't have any roots. There's nothing connecting me to this part of the city.

I could vanish overnight (disappear in Upper Foxville on a *caza de grillos*), and it wouldn't cause much more than a ripple. Back home, the *abuelas* are *still* talking about how Donita's youngest girl moved to Crowsea and when was she going to settle down?

I don't really know anybody I can talk to about this kind of thing. Neither my Anglo friends nor my own people would understand. But I think about it. Not a lot, but I think about it. And about decisions. About all kinds of things.

Ruth says I think too much.

Lori just wonders why I'm always trying to explain Poland. You'd think I was her mother or something.

6

Saturday morning, bright and early, and only a little hungover, we got off the Yoors Street subway and followed the stairs up from the underground station to where they spat us out on the corner of Gracie Street and Yoors. Gracie Street's the *frontera* between Upper Foxville and Foxville proper. South of Gracie it's all low-rent apartment buildings and tenements, shabby old *viviendas* that manage to hang on to an old world feel, mostly because it's still families living here, just like it's been for a hundred years. The people take care of their neighborhood, no differently than their parents did before them.

North of Gracie a bunch of developers got together and planned to give the area a new facelift. I've seen the plans—condominiums, shopping malls, parks. Basically what they wanted to do was shove a high class suburb into the middle of the city. Only what happened was their backers pulled out while they were in the middle of leveling about a square mile of city blocks, so now the whole area's just a mess of empty buildings and rubble-strewn lots.

It's creepy, looking out on it from Gracie Street. It's like standing on the line of a map that divides civilization from no-man's-land. You almost expect some graffiti to say, "Here there be dragons." And maybe they wouldn't be so far off. Because you can find dragons in Upper Foxville—the *muy malo* kind that ride chopped-down Harleys. The Devil's Dragon. Bikers making deals with their junkies. I think I'd prefer the kind that breathe fire.

I don't like the open spaces of rubble in Upper Foxville. My true self—the way I see me—is like an alley cat, crouching for shelter under a car, watching the world go by. I'm comfortable in Crowsea's narrow streets and alleyways. They're like the barrio where I got my street smarts. It's easy to duck away from trouble, to get lost in the shadows. To hang out and watch, but not be seen. Out there, in those desolate blocks north of Gracie, there's no place to hide, and too many places—all at the same time.

If that kind of thing bothered Lori, she sure wasn't showing it. She was all decked out in fatigues, hiking boots and a khaki-colored shoulderbag like she was in the Army Reserves and going out on maneuvers or something. Ruth was almost as bad, only she went to the other extreme. She was wearing baggy white cotton pants with a puffed sleeve blouse and a trendy vest, low-heeled sandals and a matching purse.

Me? That morning I dressed with survival in mind, not fashion. I had my yellow jeans and my red hightops, an old black Motorhead T-shirt and a scuffed leather jacket that I hoped would make me look tough. I had some of my hair up in a top-knot, the rest all *loco,* and went heavy on the makeup. My camera—a *barato* little Vitoret that I'd borrowed from Pipo last fall and still hadn't returned yet—was stuffed in a shapeless canvas shoulderbag. All I wanted to do was fit in.

Checking out the skateboarders and other kids already clogging up Gracie's sidewalks, I didn't think I was doing too bad a job. Especially when this little *muchacho* with a pink Mohawk came whipping over on his board and tried to put the moves on me. I felt like I was sixteen again.

"Well, I'm going straight up Yoors," Lori said. "Everybody got their cameras and some film?"

Ruth and I dutifully patted our purse and shoulderbag respectively.

"I guess I'll try the Tombs," I said.

It only took a week after the machines stopped pushing over the buildings for people to start dumping everything from old car parts to bags of trash in the blocks between Lanois and Flood north of MacNeil. People took to calling it the Tombs because of all the wrecked vehicles.

I'd had some time to think things through over a breakfast of black coffee this morning—a strangely lucid moment, considering the night before. I'd almost decided on getting my friend Izzy from the apartment downstairs to hide out in an ape suit somewhere in the rubble, and then it hit me. Lori probably had something similar planned. She'd have Ruth and I tramping around through the rubble, getting all hot and sweaty, and more than a little tense, and then she'd produce a photo of some friend of *hers* in an ape suit, snapped slightly out of focus as he was ducking into some run-down old building. It'd be good for a laugh and a free dinner and it was just the kind of stunt Lori'd pull. I mean, we could have been doing some serious shopping today. . . .

My new plan was to head out towards the Tombs, then work my way over to Yoors where I'd follow Lori and take my picture of her and her pal in his monkeysuit. *Mama* didn't raise any stupid kids, no matter what her neighbors thought.

So I gave them both a jaunty wave and set off down Gracie to where Lanois would take me north into the Tombs. Lori went up Yoors. Ruth was still standing by the stairs going down to the subway station by the time I lost sight of her, looking back through the crowds. My pink Mohawked admirer followed me until I turned up towards the Tombs, then he went whizzing back to his friends, expertly guiding his skateboard down the congested sidewalk like the pro he was. He couldn't have been more than thirteen.

7

When you're a *niña*—and maybe twenty-one is still being a kid to some people—it's not so weird to be worrying about who you are and how you're ever going to fit in. But then you're supposed to get a handle on things and by the time you're my age, you've got it all pretty well figured out. At least that's the impression I got when I was a *niña* and twenty-one looked like it was about as old as you ever wanted to get.

Verdad, I still don't know who I am or where I fit in. I stand in front of the mirror and the *muchacha* I see studying me just as carefully as I'm studying her *looks* older. But I don't feel any different from when I was fifteen.

So when does it happen?

Maybe it never does.

Maybe that explains Poland.

8

All things considered—I mean, this *was* Upper Foxville—it wasn't a bad day to be scuffling around in the Tombs. The sun was bright in a sky so blue it hurt to look at it. Good thing I hadn't forgotten my shades. Broken glass shimmered and gleamed in the light and crunched underfoot.

What's this thing people have for busting windows and bottles and the like? It seems like all you need is an unbroken piece of glass and rocks just sort of pop into people's hands. Of course it makes such an interesting sound when it breaks. And it gives you such a feeling of . . . oh, I don't know. Having *cojones,* I suppose. What's that song by Nick Lowe? "I Love the Sound of Breaking Glass." Not that I'm into that kind of thing—okay, at least not anymore. And better it be in a place like this than on the sidewalk or streets where people have to walk or go wheeling by on their bikes.

I was feeling pretty punky by the time I'd been in the Tombs for an hour or so. That always happens when I wear my leather jacket. I may not be a real *machona*—or at least not capable of violence, let's say—but the jacket makes me *feel* tough anyway. It says don't mess with me all over it. Not that there was anybody there to mess around with me.

I spotted a few dogs—feral, mangy-looking *perros* that kept their distance. The rat that surprised me as I came around a corner was a lot less forgiving about having its morning disturbed. It stood its ground until I pitched a rock at it, then it just sort of melted away, slinky and fast.

It was early for the junkies and other lowlifes that were out in full force come late afternoon, but the bag ladies were making their rounds, all bundled up in layers of coats and dresses, pushing their homes and belongings around in shopping carts or carrying it all about in plastic shopping bags. I passed winos, sleeping off last night's booze, and hoboes huddled around small fires, taking their time about waking up before they hit the streets of Foxville and Crowsea to panhandle the Saturday crowds. They gave me the creeps, staring at me like I didn't belong—fair enough, I guess, since I didn't—obviously thinking what the hell was I doing here? Would you believe looking for Bigfoot? Didn't think so.

Did I mention the smell? If you've ever been to a dump, you'll know what I mean. It's a sweet-sour cloying smell that gets into your clothes and hair and just hangs in there. You could get used to it, I guess—it stopped bothering me after the first fifteen minutes or so—but I wouldn't want to have to be sitting next to me on El Sub going home.

I guess I killed an hour or so before I worked my way west towards Yoors Street to look for Lori. It was kind of fun, playing Indian scout in the rubble. I got so involved in sneaking around that I almost ran right into them.

Them. Yeah, I was right. Lori was sitting on what was left of some building's front steps, sharing a beer with a guy named Byron Murphy. Near Byron's knee was a plastic shopping bag out of which spilled something that looked remarkably like a flat ape's arm. I mean the arm was flat, because it was part of a costume and there was nobody in it at the moment. Come to think of it, that *would* make it a flat ape, wouldn't it?

Byron worked at the sports clinic at Butler U. as a therapist. Like most of Lori's old boyfriends, he'd stayed her friend after they broke up. That kind of thing never happens to me. When I break up with a guy it usually involves various household objects flying through the air aimed for his head. You'd think I had a Latin temper or something.

I backed up quickly, but I shouldn't have worried. Neither of them had spotted me. I thought about trying to find Ruth, then realized that I'd have to wait until later to let her in on the joke. What I didn't want to do was miss getting this all down on film. Byron putting on the apesuit. The two of them setting up the shot. I wanted the whole thing. Maybe I could even sell my photos to *The Daily Journal*—

"bigfoot hoaxers caught in the act"—and really play the trick back on her.

Circling around them, I made my way to an old deserted brownstone and went in. After checking around first to make sure I was alone, I got comfortable by a window where I had a perfect view of Lori and Byron and settled down to wait.

Gotcha now, Lori.

9

The best kinds of practical jokes are those that backfire on whoever's playing the trick. Didn't you ever want to get a camera on Alan Funt and catch *him* looking silly for a change? I didn't get many opportunities to catch Lori—and don't think I haven't tried. (Remind me to tell you the story of the thirty-five pizzas and the priest sometime.) The trouble with Lori is that she doesn't think linearly or even in intuitive leaps. Her mind tends to move sideways in its thinking, which makes it hard to catch her out, since you haven't a clue what she's on about in the first place.

She gets it from her mother, I guess.

It might not explain Poland, but it says volumes about genetics.

10

I had to wait a half hour before they finally pulled the gorilla suit out of the bag. It didn't fit Byron all that well, but did an okay job from a distance. I figured Lori would put him in the shadows of the building on the other side of the street and move the camera a bit while she was taking her shot. Nothing's quite so effective as a slightly blurry, dark shot when you're dealing with whacko things like a Bigfoot or flying saucers.

Me, I was wishing for a telephoto lens and a decent camera, but I was pretty sure the Vitoret would work fine. We weren't talking high art here. Anyway, I could always have the prints blown up—and no, smart guy, I'm not talking about dynamite.

I got the whole thing on film. Byron putting on the costume. Lori posing him, taking her shots. Byron taking the costume off and stashing it away. The two of them leaving. All I wanted to do was lean out the window and shout, "Nya nya!," but I kept my mouth shut and let them go. Then, camera in hand, I left the building by the back, heading for the Tombs.

There were no steps, so I had to jump down a three-foot drop. I paused at the top to put away my camera, and then I froze.

Not twenty yards away, a huge figure in a bulky overcoat and slouched down hat was shuffling through the rubble. Before I could duck away, the figure turned and I was looking straight into this hairy face.

I don't quite know how to describe him to you. You're not going to believe me anyway and words just don't quite do justice to the *feeling* of the moment.

He wasn't wearing anything under the overcoat and the sun was bright enough so that I could see he was covered with hair all over. It was a fine pelt—more like an ape's than a bear's—a rich dark brown that was glossy where it caught the sun. His feet were huge, his chest like a barrel, his arms like a weightlifter's. But his face . . . It was human, and it wasn't. It was like an ape's, but it wasn't. The nose was flat, but the cheekbones were delicate under the fine covering of hair. His lips were thin, chin square. And his eyes . . . They were a warm brown liquid color, full of smarts, no question about it. And they were looking straight at me, thinking about what kind of a threat I posed for him.

Let me tell you, my heart stopped dead in my chest. It was all a joke, right? Lori's gag that I was playing back on her. Except there *had* been that article in the newspaper, and right now I was staring at Bigfoot and there were no ifs, ands, or buts about it. I had my camera in my hand. All I had to do was lift it, snap a shot, and take off running.

But I thought about what it would mean if I did that. If there was a photo to *really* prove this guy existed, they'd be sending in teams to track him down. When they caught him, they'd keep him locked up, maybe dissect him to see what made him work. . . . Like everybody else, I've seen *E.T.*

I don't want to sound all mushy or anything, but there was something in those eyes that I didn't ever want to see locked away. I moved really slowly, putting the camera away in my bag, then I held my hands out to him so that he could see that I wasn't going to hurt him.

(Me hurt *him*—there's a laugh. The *size* of him . . .)

"You don't want to hang around this city too long," I told him. "If they catch you, nobody's going to be nice about it."

I was surprised at how calm I sounded.

He didn't say anything. He just stood there, looking at me with those big browns of his. Then he grinned—proof positive, as if I needed it, that he wasn't some guy in a suit like Byron, because there was no way they'd made a mask yet that could move like his features did right then. His whole face was animated—filled with a big silly lopsided grin that made me grin right back when it reached his eyes. He tipped a hairy finger to the brim of his hat, and then he just sort of faded away into the rubble—as quick and smooth as the rat had earlier, but there was nothing sneaky or sly about the way he moved.

One minute he was there, grinning like a loon, and the next he was gone.

I sank down and sat in the doorway, my legs swinging in the space below, and looked at where he'd been. I guess I was there for awhile, just trying to take it all in. I remembered a time when I'd been camping with my brother and a couple of friends from the neighborhood. I woke early the first morning and stuck my head out of the tent to find myself face to face with a deer. We both held our breath for what seemed like hours. When I finally breathed, she took off like a shot, but left me with a warm feeling that stayed with me for the rest of that weekend.

That's kind of what I was feeling right now. Like I'd lucked into a peek at one of the big mysteries of the world and if I kept it to myself, then I'd always be a part of it. It'd be our secret. Something nobody could ever take away from me.

11

So we all survived our *casa de grillos* in Upper Foxville. Ruth had gotten bored walking around in the rubble and gone back to Gracie Street, where she'd spent the better part of the day hanging around with some graffiti artists that she'd met while she was waiting for us. I got my film processed at one of those one-hour places and we made Lori pay up with a fancy dinner for trying to pull another one over on us.

Some reporters were in the area too, we found out later, trying to do a follow-up on the piece in the *Journal* yesterday, but nobody came back with a photo of Bigfoot, except for me, and mine's just a snapshot sitting there in the back of my head where I can take it out from time to time whenever I'm feeling blue and looking for a good memory.

It's absurd when you think about it—Bigfoot wandering around in the city, poorly disguised in an oversized trenchcoat and battered slouch hat—but I like the idea of it. Maybe he was trying to figure out who he was and where he fit in. Maybe it was all a laugh for him too. Maybe he really was just this hairy *muchacho,* making do in the Tombs. I don't know. I just think of him and smile.

Maybe that explains Poland.

Romano Drom

*The road leading to a goal does not separate you from the destination;
it is essentially a part of it.*
—Romany saying

A light Friday night drizzle had left a glistening sheen on Yoors Street when Lorio Munn stepped out of the club. She hefted her guitar case and looked down at her running shoes with a frown. The door opened and closed behind her and Terry Dixon joined her on the sidewalk, carrying his bass.

"What's the problem?" he asked.

Lorio lifted a shoe to show him the hole in its sole. "It's going to be a wet walk."

"You want a lift? Jane's meeting me at the Fan—we can give you a lift home after, if you want."

"No. I'm not much in the mood for socializing tonight."

"Hey, come on. It was a great night. We packed the place."

"Yeah. But they weren't really listening."

"They were dancing, weren't they? All of a sudden, that's not enough? You used to complain that all they'd do is just sit there."

"I know. I like it when they dance. It's just—"

Terry caught her arm. Putting a finger to his lips, he nodded to a pair of women who were walking by, neither of whom noticed Lorio and Terry standing in the club's doorway. One of them was humming the chorus to the band's last number under her breath:

> *I don't need nobody staring at me,*
> *stripping me down with their 1-2-3,*
> *I got a right to my own dignity*
> *—who needs pornography?*

"Okay," Lorio said when the women had passed them. "So somebody's listening. But when I went to get our money, Slimy Ted—"

"Slimy Toad."

Lorio smiled briefly. "He told me I could make a few extra bucks if I'd go out with a couple of his friends who, quote, 'liked my moves,' unquote. What does that tell you?"

"That I ought to break his head."

"It means the people that I want to reach *aren't* listening."

"Maybe we should be singing louder?"

"Sure." Lorio shook her head. "Look, say hi to Jane for me, would you? Maybe I'll make it next time."

She watched him go, then set off in the opposite direction towards Stanton Street. Maybe she shouldn't be complaining. No Nuns Here was starting to get the decent gigs. *In the City* had run an article on them—even spent a paragraph or two on what was behind the band, instead of just dismissing what they were trying to say as post-punk jingoism like their one two-line review in *The Newford Star* had.

Oh, it was still very in to sing about women's rights, gay rights, *people*'s rights, for God's sake, but the band still got the "aren't you limiting yourselves?" thrown at them by people who should know better. Still, at least they were getting some attention and, more importantly, what they were trying to say was getting some attention. It might bore the pants off of Joe Average Jock—but that was just the person they were trying to reach. So where did you go? If they could only get a decent gig. A big one where they could really reach more—

She paused in mid-step, certain she'd heard a moan from the alleyway she was passing. As she peered into it, the sound was repeated. Definitely a moan. She looked up and down Yoors Street, but there was no one close to her.

"Hey!" she called softly into the alley. "Is there someone in there?"

She caught a glimpse of eyes, gleaming like a cat's caught in the headbeams of a car—just a shivery flash and they were gone. Animal's eyes. But the sound she'd heard had seemed human.

"Hey!"

Swallowing thickly, she edged into the alley, her guitar case held out in front of her. As she moved down its length, her eyes began to adjust to the poor light.

Why was she doing this? She had to be nuts.

The moan came a third time then and she saw what she took to be a small man lying in some refuse.

"Oh, jeez." She moved forward, fear forgotten. "Are you okay?"

She laid her guitar case down and knelt beside the figure, but when she reached out a hand to his shoulder, she touched fur instead of clothing. Muscles moved under her fingers—weakly, but enough to tell her that it wasn't a fur coat. She snatched back her hand as a broad face turned towards her.

She froze, looking into that face. The first thing she thought of were the orangutans in the Metro Zoo. The features had a simian cast with their close-set eyes, broad overhanging brow and protruding lower jaw. Reddish fur surrounded the face—the same fur that covered the creature's body.

It had to be a costume, she thought. Except it was too real. She began to back away.

"Help . . . me. . . ."

This *couldn't* be real.

"When they track me down again . . . this time . . . they will . . . they will kill me. . . ."

The gaze that met her own was cloudy with pain, but it wasn't an animal's. Intelligence lay in its depth, behind the pain. But this wasn't a man wearing a costume either.

"Who will?" she asked at last.

For the first time, the gaze appeared to really focus on her.

"You . . . you're a Gypsy," the creature said. *"Sarishan, Romani chi."*

Lorio shook her head, unable to accept what she was hearing.

"The blood's awfully thin," she said finally. "And I don't speak Romany."

Though she knew it to hear it and remembered the odd word. The last person to speak it in her presence had been her uncle Palko, but that was a long time ago now.

"You are strangely garbed," the creature said, "but I know a Gypsy when I see one."

Strangely garbed? Well, it all depended, Lorio thought.

Her long curly hair was dyed a black too deep to be natural and grew from a three-inch swatch down the center of her head. Light brown stubble grew on either side of the mohawk where the sides of her head had been shaved. She wore a brown leather bomber's jacket over a bright red and black Forties dress, net stockings, and her running shoes. A strand of plastic pearls hung around her neck. Six earrings, from a rhinestone stud to threaded beads, hung from her right ear. In her left lobe was a stud in the shape of an Anarchy symbol.

"My mother was a Gypsy," she said, "but my father—"

She shook her head. What was she doing? Arguing with a ragged bundle of orange fur did not make much bloody sense.

"Your people know the roads," the creature said. "The roads of this world and those roads beyond that bind the balance. You . . . you can help me. Take my place. The hound caught me before—before I could complete my journey. The boundaries grow thin . . . frail. You must—"

"I don't know what you're talking about," Lorio said. "God, I don't even know what you are."

"My name is Elderee and this time Mahail's hound did its job too well. It will be back . . . once it scents my weakness. . . ." He coughed and Lorio stared at the blood speckling the hand-like paw that went up to his mouth.

"Look, you shouldn't be talking. You need a doctor."

Right. Maybe a vet would be more like it. She started to take off her jacket to lay it over him, but Elderee reached out and touched her arm.

"You need only walk it," he said. "That's all it takes. Walk it with intent. An old straight track . . . there for those who know to see it. Like a Gypsy road—*un Romano drom.* It will take you home."

"How do you know where I live?"

And why, she asked herself, am I taking this all so calmly? Probably because any minute she expected Steven Spielberg to step out and say, "Cut! That's a take."

"Not where you live—but *home.* Where all roads meet. Jacca calls it Lankelly— because of the sacred grove in the heart of the valley—but I just think of it as the Wood."

Lorio shook her head. "This is a joke, right? You're just wearing a . . . a costume, right? A really good one."

"No, I—"

"Sure. It's almost Halloween. You were at a party and you got mugged. The Gypsy bit was a good guess. I can handle this—no problem. Now we've got to get you to a hospital."

"Too . . . too late. . . ."

"Jeez, don't fade out on me now. I can . . ."

Her voice trailed off as she realized that the man in the monkey suit was looking behind her. She turned just in time to see a dog-like creature materialize out of nowhere. It came with a *whufft* of displaced air, bringing an unpleasant reek in its wake. Crouching on powerful legs, it looked like a cross between a hyena and a wolf, except for the protruding canines that Lorio had only seen in zoological texts on extinct species such as the saber-toothed tiger.

"Flee!" Elderee croaked. "You can't hope to face a polrech. . . ."

His warning came too late. With a rumbling growl that came from deep in its chest, the creature charged. Lorio didn't even stop to think of what she was doing. She just hoisted her guitar case and swung it in a flailing arc as hard as she could. The end of the case holding the body of her guitar struck the creature with such force that it snapped the beast's neck with an audible crack.

Lorio lost her hold on the case and it flew from her hands to land in a skidding crash well beyond the polrech that had dropped in its tracks. She stared at the dying creature, numb with fright. Adrenaline roared through her, bringing a buzz to her ears.

Saliva dripped from the creature's open mouth. The pavement of the alley smoked at its acidic touch. A pair of red fiery eyes glared at her. Taloned paws twitched, trying to reach her. When the light died in the creature's eyes, its shape wavered, then came apart, drifting away like smoke. A spark or two, like coals in a dying fire, hissed on the pavement, then there was nothing except for the small hole where the creature's saliva had pooled.

Lorio hugged herself to keep from shaking. Slowly she turned to look at her companion, but he lay very still now.

"Uh . . . Elderee?" she tried.

She moved forward, keeping half an eye on the alley behind her in case there were more of the hounds coming. Gingerly she touched Elderee. His eyes flickered open and something sparked between them, leaving Lorio momentarily dizzy. When her gaze cleared, she saw that the life-light was fading in his eyes now.

He had been holding his left arm across his lower torso. It fell free, revealing a gaping wound. Blood had matted in the fur around it. A queasy feeling started up in Lorio's stomach, but she forced it down. She tried to be calm. Something weird was going on—no doubt about that—but first things first.

"You must . . ." Elderee began in a weak voice.

"Uh-uh," Lorio interrupted. "You listen to me. You're hurt. I don't know what you are and I can't take you to a regular hospital, but you look enough like a . . . like an orangutan that the Zoo might take you in and hopefully patch you up. Now what I want you to do is keep your mouth shut and pretend you're an animal, okay? Otherwise they'll probably dissect you, just to see what makes you tick. We'll figure out how to get you out of the Zoo again when that problem comes up."

"But . . ."

"Take it easy. I'm going to get us a ride."

Without letting him reply, she bolted from the alleyway and ran down Yoors Street. She didn't know how she was going to explain this to Terry—she wasn't sure she could explain it to herself—but that didn't matter. First she had to get Elderee to a place where his injury could be treated. Everything else had to wait until then. The Fan loomed up on her left and she charged into the restaurant, ignoring the stares she was getting as she pushed her way to Terry and Jane's table.

"Lorio!" Terry said, looking up with a smile. "So you changed your—"

"No time to talk, Terry. I'm taking you up on that offer of a ride—only I need it right away."

"What's the big—"

"We're talking desperate here, Terry. Please?"

The bass player of No Nuns Here exchanged a glance with his girlfriend. Jane shrugged, so he dumped a handful of bills on the table and hurried out of the restaurant with her, trying to catch up to Lorio who was already running back to the alleyway where she'd left her monkeyman.

It was a twenty minute drive from downtown Newford to the Metro Zoo, and another twenty minutes back again. Terry pulled his Toyota over to the curb in front of Lorio's apartment building on Lee Street in Crowsea. She shared a second floor loft with a traditional musician named Angie Tichell in the old three-story brick building. The loft retained a consistent smell of Chinese food because of the ground floor that specialized in Mainland dishes.

Terry looked back between the bucket seats and studied Lorio for a moment.

"Are you going to be okay?" he asked.

Lorio nodded. "At least they took him in," she said.

They'd stayed in the Zoo parking lot long enough to be sure of that.

"I'm sure they'll do the best they can for him."

"But what if they can't help him? I mean, he *looks* like an orangutan, but what if he's too alien for them to help him?"

Terry had no answer for her. He'd been shocked enough to see the ape with its orange-red fur lying there in the alleyway, but when he'd heard it talk . . .

"Just what *is* he?" Jane asked.

Lorio wore a mournful expression. "I don't know." She sat there a moment longer, then stepped out of the car. "Thanks for the lift," she told Terry as he got her guitar out of the back for her. "I'll see you tomorrow night. You too, Jane," she added, leaning into the open window on the passenger's side of the car for a moment.

Jane touched her arm. "You take care of yourself," she said.

Lorio nodded. She stepped back as the Toyota pulled away and stood watching its taillights until it turned west on McKennitt and was lost from view. Turning, she faced the door to her building and wished her roommate wasn't away for the weekend. Being on her own in the loft tonight didn't hold very much appeal.

That's because you're scared, she chided herself. Don't be a baby. Just go to sleep.

She gave the night street one last look. A cab went by, but then the street was quiet again. No pedestrians at this time of night; everybody was sensibly in bed and asleep. The rain had stopped, the streetlights reflected in the puddles that it had left behind. Up and down the street the second floor windows were dark above the soft glow of the lit-up display windows of the stores on the ground floors.

Everything seemed normal. There wasn't even a hint that behind the facade there was another world that held talking monkeymen and bizarre dogs that appeared out of nowhere.

Sighing, Lorio squared her shoulders and went upstairs to bed, trying not to think about the weird turn the night had taken. She didn't have much luck.

She kept seeing that dog-like creature and worried about one finding its way into her apartment. Or to the Zoo where Elderee was. Then she worried about Elderee. When she finally nodded off, she fell into a fitful sleep, all too full of disturbing dreams.

At first she was in the alleyway again. For all that it was very real around her, there was a distancing sense, a feeling of dislocation in her being there. As she looked around, the pavement underfoot began to fracture. Cracks went up and down its length, then webbed the sides of the buildings. She started to back away onto Yoors Street when everything shattered like a piece of dropped glass.

Shards of the alley, like images reflected in a broken mirror, whirled and spun around her. When they settled down, drifting slowly around her like feathers after a pillow fight, she found herself on a roadway—more of a farmer's track, really—that stretched on to either horizon. On both sides of the track were rolling hills dotted with stands of trees.

"A pretty scene," a voice said from behind her. "Though not for long."

The man she saw, when she turned around, was a good head taller than her own five-four. His hair was black, his eyes glittery bright, his mouth an arrogant slash in a pale face. He was dressed all in browns and blacks, his clothing hanging in a poor fit from his too-thin frame.

"Who're—" Lorio began, but the man cut her off.

"This I claim for the Dark, while you—" he shook his head, taking in her hair, her clothes, with a disdainful look "—will be my gift to Mahail."

He made a motion towards her with his hand and sparks flew from his fingertips. She stumbled as the road dissolved under her and she began to drop through grey space. There was light far below her. In it was a writhing mass of tentacles that reached up for her from a dark heart of shadow. As she rushed down to meet it, the darkness resolved into a monstrous bloated shape with coal-eyes and a gaping maw.

It didn't take much speculation to realize that this thing had to be Mahail.

"Tell him Dorn sent you!" the pale-faced man cried after her.

She dropped like a bullet, straight for Mahail, her mouth open, but the scream dying before it left her throat. The monster's oozing tentacles snatched her out of the air. They squeezed her, shook her, held her up for inspection to one eye, then the other.

The soul studying her behind those eyes was like something dead. The air was filled with a reek of decay and rot. The tentacles tightened around her chest and lower torso, squeezing the breath from her as they brought her up to the monster's mouth. Slime covered her, burning and painful where it touched her bare skin. She flailed her arms, slapped at the creature's rubbery lips. The scream building up in her throat finally broke free, shrill and rattling and—

—it woke her to a tangle of bedclothes that were wrapped around her. Cold sweat covered her from head to toe.

She lay gasping, pushed aside the sheet and blankets, and stared up at the dark ceiling of her bedroom. Her heart beat a wild tattoo. Slowly the fear drained away.

Just a dream, she thought. That was all. Maybe the whole night had been just a dream. But as she finally drifted off again, she remembered Elderee's warm eyes and the long winding track of a road that went uphill and down, and this time she smiled and her sleep was dreamless.

The next day it all did seem like a dream. She checked the papers, tried the news on both TV and radio, but there was no mention of the Zoo acquiring a mysterious new animal. It wasn't until she called Terry to confirm that they *had* taken Elderee to the Zoo that she was willing to believe that she hadn't gone crazy. Things were weird, sure, but at least she hadn't totally lost it herself.

She spent the day in a state of anxiety that didn't go away until she got on stage at the club and No Nuns Here went into their first set. The chopping rhythms of the music, her guitar humming in her hands, her voice soaring over the blast of the instruments, let her escape that feeling of being lost. By the time they got to the last song of the night, she was filled with a crackling energy that let her rip through the song and make it not just a statement, but an anthem.

> *I hear your whistle when I cross the park,*
> *you make me nervous when I walk in the dark,*
> *but I won't listen—I won't scream,*
> *you won't find me in your magazines*
> *'cos*
> *I don't need nobody staring at me,*
> *stripping me down with their 1-2-3. . . .*

The song ended with a thunderous chord that shook the stage underfoot. She helped pack up the gear once the crowd was gone, but left on her own, not even taking her guitar with her. Terry promised to drop it off on Sunday afternoon, but she only nodded and made her way out onto Yoors Street.

The sidewalks were crowded, overfilled with a strutting array of humanity from the trendy to punks to burnouts, everyone on their own personal course and all of them the same. They made the city come to life, but at the same time they drowned it with postures, and images like costumes. It was all artifice, lacking depth. Lorio turned to look at her own reflection in a store window. She was no different. Any meaning she meant to communicate was lost behind a shuffle of makeup, styling and pose.

Mahail fed on hearts, she thought, not knowing where the thought had come from. He fed on them and left the shells to walk around just like we walk around.

She turned from the window and made her way through the people to the alley where she'd found Elderee. Without a pause, she turned into it and walked straight to its end. There she stopped and looked back at the sidewalk she'd just left. Cars flickered by on the street beyond it. On the sidewalk itself, every size and shape of Yoors Street poseur walked by the mouth of the alley, leaving echoing spills of conversation or laughter in their wake. But here it was quiet, like a world apart. Here it was . . . different.

Your people know the roads. . . .
You need only walk it . . . with intent. . . .

She sighed. Maybe the Rom of old had known hidden roads, but nobody had taken the time to show her any—not even Palko. Besides, her Gypsy blood was thin, a matter of chance rather than upbringing, and these days there were as many Gypsies in business suits as there were those following the old ways. Gypsy magic was just something the Rom used to baffle the *Gaje,* the non-Gypsies. Magic itself was just parlor tricks. Except . . .

She remembered the polrech, appearing out of nowhere, dissolving into smoke when she'd killed it. And Elderee . . . like an orangutan, only he could talk.

Magic.

She moved closer to one side of the alley, studying the brick wall of the building there. This alleyway was the last place in the world that she would ever expect to find a marvel. The grime and the dirt, the plastic garbage bags torn open in their corners, the refuse heaped against the walls—this wasn't the stuff of magic. Magic was Tolkien's Middle Earth. Cat Midhir's Borderlands. This was . . . She ran a hand down the side of the wall and looked at the smudge it left on her fingers. This was an armpit of the real world.

Turning, she faced the mouth of the alley again, only to find a tall figure standing there, watching her. Fear made her blood pump quicker through her veins and for the first time in her life she knew what it meant to have one's heart in one's mouth. She knew who this was.

"Dorn."

The name came out of her mouth in a spidery croak. The man's face was in shadow, but she could still see, no, sense his grin.

"I warned you not to involve yourself further in what doesn't concern you."

He'd warned her? Then she remembered the dream. The thought of his sending her that dream, of his being inside her head like that, made her skin crawl.

"You should not have come back," he said.

"You don't . . . you don't scare me," she said.

No. He terrified her. How could something she'd only dreamed be real? She took a step back and the heel of her shoe came up against a garbage bag.

"Elderee's road is *mine,*" he said, moving closer. "*I* took it from him. *I* set the hound on him."

"You—"

"But I felt you drawing on its power, and then I knew you would try to take it from me."

"I think you're making a—"

"No mistake." He touched his chest. "I can *feel* the bond between you and that damned monkey. He gave it to you, didn't he? Heart's shadow, look at you!"

He stood very close to her now. A hand went up and flicked a finger against the stubble on the shaved part of her scalp. Lorio flinched at the touch, but couldn't seem to move away. She was weak with fear. Sparks flickered around Dorn's fingers. She stared at them with widening eyes.

"You're nothing better than an animal yourself," he told her.

Strangely enough, Lorio took comfort in that remark. She looked up into his eyes and saw that they were as dead as Mahail's had been in her nightmare. Nightmare. If

Dorn was real, did that mean the road was too? Could she shatter this alleyway, as she had in her dream, to find the road lying underfoot—behind its facade?

An old straight track . . . there for those who know to see it.

Something sparked in his eyes. It wasn't until he spoke that Lorio realized it had been amusement.

"You don't know, do you?" he mocked. "You couldn't find a road if your life depended on it."

"I . . ."

"Let me show you."

Before she could do anything, he grabbed her, one hand on either lapel of her bomber's jacket, and slammed her against the wall of the alley. The impact knocked the breath out of her and brought tears to her eyes.

"Watch," he grinned, his face inches from hers.

He held her straight-armed and slowly turned from the wall. He made one full circuit, then dumped her on the ground. Lorio's legs gave away from under her and she tumbled to the dirt.

Dirt?

Slowly the realization settled in her. He'd taken her back into her dream.

The silence came to her first, a sudden cessation of all sound so that her breathing sounded ragged to her ears. Then she looked around. The city was gone. She was crouching on a dirt road, under a starry sky. The hills of her dream were on either side, the road running between them like a straight white ribbon.

Dorn grabbed a handful of her hair and hauled her to her feet. She blinked with the pain, eyes tearing, but as she turned slowly to face her captor she could feel something shift inside her. She had no more doubt that magic was real, that the road existed, that Elderee had offered her something precious beyond compare. There was no way she was going to let Dorn with his dead eyes take this from her.

On the heels of that realization, knowledge filled her like a flower sprouting from a seed in time-lapse photography. Eye to eye, mind to mind, Elderee had left that seed in her mind until something—the promise of this place, the magic of this road, her own understanding of it, perhaps—woke it and set it spinning through her.

There was not one road, but a countless number of them. They made a pattern that webbed not only her own world, but all worlds; not only her own time, but all times. They upheld a fragile balance between light and dark, order and chaos, while at the center of the web lay a sacred grove in that valley that Elderee had called Lankelly.

And I know how to get there, she realized.

I know that Wood. And it was home.

Her understanding of the roads and all they meant took only a moment to flash through her. In the same breath she knew that the magic that Elderee and others like him used was drawn from the pattern of the roads. A being like Dorn was a destroyer and gained his power from what he destroyed. It was a power that came quickly, draining as it ravaged, leaving the user hungry for more, while the power Elderee used worked in harmony with the pattern, built on it, drew from it, then gave back more than it took. It was a slower magic, but a more enduring one.

Dorn saw the understanding come into her eyes. Its suddenness, the depth of it filling her, shocked him. His grip on her hair slackened for a moment and Lorio brought her knee up into his groin. His hand dropped from her hair as he folded over.

Lorio stood over him, staring at his bent figure. She raised her hands and gold sparks flickered between her fingers. But she didn't need magic to deal with him. She brought doubled fists down on the nape of his neck and he sprawled face forward in the dirt. He turned pained eyes to her, hands scrabbling at the surface of the road. His magic glimmered dully between his fingers, but Lorio shook her head.

He wouldn't look at her. Instead he concentrated, brow furrowed, as he called up his magic. Whatever spell he was trying to work made the light between his fingers gleam more sharply. Lorio stepped quickly forward and stamped down hard on his hand. She was wearing boots tonight. Bones crunched under the impact of her heel.

"That's for Elderee," she said, her voice soft but grim.

Dorn bit back a scream and glared at her. He sat up and scuttled a few paces away, moving on two bent legs and one arm, sideways like a crab. When he stopped, he cradled his hurt hand against his chest.

Silently they faced each other. Dorn knew that she was stronger than he was at this moment. Her will was too focused, the cloak of knowledge that Elderee had given her was too powerful in its newness. She'd hurt him. Among humanoids, hands were needed to spark spells—fingers and voice. She'd effectively cut him off from the use of his own spells, from calling up a polrech, from anything he might have done to hurt her. In her eyes, he could see that she knew too.

She took a step towards him and he called up the one magic he could use, that which would take him from the road to safety in any one of the myriad worlds touched by the roads.

"There will be another time," he muttered, and then he was gone.

Displaced air *whuff*ed where he'd stood and Lorio found herself alone on the road.

She let out a long breath and looked around.

The road. The Chinese called it a dragon track. Alfred Watkins, in England, had discovered the old straight tracks there and called them leys. Secret ways, hidden roads. The Native Americans had them. African tribesmen and the aborigines of Australia. Even her own people had secret roads unknown to the non-Gypsy. In every culture, the wise people, the shamans and magicians and the outsiders knew these ways, and it made sense, didn't it? It was by following such roads that they could grow strong themselves.

But not like Dorn, she thought. Not the kind of strength that destroys, but rather the kind of strength that gives back more than it takes. Like . . . like playing on stage with No Nuns Here. Having something to say and putting it across as honestly as possible. When it worked, when something sparked between herself and the audience, a strength went back and forth between them, each of them feeding the other, the sensation so intense that she often came off the stage just vibrating.

Lorio smiled. She started to walk the road, giving herself to it as step followed step. She walked and a hum built up in her mind. Time went spilling down other corridors, leaving her to stride through a place where hours moved to a different step. The stars in their unfamiliar constellations wheeled above her. The landscape on either side of the road changed from hills to woodlands to deserts to mountainsides to seashores until she found herself back in the hills once more.

She paused there. A thrumming sensation filled her, giving her surroundings a sparkle. Rich scents filled her nostrils. The wind coming down from the hills was a sigh like a synthesizer, dreamy and distant. And underfoot, the road glimmered faintly as though in response to what she'd given it by walking its length.

There's no end to it, she realized. It just goes around and around. Sometimes it'll be longer, sometimes shorter. It just goes on. Because it wasn't where she was coming from, nor where she was going to that was important, but the road itself and how she walked it. And it would never be the same.

She ruffled through the knowledge that Elderee had planted in her and found a way to step off the road. But when she moved back into her own world, she didn't return to the alleyway where it had all begun. Instead she chose a different exit point and stepped towards it. The road and surrounding hills shimmered around her and then were gone.

It was more a room than a cage, the concrete floor and walls smelling strongly of disinfectant and the unmistakable odor of a zoo's monkey house. The only light came through the barred front of the cage, but it was enough for Lorio to see Elderee glance up at her sudden appearance. A look of fatherly pride came over his simian features. Lorio stood self-consciously in the middle of the floor for a long moment, then after a quick look around to make sure they were alone, she walked over to where Elderee lay, her boots scuffing quietly on the concrete.

"Hi," she said, crouching down beside him.

"Hello, yourself."

"How're you feeling?"

A faint smile touched his lips. "I've felt better."

"The doctors fixed you up?"

"Oh, yes. And a remarkable job they've done. I'm alive, am I not?" He paused, then laid a hand gently on her shoulder. "You found the road?"

Lorio smiled. "Along with everything else you stuck in my head. How did you do that?"

She didn't ask why. Having walked the road, she knew that someone had to assume his responsibility of it. He'd chosen her.

"I'll show you sometime—when I'm better. Did you go to the Wood?"

"No. I thought I'd save that for when I could go with you."

"Did you have any . . . trouble?"

Her dream of Mahail flashed into her mind. And Dorn's very real presence. The hounds that he could have called down on her if he hadn't been so sure of himself.

"Ah," Elderee said, catching the images. "Dorn. I wish I'd been there to see you deal with him."

"Are you reading my mind?"

"Only what you're projecting to me."

"Oh." Lorio settled down into a more comfortable position. "He folded pretty easily, didn't he? Just like the polrech that attacked us in the alley."

Elderee shrugged. "Dorn is a lesser evil. He could control one hound at a time, no more. But like most of his kind, he liked to think of himself as far more than he was. You did well. As for the polrech—you were simply stronger. And quicker."

Lorio flushed at the praise.

"And now?" Elderee asked. "What will you do?"

"Jeez, I . . . I don't know. Take care of your part of the road until you get better, I guess."

"I'm getting old," Elderee said. "I could use your help—even when I'm better. There are more of them—" he didn't need to name Mahail and his minions for Lorio to know whom he meant "—than there ever are of us. And there are many roads."

"We'll handle it," Lorio said, still buzzing from her time on the road. "No problem."

"It can be dangerous," Elderee warned, "if a polrech catches you unaware—or if you run into a pack of them. And there are others like Dorn—only stronger, fiercer. But," he added as Lorio's humor began to drain away, "there are good things, too. Wait until you see the monkey puzzle tree—there are more birds in it, and from stranger worlds, than you could ever imagine. And there are friends in the Wood that I'd like you to meet—Jacca and Mabena and . . ."

His voice began to drift a bit.

"You're wearing yourself out," Lorio said.

Elderee nodded.

"I'll come back and see you tomorrow night," she said. "You should rest now. There'll be time enough to meet all your friends and for us to get to know each other better later on."

She stood up and smiled down at him. Elderee's gaze lifted to meet hers.

"Bahtalo drom," he said in Romany. Roughly translated it meant, follow a good road.

"I will," Lorio said. "Maybe not a Gypsy road, but a good road all the same."

"Not a Gypsy road? Then what are you?"

"Part Rom," Lorio replied with a grin. "But mostly just a punker."

Elderee shook his head. Lorio lifted a hand in farewell, then reached for and found the road that would take her home. She stepped onto it and disappeared. Elderee lay back with a contented smile on his lips and let sleep rise up to claim him once again.

The Sacred Fire

> No one lives forever,
> and dead men rise up never,
> and even the longest river
> winds somewhere safe to sea.
> —from British folklore;
> collected by Stephen Gallagher

There were ten thousand maniacs on the radio—the band, not a bunch of lunatics; playing their latest single, Natalie Merchant's distinctive voice rising from the music like a soothing balm.

Trouble me. . . .

Sharing your problems . . . sometimes talking a thing through was enough to ease the burden. You didn't need to be a shrink to know it could work. You just had to find someone to listen to you.

Nicky Straw had tried talking. He'd try anything if it would work, but nothing did. There was only one way to deal with his problems and it took him a long time to accept that. But it was hard, because the job was never done. Every time he put one of them down, another of the freaks would come buzzing in his face like a fly on a corpse.

He was getting tired of fixing things. Tired of running. Tired of being on his own.

Trouble me. . . .

He could hear the music clearly from where he crouched in the bushes. The boom box pumped out the song from one corner of the blanket on which she was sitting, reading a paperback edition of Christy Riddell's *How to Make the Wind Blow*. She even looked a little like Natalie Merchant. Same dark eyes, same dark hair; same slight build. Better taste in clothes, though. None of those thrift shop dresses and the like that made Merchant look like she was old before her time; just a nice white Butler U. T-shirt and a pair of bright yellow jogging shorts. White Reeboks with laces to match the shorts; a red headband.

The light was leaking from the sky. Be too dark to read soon. Maybe she'd get up and go.

Nicky sat back on his haunches. He shifted his weight from one leg to the other.

Maybe nothing would happen, but he didn't see things working out that way. Not with how his luck was running.

All bad.

Trouble me. . . .

I did, he thought. I tried. But it didn't work out, did it?

So now he was back to fixing things the only way he knew how.

Her name was Luann. Luann Somerson.

She'd picked him up in the Tombs—about as far from the green harbor of Fitzhenry Park as you could get in Newford. It was the lost part of the city—a wilderness of urban decay stolen back from the neon and glitter. Block on block of decaying tenements and run-down buildings. The kind of place to which the homeless gravitated, looking for squats; where the kids hung out to sneak beers and junkies made their deals, hands twitching as they exchanged rumpled bills for little packets of short-lived empyrean; where winos slept in doorways that reeked of puke and urine and the cops only went if they were on the take and meeting the moneyman.

It was also the kind of place where the freaks hid out, waiting for Lady Night to start her prowl. Waiting for dark. The freaks liked her shadows and he did too, because he could hide in them as well as they could. Maybe better. He was still alive, wasn't he?

He was looking for the freaks to show when Luann approached him, sitting with his back against the wall, right on the edge of the Tombs, watching the rush hour slow to a trickle on Gracie Street. He had his legs splayed out on the sidewalk in front of him, playing the drunk, the bum. Three-days' stubble, hair getting ragged, scruffy clothes, two dimes in his pocket—it wasn't hard to look the part. Commuters stepped over him or went around him, but nobody gave him a second glance. Their gazes just touched him, then slid on by. Until she showed up.

She stopped, then crouched down so that she wasn't standing over him. She looked too healthy and clean to be hanging around this part of town.

"You look like you could use a meal," she said.

"I suppose you're buying?"

She nodded.

Nicky just shook his head. "What? You like to live dangerously or something, lady? I could be anybody."

She nodded again, a half smile playing on her lips.

"Sure," she said. "Anybody at all. Except you're Nicky Straw. We used to take English 201 together, remember?"

He'd recognized her as well, just hoped she hadn't. The guy she remembered didn't exist anymore.

"I know about being down on your luck," she added when he didn't respond. "Believe me, I've been there."

You haven't been anywhere, he thought. You don't want to know about the places I've been.

"You're Luann Somerson," he said finally.

Again that smile. "Let me buy you a meal, Nicky."

He'd wanted to avoid this kind of a thing, but he supposed he'd known all along that he couldn't. This was what happened when the hunt took you into your hometown. You didn't disappear into the background like all the other bums. Someone was always there to remember.

Hey, Nicky. How's it going? How's the wife and that kid of yours?

Like they cared. Maybe he should just tell the truth for a change. You know those things we used to think were hiding in the closet when we were too young to know any better? Well, surprise. One night one of those monsters came out of the closet and chewed off their faces. . . .

"C'mon," Luann was saying.

She stood up, waiting for him. He gave it a heartbeat, then another. When he saw she wasn't going without him, he finally got to his feet.

"You do this a lot?" he asked.

She shook her head. "First time," she said.

All it took was one time. . . .

"I'm like everyone else," she said. "I pretend there's no one there, lying half-starved in the gutter, you know? But when I recognized you, I couldn't just walk by."

You should have, he thought.

His silence was making her nervous and she began to chatter as they headed slowly down Yoors Street.

"Why don't we just go back to my place?" she said. "It'll give you a chance to clean up. Chad—that's my ex—left some clothes behind that might fit you. . . ."

Her voice trailed off. She was embarrassed now, finally realizing how he must feel, having her see him like this.

"Uh . . ."

"That'd be great," he said, relenting.

He got that smile of hers as a reward. A man could get lost in its warmth, he thought. It'd feed a freak for a month.

"So this guy," he said. "Chad. He been gone long?"

The smile faltered.

"Three and a half weeks now," she said.

That explained a lot. Nothing made you forget your own troubles so much as running into someone who had them worse.

"Not too bright a guy, I guess," he said.

"That's . . . Thank you, Nicky. I guess I need to hear that kind of thing."

"Hey, I'm a bum. We've got nothing better to do than to think up nice things to say."

"You were never a bum, Nicky."

"Yeah. Well, things change."

She took the hint. As they walked on, she talked about the book she'd started reading last night instead.

It took them fifteen minutes or so to reach her apartment on McKennitt, right in the heart of Lower Crowsea. It was a walk-up with its own stairwell—a narrow, winding affair that started on the pavement by the entrance of a small Lebanese groceria and then deposited you on a balcony overlooking the street.

Inside, the apartment had the look of a recent split-up. There was an amplifier on a wooden orange crate by the front window, but no turntable or speakers. The bookcase to the right of the window had gaps where apparently random volumes had been removed. A pair of rattan chairs with bright slipcovers stood in the middle of the room, but there were no end tables to go with them, nor a coffee table. She was making do with another orange crate, this one cluttered with magazines, a couple of plates stacked on top of each other and what looked like every coffee mug she owned squeezed into the remaining space. A small portable black-and-white Zenith TV stood at the base of the bookcase, alongside a portable cassette deck. There were a couple of rectangles on the wall where paintings had obviously been removed. A couple of weeks' worth of newspapers were in a pile on the floor by one of the chairs.

She started to apologize for the mess, then smiled and shrugged.

Nicky had to smile with her. Like he was going to complain about the place, looking like he did.

She showed him to the bathroom. By the time he came out again, showered and shaved, dressed in a pair of Chad's corduroys and a white linen shirt, both of which were at least a size too big, she had a salad on the tiny table in the kitchen, wine glasses out, the bottle waiting for him to open it, breaded pork chops and potatoes on the stove, still cooking.

Nicky's stomach grumbled at the rich smell that filled the air.

She talked a little about her failed marriage over dinner—sounding sad rather than bitter—but more about old times at the university. As she spoke, Nicky realized that the only thing they had shared back then had been that English class; still he let her ramble on about campus events he only half-remembered and people who'd meant nothing to him then and even less now.

But at least they hadn't been freaks.

He corrected himself. He hadn't been able to *recognize* the freaks among them back then.

"God, listen to me," Luann said suddenly.

They were finished their meal and sitting in her living room having coffee. He'd been wrong; there were still two clean mugs in her cupboard.

"I am," he said.

She gave him that smile of hers again—this time it had a wistfulness about it.

"I know you are," she said. "It's just that all I've been talking about is myself. What about you, Nicky? What happened to you?"

"I . . ."

Where did he start? Which lie did he give her?

That was the one good thing about street people. They didn't ask questions. Whatever put you there, that was your business. But citizens always wanted whys and hows and wherefores.

As he hesitated, she seemed to realize her faux pas.

"I'm sorry," she said. "If you don't want to talk about it . . ."

"It's not that," Nicky told her. "It's just . . ."

"Hard to open up?"

Try impossible. But oddly enough, Nicky found himself wanting to talk to her about it. To explain. To ease the burden. Even to warn her, because she was just the kind of person the freaks went for.

The fire inside her shimmered off her skin like a high voltage aura, sending shadows skittering. It was a bright shatter of light and a deep golden glow like honey, all at the same time. It sparked in her eyes; blazed when she smiled. Sooner or later it was going to draw a nest of the freaks to her, just as surely as a junkie could sniff out a fix.

"There's these . . . things," he said slowly. "They look enough like you or me to walk among us—especially at night—but they're . . . they're not human."

She got a puzzled look on her face which didn't surprise him in the least.

"They're freaks," he said. "I don't know what they are, or where they came from, but they're not natural. They feed on us, on our hopes and our dreams, on our vitality. They're like . . . I guess the best analogy would be that they're like vampires. Once they're on to you, you can't shake them. They'll keep after you until they've bled you dry."

Her puzzlement was turning to a mild alarm, but now that he'd started, Nicky was determined to tell it all through, right to the end.

"What," she began.

"What I do," he said, interrupting her, "is hunt them down."

The song by 10,000 Maniacs ended and the boom box's speakers offered up another to the fading day. Nicky couldn't name the band this time, but he was familiar with the song's punchy rhythm. The lead singer was talking about burning beds. . . .

Beside the machine, Luann put down her book and stretched.

Do it, Nicky thought. Get out of here. Now. While you still can.

Instead, she lay down on the blanket, hands behind her head, and looked up into the darkening sky, listening to the music. Maybe she was looking for the first star of the night.

Something to wish upon.

The fire burned in her brighter than any star. Flaring and ebbing to the pulse of her thoughts.

Calling to the freaks.

Nicky's fingers clenched into fists. He made himself look away. But even closing his eyes, he couldn't ignore the fire. Its heat sparked the distance between them as though he lay beside her on the blanket, skin pressed to skin. His pulse drummed, twinning her heartbeat.

This was how the freaks felt. This was what they wanted, what they hungered for, what they fed on. This was what he denied them.

The spark of life.

The sacred fire.

He couldn't look away any longer. He had to see her one more time, her fire burning, burning . . .

He opened his eyes to find that the twilight had finally found Fitzhenry Park. And Luann—she was blazing like a bonfire in its dusky shadows.

"What do you mean, you hunt them down?" she asked.

"I kill them," Nicky told her.

"But—"

"Understand, they're not human. They just *look* like us, but their faces don't fit quite right and they wear our kind of a body like they've put on an unfamiliar suit of loose clothing."

He touched his borrowed shirt as he spoke. She just stared at him—all trace of that earlier smile gone. Fear lived in her eyes now.

That's it, he told himself. You've done enough. Get out of here.

But once started, he didn't seem to be able to stop. All the lonely years of the endless hunt came spilling out of him.

"They're out there in the night," he said. "That's when they can get away with moving among us. When their shambling walk makes you think of drunks or some feeble old homeless bag lady—not of monsters. They're freaks and they live on the fire that makes us human."

"The . . . the fire . . . ?

He touched his chest.

"The one in here," he said. "They're drawn to the ones whose fires burn the brightest," he added. "Like yours does."

She edged her chair back from the table, ready to bolt. Then he saw her realize that there was no place to bolt to. The knowledge sat there in her eyes, fanning the fear into an ever-more debilitating panic. Where was she going to go that he couldn't get to her first?

"I know what you're thinking," he said. "If someone had come to me with this story before I . . . found out about them—"

("Momma! Daddy!" he could hear his daughter crying. "The monsters are coming for me!"

Soothing her. Showing her that the closet was empty. But never thinking about the window and the fire escape outside it. Never thinking for a minute that the freaks would come in through the window and take them both when he was at work.

But that was before he'd known about the freaks, wasn't it?)

He looked down at the table and cleared his throat. There was pain in his eyes when his gaze lifted to meet hers again—pain as intense as her fear.

"If someone had told me," he went on, "I'd have recommended him for the Zeb, too—just lock him up in a padded cell and throw away the key. But I don't think that way now. Because I can see them. I can recognize them. All it takes is one time and you'll never disbelieve again.

"And you'll never forget."

"You . . . you just kill these people . . . ?" she asked.

Her voice was tiny—no more than a whisper. Her mind was tape looped around the one fact. She wasn't hearing anything else.

"I told you—they're not people," he began, then shook his head.

What was the point? What had he thought was going to happen? She'd go, yeah, right, and jump in to help him? Here, honey, let me hold the stake. Would you like another garlic clove in your lunch?

But they weren't vampires. He didn't know what they were, just that they were dangerous.

Freaks.

"They know about me," he said. "They've been hunting me for as long as I've been hunting them, but I move too fast for them. One day, though, I'll make a mistake and then they'll have me. It's that, or the cops'll pick me up and I wouldn't last the night in a cell. The freaks'd be on me so fast . . ."

He let his voice trail off. Her lower lip was trembling. Her eyes looked like those of some small panicked creature, caught in a trap, the hunter almost upon her.

"Maybe I should go," he said.

He rose from the table, pretending he didn't see the astonished relief in her eyes. He paused at the door that would let him out onto the balcony.

"I didn't mean to scare you," he said.

"I . . . you . . ."

He shook his head. "I should never have come."

"I . . ."

She still couldn't string two words together. Still didn't believe that she was getting out of this alive. He felt bad for unsettling her the way he had, but maybe it was for the best. Maybe she wouldn't bring any more strays home the way she had him. Maybe the freaks'd never get to her.

"Just think about this," he said, before he left. "What if I'm right?"

Then he stepped outside and closed the door behind him.

He could move fast when he had to—it was what had kept him alive through all these years. By the time she reached her living room window, he was down the stairs and across the street, looking back at her from the darkened mouth of an alleyway nestled between a yuppie restaurant and a bookstore, both of which were closed. He could see her, studying the street, looking for him.

But she couldn't see him.

And that was the way he'd keep it.

He came out of the bushes, the mask of his face shifting and unsettled in the poor light. Luann was sitting up, fiddling with the dial on her boom box, flipping through the channels. She didn't hear him until he was almost upon her. When she turned, her face drained of color. She sprawled backwards in her attempt to escape and then could only lie there and stare, mouth working, but no sound coming out. He lunged for her—

But then Nicky was there. The hunting knife that he carried in a sheath under his shirt was in his hand, cutting edge up. He grabbed the freak by the back of his collar and hauled him around. Before the freak could make a move, Nicky rammed the knife home in the freak's stomach and ripped it up. Blood sprayed, showering them both.

He could hear Luann screaming. He could feel the freak jerking in his grip as he died. He could taste the freak's blood on his lips. But his mind was years and miles away, falling back and back to a small apartment where his wife and daughter had fallen prey to the monsters his daughter told him were living in the closet. . . .

The freak slipped from his grip and sprawled on the grass. The knife fell from Nicky's hand. He looked at Luann, finally focusing on her. She was on her knees, staring at him and the freak like they were both aliens.

"He . . . his face . . . he . . ."

She could barely speak.

"I can't do it anymore," he told her.

He was empty inside. Couldn't feel a thing. It was as though all those years of hunting down the freaks had finally extinguished his own fire.

In the distance he could hear a siren. Someone must have seen what went down.

Had to have been a citizen, because street people minded their own business, didn't matter what they saw.

"It ends here," he said.

He sat down beside the freak's corpse to wait for the police to arrive.

"For me, it ends here."

Late the following day, Luann was still in shock.

She'd finally escaped the endless barrage of questions from both the police and the press, only to find that being alone brought no relief. She kept seeing the face of the man who had attacked her. Had it really seemed to *shift* about like an ill-fitting mask, or had that just been something she'd seen as a result of the poor light and what Nicky had told her?

Their faces don't fit quite right. . . .

She couldn't get it out of her mind. The face. The blood. The police dragging Nicky away. And all those things he'd told her last night.

They're freaks. . . .

Crazy things.

They live on the fire that makes us human.

Words that seemed to well up out of some great pain he was carrying around inside him.

They're not human . . . they just look *like us. . . .*

A thump on her balcony had her jumping nervously out of her chair until she realized that it was just the paperboy tossing up today's newspaper. She didn't want to look at what *The Daily Journal* had to say, but couldn't seem to stop herself from going out to get it. She took the paper back inside and spread it out on her lap.

Naturally enough, the story had made the front page. There was a picture of her, looking washed out and stunned. A shot of the corpse being taken away in a body bag. A head and shoulders shot of Nicky . . .

She stopped, her pulse doubling its tempo as the headline under Nicky's picture sank in.

"killer found dead in cell—police baffled."

"No," she said.

They know about me.

She pushed the paper away from her until it fell to the floor. But Nicky's picture continued to look up at her from where the paper lay.

They've been hunting me.

None of what he'd told her could be true. It had just been the pitiful ravings of a very disturbed man.

I wouldn't last the night in a cell. The freaks'd be on me so fast . . .

But she'd known him once—a long time ago—and he'd been as normal as anybody then. Still, people changed. . . .

She picked up the paper and quickly scanned the story, looking for a reasonable explanation to put to rest the irrational fears that were reawakening her panic. But the police knew nothing. Nobody knew a thing.

"I suppose that at this point, only Nicky Straw knows what really happened," the police spokesman was quoted as saying.

Nicky and you, a small worried voice said in the back of Luann's mind.

She shook her head, unwilling to accept it.

They're drawn to the ones whose fires burn the brightest.

She looked to her window. Beyond its smudged panes, the night was gathering. Soon it would be dark. Soon it would be night. Light showed a long way in the dark; a bright light would show further.

The ones whose fires burn the brightest . . . like yours does.

"It . . . it wasn't true," she said, her voice ringing hollowly in the room. "None of it. Tell me it wasn't true, Nicky."

But Nicky was dead.

She let the paper fall again and rose to her feet, drifting across the room to the window like a ghost. She just didn't seem to feel connected to anything anymore.

It seemed oddly quiet on the street below. Less traffic than usual—both vehicular and pedestrian. There was a figure standing in front of the bookstore across the street, back to the window display, leaning against the glass. He seemed to be looking up at her window, but it was hard to tell because the brim of his hat cast a shadow on his face.

Once they're on to you, you can't shake them.

That man in the park. His face. Shifting. The skin seeming too loose.

They'll keep after you until they bleed you dry.

It wasn't real.

She turned from the window and shivered, hugging her arms around herself as she remembered what Nicky had said when he'd left the apartment last night.

What if I'm right?

She couldn't accept that. She looked back across the street, but the figure was gone. She listened for a footstep on the narrow, winding stairwell that led up to her balcony. Waited for the movement of a shadow across the window.

Winter Was Hard

I pretty much try to stay in a constant state of confusion just because of the expression it leaves on my face.
—Johnny Depp

It was the coldest December since they'd first started keeping records at the turn of the century, though warmer, Jilly thought, than it must have been in the ice ages of the Pleistocene. The veracity of that extraneous bit of trivia gave her small comfort, for it did nothing to lessen the impact of the night's bitter weather. The wind shrieked through the tunnel-like streets created by the abandoned buildings of the Tombs, carrying with it a deep, arctic chill. It spun the granular snow into dervishing whirligigs that made it almost impossible to see at times and packed drifts up against the sides of the buildings and derelict cars.

Jilly felt like a little kid, bundled up in her boots and parka, with longjohns under her jeans, a woolen cap pushing down her unruly curls and a long scarf wrapped about fifty times around her neck and face, cocooning her so completely that only her eyes peered out through a narrow slit. Turtle-like, she hunched her shoulders, trying to make her neck disappear into her parka, and stuffed her mittened hands deep in its pockets.

It didn't help. The wind bit through it all as though unhindered, and she just grew colder with each step she took as she plodded on through the deepening drifts. The work crews were already out with their carnival of flashing blue and amber lights, removing the snow on Gracie Street and Williamson, but here in the Tombs it would just lie where it fell until the spring melt. The only signs of humanity were the odd little trails that the derelicts and other inhabitants of the Tombs made as they went about their business, but even those were being swallowed by the storm.

Only fools or those who had no choice were out tonight. Jilly thought she should be counted among the latter, though Geordie had called her the former when she'd left the loft earlier in the evening.

"This is just craziness, Jilly," he'd said. "Look at the bloody weather."

"I've got to go. It's important."

"To you and the penguins, but nobody else."

Still, she'd had to come. It was the eve of the solstice, one year exactly since the gemmin went away, and she didn't feel as though she had any choice in the matter. She was driven to walk the Tombs tonight, never mind the storm. What sent her out from the warm comfort of her loft was like what Professor Dapple said they used to call a geas in the old days—something you just had to do.

So she left Geordie sitting on her Murphy bed, playing his new Copeland whistle, surrounded by finished and unfinished canvases and the rest of the clutter that her motley collection of possessions had created in the loft, and went out into the storm.

She didn't pause until she reached the mouth of the alley that ran along the south side of the old Clark Building. There, under the suspicious gaze of the building's snow-swept gargoyles, she hunched her back against the storm and pulled her scarf down a little, widening the eye-slit so that she could have a clearer look down the length of the alley. She could almost see Babe, leaning casually against the side of the old Buick that was still sitting there, dressed in her raggedy T-shirt, black body stocking and raincoat, Doc Martin's dark against the snow that lay underfoot. She could almost hear the high husky voices of the other gemmin, chanting an eerie version of a rap song that had been popular at the time.

She could almost—

But no. She blinked as the wind shifted, blinding her with snow. She saw only snow, heard only the wind. But in her memory . . .

By night they nested in one of those abandoned cars that could be found on any street or alley of the Tombs—a handful of gangly teenagers burrowed under blankets, burlap sacks and tattered jackets, bodies snugly fit into holes that seemed to have been chewed from the ragged upholstery. This morning they had built a fire in the trunk of the Buick, scavenging fuel from the buildings, and one of them was cooking their breakfast on the heated metal of its hood.

Babe was the oldest. She looked about seventeen—it was something in the way she carried herself—but otherwise had the same thin androgynous body as her companions. The other gemmin all had dark complexions and feminine features, but none of them had Babe's short mauve hair, nor her luminous violet eyes. The hair coloring of the others ran more to various shades of henna red; their eyes were mostly the same electric blue that Jilly's were.

That December had been as unnaturally warm as this one was cold, but Babe's open raincoat with the thin T-shirt and body stocking underneath still made Jilly pause with concern. There was such a thing as carrying fashion too far, she thought—had they never heard of pneumonia?—but then Babe lifted her head, her large violet eyes fixing their gaze as curiously on Jilly as Jilly's did on her. Concern fell by the wayside, shifting into a sense of frustration as Jilly realized that all she had in the pocket of her coat that day was a stub of charcoal and her sketchbook instead of the oils and canvas which was the only medium that could really do justice in capturing the startling picture Babe and her companions made.

For long moments none of them spoke. Babe watched her, a half-smile teasing one corner of her mouth. Behind her, the cook stood motionless, a makeshift spatula held negligently in a delicate hand. Eggs and bacon sizzled on the trunk hood in front of her, filling the air with their unmistakable aroma. The other gemmin peered up over the dash of the Buick, supporting their narrow chins on their folded arms.

All Jilly could do was look back. A kind of vertigo licked at the edges of her mind, making her feel as though she'd just stepped into one of her own paintings—the ones that made up her last show, an urban faerie series: twelve enormous canvases, all in oils, one for each month, each depicting a different kind of mythological being transposed from its traditional folkloric rural surroundings onto a cityscape.

Her vague dizziness wasn't caused by the promise of magic that seemed to decorate the moment with a sparkling sense of impossible possibilities as surely as the bacon filled the air with its come-hither smell. It was rather the unexpectedness of coming across a moment like this—in the Tombs, of all places, where winos and junkies were the norm.

It took her awhile to collect her thoughts.

"Interesting stove you've got there," she said finally.

Babe's brow furrowed for a moment, then cleared as a radiant smile first lifted the corners of her mouth, then put an infectious humor into those amazing eyes of hers.

"Interesting, yes," she said. Her voice had an accent Jilly couldn't place and an odd tonality that was at once both husky and high-pitched. "But we—" she frowned prettily, searching for what she wanted to say "—make do."

It was obvious to Jilly that English wasn't her first language. It was also obvious, the more Jilly looked, that while the girl and her companions weren't at all properly dressed for the weather, it really didn't seem to bother them. Even with the fire in the trunk of the Buick, and mild winter or not, they should still have been shivering, but she couldn't spot one goosebump.

"And you're not cold?" she asked.

"Cold is . . . ?" Babe began, frowning again, but before Jilly could elaborate, that dazzling smile returned. "No, we have comfort. Cold is no trouble for us. We like the winter; we like any weather."

Jilly couldn't help but laugh.

"I suppose you're all snow elves," she said, "so the cold doesn't bother you?"

"Not elves—but we are good neighbors. Would you like some breakfast?"

A year and three days later, the memory of that first meeting brought a touch of warmth to Jilly where she stood shivering in the mouth of the alleyway. Gemmin. She'd always liked the taste of words and that one had sounded just right for Babe and her companions. It reminded Jilly of gummy bears, thick cotton quilts and the sound that the bass strings of Geordie's fiddle made when he was playing a fast reel. It reminded her of tiny bunches of fresh violets, touched with dew, that still couldn't hope to match the incandescent hue of Babe's eyes.

She had met the gemmin at a perfect time. She was in need of something warm and happy just then, being on the wrong end of a three-month relationship with a guy who, throughout the time they'd been together, turned out to have been married all along. He wouldn't leave his wife, and Jilly had no taste to be someone's—anyone's—mistress, all of which had been discussed in increasingly raised voices in The Monkey Woman's Nest the last time she saw him. She'd been mortified when she realized that a whole restaurant full of people had been listening to their breaking-up argument, but unrepentant.

She missed Jeff—missed him desperately—but refused to listen to any of the subsequent phonecalls or answer any of the letters that had deluged her loft over the next couple of weeks, explaining how they could "work things out." She wasn't interested in working things out. It wasn't just the fact that he had a wife, but that he'd kept it from her. The thing she kept asking her friend Sue was: having been with him for all that time, how could she not have *known*?

So she wasn't a happy camper, traipsing aimlessly through the Tombs that day. Her normally high-spirited view of the world was overhung with gloominess and there was a sick feeling in the pit of her stomach that just wouldn't go away.

Until she met Babe and her friends.

Gemmin wasn't a name that they used; they had no name for themselves. It was Frank Hodgers who told Jilly what they were.

Breakfast with the gemmin on that long gone morning was . . . odd. Jilly sat behind the driver's wheel of the Buick, with the door propped open and her feet dangling outside. Babe sat on a steel drum set a few feet from the car, facing her. Four of the other gemmin were crowded in the back seat; the fifth was beside Jilly in the front, her back against the passenger's door. The eggs were tasty, flavored with herbs that Jilly couldn't recognize; the tea had a similarly odd tang about it. The bacon was fried to a perfect crisp. The toast was actually muffins, neatly sliced in two and toasted on coat hangers rebent into new shapes for that purpose.

The gemmin acted like they were having a picnic. When Jilly introduced herself, a chorus of odd names echoed back in reply: Nita, Emmie, Callio, Yoon, Purspie. And Babe.

"Babe?" Jilly repeated.

"It was a present—from Johnny Defalco."

Jilly had seen Defalco around and talked to him once or twice. He was a hash dealer who'd had himself a squat in the Clark Building up until the end of the summer when he'd made the mistake of selling to a narc and had to leave the city just one step ahead of a warrant. Somehow, she couldn't see him keeping company with this odd little gaggle of street girls. Defalco's taste seemed to run more to what her bouncer friend Percy called the three B's—bold, blonde and built—or at least it had whenever she'd seen him in the clubs.

"He gave all of you your names?" Jilly asked.

Babe shook her head. "He only ever saw me, and whenever he did, he'd say, 'Hey Babe, how're ya doin'?' "

Babe's speech patterns seemed to change the longer they talked, Jilly remembered thinking later. She no longer sounded like a foreigner struggling with the language; instead, the words came easily, sentences peppered with conjunctions and slang.

"We miss him," Purspie—or perhaps it was Nita—said. Except for Babe, Jilly was still having trouble telling them all apart.

"He talked in the dark." That was definitely Emmie—her voice was slightly higher than those of the others.

"He told stories to the walls," Babe explained, "and we'd creep close and listen to him."

"You've lived around here for awhile?" Jilly asked.

Yoon—or was it Callio?—nodded. "All our lives."

Jilly had to smile at the seriousness with which that line was delivered. As though, except for Babe, there was one of them older than thirteen.

She spent the rest of the morning with them, chatting, listening to their odd songs, sketching them whenever she could get them to sit still for longer than five seconds. Thanks goodness, she thought more than once as she bent over her sketchbook, for life drawing classes and Albert Choira, one of her art instructors at Butler U., who had instilled in her and every one of his students the ability to capture shape and form in just a few quick strokes of charcoal.

Her depression and the sick feeling in her stomach had gone away, and her heart didn't feel nearly so fragile anymore, but all too soon it was noon and time for her to go. She had Christmas presents to deliver at St. Vincent's Home for the Aged, where she did volunteer work twice a week. Some of her favorites were going to stay with family during the holidays and today would be her last chance to see them.

"We'll be going soon, too," Babe told her when Jilly explained she had to leave.

"Going?" Jilly repeated, feeling an odd tightness in her chest. It wasn't the same kind of a feeling that Jeff had left in her, but it was discomforting all the same.

Babe nodded. "When the moon's full, we'll sail away."

"Away, away, away," the others chorused.

There was something both sweet and sad in the way they half spoke, half chanted the words. The tightness in Jilly's chest grew more pronounced. She wanted to ask, Away to where?, but found herself only saying, "But you'll be here tomorrow?"

Babe lifted a delicate hand to push back the unruly curls that were forever falling in Jilly's eyes. There was something so maternal in the motion that it made Jilly wish she could just rest her head on Babe's breast, to be protected from all that was fierce and mean and dangerous in the world beyond the enfolding comfort that that motherly embrace would offer.

"We'll be here," Babe said.

Then, giggling like schoolgirls, the little band ran off through the ruins, leaving Jilly to stand alone on the deserted street. She felt giddy and lost, all at once. She wanted to run with them, imagining Babe as a kind of archetypal Peter Pan who could take her away to a place where she could be forever young. Then she shook her head, and headed back downtown to St. Vincent's.

She saved her visit with Frank for last, as she always did. He was sitting in a wheelchair by the small window in his room that overlooked the alley between St. Vincent's and the office building next door. It wasn't much of a view, but Frank never seemed to mind.

"I'd rather stare at a brick wall, anytime, than watch that damn TV in the lounge," he'd told Jilly more than once. "That's when things started to go wrong—with the invention of television. Wasn't till then that we found out there was so much wrong in the world."

Jilly was one of those who preferred to know what was going on and try to do something about it, rather than pretend it wasn't happening and hoping that, by ignoring what was wrong, it would just go away. Truth was, Jilly had long ago learned, trouble never went away. It just got worse—unless you fixed it. But at eighty-seven, she felt that Frank was entitled to his opinions.

His face lit up when she came in the door. He was all lines and bones, as he liked to say; a skinny man, made almost cadaverous by age. His cheeks were hollowed, eyes sunken, torso collapsed in on itself. His skin was wrinkled and dry, his hair just a few white tufts around his ears. But whatever ruin the years had brought to his body, they hadn't managed to get even a fingerhold on his spirit. He could be cantankerous, but he was never bitter.

She'd first met him last spring. His son had died, and with nowhere else to go, he'd come to live at St. Vincent's. From the first afternoon that she met him in his room, he'd become one of her favorite people.

"You've got that look," he said after she'd kissed his cheek and sat down on the edge of his bed.

"What look?" Jilly asked, pretending ignorance.

She often gave the impression of being in a constant state of confusion—which was what gave her her charm, Sue had told her more than once—but she knew that Frank wasn't referring to that. It was that strange occurrences tended to gather around her; mystery clung to her like burrs on an old sweater.

At one time when she was younger, she just collected folktales and odd stories, magical rumors and mythologies—much like Geordie's brother Christy did, although she never published them. She couldn't have explained why she was drawn to that kind of story; she just liked the idea of what they had to say. But then one day she discovered that there *was* an alternate reality, and her view of the world was forever changed.

It had felt like a curse at first, knowing that magic was real, but that if she spoke of it, people would think her mad. But the wonder it woke in her could never be considered a curse and she merely learned to be careful with whom she spoke. It was in her art that she allowed herself total freedom to express what she saw from the corner of her eye. An endless stream of faerie folk paraded from her easel and sketch-book, making new homes for themselves in back alleys and city parks, on the wharves down by the waterfront or in the twisty lanes of Lower Crowsea.

In that way, she and Frank were much alike. He'd been a writer once, but, "I've told all the tales I have to tell by now," he explained to Jilly when she asked him why he'd stopped. She disagreed, but knew that his arthritis was so bad that he could neither hold a pencil nor work a keyboard for any length of time.

"You've seen something magic," he said to her now.

"I have," she replied with a grin and told him of her morning.

"Show me your sketches," Frank said when she was done.

Jilly dutifully handed them over, apologizing for the rough state they were in until Frank told her to shush. He turned the pages of the sketchbook, studying each quick drawing carefully before going on to the next one.

"They're gemmin," he pronounced finally.

"I've never heard of them."

"Most people haven't. It was my grandmother who told me about them—she saw them one night, dancing in Fitzhenry Park—but I never did."

The wistfulness in his voice made Jilly want to stage a breakout from the old folk's home and carry him off to the Tombs to meet Babe, but she knew she couldn't. She couldn't even bring him home to her own loft for the holidays because he was too dependent on the care that he could only get here. She'd never even be able to carry him up the steep stairs to her loft.

"How do you know that they're gemmin and whatever *are* gemmin?" she asked.

Frank tapped the sketchbook. "I know they're gemmin because they look just like the way my gran described them to me. And didn't you say they had violet eyes?"

"But only Babe's got them."

Frank smiled, enjoying himself. "Do you know what violet's made up of?"

"Sure. Blue and red."

"Which, symbolically, stand for devotion and passion; blended into violet, they're a symbol of memory."

"That still doesn't explain anything."

"Gemmin are the spirits of place, just like hobs are spirits of a house. They're what make a place feel good and safeguard its positive memories. When they leave, that's when a place gets a haunted feeling. And then only the bad feelings are left—or no feelings, which is just about the same difference."

"So what makes them go?" Jilly asked, remembering what Babe had said earlier.

"Nasty things happening. In the old days, it might be a murder or a battle. Nowadays we can add pollution and the like to that list."

"But—"

"They store memories you see," Frank went on. "The one you call Babe is the oldest, so her eyes have turned violet."

"So," Jilly asked with a grin. "Does it make their hair go mauve, too?"

"Don't be impudent."

They talked some more about the gemmin, going back and forth between, "Were they really?" and "What else could they be?" until it was time for Frank's supper and Jilly had to go. But first she made him open his Christmas present. His eyes filmed when he saw the tiny painting of his old house that Jilly had done for him. Sitting on the stoop was a younger version of himself with a small faun standing jauntily behind him, elbow resting on his shoulder.

"Got something in my eye," he muttered as he brought his sleeve up to his eyes.

"I just wanted you to have this today, because I brought everybody else their presents," Jilly said, "but I'm coming back on Christmas—we'll do something fun. I'd come Christmas eve, but I've got to work at the restaurant that night."

Frank nodded. His tears were gone, but his eyes were still shiny.

"The solstice is coming," he said. "In two days."

Jilly nodded, but didn't say anything.

"That's when they'll be going," Frank explained. "The gemmin. The moon'll be full, just like Babe said. Solstices are like May Eve and Halloween—the borders between this world and others are thinnest then." He gave Jilly a sad smile. "Wouldn't I love to see them before they go."

Jilly thought quickly, but she still couldn't think of any way she could maneuver him into the Tombs in his chair. She couldn't even borrow Sue's car, because the streets there were too choked with rubble and refuse. So she picked up her sketchbook and put it on his lap.

"Keep this," she said.

Then she wheeled him off to the dining room, refusing to listen to his protests that he couldn't.

* * *

A sad smile touched Jilly's lips as she stood in the storm, remembering. She walked down the alleyway and ran her mittened hand along the windshield of the Buick, dislodging the snow that had gathered there. She tried the door, but it was rusted shut. A back window was open, so she crawled in through it, then clambered into the front seat, which was relatively free of snow.

It was warmer inside—probably because she was out of the wind. She sat looking out the windshield until the snow covered it again. It was like being in a cocoon, she thought. Protected. A person could almost imagine that the gemmin were still around, not yet ready to leave. And when they did, maybe they'd take her with them. . . .

A dreamy feeling stole over her and her eyes fluttered, grew heavy, then closed. Outside the wind continued to howl, driving the snow against the car; inside, Jilly slept, dreaming of the past.

The gemmin were waiting for her the day after she saw Frank, lounging around the abandoned Buick beside the old Clark Building. She wanted to talk to them about what they were and why they were going away and a hundred other things, but somehow she just never got around to any of it. She was too busy laughing at their antics and trying to capture their portraits with the pastels she'd brought that day. Once they all sang a long song that sounded like a cross between a traditional ballad and rap, but was in some foreign language that was both flutelike and gritty. Babe later explained that it was one of their traditional song cycles, a part of their oral tradition that kept alive the histories and genealogies of their people and the places where they lived.

Gemmin, Jilly thought. Storing memories. And then she was clearheaded long enough to ask if they would come with her to visit Frank.

Babe shook her head, honest regret in her luminous eyes.

"It's too far," she said.

"Too far, too far," the other gemmin chorused.

"From home," Babe explained.

"But," Jilly began, except she couldn't find the words for what she wanted to say.

There were people who just made other people feel good. Just being around them, made you feel better, creative, uplifted, happy. Geordie said that she was like that herself, though Jilly wasn't so sure of that. She tried to be, but she was subject to the same bad moods as anybody else, the same impatience with stupidity and ignorance which, parenthetically speaking, were to her mind the prime causes of all the world's ills.

The gemmin didn't seem to have those flaws. Even better, beyond that, there was magic about them. It lay thick in the air, filling your eyes and ears and nose and heart with its wild tang. Jilly desperately wanted Frank to share this with her, but when she tried to explain it to Babe, she just couldn't seem to make herself understood.

And then she realized the time and knew she had to go to work. Art was well and fine to feed the heart and mind, and so was magic, but if she wanted to pay the rent on the loft and have anything to eat next month—never mind the endless drain that art supplies made on her meager budget—she had to go.

As though sensing her imminent departure, the gemmin bounded around her in an abandoned display of wild monkeyshines, and then vanished like so many will-o'-the-wisps in among the snowy rubble of the Tombs, leaving her alone once again.

The next day was much the same, except that tonight was the night they were leaving. Babe never made mention of it, but the knowledge hung ever heavier on Jilly as the hours progressed, coloring her enjoyment of their company.

The gemmin had washed away most of the residue of her bad breakup with Jeff, and for that Jilly was grateful. She could look on it now with that kind of wistful remembering one held for high school romances, long past and distanced. But in its place they had left a sense of abandonment. They were going, would soon be gone, and the world would be that much the emptier for their departure.

Jilly tried to find words to express what she was feeling, but as had happened yesterday when she'd tried to explain Frank's need, she couldn't get the first one past her tongue.

And then again, it was time to go. The gemmin started acting wilder again, dancing and singing around her like a pack of mad imps, but before they could all vanish once more, Jilly caught Babe's arm. Don't go, don't go, she wanted to say, but all that came out was, "I . . . I don't . . . I want . . ."

Jilly, normally never at a loss for something to say, sighed with frustration.

"We won't be gone forever," Babe said, understanding Jilly's unspoken need. She touched a long delicate finger to her temple. "We'll always be with you in here, in your memories of us, and in here—" she tapped the pocket in Jilly's coat that held her sketchbook "—in your pictures. If you don't forget us, we'll never be gone."

"It . . . it won't be the same," Jilly said.

Babe smiled sadly. "Nothing is ever the same. That's why we must go now."

She ruffled Jilly's hair—again the motion was like one made by a mother, rather than someone who appeared to be a girl only half Jilly's age—then stepped back. The other gemmin approached, and touched her as well—featherlight fingers brushing against her arms, tousling her hair like a breeze—and then they all began their mad dancing and pirouetting like so many scruffy ballerinas.

Until they were gone.

Jilly thought she would just stay here, never mind going in to work, but somehow she couldn't face a second parting. Slowly, she headed south, towards Gracie Street and the subway that would take her to work. And oddly enough, though she was sad at their leaving, it wasn't the kind of sadness that hurt. It was the kind that was like a singing in the soul.

Frank died that night, on the winter solstice, but Jilly didn't find out until the next day. He died in his sleep, Jilly's painting propped up on the night table beside him, her sketchbook with her initial rough drawings of the gemmin in it held against his thin chest. On the first blank page after her sketches of the gemmin, in an awkward script that must have taken him hours to write, he'd left her a short note:

"I have to tell you this, Jilly. I never saw any real magic—I just pretended that I did. I only knew it through the stories I got from my gran and from you. But I always believed. That's why I wrote all those stories when I was younger, because I wanted others to believe. I thought if enough of us did, if we learned to care again about the wild places from which we'd driven the magic away, then maybe it would return.

"I didn't think it ever would, but I'm going to open my window tonight and call to them. I'm going to ask them to take me with them when they go. I'm all used up—at least the man I am in this world is—but maybe in another world I'll have something to give. I hope they'll give me the chance.

"The faerie folk used to do that in the old days, you know. That was what a lot of the stories were about—people like us, going away, beyond the fields we know.

"If they take me, don't be sad, Jilly. I'll be waiting for you there."

The script was almost illegible by the time it got near the end, but Jilly managed to decipher it all. At the very end, he'd just signed the note with an "F" with a small flower drawn beside it. It looked an awful lot like a tiny violet, though maybe that was only because that was what Jilly wanted to see.

You saw real magic, she thought when she looked up from the sketchbook. You *were* real magic.

She gazed out the window of his room to where a soft snow was falling in the alley between St. Vincent's and the building next door. She hoped that on their way to wherever they'd gone, the gemmin had been able to include the tired and lonely spirit of one old man in their company.

Take care of him, Babe, she thought.

That Christmas was a quiet period in Jilly's life. She had gone to a church service for the first time since she was a child to attend the memorial service that St. Vincent's held for Frank. She and Geordie and a few of the staff of the home were the only ones in attendance. She missed Frank and found herself putting him in crowd scenes in the paintings she did over the holidays—Frank in the crowds, and the thin ghostly shapes of gemmin peering out from behind cornices and rooflines and the corners of alley-ways.

Often when she went out on her night walks—after the restaurant was closed, when the city was half-asleep—she'd hear a singing in the quiet snow-muffled streets; not an audible singing, something she could hear with her ears, but one that only her heart and spirit could feel. Then she'd wonder if it was the voices of Frank and Babe and the others she heard, singing to her from the faraway, or that of other gemmin, not yet gone.

She never thought of Jeff, except with distance.

Life was subdued. A hiatus between storms. Just thinking of that time, usually brought her a sense of peace, if not completion. So why . . . remembering now . . . this time . . . ?

There was a ringing in her ears—sharp and loud, like thunderclaps erupting directly above her. She felt as though she was in an earthquake, her body being violently shaken. Everything felt topsy-turvy. There was no up and no down, just a sense of vertigo and endless spinning, a roar and whorl of shouting and shaking until—

She snapped her eyes open to find Geordie's worried features peering out at her from the circle that the fur of his parka hood made around his face. He was in the Buick with her, on the front seat beside her. It was his hands on her shoulders, shaking her; his voice that sounded like thunder in the confines of the Buick.

The Buick.

And then she remembered: walking in the Tombs, the storm, climbing into the car, falling asleep . . .

"Jesus, Jilly," Geordie was saying. He sat back from her, giving her a bit of space, but the worry hadn't left his features yet. "You really are nuts, aren't you? I mean, falling asleep out here. Didn't you ever hear of hypothermia?"

She could have died, Jilly realized. She could have just slept on here until she froze to death and nobody'd know until the spring thaw, or until some poor homeless bugger crawled in to get out of the wind and found himself sharing space with Jilly, the Amazing Dead Woman.

She shivered, as much from dread as the storm's chill.

"How . . . how did you find me?" she asked.

Geordie shrugged. "God only knows. I got worried, the longer you were gone, until finally I couldn't stand it and had to come looking for you. It was like there was a nagging in the back of my head—sort of a Lassie kind of a thought, you know?"

Jilly had to smile at the analogy.

"Maybe I'm getting psychic—what do you think?" he asked.

"Finding me the way you did, maybe you are," Jilly said.

She sat up a little straighter, then realized that sometime during her sleep, she had unbuttoned her parka enough to stick a hand in under the coat. She pulled it out and both she and Geordie stared at what she held in her mittened hand.

It was a small violet flower, complete with roots.

"Jilly, where did you . . . ?" Geordie began, but then he shook his head. "Never mind. I don't want to know."

But Jilly knew. Tonight was the anniversary, after all. Babe or Frank, or maybe both of them, had come by as well.

If you don't forget us, we'll never be gone.

She hadn't.

And it looked like they hadn't either, because who else had left her this flower, and maybe sent Geordie out into the storm to find her? How else could he have lucked upon her the way he had with all those blocks upon blocks of the Tombs that he would have to search?

"Are you going to be okay?" Geordie asked.

Jilly stuck the plant back under her parka and nodded.

"Help me home, would you? I feel a little wobbly."

"You've got it."

"And Geordie?"

He looked at her, eyebrows raised.

"Thanks for coming out to look for me."

It was a long trek back to Jilly's loft, but this time the wind was helpful, rather than hindering. It rose up at their backs and hurried them along so that it seemed to only take them half the time it should have to return. While Jilly changed, Geordie made great steaming mugs of hot chocolate for both of them. They sat together on the old sofa by the window, Geordie in his usual rumpled sweater and old jeans, Jilly bundled up in two pairs of sweatpants, fingerless gloves and what seemed like a half-dozen shirts and socks.

Jilly told him her story of finding about the gemmin, and how they went away. When she was done, Geordie just said, "Wow. We should tell Christy about them—he'd put them in one of his books."

"Yes, we should," Jilly said. "Maybe if more people knew about them, they wouldn't be so ready to go away."

"What about Mr. Hodgers?" Geordie asked. "Do you really think they took him away with them?"

Jilly looked at the newly potted flower on her windowsill. It stood jauntily in the dirt and looked an awful lot like a drawing in one of her sketchbooks that she hadn't drawn herself.

"I like to think so," she said. "I like to think that St. Vincent's was on the way to wherever they were going." She gave Geordie a smile, more sweet than bitter. "You couldn't see it to look at him," she added, "but Frank had violet eyes, too; he had all kinds of memories stored away in that old head of his—just like Babe did."

Her own eyes took on a distant look, as though she was looking into the faraway herself, through the gates of dream and beyond the fields we know.

"I like to think they're getting along just fine," she said.

Pity the Monsters

> *We are standing in the storm of our own being.*
> —Michael Ventura

"I was a beauty once," the old woman said. "The neighborhood boys were forever standing outside my parents' home, hoping for a word, a smile, a kiss, as though somehow my unearned beauty gave me an intrinsic worth that far overshadowed Emma's cleverness with her schoolwork, or Betsy's gift for music. It always seemed unfair to me. My value was based on an accident of birth; theirs was earned."

The monster made no reply.

"I would have given anything to be clever or to have had some artistic ability," the old woman added. "Those are assets with which a body can grow old."

She drew her tattery shawl closer, hunching her thin shoulders against the cold. Her gaze went to her companion. The monster was looking at the blank expanse of wall above her head, eyes unfocused, scars almost invisible in the dim light.

"Yes, well," she said. "I suppose we all have our own cross to bear. At least I have good memories to go with the bad."

The snow was coming down so thickly that visibility had already become all but impossible. The fat wet flakes whirled and spun in dervishing clouds, clogging the sidewalks and streets, snarling traffic, making the simple act of walking an epic adventure. One could be anywhere, anywhen. The familiar was suddenly strange; the city transformed. The wind and the snow made even the commonest landmarks unrecognizable.

If she hadn't already been so bloody late, Harriet Pierson would have simply walked her mountain bike through the storm. She only lived a mile or so from the library and the trip wouldn't have taken *that* long by foot. But she was late, desperately late, and being sensible had never been her forte, so there she was, pedaling like a madwoman in her highest gear, the wheels skidding and sliding for purchase on the slippery street as she biked along the narrow passageway between the curb and the crawling traffic.

The so-called waterproof boots that she'd bought on sale last week were already soaked, as were the bottoms of her jeans. Her old camel hair coat was standing up to the cold, however, and her earmuffs kept her ears warm. The same couldn't be said for her hands and face. The wind bit straight through her thin woolen mittens, her cheeks were red with the cold, while her long, brown hair, bound up into a vague bun on the top of her head, was covered with an inch of snow that was already leaking its wet chill into her scalp.

Why did I move to this bloody country? she thought. It's too hot in the summer, too cold in the winter . . .

England looked very good right at that moment, but it hadn't always been so. England hadn't had Brian whom she'd met while on holiday here in Newford three years ago, Brian who'd been just as eager for her to come as she had been to emigrate, Brian who walked out on her not two months after she'd arrived and they had gotten an apartment together. She'd refused to go back. Deciding to make the best of her new homeland, she had stuck it out surprisingly well, not so much because she led such an ordered existence, as that she'd refused to run back home and have her mother tell her, ever so patronizingly, "Well, I told you so, dear."

She had a good job, if not a great one, a lovely little flat that was all her own, a fairly busy social life—that admittedly contained more friends than it did romantic interests—and liked everything about her new home. Except for the weather.

She turned off Yoors Street onto Kelly, navigating more by instinct than vision, and was just starting to congratulate herself on having completed her journey all in one piece, with time to spare, when a tall shape loomed suddenly up out of the whirling snow in front of her. Trying to avoid a collision, she turned the handlebars too quickly— and the wrong way.

Her front wheel hit the curb and she sailed over the handlebars, one more white airborne object defying gravity, except that unlike the lighter snowflakes with which she momentarily shared the sky, her weight brought her immediately down with a jarring impact against a heap of refuse that someone had set out in anticipation of tomorrow's garbage pickup.

She rose spluttering snow and staggered back towards her bike, disoriented, the suddenness of her accident not yet having sunk in. She knelt beside the bike and stared with dismay at the bent wheel frame. Then she remembered what had caused her to veer in the first place.

Her gaze went to the street, but then traveled up, and up, to the face of the tall shape that stood by the curb. The man was a giant. At five-one, Harriet wasn't tall, and perhaps it had something to do with her low perspective, but he seemed to be at least seven feet high. And yet it wasn't his size that brought the small gasp to her lips.

That face . . .

It was set in a squarish head which was itself perched on thick broad shoulders. The big nose was bent, the left eye was slightly higher than the right, the ears were like huge cauliflowers, the hairline high and square. Thick white scars crisscrossed his features, giving the impression that he'd been sewn together by some untalented seamstress who was too deep in her cups to do a proper job. An icon from an old horror movie flashed in Harriet's mind and she found herself looking for the bolts in the man's neck before she even knew what she was doing.

Of course they weren't there, but the size of the man and the way he was just standing there, staring at her, made Harriet unaccountably nervous as though this really was Victor Frankenstein's creation standing over her in the storm. She stood quickly, wanting to lessen the discrepancy of their heights. The sudden movement woke a wave of dizziness.

"I'm dreadfully sorry," she meant to say, but the words slurred, turning to mush in her mouth and what came out was, "Redfolly shurry."

Vertigo jellied her legs and made the street underfoot so wobbly that she couldn't keep her balance. The giant took a quick step towards her, huge hands outstretched, as a black wave swept over her and she pitched forward.

Bloody hell, she had time to think. I'm going all faint. . . .

Water bubbled merrily in the tin can that sat on the Coleman stove's burner. The old woman leaned forward and dropped in a tea bag, then moved the can from the heat with a mittened hand.

Only two more bags left, she thought.

She held her hands out to the stove and savored the warmth.

"I married for money, not love," she told her companion. "My Henry was not a handsome man."

The monster gaze focused and tracked down to her face.

"But I grew to love him. Not for his money, nor for the comfort of his home and the safety it offered to a young woman whose future, for all her beauty, looked to take her no further than the tenements in which she was born and bred."

The monster made a querulous noise, no more than a grunt, but the old woman could hear the question in it. They'd been together for so long that she could read him easily, without his needing to speak.

"It was for his kindness," she said.

Harriet woke to the cold. Shivering, she sat up to find herself in an unfamiliar room, enwrapped in a nest of blankets that carried a pungent, musty odor in their folds. The room itself appeared to be part of some abandoned building. The walls were unadorned except for their chipped paint and plaster and a cheerful bit of graffiti suggesting that the reader of it do something that Harriet didn't think was anatomically possible.

There were no furnishings at all. The only light came from a short, fat candle which sat on the windowsill in a puddle of cooled wax. Outside, the wind howled. In the room, in the building itself, all was still. But as she cocked her head to listen, she could just faintly make out a low murmur of conversation. It appeared to be a monologue, for it was simply one voice, droning on.

She remembered her accident and the seven-foot tall giant as though they were only something she'd experienced in a dream. The vague sense of dislocation she'd felt upon awakening had grown into a dreamy kind of muddled feeling. She was somewhat concerned over her whereabouts, but not in any sort of a pressing way. Her mind seemed to be in a fog.

Getting up, she hesitated for a moment, then wrapped one of the smelly blankets about her shoulders like a shawl against the cold and crossed the room to its one doorway. Stepping outside, she found herself in a hall as disrepaired and empty as the room she'd just quit. The murmuring voice led her down the length of the hall into what proved to be a foyer. Leaning against the last bit of wall, there where the hallway opened up into the larger space, she studied the odd scene before her.

Seven candles sat in their wax on wooden orange crates that were arranged in a half circle around an old woman. She had her back to the wall, legs tucked up under what appeared to be a half-dozen skirts. A ratty shawl covered her grey hair and hung down over her shoulders. Her face was a spiderweb of lines, all pinched and thin. Water steamed in a large tin can on a Coleman stove that stood on the floor in front of her. She had another, smaller tin can in her hand filled with, judging by the smell that filled the room, some kind of herbal tea. She was talking softly to no one that Harriet could see.

The old woman looked up just as Harriet was trying to decide how to approach her. The candlelight woke an odd glimmer in the woman's eyes, a reflective quality that reminded Harriet of a cat's gaze caught in a car's headbeams.

"And who are you, dear?" the woman asked.

"I . . . my name's Harriet. Harriet Pierson." She got the odd feeling that she should curtsy as she introduced herself.

"You may call me Flora," the old woman said. "My name's actually Anne Boddeker, but I prefer Flora."

Harriet nodded absently. Under the muddle of her thoughts, the first sharp wedge of concern was beginning to surface. She remembered taking a fall from her bike . . . had she hit her head?

"What am I doing here?" she asked.

The old woman's eyes twinkled with humor. "Now how would I know?"

"But . . ." The fuzz in Harriet's head seemed to thicken. She blinked a couple of times and then cleared her throat. "Where are we?" she tried.

"North of Gracie Street," Flora replied, "in that part of town that, I believe, people your age refer to as Squatland. I'm afraid I don't know the exact address. Vandals have played havoc with the street signs, as I'm sure you know, but I believe we're not far from the corner of Flood and MacNeil where I grew up."

Harriet's heart sank. She was in the Tombs, an area of Newford that had once been a developer's bright dream. The old, tired blocks of tenements, office buildings and factories were to be transformed into a yuppie paradise and work had already begun on tearing down the existing structures when a sudden lack of backing had left the developer scrambling for solvency. All that remained now of the bright dream was block upon block of abandoned buildings and rubble-strewn lots generally referred to as the Tombs. It was home to runaways, the homeless, derelicts, bikers, drug addicts and the like who squatted in its buildings.

It was also probably one of the most dangerous parts of Newford.

"I . . . how did I get here?" Harriet tried again.

"What do you remember?" Flora said.

"I was biking home from work," Harriet began and then proceeded to relate what she remembered of the storm, the giant who'd loomed up so suddenly out of the snow, her accident . . . "And then I suppose I must have fainted."

She lifted a hand to her head and searched about for a tender spot, but couldn't find a lump or a bruise.

"Did he speak to you?" Flora asked. "The . . . man who startled you?"

Harriet shook her head.

"Then it was Frank. He must have brought you here."

Harriet thought about what the old woman had just said.

"Does that mean there's more than one of him?" she asked. She had the feeling that her memory was playing tricks on her when she tried to call up the giant's scarred and misshapen features. She couldn't imagine there being more than one of him.

"In a way," Flora said.

"You're not being very clear."

"I'm sorry."

But she didn't appear to be, Harriet realized.

"So . . . he, this Frank . . . he's mute?" she asked.

"Terrible, isn't it?" Flora said. "A great big strapping lad like that."

Harriet nodded in agreement. "But that doesn't explain what you meant by there being more than one of him. Does he have a brother?"

"He . . ." The old woman hesitated. "Perhaps you should ask him yourself."

"But you just said that he was a mute."

"I think he's down that hall," Flora said, ignoring Harriet. She pointed to a doorway opposite from the one that Harriet had used to enter the foyer. "That's usually where he goes to play."

Harriet stood there for a long moment, just looking at the old woman. Flora, Anne, whatever her name was—she was obviously senile. That had to explain her odd manner.

Harriet lifted her gaze to look in the direction Flora had pointed. Her thoughts still felt muddy. She found standing as long as she had been was far more tiring than it should have been and her tongue felt all fuzzy.

All she wanted to do was to go home. But if this *was* the Tombs, then she'd need directions. Perhaps even protection from some of the more feral characters who were said to inhabit these abandoned buildings. Unless, she thought glumly, this "Frank" was the danger himself. . . .

She looked back at Flora, but the old woman was ignoring her. Flora drew her shawl more tightly around her shoulders and took a sip of tea from her tin can.

Bother, Harriet thought and started across the foyer.

Halfway down the new hallway, she heard a child's voice singing softly. She couldn't make out the words until she'd reached the end of the hall where yet another candlelit room offered up a view of its bizarre occupant.

Frank was sitting cross-legged in the middle of the room, the contents of Harriet's purse scattered on the floor by his knees. Her purse itself had been tossed into a corner. Harriet would have backed right out of the room before Frank looked up except that she was frozen in place by the singing. The child's voice came from Frank's twisted lips—a high, impossibly sweet sound. It was a little girl's voice, singing a skipping song:

> *Frank and Harriet, sitting in a tree*
> *K-I-S-S-I-N-G*
> *First comes love, then comes marriage*
> *Here comes Frank with a baby's carriage*

Frank's features seemed more monstrous than ever with that sweet child's voice issuing from his throat. He tossed the contents of Harriet's wallet into the air, juggling them. Her ID, a credit card, some photos from back home, scraps of paper with addresses or phone numbers on them, paper money, her bank card . . . they did a fluttering fandango as he sang, the movement of his hands oddly graceful for all the scarred squat bulk of his fingers. Her makeup, keys and loose change were lined up in rows like toy soldiers on parade in front of him. A half-burned ten dollar bill lay beside a candle on the wooden crate to his right. On the crate to his left lay a dead cat, curled up as though it was only sleeping, but the glassy dead eyes and swollen tongue that pushed open its jaws gave lie to the pretense.

Harriet felt a scream build up in her throat. She tried to back away, but bumped into the wall. The child's voice went still and Frank looked up. Photos, paper money, paper scraps and all flittered down upon his knees. His gaze locked on hers.

For one moment, Harriet was sure it was a child's eyes that regarded her from that ruined face. They carried a look of pure, absolute innocence, utterly at odds with the misshapen flesh and scars that surrounded them. But then they changed, gaining a feral, dark intelligence.

Frank scattered the scraps of paper and money in front of him away with a sweep of his hands.

"Mine," he cried in a deep, booming voice. "Girl is mine!"

As he lurched to his feet, Harriet fled back the way she'd come.

"The hardest thing," the old woman said, "is watching everybody die. One by one, they all die: your parents, your friends, your family. . . ."

Her voice trailed off, rheumy eyes going sad. The monster merely regarded her.

"It was hardest when Julie died," she went on after a moment. There was a hitch in her voice as she spoke her daughter's name. "It's not right that parents should outlive their children." Her gaze settled on the monster's face. "But then you'll never know that particular pain, will you?"

The monster threw back his head and a soundless howl tore from his throat.

As Harriet ran back into the room where she'd left Flora, she saw that the old woman was gone. Her candles, the crates and stove remained. The tin can half full of tea sat warming on the edge of the stove, not quite on the lit burner.

Harried looked back down the hall where Frank's shambling bulk stumbled towards her.

She had to get out of this place. Never mind the storm still howling outside the building, never mind the confusing maze of abandoned buildings and refuse-choked streets of the Tombs. She just had to—

"There you are," a voice said from directly behind her.

Harriet heart skipped a beat. A sharp, small inadvertent squeak escaped her lips as she flung herself to one side and then backed quickly away from the shadows by the door from which the voice had come. When she realized it was only the old woman, she kept right on backing up. Whoever, whatever, Flora was, Harriet knew she wasn't a friend.

Frank shambled into the foyer then, the queer lopsided set of his gaze fixed hungrily upon her. Harriet's heartbeat kicked into double-time. Her throat went dry. The muscles of her chest tightened, squeezing her lungs so that she found it hard to breathe.

Oh god, she thought. Get out of here while you can.

But she couldn't seem to move. Her limbs were deadened weights and she was starting to feel faint again.

"Now, now," the old woman said. "Don't carry on so, Samson, or you'll frighten her to death."

The monster obediently stopped in the doorway, but his hungry gaze never left Harriet.

"Sam-samson?" Harriet asked in a weak voice.

"Oh, there's all sorts of bits and pieces of people inside that poor ugly head," Flora replied. "Comes from traumas he suffered as a child. He suffers from—what was it that Dr. Adams called him? Dissociation. I think, before the accident, the doctor had documented seventeen people inside him. Some are harmless, such as Frank and little Bessie. Others, like Samson, have an unfortunate capacity for violence when they can't have their way."

"Doctor?" Harriet asked. All she seemed capable of was catching a word from the woman's explanation and repeating it as a question.

"Yes, he was institutionalized as a young boy. The odd thing is that he's somewhat aware of all the different people living inside him. He thinks that when his father sewed him back together, he used parts of all sorts of different people to do so and those bits of alien skin and tissue took hold of his mind and borrowed parts of it for their own use."

"That . . ." Harriet cleared her throat. "That was the . . . accident?"

"Oh, it wasn't any accident," Flora said. "And don't let anyone try to tell you different. His father knew exactly what he was doing when he threw him through that plate glass window."

"But . . ."

"Of course, the father was too poor to be able to afford medical attention for the boy, so he patched him up on his own."

Harriet stared at the monstrous figure with growing horror.

"This . . . none of this can be true," she finally managed.

"It's all documented at the institution," Flora told her. "His father made a full confession before they locked him away. Poor Frank, though. It was too late to do anything to help him by that point, so he ended up being put away as well, for all that his only crime was the misfortune of being born the son of a lunatic."

Harriet tore her gaze from Frank's scarred features and turned to the old woman.

"How do you know all of this?" she asked.

"Why, I lived there as well," Flora said. "Didn't I tell you?"

"No. No, you didn't."

Flora shrugged. "It's old history. Mind you, when you get to be my age, everything's old history."

Harriet wanted to ask why Flora had been in the institution herself, but couldn't find the courage to do so. She wasn't even sure she *wanted* to know. But there was something she had no choice but to ask. She hugged her blanket closer around her, no longer even aware of its smell, but the chill that was in her bones didn't come from the cold.

"What happens now?" she said.

"I'm not sure I understand the question," Flora replied with a sly smile in her eyes that said she understood all too well.

Harriet pressed forward. "What happens to me?"

"Well, now," Flora said. She shot the monster an affectionate look. "Frank wants to start a family."

Harriet shook her head. "No," she said, her voice sounding weak and ineffectual even to her own ears. "No way."

"You don't exactly have a say in the matter, dear. It's not as though there's anyone coming to rescue you—not in this storm. And even if someone did come searching, where would they look? People disappear in this city all of the time. It's a sad, but unavoidable fact in these trying times that we've brought upon ourselves."

Harriet was still shaking her head.

"Oh, think of someone else for a change," the old woman told her. "I know your type. You're filled with your own self-importance; the whole world revolves around you. It's a party here, an evening of dancing there, theatre, clubs, cabaret, with never a thought for those less fortunate. What would it hurt you to give a bit of love and affection to a poor, lonely monster?"

I've gone all demented, Harriet thought. All of this—the monster, the lunatic calm of the old woman—none of it was real. None of it *could* be real.

"Do you think he *likes* being this way?" Flora demanded.

Her voice grew sharp and the monster shifted nervously at the tone of her anger, the way a dog might bristle, catching its master's mood.

"It's got nothing to do with me," Harriet said, surprising herself that she could still find the courage to stand up for herself. "I'm not like you think I am and I had nothing to do with what happened to that—to Frank."

"It's got everything to do with you," the old woman replied. "It's got to do with caring and family and good Samaritanism and decency and long, lasting relationships."

"You can't force a person into something like that," Harriet argued.

Flora sighed. "Sometimes, in *these* times, it's the only way. There's a sickness abroad in the world, child; your denial of what's right and true is as much a cause as a symptom."

"You're the one that's sick!" Harriet cried.

She bolted for the building's front doors, praying they weren't locked. The monster was too far away and moved too slowly to stop her. The old woman was closer and quicker, but in her panic, Harriet found the strength to fling her bodily away. She raced for the glass doors that led out of the foyer and into the storm.

The wind almost drove her back inside when she finally got a door open, but she pressed against it, through the door and out onto the street. The whirling snow, driven by the mad, capricious wind, soon stole away all sense of direction, but she didn't dare stop. She plowed through drifts, blinded by the snow, head bent against the howling wind, determined to put as much distance between herself and what she fled.

Oh god, she thought at one point. My purse was back there. My ID. They know where I live. They can come and get me at home, or at work, anytime they want.

But mostly she fought the snow and wind. How long she fled through the blizzard, she had no way of knowing. It might have been an hour, it might have been the whole night. She was shaking with cold and fear when she stumbled to the ground one last time and couldn't get up.

She lay there, a delicious sense of warmth enveloping her. All she had to do was let go, she realized. Just let go and she could drift away into that dark, warm place that beckoned to her. She rolled over on her side and stared up into the white sky. Snow immediately filmed her face. She rubbed it away with her hand, already half-frozen with the cold.

She was ready to let go. She was ready to just give up the struggle, because she was only so strong and she'd given it her all, hadn't she? She—

A tall dark figure loomed up suddenly, towering over her. Snow blurred her sight so that it was only a shape, an outline, against the white.

No, she pleaded. Don't take me back. I'd rather die than go back.

As the figure bent down beside her, she found the strength to beat at it with her frozen hands.

"Easy now," a kind voice said, blocking her weak blows. "We'll get you out of here."

She stopped trying to fight. It wasn't the monster, but a policeman. Somehow, in her aimless flight, she'd wandered out of the Tombs.

"What are you doing out here?" the policeman said.

Monster, she wanted to say. There's a monster. It attacked me. But all that came out from her frozen lips was, "Muh . . . tacked me . . ."

"First we'll get you out of this weather," he told her, "then we'll deal with the man who assaulted you."

The hours that followed passed in a blur. She was in a hospital, being treated for frostbite. A detective interviewed her, calmly, patiently sifting through her mumbled replies for a description of what had happened to her, and then finally she was left alone.

At one point she came out of her dozing state and thought she saw two policeman standing at the end of her bed. She wasn't sure if they were actually present or not, but like Agatha Christie characters, gathered at the denouement of one of the great mystery writer's stories, their conversation conveniently filled in some details concerning her captors of which she hadn't been aware.

"Maybe it was before your time," one of the policemen was saying, "but that description she gave fits."

"No, I remember," the other replied. "They were residents in the Zeb's criminal ward and Cross killed their shrink during a power failure."

The first officer nodded. "I don't know which of them was worse: Cross with that monstrous face, or Boddeker."

"Poisoned her whole family, didn't she?"

"Yeah, but I remember seeing what Cross did to the shrink—just about tore the poor bastard in two."

"I heard that it was Boddeker who put him up to it. The poor geek doesn't have a mind of his own."

Vaguely, as though observing the action from a vast distance, Harriet could sense the first officer looking in her direction.

"She's lucky she's still alive," he added, looking back at his companion.

In the days that followed, researching old newspapers at the library, Harriet found out that all that the two men had said, or that she'd dreamed they had said, was true, but she couldn't absorb any of it at the moment. For now she just drifted away once more, entering a troubled sleep that was plagued with dreams of ghosts and monsters. The latter wore masks to hide the horror inside them, and they were the worst of all.

She woke much later, desperately needing to pee. It was still dark in her room. Outside she could hear the wind howling.

She fumbled her way into the bathroom and did her business, then stared into the mirror after she'd flushed. There was barely enough light for the mirror to show her reflection. What looked back at her from the glass was a ghostly face that she almost didn't recognize.

"Monsters," she said softly, not sure if what she felt was pity or fear, not sure if she recognized one in herself, or if it was just the old woman's lunatic calm still pointing an accusing finger.

She stared at that spectral reflection for a very long time before she finally went back to bed.

"We'll find you another," the old woman said.

Her tea had gone cold but she was too tired to relight the stove and make herself another cup. Her hand were folded on her lap, her gaze fixed on the tin can of cold water that still sat on the stove. A film of ice was forming on the water.

"You'll see," she added. "We'll find another, but this time we'll put her together ourselves, just the way your father did with you. We'll take a bit from one and a bit from another and we'll make you the perfect mate, just see if we don't. I always was a fair hand with a needle and thread, you know—a necessary quality for a wife in my time. Of course everything's different now, everything's changed. Sometimes I wonder why we bother to go on. . . ."

The monster stared out the window to where the snow still fell, quietly now, the blizzard having moved on, leaving only this calm memory of its storm winds in its wake. He gave no indication that he was listening to the old woman, but she went on talking all the same.

Ghosts of Wind
and Shadow

*There may be great and undreamed of possibilities
awaiting mankind; but because of our line of descent there are also
queer limitations.*
—Clarence Day, from *This Simian World*

Tuesday and Thursday afternoons, from two to four, Meran Kelledy gave flute lessons at the Old Firehall on Lee Street which served as Lower Crowsea's community center. A small room in the basement was set aside for her at those times. The rest of the week it served as an office for the editor of *The Crowsea Times,* the monthly community newspaper.

The room always had a bit of a damp smell about it. The walls were bare except for two old posters: one sponsored a community rummage sale, now long past; the other was an advertisement for a Jilly Coppercorn one-woman show at the The Green Man Gallery featuring a reproduction of the firehall that had been taken from the artist's *In Lower Crowsea* series of street scenes. It, too, was long out of date.

Much of the room was taken up by a sturdy oak desk. A computer sat on its broad surface, always surrounded by a clutter of manuscripts waiting to be put on diskette, spot art, advertisements, sheets of Lettraset, glue sticks, pens, pencils, scratch pads and the like. Its printer was relegated to an apple crate on the floor. A large cork board in easy reach of the desk held a bewildering array of pinned-up slips of paper with almost indecipherable notes and appointments jotted on them. Post-its laureled the frame of the cork board and the sides of the computer like festive yellow decorations. A battered metal filing cabinet held back issues of the newspaper. On top of it was a vase with dried flowers—not so much an arrangement as a forgotten bouquet. One week of the month, the entire desk was covered with the current issue in progress in its various stages of layout.

It was not a room that appeared conducive to music, despite the presence of two small music stands taken from their storage spot behind the filing cabinet and set out in the open space between the desk and door along with a pair of straight-backed wooden chairs, salvaged twice a week from a closet down the hall. But music has its own enchantment and the first few notes of an old tune are all that it requires to transform any site into a place of magic, even if that location is no more than a windowless office cubicle in the Old Firehall's basement.

Meran taught an old style of flute-playing. Her instrument of choice was that enduring cousin of the silver transverse orchestral flute: a simpler wooden instrument, side-blown as well, though it lacked a lip plate to help direct the airstream; keyless with only six holes. It was popularly referred to as an Irish flute since it was used for the playing of traditional Irish and Scottish dance music and the plaintive slow airs native to those same countries, but it had relatives in most countries of the world as well as in baroque orchestras.

In one form or another, it was one of the first implements created by ancient people to give voice to the mysteries that words cannot encompass, but that they had a need to express; only the drum was older.

With her last student of the day just out the door, Meran began the ritual of cleaning her instrument in preparation to packing it away and going home herself. She separated the flute into its three parts, swabbing dry the inside of each piece with a piece of soft cotton attached to a flute-rod. As she was putting the instrument away in its case, she realized that there was a woman standing in the doorway, a hesitant presence, reluctant to disturb the ritual until Meran was ready to notice her.

"Mrs. Batterberry," Meran said. "I'm sorry. I didn't realize you were there."

The mother of her last student was in her late thirties, a striking, well-dressed woman whose attractiveness was undermined by an obvious lack of self-esteem.

"I hope I'm not intruding . . . ?"

"Not at all; I'm just packing up. Please have a seat."

Meran indicated the second chair, which Mrs. Batterberry's daughter had so recently vacated. The woman walked gingerly into the room and perched on the edge of the chair, handbag clutched in both hands. She looked for all the world like a bird that was ready at any moment to erupt into flight and be gone.

"How can I help you, Mrs. Batterberry?" Meran asked.

"Please, call me Anna."

"Anna it is."

Meran waited expectantly.

"I . . . . it's about Lesli," Mrs. Batterberry finally began.

Meran nodded encouragingly. "She's doing very well. I think she has a real gift."

"Here perhaps, but . . . well, look at this."

Drawing a handful of folded papers from her handbag, she passed them over to Meran. There were about five sheets of neat, closely-written lines of what appeared to be a school essay. Meran recognized the handwriting as Lesli's. She read the teacher's remarks, written in red ink at the top of the first page—"Well written and imaginative, but the next time, please stick to the assigned topic"—then quickly scanned through the pages. The last two paragraphs bore rereading:

"The old gods and their magics did not dwindle away into murky memories of brownies and little fairies more at home in a Disney cartoon; rather, they changed. The coming of Christ and Christians actually freed them. They were no longer bound to people's expectations but could now become anything that they could imagine themselves to be.

"They are still here, walking among us. We just don't recognize them anymore."

Meran looked up from the paper. "It's quite evocative."

"The essay was supposed to be on one of the ethnic minorities of Newford," Mrs. Batterberry said.

"Then, to a believer in Faerie," Meran said with a smile, "Lesli's essay would seem most apropos."

"I'm sorry," Mrs. Batterberry said, "but I can't find any humor in this situation. This—" she indicated the essay "—it just makes me uncomfortable."

"No, I'm the one who's sorry," Meran said. "I didn't mean to make light of your worries, but I'm also afraid that I don't understand them."

Mrs. Batterberry looked more uncomfortable than ever. "It . . . it just seems so obvious. She must be involved with the occult, or drugs. Perhaps both."

"Just because of this essay?" Meran asked. She only just managed to keep the incredulity from her voice.

"Fairies and magic are all she ever talks about—or did talk about, I should say. We don't seem to have much luck communicating anymore."

Mrs. Batterberry fell silent then. Meran looked down at the essay, reading more of it as she waited for Lesli's mother to go on. After a few moments, she looked up to find Mrs. Batterberry regarding her hopefully.

Meran cleared her throat. "I'm not exactly sure why it is that you've come to me," she said finally.

"I was hoping you'd talk to her—to Lesli. She adores you. I'm sure she'd listen to you."

"And tell her what?"

"That this sort of thinking—" Mrs. Batterberry waved a hand in the general direction of the essay that Meran was holding "—is wrong."

"I'm not sure that I can—"

Before Meran could complete her sentence with "do that," Mrs. Batterberry reached over and gripped her hand.

"Please," the woman said. "I don't know where else to turn. She's going to be sixteen in a few days. Legally, she can live on her own then and I'm afraid she's just going to leave home if we can't get this settled. I won't have drugs or . . . or occult things in my house. But I . . ." Her eyes were suddenly swimming with unshed tears. "I don't want to lose her. . . ."

She drew back. From her handbag, she fished out a handkerchief which she used to dab at her eyes.

Meran sighed. "All right," she said. "Lesli has another lesson with me on Thursday—a makeup one for having missed one last week. I'll talk to her then, but I can't promise you anything."

Mrs. Batterberry looked embarrassed, but relieved. "I'm sure you'll be able to help."

Meran had no such assurances, but Lesli's mother was already on her feet and heading for the door, forestalling any attempt Meran might have tried to muster to back out of the situation. Mrs. Batterberry paused in the doorway and looked back.

"Thank you so much," she said, and then she was gone.

Meran stared sourly at the space Mrs. Batterberry had occupied.

"Well, isn't this just wonderful," she said.

From Lesli's diary, entry dated October 12th:

I saw another one today! It wasn't at all the same as the one I spied on the Common last week. That one was more like a wizened little monkey, dressed up like an Arthur Rackham leprechaun. If I'd told anybody about him, they'd say that it *was* just a dressed-up monkey, but we know better, don't we?

This is just so wonderful. I've always known they were there, of course. All around. But they were just hints, things I'd see out of the corner of my eye, snatches of music or conversation that I'd hear in a park or the backyard, when no one else was around. But ever since Midsummer's Eve, I've actually been able to see them.

I feel like a birder, noting each new separate species I spot down here on your pages, but was there ever a birdwatcher that could claim to have seen the marvels I have? It's like, all of a sudden, I've finally learned how to *see*.

This one was at the Old Firehall of all places. I was having my weekly lesson with Meran—I get two this week because she was out of town last week. Anyway, we were playing my new tune—the one with the arpeggio bit in the second part that I'm supposed to be practicing but can't quite get the hang of. It's easy when Meran's playing along with me, but when I try to do it on my own, my fingers get all fumbly and I keep muddling up the middle D.

I seem to have gotten sidetracked. Where was I? Oh yes. We were playing "Touch Me If You Dare" and it really sounded nice with both of us playing. Meran just seemed to pull my playing along with hers until it got lost in her music and you couldn't tell which instrument was which, or even how many there were playing.

It was one of those perfect moments. I felt like I was in a trance or something. I had my eyes closed, but then I felt the air getting all thick. There was this weird sort of pressure on my skin, as though gravity had just doubled or something. I kept on playing, but I opened my eyes and that's when I saw her—hovering up behind Meran's shoulders.

She was the neatest thing I've ever seen—just the tiniest little faerie, ever so pretty, with gossamer wings that moved so quickly to keep her aloft that they were just a blur. They moved like a hummingbird's wings. She looked just like the faeries on a pair of earrings I got a few years ago at a stall in the Market—sort of a Mucha design and all delicate and airy. But she wasn't two-dimensional or just one color.

Her wings were like a rainbow blaze. Her hair was like honey, her skin a soft-burnished gold. She was wearing—now don't blush, diary—nothing at all on top and just a gauzy skirt that seemed to be made of little leaves that kept changing colour, now sort of pink, now mauve, now bluish.

I was so surprised that I almost dropped my flute. I didn't—wouldn't that give Mom something to yell at me for if I broke it!—but I did muddle the tune. As soon as the music faltered—just like that, as though the only thing that was keeping her in this world was that tune—she disappeared.

I didn't pay a whole lot of attention to what Meran was saying for the rest of the lesson, but I don't think she noticed. I couldn't get the faerie out of my mind. I still can't. I wish Mom had been there to see her, or stupid old Mr. Allen. They couldn't say it was just my imagination then!

Of course they probably wouldn't have been able to see her anyway. That's the thing with magic. You've got to know it's still here, all around us, or it just stays invisible for you.

After my lesson, Mom went in to talk to Meran and made me wait in the car. She wouldn't say what they'd talked about, but she seemed to be in a way better mood than usual when she got back. God, I wish she wouldn't get so uptight.

"So," Cerin said finally, setting aside his book. Meran had been moping about the house for the whole of the hour since she'd gotten home from the Firehall. "Do you want to talk about it?"

"You'll just say I told you so."

"Told you so how?"

Meran sighed. "Oh, you know. How did you put it? 'The problem with teaching children is that you have to put up with their parents.' It was something like that."

Cerin joined her in the windowseat, where she'd been staring out at the garden. He looked out at the giant old oaks that surrounded the house and said nothing for a long moment. In the fading afternoon light, he could see little brown men scurrying about in the leaves like so many monkeys.

"But the kids are worth it," he said finally.

"I don't see you teaching children."

"There's just not many parents that can afford a harp for their prodigies."

"But still . . ."

"Still," he agreed. "You're perfectly right. I don't like dealing with their parents; never did. When I see children put into little boxes, their enthusiasms stifled . . . Everything gets regimented into what's proper and what's not, into recitals and passing examinations instead of just playing—" he began to mimic a hoity-toity voice "—I don't care if you want to play in a rock band, you'll learn what I tell you to learn. . . ."

His voice trailed off. In the back of his eyes, a dark light gleamed—not quite anger, more frustration.

"It makes you want to give them a good whack," Meran said.

"Exactly. So did you?"

Meran shook her head. "It wasn't like that, but it was almost as bad. No, maybe it was worse."

She told her husband about what Lesli's mother had asked of her, handing over the English essay when she was done so that he could read it for himself.

"This is quite good, isn't it?" he said when he reached the end.

Meran nodded. "But how can I tell Lesli that none of it's true when I know it is?"

"You can't."

Cerin laid the essay down on the windowsill and looked out at the oaks again. The twilight had crept up on the garden while they were talking. All the trees wore thick mantles of shadow now—poor recompense for the glorious cloaks of leaves that the season had stolen from them over the past few weeks. At the base of one fat trunk, the little monkeymen were roasting skewers of mushrooms and acorns over a small, almost smokeless fire.

"What about Anna Batterberry herself?" he asked. "Does she remember anything?"

Meran shook her head. "I don't think she even realizes that we've met before, that she changed but we never did. She's like most people; if it doesn't make sense, she'd rather convince herself that it simply never happened."

Cerin turned from the window to regard his wife.

"Perhaps the solution would be to remind her, then," he said.

"I don't think that's such a good idea. It'd probably do more harm than good. She's just not the right sort of person . . ."

Meran sighed again.

"But she could have been," Cerin said.

"Oh yes," Meran said, remembering. "She could have been. But it's too late for her now."

Cerin shook his head. "It's never too late."

From Lesli's diary, addendum to the entry dated October 12th:

I hate living in this house! I just hate it! How could she do this to me? It's bad enough that she never lets me so much as breathe without standing there behind me to determine that I'm not making a vulgar display of myself in the process, but this really isn't fair.

I suppose you're wondering what I'm talking about. Well, remember that essay I did on ethnic minorities for Mr. Allen? Mom got her hands on it and it's convinced her that I've turned into a Satan-worshipping drug fiend. The worst thing is that she gave it to Meran and now Meran's supposed to "have a talk with me to set me straight" on Thursday.

I just hate this. She had no right to do that. And how am I supposed to go to my lesson now? It's so embarrassing. Not to mention disappointing. I thought Meran would understand. I never thought she'd take Mom's side—not on something like this.

Meran's always seemed so special. It's not just that she wears all those funky clothes and doesn't talk down to me and looks just like one of those Pre-Raphaelite women, except that she's got those really neat green streaks in her hair. She's just a great person. She makes playing music seem so effortlessly magical and she's got all these really great stories about the origins of the tunes. When she talks about things like where "The Gold Ring" came from, it's like she really believes it was the faeries that gave that piper the tune in exchange for the lost ring he returned to them. The way she tells it, it's like she was there when it happened.

I feel like I've always known her. From the first time I saw her, I felt like I was meeting an old friend. Sometimes I think that she's magic herself—a kind of oak-tree faerie princess who's just spending a few years living in the Fields We Know before she goes back home to the magic place where she really lives.

Why would someone like that involve themselves in my mother's crusade against Faerie?

I guess I was just being naive. She's probably no different from Mom or Mr. Allen and everybody else who doesn't believe. Well, I'm not going to any more stupid flute lessons, that's for sure.

I hate living here. Anything'd be better.

Oh, why couldn't I just have been stolen by the faeries when I was a baby? Then I'd *be* there and there'd just be some changeling living here in my place. Mom could turn *it* into a good little robot instead. Because that's all she wants. She doesn't want a daughter who can think on her own, but a boring, closed-minded junior model of herself. She should have gotten a dog instead of having a kid. Dogs are easy to train and they like being led around on a leash.

I wish Granny Nell was still alive. She would never, ever have tried to tell me that I had to grow up and stop imagining things. Everything seemed magic when she was around. It was like she was magic—just like Meran. Sometimes when Meran's playing her flute, I almost feel as though Granny Nell's sitting there with us, just listening to the music with that sad wise smile of hers.

I know I was only five when she died, but lots of the time she seems more real to me than any of my relatives that are still alive. If she was still alive, I could be living with her right now and everything'd be really great.

Jeez, I miss her.

Anna Batterberry was in an anxious state when she pulled up in front of the Kelledy house on McKennitt Street. She checked the street number that hung beside the wrought-iron gate where the walkway met the sidewalk and compared it against the address she'd hurriedly scribbled down on a scrap of paper before leaving home. When she was sure that they were the same, she slipped out of the car and approached the gate.

Walking up to the house, the sound of her heels was loud on the walkway's flagstones. She frowned at the thick carpet of fallen oak leaves that covered the lawn. The Kelledys had better hurry in cleaning them up, she thought. The city work crews would only be collecting leaves for one more week and they had to be neatly bagged and sitting at the curb for them to do so. It was a shame that such a pretty estate wasn't treated better.

When she reached the porch, she spent a disorienting moment trying to find a doorbell, then realized that there was only the small brass door knocker in the middle of the door. It was shaped like a Cornish piskie.

The sight of it gave her a queer feeling. Where had she seen that before? In one of Lesli's books, she supposed.

Lesli.

At the thought of her daughter, she quickly reached for the knocker, but the door swung open before she could use it. Lesli's flute teacher stood in the open doorway and regarded her with a puzzled look.

"Anna," Meran said, her voice betraying her surprise. "Whatever are you—"

"It's Lesli," Anna said, interrupting. "She's . . . she . . ."

Her voice trailed off as what she could see of the house's interior behind Meran registered. A strange dissonance built up in her mind at the sight of the long hallway, paneled in dark wood, the thick Oriental carpet on the hardwood floor, the old photographs and prints that hung from the walls. It was when she focused on the burnished metal umbrella stand, which was, itself, in the shape of a partially-opened umbrella, and the sidetable on which stood a cast-iron, grinning gargoyle bereft of its roof gutter home, that the curious sense of familiarity she felt delved deep into the secret recesses of her mind and connected with a swell of long-forgotten memories.

She put out a hand against the doorjamb to steady herself as the flood rose up inside her. She saw her mother-in-law standing in that hallway with a kind of glow around her head. She was older than she'd been when Anna had married Peter, years older, her body wreathed in a golden Botticelli nimbus, that beatific smile on her lips, Meran Kelledy standing beside her, the two of them sharing some private joke, and all around them . . . presences seemed to slip and slide across one's vision.

No, she told herself. None of that was real. Not the golden glow, nor the flickering twig-thin figures that teased the mind from the corner of the eye.

But she'd thought she'd seen them. Once. More than once. Many times. Whenever she was with Helen Batterberry . . .

Walking in her mother-in-law's garden and hearing music, turning the corner of the house to see a trio of what she first took to be children, then realized were midgets, playing fiddle and flute and drum, the figures slipping away as they approached, winking out of existence, the music fading, but its echoes lingering on. In the mind. In memory. In dreams.

"Faerie," her mother-in-law explained to her, matter-of-factly.

Lesli as a toddler, playing with her invisible friends that could actually be *seen* when Helen Batterberry was in the room.

No. None of that was possible.

That was when she and Peter were going through a rough period in their marriage. Those sights, those strange ethereal beings, music played on absent instruments, they were all part and parcel of what she later realized had been a nervous breakdown. Her analyst had agreed.

But they'd seemed so real.

In the hospital room where her mother-in-law lay dying, her bed a clutter of strange creatures, tiny wizened men, small perfect women, all of them flickering in and out of sight, the wonder of their presences, the music of their voices, Lesli sitting wide-eyed by the bed as the courts of Faerie came to bid farewell to an old friend.

"Say you're going to live forever," Leslie had said to her grandmother.

"I will," the old woman replied. "But you have to remember me. You have to promise never to close your awareness to the Otherworld around you. If you do that, I'll never be far."

All nonsense.

But there in the hospital room, with the scratchy sound of the IVAC pump, the clean white walls, the incessant beep of the heart monitor, the antiseptic sting in the air, Anna could only shake her head.

"None . . . none of this is real. . . ." she said.

Her mother-in-law turned her head to look at her, an infinite sadness in her dark eyes.

"Maybe not for you," she said sadly, "but for those who will see, it will always be there."

And later, with Lesli at home, when just she and Peter were there, she remembered Meran coming into that hospital room, Meran and her husband, neither of them having aged since the first time Anna had seen them at her mother-in-law's house, years, oh now years ago. The four of them were there when Helen Batterberry died. She and Peter had bent their heads over the body at the moment of death, but the other two, the unaging musicians who claimed Faerie more silently, but as surely and subtly as ever Helen Batterberry had, stood at the window and watched the twilight grow across the hospital lawn as though they could see the old woman's spirit walking off into the night.

They didn't come to the funeral.

They—

She tried to push the memories aside, just as she had when the events had first occurred, but the flood was too strong. And worse, she knew they were true memories. Not the clouded rantings of a stressful mind suffering a mild breakdown.

Meran was speaking to her, but Anna couldn't hear what she was saying. She heard a vague, disturbing music that seemed to come from the ground underfoot. Small figures seemed to caper and dance in the corner of her eye, humming and buzzing like summer bees. Vertigo gripped her and she could feel herself falling. She realized that Meran was stepping forward to catch her, but by then the darkness had grown too seductive and she simply let herself fall into its welcoming depths.

From Lesli's diary, entry dated October 13th:

I've well and truly done it. I got up this morning and instead of my school books, I packed my flute and some clothes and you, of course, in my knapsack; and then I just left. I couldn't live there anymore. I just couldn't.

Nobody's going to miss me. Daddy's never home anyway and Mom won't be looking for me—she'll be looking for her idea of me and that person doesn't exist. The city's so big that they'll never find me.

I was kind of worried about where I was going to stay tonight, especially with the sky getting more and more overcast all day long, but I met this really neat girl in Fitzhenry Park this morning. Her name's Susan and even though she's just a year older than me, she lives with this guy in an apartment in Chinatown. She's gone to ask him if I can stay with them for a couple of days. His name's Paul. Susan says he's in his late twenties, but he doesn't act at all like an old guy. He's really neat and treats her like she's an adult, not a kid. She's his *girlfriend*!

I'm sitting in the park waiting for her to come back as I write this. I hope she doesn't take too long because there's some weird-looking people around here. This one guy sitting over by the War Memorial keeps giving me the eye like he's going to hit on me or something. He really gives me the creeps. He's got this kind of dark aura that flickers around him so I know he's bad news.

I know it's only been one morning since I left home, but I already feel different. It's like I was dragging around this huge weight and all of a sudden it's gone. I feel light as a feather. Of course, we all know what that weight was: neuro-mother.

Once I get settled in at Susan and Paul's, I'm going to go look for a job. Susan says Paul can get me some fake ID so that I can work in a club or something and make some real money. That's what Susan does. She said that there's been times when she's made fifty bucks in tips in just one night!

I've never met anyone like her before. It's hard to believe she's almost my age. When I compare the girls at school to her, they just seem like a bunch of kids. Susan dresses so cool, like she just stepped out of an MTV video. She's got short funky black hair, a leather jacket and jeans so tight I don't know how she gets into them. Her T-shirt's got this really cool picture of a Brian Froud faery on it that I'd never seen before.

When I asked her if she believes in Faerie, she just gave me this big grin and said, "I'll tell you, Lesli, I'll believe in anything that makes me feel good."

I think I'm going to like living with her.

When Anna Batterberry regained consciousness, it was to find herself inside that disturbingly familiar house. She lay on a soft, overstuffed sofa, surrounded by the crouching presences of far more pieces of comfortable-looking furniture than the room was really meant to hold. The room simply had a too-full look about it, aided and abetted by a bewildering array of knickknacks that ranged from dozens of tiny porcelain miniatures on the mantel, each depicting some anthropomorphized woodland creature playing a harp or a fiddle or a flute, to a life-sized fabric mâché sculpture of a grizzly-bear in top hat and tails that reared up in one corner of the room.

Every square inch of wall space appeared to be taken up with posters, framed photographs, prints and paintings. Old-fashioned curtains—the print was large dusky roses on a black background—stood guard on either side of a window seat. Underfoot was a thick carpet that had been woven into a semblance of the heavily-leafed yard outside.

The more she looked around herself, the more familiar it all looked. And the more her mind filled with memories that she'd spent so many years denying.

The sound of a footstep had her sitting up and half-turning to look behind the sofa at who—or maybe even, what—was approaching. It was only Meran. The movement brought back the vertigo and she lay down once more. Meran sat down on an ottoman that had been pulled up beside the sofa and laid a deliciously cool damp cloth against Anna's brow.

"You gave me a bit of a start," Meran said, "collapsing on my porch like that."

Anna had lost her ability to be polite. Forsaking small talk, she went straight for the heart of the matter.

"I've been here before," she said.

Meran nodded.

"With my mother-in-law—Helen Batterberry."

"Nell," Meran agreed. "She was a good friend."

"But why haven't I *remembered* that I'd met you before until today?"

Meran shrugged. "These things happen."

"No," Anna said. "People forget things, yes, but not like this. I didn't just meet you in passing, I knew you for years—from my last year in college when Peter first began dating me. You were at his parents' house the first time he took me home. I remember thinking how odd that you and Helen were such good friends, considering how much younger you were than her."

"Should age make a difference?" Meran asked.

"No. It's just . . . you haven't changed at all. You're still the same age."

"I know," Meran said.

"But . . ." Anna's bewilderment accentuated her nervous bird temperament. "How can that be possible?"

"You said something about Lesli when you first arrived," Meran said, changing the subject.

That was probably the only thing that could have drawn Anna away from the quagmire puzzle of agelessness and hidden music and twitchy shapes moving just beyond the grasp of her vision.

"She's run away from home," Anna said. "I went into her room to get something and found that she'd left all her schoolbooks just sitting on her desk. Then when I called the school, they told me that she'd never arrived. They were about to call me to ask if she was ill. Lesli never misses school, you know."

Meran nodded. She hadn't, but it fit with the image of the relationship between Lesli and her mother that was growing in her mind.

"Have you called the police?" she asked.

"As soon as I got off the phone. They told me it was a little early to start worrying—can you imagine that? The detective I spoke to said that he'd put out her description so that his officers would keep an eye out for her, but basically he told me that she must just be skipping school. Lesli would *never* do that."

"What does your husband say?"

"Peter doesn't know yet. He's on a business trip out east and I won't be able to talk to him until he calls me tonight. I don't even know what hotel he'll be staying in until he calls." Anna reached out with a bird-thin hand and gripped Meran's arm. "What am I going to *do*?"

"We could go looking for her ourselves."

Anna nodded eagerly at the suggestion, but then the futility of that course of action hit home.

"The city's so big," she said. "It's too big. How would we ever find her?"

"There is another way," Cerin said.

Anna started at the new voice. Meran removed the damp cloth from Anna's brow and moved back from the sofa so that Anna could sit up once more. She looked at the tall figure standing in the doorway, recognizing him as Meran's husband. She didn't remember him seeming quite so intimidating before.

"What . . . what way is that?" Anna said.

"You could ask for help from Faerie," Cerin told her.

"So—you're gonna be one of Paulie's girls?"

Lesli looked up from writing in her diary to find that the creepy guy by the War Memorial had sauntered over to stand beside her bench. Up close, he seemed even tougher than he had from a distance. His hair was slicked back on top, long at the back. He had three earrings in his left earlobe, one in the right. Dirty jeans were tucked into tall black cowboy boots, his white shirt was half open under his jean jacket. There was an oily look in his eyes that made her shiver.

She quickly shut the diary, keeping her place with a finger, and looked around hopefully to see if Susan was on her way back, but there was no sign of her new friend. Taking a deep breath, she gave him what she hoped was a look of appropriate streetwise bravado.

"I . . . I don't know what you're talking about," she said.

"I saw you talking to Susie," he said, sitting down beside her on the bench. "She's Paulie's recruiter."

Lesli started to get a bad feeling right about then. It wasn't just that this guy was so awful, but that she might have made a terrible misjudgment when it came to Susan.

"I think I should go," she said.

She started to get up, but he grabbed her arm. Off balance, she fell back onto the bench.

"Hey, look," he said. "I'm doing you a favor. Paulie's got ten or twelve girls in his string and he works them like they're dogs. You look like a nice kid. Do you really want to spend the next ten years peddling your ass for some homeboy who's gonna have you hooked on junk before the week's out?"

"I—"

"See, I run a clean shop. No drugs, nice clothes for the girls, nice apartment that you're gonna share with just one other girl, not a half dozen the way Paulie run his biz. My girls turn maybe two, three tricks a night and that's it. Paulie'll have you on the street nine, ten hours a pop, easy."

His voice was calm, easygoing, but Leslie had never been so scared before in her life.

"Please," she said. "You're making a mistake. I really have to go."

She tried to rise again, but he kept a hand on her shoulder so that she couldn't get up. His voice, so mild before, went hard.

"You go anywhere, babe, you're going with me," he said. "There are no other options. End of conversation."

He stood up and hauled her to her feet. His hand held her in a bruising grip. Her diary fell from her grip, and he let her pick it up and stuff it into her knapsack, but then he pulled her roughly away from the bench.

"You're hurting me!" she cried.

He leaned close to her, his mouth only inches from her ear.

"Keep that up," he warned her, "and you're really gonna find out what pain's all about. Now make nice. You're working for me now."

"I . . ."

"Repeat after me, sweet stuff: I'm Cutter's girl."

Tears welled in Lesli's eyes. She looked around the park, but nobody was paying any attention to what was happening to her. Cutter gave her a painful shake that made her teeth rattle.

"C'mon," he told her. "Say it."

He glared at her with the promise of worse to come in his eyes if she didn't start doing what he said. His grip tightened on her shoulder, fingers digging into the soft flesh of her upper arm.

"Say it!"

"I . . . I'm Cutter's . . . girl."

"See? That wasn't so hard."

He gave her another shove to start her moving again. She wanted desperately to break free of his hand and just run, but as he marched her across the park, she discovered that she was too scared to do anything but let him lead her away.

She'd never felt so helpless or alone in all her life. It made her feel ashamed.

"Please don't joke about this," Anna said in response to Cerin's suggestion that they turn to Faerie for help in finding Lesli.

"Yes," Meran agreed, though she wasn't speaking of jokes. "This isn't the time."

Cerin shook his head. "This seems a particularly appropriate time to me." He turned to Anna. "I don't like to involve myself in private quarrels, but since it's you that's come to us, I feel I have the right to ask you this: Why is it, do you think, that Lesli ran away in the first place?"

"What are you insinuating? That I'm not a good mother?"

"Hardly. I no longer know you well enough to make that sort of a judgment. Besides, it's not really any of my business, is it?"

"Cerin, please," Meran said.

A headache was starting up between Anna's temples.

"I don't understand," Anna said. "What is it that you're saying?"

"Meran and I loved Nell Batterberry," Cerin said. "I don't doubt that you held some affection for her as well, but I do know that you thought her a bit of a daft old woman. She told me once that after her husband—after Philip—died, you tried to convince Peter that she should be put in a home. Not in a home for the elderly, but for the, shall we say, gently mad?"

"But she—"

"Was full of stories that made no sense to you," Cerin said. "She heard and saw what others couldn't, though she had the gift that would allow such people to see into the invisible world of Faerie when they were in her presence. You saw into that world once, Anna. I don't think you ever forgave her for showing it to you."

"It . . . it wasn't real."

Cerin shrugged. "That's not really important at this moment. What's important is that, if I understand the situation correctly, you've been living in the fear that Lesli would grow up just as fey as her grandmother. And if this is so, your denying her belief in Faerie lies at the root of the troubles that the two of you share."

Anna looked to Meran for support, but Meran knew her husband too well and kept her own council. Having begun, Cerin wouldn't stop until he said everything he meant to.

"Why are you doing this to me?" Anna asked. "My daughter's run away. All of . . . all of this . . ." She waved a hand that was perhaps meant to take in just the conversation, perhaps the whole room. "It's not real. Little people and fairies and all the things my mother-in-law reveled in discussing just aren't real. She could make them *seem* real, I'll grant you that, but they could never exist."

"In your world," Cerin said.

"In the real world."

"They're not one and the same," Cerin told her.

Anna began to rise from the sofa. "I don't have to listen to any of this," she said. "My daughter's run away and I thought you might be able to help me. I didn't come here to be mocked."

"The only reason I've said anything at all," Cerin told her, "is for Lesli's sake. Meran talks about her all the time. She sounds like a wonderful, gifted child."

"She is."

"I hate the thought of her being forced into a box that doesn't fit her. Of having her wings cut off, her sight blinded, her hearing muted, her voice stilled."

"I'm not doing any such thing!" Anna cried.

"You just don't realize what you're doing," Cerin replied.

His voice was mild, but dark lights in the back of his eyes were flashing.

Meran realized it was time to intervene. She stepped between the two. Putting her back to her husband, she turned to face Anna.

"We'll find Lesli," she said.

"How? With *magic*?"

"It doesn't matter how. Just trust that we will. What you have to think of is of what you were telling me yesterday: her birthday's coming up in just a few days. Once she turns sixteen, so long as she can prove that she's capable of supporting herself, she can legally leave home and nothing you might do or say then can stop her."

"It's you, isn't it?" Anna cried. "You're the one who's been filling up her head with all these horrible fairy tales. I should never have let her take those lessons."

Her voice rose ever higher in pitch as she lunged forward, arms flailing. Meran slipped to one side, then reached out one quick hand. She pinched a nerve in Anna's neck and the woman suddenly went limp. Cerin caught her before she could fall and carried her back to the sofa.

"Now do you see what I mean about parents?" he said as he laid Anna down.

Meran gave him a mock-serious cuff on the back of his head.

"Go find Lesli," she said.

"But—"

"Or would you rather stay with Anna and continue your silly attempt at converting her when she wakes up again?"

"I'm on my way," Cerin told her and was out the door before she could change her mind.

Thunder cracked almost directly overhead as Cutter dragged Lesli into a brownstone just off Palm Street. The building stood in the heart of what was known as Newford's Combat Zone, a few square blocks of night clubs, strip joints and bars. It was a tough part of town with hookers on every corner, bikers cruising the streets on chopped-down Harleys, bums sleeping in doorways, winos sitting on the curbs, drinking cheap booze from bottles vaguely hidden in paper bags.

Cutter had an apartment on the top floor of the brownstone, three stories up from the street. If he hadn't told her that he lived here, Leslie would have thought that he'd taken her into an abandoned building. There was no furniture except a vinyl-topped table and two chairs in the dirty kitchen. A few mangy pillows were piled up against the wall in what she assumed was the living room.

He led her down to the room at the end of the long hall that ran the length of the apartment and pushed her inside. She lost her balance and went sprawling onto the mattress that lay in the middle of the floor. It smelled of mildew and, vaguely, of old urine. She scrambled away from it and crouched up against the far wall, clutching her knapsack against her chest.

"Now, you just relax, sweet stuff," Cutter told her. "Take things easy. I'm going out for a little while to find you a nice guy to ease you into the trade. I'd do it myself, but there's guys that want to be first with a kid as young and pretty as you are and I sure could use the bread they're willing to pay for the privilege."

Lesli was prepared to beg him to let her go, but her throat was so tight she couldn't make a sound.

"Don't go away now," Cutter told her.

He chuckled at his own wit, then closed the door and locked it. Lesli didn't think she'd ever heard anything so final as the sound of that lock catching. She listened to

Cutter's footsteps as they crossed the apartment, the sound of the front door closing, his footsteps receding on the stairs.

As soon as she was sure he was far enough away, she got up and ran to the door, trying it, just in case, but it really was locked and far too solid for her to have any hope of breaking through its panels. Of course there was no phone. She crossed the room to the window and forced it open. The window looked out on the side of another building, with an alleyway below. There was no fire escape outside the window and she was far too high up to think of trying to get down to the alley.

Thunder rumbled again, not quite overhead now, and it started to rain. She leaned by the window, resting her head on its sill. Tears sprang up in her eyes again.

"Please," she sniffed. "Please, somebody help me. . . ."

The rain coming in the window mingled with the tears that streaked her cheek.

Cerin began his search at the Batterberry house, which was in Ferryside, across the Stanton Street Bridge on the west side of the Kickaha river. As Anna Batterberry had remarked, the city was large. To find one teenage girl, hiding somewhere in the confounding labyrinth of its thousands of crisscrossing streets and avenues, was a daunting task, but Cerin was depending on help.

To anyone watching him, he must have appeared to be slightly mad. He wandered back and forth across the streets of Ferryside, stopping under trees to look up into their bare branches, hunkering down at the mouths of alleys or alongside hedges, apparently talking to himself. In truth, he was looking for the city's gossips:

Magpies and crows, sparrows and pigeons saw everything, but listening to their litanies of the day's events was like looking something up in an encyclopedia that was merely a confusing heap of loose pages, gathered together in a basket. All the information you wanted was there, but finding it would take more hours than there were in a day.

Cats were little better. They liked to keep most of what they knew to themselves, so what they did offer him was usually cryptic and sometimes even pointedly unhelpful. Cerin couldn't blame them; they were by nature secretive and, like much of Faerie, capricious.

The most ready to give him a hand were those little sprites commonly known as the flower faeries. They were the little winged spirits of the various trees and bushes, flowers and weeds, that grew tidily in parks and gardens, rioting only in the odd empty lot or wild place, such as the riverbanks that ran down under the Stanton Street Bridge to meet the water. Years ago, Cicely Mary Barker had catalogued any number of them in a loving series of books; more recently the Boston artist, Terri Windling, had taken up the task, specializing in the urban relations of those Barker had already noted.

It was late in the year for the little folk. Most of them were already tucked away in Faerie, sleeping through the winter, or else too busy with their harvests and other seasonal preoccupations to have paid any attention at all to what went on beyond the task at hand. But a few had seen the young girl who could sometimes see them. Meran's cousins were the most helpful. Their small pointed faces would regard Cerin gravely from under acorn caps as they pointed this way down one street, or that way down another.

It took time. The sky grew darker, and then still darker as the clouds thickened with an approaching storm, but slowly and surely, Cerin traced Lesli's passage over the Stanton Street Bridge all the way across town to Fitzhenry Park. It was just as he reached the bench where she'd been sitting that it began to rain.

There, from two of the wizened little monkey-like bodachs that lived in the park, he got the tale of how she'd been accosted and taken away.

"She didn't want to go, sir," said the one, adjusting the brim of his little cap against the rain.

All faerie knew Cerin, but it wasn't just for his bardic harping that they paid him the respect that they did. He was the husband of the oak king's daughter, she who could match them trick for trick and then some, and they'd long since learned to treat her, and those under her protection, with a wary deference.

"No sir, she didn't," added the other, "but he led her off all the same."

Cerin hunkered down beside the bench so that he wasn't towering over them.

"Where did he take her?" he asked.

The first bodach pointed to where two men were standing by the War Memorial, shoulders hunched against the rain, heads bent together as they spoke. One wore a thin raincoat over a suit; the other was dressed in denim jacket, jeans and cowboy boots. They appeared to be discussing a business transaction.

"You could ask him for yourself," the bodach said. "He's the one all in blue."

Cerin's gaze went to the pair and a hard look came over his features. If Meran had been there, she might have laid a hand on his arm, or spoken a calming word, to bank the dangerous fire that grew in behind his eyes. But she was at home, too far away for her quieting influence to be felt.

The bodachs scampered away as Cerin rose to his feet. By the War Memorial, the two men seemed to come to an agreement and left the park together. Cerin fell in behind them, the rain that slicked the pavement underfoot muffling his footsteps. His fingers twitched at his side, as though striking a harp's strings.

From the branches of the tree where they'd taken sanctuary, the bodachs thought they could hear the sound of a harp, its music echoing softly against the rhythm of the rain.

Anna came to once more just as Meran was returning from the kitchen with a pot of herb tea and a pair of mugs. Meran set the mugs and pot down on the table by the sofa and sat down beside Lesli's mother.

"How are you feeling?" she asked as she adjusted the cool cloth she'd laid upon Anna's brow earlier.

Anna's gaze flicked from left to right, over Meran's shoulder and down to the floor, as though tracking invisible presences. Meran tried to shoo away the inquisitive faerie, but it was a useless gesture. In this house, with Anna's presence to fuel their quenchless curiosity, it was like trying to catch the wind.

"I've made us some tea," Meran said. "It'll make you feel better."

Anna appeared docile now, her earlier anger fled as though it had never existed. Outside, rain pattered gently against the window panes. The face of a nosy hob was pressed against one lower pane, its breath clouding the glass, its large eyes glimmering with their own inner light.

"Can . . . can you make them go away?" Anna asked.

Meran shook her head. "But I can make you forget again."

"Forget." Anna's voice grew dreamy. "Is that what you did before? You made me forget?"

"No. You did that on your own. You didn't want to remember, so you simply forgot."

"And you . . . you didn't do a thing?"

"We do have a certain . . . aura," Meran admitted, "which accelerates the process. It's not even something we consciously work at. It just seems to happen when we're around those who'd rather not remember what they see."

"So I'll forget, but they'll all still be there?"

Meran nodded.

"I just won't be able to see them?"

"It'll be like it was before," Meran said.

"I . . . I don't think I like that. . . ."

Her voice slurred. Meran leaned forward with a worried expression. Anna seemed to regard her through blurring vision.

"I think I'm going . . . away . . . now. . . ." she said.

Her eyelids fluttered, then her head lolled to one side and she lay still. Meran called Anna's name and gave her a little shake, but there was no response. She put two fingers to Anna's throat and found her pulse. It was regular and strong, but try though she did, Meran couldn't rouse the woman.

Rising from the sofa, she went into the kitchen to phone for an ambulance. As she was dialing the number, she heard Cerin's harp begin to play by itself up in his study on the second floor.

Lesli's tears lasted until she thought she saw something moving in the rain on the other side of the window. It was a flicker of movement and color, just above the outside windowsill, as though a pigeon had come in for a wet landing, but it had moved with far more grace and deftness than any pigeon she'd ever seen. And that memory of color was all wrong, too. It hadn't been the blue/white/grey of a pigeon; it had been more like a butterfly—

doubtful, she thought, in the rain and this time of year

—or a hummingbird—

even more doubtful

—but then she remembered what the music had woken at her last flute lesson. She rubbed at her eyes with her sleeve to remove the blur of her tears and looked more closely into the rain. Face-on, she couldn't see anything, but as soon as she turned her head, there it was again, she could see it out of the corner of her eye, a dancing dervish of color and movement that flickered out of her line of sight as soon as she concentrated on it.

After a few moments, she turned from the window. She gave the door a considering look and listened hard, but there was still no sound of Cutter's return.

Maybe, she thought, maybe magic can rescue me. . . .

She dug out her flute from her knapsack and quickly put the pieces together. Turning back to the window, she sat on her haunches and tried to start up a tune, but to no avail. She was still too nervous, her chest felt too tight, and she couldn't get the air to come up properly from her diaphragm.

She brought the flute down from her lip and laid it across her knees. Trying not to think of the locked door, of why it was locked and who would be coming through it, she steadied her breathing.

In, slowly now, hold it, let it out, slowly. And again.

She pretended she was with Meran, just the two of them in the basement of the Old Firehall. There. She could almost hear the tune that Meran was playing, except it sounded more like the bell-like tones of a harp than the breathy timbre of a wooden flute. But still, it was there for her to follow, a path marked out on a roadmap of music.

Lifting the flute back up to her lip, she blew again, a narrow channel of air going down into the mouth hole at an angle, all her fingers down, the low D note ringing in the empty room, a deep rich sound, resonant and full. She played it again, then caught the music she heard, that particular path laid out on the roadmap of all tunes that are or yet could be, and followed where it led.

It was easier to do than she would have thought possible, easier than at all those lessons with Meran. The music she followed seemed to allow her instrument to almost play itself. And as the tune woke from her flute, she fixed her gaze on the rain falling just outside the window where a flicker of color appeared, a spin of movement.

Please, she thought. Oh please . . .

And then it was there, hummingbird wings vibrating in the rain, sending incandescent sprays of water arcing away from their movement; the tiny naked upper torso, the lower wrapped in tiny leaves and vines; the dark hair gathered wetly against her miniature cheeks and neck; the eyes, tiny and timeless, watching her as she watched back and all the while, the music played.

Help me, she thought to that little hovering figure. Won't you please—

She had been oblivious to anything but the music and the tiny faerie outside in the rain. She hadn't heard the footsteps on the stairs, nor heard them crossing the apartment. But she heard the door open.

The tune faltered, the faerie flickered out of sight as though it had never been there. She brought the flute down from her lip and turned, her heart drumming wildly in her chest, but she refused to be scared. That's all guys like Cutter wanted. They wanted to see you scared of them. They wanted to be in control. But no more.

I'm not going to go without a fight, she thought. I'll break my flute over his stupid head. I'll . . .

The stranger standing in the doorway brought her train of thought to a scurrying halt. And then she realized that the harping she'd heard, the tune that had led her flute to join it, had grown in volume, rather than diminished.

"Who . . . who are you?" she asked.

Her hands had begun to perspire, making her flute slippery and hard to hold. The stranger had longer hair than Cutter. It was drawn back in a braid that hung down one side of his head and dangled halfway down his chest. He had a full beard and wore clothes that, though they were simple jeans, shirt and jacket, seemed to have a timeless cut to them, as though they could have been worn at any point in history and not seemed out of place. Meran dressed like that as well, she realized.

But it was his eyes that held her—not their startling brightness, but the fire that seemed to flicker in their depths, a rhythmic movement that seemed to keep time to the harping she heard.

"Have you come to . . . rescue me?" she found herself asking before the stranger had time to reply to her first question.

"I'd think," he said, "with a spirit so brave as yours, that you'd simply rescue yourself."

Lesli shook her head. "I'm not really brave at all."

"Braver than you know, fluting here while a darkness stalked you through the storm. My name's Cerin Kelledy; I'm Meran's husband and I've come to take you home."

He waited for her to disassemble her flute and stow it away, then offered her a hand up from the floor. As she stood up, he took the knapsack and slung it over his shoulder and led her towards the door. The sound of the harping was very faint now, Lesli realized.

When they walked by the hall, she stopped in the doorway leading to the living room and looked at the two men that were huddled against the far wall, their eyes wild with terror. One was Cutter; the other a business man in suit and raincoat whom she'd never seen before. She hesitated, fingers tightening on Cerin's hand, as she turned to see what was frightening them so much. There was nothing at all in the spot that their frightened gazes were fixed upon.

"What . . . what's the matter with them?" she asked her companion. "What are they looking at?"

"Night fears," Cerin replied. "Somehow the darkness that lies in their hearts has given those fears substance and made them real."

The way he said "somehow" let Lesli know that he'd been responsible for what the two men were undergoing.

"Are they going to die?" she asked.

She didn't think she was the first girl to fall prey to Cutter so she wasn't exactly feeling sorry for him at that point.

Cerin shook his head. "But they will always have the *sight*. Unless they change their ways, it will show them only the dark side of Faerie."

Lesli shivered.

"There are no happy endings," Cerin told her. "There are no real endings ever—happy or otherwise. We all have our own stories which are just a part of the one Story that binds both this world and Faerie. Sometimes we step into each others' stories—perhaps just for a few minutes, perhaps for years—and then we step out of them again. But all the while, the Story just goes on."

That day, his explanation only served to confuse her.

From Lesli's diary, entry dated November 24th:

Nothing turned out the way I thought it would.

Something happened to Mom. Everybody tells me it's not my fault, but it happened when I ran away, so I can't help but feel that I'm to blame. Daddy says she had a nervous breakdown and that's why she's in the sanitarium. It happened to her before and it had been coming again for a long time. But that's not the way Mom tells it.

I go by to see her every day after school. Sometimes she's pretty spaced from the drugs they give her to keep her calm, but on one of her good days, she told me about Granny Nell and the Kelledys and Faerie. She says the world's just like I said it was in that essay I did for English. Faerie's real and it didn't go away; it just got freed from people's preconceptions of it and now it's just whatever it wants to be.

And that's what scares her.

She also thinks the Kelledys are some kind of earth spirits.

"I can't forget this time," she told me.

"But if you know," I asked her, "if you believe, then why are you in this place? Maybe I should be in here, too."

And you know what she told me? "I don't want to believe in any of it; it just makes me feel sick. But at the same time, I can't stop knowing it's all out there: every kind of magic being and nightmare. They're all real."

I remember thinking of Cutter and that other guy in his apartment and what Cerin said about them. Did that make my Mom a bad person? I couldn't believe that.

"But they're not *supposed* to be real," Mom said. "That's what's got me feeling so crazy. In a sane world, in the world that was the way I'd grown up believing it to be, that *wouldn't* be real. The Kelledys could fix it so that I'd forget again, but then I'd be back to going through life always feeling like there was something important that I couldn't remember. And that just leaves you with another kind of craziness—an ache that you can't explain and it doesn't ever go away. It's better this way, and my medicine keeps me from feeling too crazy."

She looked away then, out the window of her room. I looked, too, and saw the little monkeyman that was crossing the lawn of the sanitarium, pulling a pig behind him. The pig had a load of gear on its back like it was a pack horse.

"Could you . . . could you ask the nurse to bring my medicine," Mom said.

I tried to tell her that all she had to do was accept it, but she wouldn't listen. She just kept asking for the nurse, so finally I went and got one.

I still think it's my fault.

I live with the Kelledys now. Daddy was going to send me away to a boarding school, because he felt that he couldn't be home enough to take care of me. I never really thought about it before, but when he said that, I realized that he didn't know me at all.

Meran offered to let me live at their place. I moved in on my birthday.

There's a book in their library—ha! There's like ten million books in there. But the one I'm thinking of is by a local writer, this guy named Christy Riddell.

In it, he talks about Faerie, how everybody just thinks of them as ghosts of wind and shadow.

"Faerie music is the wind," he says, "and their movement is the play of shadow cast by moonlight, or starlight, or no light at all. Faerie lives like a ghost beside us, but only the city remembers. But then the city never forgets anything."

I don't know if the Kelledys are part of that ghostliness. What I do know is that, seeing how they live for each other, how they care so much about each other, I find myself feeling more hopeful about things. My parents and I didn't so much not get along, as lack interest in each other. It got to the point where I figured that's how everybody was in the world, because I never knew any different.

So I'm trying harder with Mom. I don't talk about things she doesn't want to hear, but I don't stop believing in them either. Like Cerin said, we're just two threads of the Story. Sometimes we come together for awhile and sometimes we're apart. And no matter how much one or the other of us might want it to be different, both our stories are true.

But I can't stop wishing for a happy ending.

The Conjure Man

I do not think it had any friends, or mourners, except myself and a pair of owls.
—J. R. R. Tolkien, from the introductory
note to *Tree and Leaf*

You only see the tree by the light of the lamp. I wonder when
you would ever see the lamp by the light of the tree.
—G. K. Chesterton, from The Man Who Was Thursday

The conjure man rode a red, old-fashioned bicycle with fat tires and only one, fixed gear. A wicker basket in front contained a small mongrel dog that seemed mostly terrier. Behind the seat, tied to the carrier, was a battered brown satchel that hid from prying eyes the sum total of all his worldly possessions.

What he had was not much, but he needed little. He was, after all, the conjure man, and what he didn't have, he could conjure for himself.

He was more stout than slim, with a long grizzled beard and a halo of frizzy grey hair that protruded from under his tall black hat like ivy tangled under an eave. Nesting in the hatband were a posy of dried wildflowers and three feathers: one white, from a swan; one black, from a crow; one brown, from an owl. His jacket was an exhilarating shade of blue, the color of the sky on a perfect summer's morning. Under it he wore a shirt that was as green as a fresh-cut lawn. His trousers were brown corduroy, patched with leather and plaid squares; his boots were a deep golden yellow, the color of buttercups past their prime.

His age was a puzzle, somewhere between fifty and seventy. Most people assumed he was one of the homeless—more colorful than most, and certainly more cheerful, but a derelict all the same—so the scent of apples that seemed to follow him was always a surprise, as was the good humor that walked hand in hand with a keen intelligence in his bright blue eyes. When he raised his head, hat brim lifting, and he met one's gaze, the impact of those eyes was a sudden shock, a diamond in the rough.

His name was John Windle, which could mean, if you were one to ascribe meaning to names, "favored of god" for his given name, while his surname was variously defined as "basket," "the red-winged thrush," or "to lose vigor and strength, to dwindle." They could all be true, for he led a charmed life; his mind was a treasure trove storing equal amounts of experience, rumor and history; he had a high clear singing voice; and though he wasn't tall—he stood five-ten in his boots—he had once been a much larger man.

"I was a giant once," he liked to explain, "when the world was young. But conjuring takes its toll. Now John's just an old man, pretty well all used up. Just like the world," he'd add with a sigh and a nod, bright eyes holding a tired sorrow. "Just like the world."

There were some things even the conjure man couldn't fix.

Living in the city, one grew used to its more outlandish characters, eventually noting them in passing with an almost familial affection: The pigeon lady in her faded Laura Ashley dresses with her shopping cart filled with sacks of birdseed and bread crumbs. Paperjack, the old black man with his Chinese fortune-teller and deft origami sculptures. The German cowboy who dressed like an extra from a spaghetti western and made long declamatory speeches in his native language to which no one listened.

And, of course, the conjure man.

Wendy St. James had seen him dozens of times—she lived and worked downtown, which was the conjure man's principal haunt—but she'd never actually spoken to him until one day in the fall when the trees were just beginning to change into their cheerful autumnal party dresses.

She was sitting on a bench on the Ferryside bank of the Kickaha River, a small, almost waif-like woman in jeans and a white T-shirt, with an unzipped brown leather bomber's jacket and hightops. In lieu of a purse, she had a small, worn knapsack sitting on the bench beside her and she was bent over a hardcover journal which she spent more time staring at than actually writing in. Her hair was thick and blonde, hanging down past her collar in a grown-out pageboy with a half-inch of dark roots showing. She was chewing on the end of her pen, worrying the plastic for inspiration.

It was a poem that had stopped her in mid-stroll and plunked her down on the bench. It had glimmered and shone in her head until she got out her journal and pen. Then it fled, as impossible to catch as a fading dream. The more she tried to recapture the impulse that had set her wanting to put pen to paper, the less it seemed to have ever existed in the first place. The annoying presence of three teenage boys clowning around on the lawn a half-dozen yards from where she sat didn't help at all.

She was giving them a dirty stare when she saw one of the boys pick up a stick and throw it into the wheel of the conjure man's bike as he came riding up on the park path that followed the river. The small dog in the bike's wicker basket jumped free, but the conjure man himself fell in a tangle of limbs and spinning wheels. The boys took off, laughing, the dog chasing them for a few feet, yapping shrilly, before it hurried back to where its master had fallen.

Wendy had already put down her journal and pen and reached the fallen man by the time the dog got back to its master's side.

"Are you okay?" Wendy asked the conjure man as she helped him untangle himself from the bike.

She'd taken a fall herself in the summer. The front wheel of her ten-speed struck a pebble, the bike wobbled dangerously and she'd grabbed at the brakes, but her fingers closed over the front ones first, and too hard. The back of the bike went up, flipping her right over the handlebars, and she'd had the worst headache for at least a week afterwards.

The conjure man didn't answer her immediately. His gaze followed the escaping boys.

"As you sow," he muttered.

Following his gaze, Wendy saw the boy who'd thrown the stick trip and go sprawling in the grass. An odd chill danced up her spine. The boy's tumble came so quickly on the heels of the conjure man's words, for a moment it felt to her as though he'd actually caused the boy's fall.

As you sow, so shall you reap.

She looked back at the conjure man, but he was sitting up now, fingering a tear in his corduroys, which already had a quiltwork of patches on them. He gave her a quick smile that traveled all the way up to his eyes and she found herself thinking of Santa Claus. The little dog pressed its nose up against the conjure man's hand, pushing it away from the tear. But the tear was gone.

It had just been a fold in the cloth, Wendy realized. That was all.

She helped the conjure man limp to her bench, then went back and got his bike. She righted it and wheeled it over to lean against the back of the bench before sitting down herself. The little dog leaped up onto the conjure man's lap.

"What a cute dog," Wendy said, giving it a pat. "What's her name?"

"Ginger," the conjure man replied as though it was so obvious that he couldn't understand her having to ask.

Wendy looked at the dog. Ginger's fur was as grey and grizzled as her master's beard without a hint of the spice's strong brown hue.

"But she's not at all brown," Wendy found herself saying.

The conjure man shook his head. "It's what she's made of—she's a gingerbread dog. Here." He plucked a hair from Ginger's back which made the dog start and give him a sour look. He offered the hair to Wendy. "Taste it."

Wendy grimaced. "I don't think so."

"Suit yourself," the conjure man said. He shrugged and popped the hair into his own mouth, chewing it with relish.

Oh boy, Wendy thought. She had a live one on her hands.

"Where do you think ginger comes from?" the conjure man asked her.

"What, do you mean your dog?"

"No, the spice."

Wendy shrugged. "I don't know. Some kind of plant, I suppose."

"And that's where you're wrong. They shave gingerbread dogs like our Ginger here and grind up the hair until all that's left is a powder that's ever so fine. Then they leave it out in the hot sun for a day and half—which is where it gets its brownish colour."

Wendy only just stopped herself from rolling her eyes. It was time to extract herself from this encounter, she realized. Well past the time. She'd done her bit to make sure he was all right and since the conjure man didn't seem any worse for the wear from his fall—

"Hey!" she said as he picked up her journal and started to leaf through it. "That's personal."

He fended off her reaching hand with his own and continued to look through it.

"Poetry," he said. "And lovely verses they are, too."

"Please . . ."

"Ever had any published?"

Wendy let her hand drop and leaned back against the bench with a sigh.

"Two collections," she said, adding, "and a few sales to some of the literary magazines."

Although, she corrected herself, "sales" was perhaps a misnomer since most of the magazines only paid in copies. And while she did have two collections in print, they were published by the East Street Press, a small local publisher, which meant the bookstores of Newford were probably the only places in the world where either of her books could be found.

"Romantic, but with a very optimistic flavor," the conjure man remarked as he continued to look through her journal where all her false starts and incomplete drafts were laid out for him to see. "None of that *Sturm und drang* of the earlier romantic era and more like Yeats' Celtic twilight or, what did Chesterton call it? *Mooreeffoc*—that queerness that comes when familiar things are seen from a new angle."

Wendy couldn't believe she was having this conversation. What was he? A renegade English professor living on the street like some hedgerow philosopher of old? It seemed absurd to be sitting here, listening to his discourse.

The conjure man turned to give her a charming smile. "Because that's our hope for the future, isn't it? That the imagination reaches beyond the present to glimpse not so much a sense of meaning in what lies all around us, but to let us simply see it in the first place?"

"I . . . I don't know what to say," Wendy replied.

Ginger had fallen asleep on his lap. He closed her journal and regarded her for a long moment, eyes impossibly blue and bright under the brim of his odd hat.

"John has something he wants to show you," he said.

Wendy blinked. "John?" she asked, looking around.

The conjure man tapped his chest. "John Windle is what those who know my name call me."

"Oh."

She found it odd how his speech shifted from that of a learned man to a much simpler idiom, even referring to himself in the third person. But then, if she stopped to consider it, everything about him was odd.

"What kind of something?" Wendy asked cautiously.

"It's not far."

Wendy looked at her watch. Her shift started at four, which was still a couple of hours away, so there was plenty of time. But she was fairly certain that interesting though her companion was, he wasn't at all the sort of person with whom she wanted to involve herself any more than she already had. The dichotomy between the nonsense and substance that peppered his conversation made her uncomfortable.

It wasn't so much that she thought him dangerous. She just felt as though she was walking on boggy ground that might at any minute dissolve into quicksand with a wrong turn. Despite hardly knowing him at all, she was already sure that listening to him would be full of the potential for wrong turns.

"I'm sorry," she said, "but I don't have the time."

"It's something that I think only you can, if not understand, then at least appreciate."

"I'm sure it's fascinating, whatever it is, but—"

"Come along, then," he said.

He handed her back her journal and stood up, dislodging Ginger, who leapt to the ground with a sharp yap of protest. Scooping the dog up, he returned her to the wicker basket that hung from his handlebars, then wheeled the bike in front of the bench where he stood waiting for Wendy.

Wendy opened her mouth to continue her protest, but then simply shrugged. Well, why not? He really didn't look at all dangerous and she'd just make sure that she stayed in public places.

She stuffed her journal back into her knapsack and then followed as he led the way south along the park path up to where the City Commission's lawns gave way to Butler University's common. She started to ask him how his leg felt, since he'd been limping before, but he walked at a quick, easy pace—that of someone half his apparent age—so she just assumed he hadn't been hurt that badly by his fall after all.

They crossed the common, eschewing the path now to walk straight across the lawn towards the G. Smithers Memorial Library, weaving their way in between islands of students involved in any number of activities, none of which included studying. When they reached the library, they followed its ivy-hung walls to the rear of the building, where the conjure man stopped.

"There," he said, waving his arm in a gesture that took in the entire area behind the library. "What do you see?"

The view they had was of an open space of land backed by a number of other buildings. Having attended the university herself, Wendy recognized all three: the Student Center, the Science Building and one of the dorms, though she couldn't remember which one. The landscape enclosed by their various bulking presences had the look of recently having undergone a complete overhaul. All the lilacs and hawthorns had been cut back, brush and weeds were now just an uneven stubble of ground covering, there were clumps of raw dirt, scattered here and there, where trees had obviously been removed, and right in the middle was an enormous stump.

It had been at least fifteen years since Wendy had had any reason to come here behind the library. But it was so different now. She found herself looking around with a "what's wrong with this picture?" caption floating in her mind. This had been a little cranny of wild wood when she'd attended Butler, hidden away from all the trimmed lawns and shrubbery that made the rest of the university so picturesque. But she could remember slipping back here, journal in hand, and sitting under that huge . . .

"It's all changed," she said slowly. "They cleaned out all the brush and cut down the oak tree. . . ."

Someone had once told her that this particular tree was—had been—a rarity. It had belonged to a species not native to North America—the *Quercus robur,* or common oak of Europe—and was supposed to be over four hundred years old, which made it older than the university, older than Newford itself.

"How could they just . . . cut it down . . . ?" she asked.

The conjure man jerked a thumb over his shoulder towards the library.

"Your man with the books had the work done—didn't like the shade it was throwing on his office. Didn't like to look out and see an untamed bit of the wild hidden in here disturbing his sense of order."

"The head librarian?" Wendy asked.

The conjure man just shrugged.

"But—didn't anyone complain? Surely the students . . ."

In her day there would have been protests. Students would have formed a human chain around the tree, refusing to let anyone near it. They would have camped out, day and night. They . . .

She looked at the stump and felt a tightness in her chest as though someone had wrapped her in wet leather that was now starting to dry out and shrink.

"That tree was John's friend," the conjure man said. "The last friend I ever had. She was ten thousand years old and they just cut her down."

Wendy gave him an odd look. Ten thousand years old? Were we exaggerating now or what?

"Her death is a symbol," the conjure man went on. "The world has no more time for stories."

"I'm not sure I follow you," Wendy said.

He turned to look at her, eyes glittering with a strange light under the dark brim of his hat.

"She was a Tree of Tales," he said. "There are very few of them left, just as there are very few of me. She held stories, all the stories the wind brought to her that were of any worth, and with each such story she heard, she grew."

"But there's always going to be stories," Wendy said, falling into the spirit of the conversation even if she didn't quite understand its relevance to the situation at hand. "There are more books being published today than there ever have been in the history of the world."

The conjure man gave her a sour frown and hooked his thumb towards the library again. "Now you sound like him."

"But—"

"There's stories and then there's stories," he said, interrupting her. "The ones with any worth change your life forever, perhaps only in a small way, but once you've heard them, they are forever a part of you. You nurture them and pass them on and the giving only makes you feel better.

"The others are just words on a page."

"I know that," Wendy said.

And on some level she did, though it wasn't something she'd ever really stopped to think about. It was more an instinctive sort of knowledge that had always been present inside her, rising up into her awareness now as though called forth by the conjure man's words.

"It's all machines now," the conjure man went on. "It's a—what do they call it?—high-tech world. Fascinating, to be sure, but John thinks that it estranges many people, cheapens the human experience. There's no more room for the stories that matter, and that's wrong, for stories are a part of the language of dream—they grow not from one writer, but from a people. They become the voice of a country, or a race. Without them, people lose touch with themselves."

"You're talking about myths," Wendy said.

The conjure man shook his head. "Not specifically—not in the classical sense of the word. Such myths are only a part of the collective story that is harvested in a Tree of Tales. In a world as pessimistic as this has become, that collective story is all that's left to guide people through the encroaching dark. It serves to create a sense of options, the possibility of permanence out of nothing."

Wendy was really beginning to lose the thread of his argument now.

"What exactly is it that you're saying?" she asked.

"A Tree of Tales is an act of magic, of faith. Its existence becomes an affirmation of the power that the human spirit can have over its own destiny. The stories are just stories—they entertain, they make one laugh or cry—but if they have any worth, they carry within them a deeper resonance that remains long after the final page is turned, or the storyteller has come to the end of her tale. Both aspects of the story are necessary for it to have any worth."

He was silent for a long moment, then added, "Otherwise the story goes on without you."

Wendy gave him a questioning look.

"Do you know what 'ever after' means?" he asked.

"I suppose."

"It's one bookend of a tale—the kind that begins with 'once upon a time.' It's the end of the story when everybody goes home. That's what they said at the end of the story John was in, but John wasn't paying attention, so he got left behind."

"I'm not sure I know what you're talking about," Wendy said.

Not sure? she thought. She was positive. It was all so much . . . well, not exactly nonsense, as queer. And unrelated to any working of the world with which she was familiar. But the oddest thing was that everything he said continued to pull a kind of tickle out from deep in her mind so that while she didn't completely understand him, some part of her did. Some part, hidden behind the person who took care of all the day-to-day business of her life, perhaps the same part of her that pulled a poem into the empty page where no words had ever existed before. The part of her that was a conjurer.

"John took care of the Tale of Trees," the conjure man went on. "Because John got left behind in his own story, he wanted to make sure that the stories themselves would at least live on. But one day he went wandering too far—just like he did when his story was ending—and when he got back she was gone. When he got back, they'd done *this* to her."

Wendy said nothing. For all that he was a comical figure in his bright clothes and with his Santa Claus air, there was nothing even faintly humorous about the sudden anguish in his voice.

"I'm sorry," she said.

And she was. Not just in sympathy with him, but because in her own way she'd loved that old oak tree as well. And—just like the conjure man, she supposed—she'd wandered away as well.

"Well then," the conjure man said. He rubbed a sleeve up against his nose and looked away from her. "John just wanted you to see."

He got on his bike and reached forward to tousle the fur around Ginger's ears. When he looked back to Wendy, his eyes glittered like tiny blue fires.

"I knew you'd understand," he said.

Before Wendy could respond, he pushed off and pedaled away, bumping across the uneven lawn to leave her standing alone in that once wild place that was now so dispiriting. But then she saw something stir in the middle of the broad stump.

At first it was no more than a small flicker in the air like a heat ripple. Wendy took a step forward, stopping when the flicker resolved into a tiny sapling. As she watched, it took on the slow stately dance of time-lapse photography: budded, unfurled leaves, grew taller, its growth like a rondo, a basic theme that brackets two completely separate tunes. Growth was the theme, while the tunes on either end began with the tiny sapling and ended with a full-grown oak tree as majestic as the behemoth that had originally stood there. When it reached its full height, light seemed to emanate from its trunk, from the roots underground, from each stalkless, broad saw-toothed leaf.

Wendy stared, wide-eyed, then stepped forward with an outstretched hand. As soon as her fingers touched the glowing tree, it came apart, drifting like mist until every trace of it was gone. Once more, all that remained was the stump of the original tree.

The vision, combined with the tightness in her chest and the sadness the conjure man had left her, transformed itself into words that rolled across her mind, but she didn't write them down. All she could do was stand and look at the tree stump for a very long time, before she finally turned and walked away.

Kathryn's Cafe was on Battersfield Road in Lower Crowsea, not far from the university but across the river and far enough that Wendy had to hurry to make it to work on time. But it was as though a black hole had swallowed the two hours from when she'd met the conjure man to when her shift began. She was late getting to work—not by much, but she could see that Jilly had already taken orders from two tables that were supposed to be her responsibility.

She dashed into the restaurant's washroom and changed from her jeans into a short black skirt. She tucked her T-shirt in, pulled her hair back into a loose bun, then bustled out to stash her knapsack and pick up her order pad from the storage shelf behind the employee's coat rack.

"You're looking peaked," Jilly said as she finally got out into the dining area.

Jilly Coppercorn and Wendy were spiritual sisters and could almost pass as physical ones as well. Both women were small, with slender frames and attractive delicate features, though Jilly's hair was a dark curly brown—the same as Wendy's natural hair color. They both moonlighted as waitresses, saving their true energy for creative pursuits: Jilly for her art, Wendy her poetry.

Neither had known the other until they began to work at the restaurant together, but they'd become fast friends from the very first shift they shared.

"I'm feeling confused," Wendy said in response to Jilly's comment.

"You're confused? Check out table five—he's changed his mind three times since he first ordered. I'm going to stand here and wait five minutes before I give Frank his latest order, just in case he decides he wants to change it again."

Wendy smiled. "And then he'll complain about slow service and won't leave you much of a tip."

"If he leaves one at all."

Wendy laid a hand on Jilly's arm. "Are you busy tonight?"

Jilly shook her head. "What's up?"

"I need to talk to someone."

"I'm yours to command," Jilly said. She made a little curtsy which had Wendy quickly stifle a giggle, then shifted her gaze to table five. "Oh bother, he's signaling me again."

"Give me his order," Wendy said. "I'll take care of him."

It was such a nice night that they just went around back of the restaurant when their shift was over. Walking the length of a short alley, they came out on small strip of lawn and made their way down to the river. There they sat on a stone wall, dangling their feet above the sluggish water. The night felt still. Through some trick of the air, the traffic on nearby Battersfield Road was no more than a distant murmur, as though there was more of a sound baffle between where they sat and the busy street than just the building that housed their workplace.

"Remember that time we went camping?" Wendy said after they'd been sitting for awhile in a companionable silence. "It was just me, you and LaDonna. We sat around the campfire telling ghost stories that first night."

"Sure," Jilly said with a smile in her voice. "You kept telling us ones by Robert Aickman and the like—they were all taken from books."

"While you and LaDonna claimed that the ones you told were real and no matter how much I tried to get either of you to admit they weren't, you wouldn't."

"But they were true," Jilly said.

Wendy thought of LaDonna telling them that she'd seen Bigfoot in the Tombs and Jilly's stories about a kind of earth spirit called a gemmin that she'd met in the same part of the city and of a race of goblin-like creatures living in the subterranean remains of the old city that lay beneath Newford's subway system.

She turned from the river to regard her friend. "Do you really believe those things you told me?"

Jilly nodded. "Of course I do. They're true." She paused a moment, leaning closer to Wendy as though trying to read her features in the gloom. "Why? What's happened, Wendy?"

"I think I just had my own close encounter of the weird kind this afternoon."

When Jilly said nothing, Wendy went on to tell her of her meeting with the conjure man earlier in the day.

"I mean, I know why he's called the conjure man," she finished up. "I've seen him pulling flowers out of people's ears and all those other stage tricks he does, but this was different. The whole time I was with him I kept feeling like there really was a kind of magic in the air, a *real* magic just sort of humming around him, and then when I saw the . . . I guess it was a vision of the tree . . .

"Well, I don't know what to think."

She'd been looking across the river while she spoke, gaze fixed on the darkness of the far bank. Now she turned to Jilly.

"Who is he?" she asked. "Or maybe I should be asking *what* is he?"

"I've always thought of him as a kind of anima," Jilly said. "A loose bit of myth that got left behind when all the others went on to wherever it is that myths go when we don't believe in them anymore."

"That's sort of what he said. But what does it mean? What is he really?"

Jilly shrugged. "Maybe what he is isn't so important as *that* he is." At Wendy's puzzled look, she added, "I can't explain it any better. I . . . Look, it's like it's not so important that he is or isn't what he says he is, but *that* he says it. That he believes it."

"Why?"

"Because it's just like he told you," Jilly said. "People are losing touch with themselves and with each other. They need stories because they really are the only thing that brings us together. Gossip, anecdotes, jokes, stories—these are the things that we used to exchange with each other. It kept the lines of communication open, let us touch each other on a regular basis.

"That's what art's all about, too. My paintings and your poems, the books Christy writes, the music Geordie plays—they're all lines of communication. But they're harder to keep open now because it's so much easier for most people to relate to a TV set than it is to another person. They get all this data fed into them, but they don't know what to do with it anymore. When they talk to other people, it's all surface. How ya doing, what about the weather. The only opinions they have are those that they've gotten from people on the TV. They think they're informed, but all they're doing is repeating the views of talk show hosts and news commentators.

"They don't know how to listen to real people anymore."

"I know all that," Wendy said. "But what does any of it have to do with what the conjure man was showing me this afternoon?"

"I guess what I'm trying to say is that he validates an older kind of value, that's all."

"Okay, but what did he want from me?"

Jilly didn't say anything for a long time. She looked out across the river, her gaze caught by the same darkness as Wendy's had earlier when she was relating her afternoon encounter. Twice Wendy started to ask Jilly what she was thinking, but both times she forbore. Then finally Jilly turned to her.

"Maybe he wants you to plant a new tree," she said.

"But that's silly. I wouldn't know how to begin to go about something like that." Wendy sighed. "I don't even know if I believe in a Tree of Tales."

But then she remembered the feeling that had risen in her when the conjure man spoke to her, that sense of familiarity as though she was being reminded of something she already knew, rather than being told what she didn't. And then there was the vision of the tree . . .

She sighed again.

"Why me?" she asked.

Her words were directed almost to the night at large, rather than just her companion, but it was Jilly who replied. The night held its own counsel.

"I'm going to ask you something," Jilly said, "and I don't want you to think about the answer. Just tell me the first thing that comes to mind—okay?"

Wendy nodded uncertainly. "I guess."

"If you could be granted one wish—anything at all, no limits—what would you ask for?"

With the state the world was in at the moment, Wendy had no hesitation in answering: "World peace."

"Well, there you go," Jilly told her.

"I don't get it."

"You were asking why the conjure man picked you and there's your reason. Most people would have started out thinking of what they wanted for themselves. You know, tons of money, or to live forever—that kind of thing."

Wendy shook her head. "But he doesn't even know me."

Jilly got up and pulled Wendy to her feet.

"Come on," she said. "Let's go look at the tree."

"It's just a stump."

"Let's go anyway."

Wendy wasn't sure why she felt reluctant, but just as she had this afternoon, she allowed herself to be led back to the campus.

Nothing had changed, except that this time it was dark, which gave the scene, at least to Wendy's way of thinking, an even more desolate feeling.

Jilly was very quiet beside her. She stepped ahead of Wendy and crouched down beside the stump, running her hand along the top of it.

"I'd forgotten all about this place," she said softly.

That's right, Wendy thought. Jilly'd gone to Butler U. just as she had—around the same time, too, though they hadn't known each other then.

She crouched down beside Jilly, starting slightly when Jilly took her hand and laid it on the stump.

"Listen," Jilly said. "You can almost feel the whisper of a story . . . a last echo . . ."

Wendy shivered, though the night was mild. Jilly turned to her. At that moment, the starlight flickering in her companion's blue eyes reminded Wendy very much of the conjure man.

"You've got to do it," Jilly said. "You've got to plant a new tree. It wasn't just the conjure man choosing you—the tree chose you, too."

Wendy wasn't sure what was what anymore. It all seemed more than a little mad, yet as she listened to Jilly, she could almost believe in it all. But then that was one of Jilly's gifts: she could make the oddest thing seem normal. Wendy wasn't sure if you could call a thing like that a gift, but whatever it was, Jilly had it.

"Maybe we should get Christy to do it," she said. "After all, he's the story writer."

"Christy is a lovely man," Jilly said, "but sometimes he's far more concerned with how he says a thing, rather than with the story itself."

"Well, I'm not much better. I've been known to worry for hours over a stanza—or even just a line."

"For the sake of being clever?" Jilly asked.

"No. So that it's right."

Jilly raked her fingers through the short stubble of the weeds that passed for a lawn around the base of the oak stump. She found something and pressed it into Wendy's hand. Wendy didn't have to look at it to know that it was an acorn.

"You have to do it," Jilly said. "Plant a new Tree of Tales and feed it with stories. It's really up to you."

Wendy looked from the glow of her friend's eyes to the stump. She remembered her conversation with the conjure man and her vision of the tree. She closed her fingers around the acorn, feeling the press of the cap's bristles indent her skin.

Maybe it *was* up to her, she found herself thinking.

* * *

The poem that came to her that night after she left Jilly and got back to her little apartment in Ferryside, came all at once, fully formed and complete. The act of putting it to paper was a mere formality.

She sat by her window for a long time afterward, her journal on her lap, the acorn in her hand. She rolled it slowly back and forth on her palm. Finally, she laid both journal and acorn on the windowsill and went into her tiny kitchen. She rummaged around in the cupboard under the sink until she came up with an old flowerpot, which she took into the backyard and filled with dirt—rich loam, as dark and mysterious as that indefinable place inside herself that was the source of the words that filled her poetry and had risen in recognition to the conjure man's words.

When she returned to the window, she put the pot between her knees. Tearing the new poem out of her journal, she wrapped the acorn up in it and buried it in the pot. She watered it until the surface of the dirt was slick with mud, then placed the flowerpot on her windowsill and went to bed.

That night she dreamed of Jilly's gemmin—slender earth spirits that appeared outside the old three-story building that housed her apartment and peered in at the flowerpot on the windowsill. In the morning, she got up and told the buried acorn her dream.

Autumn turned to winter and Wendy's life went pretty much the way it always had. She took turns working at the restaurant and on her poems, she saw her friends, she started a relationship with a fellow she met at a party in Jilly's loft, but it floundered after a month.

Life went on.

The only change was centered around the contents of the pot on her windowsill. As though the tiny green sprig that pushed up through the dark soil was her lover, every day she told it all the things that had happened to her and around her. Sometimes she read it her favorite stories from anthologies and collections, or interesting bits from magazines and newspapers. She badgered her friends for stories, sometimes passing them on, speaking to the tiny plant in a low, but animated voice, other times convincing her friends to come over and tell the stories themselves.

Except for Jilly, LaDonna and the two Riddell brothers, Geordie and Christy, most people thought she'd gone just a little daft. Nothing serious, mind you, but strange all the same.

Wendy didn't care.

Somewhere out in the world, there were other Trees of Tales, but they were few—if the conjure man was to be believed. And she believed him now. She had no proof, only faith, but oddly enough, faith seemed enough. But since she believed, she knew it was more important than ever that her charge should flourish.

With the coming of winter, there were less and less of the street people to be found. They were indoors, if they had such an option, or perhaps they migrated to warmer climes like the swallows. But Wendy still spied the more regular ones in their usual haunts. Paperjack had gone, but the pigeon lady still fed her charges every day, the German cowboy continued his bombastic monologues—though mostly on the subway platforms now. She saw the conjure man, too, but he was never near enough for her to get a chance to talk to him.

By the springtime, the sprig of green in the flowerpot grew into a sapling that stood almost a foot high. On warmer days, Wendy put the pot out on the backporch steps, where it could taste the air and catch the growing warmth of the afternoon sun. She still wasn't sure what she was going to do with it once it outgrew its pot.

But she had some ideas. There was a part of Fitzhenry Park called the Silenus Gardens that was dedicated to the poet Joshua Stanhold. She thought it might be appropriate to plant the sapling there.

One day in late April, she was leaning on the handlebars of her ten-speed in front of the public library in Lower Crowsea, admiring the yellow splash the daffodils made against the building's grey stone walls, when she sensed, more than saw, a red bicycle pull up onto the sidewalk behind her. She turned around to find herself looking into the conjure man's merry features.

"It's spring, isn't it just," the conjure man said. "A time to finally forget the cold and bluster and think of summer. John can feel the leaf buds stir, the flowers blossoming. There's a grand smile in the air for all the growing."

Wendy gave Ginger a pat, before letting her gaze meet the blue shock of his eyes.

"What about a Tree of Tales?" she asked. "Can you feel her growing?"

The conjure man gave her a wide smile. "Especially her." He paused to adjust the brim of his hat, then gave her a sly look. "Your man Stanhold," he added. "Now there was a fine poet—and a fine storyteller."

Wendy didn't bother to ask how he knew of her plan. She just returned the conjure man's smile and then asked, "Do you have a story to tell me?"

The conjure man polished one of the buttons of his bright blue jacket.

"I believe I do," he said. He patted the brown satchel that rode on his back carrier. "John has a thermos filled with the very best tea, right here in his bag. Why don't we find ourselves a comfortable place to sit and he'll tell you how he got this bicycle of his over a hot cuppa."

He started to pedal off down the street, without waiting for her response. Wendy stared after him, her gaze catching the little terrier, sitting erect in her basket and looking back at her.

There seemed to be a humming in the air that woke a kind of singing feeling in her chest. The wind rose up and caught her hair, pushing it playfully into her eyes. As she swept it back from her face with her hand, she thought of the sapling sitting in its pot on her back steps, thought of the wind, and knew that stories were already being harvested without the necessity of her having to pass them on.

But she wanted to hear them all the same.

Getting on her ten-speed, she hurried to catch up with the conjure man.

Small Deaths

What unites us universally is our emotions, our feelings in the face of experience, and not necessarily the actual experiences themselves.

—Anaïs Nin

"I feel like I should know you."

Zoe Brill looked up. The line was familiar, but it usually came only after she'd spoken—that was the down side of being an all-night DJ in a city with too many people awake and having nothing to do between midnight and dawn. Everybody felt they knew you, everybody was your friend. Most of the time that suited her fine, since she genuinely liked people, but as her mother used to tell her, every family has its black sheep. Sometimes it seemed that every one of them tended to gravitate to her at one point or another in their lives.

The man who'd paused by the cafe railing to speak to Zoe this evening reminded her of a fox. He had lean, pointy features, dark eyes, the corners of his lips constantly lifted in a sly smile, hair as red as her own, if not as long. Unlike her, he had a dark complexion, as though swimming somewhere back in the gene pool of his forebears was an Italian, an Arab, or a Native American. His self-assurance radiated a touch too shrill for Zoe's taste, but he seemed basically harmless. Just your average single male yuppie on the prowl, heading out for an evening in clubland—she could almost hear the Full Force-produced dance number kick up as a soundtrack to the moment. Move your body all night long.

He was well-dressed, as all Lotharios should be, casual, but with flair; she doubted there was a single item in his wardrobe worth under two hundred dollars. Maybe the socks.

"I think I'd remember if we'd met before," she said.

He ignored the wryness in her voice and took what she'd said as a compliment.

"Most people do," he agreed.

"Lucky them."

It was one of those rare, supernaturally perfect November evenings, warm with a light breeze, wedged in between a week of sub-zero temperatures with similar weather to follow. All up and down Lee Street, from one end of the Market to the other, the restaurants and cafes had opened their patios for one last outdoor fling.

"No, no," the man said, finally picking up on her lack of interest. "It's not like what you're thinking."

Zoe tapped a long finger lightly against the page of the opened book that lay on her table beside a glass of red wine.

"I'm kind of busy," she said. "Maybe some other time."

He leaned closer to read the running head at the top of the book's left-hand page: *Disappearing Through the Skylight.*

"That's by O. B. Hardison, isn't it?" he asked. "Didn't he also write *Entering the Maze?*"

Zoe gave a reluctant nod and upgraded her opinion of him. Fine. So he was a well-read single male yuppie on the prowl, but she still wasn't interested.

"Technology," he said, "is a perfect example of evolution, don't you think? Take the camera. If you compare present models to the best they had just thirty years ago, you can see—"

"Look," Zoe said. "This is all very interesting, and I don't mean to sound rude, but why don't you go hit on someone else? If I'd wanted company, I would've gone out with a friend."

He shook his head. "No, no. I told you, I'm not trying to pick you up." He put out his hand. "My name's Gordon Wolfe."

He gave her his name with the simple assurance inherent in his voice that it was impossible that she wouldn't recognize it.

Zoe ignored the hand. As an attractive woman living on her own in a city the size of Newford, she'd long ago acquired a highly developed sense of radar, a kind of mental dah-*dum,* dah-*dum* straight out of *Jaws,* that kicked in whenever that sixth sense hiding somewhere in her subconscious decided that the situation carried too much of a possibility of turning weird, or a little too intense.

Gordon Wolfe had done nothing yet, but the warning bell was sounding faintly in her mind.

"Then what do you want?" she asked.

He lifted his hand and ran it through his hair, the movement so casual it was as though he'd never been rebuffed. "I'm just trying to figure out why I feel like I should know you."

So they were back to that again.

"The world's full of mysteries," Zoe told him. "I guess that's just going to be another one."

She turned back to her book, but he didn't leave the railing. Looking up, she tried to catch the eye of the waiter, to let him know that she was being bothered, but naturally neither he nor the two waitresses were anywhere in sight. The patio held only the usual bohemian mix of Lower Crowsea's inhabitants and hangers-on—a well-stirred stew of actors, poets, artists, musicians and those who aspired, through their clothing or attitude, to be counted in that number. Sometimes it was all just a little too trendy.

She turned back to her unwelcome visitor who still stood on the other side of the cafe's railing.

"It's nothing personal," she began. "I just don't—"

"You shouldn't mock me," he said, cutting in. "I'm the bringer of small deaths." His dark eyes flashed. "Remember me the next time you die a little."

Then he turned and walked away, losing himself in among the crowd of pedestrians that filled the sidewalk on either side of Lee Street.

Zoe sighed. Why were they always drawn to her? The weird and the wacky. Why not the wonderful for a change? When was the last time a nice normal guy had tried to chat her up?

It wasn't as though she looked particularly exotic: skin a little too pale, perhaps, due to the same genes that had given her her shoulder-length red hair and green eyes, but certainly not the extreme vampiric pallor affected by so many fans of the various British Gothic bands that jostled for position on the album charts of college radio and independent record stores; clothing less thrift-shop than most of those with whom she shared the patio this evening: ankle-high black lace-up boots, dark stockings, a black dress that was somewhat tight and a little short, a faded jean jacket that was a couple of sizes too big.

Just your basic semi-hip working girl, relaxing over a glass of wine and a book before she had to head over to the studio. So where were all the nice semi-hip guys for her to meet?

She took a sip of her wine and went back to her book, but found herself unable to concentrate on what she was reading. Gordon Wolfe's parting shot kept intruding on the words that filled the page before her.

Remember me the next time you die a little.

She couldn't suppress the small shiver that slithered up her spine.

Congratulations, she thought to her now-absent irritant. You've succeeded in screwing up my evening anyway.

Paying her bill, she decided to go home and walk Rupert, then head in to work early. An electronic score with lots of deep, low bass notes echoed in her head as she went home, Tangerine Dream crossed with B-movie horror themes. She kept thinking Wolfe was lurking about, following her home, although whenever she turned, there was no one there. She hated this mild anxiety he'd bestowed upon her like some spiteful parting gift.

Her relief at finally getting home to where Rupert waited for her far outweighed the dog's slobbery enthusiasm at the thought of going out for their evening ramble earlier than usual. Zoe took a long roundabout way to the station, letting Rupert's ingenuous affection work its magic. With the big galoot at her side, it was easy to put the bad taste of her encounter with Wolfe to rest.

An old Lovin' Spoonful song provided backdrop to the walk, bouncing and cheerful. It wasn't summer yet, but it was warmer than usual and Newford had always been a hot town.

The phone call came in during the fourth hour of her show, "Nightnoise." As usual, the music was an eclectic mix. An Italian aria by Kiri Te Kanawa was segueing into a cut by the New Age Celtic group from which the show had gotten its name, with Steve Earle's "The Hard Way" cued up next, when the yellow light on the studio's phone began to blink with an incoming call.

"Nightnoise," she said into the receiver. "Zoe B. here."

"Are we on the air?"

It was a man's voice—an unfamiliar voice, warm and friendly with just the vaguest undercurrent of tension.

"I'm sorry," she said. "We don't take call-ins after three."

From one to three A.M. she took on-air calls for requests, commentaries, sometimes just to chat; during that time period she also conducted interviews, if she had any slated. Experience had proven that the real fruitcakes didn't come out of the woodwork until the show was into its fourth hour, creeping up on dawn.

"That's all right," her caller said. "It's you I wanted to talk to."

Zoe cradled the receiver between her shoulder and ear and checked the studio clock. As the instrumental she was playing ended, she brought up the beginning of the Steve Earle cut and began to cue up her next choice, Concrete Blonde's cover of a Leonard Cohen song from the *Pump Up the Volume* soundtrack.

"So talk," she said, shifting the receiver back to her hand.

She could almost feel the caller's hesitation. It happened a lot. They got up the nerve to make the call, but once they were connected, their mouths went dry and all their words turned to sand.

"What's your name?" she added, trying to make it easier on him.

"Bob."

"Not the one from *Twin Peaks* I hope."

"I'm sorry?"

Obviously not a David Lynch fan, Zoe thought.

"Nothing," she said. "What can I do for you tonight, Bob?" Maybe she'd make an exception, she thought, and added: "Did you have a special song you wanted me to play for you?"

"No, I . . . It's about Gordon."

Zoe went blank for a moment. The first Gordon that came to mind was Gordon Waller from the old UK band, Peter & Gordon, rapidly followed by rockabilly great Robert Gordon and then Jim Gordon, the drummer who'd played with everybody from Baez to Clapton, including a short stint with Bread.

"Gordon Wolfe," Bob said, filling in the blank for her. "You were talking to him earlier tonight on the patio of The Rusty Lion."

Zoe shivered. From his blanket beside the studio door, Rupert lifted his head and gave an anxious whine, sensing her distress.

"You . . ." she began. "How could you know? What were you doing, following me?"

"No. I was following him."

"Oh."

Recovering her equilibrium, Zoe glanced at the studio clock and cued up the first cut from her next set in the CD player, her fingers going through the procedure on automatic.

"Why?" she asked.

"Because he's dangerous."

He'd given her the creeps, Zoe remembered, but she hadn't really thought of him as dangerous—at least not until his parting shot.

Remember me the next time you die a little.

"Who is he?" she asked. "Better yet, who are you? Why are you following this Wolfe guy around?"

"That's not his real name," Bob said.

"Then what is?"

"I can't tell you."

"Why the hell not?"

"Not won't," Bob said quickly. "*Can't.* I don't know it myself. All I know is he's dangerous and you shouldn't have gotten him mad at you."

"Jesus," Zoe said. "I really need this." Her gaze flicked back to the studio clock; the Steve Earle cut was heading into its fade-out. "Hang on a sec, Bob. I've got to run some commercials."

She put him on hold and brought up the volume on her mike.

"That was Steve Earle," she said, "with the title cut from his latest album, and you're listening to Nightnoise on WKPN. Zoe B. here, spinning the tunes for all you night birds and birdettes. Coming up we've got a hot and heavy metal set, starting off with the classic "Ace of Spades' by Motorhead. These are *not* new kids on the block, my friends. But first, oh yes, even at this time of night, a word from some sponsors."

She punched up the cassette with its minute of ads for this half hour and brought the volume down off her mike again. But when she turned back to the phone, the on-line light was dead. She tried it anyway, but Bob had hung up.

"Shit," she said. "Why are you doing this to me?"

Rupert looked up again, then got up from his blanket and padded across the floor to press his wet nose up against her hand. He was a cross between a golden lab and a German shepherd, seventy pounds of big-hearted mush.

"No, not you," she told him, taking his head in both of her hands and rubbing her nose against the tip of his muzzle. "You're Zoe's big baby, aren't you?"

The ads cassette ran its course and she brought up Motorhead. As she cued up the rest of the pieces for this set, she kept looking at the phone, but the on-line light stayed dead.

"Weird," Hilary Carlisle agreed. She brushed a stray lock of hair away from her face and gave Zoe a quick smile. "But par for the course, don't you think?"

"Thanks a lot."

"I didn't say you egged them on, but it seems to be the story of your life: put you in a roomful of strangers and you can almost guarantee that the most oddball guy there will be standing beside you within ten minutes. It's—" she grinned "—just a gift you have."

"Well, this guy's really given me a case of the creeps."

"Which one—Gordon or Bob?"

"Both of them, if you want the truth."

Hilary's smile faded. "This is really getting to you, isn't it?"

"I could've just forgotten my delightful encounter at The Rusty Lion if it hadn't been for the follow-up call."

"You think it's connected?"

"Well, of course it's connected."

"No, not like that," Hilary said. "I mean, do you think the two of them have worked this thing up together?"

That was just what Zoe had been thinking. She didn't really believe in coincidence.

To her mind, there was always connections; they just weren't always that easy to work out.

"But what would be the point?" she asked.

"You've got me," Hilary said. "You can stay here with me for a few days if you like," she added.

They were sitting in the front room of Hilary's downstairs apartment which was in the front half of one of the old Tudor buildings on the south side of Stanton Street facing the estates. Hilary in this room always reminded Zoe of Mendelssohn's "Concerto in E Minor," a perfect dialogue between soloist and orchestra. Paintings, curtains, carpet and furniture all reflected Hilary's slightly askew worldview so that Impressionists hung side-by-side with paintings that seemed more the work of a camera; an antique sideboard housed a state-of-the-art stereo, glass shelves held old books; the curtains were dark antique flower prints, with sheers trimmed in lace, the carpet a riot of symmetrical designs and primary colors. The recamier on which Hilary was lounging had a glory of leaf and scrollwork in its wood; Zoe's club chair looked as though a bear had been hibernating in it.

Hilary herself was as tall as Zoe's five-ten, but where Zoe was more angular and big-boned, Hilary was all graceful lines with tanned skin that accentuated her blue eyes and the waterfall of her long straight blonde hair. She was dressed in white this morning, wearing a simple cotton shirt and trousers with the casual elegance of a model, and appeared, as she always did, as the perfect centerpiece to the room.

"I think I'll be okay," Zoe said. "Besides, I've always got Rupert to protect me."

At the sound of his name, Rupert lifted his head from the floor by Zoe's feet and gave her a quick, searching glance.

Hilary laughed. "Right. Like he isn't scared of his own shadow."

"He can't help being nervous. He's just—"

"I know. High-strung."

"Did I ever tell you how he jumped right—"

"Into the canal and saved Tommy's dog from drowning when it fell in? Only about a hundred times since it happened."

Zoe's lips shaped a moue.

"Oh God," Hilary said, starting to laugh. "Don't pout. You know what it does to me when you pout."

Hilary was a talent scout for WEA Records. They'd met three years ago at a record launch party when Hilary had made a pass at her. Once they got past the fact that Zoe preferred men and wasn't planning on changing that preference, they discovered that they had far too much in common not to be good friends. But that didn't stop Hilary from occasionally teasing her, especially when Zoe was complaining about man troubles.

Such troubles were usually far simpler than the one currently in hand.

"What do you think he meant by small deaths?" Zoe asked. "The more I think of it, the more it gives me the creeps."

Hilary nodded. "Isn't sleep sometimes referred to as the little death?"

Zoe could hear Wolfe's voice in her head. *I'm the bringer of small deaths.*

"I don't think that's what he was talking about," she said.

"Maybe it's just his way of saying you're going to have bad dreams. You know, he freaks you out a little, makes you nervous, then bingo—he's a success."

"But why?"

"Creeps don't need reasons for what they do; that's why they're creeps."

Remember me the next time you die a little.

Zoe was back to shivering again.

"Maybe I will stay here," she said, "if you're sure I won't be in your way."

"Be in my way?" Hilary glanced at her watch. "I'm supposed to be at work right now—I've got a meeting in an hour—so you'll have the place to yourself."

"I just hope I can get to sleep."

"Do you want something to help you relax?"

"What, like a sleeping pill?"

Hilary shook her head. "I was thinking more along the lines of some hot milk."

"That'd be lovely."

Zoe didn't sleep well. It wasn't her own bed and the daytime street noises were different from the ones outside her own apartment, but it was mostly the constant replay of last night's two conversations that kept her turning restlessly from one side of the bed to the other. Finally, she just gave up and decided to face the day on less sleep than she normally needed.

She knew she'd been having bad dreams during the few times when she had managed to sleep, but couldn't remember one of them. Padding through the apartment in an oversize T-shirt, she found herself drawn to the front window. She peeked out through the curtains, gaze traveling up and down the length of Stanton Street. When she realized what she was doing—looking for a shock of red hair, dark eyes watching the house—she felt more irritable than ever.

She was not going to let it get to her, she decided. At least not anymore.

A shower woke her up, while breakfast and a long afternoon ramble with Rupert through the grounds of Butler University made her feel a little better, but by the time she got to work at a quarter to twelve that night and started to go through the station's library to collect the music she needed for the show, she was back to being tense and irritable. Halfway through the first hour of the show, she interrupted a Bobby Brown/Ice T/Living Colour set and brought up her voice mike.

"Here's a song for Gordon Wolfe," she said as she cued up an album cut by the local band No Nuns Here. "Memories are made of this, Wolfe."

The long wail of an electric guitar went out over the air waves, a primal screech as the high E string was fingered down around the fourteenth fret and pushed up past the G string, then the bass and drums caught and settled into a driving back beat. The wailing guitar broke into chunky bar chords as Lorio Munn's voice cut across the music like the punch of a fist.

> *I don't want your love, baby*
> *So don't come on so sweet*
> *I don't need a man, baby*
> *Treats me like I'm meat*
>
> *I'm coming to your house, baby*
> *Coming to your door*
> *Gonna knock you down, right where you stand*
> *And stomp you on the floor*

* * *

Zoe eyed the studio phone. She picked up the handset as soon as the on-line light began to flash. Which one was it going to be? she thought as she spoke into the phone.

"Nightnoise. Zoe B. here."

She kept the call off the air, just in case.

"What the hell do you think you're doing?"

Bingo. It was Bob.

"Tell me about small deaths," she said.

"I *told* you he was dangerous, but you just—"

"You'll get your chance to natter on," Zoe interrupted, "but first I want to know about these small deaths."

Silence on the line was the only reply.

"I don't hear a dial tone," she said, "so I know you're still there. Talk to me."

"I . . . Jesus," Bob said finally.

"Small deaths," Zoe repeated.

After another long hesitation, she heard Bob sigh. "They're those pivotal moments in a person's life that change it forever: a love affair gone wrong, not getting into the right post-graduate program, stealing a car on a dare and getting caught, that kind of thing. They're the moments that some people brood on forever; right now they could have the most successful marriage or career, but they can't stop thinking about the past, about what might have happened if things had gone differently.

"It sours their success, makes them bitter. And usually it leads to more small deaths: depression, stress, heavy drinking or drug use, abusing their spouse or children."

"What are you saying?" Zoe asked. "That a small death's like disappointment?"

"More like a pain, a sorrow, an anger. It doesn't have to be something you do to yourself. Maybe one of your parents died when you were just a kid, or you were abused as a child; that kind of trauma changes a person forever. You can't go through such an experience and grow up to be the same person you would have been without it."

"It sounds like you're just talking about life," Zoe said. "It's got its ups and its downs; to stay sane, you've got to take what it hands you. Ride the punches and maybe try to leave the place in a little better shape than it was before you got there."

What was *with* this conversation? Zoe thought as she was speaking.

As the No Nuns Here cut came to an end, she cued in a version of Carly Simon's "You're So Vain" by Faster Pussycat.

"Jesus," Bob said as the song went out over the air. "You really have a death wish, don't you?"

"Tell me about Gordon Wolfe."

The man's voice echoed in her mind as she spoke his name.

I'm the bringer of small deaths.

"What's he got to do with all of this?" she added.

Remember me the next time you die a little.

"He's a catalyst for bad luck," Bob said. "It's like, being in his company—just being in proximity to him—can bring on a small death. It's like . . . do you remember that character in the *L'il Abner* comic strip—the one who always had a cloud hanging over his head. What was his name?"

"I can't remember."

"Everywhere he went he brought bad luck."

"What about him?" Zoe asked.

"Gordon Wolfe's like that, except you don't see the cloud. You don't get any warning at all. I guess the worst thing is that his effects are completely random—unless he happens to take a dislike to you. Then it's personal."

"A serial killer of people's hopes," Zoe said, half jokingly.

"Exactly."

"Oh, give me a break."

"I'm trying to."

"Yeah, right," Zoe said. "You feed me a crock of shit and then expect me to—"

"I don't think he's human," Bob said then.

Zoe wasn't sure what she'd been expecting from this conversation—a confession, perhaps, or even just an apology, but it wasn't this.

"And I don't think you are either," he added.

"Oh, please."

"Why else do you think he was so attracted to you? He recognized something in you—I'm sure of it."

Wolfe's voice was back in her head.

I feel like I should know you.

"I think we've taken this about as far as it can go," Zoe said.

This time she was the one to cut the connection.

The phone's on-line light immediately lit up once more. She hesitated for a long moment, then brought the handset up to her ear.

"I am not bullshitting you," Bob said.

"Look, why don't you take it to the tabloids—they'd eat it up."

"You don't think I've tried? I'd do anything to see him stopped."

"Why?"

"Because the world's tough enough without having something like him wandering through it, randomly shooting down people's hopes. He's the father of fear. You know what fear stands for? Fuck Everything And Run. You want the whole world to be like that? People screw up their lives enough on their own; they don't need a . . . a *thing* like Wolfe to add to their grief."

The scariest thing, Zoe realized, was that he really sounded sincere.

"So what am I then?" she asked. "The mother of hope?"

"I don't know. But I think you scare *him*."

Zoe had to laugh. Wolfe had her so creeped out she hadn't even been able to go to her own apartment last night, and Bob thought she was the scary one?

"Look, could we meet somewhere?" Bob said.

"I don't think so."

"Somewhere public. Bring along a friend—bring a dozen friends. Face to face, I know I can make you understand."

Zoe thought about it.

"It's important," Bob said. "Look at it this way: if I'm a nut, you've got nothing to lose except some time. But if I'm right, then you'd really be—how did you put it?—leaving the world in a little better shape than it was before you got there. A lot better shape."

"Okay," Zoe said. "Tomorrow noon. I'll be at the main entrance of the Williamson Street Mall."

"Great." Zoe started to hang up, pausing when he added: "And Zoe, cool it with the on-air digs at Wolfe, would you? You don't want to see him pissed."

Zoe hung up.

"Your problem," Hilary said as the two of them sat on the edge of the indoor fountain just inside the main entrance of the Williamson Street Mall, "is that you keep expecting to find a man who's going to solve all of your problems for you."

"Of course. Why didn't I realize that was the problem?"

"You know," Hilary went on, ignoring Zoe's sarcasm. "Like who you are, where you're going, who you want to be."

Rupert sat on his haunches by Zoe's knee, head leaning in towards her as she absently played with the hair on the top of his head.

"So what're you saying?" she asked. "That I should be looking for a woman instead?"

Hilary shook her head. "You've got to find yourself first. Everything else'll follow."

"I'm not looking for a man."

"Right."

"Well, not actively. And besides, what's that got to do with anything?"

"Everything. You wouldn't be in this situation, you wouldn't have all these weird guys coming on to you, if you didn't exude a kind of confusion about your identity. People pick up on that kind of thing, even if the signals are just subliminal. Look at yourself: You're a nice normal-looking woman with terrific skin and hair and great posture. The loony squad shouldn't be hitting on you. Who's that actor you like so much?"

"Mel Gibson."

"Guys like him should be hitting on you. Or at least, guys like your idolized version of him. Who knows what Gibson's really like?"

Over an early breakfast, Zoe had laid out the whole story for her friend. Hilary had been skeptical about meeting with Bob, but when she realized that Zoe was going to keep the rendezvous, with or without her, she'd allowed herself to be talked into coming along. She'd left work early enough to return to her apartment to wake Zoe and then the two of them had taken the subway over to the Mall.

"You think this is all a waste of time, don't you?" Zoe said.

"Don't you?"

Zoe shrugged. A young security guard walked by and eyed the three of them, his gaze lingering longest on Rupert, but he didn't ask them to leave. Maybe he thought Rupert was a seeing-eye dog, Zoe thought. Maybe he just liked the look of Hilary. Most guys did.

Hilary glanced at her watch. "He's five minutes late. Want to bet he's a no-show?"

But Zoe wasn't listening to her. Her gaze was locked on the red-haired man who had just come in off the street.

"What's the matter?" Hilary asked.

"That's him—the red-haired guy."

"I thought you'd never met this Bob."

"I haven't," Zoe said. "That's Gordon Wolfe."

Or was it? Wolfe was still decked out like a highroller on the make, but there was something subtly different about him this afternoon. His carriage, his whole body language had changed.

Zoe was struck with a sudden insight. A long shiver went up her spine. It started out as a low thrum and climbed into a high-pitched, almost piercing note, like Mariah Carey running through all seven of her octaves.

"Hello, Zoe," Wolfe said as he joined them.

Zoe looked up at him, trying to find a physical difference. It was Wolfe, but it wasn't. The voice was the same as the one on the phone, but people could change their voices; a good actor could look like an entirely different person just through the use of his body language.

Wolfe glanced at Hilary, raising his eyebrows questioningly.

"You . . . you're Bob?" Zoe asked.

He nodded. "I know what you're thinking."

"You're twins?"

"It's a little more complicated than that." His gaze flicked to Hilary again. "How much does your friend know?"

"My name's Hilary and Zoe's pretty well filled me in on the whole sorry business."

"That's good."

Hilary shook her head. "No, it isn't. The whole thing sucks. Why don't you just pack up your silly game and take it someplace else?"

Rupert stirred by Zoe's feet. The sharpness in Hilary's voice and Zoe's tension brought the rumbling start of a growl to his chest.

"I didn't start anything," Bob said. "Keep your anger for someone who deserves it."

"Like Wolfe," Zoe said.

Bob nodded.

"Your twin."

"It's more like he's my other half," Bob said. "We share the same body, except he doesn't know it. Only I'm aware of the relationship."

"Jesus, would you give us a break," Hilary said. "This is about as lame as that episode of—"

Zoe laid a hand on her friend's knee. "Wait a minute," she said. "You're saying Wolfe's a schizophrene?"

"I'm not sure if that's technically correct," Bob replied.

He sat down on the marble floor in front of them. It made for an incongruous image: an obviously well-heeled executive type sitting cross-legged on the floor like some panhandler.

"I just know that there's two of us in here," he added, touched a hand to his chest.

"You said you went to the tabloids with this story, didn't you?" Zoe asked.

"I tried."

"I can't believe that they weren't interested. When you think of the stuff that they do print . . ."

"Something . . . happened to every reporter I approached. I gave up after the third one."

"What kind of something?" Hilary asked.

Bob sighed. He lifted a hand and began to count on his fingers. "The first one's wife died in a freak traffic accident; the second had a miscarriage; the third lost his job in disgrace."

"That kind of thing just happens," Zoe said. "It's awful, but there's no way you or Wolfe could be to blame for any of it."

"I'd like to believe you, but I know better."

"Wait a sec," Hilary said. "This happened after you talked to these reporters? What's to stop something from happening to us?"

Zoe glanced at her. "I thought you didn't believe any of this."

"I don't. Do you?"

Zoe just didn't know anymore. The whole thing sounded preposterous, but she couldn't shake the nagging possibility that he wasn't lying to her. It was the complete sincerity with which he—Bob, Wolfe, whatever his name was—spoke that had her mistrusting her logic. Somehow she just couldn't see that sincerity as being faked. She felt that she was too good a judge of character to be taken in so easily by an act, no matter how good; ludicrous as the situation was, she realized that she'd actually feel better if it was true. At least her judgment wouldn't be in question then.

Of course, if Bob was telling the truth, then that changed all the rules. The world could never be the same again.

"I don't know," she said finally.

"Yeah, well better safe than sorry," Hilary said. She turned her attention back to Bob. "Well?" she asked. "*Are* we in danger?"

"Not at the moment. Zoe negates Wolfe's abilities."

"Whoa," Hilary said. "I can already see where this is going. You want her to be your shadow so that the big bad Wolfe won't hurt anybody else—right? Jesus, I've heard some lame pick-up lines in my time, but this beats them all, hands down."

"That's not it at all," Bob said. "He can't hurt Zoe, that's true. And he's already tried. He's exerted tremendous amounts of time and energy since last night in making her life miserable and hasn't seen any success."

"I don't know about that," Zoe said. "I haven't exactly been having a fun time since I ran into him last night."

"What I'm worried about," Bob said, going on as though Zoe hadn't spoken, "is that he's now going to turn his attention on her friends."

"Okay," Zoe said. "This has gone far enough. I'm going to the cops."

"I'm not threatening you," Bob said as she started to stand up. "I'm just warning you."

"It sounds like a threat to me, pal."

"I've spent years looking for some way to stop Wolfe," Bob said. The desperation in his eyes held Zoe captive. "You're the first ray of hope I've found in all that time. He's scared of you."

"Why? I'm nobody special."

"I could give you a lecture on how we're all unique individuals, each important in his or her own way," Bob said, "but that's not what we're talking about here. What you are goes beyond that. In some ways, you and Wolfe are much the same, except where he brings pain into people's lives, you heal."

Zoe shook her head. "Oh, please."

"I don't think the world is the way we like to think it is," Bob went on. "I don't think it's one solid world, but many, thousands upon thousands of them—as many as there are people—because each person perceives the world in his or her own way; each lives in his or her own world. Sometimes they connect, for a moment, or more rarely, for a lifetime, but mostly we are alone, each living in our own world, suffering our small deaths."

"This is stupid," Zoe said.

But she was still held captive by his sincerity. She heard a kind of mystical backdrop to what he was saying, a breathy sound that reminded her of an LP they had in the station's library of R. Carlos Nakai playing a traditional Native American flute.

"I believe you're an easy person to meet," Bob said. "The kind of person that people are drawn to talk to—especially by those who are confused, or hurt, or lost. You give them hope. You help them heal."

Zoe continued to shake her head. "I'm not any of that."

"I'm not so sure he's wrong," Hilary said.

Zoe gave her friend a sour look.

"Well, think about it," Hilary said. "The weird and the wacky are always drawn to you. And that show of yours. There's no way that Nightnoise should work—it's just too bizarre a mix. I can't see headbangers sitting through the opera you play, classical buffs putting up with rap, but they do. It's the most popular show in its time slot."

"Yeah, right. Like it's got so much competition at that hour of the night."

"That's just it," Hilary said. "It does have competition, but people still tune in to you."

"Not fifteen minutes ago, you were telling me that the reason I get all these weird people coming on to me is because I'm putting out confused vibes."

Hilary nodded. "I think I was wrong."

"Oh, for God's sake."

"You do help people," Hilary said. "I've seen some of your fan mail and then there's all of those people who are constantly calling in. You help them, Zoe. You really do."

This was just too much for Zoe.

"Why are you saying all of this?" she asked Hilary. "Can't you hear what it sounds like?"

"I know. It sounds ridiculous. But at the same time, I think it makes its own kind of sense. All those people are turning to you for help. I don't think they expect you to solve all of their problems; they just want that touch of hope that you give them."

"I think Wolfe's asking for your help, too," Bob said.

"Oh, really?" Zoe said. "And how am I supposed to do that? Find you and him a good shrink?"

"In the old days," Hilary said, "there were people who could drive out demons just by a laying on of the hands."

Zoe looked from Hilary to Bob and realized that they were both serious. A smartass remark was on the tip of her tongue, but this time she just let it die unspoken.

A surreal quality had taken hold of the afternoon, as though the Academy of St. Martin-in-the-Fields was playing Hendrix, or Captain Beefheart was doing a duet with Tiffany. The light in the Mall seemed incandescent. The air was hot on her skin, but she could feel a chill all the way down to the marrow of her bones.

I don't want this to be real, she realized.

But she knelt down in front of Bob and reached out her hands, laying a palm on either temple.

What now? she thought. Am I supposed to reel off some gibberish to make it sound like a genuine exorcism?

She felt so dumb, she—

The change caught her completely by surprise, stunning her thoughts and the ever-playing soundtrack that ran through her mind into silence. A tingle like static electricity built up in her fingers.

She was looking directly at Bob, but suddenly it seemed as though she was looking through him, directly into him, into the essence of him. It was flesh and blood that lay under her hands, but rainbowing swirls of light were all she could see. A small sound of wonder sighed from between her lips at the sight.

We're all made of light, she thought. Sounds and light, cells vibrating . . .

But when she looked more closely, she could see that under her hands the play of lights was threaded with discordances. As soon as she noticed them, the webwork of dark threads coalesced into a pebble-sized oval of shadow that fell through the swirl of lights, down, down, until it was gone. The rainbowing pattern of the lights was unblemished now, the lights faded, became flesh and bone and skin, and then she was just holding Bob's head in her hands once more.

The tingle left her fingers and she dropped her hands. Bob smiled at her.

"Thank you," he said.

That sense of sincerity remained, but it wasn't Bob's voice anymore. It was Wolfe's.

"Be careful," he added.

"What do you mean?" she asked.

"I was like you once."

"Like me how?"

"Just be careful," he said.

She tilted her head back as he rose to his feet, gaze tracking him as he walked away, across the marble floor and through the doors of the Mall. He didn't open the doors, he just stepped through the glass and steel out into the street and continued off across the pavement. A half-dozen yards from the entrance, he simply faded away like a video effect and was gone.

Zoe shook her head.

"No," she said softly. "I don't want to believe this."

"Believe what?" Hilary asked.

Zoe turned to look at her. "You didn't see what happened?"

"Happened where?"

"Bob."

"He's finally here?" Hilary looked around at the passersby. "I was so sure he was going to pull a no-show."

"No, he's not here," Zoe said. "He . . ."

Her voice trailed off as the realization hit home. She was on her own with this. What had happened? If she took it all at face value, she realized that meeting Wolfe *had* brought her a small death after all—the death of the world the way it had been to the way she now knew it to be. It was changed forever. *She* was changed forever. She carried a responsibility now of which she'd never been aware before.

Why didn't Hilary remember the encounter? Probably because it would have been the same small death for her as it had been for Zoe herself; her world would have been changed forever.

But I've negated that for her, Zoe thought. Just like I did for Wolfe, or Bob, or whoever he really was.

Her gaze dropped to the floor where he'd been sitting and saw a small black pebble lying on the marble. She hesitated for a moment, then reached over and picked it up. Her fingers tingled again and she watched in wonder as the pebble went from black, through grey, until it was a milky white.

"What've you got there?" Hilary asked.

Zoe shook her head. She closed her fingers around the small smooth stone, savoring its odd warmth.

"Nothing," she said. "Just a pebble."

She got up and sat beside Hilary again.

"Excuse me, miss?"

The security guard had returned and this time he wasn't ignoring Rupert.

"I'm sorry," he said, "but I'm afraid you'll have to take your dog outside. It's the mall management's rules."

"Yes," Zoe said. "Of course."

She gave him a quick smile which the guard returned with more warmth than Zoe thought was warranted. It was as though she'd propositioned him or something.

Jesus, she thought. Was she going to go through the rest of her life second-guessing every encounter she ever had? Does he know, does she? Life was tough enough without having to feel self-conscious every time she met somebody. Maybe this was what Wolfe had meant when he said that he had been just like her once. Maybe the pressure just got to be too much for him and it turned him from healing to hurting.

Just be careful.

It seemed possible. It seemed more than possible when she remembered the gratitude she'd seen in his eyes when he'd thanked her.

Beside her, Hilary looked at her watch. "We might as well go," she said. "This whole thing's a washout. It's almost twelve-thirty. If he was going to come, he'd've been here by now."

Zoe nodded her head.

"See the thing is," Hilary said as they started for the door, Rupert walking in between them, "a guy like that can't face an actual confrontation. If you ask me, you're never going to hear from him again."

"I think you're right," Zoe said.

But there might be others, changing, already changed. She might become one of them herself if she wasn't—

just be

Her fingers tightened around the white pebble she'd picked up. She stuck it in the front pocket of her jeans as a token to remind her of what had happened to Wolfe, of how it could just as easily happen to her if she wasn't

—careful.

The Moon Is Drowning
While I Sleep

If you keep your mind sufficiently open, people will throw a lot of rubbish into it.
—William A. Orton

1

Once upon a time there was what there was, and if nothing had happened there would be nothing to tell.

2

It was my father who told me that dreams want to be real. When you start to wake up, he said, they hang on and try to slip out into the waking world when you don't notice. Very strong dreams, he added, can almost do it; they can last for almost half a day, but not much longer.

I asked him if any ever made it. If any of the people our subconscious minds toss up and make real while we're sleeping had ever actually stolen out into this world from the dream world.

He knew of at least one that had, he said.

He had that kind of lost look in his eyes that made me think of my mother. He always looked like that when he talked about her, which wasn't often.

Who was it? I asked, hoping he'd dole out another little tidbit about my mother. Is it someone I know?

Even as I asked, I was wondering how he related my mother to a dream. He'd at least known her. I didn't have any memories, just imaginings. Dreams.

But he only shook his head. Not really, he told me. It happened a long time ago. But I often wondered, he added almost to himself, what did *she* dream of?

That was a long time ago and I don't know if he ever found out. If he did, he never told me. But lately I've been wondering about it. I think maybe they don't dream. I think that if they do, they get pulled back into the dream world.

And if we're not too careful, they can pull us back with them.

3

"I've been having the strangest dreams," Sophie Etoile said, more as an observation than a conversational opener.

She and Jilly Coppercorn had been enjoying a companionable silence while they sat on the stone river wall in the old part of Lower Crowsea's Market. The wall is by a small public courtyard, surrounded on three sides by old three-story brick and stone town houses, peaked with mansard roofs, the dormer windows thrusting out from the walls like hooded eyes with heavy brows. The buildings date back over a hundred years, leaning against each other like old friends too tired to talk, just taking comfort from each other's presence.

The cobblestoned streets that web out from the courtyard are narrow, too tight a fit for a car, even the small imported makes. They twist and turn, winding in and around the buildings more like back alleys than thoroughfares. If you have any sort of familiarity with the area you can maze your way by those lanes to find still smaller courtyards, hidden and private, and deeper still, secret gardens.

There are more cats in Old Market than anywhere else in Newford and the air smells different. Though it sits just a few blocks west of some of the city's principal thorough-fares, you can hardly hear the traffic, and you can't smell it at all. No exhaust, no refuse, no dead air. In Old Market it always seems to smell of fresh bread baking, cabbage soups, frying fish, roses and those tart, sharp-tasting apples that make the best strudels.

Sophie and Jilly were bookended by stairs going down to the Kickaha River on either side of them. Pale yellow light from the streetlamp behind them put a glow on their hair, haloing each with her own nimbus of light—Jilly's darker, all loose tangled curls, Sophie's a soft auburn, hanging in ringlets. They each had a similar slim build, though Sophie was somewhat bustier.

In the half-dark of the streetlamp's murky light, their small figures could almost be taken for each other, but when the light touched their features as they turned to talk to each other, Jilly could be seen to have the quick, clever features of a Rackham pixie, while Sophie's were softer, as though rendered by Rossetti or Burne-Jones.

Though similarly dressed with paint-stained smocks over loose T-shirts and baggy cotton pants, Sophie still managed to look tidy, while Jilly could never seem to help a slight tendency towards scruffiness. She was the only one of the two with paint in her hair.

"What sort of dreams?" she asked.

It was almost four o'clock in the morning. The narrow streets of Old Market lay empty and still about them, except for the odd prowling cat, and cats can be like the hint of a whisper when they want, ghosting and silent, invisible presences. The two women had been working at Sophie's studio on a joint painting, a collaboration that was going to combine Jilly's precise delicate work with Sophie's current penchant for bright flaring colors and loosely rendered figures.

Neither was sure the experiment would work, but they'd been enjoying themselves immensely with it, so it really didn't matter.

"Well, they're sort of serial," Sophie said. "You know, where you keep dreaming about the same place, the same people, the same events, except each night you're a little further along in the story."

Jilly gave her an envious look. "I've always wanted to have that kind of dream. Christy's had them. I think he told me that it's called lucid dreaming."

"They're anything but lucid," Sophie said. "If you ask me, they're downright strange."

"No, no. It just means that you know you're dreaming, *when* you're dreaming, and have some kind of control over what happens in the dream."

Sophie laughed. "I wish."

4

I'm wearing a long pleated skirt and one of those white cotton peasant blouses that's cut way too low in the bodice. I don't know why. I hate that kind of bodice. I keep feeling like I'm going to fall out whenever I bend over. Definitely designed by a man. Wendy likes to wear that kind of thing from time to time, but it's not for me.

Nor is going barefoot. Especially not here. I'm standing on a path, but it's muddy underfoot, all squishy between my toes. It's sort of nice in some ways, but I keep getting the feeling that something's going to sidle up to me, under the mud, and brush against my foot, so I don't want to move, but I don't want to just stand here either.

Everywhere I look it's all marsh. Low flat fens, with just the odd crack willow or alder trailing raggedy vines the way you see Spanish moss do in pictures of the Everglades, but this definitely isn't Florida. It feels more Englishy, if that makes sense.

I know if I step off the path I'll be in muck up to my knees.

I can see a dim kind of light off in the distance, way off the path. I'm attracted to it, the way any light in the darkness seems to call out, welcoming you, but I don't want to brave the deeper mud or the pools of still water that glimmer in the pale starlight.

It's all mud and reeds, cattails, bulrushes and swamp grass and I just want to be back home in bed, but I can't wake up. There's a funny smell in the air, a mix of things rotting and stagnant water. I feel like there's something horrible in the shadows under those strange overhung trees—especially the willows, the tall sharp leaves of sedge and water plantain growing thick around their trunks. It's like there are eyes watching me from all sides, dark misshapen heads floating frog-like in the water, only the eyes showing, staring. Quicks and bogles and dark things.

I hear something move in the tangle of bulrushes and bur reeds just a few feet away. My heart's in my throat, but I move a little closer to see that it's only a bird caught in some kind of a net.

Hush, I tell it and move closer.

The bird gets frantic when I put my hand on the netting. It starts to peck at my fingers, but I keep talking softly to it until it finally settles down. The net's a mess of knots and tangles and I can't work too quickly because I don't want to hurt the bird.

You should leave him be, a voice says, and I turn to find an old woman standing on the path beside me. I don't know where she came from. Every time I lift one of my feet it makes this creepy sucking sound, but I never even heard her approach.

She looks like the wizened old crone in that painting Jilly did for Geordie when he got onto this kick of learning fiddle tunes with the word "hag" in the title: "The Hag in the Kiln," "Old Hag You Have Killed Me," "The Hag With the Money" and god knows how many more.

Just like in the painting, she's wizened and small and bent over and . . . dry. Like kindling, like the pages of an old book. Like she's almost all used up. Hair thin, body thinner. But then you look into her eyes and they're so alive it makes you feel a little dizzy.

Helping such as he will only bring you grief, she says.

I tell her that I can't just leave it.

She looks at me for a long moment, then shrugs. So be it, she says.

I wait a moment, but she doesn't seem to have anything else to say, so I go back to freeing the bird. But now, where a moment ago the netting was a hopeless tangle, it just seems to unknot itself as soon as I lay my hand on it. I'm careful when I put my fingers around the bird and pull it free. I get it out of the tangle and then toss it up in the air. It circles above me in the air, once, twice, three times, cawing. Then it flies away.

It's not safe here, the old lady says then.

I'd forgotten all about her. I get back onto the path, my legs smeared with smelly dark mud.

What do you mean? I ask her.

When the Moon still walked the sky, she says, why it was safe then. The dark things didn't like her light and fair fell over themselves to get away when she shone. But they're bold now, tricked and trapped her, they have, and no one's safe. Not you, not me. Best we were away.

Trapped her? I repeat like an echo. The moon?

She nods.

Where?

She points to the light I saw earlier, far out in the fens.

They've drowned her under the Black Snag, she says. I will show you.

She takes my hand before I realize what she's doing and pulls me through the rushes and reeds, the mud squishing awfully under my bare feet, but it doesn't seem to bother her at all. She stops when we're at the edge of some open water.

Watch now, she says.

She takes something from the pocket of her apron and tosses it into the water. It's like a small stone, or a pebble or something, and it enters the water without a sound, without making a ripple. Then the water starts to glow and a picture forms in the dim flickering light.

It's like we have a bird's eye view of the fens for a moment, then the focus comes in sharp on the edge of a big still pool, sentried by a huge dead willow. I don't know how I know it, because the light's still poor, but the mud's black around its shore. It almost swallows the pale wan glow coming up from out of the water.

Drowning, the old woman says. The moon is drowning.

I look down at the image that's formed on the surface and I see a woman floating there. Her hair's all spread out from her, drifting in the water like lily roots. There's a great big stone on top of her torso so she's only really visible from the breasts up. Her shoulders are slightly sloped, neck slender, with a swan's curve, but not so long. Her face is in repose, as though she's sleeping, but she's underwater, so I know she's dead.

She looks like me.

I turn to the old woman, but before I can say anything, there's movement all around us. Shadows pull away from trees, rise from the stagnant pools, change from vague blotches of darkness, into moving shapes, limbed and headed, pale eyes glowing with menace. The old woman pulls me back onto the path.

Wake quick! she cries.

She pinches my arm—hard, sharp. It really hurts. And then I'm sitting up in my bed.

5

"And did you have a bruise on your arm from where she pinched you?" Jilly asked.

Sophie shook her head and smiled. Trust Jilly. Who else was always looking for the magic in a situation?

"Of course not," she said. "It was just a dream."

"But . . ."

"Wait," Sophie said. "There's more."

Something suddenly hopped onto the wall between them and they both started, until they realized it was only a cat.

"Silly puss," Sophie said as it walked towards her and began to butt its head against her arm. She gave it a pat.

6

The next night I'm standing by my window, looking out at the street, when I hear movement behind me. I turn and it isn't my apartment any more. It's like the inside of an old barn, heaped up with straw in a big tidy pile against one wall. There's a lit lantern swinging from a low rafter beam, a dusty but pleasant smell in the air, a cow or maybe a horse making some kind of nickering sound in a stall at the far end.

And there's a guy standing there in the lantern light, a half dozen feet away from me, not doing anything, just looking at me. He's drop-down gorgeous. Not too thin, not too muscle-bound. A friendly open face with a wide smile and eyes to kill for—long moody lashes, and the irises are the color of violets. His hair's thick and dark, long in the back with a cowlick hanging down over his brow that I just want to reach out and brush back.

I'm sorry, he says. I didn't mean to startle you.

That's okay, I tell him.

And it is. I think maybe I'm already getting used to all the to-and-froing.

He smiles. My name's Jeck Crow, he says.

I don't know why, but all of a sudden I'm feeling a little weak in the knees. Ah, who am I kidding? I know why.

What are you doing here? he asks.

I tell him I was standing in my apartment, looking for the moon, but then I remembered that I'd just seen the last quarter a few nights ago and I wouldn't be able to see it tonight.

He nods. She's drowning, he says, and then I remember the old woman from last night.

I look out the window and see the fens are out there. It's dark and creepy and I can't see the distant glow of the woman drowned in the pool from here the way I could last night. I shiver and Jeck comes over all concerned. He's picked up a blanket that was hanging from one of the support beams and he lays it across my shoulders. He leaves his arm there, to keep it in place, and I don't mind. I just sort of lean into him, like we've always been together. It's weird. I'm feeling drowsy and safe and incredibly aroused, all at the same time.

He looks out the window with me, his hip against mine, the press of his arm on my shoulder a comfortable weight, his body radiating heat.

It used to be, he says, that she would walk every night until she grew so weak that her light was almost failing. Then she would leave the world to go to another, into Faerie, it's said, or at least to a place where the darkness doesn't hide quicks and bogles, and there she would rejuvenate herself for her return. We would have three nights of darkness, when evil owned the night, but then we'd see the glow of her lantern approaching and the haunts would flee her light and we could visit with one another again when the day's work was done.

He leans his head against mine, his voice going dreamy.

I remember my mam saying once, how the Moon lived another life in those three days. How time moves differently in Faerie so that what was a day for us, might be a month for her in that place.

He pauses, then adds, I wonder if they miss her in that other world.

I don't know what to say. But then I realize it's not the kind of conversation in which I have to say anything.

He turns to me, head lowering until we're looking straight into each other's eyes. I get lost in the violet and suddenly I'm in his arms and we're kissing. He guides me, step by sweet step, backward towards that heap of straw. We've got the blanket under us and this time I'm glad I'm wearing the long skirt and peasant blouse again, because they come off so easily.

His hands and his mouth are so gentle and they're all over me like moth wings brushing my skin. I don't know how to describe what he's doing to me. It isn't anything that other lovers haven't done to me before, but the way Jeck does it has me glowing, my skin all warm and tingling with this deep slow burn starting up deep between my legs and just firing up along every one of my nerve ends.

I can hear myself making moaning sounds and then he's inside me, his breathing heavy in my ear. All I can feel and smell is him. My hips are grinding against his and we're synched into this perfect rhythm and then I wake up in my own bed and I'm all tangled up in the sheets with my hand between my legs, finger tip right on the spot, moving back and forth and back and forth. . . .

7

Sophie fell silent.

"Steamy," Jilly said after a moment.

Sophie gave a little bit of an embarrassed laugh. "You're telling me. I get a little squirmy just thinking about it. And that night—I was still so fired up when I woke that I couldn't think straight. I just went ahead and finished and then lay there afterwards, completely spent. I couldn't even move."

"You know a guy named Jack Crow, don't you?" Jilly asked.

"Yeah, he's the one who's got that tattoo parlor down on Palm Street. I went out with him a couple of times, but—" Sophie shrugged "—you know. Things just didn't work out."

"That's right. You told me that all he ever wanted to do was to give you tattoos."

Sophie shook her head, remembering. "In private places so only he and I would know they were there. Boy."

The cat had fallen asleep, body sprawled out on her lap, head pressed tight up against her stomach. A deep resonant purr rose up from him. Sophie just hoped he didn't have fleas.

"But the guy in my dream was nothing like Jack," she said. "And besides, his name was Jeck."

"What kind of a name *is* that?"

"A dream name."

"So did you see him again—the next night?"

Sophie shook her head. "Though not from lack of interest on my part."

8

The third night I find myself in this one-room cottage out of a fairy tale. You know, there's dried herbs hanging everywhere, a big hearth considering the size of the place, with black iron pots and a kettle sitting on the hearth stones, thick hand-woven rugs underfoot, a small tidy little bed in one corner, a cloak hanging by the door, a rough set of a table and two chairs by a shuttered window.

The old lady is sitting on one of the chairs.

There you are, she says. I looked for you to come last night, but I couldn't find you.

I'm getting so used to this dreaming business by now that I'm not at all weirded out, just kind of accepting it all, but I am a little disappointed to find myself here, instead of in the barn.

I was with Jeck, I say and then she frowns, but she doesn't say anything.

Do you know him? I ask.

Too well.

Is there something wrong with him?

I'm feeling a little flushed, just talking about him. So far as I'm concerned, there's nothing wrong with him at all.

He's not trustworthy, the old lady finally says.

I shake my head. He seems to be just as upset about the drowned lady as you are. He told me all about her—how she used to go into Faerie and that kind of thing.

She never went into Faerie.

Well then, where did she go?

The old lady shakes her head. Crows talk too much, she says and I can't tell if she means the birds, or a whole bunch of Jecks. Thinking about the latter gives me goosebumps. I can barely stay clear-headed around Jeck; a whole crowd of him would probably overload all my circuits and leave me lying on the floor like a little pool of jelly.

I don't tell the old lady any of this. Jeck inspired confidences, as much as sensuality; she does neither.

Will you help us? she says instead.

I sit down at the table with her and ask, Help with what?

The Moon, she says.

I shake my head. I don't understand. You mean the drowned lady in the pool?

Drowned, the old lady says, but not dead. Not yet.

I start to argue the point, but then realize where I am. It's a dream and anything can happen, right?

It needs you to break the bogles' spell, the old lady goes on.

Me? But—

Tomorrow night, go to sleep with a stone in your mouth and a hazel twig in your hands. Now mayhap, you'll find yourself back here, mayhap with your crow, but guard you don't say a word, not one word. Go out into the fen until you find a coffin, and on that coffin a candle, and then look sideways and you'll see that you're in the place I showed you yesternight.

She falls silent.

And then what am I supposed to do? I ask.

What needs to be done.

But—

I'm tired, she says.

She waves her hand at me and I'm back in my own bed again.

9

"And so?" Jilly asked. "Did you do it?"

"Would you have?"

"In a moment," Jilly said. She sidled closer along the wall until she was right beside Sophie and peered into her friend's face. "Oh don't tell me you didn't do it. Don't tell me that's the whole story."

"The whole thing just seemed silly," Sophie said.

"Oh, please!"

"Well, it did. It was all too oblique and riddlish. I know it was just a dream, so that it didn't have to make sense, but there was so much of a coherence to a lot of it that when it did get incomprehensible, it just didn't seem . . . oh, I don't know. Didn't seem fair, I suppose."

"But you *did* do it?"

Sophie finally relented.

"Yes," she said.

10

I go to sleep with a small smooth stone in my mouth and have the hardest time getting to sleep because I'm sure I'm going to swallow it during the night and choke. And I have the hazel twig as well, though I don't know what help either of them is going to be.

Hazel twig to ward you from quicks and bogles, I hear Jeck say. And the stone to remind you of your own world, of the difference between waking and dream, else you might find yourself sharing the Moon's fate.

We're standing on a sort of grassy knoll, an island of semi-solid ground, but the footing's still spongy. I start to say hello, but he puts his finger to his lips.

She's old, is Granny Weather, he says, and cranky, too, but there's more magic in one of her toenails than most of us will find in a lifetime.

I never really thought about his voice before. It's like velvet, soft and smooth, but not effeminate. It's too resonant for that.

He puts his hands on my shoulders and I feel like melting. I close my eyes, lift my face to his, but he turns me around until I'm leaning against his back. He cups his hands around my breasts and kisses me on the nape of my neck. I lean back against him, but he lifts his mouth to my ear.

You must go, he says softly, his breath tickling the inside of my ear. Into the fens.

I pull free from his embrace and face him. I start to say, Why me? Why do I have to go alone? But before I can get a word out he has his hand across my mouth.

Trust Granny Weather, he says. And trust me. This is something only you can do. Whether you do it or not, is your choice. But if you mean to try tonight, you mustn't speak. You must go out into the fens and find her. They will tempt you and torment you, but you must ignore them, else they'll have you drowning too, under the Black Snag.

I look at him and I know he can see the need I have for him because in his eyes I can see the same need for me reflected in their violet depths.

I will wait for you, he says. If I can.

I don't like the sound of that. I don't like the sound of any of it, but I tell myself again, it's just a dream, so I finally nod. I start to turn away, but he catches hold of me for a last moment and kisses me. There's a hot rush of tongues touching, arms tight around each other, before he finally steps back.

I love the strength of you, he says.

I don't want to go, I want to change the rules of the dream, but I get this feeling that if I do, if I change one thing, everything'll change, and maybe he won't even exist in whatever comes along to replace it. So I lift my hand and run it along the side of his face, I take a long last drink of those deep violet eyes that just want to swallow me, then I get brave and turn away again.

And this time I go into the fens.

I'm nervous, but I guess that goes without saying. I look back, but I can't see Jeck anymore. I can just feel I'm being watched, and it's not by him. I clutch my little hazel twig tighter, roll the stone around from one side of my mouth to the other, and keep going.

It's not easy. I have to test each step to make sure I'm not just going to sink away forever into the muck. I start thinking of what you hear about dreams, how if you die in a dream, you die for real, that's why you always wake up just in time. Except for those people who die in their sleep, I guess.

I don't know how long I'm slogging through the muck. My arms and legs have dozens of little nicks and cuts—you never think of how sharp the edge of a reed can be until your skin slides across one. It's like a paper cut, sharp and quick, and it stings like hell. I don't suppose all the muck's doing the cuts much good either. The only thing I can be happy about is that there aren't any bugs.

Actually, there doesn't seem to be the sense of anything living at all in the fens, just me, on my own. But I know I'm not alone. It's like a word sitting on the tip of your tongue. I can't see or hear or sense anything, but I'm being watched.

I think of Jeck and Granny Weather, of what they say the darkness hides. Quicks and bogles and haunts.

After awhile I almost forget what I'm doing out here. I'm just stumbling along with a feeling of dread hanging over me that just won't go away. Bogbean and water mint leaves feel like cold wet fingers sliding along my legs. I hear the occasional flutter of wings, and sometimes a deep kind of sighing moan, but I never see anything.

I'm just about played out when suddenly I come up upon this tall rock under the biggest crack willow I've seen so far. The tree's dead, drooping leafless branches into the still water around the stone. The stone rises out of the water at a slant, the mud's all really black underfoot, the marsh is, if anything, even quieter here, expectant, almost, and I get the feeling like something—some*things* are closing in all around me.

I start to walk across the dark mud to the other side of the rock until I hit a certain vantage point. I stop when I can see that it's shaped like a big strange coffin and I remember what Granny Weather told me. I look for the candle and I see a tiny light flickering at the very top of the black stone, right where it's pushed up and snagged among the dangling branches of the dead willow. It's no brighter than a firefly's glow, but it burns steady.

I do what Granny Weather told me and look around myself using my peripheral vision. I don't see anything at first, but as I slowly turn towards the water, I catch just a hint of a glow in the water. I stop and then I wonder what to do. Is it still going to be there if I turn to face it?

Eventually, I move sideways towards it, always keeping it in the corner of my eye. The closer I get, the brighter it starts to glow, until I'm standing hip deep in the cold water, the mud sucking at my feet, and it's all around me, this dim eerie glowing. I look down into the water and I see my own face reflected back at me, but then I realize that it's not me I'm seeing, it's the drowned woman, the moon, trapped under the stone.

I stick my hazel twig down the bodice of my blouse and reach into the water. I have to bend down, the dark water licking at my shoulders and chin and smelling something awful, but I finally touch the woman's shoulder. Her skin's warm against my fingers and for some reason that makes me feel braver. I get a grip with one hand on her shoulder, then the other, and give a pull.

Nothing budges.

I try some more, moving a little deeper into the water. Finally I plunge my head under and get a really good hold, but she simply won't move. The rock's got her pressed down tight, and the willow's got the rock snagged, and dream or no dream, I'm not some kind of superwoman. I'm only so strong and I have to breathe.

I come up spluttering and choking on the foul water.

And then I hear the laughter.

I look up and there's these things all around the edge of the pool. Quicks and bogles and small monsters. All eyes and teeth and spindly black limbs and crooked hands with too many joints to the fingers. The tree is full of crows and their cawing adds to the mocking hubbub of sound.

First got one, now got two, a pair of voices chant. Boil her up in a tiddy stew.

I'm starting to shiver—not just because I'm scared, which I am, but because the water's so damn cold. The haunts just keep on laughing and making up these creepy little rhymes that mostly have to do with little stews and barbecues. And then suddenly, they all fall silent and these three figures come swinging down from the willow's boughs.

I don't know where they came from, they're just there all of a sudden. These aren't haunts, nor quicks nor bogles. They're men and they look all too familiar.

Ask for anything, one of them says, and it will be yours.

It's Jeck, I realize. Jeck talking to me, except the voice doesn't sound right. But it looks just like him. All three look like him.

I remember Granny Weather telling me that Jeck was untrustworthy, but then Jeck told me to trust her. And to trust him. Looking at these three Jecks, I don't know what to think anymore. My head starts to hurt and I just wish I could wake up.

You need only tell us what it is you want, one of the Jecks says, and we will give it to you. There should be no enmity between us. The woman is drowned. She is dead. You have come too late. There is nothing you can do for her now. But you can do something for yourself. Let us gift you with your heart's desire.

My heart's desire, I think.

I tell myself, again, it's just a dream, but I can't help the way I start thinking about what I'd ask for if I could really have anything I wanted, anything at all.

I look down into the water at the drowned woman and I think about my dad. He never liked to talk about my mother. It's like she was just a dream, he said once.

And maybe she was, I find myself thinking as my gaze goes down into the water and I study the features of the drowned woman who looks so much like me. Maybe she was the Moon in this world and she came to ours to rejuvenate, but when the time came for her to go back, she didn't want to leave because she loved me and dad too much. Except she didn't have a choice.

So when she returned, she was weaker, instead of stronger like she was supposed to be, because she was so sad. And that's how the quicks and the bogles trapped her.

I laugh then. What I'm making up, as I stand here waist-deep in smelly dream water, is the classic abandoned child's scenario. They always figure that there was just a mix-up, that one day their real parents are going to show up and take them away to some place where everything's magical and loving and perfect.

I used to feel real guilty about my mother leaving us—that's something else that happens when you're just a kid in that kind of a situation. You just automatically feel guilty when something bad happens, like it's got to be your fault. But I got older. I learned to deal with it. I learned that I was a good person, that it hadn't been my fault, that my dad was a good person, too, and it wasn't his fault either.

I'd still like to know why my mother left us, but I came to understand that whatever the reasons were for her going, they had to do with her, not with us. Just like I know this is only a dream and the drowned woman might look like me, but that's just something I'm projecting onto her. I *want* her to be my mother. I want her having abandoned me and dad not to have been her fault either. I want to come to her rescue and bring us all back together again.

Except it isn't going to happen. Pretend and real just don't mix.

But it's tempting all the same. It's tempting to let it all play out. I know the haunts just want me to talk so that they can trap me as well, that they wouldn't follow through on any promise they made, but this is *my* dream. I can *make* them keep to their promise. All I have to do is say what I want.

And then I understand that it's all real after all. Not real in the sense that I can be physically harmed in this place, but real in that if I make a selfish choice, even if it's just in a dream, I'll still have to live with the fact of it when I wake up. It doesn't matter that I'm dreaming, I'll *still* have done it.

What the bogles are offering is my heart's desire, if I just leave the Moon to drown. But if I do that, I'm responsible for her death. She might not be real, but it doesn't change anything at all. It'll still mean that I'm willing to let someone die, just so I can have my own way.

I suck on the stone and move it back and forth from one cheek to the other. I reach down into my wet bodice and pluck out the hazel twig from where it got pushed down between my breasts. I lift a hand to my hair and brush it back from my face and then I look at those sham copies of my Jeck Crow and I smile at them.

My dream, I think. What I say goes.

I don't know if it's going to work, but I'm fed up with having everyone else decide what happens in my dream. I turn to the stone and I put my hands upon it, the hazel twig sticking out between the fingers of my right hand, and I give the stone a shove. There's this great big outcry among the quicks and bogles and haunts as the stone starts to topple over. I look down at the drowned woman and I see her eyes open, I see her smile, but then there's too much light and I'm blinded.

When my vision finally clears, I'm alone by the pool. There's a big fat full moon hanging in the sky, making the fens almost as bright as day. They've all fled, the monsters, the quicks and bogles and things. The dead willow's still full of crows, but as soon as I look up, they lift from the tree in an explosion of dark wings, a circling murder, cawing and crying, until they finally go away. The stone's lying on its side, half in the water, half out.

And I'm still dreaming.

I'm standing here, up to my waist in the smelly water, with a hazel twig in my hand and a stone in my mouth, and I stare up at that big full moon until it seems I can feel her light just singing through my veins. For a moment it's like being back in the barn with Jeck, I'm just on fire, but it's a different kind of fire, it burns away the darknesses that have gotten lodged in me over the years, just like they get lodged in everybody, and just for that moment, I'm solid light, innocent and newborn, a burning Midsummer fire in the shape of a woman.

And then I wake up, back home again.

I lie there in my bed and look out the window, but it's still the dark of the moon in our world. The streets are quiet outside, there's a hush over the whole city, and I'm lying here with a hazel twig in my hand, a stone in my mouth, pushed up into one cheek, and a warm burning glow deep inside.

I sit up and spit the stone out into my hand. I walk over to the window. I'm not in some magical dream now; I'm in the real world. I know the lighted moon glows with light borrowed from the sun. That she's still out there in the dark of the moon, we just can't see her tonight because the earth is between her and the sun.

Or maybe she's gone into some other world, to replenish her lantern before she begins her nightly trek across the sky once more.

I feel like I've learned something, but I'm not sure what. I'm not sure what any of it means.

11

"How can you say that?" Jilly said. "God, Sophie, it's so obvious. She really *was* your mother and you really *did* save her. As for Jeck, he was the bird you rescued in your first dream. Jeck *Crow*—don't you get it? One of the bad guys, only you won him over with an act of kindness. It all makes perfect sense."

Sophie slowly shook her head. "I suppose I'd like to believe that, too," she said, "but what we want and what really is aren't always the same thing."

"But what about Jeck? He'll be waiting for you. And Granny Weather? They both knew you were the Moon's daughter all along. It all means something."

Sophie sighed. She stroked the sleeping cat on her lap, imagining for a moment that it was the soft dark curls of a crow that could be a man, in a land that only existed in her dreams.

"I guess," she said, "it means I need a new boyfriend."

12

Jilly's a real sweetheart, and I love her dearly, but she's naive in some ways. Or maybe it's just that she wants to play the ingenue. She's always so ready to believe anything that anyone tells her, so long as it's magical.

Well, I believe in magic, too, but it's the magic that can turn a caterpillar into a butterfly, the natural wonder and beauty of the world that's all around me. I can't believe in some dreamland being real. I can't believe what Jilly now insists is true: that I've got faerie blood, because I'm the daughter of the Moon.

Though I have to admit that I'd like to.

I never do get to sleep that night. I prowl around the apartment, drinking coffee to keep me awake. I'm afraid to go to sleep, afraid I'll dream and that it'll all be real.

Or maybe that it won't.

When it starts to get light, I take a long cold shower, because I've been thinking about Jeck again. I guess if my making the wrong decision in a dream would've had ramifications in the waking world, then there's no reason that a rampaging libido shouldn't carry over as well.

I get dressed in some old clothes I haven't worn in years, just to try to recapture a more innocent time. White blouse, faded jeans, and hightops with this smoking jacket overtop that used to belong to my dad. It's made of burgundy velvet with black satin lapels. A black hat, with a flat top and a bit of a curl to its brim, completes the picture.

I look in the mirror and I feel like I'm auditioning to be a stage magician's assistant, but I don't much care.

As soon as the hour gets civilized, I head over to Christy Riddell's house. I'm knocking on his door at nine o'clock, but when he comes to let me in, he's all sleepy-eyed and disheveled and I realize that I should've given him another couple of hours. Too late for that now.

I just come right out with it. I tell him that Jilly said he knew all about lucid dreaming and what I want to know is, is any of it real—the place you dream of, the people you meet there?

He stands there in the doorway, blinking like an owl, but I guess he's used to stranger things, because after a moment he leans against the door jamb and asks me what I know about consensual reality.

It's where everything that we see around us only exists because we all agree it does, I say.

Well, maybe it's the same in a dream, he replies. If everyone in the dream agrees that what's around them is real, then why shouldn't it be?

I want to ask him about what my dad had to say about dreams trying to escape into the waking world, but I decide I've already pushed my luck.

Thanks, I say.

He gives me a funny look. That's it? he asks.

I'll explain it some other time, I tell him.

Please do, he says without a whole lot of enthusiasm, then goes back inside.

When I get home, I go and lie down on the old sofa that's out on my balcony. I close my eyes. I'm still not so sure about any of this, but I figure it can't hurt to see if Jeck and I can't find ourselves one of those happily-ever-afters with which fairy tales usually end.

Who knows? Maybe I really am the daughter of the Moon. If not here, then someplace.

In the House
of My Enemy

*We have not inherited the earth from our fathers, we are borrowing it
from our children.*
—Native American saying

1

The past scampers like an alleycat through the present, leaving the pawprints of memories scattered helter-skelter—here ink is smeared on a page, there lies an old photograph with a chewed corner, elsewhere still, a nest has been made of old newspapers, the headlines running one into the other to make strange declarations. There is no order to what we recall, the wheel of time follows no straight line as it turns in our heads. In the dark attics of our minds, all times mingle, sometimes literally.

I get so confused. I've been so many people; some I didn't like at all. I wonder that anyone could. Victim, hooker, junkie, liar, thief. But without them, I wouldn't be who I am today. I'm no one special, but I like who I am, lost childhood and all.

Did I have to be all those people to become the person I am today? Are they still living inside me, hiding in some dark corner of my mind, waiting for me to slip and stumble and fall and give them life again?

I tell myself not to remember, but that's wrong, too. Not remembering makes them stronger.

2

The morning sun came in through the window of Jilly Coppercorn's loft, playing across the features of her guest. The girl was still asleep on the Murphy bed, sheets all tangled around her skinny limbs, pulled tight and smooth over the rounded swell of her abdomen. Sleep had gentled her features. Her hair clouded the pillow around her head. The soft morning sunlight gave her a Madonna quality, a nimbus of Botticelli purity that the harsher light of the later day would steal away once she woke.

She was fifteen years old. And eight months pregnant.

Jilly sat in the windowseat, feet propped up on the sill, sketchpad on her lap. She caught the scene in charcoal, smudging the lines with the pad of her middle finger to soften them. On the fire escape outside, a stray cat climbed up the last few metal steps until it was level with where she was sitting and gave a plaintive meow.

Jilly had been expecting the black and white tabby. She reached under her knees and picked up a small plastic margarine container filled with dried kibbles, which she set down on the fire escape in front of the cat. As the tabby contentedly crunched its breakfast, Jilly returned to her portrait.

"My name's Annie," her guest had told her last night when she stopped Jilly on Yoors Street just a few blocks south of the loft. "Could you spare some change? I really need to get some decent food. It's not so much for me. . . ."

She put her hand on the swell of her stomach as she spoke. Jilly had looked at her, taking in the stringy hair, the ragged clothes, the unhealthy color of her complexion, the too-thin body that seemed barely capable of sustaining the girl herself, little say nourishing the child she carried.

"Are you all on your own?" Jilly asked.

The girl nodded.

Jilly put her arm around the girl's shoulder and steered her back to the loft. She let her take a shower while she cooked a meal, gave her a clean smock to wear, and tried not to be patronizing while she did it all.

The girl had lost enough dignity as it was and Jilly knew that dignity was almost as hard to recover as innocence. She knew all too well.

3

Stolen Childhood, by Sophie Etoile. Copperplate engraving. Five Coyotes Singing Studio, Newford, 1988.

> *A child in a ragged dress stands in front of a ramshackle farmhouse. In one hand she holds a doll—a stick with a ball stuck in one end and a skirt on the other. She wears a lost expression, holding the doll as though she doesn't quite know what to do with it.*
>
> *A shadowed figure stands behind the screen door, watching her.*

* * *

I guess I was around three years old when my oldest brother started molesting me. That'd make him eleven. He used to touch me down between my legs while my parents were out drinking or sobering up down in the kitchen. I tried to fight him off, but I didn't really know that what he was doing was wrong—even when he started to put his cock inside me.

I was eight when my mother walked in on one of his rapes and you know what she did? She walked right out again until my brother was finished and we both had our clothes on again. She waited until he'd left the room, then she came back in and started screaming at me.

"You little slut! Why are you doing this to your own brother?"

Like it was my fault. Like I *wanted* him to rape me. Like the three-year-old I was when he started molesting me had any idea about what he was doing.

I think my other brothers knew what was going on all along, but they never said anything about it—they didn't want to break that macho code-of-honor bullshit. When my dad found out about it, he beat the crap out of my brother, but in some ways it just got worse after that.

My brother didn't molest me anymore, but he'd glare at me all the time, like he was going to pay me back for the beating he got soon as he got a chance. My mother and my other brothers, every time I'd come into a room, they'd all just stop talking and look at me like I was some kind of bug.

I think at first my dad wanted to do something to help me, but in the end he really wasn't any better than my mother. I could see it in his eyes: he blamed me for it, too. He kept me at a distance, never came close to me anymore, never let me feel like I was normal.

He's the one who had me see a psychiatrist. I'd have to go and sit in his office all alone, just a little kid in this big leather chair. The psychiatrist would lean across his desk, all smiles and smarmy understanding, and try to get me to talk, but I never told him a thing. I didn't trust him. I'd already learned that I couldn't trust men. Couldn't trust women either, thanks to my mother. Her idea of working things out was to send me to confession, like the same God who let my brother rape me was now going to make everything okay so long as I owned up to seducing him in the first place.

What kind of a way is that for a kid to grow up?

4

"Forgive me, Father, for I have sinned. I let my brother . . ."

5

Jilly laid her sketchpad aside when her guest began to stir. She swung her legs down so that they dangled from the windowsill, heels banging lightly against the wall, toes almost touching the ground. She pushed an unruly lock of hair from her brow, leaving behind a charcoal smudge on her temple.

Small and slender, with pixie features and a mass of curly dark hair, she looked almost as young as the girl on her bed. Jeans and sneakers, a dark T-shirt and an oversized peach-colored smock only added to her air of slightness and youth. But she was halfway through her thirties, her own teenage years long gone; she could have been Annie's mother.

"What were you doing?" Annie asked as she sat up, tugging the sheets up around herself.

"Sketching you while you slept. I hope you don't mind."

"Can I see?"

Jilly passed the sketchpad over and watched Annie study it. On the fire escape behind her, two more cats had joined the black and white tabby at the margarine container. One was an old alleycat, its left ear ragged and torn, ribs showing like so many hills and valleys against the matted landscape of its fur. The other belonged to an upstairs neighbor; it was making its usual morning rounds.

"You made me look a lot better than I really am," Annie said finally.

Jilly shook her head. "I only drew what was there."

"Yeah, right."

Jilly didn't bother to contradict her. The self-worth speech would keep.

"So is this how you make your living?" Annie asked.

"Pretty well. I do a little waitressing on the side."

"Beats being a hooker, I guess."

She gave Jilly a challenging look as she spoke, obviously anticipating a reaction.

Jilly only shrugged. "Tell me about it," she said.

Annie didn't say anything for a long moment. She looked down at the rough portrait with an unreadable expression, then finally met Jilly's gaze again.

"I've heard about you," she said. "On the street. Seems like everybody knows you. They say . . ."

Her voice trailed off.

Jilly smiled. "What do they say?"

"Oh, all kinds of stuff." She shrugged. "You know. That you used to live on the street, that you're kind of like a one-woman social service, but you don't lecture. And that you're—" she hesitated, looked away for a moment "—you know, a witch."

Jilly laughed. "A witch?"

That was a new one on her.

Annie waved a hand towards the wall across from the window where Jilly was sitting. Paintings leaned up against each other in untidy stacks. Above them, the wall held more, a careless gallery hung frame to frame to save space. They were part of Jilly's ongoing "Urban Faerie" series, realistic city scenes and characters to which were added the curious little denizens of lands which never were. Hobs and fairies, little elf men and goblins.

"They say you think all that stuff's real," Annie said.

"What do you think?"

When Annie gave her a "give me a break" look, Jilly just smiled again.

"How about some breakfast?" she asked to change the subject.

"Look," Annie said. "I really appreciate your taking me in and feeding me and everything last night, but I don't want to be freeloader."

"One more meal's not freeloading."

Jilly pretended to pay no attention as Annie's pride fought with her baby's need.

"Well, if you're sure it's okay," Annie said hesitantly.

"I wouldn't have offered if it wasn't," Jilly said.

She dropped down from the windowsill and went across the loft to the kitchen corner. She normally didn't eat a big breakfast, but twenty minutes later they were both sitting down to fried eggs and bacon, home fries and toast, coffee for Jilly and herb tea for Annie.

"Got any plans for today?" Jilly asked as they were finishing up.

"Why?" Annie replied, immediately suspicious.

"I thought you might want to come visit a friend of mine."

"A social worker, right?"

The tone in her voice was the same as though she was talking about a cockroach or maggot.

Jilly shook her head. "More like a storefront counselor. Her name's Angelina Marceau. She runs that drop-in center on Grasso Street. It's privately funded, no political connections."

"I've heard of her. The Grasso Street Angel."

"You don't have to come," Jilly said, "but I know she'd like to meet you."

"I'm sure."

Jilly shrugged. When she started to clean up, Annie stopped her.

"Please," she said. "Let me do it."

Jilly retrieved her sketchpad from the bed and returned to the windowseat while Annie washed up. She was just adding the finishing touches to the rough portrait she'd started earlier when Annie came to sit on the edge of the Murphy bed.

"That painting on the easel," Annie said. "Is that something new you're working on?"

Jilly nodded.

"It's not like your other stuff at all."

"I'm part of an artist's group that calls itself the Five Coyotes Singing Studio," Jilly explained. "The actual studio's owned by a friend of mine named Sophie Etoile, but we all work in it from time to time. There's five of us, all women, and we're doing a group show with a theme of child abuse at the Green Man Gallery next month."

"And that painting's going to be in it?" Annie asked.

"It's one of three I'm doing for the show."

"What's that one called?"

" 'I Don't Know How To Laugh Anymore.' "

Annie put her hands on top of her swollen stomach.

"Me, neither," she said.

6

I Don't Know How to Laugh Anymore, by Jilly Coppercorn. Oils and mixed media. Yoors Street Studio, Newford, 1991.

A life-sized female subject leans against an inner city wall in the classic pose of a prostitute waiting for a customer. She wears high heels, a micro-miniskirt, tube-top and short jacket, with a purse slung over one shoulder, hanging against her hip from a narrow strap. Her hands are thrust into the pockets of her jacket. Her features are tired, the lost look of a junkie in her eyes undermining her attempt to appear sultry.

Near her feet, a condom is attached to the painting, stiffened with gesso. The subject is thirteen years old.

I started running away from home when I was ten. The summer I turned eleven I managed to make it to Newford and lived on its streets for six months. I ate what I could find in the dumpsters behind the McDonald's and other fast food places on Williamson Street—there was nothing wrong with the food. It was just dried out from having been under the heating lamps for too long.

I spent those six months walking the streets all night. I was afraid to sleep when it was dark because I was just a kid and who knows what could've happened to me. At least being awake I could hide whenever I saw something that made me nervous. In the daytime I slept where I could—in parks, in the back seats of abandoned cars, wherever I didn't think I'd get caught. I tried to keep myself clean, washed up in restaurant bathrooms and at this gas bar on Yoors Street where the guy running the pumps took a liking to me. Paydays he'd spot me for lunch at the grill down the street.

I started drawing back then and for awhile I tried to hawk my pictures to the tourists down by the Pier, but the stuff wasn't all that good and I was drawing with pencils on foolscap or pages torn out of old school notebooks—not exactly the kind of art that looks good in a frame, if you know what I mean. I did a lot better panhandling and shoplifting.

I finally got busted trying to boost a tape deck from Kreiger's Stereo—it used to be where Gypsy Records is. Now it's out on the strip past the Tombs. I've always been small for my age, which didn't help when I tried to convince the cops that I was older than I really was. I figured juvie would be better than going back to my parents' place, but it didn't work. My parents had a missing persons out on me, God knows why. It's not like they could've missed me.

But I didn't go back home. My mother didn't want me and my dad didn't argue, so I guess he didn't either. I figured that was great until I started making the rounds of foster homes, bouncing back and forth between them and the Home for Wayward Girls. It's just juvie with an old-fashioned name.

I guess there must be some good foster parents, but I never saw any. All mine ever wanted was to collect their check and treat me like I was a piece of shit unless my case worker was coming by for a visit. Then I got moved up from the mattress in the basement to one of their kids' rooms. The first time I tried to tell the worker what was going down, she didn't believe me and then my foster parents beat the crap out of me once she was gone. I didn't make that mistake again.

I was thirteen and in my fourth or fifth foster home when I got molested again. This time I didn't take any crap. I booted the old pervert in the balls and just took off out of there, back to Newford.

I was older and knew better now. Girls I talked to in juvie told me how to get around, who to trust and who was just out to peddle your ass.

See, I never planned on being a hooker. I don't know what I thought I'd do when

I got to the city—I wasn't exactly thinking straight. Anyway, I ended up with this guy—Robert Carson. He was fifteen.

I met him in back of the Convention Center on the beach where all the kids used to all hang out in the summer and we ended up getting a room together on Grasso Street, near the high school. I was still pretty fucked up about getting physical with a guy but we ended up doing so many drugs—acid, MDA, coke, smack, you name it—that half the time I didn't know when he was putting it to me.

We ran out of money one day, rent was due, no food in the place, no dope, both of us too fucked up to panhandle, when Rob gets the big idea of selling my ass to bring in a little money. Well, I was screwed up, but not that screwed up. But then he got some guy to front him some smack and next thing I know I'm in this car with some guy I never saw before and he's expecting a blow job and I'm crying and all fucked up from the dope and then I'm doing it and standing out on the street corner where he's dumped me some ten minutes later with forty bucks in my hand and Rob's laughing, saying how we got it made, and all I can do is crouch on the sidewalk and puke, trying to get the taste of that guy's come out of my mouth.

So Rob thinks I'm being, like, so fucking weird—I mean, it's easy money, he tells me. Easy for him maybe. We have this big fight and then he hits me. Tells me if I don't get my ass out on the street and make some more money, he's going to do worse, like cut me.

My luck, I guess. Of all the guys to hang out with, I've got to pick one who suddenly realizes it's his ambition in life to be a pimp. Three years later he's running a string of five girls, but he lets me pay my respect—two grand which I got by skimming what I was paying him—and I'm out of the scene.

Except I'm not, because I'm still a junkie and I'm too fucked up to work, I've got no ID, I've got no skills except I can draw a little when I'm not fucked up on smack which is just about all the time. I start muling for a couple of dealers in Fitzhenry Park, just to get my fixes, and then one night I'm so out of it, I just collapse in a doorway of a pawn shop up on Perry Street.

I haven't eaten in, like, three days. I'm shaking because I need a fix so bad I can't see straight. I haven't washed in Christ knows how long, so I smell and the clothes I'm wearing are worse. I'm at the end of the line and I know it, when I hear footsteps coming down the street and I know it's the local cop on his beat, doing his rounds.

I try to crawl deeper into the shadows but the doorway's only so deep and the cop's coming closer and then he's standing there, blocking what little light the street-lamps were throwing and I know I'm screwed. But there's no way I'm going back into juvie or a foster home. I'm thinking of offering him a blow job to let me go—so far as the cops're concerned, hookers're just scum, but they'll take a freebie all the same—but I see something in this guy's face, when he turns his head and the streetlight touches it, that tells me he's an honest joe. A rookie, true blue, probably his first week on the beat and full of wanting to help everybody and I know for sure I'm screwed. With my luck running true, he's going to be the kind of guy who thinks social workers really want to help someone like me instead of playing bureaucratic mind-fuck games with my head.

I don't think I can take anymore.

I find myself wishing I had Rob's switchblade—the one he liked to push up against my face when he didn't think I was bringing in enough. I just want to cut something. The cop. Myself. I don't really give a fuck. I just want out.

He crouches down so he's kind of level with me, lying there scrunched up against the door, and says, "How bad is it?"

I just look at him like he's from another planet. How bad is it? Can it get any worse I wonder?

"I . . . I'm doing fine," I tell him.

He nods like we're discussing the weather. "What's your name?"

"Jilly," I say.

"Jilly what?"

"Uh. . . ."

I think of my parents, who've turned their backs on me. I think of juvie and foster homes. I look over his shoulder and there's a pair of billboards on the building behind me. One's advertising a suntan lotion—you know the one with the dog pulling the kid's pants down? I'll bet some old pervert thought that one up. The other's got the Jolly Green Giant himself selling vegetables. I pull a word from each ad and give it to the cop.

"Jilly Coppercorn."

"Think you can stand, Jilly?"

I'm thinking, If I could stand, would I be lying here? But I give it a try. He helps me the rest of the way up, supports me when I start to sway.

"So . . . so am I busted?" I ask him.

"Have you committed a crime?"

I don't know where the laugh comes from, but it falls out of my mouth all the same. There's no humor in it.

"Sure," I tell him. "I was born."

He sees my bag still lying on the ground. He picks it up while I lean against the wall and a bunch of my drawings fall out. He looks at them as he stuffs them back in the bag.

"Did you do those?"

I want to sneer at him, ask him why the fuck should he care, but I've got nothing left in me. It's all I can do to stand. So I tell him, yeah, they're mine.

"They're very good."

Right. I'm actually this fucking brilliant artist, slumming just to get material for my art.

"Do you have a place to stay?" he asks.

Whoops, did I read him wrong? Maybe he's planning to get me home, clean me up, and then put it to me.

"Jilly?" he asks when I don't answer.

Sure, I want to tell him. I've got my pick of the city's alleyways and doorways. I'm welcome wherever I go. World treats me like a fucking princess. But all I do is shake my head.

"I want to take you to see a friend of mine," he says.

I wonder how he can stand to touch me. I can't stand myself. I'm like a walking sewer. And now he wants to bring me to meet a friend?

"Am I busted?" I ask him again.

He shakes his head. I think of where I am, what I got ahead of me, then I just shrug. If I'm not busted, then whatever he's got planned for me's got to be better. Who knows, maybe his friend'll front me with a fix to get me through the night.

"Okay," I tell him. "Whatever."

"C'mon," he says.

He puts an arm around my shoulder and steers me off down the street and that's how I met Lou Fucceri and his girlfriend, the Grasso Street Angel.

7

Jilly sat on the stoop of Angel's office on Grasso Street, watching the passersby. She had her sketchpad on her knee, but she hadn't opened it yet. Instead, she was amusing herself with one of her favorite pastimes: making up stories about the people walking by. The young woman with the child in a stroller, she was a princess in exile, disguising herself as a nanny in a far distant land until she could regain her rightful station in some suitably romantic dukedom in Europe. The old black man with the cane was a physicist studying the effects of Chaos theory in the Grasso Street traffic. The Hispanic girl on her skateboard was actually a mermaid, having exchanged the waves of her ocean for concrete.

She didn't turn around when she heard the door open behind her. There was a scuffle of sneakers on the stoop, then the sound of the door closing again. After a moment, Annie sat down beside her.

"How're you doing?" Jilly asked.

"It was weird."

"Good weird, or bad?" Jilly asked when Annie didn't go on. "Or just uncomfortable?"

"Good weird, I guess. She played the tape you did for her book. She said you knew, that you'd said it was okay."

Jilly nodded.

"I couldn't believe it was you. I mean, I recognized your voice and everything, but you sounded so different."

"I was just a kid," Jilly said. "A punky street kid."

"But look at you now."

"I'm nothing special," Jilly said, suddenly feeling self-conscious. She ran a hand through her hair. "Did Angel tell you about the sponsorship program?"

Annie nodded. "Sort of. She said you'd tell me more."

"What Angel does is coordinate a relationship between kids that need help and people who want to help. It's different every time, because everybody's different. I didn't meet my sponsor for the longest time; he just put up the money while Angel was my contact. My lifeline, if you want to know the truth. I can't remember how many times I'd show up at her door and spend the night crying on her shoulder."

"How did you get, you know, cleaned up?" Annie asked. Her voice was shy.

"The first thing is I went into detox. When I finally got out, my sponsor paid for my room and board at the Chelsea Arms while I went through an accelerated high school program. I told Angel I wanted to go on to college, so he cosigned my student loan and helped me out with my books and supplies and stuff. I was working by that point. I had part-time jobs at a couple of stores and with the Post Office, and then I started waitressing, but that kind of money doesn't go far—not when you're carrying a full course load."

"When did you find out who your sponsor was?"

"When I graduated. He was at the ceremony."

"Was it weird finally meeting him?"

Jilly laughed. "Yes and no. I'd already known him for years—he was my art history professor. We got along really well and he used to let me use the sunroom at the back of his house for a studio. Angel and Lou had shown him some of that bad art I'd been doing when I was still on the street and that's why he sponsored me—because he thought I had a lot of talent, he told me later. But he didn't want me to know it was him putting up the money because he thought it might affect our relationship at Butler U." She shook her head. "He said he *knew* I'd be going the first time Angel and Lou showed him the stuff I was doing."

"It's sort of like a fairy tale, isn't it?" Annie said.

"I guess it is. I never thought of it that way."

"And it really works, doesn't it?"

"If you want it to," Jilly said. "I'm not saying it's easy. There's ups and downs—lots more downs at the start."

"How many kids make it?"

"This hasn't got anything to do with statistics," Jilly said. "You can only look at it on a person to person basis. But Angel's been doing this for a long, long time. You can trust her to do her best for you. She takes a lot of flak for what she does. Parents get mad at her because she won't tell them where their kids are. Social services says she's undermining their authority. She's been to jail twice on contempt of court charges because she wouldn't tell where some kid was."

"Even with her boyfriend being a cop?"

"That was a long time ago," Jilly said. "And it didn't work out. They're still friends but—Angel went through an awful bad time when she was a kid. That changes a person, no matter how much they learn to take control of their life. Angel's great with people, especially kids, and she's got a million friends, but she's not good at maintaining a personal relationship with a guy. When it comes down to the crunch, she just can't learn to trust them. As friends, sure, but not as lovers."

"She said something along the same lines about you," Annie said. "She said you were full of love, but it wasn't sexual or romantic so much as a general kindness towards everything and everybody."

"Yeah, well . . . I guess both Angel and I talk too much."

Annie hesitated for a few heartbeats, then said, "She also told me that you want to sponsor me."

Jilly nodded. "I'd like to."

"I don't get it."

"What's to get?"

"Well, I'm not like you or your professor friend. I'm not, you know, all that creative. I couldn't make something beautiful if my life depended on it. I'm not much good at anything."

Jilly shook her head. "That's not what it's about. Beauty isn't what you see on TV or in magazine ads or even necessarily in art galleries. It's a lot deeper and a lot simpler than that. It's realizing the goodness of things, it's leaving the world a little better than it was before you got here. It's appreciating the inspiration of the world around you and trying to inspire others.

"Sculptors, poets, painters, musicians—they're the traditional purveyors of Beauty. But it can as easily be created by a gardener, a farmer, a plumber, a careworker. It's the intent you put into your work, the pride you take in it—whatever it is."

"But still. . . . I really don't have anything to offer."

Annie's statement was all the more painful for Jilly because it held no self-pity, it was just a laying out of facts as Annie saw them.

"Giving birth is an act of Beauty," Jilly said.

"I don't even know if I want a kid. I . . . I don't know what I want. I don't know who I am."

She turned to Jilly. There seemed to be years of pain and confusion in her eyes, far more years than she had lived in the world. When had that pain begun? Jilly thought. Who could have done it to her, beautiful child that she must have been? Father, brother, uncle, family friend?

Jilly wanted to just reach out and hold her, but knew too well how the physical contact of comfort could too easily be misconstrued as an invasion of the private space an abused victim sometimes so desperately needed to maintain.

"I need help," Annie said softly. "I know that. But I don't want charity."

"Don't think of this sponsorship program as charity," Jilly said. "What Angel does is simply what we all should be doing all of the time—taking care of each other."

Annie sighed, but fell silent. Jilly didn't push it any further. They sat for awhile longer on the stoop while the world bustled by on Grasso Street.

"What was the hardest part?" Annie asked. "You know, when you first came off the street."

"Thinking of myself as normal."

8

Daddy's Home, by Isabelle Copley. Painted Wood. Adjani Farm, Wren Island, 1990.

> *The sculpture is three feet high, a flat rectangle of solid wood, standing on end with a child's face, upper torso and hands protruding from one side, as though the wood is gauze against which the subject is pressing.*
> *The child wears a look of terror.*

Annie's sleeping again. She needs the rest as much as she needs regular meals and the knowledge that she's got a safe place to stay. I took my Walkman out onto the fire escape and listened to a copy of the tape that Angel played for her today. I don't much recognize that kid either, but I know it's me.

It's funny, me talking about Angel, Angel talking about me, both of us knowing what the other needs, but neither able to help herself. I like to see my friends as couples. I like to see them in love with each other. But it's not the same for me.

Except who am I kidding? I want the same thing, but I just choke when a man gets too close to me. I can't let down that final barrier, I can't even tell them why.

Sophie says I expect them to just instinctively know. That I'm waiting for them to be understanding and caring without ever opening up to them. If I want them to follow the script I've got written out in my head, she says I have to let them in on it.

I know she's right, but I can't do anything about it.

I see a dog slink into the alleyway beside the building. He's skinny as a whippet, but he's just a mongrel that no one's taken care of for awhile. He's got dried blood on his shoulders, so I guess someone's been beating him.

I go down with some cat food in a bowl, but he won't come near me, no matter how soothingly I call to him. I know he can smell the food, but he's more scared of me than he's hungry. Finally I just leave the bowl and go back up the fire escape. He waits until I'm sitting outside my window again before he goes up to the bowl. He wolfs the food down and then he takes off like he's done something wrong.

I guess that's the way I am when I meet a man I like. I'm really happy with him until he's nice to me, until he wants to kiss me and hold me, and then I just run off like I've done something wrong.

9

Annie woke while Jilly was starting dinner. She helped chop up vegetables for the vegetarian stew Jilly was making, then drifted over to the long worktable that ran along the back wall near Jilly's easel. She found a brochure for the Five Coyotes Singing Studio show in amongst the litter of paper, magazines, sketches and old paint brushes and brought it over to the kitchen table where she leafed through it while Jilly finished up the dinner preparations.

"Do you really think something like this is going to make a difference?" Annie asked after she'd read through the brochure.

"Depends on how big a difference you're talking about," Jilly said. "Sophie's arranged for a series of lectures to run in association with the show and she's also organized a couple of discussion evenings at the gallery where people who come to the show can talk to us—about their reactions to the show, about their feelings, maybe even share their own experiences if that's something that feels right to them at the time."

"Yeah, but what about the kids that this is all about?" Annie asked.

Jilly turned from the stove. Annie didn't look at all like a young expectant mother, glowing with her pregnancy. She just looked like a hurt and confused kid with a distended stomach, a kind of Ralph Steadman aura of frantic anxiety splattered around her.

"The way we see it," Jilly said, "is if only one kid gets spared the kind of hell we all went through, then the show'll be worth it."

"Yeah, but the only kind of people who are going to go to this kind of thing are those who already know about it. You're preaching to the converted."

"Maybe. But there'll be media coverage—in the papers for sure, maybe a spot on the news. That's where—if we're going to reach out and wake someone up—that's where it's going to happen."

"I suppose."

Annie flipped over the brochure and looked at the four photographs on the back.

"How come there isn't a picture of Sophie?" she asked.

"Cameras don't seem to work all that well around her," Jilly said. "It's like—"
she smiled "—an enchantment."

The corner of Annie's mouth twitched in response.

"Tell me about, you know . . ." She pointed to Jilly's Urban Faerie paintings.
"Magic. Enchanted stuff."

Jilly put the stew on low to simmer then fetched a sketchbook that held some of
the preliminary pencil drawings for the finished paintings that were leaning up against
the wall. The urban settings were barely realized—just rough outlines and shapes—but
the faerie were painstakingly detailed.

As they flipped through the sketchbook, Jilly talked about where she'd done the
sketches, what she'd seen, or more properly glimpsed, that led her to make the drawings
she had.

"You've really seen all these . . . little magic people?" Annie asked.

Her tone of voice was incredulous, but Jilly could tell that she wanted to believe.

"Not all of them," Jilly said. "Some I've only imagined, but others . . . like this
one." She pointed to a sketch that had been done in the Tombs where a number of fey
figures were hanging out around an abandoned car, pre-Raphaelite features at odds
with their raggedy clothing and setting. "They're real."

"But they could just be people. It's not like they're tiny or have wings like some
of the others."

Jilly shrugged. "Maybe, but they weren't just people."

"Do you have to be magic yourself to see them?"

Jilly shook her head. "You just have to pay attention. If you don't you'll miss
them, or see something else—something you expected to see rather than what was
really there. Fairy voices become just the wind, a bodach, like this little man here—"
she flipped to another page and pointed out a small gnomish figure the size of a cat,
darting off a sidewalk "—scurrying across the street becomes just a piece of litter
caught in the backwash of a bus."

"Pay attention," Annie repeated dubiously.

Jilly nodded. "Just like we have to pay attention to each other, or we miss the
important things that are going on there as well."

Annie turned another page, but she didn't look at the drawing. Instead she studied
Jilly's pixie features.

"You really, really believe in magic, don't you?" she said.

"I really, really do," Jilly told her. "But it's not something I just take on faith. For
me, art is an act of magic. I pass on the spirits that I see—of people, of places,
mysteries."

"So what if you're not an artist? Where's the magic then?"

"Life's an act of magic, too. Claire Hamill sings a line in one of her songs that really
sums it up for me: 'If there's no magic, there's no meaning.' Without magic—or call it
wonder, mystery, natural wisdom—nothing has any depth. It's all just surface. You know:
what you see is what you get. I honestly believe there's more to everything than that,
whether it's a Monet hanging in a gallery or some old vagrant sleeping in an alley."

"I don't know," Annie said. "I understand what you're saying, about people and
things, but this other stuff—it sounds more like the kinds of things you see when
you're tripping."

Jilly shook her head. "I've done drugs and I've seen Faerie. They're not the same."

She got up to stir the stew. When she sat down again, Annie had closed the sketch-book and was sitting with her hands flat against her stomach.

"Can you feel the baby?" Jilly asked.

Annie nodded.

"Have you thought about what you want to do?"

"I guess. I'm just not sure I even want to keep the baby."

"That's your decision," Jilly said. "Whatever you want to do, we'll stand by you. Either way we'll get you a place to stay. If you keep the baby and want to work, we'll see about arranging daycare. If you want to stay home with the baby, we'll work something out for that as well. That's what this sponsorship's all about. It's not us telling you what to do; we just want to help you be the person you were meant to be."

"I don't know if that's such a good person," Annie said.

"Don't think like that. It's not true."

Annie shrugged. "I guess I'm scared I'll do the same thing to my baby that my mother did to me. That's how it happens, doesn't it? My mom used to beat the crap out of me all the time, didn't matter if I did something wrong or not, and I'm just going to end up doing the same thing to my kid."

"You're only hurting yourself with that kind of thinking," Jilly said.

"But it *can* happen, can't it? Jesus, I . . . You know I've been gone from her for two years now, but I still feel like she's standing right next to me half the time, or waiting around the corner for me. It's like I'll never escape. When I lived at home, it was like I was living in the house of an enemy. But running away didn't change that. I still feel like that, except now it's like everybody's my enemy."

Jilly reached over and laid a hand on hers.

"Not everybody," she said. "You've got to believe that."

"It's hard not to."

"I know."

10

This Is Where We Dump Them, *by Meg Mullally. Tinted photograph. The Tombs, Newford, 1991.*

> *Two children sit on the stoop of one of the abandoned buildings in the Tombs. Their hair is matted, faces smudged, clothing dirty and ill-fitting. They look like turn-of-the-century Irish tinkers. There's litter all around them: torn garbage bags spewing their contents on the sidewalk, broken bottles, a rotting mattress on the street, half-crushed pop cans, soggy newspapers, used condoms.*
>
> *The children are seven and thirteen, a boy and a girl. They have no home, no family. They only have each other.*

The next month went by awfully fast. Annie stayed with me—it was what she wanted. Angel and I did get her a place, a one-bedroom on Landis that she's going to move into after she's had the baby. It's right behind the loft—you can see her back window from mine. But for now she's going to stay here with me.

She's really a great kid. No artistic leanings, but really bright. She could be anything she wants to be if she can just learn to deal with all the baggage her parents
dumped on her.

She's kind of shy around Angel and some of my other friends—I guess they're
all too old for her or something—but she gets along really well with Sophie and me.
Probably because, whenever you put Sophie and me together in the same room for
more than two minutes, we just start giggling and acting about half our respective
ages, which would make us, mentally at least, just a few years Annie's senior.

"You two could be sisters," Annie told me one day when we got back from Sophie's
studio. "Her hair's lighter, and she's a little chestier, and she's *definitely* more organized
than you are, but I get a real sense of family when I'm with the two of you. The way
families are supposed to be."

"Even though Sophie's got faerie blood?" I asked her.

She thought I was joking.

"If she's got magic in her," Annie said, "then so do you. Maybe that's what makes
you seem so much like sisters."

"I just pay attention to things," I told her. "That's all."

"Yeah, right."

The baby came right on schedule—three-thirty, Sunday morning. I probably would've
panicked if Annie hadn't been doing enough of that for both of us. Instead I got on
the phone, called Angel, and then saw about helping Annie get dressed.

The contractions were really close by the time Angel arrived with the car. But
everything worked out fine. Jillian Sophia Mackle was born two hours and forty-five
minutes later at the Newford General Hospital. Six pounds and five ounces of red-faced
wonder. There were no complications.

Those came later.

11

The last week before the show was simple chaos. There seemed to be a hundred and
one things that none of them had thought of, all of which had to be done at the last
moment. And to make matters worse, Jilly still had one unfinished canvas haunting her
by Friday night.

It stood on her easel, untitled, barely-sketched in images, still in monochrome.
The colors eluded her. She knew what she wanted, but every time she stood before
her easel, her mind went blank. She seemed to forget everything she'd ever known
about art. The inner essence of the canvas rose up inside her like a ghost, so close she
could almost touch it, but then fled daily, like a dream lost upon waking. The outside
world intruded. A knock on the door. The ringing of the phone.

The show opened in exactly seven days.

Annie's baby was almost two weeks old. She was a happy, satisfied infant, the
kind of baby that was forever making contented little gurgling sounds, as though
talking to herself; she never cried. Annie herself was a nervous wreck.

"I'm scared," she told Jilly when she came over to the loft that afternoon. "Everything's going too well. I don't deserve it."

They were sitting at the kitchen table, the baby propped up on the Murphy bed between two pillows. Annie kept fidgeting. Finally she picked up a pencil and started drawing stick figures on pieces of paper.

"Don't say that," Jilly said. "Don't even think it."

"But it's true. Look at me. I'm not like you or Sophie. I'm not like Angel. What have I got to offer my baby? What's she going to have to look up to when she looks at me?"

"A kind, caring mother."

Annie shook her head. "I don't feel like that. I feel like everything's sort of fuzzy and it's like pushing through cobwebs just to make it through the day."

"We'd better make an appointment with you to see a doctor."

"Make it a shrink," Annie said. She continued to doodle, then looked down at what she was doing. "Look at this. It's just crap."

Before Jilly could see, Annie swept the sheaf of papers to the floor.

"Oh, jeez," she said as they went fluttering all over the place. "I'm sorry. I didn't mean to do that."

She got up before Jilly could and tossed the lot of them in the garbage container beside the stove. She stood there for a long moment, taking deep breaths, holding them, slowly letting them out.

"Annie . . . ?"

She turned as Jilly approached her. The glow of motherhood that had seemed to revitalize her in the month before the baby was born had slowly worn away. She was pale again. Wan. She looked so lost that all Jilly could do was put her arms around her and offer a wordless comfort.

"I'm sorry," Annie said against Jilly's hair. "I don't know what's going on. I just . . . I know I should be really happy, but I just feel scared and confused." She rubbed at her eyes with a knuckle. "God, listen to me. All it seems I can do is complain about my life."

"It's not like you've had a great one," Jilly said.

"Yeah, but when I compare it to what it was like before I met you, it's like I moved up into heaven."

"Why don't you stay here tonight?" Jilly said.

Annie stepped back out of her arms. "Maybe I will—if you really don't mind . . . ?"

"I really don't mind."

"Thanks."

Annie glanced towards the bed, her gaze pausing on the clock on the wall above the stove.

"You're going to be late for work," she said.

"That's all right. I don't think I'll go in tonight."

Annie shook her head. "No, go on. You've told me how busy it gets on a Friday night."

Jilly still worked part-time at Kathryn's Cafe on Battersfield Road. She could just imagine what Wendy would say if she called in sick. There was no one else in town this weekend to take her shift, so that would leave Wendy working all the tables on her own.

"If you're sure," Jilly said.

"We'll be okay," Annie said. "Honestly."

She went over to the bed and picked up the baby, cradling her gently in her arms.

"Look at her," she said, almost to herself. "It's hard to believe something so beautiful came out of me." She turned to Jilly, adding before Jilly could speak, "That's a kind of magic all by itself, isn't it?"

"Maybe one of the best we can make," Jilly said.

12

How Can You Call This Love? by Claudia Feder. Oils. Old Market Studio, Newford, 1990.

 A fat man sits on a bed in a cheap hotel room. He's removing his shirt. Through the ajar door of the bathroom behind him, a thin girl in bra and panties can be seen sitting on the toilet, shooting up.

 She appears to be about fourteen.

I just pay attention to things, I told her. I guess that's why, when I got off my shift and came back to the loft, Annie was gone. Because I pay such good attention. The baby was still on the bed, lying between the pillows, sleeping. There was a note on the kitchen table:

 I don't know what's wrong with me. I just keep wanting to hit something. I look at little Jilly and I think about my mother and I get so scared. Take care of her for me. Teach her magic.

 Please don't hate me.

I don't know how long I sat and stared at those sad, piteous words, tears streaming from my eyes.

I should never have gone to work. I should never have left her alone. She really thought she was just going to replay her own childhood. She told me, I don't know how many times she told me, but I just wasn't paying attention, was I?

Finally I got on the phone. I called Angel. I called Sophie. I called Lou Fucceri. I called everybody I could think of to go out and look for Annie. Angel was at the loft with me when we finally heard. I was the one who picked up the phone.

I heard what Lou said: "A patrolman brought her into the General not fifteen minutes ago, ODing on Christ knows what. She was just trying to self-destruct, is what he said. I'm sorry, Jilly. But she died before I got there."

I didn't say anything. I just passed the phone to Angel and went to sit on the bed. I held little Jilly in my arms and then I cried some more.

I was never joking about Sophie. She really does have faerie blood. It's something I can't explain, something we've never really talked about, something I just know and she's never denied. But she did promise me that she'd bless Annie's baby, just the way fairy godmothers would do it in all those old stories.

"I gave her the gift of a happy life," she told me later. "I never dreamed it wouldn't include Annie."

But that's the way it works in fairy tales, too, isn't it? Something always goes wrong, or there wouldn't be a story. You have to be strong, you have to earn your happily ever after.

Annie was strong enough to go away from her baby when she felt like all she could do was just lash out, but she wasn't strong enough to help herself. That was the awful gift her parents gave her.

I never finished that last painting in time for the show, but I found something to take its place. Something that said more to me in just a few rough lines than anything I've ever done.

I was about to throw out my garbage when I saw those crude little drawings that Annie had been doodling on my kitchen table the night she died. They were like the work of a child.

I framed one of them and hung it in the show.

"I guess we're five coyotes and one coyote ghost now," was all Sophie said when she saw what I had done.

13

In the House of My Enemy, *by Annie Mackle. Pencils. Yoors Street Studio, Newford, 1991.*

The images are crudely rendered. In a house that is merely a square with a triangle on top, are three stick figures, one plain, two with small "skirt" triangles to represent their gender. The two larger figures are beating the smaller one with what might be crooked sticks, or might be belts.

The small figure is cringing away.

14

In the visitor's book set out at the show, someone wrote: "I can never forgive those responsible for what's been done to us. I don't even want to try."

"Neither do I," Jilly said when she read it. "God help me, but neither do I."

But for the Grace
Go I

*You can only predict things
after they've happened.*
—Eugene Ionesco

I inherited Tommy the same way I did the dogs. Found him wandering lost and alone, so I took him home. I've always taken in strays—maybe because a long time ago I used to hope that someone'd take me in. I grew out of that idea pretty fast.

Tommy's kind of like a pet, I guess, except he can talk. He doesn't make a whole lot of sense, but then I don't find what most people have to say makes much sense. At least Tommy's honest. What you see is what you get. No games, no hidden agendas. He's only Tommy, a big guy who wouldn't hurt you even if you took a stick to him. Likes to smile, likes to laugh—a regular guy. He's just a few bricks short of a load, is all. Hell, sometimes I figure all he's got is bricks sitting back in there behind his eyes.

I know what you're thinking. A guy like him should be in an institution, and I suppose you're right, except they pronounced him cured at the Zeb when they needed his bed for somebody whose family had money to pay for the space he was taking up and they're not exactly falling over themselves to get him back.

We live right in the middle of that part of Newford that some people call the Tombs and some call Squatland. It's the dead part of the city—a jungle of empty lots filled with trash and abandoned cars, gutted buildings and rubble. I've seen it described in the papers as a blight, a disgrace, a breeding ground for criminals and racial strife, though we've got every color you can think of living in here and we get along pretty well together, mostly because we just leave each other alone. And we're not so much criminals as losers.

Sitting in their fancy apartments and houses, with running water and electricity and no worry about where the next meal's coming from, the good citizens of Newford have got a lot of names and ways to describe this place and us, but those of us who actually live here just call it home. I think of it as one of those outlaw roosts like they used to have in the Old West—some little ramshackle town, way back in the badlands, where only the outlaws lived. Of course those guys like L'Amour and Short who wrote about places like that probably just made them up. I find that a lot of people have this thing about making crap romantic, the way they like to blur outlaws and heroes, the good with the bad.

I know that feeling all too well, but I broke the only pair of rose-colored glasses I had the chance to own a long time ago. Sometimes I pretend I'm here because I want to be, because it's the only place I can be free, because I'm judged by who I am and what I can do, not by how screwed up my family is and how dirt poor looked pretty good from the position we were in.

I'm not saying this part of town's pretty. I'm not even saying I like living here. We're all just putting in time, trying to make do. Every time I hear about some kid ODing, somebody getting knifed, somebody taking that long step off a building or wrapping their belt around their neck, I figure that's just one more of us who finally got out. It's a war zone in here, and just like in Vietnam, they either carry you out in a box, or you leave under your own steam carrying a piece of the place with you—a kind of cold shadow that sits inside your soul and has you waking up in a cold sweat some nights, or feeling closed in and crazy in your new workplace, home, social life, whatever, for no good reason except that it's the Tombs calling to you, telling you that maybe you don't deserve what you've got now, reminding you of all those people you left behind who didn't get the break you did.

I don't know why we bother. Let's be honest. I don't know why *I* bother. I just don't know any better, I guess. Or maybe I'm just too damn stubborn to give up.

Angel—you know, the do-gooder who runs that program out of her Grasso Street office to get kids like me off the streets? She tells me I've got a nihilistic attitude. Once she explained what that meant, all I could do was laugh.

"Look at where I'm coming from," I told her. "What do you expect?"

"I can help you."

I just shook my head. "You want a piece of me, that's all, but I've got nothing left to give."

That's only partly true. See, I've got responsibilities, just like a regular citizen. I've got the dogs. And I've got Tommy. I was joking about calling him my pet. That's just what the bikers who're squatting down the street from us call him. I think of us all—me, the dogs and Tommy—as family. Or about as close to family as any of us are ever going to get. I can't leave, because what would they do without me? And who'd take the whole pack of us, which is the only way I'd go?

Tommy's got this thing about magazines, though he can't read a word. Me, I love to read. I've got thousands of books. I get them all from the dump bins in back of bookstores—you know, where they tear off the covers to get their money back for the ones they don't sell and just throw the book away? Never made any sense to me, but you won't catch me complaining.

I'm not that particular about what I read. I just like the stories. Danielle Steel or Dostoyevsky, Somerset Maugham or King—doesn't make much difference. Just so long as I can get away in the words.

But Tommy likes his magazines, and he likes them with his name on the cover—you know, the subscription sticker? There's two words he can read: Thomas and Flood.

I know his first name's Tommy, because he knows that much and that's what he told me. I made up the last name. The building we live in is on Flood Street.

He likes *People* and *Us* and *Entertainment Weekly* and *Life* and stuff like that. Lots of pictures, not too many words. He gets me to cut out the pictures of the people and animals and ads and stuff he likes and then he plays with them like they were paper dolls. That's how he gets away, I guess. Whatever works.

Anyway, I've got a post office box down on Grasso Street near Angel's office and that's where I have the subscriptions sent. I go down once a week to pick them up—usually on Thursday afternoons. It's all a little more than I can afford—makes me work a little harder at my garbage picking, you know?—but what am I going to do? Cut him off from his only pleasure? People think I'm hard—when they don't just think I'm crazy—and maybe I am, but I'm not mean.

The thing about having a post office box is that you get some pretty interesting junk mail—well at least Tommy finds it interesting. I used to throw it out, but he came down with me to the box one time and got all weirded out when he saw me throwing it out so I bring most of it back now. He calls them his surprises. First thing he asks when I get back is, "Were there any surprises?"

I went in the Thursday this all started and gave the clerk my usual glare, hoping that one day he'll finally get the message, but he never does. He was the one who sicced Angel on me in the first place. Thought nineteen was too young to be a bag lady, pretty girl like me. Thought he could help.

I didn't bother to explain that I'd chosen to live this way. I've been living on my own since I was twelve. I don't sell my bod' and I don't do drugs. My clothes may be worn down and patched, but they're clean. I wash every day, which is more than I can say for some of the real citizens I pass by on the street. You can smell their B.O. a half block away. I look pretty regular except on garbage day when Tommy and I hit the streets with our shopping carts, the dogs all strung out around us like our own special honor guard.

There's nothing wrong with garbage picking. Where do you think all those fancy antique shops get most of their high-priced merchandise?

I do okay, without either Angel's help or his. He was probably just hard up for a girlfriend.

"How's it going, Maisie?" he asked when I came in, all friendly, like we're pals. I guess he got my name from the form I filled out when I rented the box.

I ignored him, like I always do, and gathered the week's pile up. It was a fairly thick stack—lots of surprises for Tommy. I took it all outside where Rexy was waiting for me. He's the smallest of the dogs, just a small little mutt with wiry brown hair and a real insecurity problem. He's the only one who comes everywhere with me because he just falls apart if I leave him at home.

I gave Rexy a quick pat, then sat on the curb, sorting through Tommy's surprises. If the junk mail doesn't have pictures, I toss it. I only want to carry so much of this crap back with me.

It was while I was going through the stack that this envelope fell out. I just sat and stared at it for the longest time. It looked like one of those ornate invitations they're always making a fuss over in the romance novels I read: almost square, the paper really thick and cream-colored, ornate lettering on the outside that was real high-class calligraphy, it was so pretty. But that wasn't what had me staring at it, unwilling to pick it up.

The lettering spelled out my name. Not the one I use, but my real name. Margaret. Maisie's just a diminutive of it that I read about in this book about Scotland. That was all that was there, just "Margaret," no surname. I never use one except for when the cops decide to roust the squatters in the Tombs, like they do from time to time—I think it's like some kind of training exercise for them—and then I use Flood, same as I gave Tommy.

I shot a glance back in through the glass doors because I figured it had to be from the postal clerk—who else knew me?—but he wasn't even looking at me. I sat and stared at it a little longer, but then I finally picked it up. I took out my pen knife and slit the envelope open, and carefully pulled out this card. All it said on it was, "Allow the dark-robed access tonight and they will kill you."

I didn't have a clue what it meant, but it gave me a royal case of the creeps. If it wasn't a joke—which I figured it had to be—then who were these black-robed and why would they want to kill me?

Every big city like this is really two worlds. You could say it's divided up between the haves and the have-nots, but it's not that simple. It's more like some people are citizens of the day and others of the night. Someone like me belongs to the night. Not because I'm bad, but because I'm invisible. People don't know I exist. They don't know and they don't care, except for Angel and the postal clerk, I guess.

But now someone did.

Unless it was a joke. I tried to laugh it off, but it just didn't work. I looked at the envelope again, checking it out for a return address, and that's when I realized something I should have noticed straightaway. The envelope didn't have my box number on it, it didn't have anything at all except for my name. So how the hell did it end up in my box? There was only one way.

I left Rexy guarding Tommy's mail—just to keep him occupied—and went back inside. When the clerk finished with the customer ahead of me, he gave me a big smile but I laid the envelope down on the counter between us and didn't smile back.

Actually, he's a pretty good-looking guy. He's got one of those flat-top haircuts— shaved sides, kinky black hair standing straight up on top. His skin's the color of coffee and he's got dark eyes with the longest lashes I ever saw on a guy. I could like him just fine, but the trouble is he's a regular citizen. It'd just never work out.

"How'd this get in my box?" I asked him. "All it's got is my name on it, no box number, no address, nothing."

He looked down at the envelope. "You found it in your box?"

I nodded.

"I didn't put it in there and I'm the one who sorts all the mail for the boxes."

"I still found it in there."

He picked it up and turned it over in his hands.

"This is really weird," he said.

"You into occult shit?" I asked him.

I was thinking of dark robes. The only people I ever saw wear them were priests or people dabbling in the occult.

He blinked with surprise. "What do you mean?"

"Nothing."

I grabbed the envelope back and headed back to where Rexy was waiting for me.

"Maisie!" the clerk called after me, but I just ignored him.

Great, I thought as I collected the mail Rexy'd been guarding for me. First Joe postal clerk's got a good Samaritan complex over me—probably fueled by his dick—now he's going downright weird. I wondered if he knew where I lived. I wondered if he knew about the dogs. I wondered about magicians in dark robes and whether he thought he had some kind of magic that was going to deal with the dogs and make me go all gooshy for him—just before he killed me.

The more I thought about it, the more screwed up I got. I wasn't so much scared as confused. And angry. How was I supposed to keep coming back to get Tommy's mail, knowing he was there? What would he put in the box next? A dead rat? It wasn't like I could complain to anybody. People like me, we don't have any rights.

Finally I just started for home, but I paused as I passed the door to Angel's office.

Angel's a little cool with me these days. She still says she wanted to help me, but she doesn't quite trust me anymore. It's not really her fault.

She had me in her office one time—I finally went, just to get her off my back—and we sat there for awhile, looking at each other, drinking this crappy coffee from the machine that someone donated to her a few years ago. I wouldn't have picked it up on a dare if I'd come across it on my rounds.

"What do you want from me?" I finally asked her.

"I'm just trying to understand you."

"There's nothing to understand. What you see is what I am. No more, no less."

"But why do you live the way you do?"

Understand, I admire what Angel does. She's helped a lot of kids that were in a really bad way and that's a good thing. Some people need help because they can't help themselves.

She's an attractive woman with a heart-shaped face, the kind of eyes that always look really warm and caring and long dark hair that seems to go on forever down her back. I always figured something really bad must have happened to her as a kid, for her to do what she does. It's not like she makes much of a living. I think the only thing she really and honestly cares about is helping people through this sponsorship program she's developed where straights put up money and time to help the down-and-outers get a second chance.

I don't need that kind of help. I'm never going to be much more than what I am, but that's okay. It beats what I had before I hit the streets.

I've told Angel all of this a dozen times, but she sat there behind her desk, looking at me with those sad eyes of hers, and I knew she wanted a piece of me, so I gave her one. I figured maybe she'd leave me alone then.

"I was in high school," I told her, "and there was this girl who wanted to get back at one of the teachers—a really nice guy named Mr. Hammond. He taught math. So she made up this story about how he'd molested her and the shit really hit the fan. He got suspended while the cops and the school board looked into the matter and all the time this girl's laughing her head off behind everybody's back, but looking real sad and screwed up whenever the cops and the social workers are talking to her.

"But I knew he didn't do it. I knew where she was, the night she said it happened, and it wasn't with Mr. Hammond. Now I wasn't exactly the best-liked kid in that school, and I knew what this girl's gang was going to do to me, but I went ahead and told the truth anyway.

"Things worked out pretty much the way I expected. I got the cold shoulder from everybody, but at least Mr. Hammond got his name cleared and his job back.

"One afternoon he asks me to see him after school and I figure it's to thank me for what I've done, so I go to his classroom. The building's pretty well empty and the scuff of my shoes in the hallway is the only sound I hear as I go to see him. I get to the math room and he takes me back into his office. Then he locks the door and he rapes me. Not just once, but over and over again. And you know what he says to me while he's doing it?

" 'Nobody's going to believe a thing you say,' he says. 'You try to talk about this and they're just going to laugh in your face.' "

I looked over at Angel and there were tears swimming in her eyes.

"And you know what?" I said. "I knew he was right. I was the one that cleared his name. There was *nobody* going to believe me and I didn't even try."

"Oh, Jesus," Angel said. "You poor kid."

"Don't take it so hard," I told her. "It's past history. Besides, it never really happened. I just made it up because I figured it was the kind of thing you wanted to hear."

I'll give her this: she took it well. Didn't yell at me, didn't pitch me out onto the street. But you can see why maybe I'm not on her list of favorite people these days. On the other hand, she doesn't hold a grudge—I know that too.

I felt like a hypocrite going in to see her with this problem, but I didn't have anyone else to turn to. It's not like Tommy or the dogs could give me any advice. I hesitated for the longest moment in the doorway, but then she looked up and saw me standing there, so I went ahead in.

I took off my hat—it's this fedora that I actually bought new because it was just too cool to pass up. I wear it all the time, my light brown hair hanging down from it, long and straight, though not as long as Angel's. I like the way it looks with my jeans and sneakers and this cotton shirt I found at a rummage sale that only needed a tear fixed on one of its shirttails.

I know what you're thinking, but hey, I never said I wasn't vain. I may be a squatter, but I like to look my best. It gets me into places where they don't let in bums.

Anyway I took off my hat and slouched in the chair on this side of Angel's desk.

"Which one's that?" she asked, pointing to Rexy who was sitting outside by the door like the good little dog he is.

"Rexy."

"He can come in if you'd like."

I shook my head. "No. I'm not staying long. I just had this thing I wanted to ask you about. It's . . . ."

I didn't know where to begin, but finally I just started in with finding the envelope. It got easier as I went along. That's one thing you got to hand to Angel—there's nobody can listen like she does. You take up *all* of her attention when you're talking to her. You never get the feeling she's thinking of something else, or of what she's going to say back to you, or anything like that.

Angel didn't speak for a long time after I was done. When I stopped talking, she looked past me, out at the traffic going by on Grasso Street.

"Maisie," she said finally. "Have you ever heard the story of the boy who cried wolf?"

"Sure, but what's that got to do with—oh, I get it." I took out the envelope and slid it across the desk to her. "I didn't have to come in here," I added.

And I was wishing I hadn't, but Angel seemed to give herself a kind of mental shake. She opened the envelope and read the message, then her gaze came back to me.

"No," she said. "I'm glad you did. Do you want me to have a talk with Franklin?"

"Who's that?"

"The fellow behind the counter at the post office. I don't mind doing it, although I have to admit that it doesn't sound like the kind of thing he'd do."

So that was his name. Franklin. Franklin the creep.

I shrugged. "What good would that do? Even if he did do it—" and the odds looked good so far as I was concerned "—he's not going to admit to it."

"Maybe we can talk to his supervisor." She looked at her watch. "I think it's too late to do it today, but I can try first thing tomorrow morning."

Great. In the meantime, I could be dead.

Angel must have guessed what I was thinking, because she added, "Do you need a place to stay for tonight? Some place where you'll feel safe?"

I thought of Tommy and the dogs and shook my head.

"No, I'll be okay," I said as I collected my envelope and stuck it back in with Tommy's mail. "Thanks for, you know, listening and everything."

I waited for her to roll into some spiel about how she could do more, could get me off the street, that kind of thing, but it was like she was tuned right into my wavelength because she didn't say a word about any of that. She just knew, I guess, that I'd never come back if every time I talked to her that was all I could look forward to.

"Come see me tomorrow," was all she said as I got to my feet. "And Maisie?"

I paused in the doorway where Rexy was ready to start bouncing off my legs as if he hadn't seen me in weeks.

"Be careful," Angel added.

"I will."

I took a long route back to the squat, watching my back the whole time, but I never saw anybody that looked like he was following me, and not a single person in a dark robe. I almost laughed at myself by the time I got back. There were Tommy and the dogs, all sprawled out on the steps of our building until Rexy yelped and then the whole pack of them were racing down the street towards me.

Okay, big as he was, Tommy still couldn't hurt a flea even if his life depended on it and the dogs were all small and old and pretty well used up, but Franklin would still have to be crazy to think he could mess with us. He didn't *know* my family. You get a guy as big as Tommy and all those dogs . . . well, they just looked dangerous. What did I have to worry about?

The dogs were all over me then with Tommy right behind them. He grinned from ear to ear as I handed him his mail.

"Surprises!" he cried happily, in that weird high voice of his. "Maisie bring surprises!"

We went inside to our place up on the second floor. It's got this big open space that we use in the summer when we want the air to have a chance to move around.

There's books everywhere. Tommy's got his own corner with his magazines and all the little cut-out people and stuff that he plays with. There's a couple of mismatched kitchen chairs and a card table. A kind of old cabinet that some hoboes helped me move up the one flight from the street holds our food and the Coleman stove I use for cooking.

We sleep on the mattresses over in another corner, the whole pack together, except for Chuckie. He's this old lab that likes to guard the doorway. I usually think he's crazy for doing so, but I wouldn't mind tonight. Chuckie can look real fierce when he wants to. There's a couple of chests by the bed area. I keep our clothes in one and dry kibbles for the dogs in another. They're pretty good scavengers, but I like to see that they're eating the right kind of food. I wouldn't want anything to happen to them. One thing I can't afford is vet bills.

First off I fed the dogs, then I made supper for Tommy and me—lentil soup with day-old buns I'd picked up behind a bakery in Crowsea. We'd been eating the soup for a few days, but we had to use it up because, with the spring finally here, it was getting too warm for food to keep. In the winter we've got smaller quarters down the hall, complete with a cast-iron stove that I salvaged from this place they were wrecking over in Foxville. Tommy and I pretty near killed ourselves hauling it back. One of the bikers helped us bring it upstairs.

We fell into our usual Thursday night ritual once we'd finished supper. After hauling down tomorrow's water from the tank I'd set up on the roof to catch rainwater, I lit the oil lamp, then Tommy and I sat down at the table and went through his new magazines and ads. Every time he'd point out something that he liked in a picture, I'd cut it out for him. I do a pretty tidy job, if I say so myself. Getting to be an old hand at it. By the time we finished, he had a big stack of new cut-out people and stuff for his games that he just had to go try out right away. I went and got the book I'd started this morning and brought it back to the table, but I couldn't read.

I could hear Tommy talking to his new little friends. The dogs shifting and moving about the way they do. Down the street a Harley kicked over and I listened to it go through the Tombs until it faded in the distance. Then there was only the sound of the wind outside the window.

I'd been able to keep that stupid envelope with its message out of my head just by staying busy, but now it was all I could think about. I looked out the window. It was barely eight, but it was dark already. The real long days of summer were still to come.

So is Franklin out there? I asked myself. Is he watching the building, scoping things out, getting ready to make his move? Maybe dressed up in some black robe, him and a bunch of his pals?

I didn't really believe it. I didn't know him, but like Angel had said, it didn't seem like him and I could believe it. He might bug me, being all friendly and wanting to play Pygmalion to my Eliza Doolittle, but I didn't think he had a mean streak in him.

So where *did* the damn message come from? What was it supposed to mean? And, here was the scary part: if it wasn't a joke, and if Franklin wasn't responsible for it, then who was?

I kept turning that around and around in my mind until my head felt like it was spinning. Everybody started picking up on my mood. The dogs became all anxious and when I walked near them got to whining and shrinking away like I was going to hit them. Tommy got the shakes and his little people started tearing and then he was crying and the dogs started in howling and I just wanted to get the hell out of there.

But I didn't. It took me a couple of hours to calm Tommy down and finally get him to fall asleep. I told him the story he likes the best, the one where this count from some place far away shows up and tells us that we're really his kids and he takes us away, dogs and all, to our real home where we all live happily ever after. Sometimes I use his little cut-outs to tell the story, but I didn't do that tonight. I didn't want to remind him of how a bunch'd gotten torn.

By the time Tommy was sleeping, the dogs had calmed down again and were sleeping too. I couldn't. I sat up all night worrying about that damned message, about what would happen to Tommy and the dogs if anything ever did happen to me, about all kinds of crap that I usually don't let myself think about.

Come the morning, I felt like I'd crawled up out of a sewer. You know what it's like when you pull an all-nighter? Your eyes have this burning behind them, you'd kill for a shower and everything seems a little on edge? I saw about getting breakfast for everyone, let the dogs out for a run, then I told Tommy I had to go back downtown.

"You don't go out today," I told him. "You understand? You don't go out and you don't let anybody in. You and the dogs play inside today, okay? Can you do that for Maisie?"

"Sure," Tommy said, like I was the one with bricks for brains. "No problem, Maisie."

God I love him.

I gave him a big hug and a kiss, patted each of the dogs, then headed back down to Grasso Street with Rexy. I was about half a block from Angel's office when the headlines of a newspaper outside a drugstore caught my eye. I stopped dead in my tracks and just stared at it. The words swam in my sight, headlines blurring with the subheadings. I picked up the paper and unfolded it so that I could see the whole front page, then I started reading from the top.

```
grierson slain by satanists.
director of the city's new aids clinic found dead in ferryside graveyard
amid occult paraphernalia.
police baffled.
mayor says, 'this is an outrage.'
```

"Hey, this isn't a library, kid."

Rexy growled and I looked up to find the drugstore owner standing over me. I dug in my pocket until it coughed up a quarter, then handed it over to him. I took the paper over to the curb and sat down.

It was the picture that got to me. It looked like one of the buildings in the Tombs in which kids had been playing at ritual magic a few years ago. All the same kinds of candles and inverted pentacles and weird graffiti. Nobody squatted in that building anymore, though the kids hadn't been back for over a year. There was still something wrong about the place, like the miasma of whatever the hell it was that they'd been doing was still there, hanging on.

It was a place to give you the creeps. But this picture had something worse. It had a body, covered up by a blanket, right in the middle of it. The tombstones around it were all scorched and in pieces, like someone had set off a bomb. The police couldn't explain what had happened, except they did say it hadn't been a bomb, because no one nearby had heard a thing.

Pinpricks of dread went crawling up my spine as I reread the first paragraph. The victim, Grierson. Her first name was Margaret.

I folded the paper and got up, heading for the post office. Franklin was alone behind the counter when I got inside.

"The woman who died last night," I said before he had a chance to even say hello. "Margaret Grierson. The Director of the AIDS Clinic. Did she have a box here?"

Franklin nodded. "It's terrible, isn't it? One of my friends says the whole clinic's going to fall apart without her there to run it. God, I hope it doesn't change anything. I know a half-dozen people that are going to it."

I gave him a considering look. A half dozen friends? He had this real sad look in his eyes, like . . . Jesus, I thought. Was Franklin gay? Had he really been just making nice and not trying to jump my bones?

I reached across the counter and put my hand on his arm.

"They won't let this screw it up," I told him. "The clinic's too important."

The look of surprise in his face had me backing out the door fast. What the hell was I doing?

"Maisie!" he cried.

I guess I felt like a bit of a shit for having misjudged him, but all the same, I couldn't stick around. I followed my usual rule of thumb when things get heavy or weird: I fled.

I just started wandering aimlessly, thinking about what I'd learned. That message hadn't been for me, it had been for Grierson. Margaret, yeah, but Margaret *Grierson,* not Flood. Not me. Somehow it had gotten in the wrong box. I don't know who put it there, or how he knew what was going to happen last night before it happened, but whoever he was, he'd screwed up royally.

Better it had been me, I thought. Better a loser from the Tombs, than someone like Grierson who was really doing something worthwhile.

When I thought that, I realized something that I guess I'd always known, but I just didn't ever let myself think about. You get called a loser often enough and you start to believe it. I know I did. But it didn't have to be true.

I guess I had what they call an epiphany in some of the older books I've read. Everything came together and made sense—except for what I was doing with myself.

I unfolded the paper again. There was a picture of Grierson near the bottom—one of those shots they keep on file for important people and run whenever they haven't got anything else. It was cropped down from one that had been taken when she cut the ribbon at the new clinic a few months back. I remembered seeing it when they ran coverage of the ceremony.

"This isn't going to mean a whole lot to you," I told her picture, "but I'm sorry about what happened to you. Maybe it should've been me, but it wasn't. There's not much I can do about that. But I can do something about the rest of *my* life."

I left the paper on a bench near a bus stop and walked back to Grasso Street to Angel's office. I sat down in the chair across from her desk, holding Rexy on my lap to give me courage, and I told her about Tommy and the dogs, about how they needed me and that was why I'd never wanted to take her up on her offers to help.

She shook her head sadly when I was done. She was looking a little weepy again—like she had when I told her that story before—but I was feeling a little weepy myself this time.

"Why didn't you tell me?" she asked.

I shrugged. "I guess I thought you'd take them away from me."

I surprised myself. I hadn't lied, or made a joke. Instead I'd told her the truth. It wasn't much, but it was a start.

"Oh, Maisie," she said. "We can work something out."

She came around the desk and I let her hold me. It's funny. I didn't mean to cry, but I did. And so did she. It felt good, having someone else be strong for a change. I haven't had someone be there for me since my grandma died in 1971, the year I turned eight. I hung in for a long time, all things considered, but the day that Mr. Hammond asked me to come see him after school was the day I finally gave up my nice little regulated slot as a citizen of the day and became a part of the night world instead.

I knew it wasn't going to be easy, trying to fit into the day world—I'd probably never fit in completely, and I don't think I'd want to. I also knew that I was going to have a lot of crap to go through and to put up with in the days to come, and maybe I'd regret the decision I'd made today, but right now it felt good to be back.

Bridges

She watched the taillights dwindle until, far down the dirt road, the car went around a curve. The two red dots winked out and then she was alone.

Stones crunched underfoot as she shifted from one foot to another, looking around herself. Trees, mostly cedar and pine, crowded the narrow verge on either side. Above her, the sky held too many stars, but for all their number, they shed too little light. She was used to city streets and pavement, to neon and streetlights. Even in the 'burbs there was always some manmade light.

The darkness and silence, the loneliness of the night as it crouched in the trees, spooked her. It chipped at the veneer of her streetsmart toughness. She was twenty miles out of the city, up in the hills that backed onto the Kickaha Reserve. Attitude counted for nothing out here.

She didn't bother cursing Eddie. She conserved her breath for the long walk back to the city, just hoping she wouldn't run into some pickup truck full of redneck hillbillies who might not be quite as ready to just cut her loose as Eddie had when he realized he wasn't going to get his way. For too many men, no meant yes. And she'd heard stories about some of the good old boys who lived in these hills.

She didn't even hate Eddie, for all that he was eminently hateful. She saved that hatred for herself, for being so trusting when she knew—when she *knew*—how it always turned out.

"Stupid bloody cow," she muttered as she began to walk.

High school was where it had started.

She'd liked to party, she'd liked to have a good time, she hadn't seen anything wrong with making out because it was fun. Once you got a guy to slow down, sex was the best thing around.

She went with a lot of guys, but it took her a long time to realize just how many and that they only wanted one thing from her. She was slow on the uptake because she didn't see a problem until that night with Dave. Before that, she'd just seen herself as popular. She always had a date; someone was always ready to take her out and have some fun. The guy she'd gone out with on the weekend might ignore her the next Monday at school, but there was always someone else there, leaning up against her locker, asking her what was she doing tonight, so that she never really had time to think it through.

Never *wanted* to think it through, she'd realized in retrospect.

Until Dave wanted her to go to the drive-in that Saturday night.

"I'd rather go to the dance," she told him.

It was just a disco with a DJ, but she was in the mood for loud music and stepping out, not a movie. First Dave tried to convince her to go to the drive-in, then he said that if she wanted to go dancing, he knew some good clubs. She didn't know where the flash of insight came from—it just flared there inside her head, leaving a sick feeling in the pit of her stomach, a tightness in her chest.

"You don't want to be seen with me at the dance," she said.

"It's not that. It's just . . . well, all the guys . . ."

"Told you what? That I'm a cheap lay?"

"No, it's just, well . . ."

The knowing looks she got in the hall, the way guys would talk to her before they went out, but avoided her later—it all came together.

Jesus, how could she have been so stupid?

She got out of his car, which was still parked in front of her dad's house. Tears were burning the back of her eyes, but she refused to let them come. She never talked to Dave again. She swore that things were going to change.

It didn't matter that she didn't go out with another guy for her whole senior year; everyone still thought of her as the school tramp. Two months ago, she'd finally finished school. She didn't even wait to get her grades. With money she'd saved up through the years, she moved from her dad's place in the 'burbs to her own apartment in Lower Crowsea, got a job as a receptionist in an office on Yoors Street and was determined that things were going to be different. She had no history where she lived or where she worked; no one to snigger at her when she went down a hall.

It was a new start and it wasn't easy. She didn't have any friends, but then she hadn't really had any before either—she just hadn't had the time or good sense to realize that. But she was working on it now. She'd gotten to know Sandra who lived down the hall in her building, and they'd hung out together, watching videos or going to one of the bars in the Market—girls night out, men need not apply.

She liked having a girl for a friend. She hadn't had one since she lost her virginity just a few days before her fifteenth birthday and discovered that boys could make her feel really good in ways that a girl couldn't.

Besides Sandra, she was starting to get to know the people at work, too—which was where she met Eddie. He was the building's mail clerk, dropping off a bundle of mail on her desk every morning, hanging out for a couple of minutes, finally getting the courage up to ask her for a date. Her first one in a very long time.

He seemed like a nice guy, so she said yes. A friend of his was having a party at his cottage, not far from town. There'd be a bonfire on the beach, some people would be bringing their guitars and they'd sing old Buddy Holly and Beatles tunes. They'd barbecue hamburgers and hotdogs. It'd be fun.

Fifteen minutes ago, Eddie had pulled the car over to the side of the road. Killing the engine, he leaned back against the driver's door, gaze lingering on how her T-shirt molded to her chest. He gave her a goofy grin.

"Why are we stopping?" she'd asked, knowing it sounded dumb, knowing what was coming next.

"I was thinking," Eddie said. "We could have our private party."

"No thanks."

"Come on. Chuck said—"

"Chuck? Chuck who?"

"Anderson. He used to go to Mawson High with you."

A ghost from the past, rising to haunt her. She knew Chuck Anderson.

"He just moved into my building. We were talking and when I mentioned your name, he told me all about you. He said you liked to party."

"Well, he's full of shit. I think you'd better take me home."

"You don't have to play hard to get," Eddie said.

He started to reach for her, but her hand was quicker. It went into her purse and came out with a switchblade. She touched the release button and its blade came out of the handle with a wicked-sounding *snick*. Eddie moved back to his own side of the car.

"What the hell are you trying to prove?" he demanded.

"Just take me home."

"Screw you. Either you come across, or you walk."

She gave him a long hard stare, then nodded. "Then I walk."

The car's wheels spat gravel as soon as she was out, engine gunning as Eddie maneuvered a tight one-eighty. She closed up her knife and dropped it back into her purse as she watched the taillights recede.

Her legs were aching by the time she reached the covered bridge that crossed Stickers Creek just before it ran into the Kickaha River. She'd walked about three miles since Eddie had dumped her; only another seventeen to go.

Twice she'd hidden in the trees as a vehicle passed her. The first one had looked so innocent that she'd berated herself for not trying to thumb a ride. The second was a pickup with a couple of yahoos in it. One of them had tossed out a beer bottle that just missed hitting her—he hadn't known she was hiding in the cedars there and she was happy that it had stayed that way. Thankfully, she had let nervous caution overrule the desire to just get the hell out of here and home.

She sat down on this side of the bridge to rest. She couldn't see much of the quick-moving creek below her—just white tops that flashed in the starlight—but she could hear it. It was a soothing sound.

She thought about Eddie.

She should have been able to see it in him, shouldn't she? It wasn't as though she didn't know what to be looking out for.

And Chuck Anderson. Jesus.

What was the point in trying to make a new start when nobody gave you a break?

She sighed and rose to her feet. There was no sense in railing against it. The world wasn't fair, and that was that. But god it was lonely. How could you carry on, always by yourself? What was the *point*?

Her footsteps had a hollow ring as she walked across the covered bridge and she started to get spooked again. What if a car came, right *now*? There was nowhere to run to, nowhere to hide. Just the dusty insides of the covered bridge, its wood so old she was surprised it was still standing.

Halfway across she felt an odd dropping sensation in her stomach, like being in an elevator that was going down too quickly. Vertigo had her leaning against the wooden planks that sided the bridge. She knew a moment's panic—oh, Jesus, she was falling—but then the feeling went away and she could walk without feeling dizzy to the far end of the bridge.

She stepped outside and stopped dead in her tracks. Her earlier panic was mild in comparison to what she felt now as she stared ahead in disbelief.

Everything familiar was gone. Road, trees, hills—all gone. She wasn't in the same country anymore—wasn't in the country at all. A city like something out of an Escher painting lay spread out in front of her. Odd buildings, angles all awry, leaned against and pushed away from each other, all at the same time. Halfway up their lengths, there seemed to be a kind of vortal shift so that the top halves appeared to be reflections of the lower.

And then there were the bridges.

Everywhere she looked there were bridges. Bridges connecting the buildings, bridges connecting bridges, bridges that went nowhere, bridges that folded back on themselves so that you couldn't tell where they started or ended. Too many bridges to count.

She started to back up the way she'd come but got no further than two steps when a hand reached out of the shadows and pulled her forward. She flailed against her attacker who swung her about and then held her with her arms pinned against her body.

"Easy, easy," a male voice said in her ear.

It had a dry, dusty sound to it, like the kind you could imagine old books in a library's stacks have when they talk to each other late at night.

"Let me go, let me *GO!*" she cried.

Still holding her, her assailant walked her to the mouth of the covered bridge.

"Look," he said.

For a moment she was still too panicked to know what he was talking about. But then it registered. The bridge she'd walked across to get to this nightmare city no longer had a roadway. There was just empty space between its wooden walls now. If her captor hadn't grabbed her when he did, she would have fallen god knew how far.

She stopped struggling and he let her go. She moved gingerly away from the mouth of the covered bridge, then stopped again, not knowing where to go, what to do. Everywhere she looked there were weird tilting buildings and bridges.

It was impossible. None of this was happening, she decided. She'd fallen asleep on the other side of the bridge and was just dreaming all of this.

"Will you be all right?" her benefactor asked.

"I . . . I . . ."

She turned to look at him. The moonlight made him out to be a harmless-looking guy. He was dressed in faded jeans and an off-white flannel shirt, cowboy boots and a jean jacket. His hair was dark and short. It was hard to make out his features, except for his eyes. They seemed to take in the moonlight and then send it back out again, twice as bright.

Something about him calmed her—until she tried to speak.

"Whoareyou?" she asked. "WhatisthisplacehowdidIgethere?"

As soon as the first question came out, a hundred others came clamoring into her mind, each demanding to be voiced, to be answered. She shut her mouth after the first few burst out in a breathless spurt, realizing that they would just feed the panic that she was only barely keeping in check.

She took a deep breath, then tried again.

"Thank you," she said. "For saving me."

"You're welcome."

Again that dry, dusty voice. But the air itself was dry, she realized. She could almost feel the moisture leaving her skin.

"Who are you?" she asked.

"You can call me Jack."

"My name's Moira—Moira Jones."

Jack inclined his head in a slight nod. "Are you all right now, Moira Jones?" he asked.

"I think so."

"Good, well—"

"Wait!" she cried, realizing that he was about to leave her. "What is this place? Why did you bring me here?"

He shook his head. "I didn't," he said. "No one comes to the City of Bridges unless it's their fate to do so. In that sense, you brought yourself."

"But . . . ?"

"I know. It's all strange and different. You don't know where to turn, who to trust."

There was the faintest hint of mockery under the dry tones of his voice.

"Something like that," Moira said.

He seemed to consider her for the longest time.

"I don't know you," he said finally. "I don't know why you brought yourself here or where you come from. I don't know how, or even if, you'll ever find your way home again."

Bizarre though her situation was, oddly enough, Moira found herself adjusting to it far more quickly than she would have thought possible. It was almost like being in a dream where you just accept things as they come along, except she knew this wasn't a dream—just as she knew that she was getting the brush off.

"Listen," she said. "I appreciate your help a moment ago, but don't worry about me. I'll get by."

"What I do know, however," Jack went on as though she hadn't spoken, "is that this is a place for those who have no other place to go."

"What're you saying? That's it's some kind of a dead end place?"

The way her life was going, it sounded like it had been made for her.

"It's a forgotten place."

"Forgotten by who?"

"By the world in which it exists," Jack said.

"How can a place this weird be forgotten?" she asked.

Moira looked around at the bridges as she spoke. They were everywhere, of every size and shape and persuasion. One that looked like it belonged in a Japanese tea garden stood side by side with part of what had to be an interstate overpass, but somehow the latter didn't overshadow the former, although both their proportions were precise. She saw rope bridges, wooden bridges and old stone bridges like the Kelly Street Bridge that crossed the Kickaha River in that part of Newford called the Rosses.

She wondered if she'd ever see Newford again.

"The same way people forget their dreams," Jack replied. He touched her elbow, withdrawing his hand before she could take offense. "Come walk with me if you like. I've a previous appointment, but I can show you around a bit on the way."

Moira hesitated for a long moment, then fell into step beside him. They crossed a metal bridge, the heels of their boots ringing. Of course, she thought, they couldn't go anywhere without crossing a bridge. Bridges were the only kind of roads that existed in this place.

"Do you live here?" she asked.

Jack shook his head. "But I'm here a lot. I deal in possibilities and that's what bridges are in a way—not so much the ones that already exist to take you from one side of something to another, but the kind we build for ourselves."

"What are you talking about?"

"Say you want to be an artist—a painter, perhaps. The bridge you build between when you don't know which end of the brush to hold to when you're doing respected work can include studying under another artist, experimenting on your own, whatever. You build the bridge and it either takes you where you want it to, or it doesn't."

"And if it doesn't?"

His teeth flashed in the moonlight. "Then you build another one and maybe another one until one of them does."

Moira nodded as though she understood, all the while asking herself, what am I *doing* here?

"But this," he added, "is a place of failed dreams. Where bridges that go nowhere find their end."

Wonderful, Moira thought. A forgotten place. A dead end.

They started across an ornate bridge, its upper chords were all filigreed metal, its roadway cobblestone. Two thirds of the way across, what she took to be a pile of rags shifted and sat up. It was a beggar with a tattered cloak wrapped around him or her—Moira couldn't tell the sex of the poor creature. It seemed to press closer against the railing as they came abreast of it.

"Cancer victim," Jack said, as they passed the figure. "Nothing left to live for, so she came here."

Moira shivered. "Can't you—can't we do anything for her?"

"Nothing to be done for her," Jack replied.

The dusty tones of his voice made it impossible for her to decide if that was true, or if he just didn't care.

"But—"

"She wouldn't be here if there was," he said.

Wood underfoot now—a primitive bridge of rough timbers. The way Jack led her was a twisting path that seemed to take them back the way they'd come as much as forward. As they crossed an arched stone walkway, Moira heard a whimper. She paused and saw a child huddled up against a doorway below.

Jack stopped, waiting for her to catch up.

"There's a child," she began.

"You'll have to understand," Jack said, "that there's nothing you can do for anyone here. They've long since given up Hope. They belong to Despair now."

"Surely—"

"It's an abused child," Jack said. He glanced at his wrist watch. "I've time. Go help it."

"God, you're a cold fish."

Jack tapped his watch. "Time's slipping away."

Moira was trapped between just wanting to tell him to shove off and her fear of being stuck in this place by herself. Jack wasn't much, but at least he seemed to know his way around.

"I'll be right back," she said.

She hurried back down the arched path and crossed a rickety wooden bridge to the doorway of the building. The child looked up at her approach, his whimpers muting as he pushed his face against his shoulder.

"There, there," Moira said. "You're going to be okay."

She moved forward, pausing when the child leapt to his feet, back against the wall. He held his hands out before him, warding her away.

"No one's going to hurt you."

She took another step, and he started to scream.

"Don't cry!" she said, continuing to move forward. "I'm here to help you."

The child bolted before she could reach him. He slipped under her arm and was off and away, leaving a wailing cry in his wake. Moira stared after him.

"You'll never catch him now," Jack called down from above.

She looked up at him. He was sitting on the edge of the arched walkway, legs dangling, heels tapping against the stonework.

"I wasn't going to hurt him," she said.

"He doesn't know that. I told you, the people here have long since given up hope. You can't help them—nobody can. They can't even help themselves anymore."

"What are they doing here?"

Jack shrugged. "They've got to go somewhere, don't they?"

Moira made her way back to where he was waiting for her, anger clouding her features.

"Don't you even *care*?" she demanded.

His only reply was to start walking again. She hesitated for a long moment, then hurried to catch up. She walked with her arms wrapped around herself, but the chill she felt came from inside and it wouldn't go away.

They crossed bridges beyond her ability to count as they made their way into the central part of the city. From time to time they passed the odd streetlight, its dim glow making a feeble attempt to push back the shadows; in other places, the ghosts of flickering neon signs crackled and hissed more than they gave off light. In some ways the lighting made things worse for it revealed the city's general state of decay—cracked walls, rubbled streets, refuse wherever one turned.

Under one lamp post, she got a better look at her companion. His features were strong rather than handsome; none of the callousness she sensed in his voice was reflected in them. He caught her gaze and gave her a thin smile, but the humor in his eyes was more mocking than companionable.

They continued to pass by dejected and lost figures that hunched in the shadows, huddled against buildings, or bolted at their approach. Jack listed their despairs for her—AIDS victim, rape victim, abused wife, paraplegic—until Moira begged him to stop.

"I can't take anymore," she said.

"I'm sorry. I thought you wanted to know."

They went the rest of the way in silence, the bridges taking them higher and higher until they finally stood on the top of an enormous building that appeared to be the largest and most centrally placed of the city's structures. From its heights, the city was spread out around them on all sides.

It made for an eerie sight. Moira stepped back from the edge of the roof, away from the pull of vertigo that came creeping up the small of her back to whisper in her ear. She had only to step out, into the night sky, it told her. Step out and all her troubles would be forever eased.

At the sound of a footstep, she turned gratefully away from the disturbing view. A woman was walking towards them, pausing when she was a few paces away. Unlike the other inhabitants of the city, she gave the impression of being self-assured, of being in control of her destiny.

She had pale skin, and short spiky red hair. A half dozen silver earrings hung from one ear; the other had a small silver stud in the shape of a star. Like Jack, she was dressed casually: black jeans, black boots, white tank-top, a black leather jacket draped over one shoulder. And like Jack, her eyes, too, seemed like a reservoir for the moonlight.

"You're not alone," she said to Jack.

"I never am," Jack replied. "You know that. My sister, Diane," he added to Moira, then introduced her to Diane.

The woman remained silent, studying Moira with her moon-bright eyes until Moira couldn't help but fidget. The dreamlike quality of her situation was beginning to filter away. Once again a panicked feeling was making itself felt in the pit of her stomach.

"Why are you here?" Diane asked her finally.

Her voice had a different quality from her brother's. It was a warm, rounded sound that carried in it a sweet scent like that of cherry blossoms or rose buds. It took away Moira's panic, returning her once more to that sense of it all just being a dream.

"I . . . I don't know," she said. "I was just crossing a bridge on my way home and the next thing I knew I was . . . here. Wherever here is. I—look. I just want to go home. I don't want any of this to be real."

"It's very real," Diane said.

"Wonderful."

"She wants to help the unhappy," Jack offered, "but they just run away from her."

Moira shot him a dirty look.

"Do be still," Diane told him, frowning as she spoke. She returned her attention to Moira. "Why don't you go home?"

"I—I don't know *how* to. The bridge that brought me here . . . when I went to go back across it, its roadway was gone."

Diane nodded. "What has my brother told you?"

Nothing that made sense, Moira wanted to say, but she related what she remembered of her conversations with Jack.

"And do you despair?" Diane asked.

"I . . ."

Moira hesitated. She thought of the hopeless, dejected people she'd passed on the way to this rooftop.

"Not really, I guess. I mean, I'm not happy or anything, but . . ."

"You have hope? That things will get better for you?"

A flicker of faces passed through her mind. Ghosts from the distant and recent past. Boys from high school. Eddie. She heard Eddie's voice.

Either you come across, or you walk. . . .

She just wanted a normal life. She wanted to find something to enjoy in it. She wanted to find somebody she could have a good relationship with, she wanted to enjoy making love with him without worrying about people thinking she was a tramp. She wanted him to be there the next morning. She wanted there to be more to what they had than just a roll in the hay.

Right now, none of that seemed very possible.

"I don't know," she said finally. "I want it to. I'm not going to give up, but . . ."

Again, faces paraded before her—this time they belonged to those lost souls of the city. The despairing.

"I know there are people a lot worse off than I am," she said. "I'm not sick, I've got the use of my body and my mind. But I'm missing something, too. I don't know how it is for other people—maybe they feel the same and just handle it better—but I feel like there's a hole inside me that I just can't fill. I get so lonely . . ."

"You see," Jack said then. "She's mine."

Moira turned to him. "What are you talking about?"

It was Diane who answered. "He's laying claim to your unhappiness," she said.

Moira looked from one to the other. There was something going on here, some undercurrent, that she wasn't picking up on.

"What are you *talking* about?" she asked.

"This city is ours," Diane said. "My brother's and mine. We are two sides to the same coin. In most people, that coin lies with my face up, for you are an optimistic race. But optimism only carries some so far. When my brother's face lies looking skyward, all hope is gone."

Moira centered on the words, "you are an optimistic race," realizing from the way Diane spoke it was as though she and her brother weren't human. She looked away, across the cityscape of bridges and tilting buildings. It was a dreamscape—not exactly a nightmare, but not at all pleasant either. And she was trapped in it; trapped in a dream.

"Who are you people?" she asked. "I don't buy this 'Jack and Diane' bit—that's like out of that John Mellencamp song. Who are you *really?* What is this place?"

"I've already told you," Jack said.

"But you only gave her half the answer," Diane added. She turned to Moira. "We are Hope and Despair," she said. She touched a hand to her breast. "Because of your need for us, we are no longer mere allegory, but have shape and form. This is our city."

Moira shook her head. "Despair I can understand—this place reeks of it. But not Hope."

"Hope is what allows the strong to rise above their despair," Diane said. "It's what makes them strong. Not blind faith, not the certain knowledge that someone will step in and help them, but the understanding that through their own force of will they cannot merely survive, but succeed. Hope is what tempers that will and gives it the strength to carry on, no matter what the odds are ranked against them."

"Don't forget to tell her how too much hope will turn her into a lazy cow," her brother said.

Diane sighed, but didn't ignore him. "It's true," she said. "Too much hope can also be harmful. Remember this: Neither hope nor despair have power of their own; they can only provide the fuel that you will use to prevail or be defeated."

"Pop psychology," Moira muttered.

Diane smiled. "Yet, like old wives' tales, it has within it a kernel of truth, or why would it linger?"

"So what am I doing here?" Moira asked. "I never gave up. I'm still trying."

Diane looked at her brother. He shrugged his shoulders.

"I admit defeat," he said. "She is yours."

Diane shook her head. "No. She is her own. Let her go."

Jack turned to Moira, the look of a petulant child marring his strong features before they started to become hazy.

"You'll be back," he said. That dry voice was like a desert wind, its fine sand filling her heart with an aching forlornness. "Hope is sweet, I'll admit that readily, but once Despair has touched you, you can never be wholly free of its influence."

A hot flush ran through Moira. She reeled, dizzy, vision blurring, only half hearing what was being said. Her head was thick with a heavy buzz of pain.

But Hope is stronger.

Moira wasn't sure if she'd actually heard that, the sweet scent of blossoms clearing her heart of Despair's dust, or if it came from within herself—something she wanted—*had* to believe. But it overrode Despair's dry voice. She no longer fought the vertigo, but just let it take her away.

Moira was suddenly aware that she was on her hands and knees, with dirty wood under her. Where . . . ?

Then she remembered: Walking across the covered bridge. The city. Hope and Despair.

She sat back on her haunches and looked around herself. She was back in her own world. Back—if she'd ever even gone anywhere in the first place.

A sudden roaring filled her head. Lights blinded her as a car came rushing up on the far side of the bridge. She remembered Eddie, her fear of some redneck hillbillies, but there was nowhere to run to. The car screeched to a halt on the wood, a door opened. A man stepped out onto the roadway of the bridge and came towards her.

Backlit by the car's headbeams, he seemed huge—a monstrous shape. She wanted to bolt. She wanted to scream. She couldn't seem to move, not even enough to reach into her purse for her switchblade.

"Jesus!" the stranger said. "Are you okay?"

He was bent down beside her now, features pulled tight with concern.

She nodded slowly. "I just . . . felt dizzy, I guess."

"Here. Let me help you up."

She allowed him to do that. She let him walk her to his car. He opened up the passenger's door and she sank gratefully onto the seat. The man looked down to the end of the bridge by which she'd entered it what seemed like a lifetime ago.

"Did you have some car trouble?" the man asked.

"You could say that," she said. "The guy I was with dumped me from his car a few miles back."

"Are you hurt?"

She shook her head. "Just my feelings."

"Jesus. What a crappy thing to do."

"Yeah. Thanks for stopping."

"No problem. Can I give you a lift somewhere?"

Moira shook her head. "I'm going back to Newford. I think that's a little far out of your way."

"Well, I'm not just going to leave you here by yourself."

Before she could protest, he closed the door and went back around to the driver's side.

"Don't worry," he said as he got behind the wheel. "After what you've been through, a guy'd have to be a real heel to—well, you know."

Moira had to smile. He actually seemed embarrassed.

"We'll just drive to the other side of the bridge and turn around and then—"

Moira touched his arm. She remembered what had happened the last time she'd tried to go through this bridge.

"Do me a favor, would you?" she asked. "Could you just back out instead?"

Her benefactor gave her a funny look, then shrugged. Putting the car into reverse, he started backing up. Moira held her breath until they were back out on the road again. There were pines and cedars pushing up against the verge, stars overhead. No weird city. No bridges.

She let out her breath.

"What's your name?" she asked as he maneuvered the car back and forth on the narrow road until he had its nose pointed towards Newford.

"John—John Fraser."

"My name's Moira."

"My grandmother's name was Moira," John said.

"Really?"

He nodded.

He seemed like a nice guy, Moira thought. Not the kind who'd try to pull anything funny.

The sweet scent of blossoms came to her for just a moment, then it was gone.

John's showing up so fortuitously as he had—that had to be Hope's doing, she decided. Maybe it was a freebie of good luck to make up for her brother's bad manners. Or maybe it was true: if you had a positive attitude, you had a better chance that things would work out.

"Thanks," she said. She wasn't sure if Hope could hear her, but she wanted to say it all the same.

"You're welcome," John said from beside her.

Moira glanced at him, then smiled.

"Yeah," she said. "You, too."

His puzzled look made her smile widen.

"What's so funny?" he asked.

She just shrugged and settled back into her seat. "It's a long weird story and you wouldn't believe me anyway."

"Try me."

"Maybe some other time," she said.

"I might just hold you to that," he said.

Moira surprised herself with the hope that maybe he would.

Our Lady of the Harbour

People don't behave the way they should; they behave the way they do.
—Jim Beaubien and Karen Caesar

She sat on her rock, looking out over the lake, her back to the city that reared up behind her in a bewildering array of towers and lights. A half mile of water separated her island from Newford, but on a night such as this, with the moon high and the water still as glass, the city might as well have been on the other side of the planet.

Tonight, an essence of *Marchen* prevailed in the darkened groves and on the moon-lit lawns of the island.

For uncounted years before Diederick van Yoors first settled the area in the early part of the nineteenth century, the native Kickaha called the island Myeengun. By the turn of the century, it had become the playground of Newford's wealthy, its bright facade first beginning to lose its luster with the Great Depression when wealthy land-owners could no longer keep up their summer homes; by the end of the Second World War it was an eyesore. It wasn't turned into a park until the late 1950s. Today most people knew it only by the anglicized translation of its Kickaha name: Wolf Island.

Matt Casey always thought of it as *her* island.

The cast bronze statue he regarded had originally stood in the garden of an ex-patriate Danish businessman's summer home, a faithful reproduction of the well-known figure that haunted the waterfront of the Dane's native Copenhagen. When the city expropriated the man's land for the park, he was generous enough to donate the statue, and so she sat now on the island, as she had for fifty years, looking out over the lake, motionless, always looking, the moonlight gleaming on her bronze features and slender form.

The sharp blast of a warning horn signaling the last ferry back to the city cut through the night's contemplative mood. Matt turned to look to the far side of the island where the ferry was docked. As he watched, the lights on the park's winding paths winked out, followed by those in the island's restaurant and the other buildings near the dock. The horn gave one last blast. Five minutes later, the ferry lurched away from the dock and began the final journey of the day back to Newford's harbour.

Now, except for a pair of security guards who, Matt knew, would spend the night watching TV and sleeping in the park's offices above the souvenir store, he had the island to himself. He turned back to look at the statue. It was still silent, still motionless, still watching the unfathomable waters of the lake.

He'd been here one afternoon and watched a bag lady feeding gulls with bits of bread that she probably should have kept for herself. The gulls here were all overfed. When the bread was all gone, she'd walked up to the statue.

"Our Lady of the Harbour," she'd said. "Bless me."

Then she'd made the sign of the cross, as though she was a Catholic stepping forward into the nave of her church. From one of her bulging shopping bags, she took out a small plastic flower and laid it on the stone by the statue's feet, then turned and walked away.

The flower was long gone, plucked by one of the cleaning crews no doubt, but the memory remained.

Matt moved closer to the statue, so close that he could have laid his palm against the cool metal of her flesh.

"Lady," he began, but he couldn't go on.

Matt Casey wasn't an easy man to like. He lived for one thing, and that was his music. About the only social intercourse he had was with the members of the various bands he had played in over the years, and even that was spotty. Nobody he ever played with seemed willing to just concentrate on the music; they always wanted to hang out together as though they were all friends, as though they were in some kind of social club.

Music took the place of people in his life. It was his friend and his lover, his confidant and his voice, his gossip and his comfort.

It was almost always so.

From his earliest years he suffered from an acute sense of xenophobia: everyone was a stranger to him. All were foreigners to the observer captured in the flesh, blood and bone of his body. It was not something he understood, in the sense that one might be aware of a problem one had; it was just the way he was. He could trust no one—perhaps because he had never learned to trust himself.

His fellow musicians thought of him as cold, aloof, cynical—descriptions that were completely at odds with the sensitivity of his singing and the warmth that lay at the heart of his music. The men he played with sometimes thought that all he needed was a friend, but his rebuffs to even the most casual overtures of friendship always cured such notions. The women he played with sometimes thought that all he needed was a lover, but though he slept with a few, the distance he maintained eventually cooled the ardor of even the most persistent.

Always, in the end, there was only the music. To all else, he was an outsider.

He grew up in the suburbs north of the city's center, part of a caring family. He had an older brother and two younger sisters, each of them outgoing and popular in their own way. Standing out in such contrast to them, even at an early age, his parents had sent him to a seemingly endless series of child specialists and psychologists, but no one could get through except for his music teachers—first in the school orchestra, then the private tutors that his parents were only too happy to provide for him.

They saw a future in music for him, but not the one he chose. They saw him studying music at a university, taken under the wing of some master whenever he finally settled on a chosen instrument, eventually playing concert halls, touring the world with famous orchestras. Instead he left home at sixteen. He turned his back on formal studies, but not on learning, and played in the streets. He traveled all over North America, then to Europe and the Middle East, finally returning home to busk on Newford's streets and play in her clubs.

Still the outsider; more so, perhaps, rather than less.

It wasn't that he was unfriendly; he simply remained uninvolved, animated only in the presence of other musicians and then only to discuss the esoterics of obscure lyrics and tunes and instruments, or to play. He never thought of himself as lonely, just as alone; never considered himself to be a social misfit or an outcast from the company of his fellow men, just an observer of the social dance to which most men and women knew the steps rather than one who would join them on the dance floor.

An outsider.

A gifted genius, undoubtedly, as any who heard him play would affirm, but an outsider all the same.

It was almost always so.

In the late seventies, the current band was Marrowbones and they had a weekend gig at a folk club in Lower Crowsea called Feeney's Kitchen—a popular hangout for those Butler University students who shunned disco and punk as well as the New Wave. The line-up was Matt on his usual bouzouki and guitar and handling the vocals, Nicky Doyle on fiddle, Johnny Ryan on tenor banjo, doubling on his classic Gibson mando-cello for song accompaniments, and Matt's long-time musical associate Amy Scallan on Uillean pipes and whistles.

They'd been playing together for a year and a half now and the band had developed a big, tight sound that had recently brought in offers for them to tour the college and festival circuits right across the country.

But it'd never happen, Amy thought as she buckled on her pipes in preparation for the selection of reels with which they were going to end the first set of the evening.

The same thing was going to happen that always happened. It was already starting. She'd had to listen to Nicky and Johnny going on about Matt earlier this afternoon when the three of them had gotten together to jam with a couple of other friends at The Harp. They couldn't deal with the dichotomy of Matt offstage and on. Fronting the band, Matt projected the charming image of a friendly and outgoing man that you couldn't help but want to get to know; offstage, he was taciturn and withdrawn, un-interested in anything that didn't deal with the music.

But that was Matt, she'd tried to explain. You couldn't find a better singer or musician to play with and he had a knack for giving even the simplest piece a knockout arrangement. Nobody said you had to like him.

But Nicky had only shaken his head, brown curls bobbing. "Your man's taking all the *craic* from playing in a band."

Johnny nodded in agreement. "It's just not fun anymore. He'll barely pass the time of day with you, but on stage he's all bloody smiles and jokes. I don't know how you put up with him."

Amy hadn't been able to come up with an explanation then and looking across the stage now to where Matt was raising his eyebrows to ask if she was ready, then winking when she nodded back that she was, she couldn't explain it any better. She'd just learned over the years that what they shared was the music—and the music was very good; if she wanted more, she had to look for it elsewhere.

She'd come to terms with it where most people wouldn't, or couldn't, but then there was very little in the world that ever fazed her.

Matt started a G-drone on his bouzouki. He leaned close to the mike, just a touch of a welcoming smile tugging the corner of his mouth as a handful of dancers, anticipating what was to come, stepped onto the tiny wooden dance floor in front of the stage. Amy gave him a handful of bars to lock in the tempo, then launched into the first high popping notes of "The Road West," the opening salvo in this set of reels.

She and Matt played the tune through twice on their own and room on the dance floor grew to such a premium that the dancers could do little more than jig in one spot. Their elbows and knees could barely jostle against one another.

It wasn't quite a sea of bobbing heads, Amy thought, looking down from the stage. More like a small lake, or even a puddle.

The analogy made her smile. She kicked in her pipe drones as the fiddle and tenor banjo joined in on "The Glen Allen." It was halfway through that second tune that she became aware of the young woman dancing directly in front of Matt's microphone.

She was small and slender, with hair that seemed to be made of spun gold and eyes such a deep blue that they glittered like sapphires in the light spilling from the stage. Her features reminded Amy of a fox—pointed and tight like a Rackham sprite, but no less attractive for all that.

The other dancers gave way like reeds before a wind, drawing back to allow her the room to swirl the skirt of her unbelted flowered dress, her tiny feet scissoring intricate steps in their black Chinese slippers. Her movements were at once sensual and innocent. Amy's first impression was that the young woman was a professional dancer, but as she watched more closely, she realized that the girl's fluidity and grace were more an inherent talent than a studied skill.

The dancer's gaze caught and held on Matt, no matter how her steps turned her about, her attention fixed and steady as though he had bewitched her, while Matt, to Amy's surprise, seemed just as entranced. When they kicked into "Sheehan's Reel," the third and final tune of the set, she almost thought Matt was going to leave the stage to dance with the girl.

"Again!" Matt cried out as they neared the usual end of the tune.

Amy didn't mind. She pumped the bellows of her pipes, long fingers dancing on the chanter, more than happy to play the piece all night if the dancer could keep up. But the tune unwound to its end, they ended with a flourish, and suddenly it was all over. The dance floor cleared, the girl was swallowed by the crowd.

When the applause died down, an odd sort of hush fell over the club. Amy unbuckled her pipes and looked over to see that Matt had already left the stage. She hadn't even seen him go. She tugged her chanter mike up to mouth level.

"We're, uh, going to take a short break, folks," she said into the mike. Her voice seemed to boom in the quiet. "Then," she added, "we'll be right back with some more music, so don't go away."

The patter bookending the tunes and songs was Matt's usual job. Since Amy didn't feel she had his natural stage charm, she just kept it simple.

There was an another smatter of applause that she acknowledged with a smile. The house system came on, playing a Jackson Browne tune, and she turned to Nicky, who was putting his fiddle in its case.

"Where'd Matt go?" she asked.

He gave her a "who cares?" shrug. "Probably chasing that bird who was shaking her tush at him all through the last piece."

"I don't envy her," Johnny added.

Amy knew exactly what he meant. Over the past few months they'd all seen the fallout of casualties who gathered like moths around the bright flame of Matt's stage presence only to have their wings burnt with his indifference. He'd charm them in a club, sometimes sleep with them, but in the end, the only lover he kept was the music.

Amy knew all too well. There was a time . . .

She pushed the past away with a shake of her head. Putting a hand above her eyes to shade them from the lights, she scanned the crowd as the other two went to get themselves a beer but she couldn't spot either Matt or the girl. Her gaze settled on a black-haired Chinese woman sitting alone at at small table near the door and she smiled as the woman raised her hand in a wave. She'd forgotten that Lucia had arrived halfway through their first set—fashionably late, as always—and now that she thought about it, hadn't she seen the dancer come in about the same time? They might even have come in together.

Lucia Han was a performance artist based in Upper Foxville and an old friend of Amy's. When they'd first met, Amy had been told by too many people to be careful because Lucia was gay and would probably make a pass at her. Amy just ignored them. She had nothing against gays to begin with and she soon learned that the gossips' reasoning for their false assumption was just that Lucia only liked to work with other women. But as Lucia had explained to Amy once, "There's just not enough women involved in the arts and I want to support those who do make the plunge—at least if they're any good."

Amy understood perfectly. She often wished there were more women players in traditional music. She was sick to death of going to a music session where she wasn't known. All too often she'd be the only woman in a gathering of men and have to play rings around them on her pipes just to prove that she was as good as them. Irish men weren't exactly noted for their liberated standards.

Which didn't mean that either she or Lucia weren't fond of the right sort of man. *"Au contraire,"* as Lucia would say in the phony Parisian accent she liked to affect, "I am liking them too much."

Amy made her way to the bar, where she ordered a beer on her tab, then took the brimming draught glass through the crowd to Lucia's table, trying to slosh as little of the foam as she could on her new jeans.

"Bet you thought I wouldn't come," Lucia said as Amy sat down with her stein relatively full. The only spillage had joined the stickiness of other people's spills that lay underfoot.

Lucia was older than Amy by at least six or seven years, putting her in her mid-thirties. She had her hair in a wild spiky do tonight—to match the torn white T-shirt and leather jeans, no doubt. The punk movement had barely begun to trickle across the Atlantic as yet, but it was obvious that Lucia was already an eager proponent. A strand of safety pins dangled from one earlobe; others held the tears of her T-shirt closed in strategic places.

"I don't even remember telling you about the gig," Amy said.

Lucia waved a negligent hand towards the small poster on the wall behind her that advertised the band's appearance at Feeney's Kitchen this weekend.

"But you are famous now, *ma cherie*," she said. "How could I *not* know?" She dropped the accent to add, "You guys sound great."

"Thanks."

Amy looked at the tabletop. She set her stein down beside a glass of white wine, Lucia's cigarettes and matches and a half-filled ashtray. There was also an empty teacup with a small bright steel teapot on one side of it and a used tea bag on the lip of its saucer.

"Did you come alone?" she asked.

Lucia shook her head. "I brought a foundling—fresh from who really knows where. You probably noticed her and Matt making goo-goo eyes at each other all through the last piece you did." She brought a hand to her lips as soon as she'd made the last comment. "Sorry. I forgot about the thing you used to have going with him."

"Old history," Amy said. "I've long since dealt with it. I don't know that Matt ever even knew anything existed between us, but I'm cool now."

"It's for the better."

"Definitely," Amy agreed.

"I should probably warn my little friend about him," Lucia said, "but you know what they're like at that age—it'd just egg her on."

"Who *is* your little friend? She moves like all she was born to do was dance."

"She's something, isn't she? I met her on Wolf Island about a week ago, just before the last ferry—all wet and bedraggled like she'd fallen off a boat and been washed to shore. She wasn't wearing a stitch of clothing and I thought the worst, you know? Some asshole brought her out for a quick wham, bam, and then just dumped her."

Lucia paused to light a cigarette.

"And?" Amy asked.

Lucia shrugged, blowing out a wreath of blue-grey smoke. "Seems she fell off a boat and took off her clothes so that they wouldn't drag her down while she swam to shore. Course, I got that from her later."

Just then the door to the club opened behind Lucia and a gust of cool air caught the smoke from Lucia's cigarette, giving it a slow dervishing whirl. On the heels of the wind, Amy saw Matt and the girl walk in. The seemed to be in the middle of an animated discussion—or at least Matt was, so they had to be talking about music.

Amy felt the same slight twinge of jealousy watching him with the dancer as she did in the first few moments of every one of the short relationships that came about from some girl basically flinging herself at him halfway through a gig. Though perhaps "relationship" was too strong a word, since any sense of responsibility to a partner was inevitably one-sided.

The girl laughed at what he was saying—but it was a silent laugh. Her mouth was open, her eyes sparkled with a humored appreciation, but there was no sound. She began to move her hands in an intricate pattern that, Amy realized, was the American Sign Language used by deaf-mutes.

"Her problem right then," Lucia was saying, "was finding something to wear so that she could get into town. Luckily I was wearing my duster—you know, from when I was into my Sergio Leone phase—so she could cover herself up."

"She took off everything while she was in the water?" Amy asked, her gaze returning to her friend. "Even her underwear?"

"I guess. Unless she wasn't wearing any in the first place."

"Weird."

"I don't see you wearing a bra."

"You know what I meant," Amy said with a laugh.

Lucia nodded. "So anyway, she came on the ferry with me—I paid her fare—and then I brought her back to my place because it turned out she didn't have anywhere else to go. Doesn't know a soul in town. To be honest, I wasn't even sure she spoke English at first."

Amy looked over Lucia's shoulder to where Matt was answering whatever it was that the girl's hands had told him. Where had he learned sign language? she wondered. He'd never said anything about it before, but then she realized that for all the years she'd known him, she really didn't *know* much about him at all except that he was a brilliant musician and good in bed, related actions, perhaps, since she didn't doubt that they both were something he'd regard as a performance.

Meow, she thought.

"She's deaf-mute, isn't she?" she added aloud.

Lucia looked surprised. "Mute, but not deaf. How you'd know?"

"I'm watching her talk to Matt with her hands right now."

"She couldn't even do that when I first met her," Lucia said.

Amy returned her attention to Lucia once more. "What do you mean?"

"Well, I know sign language—I learned it when I worked at the Institute for the Deaf up on Gracie Street when I first got out of college—so when I realized she was mute, it was the first thing I tried. But she's not deaf—she just can't talk. She didn't even try to communicate at first. I thought she was in shock. She just sat beside me, looking out over the water, her eyes getting bigger and bigger as we approached the docks.

"When we caught a bus back to my place, it was like she'd never been in a city before. She just sat beside me all wide-eyed and then took my hand—not like she was scared, it was more like she just wanted to share the wonder of it all with me. It wasn't until we got back to my place that she asked for pen and paper." Lucia mimed the action as she spoke.

"It's all kind of mysterious, isn't it?" Amy said.

"I'll say. Anyway, her name's Katrina Ludvigsen and she's from one of those little towns on the Islands further down the lake—the ones just past the mouth of the Dulfer River, you know?"

Amy nodded.

"Her family came over from Norway originally," Lucia went on. "They were Lapps—as in Lapland—except she doesn't like to be called that. Her people call themselves Sami."

"I've heard about that," Amy said. "Referring to them as Lapps is a kind of insult."

"Exactly." Lucia took a final drag from her cigarette and butted it out in the ashtray. "Once she introduced herself, she asked me to teach her sign language. Would you believe she picked it up in *two* days?"

"I don't know," Amy said. "Is that fast?"

"Try *fantastique, ma cherie*."

"So what's she doing here?"

Lucia shrugged. "She told me she was looking for a man—like, aren't we all, ha ha—only she didn't know his name, just that he lived in Newford. She just about had a fit when she spotted the picture of Matt in the poster for this gig."

"So she knows him from before."

"You tell me," Lucia said.

Amy shook her head. "Only Matt knows whatever it is that Matt knows."

"Katrina says she's twenty-two," Lucia went on, "but if you ask me, I think she's a lot younger. I'll bet she ran away from home—maybe even stowed away on some tourist's powerboat and jumped ship just outside the harbour because they were about to catch her and maybe take her back home."

"So what are you going to do about it?"

"Not a damn thing. She's a nice kid and besides," she added as Katrina and Matt walked by their table, heading for the bar, "I've got the feeling she's not even going to be my responsibility for much longer."

"Don't count on it," Amy said. "She'll be lucky if she lasts the night."

Although maybe not. Katrina *was* pretty, and she certainly could dance, so there was the musical connection, just as there had been with her.

Amy sighed. She didn't know why she got to feeling the way she did at times like this. She wouldn't even *want* to make a go at it with Matt again.

Lucia reached across the table and put her hand on Amy's, giving it a squeeze. "How're you handling this, Amy? I remember you were pretty messed up about him at one point."

"I can deal with it."

"Well—what's that line of yours? More power to your elbow then if you can, though I still can't figure out how you got past it enough to still be able to play with him."

Amy looked over to the bar where Matt was getting the girl a cup of tea. She wished the twinge of not so much jealousy, as hurt, would go away.

Patience, she told herself. She'd seen Matt with who knew how many women over the years, all of them crazy over him. The twinge only lasted for a little while—a reminder of a bad time, not the bad time itself. She was past that now.

Well, mostly.

"You just change your way of thinking about a person," she said after a few moments, trying to convince herself as much as Lucia. "You change what you need from them, your expectations. That's all."

"You make it sound easy."

Amy turned back to her friend. "It's not," she said in a quiet voice.

Lucia gave her hand a squeeze.

* * *

The girl was drunk on Matt, Amy realized. There was no other explanation for the way she was carrying on.

For the rest of the night, Amy could see Katrina sitting with Lucia at the back of the club, chin cupped in her hands as she listened to Matt sing. No, not just listening. She drank in the songs, swallowed them whole. And with every dance set they played, she was up on her feet at the front of the stage, the sinuous grace of her movement, the swirl and the lift and the rapid fire steps of her small feet capturing each tune to perfection.

Matt was obviously complimented by her attention—or at least whatever it was that he'd feel that would be close to flattered—and why not? Next to Lucia, she was the best looking woman in the club, and Lucia wasn't exactly sending out "available" signals, not dressed the way she was.

Matt and the girl talked between each set, filling up the twenty minutes or so of canned music and patron conversation with a forest of words, his spoken, hers signed, each of them oblivious to their surroundings, to everything except for each other.

Maybe Katrina will be the one, Amy thought.

Once she got past her own feelings, that was what she usually found herself hoping. Although Matt could be insensitive once he stepped off the stage, she still believed that all he really needed was someone to care about to turn him around. Nobody who put such heart into his music, could be completely empty inside. She was sure that he just needed someone—the right someone. It hadn't been her, fine. But somewhere there had to be a woman for him—a catalyst to take down the walls through which only his music dared forth to touch the world.

The way he'd been so attentive towards Katrina all night, Amy was sure he was going to take her home with him, but all he did was ask her out tomorrow.

Okay, she thought standing beside Lucia while Matt and Katrina "talked." That's a start and maybe a good one.

Katrina's hands moved in response to Matt's question.

"What's she saying?" Amy asked, leaning close to whisper to Lucia.

"Yes," Lucia translated. "Now she's asking him if they can ride the ferry."

"The one to Wolf Island?" Amy said. "That's where you found her."

"Whisht," Lucia told her.

"We'll do whatever you want," Matt was saying.

And then Katrina was gone, trailing after Lucia with a last lingering wave before the world outside the club swallowed her and the door closed behind the pair of them.

Matt and Amy returned to the stage to pack up their instruments.

"I was thinking of heading up to The Harp to see if there's a session on," Matt said. He looked around at the other three. "Anyone feel like coming?"

If there were enough musicians up for the music, Joe Breen, the proprietor of The Harp, would lock the doors to the public after closing hours and just let the music flow until the last musician packed it in, acting no different on this side of the Atlantic than he had with the pub he'd run back home in Ireland.

Johnny shook his head. "I'm beat. It's straight to bed for me tonight."

"It's been a long night," Nicky agreed.

Nicky looked a little sullen, but Amy doubted that Matt even noticed. He just shrugged, then looked to her.

Well, and why not? she thought.

"I'll give it a go," she told him.

Saying their goodbyes to the other two outside the club, she and Matt walked north to the Rosses where The Harp stood in the shadow of the Kelly Street Bridge.

"Katrina seemed nice," Amy said after a few blocks.

"I suppose," he said. "A little intense, maybe."

"I think she's a little taken with you."

Matt nodded unself-consciously. "Maybe too much. But she sure can dance, can't she?"

"Like an angel," Amy agreed.

Conversation fell flat then, just as it always did.

"I got a new tune from Geordie this afternoon," Amy said finally. "He doesn't remember where he picked it up, but it fits onto the end of 'The Kilavel Jig' like it was born to it."

Matt's eyes brightened with interest. "What's it called?"

"He didn't know. It had some Gaelic title that he'd forgotten, but it's a lovely piece. In G-major, but the first part has a kind of a modal flavor so that it almost feels as though it's being played out of C. It'd be just lovely on the bouzouki."

The talk stayed on tunes the rest of the way to The Harp—safe ground. At one point Amy found herself remembering a gig they'd played a few months ago and the story that Matt had used to introduce a song called "Sure, All He Did Was Go" that they'd played that night.

"He couldn't help himself," Matt had said, speaking of the fiddler in the song who gave up everything he had to follow a tune. "Music can be a severe mistress, demanding and jealous, and don't you doubt it. Do her bidding and isn't it just like royalty that she'll be treating you, but turn your back on her and she can take back her gift as easily as it was given. Your man could find himself holding only the tattered ribbons of a tune and song ashes and that's the God's own truth. I've seen it happen."

And then he'd laughed, as though he'd been having the audience on, and they'd launched into the song, but Amy had seen more than laughter in Matt's eyes as he started to sing. She wondered then, as she wondered now, if he didn't half believe that little bit of superstition, picked up somewhere on his travels, God knew where.

Maybe that was the answer to the riddle that was Matt Casey: he thought he'd lose his gift of music if he gave his heart to another. Maybe he'd even written that song himself, for she'd surely never heard it before. Picked it up in Morocco, he'd told her once, from one of the Wild Geese, the many Irish-in-exile, but she wasn't so sure.

Did you write it? She was ready to ask him right now, but then they were at The Harp and there was old Joe Breen flinging open the door to welcome them in and the opportunity was gone.

Lucia put on a pot of tea when she and Katrina returned to the apartment. While they waited for it to steep, they sat on the legless sofa pushed up against one wall of the long open loft that took up the majority of the apartment's floor space.

There was a small bedroom and a smaller bathroom off this main room. The kitchen area was in one corner—a battered fridge, its paint peeling, a sink and a counter with a hot plate on it and storage cupboards underneath and a small wooden kitchen table with five mismatching chairs set around it.

A low coffee table made of a plank of wood set on two apple crates crouched before the couch, laden with magazines and ashtrays. Along a far wall, three tall old mirrors had been fastened to the wall with a twelve-foot long support bar set out in front of them. The other walls were adorned with posters of the various shows in which Lucia had performed. In two she had headlined—one a traditional ballet, while the other had been a very outre multimedia event written and choreographed by a friend of hers.

When the tea was ready, Lucia brought the pot and two cups over to the sofa and set them on a stack of magazines. She poured Katrina a cup, then another for herself.

"So you found him," Lucia said as she returned to her seat on the sofa.

Katrina nodded happily.

He's just the way I remember him, she signed.

"Where did you meet him?" Lucia asked.

Katrina gave a shy smile in response, then added, *Near my home. He was playing music.*

The bright blue fire of her eyes grew unfocused as she looked across the room, seeing not plaster walls and the dance posters upon them, but the rough rocky shore of a coastline that lay east of the city by the mouth of the Dulfer River. She went into the past, and the past was like a dream.

She'd been underlake when the sound of his voice drew her up from the cold and the dark, neither of which she felt except as a kind of malaise in her spirit; up into the moonlight, bobbing in the white-capped waves; listening, *swallowing* that golden sound of strings and voice, and he so handsome and all alone on the shore. And sad. She could hear it in his song, feel the timbre of his loneliness in his voice.

Always intrigued with the strange folk who moved on the shore with their odd stumpy legs, this time she was utterly smitten. She swam closer and laid her arms on a stone by the shore, her head on her arms, to watch and listen.

It was his music that initially won her, for music had been her first love. Each of her four sisters was prettier than the next, and each had a voice that could charm moonlight from a stone, milk from a virgin, a ghost from the cold dark depths below, but her voice was better still, as golden as her hair and as rich and pure as the first larksong at dawn.

But if it was his music that first enchanted her, then he himself completed the spell. She longed to join her voice to his, to hold him and be held, but she never moved from her hiding place. One look at her, and he would be driven away, for he'd see only that which was scaled, and she had no soul, not as did those who walked ashore.

No soul, no soul. A heart that broke for want of him, but no immortal soul. That was the curse of the lake-born.

When he finally put away his instrument and walked further inland, up under the pines where she couldn't follow, she let the waves close over her head and returned to her home underlake.

For three nights she returned to the shore and for two of them he was there, his voice like honey against the beat of the waves that the wind pushed shoreward and she only loved him more. But on the fourth night, he didn't come, nor on the fifth night, nor the sixth, and she despaired, knowing he was gone, away in the wide world, lost to her forever.

Her family couldn't help her; there was no one to help her. She yearned to be rid of scales, to walk on shore, no matter the cost, just so that she could be with him, but as well ask the sun not rise, or the wind to cease its endless motion.

"No matter the cost," she whispered. Tears trailed down her cheek, a sorrowful tide that would not ebb.

"Maraghreen," the lake replied as the wind lifted one of its waves to break upon the land.

She lifted her head, looked over the white caps, to where the lake grew darker still as it crept under the cliffs into the hidden cave where the lake witch lived.

She was afraid, but she went. To Maraghreen. Who took her scales and gave her legs with a bitter potion that tasted of witch blood; satisfied her impossible need, but took Katrina's voice in payment.

"A week and a day," the lake witch told her before she took Katrina's voice. "You have only so long to win him and your immortal soul, or to foam you will return."

"But without my voice . . ." It was through song, she'd thought to win him, voices joined in a harmony so pure how could he help but love her? "Without it . . ."

"He must speak of his love first, or your soul will be forfeit."

"But without my voice . . ."

"You will have your body; that will need be enough."

So she drank the blood, bitter on her tongue; gained legs, and each step she took was fiery pain and would be so until she'd gained a soul; went in search of he who held her love, for whose love she had paid such a dear price. Surely he would speak the words to her before the seven days were past and gone?

"Penny for your thoughts," Lucia said.

Katrina only smiled and shook her head. She could tell no one. The words must come unbidden from him or all would be undone.

Matt was late picking Katrina up on Sunday. It was partly his own fault—he'd gotten caught up with a new song that he was learning from a tape a friend had sent him from Co. Cork and lost track of the time—and partly from trying to follow the Byzantine directions that Lucia had used to describe the route to her Upper Foxville apartment.

Katrina didn't seem to mind at all; she was just happy to see him, her hands said, moving as graceful in speech as the whole of her did when she danced.

You didn't bring your guitar, she signed.

"I've been playing it all day. I thought I'd leave it at home."

Your voice . . . your music. They are a gift.

"Yeah, well . . ."

He looked around the loft, recognizing a couple of the posters from having seen them around town before, pasted on subway walls or stuck in amongst the clutter of dozens of other ads in the front of restaurants and record stores. He'd never gone to any of the shows. Dance wasn't his thing, especially not modern dance or the performance art that Lucia was into. He'd seen a show of hers once. She'd spent fifteen minutes rolling back and forth across the stage, wrapped head to toe in old brown paper shopping bags to a soundtrack that consisted of water dripping for its rhythm, the hypnotic drone only occasionally broken by the sound of footsteps walking through broken glass.

Definitely not his thing.

Lucia was not his idea of what being creative was all about. In his head, he filed her type of artist under the general heading of lunatic fringe. Happily, she was out for the day.

"So," he said, "do you want to head out to the island?"

Katrina nodded. *But not just yet,* her hands added.

She smiled at him, long hair clouding down her back. She was wearing clothes borrowed from Lucia—cotton pants a touch too big and tied closed with a scarf through the belt loops, a T-shirt advertising a band that he'd never heard of and the same black Chinese slippers she'd been wearing last night.

"So what do you want—" he began.

Katrina took his hands before he could finish and placed them on her breasts. They were small and firm against his palms, her heartbeat echoing through the thin fabric, fluttering against his skin. Her own hands dropped to his groin, one gently cupping him through his jeans, the other pulling down the zipper.

She was gentle and loving, each motion innocent of artifice and certainly welcome, but she'd caught Matt off-guard.

"Look," he said, "are you sure you . . . ?"

She raised a hand, laying a finger against his lips. No words. Just touch. He grew hard, his penis uncomfortably bent in the confines of his jeans until she popped the top button and pulled it out. She put her small hand around it, fingers tight, hand moving slowly up and down. Speaking without words, her emotions laid bare before him.

Matt took his hands from her breasts and lifted the T-shirt over her head. He let it drop behind her as he enfolded her in an embrace. She was like liquid against him, a shimmer of movement and soft touches.

No words, he thought.

She was right. There was no need for words.

He let her lead him into Lucia's bedroom.

Afterwards, he felt so still inside it was as though the world had stopped moving, time stalled, no one left but the two of them, wrapped up together, here in the dusky shadows that licked across the bed. He raised himself up on one elbow and looked down at her.

She seemed to be made of light. An unearthly radiance lay upon her pale skin like an angelic nimbus, except he doubted that any angel in heaven knew how to give and accept pleasure as she did. Not unless heaven was a very different place from the one he'd heard about in Sunday school.

There was a look in her eyes that promised him everything—not just bodily pleasures, but heart and soul—and for a moment he wanted to open up to her, to give to her what he gave his music, but then he felt something close up thick inside him. He found himself remembering a parting conversation he'd had with another woman. Darlene Flatt, born Darlene Johnston. Belying her stage name, she was an extraordinarily well-endowed singer in one of the local country bands. Partial to slow-dancing on sawdusted floors, bolo ties, fringed jackets and, for the longest time, to him.

"You're just a hollow man," she told him finally. "A sham. The only place you're alive is on stage, but let me tell you something, Matt, the whole world's a stage if you'd just open your eyes and see."

Maybe in Shakespeare's day, he thought, but not now, not here, not in this world. Here you only get hurt.

"If you gave a fraction of your commitment to music to another person, you'd be . . ."

He didn't know what Darlene thought he'd be because he tuned her out. Stepped behind the wall and followed the intricate turns of a song he was working on at the time until she finally got up and left his apartment.

Got up and left.

He swung his feet to the floor and looked for his clothes. Katrina caught his arm. *What's wrong?* she signed. *What have I done?*

"Nothing," he said. "It's not you. It's not anything. It's just . . . I've just got to go, okay?"

Please, she signed. *Just tell me . . .*

But he turned away so that he couldn't see her words. Got dressed. Paused in the doorway of the bedroom, choking on words that tried to slip through the wall. Turned finally, and left. The room. The apartment. Her, crying.

Lucia found Katrina when she came home later, red-eyed and sitting on the sofa in just a T-shirt, staring out the window, unable or unwilling to explain what was wrong. So Lucia thought the worst.

"That sonuvabitch," she started. "He never even showed up, did he? I should have warned you about what a prick he can be."

But Katrina's hands said, *No. It wasn't his fault. I want too much.*

"He was here?" Lucia asked.

She nodded.

"And you had a fight?"

The shrug that came in response said, sort of, and then Katrina began to cry again. Lucia enfolded her in her arms. It was small, cold comfort, she knew, for she'd had her own time in that lonely place in which Katrina now found herself, but it was all Lucia had to offer.

Matt found himself on the ferry, crossing from the city over to Wolf Island, as though, by doing so, he was completing some unfinished ritual to which neither he nor Katrina had quite set the parameters. He stood at the rail on the upper deck with the wind in his face and let the words to long-dead ballads run through his mind so that he wouldn't have to think about people, about relationships, about complications, about Katrina.

But in the dusking sky and in the wake that trailed behind the ferry, and later on the island, in the shadows that crept across the lawn and in the tangle that branches made against the sky, he could see only her face. Not all the words to all the songs he knew could free him from the burden of guilt that clung to him like burrs gathered on a sweater while crossing an autumn field.

He stopped at the statue of the little mermaid, and of course even she had Katrina's face.

"I didn't ask to start anything," he told the statue, saying now what he should have said in Lucia's bedroom. "So why the hell do I have to feel so guilty?"

It was the old story, he realized. Everything, everybody wanted to lay claim to a piece of your soul. And if they couldn't have it, they made you pay for it in guilt.

"I'm not a hollow man," he told the statue, saying what he should have said to Darlene. "I just don't have what you want me to give."

The statue just looked out across the lake. The dusk stretched for long impossible moments, then the sun dropped completely behind the horizon and the lamps lit up along the island's pathways. Matt turned and walked back to where the ferry waited to return him to Newford.

He didn't see Katrina again for two days.

I'm sorry, was the first thing she said to him, her hands moving quickly before he could speak.

He stood in the hallway leading into Lucia's apartment, late on a Wednesday afternoon, not even sure what he was doing here. Apologizing. Explaining. Maybe just trying to understand.

"It wasn't your fault," he said. "It's just . . . everything happened too fast."

She nodded. *Do you want to come in?*

Matt regarded her. She was barefoot, framed by the doorway. The light behind her turned the flowered dress she was wearing into gossamer, highlighting the shape of her body under it. Her hair was the colour of soft gold. He remembered her lying on the bed, radiant in the afterglow of their lovemaking.

"Could we go out instead?" he said. "Just for a walk or something?"

Let me get my shoes.

He took her to the lakefront and they walked the length of the boardwalk and the Pier, and then, when the jostle of the crowds became too much, they made their way down to the sand and sat near the shoreline. For the most part, his voice, her hands, were still. When they did talk, it was to make up stories about the more colorful characters with whom they shared the beach, both using their hands to speak so that they wouldn't be overheard, laughing as each tried to outdo the other with an outrageous background for one person or another.

Where did you learn sign language? she asked him at one point.

My cousin's deaf, he replied, his hands growing more deft, remembering old patterns, the longer they spoke. *Our parents were pretty close and we all saw a lot of each other, so everybody in the family learned.*

They had dinner at Kathryn's Cafe. Afterwards, they went to the Owlnight, another of Newford's folk clubs, but this one was on the Butler University campus itself, in the Student Center. Garve MacCauley was doing a solo act, just guitar and gravely voice, mostly his own material.

You're much better, Katrina signed to Matt after the first few songs.

"Just different," he said.

Katrina only smiled and shook her head.

After the last set, he took her back to Upper Foxville and left her at Lucia's door with a chaste kiss.

Thursday evening they took in a play at the Standish, a small concert hall that divided its evenings between repertory theatre and music concerts. Katrina was entranced. She'd never seen live actors before, but then there was so much she didn't know about this new world in which she found herself and still more that she hadn't experienced in his company.

It was just past eleven by the time they got back to the apartment. Lucia had gone out, so they could have the place to themselves but when Katrina invited Matt in, he begged off. His confused mumble of an explanation made little sense. All Katrina knew was that the days were slipping away. Saturday night, the lake witch's deadline, was blurring all too close, all too fast.

When he bent to kiss her on the forehead as he had the night before, she lifted her head so that their lips met. The kiss lasted a long time, a tangle of tongues. She pressed in close to him, hands stroking his back, but he pulled away with a confused panic fluttering in his eyes.

Why do I frighten you? she wanted to ask, but she had already guessed that it wasn't just her. It was any close relationship. Responsibility frightened him and perhaps more to the point, he just didn't love her. Maybe he would, given time, but by then it would be too late. Days went by quickly; hours were simply a rush, one tumbling into the other.

She gave him a sad smile and let him go, listened to his footsteps in the stairwell, then slowly went into the apartment and closed the door behind her. Each step she took, as it always did since she stepped onto the land, was like small knives cutting through her feet. She remembered the freedom of the waves, of movement without pain, but she had turned her back on scales and water. For better or worse, she belonged on the land now.

But that night her dreams were of foam. It gathered against the craggy shore near her home as the wind drove the lake water onto the rocks. Her sisters swam nearby, weeping.

Late Friday afternoon, Amy and Lucia were sitting on a bench in Fitzhenry Park, watching the traffic go by on Palm Street. They'd been to the Y to swim laps and they each nursed a coffee now, bought from one of the vendors in the little parade of carts that set up along the sidewalk first thing every morning. The sky was overcast, with the scent of rain in the air, but for all the weather report's warnings, it had held off all day.

"So how's Katrina doing?" Amy asked.

An expression that was more puzzlement than a frown touched Lucia's features. She took a sip of her coffee then set it down on the bench between them and took out her cigarettes.

"Well, they started off rocky on Sunday," she said. "He left her crying."

"God, so soon?"

"It's not as bad as it sounds," Lucia said.

She got her cigarette lit and blew out a wreath of smoke. Amy coughed.

"Sorry," Lucia said. She moved the cigarette away.

"It's not the smoke," Amy told her, lifting a hand to rub her throat. "I've had a tickle in my throat all day. I just hope I'm not coming down with something." She took a sip of her coffee and wished she had a throat lozenge. "So what did happen?" she asked.

"He didn't show up for a couple of days, didn't call—well, I guess he wouldn't want to speak to me, would he?—but then he's been real nice ever since he did show up on Wednesday. Took her to see your friend MacCauley over at the Owlnight, the next night they went to that production of Lizzie's play that's running at the Standish and earlier today they were out just mooching around town, I guess."

"He really needs someone," Amy said.

"I suppose. But knowing your history with him, I don't know if I wish him on Katrina."

"But at least they're doing things. He's *talking* to her."

"Yeah, but then he told her today that he's going to be away this weekend."

"That's right. He canceled Saturday morning band practice because he's got a gig at that little bar in Hartnett's Point. What's the problem with that? That's his job. She must know that."

Lucia shrugged. "I just think he should've taken her with him when he left this afternoon."

Amy sighed in sympathy. "Matt's not big on bringing his current belle to a gig. I remember how it used to really piss me off when we were going together."

"Well, she's heartbroken that he didn't ask her to come along. I told her she should just go anyway—show up and meet him there; I even offered to lend her the money for the bus—but she thinks he'd get mad."

"I don't know. He seemed to like her dancing when we played at Feeney's last weekend." Amy paused. "Of course he'll just be doing songs on his own. There won't be anything for her to dance to."

"She likes his songs, too," Lucia said.

Amy thought of the intensity with which Katrina had listened to Matt's singing that night at Feeney's and she knew exactly why Matt hadn't asked Katrina along to the gig.

"Maybe she likes them too much," she said. "Matt puts a lot into his music, and you know how bloody brilliant he is, but he's pretty humble about it all at the same time. He probably thinks it'd freak him too much having her sitting there just kind of—" her shoulders lifted and fell "—I don't know, swallowing the songs."

"Well, I wish he'd given it a try all the same. I've got to help Sharon with some set decorations, so Katrina's going to be on her own all night, just moping about the apartment. I asked her to come along, but she didn't want to go out."

"I could drop by your place," Amy said.

Lucia grinned. "I thought you'd never offer."

Amy punched her lightly on the arm. "You set me up!"

"Has she still got it or what?" Lucia asked, blowing on her fingernails.

Amy laughed and they went through a quick little flurry of slapping at each other's hands until they were too giddy to continue. They both leaned back on the park bench.

"I bet I'll have a better time," Amy said after a moment. "I've helped Sharon before. If she's got anything organized at all, it'll only be because someone else did it."

Lucia nodded glumly. "Don't I know it."

Amy went home to change and have a bite to eat before she took the subway north to Upper Foxville. Looking in the mirror as she put on her makeup, she saw that she was looking awfully pale. Thinking about feeling sick made her throat tickle again and she coughed. She stopped for some lozenges at a drug store that was on her way. They helped her throat, but she felt a little light-headed now.

She should just go home, she thought, but she'd promised Lucia and she couldn't help but be sympathetic towards Katrina. She'd just stay a little while, that was all.

It was just going on nightfall when she reached Lucia's street. She paused at the corner, as she saw a small familiar figure step from the stoop of Lucia's building and head off the other way down the street. She almost called Katrina by name, but something stopped her. Curiosity got the better of her and she kept still, following along behind instead.

It was easy to keep track of her—Katrina's cloud of gold hair caught the light of every streetlamp she passed under and seemed to reflect a burnished glow up into the night. She led Amy down to MacNeil Street, turning west once she reached it. Her stride was both purposeful and wearied, but always graceful.

Poor kid, Amy thought.

More than once she started to hurry to catch up with Katrina, but then her curiosity would rise to the fore and she'd tell herself to be patient just a little longer. Since Katrina didn't know anyone in Newford—according to Lucia she didn't even know the city—Amy couldn't figure out where Katrina might be going.

Where MacNeil ended at Lee Street, Katrina crossed over and went down to the bank of the Kickaha River. She followed the riverbank southward, pausing only when she came near the Gracie Street Bridge. There the fenced-off ruins of the old L & B sawmill reared up in the darkness, ill-lit, drowning the riverbank with its shadow. It took up enough room that a person walking along the river by its chain-link fence would be almost invisible from any of the more peopled areas roundabout. Even across the river there were only empty warehouses.

Amy started to hurry again, struck by the sudden fear that Katrina meant to do herself harm. The river ran quicker here, rapiding over a descending shelf of broken stone slabs from where an old railway bridge had collapsed a few years ago. The city had cleared a channel through the debris, but that just made the river run more quickly through the narrower course. More than one person had drowned on this stretch of water—and not always by accident.

Matt's not worth it, she wanted to tell Katrina. Nobody's worth it.

Before she could reach Katrina, she came to an abrupt halt again. She stifled a cough that reared up in her throat and leaned against a fence post, suddenly dizzy. But it wasn't the escalating onset of a flu bug that had made her stop. Rather it was what she had spied, bobbing in the swift-moving water.

The light was bad, just a diffused glow from the streets a block or so over, but it was enough for her to make out four white shapes in the dark water. They each seemed as slender and graceful as Katrina, with the same spun gold hair, except theirs was cut short to their skulls, highlighting the fox-like shape of their features. They probably had, Amy thought, the same blue eyes, too.

What were they *doing* there?

Another wave of dizziness came over her. She slid down the side of the fence pole until she was crouched on the ground. She remembered thinking that this way she wouldn't have as far to fall if she fainted. Clutching the pole for support, she looked back to the river.

Katrina had moved closer to the shore and was holding her arms out to the women. As their shapes moved closer, Amy's heartbeat drummed into overtime for she realized that they had no legs. They were propelling themselves through the water with scaled fish tails. There was no mistaking the shape of them as the long tail fins broke the surface of the water.

Mermaids, Amy thought, no longer able to breathe. They were mermaids.

It wasn't possible. *How* could it be possible?

And what did it make Katrina?

The sight of them blurred. For a moment she was looking through a veil, then it was like looking through a double-paned window at an angle, images all duplicated and laid over each other.

She blinked hard. She started to lift her hand to rub at her eyes, but she was suddenly so weak it was all she could do to just crouch beside the pole and not tumble over into the weeds.

The women in the river drew closer as Katrina stepped to the very edge of the water. Katrina lifted her hair, then let it drop in a clouding fall. She pointed at the women.

"Cut away and gone," one of the women said.

"All gone."

"We gave it to Maraghreen."

"For you, sister."

"We traded, gold for silver."

Amy pressed her face against the pole as the mermaids spoke. Through her dizziness, their voices seemed preternaturally enhanced. They chorused, one beginning where another ended, words molten, bell-like, sweet as honey, and so very, very pure.

"She gave us this."

The foremost of the women in the river reached up out of the water. Something glimmered silver and bright in her hand. A knife.

"Pierce his heart."

"Bathe in his blood."

"Your legs will grow together once more."

"You'll come back to us."

"Oh, sister."

Katrina went down on her knees at the water's edge. She took the knife from the mermaid's hand and laid it gingerly on her lap.

"He doesn't love you."

"He will never love you."

The women all drew close. They reached out of the water, stroking Katrina's arms and her face with gentling hands.

"You must do it—before the first dawn light follows tomorrow night."

"Or foam you'll be."

"Sister, please."

"Return to those who love you."

Katrina bowed her head, making no response. One by one the women dove into the river deeps and were gone. From her hiding place, Amy tried to rise—she knew Katrina would be coming back soon, coming back this way, and she didn't want to be caught—but she couldn't manage it, even with the help of the pole beside her. Then Katrina stepped away from the river and walked towards her, the knife held gingerly in one hand.

As their gazes met, another wave of dizziness rose in Amy, this one a tsunami, and in its wake she felt the ground tremble underfoot, but it was only herself, tumbling into the dirt and weeds. She closed her eyes and let the darkness take her away.

It was late afternoon when Amy awoke on the sofa in Lucia's loft. Her surroundings and the wrong angle of the afternoon light left her disoriented and confused, but no longer feeling sick. It must have been one of those 24-hour viruses, she thought as she swung her legs to the floor, then leaned back against the sofa's cushions.

Lucia looked up from the magazine she was reading at the kitchen table. Laying it down she walked over and joined Amy on the sofa.

"I was *tres* surprised to find you sleeping here when I got in last night," she said. "Katrina said you got sick, so she put you to bed on the sofa and slept on the floor herself. How're you feeling now, *ma cherie*?"

Amy worked through what Lucia had just said. None of it quite jibed with her own muddled memory of the previous evening.

"Okay . . . I guess," she said finally. She looked around the loft. "Where's Katrina?"

"She borrowed the bus money from me and went to Hartnett's Point after all. True love wins over all, *n'est-ce pas*?"

Amy thought of mermaids swimming in the Kickaha River, of Katrina kneeling by the water, of the silver knife.

"Oh, shit," she said.

"What's the matter?"

"I . . ."

Amy didn't know what to say. What she'd seen hadn't made any sense. She'd been sick, dizzy, probably delirious. But it had seemed so real.

Pierce his heart . . . bathe in his blood. . . .

She shook her head. None of it could have happened. There were no such things as mermaids. But what if there were? What if Katrina was carrying that silver knife as she made her way to Matt's gig? What if she did just what those . . . mermaids had told her . . .

You must do it—before the first dawn light that follows tomorrow night. . . .

What if—

Or foam you'll be . . .

—it was real?

She bent down and looked for her shoes, found them pressed up against one of the coffee table's crate supports. She put them on and rose from the sofa.

"I've got to go," she told Lucia.

"Go where? What's going on?"

"I don't know. I don't have time to explain. I'll tell you later."

Lucia followed her across the loft to the door. "Amy, you're acting really weird."

"I'm fine," Amy said. "Honest."

Though she still didn't feel quite normal. She was weak and didn't want to look in a mirror for fear of seeing the white ghost of her own face looking back at her. But she didn't feel that she had any choice.

If what she'd seen last night *had* been real . . .

Lucia shook her head uncertainly. "Are you sure you're—"

Amy paused long enough to give her friend a quick peck on the cheek, then she was out the door.

Borrowing a car was easy. Her brother Pete had two and was used to her sudden requests for transportational needs, relieved that he wasn't required to provide a chauffeur service along with it. She was on the road by seven, tooling west along the old lakeside highway in a gas-guzzling Chev, stopping for a meal at a truck stop that marked the halfway point and arriving at Harnett's Point just as Matt would be starting his first set.

She pulled in beside his VW van—a positive antique by now, she liked to tease him—and parked. The building that housed Murphy's Bar where Matt had his gig was a ramshackle affair, log walls here in back, plaster on cement walls in front. The bar sat on the edge of the point from which the village got its name, with a long pier out behind the building, running into the lake. The water around the pier was thick with moored boats.

She went around front to where the neon sign spelling the name of the bar crackled and spat an orange glow and stepped inside to the familiar sound of Matt singing Leon Rosselson's "World Turned Upside Down." The audience, surprisingly enough for a backwoods establishment such as this, was actually paying attention to the music. Amy thought that only a third of them were probably even aware of the socialist message the song espoused.

The patrons were evenly divided between the back-to-the-earth hippies who tended organic farms west of the village, all jeans and unbleached cotton, long hair and flower-print dresses; the locals who'd grown up in the area and would probably die here, heavier drinkers, also in jeans, but tending towards flannel shirts and baseball caps, T-shirts and workboots; and then those cottagers who hadn't yet closed their places up for the year, a hodgepodge of golf shirts and cotton blends, short skirts and, yes, even one dark blue captain's cap, complete with braided rope trim.

She shaded her eyes and looked for Katrina, but didn't spot her. After a few moments, she got herself a beer from the bar and found a corner table to sit at that she shared with a pair of earth-mothers and a tall skinny man with drooping eyes and hair longer than that of either of his companions, pulled back into a ponytail that fell to his waist. They made introductions all around, then settled back into their chairs to listen to the music.

As Matt's set wound on, Amy began to wonder just exactly what it was that she was doing here. Even closing her eyes and concentrating, she could barely call up last night's fantastic images with any sort of clarity. What if the whole thing *had* just been a delirium? What if she'd made her way to Lucia's apartment only to pass out on the sofa and have dreamt it all?

Matt stopped by the table when he ended his set.

"What brings you up here, Scallan?" he asked.

She shrugged. "Just thought I'd check out how you do without the rest of us to keep you honest."

A touch of humor crinkled around his eyes. "So what's the verdict?"

"You're doing good." She introduced him to her companions, then asked, "Do you want to get a little air?"

He nodded and let her lead the way outside. They leaned against the back of somebody's Bronco looked up and down the length of one of the village's two streets. This one cut north and south, from the bush down to the lake. The other was merely the highway as it cut through the village.

"So have you seen Katrina?" Amy asked.

Matt nodded. "Yeah, we walked around the Market for awhile yesterday afternoon."

"You mean, she's not up here?"

"Not so's I know."

Amy sighed. So much for her worries. But if Katrina hadn't borrowed the money from Lucia to come up here, then where *had* she gone?

"Why are you so concerned about Katrina?" Matt asked.

Amy started to make up some excuse, but then thought, screw it. One of them might as well be up front.

"I'm just worried about her."

Matt nodded. He kicked at the gravel underfoot, but didn't say anything.

"I know it's none of my business," Amy said.

"You're right. It's not." There was no rancor in Matt's voice. Just a kind of weariness.

"It's just that—"

"Look," he said, turning to Amy, "she seems nice, that's all. I think maybe we started out on the wrong foot, but I'm trying to fix that. For now, I just want to be her friend. If something else comes up later, okay. But I want to take it as it comes. Slowly. Is that so wrong?"

Amy shook her head. And then it struck her. For the first time that they weren't on stage together, or working out an arrangement, Matt actually seemed to focus on her. To listen to what she was saying, and answer honestly. Protective walls maybe not completely down, but there *was* a little breach in them.

"I think she loves you," Amy said.

Matt sighed. "It's kind of early for that—don't you think? I think it's more a kind of infatuation. She'll probably grow out of it just as fast as she fell into it."

"I don't know about that. Seems to me that if you're going to be at all fair, you'd be just a little bit more—"

"Don't talk to me about responsibility," Matt said, breaking in. "Just because someone falls in love with you, it doesn't mean you owe them anything. I've got no control over how other people feel about me—"

That's where you're wrong, Amy thought. If you'd just act more human, more like this . . .

"—and I'm sure not going to run my life by their feelings and schedules. I'm not trying to sound self-centered, I'm just trying to . . . I don't know. Protect my privacy."

"But if you don't give a little, how will you ever know what you might be missing?"

"Giving too much, too fast—that just leaves you open to being hurt."

"But—"

"Oh, shit," Matt said, glancing at his watch. "I've got another set to do." He pushed away from the Bronco. "Look, I'm sorry if I don't measure up to how people want me to be, but this is just the way I am."

Why didn't you open yourself up even this much while we were going out together? Amy wanted to ask. But all she did was nod and say, "I know."

"Are you coming in?"

She shook her head. "Not right away."

"Well, I've got—"

"I know." She waved him off. "Break a leg or whatever."

She moved away from the Bronco once he'd gone inside and crossed the parking lot, gravel crunching underfoot until she reached the grass verge. She followed it around to the lawn by the side of the building and down to the lakefront. There she stood, listening to the vague sound of Matt's voice and guitar as it carried through an open window. She looked at all the boats clustered around the pier. A splash drew her attention to the far end of the wooden walkway where a figure sat with its back to the shore having just thrown something into the lake.

Amy had one of those moments of utter clarity. She knew immediately that it was Katrina sitting there, feet dangling in the water, long hair clouding down her back, knew as well that it was the silver knife she'd thrown into the lake. Amy could almost see it, turning end on slow end as it sank in the water.

She hesitated for the space of a few long breaths, gaze tracking the surface of the lake for Katrina's sisters, then she slowly made her way down to the pier. Katrina turned at the sound of Amy's shoes on the wooden slats of the walkway. She nodded once, then looked back out over the lake.

Amy sat beside her. She hesitated again, then put her arm comfortingly around Katrina's small shoulders. They sat like that for a long time. The water lapped against the pilings below them. An owl called out from the woods to their left, a long mournful sound. A truck pulled into the bar's parking lot. Car doors slammed, voices rose in laughter, then disappeared into the bar.

Katrina stirred beside Amy. She began to move her hands, but Amy shook her head.

"I'm sorry," she said. "I can't understand what you're saying."

Katrina mimed steering, both hands raised up in front of her, fingers closed around an invisible steering wheel.

Amy nodded. "I drove up in my brother's car."

Katrina pointed to herself then to Amy and again mimed turning a steering wheel.

"You want me to drive you somewhere?"

Katrina nodded.

Amy looked back towards the bar. "What about Matt?"

Katrina shook her head. She put her hands together, eyes eloquent where her voice was silent. Please.

Amy looked at her for a long moment, then she slowly nodded. "Sure. I can give you a lift. Is there someplace specific you want to go?"

Katrina merely rose to her feet and started back down the pier towards shore. Once they were in the Chev, she pointed to the glove compartment.

"Go ahead," Amy said.

As she started the car, Katrina pulled out a handful of roadmaps. She sorted through them until she came to one that showed the whole north shore of the lake. She unfolded it and laid it on the dashboard between them and pointed to a spot west of Newford. Amy looked more closely. The place where Katrina had her finger was where the Dulfer River emptied into the lake. The tip of her small finger was placed directly on the lakeside campgrounds of the State Park there.

"Jesus," Amy said. "It'll take us all night to get there. We'll be lucky to make it before dawn."

As Katrina shrugged, Amy remembered what Katrina's sisters had said last night. *Before the first dawn light follows tomorrow night.*

That was tonight. *This* morning.

Or foam you'll be.

She shivered and looked at Katrina.

"Tell me what's going on," she said. "Please, Katrina. Maybe I can help you."

Katrina just shook her head sadly. She mimed driving, hands around the invisible steering wheel again.

Amy sighed. She put the car in gear and pulled out of the parking lot. Katrina reached towards the radio, eyebrows raised quizzically. When Amy nodded, she turned it on and slowly wound through the stations until she got Newford's WKPN–FM. It was too early for Zoe B.'s "Nightnoise" show, so they listened to Mariah Carey, the Vaughan Brothers and the like as they followed the highway east.

Neither of them spoke as they drove; Katrina couldn't and Amy was just too depressed. She didn't know what was going on. She just felt as though she'd become trapped in a Greek tragedy. The storyline was already written, everything was predestined to a certain outcome and there was nothing she could do about it. Only Matt could have, if he'd loved Katrina, but she couldn't even blame him. You couldn't force a person to love somebody.

She didn't agree with his need to protect his privacy. Maybe it stopped him from being hurt, but it also stopped him from being alive. But he was right about one thing: he couldn't be held responsible for who chose to love him.

They crossed over the Dulfer River just as dawn was starting to pink the eastern horizon. When Amy pulled into the campgrounds, Katrina directed her down a narrow dirt road that led to the park's boat launch.

They had the place to themselves. Amy pulled up by the water and killed the engine. The pines stood silent around them when they got out of the car. There was birdsong, but it seemed strangely muted. Distant. As though heard through gauze.

Katrina lifted a hand and touched Amy's cheek, then walked towards the water. She headed to the left of the launching area where a series of broad flat rocks staircased down into the water. After a moment's hesitation, Amy followed after. She sat down beside Katrina, who was right by the edge of the water, arms wrapped around her knees.

"Katrina," she began. "Please tell me what's going on. I—"

She fussed in her purse, looking for pen and paper. She found the former, and pulled out her checkbook to use the back of a check as a writing surface.

"I want to help," she said, holding the pen and checkbook out to her companion.

Katrina regarded her for a long moment, a helpless look in her eyes, but finally she took the proffered items. She began to write on the back of one of the checks, but before she could hand it back to Amy, a wind rose up. The pine trees shivered, needles whispering against each other.

An electric tingle sparked across every inch of Amy's skin. The hairs at the nape of her neck prickled and goosebumps traveled up her arms. It was like that moment before a storm broke, when the air is so charged with ions that it seems anything might happen.

"What . . . ?" she began.

Her voice died in her throat as the air around them thickened. Shapes formed in the air, pale diffused airy shapes, slender and transparent. Their voices were like the sound of the wind in the pines.

"Come with us," they said, beckoning to Katrina.

"Be one with us."

"We can give you what you lack."

Katrina stared at the misty apparitions for the longest time. Then she let pen and checkbook fall to the rock and stood up, stretching her arms towards the airy figures. Her own body began to lose its definition. She was a spiderweb in the shape of a woman, gossamer, smoke and mist. Her clothing fell from her transparent form to fall into a tangle beside Amy.

And then she was gone. The wind died. The whisper stilled in the pines.

Amy stared open-mouthed at where Katrina had disappeared. All that lay on the rock were Katrina's clothes, the pen and the checkbook. Amy reached out towards the clothes. They were damp to the touch.

Or foam you'll be.

Amy looked up into the lightening sky. But Katrina hadn't just turned to foam, had she? Something had come and taken her away before that happened. If any of this had even been real at all. If she hadn't just lost it completely.

She heard weeping and lowered her gaze to the surface of the lake. There were four women's heads there, bobbing in the unruly water. Their hair was short, cropped close to their heads, untidily, as though cut with garden shears or a knife. Their eyes were red with tears. Each could have been Katrina's twin.

Seeing her gaze upon them, they sank beneath the waves, one by one, and then Amy was alone again. She swallowed thickly, then picked up her checkbook to read what Katrina had written before what could only have been angels came to take her away:

"Is this what having a soul means, to know such bittersweet pain? But still, I cherish the time I had. Those who live forever, who have no stake in the dance of death's inevitable approach, can never understand the sanctity of life."

It sounded stiff, like a quote, but then Amy realized she'd never heard how Katrina would speak, not the cadence of her voice, nor its timbre, nor her diction.

And now she never would.

The next day, Matt found Amy where her brother Pete said she was going. She was by the statue of the little mermaid on Wolf Island, just sitting on a bench and staring out at the lake. She looked haggard from a lack of sleep.

"What happened to you last night?" he asked.

She shrugged. "I decided to go for a drive."

Matt nodded as though he understood, though he didn't pretend to have a clue. The complexities that made up people's personalities were forever a mystery to him.

He sat down beside her.

"Have you seen Katrina?" he asked. "I went by Lucia's place looking for her, but she was acting all weird—" not unusual for Lucia, he added to himself "—and told me I should ask you."

"She's gone," Amy said. "Maybe back into the lake, maybe into the sky. I'm not really sure."

Matt just looked at her. "Come again?" he said finally.

So Amy told him about it all, of what she'd seen two nights ago by the old L & N sawmill, of what had happened last night.

"It's like in that legend about the little mermaid," she said as she finished up. She glanced at the statue beside them. "The real legend—not what you'd find in some kid's picturebook."

Matt shook his head. " 'The Little Mermaid' isn't a legend," he said. "It's just a story, made up by Hans Christian Andersen, like 'The Emperor's New Clothes' and 'The Ugly Duckling.' They sure as hell aren't real."

"I'm just telling you what I saw."

"Jesus, Amy. Will you listen to yourself?"

When she turned to face him, he saw real anguish in her features.

"I can't help it," she said. "It really happened."

Matt started to argue, but then he shook his head. He didn't know what had gotten into Amy to go on like this. He expected this kind of thing from Geordie's brother who made his living gussying up fantastical stories from nothing, but Amy?

"It looks like her, doesn't it?" Amy said.

Matt followed her gaze to the statue. He remembered the last time he'd been on the island, the night when he'd walked out on Katrina, when everything had looked like her. He got up from the bench and stepped closer. The statue's bronze features gleamed in the sunlight.

"Yeah," he said. "I guess it does."

Then he walked away.

He was pissed off with Amy for going on the way she had and brooded about her stupid story all the way back to the city. He had a copy of the Andersen Fairy Tales at home. When he got back to his apartment, he took it down from the shelf and read the story again.

"Aw, shit," he said as he closed the book.

It was just a story. Katrina would turn up. They'd all share a laugh at how Amy was having him on.

But Katrina didn't turn up. Not that day, nor the next, nor by the end of the week. She'd vanished from his life as mysteriously as she'd come into it.

That's why I don't want to get involved with people, he wanted to tell Amy. Because they just walk out of your life if you don't do what they want you to do.

No way it had happened as Amy had said it did. But he found himself wondering about what it would be like to be without a soul, wondering if he even had one.

Friday of that week, he found himself back on the island, standing by the statue once again. There were a couple of tattered silk flowers on the stone at its base. He stared at the mermaid's features for a long time, then he went home and started to phone the members of Marrowbones.

* * *

"Well, I kind of thought this was coming," Amy said when he called to tell her that he was breaking up the band, "except I thought it'd be Johnny or Nicky quitting."

She was sitting in the windowseat of her apartment's bay window, back against one side, feet propped up against the other. She was feeling better than she had when she'd seen him on Sunday, but there was still a strangeness inside her. A lost feeling, a sense of the world having shifted underfoot and the rules being all changed.

"So what're you going to do?" she added when he didn't respond.

"Hit the road for awhile."

"Gigging, or just traveling?"

"Little of both, I guess."

There was another long pause and Amy wondered if he was waiting for her to ask if she could come. But she was really over him now. Had been for a long time. She wasn't looking to be anybody's psychiatrist, or mother. Or matchmaker.

"Well, see you then," he said.

"Bon voyage," Amy said.

She cradled the phone. She thought of how he had talked with her the other night up at Hartnett's Point, opening up, actually *relating* to her. And now . . . She realized that the whole business with Katrina had just wound him up tighter than ever before.

Well, somebody else was going to have to work on those walls and she knew who it had to be. A guy named Matt Casey.

She looked out the window again.

"Good luck," she said.

Matt was gone for a year. When he came back, the first place he went to was Wolf Island. He stood out by the statue for a long time, not saying anything, just trying to sort out why he was here. He didn't have much luck, not that year, nor each subsequent year that he came. Finally, almost a decade after Katrina was gone—walked out of his life, turned into a puddle of lake water, went sailing through the air with angels, whatever—he decided to stay overnight, as though being alone in the dark would reveal something that was hidden from the day.

"Lady," he said, standing in front of the statue, drowned in the thick silence of the night.

He hadn't brought an offering for the statue—Our Lady of the Harbour, as the bag lady had called her. He was just here, looking for something that remained forever out of reach. He wasn't trying to understand Katrina or the story that Amy had told of her. Not anymore.

"Why am I so empty inside?" he asked.

"I can't believe you're going to play with him again," Lucia said when Amy told her about her new band, Johnny Jump Up.

Amy shrugged. "It'll just be the three of us—Geordie's going to be playing fiddle."

"But he hasn't changed at all. He's still so—cold."

"Not on stage."

"I suppose not," Lucia said. "I guess all he's got going for him is his music."

Amy nodded sadly.

"I know," she said.

Paperjack

*If you think education is
expensive, try ignorance.*
—Derek Bok

Churches aren't havens of spiritual enlightenment; they enclose the spirit. The way Jilly explains it, organizing Mystery tends to undermine its essence. I'm not so sure I agree, but then I don't really know enough about it. When it comes to things that can't be logically explained, I take a step back and leave them to Jilly or my brother Christy—they thrive on that kind of thing. If I had to describe myself as belonging to any church or mystical order, it'd be one devoted to secular humanism. My concerns are for real people and the here and now; the possible existence of God, faeries, or some metaphysical Otherworld just doesn't fit into my worldview.

Except . . .

You knew there'd be an "except," didn't you, or else why would I be writing this down?

It's not like I don't have anything to say. I'm all for creative expression, but my medium's music. I'm not an artist like Jilly, or a writer like Christy. But the kinds of things that have been happening to me can't really be expressed in a fiddle tune—no, that's not entirely true. I can express them, but the medium is such I can't be assured that, when I'm playing, listeners hear what I mean them to hear.

That's how it works with instrumental music, and it's probably why the best of it is so enduring: the listener takes away whatever he or she wants from it. Say the composer was trying to tell us about the aftermath of some great battle. When we hear it, the music might speak to us of a parent we've lost, a friend's struggle with some debilitating disease, a doe standing at the edge of a forest at twilight, or any of a thousand other unrelated things.

Realistic art like Jilly does—or at least it's realistically rendered; her subject matter's right out of some urban update of those Andrew Lang color-coded fairy tale books that most of us read when we were kids—and the collections of urban legends and stories that my brother writes don't have that same leeway. What goes down on the canvas or on paper, no matter how skillfully drawn or written, doesn't allow for much in the way of an alternate interpretation.

So that's why I'm writing this down: to lay it all out in black and white where maybe I can understand it myself.

For the past week, every afternoon after busking up by the Williamson Street Mall for the lunchtime crowds, I've packed up my fiddle case and headed across town to come here to St. Paul's Cathedral. Once I get here, I sit on the steps about halfway up, take out this notebook, and try to write. The trouble is, I haven't been able to figure out where to start.

I like it out here on the steps. I've played inside the cathedral—just once, for a friend's wedding. The wedding was okay, but I remember coming in on my own to test the acoustics an hour or so before the rehearsal; ever since then I've been a little unsure about how Jilly views this kind of place. My fiddling didn't feel enclosed. Instead the walls seemed to open the music right up; the cathedral gave the reel I was playing a stately grace—a spiritual grace—that it had never held for me before. I suppose it had more to do with the architect's design than the presence of God, still I could've played there all night only—

But I'm rambling again. I've filled a couple of pages now, which is more than I've done all week, except after just rereading what I've written so far, I don't know if any of it's relevant.

Maybe I should just tell you about Paperjack. I don't know that it starts with him exactly, but it's probably as good a place as any to begin.

It was a glorious day, made all the more precious because the weather had been so weird that spring. One day I'd be bundled up in a jacket and scarf, cloth cap on my head, with fingerless gloves to keep the cold from my finger joints while I was out busking, the next I'd be in a T-shirt, breaking into a sweat just thinking about standing out on some street corner to play tunes.

There wasn't a cloud in the sky, the sun was halfway home from noon to the western horizon, and Jilly and I were just soaking up the rays on the steps of St. Paul's. I was slouched on the steps, leaning on one elbow, my fiddlecase propped up beside me, wishing I had worn shorts because my jeans felt like leaden weights on my legs. Sitting beside me, perched like a cat about to pounce on something terribly interesting that only it could see, Jilly was her usual scruffy self. There were flecks of paint on her loose cotton pants and her short-sleeved blouse, more under her fingernails, and still more half-lost in the tangles of her hair. She turned to look at me, her face miraculously untouched by her morning's work, and gave me one of her patented smiles.

"Did you ever wonder where he's from?" Jilly asked.

That was one of her favorite phrases: "Did you ever wonder . . . ?" It could take you from considering if and when fish slept, or why people look up when they're thinking, to more arcane questions about ghosts, little people living behind wallboards, and the like. And she loved guessing about people's origins. Sometimes when I was busking she'd tag along and sit by the wall at my back, sketching the people who were listening to me play. Invariably, she'd come up behind me and whisper in my ear— usually when I was in the middle of a complicated tune that needed all my attention— something along the lines of, "The guy in the polyester suit? Ten to one he rides a big chopper on the weekends, complete with a jean vest."

So I was used to it.

Today she wasn't picking out some nameless stranger from a crowd. Instead her attention was on Paperjack, sitting on the steps far enough below us that he couldn't hear what we were saying.

Paperjack had the darkest skin I'd ever seen on a man—an amazing ebony that seemed to swallow light. He was in his mid-sixties, I'd guess, short corkscrew hair all gone grey. The dark suits he wore were threadbare and out of fashion, but always clean. Under his suit jacket he usually wore a white T-shirt that flashed so brightly in the sun it almost hurt your eyes—just like his teeth did when he gave you that lopsided grin of his.

Nobody knew his real name and he never talked. I don't know if he was mute, or if he just didn't have anything to say, but the only sounds I ever heard him make were a chuckle or a laugh. People started calling him Paperjack because he worked an origami gig on the streets.

He was a master at folding paper into shapes. He kept a bag of different colored paper by his knee; people would pick their color and then tell him what they wanted, and he'd make it—no cuts, just folding. And he could make anything. From simple flower and animal shapes to things so complex it didn't seem possible for him to capture their essence in a piece of folded paper. So far as I know, he'd never disappointed a single customer.

I'd seen some of the old men come down from Little Japan to sit and watch him work. They called him *sensei,* a term of respect that they didn't exactly bandy around.

But origami was only the most visible side of his gig. He also told fortunes. He had one of those little folded paper Chinese fortune-telling devices that we all played around with when we were kids. You know the kind: you fold the corners in to the center, turn it over, then fold them in again. When you're done you can stick your index fingers and thumbs inside the little flaps of the folds and open it up so that it looks like a flower. You move your fingers back and forth, and it looks like the flower's talking to you.

Paperjack's fortune-teller was just like that. It had the names of four colors on the outside and eight different numbers inside. First you picked a color—say, red. The fortune-teller would seem to talk soundlessly as his fingers moved back and forth to spell the word, R-E-D, opening and closing until there'd be a choice from four of the numbers. Then you picked a number, and he counted it out until the fortune-teller was open with another or the same set of numbers revealed. Under the number you choose at that point was your fortune.

Paperjack didn't read it out—he just showed it to the person, then stowed the fortune-teller back into the inside pocket of his jacket from which he'd taken it earlier. I'd never had my fortune read by him, but Jilly'd had it done for her a whole bunch of times.

"The fortunes are always different," she told me once. "I sat behind him while he was doing one for a customer, and I read the fortune over her shoulder. When she'd paid him, I got mine done. I picked the same number she did, but when he opened it, there was a different fortune there."

"He's just got more than one of those paper fortune-tellers in his pocket," I said, but she shook her head.

"He never put it away," she said. "It was the same fortune-teller, the same number, but some time between the woman's reading and mine, it changed."

I knew there could be any number of logical explanations for how that could have happened, starting with plain sleight of hand, but I'd long ago given up continuing arguments with Jilly when it comes to that kind of thing.

Was Paperjack magic? Not in my book, at least not the way Jilly thought he was. But there was a magic about him, the magic that always hangs like an aura about someone who's as good an artist as Paperjack was. He also made me feel good. Around him, an overcast day didn't seem half so gloomy, and when the sun shone, it always seemed brighter. He just exuded a glad feeling that you couldn't help but pick up on. So in that sense, he was magic.

I'd also wondered where he'd come from, how he'd ended up on the street. Street people seemed pretty well evenly divided between those who had no choice but to be there, and those who chose to live there like I do. But even then there's a difference. I had a little apartment not far from Jilly's. I could get a job when I wanted one, usually in the winter when the busking was bad and club gigs were slow.

Not many street people have that choice, but I thought that Paperjack might be one of them.

"He's such an interesting guy," Jilly was saying.

I nodded.

"But I'm worried about him," she went on.

"How so?"

Jilly's brow wrinkled with a frown. "He seems to be getting thinner, and he doesn't get around as easily as he once did. You weren't here when he showed up today—he walked as though gravity had suddenly doubled its pull on him."

"Well, he's an old guy, Jilly."

"That's exactly it. Where does he live? Does he have someone to look out for him?"

That was Jilly for you. She had a heart as big as the city, with room in it for everyone and everything. She was forever taking in strays, be they dogs, cats, or people.

I'd been one of her strays once, but that was a long time ago.

"Maybe we should ask him," I said.

"He can't talk," she reminded me.

"Maybe he just doesn't *want* to talk."

Jilly shook her head. "I've tried a zillion times. He hears what I'm saying, and somehow he manages to answer with a smile or a raised eyebrow or whatever, but he doesn't talk." The wrinkles in her brow deepened until I wanted to reach over and smooth them out. "These days," she added, "he seems haunted to me."

If someone else had said that, I'd know that they meant Paperjack had something troubling him. With Jilly though, you often had to take that kind of a statement literally.

"Are we talking ghosts now?" I asked.

I tried to keep the skepticism out of my voice, but from the flash of disappointment that touched Jilly's eyes, I knew I hadn't done a very good job.

"Oh, Geordie," she said. "Why can't you just *believe* what happened to us?"

Here's one version of what happened that night, some three years ago now, to which Jilly was referring:

We saw a ghost. He stepped out of the past on a rainy night and stole away the woman I loved. At least that's the way I remember it. Except for Jilly, no one else does.

Her name was Samantha Rey. She worked at Gypsy Records and had an apartment on Stanton Street, except after that night, when the past came up to steal her away, no one at Gypsy Records remembered her anymore, and the landlady of her Stanton Street apartment had never heard of her. The ghost hadn't just stolen her, he'd stolen all memory of her existence.

All I had left of her was an old photograph that Jilly and I found in Moore's Antiques a little while later. It had a photographer's date on the back: 1912. It was Sam in the picture, Sam with a group of strangers standing on the front porch of some old house.

I remembered her, but she'd never existed. That's what I had to believe. Because nothing else made sense. I had all these feelings and memories of her, but they had to be what my brother called *jamais vu*. That's like *déjà vu,* except instead of having felt you'd been somewhere before, you remembered something that had never happened. I'd never heard the expression before—he got it from a David Morrell thriller that he'd been reading—but it had an authentic ring about it.

Jamais vu.

But Jilly remembered Sam, too.

Thinking about Sam always brought a tightness to my chest; it made my head hurt trying to figure it out. I felt as if I were betraying Sam by trying to convince myself she'd never existed, but I had to convince myself of that, because believing that it really *had* happened was even scarier. How do you live in a world where anything can happen?

"You'll get used to it," Jilly told me. "There's a whole invisible world out there, lying side by side with our own. Once you get a peek into it, the window doesn't close. You're always going to be *aware* of it."

"I don't want to be," I said.

She just shook her head. "You don't really get a lot of choice in this kind of thing," she said.

You always have a choice—that's what I believe. And I chose to not get caught up in some invisible world of ghosts and spirits and who knew what. But I still dreamed of Sam, as if she'd been real. I still kept her photo in my fiddlecase.

I could feel its presence right now, glimmering through the leather, whispering to me.

Remember me . . .

I couldn't forget. *Jamais vu.* But I wanted to.

Jilly scooted a little closer to me on the step and laid a hand on my knee.

"Denying it just makes things worse," she said, continuing an old ongoing argument that I don't think we'll ever resolve. "Until you accept that it really happened, the memory's always going to haunt you, undermining everything that makes you who you are."

"Haunted like Paperjack?" I asked, trying to turn the subject back onto more comfortable ground, or at least focus the attention onto someone other than myself. "Is that what you think's happened to him?"

Jilly sighed. "Memories can be just like ghosts," she said.

Didn't I know it.

I looked down the steps to where Paperjack had been sitting, but he was gone, and now a couple of pigeons were waddling across the steps. The wind blew a candy bar wrapper up against a riser. I laid my hand on Jilly's and gave it a squeeze, then picked up my fiddlecase and stood up.

"I've got to go," I told her.

"I didn't mean to upset you . . ."

"I know. I've just got to walk for a bit and think."

She didn't offer to accompany me and for that I was glad. Jilly was my best friend, but right then I had to be alone.

I went rambling; just let my feet take me wherever they felt like going, south from St. Paul's and down Battersfield Road, all the way to the Pier, my fiddlecase banging against my thigh as I walked. When I got to the waterfront, I leaned up against the fieldstone wall where the Pier met the beach. I stood and watched the fishermen work their lines farther out over the lake. Fat gulls wheeled above, crying like they hadn't been fed in months. Down on the sand, a couple was having an animated discussion, but they were too far away for me to make out what they were arguing about. They looked like figures in some old silent movie; caricatures, their movements larger than life, rather than real people.

I don't know what I was thinking about; I was trying *not* to think, I suppose, but I wasn't having much luck. The arguing couple depressed me.

Hang on to what you've got, I wanted to tell them, but it wasn't any of my business. I thought about heading across town to Fitzhenry Park—there was a part of it called the Silenus Gardens filled with stone benches and statuary where I always felt better—when I spied a familiar figure sitting down by the river west of the Pier: Paperjack.

The Kickaha River was named after that branch of the Algonquin language family that originally lived in this area before the white men came and took it all away from them. All the tribe had left now was a reservation north of the city and this river named after them. The Kickaha had its source north of the reserve and cut through the city on its way to the lake. In this part of town it separated the business section and commercial waterfront from the Beaches where the money lives.

There are houses in the Beaches that make the old stately homes in Lower Crowsea look like tenements, but you can't see them from here. Looking west, all you see is green—first the City Commission's manicured lawns on either side of the river, then the treed hills that hide the homes of the wealthy from the rest of us plebes. On the waterfront itself are a couple of country clubs and the private beaches of the *really* wealthy whose estates back right onto the water.

Paperjack was sitting on this side of the river, doing I don't know what. From where I stood, I couldn't tell. He seemed to be just sitting there on the riverbank, watching the slow water move past. I watched him for awhile, then hoisted my fiddlecase from where I'd leaned it against the wall and hopped down to the sand. When I got to where he was sitting, he looked up and gave me an easy, welcoming grin, as if he'd been expecting me to show up.

Running into him like this was fate, Jilly would say. I'll stick to calling it coincidence. It's a big city, but it isn't that big.

Paperjack made a motion with his hand, indicating I should pull up a bit of lawn beside him. I hesitated for a moment—right up until then, I realized later, everything could have worked out differently. But I made the choice and sat beside him.

There was a low wall, right down by the water, with rushes and lilies growing up against it. Among the lilies was a family of ducks—mother and a paddling of duck-lings—and that was what Paperjack had been watching. He had an empty plastic bag in his hand, and the breadcrumbs that remained in the bottom told me he'd been feeding the ducks until his bread ran out.

He made another motion with his hand, touching the bag, then pointing to the ducks.

I shook my head. "I wasn't planning on coming down," I said, "so I didn't bring anything to feed them."

He nodded, understanding.

We sat quietly awhile longer. The ducks finally gave up on us and paddled farther up the river, looking for better pickings. Once they were gone, Paperjack turned to me again. He laid his hand against his heart, then raised his eyebrows questioningly.

Looking at that slim black hand with its long narrow fingers lying against his dark suit, I marveled again at the sheer depth of his ebony coloring. Even with the bit of a tan I'd picked up busking the last few weeks, I felt absolutely pallid beside him. Then I lifted my gaze to his eyes. If his skin swallowed light, I knew where it went: into his eyes. They were dark, so dark you could barely tell the difference between pupil and cornea, but inside their darkness was a kind of glow—a shine that resonated inside me like the deep hum that comes from my fiddle's bass strings whenever I play one of those wild Shetland reels in A minor.

I suppose it's odd, describing something visual in terms of sound, but right then, right at that moment, I *heard* the shine of his eyes, singing inside me. And I understood immediately what he'd meant by his gesture.

"Yeah," I said. "I'm feeling a little low."

He touched his chest again, but it was a different, lighter gesture this time. I knew what that meant as well.

"There's not much anybody can do about it," I said.

Except Sam. She could come back. Or maybe if I just knew she'd been *real* . . . But that opened a whole other line of thinking that I wasn't sure I wanted to get into again. I wanted her to have been real, I wanted her to come back, but if I accepted that, I also had to accept that ghosts were real and that the past could sneak up and steal someone from the present, taking them back into a time that had already been and gone.

Paperjack took his fortune-telling device out of the breast pocket of his jacket and gave me a questioning look. I started to shake my head, but before I could think about what I was doing, I just said, "What the hell," and let him do his stuff.

I chose blue from the colors, because that was the closest to how I was feeling; he didn't have any colors like confused or lost or foolish. I watched his fingers move the paper to spell out the color, then chose four from the numbers, because that's how many strings my fiddle has. When his fingers stopped moving the second time, I picked seven for no particular reason at all.

He folded back the paper flap so I could read my fortune. All it said was: "Swallow the past."

I didn't get it. I thought it'd say something like that Bobby McFerrin song, "Don't Worry, Be Happy." What it did say didn't make any sense at all.

"I don't understand," I told Paperjack. "What's it supposed to mean?"

He just shrugged. Folding up the fortune-teller, he put it back in his pocket.

Swallow the past. Did that mean I was supposed to forget about it? Or . . . well, swallow could also mean believe or accept. Was that what he was trying to tell me? Was he echoing Jilly's argument?

I thought about that photo in my fiddlecase, and then an idea came to me. I don't know why I'd never thought of it before. I grabbed my fiddlecase and stood up.

"I . . ." I wanted to thank him, but somehow the words just escaped me. All that came out was, "I've gotta run."

But I could tell he understood my gratitude. I wasn't exactly sure what he'd done, except that that little message on his fortune-teller had put together a connection for me that I'd never seen before.

Fate, I could hear Jilly saying.

Paperjack smiled and waved me off.

I followed coincidence away from Paperjack and the riverbank and back up Battersfield Road to the Newford Public Library in Lower Crowsea.

Time does more than erode a riverbank or wear mountains down into tired hills. It takes the edge from our memories as well, overlaying everything with a soft focus so that it all blurs together. What really happened gets all jumbled up with the hopes and dreams we once had and what we wish had really happened. Did you ever run into someone you went to school with—someone you never really hung around with, but just passed in the halls, or had a class with—and they act like you were the best of buddies, because that's how they remember it? For that matter, maybe you *were* buddies, and it's you that's remembering it wrong. . . .

Starting some solid detective work on what happened to Sam took the blur from my memories and brought her back into focus for me. The concepts of ghosts or people disappearing into the past just got pushed to one side, and all I thought about was Sam and tracking her down; if not the Sam I had known, then the woman she'd become in the past.

My friend Amy Scallan works at the library. She's a tall, angular woman with russet hair and long fingers that would have stood her in good stead at a piano keyboard. Instead she took up the Uillean pipes, and we play together in an on-again, off-again band called Johnny Jump Up. Matt Casey, our third member, is the reason we're not that regular a band.

Matt's a brilliant bouzouki and guitar player and a fabulous singer, but he's not got much in the way of social skills, and he's way too cynical for my liking. Since he and I don't really get along well, it makes rehearsals kind of tense at times. On the other hand, I love playing with Amy. She's the kind of musician who has such a good time playing that you can't help but enjoy yourself as well. Whenever I think of Amy, the first image that always comes to mind is of her rangy frame folded around her pipes, right elbow moving back and forth on the bellows to fill the bag under her left arm, those long fingers just dancing on the chanter, foot tapping, head bobbing, a grin on her face.

She always makes sure that the gig goes well, and we have a lot of fun, so it balances out I guess.

I showed her the picture I had of Sam. There was a street number on the porch's support pillar to the right of the steps and enough of the house in the picture that I'd be able to match it up to the real thing. If I could find out what street it was on. If the house still existed.

"This could take forever," Amy said as she laid the photo down on the desk.

"I've got the time."

Amy laughed. "I suppose you do. I don't know how you do it, Geordie. Everyone else in the world has to bust their buns to make a living, but you just cruise on through."

"The trick's having a low overhead," I said.

Amy just rolled her eyes. She'd been to my apartment, and there wasn't much to see: a spare fiddle hanging on the wall with a couple of Jilly's paintings; some tune books with tattered covers and some changes of clothing; one of those old-fashioned record players that had the turntable and speakers all in one unit and a few albums leaning against the side of the apple crate it sat on; a couple of bows that desperately needed rehairing; the handful of used paperbacks I'd picked up for the week's reading from Duffy's Used Books over on Walker Street; and a little beat-up old cassette machine with a handful of tapes.

And that was it. I got by.

I waited at the desk while Amy got the books we needed. She came back with an armload. Most had Newford in the title, but a few also covered that period of time when the city was still called Yoors, after the Dutchman Diederick van Yoors, who first settled the area in the early 1800s. It got changed to Newford back around the turn of the century, so all that's left now to remind the city of its original founding father is a street name.

Setting the books down before me on the desk, Amy went off into the stacks to look for some more obscure titles. I didn't wait for her to get back, but went ahead and started flipping through the first book on the pile, looking carefully at the pictures.

I started off having a good time. There's a certain magic in old photos, especially when they're of the place where you grew up. They cast a spell over you. Dirt roads where now there was pavement, sided by office complexes. The old Brewster Theatre in its heyday—I remembered it as the place where I first saw Phil Ochs and Bob Dylan, and later all-night movie festivals, but the Williamson Street Mall stood there now. Boating parties on the river. Old City Hall—it was a youth hostel these days.

But my enthusiasm waned with the afternoon. By the time the library closed, I was no closer to getting a street name for the house in Sam's photo than I had been when I came in. Amy gave me a sympathetic "I told you so" look when we separated on the front steps of the library. I just told her I'd see her tomorrow.

I had something to eat at Kathryn's Cafe. I'd gone there hoping to see Jilly, only I'd forgotten it was her night off. I tried calling her when I'd finished eating, but she was out. So I took my fiddle over to the theatre district and worked the crowds waiting in line there for an hour or so before I headed off for home, my pockets heavy with change.

That night, just before I fell asleep, I felt like a hole sort of opened in the air above my bed. Lying there, I found myself touring Newford—just floating through its streets. Though the time was the present, there was no color. Everything appeared in the same sepia tones as in my photo of Sam.

I don't remember when I finally did fall asleep.

The next morning I was at the library right when it opened, carrying two cups of take-out coffee in a paper bag, one of which I offered to Amy when I got to her desk. Amy muttered something like, "when owls prowl the day, they shouldn't look so bloody cheerful about it," but she accepted the coffee and cleared a corner of her desk so that I could get back to the books.

In the photo I had of Sam there was just the edge of a bay window visible beside the porch, with fairly unique rounded gingerbread trim running off from either side of its keystone. I'd thought it would be the clue to tracking down the place. It looked almost familiar, but I was no longer sure if that was because I'd actually seen the house at some time, or it was just from looking at the photo so much.

Unfortunately, those details weren't helping at all.

"You know, there's no guarantee you're going to find a picture of the house you're looking for in those books," Amy said around mid-morning when she was taking her coffee break. "They didn't exactly go around taking pictures of everything."

I was at the last page of *Walks Through Old Crowsea.* Closing the book, I set it on the finished pile beside my chair and then leaned back, lacing my fingers behind my head. My shoulders were stiff from sitting hunched over a desk all morning.

"I know. I'm going to give Jack a call when I'm done here to see if I can borrow his bike this afternoon."

"You're going to pedal all around town looking for this house?"

"What else can I do?"

"There's always the archives at the main library."

I nodded, feeling depressed. It had seemed like such a good idea yesterday. It was still a good idea. I just hadn't realized how long it would take.

"Or you could go someplace like the Market and show the photo around to some of the older folks. Maybe one of them will remember the place."

"I suppose."

I picked up the next book, *The Architectural Heritage of Old Yoors,* and went back to work.

And there it was, on page thirty-eight. The house. There were three buildings in a row in the photo; the one I'd been looking for was the middle one. I checked the caption: "Grasso Street, circa 1920."

"I don't believe it," Amy said. I must have made some kind of a noise, because she was looking up at me from her own work. "You found it, didn't you?" she added.

"I think so. Have you got a magnifying glass?"

She passed it over, and I checked out the street number of the middle house. One-forty-two. The same as in my photo.

Amy took over then. She phoned a friend who worked in the land registry office. He called back a half hour later and gave us the name of the owner in 1912, when my photo had been taken: Edward Dickenson. The house had changed hands a number of times since the Dickensons had sold it in the forties.

We checked the phone book, but there were over a hundred Dickensons listed, twelve with just an initial "E" and one Ed. None of the addresses were on Grasso Street.

"Which makes sense," Amy said, "since they sold the place fifty years ago."

I wanted to run by that block on Grasso where the house was—I'd passed it I don't know how many times, and never paid much attention to it or any of its neighbors—but I needed more background on the Dickensons first. Amy showed me how to run the microfiche, and soon I was going through back issues of *The Newford Star* and *The Daily Journal,* concentrating on the local news sections and the gossip columns.

The first photo of Edward Dickenson that came up was in *The Daily Journal,* the June 21st, 1913, issue. He was standing with the Dean of Butler University at some opening ceremony. I compared him to the people with Sam in my photo and found him standing behind her to her left.

Now that I was on the right track, I began to work in a kind of frenzy. I whipped through the microfiche, making notes of every mention of the Dickensons. Edward turned out to have been a stockbroker, one of the few who didn't lose his shirt in subsequent market crashes. Back then the money lived in Lower Crowsea, mostly on McKennitt, Grasso, and Stanton Streets. Edward made the papers about once a month—business deals, society galas, fund-raising events, political dinners, and the like. It wasn't until I hit the October 29, 1915, issue of *The Newford Star* that I had the wind knocked out of my sails.

It was the picture that got to me: Sam and a man who was no stranger. I'd seen him before. He was the ghost that had stepped out of the past and stolen her away. Under the photo was a caption announcing the engagement of Thomas Edward Dickenson, son of the well-known local businessman, to Samantha Rey.

In the picture of Sam that I had, Dickenson wasn't there with the rest of the people—he'd probably taken it. But here he was. Real. With Sam. I couldn't ignore it.

Back then they didn't have the technology to make a photograph lie.

There was a weird buzzing in my ears as that picture burned its imprint onto my retinas. It was hard to breathe, and my T-shirt suddenly seemed too tight.

I don't know what I'd been expecting, but I knew it wasn't this. I suppose I thought I'd track down the people in the picture and find out that the woman who looked like Sam was actually named Gertrude something-or-other, and she'd lived her whole life with that family. I didn't expect to find Sam. I didn't expect the ghost to have been real.

I was in a daze as I put away the microfiche and shut down the machine.

"Geordie?" Amy asked as I walked by her desk. "Are you okay?"

I remember nodding and muttering something about needing a break. I picked up my fiddle and headed for the front door. The next thing I remember is standing in front of the address on Grasso Street and looking at the Dickensons' house.

I had no idea who owned it now; I hadn't been paying much attention to Amy after she told me that the Dickensons had sold it. Someone had renovated it fairly recently, so it didn't look at all the same as in the photos, but under its trendy additions, I could see the lines of the old house.

I sat down on the curb with my fiddlecase across my knees and just stared at the building. The buzzing was back in my head. My shirt still felt too tight.

I didn't know what to do anymore, so I just sat there, trying to make sense out of what couldn't be reasoned away. I no longer had any doubt that Sam had been real, or that a ghost had stolen her away. The feeling of loss came back all over again, as if it had happened just now, not three years ago. And what scared me was, if she and the ghost were real, then what else might be?

I closed my eyes, and headlines of supermarket tabloids flashed across my eyes, a strobing flicker of bizarre images and words. That was the world Jilly lived in—one in which anything was possible. I didn't know if I could handle living in that kind of world. I needed rules and boundaries. Patterns.

It was a long time before I got up and headed for Kathryn's Cafe.

The first thing Jilly asked when I got in the door was, "Have you seen Paperjack?"

It took me a few moments to push back the clamor of my own thoughts to register what she'd asked. Finally I just shook my head.

"He wasn't at St. Paul's today," Jilly went on, "and he's always there, rain or shine, winter or summer. I didn't think he was looking well yesterday, and now . . ."

I tuned her out and took a seat at an empty table before I could fall down. That feeling of dislocation that had started up in me when I first saw Sam's photo in the microfiche kept coming and going in waves. It was cresting right now, and I found it hard to just sit in the chair, let alone listen to what Jilly was saying. I tuned her back in when the spaciness finally started to recede.

". . . heart attack, who would he call? He can't *speak*."

"I saw him yesterday," I said, surprised that my voice sounded so calm. "Around mid-afternoon. He seemed fine."

"He did?"

I nodded. "He was down by the Pier, sitting on the riverbank, feeding the ducks. He read my fortune."

"He *did*?"

"You're beginning to sound like a broken record, Jilly."

For some reason, I was starting to feel better. That sense of being on the verge of a panic attack faded and then disappeared completely. Jilly pulled up a chair and leaned across the table, elbows propped up, chin cupped in her hands.

"So tell me," she said. "What made you do it? What was your fortune?"

I told her everything that had happened since I had seen Paperjack. That sense of dislocation came and went again a few times while I talked, but mostly I was holding firm.

"Holy shit!" Jilly said when I was done.

She put her hand to her mouth and looked quickly around, but none of the customers seemed to have noticed. She reached a hand across the table and caught one of mine.

"So now you believe?" she asked.

"I don't have a whole lot of choice, do I?"

"What are you going to do?"

I shrugged. "What's to do? I found out what I needed to know—now I've got to learn to live with it and all the other baggage that comes with it."

Jilly didn't say anything for a long moment. She just held my hand and exuded comfort as only Jilly can.

"You could find her," she said finally.

"Who? Sam?"

"Who else?"

"She's probably—" I stumbled over the word dead and settled for "—not even alive anymore."

"Maybe not," Jilly said. "She'd definitely be old. But don't you think you should find out?"

"I . . ."

I wasn't sure I wanted to know. And if she were alive, I wasn't sure I wanted to meet her. What could we say to each other?

"Think about it, anyway," Jilly said.

That was Jilly; she never took no for an answer.

"I'm off at eight," she said. "Do you want to meet me then?"

"What's up?" I asked, halfheartedly.

"I thought maybe you'd help me find Paperjack."

I might as well, I thought. I was becoming a bit of an expert in tracking people down by this point. Maybe I should get a card printed: Geordie Riddell, Private Investigations and Fiddle Tunes.

"Sure," I told her.

"Great," Jilly said.

She bounced up from her seat as a couple of new customers came into the cafe. I ordered a coffee from her after she'd gotten them seated, then stared out the window at the traffic going by on Battersfield. I tried not to think of Sam—trapped in the past, making a new life for herself there—but I might as well have tried to jump to the moon.

By the time Jilly came off shift I was feeling almost myself again, but instead of being relieved, I had this great load of guilt hanging over me. It all centered around Sam and the ghost. I'd denied her once. Now I felt as though I was betraying her all over again. Knowing what I knew—the photo accompanying the engagement notice in that old issue of *The Newford Star* flashed across my mind—the way I was feeling at the moment didn't seem right. I felt too normal; and so the guilt.

"I don't get it," I said to Jilly as we walked down Battersfield towards the Pier. "This afternoon I was falling to pieces, but now I just feel . . ."

"Calm?"

"Yeah."

"That's because you've finally stopped fighting yourself and accepted that what you saw—what you remember—really happened. It was denial that was screwing you up."

She didn't add, "I told you so," but she didn't have to. It echoed in my head anyway, joining the rest of the guilt I was carrying around with me. If I'd only listened to her with an open mind, then . . . what?

I wouldn't be going through this all over again?

We crossed Lakeside Drive and made our way through the closed concession and souvenir stands to the beach. When we reached the Pier, I led her westward to where I'd last seen Paperjack, but he wasn't sitting by the river anymore. A lone duck regarded us hopefully, but neither of us had thought to bring any bread.

"So I track down Sam," I said, still more caught up in my personal quest than in looking for Paperjack. "If she's not dead, she'll be an old lady. If I find her—then what?"

"You'll complete the circle," Jilly said. She looked away from the river and faced me, her pixie features serious. "It's like the Kickaha say: everything is on a wheel. You stepped off the one that represents your relationship with Sam before it came full circle. Until you complete your turn on it, you'll never have peace of mind."

"When do you know you've come full circle?" I asked.

"You'll know."

She turned away before I could go on and started back towards the Pier. By day the place was crowded and full of noise, alive with tourists and people out relaxing, just looking to have a good time; by night, its occupancy was turned over to gangs of kids, fooling around on skateboards or simply hanging out, and the homeless: winos, bag ladies, hoboes, and the like.

Jilly worked the crowd, asking after Paperjack, while I followed in her wake. Everybody knew him, or had seen him in the past week, but no one knew where he was now, or where he lived. We were about to give up and head over to Fitzhenry Park to start over again with the people hanging out there, when we heard the sound of a harmonica. It was playing the blues, a soft, mournful sound that drifted up from the beach.

We made for the nearest stairs and then walked back across the sand to find the Bossman sitting under the boardwalk, hands cupped around his instrument, head bowed down, eyes closed. There was no one listening to him except us. The people with money to throw in his old cloth cap were having dinner now in the fancy restaurants across Lakeside Drive or over in the theatre district. He was just playing for himself.

When he was busking, he stuck to popular pieces—whatever was playing on the radio mixed with old show tunes, jazz favorites, and that kind of thing. The music that came from his harmonica now was pure magic. It transformed him, making him larger than life. The blues he played held all the world's sorrows in its long sliding notes and didn't so much change it, as make it bearable.

My fingers itched to pull out my fiddle and join him, but we hadn't come to jam. So we waited until he was done. The last note hung in the air for far longer than seemed possible, then he brought his hands away from his mouth and cradled the harmonica on his lap. He looked up at us from under drooping eyelids, the magic disappearing now that he'd stopped playing. He was just an old, homeless black man now, with the faint trace of a smile touching his lips.

"Hey, Jill—Geordie," he said. "What's doin'?"

"We're looking for Paperjack," Jilly told him.

The Bossman nodded. "Jack's the man for paperwork, all right."

"I've been worried about him," Jilly said. "About his health."

"You a doctor now, Jill?"

She shook her head.

"Anybody got a smoke?"

This time we both shook our heads.

From his pocket he pulled a half-smoked butt that he must have picked up off the boardwalk earlier, then lit it with a wooden match that he struck on the zipper of his jeans. He took a long drag and let it out so that the blue-grey smoke wreathed his head, studying us all the while.

"You care too much, you just get hurt," he said finally.

Jilly nodded. "I know. But I can't help it. Do you know where we can find him?"

"Well now. Come winter, he lives with a Mex family down in the Barrio."

"And in the summer?"

The Bossman shrugged. "I heard once he's got himself a camp up behind the Beaches."

"Thanks," Jilly said.

"He might not take to uninvited guests," the Bossman added. "Body gets himself an out-of-the-way squat like that, I'd think he be lookin' for privacy."

"I don't want to intrude," Jilly assured him. "I just want to make sure he's okay."

The Bossman nodded. "You're a stand-up kind of lady, Jill. I'll trust you to do what's right. I've been thinkin' old Jack's lookin' a little peaked myself. It's somethin' in his eyes—like just makin' do is gettin' to be a chore. But you take care, goin' back up in there. Some of the 'boes, they're not real accommodatin' to havin' strangers on their turf."

"We'll be careful," Jilly said.

The Bossman gave us both another long, thoughtful look, then lifted his harmonica and started to play again. Its mournful sound followed us back up to the boardwalk and seemed to trail us all the way to Lakeside Drive where we walked across the bridge to get to the other side of the Kickaha.

I don't know what Jilly was thinking about, but I was going over what she'd told me earlier. I kept thinking about wheels and how they turned.

Once past the City Commission's lawns on the far side of the river, the land starts to climb. It's just a lot of rough scrub on this side of the hills that make up the Beaches and every summer some of the hoboes and other homeless people camp out in it. The cops roust them from time to time, but mostly they're left alone, and they keep to themselves.

Going in there I was more nervous than Jilly; I don't think she's scared of anything. The sun had gone down behind the hills, and while it was twilight in the city, here it was already dark. I know a lot of the street people and get along with them better than most—everyone likes a good fiddle tune—but some of them could look pretty rough, and I kept anticipating that we'd run into some big wild-eyed hillbilly who'd take exception to our being there.

Well, we did run into one, but—like ninety percent of the street people in Newford—he was somebody that Jilly knew. He seemed pleased, if a little surprised to find her here, grinning at us in the fading light. He was a tall, big-shouldered man, dressed in dirty jeans and a flannel shirt, with big hobnailed boots on his feet and a shock of red hair that fell to his neck and stood up on top of his head in matted tangles. His name, appropriately enough, was Red. The smell that emanated from him made me want to shift position until I was standing upwind.

He not only knew where Paperjack's camp was, but took us there, only Paperjack wasn't home.

The place had Paperjack stamped all over it. There was a neatly rolled bedroll pushed up against a knapsack which probably held his changes of clothing. We didn't check it out, because we weren't there to go through his stuff. Behind the pack was a food cooler with a Coleman stove sitting on top of it, and everywhere you could see small origami stars that hung from the tree branches. There must have been over a hundred of them. I felt as if I were standing in the middle of space with stars all around me.

Jilly left a note for Paperjack, then we followed Red back out to Lakeside Drive. He didn't wait for our thanks. He just drifted away as soon as we reached the mown lawns that bordered the bush.

We split up then. Jilly had work to do—some art for Newford's entertainment weekly, *In the City*—and I didn't feel like tagging along to watch her work at her studio. She took the subway, but I decided to walk. I was bone-tired by then, but the night was one of those perfect ones when the city seems to be smiling. You can't see the dirt or the grime for the sparkle over everything. After all I'd been through today, I didn't want to be cooped up inside anywhere. I just wanted to enjoy the night.

I remember thinking about how Sam would've loved to be out walking with me on a night like this—the old Sam I'd lost, not necessarily the one she'd become. I didn't know that Sam at all, and I still wasn't sure I wanted to, even if I could track her down.

When I reached St. Paul's, I paused by the steps. Even though it was a perfect night to be out walking, something drew me inside. I tried the door, and it opened soundlessly at my touch. I paused just inside the door, one hand resting on the back pew, when I heard a cough.

I froze, ready to take flight. I wasn't sure how churches worked. Maybe my creeping around here at this time of night was . . . I don't know, sacrilegious or something.

I looked up to the front and saw that someone was sitting in the foremost pew. The cough was repeated, and I started down the aisle.

Intuitively, I guess I knew I'd find him here. Why else had I come inside?

Paperjack nodded to me as I sat down beside him on the pew. I laid my fiddlecase by my feet and leaned back. I wanted to ask after his health, to tell him how worried Jill was about him, but my day caught up with me in a rush. Before I knew it, I was nodding off.

I knew I was dreaming when I heard the voice. I had to be dreaming, because there was only Paperjack and I sitting on the pew, and Paperjack was mute. But the voice had the sound that I'd always imagined Paperjack's would have if he could speak. It was like the movement of his fingers when he was folding origami—quick, but measured and certain. Resonant, like his finished paper sculptures that always seemed to have more substance to them than just their folds and shapes.

"No one in this world views it the same," the voice said. "I believe that is what amazes me the most about it. Each person has his or her own vision of the world, and whatever lies outside that worldview becomes invisible. The rich ignore the poor. The happy can't see those who are hurting."

"Paperjack . . . ?" I asked.

There was only silence in reply.

"I . . . I thought you couldn't talk."

"So a man who has nothing he wishes to articulate is considered mute," the voice went on as though I hadn't interrupted. "It makes me weary."

"Who . . . who are you?" I asked.

"A mirror into which no one will look. A fortune that remains forever unread. My time here is done."

The voice fell silent again.

"Paperjack?"

Still silence.

It was just a dream, I told myself. I tried to wake myself from it. I told myself that the pew was made of hard, unyielding wood, and far too uncomfortable to sleep on. And Paperjack needed help. I remembered the cough and Jilly's worries.

But I couldn't wake up.

"The giving itself is the gift," the voice said suddenly. It sounded as though it came from the back of the church, or even farther away. "The longer I remain here, the more I forget."

Then the voice went away for good. I lost it in a dreamless sleep.

I woke early, and all my muscles were stiff. My watch said it was ten to six. I had a moment's disorientation—where the hell *was* I?—and then I remembered. Paperjack. And the dream.

I sat up straighter in the pew, and something fell from my lap to the floor. A piece of folded paper. I bent stiffly to retrieve it, turning it over and over in my hands, holding it up to the dim grey light that was creeping in through the windows. It was one of Paperjack's Chinese fortune-tellers.

After awhile I fit my fingers into the folds of the paper and looked down at the colors. I chose blue, same as I had the last time, and spelled it out, my fingers moving the paper back and forth so that it looked like a flower speaking soundlessly to me. I picked numbers at random, then unfolded the flap to read what it had to say.

"The question is more important than the answer," it said.

I frowned, puzzling over it, then looked at what I would have gotten if I'd picked another number, but all the other folds were blank when I turned them over. I stared at it, then folded the whole thing back up and stuck it in my pocket. I was starting to get a serious case of the creeps.

Picking up my fiddlecase, I left St. Paul's and wandered over to Chinatown. I had breakfast in an all-night diner, sharing the place with a bunch of blue-collar workers who were all talking about some baseball game they'd watched the night before. I thought of calling Jilly, but knew that if she'd been working all night on that *In the City* assignment, she'd be crashed out now and wouldn't appreciate a phone call.

I dawdled over breakfast, then slowly made my way up to that part of Foxville that's called the Rosses. That's where the Irish immigrants all lived in the forties and fifties. The place started changing in the sixties when a lot of hippies who couldn't afford the rents in Crowsea moved in, and it changed again with a new wave of immigrants from Vietnam and the Caribbean in the following decades. But the area, for all its changes, was still called the Rosses. My apartment was in the heart of it, right where Kelly Street meets Lee and crosses the Kickaha River. It's two doors down from The Harp, the only real Irish pub in town, which makes it convenient for me to get to the Irish music sessions on Sunday afternoons.

My phone was ringing when I got home. I was half expecting it to be Jilly, even though it was only going on eight, but found myself talking to a reporter from *The Daily Journal* instead. His name was Ian Begley, and it turned out he was a friend of Jilly's. She'd asked him to run down what information he could on the Dickensons in the paper's morgue.

"Old man Dickenson was the last real businessman of the family," Begley told me. "Their fortunes started to decline when his son Tom took over—he's the one who married the woman that Jilly said you were interested in tracking down. He died in 1976. I don't have an obit on his widow, but that doesn't necessarily mean she's still alive. If she moved out of town, the paper wouldn't have an obit for her unless the family put one in."

He told me a lot of other stuff, but I was only half listening. The business with Paperjack last night and the fortune-telling device this morning were still eating away at me. I did take down the address of Sam's granddaughter when it came up. Begley ran out of steam after another five minutes or so.

"You got enough there?" he asked.

I nodded, then realized he couldn't see me. "Yeah. Thanks a lot."

"Say hello to Jilly for me and tell her she owes me one."

After I hung up, I looked out the window for a long time. I managed to shift gears from Paperjack to thinking about what Begley had told me, about wheels, about Sam. Finally I got up and took a shower and shaved. I put on my cleanest jeans and shirt and shrugged on a sports jacket that had seen better days before I bought it in a retro fashion shop. I thought about leaving my fiddle behind, but knew I'd feel naked without it—I couldn't remember the last time I'd gone somewhere without it. The leather handle felt comforting in my hand as I hefted the case and went out the door.

All the way over to the address Begley had given me I tried to think of what I was going to say when I met Sam's granddaughter. The truth would make me sound like I was crazy, but I couldn't seem to concoct a story that would make sense.

I remember wondering—where was my brother when I needed him? Christy was never at a loss for words, no matter what the situation.

It wasn't until I was standing on the sidewalk in front of the house that I decided to stick as close to the truth as I could—I was an old friend of her grandmother's, could she put me in touch with her?—and take it from there. But even my vague plans went out the door when I rang the bell and stood face-to-face with Sam's granddaughter.

Maybe you saw this coming, but it was the last thing I'd expected. The woman had Sam's hair, Sam's eyes, Sam's face . . . to all intents and purposes it *was* Sam standing there, looking at me with that vaguely uncertain expression that most of us wear when we open the door to a stranger standing on our steps.

My chest grew so tight I could barely breathe, and suddenly I could hear the sound of rain in my memory—it was always raining when Sam saw the ghost; it was raining the night he stole her away into the past.

Ghosts. *I* was looking at a ghost.

The woman's expression was starting to change, the uncertainty turning into nervousness. There was no recognition in her eyes. As she began to step back—in a moment she'd close the door in my face, probably call the cops—I found my voice. I knew what I was going to say—I was going to ask about her grandmother—but all that came out was her name: "Sam."

"Yes?" she said. She looked at me a little more carefully. "Do I know you?"

Jesus, even the name was the same.

A hundred thoughts were going through my head, but they all spiraled down into one mad hope: this was Sam. We could be together again. Then a child appeared behind the woman. She was a little girl no more than five, blonde-haired, blue-eyed, just like her mother—just like her *mother's* grandmother. Reality came crashing down around me.

This Sam wasn't the woman I knew. She was married, she had children, she had a life.

"I . . . I knew your grandmother," I said. "We were . . . we used to be friends."

It sounded so inane to my ears, almost crazy. What would her grandmother—a woman maybe three times my age if she was still alive—have to do with a guy like me?

The woman's gaze traveled down to my fiddlecase. "Is your name Geordie? Geordie Riddell?"

I blinked in surprise, then nodded slowly.

The woman smiled a little sadly, mostly with her eyes.

"Granny said you'd come by," she said. "She didn't know when, but she said you'd come by one day." She stepped away from the door, shooing her daughter down the hall. "Would you like to come in?"

"I . . . uh, sure."

She led me into a living room that was furnished in mismatched antiques that, taken all together, shouldn't have worked, but did. The little girl perched in a Morris chair and watched me curiously as I sat down and set my fiddlecase down by my feet. Her mother pushed back a stray lock with a mannerism so like Sam's that my chest tightened up even more.

"Would you like some coffee or tea?" she asked.

I shook my head. "I don't want to intrude. I . . ." Words escaped me again.

"You're not intruding," she said. She sat down on the couch in front of me, that sad look back in her eyes. "My grandmother died a few years ago—she'd moved to New England in the late seventies, and she died there in her sleep. Because she loved it so much, we buried her there in a small graveyard overlooking the sea."

I could see it in my mind as she spoke. I could hear the sound of the waves breaking on the shore below, the spray falling on the rocks like rain.

"She and I were very close, a lot closer than I ever felt to my mother." She gave me a rueful look. "You know how it is."

She didn't seem to be expecting a response, but I nodded anyway.

"When her estate was settled, most of her personal effects came to me. I . . ." She paused, then stood up. "Excuse me for a moment, would you?"

I nodded again. She'd looked sad, talking about Sam. I hoped that bringing it all up hadn't made her cry.

The little girl and I sat in silence, looking at each other until her mother returned. She was such a serious kid, her big eyes taking everything in; she sat quietly, not running around or acting up like most kids do when there's someone new in the house that they can show off to. I didn't think she was shy; she was just . . . well, serious.

Her mother had a package wrapped in brown paper and twine in her hands when she came back. She sat down across from me again and laid the package on the table between us.

"Granny told me a story once," she said, "about her first and only real true love. It was an odd story, a kind of ghost story, about how she'd once lived in the future until granddad's love stole her away from her own time and brought her to his." She gave me an apologetic smile. "I knew it was just a story because, when I was growing up I'd met people she'd gone to school with, friends from her past before she met granddad. Besides, it was too much like some science fiction story.

"But it was true, wasn't it?"

I could only nod. I didn't understand how Sam and everything about her except my memories of her could vanish into the past, how she could have a whole new set of memories when she got back there, but I knew it was true.

I accepted it now, just as Jilly had been trying to get me to do for years. When I looked at Sam's granddaughter, I saw that she accepted it as well.

"When her effects were sent to me," she went on, "I found this package in them. It's addressed to you."

I had seen my name on it, written in a familiar hand. My own hand trembled as I reached over to pick it up.

"You don't have to open it now," she said.

I was grateful for that.

"I . . . I'd better go," I said and stood up. "Thank you for taking the time to see me."

That sad smile was back as she saw me to the door.

"I'm glad I got the chance to meet you," she said when I stepped out onto the porch.

I wasn't sure I could say the same. She looked so much like Sam, *sounded* so much like Sam, that it hurt.

"I don't think we'll be seeing each other again," she added.

No. She had her husband, her family. I had my ghosts.

"Thanks," I said again and started off down the walk, fiddlecase in one hand, the brown paper package in the other.

I didn't open the package until I was sitting in the Silenus Gardens in Fitzhenry Park, a place that always made me feel good; I figured I was going to need all the help I could get. Inside there was a book with a short letter. The book I recognized. It was the small J. M. Dent & Sons edition of Shakespeare's *A Midsummer Night's Dream* that I'd given Sam because I'd known it was one of her favorite stories.

There was nothing special about the edition, other than its size—it was small enough for her to carry around in her purse, which she did. The inscription I'd written to her was inside, but the book was far more worn than it had been when I'd first given it to her. I didn't have to open the book to remember that famous quotation from Puck's final lines:

> *If we shadows have offended,*
> *Think but this, and all is mended,*
> *That you have but slumber'd here,*
> *While these visions did appear.*
> *And this weak and idle theme,*
> *No more yielding but a dream . . .*

But it hadn't been a dream—not for me, and not for Sam. I set the book down beside me on the stone bench and unfolded the letter.

"Dear Geordie," it said. "I know you'll read this one day, and I hope you can forgive me for not seeing you in person, but I wanted you to remember me as I was, not as I've become. I've had a full and mostly happy life; you know my only regret. I can look back on our time together with the wisdom of an old woman now and truly know that all things have their time. Ours was short—too short, my heart—but we did have it.

"Who was it that said, 'better to have loved and lost, than never to have loved at all'? We loved and lost each other, but I would rather cherish the memory than rail against the unfairness. I hope you will do the same."

I sat there and cried. I didn't care about the looks I was getting from people walking by, I just let it all out. Some of my tears were for what I'd lost, some were for Sam and her bravery, and some were for my own stupidity at denying her memory for so long.

I don't know how long I sat there like that, holding her letter, but the tears finally dried on my cheeks. I heard the scuff of feet on the path and wasn't surprised to look up and find Jilly standing in front of me.

"Oh Geordie, me lad," she said.

She sat down at my side and leaned against me. I can't tell you how comforting it was to have her there. I handed her the letter and book and sat quietly while she read the first and looked at the latter. Slowly she folded up the letter and slipped it inside the book.

"How do you feel now?" she asked finally. "Better or worse?"

"Both."

She raised her eyebrows in a silent question.

"Well, it's like what they say funerals are for," I tried to explain. "It gives you the chance to say goodbye, to settle things, like taking a—" I looked at her and managed to find a small smile "—final turn on a wheel. But I feel depressed about Sam. I know what we had was real, and I know how it felt for me, losing her. But I only had to deal with it for a few years. She carried it for a lifetime."

"Still, she carried on."

I nodded. "Thank god for that."

Neither of us spoke for awhile, but then I remembered Paperjack. I told her what I thought had happened last night, then showed her the fortune-telling device that he'd left with me in St. Paul's. She read my fortune with pursed lips and the start of a wrinkle on her forehead, but didn't seem particularly surprised by it.

"What do you think?" I asked her.

She shrugged. "Everybody makes the same mistake. Fortune-telling doesn't reveal the future; it mirrors the present. It resonates against what your subconscious already knows and hauls it up out of the darkness so that you can get a good look at it."

"I meant about Paperjack."

"I think he's gone—back to wherever it was that he came from."

She was beginning to exasperate me in that way that only she could.

"But who was he?" I asked. "No, better yet, *what* was he?"

"I don't know," Jilly said. "I just know it's like your fortune said. It's the questions we ask, the journey we take to get where we're going that's more important than the actual answer. It's good to have mysteries. It reminds us that there's more to the world than just making do and having a bit of fun."

I sighed, knowing I wasn't going to get much more sense out of her than that.

* * *

It wasn't until the next day that I made my way alone to Paperjack's camp in back of the Beaches. All his gear was gone, but the paper stars still hung from the trees. I wondered again about who he was. Some oracular spirit, a kind of guardian angel, drifting around, trying to help people see themselves? Or an old homeless black man with a gift for folding paper? I understood then that my fortune made a certain kind of sense, but I didn't entirely agree with it.

Still, in Sam's case, knowing the answer had brought me peace.

I took Paperjack's fortune-teller from my pocket and strung it with a piece of string I'd brought along for that purpose. Then I hung it on the branch of a tree so that it could swing there, in among all those paper stars, and I walked away.

Tallulah

*Nothing is too wonderful
to be true.*
—Michael Faraday

For the longest time, I thought she was a ghost, but I know what she is now. She's come to mean everything to me; like a lifeline, she keeps me connected to reality, to this place and this time, by her very capriciousness.

I wish I'd never met her.

That's a lie, of course, but it comes easily to the tongue. It's a way to pretend that the ache she left behind in my heart doesn't hurt.

She calls herself Tallulah, but I know who she really is. A name can't begin to encompass the sum of all her parts. But that's the magic of names, isn't it? That the complex, contradictory individuals we are can be called up complete and whole in another mind through the simple sorcery of a name. And connected to the complete person we call up in our mind with the alchemy of their name comes all the baggage of memory: times you were together, the music you listened to this morning or that night, conversation and jokes and private moments—all the good and bad times you've shared.

Tally's name conjures up more than just that for me. When the *gris-gris* of the memories that hold her stir in my mind, she guides me through the city's night like a totem does a shaman through Dreamtime. Everything familiar is changed; what she shows me goes under the skin, right to the marrow of the bone. I see a building and I know not only its shape and form, but its history. I can hear its breathing, I can almost read its thoughts.

It's the same for a street or a park, an abandoned car or some secret garden hidden behind a wall, a late night cafe or an empty lot. Each one has its story, its secret history, and Tally taught me how to read each one of them. Where once I guessed at those stories, chasing rumors of them like they were errant fireflies, now I know.

I'm not as good with people. Neither of us are. Tally, at least, has an excuse. But me . . .

I wish I'd never met her.

My brother Geordie is a busker—a street musician. He plays his fiddle on street corners or along the queues in the theatre district and makes a kind of magic with his music that words just can't describe. Listening to him play is like stepping into an old Irish or Scottish fairy tale. The slow airs call up haunted moors and lonely coastlines; the jigs and reels wake a fire in the soul that burns with the awesome wonder of bright stars on a cold night, or the familiar warmth of red coals glimmering in a friendly hearth.

The funny thing is, he's one of the most pragmatic people I know. For all the enchantment he can call up out of that old Czech fiddle of his, I'm the one with the fey streak in our family.

As far as I'm concerned, the only difference between fact and what most people call fiction is about fifteen pages in the dictionary. I've got such an open mind that Geordie says I've got a hole in it, but I've been that way for as long as I can remember. It's not so much that I'm gullible—though I've been called that and less charitable things in my time; it's more that I'm willing to just suspend my disbelief until whatever I'm considering has been thoroughly debunked to my satisfaction.

I first started collecting oddities and curiosities as I heard about them when I was in my teens, filling page after page of spiral-bound notebooks with little notes and jottings—neat inky scratches on the paper, each entry opening worlds of possibility for me whenever I reread them. I liked things to do with the city the best because that seemed the last place in the world where the delicate wonders that are magic should exist.

Truth to tell, a lot of what showed up in those notebooks leaned towards a darker side of the coin, but even that darkness had a light in it for me because it still stretched the realms of what was into a thousand variable what-might-be's. That was the real magic for me: the possibility that we only have to draw aside a veil to find the world a far more strange and wondrous place than its mundaneness allowed it could be.

It was my girlfriend back then—Katie Deren—who first convinced me to use my notebooks as the basis for stories. Katie was about as odd a bird as I was in those days. We'd sit around with the music of obscure groups like the Incredible String Band or Dr. Strangely Strange playing on the turntable and literally talk away whole nights about anything and everything. She had the strangest way of looking at things; everything had a soul for her, be it the majestic old oak tree that stood in her parents' back yard, or the old black iron kettle that she kept filled with dried weeds on the sill of her bedroom window.

We drifted apart, the way it happens with a lot of relationships at that age, but I kept the gift she'd woken in me: the stories.

I never expected to become a writer, but then I had no real expectations whatsoever as to what I was going to be when I "grew up." Sometimes I think I never did—grow up that is.

But I did get older. And I found I could make a living with my stories. I called them urban legends—independently of Jan Harold Brunvand, who also makes a living collecting them. But he approaches them as a folklorist, cataloguing and comparing them, while I retell them in stories that I sell to magazines and then recycle into book collections.

I don't feel we're in any kind of competition with each other, but then I feel that way about all writers. There are as many stories to be told as there are people to tell them about; only the mean-spirited would consider there to be a competition at all. And Brunvand does such a wonderful job. The first time I read his *The Vanishing Hitchhiker,* I was completely smitten with his work and, like the hundreds of other correspondents Brunvand has, made a point of sending him items I thought he could use for his future books.

But I never wrote to him about Tally.

I do my writing at night—the later the better. I don't work in a study or an office and I don't use a typewriter or computer, at least not for my first drafts. What I like to do is go out into the night and just set up shop wherever it feels right: a park bench, the counter of some all-night diner, the stoop of St. Paul's Cathedral, the doorway of a closed junk shop on Grasso Street.

I still keep notebooks, but they're hardcover ones now. I write my stories in them as well. And though the stories owe their existence to the urban legends that give them their quirky spin, what they're really about is people: what makes them happy or sad. My themes are simple. They're about love and loss, honor and the responsibilities of friendship. And wonder . . . always wonder. As complex as people are individually, their drives are universal.

I've been told—so often I almost believe it myself—that I've got a real under-standing of people. However strange the situations my characters find themselves in, the characters themselves seem very real to my readers. That makes me feel good, naturally enough, but I don't understand it because I don't feel that I know people very well at all.

I'm just not good with them.

I think it comes from being that odd bird when I was growing up. I was distanced from the concerns of my peers, I just couldn't get into so many of the things that they felt was important. The fault was partly the other kids—if you're different, you're fair game. You know how it can be. There are three kinds of kids: the ones that are the odd birds, the ones that pissed on them, and the ones that watched it happen.

It was partly my fault, too, because I ostracized them as much as they did me. I was always out of step; I didn't really care about belonging to this gang or that clique. A few years earlier and I'd have been a beatnik, a few years later, a hippie. I got into drugs before they were cool; found out they were messing up my head and got out of them when everybody else starting dropping acid and MDA and who knows what all.

What it boiled down to was that I had a lot of acquaintances, but very few friends. And even with the friends I did have, I always felt one step removed from the rela-tionship, as though I was observing what was going on, taking notes, rather than just being there.

That hasn't changed much as I've grown older.

How that—let's call it aloofness, for lack of a better word—translated into this so-called gift for characterization in my fiction, I can't tell you. Maybe I put so much into the stories, I had nothing left over for real life. Maybe it's because each one of us, no matter how many or how close our connections to other people, remains in the end, irrevocably on his or her own, solitary islands separated by expanses of the world's sea, and I'm just more aware of it than others. Maybe I'm just missing the necessary circuit in my brain.

Tally changed all of that.

I wouldn't have thought it, the first time I saw her.

There's a section of the Market in Lower Crowsea, where it backs onto the Kickaha River, that's got a kind of Old World magic about it. The roads are too narrow for normal vehicular traffic, so most people go through on bicycles or by foot. The buildings lean close to each other over the cobblestoned streets that twist and wind in a confusion that not even the city's mapmakers have been able to unravel to anyone's satisfaction.

There are old shops back in there and some of them still have signage in Dutch dating back a hundred years. There are buildings tenanted by generations of the same families, little courtyards, secret gardens, any number of sly-eyed cats, old men playing dominoes and checkers and their gossiping wives, small gales of shrieking children by day, mysterious eddies of silence by night. It's a wonderful place, completely untouched by the yuppie renovation projects that took over the rest of the Market.

Right down by the river there's a public courtyard surrounded on all sides by three-story brick and stone town houses with mansard roofs and dormer windows. Late at night, the only manmade sound comes from the odd bit of traffic on the McKennitt Street Bridge a block or so south, the only light comes from the single streetlamp under which stands a bench made of cast iron and wooden slats. Not a light shines from the windows of the buildings that enclose it. When you sit on that bench, the river murmurs at your back and the streetlamp encloses you in a comforting embrace of warm yellow light.

It's one of my favorite places to write. I'll sit there with my notebook propped up on my lap and scribble away for hours, my only companion, more often than not, a tattered-eared tom sleeping on the bench beside me. I think he lives in one of the houses, though he could be a stray. He's there most times I come—not waiting for me. I'll sit down and start to work and after a half-hour or so he'll come sauntering out of the shadows, stopping a half-dozen times to lick this shoulder, that hind leg, before finally settling down beside me like he's been there all night.

He doesn't much care to be patted, but I'm usually too busy to pay that much attention to him anyway. Still, I enjoy his company. I'd miss him if he stopped coming.

I've wondered about his name sometimes. You know that old story where they talk about a cat having three names? There's the one we give them, the one they use among themselves and then the secret one that only they know.

I just call him Ben; I don't know what he calls himself. He could be the King of the Cats, for all I know.

He was sleeping on the bench beside me the night she showed up. He saw her first. Or maybe he heard her.

It was early autumn, a brisk night that followed one of those perfect crisp autumn days—clear skies, the sunshine bright on the turning leaves, a smell in the air of a change coming, the wheel of the seasons turning. I was bundled up in a flannel jacket and wore half-gloves to keep my hands from getting too cold as I wrote.

I looked up when Ben stirred beside me, fur bristling, slit-eyed gaze focused on the narrow mouth of an alleyway that cut like a tunnel through the town houses on the north side of the courtyard. I followed his gaze in time to see her step from the shadows.

She reminded me of Geordie's friend Jilly, the artist. She had the same slender frame and tangled hair, the same pixie face and wardrobe that made her look like she did all her clothes buying at a thrift shop. But she had a harder look than Jilly, a toughness that was reflected in the sharp lines that modified her features and in her gear: battered leather jacket, jeans stuffed into low-heeled black cowboy boots, hands in her pockets, a kind of leather carryall hanging by its strap from her shoulder.

She had a loose, confident gait as she crossed the courtyard, boot heels clicking on the cobblestones. The warm light from the streetlamp softened her features a little.

Beside me, Ben turned around a couple of times, a slow chase of his tail that had no enthusiasm to it, and settled back into sleep. She sat down on the bench, the cat between us, and dropped her carryall at her feet. Then she leaned back against the bench, legs stretched out in front of her, hands back in the pockets of her jeans, head turned to look at me.

"Some night, isn't it?" she said.

I was still trying to figure her out. I couldn't place her age. One moment she looked young enough to be a runaway and I waited for the inevitable request for spare change or a place to crash, the next she seemed around my age—late twenties, early thirties—and I didn't know what she might want. One thing people didn't do in the city, even in this part of it, was befriend strangers. Not at night. Especially not if you were young and as pretty as she was.

My lack of a response didn't seem to faze her in the least.

"What's your name?" she asked.

"Christy Riddell," I said. I hesitated for a moment, then reconciled myself to a conversation. "What's yours?" I added as I closed my notebook, leaving my pen inside it to keep my place.

"Tallulah."

Just that, the one name. Spoken with the brassy confidence of a Cher or a Madonna.

"You're kidding," I said.

Tallulah sounded like it should belong to a '20s flapper, not some punky street kid.

She gave me a smile that lit up her face, banishing the last trace of the harshness I'd seen in her features as she was walking up to the bench.

"No, really," she said. "But you can call me Tally."

The melody of the ridiculous refrain from that song by—was it Harry Belafonte?—came to mind, something about tallying bananas.

"What're you doing?" she asked.

"Writing."

"I can *see* that. I meant, what kind of writing?"

"I write stories," I told her.

I waited then for the inevitable questions: Have you ever been published? What name do you write under? Where do you get your ideas? Instead she turned away and looked up at the sky.

"I knew a poet once," she said. "He wanted to capture his soul on a piece of paper—really capture it." She looked back at me. "But of course, you can't do that, can you? You can try, you can bleed honesty into your art until it feels like you've wrung your soul dry, but in the end, all you've created is a possible link between minds. An attempt at communication. If a soul can't be measured, then how can it be captured?"

I revised my opinion of her age. She might look young, but she spoke with too much experience couched in her words.

"What happened to him?" I found myself asking. "Did he give up?"

She shrugged. "I don't know. He moved away." Her gaze left mine and turned skyward once more. "When they move away, they leave my life because I can't follow them."

She mesmerized me—right from that first night. I sensed a portent in her casual appearance into my life, though a portent of what, I couldn't say.

"Did you ever want to?" I asked her.

"Want to what?"

"Follow them." I remember, even then, how the plurality bothered me. I was jealous and I didn't even know of what.

She shook her head. "No. All I ever have is what they leave behind."

Her voice seemed to diminish as she spoke. I wanted to reach out and touch her shoulder with my hand, to offer what comfort I could to ease the sudden malaise that appeared to have gripped her, but her moods, I came to learn, were mercurial. She sat up suddenly and stroked Ben until the motor of his purring filled the air with its resonance.

"Do you always write in places like this?" she asked.

I nodded. "I like the night; I like the city at night. It doesn't seem to belong to anyone then. On a good night, it almost seems as if the stories write themselves. It's almost as though coming out here plugs me directly into the dark heart of the city night and all of its secrets come spilling from my pen."

I stopped, suddenly embarrassed by what I'd said. It seemed too personal a disclosure for such short acquaintance. But she just gave me a low-watt version of her earlier smile.

"Doesn't that bother you?" she asked.

"Does what bother me?"

"That perhaps what you're putting down on paper doesn't belong to you."

"Does it ever?" I replied. "Isn't the very act of creation made up of setting a piece of yourself free?"

"What happens when there's no more pieces left?"

"That's what makes it special—I don't think you ever run out of the creative spark. Just doing it, replenishes the well. The more I work, the more ideas come to me. Whether they come from my subconscious or some outside source, isn't really relevant. What is relevant is what I put into it."

"Even when it seems to write itself?"

"Maybe especially so."

I was struck—not then, but later, remembering—by the odd intensity of the conversation. It wasn't a normal dialogue between strangers. We must have talked for three hours, never about ourselves, our histories, our pasts, but rather about what we were now, creating an intimacy that seemed surreal when I thought back on it the next day. Occasionally, there were lulls in the conversation, but they, too, seemed to add to the sense of bonding, like the comfortable silences that are only possible between good friends.

I could've kept right on talking, straight through the night until dawn, but she rose during one of those lulls.

"I have to go," she said, swinging the strap of her carryall onto her shoulder.

I knew a moment's panic. I didn't know her address or her phone number. All I had was her first name.

"When can I see you again?" I asked.

"Have you ever been down to those old stone steps under the Kelly Street Bridge?"

I nodded. They dated back from when the river was used to haul goods from upland, down to the lake. The steps under the bridge were all that was left of an old dock that had serviced the Irish-owned inn called The Harp. The dock was long abandoned, but The Harp still stood. It was one of the oldest buildings in the city. Only the solid stone structures of the city's Dutch founding fathers, like the ones that encircled us, were older.

"I'll meet you there tomorrow night," she said. She took a few steps, then paused, adding, "Why don't you bring along one of your books?"

The smile she gave me, before she turned away again, was intoxicating. I watched her walk back across the courtyard, disappearing into the narrow mouth of the alleyway from which she'd first come. Her footsteps lingered on, an echoing tap-tap on the cobblestones, but then that too faded.

I think it was at that moment that I decided she was a ghost.

I didn't get much writing done over the next few weeks. She wouldn't—she said she couldn't—see me during the day, but she wouldn't say why. I've got such a head filled with fictions that I honestly thought it was because she was a ghost, or maybe a succubus or a vampire. The sexual attraction was certainly there. If she'd sprouted fangs one night, I'd probably just have bared my neck and let her feed. But she didn't, of course. Given a multiple-choice quiz, in the end I realized the correct answer was none of the above.

I was also sure that she was at least my own age, if not older. She was widely read and, like myself, had eclectic tastes that ranged from genre fiction to the classics. We talked for hours every night, progressed to walking hand in hand through our favorite parts of the benighted city and finally made love one night in a large, cozy sleeping bag in Fitzhenry Park.

She took me there on one of what we called our rambles and didn't say a word, just stripped down in the moonlight and then drew me down into the sweet harbor of her arms. Above us, I heard geese heading south as, later, I drifted into sleep. I remember thinking it was odd to hear them so late at night, but then what wasn't in the hours I spent with Tally?

I woke alone in the morning, the subject of some curiosity by a couple of old winos who casually watched me get dressed inside the bag as though they saw this kind of thing every morning.

Our times together blur in my mind now. It's hard for me to remember one night from another. But I have little fetish bundles of memory that stay whole and complete in my mind, the *gris-gris* that collected around her name in my mind, like my nervousness that second night under the Kelly Street Bridge, worried that she wouldn't show, and three nights later when, after not saying a word about the book of my stories I'd given her when we parted on the old stone steps under the bridge, she told me how much she'd liked them.

"These are my stories," she said as she handed the book back to me that night.

I'd run into possessive readers before, fans who laid claim to my work as their own private domain, who treated the characters in the stories as real people, or thought that I carried all sorts of hidden and secret knowledge in my head, just because of the magic and mystery that appeared in the tales I told. But I'd never had a reaction like Tally's before.

"They're about me," she said. "They're your stories, I can taste your presence in every word, but each of them's a piece of me, too."

I told her she could keep the book and the next night, I brought her copies of my other three collections, plus photocopies of the stories that had only appeared in magazines to date. I won't say it's because she liked the stories so much, that I came to love her; that would have happened anyway. But her pleasure in them certainly didn't make me think any the less of her.

Another night she took a photograph out of her carryall and showed it to me. It was a picture of her, but she looked different, softer, not so much younger as not so tough. She wore her hair differently and had a flower print dress on; she was standing in sunlight.

"When . . . when was this taken?" I asked.

"In happier times."

Call me small-minded that my disappointment should show so plain, but it hurt that what were the happiest nights of my life, weren't the same for her.

She noticed my reaction—she was always quick with things like that—and laid a warm hand on mine.

"It's not you," she said. "I love our time together. It's the rest of my life that's not so happy."

Then be with me all the time, I wanted to tell her, but I already knew from experience that there was no talking about where she went when she left me, what she did, who she was. I was still thinking of ghosts, you see. I was afraid that some taboo lay upon her telling me, that if she spoke about it, if she told me where she was during the day, the spell would break and her spirit would be banished forever like in some hokey B-movie.

I wanted more than just the nights, I'll admit freely to that, but not enough to risk losing what I had. I was like the wife in "Bluebeard," except I refused to allow my curiosity to turn the key in the forbidden door. I could have followed her, but I didn't. And not just because I was afraid of her vanishing on me. It was because she trusted me not to.

We made love three times, all told, every time in that old sleeping bag of hers, each time in a different place, each morning I woke alone. I'd bring back her sleeping bag when we met that night and she'd smile to see its bulk rolled under my arm.

The morning after the first time, I realized that I was changing; that she was changing me. It wasn't by anything she said or did, or rather it wasn't that she was making me change, but that our relationship was stealing away that sense of distancing I had carried with me through my life.

And she was changing, too. She still wore her jeans and leather jacket most of the time, but sometimes she appeared wearing a short dress under the jacket, warm leggings, small trim shoes instead of her boots. Her face kept its character, but the tension wasn't so noticeable anymore, the toughness had softened.

I'd been open with her from the very first night, more open than I'd ever been with friends I'd known for years. And that remained. But now it was starting to spill over to my other relationships. I found my brother and my friends were more comfortable with me, and I with them. None of them knew about Tally; so far as they knew I was still prowling the nocturnal streets of the city in search of inspiration. They didn't know that I wasn't writing, though Professor Dapple guessed.

I suppose it was because he always read my manuscripts before I sent them off. We had the same interests in the odd and the curious—it was what had drawn us together long before Jilly became his student, before he retired from the university. Everybody still thought of him as the Professor; it was hard not to.

He was a tiny wizened man with a shock of frizzy white hair and glasses who delighted in long conversations conducted over tea, or if the hour was appropriate, a good Irish whisky. At least once every couple of weeks the two of us would sit in his cozy study, he reading one of my stories while I read his latest article before it was sent off to some journal or other. When the third visit went by in which I didn't have a manuscript in hand, he finally broached the subject.

"You seem happy these days, Christy."

"I am."

He'd smiled. "So is it true what they say—an artist must suffer to produce good work?"

I hadn't quite caught on yet to what he was about.

"Neither of us believe that," I said.

"Then you must be in love."

"I . . ."

I didn't know what to say. An awful sinking feeling had settled in my stomach at his words. Lord knew, he was right, but for some reason, just as I knew I shouldn't follow Tally when she left me after our midnight trysts, I had this superstitious dread that if the world discovered our secret, she would no longer be a part of my life.

"There's nothing wrong with being in love," he said, mistaking my hesitation for embarrassment.

"It's not that," I began, knowing I had nowhere to go except a lie and I couldn't lie to the Professor.

"Never fear," he said. "You're allowed your privacy—and welcome to it, I might add. At my age, any relating of your escapades would simply make me jealous. But I worry about your writing."

"I haven't stopped," I told him. And then I had it. "I've been thinking of writing a novel."

That wasn't a lie. I was always thinking of writing a novel; I just doubted that I ever would. My creative process could easily work within the perimeters of short fiction, even a connected series of stories such as *The Red Crow* had turned out to be, but a novel was too massive an undertaking for me to understand, little say attempt. I had to have the whole of it in my head and to do so with anything much longer than a short novella was far too daunting a process for me to begin. I had discovered, to my disappointment because I did actually *want* to make the attempt, that the longer a piece of mine was, the less . . . substance it came to have. It was as though the sheer volume of a novel's wordage would somehow dissipate the strengths my work had to date.

My friends who did write novels told me I was just being a chickenshit; but then they had trouble with short fiction and avoided it like the plague. It was my firm belief that one should stick with what worked, though maybe that was just a way of rationalizing a failure.

"What sort of a novel?" the Professor asked, intrigued since he knew my feelings on the subject.

I gave what I hoped was a casual shrug.

"That's what I'm still trying to decide," I said, and then turned the conversation to other concerns.

But I was nervous leaving the Professor's house, as though the little I had said was enough to turn the key in the door that led into the hidden room I shouldn't enter. I sensed a weakening of the dam that kept the mystery of our trysts deep and safe. I feared for the floodgate opening and the rush of reality that would tear my ghostly lover away from me.

But as I've already said, she wasn't a ghost. No, something far stranger hid behind her facade of pixie face and tousled hair.

I've wondered before, and still do, how much of what happens to us we bring upon ourselves. Did my odd superstition concerning Tally drive her away, or was she already leaving before I ever said as much as I did to the Professor? Or was it mere coincidence that she said goodbye that same night?

I think of the carryall she'd had on her shoulder the first time we met and have wondered since if she wasn't already on her way then. Perhaps I had only interrupted a journey already begun.

"You know, don't you?" she said when I saw her that night.

Did synchronicity reach so far that we would part that night in that same courtyard by the river where we had first met?

"You know I have to go," she added when I said nothing.

I nodded. I did. What I didn't know was—

"Why?" I asked.

Her features seemed harder again—like they had been that first night. The softness that had grown as our relationship had was more memory than fact, her features seemed to be cut to the bone once more. Only her eyes still held a touch of warmth, as did her smile. A tough veneer masked the rest of her.

"It's because of how the city is used," she said. "It's because of hatred and spite and bigotry; it's because of homelessness and drugs and crime; it's because the green quiet places are so few while the dark terrors multiply; it's because what's old and comfortable and rounded must make way for what's new and sharp and brittle; it's because a mean spirit grips its streets and that meanness cuts inside me like a knife.

"It's changing me, Christy, and I don't want you to see what I will become. You wouldn't recognize me and I wouldn't want you to.

"That's why I have to go."

When she said go, I knew she meant she was leaving me, not the city.

"But—"

"You've helped me keep it all at bay, truly you have, but it's not enough. Neither of us have enough strength to hold that mean spirit at bay forever. What we have was stolen from the darkness. But it won't let us steal any more."

I started to speak, but she just laid her fingers across my lips. I saw that her sleeping bag was stuffed under the bench. She pulled it out and unrolled it on the cobblestones. I thought of the dark windows of the town houses looking into the courtyard. There could be a hundred gazes watching as she gently pulled me down onto the sleeping bag, but I didn't care.

I tried to stay awake. I lay beside her, propped up on an elbow and stroked her shoulder, her hair. I marveled at the softness of her skin, the silkiness of her hair. In repose, the harsh lines were gone from her face again. I wished that there was some way I could just keep all her unhappiness at bay, that I could stay awake and protect her forever, but sleep snuck up on me all the same and took me away.

Just as I went under, I thought I heard her say, "You'll know other lovers."

But not like her. Never like her.

When I woke the next morning, I was alone on the sleeping bag, except for Ben who lay purring on the bag where she had lain.

It was early, too early for anyone to be awake in any of the houses, but I wouldn't have cared. I stood naked in the frosty air and slowly got dressed. Ben protested when I shooed him off the sleeping bag and rolled it up.

The walk home, with the sleeping bag rolled up under my arm, was never so long.

No, Tally wasn't a ghost, though she haunts the city's streets at night—just as she haunts my mind.

I know her now. She's like a rose bush grown old, gone wild; untrimmed, neglected for years, the thorns become sharper, more bitter; her foliage spreading, grown out of control, reaching high and wide, while the center chokes and dies. The blossoms that remain are just small now, hidden in the wild growth, memories of what they once were.

I know her now. She's the spirit that connects the notes of a tune—the silences in between the sounds; the resonance that lies under the lines I put down on a page. Not a ghost, but a spirit all the same: the city's heart and soul.

I don't wonder about her origin. I don't wonder whether she was here first, and the city grew around her, or if the city created her. She just is.

Tallulah. Tally. A reckoning of accounts.

I think of the old traveling hawkers who called at private houses in the old days and sold their wares on the tally system—part payment on account, the other part due when they called again. Tallymen.

The payments owed her were long overdue, but we no longer have the necessary coin to settle our accounts with her. So she changes; just as we change. I can remember a time when the city was a safer place, how when I was young, we never locked our doors and we knew every neighbor on our block. Kids growing up today wouldn't even know what I'm talking about; the people my own age have forgotten. The old folks remember, but who listens to them? Most of us wish that they didn't exist; that they'd just take care of themselves so that we can get on with our own lives.

Not all change is for the good.

I still go out on my rambles, most every night. I hope for a secret tryst, but all I do is write stories again. As the new work fills my notebooks, I've come to realize that the characters in my stories were so real because I really did want to get close to people, I really did want to know them. It was just easier to do it on paper, one step removed.

I'm trying to change that now.

I look for her on my rambles. She's all around me, of course, in every brick of every building, in every whisper of wind as it scurries down an empty street. She's a cab's lights at 3:00 am, a siren near dawn, a shuffling bag lady pushing a squeaky grocery cart, a dark-eyed cat sitting on a shadowed stoop.

She's all around me, but I can't find her. I'm sure I'd recognize her—

I don't want you to see what I will become.

—but I can't be sure. The city can be so many things. It's a place where the familiar can become strange with just the blink of an eye. And if I saw her—

You wouldn't recognize me and I wouldn't want you to.

—what would I do? If she could, she'd come to me, but that mean spirit still grips the streets. I see it in people's faces; I feel it in the coldness that's settled in their hearts. I don't think I would recognize her; I don't think I'd want to. I have the *gris-gris* of her memory in my mind; I have an old sleeping bag rolled up in a corner of my hall closet; I'm here if she needs me.

I have this fantasy that it's still not too late; that we can still drive that mean spirit away and keep it at bay. The city would be a better place to live in if we could and I think we owe it to her. I'm doing my part. I write about her—

They're about me. They're your stories, I can taste your presence in every word, but each of them's a piece of me, too.

—about her strange wonder and her magic and all. I write about how she changed me, how she taught me that getting close can hurt, but not getting close is an even lonelier hurt. I don't preach; I just tell the stories.

But I wish the ache would go away. Not the memories, not the *gris-gris* that keeps her real inside me, but the hurt. I could live without that hurt.

Sometimes I wish I'd never met her.

Maybe one day I'll believe that lie, but I hope not.

The
Ivory
and the
Horn

for
Jane Yolen,
who showed me how to touch magic
and pass it on

ACKNOWLEDGMENTS

As anyone involved knows, contrary to the belief that artists create in the isolation of their workspaces, the act of creation is not a solitary endeavor. Without the inspiration and support I've received over the years, these stories wouldn't exist, so this time out I'd like to thank:

My wife, MaryAnn, for her help in the genesis of many of these stories and in their fine-tuning, always knowing when and where to say the right thing;

My editors at Tor, Terri Windling, Patrick Nielsen Hayden, Donald G. Keller and Greg Cox, for having enough faith in these stories to request a second volume sight unseen, and for making the publishing process so painless;

My agent, Richard Curtis, for finding me the spaces between novels when I could write these stories;

Altan, Tori Amos, Sarah Bauhan, Lisa Germano, Kiya Heartwood, Maria Kalaniemi, Peter Kater, Jon Mark, R. Carlos Nakai, Johnette Napolitano, Happy Rhodes and Ian Tamblyn, whose music keeps me sane;

All those editors who first asked for the stories collected herein: Kurt Busiak, Richard Chizmar, Pete Crowther, Bob Garcia, Marty Greenberg, David Hartwell, Kit Kerr, Greg Ketter, Andre Norton, Jan and George O'Nale, Kris Rusch, Darrell Schweitzer, Erik Secker, Carol Serling and Dean Smith.

A few notes concerning individual stories:

In "The Bone Woman," the idea of *La Huesera* comes from the folklore of the American Southwest. My thanks to Clarissa Pinkola Estes for making me aware of the tale.

In "Where Desert Spirits Crowd the Night" the story of Coyote and the Buzzard is based upon traditional Kickapoo folklore.

"The Wishing Well" was written for MaryAnn, who wanted to know what was in the well, and for Jane Siberry, for her own "strange well" of songs. Special thanks to Dr. Sean Costello (a fine author in his own right) for technical advice.

—Charles de Lint
Ottawa, Canada

CONTENTS

Father, O father, what do we here
In this land of unbelief and fear?
The Land of Dreams is better far,
Above the light of the morning star.

—William Blake

We are all in the gutter, but some
of us are looking at the stars.

—Oscar Wilde

Waifs and Strays

Do I have to dig,
Do I have to prod;
Reach into your chest
And pull your feelings out?
—Happy Rhodes, from "Words
Weren't Made for Cowards"

1

There's a big moon glowing in the sky, a swollen circle of silvery-gold light that looks as though it's sitting right on top of the old Clark Building, balancing there on the northeast corner where the twisted remains of a smokestack rises up from the roof like a long, tottery flagpole, colors lowered for the night, or maybe like a tin giant's arm making some kind of semaphore that only other tin giants can understand. I sure don't.

But that doesn't stop me from admiring the silhouette of the smokestack against that fat moon as I walk through the rubble-strewn streets of the Tombs. I feel like a stranger and I think, That moon's a stranger, too. It doesn't seem real; it's more like the painted backdrop from some forties soundstage, except there's no way anybody ever gave paint and plywood this kind of depth. We're both strangers. That moon looks like it might be out of place anywhere, but I belonged here once.

Not anymore, though. I'm not even supposed to be here. I've got responsibilities now. I've got duties to fulfill. I should be Getting Things Done like the good little taxpaying citizen I'm trying to be, but instead I'm slumming, standing in front of my old squat, and I couldn't tell you why I've come. No, that's not quite right. I know, I guess; I just can't put it into words.

"You've got to see the full moon in a country sky sometime," Jackie told me the other day when she got back from her girlfriend's cottage. "It just takes over the sky."

I look up at it again and don't feel that this moon's at all diminished by being here. Maybe because in many respects this part of the city's just like a wilderness—

about as close to the country as you can get in a place that's all concrete and steel. Some people might say you'd get that feeling more in a place like Fitzhenry Park, or on the lakefront where it follows the shoreline beyond the Pier, westward, out past the concession stands and hotels, but I don't think it's quite the same. Places like that are where you can only pretend it's wild; they look right, but they were tamed a long time ago. The Tombs, though, is like a piece of the city gone feral, the wild reclaiming its own—not asking, just taking.

In this kind of moonlight, you can feel the wilderness hiding in back of the shadows, lips pulled in an uncurbed, savage grin.

I think about that as I step a little closer to my old squat and it doesn't spook me at all. I find the idea kind of liberating. I look at the building and all I see is a big, dark, tired shape hulking in the moonlight. I like the idea that it's got a secret locked away behind its mundane façade, that's there's more to it than something that's been used up and then just tossed away.

Abandoned things make me feel sad. For as long as I can remember I've made up histories for them, cloaked them in stories, seen them as frog princes waiting for that magic kiss, princesses being tested with a pea, little engines that could if only they were given half a chance again.

But I'm pragmatic, too. Stories in my head are all well and fine, but they don't do much good for a dog that some guy's tossed out of a car when he's speeding through the Tombs and the poor little thing breaks a leg when it hits the pavement so it can't even fend for itself—just saying the feral dogs that run in these streets give it half a chance. When I can—if I get to it in time—I'm the kind of person who'll take it in.

People have tried to take me in, but it never quite works out right. Bad genes, I guess. Bad attitude. It's not the kind of thing I ever worried about much till the past few weeks.

I don't know how long I've been standing on the street, not even seeing the building anymore. I'm just here, a small shape in the moonlight, a stray dream from the safe part of the city that got lost and found itself wandering in this nightland that eats small dreams, feeds on hopes. A devouring landscape that fed on itself first and now preys on anything that wanders into its domain.

I never let it have me, but these days I wonder why I bothered. Living in the Tombs isn't much of a life, but what do you do when you don't fit in anywhere else?

I start to turn away, finally. The moon's up above the Clark Building now, hanging like a fat round flag on the smokestack, and the shadows it casts are longer. I don't want to go, but I can't stay. Everything that's important to me isn't part of the Tombs anymore.

The voice stops me. It's a woman's voice, calling softly from the shadows of my old squat.

"Hey, Maisie," she says.

I feel like I should know her, this woman sitting in the shadows, but the sense of familiarity I get from those two words keeps sliding away whenever I reach for it.

"Hey, yourself," I say.

She moves out into the moonlight, but she's still just a shape. There's no definition, nothing I can pin the sliding memories onto. I get an impression of layers of clothing that make a skinny frame seem bulky, a toque pulled down over hair that might be any color or length. She's dressed for winter though the night's warm and she's got a pair of shopping bags in each hand.

I've known a lot of street people like that. Hottest day of the summer and they still have to wear everything they own, all at once. Sometimes it's to protect themselves from space rays; sometimes it's just so that no one'll steal the little they've got to call their own.

"Been a long time," she says, and then I place her.

It's partly the way she moves, partly the voice, partly just the shape of her, though in this light she doesn't look any different from a hundred other bagladies.

The trouble is, she can't possibly wear the name I call up to fit her because the woman it used to belong to has been dead for four years. I know this, logically, intellectually, but I can't help trying it on for size all the same.

"Shirl?" I say. "Is that you?"

Shirley Jones, who everybody on the street knew as Granny Buttons because she carried hundreds of them around in the many pockets of her dresses and coats.

The woman on the street in front of me bobs her head, sticks her hands in the pockets of the raincoat she's wearing over all those layers of clothing, and I hear the familiar rattle of plastic against wood against bone, a soft *clickety-clickety-click* that I never thought I'd hear again.

"Jesus, Shirley—"

"I know, child," she says. "What am I doing here when I'm supposed to be dead?"

I'm still not spooked. It's like I'm in a dream and none of this is real, or at least it's only as real as the dream wants it to be. I'm just happy to see her. Granny Buttons was the person who first taught me that "family" didn't have to be an ugly word.

She's close enough now that I can even see some of her features. She doesn't look any different than she did when she died. She's got the same twinkle in her brown eyes—part charm and part crazy. Her coffee-colored skin's as wrinkled as a piece of brown wrapping paper that you've had in your back pocket for a few days. I see it isn't a toque she's wearing, but that same almost conical velour cap she always wore, her hair hanging out from below in dozens of unwashed, uncombed dreadlocks festooned with tiny buttons of every shape and description. She still smells the same as well—a combination of rosehip sachet and licorice.

I want to hug her, but I'm afraid if I touch her she'll just drift apart like smoke.

"I've missed you," I say.

"I know, child."

"But how . . . how can you *be* here . . . ?"

"It's like a riddle," she says. "Remember our treasure hunts?"

I nod my head. How can I forget? That's where I first learned about the freebies you can find in behind the bookstores, where I was initiated into what Shirley liked to call the rehab biz.

"If you cherish something enough," she told me, "it doesn't matter how old, or worn, or useless it's become; your caring for it immediately raises its value in somebody else's eyes. It's just like rehab—a body's got to believe in their own worth before anybody can start fixing them, but most people need someone to believe in them before they can start believing in themselves.

"You know, I've seen people pay five hundred dollars for something I took out of their trash just the week before—*only* because they saw it sitting on the shelf of some fancy antique shop. They don't even remember that it once was theirs.

" 'Course the dealer only paid me fifty bucks for it, but who's complaining? Two hours before I came knocking on his back door, it was sitting at the end of the curb in a garbage can."

Garbage days we went on our treasure hunts. Shirley probably knew more about collection days than the city crews did themselves: when each borough had its pickup, what the best areas were depending on the time of year, when you had to make your rounds in certain areas to beat the flea market dealers on their own night runs. We had dozens of routes, from Foxville down into Crowsea, across the river to Ferryside and the Beaches, from Chinatown over to the East End.

We'd head out with our shopping carts, sensei baglady and her apprentice, on a kind of Grail quest. But what we found was never as important as the zen of our being out there in the first place. Each other's company. The conversation. The night's journey as we zigzagged from one block to another, checking out this alleyway, that bin, those Dumpsters.

We were like urban coyotes prowling the city's streets. At that time of night, nobody bothered us, not the cops, not muggers, not street toughs. We became invisible knights tilting against the remnants of other people's lives.

After Shirley died, it took me over a month to go out on my own and it was never quite the same again. Not bad, just not the same.

"I remember," I tell her.

"Well, it's something like that," she says, "only it's not entirely happenstance."

I shake my head, confused. "What are you trying to tell me, Shirley?"

"Nothing you don't already know."

Back of me, something knocks a bottle off a heap of trash—I don't know what it is. A cat, maybe. A dog. A rat. I can't help myself. I have to have a look. When I turn back to Shirley—you probably saw this coming—she's gone.

2

Pride goes before a fall, I read somewhere, and I guess whoever thought up that little homily had her finger on the pulse of how it all works.

There was a time when I wouldn't have had far to fall; by most people's standards, at seventeen, I was already on the bottom rung of the ladder, and all the rungs going up were broken as far as I'd ever be able to reach. I lived in a squat. I made my living picking garbage and selling the better stuff off to junk shops and the fancy antique places—only through the back door, if you would, yes it's a lovely piece but terribly worn, sorry that's my best offer, many thanks and do come again. I had a family that consisted of a bunch of old dogs so worn out that nobody wanted them, not to mention Tommy who's—what's the current euphemism? I lose track. Mentally handicapped, I guess you'd call him. I just call him Tommy and it doesn't matter how dim the bulb is burning in behind his eyes; like the dogs, he became family when I took him in and I love him.

I never thought much about pride back in those days, though I guess I had my share. Maybe I was just white trash to whoever passed me on the street, but I kept myself cleaner than a lot of those paying taxes and what I had then sure beat the hell hole I grew up in.

I hit the road when I was twelve and never looked back because up until then family was just another word for pain. Physical pain, and worse, the kind that just leaves your heart feeling like some dead thing is caught inside your chest. You know what pigeons look like once the traffic's been running over them for a couple of weeks and there's not much left except for a flat bundle of dried feathers that hasn't even got flies buzzing around it anymore?

That's like what I had in my chest until I ran away.

I was one of the lucky ones. I survived. I didn't get done in by drugs or selling my body. Shirley took me in under her wing before the lean men with the flashy suits and too much jewelry could get their hands on me. Don't know why she helped me—maybe when she saw me she was remembering the day she was just a kid stepping off a bus in some big city herself. Maybe, just looking at me, she could tell I'd make a good apprentice.

And then, after five years, I got luckier still—with a little help from the Grasso Street Angel and my own determination.

And that pride.

I was so proud of myself for doing the right thing: I got the family off the street. I was straightening out my life. I rejoined society—not that society seemed to care all that much, but I wasn't doing it for them anyway. I was doing it for Tommy and the dogs, for myself, and so that one day maybe I could be in a position to help somebody else, the way that Angel does out of her little storefront office on Grasso, the way that Shirley helped me.

I should've known better.

We've got a real place to live in—a tenement on Flood Street just before it heads on into the Tombs, instead of a squat. I had a job as a messenger for the QMS—the Quicksilver Messenger Service, run by a bunch of old hippies who got the job done, but lived in a tie-dyed past. Evenings, four times a week, I was going to night school to get my high school diploma.

But I just didn't see it as being better than what we'd had before. Paying for rent and utilities, food and for someone to come in to look after Tommy, sucked away every cent I made. Maybe I could've handled that, but all my time was gone too. I never really saw Tommy anymore, except on the weekends and even then I'd have to be studying half the time. I had it a little easier than a lot of the other people in my class because I always read a lot. It was my way of escaping—even before I came here to live on the streets.

Before I ran away I was a regular at the local library—it was both a source of books and refuge from what was happening at home. Once I got here, Shirley told me about how the bookstores'd strip the covers off paperbacks and just throw the rest of the book away, so I always made sure I stopped by the alleys in back of their stores on garbage days.

I hadn't read a book in months. The dogs were pining—little Rexy taking it the worst. He's just a cat-sized wiry-haired mutt with a major insecurity problem. I think someone used to beat on him, which made me feel close to him, because I knew what that was all about. Used to be Rexy was like my shadow; nervous, sure, but so long as I was around, he was okay. These days, he's just a wreck, because he can't come on my bike when I'm working and they won't let me bring him into the school.

The way things stand, Tommy's depressed, the other dogs are depressed, Rexy's almost suicidal, and I'm not in any great shape myself. Always tired, impatient, unhappy.

So I really needed to meet a ghost in the Tombs right about now. It's doing wonders for my sense of sanity—or rather lack thereof, because I know I wasn't dreaming that night, or at least I wasn't asleep.

3

Everybody's worried about me when I finally get home—Rexy, the other dogs, Tommy, my landlady, Aunt Hilary, who looks after Tommy—and I appreciate it, but I don't talk about where I've been or what I've seen. What's the point? I'm kind of embarrassed about anybody knowing that I'm feeling nostalgic for the old squat and I'm not quite sure I believe who I saw there anyway, so what's to tell?

I make nice with Aunt Hilary, calm down the dogs, put Tommy to bed, then I've got homework to do for tomorrow night's class and work in the morning, so by the time I finally get to bed myself, Shirley's maybe-ghost is pretty well out of my mind. I'm so tired that I'm out like a light as soon as my head hits the pillow.

Where do they get these expressions we all use, anyway? Why out like a light and not on like one? Why do we hit the pillow when we go to sleep? Logs don't have a waking/sleeping cycle, so how can we sleep like one?

Sometimes I think about what this stuff must sound like when it gets literally translated into some other language. Yeah, I know. It's not exactly Advanced Philosophy 101 or anything, but it sure beats thinking about ghosts, which is what I'm trying not to think about as I walk home from the subway that night after my classes. I'm doing a pretty good job, too, until I get to my landlady's front steps.

Aunt Hilary is like the classic tenement landlady. She's a widow, a small but robust grey-haired woman with more energy than half the messengers at QMS. She's got lace hanging in her windows, potted geraniums on the steps going down to the pavement, an old black-and-white tabby named Frank that she walks on a leash. Rexy and Tommy are the only ones in my family that Frank'll tolerate.

Anyway, I come walking down the street, literally dragging my feet I'm so tired, and there's Frank sitting by one of the geranium pots giving me the evil eye—which is not so unusual—while sitting one step up is Shirley—which up until last night I would have thought was damned well impossible. Tonight I don't even question her presence.

"How's it going, Shirl?" I say as I collapse beside her on the steps.

Frank arches his back when I go by him, but deigns to give my shoulder bag a sniff before he realizes it's only got my school books in it. The look he gives me as he settles down again is less than respectful.

Shirley's leaning back against a higher step. She's got her hands in her pockets, *clickety-clickety-click,* her hat pushed back from her forehead. Her rosehip-and-licorice scent has to work a little harder against the cloying odor of the geraniums, but it's still there.

"Ever wonder why there's a moon?" she asks me, her voice all dreamy and distant.

I follow her gaze to where the fat round globe is ballooning in the sky above the buildings on the opposite side of the street. It looks different here than it did in the Tombs—safer, maybe—but then everything does. It's the second night that it's full, and I find myself wondering if ghosts are like werewolves, called up by the moon's light, only nobody's quite clued to it yet. Or at least Hollywood and the authors of cheap horror novels haven't.

I decide not to share this with Shirley. I knew her pretty well, but who knows what's going to offend a ghost? She doesn't wait for me to answer anyway.

"It's to remind us of Mystery," she says, "and that makes it both a Gift and a Curse."

She's talking like Pooh in the Milne books, her inflection setting capital letters at the beginning of certain words. I've never been able to figure out how she does that. I've never been able to figure out how she knows so much about books, because I never even saw her read a newspaper all the time we were together.

"How so?" I ask.

"Grab an eyeful," she says. "Did you ever see anything so mysteriously beautiful? Just looking at it, really Considering it, has got to fill the most jaded spirit with awe."

I think about how ghosts have that trick down pretty good, too, but all I say is, "And what about the curse?"

"We all know it's just an over-sized rock hanging there in the sky. We've sent men to walk around on it, left trash on its surface, photographed it and mapped it. We know what it weighs, its size, its gravitational influence. We've sucked all the Mystery out of it, but it still maintains its hold on our imaginations.

"No matter how much we try to deny it, that's where poetry and madness were born."

I still don't get the curse part of it, but Shirley's already turned away from this line of thought. I can almost see her ghostly mind unfolding a chart inside her head and plotting a new course for our conversation. She looks at me.

"What's more important?" she asks. "To be happy or to bring happiness to others?"

"I kind of like to think they go hand in hand," I tell her. "That you can't really have one without the other."

"Then what have you forgotten?"

This is another side of Shirley I remember well. She gets into this one-hand-clapping mode, asking you simple stuff that gets more and more complicated the longer you think about it, but if you keep worrying at it, the way Rexy'll take on an old slipper, it gets back to being simple again. To get there, though, you have to work through a forest of words and images that can be far too zen-deep and confusing—especially when you're tired and your brain's in neutral the way mine is tonight.

"Is this part of the riddle you were talking about last night?" I ask.

She sort of smiles—lines crinkle around her eyes, fingers work the pocketed buttons, *clickety-clickety-click*. There's a feeling in the air like there was last night just before she vanished, but this time I'm not looking away. I hear a car turn onto this block, its headbeams washing briefly over us, bright lights flicker, then it's dark again, with one solid flash of real deep dark just before my eyes adjust to the change in illumination.

Of course she's gone once I can see properly again and there's only me and Frank sitting on the steps. I forget for a moment about where our relationship stands and reach out to give him a pat. I'm just trying to touch base with reality, I realize as I'm doing it, but that doesn't matter to him. He doesn't quite hiss as he gets up and jumps down to the sidewalk.

I watch him swagger off down the street, watch the empty pavement for a while longer, then finally I get up myself and go inside.

4

There's a wariness in Angel's features when I step into her Grasso Street office. It's a familiar look. I asked her about it once, and she was both precise and polite with her explanation: "Well, Maisie. Things just seem to get complicated whenever you're around."

It's nothing I plan.

Her office is a one-room walk-in storefront off Grasso Street, shabby in a genteel sort of way. She has a rack of filing cabinets along one wall, an old beat-up sofa with a matching chair by the bay window, a government surplus desk—one of those massive oak affairs with about ten million scratches and dents—a swivel chair behind the desk and a couple of matching oak straightbacks sitting to one side. I remember thinking they looked like a pair I'd sold a few years ago to old man Kemps down the street, and it turns out that's where she picked them up.

A little table beside the filing cabinets holds a hot plate, a kettle, a bunch of mismatched mugs, a teapot and the various makings for coffee, hot chocolate and tea. The walls have cheerful posters—one from a travel agency that shows this wild New Orleans street scene where there's a carnival going on, one from a Jilly Coppercorn show—cutesy little flower fairies fluttering around in a junkyard.

I like the one of Bart Simpson best. I've never seen the show, but I don't think you have to to know what he's all about.

The nicest thing about the office is the front porch and steps that go down from it to the pavement. It's a great place from which to watch the traffic go by, vehicular and pedestrian, or just to hang out. No, that's not true. The nicest thing is Angel herself.

Her real name's Angelina Marceau, but everyone calls her Angel, partly on account of her name, I guess, but mostly because of the salvage work she does with street kids. The thing is, she looks like an angel. She tries to hide it with baggy pants and plain T-shirts and about as little makeup as you can get away with wearing and still not be considered a Baptist, but she's gorgeous. Heart-shaped face, hair to kill for—a long, dark waterfall that just seems to go forever down her back—and soft warm eyes that let you know straight-away that here's someone who genuinely cares about you. Not as a statistic to add to her list of rescued souls, but as an individual. A real person.

Unless she's giving you the suspicious once-over she's giving me as I come in. It's a look you have to earn, because normally she'll bend over backwards to give you the benefit of the doubt.

I have to admit, there was a time when I'd push her, just to test the limits of her patience. It's not something I was particularly prone to, but we used to have a history of her trying to help me and me insisting I didn't need any help. We worked through all of that, eventually, but I keep finding myself in circumstances that make her feel as though I'm still testing the limits.

Like the time I punched out the booking agent at the Harbour Ritz my first day on the job that Angel had gotten for me at QMS.

I'm not the heartstopper that Angel is, but I do okay in the looks department. My best feature, I figure, is my hair. It's not as long as Angel's, but it's as thick. Jackie, the dispatch girl at QMS, says it reminds her of the way they all wore their hair in the sixties—did I mention that these folks are living in a time warp? I've never bothered to tell them that the sixties have been and gone, it's only the styles that are making yet another comeback.

Anyway, my hair's a nice shade of light golden brown and hangs halfway down my back. I do okay in the figure department, too, though I lean more towards Winona Ryder, say, than Kim Basinger. Still, I've had guys hit on me occasionally, especially these days, since I don't put out the impression that I'm some assistant baglady-in-training anymore.

The Harbour Ritz booking agent doesn't know any of this. He just sees a messenger girl delivering some documents and figures he'll give me a thrill. I guess he's either hard up, or figures anyone without his equipment between their legs is just dying to have him paw them, because that's what he does to me when I try to get him to sign for his envelope. He ushers me into his office and then closes the door, leans back against it and pulls me toward him.

What was I supposed to do? I just cocked back a fist and broke his nose.

Needless to say, he raised a stink, it's his word against mine, etcetera, etcetera. Except the folks at QMS turn out to be real supportive and Angel comes down on this guy like he's some used condom she's found stuck to the bottom of her shoe when she's walking through the Combat Zone. I keep my job, and don't get arrested for assault like the guy's threatening, but it's a messy situation, right?

The look Angel's wearing says, "I hope this isn't more of the same, but just seeing you kicks in this bad feeling. . . ."

It's not more of the same, I want to tell her, but that's about as far as my reasoning can take it. What's bothering me isn't exactly something I can just put my finger on. Do I tell her about Shirley, do I tell her about the malaise I've got eating away at me, or what?

I'd been tempted to bring the whole family with me—I spend so little time with them as it is—but settled on Rexy, mostly because he's easier to control. It's hard to think when you're trying to keep your eye on six of them and Tommy, too.

Today I could be alone in a padded cell and I'd still find it hard to think.

I take a seat on the sofa and after a moment Angel comes around from behind her desk and settles on the other end. Rexy's being real good. He licks her hand when she reaches out to pet him, then curls up on my lap and pretends to go to sleep. I know he's faking it because his ears twitch in a way they don't when he's really conked out.

Angel and I do some prelims—small talk which is always relaxed and easy around her, but eventually we get to the nitty-gritty of why I'm here.

"I've got this problem," I say, thinking of Shirley, but I know it's not her. I kind of like having her around again, dead or not.

"At work?" Angel tries when I'm not more forthcoming.

"Not exactly."

Angel's looking a little puzzled, but curious, too.

"Your grades are good," she says.

"It's not got anything to do with grades," I tell her. Well, it does, but only because the high school diploma's part and parcel of the whole problem.

"Then what *does* it have to do with?" Angel wants to know.

It's a reasonable request—more so because I'm the one who's come to her, taking up her time. I know what I want to say, but I don't know how to phrase it.

My new life's like a dress I might have wished after in a store window, saved for, finally bought, only to find out that while it's the right size, it still doesn't quite fit properly. It's the wrong color. The sleeves are too long, or maybe too short. The skirt's too tight.

It's not something Angel would understand. Intellectually, maybe, but not how I feel about it. Angel's one of those people that sees everyone having a purpose in life, you've just got to figure out what it is. I don't even know where to begin figuring out that kind of stuff.

"Nothing really," I say after a few moments.

I get up suddenly, startling Rexy who jumps to the floor and then gives me this put-upon expression of his—he should take out a patent on it.

"I've got to go," I tell Angel.

"Maisie," she starts, rising herself, but I'm already heading for the door.

I pretend I don't hear her. I pretend she's not following me to the street and calling after me as I head down the block at a quick walk that you might as well call running.

I'm not in good shape, I realize. Angel's the only person I know that I could have talked with about something like this, but I couldn't do it. I couldn't even start.

All I felt like doing was crying, and that really would have freaked her, because I never cry.

Not where people can see.

5

"So what are you really doing here?" I ask.

We're sitting on a bench in the subway station at Williamson and Stanton, Shirley and I, with little Rexy sleeping on the toes of my running shoes. We're at the far end of the platform. It's maybe ten o'clock and there's hardly anybody else down here with us. I see a couple of yuppies, probably coming back from an early show. A black guy in a three-piece checking out papers in his briefcase. Two kids slouched against a wall, watching a companion do tricks with her skateboard that bring her perilously close to the edge of the platform. My heart's in my throat watching her, but her friends just look bored.

I wonder what they see when they look down this way. A baglady and me, with my dog dozing on my feet, or just me and Rexy on our own?

Shirley's gaze is on the subway system grid that's on the opposite side of the tracks, but I doubt she's really seeing it. She always needed glasses but never got herself a pair, even when she could afford them.

"When I first got to the city," she says, "I always thought that one day I'd go back home and show everybody what an important person I had become. I wanted to prove that just because everyone from my parents to my teachers treated me like I was no good, didn't mean I really was no good.

"But I never went back."

Ghosts always want to set something right, I remember from countless books and stories. Revenge, mistakes, that kind of thing. Sometimes just to say goodbye. They're here because of unfinished business.

This is the first time I ever realized that Shirley'd had any.

I mean, I wasn't stupid, even when I was twelve and she first took me in under her wing. Even then I knew that normal people didn't live on the streets wearing their entire wardrobe on their backs. But I never really thought about why she was there. She always seemed like a part of the street, so full of smarts and a special kind of wisdom, that it simply never occurred to me that she'd been running away from something, too. That she'd had dreams and aspirations once, but all they came to was a homeless wandering to which the only end was a mishap like falling down the stairs in some run-down squat and breaking your neck.

That's what your life'll be like, I tell myself, if you don't follow through on what Angel's trying to do for you.

Maybe. But I'd respected Shirley, for all her quirks, for all that I knew she wasn't what anybody else would call a winner. I'd just always thought that whatever she lacked, she had inner peace to make up for it.

I slouch lower on the bench, legs crossed at the ankles, the back of my head leaning against the top of the bench. I'm wearing my fedora and the movement pushes it forward so that the brim hangs low over my eyes.

"Is that why you're back?" I ask Shirley. "Because you still had things left to do here?"

She shrugs, an eloquent Shirley-like gesture, for all the layers of clothes she's wearing.

"I don't really feel I ever went anywhere or came back," she says.

"But you died," I say.

"I guess so."

I try a different tack. "So what's it like?"

She smiles. "I don't really know. When I'm here, I don't feel any different from before I died. When I'm not here, I'm . . . I don't know where I am. A kind of limbo, I suppose. A place where nothing moves, nothing changes, months are minutes."

I don't say anything.

"I guess it's like the bus I never took back home," she adds after a moment. "I missed out on wherever it was I was supposed to go, and I don't know how to go on, where to catch the next bus, or if they're even running anymore. For me at least. They don't leave a schedule lying around for people like me who arrive too late.

"Story of my life, I guess."

I start to feel so bad for her that I almost wish she'd go back to throwing cryptic little riddles at me the way she'd done the first couple of times we'd met.

"Is there anything I can do?" I say, but the subway roars into the station at the same time as I speak, swallowing my words with its thunder.

I'm about to repeat what I said but when I turn to look at Shirley, she's not there anymore. I only just make it through the doors of the car, Rexy under my arm, before they hiss closed behind me and the train goes roaring off again into the darkness.

The story of her life, I think. I wonder, what's the story of mine?

6

I should tell you about Tommy.

He's a big guy, maybe six feet tall and running close to a hundred and eighty pounds. And he's strong. He's got brown hair, a dirtier shade than mine, though I try to keep it looking clean, and guileless eyes. He couldn't keep a secret if he knew one.

The thing is, he's simple. A ten-year-old in an adult's body. I'm not sure how old he is, but the last time I took him in for a checkup at the clinic, the doctor told me he was in his early thirties, which makes him older than me.

When I say simple, I don't mean stupid, though I'll admit Tommy's not all that bright by the way society reckons intelligence. I like to think of him as more basic than the rest of us. He's open with his feelings, likes to smile, likes to laugh. He's the happiest person I know, which is half the reason I love him the way I do. He may be mentally impaired, but sometimes I figure the world would be a better place if we all maintained some of that sweet innocence that makes him so endearing.

I inherited Tommy the same way I did the rest of my family: I found him on the streets, abandoned. I worried some at first about keeping him with me, but when I started asking around about institutions, I realized he'd have something with me and the dogs that he couldn't get anywhere else: a family. All a guy like Tommy needs is someone willing to put the time into loving him. You don't get that in places like the Zeb, which is where he lived until they discharged him so that someone with more pressing problems, read money, could have his bed.

One of the things I hate about the way my life's going now is that I hardly ever see him anymore. Our landlady knows him better than I do these days and that's depressing.

The day after I talk to Shirley in the subway, I get off early from work. There's a million things I should be doing—like the week's grocery shopping and research for a history essay at the library—but I decide the hell with it. It's a beautiful day, so I'm going to pack up a picnic lunch and take the family to the park.

I find Tommy and Aunt Hilary in the backyard. She's working on her garden, which for a postage-sized tenement lot is a work of art, a miniature farm and English garden all rolled into about a twenty by twenty foot yard of sunflowers, rosebushes, corn, peas, every kind of squash, tomatoes and flowerbeds aflame with color and scent. Tom's playing with the paper people that I cut out of magazines and then stick onto cardboard backings for him. The dogs are sprawled all over the place, except for Rexy, who's dogging Aunt Hilary's heels. You don't understand how apt an expression like that is until you see Rexy do his I-always-have-to-be-two-inches-away-from-you thing.

Tommy looks up when he hears the dogs starting to yap, and suddenly I'm inundated with my family, everybody trying to get a piece of hello from me at the same time. But the best thing is seeing that kind of sad expression that Tommy's wearing too much these days broaden into the sweetest, happiest smile you can imagine. I don't figure

I've ever done anything to deserve all this unadulterated love, but I accept it—on credit, I guess. It makes me try harder to be good to them, to be worthy of that love.

I've got the trick down pat by now, ruffling the fur of six dogs and giving Tommy a hug without ever letting anybody feel left out. Aunt Hilary's straightening up from her garden, hands at the small of her back as she stretches the kinks from her muscles. She's smiling, too.

"We had a visitor," she tells me when the pandemonium settles down into simple chaos.

Tommy's leading me over to the big wooden tray on a patch of grass to show me what his paper people have been up to while I was gone this morning, and the dogs sort of mooch along beside us in an undulating wave.

"Anybody I know?" I ask Aunt Hilary.

"I suppose you must," my landlady says, "but she didn't leave a name. She just said she wanted to drop by to see how your family was making out—especially your son."

I blink with surprise at that. "You mean Tommy?"

"Who else?"

Well, I guess he is like my kid, I think.

"What did she look like?" I ask, half-anticipating the answer.

"A bit like a homeless person, if you want to know the truth," Aunt Hilary says. "She must have been wearing three or four dresses under her overcoat."

"Was she black?"

"Yes, how did you—"

"Hair in dreadlocks with lots of buttons attached to them?"

Aunt Hilary nods. "And she kept fiddling with something in her pockets that made a rattle-y sort of sound."

"That's Shirley," I say.

"So you do know her."

"She's an old friend."

Aunt Hilary starts to say something else, but I lose the thread of her conversation because all I'm thinking is, I'm not crazy. Other people *can* see her. I was being pretty cool whenever Shirley showed up, but I have to admit to worrying that her presence was just the first stage of a nervous breakdown.

Suddenly I realize that I'm missing everything my landlady's telling me about Shirley's visit.

"I'm sorry," I tell her. "What did you say?"

Aunt Hilary smiles. She's used to my spacing out from time to time.

"Your friend didn't stay long," she says. "She just told Tommy what a handsome young man he was and patted each of the dogs with utter concentration, as though she wanted to remember them, and then she left. I asked her to stay for some lunch, or at least a cup of tea, because she looked so—well, hungry, I suppose. But she just shook her head and said, 'That's very kind of you, but I don't indulge anymore.'"

Aunt Hilary frowns. "At least I think that's what she said. It doesn't really make a lot of sense, when you consider it."

"That's just Shirley," I tell her.

I can tell Aunt Hilary wants to talk some more about it, but I turn the conversation to my plan for an outing to the park, inviting her along. She hasn't got the time, she says—is probably looking forward to a few hours by herself, is what I hear, and I don't blame her—but she gets right into helping me get a knapsack of goodies organized.

We have a great day. Nothing's changed. I've still got to deal with my malaise, I've still got the ghost of a dead friend hanging around, but for a few hours I manage to put it all aside and it's like old times again.

I haven't seen Tommy this happy since I can't remember when, and that makes me feel both glad and depressed.

There's got to be a better way to live.

7

I decide it's time to get some expert advice, so the next day I call in sick at work and head off down to Fitzhenry Park instead.

Everybody who spends most of their time on the streets isn't necessarily a bum. Newford's got more than its share of genuinely homeless people—the ones who don't have any choice: winos, losers, the hopeless and the helpless, runaways, and far too many ordinary people who've lost their jobs, their homes, their future through no fault of their own. But it's also got a whole subculture, if you will, of street musicians, performance artists, sidewalk vendors and the like.

Some are like me: They started out as runaways and then evolved into something like when I was making cash from trash. Others have a room in a boarding house or some old hotel and work the streets because that's where their inclination lies. There's not a whole lot of ways to make a living playing fiddle tunes or telling fortunes in other outlets, and the overhead is very affordable.

Fitzhenry Park is where a lot of that kind of action lies. It's close to the Combat Zone, so you get a fair amount of hookers and even less-reputable types drifting down when they're, let's say, off-shift. But it's also close to the Barrio, so the seedy element is balanced out with mothers walking in pairs and pushing strollers, old women gossiping in tight clusters, old men playing dominoes and checkers on the benches. Plus you get the lunch crowds from the downtown core which faces the west side of the park.

The other hot spot is down by the Pier, on the lakefront, but that's geared more to the tourists, and the cops are tight-assed about permits and the like. If you're going to get arrested for busking or hawking goods from a sidewalk cart or just plain pan-handling, that's the place it'll happen.

The kind of person I was looking for now would work the park crowds and I found him without hardly even trying. He was just setting up for the day.

Bones is a Native American—a full-blooded Kickaha with dark coppery skin, broad features and a braid hanging down his back that's almost as long as Angel's hair. He got his name from the way he tells fortunes. He'll toss a handful of tiny bones onto a piece of deerskin and read auguries from the pattern they make. He doesn't really dress for the part, eschewing buckskins and beads for scuffed old workboots, faded blue jeans and a white T-shirt with the arms torn off, but it doesn't seem to hurt business.

I don't really hold much with any of this mumbo-jumbo stuff—not Bones's gig, nor what his girlfriend Cassie does with Tarot cards, nor Paperjack's Chinese fortune-telling devices. But while I don't believe that any of them can foretell the future, I still have to admit there's something different about some of the people who work this schtick.

Take Bones.

The man has crazy eyes. Not crazy, you-better-lock-him-up kind of eyes, but crazy because maybe he sees something we can't. Like there really is some other world lying draped across ours, and he can see right into it. Maybe he's even been there. Lots of times, I figure he's just clowning around, but sometimes that dark gaze of his locks onto you and then you see this seriousness lying behind the laughter and it's like the Tombs all over again—a piece of the wilderness biding on a city street, a dislocating sensation like not only is anything possible, but it probably already exists.

Besides, who am I to make judgments these days? I'm being haunted by a ghost.

"How do, Maisie?" he says when I wheel my mountain bike up to the edge of the fountain where he's sitting.

I prop the bike up on its kickstand, hang my helmet from one of the handlebars and sit down beside him. He's fiddling with his bones, letting them tumble from one hand to the other. They make a sound like Shirley's buttons, only more muted. I find myself wondering what kind of an animal they came from. Mice? Birds? I look up from his hands and see the clown is sitting in his eyes, laughing. Maybe with me, maybe at me—I can never tell.

"Haven't seen you around much these days," he adds.

"I'm going to school," I tell him.

"Yeah?"

"And I've got a job."

He looks at me for this long heartbeat and I get that glimpse of otherness that puts a weird shifting sensation in the pit of my stomach.

"So are you happy?" he asks.

That's something no one ever asks when I tell them what I'm doing now. I pick at a piece of lint that's stuck to the cuff of my shorts.

"Not really," I tell him.

"Want to see what Nanabozo's got in store for you?" he asks, holding up his bones.

I don't know who Nanabozo is, but I get the idea.

"No," I say. "I want to ask you about ghosts."

He doesn't even blink an eye. Just grins.

"What about them?"

"Well, what are they?" I ask.

"Souls that got lost," he tells me, still smiling, but serious now, too.

I feel weird talking about this. It's a sunny day, the park's full of people, joggers, skateboarders, women with baby carriages, a girl on the bench just a few steps away who probably looks sexy at night under a streetlight, the way she's all tarted up, but now she just looks used. Nothing out of the ordinary, and here we are, talking about ghosts.

"What do you mean?" I ask. "How do they get lost?"

"There's a Path of Souls, all laid out for us to follow when we die," he tells me. "But some spirits can't see it, so they wander the earth instead. Others can't accept the fact that they're dead yet, and they hang around too."

"A path."

He nods.

"Like something you walk along."

"Inasmuch as a spirit walks," Bones says.

"My ghost says she missed a bus," I tell him.

"Maybe it's different for white people."

"She's black."

He sits there, not looking at me, bones trailing from one hand to the other, making their tiny rattling sound.

"What do you really want to know?" he asks me.

"How do I help her?"

"Why don't you try asking her?"

"I did, but all she gives me back are riddles."

"Maybe you're just not listening properly," he says.

I think back on the conversations I've had with Shirley since I first saw her in the Tombs a few nights ago, but I can't seem to focus on them. I remember being with her, I remember the feeling of what we talked about, but the actual content is muddy now. It seems to shift away as soon as I try to think about it.

"I've really seen her," I tell Bones. "I was there when she died—almost four years ago—but she's back. And other people have seen her, too."

"I know you have," he says.

I don't even know why I was trying to convince him—it's not like he'd be a person that needed convincing—but what he says, stops me.

"What do you mean?" I ask. It's my question for the day.

"It's in your eyes," he says. "The Otherworld has touched you. Think of it as a blessing."

"I don't know if I like the idea," I tell him. "I mean, I miss Shirley, and I actually feel kind of good about her being back, even if she is just a ghost, but it doesn't seem right somehow."

"Often," he says, "what we take from the spirit world is only a reflection of what lies inside ourselves."

There's that look in his eyes, a feral seriousness, like it's important, not so much that I understand, or even believe what he's saying, but *that* he's saying it.

"What . . . ?" I start, but then I figure it out. Part of it anyway.

When I first came to the city, I was pretty messed up, but then Shirley was there to help me. I'm messed up again, so. . . .

"So I'm just projecting her ghost?" I ask. "I need her help, so I've made myself a ghost of her?"

"I didn't say that."

"No, but—"

"Ghosts have their own agendas," he tells me. "Maybe you both have something to give to each other."

We sit for awhile, neither of us speaking. I play with the whistle that hangs from a cord around my neck—all the messengers have them to blow at cars that're trying to cut us off. Finally, I get up and take my bike off its kickstand. I look at Bones and that feral quality is still lying there in his grin. His eyes seem to be all pupil, dark, dark. I'm about to say thanks, but the words lock up in my throat. Instead I just nod, put on my helmet and go away to think about what he's told me.

8

Tommy's got this new story that he tells me after we've cleaned up the dinner dishes. We sit together at the kitchen table and he has his little paper people act it out for me. It's about this Chinese man who falls down the crack in the pavement outside Aunt Hilary's house and finds himself in this magic land where everybody's a beautiful model or movie star and they all want to marry the Chinese guy except he misses his family too much, so he just tells them he can't marry any of them—not even the woman who won the Oscar for her part in *Misery,* who for some reason, Tommy's really crazy about.

I've got the old black lab Chuckie lying on my feet, Rexy snuggled up in my lap. Mutt and Jeff are tangled up in a heap on the sofa so that it's hard to tell which part of them's which. They're a cross between a German Shepherd and who knows what; I found Jeff first and gave the other old guy his name because the two were immediately inseparable. Jimmie's part dachshund, part collie—I know, go figure—and his long, furry body is stretched out in front of the door like he's a dust puppy. Patty's mostly poodle, but there's some kind of placid mix in there as well because she's not at all high-strung. Right now she's sitting in the bay window, checking the traffic and pretending to be a cat.

The sad thing, Tommy tells me, is that the Chinese man knows that he'll never be able to get back home, but he's going to stay faithful to his family anyway.

"Where'd you get that story?" I ask Tommy.

He just shrugs, then he says, "I really miss you, Maisie."

How can I keep leaving him?

I feel like a real shit. I know it's not my fault, I know I'm trying to do my best for all of us, for our future, but Tommy's mind doesn't work very well considering the long term and my explanations don't really register. It's just me going out all the time, and not taking him or the dogs with me.

There's a knock on the door. Jimmie gets laboriously to his feet and moves aside as Aunt Hilary comes in. She gives her wristwatch an obvious look.

"You're going to be late for school," she says, not really nagging, she just knows me too well.

I feel like saying, Fuck school, but I put Rexy down, shift Chuckie from my feet and stand up. Six dogs and Tommy all give me a hopeful look, like we're going out for a walk, faces all dropping when I pick up my knapsack, heavy with school books.

I give Tommy a hug and kiss then make the goodbye rounds of the dogs. They're like Tommy; long term means nothing to them. All they know is I'm going out and they can't come. Rexy takes a few hopeful steps in the direction of the door, but Aunt Hilary scoops him up.

"Now, now, Rexy," she tells him. "You know Margaret's got to go to school and she can't take you."

Margaret. She's the one who goes to school and works at QMS and deserts her family five days and four nights a week. She's the traitor.

I'm Maisie, but I'm Margaret, too.

I say goodbye, trying not to look anyone in the eye, and head for the subway. My eyes are pretty well dry by the time I get there. I pause on the platform. When the southbound train comes, I don't get off at the stop for my school, but ride it all the way downtown. I walk the six blocks to the bus depot.

I get a piece of gum stuck to the bottom of my sneaker while I'm waiting in line at the ticket counter. I'm still trying to get it off with an old piece of tissue I find in my pocket—not the most useful tool for the job—when the guy behind the counter says, "Next," in this really tired voice.

Who's he got waiting at home for him? I wonder as I move toward the counter, sort of shuffling the foot with the gum stuck on it so it doesn't trap me to another spot.

"How much for a ticket?" I ask him.

"Depends where you're going."

He's got thinning hair lying flat against his head, parted way over on the left side. Just a skinny little guy in a faded shirt and pants that are too baggy for him, trying to do his job. He's got a tic in one eye and I keep thinking that he's giving me a wink.

"Right," I say.

My mind's out of sync. Of course he needs the destination. I let my thoughts head back into the past, looking for the name of the place I want, trying to avoid the bad times that are hiding there in my memories, just waiting to jump me, but it's impossible to do.

That's another thing about street people, whether they put the street behind them or not: The past holds pain. The present may not be all that great, but it's usually better than what went before. That goes for me, for Shirley, for pretty well everybody I know. You try to live here and now, like the people who go through twelve-step, taking it day by day.

Mostly, you try not to think at all.

"Rockcastle," I tell the guy behind the counter.

He does something mysterious with his computer before he looks up.

"Return or one-way?"

"One-way."

More fiddling with the computer before he tells me the price. I pay him and a couple of minutes later I'm hop-stepping my way out of the depot with a one-way ticket to Rockcastle in my pocket. I sit on a bench outside and scrape off the gum with a popsicle stick I find on the sidewalk, and then I'm ready.

I don't go to my class; I don't go home, either. Instead I take the subway up to Gracie Street. When I come up the steps from the station I stand on the pavement for a long time before I finally cross over and walk into the Tombs.

9

The moon seems smaller tonight. It's not just that it's had a few slivers shaved off one side because its waning; it's like it got tamed somehow.

I can't say the same for the Tombs. I see kids sniffing glue, shooting up, some just sprawled with their backs against a pile of rubble, legs splayed out in front of them, eyes staring into nothing. I pass a few 'bos cooking God-knows-what over a fire they've got rigged up in an old jerry can. A baglady comes lurching out between the sagging doors of an old office building and starts to yell at me. Her voice follows me as I pick a way through the litter and abandoned cars.

The bikers down the street are having a party. The buckling pavement in front of their building has got about thirty-five chopped-down street hogs parked in front of it. The place is lit up with Coleman lights and I can hear the music and laughter from where I'm sitting in the bay window of my old squat in the Clark Building.

They don't bother me; I never exactly hung out with them or anything, but they used to consider me a kind of mascot after Shirley died and let the word get out that I was under their protection. It's not the kind of thing that means a lot everywhere, but it helped me more than once.

No one's taken over the old squat yet, but after five months it's already got the same dead feel to it that hits you anywhere in the Tombs. It's not exactly dirty, but it's dusty and the wind's been blowing crap in off the street. There's a smell in the air; though it's not quite musty, it's getting there.

But I'm not really thinking about any of that. I'm just passing time. Sitting here, waiting for a piece of the past to catch up to me.

I used to sit here all the time once I'd put Tommy to bed, looking out the window when I wasn't reading, Rexy snuggled close, the other dogs sprawled around the room, a comforting presence of soft snores and twitching bodies as they chased dream-rabbits in their sleep.

There's no comfort here now.

I look back out the window and see a figure coming up the street, but it's not who I was expecting. It's Angel, with Chuckie on a leash, his black shadow shape stepping out front, leading the way. As I watch them approach, some guy moves from out of the shadows that've collected around the building across the street and Chuckie, worn out and old though he is, lunges at him. The guy makes a fast fade.

I listen to them come into the building, Chuckie's claws clicking on the scratched marble, the leather soles of Angel's shoes making a scuffley sound as she comes up the stairs. I turn around when they come into the squat.

"I thought I'd find you here," Angel says.

"I didn't know you were looking."

I don't mean to sound put off, but I can't keep the punkiness out of my voice.

"I'm not checking up on you, Maisie. I was just worried."

"Well, here I am."

She undoes the lead from Chuckie's collar and he comes across the room and sticks his face up against my knees. The feel of his fur under my hand is comforting.

"You really shouldn't be out here," I tell Angel. "It's not safe."

"But it's okay for you?"

I shrug. "This was my home."

She crosses the room as well. The window sill's big enough to hold us both. She scoots up and then sits across from me, arms wrapped around her legs.

"After you came by the office, I went by your work to see you, then to your apartment, then to the school."

I shrug again.

"Do you want to talk about it?" she asks.

"What's to say?"

"Whatever's in your heart. I'm here to listen. Or I can just go away, if that's what you prefer, but I don't really want to do that."

"I . . ."

The words start locking up inside me again. I take a deep breath and start over.

"I'm not really happy, I guess," I tell her.

She doesn't say anything, just nods encouragingly.

"It's . . . I never really told you why I came to see you about school and the job and everything. You probably just thought that you'd finally won me over, right?"

Angel shakes her head. "It was never a matter of winning or losing. I'm just there for the people who need me."

"Yeah, well, what happened was—do you remember when Margaret Grierson died?"

Angel nods.

"We shared the same postal station," I tell her, "and the day before she was killed, I got a message in my box warning me to be careful, that someone was out to do a serious number on me. I spent the night in a panic and I was so relieved when the morning finally came and nothing had happened, because what'd happen to Tommy and the dogs if anything ever happened to me, you know?"

"What does that have to do with Margaret Grierson?" Angel asks.

"The note I got was addressed to 'Margaret'—just that, nothing else. I thought it was for me, but I guess whoever sent it got his boxes mixed up and it ended up in mine instead of hers."

"But I still don't see what—"

I can't believe she doesn't get it.

"Margaret Grierson was an important person," I say. "She was heading up that AIDS clinic, she was doing things for people. She was making a difference."

"Yes, but—"

"I'm nobody," I say. "It should've been me that died. But it wasn't, so I thought well, I better do something with myself, with my life, you know? I better make my having survived meaningful. But I can't cut it.

"I've got the straight job, the straight residence, I'm going back to school and it's like it's all happening to someone else. The things that are important to me—Tommy and the dogs—it's like they're not even a part of my life anymore."

I remember something Shirley's ghost asked me, and add, "Maybe it's selfish, but I figure charity should start at home, you know? I can't do much for other people if I'm feeling miserable myself."

"You should've come to me," Angel says.

I shake my head. "And tell you what? It sounds so whiny. I mean there's people starving not two blocks from where we're sitting, and I should be worried about being happy or not? The important stuff's covered—I'm providing for my family, putting a roof over their heads and making sure they have enough to eat—that should be enough, right? But it doesn't feel that way. It feels like the most important things are missing.

"I used to have time to spend with Tommy and the dogs; now I have to steal a minute here, another there. . . ."

My voice trails off. I think of how sad they all looked when I left the apartment tonight, like I was deserting them, not just for the evening, but forever. I can't bear that feeling, but how do you explain yourself to those who can't possibly understand?

"We could've worked something out," Angel says. "We still can."

"Like what?"

Angel smiles. "I don't know. We'll just have to think it through better than we have so far. You'll have to try to open up a bit more, tell me what you're *really* feeling, not just what you think I want to hear."

"It's that obvious, huh?"

"Let's just say I have a built-in bullshit detector."

We don't say anything for awhile then. I think about what she's said, wondering if something could be worked out. I don't want special dispensation because I'm some kind of charity case—I've *always* earned my own way—but I know there've got to be some changes or the little I've got is going to fall apart.

I can't get the image out of my mind—Tommy with his sad eyes as I'm going out the door—and I know I've got to make the effort. Find a way to keep what was good about the past and still make a decent future for us.

I put my hand in my pocket and feel the bus ticket I bought earlier.

I have to open up a bit more? I think, looking at Angel, What would her bullshit detector do if I told her about Shirley?

Angel stretches out her legs, then lowers them to the floor.

"Come on," she says, offering me her hand. "Let's go talk about this some more."

I look around the squat and compare it to Aunt Hilary's apartment. There's no comparison. What made this place special, we took with us.

"Okay," I tell Angel.

I take her hand and we leave the building. I know it's not going to be easy, but then nothing ever is. I'm not afraid to work my butt off; I just don't want to lose sight of what's really important.

When we're outside, I look back up to the window where we were sitting. I wonder about Shirley, how's she's going to work out whatever it is that she's got to do to regain her own sense of peace. I hope she finds it. I don't even mind if she comes to see me again, but I don't think that'll be part of the package.

I left the bus ticket for her, on the window sill.

10

I don't know if we've worked everything out, but I think we're making a good start. Angel's fixed it so that I've dropped a few courses which just means that it'll take me longer to get my diploma. I'm only working a couple of days a week at QMS—the Saturday shift that nobody likes and a rotating day during the week.

The best thing is I'm back following my trade again, trash for cash. Aunt Hilary lets me store stuff in her garage because she doesn't have a car anyway. A couple of nights a week, Tommy and I head out with our carts, the dogs on our heels, and we work the bins. We're spending a lot more time together and everybody's happier.

I haven't seen Shirley again. If it hadn't been for Aunt Hilary telling me about her coming by the house, I'd just think I made the whole thing up.

I remember what Bones told me about ghosts having their own agendas and how maybe we both had something to give each other. Seeing Shirley was the catalyst for me. I hope I helped her some, too. I remember her telling me once that she came from Rockcastle. I think wherever she was finally heading, Rockcastle was still on the way.

There isn't a solution to every problem, but at the very least, you've got to try.

I went back to the squat the day after I was there with Angel, and the bus ticket was gone. Logic tells me that someone found it and cashed it in for a quick fix or a bottle of cheap wine. I'm pretty sure I just imagined the lingered scent of rosehip and licorice, and the button I found on the floor was probably from one of Tommy's shirts, left behind when we moved.

But I'd like to think that it was Shirley who picked the ticket up, that this time she got to the depot on time.

Mr. Truepenny's Book Emporium and Gallery

The constellations were consulted
for advice, but no one understood them.
—attributed to Elias Canetti

My name's Sophie and my friend Jilly says I have faerie blood. Maybe she's right.

Faeries are supposed to have problems dealing with modern technology and I certainly have trouble with anything technological. The simplest appliances develop horrendous problems when I'm around. I can't wear a watch because they start to run backwards, unless they're digital; then they just flash random numbers as though the watch's inner workings have taken to measuring fractals instead of time. If I take a subway or bus, it's sure to be late. Or it'll have a new driver who takes a wrong turn and we all get lost.

This actually happened to me once. I got on the number 3 at the Kelly Street Bridge and somehow, instead of going downtown on Lee, we ended up heading north into Foxville.

I also have strange dreams.

I used to think they were the place that my art came from, that my subconscious was playing around with images, tossing them up in my sleep before I put them down on canvas or paper. But then a few months ago I had this serial dream that ran on for a half dozen nights in a row, a kind of fairy tale that was either me stepping into faerie, and therefore real within its own parameters—which is what Jilly would like me to believe—or it was just my subconscious making another attempt to deal with the way my mother abandoned my father and me when I was a kid. I don't really know which I believe anymore, because I still find myself going back to that dream world from time to time and meeting the people I first met there.

I even have a boyfriend in that place, which probably tells you more about my usual ongoing social status than it does my state of mind.

Rationally, I know it's just a continuation of that serial dream. And I'd let it go at that, except it feels so damn real. Every morning when I wake up from the latest installment, my head's filled with memories of what I've done that seem as real as anything I do during the day—sometimes more so.

But I'm getting off on a tangent. I started off meaning just to introduce myself, and here I am, giving you my life story. What I really wanted to tell you about was Mr. Truepenny.

The thing you have to understand is that I made him up. He was like one of those invisible childhood friends, except I deliberately created him.

We weren't exactly well-off when I was growing up. When my mother left us, I ended up being one of those latchkey kids. We didn't live in the best part of town; Upper Foxville is a rough part of the city and it could be a scary place for a little girl who loved art and books and got teased for that love by the other neighborhood kids, who couldn't even be bothered to learn how to read. When I got home from school, I went straight in and locked the door.

I'd get supper ready for my dad, but there were always a couple of hours to kill in between my arriving home and when he finished work—longer if he had to work late. We didn't have a TV, so I read a lot, but we couldn't afford to buy books. On Saturday mornings, we'd go to the library and I'd take out my limit—five books—which I'd finish by Tuesday, even if I tried to stretch them out.

To fill the rest of the time, I'd draw on shopping bags or the pads of paper that dad brought me home from work, but that never seemed to occupy enough hours. So one day I made up Mr. Truepenny.

I'd daydream about going to his shop. It was the most perfect place that I could imagine: all dark wood and leaded glass, thick carpets and club chairs with carved wooden-based reading lamps strategically placed throughout. The shelves were filled with leather-bound books and folios, and there was a small art gallery in the back.

The special thing about Mr. Truepenny's shop was that all of its contents existed only within its walls. Shakespeare's *The Storm of Winter. The Chapman's Tale* by Chaucer. *The Blissful Stream* by William Morris. Steinbeck's companion collection to *The Long Valley, Salinas. North Country Stoic* by Emily Brontë.

None of these books existed, of course, but being the dreamy sort of kid that I was, not only could I daydream of visiting Mr. Truepenny's shop, but I could actually read these unwritten stories. The gallery in the back of the shop was much the same. There hung works by the masters that saw the light of day only in my imagination. Van Goghs and Monets and da Vincis. Rossettis and Homers and Cézannes.

Mr. Truepenny himself was a wonderfully eccentric individual who never once chased me out for being unable to make a purchase. He had a Don Quixote air about him, a sense that he was forever tilting at windmills. He was tall and thin with a thatch of mouse-brown hair and round spectacles, a rumpled tweed suit and a huge briar pipe that he continually fussed with but never actually lit. He always greeted me with genuine affection and seemed disappointed when it was time for me to go.

My imagination was so vivid that my daydream visits to his shop were as real to me as when my dad took me to the library or to the Newford Gallery of Fine Art. But it didn't last. I grew up, went to Butler University on student loans and the money from far too many menial jobs—"got a life," as the old saying goes. I made friends,

I was so busy, there was no time, no *need* to visit the shop anymore. Eventually I simply forgot all about it.

Until I met Janice Petrie.

Wendy and I were in the Market after a late night at her place the previous evening. I was on my way home, but we'd decided to shop for groceries together before I left. Trying to make up my mind between green beans and a head of broccoli, my gaze lifted above the vegetable stand and met that of a little girl standing nearby with her parents. Her eyes widened with recognition though I'd never seen her before.

"You're the woman!" she cried. "You're the woman who's evicting Mr. Truepenny. I think it's a horrible thing to do. You're a horrible woman!"

And then she started to cry. Her mother shushed her and apologized to me for the outburst before bustling the little girl away.

"What was all *that* about, Sophie?" Wendy asked me.

"I have no idea," I said.

But of course I did. I was just so astonished by the encounter that I didn't know what to say. I changed the subject and that was the end of it until I got home. I dug out an old cardboard box from the back of my hall closet and rooted about in it until I came up with a folder of drawings I'd done when I still lived with my dad. Near the back I found the ones I was looking for.

They were studies of Mr. Truepenny and his amazing shop.

God, I thought, looking at these awkward drawings, pencil on brown grocery-bag paper, ballpoint on foolscap. The things we forget.

I took the drawings out onto my balcony and lay down on the old sofa I kept out there, studying them, one by one. There was Mr. Truepenny, writing something in his big leather-bound ledger. Here was another of him, holding his cat, Dodger, the two of them looking out the leaded glass windows of the shop. There was a view of the main aisle of the shop, leading down to the gallery, the perspective slightly askew, but not half bad considering I was no older when I did them than was the little girl in the Market today.

How could she have *known?* I found myself thinking. Mr. Truepenny and his shop were something I'd made up. I couldn't remember ever telling anyone else about them—not even Jilly. And what did she mean about my evicting him from the shop?

I could think of no rational response. After a while, I just set the drawings aside and tried to forget about it. Exhaustion from the late night before soon had me nodding off, and I fell asleep only to find myself, not in my boyfriend's faerie dream world, but on the streets of Mabon, the made-up city in which I'd put Mr. Truepenny's Book Emporium and Gallery.

I'm half a block from the shop. The area's changed. The once-neat cobblestones are thick with grime. Refuse lies everywhere. Most of the storefronts are boarded up, their walls festooned with graffiti. When I reach Mr. Truepenny's shop, I see a sign in the window that reads, CLOSING SOON DUE TO LEASE EXPIRATION.

Half-dreading what I'll find, I open the door and hear the familiar little bell tinkle as I step inside. The shop's dusty and dim, and much smaller than I remember it. The shelves are almost bare. The door leading to the gallery is shut and has a CLOSED sign tacked onto it.

"Ah, Miss Etoile. It's been so very long."

I turn to find Mr. Truepenny at his usual station behind the front counter. He's smaller than I remember as well, and looks a little shabby now. Hair thinning, tweed suit threadbare and more shapeless than ever.

"What . . . what's happened to the shop?" I ask.

I've forgotten that I'm asleep on the sofa out on my balcony. All I know is this awful feeling I have inside as I look at what's become of my old childhood haunt.

"Well, times change," he says. "The world moves on."

"This—is this my doing?"

His eyebrows rise quizzically.

"I met this little girl and she said I was evicting you."

"I don't blame you," Mr. Truepenny says, and I can see in his sad eyes that it's true. "You've no more need for me or my wares, so it's only fair that you let us fade."

"But you . . . that is . . . well, you're not real."

I feel weird saying this, because while I remember now that I'm dreaming, this place is like one of my faerie dreams that feel as real as the waking world.

"That's not strictly true," he tells me. "You did conceive of the city and this shop, but we were drawn to fit the blueprint of your plan from . . . elsewhere."

"What elsewhere?"

He frowns, brow furrowing as he thinks.

"I'm not really sure myself," he tells me.

"You're saying I didn't make you up, I just drew you here from somewhere else?" He nods.

"And now you have to go back?"

"So it would seem."

"And this little girl—how can she know about you?"

"Once a reputable establishment is open for business, it really can't deny any customer access, regardless of their age or station in life."

"She's visiting my daydream?" I ask. This is too much to accept, even for a dream.

Mr. Truepenny shakes his head. "You brought this world into being through your single-minded desire, but now it has a life of its own."

"Until I forgot about it."

"You had a very strong will," he says. "You made us so real that we've been able to hang on for decades. But now we really have to go."

There's a very twisty sort of logic involved here, I can see. It doesn't make sense by way of the waking world's logic, but I think there are different rules in a dreamscape. After all, my faerie boyfriend can turn into a crow.

"Do you have more customers, other than that little girl?" I ask.

"Oh yes. Or at least, we did." He waves a hand to encompass the shop. "Not much stock left, I'm afraid. That was the first to go."

"Why doesn't *their* desire keep things running?"

"Well, they don't have faerie blood, now do they? They can visit, but they haven't the magic to bring us across or keep us here."

It figures. I think. We're back to that faerie-blood thing again. Jilly would love this.

I'm about to ask him to explain it all a little more clearly when I get this odd jangling sound in my ears and wake up back on the sofa. My doorbell's ringing. I go inside the apartment to accept what turns out to be a FedEx package.

"Can dreams be real?" I ask the courier. "Can we invent something in a dream and have it turn out to be a real place?"

"Beats me, lady," he replies, never blinking an eye. "Just sign here."

I guess he gets all kinds.

So now I visit Mr. Truepenny's shop on a regular basis again. The area's vastly improved. There's a café nearby where Jeck—that's my boyfriend that I've been telling you about—and I go for tea after we've browsed through Mr. Truepenny's latest wares. Jeck likes this part of Mabon so much that he's now got an apartment on the same street as the shop. I think I might set up a studio nearby.

I've even run into Janice—the little girl who brought me back here in the first place. She's forgiven me, of course, now that she knows it was all a misunderstanding, and lets me buy her an ice cream from the soda fountain sometimes before she goes home.

I'm very accepting of it all—you get that way after a while. The thing that worries me now is, what happens to Mabon when I die? Will the city get run down again and eventually disappear? And what about its residents? There's all these people here; they've got family, friends, lives. I get the feeling it wouldn't be the same for them if they have to go back to that elsewhere place Mr. Truepenny was so vague about.

So that's the reason I've written all this down and had it printed up into a little folio by one of Mr. Truepenny's friends in the waking world. I'm hoping somebody out there's like me. Someone's got enough faerie blood not only to visit, but to keep the place going. Naturally, not just anyone will do. It has to be the right sort of person, a book lover, a lover of old places and tradition, as well as the new.

If you think you're the person for the position, please send a résumé to me care of Mr. Truepenny's Book Emporium and Gallery, Mabon. I'll get back to you as soon as I can.

The Forest Is Crying

*There are seven million homeless children
on the streets of Brazil. Are vanishing
trees being reborn as unwanted children?*
—Gary Snyder, from *The Practice of the Wild*

The real problem is, people think life
is a ladder, and it's really a wheel.
—Pat Cadigan, from "Johnny Come Home"

Two pairs of footsteps, leather soles on marble floors. Listening to the sound they made, Dennison felt himself wondering, What was the last thing that Ronnie Egan heard before he died? The squeal of tires on wet pavement? Some hooker or an old wino shouting, "Look out!" Or was there no warning, no warning at all? Just the sudden impact of the car as it hit him and flung his body ten feet in the air before it was smeared up against the plate glass window of the pawn shop?

"You don't have to do this," Stone said as they paused at the door. "One of the neighbors already IDed the body."

"I know."

Looking through the small window, glass reinforced with metal mesh, Dennison watched the morgue attendant approach to let them in. Like the detective at Dennison's side, the attendant was wearing a sidearm. Was the security to keep people out or keep them in? he wondered morbidly.

"So why—" Stone began, then he shook his head. "Never mind."

It wasn't long before they were standing on either side of a metal tray that the attendant had pulled out from the wall at Stone's request. It could easily hold a grown man, twice the 170 pounds Dennison carried on his own six-one frame. The small body laid out upon the metal surface was dwarfed by the expanse of stainless steel that surrounded it.

"His mother's a heavy user," Dennison said. "She peddles her ass to feed the habit. Sometimes she brings the man home—she's got a room at the Claymore. If the guy didn't like having a kid around, she'd get one of the neighbors to look after him. We've had her in twice for putting him outside to play in the middle of the night when she couldn't find anybody to take him in. Trouble is, she always put on such a good show for the judge that we couldn't make the neglect charges stick."

He delivered the brief summary in a monotone. It didn't seem real. Just like Ronnie Egan's dead body didn't seem real. The skin so ashen, the bruises so dark against its pallor.

"I read the file," Stone said.

Dennison looked up from the corpse of the four-year-old boy.

"Did you bring her in?" he asked.

Stone shook his head. "Can't track her down. We've got an APB out on her, but . . ." He sighed. "Who're we kidding, Chris? Even when we do bring her in, we're not going to be able to find a charge that'll stick. She'll just tell the judge what she's told them before."

Dennison nodded heavily. I'm sorry, Your Honor, but I was asleep and I never even heard him go out. He's a good boy, but he doesn't always listen to his momma. He likes to wander. If Social Services could give her enough to raise him in a decent neighborhood, this kind of thing would never happen. . . .

"I should've tried harder," he said.

"Yeah, like your caseload's any lighter than mine," Stone said. "Where the fuck would you find the time?"

"I still should've . . ."

Done something, Dennison thought. Made a difference.

Stone nodded to the attendant, who zipped up the heavy plastic bag, then slid the drawer back into the wall. Dennison watched until the drawer closed with a metal click, then finally turned away.

"You're taking this too personally," Stone said.

"It's always personal."

Stone put his arm around Dennison's shoulders and steered him toward the door.

"It gets worse every time something like this happens," Dennison went on. "For every one I help, I lose a dozen. It's like pissing in the wind."

"I know," Stone said heavily.

The bright daylight stung Dennison's eyes when he stepped outside. He hadn't had breakfast yet, but he had no appetite. His pager beeped, but he didn't bother to check the number he was supposed to call. He just shut off the annoying sound. He couldn't deal with whatever the call was about. Not today. He couldn't face going into the office either, couldn't face all those hopeless faces of people he wanted to help; there just wasn't enough time in a day, enough money in the budget, enough of anything to make a real difference.

Ronnie Egan's lifeless features floated up in his mind.

He shook his head and started to walk. Aimlessly, but at a fast pace. Shoe leather on pavement now, but he couldn't hear it for the sound of the traffic, vehicular and pedestrian. Half an hour after leaving the morgue he found himself on the waterfront, staring out over the lake.

He didn't think he could take it anymore. He'd put in seven years as a caseworker for Social Services, but it seemed as though he'd finally burned out. Ronnie Egan's stupid, senseless death was just too much to bear. If he went into the office right now, it would only be to type up a letter of resignation. He decided to get drunk instead.

Turning, he almost bumped into the attractive woman who was approaching him. She might be younger, but he put her at his own twenty-nine; she just wore the years better. A soft fall of light-brown hair spilled down to her shoulders in untidy tangles. Her eyes were a little too large for the rest of her features, but they were such an astonishing grey-green that it didn't matter. She was wearing jeans and a "Save the Rainforests" T-shirt, a black cotton jacket overtop.

"Hi there," she said.

She offered him a pamphlet that he reached for automatically, before he realized what he was doing. He dropped his hand and stuck it in his pocket, leaving her with the pamphlet still proffered.

"I don't think so," he said.

"It's a serious issue," she began.

"I've got my own problems."

She tapped the pamphlet. "This is everybody's problem."

Dennison sighed. "Look, lady," he said. "I'm more interested in helping people than trees. Sorry."

"But without the rainforests—"

"Trees don't have feelings," he said, cutting her off. "Trees don't cry. Kids do."

"Maybe you just can't hear them."

Her gaze held his. He turned away, unable to face her disappointed look. But what was he supposed to do? If he couldn't even be there for Ronnie Egan when the kid had needed help the most, what the hell did she expect him to do about a bunch of trees? There were other people, far better equipped, to deal with that kind of problem.

"You caught me on a bad day," he said. "Sorry."

He walked away before she could reply.

Dennison wasn't much of a drinker. A beer after work a couple of times a week. Wine with a meal even more occasionally. A few brews with the guys after one of their weekend softball games—that was just saying his pager left him alone long enough to get through all the innings. His clients' needs didn't fit into a tidy nine-to-five schedule, with weekends off. Crises could arise at any time of the day or night—usually when it was most inconvenient. But Dennison had never really minded. He'd bitch and complain about it like everybody else he worked with, but he'd always be there for whoever needed the help.

Why hadn't Sandy Egan called him last night? He'd told her to phone him, instead of just putting Ronnie outside again. He'd promised her, no questions. He wouldn't use the incident as pressure to take the boy away from her. Ronnie was the first priority, plain and simple.

But she hadn't called. She hadn't trusted him, hadn't wanted to chance losing the extra money Social Services gave her to raise the boy. And now he was dead.

Halfway through his fourth beer, Dennison started ordering shots of whiskey on the side. By the time the dinner hour rolled around, he was too drunk to know where he was anymore. He'd started out in a run-down bar somewhere on Palm Street; he could be anywhere now.

The smoky interior of the bar looked like every other place he'd been in this afternoon. Dirty wooden floors, their polish scratched and worn beyond all redemption. Tables in little better condition, chairs with loose legs that wobbled when you sat on them, leaving you unsure if it was all the booze you'd been putting away that made your seat feel so precarious, or the rickety furniture that the owner was too cheap to replace until it actually fell apart under someone. A TV set up in a corner of the bar where game shows and soap operas took turns until they finally gave way to the six o'clock news.

And then there was the clientele.

The thin afternoon crowd was invariably composed of far too many lost and hopeless faces. He recognized them from his job. Today, as he staggered away from the urinal to blink at the reflection looking back at him from the mirror, he realized that he looked about the same. He couldn't tell himself apart from them if he tried, except that maybe they could hold their drink better.

Because he felt sick. Unable to face the squalor of one of the cubicles, he stumbled out of the bar, hoping to clear his head. The street didn't look familiar, and the air didn't help. It was filled with exhaust fumes and the tail end of rush-hour noise. His stomach roiled and he made his slow way along the pavement in front of the bar, one hand on the wall to keep his balance.

When he reached the alleyway, it was all he could do to take a few floundering steps inside before he fell to his hands and knees and threw up. Vomiting brought no relief. He still felt the world doing a slow spin and the stink just made his nausea worse.

Pushing himself away from the noxious puddle, the most he could manage was to fall back against the brick wall on this side of the alley. He brought his knees slowly up, wrapped his arms around them and leaned his head on top. He must have inadvertently turned his pager back on at some point in the afternoon, because it suddenly went off, its insistent beep piercing his aching head.

He unclipped it from his belt and threw it against the far wall. The sound of it smashing was only slightly more satisfying than the blessed relief from its shrill beeping.

"You don't look so good."

He lifted his head at the familiar voice, half-expecting that one of his clients had found him in this condition, or worse, one of his coworkers. Instead he met the greygreen gaze of the woman he'd briefly run into by the lakefront earlier in the day.

"Jesus," he said. "You . . . you're like a bad penny."

He lowered his head back onto his knees again and just hoped she'd go away. He could feel her standing there, looking down at him for a long time before she finally went down on one knee beside him and gave his arm a tug.

"C'mon," she said. "You can't stay here."

"Lemme alone."

"I don't just care about trees, either," she said.

"Who gives a fuck."

But it was easier to let her drag him to his feet than to fight her offer of help. She slung his arm over her shoulder and walked him back to the street where she flagged down a cab. He heard her give his address to the cabbie and wondered how she knew it, but soon gave up that train of thought as he concentrated on not getting sick in the back of the cab.

He retained the rest of the night in brief flashes. At some point they were in the stairwell of his building, what felt like a month later he was propped up beside the door to his apartment while she worked the key in the lock. Then he was lying on his bed while she removed his shoes.

"Who . . . who are you?" he remembered asking her.

"Debra Eisenstadt."

The name meant nothing to him. The bed seemed to move under him. I don't have a water bed, he remembered thinking, and then he threw up again. Debra caught it in his wastepaper basket.

A little later still, he came to again to find her sitting in one of his kitchen chairs that she'd brought into the bedroom and placed by the head of the bed. He remembered thinking that this was an awful lot to go through just for a donation to some rainforest fund.

He started to sit up, but the room spun dangerously, so he just let his head fall back against the pillow. She wiped his brow with a cool, damp washcloth.

"What do you want from me?" he managed to ask.

"I just wanted to see what you were like when you were my age," she said.

That made so little sense that he passed out again trying to work it out.

She was still there when he woke up the next morning. If anything, he thought he actually felt worse than he had the night before. Debra came into the room when he stirred and gave him a glass of Eno that helped settle his stomach. A couple of Tylenol started to work on the pounding behind his eyes.

"Someone from your office called and I told her you were sick," she said. "I hope that was okay."

"You stayed all night?"

She nodded, but Dennison didn't think she had the look of someone who'd been up all night. She had a fresh-scrubbed glow to her complexion and her head seemed to catch the sun, spinning it off into strands of light that mingled with the natural highlights already present in her light-brown hair. Her hair looked damp.

"I used your shower," she said. "I hope you don't mind."

"No, no. Help yourself."

He started to get up, but she put a palm against his chest to keep him lying down.

"Give the pills a chance to work," she said. "Meanwhile, I'll get you some coffee. Do you feel up to some breakfast?"

The very thought of eating made his stomach churn.

"Never mind," she said, taking in the look on his face. "I'll just bring the coffee."

Dennison watched her leave, then straightened his head and stared at the ceiling. After meeting her, he thought maybe he believed in angels for the first time since Sunday school.

It was past ten before he finally dragged himself out of bed and into the shower. The sting of hot water helped to clear his head; being clean and putting on fresh clothes helped some more. He regarded himself in the bathroom mirror. His features were still puffy from alcohol poisoning and his cheeks looked dirty with twenty-four hours worth of dark stubble. His hands were unsteady, but he shaved all the same. Neither mouthwash nor brushing his teeth could quite get rid of the sour taste in his mouth.

Debra had toast and more coffee waiting for him in the kitchen.

"I don't get it," he said as he slid into a chair across the table from her. "I could be anyone—some maniac for all you know. Why're you being so nice to me?"

She just shrugged.

"C'mon. It's not like I could have been a pretty sight when you found me in the alley, so it can't be that you were attracted to me."

"Were you serious about what you said last night?" she asked by way of response. "About quitting your job?"

Dennison paused before answering to consider what she'd asked. He couldn't remember telling her that, but then there was a lot about yesterday he couldn't remember. The day was mostly a blur except for one thing. Ronnie Egan's features swam up in his mind until he squeezed his eyes shut and forced the image away.

Serious about quitting his job?

"Yeah," he said with a slow nod. "I guess I was. I mean, I am. I don't think I can even face going into the office. I'll just send them my letter of resignation and have somebody pick up my stuff from my desk."

"You do make a difference," she said. "It might not seem so at a time like this, but you've got to concentrate on all the people you have helped. That's got to count for something, doesn't it?"

"How would you know?" Dennison asked her. No sooner did the question leave his mouth, than it was followed by a flood of others. "Where did you come from? What are you doing here? It's got to be more than trying to convince me to keep my job so that I can afford to donate some money to your cause."

"You don't believe in good Samaritans?"

Dennison shook his head. "Nor Santa Claus."

But maybe angels, he added to himself. She was so fresh and pretty—light years different from the people who came into his office, their worn and desperate features eventually all bleeding one into the other.

"I appreciate your looking after me the way you did," he said. "Really I do. And I don't mean to sound ungrateful. But it just doesn't make a lot of sense."

"You help people all the time."

"That's my job—was my job." He looked away from her steady gaze. "Christ, I don't know anymore."

"And that's all it was?" she asked.

"No. It's just . . . I'm tired, I guess. Tired of seeing it all turn to shit on me. This little kid who died yesterday . . . I could've tried harder. If I'd tried harder, maybe he'd still be alive."

"That's the way I feel about the environment, sometimes," she said. "There are times when it just feels so hopeless, I can't go on."

"So why do you?"

"Because the bottom line is I believe I can make a difference. Not a big one. What I do is just a small ripple, but I know it helps. And if enough little people like me make our little differences, one day we're going to wake up to find that we really did manage to change the world."

"There's a big distinction between some trees getting cut down and a kid dying," Dennison said.

"From our perspective, sure," she agreed. "But maybe not from a global view.

We have to remember that everything's connected. The real world's not something that can be divided into convenient little compartments, like we'll label this, 'the child abuse problem,' this'll go under 'depletion of the ozone layer.' If you help some homeless child on these city streets, it has repercussions that touch every part of the world."

"I don't get it."

"It's like a vibe," she said. "If enough people think positively, take positive action, then it snowballs all of its own accord and the world can't help but get a little better."

Dennison couldn't stop from voicing the cynical retort that immediately came into his mind.

"How retro," he said.

"What do you mean?"

"It sounds so sixties. All this talk about vibes and positive mumbo-jumbo."

"Positive thinking brought down the Berlin Wall," she said.

"Yeah, and I'm sure some fortune teller predicted it in the pages of a supermarket tabloid, although she probably got the decade wrong. Look, I'm sorry, but I don't buy it. If the world really worked on 'vibes,' I think it'd be in even worse shape than it already is."

"Maybe that's what *is* wrong with it: too much negative energy. So we've got to counteract it with positive energy."

"Oh, please."

She got a sad look on her face. "I believe it," she said. "I learned that from a man that I came to love very much. I didn't believe him when he told me, either, but now I know it's true."

"*How* can you know it's true?"

Debra sighed. She put her hand in the back pocket of her jeans and pulled out a piece of paper.

"Talk to these people," she said. "They can explain it a whole lot better than I can."

Dennison looked at the scrap of paper she'd handed him. "Elders' Council" was written in ballpoint. The address given was City Hall's.

"Who are they?"

"Elders from the Kickaha Reservation."

"They've got an office at City Hall?"

Debra nodded. "It's part of a program to integrate alternative methods of dealing with problems with the ones we would traditionally use."

"What? People go to these old guys and ask them for advice?"

"They're not just men," she said. "In fact, among the Kickaha—as with many native peoples—there are more women than men sitting on an elders' council. They're the grandmothers of the tribe who hold and remember all the wisdoms. The Kickaha call them 'the Aunts.' "

Dennison started to shake his head. "I know you mean well, Debra, but—"

"Just go talk to them—please? Before you make your decision."

"But nothing they say is going to—"

"Promise me you will. You asked me why I helped you last night, well, let's say this is what I want in return: for you just to talk to them."

"I . . ."

The last thing Dennison wanted was to involve himself with some nut-case situation like this, but he liked the woman, despite her flaky beliefs, and he did owe her something. He remembered throwing up last night and her catching the vomit in his garbage can. How many people would do that for a stranger?

"Okay," he said. "I promise."

The smile that she gave him seemed to make her whole face glow.

"Good," she said. "Make sure you bring a present. A package of tobacco would be good."

"Tobacco."

She nodded. "I've got to go now," she added. She stood up and shook his hand. "I'm really glad I got the chance to meet you."

"Wait a minute," Dennison said as she left the kitchen.

He followed her into the living room where she was putting on her jacket.

"Am I going to see you again?" he asked.

"I hope so."

"What's your number?"

"Do you have a pen?"

He went back into the kitchen and returned with a pencil and the scrap of paper she'd given him. She took it from him and quickly scribbled a phone number and address on it. She handed it back to him, gave him a quick kiss on the cheek, and then she was out the door and gone.

Dennison stood staring at the door after it had closed behind her. The apartment had never seemed so empty before.

Definitely flaky, he thought as he returned to the kitchen. But he thought maybe he'd fallen in love with her, if that was something you were allowed to do with angels.

He finished his coffee and cleaned up the dishes, dawdling over the job. He didn't know anything about the Kickaha except for those that he saw in his office, applying for welfare, and what he'd seen on the news a couple of years ago when the more militant braves from the reservation had blockaded Highway 14 to protest logging on their land. So he had only two images of them: down and out, or dressed in khaki, carrying an assault rifle. Wait, make that three. There were also the pictures in the history books of them standing around in ceremonial garb.

He didn't want to go to this Elders' Council. Nothing they could tell him was going to make him look at the world any differently, so why bother? But finally he put on a lightweight sportsjacket and went out to flag a cab to take him to City Hall, because whatever else he believed or didn't believe, the one thing he'd never done yet was break a promise.

He wasn't about to start now—especially with a promise made to an angel.

Dennison left the elevator and walked down a carpeted hallway on the third floor of City hall. he stopped at the door with the neatly lettered sign that read elders' council. He felt surreal, as though he'd taken a misstep somewhere along the way yesterday and had ended up in a Fellini film. Being here was odd enough, in and of itself. But if he was going to meet a native elder, he felt it should be under pine trees with the smell of wood smoke in the air, not cloistered away in City Hall, surrounded by miles of concrete and steel.

Really, he shouldn't be here at all. What he should be doing was getting his affairs in order. Resigning from his job, getting in touch with his cousin Pete, who asked

Dennison at least every three or four months if he wanted to go into business with him. Pete worked for a small shipping firm, but he wanted to start his own company. "I've got the know-how and the money," he'd tell Dennison, "but frankly, when it comes to dealing with people, I stink. That's where you'd come in."

Dennison hesitated for a long moment, staring at the door and the sign affixed to its plain wooden surface. He knew what he should be doing, but he'd made that promise, so he knocked on the door. An old native woman answered as he was about to lift his hand to rap a second time.

Her face was wrinkled, her complexion dark; her braided hair almost grey. She wore a long brown skirt, flat-soled shoes and a plain white blouse that was decorated with a tracing of brightly coloured beadwork on its collar points and buttoned placket. The gaze that looked up to meet his was friendly, the eyes such a dark brown that it was hard to differentiate between pupil and iris.

"Hello," she said and ushered him in.

It was strange inside. He found himself standing in a conference room overlooking the parking garage behind City Hall. The walls were unadorned and there was no table, just thick wall-to-wall on the floor and a ring of chairs set in a wide circle, close to the walls. At the far side of the room, he spied a closed door that might lead into another room or a storage closet.

"Uh . . ."

Suddenly at a loss for words, he put his hand in his pocket, pulled out the package of cigarette tobacco that he'd bought on the way over and handed it to her.

"Thank you," the woman said. She steered him to a chair, then sat down beside him. "My name is Dorothy. How can I help you?"

"Dorothy?" Dennison replied, unable to hide his surprise.

The woman nodded. "Dorothy Born. You were expecting something more exotic such as Woman-Who-Speaks-With-One-Hand-Rising?"

"I didn't know what to expect."

"That was my mother's name actually—in the old language. She was called that because she'd raise her hand as she spoke, ready to slap the head of those braves who wouldn't listen to her advice."

"Oh."

She smiled. "That's a joke. My mother's name was Ruth."

"Uh . . ."

What a great conversationalist he was proving to be today. Good thing Pete couldn't hear him at this moment. But he just didn't know where to begin.

"Why don't you just tell me why you've come," Dorothy said.

"Actually, I feel a little foolish."

Her smile broadened. "Good. That is the first step on the road to wisdom." She put a hand on his knee, dark gaze locking with his. "What is your name?"

"Chris—Chris Dennison."

"Speak to me, Chris. I am here to listen."

So Dennison told her about his job, about Ronnie Egan's death, about getting drunk, about Debra Eisenstadt and how she'd come to send him here. Once he started, his awkwardness fled.

"Nothing seems worth it anymore," he said in conclusion.

Dorothy nodded. "I understand. When the spirit despairs, it becomes difficult to see clearly. Your friend's words require too much faith for you to accept them."

"I guess. I'm not sure I even understand them."

"Perhaps I can help you there."

She fell silent for a moment, her gaze still on him, but she no longer seemed to see him. It was as though she saw beyond him, or had turned to look inward.

"The Kickaha way to see the world," she finally said, "is to understand that everything is on a wheel: Day turns to night. The moon waxes and wanes. Summer turns to autumn. A man is born, he lives, he dies. But no wheel turns by itself. Each affects the other, so that when the wheel of the seasons turns to winter, the wheel of the day grows shorter. When the day grows shorter, the sweetgrass is covered with snow and the deer must forage for bark and twigs rather than feast on its delicate blades. The hunter must travel farther afield to find the deer, but perhaps the wolf finds her first."

She paused, sitting back in her chair. "Do you see?"

Dennison nodded slowly. "I see the connection in what you're saying, but not with what Debra was trying to tell me. It was so vague—all this talk about positive energy."

"But the energy we produce is very powerful medicine," Dorothy said. "It can work great good or ill."

"You make it sound like voodoo."

She frowned for a moment as though she needed to think that through.

"Perhaps it is," she said. "From the little I know of it, *voudoun* is a very basic application of the use of one's will. The results one gains from its medicine become positive or negative only depending upon one's intention."

"You're saying we make bad things happen to ourselves?"

Dorothy nodded. "And to our sacred trust, the earth."

"I still don't see how a person can be so sure he's really making a difference."

"What if the child you save grows up to be the scientist who will cure AIDS?"

"What if the child I don't get to in time was supposed to be that scientist, and so she never gets the chance to find the cure?"

Dorothy lifted her hand and tapped it against his chest. "You carry so much pain in here. It wasn't always so, was it?"

Dennison thought about how he'd been when he first got into social work. He'd been like Debra then, so sure he knew exactly what to do. He'd believed utterly in his ability to save the world. That had changed. Not because of Ronnie Egan, but slowly, over the years. He'd had to make compromises, his trust had been abused not once, or twice, but almost every day. What had happened to Ronnie had forced him to see that he fought a losing battle.

Perhaps it was worse than that. What he felt now was that the battle had been lost long ago and he was only just now realizing the futility of continuing to man the frontlines.

"If you were to see what I have to work with every day," he said, "you'd get depressed, too."

Dorothy shook her head. "That is not our way."

"So what is your way?"

"You must learn to let it go. The wheel must always turn. If you take upon yourself the sadness and despair from those you would help, you must also learn how to let it go. Otherwise it will settle inside you like a cancer."

"I don't know if I can anymore."

She nodded slowly. "That is something that only you can decide. But remember this: You have given a great deal of yourself. You have no reason to feel ashamed if you must now turn away."

She had just put her finger on what was making the decision so hard for him. Futile though he'd come to realize his efforts were, he still felt guilty at the idea of turning his back on those who needed his help. It wasn't like what Debra had been saying: The difference he made didn't have far-reaching effects. It didn't change what was happening in the Amazon, or make the hole in the ozone layer any smaller. All it did was make one or two persons' misery a little easier to bear, but only in the short term. It seemed cruel to give them hope when it would just be taken away from them again.

If only there really were something to Debra's domino theory. While the people he helped wouldn't go on to save the environment, or find that cure for AIDS, they might help somebody else a little worse off than themselves. That seemed worthwhile, except what do you do when you've reached inside yourself and you can't find anything left to give?

Dorothy was watching him with her dark gaze. Oddly enough, her steady regard didn't make him feel self-conscious. She had such a strong personality that he could feel its warmth as though he was holding his hands out to a fire. It made him yearn to find something to fill the cold that had lodged inside him since he'd looked down at Ronnie Egan's corpse.

"Maybe I should get into environmental work instead," he said. "You know, how they say that a change is as good as a rest?"

"Who says you aren't already doing environmental work?" Dorothy asked.

"What do you mean?"

"What if the dying trees of the rainforest are being reborn as unwanted children?" she asked.

"C'mon. You can't expect me to believe—"

"Why not? If a spirit is taken from its wheel before its time, it must go some-where."

Dennison had a sudden vision of a tenement building filled with green-skinned children, each of them struggling to reach the roof of the building to get their nourishment from the sun, except when they finally got up there, the smog cover was so thick that there was nothing for them. They got a paler and paler green until finally they just withered away. Died like so many weeds.

"Imagine living in a world with no more trees," Dorothy said.

Dennison had been in a clear-cut forest once. It was while he was visiting a friend in Oregon. He'd stood there on a hilltop and for as far as the eye could see, there were only tree stumps. It was a heartbreaking sight.

His friend had become an environmentalist after a trip to China. "There are almost no trees left there at all now," he'd told Dennison. "They've just used them all up. Trees clean the environment by absorbing the toxins from carbon dioxide and acid rain. Without them, the water and air become too toxic and people start to die off from liver cancer. China has an incredibly high mortality rate due to liver cancer.

"That's going to happen here, Chris. That's what's going to happen in the Amazon. It's going to happen all over the world."

Dennison had felt bad, enough so that he contributed some money to a couple of relevant causes, but his concern hadn't lasted. His work with Social Services took too much out of him to leave much energy for other concerns, no matter how worthy.

As though reading his mind, Dorothy said, "And now imagine a world with no more children."

Dennison thought they might be halfway there. So many of the children he dealt with were more like miniature adults than the kids he remembered growing up with. But then he and his peers hadn't had to try to survive on the streets, foraging out of trash cans, maybe taking care of a junkie parent.

"I have a great concern for Mother Earth," Dorothy said. "We have gravely mistreated her. But when we speak of the environment and the depletion of resources, we sometimes forget that our greatest resource is our children.

"My people have a word to describe the moment when all is in harmony—we call it Beauty. But Beauty can find no foothold in despair. If we mean to reclaim our Mother Earth from the ills that plague her, we must not forget our own children. We must work on many levels, walk many wheels, that lives may be spared—the lives of people, and the lives of all those other species with whom we share the world. Our contributions, no matter how small they might appear, carry an equal importance, for they will all contribute to the harmony that allows the world to walk the wheel of Beauty."

She closed her eyes and fell silent. Dennison sat quietly beside her for a time.

"What . . . what advice would you give me?" he asked finally.

Dorothy shrugged. Her eyes remained closed.

"You must do what you believe is right," she said. "We have inside of each of us a spirit, and that spirit alone knows what it is that we should or should not do."

"I've got to think about all of this," Dennison said.

"That would be a good thing," Dorothy told him. She opened her eyes suddenly, piercing him with her gaze. "But hold onto your feelings of foolishness," she added. "Wisdom never comes to those who believe they have nothing left to learn."

Dennison found an empty bench when he left City Hall. He sat down and cradled his face in his hands. His headache had returned, but that wasn't what was disturbing him. He'd found himself agreeing with the Kickaha elder. He also thought he understood what Debra had been telling him. The concepts weren't suspect—only the part he had to play in them.

He felt like one of those biblical prophets, requiring the proof of a burning bush or some other miracle before they'd go on with the task required of them. If he could just have the proof that he'd made a real and lasting difference for only one person, that would be enough. But it wasn't going to come.

The people he helped continued to live hand to mouth because there was no other way for them to live. Caught up in a recession that showed no sign of letting up, they considered themselves lucky just to be surviving.

And that was why his decision was going to have to stand. He'd given of himself, above and beyond what the job required, for years. The empty cold feeling inside told him that he had nothing left to give. It was time to call Pete and see about that shipping business. He wasn't sure he could bring Pete's enthusiasm to it, but he'd do his best.

But first he owed Debra a call: Yeah, I went and saw the elder, she was a wonderful woman, I understand what you were saying, but I haven't changed my mind. He knew he'd be closing the door on the possibility of a relationship with her, but then he didn't feel he had even that much of himself to give someone anyway.

He dug a quarter out of his pocket and went to the pay phone on the corner. But when he dialed the number she'd given him, he got a recorded message: "I'm sorry, but the number you have dialed is no longer in service."

"Shit," he said, stepping back from the phone.

An older woman, laden down with shopping bags, gave him a disapproving glare.

"Sorry," he muttered.

Flagging down a cab, he gave the driver the address that Debra had written down to accompany her bogus phone number, then settled back in his seat.

The building was a worn, brownstone tenement, indistinguishable from every other one on the block. They all had the same tired face to turn to the world. Refuse collected against their steps, graffiti on the walls, cheap curtains in the windows when there were any at all. Walking up the steps, the smell of urine and body odor was strong in the air. A drunk lay sleeping just inside the small foyer.

Dennison stepped over him and went up to the second floor. He knocked on the door that had a number matching the one Debra had written down for him. After a moment or two, the door opened to the length of its chain and a woman as worn down as the building itself was looking at him.

"What do you want?"

Dennison had been expecting an utter stranger, but the woman had enough of a family resemblance to Debra that he thought maybe his rescuing angel really did live here. Looking past the lines that worry and despair had left on the woman's face, he realized that she was about his own age. Too young to be Debra's mother. Maybe her sister?

"Are you . . . uh, Mrs. Eisenstadt?" he asked, trying the only name he had.

"Who wants to know?"

"My name's Chris Dennison. I'm here to see Debra."

The woman's eyes narrowed with suspicion. "What'd she do now?"

"Nothing. That is, she gave me some help yesterday and I just wanted to thank her."

The suspicion didn't leave the woman's features. "Debra!" she shouted over her shoulder. Turning back to Dennison, she added, "I've got lots of neighbors. You try anything funny, I'll give a scream that'll have them down here so fast you won't know if you're coming or going."

Dennison doubted that. In a place like this, people would just mind their own business. It wouldn't matter if somebody was getting murdered next door.

"I'm not here to cause trouble," he said.

"Deb-*ra!*" the woman hollered again.

She shut the door and Dennison could hear her unfastening the chain. When she opened the door once more, it swung open to its full width. Dennison looked down the hall behind the woman and saw a little girl of perhaps nine coming slowly down the hallway, head lowered, gaze on the floor.

"I thought you told me you were in school yesterday," the woman said to her.

The girl's gaze never lifted. "I was."

She spoke barely above a whisper.

"Man here says you were helping him—doing what, I'd like to know." She turned from her daughter back to Dennison. "Maybe you want to tell me, mister?"

The girl looked at him then. He saw the grey-green eyes first, the features that might one day grow into ones similar to those of the woman he'd met yesterday, though this couldn't be her. The discrepancy of years was too vast. Then he saw the bruises. One eye blackened. The right side of her jaw swollen. She seemed to favor one leg as well.

His training kept him silent. If he said something too soon, he wouldn't learn a thing. First he had to give the woman enough room to hang herself.

"This is Debra Eisenstadt?" he asked.

"What, you need to see her birth certificate?"

Dennison turned to the woman and saw then what he hadn't noticed before. The day was warm, but she was wearing slacks, long sleeves, her blouse buttoned all the way up to the top. But he could see a discoloration in the hollow of her throat that the collar couldn't quite hide. Abrasive or not, she was a victim, too, he realized.

"Where is your husband, Mrs. Eisenstadt?" he asked gently.

"So now you're a cop?"

Dennison pulled out his ID. "No. I'm with Social Services. I can help you, Mrs. Eisenstadt. Has your husband been beating you?"

She crossed her arms protectively. "Look, it's not like what you're thinking. We had an argument, that's all."

"And your daughter—was he having an argument with her as well?"

"No. She . . . she just fell. Isn't that right, honey?"

Dennison glanced at the girl. She was staring at the floor again. Slowly she nodded in agreement. Dennison went down on one knee until his head was level with the girl's.

"You can tell me the truth," he said. "I can help you, but you've got to help me. Tell me how you got hurt and I promise you I won't let it happen to you again."

What the hell are you doing? he asked himself. You're supposed to be quitting this job.

But he hadn't turned in his resignation yet.

And then he remembered an odd thing that the other Debra had said to him last night.

I just wanted to see what you were like when you were my age.

He remembered puzzling over that before he finally passed out. And then there was the way she'd looked at him the next morning, admiring, then sad, then disappointed. As though she already knew him. As though he wasn't matching up to her expectations.

Though of course she couldn't have any expectations because they'd never met before. But what if this girl grew up to be the woman who'd helped him last night? What if her being here, in need of help, was his prophetic sign, his burning bush?

Yeah, right. And it was space aliens who brought her back from the future to see him.

"Look," the girl's mother said. "You've got no right, barging in here—"

"No right?" Dennison said, standing up to face her. "Look at your daughter, for Christ's sake, and then tell me that I've got no right to intervene."

"It's not like what you think. It's just that times are hard, you know, and what with Sam's losing his job, well he gets a little crazy sometimes. He doesn't mean any real harm. . . ."

Dennison tuned her out. He looked back at the little girl. It didn't matter if she was a sign or not, if she'd grow up to be the woman who'd somehow come back in time to help him when his faith was flagging the most. What was important right now that he get the girl some help.

"Which of your neighbors has a working phone?" he asked.

"Why? What're you going to do? Sam's going to—"

"Not do a damned thing," Dennison said. "It's my professional opinion that this child will be in danger so long as she remains in this environment. You can either come with us, or I'll see that she's made a ward of the court, but I'm not leaving her here."

"You can't—"

"I think we'll leave that for a judge to decide."

He ignored her then. Crouching down beside the little girl, he said, "I'm here to help you—do you understand? No one's going to hurt you anymore."

"If I . . . he said if I tell—"

"Debra!"

Dennison shot the mother an angry look. "I'm losing my patience with you, lady. Look at your daughter. Look at those bruises. Is that the kind of childhood you meant for your child?"

Her defiance crumbled under his glare and she slowly shook her head.

"Go pack a bag," he told the woman. "For both of you."

As she slowly walked down the hall, Dennison returned his attention to the little girl. This could all go to hell in a hand basket if he wasn't careful. There were certain standard procedures to deal with this kind of a situation and badgering the girl's mother the way he had been wasn't one of them. But he was damned if he wasn't going to give it his best shot.

"Do you understand what's happening?" he asked the girl. "I'm going to take you and your mother someplace where you'll be safe."

She looked up at him, those so-familiar grey-green eyes wide and teary. "I'm scared."

Dennison nodded. "It's a scary situation. But tell you what. On the way to the shelter, maybe we get you a treat. What would you like?"

For one long moment the girl's gaze settled on his. She seemed to be considering whether she could trust him or not. He must have come up positive, because after that moment's hesitation, she opened right up.

"For there still to be trees when I grow up," she said. "I want to be a forest ranger. Sometimes when I'm sleeping, I wake up and I hear the trees crying because their daddies are being mean to them, I guess, and are hurting them and I just want to help stop it."

Dennison remembered himself saying to the older Debra, *Trees don't cry. Kids do.* And then Debra's response.

Maybe you just can't hear them.

Jesus, it wasn't possible, was it? But then how could they look so similar, the differences caused by the passage of years, not genetics. And the eyes—the eyes were exactly the same. And how could the old Debra have known the address, the phone number—

He got up and went over to the phone he could see sitting on a TV tray beside the battered sofa. The number was the same as on the scrap of paper in his pocket. He lifted the receiver, but there was no dial tone.

"I . . . I've packed a . . . bag."

Debra's mother stood in the hallway beside her daughter, looking as lost as the little girl did. But there was something they both had—there was a glimmer of hope in their eyes. He'd put that there. Now all he had to do was figure out a way to keep it there.

"Whose phone can we use to call a cab?" he asked.

"Laurie—she's down the hall in number six. She'd let us use her phone."

"Well, let's get going."

As he ushered them into the hall, he was no longer thinking about tendering his resignation. He had no doubt the feeling that he had to quit would rise again, but when that happened he was going to remember a girl with grey-green eyes and the woman she might grow up to be. He was going to remember the wheels that connect everything, cogs interlocked and turning to create a harmonious whole. He was going to remember the power of good vibes.

He was going to learn to believe.

I believe it. I learned that from a man that I came to love very much. I didn't believe him when he told me, either, but now I know it's true.

But most of all he was going to make sure that he earned the respect of the angel that had visited him from the days still to come.

Dennison knew there was probably a more rational explanation for it all, but right then, he wanted to believe in angels.

The Wishing Well

*Do you think it's better to do the right
thing for the wrong reason or the wrong
thing for the right reason?*
—Amy Luna, Sumner, WA,
from *Sassy,* May 1991

Beyond the mountains, more mountains.

—Haitian proverb

1

There are always ghosts in the well. I can't call them echoes, because the sounds I hear all were made too long ago.

The splash of coins in the water.

Voices whispering their wishes.

Secrets.

Nobody was supposed to hear them.

But I do.

2

"It's been almost two weeks," Brenda said, "and he still hasn't called."

She butted out a cigarette in the ashtray on the table between them and immediately lit another. Wendy sighed, but didn't say anything about her friend's chain-smoking. If you listened to Brenda, there was always something going wrong in her life, so Wendy had long ago decided that there was no point in getting on her case about yet one more negative aspect of it. Besides, she already knew the argument Brenda would counter with: "Right, quit smoking and gain twenty pounds. As if I don't already look like a pig."

Self-esteem wasn't Brenda's strong point. She was an attractive woman, overweight only in the sense that everyone was when compared to all those models who seemed to exist only in the pages of a fashion magazine. But that didn't stop Brenda from constantly worrying over her weight. Wendy never had to read the supermarket tabloids to find out about the latest diet fad—Brenda was sure to tell her about it, often before it appeared in newsprint along with stories of recent Elvis sightings, Bigfoot's genealogy and the like.

Sometimes it all drove Wendy a little crazy. In her unending quest for the perfect dress size, what Brenda seemed to forget was her gorgeous green eyes, the mane of naturally curly red-gold hair and the perfect complexion that people would kill for. She had a good job, she dressed well—perhaps too well, since her credit cards were invariably approaching, if not over, their limit—and when she wasn't beating on herself, she was fun to be around. Except Brenda just didn't see it that way, and so she invariably tried too hard. To be liked. To look better. To get a man.

"Was this the guy you met at the bus stop?" Wendy asked.

Brenda nodded. "He was so nice. He called me a couple of days later and we went out for dinner and a movie. *I* thought we had a great time."

"And I suppose you sent him flowers?"

Sending small gifts to men she'd just met was Brenda's thing. Usually it was flowers.

"I just wanted to let Jim know that I had a good time when we went out," Brenda said, "so I sent him a half-dozen roses. What's so wrong about that?"

Wendy set down her wine glass. "Nothing. It's just that you—I think maybe you come on too strong and scare guys off, that's all."

"I can't help it. I get compulsive."

"Obsessively so."

Brenda looked at the end of her cigarette, took a final drag, then ground it out. She dropped the butt on top of the half-dozen others already in the ashtray.

"I just want to be in love," she said. "I just want a guy to be in love with *me.*"

"I know," Wendy replied, her voice gentle. "But it's never going to happen if you're always trying too hard."

"I'm starting to get *old,*" Brenda said. "I'm almost thirty-five."

"Definitely middle-aged," Wendy teased.

"That's not funny."

"No. I guess it's not. It's just—"

"I know. I have to stop coming on so strong. Except with the nice guys, it seems like the woman always has to make the first move."

"This is too true."

3

Sunday afternoons, I often drive out of town, up Highway 14. Just before I get into the mountains proper, I pull off into the parking lot of a derelict motel called The Wishing Well. The pavement's all frost-buckled and there are weeds growing up through the cracks, refuse everywhere, but I still like the place. Maybe because it's so forsaken. So abandoned. Just the way I feel half the time.

The motel's all boarded up now, though I'm sure the local kids use it for parties. There are empty cans and broken beer bottles all over the place, fighting for space with discarded junk food packaging and used condoms. The rooms are set out in a horseshoe, the ends pointing back into the woods, embracing what's left of the motel's pool. Half the boards have been torn off the windows and all of the units have been broken into, their doors hanging ajar, some torn right off their hinges.

The pool has a little miniature marsh at the bottom of it—mud and stagnant water, cattails and reeds and a scum of algae covering about two feet of water. I've seen minnows in the spring—god knows how they got there—frogs, every kind of water bug you can imagine. And let's not forget the trash. There's even a box spring in the deep end with all the beer cans and broken glass.

The lawn between the pool and the forest has long since been reclaimed by the wilderness. The grass and weeds grow thigh-high and the flowerbeds have mostly been overtaken by dandelions and clover. The forest has sent a carpet of young trees out into the field, from six inches tall to twenty feet. Seen from the air, they would blur the once-distinct boundary between forest and lawn.

The reason I come here is for the motel's namesake. There really is a wishing well, out on the lawn, closer to the forest than the motel itself. The well must have been pretty once, with its fieldstone lip, the shingled roof on wooden supports, the bucket hanging down from its cast iron crank, three wrought-iron benches set facing the well and a flower garden all around.

The shingles have all pretty much blown off now; the bucket's completely disappeared—either bagged by some souvenir-hunter, or it's at the bottom of the well. The garden's rosebushes have taken over everything, twining around the wooden roof supports and covering the benches like Sleeping Beauty's thorn thicket. The first time I wandered out in back of the motel, I didn't even know the well was here, the roses had so completely overgrown it. But I found a way to worm through and by now I've worn a little path. I hardly ever get nicked by a thorn.

The fieldstone sides of the well are crumbling and I suppose they're not very safe, but every time I come, I sit on that short stone wall anyway and look down into the dark shaft below. It's so quiet here. The bulk of the motel blocks the sound of traffic from the highway and there's not another building for at least two miles in either direction.

Usually I sit there a while and just let the quiet settle inside me. Then I take out a penny—a lucky penny that I've found on the street during the week, of course, head side facing up—and I drop it into the darkness.

It takes a long time to hear the tiny splash. I figure dropping a penny in every week or so as I do, I'll be an old lady and I still won't have made a noticeable difference in the water level. But that's not why I'm here. I'm not here to make a wish either. I just need a place to go, I need—

A confessor, I guess. I'm a lapsed Catholic, but I still carry my burdens of worry and guilt. What I've got to talk about, I don't think a priest wants to hear. What does a priest know or care about secular concerns? All they want to talk about is God. All they want to hear is a tidy list of sins so that they can prescribe their penances and get on to the next customer.

Here I don't have to worry about God or Hail Marys or what the invisible face behind the screen is really thinking. Here I get to say it all out loud and not have to feel guilty about bringing down my friends. Here I can have a cathartic wallow in my misery, and then . . . then . . .

I'm not sure when I first started to hear the voices. But after I've run out of words, I start to hear them, coming up out of the well. Nothing profound. Just the ghosts of old wishes. The echoes of other people's dreams, paid for by the simple dropping of a coin, down into the water.

Splash.

I guess what I want is for Jane to love me, and for us to be happy together.

Splash.

Just a pony and I swear I'll take care of her.

Splash.

Don't let them find out that I'm pregnant.

Splash.

Make John stop running around on me and I promise I'll make him the best wife he could ever want.

Splash.

I don't know why it makes me feel better. All these ghost voices are asking for things, are dreaming, are wishing, are needing. Just like me. But I do come away with a sense of, not exactly peace, but . . . less urgency, I suppose.

Maybe it's because when I hear those voices, when I know that, just like me, they paid their pennies in hopes to make things a little better for themselves, I don't feel so alone anymore.

Does that make any sense?

4

"So what're you doing this weekend, Jim?" Scotty asked.

Jim Bradstreet cradled the phone against his ear and leaned back on his sofa.

"Nothing much," he said as he continued to open his mail. Water bill. Junk flyer. Another junk flyer. Visa bill. "I thought maybe I'd give Brenda a call."

"She the one who sent you those flowers?"

"Yeah."

"You can do better than that," Scotty said.

Jim tossed the opened mail onto his coffee table and shifted the receiver from one ear to the other.

"What's that supposed to mean?" he asked.

"I'd think it was obvious—you said she seemed so desperate."

Jim regretted having told Scotty anything about his one date with Brenda Perry. She *had* seemed clingy, especially for a first date, but he'd also realized from their conversation throughout the evening that she didn't exactly have the greatest amount of self-esteem. He'd hesitated calling her again—especially after the flowers—because he wasn't sure he wanted to get into a relationship with someone so dependent. But that wasn't exactly fair. He didn't really know her and asking her for another date wasn't exactly committing to a relationship.

"I still liked her," he said into the receiver.

Scotty laughed. "Just can't get her out of your mind, right?"

"No," Jim replied in all honesty. "I can't."

"Hey, I was just kidding, you know?" Before Jim could reply, Scotty added, "What do you say we get together for a few brews, check out the action at that new club on Lakeside."

"Some other time," Jim told him.

"I'm telling you, man, this woman's trouble. She sounds way too neurotic for you."

"You don't know her," Jim said. "For that matter, *I* don't really know her."

"Yeah, but we know her kind. You're not going to change your mind?"

"Not tonight."

"Well, it's your loss," Scotty said. "I'll give the ladies your regrets."

"You do that," Jim said before he hung up.

It took him a few moments to track down where he'd put Brenda's number. When he did find it and made the call, all he got was her answering machine. He hesitated for a brief moment, then left a message.

"Hi, this is Jim. Uh, Jim Bradstreet. I know it's late notice and all, but I thought maybe we could get together tonight, or maybe tomorrow? Call me."

He left his number and waited for a couple of hours, but she never phoned back. As it got close to eight-thirty, he considered going down to that new club that Scotty had been so keen on checking out, but settled instead on taking in a movie. The lead actress had red hair, with the same gold highlights as Brenda's. The guy playing the other lead character treated her like shit.

That just added to the depression of being alone in a theater where it seemed as though everyone else had come in couples.

5

Sometimes I feel as though there's this hidden country inside me, a landscape that's going to remain forever unexplored because I can't make a normal connection with another human being, with someone who might map it out for me. It's my land, it belongs to me, but I'm denied access to it. The only way I could ever see it is through the eyes of someone outside this body of mine, through the eyes of someone who loves me.

I think we all have these secret landscapes inside us, but I don't think that anybody else ever thinks about them. All I know is that no one visits mine. And when I'm with other people, I don't know how to visit theirs.

6

Wendy wasn't on shift yet when Brenda arrived at Kathryn's Cafe, but Jilly was there. Brenda had first met the two of them when she was a reporter for *In the City,* covering the Women in the Arts conference with which they'd been involved. Jilly Coppercorn was a successful artist, Wendy St. James a struggling poet. Brenda had enjoyed the panels that both women were on and made a point of talking to them afterwards.

Their lives seemed to be so perfectly in order compared to hers that Brenda invariably had a sense of guilt for intruding the cluttered mess of her existence into theirs. And they were both such small, enviably thin women that, when she was with them, she felt more uncomfortable than usual in her own big fat body.

This constant focusing on being overweight was a misperception on her part, she'd been told by the therapist her mother had made her go see while she was still in high school.

"If anything, you could stand to gain a few pounds," Dr. Coleman had said. "Especially considering your history."

Brenda's eating disorders, the woman had gone on to tell her, stemmed from her feelings of abandonment as a child, but no amount of lost weight was going to bring back her father.

"I *know* that," Brenda argued. "I know my father's dead and that it's not my fault he died. I'm not stupid."

"Of course you're not," Dr. Coleman had patiently replied with a sad look in her eyes.

Brenda could never figure out why they wouldn't just leave her alone. Yes, she'd had some trouble with her weight, but she'd gotten over it. Just as she knew it was a failing business that had put the gun in her father's mouth, the bitter knowledge that he couldn't provide for his family that had pulled the trigger. She'd dealt with *all* of that.

It was in the past, over and done with long ago. What wouldn't go away, though, was the extra weight she could never quite seem to take off and keep off. Nobody she knew seemed to understand how it felt, looking in a mirror and always seeing yourself on the wrong side of plump.

She'd asked Jilly once how she stayed so thin.

"Just my metabolism, I guess," Jilly had replied. "Personally, I'd like to gain a couple of pounds. I always feel kind of . . . skin-and-bonesy."

"You look perfect to me," Brenda had told her.

Perfect size, perfect life—which wasn't really true, of course. Neither Jilly nor Wendy was perfect. For one thing, Jilly was one of the messiest people Brenda had ever met. But at least she wasn't in debt. Brenda was tidy to a fault, but she couldn't handle her personal finances to save her life. She'd gone from reporter to the position of *In the City*'s advertising manager since she'd first become friends with Wendy and

Jilly. At work, she kept her books and budgeting perfectly in order. So why couldn't she do the same thing in her private life?

There was only one other customer in the restaurant, so after Jilly had served him his dinner, she brought a pot of herbal tea and a pair of mugs over to Brenda's table. She sat down with a contented sigh before pouring them each a steaming mugful. Brenda smiled her thanks and lit a cigarette.

"So whatever happened with that guy you met at the bus stop?" Jilly asked as she settled back in her chair.

"Didn't Wendy tell you?"

Jilly laughed. "You know Wendy. Telling her something personal is like putting it into a Swiss bank vault and you're the only person who's got the account number."

So Brenda filled her in.

"Then when I got home on Friday," she said as she finished up, "there was a message from him on my machine. But I decided to take Wendy's advice and play it cool. Instead of calling him back, I waited for him to call me again."

"Well, good for you."

"I suppose."

"And did he?"

Brenda nodded. "We made a date for Saturday night and he showed up at my door with a huge box of chocolates."

"That was nice of him."

"Right. Real nice. Give the blimp even more of what she doesn't need. You'd think he'd be more considerate than that. I mean, all you have to do is look at me and know that the last thing I need is chocolate."

"Jesus, Brenda. The last thing you are is fat."

"Oh, right."

Jilly just shook her head. "So what did you do?"

"I ate them."

"No, I meant where did you go?"

"Another movie. I can't even remember what we saw now. I spent the whole time trying to figure out how he felt about me."

"You should try to just relax," Jilly told her. "Let what happens, happen."

"I guess." Brenda butted out her cigarette and lit another. Blowing a wreath of blue-grey smoke away from the table, she gave Jilly a considering look, then asked, "Do you believe in wishing wells?"

Wendy took that moment to arrive in a flurry of blonde hair and grocery bags. She dumped the bags on the floor by the table and pulled up a chair.

"Better to ask, what *doesn't* she believe in," she said. "This woman's mind is a walking supermarket tabloid."

"Ah," Jilly said. "The poet arrives—only fifteen minutes late for her shift."

Wendy grinned and pointed at Jilly's tangle of brown ringlets.

"You've got paint in your hair," she said.

"You've got ink on your fingers," Jilly retorted, then they stuck out their tongues at each other and laughed.

Their easy rapport made Brenda feel left out. Where did a person learn to be so comfortable with other people? she wondered, not for the first time. She supposed it started with feeling good about yourself—like losing a little weight, getting out of debt, putting your love life in order. She sighed. Maybe it started with not always talking about your own problems all the time, but that was a hard thing to do. There were times when Brenda thought her problems were the only things she did have to talk about.

"Earth to Brenda," Jilly said. Under the table, the point of her shoe poked Brenda's calf to get her attention.

"Sorry."

"Why were you asking about wishing wells?" Jilly asked.

"Oh, I don't know. I was just wondering if anybody still believes that wishes can come true."

"I think there are magical things in the world," Wendy said, "but hocus-pocus, wishes coming true—" she shook her head "—I doubt it."

"I do," Jilly said. "It just depends on how badly you want them to."

7

Most wishing wells started out simply as springs or wells that were considered sacred. I found this out a while ago when I was supposed to be researching something else for the paper. I had just meant to look into the origin of wishing wells, but I ended up getting caught up in all the folklore surrounding water and spent most of that afternoon in the library, following one reference which led me to another. . . .

All the way back to primitive times, a lake or well was the place that the sick were taken to be healed. Water images show up in the medicinal rites of peoples at an animistic level, where those being healed are shown washing their hands, breast and head. At the water's edge, reeds grow and shells are found, both symbols of water as salvation—something that Christian symbolism took to itself with a vengeance.

But even before the spread of Christianity, the well of refreshing and purifying water had already gained all sorts of fascinating associations. It was symbolic of sublime aspirations, thought of as a "silver cord" which attached a human to the center of all things. The corn goddess Demeter or other deities would often be shown standing beside a well. The act of drawing water from a well was like fishing, drawing out and upward the numinous contents of the deeps. Looking into its still waters, like looking into a placid lake, was seen as equivalent to meditation or mystic contemplation. The well symbolized the human soul and was considered an attribute of all things feminine.

It's no wonder the Christians came to include it in their baptismal rituals; Christianity has had a long history of taking popular older beliefs and assimilating into its own—even I knew that. But there was so much here that I had never heard of before; fascinating stuff, even though it ended up taking me way off my initial topic. And anyway, the idea of making a wish at a well is tied up in all those tangled stories.

Throughout Europe sacred wells were given new names after various saints. But as the centuries passed and religious beliefs changed, many of these saints' wells became less esteemed and pilgrims no longer approached them with the same feelings of devotion they once had. People stopped offering prayers to the saints and made a wish instead.

And the associated rituals often survived. In some places the wish-maker had to dip her bare hands into the water up to her wrists, make a silent wish, then withdraw her hands and swallow the water held in them. Other places, one left a pin, often bent, or the ever-popular coin. In some ways, wishing wells are a reversion to paganism, the serious wishes made at them being reminiscent of when people approached the sacred water to make an offering or benediction to some god or other, or to the spirit of the water.

Of course water wasn't seen just as the home of benevolent spirits. Folklore throughout the world relates the dangers of water witches and sirens, kelpies and other malevolent creatures whose sole existence seems to rely on drowning those they manage to snare with their various wiles. Everybody knows the story of how Ulysses confronted the sirens and most have probably heard of the Rhine maiden Lorelei—although, oddly enough, she entered folkloric tradition through Clemens Brentano's ballad "Lore Lay." He was so convincing that people just assumed it was based on true folklore.

Among the creepiest of the water witches are the Russian *rusalki*. They're lake spirits in female form—very beautiful and very deadly. They were supposed to bring a weird kind of ecstatic death when they drowned their victims, although some stories said it wasn't actually death they brought, but rather passage to another world. Another book I read said that before their current place in folklore tradition, they were considered to be fertility spirits. I found one reference where some Russian peasants were quoted as saying that "where the *rusalki* trod when dancing, there the grass grew thicker and the wheat more abundant."

That's the weird thing about folklore. Everything gets stirred up so you don't know which story's the original one anymore. Whatever comes along, be it a church or a new government, usually assimilates into their own the traditions and beliefs that existed before they came, and that's what creates the tangle.

This bit with the *rusalki* being psychopomps—leading human souls into the afterworld—makes them reminiscent of angels or Valkyries. Certain birds and animals could also act as "good shepherd" spirits. All of which might make the *rusalki* seem less scary, except I saw a representation of one in a book, and it gave me a serious case of the willies. The picture showed a tall, scowling woman dressed in a tattered green dress, with claw-like hands and burning eyes. In another book I ran across a painting of a Scottish water-wraith that could have been the *rusalka*'s twin sister.

It's funny how the same inspirational source can make for opposite beliefs. Fertility goddess from one point of view, harbinger of death from another. Benevolent spirit or collector of souls. Weird.

Anyway, through all my reading, I never did discover anything interesting about the wishing well at the motel. It wasn't erected on some sacred site; it wasn't the central crossroad of a bunch of ley lines or the home of some Kickaha corn goddess. It was just a gimmick to get people to stop at the motel. But that makes for another funny thing—funny strange, still, not ha-ha. Jilly once told me that if you get enough people to agree that something is a certain way, then it becomes that way.

It almost makes sense. For one thing, it would explain how Elvis or JFK can be as much a spiritual avatar for some people as Jesus is for others. Or how a gimmicky wishing well could really grant wishes—just saying it did. Doesn't do much to explain the voices, though.

Or the ghosts.

Here's something I've never told anybody before: One day, about a month or so ago when I'm at the well, I get this weird compulsion to close my eyes and try to imagine the faces that once went with those long-lost voices I now hear.

All I want is for Timmy to look at me the way he looks at Jennifer.

That girl—was she pretty, or fat like me?

Please make Daddy stop shouting at Mommy the way he does.

That child—I can't tell, is it a boy or a girl?

We'll love each other forever.

Did they? They sound so young, that couple. Don't they know that nothing ever lasts? Nothing is forever. Except maybe loneliness. Or does being lonely just feel as though it lasts forever?

The air is thick with the scent of rose blossoms, the hum of bees. I look down at my legs and see them crisscrossed with the shadows of rose thorns and tiny jagged leaves. The faces rise easily in my imagination, but later I realize that maybe it wasn't such a good idea, calling them up the way I did.

Lying in bed that night, it's as though I've actually summoned their ghosts to me by imagining them. I dream about them, about their lives, about wishes that were granted and ones that weren't. About how the wishes some received weren't what they really wanted, how others are happy they never got theirs. . . .

It all seems so real.

I learn to put them aside in the morning, but lately it's gotten harder. These last few days I can feel my life tangling with theirs. They're not dead people, I think, but then I realize some of them might be. The Wishing Well closed its doors twenty years ago. A lot can happen to a person in twenty years. I really could be living with their ghosts—if there really were such things.

Jilly believes in ghosts. As Wendy says, Jilly believes in all kinds of things that nobody else would. Not exactly tabloid fodder, but close. Everything's got a ghost, she says. A spirit. And if you look closely enough, if you pay attention and really learn to *see,* you'll be able to recognize it.

While Jilly can be persuasive, I don't think I can quite believe in ghosts. But I do believe in memories.

Jilly's friend Christy Riddell—the writer—made the connection between ghosts and memories for me. He told me it's not just people that have memories; places have them, too.

"If you think of ghosts as a kind of recording," he says, "a memory that's attached itself to a certain place or an object, then they don't become quite so farfetched after all."

"So why don't we see them everywhere?" I ask. "Why doesn't everyone see them?"

"People's minds are like radio receivers," he explains. "They're not all capable of tuning into every station."

I still don't believe in ghosts and I tell him so.

"Look at the stars," he says.

This is happening in the middle of a party at Wendy's house. Christy and I are having a smoke in the backyard, thrown together because we're the only ones with the habit in Wendy's circle of friends.

"What about them?" I ask, my gaze roving from star to star in the darkness overhead.

"Did you ever think about how many of them are ghosts?"

"I don't get it."

"We're not seeing the stars as they are right now," he says. "We're seeing them as they were thousands of years ago, maybe millions of years ago—however long it took their light to reach us. Some of them don't exist anymore. What we see when we look at them right now aren't the stars themselves, but the light that they gave off—images of themselves, of what they once were."

"So . . . ?"

"So maybe that's what ghosts are."

I hate to admit it, but I can almost buy this.

"Then how come ghosts are so scary?" I ask.

"They're not always," he says. "But memories can be like wounds. They're not easily forgotten because they leave a scar as a constant reminder. It's the moments of strongest emotions that we remember the most: a love lost or won; anger, betrayal, vengeance. I think it's the same for ghosts, the strength of their emotions at the time of their death is what allows them to linger, or go on."

If strong emotions can linger on, I think, then so might desperate wishes.

8

"So I met this woman at the Carlisle," Scotty said as he and Jim were having lunch on Monday, "and she's stunning. She's so hot I can't believe she's interested in me."

"Really?" Jim asked, looking up from his soup with curiosity.

"Oh, yeah. Tight red leather miniskirt, legs like you wouldn't believe, and she snuggles right up next to me at the bar, rubbing her calf against my leg. And let me tell you, the place is *not* crowded. I'm thinking, if we don't get out of this place soon, she's going to jump me right here on the bar stool."

"So what happened?"

A sheepish look came over Scotty's features. "Turns out she's a hooker."

Jim laughed.

"Hey, it's not funny. I could've caught a *disease* or something, you know?"

"So you didn't take her up on her . . . offer."

"Get real. What about you?"

"No hookers for me, thanks all the same."

"No, I mean with what's-her-name, Brenda. Did you see her?"

Jim nodded. "She was different this time," he said. "A little cooler, I guess."

"What? Now she's playing hard to get?"

"I don't think that's it. She just wasn't all that up. I asked her if something was bothering her, but she just changed the subject. After the movie she perked up, though. We stopped for a drink at the Rusty Lion and she had me in stitches, talking about some of the weird people she met back when she was a reporter, but then when I took her home she was all withdrawn again." Jim toyed with his spoon for a moment, slowly stirring his soup. "I'm not really sure what makes her tick. But I want to find out."

"Well, good luck," Scotty said. "But just before you get in too deep, I want you to think of two words: manic depressive."

"Thanks a lot, pal."

"Don't tell me the thought hasn't crossed your mind."

Jim shrugged. "The only down side I see is that she smokes," he said, and then returned to his soup.

9

Jim calls me on Tuesday night and he's really sweet. Tells me he's been thinking about me a lot and he wants to see me again. We talk for a while and I feel good—mostly because he can't see me, I guess. After I get off the phone, I take a bath and then I look at myself in the mirror and wonder how he could possibly be interested in me.

I know what I see: a cow.

What's he going to think when he sees me naked? What's going to happen when he realizes what a fuck-up I am? He hasn't said anything yet, but I don't think he much cares for me smoking, and while he's not stingy or anything, I get the feeling he's careful with his money. What's he going to think about *my* finances?

I'm such a mess. I can't quit smoking, I can't stick to a diet, I can't stop spending money I don't have. Where does it stop? I keep thinking, if I just lose some weight, everything'll be okay. Except I never do, so I keep buying new clothes that I hope will make me look thinner, and makeup and whatever else I can spend money I haven't got on to trick myself into thinking things'll be different. I decide if I get out of debt, everything'll be okay, but first I have to lose some weight. I think if I get a man in my life . . . it goes on and on in an endless downward spiral.

I'd give anything to be like Wendy or Jilly. Maybe if I had a wish . . .

But while I might be starting to believe in ghosts, I side with Wendy on the wish question. Hocus-pocus just doesn't work. If I want to solve my problems, I'm going to have to do it by myself. And I can't keep putting it off. I have to make some real changes—*now,* not when I feel like it, because if I wait until then, I'll never do it.

First thing tomorrow I'm going to make an appointment with my bank manager. And I'll start a serious diet.

10

"Frankly, Ms. Perry," the manager of the Unity Trust said, "your finances are a mess."

Brenda nodded. The nameplate on his desk read "Brent Cameron." He'd given her That Look when she came into his office, the one that roved carelessly up her body before his gaze finally reached her face. Now he didn't seem to be interested in her looks at all.

She'd been upset when he gave her the once-over; now she was upset because he'd obviously dismissed her. She knew just what he was thinking. Too fat.

"But I think we can help you," he went on. "The first thing I want you to do is to destroy your credit cards—all of them."

He gave her an expectant look.

"Um, did you want me to do that now?" Brenda asked.

"That might be best."

He handed her a pair of scissors and one by one she clipped her credit cards in two—Visa, Mastercard, gas and department store cards. The only one she didn't touch was her second Visa card.

"You can't keep any of them, Ms. Perry."

"This isn't mine," she explained. "It's from work. I'll hand it in to them when I get back."

He nodded. "Fine. Now I know this isn't going to be easy, but if we start with making a list of all your monthly requirements, then I think we can come up with a plan that will . . ."

The rest of the meeting went by in a blur. She got the loan. She also came out with a sheaf of paper which held her financial plan for the next three years. Every bit of her income was accounted for, down to the last penny. God, it was depressing. She was going to have to do all her shopping in thrift shops—if she could even afford to do that. To make things worse, she hadn't even mentioned the six-hundred-dollar repair bill she owed her garage for work they'd done on her car last month.

What she could really use right now was a cigarette, she thought, but she hadn't had one since last night and this time she was determined to quit, once and for all. She was starving, too. She'd skipped breakfast and all she'd had for lunch was a bag of popcorn that she'd eaten on the way to her interview with Mr. Cameron.

It hadn't done much to quell the constant gnaw of hunger inside. All she could do was think of food—food and cigarettes and not necessarily in that order. She'd been feeling grumpy all morning. The interview hadn't done much to improve her mood. Her nerves were all jangled, her stomach was rumbling, her body craved a nicotine fix, she was broke for at least the next three years. . . .

How come doing the right thing felt so bad?

Her route back to the office took her by her favorite clothing store, Morning Glory, and naturally they were having a huge sale—up to 40% off everything! the banner read. She hesitated for a long moment before finally going in, just to have a look at what she could no longer afford. Then of course there were three dresses that she just had to have and the next thing she knew she was standing at the counter with them.

"Will that be cash or charge?" the sales clerk asked her.

It'd be her last splurge before the austerity program went into affect, she vowed.

But she didn't have enough money with her to pay for them. Nor could she write a check that wouldn't bounce—wouldn't *that* impress Mr. Cameron with how well she was following the guidelines of his budget? Finally she used her *In the City* Visa card.

She'd make it up from her next pay. Her first loan payment wasn't due for three weeks, and she had another paycheck due before that. Conveniently, she'd managed to forget the unpaid bill due her garage.

11

Thursday after work I drive up Highway 14 and pull into the parking lot of The Wishing Well. By the time I've walked around back and made my way through the rose bushes, the evening's starting to fall. I've never been here so late in the day before. I sit on the crumbly stone wall and lean against one of the roof supports. It's even more peaceful than on a Sunday afternoon, and I just drink in the tranquillity for a long time.

I need something good in my life right now. I've already lost a couple of pounds, and I still haven't had a cigarette since Tuesday night, but I feel terrible. My jaw aches from being clenched so much and all I can think of is cigarettes and food, food and cigarettes. Whenever I turned around at work, someone was stuffing a Danish into their mouth, chewing a sandwich, eating cookies or donuts or a bag of chips. The smoke from Keith's cigarettes—one desk over from mine—is a constant reminder of what I can't do anymore.

Sitting here, just letting the quiet soak into me, is the first real down time I feel I've had in the last two days. It's dark when I finally reach into the pocket of my dress and take out the penny I found in front of the trust company the other day.

Splash.

"So there's this guy," I say finally. My voice sounds loud, so I speak more softly. "I think I like him a lot, but I'm afraid I'm just going to get hurt again. . . ."

It's the same old litany, and even I'm getting tired of it. If the well had a wish for itself, it'd probably be for me just to go away and leave it alone.

Wishes. I don't believe in them, but I'd like to. I think of what Jilly said about them.

It just depends on how badly you want them.

To come true.

For all the times I've visited the well, I've never actually made a wish myself. I don't know why. It's not just because I don't believe in them. Because there's *something* here, isn't there? Why else would I be able to hear all those old wishes? Why else would the ghosts come walking through my sleep every night? Truth is, I've been thinking about wishes more and more lately, it's just that . . .

I don't know. Two days into my new healthy Brenda regime, yes, I'm still hanging in with the diet and not smoking, but it's like I'm conspiring against myself at the same time, trying to undermine what I am accomplishing with other messes. Can't eat, can't smoke? Then, why not blow some money you don't have?

I made the mistake of stopping at one of the sidewalk jewelry vendors on Lee Street and I used my *In the City* Visa card to buy fifty dollars' worth of earrings. I didn't even *know* those vendors took credit cards. Then, when I got back to work, there was a guy from a collection agency waiting for me. The garage got tired of waiting for the money I owed them. The collection agency guy had a talk with Rob—my boss, the paper's editor—and I had to agree to letting them garnishee my wages until the collection agency's paid off.

Which is going to leave me desperately short. *Where* am I going to get the money to pay off the bank loan I took out earlier this week, not to mention the money I borrowed on the paper's Visa card? This diet and no-smoking business is saving me money, but not *that* much money.

Whatever good I'm supposed to get out of doing the right thing still seems impossibly out of reach. Even though I haven't smoked in two days, my lungs seem more filled with phlegm than ever and my mouth still tastes terrible. All I had was popcorn again today, and a quarter of a head of lettuce. I'm losing weight, according to my bathroom scale, but I can feel the fat cells biding their time in my body, ready to multiply as soon as I stick a muffin or a piece of chocolate in my mouth. I'm worse than broke.

I guess the reason I haven't ever made a wish is that this is the only place I know where I don't feel so bad. If I make a wish it'll be like losing the genie in the bottle. You know, you've always got him in reserve—for company, if nothing else—until you make your final wish.

What would I wish for? To be happy? I'd have to become a completely different person for that to work. Maybe to be rich? But how long before I'd blow it all?

The only thing I'd really want to wish for is to see my dad again, but I know that's something that'll never happen.

12

Monday morning found Jilly sitting on the wooden bench in front of Amos & Cook's Arts Supplies, impatiently waiting for the store to open. She amused herself as she usually did in this sort of a situation by making up stories about the passersby, but it wasn't as much fun without somebody to share the stories with. She liked telling them to Geordie best, because she could invariably get the biggest rise out of him.

She'd been up all night working on the preliminary sketches for an album cover that the Broken Hearts had commissioned from her, only to discover when she finally started on the canvas that she'd used up all her blues the last time she'd worked with her oils. So here she sat, watching the minute hand on the clock outside the delicatessen across the street slowly climb to twelve, dragging the slower hour hand up to the nine as it went.

Eventually Amos & Cook's opened and she darted inside to buy her paints. It was while she was heading back up Yoors Street to her studio that she ran into Brenda coming the other way.

"You're looking good," she said when they came abreast of each other.

"Well, thanks a lot," Brenda said sarcastically.

Jilly blinked in confusion. "What's that supposed to mean?"

"You and Wendy are always telling me how I shouldn't worry about being fat—"

"We never said you were—"

"—but now as soon as I find a diet that's actually letting me lose some weight, I'm 'looking great.' "

"Whoa," Jilly said. "Time out. I have never said that you needed to lose weight."

"No, but now that I have I look so much better, right?"

"I was just being—"

Friendly, Jilly had been about to say, but Brenda interrupted her.

"Honest for a change," Brenda said. "Well, thanks for nothing."

She stalked off before Jilly could reply.

"You have a nice day, too," Jilly said as she watched Brenda go.

Wow, talk about getting up on the wrong side of the bed this morning, she thought. She'd never seen Brenda running on such a short fuse.

She was a little hurt from the confrontation until she realized that besides Brenda's bad mood, there'd been something else different about her this morning: no cigarette in her hand, no smell of stale smoke on her clothes. Knowing that Brenda must have recently quit smoking made Jilly feel less hurt about the way Brenda had snapped at her. She'd quit herself years ago and knew just how hard it was—and how cranky it made you feel. Add that to yet another new diet. . . .

Quitting cigarettes was a good thing, but Jilly wasn't so sure about the diet. Brenda didn't need to lose weight. She had a full figure, but everything was in its proper proportion and place. Truth was, she often felt envious of Brenda's fuller shape. It was so Italian Renaissance, all rounded and curved—and lovely to paint, though she had yet to get Brenda to sit for her. Perhaps if this latest diet helped raised Brenda's self-esteem enough, Brenda would finally agree to pose for some quick studies at the very least.

She knew Brenda needed a boost in the self-esteem department, so she supposed a diet that worked couldn't hurt. Just so long as she doesn't get *too* carried away with it, Jilly thought as she continued on home.

13

Even I'm getting tired of my bitchiness. I can't believe the way I jumped on Jilly this morning. Okay, I know why. I was not having a good morning. The ghosts kept me up all night, going through my head even when I wasn't asleep. By the time I ran into Jilly, I was feeling irritable and running late, and I didn't want to hear what she had to say.

Thinking it over, none of that seems like much of an excuse. It's just that, even though I knew she was just trying to be nice, I couldn't help feeling this rage toward her for being so two-faced. You'd think a friend would at least be honest right from the start.

Yes, Brenda, you are starting to seriously blimp on us. Do everybody a favor and lose some weight, would you?

Except nobody was going to say something like that to a friend. I wouldn't even say it to an enemy. It's bad enough when you've got to haul that fat body around with you, never mind having somebody rub your face in the fact of its existence.

I think the best thing I could do right now is just to avoid everybody I know so that I'll have some friends to come back to if I ever make it through this period of my life.

I wonder how long I can put Jim off. He called me three times this past weekend. I played sick on Friday and Saturday. When he called on Sunday, I told him I was going out of town. Maybe I really should go out of town, except I can't afford to travel. I don't even have transit fare this week. Too bad the paper won't pay my parking the way it does Rob's. Of course, I'm not the editor.

When it comes right down to it, I don't even know why I'm working at a newspaper—even a weekly entertainment rag like *In the City.* How did I get here?

I was going to be a serious writer like Christy, but somehow I got sidetracked into journalism—because it offered the safety of a regular paycheck, I suppose. I'm still not sure how I ended up as an advertising manager. I don't even write anymore—except for memos.

The girl I was in college wouldn't even recognize me now.

14

Jim looked up to find Scotty approaching his desk. Scotty sat down on a corner and started to play with Jim's crystal ball paperweight, tossing it from hand to hand.

"So," Scotty said. "How goes the romance?"

Jim grabbed the paperweight and replaced it on his desk. "One of these days you're going to break that," he said.

"Yeah, right. It wasn't me that missed the pop fly at the last game."

"Wasn't me who struck out."

"Ouch. I guess I deserved that." Scotty started to reach for the paperweight again, then settled for a ballpoint pen instead. He flipped it into the air, caught it again. "But seriously," he went on. "Was Brenda feeling better on Sunday?"

Jim nodded. "Except she said she's going to be out of town for a few weeks. She had to pack, so we couldn't get together."

"Too bad. Hey, did Roger tell you about the party he's throwing on Friday? He told me he's invited some seriously good-looking, *single* women."

"I think I'll pass."

Scotty raised his eyebrows. "How serious *is* this thing?" he asked. "She's out of town, so that means you have to stay in?"

"It's not like that."

"When do I get to meet her, anyway?"

Jim shrugged. "When she gets back, I guess."

Scotty gave him a long considering look, the pen still in his hands for a moment. "I think you've got it bad, pal," he said finally.

"I guess I do."

"How does she feel about you?"

"I think she likes me," Jim said.

Scotty set the pen back down on Jim's desk.

"You're a lucky stiff," he said.

15

I've decided that the ghosts are simply hallucinations, brought on by my hunger. Never mind what Jilly or Christy would say. That's all that makes sense. If anything makes sense anymore.

I've been on this diet for almost four weeks now. Popcorn and lettuce, lettuce and popcorn. A muffin on Wednesday, but I won't let that happen again because I'm *really* losing weight and I don't want to screw anything up. From a hundred and twenty-six to a hundred and four this morning.

Once I would have been delirious with joy to weigh only a hundred and four again, but when I look in the mirror I know it's not enough. All I still see is fat. I can get rid of more. I don't have to be a cow all my life.

I still haven't had a cigarette either and it hasn't added anything to my weight. It's as bad as I thought it'd be—you never realize what a physical addiction it really is until you try to quit—but at least I'm not putting on the pounds, stuffing my face with food because I miss sticking a cigarette in my mouth.

I'm so cranky, though. I guess that's to be expected. My whole body feels weird, like it doesn't belong to me anymore. But I kind of like it. There's a down side, like my clothes don't fit right anymore, but I can deal with it. Since I can't afford to buy new ones, I've been taking them in—skirts and jeans. My T-shirts and blouses are all getting really loose, but I don't mind. I feel so good about the way I'm starting to look now I know that I can never let myself get fat again. I'm just going to lose a few more pounds and then I'm going to go on a bit of a more normal diet. I'm sick of popcorn and lettuce.

The diet's probably making me cranky as well, but I know I'll get past it, just like I'll get past the constant need to have a cigarette. Already it's easier. Now all I've got to do is deal with the financial mess I'm in. I don't know *how* to handle it. I'm not spending any money at all—mine *or* the paper's—but I'm in deep. My phone got cut off yesterday. I just didn't have the money to pay the bill after covering my other expenses. I guess I should've told the bank manager about it when I went in for that loan, but I'd forgotten I was overdue and I don't want to go back to his office.

What I really want to do is just go away for awhile—the way I'm pretending to Jim that I have. Before my phone got cut off, I was calling him from these "hotels" I'm supposed to be staying in and we'd have nice long talks. It's the weirdest romance I've ever had. I can't wait to see his face when he finally sees the new and improved me.

But I'm not ready yet. I want to trim the last of the fat away and put the no-smoking jitters aside first. I know I can do it. I'm feeling a lot more confident about everything now. I guess it really is possible to take charge of your life and make the necessary changes so that you're happy with who you are. What I want now is some time to myself. Go away and come back as an entirely new person. Start my life over again.

Last night one of the ghosts gave me a really good idea.

16

Wendy slouched in the window seat of Jilly's studio while Jilly stood at her easel, painting. She had her notebook open on her lap, but she hadn't written a word in it. She alternated between watching Jilly work, which was fairly boring, and taking in the clutter of the studio. Paintings were piled up against one another along the walls. Everywhere she looked there were stacks of paper and reference books, jars and tins full of brushes,

tubes of paint and messy palettes for all the different media Jilly worked in. The walls
were hung with her own work and that of her friends.

One of the weirdest things in the room was a fabric mâché self-portrait that Jilly
had done. The life-size sculpture stood in a corner, dressed in Jilly's clothes, paint
brush in hand and wearing a Walkman. No matter how often Wendy came over, it still
made her start.

"You're being awfully quiet," Jilly said, stepping back from her canvass.

"I was thinking about Brenda."

Jilly leaned forward to add a daub of paint, then stepped back again.

"I haven't seen much of her myself," she said. "Of course I've been spending
twenty-six hours a day trying to get this art done for this album cover."

"Do they still make albums?"

Jilly shrugged. "CD, then. Or whatever. Why are you thinking about Brenda?"

"Oh, I don't know. I just haven't seen her for ages. We used to go down to the
Dutchman's Bakery for strudels every Saturday morning, but she's begged off for the
last three weeks."

"That's because she's on a diet," Jilly said.

"How do you know?"

Jilly stuck her brush behind her ear and used the edge of her smock to rub at
something on the canvass.

"I ran into her on the way to the art store the other day," she said as she fussed
with the painting. "She looked so thin that she's got to be on another diet—one that's
working, for a change."

"I don't know why she's so fixated on her weight," Wendy said. "She thinks she's
humongous, and she's really not."

Jilly shrugged. "I've given up trying to tell her. She's like your friend Andy in
some ways."

"Andy's a hypochondriac," Wendy said.

"I know. He's always talking about what's wrong with him, right?"

"So?"

"So Brenda's a little like that. Did you ever know her to not have a problem?"

"That's not really being fair," Wendy said.

Jilly looked up from her painting and shook her head. "It might not be a nice
thing to say," she said, "but it is fair."

"Things just don't work out for her," Wendy protested.

"And half of the reason is because she won't let them," Jilly said. "I think she
lives for extremes."

Putting her palette and brush down on the wooden orange crate that stood beside
her easel for that purpose, she dragged another orange crate over to the window and
sat down.

"Take the way she is with men," Jilly said. "Either nobody's interested in her, or
she's utterly convinced some guy's crazy about her. She never gives a relationship a
chance to grow. It's got to be all or nothing, right off the bat."

"Yeah, but—"

"And it's not just guys. It's everything. She either has to be able to buy the best
quality new blouse or dress, or she won't buy it at all. She either has to eat five
desserts, or not have dinner at all."

Wendy found herself reluctantly nodding in agreement. There were times when Brenda could just drive her crazy, too.

"So does it bug you?" she asked.

"Of course it bugs me," Jilly said. "But you have to put up with your friends' shortcomings—just like you hope they'll put up with yours. Under all her anxieties and compulsive behavior has got to be one of the nicest, warmest people I know. What's saddest, I suppose, is that *she* doesn't know it."

"So what should we do?"

"Just like we always do—be there for her when she needs us."

"I suppose," Wendy said. "You know, I hate to say this, but I think what she really needs is a man in her life—a good, solid, dependable man who cares about her. I think that'd straighten up half the problems in her life."

"I think she's got one," Jilly said. "That is, unless she screws this one up by going to the other extreme and suddenly playing too hard to get."

"What do you mean?"

Jilly leaned forward. "You know the guy she met at the bus stop?"

"Jim?"

"Uh-huh. Well, it turns out he works at the Newford School of Art."

"He's an artist?"

Jilly shook her head. "No, he works in admin. I dropped by to see how the registration was coming along for that drawing class I'm going to be teaching next semester, and he started talking to me about Brenda."

"How'd he know you knew her?"

"She'd talked to him about us, I suppose. Anyway, he was wondering if I knew when she'd get back and I almost blew it by saying I'd just run into her on Yoors Street that week, but I caught myself in time. Turns out, he thinks she's out of town on business. She calls him every few days—supposedly from this hotel where she's staying—but she's been very evasive about when she's due back."

"That is so not like Brenda," Wendy said.

"Ignoring a nice guy who's showing some interest in her?"

"That, too. But I meant lying."

"I thought so, too, but who knows what's going on with her sometimes. Did you know she quit smoking?"

"Go on."

"Really. And that last time at the restaurant—before you showed up—she was telling me how she was finally taking your advice to heart and wasn't going to throw herself all over some guy anymore."

"Yeah, but she always says that," Wendy said. She swung her legs down to the floor and hopped down from the window seat. "I'm going to give her a call," she added.

Jilly watched her dial, wait a moment with the receiver to her ear, then frown and hang up.

"She didn't leave her answering machine on?" she asked as Wendy slowly walked back to the window seat.

"The number's not in service anymore," Wendy said slowly. "Her phone must be disconnected."

"Really?"

Wendy nodded. "I guess she didn't pay her phone bill. You know how she's always juggling her finances."

"I don't get it," Jilly said. "If she was that short of cash, why didn't she just come to one of us? We're not rich, but we could've helped out."

"Has she *ever* asked you for a loan?"

Jilly shook her head.

"Me, neither. I think she'd die before she did that."

Wendy packed her notebook away in her knapsack. Turning from the window, she added, "I think I'm going to go by her apartment to see how she's doing."

"Let me clean my brushes," Jilly said, "and I'll come with you."

17

Well, I didn't have to ask Rob if I could get a leave of absence from the paper for a couple of weeks. After I left work last night, it came out how I'd been using *In the City*'s Visa card. Rob confronted me with it this morning, and since I couldn't tell him when, or even if, I'd be able to pay it back, he gave me my pink slip.

"You've been impossible to work with," he told me. "I realize you've just quit smoking—"

I hadn't told anybody, wanting to do it on my own without the pressure of feeling as though I were living in a fishbowl, but I suppose it was obvious.

"—and I can certainly empathize with you. I went through the same thing last year. But I've had complaints from everyone and this business with the Visa is just the final straw."

"No one said anything to me."

"Nobody felt like getting their head bitten off."

"I'm sorry—about everything. I'll make it up to you. I promise."

"It's not just about money," Rob said. "It's about trust."

"I know."

"If you needed a loan, why didn't you come talk to me about it?" he asked. "We could've worked something out."

"It . . . it just happened," I said. "Things have been getting out of control in my life lately."

He gave me a long, considering look. "Do you have a problem with drugs?" he asked.

"No!" That was one of the few areas of my life where I hadn't screwed up. "God, how could you even think that?"

"Because frankly, Brenda, you're starting to look like a junkie."

"I'm on a diet, that's all."

The concern in his eyes seemed to say that he genuinely cared. The next thing he said killed that idea dead in the water.

"Brenda, you need help."

Yeah, like he cared. If firing me was his idea of compassion, I'd hate to see what happened if he really started to be helpful. But I was smart this time and just kept my mouth shut.

"I'm sorry," was all I said. "I'll pay you back. It's just going to take some time."

I got up and left then. He called after me, but I pretended I didn't hear him. I was afraid of what I might say if he kept pushing at me.

I was lucky, I guess. He could have pressed charges—misappropriation of the paper's funds—but he didn't. I should have felt grateful. But I didn't walk out of there thinking how lucky I'd been. I felt like dirt. I'd never been so embarrassed in all my life.

That was Friday. I'm trying to put it behind me and not think about it. That's easier said than done. I've been only partially successful, but by this morning I don't feel as bad as I did yesterday. I'm still a little light-headed, but I'm down another couple of pounds and I still haven't had a cigarette. Day twenty-nine into my new life and counting.

I've moved into The Wishing Well, in unit number twelve—that's the last one on the north wing. I didn't bring much with me—just a few necessities. A few changes of clothing. Some toiletries. A sleeping bag and pillow. A kazillion packages of popcorn, a couple of heads of lettuce and some bottled water. A box of miscellaneous herb teas and a Coleman stove to boil water on. A handful of books.

I also brought along my trusty old manual typewriter that I used all through college, because I think I might try to do some writing again—creative writing like I used to do before I got my first job on the paper. I would've brought my computer, but there's no electricity here, which is also why I've got a flashlight and an oil lamp, though I wasn't sure I could use either until I checked if they could be seen from the highway at night. It turns out all I had to do was replace a couple of boards on the window facing the parking lot.

And of course I brought along my bathroom scale, so I can monitor my weight. This diet's proving to be one of the few successes of my life.

I've hidden my car by driving it across the overgrown lawn and parking it between the pool and my unit. After I got it there, I went back and did what I could with the grass and weeds the wheels had crushed to try and make it look as though no one had driven over them. A frontier woman I'm not, but I didn't do that bad a job. I doubted anybody would notice unless they really stopped to study the area.

Once I had the car stashed, I worked on cleaning up the unit. I had to keep resting because I didn't seem to have much stamina—I still don't—but by nine o'clock last night, I had my little hideaway all fixed up. It still has a musty smell, but either it's airing out, or I'm getting used to it by now. The trash is swept out and bagged in the unit next to mine, along with the mattress and a bundle of towels I found rotting in the bathroom. The plumbing doesn't work, so I'm going to have to figure out where I can get water to mop the floors—not to mention keep myself clean. I found an old ping-pong table in what must have been the motel's communal game room, and I laid that on top of the bed with my sleeping bag unrolled on top of it. It'll be hard, but at least it's off the floor.

I finally made myself a cup of tea, boiling the water on my Coleman stove, and settled down to do a little reading before I went to bed. That's when things got a little weird.

Now usually I'm asleep when the well's ghosts come visiting, but last night . . . last night . . .

I'm not really sure what she is, if you want to know the truth.

I was rereading my old journal—the one I kept when I was still a reporter—kind of enjoying all the little asides and notes I'd made to myself in between the cataloguing of a day's events, when the door to my unit opened. One of the reasons I'd chosen number twelve was because it had a working door; I just never expected anybody else to use it.

I almost died at the sound of the door. The fit's a little stiff, and the wood seemed to screech as it opened. The journal fell from my hands and I jumped to my feet, ready to do I don't know what. Run out the front door into the parking lot. Pick up something to defend myself with. Freeze on the spot and not be able to move.

I picked the latter—through no choice of my own, it just happened—and in walked this woman. The first thought that came to mind was that she was some old hillbilly, drawn down from the hills after seeing the light that spilled out of the window on the pool side of the room. When I was cleaning up the unit, I took the boards off that window and, miracle of miracles, the glass panes were still intact. I never did bother to tack the boards back up when night fell.

She had to be in her seventies at least. She looked wiry and tough, face as wrinkled as an unironed handkerchief, hair more white than grey and standing up from around her head in a wild tangle. Her eyes were her strongest feature—a pale blue, slightly protruding and bird-bright. She was wearing a faded red flannel shirt and baggy blue jeans, scuffed work boots on her feet, with a ratty-looking grey cardigan sweater draped over her shoulders, the sleeves hanging down across the front of her shirt.

She looked vaguely familiar—the way someone you might have gone to school with looks familiar: The features have changed, but not enough so as to render them unrecognizable. I couldn't place her, though. When I was a reporter I met more new people in a month than I could ever hope to remember, so my head's a jumble of people I can only vaguely recognize. Most of them were involved in the arts, mind you, and she didn't look the type. I could more easily picture her sitting on a rocking chair outside some hillbilly cabin, smoking a corncob pipe.

I wasn't thinking about ghosts, then.

She seemed to recognize me, too, because she stood there in the doorway, studying me for what seemed like the longest time, before she finally came in and shut the door behind her.

"You're the one who comes to the well on Sundays," she said as she sat down on the end of my bed. She moved like a man and sat with her legs spread wide, hands on her knees.

I nodded numbly and managed to sit back down on my chair again. I left my journal where it lay on the floor.

"Got a smoke?" she asked.

How I wished.

"No," I told her, finally finding my voice. "I don't smoke."

"Don't eat much either, seems."

"I'm on a diet."

She made a hrumphing sound. I wasn't sure if it was a comment on dieting or if she was just clearing her throat.

"Who . . . who are you?" I asked.

The sense of familiarity was still nagging at me. Having pretty well exhausted everyone I could think of that I knew, I'd actually found myself flipping through the faces of the ghosts I'd called up from the well.

"No reason to call myself much of anything anymore," she said, "but once I went by the name of Carter. Ellie Carter."

As soon as she said her name, I knew her. Or at least I knew where I'd seen her before. After I first found the motel and then started coming by more or less regularly, I'd tried looking up its history. There was nothing in the morgue at *In the City,* but that didn't surprise me once I tracked down a twenty-five-year-old feature in the back issues of *The Newford Star.*

I'd had a copy made of the article, and it was pinned up above my desk back home. There was a picture of Ellie accompanying the article, with the motel behind her. She looked about the same, except shrunk in on herself a little.

She'd been the owner until—as an article dated five years later told me—business had dropped to such an extent that she couldn't make her mortgage payments and the bank had foreclosed on her.

"So've you made yourself a wish yet?" she asked.

I shook my head.

"Well, don't. The well's cursed."

"What do you mean?"

"Don't you clean your ears, girl? Or is that a part of your diet as well?"

"My name's Brenda."

"How long are you planning to stay, Brenda?"

"I . . . I don't know."

"Well, the rate's a dollar a day. You can give me a week in advance and I'll refund what you've got coming back to you if you don't stay that long."

This was insane, I thought, but under her steady gaze I found myself digging the seven dollars out of my meager resources and handing it over to her.

"You need a receipt?"

I shook my head slowly.

"Well, have yourself a nice time," she said, standing up. "Plumbing's out, so you'll have to use the outhouse at the back of the field."

I hadn't got around to thinking much about that aspect of the lack of bathroom facilities yet. When I'd had to pee earlier, I'd just done it around the corner near some lilac bushes that had overgrown the south side of the motel.

"Wait," I said. "What about the well?"

She paused at the door. "I'd tell you to stay away from it, but you wouldn't listen to me anyway, would you? So just don't make a wish."

"Why not?"

She gave me a tired look, then opened the door and stepped out into the night.

"Listen to your elders, girl," she said.

"My name's Brenda."

"Whatever."

She closed the door before I could say anything else. By the time I had reached it and flung it open again, there was no one to be seen. I started out across the parking lot's pavement until I saw headlights approaching on the highway and quickly ducked back into my room and shut the door. Once the car had passed, I slipped out again, this time shutting the door behind me.

I walked all around the motel, but I could find no sign of the woman. I wasn't really expecting to. I hadn't found any recent sign of anyone when I'd explored the motel earlier in the day, either.

That's when I started thinking about ghosts.

So tonight I'm waiting to see if Ellie's going to show up again. I want to ask her more about the well. Funny thing is, I'm not scared at all. Ellie may be a ghost, but she's not frightening. Just a little cranky.

I wonder how and when she died. I don't have to guess where. I've read enough ghost stories to be able to figure out that much.

I also wonder if the only reason I saw her last night is because I'm so light-headed from my diet. I'd hate to find out that I've suddenly turned into one of those people that Jilly calls "sensitives." I've got enough problems in my life as it is without having to see ghosts every which way I turn when I'm awake as well as when I'm asleep.

Besides, if I'm going to meet a ghost, I wouldn't pick one from the wishing well. I'd call up my dad—just to talk to him. I know I can't bring him back to life or anything, but that doesn't stop me from wanting to know why he quit loving my mom and me.

18

Brenda's apartment was the second story of a three-floor brick house with an attached garage in Crowsea. It stood on a quiet avenue just off Waterhouse, a functional old building, unlike its renovated neighbors. The porch was cluttered with the belongings of Brenda's downstairs neighbor, who appeared to use it as a sitting room-cum-closet. At the moment it held a pair of mismatched chairs—one wooden, one wicker and well past its prime—several plastic milk crates that appeared to serve as tables or makeshift stools, three pairs of shoes and one Wellington boot, empty coffee mugs, books, magazines and any number of less recognizable items.

Jilly and Wendy picked their way to the front door and into the foyer which was, if anything, even more messy than the porch. The clutter, Jilly knew, would drive Brenda crazy, she who was so tidy herself. At the second landing, Wendy pressed Brenda's doorbell. When there was no answer after Wendy had rung the bell for the fifth time, she fished her key ring out of her pocket and unlocked the door. Jilly put her hand on Wendy's arm, holding her back.

"I don't think we should be doing this," she said.

"It's not like we're breaking in," Wendy said. "Brenda gave me a spare key herself."

"But it doesn't seem right."

"Well, I'm worried," Wendy told her. "For all we know she fell in the shower and she's been lying there unconscious for days."

"For all we know she's in bed with Jim and doesn't want to be disturbed."

"We wish," Wendy said as she went in ahead.

Jilly followed, reluctantly.

It was, of course, as tidy inside Brenda's apartment as it was messy on the porch. Everything was in its place. Magazines were neatly stacked in a squared-off pile on a table beside Brenda's reading chair. The coasters were all in their holder. There wasn't one shoe or sock off adventuring by itself on the carpet.

Her desk was polished until the wood gleamed, and the computer sitting dead center looked as though it had just come out of the showroom. If it weren't for the corkboard above the desk, bristling with the snarl of papers, pictures and the like pinned to it, Jilly might have thought that Brenda never used her desk at all.

"Brenda?" Wendy called.

Jilly's sympathies lay with the downstairs neighbor. Tidiness wasn't exactly her own strong point.

As Wendy went down the hall toward the kitchen, still calling Brenda's name, Jilly wandered over to the desk and looked at what the corkboard held. It was the only area that made her feel comfortable. Everything else in the room was just too perfect. It was as though no one lived here at all.

Old newspaper clippings vied for space with photographs of Brenda's friends, shopping lists, an invitation for an opening to one of Jilly's shows that Brenda hadn't been able to make, a letter that Jilly dutifully didn't read, although she wanted to. She liked the handwriting.

"This place gives me the creeps," she said as Wendy returned to the living room. "I feel like a burglar."

Wendy nodded. "But it's not just that."

Jilly thought about it for a moment. Being in somebody else's apartment when they weren't always gave one a certain empty feeling, but Wendy was right. This was different. The place felt abandoned.

"Maybe she really has gone out of town," Jilly said.

"Well, her toothbrush is gone, but her makeup bag is still here, so she can't have gone far."

"We should go," Jilly said.

"Just let me leave a note."

Jilly wandered over to the window to look out at the street below while Wendy foraged for paper and a pen in the desk. Jilly paused when she looked at Brenda's plants. They were all drooping. The leaves of one in particular, which grew up along the side of the window, had wilted. Jilly couldn't remember what it was called, but Geordie had once given her a plant just like it, so she knew it needed to be watered religiously, at least every day. This one looked exactly like hers had if she went away for the weekend and forgot to water it.

"This isn't like Brenda," Jilly said, pointing to the plants. "The Brenda I know would have gotten someone to look after her plants before she left."

Wendy nodded. "But she never called me."

"Her phone's been disconnected, remember?"

Jilly and Wendy exchanged worried glances.

"I'm getting a really bad feeling about this," Wendy said.

Jilly hugged herself, suddenly chilled. "Me, too. I think we should go by her office."

"She didn't tell you?" Greg said.

Both Jilly and Wendy shook their heads. Jilly leaned closer to his desk, expectantly.

"I don't know if I should be the one," he said.

"Oh, come on," Jilly said. "You owe me. Who got you backstage at the Mellen-camp show last year when you couldn't get a pass?"

"We could've been arrested for the way you got us in!"

Jilly gave him a sweet smile. "I didn't break the window—it just sort of popped open. Besides, you got your story, didn't you?"

Greg Sommer was *In the City*'s resident music critic and one of its feature writers. He was so straight-looking with his short hair, horn-rimmed glasses and slender build that Jilly often wondered how he ever got punk or metal musicians to talk to him.

"Yeah, I did," he admitted. "And I got double use of the material when I covered Lisa Germano's solo album."

"Isn't it wonderful?" Jilly said. "It's nothing like what I expected. I never knew that she sang, which is weird, considering what a really great voice she—"

"Jilly!" Wendy said.

"Oh. Sorry." It was so easy for Jilly to get distracted. She shot Wendy a slightly embarrassed look before she turned back to Greg. "You were saying about Brenda?" she prompted him.

"I wasn't, actually, but I might as well tell you. She got canned first thing yesterday morning."

"What?"

"Weird, isn't it? She's the last person I would've thought to get fired—she's usually so damn conscientious it makes the rest of us look bad. But she's been acting really strange for the past few weeks. I heard a rumor that she's got a really bad drug problem and I believe it. She looks completely strung out."

Wendy shook her head. "No way does Brenda do drugs."

"Well, she's doing something to herself, because there's not much left but skin and bones. And it's happened so fast—just over the last few weeks." He got a funny look. "Jesus, you don't think she has AIDS, do you?"

Just the mention of the disease made all of Jilly's skin go tight and her heartbeat jump. She'd had three friends die of the disease over the past year. Another two had recently tested HIV-positive. It seemed to be sweeping through the arts community, cutting down the brightest and the best.

"Oh, God, I hope not," she said.

Wendy stood up. "Brenda doesn't do drugs and she hasn't got AIDS," she said. "Come on, Jilly. We've got to go."

"But you heard what Greg said about the way she looks," Jilly said as she rose to join her.

Wendy nodded. "It sounds like she's finally found a diet that works," she said grimly. "Except it works too well."

She left Greg's office and walked briskly down the hall towards the stairwell. Jilly only had enough time to quickly thank Greg before she hurried off to catch up to her.

"I don't even know where to begin looking for her," she said as she followed Wendy down the stairs.

"Maybe we should start with this Jim guy she's been seeing."

Jilly nodded, then looked at her watch. It was past five.

"He'll be off work by now," she said. "The admin staff usually leaves at five."

"We can still call the school," Wendy said. "Somebody there will give you his number."

* * *

"I haven't seen her in over two weeks," Jim told Jilly when she got him on the line. "And she hasn't called for a couple of days now."

"That's just great."

"What's wrong? Is Brenda in some kind of trouble?"

Jilly put her hand over the mouthpiece and turned to Wendy who was standing outside the phone booth. "He wants to know what's going on. What do I tell him?"

"The truth," Wendy said. "We don't know where she is and we're worried because of what we've been hearing."

"Right. And if there's nothing the matter she's really going to appreciate our blabbing all her problems to a potential boyfriend."

"Hello?" Jim's voice was tiny in the receiver. "Jilly? Are you still there?"

"What do I tell him?" Jilly asked, hand still over the mouthpiece.

"Give it to me," Wendy said.

Jilly exchanged places with her but leaned in close so that she could listen as Wendy made up some story about needing to pick up a dress at Brenda's apartment and they were sorry to have bothered him.

"Right. Tell him the truth," Jilly said when Wendy had hung up. "I could've told him that kind of truth."

"What was I supposed to say? Once you reminded me of how Brenda would react if we did lay it all on him, I didn't have any other choice."

"You did fine," Jilly assured her.

They crossed the sidewalk and sat down on a bench. The tail end of rush hour crept by on McKennitt, making both of them happy that they didn't own a car.

"Could you imagine putting yourself through that every day?" Jilly said, indicating the crawling traffic with a lazy wave of her hand. "I'd go mad."

"But a car is still nice to have when you want to get out of the city," Wendy said. "Remember when Brenda drove us out to Isabelle's farm this spring?"

"Mmm. I could've stayed there for a month. . . ." Jilly's voice trailed off and she sat up on the bench. "We never checked if Brenda's car was in the garage."

The car was gone.

"Of course that doesn't prove anything," Jilly said.

She and Wendy walked slowly back up the driveway. When they reached the front of Brenda's building, they sat down on the bottom steps of the porch, trying to think of what to do next.

"Just because she's gone for a drive somewhere on a Saturday afternoon," Jilly tried, "doesn't mean anything sinister's going on."

"I suppose. But remember what Greg told us about how she looked?"

"She looked fine when I saw her," Jilly said. "Thinner, and a little jittery from having quit smoking, but not sickly."

"But that was a few weeks ago," Wendy said. "Now people are talking about her looking emaciated, like she's a junkie or something."

Jilly nodded. "I'm not as close to her as you are. I know she's always going on about her weight and diets, but does she actually have an eating disorder?"

The Brenda Jilly knew had never weighed under a hundred and twenty-five.

"She was in therapy in high school," Wendy said. "Which is when she first started suffering from anorexia. The one time she talked to me about it, she told me that the therapist thought her problems stemmed from her trying to get her father back: If she looked like a little girl instead of a woman, then he'll love her again."

"But her father didn't abandon his family, did he?" Jilly asked. "I thought he died when she was eight or nine."

"He did, which is a kind of abandonment, don't you think? Anyway, she doesn't buy into the idea at all, doesn't think she has a problem anymore."

"A classic symptom of denial."

Wendy nodded. "All of which makes me even more worried. The way Greg was talking, she's down to skin and bones."

"I wouldn't have thought it was possible to lose so much weight so fast," Jilly said.

"What if you just stopped eating?" Wendy said. "Your basic starvation diet."

Jilly considered that for a moment. "I suppose. You'd have to drink a lot of liquids, though, or the dehydration'd get to you."

"It's still going to leave you weak."

Jilly nodded. "And spacey."

"I wonder if we should report her as missing?" Wendy wondered aloud.

"I've been that route before," Jilly said. "There's not much the police can do until she's been gone for at least forty-eight hours."

"We don't know *how* long she's been gone."

"Let's give it until tomorrow," Jilly said. "If she's just gone somewhere for the weekend, she'll be back in the afternoon or early evening."

"And if she's not?"

"Then we'll see my pal Lou. He'll cut through the red tape for us."

"That's right, he's a cop, isn't he?"

Jilly nodded.

"I might still try calling the hospitals," Wendy said. She gave Jilly a pained look. "God, I sound like a parent, don't I?"

"You're just really worried."

Wendy sighed. "What gets me is that Brenda's always so . . . so organized. If she was going somewhere, she'd be talking about it for weeks in advance. She'd ask me to drop by to look after her plants. She'd—oh, I don't know. I thought we were close, but she's been avoiding me these past few weeks—nothing I can really point to, it's only when I look back on it I can see there was something more going on. Whenever I called, she was just on her way out, or working overtime, or doing something. I thought it was bad timing on my part, but now I'm not so sure."

She gave Jilly a worried look. "The idea that she's gone on some weird diet really scares me."

Jilly put her arm around Wendy's shoulders and gave her a hug.

"Things'll work out," she said, wishing she felt as confident as she sounded.

Wendy's anxiety had become contagious.

19

I wait until it's past ten and then realize Ellie's going to pull a no-show. Waiting for her, I find myself wondering about my reaction to all of this. From the voices rising up out of the well and their lost faces manifesting in my dreams to the ghost of the motel's old proprietor . . . I seem to accept it all so easily. Why doesn't it freak me as much as it should?

I don't have an answer—at least I don't have one that makes me feel comfortable. Because either the ghosts are all real and I'm far more resilient than I'd ever have imagined myself to be, or I'm losing it.

I'm tired, but I'm not quite ready to go to bed. Maybe weak would be a better way to put it. I've had a busy day. Since there's no maid service—along with everything else this place hasn't got—the first thing I did after I got up was go exploring for water. There was the well, of course, but it was deep and I'd no way to bring water up its shaft. I wasn't so sure I'd even want to if I could. Bad enough I called up ghosts, just by thinking of them. I didn't want to know what would show up if I took some water from that well.

Turns out I didn't have to worry. Not a half dozen yards into the forest, on this side of an old set of railway tracks, I found a stream. The water's clear and cold, even at this time of year. Using a battered tin pail that I discovered inside what must have been a tool shed, I carried water back to my unit and scrubbed the floors and walls. It sounds pretty straightforward, but it took a long time, because I had to rest a lot.

I'll be glad when I've regained my strength. I think I've caught some bug—a summer flu or something—because I keep getting these waves of dizziness that makes the room do a slow spin. It only goes away when I rest my head.

I forgot to mention: I checked my weight this morning, and I'm right at a hundred pounds even. When I look in the mirror, I still see some flab I could lose, but I really think I'm getting there. Once I hit a comfortable ninety-six or seven, I'll switch to a hold-and-maintain diet. Well, maybe ninety-five. No point in going halfway.

I just wish I didn't still want a cigarette. You'd think the urge would be gone by now.

Jim's been on my mind a lot. I'd really been enjoying our telephone conversations. I find I can relate to him so much better knowing that he can't see what I look like when we're talking. It seems to free me up and I found myself talking about all sorts of things—the kinds of conversations I had when I was in college, when we were all going to change the world.

A couple of miles back towards Newford, there's a diner and garage sitting on the corner where a county road crosses the highway. I noticed a pay phone in its parking lot when I drove by. I'm thinking of driving down tomorrow evening and giving Jim a call. This time I'll really be out of town. The only thing I worry about is moving the car too often. If I keep driving over the lawn, anyone with half a brain will be able to see that someone's staying at the motel.

Then I laugh. What am I worrying about? I'm not trespassing. I paid for my room.

I wonder what a ghost does with money.

I give Ellie a little longer to show up, but when the minute hand's crept to quarter past ten, I finally put on a jacket and go outside. I want to clear my head. It takes my eyes a few moments to adjust to the dark. The night gets absolutely black out here. The stars seem so close it's like they're hanging from a ceiling the height of the one in my unit, rather than in the sky.

But you get used to the dark. Your eyes have to work harder to take in light, but after a while you can differentiate between shapes and start to make out details.

I look around, listening to the crickets and June bugs, the frogs down at the bottom of the pool. My gaze crosses the lawn to where the rose bushes have overgrown the wishing well. After a while I cross the lawn. The tall grass and weeds make swishing noises against my jeans. My legs are damp from the dew, right up to the knee, and my sneakers are soon soaked.

I use my flashlight to light my way as I squeeze through the rose bushes, but it's a more awkward process than it is by day and I'm nursing a few thorn pricks before I make it all the way inside to the well. I shut off the light then and put a match to the candle I brought. There's not much of a wind at all, just a slight movement in the air so that the candle casts shadows that make the rose thicket seem even denser than it really is. I pretend I'm—well, not Sleeping Beauty, but one of her handmaidens, say, hidden away behind the wall of thorns. Did they all sleep straight through the hundred years? I find myself wondering. Or did they wake from time to time and glance at their watches, thinking, "When *is* that prince coming?"

It's weird what'll go through your mind when you're in a situation such as this. There are people who pay good money to go away on spiritual retreats. I always thought it was kind of weird, but now it's starting to make a little sense. When all you've got is yourself, it changes the way you think. You have the freedom to consider anything you want, for as long as you want, because there aren't any distractions. You don't have to go to work. The phone won't ring. Nobody drops by your apartment. It's just—

"So what are you hiding from, girl?" a voice asks.

I'm so startled I jump about a foot off the fieldstone wall. This is getting to be a bad habit of hers, but I've got to admit, Ellie sure knows how to make an entrance.

I see her sitting on the edge of one of the benches, the candle's light playing a thorny pattern on her white hair. She never made a sound, coming through the bushes, but then I guess a ghost would just float through.

"Who says I'm hiding?" I ask.

"Everything about you says it."

I shake my head. "I just need some time to be by myself, that's all."

"You're not a very good liar," Ellie says. "I think the only person who believes you is yourself."

"I'm not lying," I tell her, but the words ring as false to me as they obviously do to her.

If I stop to think about it, I know she's right. I have been lying—most of all to myself.

I look at her, half-hidden in the dark, and find myself telling her what's brought me here: all the messy baggage that I seem to drag around with me wherever I go. I have to laugh at myself as I'm doing it. In the stories, it's always the ghosts that unburden themselves.

"What makes you think hiding'll make it all go away?" Ellie asks when I'm done.

"It won't, I guess. There's a lot I'll have to face up to when I get back. I know that. But at least I'll be able to do it with a little self-esteem."

"Seems to me you're just going to the other extreme," she says.

Like she knows me so well.

"You don't know what I'm like," I say. "You don't know how hard it is, just trying to be normal. To fit in."

She seems to consider that. "It's easier when you're my age," she says finally. "Nobody expects you to be pretty or fashionable. You can be as pushy or as cantankerous as you want, and they don't blink an eye."

"I suppose."

"It was easier when I was younger, too," she goes on. "Oh, we had movie stars and singers to look up to, the pretty girls in the Coca-Cola adverts and all, but there didn't seem to be as desperate a need for a girl to make herself over into one of them. We all wanted to, but we didn't *have* to, if you get my meaning."

I shake my head.

"You didn't have to be pretty to land yourself a husband and raise a family. You just had to be a good person."

"Like the best looking girls didn't get the best men," I say.

"If you think the girls you see as pretty are any happier than you are, you don't know much about anything."

"Yeah, well—"

Ellie doesn't give me a chance to speak; she just barrels along over the top of what I was about to say.

"What you don't understand," she tells me, "is that all these problems you've got—none of them are your own fault."

"Oh, right. The old cop-out: Society's to blame."

"It is, girl."

"Brenda. My name's Brenda."

I hate the way she keeps calling me "girl."

"Society makes you get all these expectations for yourself and then, when you can't meet up to them, it screws up your life. You spend money you don't have because you're trying to comfort yourself. You smoke because you imagine it relieves your stress. You lose weight, not because you need to, but because you think if you can look like some woman in a magazine your life's suddenly going to be perfect. But it's not going to work that way.

"First you have to accept yourself—just as you are. Until that happens, nothing's going to get better for you."

At least she's not going on about my father, the way the therapists always do, but it still all sounds so pat. And how much did she make of her life? Working her ass off trying to keep her business afloat, having to declare bankruptcy, probably dying broke in some alleyway, one more burned-out baglady.

"What would you know about why I'm doing anything?" I say.

"Because I've been there—" she hesitates for a moment "—Brenda. I spent too much of my own life trying to be somebody that everybody else thought I should be, instead of who I am. If there's anything I regret, if there's anything that really gets me riled up still, it's all those years I wasted."

Is this my future I see sitting in front of me? I wonder. Because I know all about that feeling of having wasted my life. But then I shake my head. There's a difference. I'm *doing* something about my problems.

Still, I think maybe I know what's keeping Ellie here now. Not vengeance, not any need. Just regret.

"You really are dead, aren't you?" I say.

"Land sakes, girl. Whatever gave you that idea?"

I'm not going to let her put me off this time.

"I know you're a ghost," I tell her. "No different from the voices in the well."

"You've heard voices in the well?" she asks.

"First the voices," I say, "and then the ghosts. I dream about them. I started wondering what they looked like—the people those voices once belonged to—and now I can't get them out of my head. They've been getting stronger and stronger until now—well, here you are."

It makes sense, I think as I'm talking. The closer I am to the well, the stronger an influence the ghosts would have on me—so strong now that I'm seeing them when I'm awake. I look over at Ellie, but she's staring off into nowhere, as though she never even heard what I was saying.

"I never considered ghosts," she says suddenly. "I used to dream about spacemen coming to take me away."

This is so weird, it surprises a "You're kidding" out of me.

Ellie shakes her head. "No. I'd be vacuuming a room, or cleaning the bathroom, and suddenly I'd just get this urge to lay down. I'd stare up at the ceiling and then I'd dream about these silver saucers floating down from the hills, flying really low, almost touching the tops of the trees. They'd land out on the lawn by the wishing well here and these shapes would step out. I never quite knew what exactly they looked like; I just knew I'd be safe with them. I'd never have to worry about making ends meet again."

I wait a few moments, but she doesn't go on.

"Are there ghosts in the well?" I ask.

She looks at me and smiles. "Are there spacemen in the hills?"

I refuse to let her throw me off track again.

"Are *you* a ghost?" I ask.

Now she laughs. "Are we back to that again?"

"If you're not a ghost, then what are you doing here?"

"I live here," she says. "Just because the bank took it away from me, it didn't mean I had to go. I've got a place fixed up above the office—nothing fancy, but then I'm not a fancy person. I sleep during the day and do my walking around at night when it's quiet—except for when the kids come by for one of their hoolies. I get my water from the stream and I walk along the railway tracks out back in the woods, following them down to the general store when I run short of supplies."

I hadn't gone further into the office than the foyer, with its sagging floorboards and the front desk all falling in on itself. That part of the motel looks so decrepit I thought the building might fall in on me if I went inside. So I suppose it's possible. . . .

"What do you do in the winter?" I ask.

"Same as I always did—I go south."

She's so matter-of-fact about it all that I start to feel crazy, even though I know she's the one who's not all there. If she's not a ghost, then she's *got* to be crazy to be living here the way she does.

"And you've been doing this for twenty years?" I ask.

"Has it been that long?"

"What do you live on?"

"That's not a very polite question," she says.

I suppose it isn't. She must feel as though I'm interrogating her.

"I'm sorry," I say. "I'm just . . . curious."

She nods. "Well, I make do."

I guess it's true. She seems pretty robust for someone her age. I decide to forget about her being a ghost for the moment and get back to the other thing that's been bothering me.

"I know there's something strange about this well," I say. "You told me last night that it's cursed. . . ."

"It is."

"How?"

"It grants you your wish—can you think of anything more harmful?"

I shake my head. "I don't get it. That sounds perfect."

"Does it? How sure can you be that what you want is really the right thing for you? How do you know you haven't got your ideas all ass-backwards and the one thing you think you can't live without turns out to be the one thing that you can't live with?"

"But if it's a good wish . . ."

"Nothing's worth a damn thing unless you earn it."

"What if you wished for world peace?" I ask. "For an end to poverty? For no one ever to go hungry again? For the environment to be safe once more?"

"It only grants personal wishes," she says.

"Anybody's?"

"No. Only those of people who want—who need—a wish badly enough."

"I still don't see how that's a bad thing."

Ellie stands up. "You will if you make a wish."

She walks by me then and pushes her way through the roses. I hear the rasp of cloth against twig as she moves through the bushes, the thorns pulling at her jeans and her shirt.

"Ellie!" I call after her, but she doesn't stop.

I grab my candle, but the wind blows it out. By the time I get my flashlight out and make it out onto the lawn, there's no one there. Just me and the crickets.

Maybe she isn't a ghost, I find myself thinking. Maybe she was just sitting here all along and I never noticed her until she spoke to me. That makes a lot more sense, except it doesn't feel quite right. Do ghosts even know that they're ghosts? I wonder.

I think about the way she comes and goes. Did she have enough time to get out of sight before I got through the bushes? Who else but a ghost would hang around an abandoned motel, year after year for twenty years?

I get dizzy worrying at it. I don't know what to think anymore. All it does is make my head hurt.

I decide to follow the railway tracks through the woods to the general store where Ellie says she buys her groceries. I'll use the pay phone in the parking lot to call Jim.

And maybe, if they're still open, I'll ask them what they know about Ellie Carter and her motel.

20

Jim picked up the phone when it rang, hoping it was Brenda calling. He hadn't heard from her for a few days now, and Jilly's odd call this afternoon had left him puzzled and just a little worried. But it was Scotty on the other end of the line.

"I thought you had a date tonight," Jim said.

He carried the phone over to the sofa. Sitting down, he put his feet up on the coffee table and rested the phone on his chest.

"I did," Scotty told him, "but she stood me up."

"That's low."

He could almost see Scotty's shrug.

"I can't say's I really blame her," Scotty said, "if you really want to know the truth. I'm coming on so strong these days, I think I'd stand myself up if I was given the chance."

"What are you talking about?"

"Ah, you know. All I do is think with my cock. I should be like you—take it slow, take it easy. Be friends with a woman first instead of trying to jump her bones the minute we're alone. But I can't seem to help myself. First chance I get and I'm all over her."

"Yeah, well don't hold me up as some paradigm of virtue," Jim said. "And besides, I get the feeling I'm getting a version of the old runaround myself."

He told Jim about the call he'd gotten from Jilly this afternoon and how it had sounded as though she hadn't known Brenda was away on business.

"When you put that together with how Brenda won't even leave me the number of where she's staying, it's . . . I don't know. I just get a weird feeling about it."

"Sounds like a scam to me," Scotty said.

Jim switched the receiver from one ear to another. "What's that supposed to mean?"

"Think about it. It's obvious that she's put her friends up to call you—just to get a rise out of you. To make you more interested."

"How much more interested can I seem? Whenever she calls, we're on the phone for at least an hour. I'd take her out in a minute, but I can't seem to get the chance. She was too sick before she left and now she's out of town."

"Supposedly."

Jim sighed. "Supposedly," he repeated, somewhat reluctantly.

"Maybe she's just getting back at you for not calling her after she sent you those flowers."

"You really think so?"

"Hey, what do I know? Dear Abby I'm not. I'm just a guy who can't get a date and when I do, the girl dumps me before we even go out." He paused, then added, "Next time she calls, just ask her what's going on."

"What if there's nothing? I'd hate to screw things up. I figure not calling her back right away was already one strike against me. I don't want to add to it now because—"

A sudden beep on the line interrupted him.

"Just a sec," Jim said. "That's my call waiting. It might be Brenda calling."

"I've got to go anyway," Scotty said. "Call me tomorrow and let me know how things worked out."

"Will do," Jim told him.

Cutting the connection with Scotty, he took the other call.

21

I was really looking forward to talking to Jim tonight. I just wanted to hear his voice and connect with a world that didn't involve ghosts or diets or strange voices that come out of a haunted wishing well.

Following the railway tracks really cuts the distance to the general store. The highway takes a curve, but the tracks go straight through the woods. They're overgrown, but not so much that they're not easy to follow. I didn't even need to use my flashlight. I just stepped from wooden rail to wooden rail, one foot, then the other, but slowly, every step an effort. I was so tired.

This flu bug I've caught made it seem as though I was walking all the way back to Newford. I kept having to stop and rest. I would've given up and just gone back, but by the time I started thinking along those lines, I'd already come so far that going back no longer made much sense. And besides, I had this real *need* to step outside myself and my problems—if only for a few minutes.

But now I wish I'd never called Jim, because it seems as though all my lies are coming home tonight: the ones Ellie pointed out that I'd used on myself, and the ones I'd told Jim. He didn't come right out and say he didn't believe I was out of town, but he kept asking all these questions about what my day had been like, had I got to see the sights, that kind of thing. Innocent enough questions, but I couldn't help but feel there was an agenda behind them, as though he was trying to catch me up in my lies.

And then there was this business with Jilly calling him and Wendy wanting to pick up a dress from my apartment.

I don't have any of Wendy's dresses—God knows they'd never fit me anyway. At least they wouldn't have before the diet. I could get into one of them now, I suppose; it'd just be a little short in the skirt and sleeves. But even if I did have something of Wendy's, she's got a key to my place anyway.

As soon as Jim started talking about their having called him I knew what was really going on. They were worried about me. They'd probably found out about my phone being cut off. Or that I'd lost my job. Or both. Wendy was probably upset anyway because of the way I've been avoiding her these past few weeks. . . .

What a mess I've made of things.

I get off the phone as quickly as I can. Once I hang up, though, I don't have the energy to go back to the motel. The general store is closed, gas pumps and all, so I just sit down on the steps running up to its porch and lean my head against the railing. I want to rest for a couple of minutes.

Once I'm sitting down I feel as though I'll never be able to move again, but I know I can't stay here. It's not that I'm scared of running into the people who own the place or anything—there's no law against using a public phone and then having a rest before heading back home.

No. It's that I can't shake the feeling that I'm being watched. At first I think it's Ellie, but the watching has a hungry feeling about it, as though I'm being stalked, and I can't see Ellie wanting to hurt me. If she ever did, she's already had plenty of opportunities before now.

Logically, I know I'm safe. I'm just a little sick, weak from this flu bug I've caught. Maybe it's the flu that's making me feel paranoid. But logic doesn't help me feel any better because, logically, there shouldn't be ghost voices in the well and ghosts running through my dreams. Logically, I shouldn't keep having conversations with the deceased proprietor of an abandoned motel.

Finally, I drag myself to my feet and start back. I have to rest every fifty feet or so because I just don't have any strength left in me at all. The feeling of being watched gets stronger, but I'm feeling so sick it's as though I don't even care about it anymore. I have cramps that come and go in painful waves. I want to throw up, but I've got nothing in my stomach to bring up. I can't even remember if I had any dinner or not. When all you eat is the same thing, popcorn and lettuce, lettuce and popcorn, day in and day out, it's hard to differentiate between meals.

I don't know how I make it back to my room, but finally I do. Dawn's pinking the eastern horizon, casting long shadows as I stumble to my bed. The birds are making an incredible racket, but I almost can't hear them.

My bed seems to sway, back and forth, back and forth, as I lie on it. I keep hearing ominous sounds under the morning bird calls. A floorboard creaking. A shutter banging. I'm too sick even to turn my head to see if there's someone there. There's a wet, musty smell in the air—part stagnant water, part the smell you get when you turn over a rotting log.

I really want to turn to look now, but the cramps have come back and I double up from the pain. When they finally ease off, I fall asleep and the ghosts are waiting for me.

They're not familiar any longer—or rather, I recognize them, but they look different. It's so awful. All I can see is drowned people, bloated corpses shambling toward me. Their faces are a dead white and grotesquely swollen. Their clothes are rotting and hang in tatters, they have wet weeds hanging from them, dripping on the floor. Their hair is plastered tight against their distended faces. They have only sunken sockets, surrounded by puffs of dead white flesh where they should have eyes.

You're only dreaming, I try to tell myself. You're sick and you have a fever and this is only a dream.

I manage to come out of it. The light's bright in my eyes—must be mid-morning already. It's impossible to focus on anything. I have some dry heaves which only makes me weaker. I try to fight it, but eventually I fall back into the dreams again.

That's when I finally see her, rising up from behind the ranks of the drowned dead. She looks just like the picture of the *rusalka* in that book. A water-wraith. The deadly spirit of the well.

22

Wendy stayed over at Jilly's studio Saturday night. She slept on the Murphy bed while Jilly camped out on the sofa—over Wendy's protests. "I'll be up early working," Jilly insisted, and refused to discuss it any further. And sure enough, when Wendy woke the next morning, Jilly was already behind her easel, frowning at her current work in progress.

"I can't decide," she said when she saw that Wendy was awake. "Have I made it too dark on this side, or too light on the other?"

"Please," Wendy said. She put on the kimono that Jilly used as a bathrobe and shuffled across the studio toward the kitchen area, looking for the coffee. "At least give me a chance to wake up."

The door buzzer sounded as she was halfway to the coffee carafe sitting on the kitchen counter.

"Would you mind getting that?" Jilly asked. "It's probably Geordie coming by to mooch some breakfast."

"Wonderful," Wendy said.

She was barely awake and now she had to put up with Geordie's ebullient morning cheer on top of Jilly's. She considered writing a sign saying, "Quiet, please, some people are still half asleep," and holding it up when she opened the door, but she didn't have the energy to do more than unlock the door. When she swung it open it was to find a stranger standing there in the hallway.

"Um, is Jilly here?"

Wendy gathered the kimono more closely about her neck and looked over her shoulder. "It's for you," she told Jilly. Turning back to the stranger, she added, "Come on in."

"Thanks."

Jilly looked around the side of her easel, her welcoming smile turning puzzled.

"Jim?" she said.

"I hope I'm not interrupting anything," he said.

So this was Jim Bradstreet, Wendy thought as she continued on her quest for a caffeine hit. He wasn't as handsome as she'd imagined he'd be, but there was a warmth about him that was directly evident. Mostly, it had to do with his eyes, she decided, the laugh lines around them and the way his gaze had immediately sought her own.

Behind her, Jilly laid down the paintbrush she'd been using. Wiping her hands on her jeans, which left new streaks of a dark red on top of the other paint already on the material, she sat Jim down on the sofa and introduced him to Wendy. Wendy offered him coffee which he luckily refused, since there was barely one cup left in the carafe.

"Well, this is a pleasant surprise," Jilly said. "I didn't think you even knew where I lived."

Wendy brought her coffee over to where they were sitting and curled up on the end of the sofa opposite Jim. That was Jilly, she thought. Always happy to see anybody.

Sometimes Wendy thought Jilly must know every third person living in the city—with plans already formed to meet the rest.

"I looked the address up in the phone book," Jim said. He cleared his throat. "Uh, maybe I should get right to the point. I've been kind of worried about Brenda ever since you called yesterday. You see, I got the impression that you didn't even know she was out of town."

Jilly's eyebrows rose quizzically, but she didn't say anything. Wendy stared down at her coffee. She hated getting caught in a lie—even one so well-intentioned.

"Anyway," Jim went on, "when she called me last night, I tried to find out where she was staying, how long she'd be gone—that kind of thing. I was trying to be surreptitious, but I could tell she felt I was grilling her and she acted very evasive. We hardly talked for more than five minutes before she was off the phone."

Nice-looking and kindhearted, too, Wendy thought. Obviously concerned. She wondered if he had a brother.

Jilly sighed. "Well, it's true," she said. "We didn't know anything was wrong until yesterday when we found out her phone was cut off and she'd lost her job."

"But it's the paper that's sent her out of town," Jim began before his voice trailed off. He nodded. "I get it," he added, almost to himself. "She just didn't want to see me."

"I don't think it's quite like that," Jilly said.

"She's been avoiding everybody," Wendy said. "I haven't seen her in three weeks."

"And you say she's lost her job?"

Jilly nodded. "Brenda will probably hate us for telling you about any of this, but you seem to care for her and right now I get the feeling she needs all the people she can get to care about her."

"What—what's the matter with her?" Jim asked.

"We don't know exactly," Jilly said.

With Jilly having opened the Pandora's box, Wendy realized she couldn't hold back herself now. She just hoped that it wouldn't put Jim off and that Brenda would forgive them.

"Brenda's got a serious case of low self-esteem," she said. "Way serious. She's always had money problems, but now we think she's quit smoking *and* gone on some weird crash diet. If you've done either, you probably know how it can make you a little crazy. With everything coming down at once on top of that—losing her job, obviously way broke—God knows what she's thinking right now."

"She never said anything. . . ."

"Well, she wouldn't, would she?" Wendy said. "Do you lay all your problems on a woman you've just met—especially someone you might like a lot?"

"She said that?" Jim asked. "That she likes me a lot?"

Wendy and Jilly exchanged amused glances. It was almost like talking to Brenda, Wendy thought. That'd be the first thing she'd center on as well.

"When you were talking to Brenda," Jilly asked, "did she say where she was staying?"

Jim shook his head.

"Well, I might be able to fix that," Jilly said. "Or at least, Lou might."

She got up and dug her phone out from under a pile of newspapers and art magazines and dialed a number.

"Who's Lou?" Jim asked Wendy.

"A cop she knows."

"Yes, hello?" Jilly said into the phone. "Could I speak to Detective Fucceri, please? It's Jilly Coppercorn calling." She listened for a moment, then put her hand over the mouthpiece. "Great," she told them. "He's in." She removed her hand before either Wendy or Jim could say anything and spoke into the phone again.

"Lou? Hi. It's Jilly. I was wondering if you could do me a favor."

"That's not true—I called you just last week to ask you out for lunch but you were too busy, remember?"

"How soon we forget."

"What? Oh, right. I want to get an address to go with a phone number."

"Well, no. I don't have the number yet. I need that as well."

Wendy sat fascinated as she listened to Jilly deal with number traces and the like as though she were some TV private eye who did this all the time. Jilly passed on Jim's number and the approximate time of Brenda's call to Lou, then finally hung up and gave Jim and Wendy a look of satisfaction.

"Lou'll have the address for us in about half an hour," she said.

"Can anybody do that?" Jim asked.

Wendy just looked at him. "What do you think?" she asked.

"What's the big deal?" Jilly asked. "All I did was ask a friend to do us a favor."

"But only *you* would think of tracing Brenda's call," Wendy said.

"But everybody knows that the phone company keeps records on that kind of thing—don't they?"

"And only you would know who to ask and have them actually do it for you," Wendy finished.

Jilly waved her hand dismissively. "Anybody want some breakfast?" she asked.

Jim glanced at his watch. "But it's almost noon."

"It's also Sunday," Wendy told him. "Normal people are only just waking up about now."

"So call it brunch," Jilly said.

It took Lou closer to an hour to get back to Jilly, by which time they'd all eaten the somewhat complicated Mexican omelet that Jilly had whipped up for them with her usual careless aplomb. Wendy and Jim were cleaning the dishes and Jilly was back behind the easel when the phone finally rang.

"You're sure?" Jilly said when she had finished writing down the information he had given her. "No, no. I'd never think that. I really appreciate your doing this, Lou. It's just such a weird place. Yes, I'll tell you all about it next week. Thanks again."

She hung up the phone and then stared at what she'd written.

"*Well?*" Wendy said. "Aren't you going to tell us where she is?"

Jilly shrugged. "I don't know. The call was made from a public phone booth in the parking lot of a general store up Highway 14."

"A general store?" Wendy said.

" 'Ada & Bill's General Store.' It's almost in the mountains."

Wendy's hopes fell. "That doesn't tell us anything."

Jilly nodded her head in glum agreement.

"I've got a car," Jim said. "Anybody want to take a drive up there to see if we can find out more?"

All Jilly had to do was change her jeans for a clean pair and comb her tangled hair with her fingers. Wendy was dressed and ready to go in a record five minutes.

23

Everything stands still when the *rusalka* appears. She's tall and gaunt, a nightmare of pale flesh clad in the remains of a tattered green dress, hair matted and tangled, the color of dried blood, the eyes burning so that looking at them is like looking into the belly of a furnace.

She's what's been haunting me, I realize. She's the curse of the well. It's not her granting wishes that makes her so terrible, but that she steals your vitality as a vampire would. She sucks all the spirit out of you and then drags your body down into the bottom of the well where you lie with all the other bodies of her victims.

I can see the mound of them in the water, a mass of drowned flesh spotted with the coins that have been dropped on top of them. I know that's where I'm going, too.

She steps up to me, clawed hands reaching out. I try to scream but it's as though my mouth's full of water. And then she touches me. Her flesh is so cold it's like a frost burn. Her claws dig into my shoulders, cutting easily through the skin like sharp knives. She starts to haul me up toward her in an awful embrace and finally I can scream.

But it's too late, I know.

That's all I can think as she drags my face up toward her own. It's too late.

She's got jaws like a snake's. Her mouth opens wider than is humanly possible— but she's not human, is she? She's going to swallow me whole . . . but suddenly I'm confused. I feel like I'm standing on the edge of the wishing well and it's the mouth of the well that's going to swallow me, not the *rusalka,* except they're one and the same and all I can do is scream, and even that comes out like a jagged whisper of sound because I've got no strength in me, no strength left at all.

24

"That was it!" Jilly cried as Jim drove by a small gas bar and store on the right side of the highway. "You went right by it."

Jim pulled over to the side of the road. He waited until there was a break in the traffic, then made a U-turn and took them back into the parking lot. The name of the store was written out in tiny letters compared to the enormous GAS sign above it. The building itself was functional rather than quaint—cinderblock walls with a flat shingled roof. All that added a picturesque element was the long wooden porch running along the front length of the building. It was simply furnished, with a pair of plastic lawn chairs, newspaper racks for both *The Newford Star* and *The Daily Journal,* and an

ancient Coca-Cola machine belonging to an older time when the soft drink was sold
only in its classic short bottles.

Jim parked in front of the store, away from the pumps, and killed the engine.
Peering through the windshield, they could see an old woman at the store's counter.

"I'll go talk to her," Jilly said. "Old people always seem to like me."

"*Everybody* likes you," Wendy said with a laugh.

Jilly gave a "can I help it" shrug before she opened her door and stepped out
onto the asphalt.

"I'm coming," Wendy added, sliding over across the seat.

In the end they all trooped inside. The store lived up to its name, selling everything
from dried and canned goods and fresh produce to fishing gear, flannel shirts, hardware
and the like. The goods were displayed on shelves that stood taller than either Jilly or
Wendy, separated by narrow aisles. It was dim inside as well—the light seeming almost
nonexistent compared to the bright sunlight outside.

The old woman behind the counter—she must be Ada, Jilly decided—looked up
and smiled as they came in. She was grey-haired and on the thin side, dressed in rather
tasteless orange polyester pants and a blouse that was either an off white or a very
pale yellow—Jilly couldn't quite decide which. Her hair was done up in a handkerchief
from which stray strands protruded like so many dangling vines.

"I wish I could be of more help," Ada said when Jilly showed her the photograph
of Brenda that she'd brought along, "but I've never seen her before. She's very pretty,
isn't she?"

Jilly nodded. "Are there any motels or bed-and-breakfasts nearby?" she asked.

"The closest would be Pine Mountain Cabins up by Sumac Lake," Ada told her.
"But that's another fifteen or so miles up the highway."

"Nothing closer?"

"Afraid not. Pine Mountain is certainly the closest—other than The Wishing Well,
of course, but that's been boarded up ever since the early seventies when the bank
foreclosed on Ellie Carter."

"That's the place where Brenda goes on her Sunday drives," Wendy put in.

Jilly nodded. She could remember Brenda having spoken of the place before.
"And she's got a newspaper clipping of it up above her desk in her apartment," she
added.

"I doubt your friend would be staying there," Ada said. "The place is a shambles."

"Let's try it anyway," Jilly said. "We've got nothing to lose. Thank you," she
added to Ada as she headed for the door with Jim in tow.

Wendy stopped long enough to buy a chocolate bar, before following them to the
car. Jilly had already slid in beside Jim so this time Wendy got the window seat.

"What would Brenda be doing at an abandoned motel?" Wendy asked as Jim
started up the car.

"Who knows?" he said.

"Besides," Jilly said, "with the way this idea panned out, our only other option
is to go back home."

The motel was easy to find. They followed the long curve of the highway as it led
away from the store and came upon it almost immediately as the road straightened
once more.

"I don't see a car," Jim said.

He parked close to the highway and they all piled out of his car again. The soles of their shoes scuffed on the buckling pavement as they approached the motel proper. The tumbled-down structure looked worse the closer they came to it.

"Maybe she parked it around back," Jilly said. "Out of sight of the highway."

She was trying to sound hopeful, but the place didn't look encouraging—at least not in terms of finding Brenda. It was so frustrating. She kicked at a discarded soda can and watched it skid across the parking lot until it was brought up short by a clump of weeds growing through the asphalt.

"God, it's so creepy-looking," Wendy said. "Way abandoned."

It did have a forlorn air about it, but Jilly rather liked it—maybe because of that. She'd always had a soft spot in her heart for the abandoned and unwanted.

"I think it's great," she said.

"Oh, please."

"No, really. I've got to come back here and do some paintings. Look at the way that shed's almost leaning right into the field. The angle's perfect. It's like it's pointing back at the motel sign. And the lattice work on that roofline—over there. It's just—"

"What's that weird *sound?*" Jim broke in.

Jilly fell silent and then both she and Wendy both heard it as well—an eerie mix of a high-pitched moan and a broken whisper. It was so quiet that it disappeared completely when a car passed on the highway behind them. Once the car was gone, though, they could hear it again.

"It . . . it must be some kind of animal," Wendy said. "Caught in a trap or something."

Jilly nodded and set off around the side of the motel at a run, quickly followed by the other two.

"Oh, shit," Wendy said. "That's Brenda's car."

Jilly had recognized it as well, but she didn't bother replying. She had a bad feeling about all of this—the motel, Brenda's car, that *sound.* Worry formed a knot in the pit of her stomach, but she ignored the discomfort as best she could. Head cocked, she tried to place where the sound originated. It made her shiver, crawling up her spine like a hundred little clawed feet.

"It's coming from over there," Jim said, pointing toward a thick tangle of rose bushes.

"That's where Brenda said the well is," Wendy said.

But Jilly wasn't listening. She'd already taken the lead again and so it was she who, after pushing her way through a worn path in the rose bush tangle, first found Brenda.

Jilly almost didn't recognize her. Brenda was wasted to the point of emaciation—a gaunt scarecrow version of the woman Jilly had known. Her clothes hung on her as though they were a few sizes too large, her hair seemed to have lost its vibrancy and was matted against her scalp and neck. She was leaning over a crumbling stone wall, head and shoulders in the well, thin arms pushing on the stones as though something was dragging her down. But there was nothing there. Only Brenda and the terrible soft keening sound she was making.

Afraid of startling her, Jilly waited until Jim and Wendy had pushed through the roses as well so that they could lend her a hand in case Brenda fell forward when she was touched. Speaking softly—just uttering meaningless comforting sounds, really—Jilly pulled Brenda back from the well with Jim's help. When they laid her on the ground, Brenda's eyes gazed sightless up at them, vision turned inward. But the sound she'd been making slowly faded away.

"Oh my God," Wendy said as she took in the change that had been wrought on Brenda in just a few weeks. "There's nothing left of her."

Jilly nodded grimly. "We have to get her to a hospital."

She and Wendy took Brenda's legs, Jim her shoulders, then they carried her back through the rose bushes, all of them suffering scratches and cuts from the sharp thorns since the path was too narrow for this sort of maneuver. Brenda seemed to weigh nothing at all. Once they had her out on the lawn, Jim hoisted her up in his arms and they hurried back to his car.

"What about Brenda's car?" Wendy said as they passed it on the way back to the motel's parking lot.

"We'll come back for it," Jilly said.

25

I don't remember much about the hospital. I feel like I was underwater the whole time—from when I hung up the phone on Jim Saturday night until a few days later, when I found myself in a hospital bed in Newford General. I don't know where the lost time went—down some dark well, I guess.

The doctor told me I'd been starving myself to death.

I was in the hospital forever and I've been in therapy ever since I got out. I'm really just starting to come to grips with the fact that I have an eating disorder. Have one, had one, and always have to guard against its recurrence.

Thank god I had my health insurance premiums paid up.

The thing that's hardest to accept is that it's not my fault. This is something Ellie told me and my therapist keeps returning to. Yes, I'm responsible for the messes I've made in my life, but I have to understand where the self-destructive impulses come from. The reason I feel so inadequate, so fat, so ugly, so mixed up, is because all my life I've had certain images pounded into my head—the same way that everybody does. Perfect ideals that no one can match. Roles to play that—for whatever reason—we can't seem to adjust to. When you don't toe the line, it's not just the outside world that looks askance at you; you feel in your own head that you've let yourself down.

Logically, it all makes sense, but it's still a hard leap of faith to accept that the person I am is a good person and deserves recognition for that, rather than trying to be somebody I'm not, that I can never be, that it would even be wrong to be.

But though that's part of my problem, it's not the real root of it. Every woman has to deal with those same social strikes against her. For me, it all comes back to my dad, to this belief that if I'd been better, prettier, he wouldn't have killed himself; that if I could somehow regain the sexless body of a child—look like a child, be the perfect child—I could win him back again.

Understanding that is even harder.

I weigh a hundred and twenty-seven pounds now, but I still haven't taken up smoking again. As for my finances—I'm working on them. I had to declare personal bankruptcy, but I'm going to pay everybody back. I have to, because I don't think anybody else should have to pay for my mistakes—no matter what the extenuating circumstances leading up to those mistakes. A friend of Jilly's got me a job at *The Daily Journal* doing proofing, copyediting, that sort of thing. The pay's not great, but there's room to move up.

Things never really worked out between Jim and me—my fault again, but I'm trying not to feel guilty about it. I just couldn't accept that he cared for me after he'd seen how screwed up I can get. I know it wasn't pity he felt—I mean, he obviously liked me before things got really weird—but I could never look at him without wondering what he was seeing: me, or that creature I became by the well. Jilly says he still asks about me. Maybe one day I'll feel confident enough to look him up again.

There was no *rusalka*—that's pretty much the general consensus, myself included. Sort of. Wendy says I must have seen a reflection of myself in the window of the motel room and just freaked out. My therapist simply says there's no such thing, but won't offer explanations for what I thought I saw except to tell me that I was in a disturbed state of mind and that people are liable to experience anything in such a situation.

I don't quite buy it. I don't know if there really was a water-wraith or not, but there's something in water that's still haunting me. Not a bad something, not a nightmare creature like the *rusalka,* but still something not of this world. When I talked about it with Jilly once, she said, "You know the way Christy talks about ghosts being a kind of audiovisual memory that a place holds? Well, water's supposedly the best conductor for that sort of a thing. And that's why there are so many holy wells and sacred lakes and the like."

I suppose. The ghosts in my head are gone, but I hear water all the time and my dreams always seem to take me underwater. I'm never scared, it's never spooky. Just . . . strange. Dark and cool. Peaceful in a way that I can't explain.

Wendy says I shouldn't let Jilly fill my head with her weird ideas, but I don't know. The interesting thing about Jilly is that she's totally impartial. She accepts everything with the same amount of interest and tolerance, just as she seems to love everybody the same—which is why I think she's never really had a steady boyfriend. She never quite has that extra amount of love it would take to make a relationship with just one person work.

Wendy disagrees with that. She says that Jilly just can't get close to a man that way. I get the feeling it's got to do with something that happened to Jilly when she was growing up, but Wendy's as closemouthed about that as she is with any bit of privileged information, and I've never quite got up the nerve to ask Jilly herself. I'd hate to remind her of some really awful thing in her past—if that's truly the case.

Whatever it was, she's moved beyond it now. Her life is so contained, so steady, for all her fey impulses. I think I envy that about her more than her thinness now.

I wonder if there's anything she envies in other people.

It's autumn now—months later. Like I said, the ghosts don't come to me anymore, but sometimes I still hear voices drifting up from out of the well when I go for my Sunday drives up to the motel. Or maybe it's only the wind. All I know is that I still like to come sit on the old stone wall here by the well and when I leave, I feel . . . different. It's as though the calmness that's hidden away in that well enclosed by its rose bushes imparts something to me: maybe no more than simply another way of seeing things.

I don't worry about it; I just appreciate it. And if I come back a little spacey, saying odd things which seem very insightful to me, but are confusing to other people, nobody seems to mind. Or at least they don't say anything about it to me.

As for Ellie, I went up into the rooms above the office where she said she lived and there was nothing there. No Ellie, no sign of anyone living there, except it was very clean, as though someone took the trouble to sweep it out regularly and maybe put some wildflowers in a vase on the window sill when they're in season. There was a glass jar with dried flowers in it when I was there, and it didn't smell musty the way the other rooms do.

I tried to find an obit for her, but as someone pointed out to me, she could have died anywhere. If she didn't die in or around the city, there wouldn't be an obit in the morgues of any of our local papers. Still, I looked.

Jilly's got another answer, of course. She says she knows what Ellie meant about the well being cursed: Ellie must have wished that she'd always be at The Wishing Well, so after she died, her ghost was forever doomed to haunt the motel. Which, as Wendy put it, is par for the course, considering the way Jilly sees the world.

I like to think Ellie's just gone south for the winter.

The first time I go back to the wishing well, I find four dollar bills held down by a stone on the wall of the well. I look at them and wonder, a refund for the days I'd paid for, but didn't stay at the motel?

I drop them down into the shaft, one after the other, but I don't make a wish. My life's not perfect, but then whose is? All I can do is forget about miracles and try to take things one day at a time. I'm the only one who can empower myself—I don't need my therapist to tell me that.

I don't think the well ever was cursed. The only curse comes from the ghosts a person brings to it.

I still think about my dad a lot. I guess we had more in common than I thought, since we both screwed up our lives pretty badly. I think he'd be proud of me for finding a solution different from the one he did.

WKPN's on the radio when I drive home. "Rock and gold, without the hard rock and rap." They're playing Buddy Holly.

Wella, wella.

I turn the dial, chasing static and stations until I hear a black woman's voice, clipped rhymes, ghetto poetry riding the back of a sliding beat that's so contagious my pulse can't help but keep time with it. She's talking about standing up for herself, being herself, facing the world with what she calls a buffalo stance.

You can keep your "rock and gold," I think. I'm tired of living in the past. I'm like the wishing well, in a lot of ways, full of old ghosts that I just can't seem to exorcise. They're what keeps dragging me down. It's when I listen to them, when I start to believe that all the unhappy things they're saying about me is true, that I'm at my worst.

What I want is what this woman's singing about, something that's here and now. What I need is my own buffalo stance.

I think I'm finally on the right road to finding it.

Dead Man's Shoes

In her office, her head rests upon her arms, her arms upon the desk. She is alone. The only sounds are those of the clock on the wall, monotonously repeating its two-syllable vocabulary, and the faint noise of the street coming in through her closed windows. Her next appointment isn't until nine pm.

She meant merely to rest her eyes for a few moments; instead, she has fallen asleep.

In her dream, the rain falls in a mist. It crouches thicker at knee level, twining across the street. The dead man approaches her through the rain with a pantherlike grace he never displayed when alive. He is nothing like Hollywood's shambling portrayals of animated corpses; confronted by the dead man, she is the one whose movements are stuttered and slow.

Because she is trapped in flesh, she thinks.

Because in this dreamscape, he is pure spirit, unfettered by gravity or body weight, while she still carries the burden of life. The world beyond this night's dreams retains a firm grip, shackling her own spirit's grace with the knowledge of its existence and her place in it.

Not so the dead man.

The rain has pressed the unruly thicket of his hair flat against his scalp. His features are expressionless, except for the need in his eyes. He carries a somewhat bulky object in his arms, bundled up in wet newspapers. She can't quite identify it. She knows what he carries is roundish, about the size of a soccer ball, but that is all. All other details have been swallowed in the play of shadow that the rain has drawn from the neon signs overhead and the streetlight on the corner.

She is not afraid of the dead man, only puzzled. Because she knows him in life.

Because she has seen him glowering from the mouths of alleyways, sleeping in doorways. He has never been truly dangerous, despite his appearance to the contrary.

What are you doing here? she wants to ask him. What do you want from me? But her voice betrays her as much as her body, and what issues forth are only sounds, unrecognizable as words.

She wakes just as he begins to hand her what he is carrying.

The dream was very much upon Angel's mind as she later looked down at the pathetic bundle of rag-covered bones Everett Hoyle's corpse made at the back of the alley. But since she had always believed that the supernatural belonged only to the realm of fiction, film and the tabloids, she refused to allow the dream to take root in her imagination.

Jilly would call what she had experienced prescience; she thought of it only as an unhappy coincidence, and let it go no further. Instead she focused her attention on the latest addition to the city's murder-victim statistics.

No one was going to miss Everett, she thought, least of all her. Still, she couldn't help but feel sorry for him. It was an alien reaction insofar as Everett was concerned.

The streets were filled with angry individuals, but the reasons behind their anger usually made sense: lost homes, lost jobs, lost families. Drink, or drugs. Institutions turning out their chronic psychiatric patients because the government couldn't afford their care. Victims of neglect or abuse who discovered too late that escaping to a life on the street wasn't the answer.

But Everett was simply mean-spirited.

He had a face that would make children cry. He wasn't deformed, he simply wore a look of rage that had frozen his features into a roadmap of constant fury. He stood a cadaverous six-four, which was more than merely intimidating to those from whom he was trying to cadge spare change; it could be downright frightening. With that manner, with his matted shock of dirty grey hair and tattered clothing, he didn't seem so much a man down on his luck as some fearsome scarecrow that had ripped itself free from its support pole and gone out to make the world around him as unpleasant as he felt himself. Which put him about one step up from those men who had to kill their families before they put the gun in their own mouth and pulled the trigger.

No, Angel corrected herself. Think in the past tense now, because Everett had terrorized his last passerby.

Surprisingly, death had brought a certain calm to his features, smoothing away the worst of the anger that normally masked them. This must be what he looked like when he was sleeping, Angel thought. Except he wasn't asleep. The blood pooled around his body bore stark testimony to that. She'd already checked for a pulse and found none. Having called the police before she left the office, now it was simply a matter of waiting for them to arrive.

The scene laid out before her held an anomaly that wouldn't stop nagging her. She took a step closer and studied the body. It was like a puzzle with one piece missing, and it took her a few minutes before she could finally pinpoint what was bothering her. She turned to the young white boy who'd come to her office twenty minutes ago and brought her back to where he'd found the body.

"What happened to his boots, Robbie?" she asked.

Everett's footwear had been distinctive: threadbare Oxfords transformed into boots by stitching the upper half of a pair of Wellingtons onto the leather of each of the shoes. Olive green with yellow trim on the left; black with red trim on the right. The Oxfords were so old and worn that they were devoid of any recognizable color themselves.

"I guess Macaulay took 'em," the boy replied.

"You never said Macaulay was here with you."

Robbie shrugged.

She waited for him to elaborate, but Robbie simply stood beside her, face washed pale by the streetlight coming in from the mouth of the alley, thin shoulders stooped, one Dr. Marten kicking at the trash underfoot. His dirty-blonde hair was so short it was no more than stubble. He wouldn't meet her gaze.

Angel sighed. "All right," she said. "I'll bite. Why did Macaulay take the boots?"

"Well, you know what the homes are saying, Miz Angel. Man gets nined, you got to take away his shoes or he's gonna go walkin' after he's dead. He'll be lookin' for who took him down, usually, but Everett now—he's so mean I suppose anybody'd do."

With all her years of working with street people, dealing with the myriad superstitions that ran rampant through the tenements and squats, Angel thought she'd heard it all. But this was a new one, even on her.

"You don't believe that, do you?" she asked.

"No, ma'am. But I'd say Macaulay surely do."

Robbie spoke casually enough, but Angel could tell there was more to what had happened here tonight than he was letting on. He was upset—a natural enough reaction, considering the circumstances. Keeping Everett's corpse company until the police arrived had upset her as well. But the tension underlying Robbie's seeming composure spoke of more.

Before she could find just the right way to persuade him to open up to her, one of the sirens that could be heard at all hours of the day or night in this part of the city disengaged itself from the general hubbub of night sounds and became more distinct. Moments later, a cruiser pulled up, blocking the mouth of the alley. The cherry-red lights of its beacons strobed inside the alley, turning the scene into a macabre funhouse. Backlit, the two officers who stepped out of the cruiser took on menacing shapes: shadows, devoid of features.

At Angel's side, Robbie began to tremble, and she knew she wouldn't get anything from him now. Hands kept carefully in view, she went to meet the approaching officers.

Angelina Marceau ran a youth distress center on Grasso Street, from which she got her nickname, the Grasso Street Angel. She looked like an angel as well: heart-shaped face surrounded by a cascade of dark curly hair, deep warm eyes, next to no makeup because she didn't need it with her clear complexion. Her trim figure didn't sport wings, and she leaned more toward baggy pants, T-shirts and hightops than she did harps and white gowns, but that didn't matter to those living on the streets of Newford. So far as they were concerned, all she lacked was a visible halo.

Angel wasn't feeling particularly angelic by the time three a m .rolled around that night. She sat wearily in her office, gratefully nursing a mug of coffee liberally spiked with a shot of whiskey, which Jilly had handed to her when she walked in the door.

"I appreciate your looking after the place while I was at the precinct," she said.

"It wasn't a problem," Jilly told her. "No one showed up."

Angel nodded. Word on the street moved fast. If the Grasso Street Angel was at the precinct, *no one* was going to keep his appointment and take the chance of running into one of the precinct bulls. The only one of her missed appointments that worried her was Patch. She'd spent weeks trying to convince him at least to look into the sponsorship program she administered, only to have this happen when she'd finally gotten him to agree. Patch was so frail now that she didn't think the boy would survive another beating at the hands of his pimp.

"So how'd it go?" Jilly asked.

It took Angel a moment to focus on what she'd been asked. She took a sip of her coffee, relaxing as the warmth from the whiskey reached her stomach.

"We were lucky," she said. "It was Lou's shift. He made sure they went easy on Robbie when they took our statements. They've got an APB out on Macaulay."

"Robbie. He's the skinny little peacenik that looks like a skinhead?"

Angel smiled. "That's one way of putting it. There's no way he could have killed Everett."

"How *did* Everett die?"

"He was stabbed to death—a half-dozen times at least."

Jilly shivered. "They didn't find the knife?"

"They didn't find the weapon and—I find this really odd—they didn't find Everett's boots either. Robbie says Macaulay took them so that Everett's ghost wouldn't be able to come after anyone." She shook her head. "I guess they just make them up when they haven't got anything better to do."

"Actually, it's a fairly old belief," Jilly said.

Angel took another sip of her whiskey-laced coffee to fortify herself against what was to come. For all her fine traits, and her unquestionable gifts as an artist, Jilly had a head filled with what could only charitably be called whimsy. Probably it was *because* she was an artist and had such a fertile imagination, Angel had eventually decided. Still, whatever the source, Jilly was ready to espouse the oddest theories at the drop of a hat, everything from Victorian-styled fairies living in refuse dumps to Bigfoot wandering through the Tombs.

Angel had learned long ago that arguing against them was a fruitless endeavor, but sometimes she couldn't help herself.

"Old," she said, "and true as well, I suppose."

"It's possible," Jilly said, plainly oblivious to Angel's lack of belief. "I mean, there's a whole literature of superstition surrounding footwear. The one you're talking about dates back hundreds of years and is based on the idea that shoes were thought to be connected with the life essence, the soul, of the person to whom they belonged. The shoes of murdered people were often buried separately to prevent hauntings. And sorcerers were known to try to persuade women to give them their left shoes. If the woman did, the sorcerer would have power over her."

"Sorcerers?" Angel repeated with a cocked eyebrow.

"Think what you want," Jilly told her, "but it's been documented in old witch trials."

"Really?"

"Well, it's been documented that they were accused of it," Jilly admitted.

Which wasn't quite the same thing as being true, Angel thought, but she kept the comment to herself.

Jilly put her feet up on a corner of Angel's desk and started to pick at the paint that freckled her fingernails. There always were smudges of paint on her clothes, or in her tangled hair. Jilly looked up to find Angel watching her work at the paint and shrugged unselfconsciously, a smile waking sparks of humor in her pale blue eyes that made them seem as electric as sapphires.

"So what're you going to do?" Jilly asked.

"Do? I'm not going to do anything. I'm a counselor, not a cop."

"But you could find Macaulay way quicker than the police could."

Angel nodded in agreement. "But what I do is based on trust—you know that. If I found Macaulay and turned him over to the police, even though it's just for questioning, who's going to trust me?"

"I guess."

"What I am going to do is have another talk with Robbie," Angel said. "He's taken all of this very badly."

"He actually liked Everett?"

Angel shook her head. "I don't think anyone liked Everett. I think it's got to do with finding the body. He's probably never seen a dead man before. I have, and I'm still feeling a little queasy."

She didn't mention that Robbie had seemed to be hiding something. That was Robbie's business, and even if he did share it with her, it would still be up to him who could know about it and who could not. She just prayed that he hadn't been any more involved in Everett's death than having stumbled upon the body.

"Actually," she said after a moment's hesitation, "there was another weird thing that happened tonight."

Although she knew she'd regret it, because it was putting a foot into the strange world Jilly inhabited, where fact mixed equally with fantasy, she told Jilly about her dream. As Angel had expected, Jilly accepted what she was told as though it were an everyday occurrence.

"Has this ever happened to you before?" she asked.

Angel shook her head. "And I hope it never happens again. It's a really creepy feeling."

Jilly seemed to be only half-listening to her. Her eyes had narrowed thoughtfully. Chewing at her lower lip, she cocked her head and studied the ceiling. Angel didn't know what Jilly saw up there, but she doubted it was the cracked plaster that anybody else would see.

"I wonder what he wanted from you," Jilly finally said. Her gaze dropped and focused on Angel's. "There has to be a reason he sent his spirit to you."

Angel shook her head. "Haven't you ever dreamed that someone you know died?"

"Well, sure. But what's that—"

"And did they turn out to be dead when you woke?"

"No, but—"

"Coincidence," Angel said. "That's all it was. Plain and simple coincidence."

Jilly looked as though she was ready to argue the point, but then she simply shrugged.

"Okay," she said, swinging her feet down from the desk. "But don't say you weren't warned when Everett's spirit comes back to haunt you again. He wants something from you and the thing with ghosts is they can be patient forever. He'll keep coming back until you figure out what he wants you to do for him and you do it."

"Of course. Why didn't I think of that?"

"I'm serious, Angel."

Angel smiled. "I'll remember."

"I just bet you will," Jilly said, returning her smile. She stood up. "Well, I've got to run. I was in the middle of a new canvas when you called."

Angel rose to her feet as well. "Thanks for filling in."

"Like I said, it was no problem. The place was dead." Jilly grimaced as the word came out of her mouth. "Sorry about that. But at least a building doesn't have shoes to lose, right?"

After Jilly left, Angel returned to her desk with another spiked coffee. She stared out the window at Grasso Street where the first touch of dawn was turning the shadows to grey, unable to get Everett's stockinged feet out of her mind. Superimposed over it was an image of Everett in the rain, holding out a shadowed bundle towards her.

One real, one from a dream. Neither made sense, but at least the dream wasn't supposed to. When it came to Everett's boots, though . . .

She disliked the idea of someone believing superstitions almost as much as she did the superstitions themselves. Taking a dead man's shoes so he wouldn't come back seeking revenge. It was so patently ludicrous.

But Macaulay had believed enough to take them.

Angel considered Jim Macaulay. At nineteen, he was positively ancient compared to the street kids such as Robbie whose company he kept, though he certainly didn't look it. His cherubic features made him seem much younger. He'd been in and out of foster homes and juvie hall since he was seven, but the experiences had done little to curb his minor criminal ways, or his good humor. Macaulay always had a smile, even when he was being arrested.

Was he good for Everett's murder? Nothing in Macaulay's record pointed to it. His crimes were always nonviolent: B&Es, minor drug dealing, trafficking in stolen goods. Nothing to indicate that he'd suddenly upscaled to murder. And where was the motive? Everett had carried nothing of value on his person—probably never had—and everyone knew it. And while it was true he'd been a royal pain in the ass, the street people just ignored him when he got on a rant.

But then why take the boots?

If Macaulay believed the superstition, why would he be afraid of Everett coming after him unless he *had* killed him?

Too tired to go home, Angel put her head down on the desk and stared out the window. She dozed off, still worrying over the problem.

Nothing has changed in her dream.

The rain continues to mist. Everett approaches her again, no less graceful, while she remains trapped in the weight of her flesh. The need is still there in Everett's eyes, the mysterious bundle still cradled against his chest as he comes up to her. But this time she finds enough of her voice to question him.

Why is he here in her dream?

"For the children," he says.

It seems such an odd thing for him to say: Everett, who's never had a kind word for anyone, so far as Angel knows.

"What do you mean?" she asks him.

But then he tries to hand the bundle to her and she wakes up again.

Angel sat up with a start. She was disoriented for a long moment—as much by her surroundings as from the dream—before she recognized the familiar confines of her office and remembered falling asleep at her desk.

She shook her head and rubbed at her tired eyes. Twice in the same night. She had to do something about these hours, but knew she never would.

The repetition of the dream was harder to set aside. She could almost hear Jilly's voice, I-told-you-so plain in its tone.

Don't say you weren't warned when Everett's spirit comes back to haunt you again.

But it had been just a dream.

He wants something from you, and the thing with ghosts is they can be patient forever.

A disturbing dream. That shadowed bundle Everett kept trying to hand to her and his enigmatic reply, "For the children."

He'll keep coming back until you figure out what it is he wants you to do for him and you do it.

She didn't need this, Angel thought. She didn't want to become part of Jilly's world, where the rules of logic were thrown out the door and nothing made sense anymore. But this dream . . . and Macaulay taking those damn boots. . . .

She remembered Jilly asking her what she was going to do and what her own reply had been. She still didn't want to get involved. Her job was helping the kids, not playing cop. But the image of the dream-Everett flashed in her mind, the need in his eyes and what he'd said when she'd asked him why he was there in her dream.

For the children.

Whether she wanted it or not, she realized that she was involved now. Not in any way that made sense, but indiscriminately, by pure blind chance, which seemed even less fair. It certainly wasn't because she and Everett had been friends. For God's sake, she'd never even *liked* Everett.

For the children.

Angel sighed. She picked up her mug and looked down at the cold mixture of whiskey and coffee. She started to call Jilly, but hung up before she'd finished dialing the number. She knew what Jilly would say.

Grimacing, she drank what was left in her mug, then left her office in search of an answer.

Macaulay had a squat in the same abandoned tenement where Robbie lived, just a few blocks north of Angel's office on the edge of the Tombs. Angel squinted at the building, then made her way across the rubble-strewn lot that sided the tenement. The front door was boarded shut, so she went around the side and climbed in through a window the way the building's illegal inhabitants did. Taking a moment to let her eyes adjust to the dimmer light inside, she listened to the silence that surrounded her. Whoever was here today, was obviously asleep.

She knew Macaulay's squat was on the top floor, so she found the stairwell by the boarded-up entrance and climbed the two flights to the third floor. She looked in through the doorways as she passed by the rooms, heart aching with what she saw. Squatters, mostly kids, were curled up in sleeping bags, under blankets or in nests of newspaper. What were they going to do when winter came and the coolness of late summer nights dropped below the freezing mark?

Macaulay's room was at the end of the hall, but he wasn't in. His squat had a door, unlike most of the other rooms, but it stood ajar. Inside it was tidier than Angel had expected. Clean, too. There was a mattress in one corner with a neatly-folded sleeping bag and pillow on top. Beside it was an oil lamp, sitting on the wooden floor, and a tidy pile of spare clothes. Two crates by the door held a number of water-swelled paperbacks with their covers removed. On another crate stood a Coleman stove, a frying pan and some utensils. Inside the crate was a row of canned goods while a cardboard box beside it served to hold garbage.

And then there were the shoes.

Although Angel didn't know Macaulay's shoe size, she doubted that any of them would fit him. She counted fifteen pairs, in all shapes and sizes, from a toddler's tiny sneakers to a woman's spike-heeled pumps. They were lined up against the wall in a neat row, a miniature mountain range, rising and falling in height, with Everett's bizarre boots standing like paired peaks at the end closest to the door.

It was a perfectly innocent sight, but Angel felt sick to her stomach as she stood there looking at them. They were all the shoes of children and women—except for Everett's. Had Macaulay killed all of their—

"Angel."

She turned to find him standing in the doorway. With the sun coming through the window, making his blonde hair look like a halo, he might have been describing himself as much as calling her name. Her gaze shifted to the line of shoes along the wall, then back to his face. His blue eyes were guileless.

Angel forwent the amenities.

"These . . . these shoes . . . ?" she began.

"Shoes carry the imprint of our souls upon their own," he replied. He paused, then added, "Get it?"

All she was getting was a severe case of the creeps. What had she been thinking to come here on her own? She hadn't told anyone where she was going. Her own hightops could be joining that line of shoes, set in place beside Everett's.

Get out while you can, she told herself, but all she could do was ask, "Did you kill him?"

"Who? Everett?"

Angel nodded.

"Do I look like a killer to you?"

No, he looked as though he was on his way to mass—not to confess, but to sing in the choir. But the shoes, something about the way the shoes stood in their tidy, innocuous line, said differently.

"Why did you take them?"

"You're thinking they're souvenirs?"

"I . . . I don't know what to think."

"So don't," he said with a shrug, then disconcertingly changed the subject. "Well, it's a good thing you're here. I was just going out to look for you."

"Why?"

"Something terrible's happened to Robbie."

The flatness of his voice was completely at odds with his choir-boy appearance. Angel's gaze dropped to his hands, but they were empty. She'd been expecting to see him holding Robbie's shoes.

"What . . . ?"

"You'd better come see."

He led the way down to the second floor, on the other side of the building, then stood aside at the open door to Robbie's room. It was as cluttered as Macaulay's was tidy, but Angel didn't notice that as she stepped inside. Her gaze was drawn and riveted to the small body hanging by a rope from the overhead light fixture. It turned slowly, as though Robbie's death throes were just moments past. On the floor under him, a chair lay on its side.

Angel turned to confront Macaulay, but he was gone. She stepped out into the hallway to find it empty. Part of her wanted to run him down, to shake the angelic smugness from his features, but she made herself go back into Robbie's room. She righted the chair and stood on it. Taking her pen knife from the back pocket of her jeans, she held Robbie against her as she sawed away at the rope. When the rope finally gave, Robbie's dead weight proved to be too much for her and he slipped from her arms, landing with a thud on the floor.

She jumped down and straightened his limbs. Forcing a finger between the rope and his neck, she slowly managed to loosen the pressure and remove the rope. Then, though she knew it was too late, though his skin was already cooling, she attempted CPR. While silently counting between breaths, she called for help, but no one stirred in the building around her. Either they were sleeping too soundly, or they just didn't want to get involved. Or maybe, a macabre part of her mind suggested, Macaulay's already killed them all. Maybe she hadn't walked by sleeping runaways and street kids on her way to Macaulay's room, but by their corpses. . . .

She forced the thought out of her mind, refusing to let it take hold.

She worked until she had no more strength left. Slumping against a nearby wall, she stared at the body, but couldn't see it for the tears in her eyes.

It was a long time before she could get to her feet. When she left Robbie's room, she didn't go downstairs and leave the building to call the police. She went upstairs, to Macaulay's room. Every room she passed was empty, the sleeping figures all woken and fled. Macaulay's room was empty as well. It looked the same as it had earlier, with one difference. The sleeping bag and the clothes were gone. The line of shoes remained.

Angel stared at them for a long time before she picked up Everett's boots. She carried them with her when she left the building and stopped at the nearest pay phone to call the police.

There was no note, but the coroner ruled it a suicide. But there was still an APB out on Macaulay, and no longer only in connection with Everett's death. Two of the pairs of shoes found in his squat were identified as belonging to recent murder victims; they could only assume that the rest did as well. The police had never connected the various killings, Lou told Angel later, because the investigations were handled by so many different precincts and, other than the missing footwear, the M.O. in each case was completely different.

Behind his cherubic features, Macaulay proved to have been a monster.

What Angel didn't understand was Robbie's suicide. She wouldn't let it go and finally, after a week of tracking down and talking to various street kids, she began to put together another picture of Macaulay. He wasn't just a killer; he'd also made a habit of molesting the street kids with whom he kept company. Their sex made no difference—just the younger the better. Coming from his background, Macaulay was a classic case of "today's victim becoming tomorrow's predator"—a theorem put forth by Andrew Vachss, a New York lawyer specializing in juvenile justice and child abuse with whom Angel had been in correspondence.

Even more startling was the realization that Macaulay probably hadn't killed Everett for whatever his usual reasons were, but because Everett had tried to help Robbie stand up to Macaulay. In a number of recent conversations Angel had with runaways, she discovered that Everett had often given them money he'd panhandled, or shown them safe places to flop for a night.

Why Everett had needed to hide this philanthropic side of himself, no one was ever going to find out, but Angel thought she now knew why Robbie had killed himself: It wasn't just the shame of being abused—a shame that kept too many victims silent—but because Everett had died trying to protect him. For the sweet soul that Robbie had been, Angel could see how he would be unable to live with himself after what had happened that night.

But the worst was that Macaulay was still free. Two weeks after Everett's death, he still hadn't been apprehended. Lou didn't hold out much hope of finding him.

"A kid like that," he told Angel over lunch the following Saturday, "he can just disappear into the underbelly of any big city. Unless he gets picked up someplace and they run his sheet, we might never hear from him again."

Angel couldn't face the idea of Macaulay in some other city, killing, sexually abusing the runaways on its streets, protected by his cherubic features, his easy smile, his guileless eyes.

"All we can hope," Lou added, "is that he picks himself the wrong victim next time—someone meaner than he is, someone quicker with a knife—so that when we do hear about him again, he'll be a number on an ID tag in some morgue."

"But this business of his taking his victims' shoes," Angel said.

"We've put it on the wire. By this time, every cop in the country has had their duty sergeant read it to them at roll call."

And that was it. People were dead. Kids already feeling hopeless carried new scars. She had a dead man visiting her in her dreams, demanding she do she didn't know what. And Macaulay went free.

Angel couldn't let it go at that, but there didn't seem to be anything more that she could do.

All week long, as soon as she goes to sleep, Everett haunts her dreams.

"I know what you were really like," she tells him. "I know you were trying to help the kids in your own way."

For the children.

"And I know why Macaulay killed you."

He stands in the misting rain, the need still plain in his eyes, the curious bundle held against his chest. He doesn't try to approach her anymore. He just stands there, half swallowed in mist and shadow, watching her.

"What I don't know is what you want from me."

The rain runs down his cheeks like tears.

"For God's sake, *talk* to me."

But all he says is, "Do it for the children. Not for me. For the children."

"Do *what?*"

But then she wakes up.

Angel dropped by Jilly's studio on that Sunday night. Telling Jilly she just wanted some company, for a long time she simply sat on the Murphy bed and watched Jilly paint.

"It's driving me insane," she finally said. "And the worst thing is, I don't even believe in this crap."

Jilly looked up from her work and pushed her hair back from her eyes, leaving a streak of Prussian blue on the errant locks.

"Even when you dream about him every night?" she asked.

Angel sighed. "Who knows what I'm dreaming, or why."

"Everett does," Jilly said.

"Everett's dead."

"True."

"And he's not telling."

Jilly laid down her brush and came over to the bed. Sitting down beside Angel, she put an arm around Angel's shoulders and gave her a comforting hug.

"This doesn't have to be scary," she said.

"Easy for you to say. This is all old hat for you. You like the fact that it's real."

"But—"

Angel turned to her. "I don't want to be part of this other world. I don't *want* to be standing at the checkout counter and have to seriously consider which of the headlines are real and which aren't. I can't deal with that. I can barely deal with this . . . this haunting."

"You don't have to deal with anything except for Everett," Jilly told her. "Most people have a very effective defensive system against paranormal experiences. Their minds just automatically find some rational explanation for the unexplainable that allows them to put it aside and carry on with their lives. You'll be able to do the same thing. Trust me on this."

"But then I'll just be denying something that's real."

Jilly shrugged. "So?"

"I don't get it. You've been trying to convince me for years that stuff like this is real and now you say just forget it?"

"Not everybody's equipped to deal with it," Jilly said. "I just always thought you would be. But I was wrong to keep pushing at you about it."

"That makes me feel inadequate."

Jilly shook her head. "Just normal."

"There's something to be said for normal," Angel said.

"It's comforting," Jilly agreed. "But you do have to deal with Everett, because it doesn't look like he's going to leave you alone until you do."

Angel nodded slowly. "But do what? He won't tell me what he wants."

"It happens like that," Jilly said. "Most times spirits can't communicate in a straightforward manner, so they have to talk in riddles, or mime, or whatever. I think that's where all the obliqueness in fairy tales comes from: They're memories of dealing with real paranormal encounters."

"That doesn't help."

"I know it doesn't," Jilly said. She smiled. "Sometimes I think I just talk to hear my own voice." She looked across her studio to where finished paintings lay stacked against the wall beside her easel, then added thoughtfully, "I think I've got an idea."

Angel gave her a hopeful look.

"When's the funeral?" Jilly asked.

"Tomorrow. I took up a collection and raised enough so that Everett won't have to be buried in a pauper's grave."

"Well, just make sure Everett's buried with his boots on," Jilly told her.

"That's *it?*"

Jilly shrugged. "It scared Macaulay enough to take them, didn't it?"

"I suppose. . . ."

For all she's learned about his hidden philanthropic nature, she still feels no warmth towards the dead man. Sympathy, yes. Even pity. But no warmth.

The need in his eyes merely replaces the anger they wore in life; it does nothing to negate it.

"You were buried today," she says. "With your boots on."

The slow smile on the dead man's face doesn't fit well. It seems more a borrowed expression than one his features ever knew. For the first time in over a week, he approaches her again.

"A gift," he says, offering up the newspaper-wrapped bundle. "For the children."

For the children.

He's turned into a broken record, she thinks, stuck on one phrase.

She watches him as he moves into the light. He peels away the soggy newspaper, then holds up Macaulay's severed head. He grips it by the haloing blonde hair, a monstrous, bloody artifact that he thrusts into her face.

Angel woke screaming. She sat bolt upright, clutching the covers to her chest. She had no idea where she was. Nothing looked right. Furniture loomed up in unfamiliar shapes, the play of shadows was all wrong. When a hand touched her shoulder, she flinched and screamed again, but it was only Jilly.

She remembered then, sleeping over, going to bed, late, late on that Sunday night, each of them taking a side of the Murphy bed.

"It's okay," Jilly was telling her. "Everything's okay."

Slowly, Angel felt the tension ease, the fear subside. She turned to Jilly and then had to smile. Jilly had been a street kid once—she was one of Angel's success stories. Now it seemed it was payback time, their roles reversed.

"What happened?" Jilly asked.

Angel trembled, remembering the awful image that had sent her screaming from her dream. Jilly couldn't suppress her own shivers as Angel told her about it.

"But at least it's over," Jilly said.

"What do you mean?"

"Everett's paid Macaulay back."

Angel sighed. "How can you *know* that?"

"I don't know it for sure. It just feels right."

"I wish everything was that simple," Angel said.

The phone rang in Angel's office at mid-morning. It was Lou on the other end of the line.

"Got some good news for you," he said.

Angel's pulse went into double-time.

"It's Macaulay," she said. "He's been found, hasn't he? He's dead."

There was a long pause before Lou asked, "Now how the hell did you know that?"

"I didn't," Angel replied. "I just hoped that was why you were calling me."

It didn't really make anything better. It didn't bring Robbie back, or take away the pain that Macaulay had inflicted on God knew how many kids. But it helped.

Sometimes her dreams still take her to that street where the neon signs and streetlights turn a misting rain into a carnival of light and shadow.

But the dead man has never returned.

Bird Bones and Wood Ash

*It's a wonder we don't dissolve
in our own bath water.*
—attributed to Pablo Picasso

1

At first, Jaime knows them only as women with the faces of animals: mare and deer, wild boar and bear, raven and toad. And others. So many others. Following her.

They smell like forest loam and open field, like wild apple blossoms and nuts crushed underfoot. Their arms are soft, but their hands are callused and hard, the palms like leather. Where they have been, they leave behind a curious residue of dried blood and rose petals, tiny bird bones and wood ashes.

In those animal faces, their eyes are disconcertingly human, but not mortal. They are eyes that have seen decades pass as we see years, that have looked upon Eden and Hades. And their voices, at times a brew of dry African veldt whispers and sweet-toned crystal bells, or half-mad, like coyotes and loons, one always rising above the others, looping through the clutter of city sound, echoing and ringing in her mind, heard only from a distance.

They never come near, they simply follow her, watching, figments of post-traumatic stress, she thinks, until they begin to leave their fetish residue in her apartment, in her car, on her pillow. They finally approach her in the graveyard, when the mourners are all gone and she's alone by Annie's grave, the mound of raw earth a sharp blade that has already left a deep scar inside her.

They give her no choice, the women. When they touch her, when they make known their voiceless need, she tells them she's already made the choice, long before they came to her.

All she lacked was the means.

"We will give you the means," one of them says.

She thinks it's the one with the wolf's head who spoke. There are so many of them, it's hard to keep track, all shapes and sizes, first one in sharp focus, then another, but never all at the same time. One like a woodcock shifts nervously from foot to foot. The rabbit woman has a nose that won't stop twitching. The one like a salmon has gills in her neck that open and close rhythmically as though the air is water.

She must have stepped into a story, she thinks—one of Annie's stories, where myths mingle with the real world and the characters never quite know which is which. Annie's stories were always about the people, but the mythic figures weren't just there to add color. They created the internal resonance of the stories, brought to life on the inner landscapes of the characters.

"It's a way of putting emotions on stage," Annie explained to her once. "A way of talking about what's going on inside us without bogging the story down with all kinds of internal dialogue and long-winded explanations. The anima are so . . . immediate."

If she closes her eyes she can picture Annie sitting in the old Morris chair by the bay window, the sunlight coming in through the window, making a pre-Raphaelite halo around the tangle of her long hennaed hair as she leans her chin on a hand and speaks.

"Or maybe it's just that I like them," Annie would add, that pixie smile of hers sliding across her lips, her eyes luminous with secrets.

Of course she would, Jaime thinks. She'd like the animal women, too.

Jaime isn't so sure that she does, but she doesn't really question the women's presence—or rather the reality of their presence. Since Annie's death, nothing is as it was. The surreal seems normal. The women don't so much make her nervous as cause her to feel unbalanced, as though the world underfoot has changed, reality curling sideways into a skein of dreams.

But if the women are real, if they can help . . .

"I'll do it," she tells them. "I'll do it for Annie."

The rat-snake woman sways her head from side to side. Her human eyes have yellow pupils, unblinking in her scaled features.

"This is not about the storyteller," she says.

"It is for all those who have need of a strong mother," explains the wild boar, lisping around her tusks.

The ground seems more unbalanced than ever underfoot. Jaime puts out a hand and steadies herself on a nearby headstone. Annie's neighbor now. The scar inside is still so raw that it's all Jaime can do to blink back the tears.

"I don't understand," she tells them. "If it's not about Annie, then why have you come to me?"

"Because you are strong," the raven says.

"Because of your need," the salmon adds.

The mountain lion bares her fangs in a predatory grin.

"Because you will never forgive them," she says.

She lays her hand on Jaime's arm. The rough palm is warm and has the give of a cat's paw. Something invisible flickers between them—more than the warmth: a glow, a spark, a fire. Jaime's eyes widen and she takes a sharp breath. The lioness's gift burns in her chest, in her heart, in her belly, in her mind. It courses through her veins, drums in her temples, sets every nerve end quivering.

One by one, the others approach. They hold her in their soft arms, touch her hands with their callused palms. Fairy godmothers in animal guises, bestowing their gifts.

2

It's a night in late July and Karl thinks he's dreaming.

He's in that private place inside his head where everything is perfect. He doesn't have to be careful here. He can be as rough as he likes, he can leave a roadmap of bruises and cuts and welts, he can do any damn thing he wants and it doesn't make a difference because it's just in his head. He doesn't have to worry about his wife finding out, about what a neighbor or a teacher might say. Nobody's going to come around asking awkward questions because it's just in his head.

Here he's hard forever and children do exactly what he tells them to do or he punishes them. How he punishes them.

Tonight's scenario has his youngest daughter tied to her bed. He's just come into the room and he's shaking his head.

"You've been a bad, bad girl, Judy," he tells her.

When she starts to cry, he brings his hand out from behind his back. He doesn't own a belt like this anywhere except for in his private place. The leather is thick, so thick the belt can barely bend, and covered with large metal studs.

Karl's problem is that it's not his daughter there on the bed tonight. He just doesn't know it yet.

I only caught the tail end of what really happened in Judy's bedroom earlier tonight. I heard her crying. I saw him zipping up his pants. I heard him remind her how if she ever told anybody about their special secret that bad people would take her and her sister away and put them in a horrible prison for bad girls. How they'd have to stay there forever and it would break their mother's heart and she would probably die.

I wanted to kill him right then and there, but I waited. I clung to the side of the tenement's wall and shivered with anger, but I've learned how to be patient. I've found a less messy way to deal with the monsters. I don't do it for them; I do it for those who are left behind. To save them the trauma of waking to find their loving husband/father/boyfriend/uncle disemboweled on the floor.

I wait until he's asleep, then I come in through his bedroom window. I pad over to the bed where he's lying beside his sleeping wife and step up, balancing my weight like a cat, so there's no give in the mattress, no indication at all that I'm crouched over the monster, hands free from their gloves, palms laid against his temples. The contact, skin to skin, makes me feel ill, but it lets me step into his private place.

It's only there, when he moves towards the bed with the belt, that I make myself known. I break the ropes tying my Judy-body to the bed as though they were tissue paper. When he looks at me he doesn't see a scared child's eyes anymore. He sees my eyes, the hot bear-rage, the unblinking snake-disdain, searing his soul.

And then I take him apart.

It's a tricky process, but I'm getting better at it with practice. The first few times

I left a vegetable behind and that's no good either. Some of these families can barely keep a roof over their heads, food in their stomachs. No way they can afford the chronic hospital care for the empty monster shells I left behind.

So I've refined the process, emasculating them, making it impossible for them ever to hurt anybody again, but still functional. Barely. Scared of everything, including their own shadow. But no more likely to regress to their former selves than I am to forgive them.

Karl's wife never wakes as I leave their bedroom through the window. I make it to the roof and I have to rest. It would be easier just to kill them, but I know this way is better. It leaves me feeling weak, with a tear in my soul as though I've lost a piece of myself. I think I leave something behind each time—more than that anima residue of dried blood and rose petals, bird bones and wood ash. I leave some part of myself that I'll never be able to regain. But it's worth it. I just have to think of the sleeping child and know that, for her, at least, the monster won't be returning.

I want a shower so bad it hurts, but the night's young and it's still full of monsters. That's what breaks my heart. There are always more monsters.

3

It's cold for a September night, colder still on the rooftop where I crouch, and the wind can find me so easily, but I don't feel the chill.

I used to laugh at the comic books Annie would read, all those impossibly proportioned characters running around in their long underwear, but I don't laugh anymore. The costumes make perfect sense now. My bodysuit has a slick black weave with enough give to let me move freely, but nothing that'll catch on a cornice or in someone's grip. The Thinsulate lining keeps me warm, even below zero. Black gloves, lined hood and runners complete the outfit. Makes me look like one of those B-movie ninjas, but I don't care. It gets the job done.

I draw the line at a cape.

I never read superhero comics when I was a kid—not because they seemed such a guy thing, but because I just couldn't believe in them. I had the same questions for Superman as I did for God: If he was so powerful, why didn't he deal with some real problems? Why didn't he stop wars, feed the starving in Ethiopia, cure cancer? At least God had the Church to do His PR work for Him—if you can buy their reasoning, they have any number of explanations ranging from how the troubles of this life build character to that inarguable catchall, "God's will." And the crap in this life sure makes heaven look good.

When I was growing up, the writers and artists of Superman never even tried to deal with the problem. And since they didn't, I could only see Superman as a monster, not a hero. I couldn't believe his battles with criminals, superpowered geniuses and the like.

I never believed in God either.

If my business wasn't so serious, I'd have to laugh to see myself wearing this getup now, climbing walls like a spider, all my senses heightened; faster, stronger, and more agile than a person has any right to be. It's like—remember the story of Gwion, when he's stirring Cerridwen's potion and it bubbles up and scorches him? He licks off those three drops, and suddenly he can understand the languages of animals and birds, he has all this understanding of the connections that make up the world, and he can change his shape into anything he wants—which proves useful when Cerridwen goes after him.

That's pretty well the way it is for me, except that I can't change my shape. What I've got are the abilities of the totem-heads the anima wore when they came to me. I just wish my fairy godmothers had made me a little smarter while they were at it. Then I wouldn't be in this mess.

I think I've figured out where they came from. I used to work for *The Newford Examiner*—I guess that makes me more like Superman than the Bat-guy, isn't that another laugh? And I guess I just blew any chance of maintaining a secret identity by revealing that much. Not that it matters. I was always pretty much a loner until I met Annie, and then most of our friends were hers. I liked them all well enough, but without our link with Annie, we've just kind of drifted apart. As for my family, well, they pretty much disowned me when I came out.

So I was working for *The Examiner,* and before you ask, it's true: We make up most of the stories. Our editor starts with a headline like "Please Adopt My Pig-Faced Son" and the writers take it from there. But sometimes we let other people make it up for us. You wouldn't believe the calls and letters that paper would get.

Anyway, a few months before Annie died, I find myself up in the mountains, interviewing this old hillbilly woman who claims to have a fairy ring on her property—you know, one of those places where the Little People are supposed to gather for dances at night? I'd brought Annie with me because she wouldn't stay home once I told her where I was going.

The interview goes a little strange—not the strange that's par for the course whenever I've been out in the field interviewing one of our loyal readers with her own take on the wild and the wacky, but strange in how it starts to make sense. Maybe it's because Annie's with me and fairy tales are her bread and butter. I don't know. But the fairy ring is amazing.

It's deep in the woods behind the old lady's trailer, this Disneylike glade surrounded by enormous old trees, with grass that's only growing about an inch high—naturally; I check to see if it's been cut and it hasn't—and the mushrooms. They form a perfect circle in the middle of the glade. These big, fat, umbrella-capped toadstools, creamy colored with blood-red spots on them standing anywhere from a foot to a foot-and-a-half high. The grass inside the mushroom ring is a dark, dark green.

I know, from having read up on them before coming out to do the interview, that fairy rings are due to the growth of certain fungi below the surface. The spawn of the fungi radiates out from the center at a similar rate every year, which is how the ring widens. The darker grass is due to the increased nitrogen produced by the fungus.

None of which explains the feeling I get from the place. Or the toadstools. The last time I saw one like that was when I was still in Brownies—you know the one the owl sits on?

"Do you have to believe in the fairies to see them?" Annie asks.

"Land's sakes, no," Betsy tells her.

She's this beautiful old woman, kind of gangly and pretty thin, but still robust and a real free spirit. I can't believe she's pushing eighty-two.

"They have to believe in you," she explains.

Annie nods like she understands, but the two of them have lost me.

"What do you mean?" I ask.

I'm not even remembering to take notes anymore.

"It's like this," Betsy says. "You don't think of them as prissy little creatures with wings. That's plain wrong. They're earth spirits—and they don't really have shapes of their own; they just show up looking the way we expect them to look. Could be you'll see 'em as your Tinkerbells, or maybe they'll come to you looking like those Japanese robot toys that my grandson likes so much."

"But the fairy ring," I say. "That's just like in the stories. . . ."

"I didn't say the stories were all lies."

"So. . . ." I pause, trying to put it all together—for myself now, never mind the interview. "What is it that you're saying? What do these earth spirits do?"

"They don't *do* anything. They just are. Mostly they mind their own business, just like we mind ours. But sometimes we catch their attention and that's when you have to be careful."

Annie doesn't say anything.

"Of what?" I ask.

"Of what you're thinking when you're around them. They like to give gifts, but when they do hand 'em out, it's word for word. Sometimes, what you're asking for isn't what you really want."

At my puzzled look Betsy goes on.

"They give you what you really want," she says. "And that can hurt, let me tell you."

I stand there, the jaded reporter, and I can't help but believe. I find myself wondering what it was that she asked for and what it was that she got.

After a while, Betsy and Annie start back towards the trailer, but I stay behind for a few moments longer, just drinking in the feel of the place. It's so . . . so innocent. The way the world was when you were a kid, before it turned all crazy-cruel and confusing. Everybody loses their innocence sooner or later; for me and Annie it was sooner.

Standing there, I feel like I'm in the middle of a fairy tale. I forget about what Betsy has just been telling us. I think about lost innocence and just wish that it doesn't have to be that way for kids, you know? That they could *be* kids for as long as possible before the world sweeps them away.

I think that's why they came to me after Annie died. They mourn that lost innocence, too. They came to me, because with Annie gone, I have no real ties to the world anymore, nothing to hold me down. I guess they just figured that, with their gifts, I'd head out into the world and do what I could to make things right; that I'd make the perfect fairy crusader.

They weren't wrong.

The trouble is, when you can do the things I can do now, you get cocky. And in this business, cocky means stupid.

Crouching there on the rooftop, all I can find myself thinking about is another bit of fairy lore.

"The way it works," Annie told me once, explaining one of her stories that I didn't get, "is that there's always a price. Nothing operates in a vacuum: not relationships, not the ecology, and especially not magic. That's what keeps everything in balance."

If there's got to be a price paid tonight, I tell the city skyline, let it be me that pays it.

I don't get any answer, but then I'm not expecting one. All I know is that it's time to get this show on the road.

4

It starts to go wrong around the middle of August, when I meet this guy on the East Side.

His name's Christopher Dennison and he works for Social Services, but I don't find that out until later. First time I see him, he's walking through the dark back alleys of the Barrio, talking in this real loud voice, having a conversation, except there's no one with him. He's tall, maybe a hundred-and-seventy pounds, and not bad looking. Clean white shirt and jeans, red windbreaker. Nikes. Dressed pretty well for a loser, which is what I figure he must be, going on the way he is.

I dismiss him as one more inner-city soul who's lost it, until I hear what it is that he's saying. Then I follow along above him, a shadow ghosting from roof to roof while he makes his way through the refuse and crap that litters the ground below. When he pauses under some graffito that reads praise god for aids, I make my way down a fire escape.

I want to tear out the heart of whoever spray-painted those words, but they're long gone, so I concentrate on the guy instead. I can see perfectly in the dark and my hearing's nothing to be ashamed of either. The wind changes and his scent comes to me. He's wearing some kind of cologne, but it's faint. Or maybe it's aftershave. I don't smell any fear.

"I just want to know how you do it," he's saying. "I've got a success rate of maybe one in thirty, but you . . . you're just shutting them down, right, left and center. And it sticks. I can tell when it's going bad. Can't always do something about it, but I can tell. The ones you help stay helped."

He's talking about me. He's talking *to* me. I don't get the impression he knows what I am—or even who I am and what exactly it is that I can do—but he knows there's something out in the city, taking back the night for those who aren't strong or old enough to do it for themselves. I've been so careful—I didn't think anybody had picked up on it yet.

"Let me in on the secret," he goes on. "I want to help. I can bring you names and addresses."

I let the silence hang for long moments. City silence. We can hear traffic from the street, the vague presences of TVs and stereos coming out of nearby windows, someone yelling at someone, a siren, but it's blocks away.

"So who died and made you my manager?" I finally say.

I hear his pulse quicken. His sudden nervousness is a sharp sting in my nostrils, but he's pretty quick at recovering. He looks above him, trying to spot me, but I'm just one more shadow in a dark alley, invisible.

"So you are real," he says.

A point for him, I think. He didn't *know* until I just confirmed it for him. How many nights has he been walking through these kinds of neighborhoods, talking to the night this way, wondering if he'll make contact or if he's just chasing a dream?

I make a deliberate noise coming down the fire escape and sit down near the bottom of it so that our heads are almost level. His heart rate quickens again, but settles fast.

"I wasn't sure," he says after I've sat there for a while not saying anything.

I've decided that I've already said enough. I'll let him do the talking. I'm in no hurry. I've got all night. I've got the rest of my life.

"Do you, ah, have a name?" he asks.

I give him nothing back.

"I mean, what do people call you?"

This is getting ridiculous.

"What?" I say. "Like the Masked Avenger?"

He takes a step closer and I tense up, but whether I'll fight back or flee if he comes at me, I'm not sure yet. The cat anima left me with a lot of curiosity.

"You're a woman," he says.

Shit. That's another bit of freebie information I've given him. I feel like just taking off, but it's too late now. I'm intrigued. I have to know what he wants from me.

"My name's Chris," he says. "Chris Dennison. I work with Social Services."

"So?"

"I want to help you."

"Why?"

He shakes his head. "Christ, you have to ask that? We're in the middle of a war and the freaks are winning—isn't that enough of a reason?"

I think of the child waiting in the dark for a boogieman that's all too real to come into her bedroom. I think of the woman whose last bruises have yet to heal, thrown across the kitchen, kicked and beaten. I think of the boy, victimized since he was an infant, turning on those weaker than himself because that's all he knows, because that's the only way he can regain any kind of self-empowerment.

It's not a war, it's a slaughter. Fought not just physically, but in the soul as well. It's about the loss of innocence. The loss of dignity and self-respect.

"What is it that you do to them?" he asks.

I don't know how to explain it. Using the abilities with which the anima have gifted me, I could literally tear the monsters apart, doesn't matter how big and strong they are—or think they are. But I don't. Instead, I pay them back, tit for tat.

But *how* do I do it? I'm not sure myself. I just know that it works. I look at this Boy Scout standing there, waiting for an answer, but I don't think he's ready to hear what I have to say, how everyone has a dreaming place inside them, a secret, private place that defines them. It's what I learned from Annie's stories. I just put that knowledge to a different use than I think Annie ever would have imagined someone could.

"I turn them off," I say finally. "I go into their heads and just turn them off."

He looks confused and I don't blame him.

"But how?" he asks.

I can tell it's not just curiosity that's driving him. What he wants is a weapon for his war—one that's more efficient than any he's had to work with so far.

"It's too weird," I tell him.

"I'm not a stranger to weird shit."

I'm not sure I want to get into wherever that came from.

"How did you figure out that I existed?" I asked to change the subject.

He takes the bait.

"I started to notice a drop of activity in some of our more habitual offenders," he says. "You know, cases where we're trying to prove that there's good reason to make the child a ward of the court, but we're still building up the evidence?"

I didn't, but I gave him an encouraging nod.

"It was weird," he goes on. "I mean we get more recants than we do testimony anyway, but when I investigated these particular cases I found that the offenders really *had* changed. Completely. I didn't make any kind of a connection, though, until I was interviewing a six-year-old boy named Peter. His mother's boyfriend had been molesting him on a regular basis, and we were working on getting a court order to deny the man access to the child and his mother as a forerunner to hopefully laying some charges.

"The mother was working with us—she was scared to death, if you want the truth, and was grasping at straws. She claimed she'd do anything to get out of this relationship. And then she suddenly retracted her offer to testify. The boyfriend had changed. He was good as gold now. Peter confirmed it when I interviewed him. He was the one who told me that he'd quote, 'seen a ninja angel who'd stolen away all of the boyfriend's badness.' "

I remembered Peter. He'd come into the room and caught me as I was getting up from his mother's bed, putting on my gloves. I almost bolted, but I didn't want to leave a different kind of night fear in the little tyke's head, so I told him what I'd done, couching the information in words I thought he'd understand. He'd been really brave and hadn't cried at all.

"He said he'd keep the secret," I say.

"Give the kid a break. He's only six."

I nod.

"Anyway," Chris says, "something clicked for me then. It seemed . . . well, impossible, but I couldn't stop thinking about it. What if there really *was* someone out there that could do what Peter had said his angel had done? I've been fighting the freaks for years with hardly anything to show for it. It's heartbreaking work."

I nod again. I've got a hundred percent success rate myself, but there's only so many places I can be at one time. I know all about heartbreak.

"I felt like a fool walking around out here, trying to get your attention, but I just had to know. And if it *was* real, I wanted a part of it."

I think of the anima that came to me all those long months ago.

"It's not something that can be shared," I tell him.

"But I can help, can't I?"

"I don't think that's such a good—"

"Look," he breaks in. "How do you figure out who to hit? I'll bet you just skulk around outside windows, hoping to get lucky. Am I right?"

Too right, but I don't answer.

"I can provide you with names and addresses," he says.

I remember him saying that earlier. It's part of what drew me down from the rooftops to hear him out.

"You won't have to waste your time guessing anymore," he goes on, voice so damn eager. "With what I give you, you can go right to the *known* offenders. Just think of how much more effective you can be."

It's tempting. Oh, who am I kidding? It's another gift, as unexpected, but as welcome, as those the anima gave me.

"Okay," I tell him. "We'll give it a try."

I barely get the words out of my mouth, then he's dragging a folded sheet of paper out of the pocket of his jacket.

"These are just some of the worst, ongoing situations that we've got on file," he begins.

My heart sinks. There must be fifty names and addresses on that one piece of paper.

So many monsters.

5

The relationship works better than I think it might. I was working blind before, hanging around on fire escapes and ledges outside windows, crawling down from rooftops, listening, watching, until I got a fix on one of the monsters. And even then I had to be careful. Not every domestic argument leads to spousal abuse. Not every child, crying in the lonely dark, has been molested.

I'm also careful with the tips I get from Chris. I may have taken on the roles of judge and jury, but I always make sure that I'm really dealing with a monster before I step into his head and turn him off. But Chris's information is usually good. We don't just use what he's collected on his own, either. He takes what we need from all the files in his office, his and the other caseworkers', as well as from Children's Aid and the like, to avoid suspicion falling on him the way it might if all the monsters I dealt with came from his caseload.

If Chris could make the connection, then so could someone else—someone perhaps not as sympathetic to my particular working methods. I've no idea how I'd deal with prison. I think the gifts of the anima would make it a thousand times worse for me. I think I'd rather die first.

A few weeks into our partnership, Chris asks me what got me started with all of this. I don't know what to say at first, but then I just tell him that I lost a good friend which leaves him with the impression that it's revenge motivating me. I let him believe that, even if it's not exactly true. What killed Annie isn't something anyone can fight against.

It's funny. I never think of Annie looking as she did when she died. It's like my mind's closed off the image of how frail she became toward the end. She was just skin and bones, a pale, pale ghost of herself lying there in the hospital ward. Chemotherapy had stolen that gorgeous head of hair, but she refused to wear a wig.

"This is who I am now," is all she'd say.

When I think of her, I see instead the woman I fell in love with. She could have been a model for one of those nineteenth-century painters whose work she so admired: Rosetti, Burne-Jones, Dixon—that crew. She was beautiful, but more importantly to me, she completed me. Until I was with Annie, I never felt whole. I was just an observer going through life, never a participant, which might be the reason I became a journalist.

I remember telling her that once and she just laughed.

"I don't think so, Jaime," she said. "If you really just wanted to report on life, you wouldn't have worked for *The Examiner*. I think, secretly, there's a novelist living inside you, just dying to get out. Why else would you be drawn to a job that has you making up such outlandish stories, day after day?"

Who knows what we secretly want—I mean, really, *seriously* want? I knew that with Annie I had everything I could ask for, so I had no more need for secrets. When I came out, it didn't raise an eyebrow among my coworkers. The only people who changed toward me were my family. Ex-family. Can you get a divorce from your flesh and blood? To all intents and purposes, I certainly have.

But that's okay. I was never close to them anyway. See, that's the real revenge motive that let me take the anima's gift: lost innocence.

Both my parents were alcoholics. I'm surprised I even survived some of the beatings I got as a kid. It was different for Annie. Instead of being beaten, her father started molesting her when she was in the cradle. The nightmare lasted until she was in her teens.

"What's scariest," she told me once, "is that I didn't even *know* it was wrong. It didn't feel right, but I never knew any different. I thought that was how it was in every family."

What are the statistics? I think it's something like two out of every three women have been sexually assaulted by the time they're in their twenties. Everything from being abused as children to being raped when they're older.

Lost innocence.

Somehow, Annie regained hers, but most people aren't that lucky. I know I never have.

But that's why I think of what I'm doing as something I'm doing for her. So many monsters, and I've barely made a dent in their numbers. I wish there was a way to get rid of them all in one fell swoop. I wish I could deal with them before the damage is done. It kills me that it's all ending for me before I've really gotten started with my work.

See, by the beginning of July my savings finally run out and I begin to lose the amenities because I can't pay my bills anymore. The phone goes first, then the power. By the time I meet Chris, I've lost my apartment.

So I become a baglady superhero—do they ever deal with that in those comics? I know I'm obsessed, but I don't have anything else to do with my life. It was bad enough when I was on my own, tracking the monsters down by trial and error. I'd deal with one, maybe two in a week—three tops. But now, with Chris's help, I can hit that same number on a good night.

I'm proud of what I'm doing, but it's starting to take its toll. That little piece of myself I was losing every time I dealt with one of the monsters has escalated to where now it feels as though what I'm losing is falling off the way clumps of dirt can be shaken from a piece of sod. The empty patches inside me just keep getting bigger. It's as though my spirit is dissolving, bit by bit. I stare down at the anima residue I leave on their beds and want to pick it up and somehow stick it back onto me. I'm so wasted come morning now that I don't care where I sleep—on a park bench, in an alleyway, in some deserted building.

Chris offers to put me up, but I don't want to get that close to him. I let him buy me meals, though. Left on my own, I forget to eat half the time. When I do remember, I'm usually scrounging something from one of the monsters' kitchens—now there's something that really helps your appetite. God.

The cramps start in September, and I begin to get these sudden spells of weakness so often that even Chris notices the change. I mean, he can't see much of me, all clothed in black and hiding in the shadows most of the time, but what he can see tells him I'm not well.

"Maybe we should ease off a bit," he says.

"I'm fine."

"You look like shit."

I know. I caught a reflection of myself in a window on my way to meet him tonight. All the meat was gone, leaving just corded animal muscles over the bones. The real emptiness is inside.

"I tell you I'm fine," I repeat, trying to convince myself as much as him. "What've you got for me tonight?"

"Nothing."

I don't even realize that the growl's rumbling in my chest until I smell the sudden sting of his fear. I force myself to calm down, but he still backs away from me.

"I'm sorry," I say and I mean it.

He nods slowly, but he keeps his distance.

"Okay," I tell him. "We'll take a break tonight. Just give me one name."

I don't know why I'm pressing him like this. I could do it on my own. Skulk around until I found a monster. I might get lucky, you never know. But I think later that I want his complicity in this. I want someone to know what I'm doing—not to feed my ego. Just to remember me when I'm gone.

"One name," he says.

"That's all."

Chris sighs. He tries to talk me out of it for a little while longer, but finally gives in. One name and address.

"This one's a little weird," he says as he hands it over. "It came in from the guidance counselor at Redding High. Something about it being a sensitive case, but I couldn't find anything in the file to say why."

"That's okay. I can handle it."

Mistake—but I don't blame him.

6

Grant Newman is awake, only I don't realize it. I pull myself in through his window, third story, nice part of town, and creep soundlessly across the hardwood floor to where he's lying. He's alone in his bed. I scouted around earlier and discovered that he and his wife have separate bedrooms. Makes it easier for when he wants to pay little Susan a night visit, I guess.

I slip up onto the bed and he grabs me. It happens so suddenly that I just freeze up in surprise. Then when I try to fight him, I can't find the strength to break free. It's not that the anima's gifts have worn off; it's that I'm worn out. I've left too many pieces of myself behind in too many monsters' lairs. The shock of my sudden helplessness makes me feel dizzy.

"What the hell've we got here?" Newman says as I struggle to break his grip.

My heightened sense of smell makes his bad breath seem worse than it must really be. I know that smell. It's the way my old man used to stink before he took the belt to me.

I try to get my legs up between us so that I can kick him, but he rolls me over and pins me to the bed with his knees.

"Some kind of little ninja fuck," he says. "So what's the deal? Yukio getting tired of paying me off?"

He reaches for my mask until his gaze locks onto my chest.

"Jesus," he says. "Your boss must be really getting hard up if he's running woman assassins now."

I'm gaunt these days, just muscle and bone and the muscles aren't working tonight. But the bodysuit still shows I'm a woman. For some men, that's excuse enough for anything. Maybe Newman thinks he's in his private place and anything goes. For all I know we *are* in his private place, and I've just lost control of the situation.

Newman forgets about the mask, and reaches for the zipper of my suit instead.

"I've never fucked a ninja before," he says. "This'll be something to—"

I'm the wolf with its leg in a trap, the bear that's been shot, the puma that's been harassed until it has its back to the wall. Panic whips my head forward and I close my teeth on his hand, biting through fingers, straight to the bone. I'll give him this: He doesn't scream. But the pain makes him loosen his grip.

I whip up a leg from behind him and manage to hook it around his neck. I pull him back, off of me, heaving myself up to help the momentum. He falls backward out of the bed and I'm out of there. I almost lose it in the window frame, but my adrenalin lets me catch my balance before I go tumbling three stories down to the pavement below. By the time Newman gets to the window, I'm two floors above his apartment, spidering my way up the wall and onto the roof.

I make the jump from his building to its neighbor, and then over one more before I collapse. The roof's covered with gravel, but I can barely feel it digging into my skin. Cramps pull me into a fetal position, and I've got the shakes so bad that my teeth start to rattle.

It's a long time before I calm down.

It's even longer before I'm scratching at Chris's window.

As I tell Chris about what happened, I start to remember things I saw in Newman's bedroom, things I hadn't noticed when I'd scouted the place out earlier.

"It's going to be okay," Chris tells me.

"But he's seen me."

By which I mean: Now the monsters know I exist.

"Don't worry," Chris says. "What's he going to do? All he saw was a masked woman. It's not like he can recognize you. It's not like there's any way he can find you. He's probably more scared of you than you are of him."

"I don't think so," I say.

On Newman's night table: The police-issue .38 in its well-worn holster. The billfold with the shape of a badge worn into the leather.

"Newman's a cop," I tell Chris.

I remember more: What he was saying about payoffs.

"A crooked cop," I add.

"Oh, shit."

We both know what can happen. Newman can have an APB put out on me. He can make up any old story he likes about why I'm wanted and they'll believe him. Christ, he can tell the truth and I'll still have every cop in the city out looking for me. The police don't take kindly to anyone assaulting one of their own.

I'm bone-tired, but I know what I have to do. Chris tries to stop me when I get up and head for the window, but I turn around and look at him.

"What else can I do?" I ask him.

"You're in no condition to—"

He's actually a really nice guy, even though he acts a bit too much like a mother. I can see why kids, even abused kids, like him and trust him.

"I know," I say. "But I don't have any choice."

I'm out the window before he can stop me. I make my way back across town to the roof of the building across from Newman's. The September wind's cold, but I can't feel it through my bodysuit. Don't need it to be chilled anyway. I've got a piece of ice inside me and that's what's making me shiver.

I know I should wait until I'm stronger, but I'm not so sure I'm ever going to get any stronger. I get the feeling that I'm wasting away, as inexorably as the cancer that took Annie.

I wait, crouching there on the rooftop, until I see the light in Newman's bedroom go off. I'm like a ghost coming down the side of the building and crossing the street. I don't feel strong, at least not physically. But I'm determined, and I hope that'll count for something.

7

When I get outside Newman's window, I realize he's not asleep. I can sense him sitting in a chair in the corner of the room, gun in hand, watching the window. He knew I'd be back.

So I go in through a window on the other side of the apartment. My entire being is focused on what I'm doing. Keeping silent. Staying strong—at least long enough to tidy up the mess I've made of things. His wife never stirs as I slip by her bed and out into the hall. I pass his daughter's bedroom and that helps. She makes a little moan in her sleep. The plaintive sound brings everything into sharper focus—why I'm here, what I'm doing—and makes it easier for me to concentrate on getting it over with.

Newman's attention is fixed on the window of his bedroom. He never hears me come in the door and sidle my way alongside the wall to where he's sitting. I'm sure of it. But something—sixth sense, cop smarts—has him turn just as I'm reaching for him.

"What the fuck *are* you?" he says as he brings up the gun. The bandage on his hand is a white flash in the dark.

Stupid, I think. I'm so stupid. I still wanted to make a try at keeping this clean. Step into his private place and shut him down instead of cutting him open. And maybe I can.

I grab his hand, the one holding the gun, skin to skin. Contact.

Everything stops. He can't shoot me, I can't claw him. We're locked in a space between our heads. Not his private place, but somewhere else. There's a sudden shift of vertigo, a crazy quilt strobing in my eyes, and then we're somewhere else again. It takes me a few moments to realize what's happened.

We're in someone's head, all right, but it's mine. This is my own dreaming place.

I've never tried to step inside when the monster was awake before. It's so easy to make the transition when they're asleep, dreaming. But Newman was so focused, his will so strong, that even though he couldn't have a clue as to what he was doing, he's managed to push me out of his head and then follow me back into my own.

I can't seem to do anything right tonight.

I try to take us back out again, but it's no good. I give Newman a shove and he goes sprawling. As soon as he hits the ground, that crazy-quilt spinning starts up again. When it finally settles down, things have changed once more.

My dreaming place looks like the kitchen in the house where I grew up. I look for Newman, but he's gone. My father there in his place. He's standing there, weaving slightly from side to side, grinning at me, smelling like a brewery.

"Time to even the score," he says, slurring the words but not so much that I can't understand them.

He takes a step toward me, mad drunk gleam in his eyes, and I lose it. This is too much for me.

I never dealt with what happened to me as a child. I just left home as soon as I could. When I remade contact with my parents—before I told them I was gay—we all just pretended that all the drinking and screaming and beatings had never happened. That was just the way it worked, I thought. Keep the family unit whole, no matter what the cost.

But I never forgot. And I never forgave. And seeing him like this now, it's like I've stepped right back into the past and all the years between were just a dream. Except I'm not powerless anymore. When he hits me, I don't have to take it. I don't have to cringe and try to hide from his fists. Not anymore. Not ever again.

With his first blow, all of my animal rage comes tearing through me and I lash back at him. My fingers are clawed, taloned, killing weapons. It's like I have rabies. I cut him down and I'm still slashing at him, long after he's fallen to the ground. Long after he's dead. There's blood everywhere. And there's this screaming that just goes on and on and on.

I think it's me screaming, I know it's me, until I fall out of my head and I'm back in Newman's bedroom. I'm crouched over his savaged corpse, snarling and growling, and then I realize how wrong I've been. It's not me screaming. It's not me at all.

I see her in the doorway, the monster's daughter. The screams stop when I turn to look at her, but then I see her go away. She folds away inside herself, going deeper and deeper, until there's just this blank-eyed child standing there, everything that ever animated her walled away against the night creature that snuck into her Daddy's bedroom and tore him apart.

Doesn't matter what he did to her. That's gone, swallowed by the more horrible image of what's been done to him.

I stagger to my feet, but I don't even think of trying to comfort her. I almost fall through the window, trying to get out. And then I just flee. Run blind. I'll do anything to get rid of those emptied eyes, their blank stare, but they follow me, out into the night.

I know I'll carry them with me for the rest of my life.

When I finally stop running, the cramps hit me. I lie on my side and throw up. I'm still dry-heaving long after my stomach's empty, but I can't get rid of what's inside me that easily. The guilt's just going to lie there and fester and never go away.

8

Nothing helps.

It comes out that Newman was on the payroll of Yukio Nakamura, the boss of Little Japan's biggest Yakuza gang.

It comes out that not only was Newman taking graft, he was using his badge to help Nakamura get rid of his competition. And when the badge didn't provide intimidation enough, Newman was happy to use his gun.

It comes out that he beat his wife, abused his daughter.

By the time the investigation's over, half the Yakuza in Little Japan are up on racketeering charges and there's not one person in the city who has an ounce of sympathy for the monster. If they knew I'd killed him, they'd probably give me a medal.

But all I can focus on is that fact that his daughter's lost to the world now, locked up inside her own head, and I put her there. I tried to help, but I all I did was make things worse.

"You can't beat yourself over this," Chris said the one time I let him find me. "It's unfortunate what happened to the girl—an awful, terrible thing—but there's still a war going on. The freaks are still out there.

"You can't walk away from the fight now."

He thinks I'm scared, but that's not it. I'm not anything. All I can think of is that little girl and what I put her through, what I made her see.

Susan Newman didn't just lose her innocence. She had any hope of a normal life torn away.

"Do you need anything?" Chris asks. "Money? Food? A place to stay?"

I shake my head.

"Give this a little time," he says. "You're suffering from trauma too, you know."

I let him talk on, but I stop listening. I've regained my strength. I can leap tall buildings with a single bound again—or at least spider my way up their walls—but I don't have the heart for it anymore. I don't have the heart to step into anybody's dreaming place and then shut him down. And I certainly can't see myself killing someone again—I don't care how much he deserves it.

After a while, Chris stops talking and I walk away. He starts to follow, but finally gives up when I keep increasing the distance between us.

I don't wear my bodysuit anymore; I don't look like some dimestore ninja. I just look like any other homeless person, wandering around the street in clothes that are more than a few weeks away from clean, looking for handouts at the shelters, cadging spare change from passersby.

A month goes by, maybe two. I don't know. I just know it's getting really cold at night. Then late one afternoon I'm standing over a grating by a used bookstore, trying to get warm, and I see, in amongst the motley selection of titles that crowd the display window, a familiar cover and byline.

When the Desert Dreams, by Anne Bourke.

I've got two dollars and eighty cents in my pocket. I'm planning to use it to get something to eat later, but I go into the bookstore. The guy behind the counter takes pity on me and sells me the book for what I've got, even though there's a price of fifteen bucks penciled in on the right-hand corner of the front endpaper.

I leave, holding the book to my chest, and I walk around like that all night, from one side of the city to the other. I don't need to read the stories. I was there when they were written—almost a lifetime ago.

Finally, I start walking up Williamson Street, just trudging on and on until the downtown stores give way to more residential blocks, which give way to drive-in fast-food joints and malls and the 'burbs, and then I'm finally out of the city. The sun's up for about an hour when I stick out my thumb.

It's a long time before someone stops, but when this guy does, he's going my way. He can take me right up into the mountains. I find myself wanting to apologize for the way I look, for the way I smell, but I don't say anything. I know if I try to say anything more than where I'm going, I'm just going to break down and cry. So I sit there and hold my book. I nod and try to smile as the guy talks to me. Mostly, I just look ahead through the windshield.

I don't know what I'm expecting or hoping to find when I get there. I don't even know why I'm going. I just know that I've run out of other options.

Without Annie, I don't know where to turn. Only she'd be able to comfort me, only she'd be able to help me reclaim my dreaming place. I've had to shut myself off from what's inside me, because when I step into my private place, I get no solace now; when I dream, I have only nightmares.

What was my only haven is home to monsters now.

9

"Are you sure this is where you want out?" my ride asks.

There's something in the tone of his voice that tells me he doesn't think it's exactly the greatest idea. I don't blame him. We're out in the middle of nowhere, and Betsy's trailer looks deserted. The lawn's overgrown and thick with leaves. Her vegetable and flower gardens are a jungle of weeds. The trailer itself was never in the greatest shape, but now shutters are hanging loose and the door stands ajar. From the road we can see that a thick carpet of forest debris has already worked its way inside.

I guess I'm not really surprised. Betsy was an old woman. It's been over a year since I was here with Annie, and anything could have happened to her in that time. She could have moved. Or died.

I don't like to think of her as dead. There are some people who deserve to live forever, and although I only met her that one afternoon, I knew that Betsy was one of them. Eternal spirits, trapped in far too transient flesh.

Like Annie.

My ride clears his throat in case I didn't hear him. This guy's so polite. I was lucky it was him that stopped for me and not some loser who thinks with his dick instead of his heart.

Or maybe, considering, it was lucky for those losers. I've still got the anima's gifts; I just don't use them anymore.

"Yeah, I'm sure," I tell him and get out. "Thanks for the ride."

I stand by the end of Betsy's overgrown driveway and watch the car until it's out of sight. There's something in the air that calms me, smoothing all my nervous edges. No longer summer, not quite winter, everything just hanging between the two. I take it all in until I hear another vehicle coming up the road, then I dart into the woods, Annie's book clutched to my chest.

The glade doesn't look anything like I remembered it, either, but I know it's just because I'm here in a different season. The surrounding trees have all lost their leaves and everything's faded and brown. Except for the fairy ring. The toadstools still stand in their circle, the grass is still a deep green, and there's not a leaf or twig lying within the circle.

I know there's probably a sound, scientific reason why this is so, but I don't have access to the paper's morgue anymore to look it up, and besides, I've seen the anima. I'm more likely to believe that fairies are keeping the ring raked and tidy.

I stand there, looking at it for a long time, before I finally step into the ring. I lay Annie's book in the middle and sit down on the grass.

I don't know what I'm doing here. Maybe I thought I could call up the anima. Or Annie's ghost. But now that I'm here, none of that matters. All the confusion and pain that's sent my life into its downward spiral after I killed Newman just fades away. My pulse takes on the slow heartbeat of the forest. I close my eyes and let myself go. I can feel myself drifting, edging up on that dreaming place inside me that I haven't been able to visit for months because I know the monsters are waiting for me there.

I'm just starting to get convinced that maybe there is a way to regain one's innocence when I realize that I'm no longer alone.

It's neither the animal-headed fairy women nor Annie's ghost that I find watching me from the edge of the ring, but Betsy. I think for a minute that maybe she's a ghost, or a fairy woman, but then I see how frail she is, the cane she's used to get here, how her face is red from the effort she's made and her breathing is way too fast. She's as real as I am—maybe more so, because I don't know where I've been these last few months.

We don't say anything for a long time. I watch her lean on her cane and slowly catch her breath. The flush leaves her face.

"I read about your friend," she says finally. "That must have been hard for you."

Tears well in my eyes and I can't seem to find my voice. I manage a nod.

"It's always hardest for those of us who get left behind," she says, filling the silence that grows up between us. "I know."

"You . . . you've lost someone close to you?" I ask.

Betsy gives me this sad smile. "At my age, girl, I've just about lost them all." She pauses for a heartbeat, then asks, "You and your friend—you were . . . lovers?"

"Does that shock you?"

"Land's sake, no. I left my own husband for a woman—though that was years ago. Folks didn't look on it with much understanding back then."

They still don't, I think.

"I think it makes it that much harder when you love someone folks don't think you're supposed to and she dies. You don't get a period of mourning. Folks are just relieved that the situation's gone and fixed itself."

"But you still mourn," I say.

"Oh yes. But you have to do your crying on the inside."

My eyes fill again, not just for Annie and me now, but for Betsy and her long-gone lover. Betsy looks like she's about to lose it too; her eyes are all shiny, and the flush is returning to her cheeks, but then she wipes her eyes on her sleeve and straightens her back.

"So," she says, trying to sound cheery. "What brings you back? Another story for your newspaper?"

I shake my head even though I know she's only being kind. She can see the state I'm in—I look like the homeless person I've become, not the reporter I was.

"Remember when you were telling me about fairy gifts?" I say.

She nods slowly.

I want to tell her about the anima and what they gave me. I want to tell her about the ninja suit and climbing walls and leaping from rooftop to rooftop, looking for prey. I want to tell her about the dreaming places, and what I did to Newman when I pulled him into mine. I want to ask what the fairy women gave her. But none of it will come out.

Instead I just say, "I liked the idea of it."

"You did a lovely job writing it all up in your article," Betsy tells me. "It had a different . . . ring to it."

"As opposed to the stories *The Examiner* usually runs," I say dryly.

Betsy smiles. "I've still got it in my scrapbook."

That reminds me.

"I didn't think you—" were still alive. "—Still lived around here," I say. "When I saw the trailer . . ."

"After I had my stroke," she says, "I went to live across the road with my friend Alice."

I don't remember there being a place across the road from hers, but when she invites me back for tea, I see that it's because the evergreens hide it so well. As we walk up the little dirt track leading to it, Betsy tells me how it's a step up for her. I look from the run-down log cabin to her, the question plain in my eyes.

"It doesn't have wheels," she explains.

I never do any of the things that might have brought me up here. I don't talk about the anima to Betsy or what their coming into my life has done to me. I don't talk about how they might have affected her. I don't meet the anima again; I don't see Annie's ghost. But when Alice's daughter drives me back to the outskirts of the city where I can catch a bus, I realize the trip was still worthwhile, because I brought away with me something I hadn't had for so long I'd forgotten it had ever existed.

I brought away some human contact.

10

In Frank Estrich's private place there's a small dog, trembling in the weeds that grow up along the dirt road where Frank's walking. The dog is just a mutt, lost and scared. You see them far too often in the country—some poor animal that's outlived its welcome in a city home, so it gets taken for a ride, the car slows down, the animal's tossed out—"returned to nature"—and the problem's solved.

Frank found a stray the summer before, but his dad killed it when Frank brought it home and tried to hide it in the barn. And then his dad took the belt to Frank. His dad does that a lot, most of the time for no other reason than because he likes to do it.

Frank always feels so helpless. Everybody's bigger than him: his father, his uncles, his brothers, the other kids. Everybody can rag on him and there's not a thing he can do about it. But this dog's not bigger than him.

Frank knows it's wrong, he knows he should feel sorry for the little fella because the dog's as unwanted as Frank feels he is most of the time, but I can see in his head that he's thinking of getting his own back. And if he can't do it to those that are hurting him, then maybe he'll just do it to the dog.

Doesn't matter how it cringes down on its belly as he approaches it, eyes hopeful, body shaking. All Frank can think of is the beating he got earlier tonight. Dad took him out to the barn, made him take down his pants, made him bend over a bale of hay as he took off his belt. . . .

I've already dealt with the father, but I know now how that's not enough. The seed's still lying inside the victim. Maybe it'll turn Frank into what his father calls a "sissy-boy," scared of his own shadow; more likely it'll make Frank grow up no different from his father, one more monster in a world that's got too many already.

So I have to teach Frank about right and wrong—not like his father did; not with arbitrary rules and punishments, but in a way that doesn't leave Frank feeling guilty for what was done to him, in a way that lets him understand that self-empowerment has got nothing to do with what you can do to someone else.

It's a long, slow process of healing that's as hard for me to put into words as it is for me to explain how I can step into other people's dreaming places. But it's worth it. Not just for the victims like Frank that I get to help, but for myself as well.

What happened to me before was that I was wearing myself out. I was putting so much out, but getting nothing back. I was living only in the shadows, living there so long that I almost forgot there was such a thing as sunlight.

That's what I do, I guess. I still step into the monsters' heads and turn them off, but then I visit the dreaming places of their victims and show them how to get back into the sunlight. The funny thing is, that when I'm with someone like Frank and he finally gets out of the shadows, I don't leave anything of myself behind. But they leave something in me.

Dried blood and rose petals.

Bird bones and wood ash.

It's all just metaphor for spirit—that's what Annie would say. I don't know. I don't need to put a name to it. I just use it all to reclaim my own dreaming place and keep it free of shadows.

A *Tempest* in Her Eyes

> *Remember all is but a poet's dream,*
> *The first he had in Phoebus' holy bower,*
> *But not the last, unless the first displease.*
> —John Lyly, from *The Woman in the Moone*

1

I've heard it said that there are always two sides to a story: There's the official history, the version that's set onto the page, then filed away in the archives where it waits for when the librarian comes to retrieve the facts to footnote some learned paper or discourse. Then there's the way an individual remembers the event; that version sits like an old woman on a lonely porch, creaking back and forth in her wicker rocker as she waits for a visitor.

I think there's a third version as well: that of the feral child, escaping from between the lines, from between how it's said the story went and how it truly took place.

I'm like that child. I'm invariably on the edge of how it goes for everyone else. I hear them tell the story of some event that I took part in and I can scarcely recognize it. I'd like to say that it's because I'm such a free spirit—the way Jilly is, always bouncing around from one moment to the next—but I know it's not true. The reason I'm not part of the official story is because I'm usually far from civilization, lost in wildernesses of my own making, unaware of either the library or the porch.

I'm just not paying attention—or at least not paying attention to the right thing. It all depends on your perspective, I suppose.

2

September was upon us and I couldn't have cared less, which is weird for me, because autumn's usually my favorite time of year. But I was living through one of those low points in my life that I guess everyone has to put up with at one time or another. I went through the summer feeling increasingly tired and discouraged. I walked hand in hand with a constant sense of foreboding, and you know what that's like: If you expect things to go wrong, they usually do.

I hadn't met a guy I liked in ages—at least not anyone who was actually available. Every time I sat down to write, my verses came out as doggerel. I was getting cranky with my friends, but I hated being home by myself. About the only thing I was still good at was waitressing. I've always liked my job, but as a lifelong career choice? I don't think so.

To cheer me up, Jilly and Sophie took me to the final performance of *A Midsummer Night's Dream* at the Standish. The play was a traditional production—Lysander and Demetrius hadn't been rewritten as bikers, say, and the actors had performed in costume, not in the nude. Being a poet myself, I lean toward less adventurous productions because they don't get in the way of the words.

I'd been especially taken with the casting of the fairy court tonight. The director had acquired the services of the Newford Ballet for their parts, which lent the characters a wonderfully fey grace. They were so light on their feet, I could almost imagine that they were flying at times, flitting about the stage, rather than constrained by gravity to walking its boards. The scene at the end where the fairies sport through the Duke's palace had been so beautifully choreographed that I was almost disappointed when the spotlight narrowed to capture Puck in his final speech, perched at the edge of the stage, fixing us in our seats with a half-mocking, half-feral gaze that seemed to belie his promise to "make amends."

The actor playing Robin Goodfellow had been my favorite among a talented cast, his mobile features perfectly capturing the fey charm and menace that the idea of fairy has always held for me. Oberon was the more handsome, but Puck had been simply magic. I found myself wishing that the play was just beginning its run, rather than ending it, so that I could go back another night, for his performance alone.

Jilly and Sophie didn't seem quite as taken with the production. They were walking a little ahead of me, arguing about the authorship of Shakespeare's works, rather than discussing the play we'd just seen.

"Oh, come on," Sophie was saying. "Just look at the names of some of these people: John Thomas Looney. S. E. Silliman. George Battey. How can anyone possibly take their theories seriously?"

"I didn't say they were necessarily right," Jilly replied. "It's just that when you consider the historical Shakespeare: a man whose father was illiterate, whose kids were illiterate, who didn't even bother to keep copies of his own work in his house . . . It's so obvious that whoever wrote the plays and sonnets, it wasn't William Shakespeare."

"I don't really see how it matters anyway," Sophie told her. "It's the work that's important, in the end. The fact that it's endured so long that we can still enjoy it today, hundreds of years after he died."

"But it's an interesting puzzle."

Sophie nodded in agreement. "I'll give you that. Personally, I like the idea that Anne Whately wrote them."

"But she was a *nun*. I can't *possibly* imagine a nun having written some of the bawdier lines."

"Maybe those are the ones old Will put in."

"I suppose. But then . . ."

Trailing along behind them, I was barely paying attention and finally just shut them out. My own thoughts were circling mothlike around Titania's final promise:

> *Hand in hand with fairy grace*
> *Will we sing and bless this place.*

That was what I needed. I needed a fairy court to bless my apartment, to lift the cloud of gloom that had been thickening over me throughout the summer until it had gotten to the point where when I looked in the mirror, I expected to see a stranger's face looking back at me. I felt that different.

I think the weather had something to do with it. It rained every weekend and day off I had this summer. It never got hot—not that I like or missed the heat. But I think we need a certain amount of sunshine just to stay sane, never mind the UV risk. Who ever heard of getting cabin fever in the middle of the summer? But that's exactly the way I felt around the end of July—the way I usually feel in early March, when I don't think I can take one more day of cold and snow.

And it's just gotten worse for me as the summer's dragged on.

The newspapers blame the weird weather on that volcano in the Philippines—Mount Pinatubo—and say that not only did the eruption mess up the weather this year, but its effects are going to be felt for a few years to come. If that's true, I think I'll just go quietly mad.

I started wondering then about how the weather affects fairies, though if they did exist, I guess it might be the other way around. Instead of a volcano causing all of this trouble, it'd be another rift in the fairy court. As Titania put it to Oberon:

> *. . . the spring, the summer,*
> *The chiding autumn, angry winter change*
> *Their wonted liveries, and the mazéd world*
> *By their increase now knows not which is which.*
> *And this same progeny of evils comes*
> *From our debate, from our dissension,*
> *We are their parents and original.*

It certainly fits the way our weather's messed up. I heard it even snowed up in Alberta a couple of weeks ago—and not just a few flurries. The skies dumped some ten inches. In *August*.

"The seasons alter," indeed.

If there were fairy courts, if they *were* having an argument, I wished they'd just kiss and make up. Though not the way they did in *A Midsummer Night's Dream*.

Ahead of me, Sophie and Jilly came to a stop and I walked right into them.

"How's our dreamwalker?" Jilly asked.

She spoke the words lightly, but the streetlights showed the concern in her eyes. Jilly worries about people—seriously, not just for show. It's nice to know that someone cares, but sometimes that kind of concern can be as much of a burden as what you're going through, however well meant it might be.

"I'm fine," I lied. "Honestly."

"So who gets *your* vote as the author of Shakespeare's works?" Sophie asked.

I thought Francis Bacon looked good for it. After all, he was known as the most erudite man of his time. The author of the plays showed through his writing that he'd had a wide knowledge of medicine and law, botany and mythology, foreign life and court manners. Where would a glove maker's son from Stratford have gotten that kind of experience? But the argument bored me.

"I'd say it was his sister," I said.

"His *sister?*"

"Did he even have a sister?" Jilly asked.

A black Cadillac pulled up to the curb beside us before I could answer. There were three Hispanic boys in it, and for a moment I thought it was LaDonna's brother Pipo and a couple of his pals. But then the driver leaned out the window to give Jilly a leer and I realized I didn't recognize any of them.

"Hey, *puta,*" he said. "Looking for a little of that kickin' action?"

Homeboys in a hot car, out for a joy ride. The oldest wasn't even fourteen. Jilly didn't hesitate. She cocked back her foot and kicked the Cadillac's door hard enough to make a dent.

"In your dreams," she told him.

If it had been anybody else, those homies would've been out of the car and all over us. We're all small women; Jilly's about my height, and I'm just topping five feet. We don't exactly look formidable. But this was Jilly, and the homie at the wheel saw something in her face that made him put the pedal to the floor and peel off.

The incident depressed all three of us. When we got to my apartment, I asked them in, but they just wanted to go home. I didn't blame them. I watched them go on off down the street, but sat down on the porch instead of going inside.

I knew I wasn't going to sleep because I started thinking about what a raw deal women always seem to get, and that always keeps me up. Even Titania in the play—sure, she and Oberon made up, but it was on *his* terms. Titania never even realized the crap he had put her through before their "reconciliation."

A Midsummer Night's Dream definitely hadn't been written by a woman.

3

A funny thing happened to me a few years ago. I caught a glimpse of the strange world that lies on the other side of the curtain we've all agreed is reality. Or at least I think I did.

The historical version of what happened is pretty straightforward: I met a street person—the old man on the bicycle that everybody calls the Conjure Man—and he got me to take an acorn from the big old tree that used to grow behind the library at Butler U. He had me nurture it over the winter, then plant it in Fitzhenry Park near the statue of the poet, Joshua Stanhold.

The version he tells is that he's this immortal who diminishes as the years go by, which is why he's only our height now. He was supposed to leave our world when its magic went away, but he got left behind. The tree that came down behind the library was a Tree of Tales, a repository of stories without which wonder is diminished in our world. The one I grew from an acorn and planted in the Silenus Gardens is supposed to be its replacement.

My version . . . I don't really know what my version is. There was something strange about the whole affair, I'll grant you that. And that little sapling I planted—it's already the size of a ten-year-old oak. Jilly told me she was talking to a botanist who was quite amazed at its appearance there. Seems that kind of oak isn't native to North America, and he was surprised to find it growing in the middle of the park that way.

"The only other one I've ever seen in the city," he told Jilly, "used to grow behind the Smithers Library, but they cut it down."

I haven't seen John—that's the Conjure Man's real name, John Windle. I haven't seen him for a while now. I like to think that he's finally made it home to wherever home is. Behind the curtain, I suppose. But I still go out to the tree and tell it stories—all kinds of stories. Happy ones, sad ones. Gossip. News. Just whatever comes to mind.

I'm not even sure why; I just do.

4

I'm not as brave—or maybe as foolish—as Jilly is. She doesn't seem to know the meaning of fear. She'll go anywhere, at any time of the day or night, and she never seems to get hurt. Like what happened earlier tonight. If I'd been on my own, or just with Sophie, when that car pulled up, who knows how it would have ended up? Not pleasant, that's for sure.

So I'm not nearly so bold—except when I'm on my bike. It's sort of like a talisman for me. It's nothing special, just an old ten-speed, but it gets me around. Sometimes I think I should become one of those messengers that wheel through the traffic on their mountain bikes, whistle between their lips, ready to let out a shrill blast if anybody gets in their way.

You think you're immortal, covering ground faster than anyone can walk, but you're not all locked up inside some motorized box that's spewing noxious fumes into the air. You feel as natural as a bird, or a deer, racing through your concrete forest. Maybe that's where John got that feeling from, riding through town on his bike, free as the wind, when all the other street people are just sort of shuffling along, gaze to the ground.

I started a poem about it once, but I couldn't get the words to fit the vision. That's been happening to me all too often this summer. Oh, who'm I kidding? Wordless pretty well sums me up these days. I look at the work I've had published, and I can't even imagine what it was like to write those verses, little say believe that it was me who did it.

Feeling sorry for myself is the one thing I have gotten good at lately. It's not a feeling I like. I hate the way it leaves me with this overpowering sense of being ineffectual. Worthless.

When I start getting into that kind of mood, I usually get on my bike and just ride. Which is how I found myself in Fitzhenry Park a few hours after Sophie and Jilly left me at my apartment.

I laid my bike down under the young Tree of Tales and sprawled on the grass beside it. I could see a handful of stars, looking up through the tree's boughs, but my mind was back in the Standish, listening to Puck warn Oberon of the coming dawn. I drifted off to the remembered sound of his voice.

5

Puck breaks off and looks at me. The play has faded, the hall is gone. It's just the two of us, alone in some copsy wood, as far from the city as the word orange is from a true rhyme.

"And who are you?" he says.

I make no reply. I'm too fascinated by his transformation. Falling asleep, the voice I heard, the face I imagined, was that of the actor from the Standish whom I'd seen earlier in the night. But he's gone along with the city and everything familiar. This Puck is more compelling still. I can't take my gaze from him. He has a beauty that no actor could replicate, but he's more inhuman, too. It's hard to say where the man ends and the animal begins. I think of Pan; I think of fauns.

"Your hair," he says, "is like moonlight, gracing your fair shoulders."

Maybe I should be thinking of satyrs. Legendary being or not, this is a come-on if ever I heard one.

"It's dyed," I tell him.

"But it looks so full of life."

"I mean, I color it. I'm not a natural blonde."

"And your eyes?" he asks. "Is that tempest of dream-starved color dyed as well?"

I have to admit, he's got a way about him. I don't know if I should assume "dream-starved" to be a compliment exactly, but the sound of his voice makes me wish he'd just take me in his arms. Maybe this is what they mean by fairy enchantment. I've only known him for the better part of a couple of minutes, and already he's got me feeling all warm and tingly inside. There's a musky odor in the air and my heartbeat has found a new, quicker rhythm.

It's a tough call, but I tell my libido to take five.

"What do you mean by "dream-starved?" " I ask him.

He sits back on his furry haunches and the sexual charge that's built up between us eases somewhat.

"I see a storm in your soul," he says, "held at bay by a grey cloud of uncomfortable reason."

"What's that supposed to mean?" I ask.

But I know. I know exactly what he's talking about: how everything that ever made me happy seems to have been washed away. I smile, but there's no light behind the smile. I laugh, but the sound is hollow. I don't know how it happened, but it all went away. I do have a storm inside me, but it can't seem to get out and I don't know how to help it. All I do know is that I don't want to feel like a robot anymore, like I took a walk-on bit as a zombie for some B-movie only to find that I can't shake the part once my scene's in the can.

"When was the last time you felt truly alive?" he asks.

I look back through my memories, but everything seems dismal and grey. It's like walking into a room where all the furniture is covered with sheets, dust lies thick on the floor, all color has been sucked away.

"I . . . I can't remember. . . ."

"It was not always so."

A statement, not a question, but I still nod my head in slow agreement.

"What bedevils you," he says, "is that you have misplaced the ability to see—to truly see behind the shadow, into the heart of a thing—and so you no longer think to look. And the more you do not look, the less able you are to see. Wait long enough, and you'll wander the world as one blind."

"I already feel that way."

"Then open your eyes and see."

"See *what?*"

Puck shrugs. "It makes no difference. You can look upon the most common thing and see the whole of the cosmos reflected within."

"Intellectually, I know what you're talking about," I tell him. "I understand—really I do. But in here—" I lay the palm of one hand between my breasts and cover it with the palm of the other "—it's not so clear. My heart just feels too heavy to even think about sunshine and light, little say look for them in anything."

"Then free your heart from your mind," he says. "Embrace wonder for one moment without the need to consider how that wonder came to be, without the need to justify if it be real or not."

"I . . . I don't know how."

His lips shape that puckish smile then. "If you would forget thought for a time, let me love you."

He cups my chin with his hand and brings his lips close to mine. At the touch, being so close to those wild eyes of his, I can feel the warmth again, the fire in my loins that rises up into my belly.

"Let the storm loose," he whispers.

I want to, I'm going to, I can't seem to stop myself, yet I manage to pull back from him.

"I'll try," I say. "But first," and I don't know where this thought comes from, "first—tell me a story."

"A . . . story."

It's all happening too fast for me. I need to slow down.

"Tell me what happened when Titania found out that Oberon had taken her changeling into his court."

He smiles. He rests his back against a tree and pulls me close so that my head's on his shoulder. I need this breathing space. I need the quiet sound of his voice, the intimacy it builds between us. Without it, fairy enchantment or not, the act of making love with him would be no different than if I did it with one of those homeboys who pulled up beside the curb earlier in the evening.

He's a good storyteller. I hope the Tree's listening.

When the story's done, he sits quietly beside me, as taken away by the story he's let unfold between us as I am. I'm the one who has to unbutton my blouse, who reaches for his hand and puts it against my breast.

6

I woke with the morning sun in my eyes, stiff and chilled from having spent the night on the damp grass. I sat up and used my fingers as a comb to pull the grass and leaves from my hair. My dream was still vivid. Puck's advice rang like a clarion bell inside my mind.

You can look upon the most common thing and see the whole of the cosmos reflected within.

But I couldn't seem to do it. I could feel the storm inside me, yearning to be freed, but the veil was over my eyes again and everything seemed to be shrouded with the fine covering of its fabric.

Free your heart from your mind. Embrace wonder for one moment without the need to consider how that wonder came to be, without the need to justify . . . if . . . it . . .

Already the advice was fading. I found myself thinking, It was only a dream. There's no more wisdom in a dream than in anything you might make up. It's just shadows. Without substance.

I tried to tell myself that it wasn't true. I might make up my poems, but when they work, when the line of communication runs true between my heart and whoever's reading them, they touch a real truth.

But the argument didn't seem worth pursuing.

Above me, the sky was grey, overcast. The morning was cool and it probably wouldn't get much warmer. So much for summer. So much for my life. But it seemed so unfair.

I remembered the dream. I remembered Puck—my Puck, not Shakespeare's, not some actor, not somebody else's interpretation of him. I remembered the magic in his voice. The gentleness in his touch. The wild enchantment in his eyes. Somehow I managed, if only in a dream, to pull aside the curtain that separates strangeness from the world we've all agreed on, and find a piece of wonder that I could bring back with me. But now that I've woken, I find that all I've brought back is more of what it seems I've always had. Greyness. Boredom. No meaning in anything.

And that seemed the most unfair thing of all.

I lay back down on the grass and stared up into the Tree of Tales, my gaze veiled with tears. I could see the gloom that had spread throughout me during the summer, just deepening and deepening until it swallowed me whole. I was so sick of feeling sorry for myself, but I just couldn't seem to stop myself.

And then a small bird landed on a branch above my head—I don't even know what kind. A sparrow? A wren? It lifted up its head and warbled a few notes and for no good reason at all, I felt happy.

I didn't see the singer as a small drab brown bird on an equally drab branch, but as a microcosm that reflected every living thing. I didn't hear its song as a few warbled notes, quickly swallowed by the sounds of traffic beyond the confines of the park, but as an echo of all the music that was ever sung.

I sat up and looked around and nothing seemed the same. It was as though someone had just told me some unbelievably good news and simply by hearing it, my perspective on everything was changed.

7

Someone once described the theory of right and left brain to me and I read up on it myself later. Basically, it boils down to this: The left brain is the logical one, the rationalist, the scientist, the one that sees us through the everyday. It's the one that lets us conduct normal business, walk safely across a busy street, that kind of thing. And it's the one we know best.

The right brain belongs to the artist and its mostly a stranger because we don't call on it very often. In the general course of our lives, we don't *need* to. But fey though it is, this stranger inside us is the one that keeps us sane. It's the one that imparts meaning to what we do, that allows us to see beyond the drone of the everyday.

It's always trying to remind us of its existence. It's the one that's responsible for synchronicities and other small wonders, strange dreams or really *seeing* a small drab brown bird. It'll do anything to shake us up. But mostly we don't pay attention to it. And when we sink low enough, we don't hear its voice at all.

And that's such a shame, because that stranger is the Puck in the midden, the part of us that makes gold out of trash, poetry out of nonsense. It calls art forth from common sights and music from ordinary sound and without it, the world would be a very grey place indeed. Trust me, I know—from my own all-too-unpleasant experience with that world. But I'm working on never going through a summer like that again.

The stranger, that Puck in my midden, showed me how.

When I think of that Puck now, I'm always reminded of how he came to me—not just from out of a dream, but from a dream that was based on someone else's dream, put to words, enacted on the stage, centuries after his death. And I believe now that Shakespeare did write the plays that bear his name.

I doubt we'll ever know for sure. In this case, the historical version's lost, while the stories everybody else has to tell contradict one another—as so often they do. But I'll pick from between the lines and say it was old Will.

Because the dream also reminds me of the Tree of Tales, and I think maybe that's what Shakespeare was: a kind of human Tree of Tales. He got told all these stories and then he reshaped them into his plays so that they wouldn't be forgotten.

It doesn't matter where he got those stories. What matters is that he was able to put them into the forms they have now so that they could and can live on: small sparks of wisdom and joy, drama and buffoonery, that touch the stranger inside us so that she'll remind us what we're all here for. Not just to plod through life, but to celebrate it.

But knowing all of that, believing in it as I do, the mystery of authorship still remains for most people, I suppose. The scholars and historians. But that's their problem; I've solved it to my own satisfaction. There's only one thing I'd ask old Will if I ever ran into him. I'd love to know who told him about Puck.

I'll bet she had a tempest in her eyes.

Saxophone Joe and
the Woman in Black

*A cat has nine lives. For three he
plays, for three he strays, and for
the last three he stays.*
—American folklore

I love this city.

Even now, with things getting worse the way they do: Too many people hungry,
or cold, or got nowhere to sleep, and here's winter creeping up on us, earlier each
year, and staying later. The warm grate doesn't do much when the sleet's coming down,
giving everything the picture-perfect prettiness of a fairy tale—just saying you've got
the wherewithal to admire a thing like that, instead of always worrying how the ends
are going to meet.

But you've got to take the time, once in a while, or what've you got? Don't be
waiting for the lotto to come in when you can't even afford the price of a ticket.

It's like all those stories that quilt the streets, untidy little threads of yarn that get
pulled together into gossiping skeins, one from here, one from there, until what you've
got in your hand isn't a book, maybe, doesn't have a real beginning or end, but it tells
you something. You can read the big splashes that make their way onto the front page,
headlines standing out one inch tall, just screaming for your attention. Sure, they're
interesting, but what interests me more is the little stories. Nothing so exciting, maybe,
about losing a job, or looking for one. Falling in or out of love. New baby coming.
Old grandad passed away. Unless the story belongs to you. Then it fills your world,
and you don't have time even to glance at those headlines.

What gets me is how everybody's looking to make sense of things. Sometimes
you don't want sense. Sometimes, the last thing in the world you need is sense. Work
a thing through till it makes sense and you lose all the possibilities.

That's what runs this city. All those possibilities. It's like the heart of the city is this old coal furnace, just smoking away under the streets, stoked with all those might-yet-bes and who'd-a-thoughts. The rich man waking up broke and he never saw it coming. The girl who figures she's so ugly she won't look in a mirror, and she finds she's got two boys fighting over her. The father who surprises himself when he finds he likes his son better, now that he knows the boy's gay.

And the thing is, the account doesn't end there. One possibility just leads straight up to the next, with handfuls of story lying in between. Stoking the furnace. Keeping the city interesting.

You just got to know where to look. You just got to know *how* to look.

Got no time?

Maybe the measurement's different from me to you to that girl who gives you your ticket at the bus depot, but the one thing we've all got is time. You can use it or lose it, your choice. That's how come we've got that old saying about how it's not having a thing that's important, but how we went about getting it. Our time's the most precious thing we've got to offer folks, and the worst thing a body can do is to take it away from us.

So don't you go wasting it.

But I was talking about possibilities and little stories, things that maybe don't even make it into the paper. Like what happened to Saxophone Joe.

I guess everybody knows how a cat's got nine lives, and I'm thinking a few more of you know how those lives are divided up: three to play, three to stray, and the last three to stay. Maybe that's a likeness for our own lives, a what-do-you-call-it, metaphor. I don't know.

But grannies used to tell their children's children how if a cat came to live with you of its own accord during one of its straying lives, why you couldn't ask for better luck in that household. And that cat'd stay, too, unless you called it by name. Not the name you gave it, or maybe the one it gave you—it comes wandering in off the fire escape with its little white paws, so you call it Boots, or maybe it's that deep orange like you'd spread on your toast, so you call it Marmalade.

I'm talking about its secret name, the one only it knows.

Anyway, Joe's playing six nights a week with a combo in the Rhatigan, a little jazz club over on Palm Street; him on sax, Tommy Morrison on skins, Rex Small bellied up to that big double bass, and Johnny Fingers tickling the ivories. The Rhatigan doesn't look like much, but it's the kind of place you never know who's going to be sitting in with the band, playing that long cool music.

Used to be people said jazz was the soul of the city, the rhythm that made it tick. A music made up of slick streets and neon lights, smoky clubs and lips that taste like whiskey. Now we've got hip hop and rap and thrash, and I hear people saying it's not music at all, but they're plain wrong. All these sounds are still true to the soul of the city; it's just changed to suit the times is all.

One night Joe's up there on the Rhatigan's stage, halfsitting on his stool, one long leg bent up, foot supported on a rung, the other pointing straight out across the stage to where Johnny's hunched over his piano, fingers dancing on the keyboard as they trade off riffs. There's something in the air that night, and they're seriously connected to it.

Joe takes a breath, head cocked as he listens to what Johnny's playing. Then, just as he tightens his lips around the reeds, he sees the woman sitting there off in a dark corner, alone at her table, black hair, black dress, skin the same midnight tone as Joe's own so that she's almost invisible, except for the whites of her eyes and her teeth, because she's looking right at him and she's smiling.

Dark eyes, she's got, like there's no pupils, watching him and not blinking, and Joe watches her back. He's got one eye that's blue and one eye that's brown, and the gaze of the two of them just about swallows her whole.

But Joe doesn't lose the music, doesn't hesitate a moment; his sax wails, coming in right when it should, only he's watching the woman now, Johnny's forgotten, and the music changes, turns slinky, like an old tomcat on the prowl. The woman smiles and lifts her glass to him.

She comes home with him that night, just moves in like she's always been there. She doesn't talk, she doesn't ever say a word, but things must be working out between them because she's there, isn't she, sharing that tiny room Joe's had in the Walker Hotel for sixteen years. Live together in a small space like that, and you soon find out if you can get along or not.

After a while, Joe starts calling her Mona because that's the name of the tune they were playing when he first saw her in the Rhatigan and, musicians being the way they are, nobody thinks it strange that she doesn't talk, that she's got no ID, that she answers to that name. It's like she's always been there, always been called Mona, always lived with Saxophone Joe and been his woman.

But if he doesn't talk to anyone else about it, Joe's still thinking about her, always thinking about her, if he's on stage or walking down a street or back in their room, who she is and where she came from, and he finds himself trying out names on her, to see which one she might've worn before he called her Mona, which one her momma and poppa called her by when she was just a little girl.

Then one day he gets it right, and the next morning she's gone, walked out of his life like the straying cat in the story the grannies tell, once someone's called her by her true, secret name. What was her name, this woman Joe started out calling Mona? I never learned. But Joe knows the story, too, cats and names, and he gets to thinking some more, he can't *stop* thinking about Mona and cats, and then he gets this crazy idea that maybe she really *was* a cat, that she could change, cat to woman, woman to cat, slipped into his life during her straying years, and now she's gone.

And then he gets an even crazier idea: The only way to get her back is if he gets himself his own cat skin.

So he goes to see the priest—not the man with the white collar, but the hoodoo man—except Papa Jo-el's dead, got himself mixed up with some kind of juju that even he couldn't handle, so when Joe goes knocking soft on Papa Jo-el's door, it's the gris-gris woman Ti Beau that answers and lets him in.

Friday night, Joe's back in the club, and he's playing a dark music now, the tone of his sax's got an undercurrent in it, like skinheaded drums played with the palm of your hand and a tap-tap of a drumstick on a bar of iron, like midnight at a crossroads and the mist's coming in from the swamp, like seven-day candles burning in the wind, but those candles don't flicker because the gateways are open and *les invisibles* are there, holding the flames still.

Saturday night, he's back again, and he's still playing music like no one's heard before—not displeasing, just unfamiliar. Tommy and Rex, they're having trouble keeping the rhythm, but Johnny's following, note for note. After the last set that Saturday night, he walks up to where Joe's putting his sax away in its case.

"You been to see the *mambo*?" Johnny asks, "playing music like that?"

Joe doesn't answer except to put his sax case in Johnny's hands.

"Hold on to this for me, would you?" he asks.

When he leaves the club that night, it's the last time anybody sees him. Sees the man. But Heber Brown, he's been working at the Walker Hotel for thirty years. When he's cleaning out Joe's room because the rent's two months due and nobody's seen him for most of that time, Heber sees an old tomcat on the fire escape, scratching at the window, trying to get in. Heber says this cat's so dark a brown it's almost black, like midnight settled in the corner of an alleyway, and it's got one blue eye, so you tell me.

You think Ti Beau's got the kind of gris-gris potion to turn a man into a cat, or maybe just an old cat skin lying about that'll work the same magic, someone says the right words over it? Or was it maybe that Joe just up and left town, nursing a broken heart?

Somebody taped that last set Joe played at the Rhatigan, and I'll tell you, when Johnny plays it for me, I hear hurting in it, but I hear something else, too, something that doesn't quite belong to this world, or maybe belonged here first but we kind of eased it out of the way once we got ourselves civilized enough. It's like one of the *loa* stepped into Joe that night, maybe freed him up, loosened his skin enough so that he could make the change, but first that spirit talked to us through Joe's sax, reminding us that we weren't here first, and maybe we won't be here the last either.

It's all part and parcel of the mystery that sits there, right under all the things we know for sure. And the thing I like about that mystery is that it doesn't show us more than a little piece at a time; but you touch it and you've just got to pass it on. So if Joe's not with Mona now, you can bet he's slipped into someone else's life and he's making them think. Sitting there on a windowsill, maybe looking lazy, but maybe looking like he knows something we don't, something important, and that person he's with, who took him in, well she stops the tumbling rush of her life for a moment to take the time to think about what lies under the stories that make up this city.

Things may be getting worse in some ways, but you can't deny that they're interesting, too, if you just stop to look at them a little closer.

Like that old man playing the clarinet in the subway station that you pass by every day. He's bent and old and his clothes are shabby and you can't figure out how he makes a living from the few coins that get tossed into the hat sitting on the pavement in front of him. So maybe he's just an old man, down on his luck, making do. Or maybe he's got a piece of magic he wants to pass on with that music he's playing.

Next time you go by, stop and give him a listen. But don't go looking for a tag to put on what you hear or, like that cat that runs off when you name her, it'll all just go away.

The Bone Woman

No one really stops to think of Ellie Spink, and why should they?

She's no one.

She has nothing.

Homely as a child, all that the passing of years did was add to her unattractiveness. Face like a horse, jaw long and square, forehead broad; limpid eyes set bird-wide on either side of a gargantuan nose; hair a nondescript brown, greasy and matted, stuffed up under a woolen toque lined with a patchwork of metal foil scavenged from discarded cigarette packages. The angularity of her slight frame doesn't get its volume from her meager diet, but from the multiple layers of clothing she wears.

Raised in foster homes, she's been used, but she's never experienced a kiss. Institutionalized for most of her adult life, she's been medicated, but never treated. Pass her on the street and your gaze slides right on by, never pausing to register the difference between the old woman huddled in the doorway and a bag of garbage.

Old woman? Though she doesn't know it, Monday, two weeks past, was her thirty-seventh birthday. She looks twice her age.

There's no point in trying to talk to her. Usually no one's home. When there is, the words spill out in a disjointed mumble, a rambling monologue itemizing a litany of misperceived conspiracies and other ills that soon leave you feeling as confused as she herself must be.

Normal conversation is impossible and not many bother to try it. The exceptions are few: The odd pitying passerby. A concerned social worker, fresh out of college and new to the streets. Maybe one of the other street people who happens to stumble into her particular haunts.

They talk and she listens, or she doesn't—she never makes any sort of a relevant response, so who can tell? Few push the matter. Fewer still, however well intentioned, have the stamina to make the attempt to do so more than once or twice. It's easier just to walk away; to bury your guilt, or laugh off her confused ranting as the excessive rhetoric it can only be.

I've done it myself.

I used to try to talk to her when I first started seeing her around, but I didn't get far. Angel told me a little about her, but even knowing her name and some of her history didn't help.

"Hey, Ellie. How're you doing?"

Pale eyes, almost translucent, turn toward me, set so far apart it's as though she can only see me with one eye at a time.

"They should test for aliens," she tells me. "You know, like in the Olympics."

"Aliens?"

"I mean, who cares who killed Kennedy? Dead's dead, right?"

"What's Kennedy got to do with aliens?"

"I don't even know why they took down the Berlin Wall. What about the one in China? Shouldn't they have worked on that one first?"

It's like trying to have a conversation with a game of Trivial Pursuit that specializes in information garnered from supermarket tabloids. After a while, I'd just pack an extra sandwich whenever I was busking in her neighborhood. I'd sit beside her, share my lunch, and let her talk if she wanted to, but I wouldn't say all that much myself.

That all changed the day I saw her with the Bone Woman.

I didn't call her the Bone Woman at first; the adjective that came more immediately to mind was fat. She couldn't have been much more than five-one, but she had to weigh in at two-fifty, leaving me with the impression that she was wider than she was tall. But she was light on her feet—peculiarly graceful for all her squat bulk.

She had a round face like a full moon, framed by thick black hair that hung in two long braids to her waist. Her eyes were small, almost lost in that expanse of face, and so dark they seemed all pupil. She went barefoot in a shapeless black dress, her only accessory an equally shapeless shoulder bag made of some kind of animal skin and festooned with dangling thongs from which hung various feathers, beads, bottle-caps and other found objects.

I paused at the far end of the street when I saw the two of them together. I had a sandwich for Ellie in my knapsack, but I hesitated in approaching them. They seemed deep in conversation, real conversation, give and take, and Ellie was—knitting? Talking *and* knitting? The pair of them looked like a couple of old gossips, sitting on the back porch of their building. The sight of Ellie acting so normal was something I didn't want to interrupt.

I sat down on a nearby stoop and watched until Ellie put away her knitting and stood up. She looked down at her companion with an expression in her features that I'd never seen before. It was awareness, I realized. She was completely *here* for a change.

As she came up the street, I stood up and called a greeting to her, but by the time she reached me she wore her usually vacuous expression.

"It's the newspapers," she told me. "They use radiation to print them and that's what makes the news seem so bad."

Before I could take the sandwich I'd brought her out of my knapsack, she'd shuffled off, around the corner, and was gone. I glanced back down the street to where the fat woman was still sitting, and decided to find Ellie later. Right now I wanted to know what the woman had done to get such a positive reaction out of Ellie.

When I approached, the fat woman was sifting through the refuse where the two of them had been sitting. As I watched, she picked up a good-sized bone. What kind,

I don't know, but it was as long as my forearm and as big around as the neck of my fiddle. Brushing dirt and a sticky candy wrapper from it, she gave it a quick polish on the sleeve of her dress and stuffed it away in her shoulderbag. Then she looked up at me.

My question died stillborn in my throat under the sudden scrutiny of those small dark eyes. She looked right through me—not the drifting, unfocused gaze of so many of the street people, but a cold, far-off seeing that weighed my presence, dismissed it, and gazed further off at something far more important.

I stood back as she rose easily to her feet. That was when I realized how graceful she was. She moved down the sidewalk as daintily as a doe, as though her bulk was filled with helium, rather than flesh, and weighed nothing. I watched her until she reached the far end of the street, turned her own corner and then, just like Ellie, was gone as well.

I ended up giving Ellie's sandwich to Johnny Rew, an old wino who's taught me a fiddle tune or two, the odd time I've run into him sober.

I started to see the Bone Woman everywhere after that day. I wasn't sure if she was just new to town, or if it was one of those cases where you suddenly see something or someone you've never noticed before and after that you see them all the time. Everybody I talked to about her seemed to know her, but no one was quite sure how long she'd been in the city, or where she lived, or even her name.

I still wasn't calling her the Bone Woman, though I knew by then that bones were all she collected. Old bones, found bones, rattling around together in her shoulderbag until she went off at the end of the day and showed up the next morning, ready to start filling her bag again.

When she wasn't hunting bones, she spent her time with the street's worst cases—people like Ellie that no one else could talk to. She'd get them making things—little pictures or carvings or beadwork, keeping their hands busy. And talking. Someone like Ellie still made no sense to anybody else, but you could tell when she was with the Bone Woman that they were sharing a real dialogue. Which was a good thing, I suppose, but I couldn't shake the feeling that there was something more going on, something if not exactly sinister, then still strange.

It was the bones, I suppose. There were so many. How could she keep finding them the way she did? And what did she do with them?

My brother Christy collects urban legends, the way the Bone Woman collects her bones, rooting them out where you'd never think they could be. But when I told him about her, he just shrugged.

"Who knows why any of them do anything?" he said.

Christy doesn't live on the streets, for all that he haunts them. He's just an observer—always has been, ever since we were kids. To him, the street people can be pretty well evenly divided between the sad cases and the crazies. Their stories are too human for him.

"Some of these are big," I told him. "The size of a human thighbone."

"So point her out to the cops."

"And tell them what?"

A smile touched his lips with just enough superiority in it to get under my skin. He's always been able to do that. Usually, it makes me do something I regret later, which I sometimes think is half his intention. It's not that he wants to see me hurt. It's just part and parcel of that air of authority that all older siblings seem to wear. You know, a raised eyebrow, a way of smiling that says "You have so much to learn, little brother."

"If you really want to know what she does with those bones," he said, "why don't you follow her home and find out?"

"Maybe I will."

It turned out that the Bone Woman had a squat on the roof of an abandoned factory building in the Tombs. She'd built herself some kind of a shed up there—just a leaning, ramshackle affair of castoff lumber and sheet metal, but it kept out the weather and could easily be heated with a woodstove in the spring and fall. Come winter, she'd need warmer quarters, but the snows were still a month or so away.

I followed her home one afternoon, then came back the next day when she was out to finally put to rest my fear about these bones she was collecting. The thought that had stuck in my mind was that she was taking something away from the street people like Ellie, people who were already at the bottom rung and deserved to be helped, or at least just left alone. I'd gotten this weird idea that the bones were tied up with the last remnants of vitality that someone like Ellie might have, and the Bone Woman was stealing it from them.

What I found was more innocuous, and at the same time creepier, than I'd expected.

The inside of her squat was littered with bones and wire and dog-shaped skeletons that appeared to be made from the two. Bones held in place by wire, half-connected ribs and skulls and limbs. A pack of bone dogs. Some of the figures were almost complete, others were merely suggestions, but everywhere I looked, the half-finished wire-and-bone skeletons sat or stood or hung suspended from the ceiling. There had to be more than a dozen in various states of creation.

I stood in the doorway, not willing to venture any further, and just stared at them all. I don't know how long I was there, but finally I turned away and made my way back down through the abandoned building and out onto the street.

So now I knew what she did with the bones. But it didn't tell me how she could find so many of them. Surely that many stray dogs didn't die, their bones scattered the length and breadth of the city like so much autumn residue?

Amy and I had a gig opening for the Kelledys that night. It didn't take me long to set up. I just adjusted my microphone, laid out my fiddle and whistles on a small table to one side, and then kicked my heels while Amy fussed with her pipes and the complicated tangle of electronics that she used to amplify them.

I've heard it said that all Uillean pipers are a little crazy—that they have to be to play an instrument that looks more like what you'd find in the back of a plumber's truck than an instrument—but I think of them as perfectionists. Every one I've ever met spends more time fiddling with their reeds and adjusting the tuning of their various chanters, drones and regulators than would seem humanly possible.

Amy's no exception. After a while I left her there on the stage, with her red hair falling in her face as she poked and prodded at a new reed she'd made for one of her drones, and wandered into the back where the Kelledys were making their own preparations for the show, which consisted of drinking tea and looking beatific. At least that's the way I always think of the two of them. I don't think I've ever met calmer people.

Jilly likes to think of them as mysterious, attributing all kinds of fairy-tale traits to them. Meran, she's convinced, with the green highlights in her nut-brown hair and her wise brown eyes, is definitely dryad material—the spirit of an oak tree come to life—while Cerin is some sort of wizard figure, a combination of adept and bard. I think the idea amuses them, and they play it up to Jilly. Nothing you can put your finger on, but they seem to get a kick out of spinning a mysterious air about themselves whenever she's around.

I'm far more practical than Jilly—actually, just about anybody's more practical than Jilly, God bless her, but that's another story. I think if you find yourself using the word magic to describe the Kelledys, what you're really talking about is their musical talent. They may seem preternaturally calm offstage, but as soon as they begin to play, that calmness is transformed into a bonfire of energy. There's enchantment then, burning on stage, but it comes from their instrumental skill.

"Geordie," Meran said after I'd paced back and forth for a few minutes. "You look a little edgy. Have some tea."

I had to smile. If the Kelledys had originated from some mysterious elsewhere, then I'd lean more toward them having come from a fiddle tune than Jilly's fairy tales.

"When sick is it tea you want?" I said, quoting the title of an old Irish jig that we all knew in common.

Meran returned my smile. "It can't hurt. Here," she added, rummaging around in a bag that was lying by her chair. "Let me see if I have something that'll ease your nervousness."

"I'm not nervous."

"No, of course not," Cerin put in. "Geordie just likes to pace, don't you?"

He was smiling as he spoke, but without a hint of Christy's sometimes annoying demeanor.

"No, really. It's just . . ."

"Just what?" Meran asked as my voice trailed off.

Well, here was the perfect opportunity to put Jilly's theories to the test, I decided. If the Kelledys were in fact as fey as she made them out to be, then they'd be able to explain this business with the bones, wouldn't they?

So I told them about the fat woman and her bones and what I'd found in her squat. They listened with far more reasonableness than I would have if someone had been telling the story to me—especially when I went on to explain the weird feeling I'd been getting from the whole business.

"It's giving me the creeps," I said, finishing up, "and I can't even say why."

"La Huesera," Cerin said when I was done.

Meran nodded. "The Bone Woman," she said, translating it for me. "It does sound like her."

"So you know her."

"No," Meran said. "It just reminds us of a story we heard when we were playing in Phoenix a few years ago. There was a young Apache man opening for us, and he and I started comparing flutes. We got on to one of the Native courting flutes which used to be made from human bone and somehow from there he started telling me about a legend they have in the Southwest about this old fat woman who wanders through the mountains and arroyos, collecting bones from the desert that she brings back to her cave."

"What does she collect them for?"

"To preserve the things that are in danger of being lost to the world," Cerin said.

"I don't get it."

"I'm not sure of the exact details," Cerin went on, "but it had something to do with the spirits of endangered species."

"Giving them a new life," Meran said.

"Or a second chance."

"But there's no desert around here," I said. "What would this Bone Woman be doing up here?"

Meran smiled. "I remember John saying that she's as often been seen riding shotgun in an eighteen-wheeler as walking down a dry wash."

"And besides," Cerin added, "any place is a desert when there's more going on underground than on the surface."

That described Newford perfectly. And who lived a more hidden life than the street people? They were right in front of us every day, but most people didn't even see them anymore. And who was more deserving of a second chance than someone like Ellie, who'd never even gotten a fair first chance?

"Too many of us live desert lives," Cerin said, and I knew just what he meant.

The gig went well. I was a little bemused, but I didn't make any major mistakes. Amy complained that her regulators had sounded too buzzy in the monitors, but that was just Amy. They'd sounded great to me, their counterpointing chords giving the tunes a real punch whenever they came in.

The Kelledys' set was pure magic. Amy and I watched them from the stage wings and felt higher as they took their final bow than we had when the applause had been directed at us.

I begged off getting together with them after the show, regretfully pleading tiredness. I *was* tired, but leaving the theater, I headed for an abandoned factory in the Tombs instead of home. When I got up on the roof of the building, the moon was full. It looked like a saucer of buttery gold, bathing everything in a warm yellow light. I heard a soft voice on the far side of the roof near the Bone Woman's squat. It wasn't exactly singing, but not chanting either. A murmuring, sliding sound that raised the hairs at the nape of my neck.

I walked a little nearer, staying in the shadows of the cornices, until I could see the Bone Woman. I paused then, laying my fiddlecase quietly on the roof and sliding down so that I was sitting with my back against the cornice.

The Bone Woman had one of her skeleton sculptures set out in front of her and she was singing over it. The dog shape was complete now, all the bones wired in place and gleaming in the moonlight. I couldn't make out the words of her song. Either there were none, or she was using a language I'd never heard before. As I watched, she stood, raising her arms up above the wired skeleton, and her voice grew louder.

The scene was peaceful—soothing, in the same way that the Kelledys' company could be—but eerie as well. The Bone Woman's voice had the cadence of one of the medicine chants I'd heard at a powwow up on the Kickaha Reservation—the same nasal tones and ringing quality. But that powwow hadn't prepared me for what came next.

At first I wasn't sure that I was really seeing it. The empty spaces between the skeleton's bones seemed to gather volume and fill out, as though flesh were forming on the bones. Then there was fur, highlighted by the moonlight, and I couldn't deny it any more. I saw a bewhiskered muzzle lift skyward, ears twitch, a tail curl up, thick-haired and strong. The powerful chest began to move rhythmically, at first in time to the Bone Woman's song, then breathing of its own accord.

The Bone Woman hadn't been making dogs in her squat, I realized as I watched the miraculous change occur. She'd been making wolves.

The newly animated creature's eyes snapped open and it leapt up, running to the edge of the roof. There it stood with its forelegs on the cornice. Arching its neck, the wolf pointed its nose at the moon and howled.

I sat there, already stunned, but the transformation still wasn't complete. As the wolf howled, it began to change again. Fur to human skin. Lupine shape, to that of a young woman. Howl to merry laughter. And as she turned, I recognized her features.

"Ellie," I breathed.

She still had the same horsy features, the same skinny body, all bones and angles, but she was beautiful. She blazed with the fire of a spirit that had never been hurt, never been abused, never been degraded. She gave me a radiant smile and then leapt from the edge of the roof.

I held my breath, but she didn't fall. She walked out across the city's skyline, out across the urban desert of rooftops and chimneys, off and away, running now, laughter trailing behind her until she was swallowed by the horizon.

I stared out at the night sky long after she had disappeared, then slowly stood up and walked across the roof to where the Bone Woman was sitting outside the door of her squat. She tracked my approach, but there was neither welcome nor dismissal in those small dark eyes. It was like the first time I'd come up to her; as far as she was concerned, I wasn't there at all.

"How did you do that?" I asked.

She looked through, past me.

"Can you teach me that song? I want to help, too."

Still no response.

"Why won't you *talk* to me?"

Finally her gaze focused on me.

"You don't have their need," she said.

Her voice was thick with an accent I couldn't place. I waited for her to go on, to explain what she meant, but once again, she ignored me. The pinpoints of black that passed for eyes in that round moon face looked away into a place where I didn't belong.

Finally, I did the only thing left for me to do. I collected my fiddlecase and went on home.

Some things haven't changed. Ellie's still living on the streets, and I still share my lunch with her when I'm down in her part of town. There's nothing the Bone Woman can do to change what this life has done to the Ellie Spinks of the world.

But what I saw that night gives me hope for the next turn of the wheel. I know now that no matter how downtrodden someone like Ellie might be, at least somewhere a piece of her is running free. Somewhere that wild and innocent part of her spirit is being preserved with those of the wolf and the rattlesnake and all the other creatures whose spirit-bones *La Huesera* collects from the desert—deserts natural and of our own making.

Spirit-bones. Collected and preserved, nurtured in the belly of the Bone Woman's song, until we learn to welcome them upon their terms, rather than our own.

Pal o' Mine

1

Gina always believed there was magic in the world. "But it doesn't work the way it does in fairy tales," she told me. "It doesn't save us. We have to save ourselves."

2

One of the things I keep coming back to when I think of Gina is walking down Yoors Street on a cold, snowy Christmas Eve during our last year of high school. We were out Christmas shopping. I'd been finished and had my presents all wrapped during the first week of December, but Gina had waited for the last minute, as usual, which was why we were out braving the storm that afternoon.

I was wrapped in as many layers of clothing as I could fit under my overcoat and looked about twice my size, but Gina was just scuffling along beside me in her usual cowboy boots and jeans, a floppy felt hat pressing down her dark curls and her hands thrust deep into the pockets of her pea jacket. She simply didn't pay any attention to the cold. Gina was good at that: ignoring inconveniences, or things she wasn't particularly interested in dealing with, much the way—I was eventually forced to admit—that I'd taught myself to ignore the dark current that was always present, running just under the surface of her exuberantly good moods.

"You know what I like best about the city?" she asked as we waited for the light to change where Yoors crosses Bunnett.

I shook my head.

"Looking up. There's a whole other world living up there."

I followed her gaze and at first I didn't know what she was on about. I looked through breaks in the gusts of snow that billowed around us, but couldn't detect anything out of the ordinary. I saw only rooftops and chimneys, multicolored Christmas decorations and the black strands of cable that ran in sagging geometric lines from the power poles to the buildings.

"What're you talking about?" I asked.

"The 'goyles," Gina said.

I gave her a blank look, no closer to understanding what she was talking about than I'd been before.

"The gargoyles, Sue," she repeated patiently. "Almost every building in this part of the city has got them, perched up there by the rooflines, looking down on us."

Once she'd pointed them out to me, I found it hard to believe that I'd never noticed them before. On that corner alone there were at least a half-dozen grotesque examples. I saw one in the archway keystone of the Annaheim Building directly across the street— a leering monstrous face, part lion, part bat, part man. Higher up, and all around, other nightmare faces peered down at us, from the corners of buildings, hidden in the frieze and cornice designs, cunningly nestled in corner brackets and the stone roof cresting. Every building had them. *Every* building.

Their presence shocked me. It's not that I was unaware of their existence—after all, I was planning on architecture as a major in college; it's just that if someone had mentioned gargoyles to me before that day, I would have automatically thought of the cathedrals and castles of Europe—not ordinary office buildings in Newford.

"I can't believe I never noticed them before," I told her.

"There are people who live their whole lives here and never see them," Gina said.

"How's that possible?"

Gina smiled. "It's because of where they are—looking down at us from just above our normal sightline. People in the city hardly ever look up."

"But still . . . ."

"I know. It's something, isn't it? It really is a whole different world. Imagine being able to live your entire life in the middle of the city and never be noticed by anybody."

"Like a baglady," I said.

Gina nodded. "Sort of. Except people wouldn't ignore you because you're some pathetic street person that they want to avoid. They'd ignore you because they simply couldn't *see* you."

That thought gave me a creepy feeling, and I couldn't suppress a shiver, but I could tell that Gina was intrigued with the idea. She was staring at that one gargoyle, above the entrance to the Annaheim Building.

"You really like those things, don't you?" I said.

Gina turned to look at me, an expression I couldn't read sitting at the back of her eyes.

"I wish I lived in their world," she told me.

She held my gaze with that strange look in her eyes for a long heartbeat. Then the light changed and she laughed, breaking the mood. Slipping her arm in mine, she started us off across the street to finish her Christmas shopping.

When we stood on the pavement in front of the Annaheim Building, she stopped and looked up at the gargoyle. I craned my neck and tried to give it a good look myself, but it was hard to see because of all the blowing snow.

Gina laughed suddenly. "It knows we were talking about it."

"What do you mean?"

"It just winked at us."

I hadn't seen anything, but then I always seemed to be looking exactly the wrong way, or perhaps *in* the wrong way, whenever Gina tried to point out some magical thing to me. She was so serious about it.

"Did you see?" Gina asked.

"I'm not sure," I told her. "I think I saw something. . . ."

Falling snow. The side of a building. And stone statuary that was pretty amazing in and of itself without the need to be animated as well. I looked up at the gargoyle again, trying to see what Gina had seen.

I wish I lived in their world.

It wasn't until years later that I finally understood what she'd meant by that.

3

Christmas wasn't the same for me as for most people—not even when I was a kid: My dad was born on Christmas day; Granny Ashworth, his mother, died on Christmas day when I was nine; and my own birthday was December 27. It made for a strange brew come the holiday season, part celebration, part mourning, liberally mixed with all the paraphernalia that means Christmas: eggnog and glittering lights, caroling, ornaments and, of course, presents.

Christmas wasn't centered around presents for me. Easy to say, I suppose, seeing how I grew up in the Beaches, wanting for nothing, but it's true. What enamored me the most about the season, once I got beyond the confusion of birthdays and mourning, was the idea of what it was supposed to be: peace and goodwill to all. The traditions. The idea of the miracle birth the way it was told in the Bible and more secular legends like the one telling how, for one hour after midnight on Christmas Eve, animals were given human voices so that they could praise the baby Jesus.

I remember staying up late the year I turned eleven, sitting in bed with my cat on my lap and watching the clock, determined to hear Chelsea speak, except I fell asleep sometime after eleven and never did find out if she could or not. By the time Christmas came around the next year I was too old to believe in that sort of thing anymore.

Gina never got too old. I remember years later when she got her dog Fritzie, she told me, "You know what I like the best about him? The stories he tells me."

"Your dog tells you stories," I said slowly.

"Everything's got a voice," Gina told me. "You just have to learn how to hear it."

4

The best present I ever got was the Christmas that Gina decided to be my friend. I'd been going to a private school and hated it. Everything about it was so stiff and proper. Even though we were only children, it was still all about money and social standing and it drove me mad. I'd see the public school kids, and they seemed so free compared to all the boundaries I perceived to be compartmentalizing my own life.

I pestered my mother for the entire summer I was nine until she finally relented and let me take the public transport into Ferryside where I attended Cairnmount Public School. By noon of my first day, I realized that I hated public school even more.

There's nothing worse than being the new kid—especially when you were busing in from the Beaches. Nobody wanted anything to do with the slumming rich kid and her airs. I didn't have airs; I was just too scared. But first impressions are everything, and I ended up feeling more left out and alone than I'd ever been at my old school. I couldn't even talk about it at home—my pride wouldn't let me. After the way I'd carried on about it all summer, I couldn't find the courage to admit that I'd been wrong.

So I did the best I could. At recess, I'd stand miserably on the sidelines, trying to look as though I was a part of the linked fence, or whatever I was standing beside at the time, because I soon learned it was better to be ignored than to be noticed and ridiculed. I stuck it out until just before Christmas break. I don't know if I would have been able to force myself to return after the holidays, but that day a bunch of boys were teasing me and my eyes were already welling with tears when Gina walked up out of nowhere and chased them off.

"Why don't you ever play with anybody?" she asked me.

"Nobody wants me to play with them," I said.

"Well, I do," she said and then she smiled at me, a smile so bright that it dried up all my tears.

After that, we were best friends forever.

5

Gina was the most outrageous, talented, wonderful person I had ever met. I was the sort of child who usually reacted to stimuli; Gina created them. She made up games, she made up stories, she made up songs. It was impossible to be bored in her company, and we became inseparable, in school and out.

I don't think a day went by that we didn't spend some part of it together. We had sleepovers. We took art and music and dance classes together, and if she won the prizes, I didn't mind, because she was my friend and I could only be proud of her. There was no limit to her imagination, but that was fine by me, too. I was happy to have been welcomed into her world, and I was more than willing to take up whatever enterprise she might propose.

I remember one afternoon we sat up in her room and made little people out of found objects: acorn heads, seed eyes, twig bodies. We made clothes for them and furniture and concocted long, extravagant family histories so that we ended up knowing more about them than we did our classmates.

"They're real now," I remember her telling me. "We've given them lives, so they'll always be real."

"What kind of real?" I asked, feeling a little confused because I was at that age when I was starting to understand the difference between what was make-believe and what was actual.

"There's only one kind of real," Gina told me. "The trouble is, not everybody can see it and they make fun of those who can."

Though I couldn't know the world through the same perspective as Gina had, there was one thing I did know. "I would never make fun of you," I said.

"I know, Sue. That's why we're friends."

I still have the little twig people I made, wrapped up in tissue and stored away in a box of childhood treasures; I don't know what ever happened to Gina's.

We had five years together, but then her parents moved out of town—not impossibly far, but far enough to make our getting together a major effort, and we rarely saw each other more than a few times a year after that. It was mainly Gina's doing that we didn't entirely lose touch with each other. She wrote me two or three times a week, long chatty letters about what she'd been reading, films she'd seen, people she'd met, her hopes of becoming a professional musician after she finished high school. The letters were decorated with fanciful illustrations of their contents and sometimes included miniature envelopes in which I would find letters from her twig people to mine.

Although I tried to keep up my side, I wasn't much of a correspondent. Usually I'd phone her, but my calls grew further and further apart as the months went by. I never stopped considering her as a friend—the occasions when we did get together were among my best memories of being a teenager—but my own life had changed, and I didn't have as much time for her anymore. It was hard to maintain a long-distance relationship when there was so much going on around me at home. I was no longer the new kid at school, and I'd made other friends. I worked on the school paper, and then I got a boyfriend.

Gina never wanted to talk about him. I suppose she thought of it as a kind of betrayal; she never again had a friend that she was as close to as she'd been with me.

I remember her mother calling me once, worried because Gina seemed to be sinking into a reclusive depression. I did my best to be there for her. I called her almost every night for a month, and went out to visit her on the weekends, but somehow I just couldn't relate to her pain. Gina had always seemed so self-contained, so perfect, that it was hard to imagine her being as withdrawn and unhappy as her mother seemed to think she was. She put on such a good face to me that eventually the worries I'd had faded and the demands of my own life pulled me away again.

6

Gina never liked Christmas.

The year she introduced me to Newford's gargoyles we saw each other twice over the holidays: once so that she could do her Christmas shopping, and then again between Christmas and New Year's when I came over to her place and stayed the night. She introduced me to her dog—Fritzie, a gangly, wirehaired, long-legged mutt that she'd found abandoned on one of the country roads near her parents' place—and played some of her new songs for me, accompanying herself on guitar.

The music had a dronal quality that seemed at odds with her clear high voice and the strange Middle Eastern decorations she used. The lyrics were strange and dark, leaving me with a sensation that was not so much unpleasant as uncomfortable, and I could understand why she'd been having so much trouble getting gigs. It wasn't just that she was so young and since most clubs served alcohol, their owners couldn't hire an underage performer; Gina's music simply wasn't what most people would think of as entertainment. Her songs went beyond introspection. They took the listener to that dark place that sits inside each and every one of us, that place we don't want to visit, that we don't even want to admit is there.

But the songs aside, there didn't seem to be any trace of the depression that had worried her mother so much the previous autumn. She appeared to be her old self, the Gina I remembered: opinionated and witty, full of life and laughter even while explaining to me what bothered her so much about the holiday season.

"I love the *idea* of Christmas," she said. "It's the hypocrisy of the season that I dislike. One time out of the year, people do what they can for the homeless, help stock the food banks, contribute to snowsuit funds and give toys to poor children. But where are they the rest of the year when their help is just as necessary? It makes me a little sick to think of all the money that gets spent on Christmas lights and parties and presents that people don't even really want in the first place. If we took all that money and gave it to the people who need it simply to survive, instead of throwing it away on ourselves, we could probably solve most of the problems of poverty and homelessness over one Christmas season."

"I suppose," I said. "But at least Christmas brings people closer together. I guess what we have to do is build on that."

Gina gave me a sad smile. "Who does it bring closer together?"

"Well . . . families, friends . . ."

"But what about those who don't have either? They look at all this closeness you're talking about, and it just makes their own situation seem all the more desperate. It's hardly surprising that the holiday season has the highest suicide rate of any time of the year."

"But what can we do?" I said. "We can't just turn our backs and pretend there's no such thing as Christmas."

Gina shrugged, then gave me a sudden grin. "We could become Christmas commandos. You know," she added at my blank look. "We'd strike from within. First we'd convince our own families to give it up and then . . ."

With that she launched into a plan of action that would be as improbable in its execution as it was entertaining in its explanation. She never did get her family to give up Christmas, and I have to admit I didn't try very hard with mine, but the next year I did go visit the residents of places like St. Vincent's Home for the Aged, and I worked in the Grasso Street soup kitchen with Gina on Christmas day. I came away with a better experience of what Christmas was all about than I'd ever had at home.

But I just couldn't maintain that commitment all year round. I kept going to St. Vincent's when I could, but the sheer despair of the soup kitchens and food banks was more than I could bear.

7

Gina dropped out of college during her second year to concentrate on her music. She sent me a copy of the demo tape she was shopping around to the record companies in hopes of getting a contract. I didn't like it at first. Neither her guitar-playing nor her vocal style had changed much, and the inner landscape the songs revealed was too bleak, the shadows it painted upon the listener seemed too unrelentingly dark, but out of loyalty I played it a few times more and subsequent listenings changed that first impression.

Her songs were still bleak, but I realized that they helped create a healing process in the listener. If I let them take me into the heart of their darkness, they took me out again as well. It was the kind of music that while it appeared to wallow in despair, in actuality it left its audience stronger, more able to face the pain and heartache that awaited them beyond the music.

She was playing at a club near the campus one weekend, and I went to see her. Sitting in front were a handful of hard-core fans, all pale-faced and dressed in black, but most of the audience didn't understand what she was offering them any more than I had the first time I sat through the demo tape. Obviously her music was an acquired taste—which didn't bode well for her career in a world where, more and more, most information was conveyed in thirty-second sound bites and audiences in the entertainment industry demanded instant gratification, rather than taking the time to explore the deeper resonances of a work.

She had Fritzie waiting for her in the claustrophobic dressing room behind the stage, so the three of us went walking in between her sets. That was the night she first told me about her bouts with depression.

"I don't know what it is that brings them on," she said. "I know I find it frustrating that I keep running into a wall with my music, but I also know that's not the cause of them either. As long as I can remember I've carried this feeling of alienation around with me; I wake up in the morning, in the middle of the night, and I'm paralyzed with all this emotional pain. The only people that have ever really helped to keep it at bay were first you, and now Fritzie."

It was such a shock to hear that her only lifelines were a friend who was hardly ever there for her and a dog. The guilt that lodged inside me then has never really gone away. I wanted to ask what had happened to that brashly confident girl who had turned my whole life around as much by the example of her own strength and resourcefulness as by her friendship, but then I realized that the answer lay in her music, in her songs that spoke of masks and what lay behind them, of puddles on muddy roads that sometimes hid deep, bottomless wells.

"I feel so . . . so stupid," she said.

This time I was the one who took charge. I steered her toward the closest bus stop and we sat down on its bench. I put my arm around her shoulders and Fritzie laid his mournful head upon her knee and looked up into her face.

"Don't feel stupid," I said. "You can't help the bad feelings."

"But why do I have to have them? Nobody else does."

"Everybody has them."

She toyed with the wiry fur between Fritzie's ears and leaned against me.

"Not like mine," she said.

"No," I agreed. "Everybody's got their own."

That got me a small smile. We sat there for a while, watching the traffic go past until it was time for her last set of the night.

"What do you think of the show?" she asked as we returned to the club.

"I like it," I told her, "but I think it's the kind of music that people have to take their time to appreciate."

Gina nodded glumly. "And who's got the time?"

"I do."

"Well, I wish you ran one of the record companies," she said. "I get the same answer from all of them. They like my voice, they like my playing, but they want me to sexy up my image and write songs that are more upbeat."

She paused. We'd reached the back door of the club by then. She put her back against the brick wall of the alley and looked up. Fritzie was pressed up against the side of her leg as though he was glued there.

"I tried, you know," Gina said. "I really tried to give them what they wanted, but it just wasn't there. I just don't have that kind of song inside me."

She disappeared inside then to retune her guitar before she went back on stage. I stayed for a moment longer, my gaze drawn up as hers had been while she'd been talking to me. There was a gargoyle there, spout-mouth open wide, a rather benevolent look about its grotesque features. I looked at it for a long time, wondering for a moment if I would see it blink or move the way Gina probably had, but it was just a stone sculpture, set high up in the wall. Finally I went back inside and found my seat.

8

I was in the middle of studying for exams the following week, but I made a point of it to call Gina at least once a day. I tried getting her to let me take her out for dinner on the weekend, but she and Fritzie were pretty much inseparable and she didn't want to leave him tied up outside the restaurant while we sat inside to eat. So I ended up having them over to the little apartment I was renting in Crowsea instead. She told me that night that she was going out west to try to shop her tape around to the big companies in L.A., and I didn't see her again for three months.

I'd been worried about her going off on her own, feeling as she was. I even offered to go with her, if she'd just wait until the semester was finished, but she assured me she'd be fine, and a series of cheerful cards and short letters—signed by either her or just a big paw print—arrived in my letterbox to prove the point. When she finally did get back, she called me up and we got together for a picnic lunch in Fitzhenry Park.

Going out to the West Coast seemed to have done her good. She came back looking radiant and tanned, full of amusing stories concerning the ups and downs of her and Fritzie's adventures out there. She'd even got some fairly serious interest from an independent record label, but they were still making up their minds when her money ran out. Instead of trying to make do in a place where she felt even more like a stranger than she did in Newford, she decided to come home to wait for their response, driving back across the country in her old station wagon, Fritzie sitting up on the passenger seat beside her, her guitar in its battered case lying across the back seat.

"By the time we rolled into Newford," she said, "the car was just running on fumes. But we made it."

"If you need some money, or a place to stay . . ." I offered.

"I can just see the three of us squeezed into that tiny place of yours."

"We'd make do."

Gina smiled. "It's okay. My dad fronted me some money until the advance from the record company comes through. But thanks all the same. Fritzie and I appreciate the offer."

I was really happy for her. Her spirits were so high now that things had finally turned around, and she could see that she was going somewhere with her music. She knew there was a lot of hard work still to come, but it was the sort of work she thrived on.

"I feel like I've lived my whole life on the edge of an abyss," she told me, "just waiting for the moment when it'd finally drag me down for good, but now everything's changed. It's like I finally figured out a way to live some place else—away from the edge. *Far* away."

I was going on to my third year at Butler U. in the fall, but we made plans to drive back to L.A. together in July, once she got the okay from the record company. We'd spend the summer together in La La Land, taking in the sights while Gina worked on her album. It's something I knew we were both looking forward to.

9

Gina was looking after the cottage of a friend of her parents' when she fell back into the abyss. She never told me how she was feeling, probably because she knew I'd have gone to any length to stop her from hurting herself. All she'd told me before she went was that she needed the solitude to work on some new songs and I'd believed her. I had no reason to worry about her. During the two weeks she was living out there I must have gotten a half-dozen cheerful cards, telling me what to add to my packing list for our trip out west and what to leave off.

Her mother told me that she'd gotten a letter from the record company, turning down her demo. She said Gina had seemed to take the rejection well when she called to give her daughter the bad news. They'd ended their conversation with Gina already making plans to start the rounds of the record companies again with the new material she'd been working on. Then she'd burned her guitar and all of her music and poetry in a firepit down by the shore, and simply walked out into the lake. Her body was found after a neighbor was drawn to the lot by Fritzie's howling. The poor dog was shivering and wet, matted with mud from having tried to rescue her. They know it wasn't an accident, because of the note she left behind in the cottage.

I never read the note. I couldn't.

I miss her terribly, but most of all, I'm angry. Not at Gina, but at this society of ours that tries to make everybody fit into the same mold. Gina was unique, but she didn't want to be. All she wanted to do was fit in, but her spirit and her muse wouldn't let her. That dichotomy between who she was and who she thought she should be was what really killed her.

All that survives of her music is that demo tape. When I listen to it, I can't understand how she could create a healing process for others through that dark music, but she couldn't use it to heal herself.

10

Tomorrow is Christmas day and I'm going down to the soup kitchen to help serve the Christmas dinners. It'll be my first Christmas without Gina. My parents wanted me to come home, but I put them off until tomorrow night. I just want to sit here tonight with

Fritzie and remember. He lives with me because Gina asked me to take care of him, but he's not the same dog he was when Gina was alive. He misses her too much.

I'm sitting by the window, watching the snow fall. On the table in front of me I've spread out the contents of a box of memories: the casing for Gina's demo tape. My twig people and the other things we made. All those letters and cards that Gina sent me over the years. I haven't been able to reread them yet, but I've looked at the drawings and I've held them in my hands, turning them over and over, one by one. The demo tape is playing softly on my stereo. It's the first time I've been able to listen to it since Gina died.

Through the snow I can see the gargoyle on the building across the street. I know now what Gina meant about wanting to live in their world and be invisible. When you're invisible, no one can see that you're different.

Thinking about Gina hurts so much, but there's good things to remember, too. I don't know what would have become of me if she hadn't rescued me in that playground all those years ago and welcomed me into her life. It's so sad that the uniqueness about her that made me love her so much was what caused her so much pain.

The bells of St. Paul's Cathedral strike midnight. They remind me of the child I was, trying to stay up late enough to hear my cat talk. I guess that's what Gina meant to me. While everybody else grew up, Gina retained all the best things about childhood: goodness and innocence and an endless wonder. But she carried the downside of being a child inside her as well. She always lived in the present moment, the way we do when we're young, and that must be why her despair was so overwhelming for her.

"I tried to save her," a voice says in the room behind me as the last echo of St. Paul's bells fades away. "But she wouldn't let me. She was too strong for me."

I don't move. I don't dare move at all. On the demo tape, Gina's guitar starts to strum the intro to another song. Against the drone of the guitar's strings, the voice goes on.

"I know she'll always live on so long as we keep her memory alive," it says, "but sometimes that's just not enough. Sometimes I miss her so much I don't think *I* can go on."

I turn slowly then, but there's only me in the room. Me and Fritzie, and one small Christmas miracle to remind me that everything magic didn't die when Gina walked into the lake.

"Me, too," I tell Fritzie.

I get up from my chair and cross the room to where he's sitting up, looking at me with those sad eyes of his. I put my arms around his neck. I bury my face in his rough fur, and we stay there like that for a long time, listening to Gina sing.

Where Desert Spirits Crowd the Night

If your mind is attuned to beauty,
you find beauty in everything.
—Jean Cooke,
in an interview in *The Artist's*
and Illustrator's Magazine,
April 1993

All I ask of you
Is that you remember me
As loving you
—traditional Sufi song

Each of us owes God a death.
—attributed to Humphrey Osmond

1

Sophie didn't attend the funeral. She hadn't met Max yet, couldn't have known that his lover had died. On the afternoon that Max stood at Peter's gravesite under a far too cheerful sky, she was in her studio in Old Market, preparing for a new show. It wasn't until the opening, two months later, that they met.

But even then, Coyote was watching.

2

There is a door in my dreams that opens into a desert. . . .

where the light is like a wash of whiskey over my vision;

where the color of the earth ranges through a spectrum of dusty browns cut with pale ochre tones and siennas;

where distant peaks jut blue-grey from the tide of hills washing up against the ragged line the mountains make at the horizon, peaks that are shadowed now as the sun sets in a geranium and violet glory behind me;

where the tall saguaro rise like sleepy green giants from the desert floor, waving lazy arms to no one in particular, with barrel cacti crouching in their shadows like smaller, shorter cousins;

where clusters of prickly pear and cholla offer a thorny embrace, and the landscape is clouded with mesquite and palo verde and smoke trees, their leaves so tiny they don't seem as much to grow from the gnarly branches as to have been dusted upon them;

where a hawk hangs in the sky high above me, a dark silhouette against the ever deepening blue, gliding effortlessly on outspread wings;

where a lizard darts into a tight crevice, its movement so quick, it only registers in the corner of my eye;

where an owl the size of my palm peers at me from the safety of its hole in a towering saguaro;

where a rattlesnake gives me one warning rattle, then fixes me with its hypnotic stare, poised to strike long after I have backed away;

where the sound of a medicine flute, breathy and soft as a secret, rises up from an arroyo, and for one moment I see the shadow of a hunchbacked man and his instrument cast upon the far wall of the gully, before the night takes the sight away, if not the sound;

where the sky, even at night, overwhelms me with its immensity;

where the stillness seems complete . . .

except for the resonance of my heartbeat that twins the distant-drum of a stag's hooves upon the dry, hard ground;

except for the incessant soughing cries of the ground-doves that feed in the brushy vegetation all around me;

except for the low sound of the flute which first brought me here.

The sweet scent of a mesquite fire in the middle of a dry wash draws me down from the higher ridges. The ground-doves break like quail with a rushing thrum of their wings as I make my way near. A figure is there by the fire, sitting motionless, head bent in shadow. I stand just beyond the circle of light, uncertain, uneasy. But finally I step forward. I sit across the fire from the figure. In the distance, I can still hear the sound of the flute. My silent companion gives neither it nor my presence any acknowledgment, but I can be patient, too.

And anyway, I've nowhere else to go.

3

Given her way in the matter, Sophie would never attend one of her own openings. She was so organized and tidy that she never really thought that she looked like the typical image of what an artist should be, and she always felt awkward trying to make nice with the gallery's clients. It wasn't that she didn't like people, or even that she wasn't prone to involved conversations. She simply felt uncomfortable around strangers, especially when she was supposed to be promoting herself and her work. But she tried.

So this evening as The Green Man Gallery filled with the guests that Albina had invited to the opening, Sophie concentrated on fulfilling what she saw as her responsibility in making the evening a success. Instead of clustering in a corner with her scruffy friends, who were doing their best not to be too rowdy and only just succeeding, she made an effort to mingle, to be sociable, the approachable artist. Whenever she felt herself gravitating to where Jilly and Wendy and the others were standing, she'd focus on someone she didn't know, walk over and strike up a conversation.

An hour or so into the opening, she picked a man in his late twenties who had just stopped in front of *Hearts Like Fire, Burning*—a small oil painting of two golden figures holding hands in a blaze of color that she'd meant to represent the fire of their consummated love.

He was tall and slender, a pale, dark-haired Pre-Raphaelite presence dressed in somber clothes: black jeans, black T-shirt, black sportsjacket, even black Nike sneakers. What attracted her to him was how he moved like a shadow through the gallery crowd and seemed completely at odds with both them and the bright, sensual colors of the paintings that made up the show. And yet he seemed more in tune with the paintings than anyone else—perhaps, she thought wryly as she noticed the intensity of his interest in the work, herself included.

Hearts Like Fire, Burning, in particular, appeared to mesmerize him. He stood longest in front of it, transfixed, his features a curious mixture of deep sadness and joy. When she approached him, he looked slowly away from the painting and smiled at her. The expression turned bittersweet by the time it reached his eyes.

"So what do you think of this piece?" he asked.

Sophie blinked in surprise. "I should probably be asking you that question."

"How so?"

"I'm the artist."

He inclined his head slightly in greeting and put out his hand. "Max Hannon," he said, introducing himself.

"I'm Sophie Etoile," she said as she took his hand. Then she laughed. "I guess that was obvious."

He laughed with her, but his laugh, like his smile, held a deep sadness by the time it reached his eyes.

"I find it very peaceful," he said, turning back to the painting.

"Now that's a description I've never heard of my work."

"Oh?" He regarded her once more. "How's it usually described?"

"Those that like it call it lively, colorful, vibrant. Those that don't call it garish, overblown. . . ." Sophie shrugged and let the words trail off.

"And how would you describe it?"

"With this piece, I agree with you. For all its flood of bright color, I find it very peaceful."

"It reminds me of my lover, Peter," Max said. "We were in Arizona a few months ago, staying with friends who have a place in the desert. We'd sit and hold hands at this table they had set up behind their house and simply let the light and the sky fill us. It felt just like this painting—full of gold and flames and the fire in our hearts, all mixed up together. When I look at this, it brings it all back."

"That's very sweet."

Max turned back to the painting. "He died a week or so after we got back."

"I'm so sorry," Sophie said, laying a hand on his arm.

Max sighed. "It doesn't hurt to talk about him, but God do I miss him."

You can say it doesn't hurt, Sophie thought, but she could see how bright his eyes had become, only just holding back a film of tears. The openness with which he'd shared his feelings with her made her want to do something special in return.

"I want you to have this painting," she said. "You can come pick it up when the show's over."

Max shook his head. "I'd love to buy it," he said, "but I don't have that kind of money."

"Who said anything about you having to pay for it?"

"I couldn't even think of . . ." he began.

But Sophie refused to listen. "Look," she said. "What would be the point of being an artist if you only did it for the money? I always feel weird about selling my work anyway. It's as though I'm selling off my children. I don't even know what kind of a home they're going to—there's no evaluation process beforehand. Someone could buy this painting just for the investment and for all I know it'll end up stuck in a closet somewhere and never be seen again. I can't tell you how good it would make me feel knowing that it was hanging in your home instead, where it would mean so much to you."

"No, I just couldn't accept it," Max told her.

"Then let me give it to Peter," Sophie said, "and you can keep it for him."

Max shook his head. "This is so strange. Things like this don't happen in the real world."

"Well, pick a world where it could happen," Sophie said, "and we'll pretend that we're there."

Max gave her a curious look. "Do you do this a lot?"

"What? Give away paintings?"

"No, pick another world to be in when you don't happen to like the way things are going in this one."

Now it was Sophie's turn to be intrigued. "Why, do you?"

"No. It's just . . . ever since you came over and started talking to me, I've felt as though we've met before. But not here. Not in this world. It's more like we met in a dream. . . ."

This was too strange, Sophie thought. For a moment the gallery and crowd about them seemed to flicker, to grow hazy and two-dimensional, as though only she and Max were real.

Like we met in a dream . . .

Slowly she shook her head. "Don't get me started on dreams," she said.

4

"There are sleeping dreams and waking dreams," Christina Rossetti says in her poem "A Ballad of Boding," as though the difference between them is absolute. My dreams aren't so clearly divided, not from one another, and not from when I'm actually awake either. My sleeping dreams bleed into the real world; actually, the place where they take place seems like a real world, too—it's just not one that's as easily accessed by most people.

The experiences I have there aren't real, of course, or at least not real in the way people normally use the word. What happens when I fall asleep and step into my dreams can't be measured or weighed—it can only be known—but that doesn't stop these experiences from influencing my life and leaving me in a state of mild confusion so much of the time.

The confusion stems from the fact that every time I turn around, the rules seem to change. Or maybe it's that every time I think I have a better understanding of what the night side of my life means, the dreams open up like a Chinese puzzle box, and I find yet another riddle lying inside the one I've just figured out. The borders blur, retreating before me, deeper and deeper into the dreamscape, walls becoming doors, and doors opening out into mysteries that often obscure the original question. I don't even know the original question anymore. I can't even remember if there ever was one.

I do remember that I went looking for my mother once. I went to a place, marshy and bogled like an old English storybook fen, where I found that she might be a drowned moon, pinned underwater by quicks and other dark creatures until I freed her from her watery tomb. But I came back from that dreamscape without a clear answer as to who she was, or what exactly it was that I had done. What I do know is that I came back with a friend: Jeck Crow, a handsome devil of a man who, I seem to remember, once bore the physical appearance of the black-winged bird that's his namesake. Is it a true memory? I don't know, he won't say, and our relationship has progressed to the point where it doesn't really matter anymore.

I only see him when I sleep. I close my eyes and step from this world to Mabon, the city that radiates from Mr. Truepenny's, the bookstore/art gallery I made up when I was a kid. Or at least I thought I'd made it up. It was the place I went when I was waiting for my dad to come home from work, a haven from my loneliness because I didn't make friends easily in those days. Not having anyone with whom I could share the fruits of my imagination, I put all that energy into making up a place where I was special, or at least had access to special things.

Faerie blood—courtesy of a mother who, Jilly is convinced, was a dream in this world, a moon in her own—is what makes it all real.

5

"Who was that guy you spent half the night talking to?" Jilly wanted to know as she and Sophie were walking home from the restaurant where they'd all gone to celebrate after the opening. Sophie had asked Max to come along, but he'd declined.

"Just this guy."

Jilly laughed. " 'Just this guy.' Oh, please. He was the best-looking man in the place and he seemed quite smitten with you."

Sophie had to smile. Only Jilly would use a word like smitten.

"His name's Max Hannon," she told Jilly, "and he's gay."

"So? This means you can't be friends?"

"Of course not. I was just pointing out that he's not potential boyfriend material."

"It's possible to be enamored with someone on an intellectual or spiritual level, you know."

"I know."

"And besides, you already have a boyfriend."

Sophie sighed. "Right. In my dreams. That doesn't exactly do much for me in the real world."

"But your dreams are like a real world for you."

"I think I need something a little more . . . substantial in my life. My biological clock is ticking away."

"But Jeck—"

"Isn't real," Sophie said. "No matter how much I pretend he is. And Mabon isn't a real city, no matter how much I want it to be, and even if it seems like other people can visit it. You can talk all you want about consensual reality, Jilly, but that doesn't change the fact that some things are real and some things aren't. There's a line drawn between the two that separates reality from fantasy."

"Yeah, but it's an imaginary line," Jilly said. "Who really decides where it gets drawn?"

They'd been through variations on this conversation many times before. Anyone who spent any amount of time with Jilly did. Her open-mindedness was either endearing or frustrating, depending on where you stood on whatever particular subject happened to be under discussion.

"Well, I'll tell you," Jilly went on when Sophie didn't respond. "A long time ago a bunch of people reached a general consensus as to what's real and what's not and most of us have been going along with it ever since."

"All of which has nothing to do with Max," Sophie said in an attempt to return to the original topic of their conversation.

"I know," Jilly said. "So are you going to see him again?"

"I hope so. There's something very intriguing about him."

"Which has nothing to do with the way he looks."

"I told you," Sophie said. "He's gay."

"Like Sue always says, the best ones are either married or gay, more's the pity."

Sophie smiled. "Only for us."

"This is true."

6

The desert dream starts in the alley behind Mr. Truepenny's shop—or at least where the alley's supposed to be. I'm in the back of the store with Jeck, poking around through the shelves of books, when I hear the sound of this flute. It goes on for a while, sort of lingering there in the back of my mind, until finally I get curious. I leave Jeck digging for treasure in a cardboard box of new arrivals and step past the door that leads into the store's small art gallery. The music is sort of atonal, and the instrument appears to have a limited range of notes, but there's something appealing about it all the same. I walk down a long narrow corridor, the walls encrusted with old portraits of thin, bearded men and women in dresses that appear far too stiff and ornately embroidered to be comfortable. The soles of my shoes squeak on the wooden floor in a rhythmic counterpoint to the music I'm following. I stop at the door at the far end of the hall. The music seems to be coming from the other side of it, so I open the door and step out, expecting to find myself in a familiar alleyway, but the alley's gone.

Instead, I'm standing in a desert. I turn around to see that the door through which I came has disappeared. All that I can see on every side of me is an endless panorama of desert, each compass point bordered by mountains. I seem to be as far from Mabon as that city is from the place where my body sleeps.

"What is this place?" I say.

My voice startles me, because I didn't realize I was speaking aloud. What startles me more is that my rhetorical question gets answered. I turn to see the oddest sight: There's a rattlesnake coiled up under a palo verde tree. The pale color of the tree's branches and twigs awakes an echoing green on the snake's scales which range through a gorgeous palette of golds and deep rusty reds. That's normal enough. What's so disconcerting is that the snake has the face of a Botticelli madonna—serene smile, rounded features enclosed by a cloud of dark ringlets. *The Virgin and Child With Singing Angels* comes immediately to mind. And she's got wings—creamy yellow wings that thrust out from the snake's body a few inches below the face. All that's lacking is a nimbus of gold light.

"A dreaming place," is what the snake has just said to me.

For all her serenity, she has an unblinking gaze which I doubt any of Botticelli's models had.

"But Mabon's already a dreaming place," I find myself replying, as though I always have conversations with snakes that have wings and human faces.

"Mabon is your dreaming place," she says. "Today you have strayed into someone else's."

"Whose?"

The snake doesn't reply.

"How do I get back to Mabon?"

Still no reply—at least not from her. Another voice answers me. This time it's that of a small owl, her feathers the color of a dead saguaro rib, streaks of silver-grey and black. She's perched on the arm of one of those tall cacti, looking down at me with another human face nestled there where an owl's beak and round eyes should be, calm madonna features surrounded by feathers. At least wings look normal on her.

"You can't return," she tells me. "You have to go on."

I hate the way that conversation can get snarled up in a dream like this: Every word an omen, every sentence a riddle.

"Go on to where?"

The owl turns her head sharply away then turns back and suddenly takes off from her perch. I catch a glimpse of a human torso in her chest feathers—breasts and a rounded belly—and then she's airborne, wings beating until she catches an updraft, and glides away. A stand of mesquite swallows her from my sight and she's gone. I turn back to the rattlesnake, but she's gone as well. The owl's advice rings in my mind. *You have to go on.*

I look around me, mountains in every direction. I know distance can be deceiving in the open desert like this, in this kind of light, with that immense sprawl of sky above me. I feel as though I could just reach any one of those ranges in a half-hour walk, but I know it would really be days.

I find my sense of direction has gone askew. Normally, I relate to a body of water. In Newford, everything's north of the lake. In Mabon, everything's south. Here, I feel displaced. There's no water—or at least none of which I'm aware. I can see the sun is setting toward the west, but it doesn't feel right. My inner compass says it's setting in the north.

I turn slowly in place, regarding the distant mountain ranges that surround me. None of them draws me more than the other, and I don't know which way to go until I remember the sound of the flute that brought me here in the first place. It's still playing, a sweet low music on the edge of my hearing that calms the panic that was beginning to lodge in my chest.

So I follow it again, hiking through what's left of the afternoon until I don't feel I can go any further. The mountains in front of me don't seem any closer, the ones behind aren't any further away. I'm thirsty and tired. Every piece of vegetation has a cutting edge or a thorn. My calves ache, my back aches, my throat holds as much moisture as the dusty ground underfoot. I don't want to be here, but I can't seem to wake up.

It's the music, I realize. The music is keeping me here.

I've figured out what kind of flute is being played now: one of those medicine flutes indigenous to the Southwest. I remember Geordie had one a couple of years ago. It was almost the size of his Irish flute, with the same six holes on top, but it had an extra thumb hole around back and it didn't have nearly the same range of notes. It also had an odd addition: up by the air hole, tied to the body of the flute with leather thongs, was a saddle holding a reed. The saddle directed the air jet up or down against the lower reed, and it was adjustable. The sound was very pretty, but the instrument had next to no volume. Geordie eventually traded it in for some whistle or other, but I picked up a tape of its music to play when I'm working—medicine flute, rattles, rainstick and synthesizers. I can't remember the last time I listened to it.

After carefully checking the area around me for snakes or scorpions or God-knows-what else might be lurking about, I sit down on some rocks and try to think things through. I'd like to believe there's a reason for my being here, but I know the dreamlands don't usually work that way. They have their own internal logic; it's only our presence in them that's arbitrary. We move through them with the same randomness as the weather in our world: basically unpredictable, for all that we'd like to think otherwise.

No, I'm here as the result of my own interference. I followed the sound of the flute out the door into the desert of my own accord. I've no one to blame but myself. There'll be no escape except for that which I can make for myself.

I'm not alone here, though. I keep sensing presences just beyond my sight, spirits hovering in the corners of my eyes. They're like the snake and the owl I saw earlier, but much more shy. I catch the hint of a face in one of the cacti, here one moment, gone the next; a ghostly shape in the bristly branches of a smoke tree; a scurry of movement and a fleeting glimpse of something with half-human skin, half-fur or -scale, darting into a burrow: little madonna faces, winged rodents and lizards, birds with human eyes and noses.

I don't know why they're so scared of me. Maybe they're naturally cautious. Maybe there's something out here in the desert that they've got good reason to hide from.

This thought doesn't lend me any comfort at all. If there's something they're scared of, I don't doubt that I should be scared of it, too. And I would be, except I'm just too exhausted to care at the moment.

I rest my arms on my knees, my head on my arms. I feel a little giddy from the sun and definitely dehydrated. I came to the desert wearing only sneakers, a pair of jeans and a white blouse. The blouse is on my head and shoulders now, to keep off the sun, but it's left my arms, my lower back and my stomach exposed. They haven't so much browned as turned the pink that's going to be a burn in another couple of hours.

Something moves in the corner of my eye and I turn my head, but not quickly enough. It was something small, a flash of pale skin and light brown fur. Winged.

"Don't be scared!" I call after it. "I won't hurt you."

But the desert lies silent around me, except for the sound of the flute. I thought I caught a glimpse of the player an hour or so ago. I was cresting a hill and saw far ahead of me a small hunched shape disappear down into the arroyo. It looked like one of those pictographs you sometimes see in Hopi or Navajo art—a little hunchbacked man with hair like dreadlocks, playing a flute. I called after him at the time, but he never reappeared.

I hate this feeling of helplessness I have at the moment, of having to react rather than do, of having to wait for answers to come to me rather than seek them out on my own. I've walked for hours, but I can't help thinking how, realistically, all that effort was only killing time. I haven't gotten anywhere, I haven't learned anything new. I'm no further ahead than I was when I first stepped through that door and found myself here. I'm thirstier, I've got the beginning of a sunburn, and that about sums it up.

The air starts to cool as the sun goes down. I take my blouse off my head and put it back on, but it doesn't help much against the growing chill. I hear something rustle in the brush on the other side of the rocks where I'm sitting, and I almost can't be bothered turning my head to see what made the noise. But I look around all the same, and then I sit very still, hoping that the Indian woman I find regarding me won't be startled off like every other creature I've met since the owl gave me her cryptic advice.

The woman is taller than I am, but that's not saying much; at just over five feet tall, I'm smaller than almost everyone I meet. Her features have a pinched, almost foxlike cast about them, and she wears her hair in two long braids into which have been woven feathers and beads and cowrie shells. She's barefoot, which strikes me as odd, since this isn't exactly the most friendly terrain I've ever had to traverse. Her buckskin dress is almost a creamy white, decorated with intricate beadwork and stitching, and she's wearing a blanket over her shoulders like a shawl, the colors of which reflect the surrounding landscape—the browns and the tans, deep shadows and burnt siennas—only they're much more vibrant.

"Don't run off on me," I say, pitching my voice low and trying to seem as unthreatening as possible.

The woman smiles. She has a smile that transforms her face; it starts on her lips and in her dark eyes, but then the whole of her solemn copper-colored features fall easily into well-worn creases of good humor. I realize that hers is the first face I've seen in this place that didn't look as though it had been rendered by a Florentine painter at the height of the Italian Renaissance. She seems indisputably of this place, as though she was birthed from the cacti and the dry hills.

"Why do you think I would do that?" she asks. Her voice is melodious and sweet.

"So far, everybody else has."

"Perhaps you confuse them."

I have to laugh. "*I* confuse *them*? Oh please."

The woman shrugs. "This is a place of spirits, a land where totem may be found, spirits consulted, lessons learned, futures explored. Those who walk its hills for these reasons have had no easy task in coming here."

"I could show them this door I found," I start to joke, but I let my voice trail off. The crease lines of her humor are still there on her face, but they're in repose. She looks too serious for jokes right now.

"You have come looking for nothing," she goes on, "so your presence is a source of agitation."

"It's not something I planned," I assure her. "If you'll show me the way out, I'll be more than happy to go. Really."

The woman shook her head. "There is no way out—except by acquiring that which you came seeking."

"But I didn't come looking for anything."

"That presents a problem."

I don't like the way this conversation is going.

"For the only way you can leave in such a case," the woman goes on, "is if you accompany another seeker when their own journeying is done."

"That . . . that doesn't seem fair."

The woman nods. "There is much unfairness—even in the spirit realms. But obstacles are set before us in order that they may be overcome." She gives me a considering look. "Perhaps you are simply unaware of what you came seeking?"

She makes a question of it.

"I heard this flute," I say. "That's what I followed to get here."

"Ah."

I wait, but she doesn't expand beyond that one enigmatic utterance.

"Could you maybe give me a little more to go on than that?" I ask.

"You are an artist?" she asks.

The question surprises me, but I nod.

"Kokopelli," she says, "the flute-player you heard. He is known for his—" she hesitates for a moment. "—inspirational qualities."

"I'm not looking for ideas," I tell her. "I have more ideas than I know what to do with. The only thing I'm ever looking for is the time to put them into practice."

"Kokopelli or Coyote," she says. "One of them is responsible for your being here."

"Can they help me get back?"

"Where either of them is concerned, anything is possible."

There's something about the way she tells me this that seems to add an unspoken "when hell freezes over," and that makes me feel even more uneasy.

"Can you tell me where I might find them?"

The woman shrugs. "Kokopelli is only found when he wishes to be, but Coyote— Coyote is always near. Look for him to be cadging a cigarette, or warming his toes by a fire."

She starts to turn away, but pauses when I call after her.

"Wait!" I say. "You can't just leave me here."

"I'm sorry," she tells me, and she really does seem sorry. "But I have duties that require my attention. I came upon you only by chance and already I have stayed too long."

"Can't I just come along with you?"

"I'm afraid that would be impossible."

There's nothing mean about the way she says it, but I can tell right away that the question is definitely not open to further discussion.

"Will you come back when you're done?" I ask.

I'm desperate. I don't want to be here on my own anymore, especially not with night falling.

"I can't make you a promise of that," she says, "but I will try. In the meantime, you would do better to look within yourself, to see if hidden somewhere within you is some secret need that might have brought you to this place."

As she starts to turn away again, I think to ask her what her name is.

"Since I am Grandmother to so many here," she says, "that would be as good a name as any. You may call me Grandmother Toad."

"My name's Sophie."

"I know, little sister."

She's walking away as she speaks. I jump to my feet and follow after her, into the dusk that's settling in between the cacti and mesquite trees, but like everyone else I've met here, she's got the trick of disappearing down pat. She steps into a shadow and she's gone.

A vast emptiness settles inside me after she's left me. The night is full of strange sounds, snuffling and rustles and weird cries in the distance that appear to be coming closer.

"Grandmother," I call softly.

I wonder, how did she know my name?

"Grandmother?"

There's no reply.

"Grandmother!"

I run to the top of another ridge, one from which I can see the last flood of light spraying up from the sunset. There's no sign, no trace at all of the Indian woman, but as I turn away, I see the flickering light of a campfire, burning there, below me in a dry wash. A figure sits in front of it. The sound of the flute is still distant, so I make the educated guess that it isn't Kokopelli hanging out down there. Grandmother's words return to my mind:

Look for him to be cadging a cigarette, or warming his toes by a fire.

I take one last look around me, then start down the hill toward Coyote's fire.

7

Sophie awoke in a tangle of sheets. She stared up at a familiar ceiling, then slowly turned her head to look at her bedside clock. The hour hand was creeping up on four. Relief flooded her.

I'm back, she thought.

She wasn't sure how it had happened, but somewhere in between leaving Grandmother Toad and starting down towards Coyote's fire, she'd managed to escape the desert dream. She lay there listening to the siren that had woken her, heard it pass her block and continue on. Sitting up, she fluffed her pillow, then lay down once more.

No more following the sound of a flute, she told herself, no matter how intriguing it might be.

Her eyelids grew heavy. Closing her eyes, she let herself drift off. Wait until she told Jeck, she thought. The desert she'd found herself in had been even stranger than the fens where she and Jeck had first met—if such a thing was possible. But when she fell asleep she bypassed Mr. Truepenny's shop and found herself scrambling down a desert incline to where a mesquite fire sent its flickering shadows along a dry wash.

8

"Little cousin," Coyote says after we've been sitting together in silence for some time. "What are you doing here?"

I can't believe I'm back here again. I would never have let myself go back to sleep if I'd thought this would happen. Still, I can't stay awake forever. That being the case, if every time I dream I'm going to find myself back here instead of in Mabon, I might as well deal with it now. But I'm not happy about it.

"I don't know," I tell him.

Coyote nods his head. He sits on his haunches, on the far side of the campfire. The pale light from the coals makes his eyes glitter and seem to be of two different colors: one brown, one blue. Except for his ears, his silhouette against the deep starry backdrop behind him belongs to a young man, long black hair braided and falling down either side of his head, body wrapped in a blanket. But the ears are those of the desert wolf whose name he bears: tall and pointed, lips quivering as they sort through the sounds drifting in from the night around them.

Wind in the mesquite. Tiny scurrying paws on the sand of the dry wash. Owl wings beating like a quickened breath. A sudden squeal. Silence. The sound of wings again, rising now. From further away, the soft grunting of javalinas feeding on prickly pear cacti.

When Coyote turns his head, a muzzle is added to his silhouette and there can be no pretending that he is other than what he is: a piece of myth set loose from old stories and come to add to the puzzle of my being here.

"So tell me," he says, a touch of amusement in his voice. "With your wise eyes so dark with secrets and insights lying thick about you like a cloak . . . what *do* you know?"

I can't tell if he's making fun of me or not.

"My name's Sophie," I tell him. "That's supposed to mean wisdom, but I don't feel very wise at the moment."

"Only fools think they're wise; the rest of us just muddle through as we can."

"I'm barely managing that."

"And yet you're here. You're alive. You breathe. You speak. Presumably, you think. You feel. The dead would give a great deal to be allowed so much."

"Look," I say. "All I know is that I stepped through a door in another dream and ended up here. I followed this Kokopelli's flute-playing and Grandmother Toad told me I have to stay here unless I either discover some secret need inside me that can be answered by the desert, or one of you help me find my way back."

"Kokopelli," Coyote says. "And Grandmother Toad. Such notable company to find oneself in."

Now I know he's mocking me, but I don't think it's meant to be malicious. It's just his way. Besides, I find that I don't really care.

"Can you help me?" I ask.

"Can I help? I'm not sure. Will I help? I'll do my best. Never let it be said that I turned my back on a friend of both the flute-player and Nokomis."

"Who?"

"The Grandmother has many names—as does anyone who lives long enough. They catch on our clothes and get all snarled up in a tangle until sometimes even we can't remember who we are anymore."

"You're confusing me."

"But not deliberately so," Coyote says. "Let it go on record that any confusion arose simply because we lacked certain commonalities of reference."

I give him a blank look.

"Besides," he adds, "it was a joke. We always know who we are; what we sometimes forget are the appellations by which we come to be known. There are, you see, so many of them."

"I just want to get out of this place."

Coyote nods. "I must say, I have to admire anyone with such a strong sense of purpose. No messing about, straight to the point. It's refreshing, really. You wouldn't have a cigarette, would you?"

"Sorry, I don't smoke."

It's hard to believe that this is the same person who sat in silence across the fire from me for the better part of an hour before he even said hello. I wonder if archetypal spirits can be schizophrenic. Then I think, just being an archetype must make you schizophrenic. Imagine if your whole existence depended on how people remember you.

"I gave it up myself," Coyote says. Then he proceeds to open up a rolling paper, sprinkle tobacco onto it and roll himself a cigarette. He lights it with a twig from the fire, then blows a contented wreath of smoke up into the air where it twists and spins before it joins the rising column of smoke from the burning mesquite.

I'm beginning to realize that my companion's not exactly the most truthful person I'm going to meet in my life. I just hope he's more reliable when it comes to getting a job done or I'm going to be stuck in this desert for a very long time.

"So where do we start?" I ask.

"With metaphor?"

"What?"

"The use of one thing to explain another," Coyote says patiently.

"I know what it means. I just don't get your point."

"I thought we were trying to find your secret need."

I shake my head. "I don't *have* any secret needs."

"Are you sure?"

"I . . ."

"Are you sexually repressed?"

I can't believe I'm having this conversation.

"What's that got to do with *anything?*"

Coyote flicks the ash from the end of his cigarette. "It's this whole flute-player business," he says. "It's riddled with sexual innuendo, don't you see? He's a fertility symbol, now, very mythopoetic and all, but it wasn't always that way. Used to be a trader, a travelling merchant, hup-two-three. That hunched back was actually his pack of trading goods, the flute his way of approaching a settlement, *tootle-toot-toot,* it's only me, no danger, except if you were some nubile young thing. Had a woman in every town, you know—they didn't call him Koke the Poke for nothing. The years go by and suddenly our randy little friend finds himself elevated to minor deity status, gets all serious, kachina material, don't you know? Becomes a kind of erotic muse, if you will."

"But—"

"Ah, yes," Coyote says. "The metaphorical bit." He grinds his cigarette out and tosses the butt into the fire. "Your following the sound of his flute—*his* particular flute, if you get my meaning—and well, I won't say he's irresistible, but if one were to be suffering for a certain particular *need,* it might be quite difficult *not* to be drawn, willy-nilly, after him."

"What are you saying? That all I have to do is have sex here, and I get to leave?"

"No, no, no, no. Nothing so crass. Nothing so obvious. At this point it's all conjecture. We're simply exploring possibilities, some more delightful than others." He pauses and gives me a considering look. "You're not a nun, are you? You haven't taken one of those absurd vows that cut you off from what might otherwise be a full and healthy human existence?"

"I don't know about nuns," I tell him, "but I'm outta here."

I stand up, expecting him to make some sort of protest, but he just looks at me, curiously, and starts to roll another cigarette. I don't really want to go out into the desert night on my own, but I don't want to sit here and listen to his lunacy either.

"I thought you were going to help me," I say finally.

"I am, little cousin. I will."

He lights his cigarette and then pointedly waits for me to sit down again.

"Well, you haven't been much help so far," I say.

"Oh, right," he says, laying a hand theatrically across his brow. "Kill the messenger, why don't you."

I lean closer to the fire and take a good long look at him. "Is there *any* relevance to anything you have to say?" I ask.

"You brought up Kokopelli. You're the one who followed the music of his randy little flute. You can't blame me for any of that. If you've got a better idea, I'm all ears."

He cups his hands around those big coyote ears of his and leans forward as well. I try to keep a straight face, but all I can do is fall back on the ground and laugh.

"I was beginning to think you didn't have any sort of a sense of humor at all," he says when I finally catch my breath.

"It's not that. I just want to get away from here. When I dream, I want to go to Mabon—to where *I* want to go."

"Mabon?" Coyote says. "Mabon's yours? Oh, I love Mabon. The first time I ever heard the Sex Pistols was in Mabon. That was years ago now, but I couldn't believe how great they were."

Whereupon he launches into a version of "My Way" that's so off-key and out of time that it makes the version Sid Vicious did sound closer to Ol' Blue Eyes than I might ever have thought possible. From the hills around us, four-legged coyote voices take up the song, and soon the night is filled with this horrible caterwauling that's so loud it's making my teeth ache. All I want to do is bury my head or scream.

"Great place, Mabon," he says when he finally breaks off and the noise from his accompanists fades away.

Wonderful, I think. Not only am I stuck with him here, but now I find out that if I ever do get out of this desert, I could run into him again in my own dreaming place.

9

"I've got to figure out a way to sleep without dreaming," Sophie told Jilly.

They were taking a break from helping out at a bazaar for St. Vincent's Home for the Aged, drinking tea and sharing a bag of potato chips on the back steps of the old stone building. The sun was shining brightly, and it made Sophie's eyes ache. She hadn't slept at all last night in protest of how she felt Coyote was wasting her time.

"Still visiting the desert every night?" Jilly asked around a mouthful of chips.

Sophie gave her a mournful nod. "Pretty much. Unless I don't go to sleep."

"But I thought you liked the desert," Jilly said. "You came back from that vacation in New Mexico just raving about how great it was, how you were going to move down there, how we were all crazy not to think of doing the same."

"This is different. All I want to do is give it up."

Jilly shook her head. "I'm so envious of the way you get to go places when you dream. I would *never* want to give it up."

"You haven't met Coyote."

"Coyote was your favorite subject when you got back."

Sophie sighed. It was true. She'd become enamored with the Trickster figure on her vacation and had even named her last studio after a painting she'd bought in Santa Fe: Five Coyotes Singing.

"This Coyote's not the same," she said. "He's not all noble and mystical and, oh I don't know, mischievous, I suppose, in a sweet sort of a way. He's more like the souvenirs in the airport gift shop—fun if you're in the right mood, but sort of tacky at the same time. And definitely not very helpful. The only agenda he pursues with any real enthusiasm is trying to convince me to have sex with him."

Jilly raised her eyebrows. "Isn't that getting kind of kinky? I mean, how would you even do it?"

"Oh please. He's not a coyote all of the time. Mostly he's a man." Sophie frowned. "Mind you, even then he'll have the odd bit of coyote about him: ears, mostly. Sometimes a muzzle. Sometimes a tail."

Jilly reached for the chip bag, but it was empty. She shook out the last few crumbs and licked them from her palm, then crumpled the bag and stuck it in the pocket of her jacket.

"What am I going to *do*?" Sophie said.

"Beats me," Jilly said. "We should go back inside. Geordie's going to think we deserted him."

"You're not being any help at all."

"If it were up to me," Jilly said, "I'd join you in a minute. But it isn't. Or at least, we've yet to find a way to make it possible."

"He's going to drive me mad."

"Maybe you should give him a taste of his own medicine," Jilly said. "You know, act just as loony."

Sophie laughed. "Only you would think of that. And only you could pull it off. I wish there *was* some way to bring you over. Then I could just watch the two of you drive each other mad."

"You could always just sleep with him."

"I've been tempted—and not simply because I think it'd drive him away. He's really quite attractive, and he can be very . . . persuasive."

"But," Jilly said.

"But, I feel as though it'd be like eating the fruit in fairyland—if I give in to him, then I'll never be able to get away."

10

So every night when I dream, I come to the desert and Coyote and I go looking for my way out. And every night's a trial. My night-nerves are shot. I'm always on edge because I never know what's going to happen next, what he's going to want to discuss, when or if he's going to put a move on me. We never do find Kokopelli, but that's not the worst of it. The worst thing is that I'm actually getting used to this: to Coyote and his mad carrying-on. Not only used to it, but enjoying it. No matter how much Coyote exasperates me, I can't stay mad at him.

And my desert time's not all bad by any means. When Coyote's being good company, you couldn't ask for a better friend. The desert spirits aren't shy around him, either. The aunts and uncles, which are what he calls the saguaro, tell us stories, or sing songs, or sometimes just gossip. All those strange madonna-faced spirits drop by to visit us, in ones and twos and threes. Women with fox-ears or antlers. Bobcat and coati spirits. Cottontails, jack rabbits and pronghorns. Vultures and grouse and hawks. Snakes and scorpions and lizards. Smoke-tree ghosts and tiny fairy-duster sprites. Twisty cholla spirits, starburst yucca bogles and mesquite dryads draped in cloaks made of a thousand perfectly shaped miniature leaves.

The mind boggles at their variety and number. They come in every shape and size, but they all have that madonna resemblance, even the males. They're all that strange mix of human with beast or plant. And they all have their own stories and songs and dances to share.

So it's not all bad. But Kokopelli's flute-playing is always there, sometimes only audible when I'm very still, a Pied Piper covenant that I don't remember agreeing to, but it keeps me here. And it's that loss of choice that won't let me ever completely relax. The knowledge that I'm here, not because I want to be, but because I have to be.

One night Coyote and I are lying on a hilltop looking up at the stars. The aunts and uncles are murmuring all around us, a kind of wordless chant like a lullaby. A black-crested phainopepla is perched on my knee, strange little Botticelli features studying mine in between groomings. Coyote is smoking a cigarette, but it doesn't smell like tobacco—more like pion. A dryad was sitting on an outcrop nearby, her skin the gorgeous green of her palo verde tree, but she's drifted away now.

"Grandmother Toad told me that this is a place where people come to find totem," I say after a while. I feel Coyote turn to look at me, but I keep my own gaze on the light show overhead. So many stars, so much sky. "Or they come to consult spirits, to learn from them."

"Nokomis is the wisest of us all. She would know."

"So how come we never see anybody else?"

"I'm nobody?" the little phainopepla warbles from my knee.

"You know what I mean. No people."

"It's a big desert," Coyote says.

"The first spirits I met here told me it was somebody else's dreaming place—the way Mabon is mine. But they wouldn't tell me whose."

"Spirits can be like that," Coyote says.

The phainopepla frowns at the both of us, then flies away.

"Is it your dreaming place?" I ask him.

"If it was my dreaming place," he says, "when I did this—" He reaches a hand over and cups my breast. I sit up and move out of his reach. "—you'd fall into my arms and we'd have glorious sex the whole night long."

"I see," I say dryly.

Coyote sits up and grins. "Well, you asked."

"Not for a demonstration."

"What is it that frightens you about having sex with me?"

"It's not a matter of being frightened," I tell him. "It's the consequences that might result from our doing it."

He reaches into his pocket and pulls out a condom. I can't *believe* this guy.

"That's not quite what I had in mind," I say.

"Ah. You're afraid of the psychic ramifications."

"Say what?"

"You're afraid that having sex with me will trap you here forever."

Am I that open a book?

"The thought has crossed my mind," I tell him.

"But maybe it'll free you instead."

I wait, but he doesn't say anything more. "Only you're not telling, right?" I ask.

"Only I don't know," he says. He rolls himself another cigarette and lights up. Blowing out a wreath of smoke, he shoots me a sudden grin. "I don't know, and you don't know, and the way things are going, I guess we never will, hey?"

I can't help but react to that lopsided grin of his. Frustrated as I'm feeling, I still have to laugh. He's got more charm than any one person deserves, and when he turns it on like this, I don't know whether to give him a hug or a bang on the ear.

11

A week after her show closed at The Green Man Gallery, Sophie appeared on Max Hannon's doorstep with *Hearts Like Fire, Burning* under her arm, wrapped in brown paper.

"You didn't pick it up," she said when he answered the bell, "so I thought I'd deliver it."

Max regarded her with surprise. "I really didn't think you were serious."

"But you will take it?" Sophie asked. She handed the package over as though there could be no question to Max's response.

"I'll treasure it forever," he said, smiling. Stepping to one side so that she could go by him, he added, "Would you like to come in?"

It was roomier inside Max's house than it looked to be from the outside. Renovations had obviously been done, since the whole of the downstairs was laid out in an open layout broken only by the necessary support beams. The kitchen was off in one corner, separated from the rest of the room by an island counter. Another corner held a desk and some bookcases. The remainder of the room consisted of a comfortable living space of sprawling sofas and armchairs, low tables, Navajo carpets and display cabinets.

There was art everywhere—on the walls, as might be expected: posters, reproductions and a few originals, but there was even more three-dimensional work. The sculptures made Sophie's heartbeat quicken. Wherever she looked there were representations of the desert spirits she'd come to know so well, those strange creatures with their human features and torsos peeping out from their feathers and fur, or their thorny cacti cloaks. Sophie was utterly entranced by them, by how faithful they were to the spirits from her desert dream.

"It's funny," Max said, laying the painting she'd given him down on a nearby table.

The two ocotillo cacti spirit statues that made up the centerpiece seemed to bend their long-branched forms toward the package, as though curious about what it held. "I was thinking about you just the other day."

"You were?"

Max nodded. "I remembered why it was that you looked so familiar to me when we met at your opening."

If her desert dream hadn't started up after that night, Sophie might have expected him to tell her now that he was one of its spirits and it was from seeing her in that otherworldly realm that he knew her. But it couldn't be so. She hadn't followed Kokopelli's flute until after she'd met Max.

"I would have remembered it if we'd ever met," she said.

"I didn't say we'd actually met."

"Now you've got me all curious."

"Maybe we should leave it a mystery."

"Don't you dare," Sophie said. "You have to tell me now."

"I'd rather show you than tell you," Max said. "Just give me a moment."

He went up a set of stairs over by the kitchen area that Sophie hadn't noticed earlier. Once he was gone, she wandered about the large downstairs room to give the statues a closer look. The resemblances were uncanny. It wasn't so much that he'd captured the exact details of her dream's desert fauna as that his sculptures contained an overall sense of the same spirit; they captured the elemental, inherent truth rather than recognizable renderings. She was crouched beside a table, peering at a statue of a desert woodrat with human hands, when Max returned with a small painting in hand.

"This is where I first saw you," he said.

Sophie had to smile. She remembered the painting. Jilly had done it years ago: a portrait of Wendy, LaDonna and her, sitting on the back steps of a Yoors Street music club, Wendy and LaDonna scruffy as always, bookending Sophie in a pleated skirt and silk blouse, the three of them caught in the circle of light cast by a nearby streetlight. Jilly had called it *The Three Muses Pause to Reconsider Their Night.*

"This was Peter's," Max said. "He loved this painting and kept it hanging in his office by his desk. The idea of the Muses having a girl's night out on the town appealed to the whimsical side of his nature. I'd forgotten all about it until I was up there the other day looking for some papers."

"I haven't thought of that painting in years," Sophie told him. "You know Jilly actually made us sit for it at night on those very steps—at least for her initial sketches, which were far more detailed than they had any need to be. I think she did them that way just to see how long we'd actually put up with sitting there."

"And how long did you sit?"

"I don't know. A few hours, I suppose. But it *seemed* like weeks. Is this your work?" she added, pointing to the statues.

Max nodded.

"I just love them," she said. "You don't show in Newford, do you? I mean, I would have remembered these if I'd seen them before."

"I used to ship all my work back to the galleries in Arizona where I first started to sell. But I haven't done any sculpting for a few years now."

"Why not? They're so good."

Max shrugged. "Different priorities. It's funny how it works, how we define ourselves. I used to think of myself as a sculptor first—everything else came second. Then when the eighties arrived, I came out and thought of myself as gay first, and only then as a sculptor. Now I define myself as an AIDS activist before anything else. Most of my time these days is taken up in editing a newsletter that deals with alternative therapies for those with HIV."

Sophie thought of the book she'd seen lying on one of the tables when she was looking at the sculptures. *Staying Healthy With HIV* by David Baker and Richard Copeland.

"Your friend Peter," she said. "Did he die of AIDS?"

"Actually, you don't die of AIDS," Max said. "AIDS destroys your immune system and it's some other illness that kills you—something your body would have been able to deal with otherwise." He gave her a sad smile. "But no. Ironically, I was the one who tested positive for HIV. Peter had leukemia. It had been in remission for a couple of years, but just before we went to the desert it came back and we had to go through it all again: the chemo treatments and the sleepless nights, the stomach cramps and awful rashes. I was sure that he'd pulled through once more, but then he died a week after we returned."

Max ran his finger along the sloped back of a statue of a horned owl whose human features seemed to echo Max's own. "I think Peter had a premonition that he was going to die, and that was why he was so insistent we visit the desert one more time. He had a spiritual awakening there after one of his bouts with the disease and afterwards, he always considered the desert as the homeground for everything he held most dear." Max smiled, remembering. "We met because of these statues. He would have moved there, except for his job. Instead, I moved here."

Sophie got a strange feeling as Max spoke of Peter's love for the desert.

"Remember we talked about dreams at the opening?" she said.

Max nodded. "Serial dreams—what a lovely conceit."

"What I was telling you wasn't something I made up. And ever since that night I've been dreaming of a desert—a desert filled up with these." Sophie included all of the statuary with a vague wave of her hand. "Except in my desert they aren't statues; they're real."

"Real."

"I know it sounds completely bizarre, but it's true. My dreams are true. I mean, they're not so much dreams as me visiting some other place."

Max gave her an odd look. "Whenever someone talked about what an imagination I must have to do such work, Peter would always insist that it was all based on reality—it was just a reality that most people couldn't see into."

"And are they?"

"I . . ." Max looked away from her to the statues. He lay his hand on the back of the owl-man again, fingers rediscovering the contours they had pulled from the clay. "I should show you Peter's office," he said when he finally looked up.

He led her up to the second floor which was laid out in a more traditional style, a hallway with doors leading off from it, two on one side, three on the other. Max opened the door at the head of the stairs and ushered her in ahead of him.

"I haven't been able to deal with any of this yet," he said. "What to keep . . . what not . . ."

A large desk stood by the window, covered with books, papers and a small computer, but Sophie didn't notice any of that at first. Her attention was caught and trapped by the rooms' other furnishings: the framed photographs of the desert and leather-skinned drums that hung on the walls; a cabinet holding kachina figures, a medicine flute, rattles, fetishes and other artifacts; the array of Max's sculptures that peered at her from every corner of the room. She turned slowly on the spot, taking it all in, until her gaze settled on the familiar face of one of the sculptures.

"Coyote," she said softly.

Max spoke up from the doorway. "Careful. You know what they say about him."

Sophie shook her head.

"Don't attract his attention."

"Why?" Sophie asked, turning to look at Max. "Is he malevolent? Or dangerous?"

"By all accounts, no. He just doesn't think things through before he takes action. But while he usually emerges intact from his misadventures, his companions aren't always quite so lucky. Spending time with Coyote is like opening your life to disorder."

Sophie smiled. "That sounds like Coyote, all right."

Her gaze went back to the cabinet and the medicine flute that lay on its second shelf between two kachinas. One was the Storyteller, her comical features the color of red clay; the other was Kokopelli. The medicine flute itself was similar to the one that Geordie had traded away, only much more beautifully crafted. But then everything in this room had a resonance of communion with more than the naked eye could see—a sense of the sacred.

"Did Peter play the flute?" she asked.

"The one in the cabinet?"

"Mmm."

"Only in the desert. It has next to no volume, but a haunting tone."

Sophie nodded. "I know."

"He'd play that flute and his drums and rattles. He'd go to sweats and drumming nights when we were down there. I used to tease him about trying to be an Indian, but he said that the Red Road was open to anyone who walked it with respect."

"The Red Road?"

"Native spiritual beliefs. I went with him sometimes, but I never really felt comfortable." He touched the nearest statue, an intricate depiction of a prickly pear spirit. "I love the desert, too, but I've never been much of a joiner."

"Did that disappoint Peter?"

Max shook his head. "Peter was one of the most open-minded, easygoing individuals you could ever have met. He always accepted people for what they were."

"Sounds like Jilly. No wonder they got along."

"You mean because of the painting?"

Sophie nodded.

"Peter never met her. I bought it for him at one of her shows. He fell in love with it on the spot—much as I did with the painting you gave me today." An awkward smile touched his lips. "I had more money in those days."

"Please don't feel guilty about it," Sophie told him, "or you'll spoil the pleasure of my giving it to you."

"I'll try."

"So did Peter have desert dreams?" Sophie asked. "Like mine?"

"He never told me that he had serial dreams, but he did dream of the desert. What are yours like?"

"This could take a while."

"I've got the time."

So while Max sat in the chair at Peter's desk, Sophie walked about the room and told him, not only about the desert dream and Coyote, but about Mabon and Jeck and the whole strange life she had when she stepped into her dreams.

"There's something odd about Coyote referring to Nokomis," Max said when she was done.

"Why's that?"

"Well, everything else in your desert relates to the Southwest except for her. Nokomis and Grandmother Toad—those are terms that relate to our part of the world. They come from the lexicon of our own local tribes like the Kickaha."

"So what are you saying?"

Max shrugged. "Maybe Coyote was the woman who sent you looking for him in the first place."

"But why would he do that?"

"Who knows why Coyote does anything? Maybe he just took a liking to you and decided to meet you in a roundabout way."

"So was he Kokopelli as well?" Sophie asked. "Because it's the flute-playing that got me there in the first place."

"I don't know."

But Sophie thought perhaps she did. She stood before the cabinet that held Peter's medicine flute. It was too much of a coincidence—Max's sculptures, Peter's interest in the desert. The feeling came to her that somehow she'd gotten caught up in unfinished business between the two, neither quite willing to let the other go, so they were haunting each other.

She turned to look at Max, but decided she needed one more night in her desert dream before she was ready to bring up that particular theory with him.

"It feels good being able to talk about this with someone," she said instead. "The only other person I've ever told it to is Jilly and frankly, she and Coyote are almost cut from the same cloth. The only difference is that Jilly's not quite as outrageous as he is, and she's not always talking about sex. Everything Coyote wants to talk about eventually relates to sex."

"And *have* you slept with him?"

Sophie smiled. "I guess there's a bit of Coyote in you, too."

"I think there's a bit of him in *every* one of us."

"Probably. But to answer your question: No, I haven't. I'll admit I've come close—he can be awfully persuasive—but I have the feeling that if I slept with him, I'd be in more trouble than I already am. I'd be trapped in those dreams forever and I can't see that being worth one night's pleasure."

Max shook his head. "I hate it when people try to divorce sex from the other aspects of their life. It's too entwined with everything we are for us to be able to do that. It's like when some people find out that I have HIV. They expect me to disavow sex. They tell me that promiscuity got me into this position in the first place, so I should just stop thinking about it, writing about it, doing it. But if I did that, then I'd be giving up. My sexuality is too much a part of who I am, as a person and as an artist, for me not to acknowledge its importance in my life. I may not be looking for a partner right now. I may not live to be forty. But I'll be damned if I'll live like a eunuch just because of the shitty hand I got dealt with this disease."

"So you think I should sleep with him."

"I'm not saying that at all," Max replied. "I'm saying that sex is the life energy, and our sexuality is how we connect to it. Whether or not you sleep with Coyote or anyone else isn't going to trap you in this faerie otherworld, or even get you infected with some disease. It's *why* you have sex with whoever you've chosen as your partner. The desire has to include some spiritual connection. You have to care enough about the other person—and that naturally includes taking all the necessary precautions.

"How often or with how many people you have sex isn't the issue at all. It's not about monogamy versus promiscuity; it's about how much love enters the equation. If there's a positive energy between you and Coyote, if you really care about him and he cares for you, then the experience can only be positive—even if you never see each other again. If that energy and caring isn't there, then you shouldn't even be thinking about having sex with him in the first place."

12

So now I'm feeling cocky. I think I've got the whole thing figured out. Those first spirits told me the truth: This isn't my dreaming place. It's either Peter's or Max's, I don't know which yet. One of them hasn't let go of the other, and whichever one of the two it is, he's trying to hang on to the other one. Maybe the desert belongs to Max and he doesn't know it. Maybe it's his way of keeping Peter alive, and I just tumbled into the place through having met him that night at my opening. Or maybe it belongs to Peter; Peter wearing Kokopelli's guise in this desert, calling me up by mistake instead of Max. He probably got me because I'm such a strong dreamer, and when he saw his mistake, he just took off, leaving me to fend for myself. Or maybe he doesn't even know I'm here. But it's got to be one or the other, and talking to Kokopelli is going to tell me which.

"No more fooling around," I tell Coyote. "I want to find Kokopelli."

"I'm doing my best," he says. "But that flute-player—he's not an easy fellow to track down."

We're sitting by another mesquite fire in another dry wash—or maybe it's the same one where we first met. Every place starts to look the same around here after a while. It's a little past noon, the sun's high. Ground-doves fill the air with their mournful *coo-ooh, coo-ooh* sound, and a hawk hangs high above the saguaro—a smudge of shadow against the blue. Coyote has coffee brewing on the fire and a cigarette dangling from the corner of his mouth. He looks almost human today, except for the coyote ears and the long stiff whiskers standing out from around his mouth. I keep expecting one of them to catch fire, but they never do.

"I'm serious, Coyote."

"There's people put chicory in with their coffee, but it just doesn't taste the same to me," he says. "I'm not looking for a smooth taste when I make coffee. I want my spoon to stand up in the cup."

He looks at me with those mismatched eyes of his, pretending he's as guileless as a newborn babe, but while my father might have made some mistakes in his life, raising me to be stupid wasn't one of them.

"If you'd wanted to," I say, "we could have found Kokopelli weeks ago."

The medicine flute is still playing, soft as a distant breeze. It's always playing when I'm here—never close by, but never so far away that I can't hear it anymore.

"You could take me to him right now . . . if you wanted to."

"The thing is," Coyote says, "nothing's as easy as we'd like it to be."

"Don't I know it," I mutter, but he's not even listening to me.

"And the real trouble comes from not knowing what we really want in the first place."

"I know what I want—to find Kokopelli, or whoever it is playing that flute."

"Did I ever tell you," Coyote says, "about the time Barking Dog was lying under a mesquite tree, just after a thunderstorm?"

"I don't want to hear another one of your stories."

13

But Coyote says:

Barking Dog looks up and the whole sky is filled with a rainbow. Now how can I get up there? he thinks. Those colors are just the paints I need for my arrows.

Then he sees Buzzard, and he cries: "Hey, Uncle! Can you take me up there so that I can get some arrow paint?"

"Sure, nephew. Climb up on my back."

Barking Dog does and Buzzard flies up and up until they reach the very edge of the sky.

"You wait here," Buzzard says, "while I get those paints for you."

So Barking Dog hangs there from the edge of the sky, and he's hanging there, but Buzzard doesn't come back. Barking Dog yells and he's making an awful racket, but he doesn't see anyone and finally he can't hang on any more and down he falls. It took Buzzard no time at all to get to the edge of the sky, but it takes Barking Dog two weeks to fall all the way back down—bang! Right into an old hollow tree and he lands so hard, he gets stuck and he can't get out.

A young woman's walking by right about then, looking for honey. She spies a hole in that old hollow tree and what does she see but Barking Dog's pubic hairs, sticking out of the hole. Oh my, she's thinking. There's a bear stuck in this tree. So she pulls out one of those hairs and goes running home to her husband with it.

"Oh, this comes from a bear, don't doubt it" her husband says.

He gets his bow and arrows and the two of them go back to the tree. The young woman, she's got an axe and she starts to chop at that tree. Her husband, he's standing by, ready to shoot that bear when the hole's big enough, but then they hear a voice come out of the tree:

"Cousin, make that hole bigger."

The young woman has to laugh. "That's no bear," she tells her husband. "That's Barking Dog, got himself stuck in a tree."

So she chops some more and soon Barking Dog crawls out of that tree and he shakes the dust and the dirt from himself.

"We thought you were a bear," the young woman says.

Her husband nods. "We could've used that meat."

Barking Dog turns back to the tree and gives it a kick. "Get out of there, you old lazy bear," he cries and when a bear comes out, he kills it and gives the meat to the young woman and her husband. Then he goes off, and you know what he's thinking? He's thinking, I wonder what ever happened to Buzzard.

14

"Was I supposed to get something out of that story," I ask "or were you just letting out some hot air?"

"Coffee's ready," he says. "You want some?"

He offers me a blue enameled mug filled with a thick, dark brown liquid. The only resemblance it bears to the coffee I'd make for myself is that it has the same smell. I take the mug from him. Gingerly, I lift it up to my lips and give it a sniff. The steam rising from it makes my eyes water.

"You didn't answer me," I say as I set the mug in the dirt down by my knee, its contents untouched.

Coyote takes a long swallow, then shrugs. "I don't know the answer to everything," he says.

"But you told me you could find him for me."

"I told you I would try."

"This is trying?" I ask. "Sitting around a campfire, drinking coffee and smoking cigarettes and telling stories that don't make any sense?"

He gives me a hurt look. "I thought you liked my company."

"I do. It's just—"

"I thought we were friends. What were you planning to do? Dump me as soon as we found the flute player?"

"No. Of course not. It's just that I want . . . I need to have some control over my dreams."

"But you do have control over your dreams."

"Then what am I doing here? How come every time I fall asleep, I end up *here*?"

"When you figure that out," Coyote says, "everything else will fall into place."

"What do you think I've been trying to do all this time?"

Coyote takes another long swallow from his mug. "The people of your world," he says, "you live two lives—an outer life that everyone can see, and another secret life inside your head. In one of those lives you can start out on a journey and reach your destination, but when you take a trip in the other, there's no end."

"What do you mean there's no end?"

Coyote shrugs. "It's the way you think. One thing leads to another and before you know it you're a thousand miles from where you thought you'd be, and you can't even remember where it was you thought you were going in the first place."

"Not everybody dreams the way I do," I tell him.

"No. But everybody's got a secret life inside their head. The difference is, you've got a stage to act yours out on."

"So none of this is real."

"I didn't say that."

"So what are you saying?"

Coyote lights another cigarette, then finishes his coffee. "Good coffee, this," he tells me.

15

"And these stories of his," Sophie said. "They just drive me crazy."

Jilly looked up from her canvas to where Sophie was slouching in the window seat of her studio. "I kind of like them. They're so zen."

"Oh please. You can keep zen. I just want something to make sense."

"Okay," Jilly said. She set her brush aside and joined Sophie in the window seat. "To start with, Barking Dog is just another one of Coyote's names."

"Really?"

Jilly nodded. "It's a literal translation of *Canis latrans,* which is Coyote's scientific name. That last story was his way of telling you that the two of you are much the same."

"I said sense," Sophie said. "You know, the way the rest of the world defines the term?"

"But it does make sense. In the story, Coyote's looking for arrow paints, but after he gets sidetracked, all he can do is wonder what happened to Buzzard."

"And?"

"You were following this flute music, but all you can think of now is finding Kokopelli."

"But *he's* the one playing the flute."

"You don't know that."

"Nokomis told me it was either Coyote or Kokopelli who tricked me into this desert dream. And she told me that it was Kokopelli's flute that I heard."

Jilly nodded. "But then think of what Max told you about how out of context she is. You've got a dream filled with desert imagery, so what's a moon deity from the eastern woodlands doing there?"

"Maybe she just got sidetracked."

"And maybe she really was Coyote in another guise. And if that's true, can you trust anything she told you?"

Sophie banged the back of her head against the window frame and let out a long sigh. "Great," she said. "That's just what I needed—to be even more confused about all of this than I already am."

"If you ask me," Jilly said, "I think it's time you left Coyote behind and struck out on your own to find your own answers."

"You don't know how good he is at sulking."

Jilly laughed. "So let him tag along. Just take the lead for a change."

So that night Sophie put on the tape she'd bought around the time Geordie was messing around with his medicine flute. *Coyote Love Medicine* by Jessita Reyes. She lay down on her bed and concentrated on the sound of Reyes's flute, letting its breathy sound fill her until its music and the music that drew her into the desert dream became one.

16

Coyote's stretched out on a rock, the brim of his hat pulled down low to shade his eyes. Today he's got human ears, a human face. He's also got a bushy tail of which he seems inordinately proud. He keeps grooming it with his long brown fingers, combing out knots that aren't there, fluffing out parts that just won't fluff out any further. He lifts the brim of his hat with a finger when he sees me start off.

"Where are you going?" he asks.

"I've got an appointment."

From lying there all languid in the sun, with only enough energy to roll himself a cigarette and groom that fine tail of his, suddenly he bounds to his feet and falls into step beside me.

"Who're you going to see?" he wants to know.

"Kokopelli."

"You know where he is?"

I shake my head. "I thought I'd let him find me."

I hold the music of the medicine flute in my mind and let it draw me through the cacti and scrub. We top one hill, scramble down the dusty slope of an arroyo, make our way up the next steep incline. We finally pull ourselves up to the top of a butte, and there he is, sitting crosslegged on the red stone, a slim, handsome man, dark hair cut in a shaggy pageboy, wearing white trousers and a white tunic, a plain wooden medicine flute lying across his knees. A worn cloth backpack lies on the stone beside him.

For the first time since I stepped into this desert dream all those weeks ago, I don't hear the flute anymore. There's just the memory of it lying there in my mind—fueled by the cassette that's playing back in that world where another part of me is sleeping.

Kokopelli looks from Coyote to me.

"Hey, Ihu," he says. "Hey, Sophie."

I shoot Coyote a dirty look, but he doesn't even have the decency to look embarrassed at how easy it was for me to track Kokopelli down.

"How do you know my name?" I ask the flute-player.

He gives me a little shrug. "The whole desert's been talking about you, walking here, walking there, looking everywhere for what's sitting right there inside you all the time."

I'm really tired of opaque conversations, and I tell him as much.

"Your problem," he says, "is that you can't seem to take anything at face value. Everything you're told doesn't necessarily have to have a hidden meaning."

"Okay," I say. "If everything's going to be so straightforward now, tell me: Which one are you? Peter or Max?"

Kokopelli smiles. "That would make everything so easy, wouldn't it?"

"What do you mean?"

"For me to be one or the other."

"You said this was going to be a straightforward conversation," I say.

I turn to Coyote, though why I expect him to back me up on this, I've no idea. Doesn't matter anyway. Coyote's not there anymore. It's just me and the flute-player, sitting up on the red stone of this butte.

"I didn't say it would be straightforward," Kokopelli tells me. "I said that sometimes you should try to take what you're told at face value."

I sigh and look away. It's some view we have. From this height, the whole desert is lain out before us.

"This isn't about Peter or Max, is it?" I say.

Kokopelli shakes his head. "It's about you. It's about what you want out of your life."

"So Coyote was telling me the truth all along."

"Ihu was telling you a piece of the truth."

"But I followed your flute to get here."

Kokopelli shakes his head again. "You were following a need that you dressed up as my music."

"So all of this—" I wave my hand to encompass everything, the butte, the desert, Kokopelli, my being here. "—Where does it fit in?"

"It's different for everyone who comes. When you travel in a dream, you can bring nothing across with you; you can bring nothing back. Only what is in your head."

And that's my real problem. I know my dream worlds are real, but it's a different kind of real from what I can find in the waking world. I work out all of my problems in my dreams—from my mother abandoning me to my never seeming to be able to maintain a good relationship. But the solutions don't have any real holding power. They don't ever seem to resonate with the same truth in the waking world as they do in my dreams. And that's because I can't bring anything tangible back with me. I have to take it all on faith and for some things, faith isn't enough.

"Perhaps you expect too much," Kokopelli says when I try to explain this to him. "We are shaped by our experiences, and no matter where those experiences occur, they are still valid. The things you have seen and done don't lose their resonance because you can only hold them in your memory. In that sense there is little difference between what you experience when you are awake or when you dream. Keepsakes, mementos, tokens . . . their real potency lies in the memories they call up, rather than what they are in and of themselves."

"But I don't always understand the things I experience."

Kokopelli smiles. "Without mysteries, life would be very dull indeed. What would be left to strive for if everything were known?"

He picks up his flute and begins to play. His music carries us through the afternoon until the shadows deepen and twilight mutes the details of the desert around us. Although I don't hear a pause in the music, at some point he's put on his pack and I look up to see him silhouetted against the sunset. For a moment I don't see a man, but a hunchbacked flute-playing kachina.

"Tell Max," he says, "to remember me as loving him."

And then he steps away, into the night, into the desert, into the sky—I don't know where. I just know he's gone, the sound of his flute is a dying echo, and I'm left with another mystery that has no answer:

If he was Peter, how did he know so much about me?

And if he wasn't, then who was he?

17

"I've been thinking a lot about the desert lately," Max said.

He and Sophie were having a late dinner in The Rusty Lion after taking in a show. They had a table by the window and could watch the bustling crowds go by on Lee Street from where they sat.

"Are you thinking of moving back to Arizona?" Sophie asked.

Max shook his head. "I probably will one day, but not yet. No, I was thinking more of the desert as a metaphor for how my life has turned out."

Sophie had often tried to imagine what it would be like to live with a terminal disease, and she thought Max was probably right. It would be very much like the desert: the barrenness, the vast empty reaches. Everything honed to its purest essence, just struggling to survive. There wouldn't be time for anything more. She wondered if she'd resent the rich forests of other people's lives, if she knew her own future could be cut short at any time.

"I think I know what you mean," she said.

Max laughed. "I can tell by the way you look that you've completely misunderstood me. You're thinking of the desert as a hopeless place, right?"

"Well, not exactly hopeless, but . . ."

"It's just the opposite," Max said. "The desert brings home how precious life is and how much we should appreciate it while we have it. That life can still flourish under such severe conditions is a miracle. It's an inspiration to me."

"You're amazing, you know that?"

"Not really. We all know we're going to die someday, but we like to pretend we won't. Given the hand I've been dealt, I don't have the luxury of that pretense. I have to live with the reality of my mortality every day of my life. Now I could just give up—and I won't pretend to you that I don't have my bad days. But when I tested positive, I made myself a promise that I was going to dedicate whatever time I have left to two things: to fight the stigmas attached to this disease, and to squeeze everything I can out of life."

The waitress came by with their orders then and for a while they were kept busy with their meals.

"You look a little gloomy," Max said later, when they were waiting for their coffees. "I hope I didn't bring you down."

"No, it's not that."

"So tell Uncle Max what's bothering you."

"My problems seem so petty compared to what you have to put up with."

"Doesn't make them any less real for you, though. So 'fess up. Are you having man trouble again? We can be such bitches, can't we?"

"I suppose," Sophie said with a smile, then her features grew serious. "I just get tired of arguing. Everything starts out fine, but it always ends up with me having to adjust my life to theirs and I'm just not ready to do that anymore. I mean, I know there's going to be compromise in a relationship, but why does it always have to be on my side?"

"Compromise is necessary," Max agreed, "so long as you never give up who you are. That isn't compromise; that's spiritual death. You have to remain true to yourself."

"That's what I keep telling myself, but it doesn't make it any easier."

"Somewhere there is someone who'll love you for who you are, not what they think you should be."

"And if there isn't?" Sophie said. "If I never connect with that person?"

"Then you'll be alone."

"Alone."

Sophie sighed. She was too familiar with what it meant to be alone.

"It's hard to be alone, isn't it?" Max said.

Sophie nodded.

"But better to be alone than to settle for less than what you need . . . less than what you deserve."

"I suppose."

"Here," Max said. He reached down under his chair for the package he'd carried into the restaurant when he'd arrived. "Maybe this'll cheer you up."

He put the package on the table between them. Sophie looked at him.

"What is it?" she asked.

"Open it up and find out."

Inside was one of Max's sculptures—a new one. Sophie recognized herself in one small figurine that made up the tableau, only she was decked out in a leather cap from which sprang a deer's antlers giving her a very mythic air. She stood in front of a saguaro on which was perched a tiny owl with a woman's face. Lounging on a rock beside her was a familiar figure in jeans, shirt and vest, coyote features under the cowboy hat. On the ground between them lay a medicine flute.

"It's beautiful," she said, looking up at Max.

"It's for you."

"I just—"

"Don't you even dare say you can't accept it."

"I just love it," Sophie said.

"Like I said," Max told her. "I've been thinking a lot about the desert lately."

"Me, too."

18

Sometimes when I'm in Mabon, walking its streets while my body's sleeping a world away, I'll get a whiff of smoke that smells like pinon and then somewhere in the crowd I'll spot a lean man who I swear has coyote ears poking up out of his hair, but he's always gone before I can get close enough to be sure.

Coyote was right about one thing: The journeys we take inside our heads never end.

I never thought I'd say this, but I miss him.

Dream Harder,
Dream True

Man is a genius when he dreams. Dream what you're capable of. The harder you dream it, the sooner it will come true.
—attributed to Akira Kurosawa

1

The best artists know what to leave out. They know how much of the support should show through as the pigment is applied, what details aren't necessary. They suggest, and let the viewer fill in whatever else is needed to make the communication complete. They aren't afraid to work with a smaller palette, to delete excess verbiage or place rests on the musical staff, for they know that almost every creative endeavor can be improved with a certain measure of understatement. For isn't it the silence between the notes that often gives music its resonance? What lies between the lines of the poem or story, the dialogue the actor doesn't speak, the pauses between the dancer's steps? The spaces can be just as important as what's distinctly portrayed.

So it's not important where the angel came from, or how she broke her wing. Only that she was there for Jean to find.

2

I'm not saying the city was perfect back then, but it was safer. There were still jobs to be had, and every neighborhood had its own sense of community. The streets and alleyways were swept clean on a regular basis, and it actually made a difference. There was crime, but its reporting was met with shock rather than a shrug. The state sanatoriums had yet to release the majority of their inmates and put them out onto the street—a seeding of homelessness that spread in the streets the way weeds will in an untended garden. Some might say it was a different world entirely through which Jean Etoile made his way home that autumn day.

Jean was a nondescript individual, neither short nor tall, neither ugly nor hand-some; the sort of man you might pass on the street even now and never give a second glance: plain grey suit, white shirt and dark tie, briefcase in hand. Brown hair and eyes, with a pleasant smile, though he showed it rarely. When he passed the time of day with his neighbors, he spoke of the weather, of baseball scores and, yes, wasn't it a pity about old Mrs. Rather down the street, may she rest in peace. Not at all the sort of person one would imagine might bring home a prostitute to live with him in his apartment.

To be fair, Jean didn't know for certain that Candida was a prostitute. It was merely the assumption he'd made when he went to put out his garbage the night before and found her hiding by the back steps of his apartment building in Lower Foxville.

Jean had a secret addiction to mystery and pulp novels—stories by Mickey Spil-lane, Richard S. Prather, Lionel White and the like; stories about tough criminals and tougher cops, hard-boiled PIs and big-hearted hookers—so he felt he knew more than most about the dark side of the city, the side ruled by the night, with its wet streets and neon lights, deals going down in alleyways and pimps running their women, broad-shouldered men with guns under their sportsjackets. And in their hearts, the need to see justice served. When he saw such a beautiful woman in her tight, short dress and stiletto heels, eyelids dark with shadow, rouged cheeks and cherry-red lips, hiding there by his back steps, of all places, he knew she was on the run. Knew she needed help. And while he had neither broad shoulders nor a gun, he did carry in his heart a need to see justice done. It was why the books appealed to him in the first place.

"Don't be frightened," he said when she realized he had seen her. "I won't hurt you."

"I'm not frightened."

Jean was too much the gentleman to point out that her hands were trembling so much that she had to make an effort to hold them still on her lap. Instead he asked, "What's your name?"

"Candida."

Jean nodded. Of course. An exotic given name—if it even was her own—and no surname. This was how the stories always started.

"Do you need some help?" he asked.

"I need a place to stay."

Jean nodded again. He put his paper bag full of garbage into the bin beside the steps, then turned back to her. She was sitting on the steps now, back straight, hands still clasped together on her lap.

"I've got an extra bed," he said. "You can use it for as long as you need."

"Really? You don't know anything about me."

"I know you need help. Isn't that enough?"

Candida gave him a long considering look, then smiled and followed him up the steps to his apartment.

3

Needless to say, Jean had a good heart. If Candida hadn't been beautiful, or even a woman, he would still have offered his help. And it was, as I said, a more innocent time. But his mystery novels about the seamier side of life were no more real than the protagonists after which he was now modeling his actions. Private detectives were rarely larger than life, and even more rarely solved murder investigations that had left the police baffled—it was as true then as it is now. Nor were real prostitutes the unblemished beauties that could be found on the covers of those same pulp novels. Walking the streets leaves scars, as many visible as hidden.

Jean's secret passion was misled, as romantic as a fairy tale. By such token, Candida might well have been something more exotic still: A faerie, perhaps, strayed from some enchanted forest glen. Or a wounded angel, fallen from heaven. For she had wings. Hidden from ordinary sight, it's true, but she did have them. When she rose to follow him up the apartment steps, they could be seen lifting from her shoulderblades, one a majestic sweep of feathers as imagined by da Vinci, or Manet; the other broken, hanging limp.

They could be seen, if you had more than ordinary sight. Or you might see only what you expected to see, what you wished to see. Jean saw a prostitute on the run, in trouble with the law, or with her pimp; perhaps both. Standing at her kitchen window, Hannah Silverstein looked up from her sinkful of dishes to see her neighbor befriend a pretty girl in a pink sweater and a modest skirt that hung just below her knees. The stranger had thick chestnut hair falling free to her shoulders, eyes that seemed as luminous as moonlight, and Hannah was happy for Jean because she had always thought of him as such a nice, pleasant man, but too old at twenty-seven to be living on his own. Too lonely. It was time he met himself a nice girl like this and settled down.

That was what Hannah saw, but then Hannah had her own preconceptions concerning what she expected to see in the world. She once met the great god Pan at the reception following Janet Carney's wedding and thought him a quaint little man who had imbibed perhaps too much wedding cheer.

"Pan is dead," he told her, lifting his glass to clink its rim against hers. "Long live Pan."

But she thought he'd said, "What a spread—long live Jan."

Perhaps it was his accent. Or perhaps, as many of us will, she used a similar filter to listen to him as the one through which she viewed the world.

4

Jean's own perception of his houseguest changed as he came to know Candida. That first autumn day when he returned home from work, not even expecting her to be in his apartment anymore, she had already undergone a slight alteration from the woman he remembered meeting the previous night. She was still sexy, he could still picture her gracing the cover of an issue of *Spicy Detective Stories,* but she no longer seemed cheap, her sexiness was no longer so blatant. She must have gone out while he was at work, he thought, for while she hadn't even been carrying a purse last night, today the tight dress and heels were gone, the makeup far more subdued. She wore, instead, a loose cotton dress with a flower print more suitable to summer than the fall.

"You look different," he said.

"So do you."

It was true. Last night he'd been wearing casual slacks and a short-sleeved polo shirt. But the difference seemed to run deeper in her—beyond a mere change in clothing.

"That's not what I meant," he began.

He was going to go on to tell her that he was dressed for work now, while last night he hadn't been, that he had a chest of drawers and closet full of different clothes into which he could change, while she'd come into his apartment with only what she was wearing, nothing more. But then he smelled the air.

"You made dinner," he said, unable to hide his delight. The last time he'd come home to dinner was when he was still living with his parents, years ago. He looked in the oven, his smile broadening. "Shepherd's pie. It's my favorite."

"I know."

And Jean forgot the anomaly of her wardrobe, never thought to ask how she might know his favorite dinner. It was as though someone had found the room in his mind that housed his curiosity and simply turned off the light and closed the door quietly behind them as they left. The riddles remained, but his questions were gone, just like that.

5

In older, more superstitious days, it might have been said that Candida had bewitched him, for theirs was a whirlwind romance—especially at that time, in that community. They met in September, but the odd circumstances of that meeting had been forgotten. They were married in January, a quiet civil ceremony, because neither had any other family. They had their first and only child late the next September and named her Sophie.

Jean didn't read his detective novels and magazines anymore—he didn't need other stories. At night when they lay in bed, Candida would tell him hers. She had an impossible storehouse of tales tucked away behind her eyes; like Scheherazade, she had so many, she never had to repeat one. In response, Jean felt an unfamiliar stirring in his own mind, a need to communicate his love for his wife and their child, a desire to share with them dreams that were his own, instead of the fantasies he had borrowed from his books and magazines.

Once he had carried a secret life inside him, an ongoing adventure in which he was the tall man in the trenchcoat with the brim of his hat pulled down low over his eyes, who acted when others stood by helpless, to whom the hurt and lost were drawn that he might find them justice, to whom men looked with respect and women with desire. Now the hat and trenchcoat were put aside. Now he had a child who had offered him her unconditional love from the moment he first saw her in the hospital. Now he had a wife who was not only his partner and his lover, but also his best friend. His life was so complete that he had no need for that old secret life.

6

But there was still something unusual about Candida, even if Jean could no longer see it. Though he wasn't alone in that particular blindness, for no one did—not in their circle of friends, not in the neighborhood, though no one ever did remember her quite the same. To some she was tall, to others she was of medium height. To some she had a classical beauty, others thought her a little plain. Some, when they looked at her, marveled at how she retained an unaffected girlishness, belying her motherhood and maturity; others were reminded of their mothers, or their grandmothers.

She was a charming conversationalist, and an even better listener, but it was only to Jean that she told her stories; stories, and cryptic remarks to which Jean never gave much thought until much later.

Because he'd been bewitched, some would say.

7

"Where does she go when she sleeps?" Candida murmured one evening, leaning on the windowsill in their bedroom, looking out at the moon where it hung above the brownstones of Upper Foxville. "Does she go into another world? Or does she only dream?"

She often watched the moon, noting its phases, her eyes not so much reflecting the light as absorbing it. But that night Jean wasn't looking at her. He sat on the bed, giving Sophie her bottle, and thought Candida spoke of the baby.

"If she's dreaming," he said, "I hope they're sweet dreams."

"Oh yes," Candida said, still looking at the moon. "We can only hope they're so sweet as mine."

8

Another time she told him, "If I should ever go, it won't be for lack of loving you—not you, not Sophie. It will be because I am called away. It will be because I will have no choice."

Jean thought she spoke of her death. He didn't like to consider death, little say speak of it. He held her closer to him.

"Don't even think about it," he told her.

He felt her sigh.

"Sometimes I can think of nothing else."

9

One time Jean asked her how she knew so many stories, and she replied that they came from her dreams.

"We have to believe in our dreams," she said, "because without them we are nothing. Dreams are how we make sense of the world, but they're also how we remember it. When your dreams are real—if only to you—when you believe in them and make them a part of the story that is your life, then anything is possible. You can go anywhere, be anyone, mend any hurt—even a broken wing."

"A broken wing?" Jean replied, puzzled.

"We fly in our dreams. But if we break a wing, we have to work that much harder to keep them real, or they fade away." She gave him a sad smile. "But the trouble is, sometimes we heal ourselves so well that we go away all the same."

Jean shook his head. "You're not making sense tonight."

"Just promise me you'll believe in your dreams. That you'll teach Sophie to believe in hers."

"But—"

"Promise me."

For a moment Jean felt as though he didn't know the woman lying in bed beside him. A sliver of moonlight came in through the window, casting strange shadows across Candida's face, reshaping the familiar planes and contours into those of a stranger.

"It's important, Jean. I need to be able to remember this."

"I . . . promise," he said slowly.

She moved out of the moonlight and the familiar features all fell back into place. The smile that touched her lips was warm and loving.

"When we look back on these days," she said, "we'll remember them as mythic times."

"What do you mean?"

"It's as though we stand in the dark of the moon and anything is possible. We're hidden from the sun's light, from anything that might try to remind us that we only borrow these lives we live, we don't own them."

"If we don't own our lives," Jean asked, "then who does?"

"The people we might become if we stop believing in our dreams."

10

Years later, Jean had trouble remembering all the stories Candida had told him. When he tried to tell them to Sophie, he got them mixed up, transposing this beginning to that ending, the characters of this story into that one, until finally he gave up and read her stories out of books the way other parents did. But he never forgot to remind her to believe in her dreams.

11

Candida went to the store to get some milk one evening, almost three years to the day that they had first met on the back steps of the brownstone, and she never came back, leaving Jean's life as mysteriously as she'd first come into it. He remembered looking at her as she turned back from the doorway to ask if there was anything else she should pick up, and being astounded at the vision he beheld. For one long glorious moment he imagined he saw her bathed in a nimbus of radiant light that shone from her every pore, gold as honey, bright as flames. Wings rose up behind her, huge magnificent feathered wings, each with a span twice her height.

The vision held, one moment, another, and then it was gone, and it was Candida standing there in the doorway, the Candida he'd married and who was the mother of their child. But it was that vision of her that he remembered—as an angel, a faerie, a shaft of moonlight, a gift of wonder that had strayed into his world from some nevernever, drawn by his need, or perhaps her own, to weave the strands of her dreams with his, his with hers. Their time together was too short, far too short, but at least they had had that time together. That was what he reminded himself whenever despair threatened to overwhelm him. The memories . . . and Sophie . . . were all that enabled him to carry on.

He remembered Candida as others remember the myths of their ancestors, and he taught their daughter to believe in her dreams. Because in time he came to understand what Candida had meant when she told him that stories begin in dreams and without the stories that we dream, we live someone else's life rather than our own. It wasn't something he realized all at once; instead, he happened upon the fragments of the puzzle, one piece at a time, finding them in the spaces that lay between his memories and his dreams, until one day, when he was sitting alone on the back steps of his apartment building after having put Sophie to bed, the puzzle pieces all came together and he understood.

He smiled then, one of his rare smiles, as sad as it was sweet, but no one was there to see. There were only the stories, the tangled skein of the city's stories, waiting to be shaped by our dreams.

The Pochade Box

1

—What's it like when you're dead?
  —You still dream.

2

One grey September day, Jilly Coppercorn decided to try to break herself of a bad habit she'd managed to acquire over the years. She'd been working on increasingly larger canvases, which was fine, she had no problem with that, but in the process she'd let herself get so finicky that the clarity of her work was getting bogged down with unnecessary detail. She stood back to look at the bewildering complexity of her latest work-in-progress and realized that, despite the near-perfect rendering of the individual sections, the painting as a whole made no sense whatsoever.

What was the point in developing an ideal composition, she thought, when the detailing eventually came to overwhelm the main point of interest to such an extent that it was subservient to all the fussy specifics around it? The viewer's eye, it was plain, could only become confused as it traveled about the canvas trying to find a point of reference amidst the barrage of detail. All she was going to succeed in doing with work such as this was make the viewer look away and walk over to the next piece hanging on the gallery wall, for relief.

So that day she stopped working in the studio, where the temptation to use big canvases would remain a constant niggle in the back of her head. Instead she took to painting on the street, using her pochade box as a studio. It held everything she needed: six tubes of paint for her limited palette, rag, tissues, a turp can, and a couple of brushes with the handles cut down so that they'd fit into the box. Out on the street, she could hold the box with one hand as though it were a palette, the thumb of her left hand poking up through a small hole in the bottom of the box. When the box was open, the lid formed an easel for the small six-by-eight-inch panels she painted. She used the box's tray for her palette, and, to make sure she didn't get too precious, the smallest brush she took with her was a number 8 oxhair filbert. Her only other equipment was a small drying box to carry her panels and a camp stool that folded flat and could be hung on her shoulder by its strap.

She gave herself thirty minutes per painting, working wet-in-wet, on-site, minimal sketching, minimal detail, looking for the heart of each composition, suggesting detail, not rendering it, concentrating on values and shapes. Most of her time was spent studying her subjects, really thinking through what was important and what wasn't, before she'd squeeze the first dollop of pigment onto her palette. She averaged three to four paintings a day, but quantity didn't interest her. All she was really trying to do at this point was get back to the place she'd been with her art before her preoccupation with detail had taken over.

The habits she'd fallen into were hard to break, but as September drifted into a chilly October and she was well into her second week out on the streets, she was finally making some progress. Rough though the finished pieces were, she was happy with the results she was beginning to get. The small six-by-eight panels forced her to ignore inconsequential details and concentrate instead on essentials: the larger shapes of light and dark, the broader color relationships and the overall composition. She was relearning the ability to portray a scene as a whole, rather than rendering its details piecemeal.

The afternoon she met Tommy Flood, she was sitting on her stool, trying to ignore the brisk nip in the wind as she painted the sweeping lines of St. Paul's Cathedral. She'd lucked into a cloudless day and this late in the afternoon, the light was wonderful. Bundled up against the chill, hands warming in fingerless wool gloves, she was so intent on the play of shadow and light on the cathedral's steps that she didn't realize she had company until Tommy spoke.

"Pretty," he said.

Jilly looked up and smiled at the large man who loomed above her. It was hard to place his age, but she thought he might be in his early thirties. He had the slack features of the simpleminded and returned her smile with one of his own, utterly charming and as innocent as a child's. Around his legs pressed an entourage of scruffy, but amazingly well-behaved dogs: an old black lab, one that looked like a cross between a dachshund and a collie, a couple that had a fair amount of German Shepherd in their mix and one that was mostly poodle.

"Thank you," Jilly told him. "It's not done yet."

"My name's Tommy," he said, thrusting out his hand.

He slurred his words a little when he spoke, but not enough so that Jilly had trouble following him. She laid her brush down on top of her palette. Gravely, she shook hands with him and introduced herself.

"Does it have a story?" Tommy asked as Jilly picked up her brush once more.

"What? This painting?"

"No. The box."

Jilly gave him an odd look. "Now how would you know that?" she asked.

"Everything has a story."

3

—So what do the dead dream about?

—I can't speak for others, only myself. Since my death, I've found myself existing in an odd state of mind, one that seems to lie somewhere between sleep and waking. In this place even my dreams don't seem to play fair with my sense of equilibrium. Often I feel that what I dream is real, while a moment such as this—conversing with you—is the dream.

—I think I know exactly what you mean.

—Do you now?

—I have a friend whose dreams are real—they're just real somewhere else.

—I see.

—But you haven't told me yet what it is that you dream about.

—*Heaven.*

—You mean like angels and the pearly gates and all?

—Hardly. *Heaven* was the name of the first painting I ever did which seemed to make the leap from mind to canvas without losing anything in the translation.

—So you're an artist.

—I *was* an artist. That was how I categorized myself, and it was through the terms of my art that I lived my life. In my present existence there appear to be only two classifications of being: the living and the dead. When you must count yourself among the latter, you soon realize that your career options are severely limited. Nonexistent, you might say.

—It sounds horrible.

—You get used to it.

—I'm an artist.

—Are you now? Well, I hope you don't let art consume your life the way I did.

—What do you mean?

—I was so single-minded in my work that the details of my life became a meaningless blur—a *sfumato* backdrop upon which I painted, but no longer experienced. In the end, when even my art was taken away from me, I had nothing left. I understood all too well how Monet, grieving at the death bed of his beloved wife Camille, could still find himself automatically studying the arrangement of colored gradations that death was imposing upon her lifeless features. Before he ever had the idea of recording the moment in a painting, his reflexes had involved him in memorizing the tonal succession. Blue, yellow, grey.

—*Camille on Her Death Bed.*

—Exactly. But while Monet went on to redeem himself in Giverny, striking a balance between the demands of his artistic genius and actually experiencing life, I painted myself into oblivion.

4

"Tommy!"

They all looked up at the figure running down the pavement toward them—Jilly, Tommy and five sleepy dogs who were suddenly almost comically alert. The approaching young woman was in her late teens or early twenties, a slim figure not much taller than Jilly with light brown hair flowing out from under an old black fedora. She wore jeans and sneakers and a short quilted jacket with white shirttails dangling below its hem. Running along beside her was a funny-looking little wirehaired dog.

It wasn't until she got closer that Jilly could see the weariness in her features, the dark circles under her eyes. The woman didn't appear so much exhausted as stretched too tightly, the way Jilly knew she looked the week before she had a show to hang and she was working day and night trying to get the last few pieces done.

"Oh-oh," Tommy said.

"Do you know her?"

Tommy nodded. "She's my sister, Maisie."

There wasn't much family resemblance between them, Jilly thought, but then whoever said everybody in a family had to look the same?

"Where have you *been*?" Maisie cried as she reached them. "I was so worried."

"Just walking, Maisie. I was just walking."

Maisie sighed. Jilly got the idea that she did that a lot when it came to Tommy.

"He wasn't bothering you, was he?" she asked, turning to Jilly.

"Not at all. He's been very sweet."

"He scares people sometimes—because he's so big and they don't understand that he's not crazy, he's just simple."

"And happy," Tommy put in.

Maisie laughed and gave him a quick hug. "And happy," she agreed.

"Jilly's going to tell me a story," Tommy informed her.

Maisie looked at Jilly, eyebrows lifting.

"It's okay," Jilly said.

Neither Maisie nor Tommy were dressed well—too busy worrying about when they were going to eat and keeping a roof over their heads to worry about buying new clothes as well, she decided. It must be especially tough making do when you had a big brother like that with special needs. The least Jilly thought she could do was entertain Tommy with a story.

"Tommy wanted to know about my pochade box," she said. "I can sit with him over on the steps there if you've got some stuff you want to do."

But Maisie's gaze had gone to the box. "Pochade," she said. "That's French for 'rapid sketch,' isn't it?"

Jilly nodded, trying to hide her surprise. Not many of her artist friends had known that—she'd had to provide the definition.

"I read a lot," Maisie explained.

Something clicked in Jilly's mind then, and she realized that she'd heard about Maisie Flood and her extended family of foundlings before.

"You know Angel, don't you?" she asked.

Maisie nodded. "Yeah, she's got me back into school and stuff."

"Welcome to the club," Jilly said. "I'm another one of her successes."

"Really?"

"Though I guess my time goes back further than yours."

"What about the story?" Tommy asked.

"There's two things Tommy loves," Maisie told Jilly. "Pictures and stories. If you can tell a story as well as you paint, you'll have a friend for life."

"Well, I'd probably argue about the criteria involved," Jilly said, "but I love making new friends."

She led the way over to the cathedral's steps, carrying the pochade box as Tommy brought along her stool and the drying box, which held the two paintings she'd done this morning along with a number of unused gessoed panels she'd prepared for other paintings. The dogs followed in what seemed like an undulating wave of fur, settling themselves around and upon Tommy, Maisie and the steps as though they were big, floppy beanbag toys instead of real dogs.

"I really don't mind looking after Tommy if you've got some things to do," Jilly said.

Maisie shook her head. "Are you kidding? Where do you think he got his love for stories from?"

"It's not that great a story—doesn't really have much of a beginning or an end. It's just sort of weird."

"You're stalling."

Jilly laughed. "Only partly. Mostly what I'm doing is offering up the apologia beforehand so that you don't ask for your money back when I'm done."

"We don't have any money to give you," Tommy said, looking disappointed, as though he thought that now they weren't going to get the story.

"It's just an expression," Maisie assured him. "Like letting the cat out of the bag—remember?" She turned to Jilly. "Tommy tends to take things pretty literally."

"I'll keep that in mind," Jilly said.

5

—What do you mean by oblivion?

—You have to be remembered. People have to think about you. If they don't, you just disappear. That's what happens to all those people who vanish mysteriously. Not enough people were thinking about them and eventually they faded away. They were simply forgotten, remembered only when they disappeared—because they disappeared—and then it was too late, of course. You can't bring back what doesn't exist anymore.

—Too late for those of us left behind, maybe, but you still exist somewhere, or I wouldn't be talking to you, would I?

—Sometimes I can't decide if I am actually dead—or alive, but somehow become invisible. Unheard, unseen, unable to taste or feel . . .

—I can't see you, but I can hear you.

—Perhaps you are imagining my voice. Perhaps you are dreaming.

—I think I'd know if I was asleep or not. Besides, I never have dreams this interesting.

—I'm happy to realize I can still be amusing.

—I'm sorry. I don't mean to trivialize your situation. Is there anything I can do to help you?

—You could riddle me this: Is it still existence, when one resides in limbo?

6

"Okay," Jilly said. "I guess it started when Geordie got back from his last trip to England. I wasn't expecting him back for another—"

"Who's Geordie?" Tommy wanted to know.

Maisie sighed. "Tommy tends to interrupt," she apologized. "He doesn't mean to be rude."

"That's all right. It's ruder to just expect everybody to know who you're talking about, without stopping to explain. Geordie's a friend of mine," she added, turning to Tommy. "He plays the fiddle and that summer—I guess it was in the mid-seventies—he went on a busking vacation of the British Isles."

"What's—"

"Busking is when you play music on the street and hope people will give you money because they like what they're hearing."

"We've seen people doing that, haven't we, Maisie?"

"We sure have."

"Is Geordie good?" Tommy wanted to know.

"Very good," Jilly assured him. "The next time he's playing somewhere, I'll take you to see him." She caught Maisie shaking her head, and realized why. "It's okay," she said. "I wouldn't make the promise unless I was going to keep it."

"It's just that people mean well . . ."

"You'll have to trust me on this," Jilly said. Maisie shrugged noncommittally, which was about as much as you could expect, Jilly thought, given how they'd only just met. "Anyway," she went on, "I'm working in my studio one morning and right out of nowhere, Geordie shows up, weeks before I thought I'd be seeing him. Seems he got caught gigging with an Irish band in a London club, except he didn't have a work permit, so he got the boot."

"They made him come back home," Maisie explained to Tommy before he could ask.

"I never got the boot until Maisie found me," Tommy said. "Before that I never had a home."

"I know what you mean," Jilly said. "It's not fun, is it?"

Tommy shook his head. "But we have fun now."

"So did Geordie bring you the box back from England?" Maisie asked.

Jilly nodded. "He got it at something called a car boot sale—it's like a flea market, except it's out in a field somewhere and everybody just sells stuff out of the trunks of their cars."

"Why do they call car trunks 'boots'?" Maisie wondered.

"I don't know. Why do we call chips French fries and crisps 'chips'? Anyway, I thought it was very sweet of him to get it for me. It was pretty grungy, with oil paint caked all over the insides and the tray you use for a palette was broken in two, but I'd never seen anything like it before. If I closed my eyes I could almost picture the turn-of-the-century artist who'd owned it, out somewhere in the English countryside painting *en plein*—outside, on location as opposed to in the studio. The pochade box is like a little studio, really, only in miniature."

She opened the box as she spoke and showed Tommy how it worked and how everything could be stowed away in it once you were done painting.

"After Geordie left that night, I cleaned it up. Scraped away all the dried paint, glued the palette tray back together again and sanded it down so I could start off fresh with my own palette. It took me most of the day before I had it all fixed up—not quite new, but certainly serviceable. I loaded it up with some tubes of paint, rags and a few old brushes cut down to fit inside, and I was ready to head out myself, just the way I imagined its original owner had. But somehow I never did. I set it up on a windowsill, and except for taking it out into the country a few times, it's been sitting there collecting dust for years. Until I started using it again a couple of weeks ago."

Tommy looked at her expectantly when she fell silent. After a few moments, he couldn't hold it in anymore.

"Is that it? Is that the whole story?"

"Well, no," Jilly said, and then she hesitated again. "It gets a little weird after that."

"We can take weird," Maisie assured her.

The wirehaired terrier sprawled out on her lap looked up at Jilly and yipped as though in agreement. Jilly laughed and roughed the stiff fur on the top of its head.

"After I was done fixing the box up," she said, "I sat with it on my lap in the window seat of my studio. I wasn't thinking of anything, just holding the box and staring out the window, watching the light change in the alley below. I can't see the sunset from there, but that alleyway seems to hold the light long after the sun's actually set. I never get tired of watching it."

"I know places like that," Maisie said. "Doesn't matter if they're in the middle of nowhere and there's trash everywhere, they just seem magical."

Jilly nodded. "I'm fascinated by what can't be explained—or at least what can't be explained through the facts most of us have decided are true. So when I had this . . . visitation, I wasn't scared or anything. Just curious."

"What kind of visitation?"

"I can't really explain it. I was alone, sitting there with the box on my lap, and then there was this ghostly presence in the studio with me, and I ended up having a long conversation with it. I can still remember most of what we talked about, word for word."

7

—I don't know about limbo, but I had a friend once—a dancer. She used to tell her boyfriends that every second step she danced, she danced for them.

—But that would only be half the dance.

—I know. She said you have to keep something for yourself. You can't give everything away.

—I'm not sure I understand how this relates to me.

—You put everything into your paintings. You didn't keep anything for yourself.

—I still don't see the relevance.

—I think you're still doing it, and that's why you're in limbo. You're not painting anymore, but even as a ghost, you're not hanging onto anything for yourself. Maybe if you did, you'd be able to let go and move on.

—I'm not sure I have the courage to move on.

—Unfortunately, I can't help you there.

8

"What happened then?" Maisie asked.

Jilly shrugged. "Nothing, really. We talked a little more and then he was just gone. He never came back—at least not so as I ever noticed. I don't know if he went on, or if he's still stuck in limbo and I just can't hear him anymore."

"Sad," Tommy said.

He looked so glum that Jilly began to regret having said anything about the pochade box having a story. But before she could think of something more cheerful to talk about, Tommy sat up straighter on the steps and suddenly brightened up on his own. He pointed down the pavement to where a vendor had set up a cart selling hot pretzels.

"Oh, look!" he cried.

He gave Maisie a long hopeful look until finally she relented. She carefully counted out the change he'd need, then stowed the remainder back in the pocket of her jacket. Jilly had been about to offer to treat them all, but reconsidered when she realized that it might be taken wrong. Maisie struck her as prideful enough to mistake generosity for charity, and Jilly didn't want to chance losing their new friendship over something like that. She was enjoying their company and wanted to get to know them better. So she sat back and let it play out, waiting there on the steps with Maisie and watching Tommy run eagerly to the pretzel cart, the dogs scrambling about at his heels.

"Do you think Tommy would like it if I gave him this painting when it's done?" she said.

Maisie shrugged. "It's hard to say. When I said he likes pictures, it's mostly stuff from magazines. He has me cut out the people in the pictures and then he uses them as dolls to make up little stories. He's never had a painting before, so I don't know what he'd do with it."

Jilly decided that she would give Tommy a painting, except it would be one of him and his sister and their dogs. She had a good enough memory that she knew she'd be able to do it back in her studio without their needing to sit for it.

"That was an odd story," Maisie said.

"What there was of it," Jilly said.

Her companion gave her a considering look. "If I didn't know better," she said, "I'd think that Angel had set this up—sort of a morality play, you know?"

Jilly shook her head.

"Well, she's always telling me I've got to get a life for myself—meet people, maybe get a boyfriend, that kind of thing. I can't seem to get her to understand that being with Tommy and the dogs is what I *want* to do."

"But she's got a point."

"And that is?"

"If you lose sight of yourself, then what've you got to offer Tommy and the dogs? You'll be as bad as my ghost, giving of yourself until there's nothing left to give and you simply fade away. You'll end up stuck in the same limbo."

"You don't get it either. I *want* to be with them."

Jilly sighed. "I do get it. But maybe it'd be good for them to have some other input as well. I'm not saying Tommy can be self-sufficient—I don't know him well enough, what his limitations might be. But if you're always there doing things for him, how's he supposed to learn to do anything for himself?"

"But that's how I found him. He was like that. He's not my brother, I just kind of adopted him. He got dumped on the streets because nobody else wanted him and let me tell you, without me, he wouldn't have survived."

"I believe you. But maybe whoever he was with before wasn't giving him any slack either." Jilly held up her hand to forestall Maisie's protest. "Look, I'm not saying you're right or wrong, just that you might want to think about it—for Tommy, if not for yourself. Maybe you need Tommy as much as he needs you. I don't know. It's not for me to say, is it?"

"That's right. It's not for you to say."

Jilly sighed. "Now you think I'm trying to tell you how to take care of Tommy."

"Aren't you? You're beginning to sound the same as everyone else I meet—you all know better."

"No, I don't," Jilly said. "The only thing I know about Tommy is that I intend to treat him like anybody else I know. I don't have some hidden agenda; I was talking about you. Maybe you know how to take care of Tommy and the dogs, but do you know how to take care of yourself? I'm not talking about making a living or going back to school, or any of that. I'm talking about what goes on in here—" she touched a hand between her breasts "—in your heart."

"What's that supposed to mean?"

"It's like my painting," Jilly said. "I'm out here on the streets with this pochade box because I was overloading my work with detail—so much so that while all the various parts of a painting would be good, the excessive details made the final painting way too busy. I was losing sight of what I was trying to say with each painting in the first place."

"So?"

"I've done the same thing with my life. Concentrated so much on the details, that I would lose sight of the overall direction of where I was going—of the fact that I even wanted to go somewhere in the first place. I've got friends who work with people with special needs. I've even done some volunteer work myself. The thing is, it's so easy to wrap your whole life around the details of theirs, that you become invisible in the process. People like Tommy can't help needing so much from us. But we've got to have something to give them, and if we spend all our time wrapped up in what we see as our responsibility, our relationships with them end up becoming burdens instead of gifts."

At first Maisie looked angry, and Jilly thought she'd gone too far. She didn't know anything about either Maisie or Tommy beyond what she'd picked up in the past hour, so who was she to be blithely handing our advice the way she was? But then Maisie's features softened and she gave another one of her sighs.

"Am I that transparent?" Maisie asked.

Jilly shook her head. "Only if you know what to look for. You seem really tired, almost worn out."

"I am. But what I said was true. I don't resent the time I spend with Tommy. I like being with him, but sometimes it gets to be too much, trying to juggle school and work and time with him. . . ." Her gaze met Jilly's. "But I can't not do it. And I don't want to just foist Tommy off somewhere so that I can have some time to myself."

"Because you think Tommy would feel hurt?"

"Partly. But I also get scared that if it looks like I can't take care of him properly, somebody'll try to take him away from me."

Jilly nodded understandingly. "Maybe you're looking at this from the wrong angle, losing the overall picture for the details. Instead of thinking of it as foisting Tommy off on other people, you should think of it as allowing Tommy to enrich their lives and for Tommy to get some different takes on the world than the way he sees it when he's only with you."

Maisie looked down the pavement to where Tommy was talking excitedly with the vendor as he waited for his pretzel.

"People don't think of time with Tommy as being enriching," she said. "I mean, even my landlady—she looks after him when I'm working or at school, and she's crazy about him—even she doesn't give me the impression that she gets anything out of the relationship."

"Have you ever asked her?"

Maisie shook her head.

"I'd like to see Tommy again," Jilly said. "I think I could learn a lot from him. And I'm sure if you talked to Angel she could help you work things out so that there'd be other people to lend you a hand without anyone thinking that you're not fit to be taking care of Tommy anymore."

"It's hard," Maisie said. "Always asking, always standing there with your hand out."

Jilly nodded. "That's one way of looking at it. But you know, the best thing I ever learned from Angel is that there's nothing wrong with asking for help. If we're not here to look out for each other, then what are we doing here?"

"Living in limbo," Maisie said.

"Exactly. Just like my ghost."

"So what do you think I should do?"

"Well, for a start, what's Tommy doing tomorrow?"

Maisie's brow furrowed. "Let's see. I've got to work until two, but after that I think—"

"Not you," Jilly told her. "Just Tommy. Do you think he'd like to come with me and see Geordie while he's busking?"

Maisie hesitated for a long moment. She looked back at the pretzel vendor to see that Tommy was on his way back, pretzel in hand, dogs running around him, hoping he'd drop a piece of it.

"I don't know," she said. "Why don't we ask him?"

9

—Since you brought up Monet earlier, maybe you should remember what he's supposed to have told Georges Clemenceau when Clemenceau was visiting him at Giverny.

—Refresh my memory.

—'Your mistake is to want to reduce the world to your measure, whereas by enlarging your knowledge of things, you will find your knowledge of self is enlarged.'

—I see. And where did a woman as young as yourself gain such wisdom?

—From making mistakes. I make a lot of them. The trick is not making excuses for them, or trying to pretend they never happened, but learning from them.

—You see the world without shades of grey.

—Hardly.

—Then how can you make it sound so effortless?

—Are you kidding? Life's like art. You have to work hard to keep it simple and still have meaning. It's so much easier just to deal with everything in how it relates to yourself. You have to really concentrate to keep an open mind, to pay attention to the broader view, to stay aware of what's going on outside your own skin.

—And if you don't?

—Think of all you've got to lose.

Coyote Stories

Four directions blow the sacred winds
We are standing at the center
Every morning wakes another chance
To make our lives a little better
—Kiya Heartwood, from "Wishing Well"

This day Coyote is feeling pretty thirsty, so he goes into Joey's Bar, you know, on the corner of Palm and Grasso, across from the Men's Mission, and he lays a nugget of gold down on the counter, but Joey he won't serve him.

"So you don't serve skins no more?" Coyote he asks him.

"Last time you gave me gold, it turned to shit on me," is what Joey says. He points to the Rolex on Coyote's wrist. "But I'll take that. Give you change and everything."

Coyote scratches his muzzle and pretends he has to think about it. "Cost me twenty-five dollars," he says. "It looks better than the real thing."

"I'll give you fifteen, cash, and a beer."

"How about a bottle of whiskey?"

So Coyote comes out of Joey's Bar and he's missing his Rolex now, but he's got a bottle of Jack in his hand and that's when he sees Albert, just around the corner, sitting on the ground with his back against the brick wall and his legs stuck out across the sidewalk so you have to step over them, you want to get by.

"Hey, Albert," Coyote says. "What's your problem?"

"Joey won't serve me no more."

"That because you're indigenous?"

"Naw. I got no money."

So Coyote offers him some of his whiskey. "Have yourself a swallow," he says, feeling generous, because he only paid two dollars for the Rolex and it never worked anyway.

"Thanks, but I don't think so," is what Albert tells him. "Seems to me I've been given a sign. Got no money means I should stop drinking."

Coyote shakes his head and takes a sip of his Jack. "You are one crazy skin," he says.

That Coyote he likes his whiskey. It goes down smooth and puts a gleam in his eye. Maybe, he drinks enough, he'll remember some good time and smile, maybe he'll get mean and pick himself a fight with a lamppost like he's done before. But one thing he knows, whether he's got money or not's got nothing to do with omens. Not for him, anyway.

But a lack of money isn't really an omen for Albert either; it's a way of life. Albert, he's like the rest of us skins. Left the reserve, and we don't know why. Come to the city, and we don't know why. Still alive, and we don't know why. But Albert, he remembers it being different. He used to listen to his grandmother's stories, soaked them up like the dirt will rain, thirsty after a long drought. And he tells stories himself, too, or pieces of stories, talk to you all night long if you want to listen to him.

It's always Coyote in Albert's stories, doesn't matter if he's making them up or just passing along gossip. Sometimes Coyote's himself, sometimes he's Albert, sometimes he's somebody else. Like it wasn't Coyote sold his Rolex and ran into him outside Joey's Bar that day, it was Billy Yazhie. Maybe ten years ago now, Billy he's standing under a turquoise sky beside Spider Rock one day, looking up, looking up for a long time, before he turns away and walks to the nearest highway, sticks out his thumb and he doesn't look back till it's too late. Wakes up one morning and everything he knew is gone and he can't find his way back.

Oh that Billy he's a dark skin, he's like leather. You shake his hand and it's like you took hold of a cowboy boot. He knows some of the old songs and he's got himself a good voice, strong, ask anyone. He used to drum for the dancers back home, but his hands shake too much now, he says. He doesn't sing much anymore, either. He's got to be like the rest of us, hanging out in Fitzhenry Park, walking the streets, sleeping in an alleyway because the Men's Mission it's out of beds. We've got the stoic faces down real good, but you look in our eyes, maybe catch us off guard, you'll see we don't forget anything. It's just most times we don't want to remember.

This Coyote he's not too smart sometimes. One day he gets into a fight with a biker, says he going to count coup like his plains brothers, knock that biker all over the street, only the biker's got himself a big hickory-handled hunting knife and he cuts Coyote's head right off. Puts a quick end to that fight, I'll tell you. Coyote he spends the rest of the afternoon running around, trying to find somebody to sew his head back on again.

"That Coyote," Jimmy Coldwater says, "he's always losing his head over one thing or another."

I tell you we laughed.

But Albert he takes that omen seriously. You see him drinking still, but he's drinking coffee now, black as a raven's wing, or some kind of tea he brews for himself in a tin can, makes it from weeds he picks in the empty lots and dries in the sun. He's living in an abandoned factory these days, and he's got this one wall, he's gluing feathers and bones to it, nothing fancy, no eagle's wings, no bear's jaw, wolf skull, just what he can find lying around, pigeon feathers and crow's, rat bones, bird bones, a necklace of mouse skulls strung on a wire. Twigs and bundles of weeds, rattles he makes from tin cans and bottles and jars. He paints figures on the wall, in between all the junk. Thunderbird. Bear. Turtle. Raven.

Everybody's starting to agree, that Albert he's one crazy skin.

Now when he's got money, he buys food with it and shares it out. Sometimes he walks over to Palm Street where the skin girls are working the trade and he gives them money, asks them to take a night off. Sometimes they take the money and just laugh, getting into the next car that pulls up. But sometimes they take the money and they sit in a coffee shop, sit there by the window, drinking their coffee and look out at where they don't have to be for one night.

And he never stops telling stories.

"That's what we are," he tells me one time. Albert he's smiling, his lips are smiling, his eyes are smiling, but I know he's not joking when he tells me that. "Just stories. You and me, everybody, we're a set of stories, and what those stories are is what makes us what we are. Same thing for whites as skins. Same thing for a tribe and a city and a nation and the world. It's all these stories and how they braid together that tells us who and what and where we are.

"We got to stop forgetting and get back to remembering. We got to stop asking for things, stop waiting for people to give us the things we think we need. All we really need is the stories. We have the stories and they'll give us the one thing nobody else can, the thing we can only take for ourselves, because there's nobody can give you back your pride. You've got to take it back yourself.

"You lose your pride and you lose everything. We don't want to know the stories, because we don't want to remember. But we've got to take the good with the bad and make ourselves whole again, be proud again. A proud people can never be defeated. They lose battles, but they'll never lose the war, because for them to lose the war you've got to go out and kill each and every one of them, everybody with even a drop of the blood. And even then, the stories will go on. There just won't be any skins left to hear them."

This Coyote he's always getting in trouble. One day he's sitting at a park bench, reading a newspaper, and this cop starts to talk big to one of the skin girls, starts talking mean, starts pushing her around. Coyote's feeling chivalrous that day, like he's in a white man's movie, and he gets into a fight with the cop. He gets beat up bad and then more cops come and they take him away, put him in jail.

The judge he turns Coyote into a mouse for a year so that there's Coyote, got that same lopsided grin, got that sharp muzzle and those long ears and the big bushy tail, but he's so small now you can hold him in the palm of your hand.

"Doesn't matter how small you make me," Coyote he says to the judge. "I'm still Coyote."

Albert he's so serious now. He gets out of jail and he goes back to living in the factory. Kids've torn down that wall of his, so he gets back to fixing it right, gets back to sharing food and brewing tea and helping the skin girls out when he can, gets back to telling stories. Some people they start thinking of him as a shaman and call him by an old Kickaha name.

Dan Whiteduck he translates the name for Billy Yazhie, but Billy he's not quite sure what he's heard. Know-more-truth, or No-more-truth?

"You spell that with a 'K' or what?" Billy he asks Albert.

"You take your pick how you want to spell it," Albert he says.

Billy he learns how to pronounce that old name and that's what he uses when he's talking about Albert. Lots of people do. But most of us we just keep on calling him Albert.

One day this Coyote decides he wants to have a powwow, so he clears the trash from this empty lot, makes the circle, makes the fire. The people come but no one knows the songs anymore, no one knows the drumming that the dancers need, no one knows the steps. Everybody they're just standing around, looking at each other, feeling sort of stupid, until Coyote he starts singing, *Ya-ha-hey, ya-ha-hey,* and he's stomping around the circle, kicking up dirt and dust.

People they start to laugh, then, seeing Coyote playing the fool.

"You are one crazy skin!" Angie Crow calls to him and people laugh some more, nodding in agreement, pointing at Coyote as he dances round and round the circle.

But Jimmy Coldwater he picks up a stick and he walks over to the drum Coyote made. It's this big metal tub, salvaged from a junkyard, that Coyote's covered with a skin and who knows where he got that skin, nobody's asking. Jimmy he hits the skin of the drum and everybody they stop laughing and look at him, so Jimmy he hits the skin again. Pretty soon he's got the rhythm to Coyote's dance and then Dan Whiteduck he picks up a stick, too, and joins Jimmy at the drum.

Billy Yazhie he starts up to singing then, takes Coyote's song and turns it around so that he's singing about Spider Rock and turquoise skies, except everybody hears it their own way, hears the stories they want to hear in it. There's more people drumming and there's people dancing and before anyone knows it, the night's over and there's the dawn poking over the roof of an abandoned factory, thinking, these are some crazy skins. People they're lying around and sitting around, eating the flatbread and drinking the tea that Coyote provided, and they're all tired, but there's something in their hearts that feels very full.

"This was one fine powwow," Coyote he says.

Angie she nods her head. She's sitting beside Coyote all sweaty and hot and she'd never looked quite so good before.

"Yeah," she says. "We got to do it again."

We start having regular powwows after that night, once, sometimes twice a month. Some of the skins they start to making dancing outfits, going back up to the reserve for visits and asking about steps and songs from the old folks. Gets to be we feel like a community, a small skin nation living here in exile with the ruins of broken-down tenements and abandoned buildings all around us. Gets to be we start remembering some of our stories and sharing them with each other instead of sharing bottles. Gets to be we have something to feel proud about.

Some of us we find jobs. Some of us we try to climb up the side of the wagon but we keep falling off. Some of us we go back to homes we can hardly remember. Some of us we come from homes where we can't live, can't even breathe, and drift here and there until we join this tribe that Albert he helped us find.

And even if Albert he's not here anymore, the stories go on. They have to go on, I know that much. I tell them every chance I get.

See, this Coyote he got in trouble again, this Coyote he's always getting in trouble, you know that by now, same as me. And when he's in jail this time he sees that it's all tribes inside, the same as it is outside. White tribes, black tribes, yellow tribes, skin tribes. He finally understands, finally realizes that maybe there can't ever be just one tribe, but that doesn't mean we should stop trying.

But even in jail this Coyote he can't stay out of trouble and one day he gets into another fight and he gets cut again, but this time he thinks maybe he's going to die.

"Albert," Coyote he says, "I am one crazy skin. I am never going to learn, am I?"

"Maybe not this time," Albert says, and he's holding Coyote's head and he's wiping the dribble of blood that comes out of the side of Coyote's mouth and is trickling down his chin. "But that's why you're Coyote. The wheel goes round and you'll get another chance."

Coyote he's trying to be brave, but he's feeling weaker and it hurts, it hurts, this wound in his chest that cuts to the bone, that cuts the thread that binds him to this story.

"There's a thing I have to remember," Coyote he says, "but I can't find it. I can't find its story. . . ."

"Doesn't matter how small they try to make you," Albert he reminds Coyote. "You're still Coyote."

"Ya-ha-hey," Coyote he says. "Now I remember."

Then Coyote he grins and he lets the pain take him away into another story.

The Forever Trees

1

In the end, what she remembers isn't her name, not at first, who she was or even how and where she lived her life. What she remembers is this:

When I was a child I had this ability to simply go somewhere. It wasn't a good place or a bad place—just *another* place. I wouldn't hide there, but when I was there, I couldn't be found. I didn't have to walk there, I'd just be there, in that ghost place.

Sometimes now I think it was a part of me, a piece of my mind where I'd go when things were bad. But then I remember: I went there when things were good, too.

2

Tasha never stops thinking, thinking. She's a visual artist but her mind's always full of words, scuttling around inside her head like mice in an old house when the sun goes down, the eyelids are drawn, the shutters fastened, the body still sleeping, but that secret part of her where the spirit candle burns the brightest is busy-busy, talking to itself, remembering, dreaming. She paints because of those words.

It's like this: She sees colors for words, like a light mottled grey touched with soft green and purple for *whisper. Free* is a Prussian blue that goes on forever, acquiring a hint of violet just before it vanishes from sight. *Cacti* is a deep fuchsia, but *cactus* is a warm buttery yellow with streaks of olive green and greenish browns. *New* is the electric color of a kingfisher's wing and *ford* is the coppery red of an old pen nib, but *Newford* is a grey with highlights of henna and purple.

Joe doesn't pretend to understand. He looks at her art. He knows that her paintings are fragments of stories, conversations, essays, all chasing down those mice in her head, trying to put them into some semblance of order, but he doesn't get the translation. All he sees is color on the canvas, random patterns that make no sense even after Tasha reads them to him.

But it doesn't stop them from being friends.

They're just friends. Good friends.

"I don't want to exchange bodily fluids with you," she tells him once. "It always spoils things."

He wonders at the time if that's how she really meant to put it, or if she just liked the way the words looked as she said them, but he understands what she means. Sex is good. Sex is fun. There's no better place to be, he thinks, than in the middle of a relationship when most of the awkwardness is gone and you're still crazy about each other. But one person always loves the other more, and the imbalance undermines the best of intentions and eventually it all falls apart. He's seen it happen. He's had it happen. Lovers have come and gone in his life, but Tasha's constant. She's not one of the guys, not even close. She brings out the best in him, the way a friend should, but too often doesn't. Asks hard questions, but doesn't answer them for him. Lets him work them out for himself. The way he does for her.

"Men always want to fix everything," she tells him another time, "and I can't figure out why. I'd settle for simply understanding things."

Gets to where he knows exactly what she means. She talks about men, he talks about women, they're generalizing, like you do, but they're not talking about each other. It's not that they're sexless. The gender thing is there, it's part of what endears them to each other, the insights they get into what each is not, but the attraction's strictly platonic. Which makes it all the more confusing when Joe finds himself thinking not about her, Tasha, his friend, but about the curve of her neck and the way her hennaed hair lies so soft against it, how she fills her sweater and jeans with perfect contours that he wants to explore, palm to skin; soft, she'd be so soft, so smooth, like silk; touching her would be like touching silk, but warm.

He'd give anything to taste her lips, and all of a sudden everything's way too complicated and he wants to fix what's going on instead of understanding it.

3

To get to that ghost place, first I'd have to find the meadow. Summer growth slaps my knees as I follow the long slope up from the bottom of the hill where the hedge is an unruly thicket tangled up in heaps of gathered fieldstone. It's been years since the slope was ploughed, but not so long that the forest has resettled the open ground. The weeds are never too tall, and there are always wildflowers in bloom, great stuttering sweeps of color that twist and wind in spiraling paths up and down the slope of the hill. Sometimes there's a hawk, high up, floating in the sky, but I don't see it right away, rarely look for the grey-brown cut of its wings against the blue. As I make my way up the slope, my gaze is always on the forest.

It's a crown of trees on the crest of the hill, trunks and fallen snags slow-dancing around the granite outcrops, a hundred-acre wood, but Pooh doesn't live there and I'm not Christopher Robin. I wouldn't even want to be. I liked being a girl and I like being a woman.

Under the trees, the air is cool and dark and rich with the wet smell of old damp wood, of ferns and mushrooms and the moss that cushions my footfalls. Not far from where the edge of the meadow and the forest blurs, a natural spring bubbles up from a leak in the granite and trickles pell-mell through the leaf mold and around the stones. The water hurries with a jigging and reeling rush that's long since cut a narrow cleft through the dark red earth as it ribbons its way down the slope. All the trees seem to lean down to listen to it as it goes by.

What kind of trees? I don't know. I never had a name for them. They're big, some of them. Bigger than redwoods. But gnarled like old oaks or elms. And kind. I can't really explain. There's a kindness about them. They always welcome me. I know they're older than the stars, thick with mystery and wind-music rustlings and shadow. Written on their bark are the histories of ancient times, long lost, and a thousand forgotten stories that they must remember, but they always have time for me. Child, girl, woman. I only ever felt kindness in that hundred-acre wood.

Nim called them the forever trees.

4

So Joe's redefined their relationship, but Tasha doesn't know. She comes over that evening to watch a video with him and feels something different in the air. Innocent in a white T-shirt and snug jeans that make her seem anything but, she looks around his apartment to see what's changed. The bookcase still stands on one wall, its shelves stuffed with paperbacks, magazines and found objects like a tattered slipper or a chipped coffee mug that have been there so long they've acquired squatters' rights and would look out of place anywhere else. The sofa still faces the old cedar chest that holds Joe's TV set and stereo. The same posters are on the wall, along with the small reproduction of a Hockney print in its narrow metal frame. The same worn Oriental carpet underfoot. The two beers Joe brings from the kitchen are given temporary refuge on the same apple crate that usually serves as his coffee table.

Nothing's different, but everything has changed. Joe seems—not edgy, but he can't stop moving. His usual stillness has dissolved, leaving behind the bare bones of nervous energy that makes his fingers twitch, his toes tap. Tasha tucks a loose lock of red hair back behind her ears and sits down on the sofa. She leans back, draws her knees up to her chin, smiles over them at Joe, who's hovering about in the middle of the carpet until finally he sits down as well.

The video he's picked is *Enchanted April*. They've seen it before, but tonight the holidaying women don't absorb him. He's constantly stealing glances at her until Tasha begins to wonder if she's got a bit of her dinner stuck to her chin or lodged in between her teeth. A scrap of egg noodle. An errant morsel of snow pea. She explores the spaces between her teeth with her tongue, surreptitiously gives her chin a wipe with the back of her hand.

When she puts her feet down for a moment to reach for her beer, Joe is suddenly right beside her. She turns to look at him, confused, their faces only inches apart. He leans closer. As their lips touch, all the clues Tasha hadn't realized were clues go tumbling through her mind, rearranged in their proper order, the mystery solved, the confusion now embracing what had brought this change to their relationship—and how could she have missed it? But then she lets the confusion go away and enjoys the moment, because Joe's a better kisser than she had ever imagined, and she finds she likes the feel of his back and shoulders as she returns his embrace, likes the press of his chest against her, especially likes the touch of his lips and the tingling that wakes in her belly as the tips of their tongues explore each other.

"This is nice," she murmurs when they finally come up for air.

Nice hangs behind her eyes, all chicory blue, like when the sun first pulls the petals awake, and speckled like a trout. The movie plays on, forgotten except for the flickering glow it throws upon their faces.

"It's weird," Joe tells her. "I just haven't been able to stop thinking about you." The parade of his words kaleidoscopes through her. "It's like we've been friends for what—eight, nine years?—and all of a sudden I'm seeing you for the first time, and I can't believe that I've ever been the least bit interested in another woman."

It takes Tasha a moment to separate the meaning of what he's saying from the colors.

"Are you saying you love me?" she asks, not sure how she wants him to answer, for all that she's been thoroughly enjoying the intimacy of the past ten minutes.

Joe gives her an odd look, as though he hadn't thought things through quite that far. But then he smiles.

"I guess I am," he says.

The words wake a warm flood of color in Tasha's mind, a mingling of rose and pale violet like a coneflower's bloom in the twilight.

"How do you feel?" he asks.

"I'm not sure," she says softly. "It's all so sudden. It's . . ." She can't find the color to tell him what she feels because she's not sure herself; she puts a hand behind his head and draws his lips back toward hers. "Kiss me again," she murmurs just before their lips meet.

The words float in their colors through her mind but Joe doesn't need the invitation.

5

I guess I have to explain everything, don't I? Nim lives in the hundred-acre wood. At least I think she does, because that's the only place I've ever seen her. Actually, I'm not even sure she's a she. I just always think of her as female, but as I try to describe her I realize she's asexual, androgynous. No breasts, but no body hair or Adam's apple either. Her long curly hair is always filled with seeds and twigs and burrs, but it's still soft as duck down. Skinny, she's so skinny you'd think she was made of sticks, but her limbs are pliant. She's the first person I've ever met who's as double-jointed as me. Maybe more. And she hears colors, too.

"But not sounds," she said when we're talking about it one time. "Just words."

Like me.

6

Joe knows he's screwed up big time. Tasha stays the night and they sleep together. They don't make out, they just sleep together, but somehow that makes everything seem more intimate instead of less. He wakes up to find her lying there beside him, still asleep. He traces the contour of her cheek with his gaze, and he sees a friend, not a lover; all the little fireworks have packed up and gone. He still thinks she's beautiful, ethereal and earthy, all mixed up in one red-topped bundle, but desire has fled. Making love to her would be like making love to a relative.

She opens her eyes and smiles at him, her warmth washing over him in a gentle pulsing tide until the guilt he's feeling registers, the smile droops, worry flits across her eyes.

"What's wrong?" she asks.

"This is a mistake," he tells her. "This is a serious mistake."

"But you said—"

"I know. I . . ."

He can't face her. He's feeling bad enough as it is. The hurt that's growing in her eyes is going to devastate him. He gets out of bed and starts dressing, fast, doesn't even look to see what he's putting on.

"I've got to get to work," he says, for all that it's a Saturday morning. He combs his hair with his hands, give her an apologetic look. "We'll talk about it," he adds, knowing how lame it sounds, but he can't seem to do any better. "Later."

And then he's gone. Tasha stares at the door of the bedroom through which he's fled. She's sitting up in the bed, has the bedclothes pulled up to her chin, but they don't do anything for the shivering chill he's left behind, the blank spot that seems to have lodged in the middle of her chest. It's hard to breathe, hard to think straight. Harder still when she starts to cry and she can't stop, she just can't stop.

7

The thing is, I don't ever have to come back if I don't want to. I could stay forever the way Nim does and never grow any older. What brings me back? It used to be my puppy—Topy. I'd come back for Topy, but then one day I let her stay and she's lived in the hundred-acre wood with Nim ever since. Nobody could understand why I wasn't sad that she'd run away, but they didn't understand that she hadn't run away from me. I could see her any time I wanted to. I still can.

What brought me back after that? I don't know. Different things. I like this world, but sometimes everything gets to be too much for me in it. Like it's hard just having simple conversations when you have to be constantly separating the meanings of what's being said from its colors. I can't argue with people. By the time I've worked out what we're fighting about, everything's usually gotten way more complicated, gotten so tangled up and knotted that it'll never make sense again. At least not for me. The hundred-acre wood gives me a break from that. Gives me a chance to catch my breath so that when I come back to this world I fit in a little easier.

Nim knows what I mean. She's never going back, she says. She wants to become a forever tree herself and sometimes, when I look at her, all twig-thin with that wild bird's-nest of hair on top, I think she's halfway there.

8

Tasha makes her way home, crawls into her own bed, pulls the covers over her head, but can't stop the chill, can't stop the tears. It hurts too much—not because Joe redefined the relationship and then, after she tentatively embraced its new parameters, he went and backed off. She enjoyed necking with him last night, but she wasn't exactly making a lifetime commitment herself. No, it's that he didn't stay to talk. To explain. She hasn't been betrayed by a lover she's just met; she's been betrayed by one of her oldest friends.

She waits for him to call, but the phone stays silent by her bed. Saturday night. All day Sunday. Maybe it's better that way. She's never been good on the phone. Without a face to concentrate on, without being able to watch the lips move, or absorb the subtext that resonates in eyes and facial tics and twitches, conversation too often turns into nothing more than a confusing porridge of color.

So Sunday evening she gets out of bed, dresses, tries to fix her face so that it doesn't look as though she's been crying for most of the weekend, sets off for Joe's apartment. Dreading it. Already knowing it'll be a disaster when she attempts to filter word-sense from the color flood of what they'll say to each other. But they've been friends too long for her not to try.

Friends, she thinks. Friends don't treat each other this way. Her ability to trust is undergoing a test of faith. Once the masks drop, anything could be waiting there. That's something she's always known. The shock is finding a mask where she didn't expect one to be. She'd never realized that Joe could have been wearing a mask all this time.

But friends make mistakes, she told herself, and she clung to those words, spoke them aloud. Saw yellow ochre veined with madder and blues. The grey underbelly of a summer cloud, winging across it, a flock of magenta and yellow-gold flowers.

But the colors couldn't disguise the fear that no matter what happened tonight, she was never going to be sure if Joe was wearing a mask or not. There was just no way to *know*.

9

I guess the hardest thing to explain is how the hundred-acre wood is a real place, that I really go there, that when I'm walking under the forever trees, I'm not here anymore. It's not like I've shut my eyes and gone to some place inside my head. That's what I thought it was at first. Well, not at first. When I first went, I was too young even to wonder about that kind of thing.

My parents knew there was something wrong with me, but no one could figure out what it was. It wasn't until years later that anyone even came up with a name for my condition: synaesthesia. Everyone just thought I was a slow learner, that the connections in my head weren't all wired the right way, which is true I guess, or I'd be like everybody else, right?

I didn't talk until I was five because it took me that long to realize that it was words people used to communicate with each other—not colors. Because I *was* communicating, you see. Right from the first. But it was with crayons and watercolor paints, and nobody could understand what I was saying. When I finally started to use words it was like having to translate everything from a foreign language.

That's what is so seductive about the hundred-acre wood. When I talk with Nim, I'm communicating directly with her. I don't feel like I'm muddling around with translations. I never get the feeling that she's impatient with the long pauses in our conversations, because she hears and sees everything the same as me. When I show her one of my paintings she knows exactly what I'm saying with it—the same way that somebody else can read a page from a book.

I guess one day I'll go and I won't come back. I'll become a raggedy wild girl like Nim with twigs and burrs in my hair. Maybe we'll both end up as forever trees. Maybe that's where they came from. Maybe we're both dryads and we just haven't matured from tree spirits into proper trees yet.

The idea of it makes me smile. If we were forever trees, we'd have *really* slow conversations, wouldn't we?

10

Joe is not a bad guy. Like Tasha said, even friends make mistakes. He never wore a mask around her, and that was part of the problem that night when he told her he thought they should be lovers *and* friends. Maybe he should have waited, kept it to himself a little longer until he'd really worked it out in his own head, dealt with it in a way that wouldn't have hurt Tasha before sharing his feelings with her. But maybe it took his sharing those feelings for him to work it out.

He knew it hadn't been fair to her, but he hadn't meant to hurt her. Not that night. Not when he fled the next morning. He'd just gotten confused, couldn't think straight, but he meant to make it right. He meant to call her and apologize for screwing up the way he had, screwing up big time, and he hoped she'd forgive him because maybe they weren't supposed to be lovers, but nothing in his life meant more to him than Tasha's friendship.

So he phones her, Sunday night, lets the phone ring and ring, but there's no answer. He keeps trying up until midnight, then he finally goes over to her apartment, lets himself in with the key she gave him so long ago, but she really isn't there, she wasn't just ignoring the phone, she really isn't home. But she isn't anywhere else either.

Days go by and she's never home, never at her studio, nobody has seen her, nobody ever sees her again.

Joe's sitting in his apartment, cradling one of Tasha's paintings on his lap, and he's remembering holding her one night when she's having a stress attack, when all the words turned into too many colors and everything inside her just shut down for a while so that she didn't even know who or where she was; he's remembering what she told him that night, about a ghost place she can visit, a hundred-acre wood of forever trees. He believed she could go there, didn't ask for proof. That's what friends do—they accept each other's secrets and marvels and hold them in trust.

So Joe knows where Tasha has gone, running up a long meadowed slope with a wild girl and a puppy, vanishing into the embrace of a forest of forever trees, and he misses her, more than anything, he misses her, and what he regrets, what he regrets the most, is that he never asked her how to get there himself, so that he could see her again.

Moonlight
and
Vines

for all those
who seek light
in the darkness

for all those
who shine light
into the darkness

CONTENTS

AUTHOR'S NOTE

I've said it before, but it bears repeating: No creative endeavor takes place in a vacuum. I've been very lucky in having incredibly supportive people in my life to help in the existence of these stories, be it in terms of the nuts and bolts of editing and the like, or on more elusive, inspirational levels. To name them all would be an impossible task, but I do want to mention at least a few:

First my wife MaryAnn, for fine-tuning the words, for asking the "What if?" behind the genesis of many of the fictional elements, and for making the writing process so much less lonely;

My longtime editor Terri Windling, and all the wonderful folks at Tor Books and at my Canadian distributor H. B. Fenn, but particularly Patrick Nielsen Hayden, Jenna Felice, Andy LeCount, Suzanne Hallsworth, and of course, Tom Doherty and Harold Fenn. Short-story collections aren't exactly the bread and butter of the publishing industry these days, but the interest and support they have shown for my previous collections, *Dreams Underfoot* and *The Ivory and the Horn,* are what helped to make them the successes that they are;

Friends such as Rodger Turner, Lisa Wilkins, Pat Caven, Andrew and Alice Vachss, Charles Saunders, Charles Vess, Karen Shaffer, Bruce McEwen, and Paul Brandon who are there to commiserate when I get whiny, and cheer me on when things are going well;

The individual editors who first commissioned these stories: Anne McCaffrey, Elizabeth Ann Scarborough, Poppy Z. Brite, Peter Crowther, Katharine Kerr, Richard Gilliam, Martin H. Greenberg, Edward E. Kramer, John DeChancie, Darrell Schweitzer, Neil Gaiman, Shawna McCarthy, Joe Lansdale, David Copperfield, Janet Berliner, Peter S. Beagle, Lawrence Schimel, Ed Gorman, James O'Barr, Bruce D. Arthurs, John Helfers, and Grant Watson;

And last, though certainly not least, my readers without whom these stories would only be soliloquies. From meeting many of you at various readings, signings, and other events, as well as the large amount of mail that arrives daily in my physical and virtual mailboxes, it's readily obvious that I'm blessed with a loyal readership made up of those for whom taking the moment for a random act of kindness is as natural as breathing. Your continued support is greatly appreciated.

If you are on the Internet, come visit my home page. The URL (address) is http://www.cyberus.ca/~cdl.

—Charles de Lint
Ottawa, Spring 1998

Sweetgrass &
City Streets

Bushes and briar,
thunder and fire.

In the ceremony
that is night,
the concrete forest
can be anywhere,
anywhen.

In the wail of a siren
rising up from the distance,
I hear a heartbeat,
a drumbeat,
a dancebeat.

I hear my own
heart
fire
beat.

I hear chanting.

> *Eagle feather, crow's caw*
> *Coyote song, cat's paw*
> *Ya-ha-hey, hip hop rapping*
> *Fiddle jig, drumbeat tapping*
> *Once a*
> *Once a*
> *Once upon a time . . .*

I smell the sweet smoke
of smudge sticks,

of tobacco,
of sweetgrass on the corner
where cultures collide
and wisdoms meet.

And in that moment of grace,
where tales branch,
bud to leaf,
where moonlight
mingles with streetlight,
I see old spirits in new skins,
bearing beadwork,
carrying spare change and charms,
walking dreams,
walking large.

They whisper.
They whisper to each other
with the sound of talking drums,
finger pads brushing taut hides.
They whisper,
their voices carrying,
deliberately,
like distant thunder,
approaching.

Bushes and briar . . .

—Wendelessen

Saskia

> *The music in my heart I bore*
> *Long after it was heard no more.*
> —Wordsworth

1

I envy the music lovers I hear.

I see them walking hand in hand, standing close to each other in a queue at a theater or subway station, heads touching while they sit on a park bench, and I ache to hear the song that plays between them: The stirring chords of romance's first bloom, the stately airs that whisper between a couple long in love. You can see it in the way they look at each other, the shared glances, the touch of a hand on an elbow, the smile that can only be so sweet for the one you love. You can almost hear it, if you listen close. Almost, but not quite, because the music belongs to them and all you can have of it is a vague echo that rises up from the bittersweet murmur and shuffle of your own memories, ragged shadows stirring restlessly, called to mind by some forgotten incident, remembered only in the late night, the early morning. Or in the happiness of others.

My own happinesses have been few and short-lived, through no choice of my own. That lack of a lasting relationship is the only thing I share with my brother besides a childhood neither of us cares to dwell upon. We always seem to fall in love with women that circumstance steals from us, we chase after ghosts and spirits and are left holding only memories and dreams. It's not that we want what we can't have; it's that we've held all we could want and then had to watch it slip away.

2

"The only thing exotic about Saskia," Aaran tells me, "is her name."

But there's more going on behind those sea-blue eyes of hers than he can see. What no one seems to realize is that she's always paying attention. She listens to you when you talk instead of waiting impatiently for her own turn to hold forth. She sees what's going on at the periphery of things, the whispers and shadows and pale might-bes that most of us only come upon in dreams.

The first time I see her, I can't look away from her.

The first time I see her, she won't even look at me—probably because of the company I'm keeping. I stand at the far end of the club, wineglass in hand, no longer paying attention to the retro-Beat standing on the stage declaiming her verses in a voice that's suddenly strident where earlier I thought it was bold. I'm not the only one Saskia distracts from the reading. She's pretty and blonde with a figure that holds your gaze even when you're trying to be polite and look away.

"Silicone," Jenny informs me. "Even her lips. And besides, her forehead's way too high. Or maybe it's just that her head's too long."

Aaran nods in agreement.

Nobody seems to like her. Men look at her, but they keep their distance. Women arch their eyebrows cattily and smile behind their hands as they whisper to each other about her. No one engages her in conversation. They treat her so strangely that I find myself studying her even more closely, wondering what it is that I'm missing. She seems so normal. Attractive, yes, but then there are any number of attractive women in the room and none of them is being ostracized. If she's had implants, she's not the first to do so, and neither that nor the size of her forehead—which I don't think is too large at all—seems to have any bearing on the reaction she seems to garner.

"She's a poseur," Aaran tries to explain. "A pretender."

"Of what?" I ask.

"Of everything. Nothing about her is the way it seems. She's supposed to be a poet. Supposed to be published, but have you ever heard of her?"

I shake my head, but what Aaran is saying doesn't mean much in this context. There are any number of fine writers that I've never heard of and—judging from what I know of Aaran's actual reading habits—the figure is even more dramatic for him.

"And then there's the way she leads you on," he goes on. "Leaning close like you're the most important person in the world, but turning a cold shoulder the moment any sort of intimacy arises."

So she turned you down? I want to ask, but I keep the question to myself, waiting for him to explain what he means.

"She's just so full of herself," Jenny says when Aaran falls silent. "The way she dresses, the way she looks down at everybody."

Saskia is wearing faded jeans, black combat boots, a short white cotton blouse that leaves a few inches of her midriff bare, and a plaid vest. Her only jewelry is a small silver Celtic cross that hangs from a chain at the base of her throat. I look at my companions, both of them overdressed in comparison. Jenny in silk blouse and skirt, heels, a clutch purse, hair piled up at the back of her head in a loose bun. Nose ring, bracelets, two earrings per ear, a ring for almost every finger. Aaran in chinos and a dark sports jacket over a white shirt, goatee, hair short on top and sides, pulled into a tiny ponytail in back. One ear double-pierced like Jenny's, the other virgin. Pinky ring on each hand.

I didn't come with either of them. Aaran's the book editor for *The Daily Journal* and Jenny's a feature writer for *In the City,* Newford's little too-cool-to-not-be-hip weekly arts-and-entertainment paper. They have many of the personality traits they attribute to Saskia and the only reason I'm standing here with them is that it's impolitic for a writer to make enemies with the press. I don't seek out their company—frankly, I don't care at all for their company—but I try to make nice when it's unavoidable. It drives my brother Geordie crazy that I can do this. But maybe that's why I can make a comfortable living, following my muse, while all too often he still has to busk on the streets to make his rent. It's not that I don't have convictions, or that I won't defend them. I save my battles for things that have meaning instead of tilting at every mild irritation that comes my way. You can fritter away your whole life with those kinds of windmills.

"So no one likes her?" I ask my companions.

"Why should they?" Jenny replies. "I mean, beyond the obvious, and that's got to wear thin once she opens her mouth."

I don't know what to reply to that, so I say, "I wonder why she comes around, then."

"Why don't you ask her yourself?" Aaran says with the same little smirk I see in too many of his reviews.

I'm thinking of doing just that, but when I look back across the club, she's no longer there. So I return my attention to the woman on the stage. She's onto a new poem now, one in which she dreams about a butcher's shop and I'm not sure if she really does, or if it's supposed to be a metaphor. Truth is, I'm not really listening to her anymore. Instead I'm thinking of Saskia and the way Aaran and Jenny have been sneering at her—physically and verbally—from the moment she walked in. I'm thinking that anyone who can call up such animosity from these two has got to have something going for her.

The poet on stage dreams of cleavers and government-approved steaks. That night I dream of Saskia and when I wake up in the morning the events of last night's reading in the club and my dream are all mixed up together. It takes the first coffee of the morning for me to sort them all out.

3

I have a friend who owns a bookstore just outside of the city and knows everything you'd ever want to know about literature, high-brow and low. She's the one who first turned me onto Michael Hannan and Jeanette Winterson. The first time I read Barry Lopez was because Holly sent me a copy of *River Notes.* We don't get together as much as either of us would like, but we've been corresponding for years—most lately by e-mail—and talk on the phone at least once a week. She's in love with books, and knows how to share that love so that when she tells you about a certain writer or book's merit, you immediately want to read it for yourself. More importantly, she's usually dead on the money. Holly's the only reason I still look at the Saturday book pages in *The Daily Journal* since Aaran took them over.

With her expertise in mind, I call Holly up after breakfast to see if she knows anything about Saskia and her poetry.

"What's her last name?" Holly asks.

I can picture her sitting at the big old rolltop desk that doubles as a sales counter in her store, a small figure in jeans and a sweater, long, dark red hair pulled back from her forehead with a pair of bobby pins, hazel eyes always bright with interest. You could come in looking for *Les Misérables* or a nurse romance and she'd treat you with the same courtesy and respect. The store is crammed with books, literally, floor to ceiling. They gather like driftwood in tall stacks at the ends of bookcases, all around and upon her desk, in boxes and bags, filling the front window display except for the small cleared area where her Jack Russell terrier, Snippet, lies watching the street when she's not ensconced on Holly's lap. The sign painted onto the window, Gothic lettering, paint flaking, simply reads, HOLLY RUE, USED BOOKS.

I think about what she's just asked me and realize I don't know.

"Well, Saskia's unusual enough," Holly tells me. "Hang on while I go online."

Holly and some friends have been creating this huge database they call the Word-wood somewhere out in the Net, assuring themselves that the Information Highway will remember the old technologies—books and printing presses were marvels of technological import in their day, after all—at the same time as it embraces the new. I don't know how many of them are involved in the project, but they've been working on it for years. The Net connects them from every part of the world, each participant adding book titles, authors, bios, publishing histories, reviews, cross-references and whatever else they might think is pertinent to this amazing forest of information they've cultivated.

I tried logging on once when I was out visiting Holly and lost an afternoon glued to the screen, following some arcane trail that started with a short story by Sherman Alexie that I was trying to track down and ended up in a thicket of dissertations on Shakespeare's identity. Holly laughed at me when I finally came up for air. "The Wordwood's like that," she tells me. "One of these days I'm going to go in there and forget to come back." The way she talks about the place it's as though she actually visits it.

"Got something," she tells me. "Her last name's Madding, but she only uses her given name for a byline. We've got three titles listed—hey, wait a minute. I think I have one of these." I hear her get up from her chair and go looking for it, roam-phone in hand, because she's still talking to me. "Yeah, here it is. It's called *Mirrors* and it's her, let me see, second collection." More shuffling noises as she makes her way back to the desk and looks through the book. "You want me to read one to you? They're all pretty short."

"Sure."

"Okay. Here, I'll just do the first one, 'Tarot.' "

> *What she said:*
> *You turn from me*
> *as I turn*
> > *from the cards*
> *refusing to face*
> *what we see.*

Holly's got this amazing speaking voice, rough and resonant, like it's been strained through years of whiskey and cigarettes, though she doesn't smoke or drink. It gives the poem an edge that I'm not sure would be there if I'd just taken the words from the page.

"Nice," I say. "It sneaks up on you, doesn't it?"

"Mmm. There's a lot of sadness in those few lines. Oh, this is cool."

The word's just come back in fashion, but Holly never gave it up. She's been known to say "far out" as well.

"What's that?" I ask.

"I was looking back at the Wordwood and I see she's involved with *Street Times*. She does some editorial work for them."

That is interesting. *Street Times* is a thin little paper produced for street people to sell in lieu of asking for spare change. You see them selling it on half the corners downtown. The vendors pay something like fifty cents an issue and whatever you give them above that is what they earn. Most of the material is produced by the street people themselves—little articles, cartoons, photographs, free classifieds. Every issue they run a profile of one of the vendors, seriously heartbreaking stories. Jilly and some of her friends do free art for it occasionally and I remember Geordie played at a benefit to raise the money to set the whole thing up a couple of years ago.

"I wonder who entered this stuff on her," Holly asks.

The question's rhetorical. Considering how many people are involved in building and maintaining the Wordwood, it could be anybody.

"So you want me to keep this book for you?" she goes on.

"Sure."

I'm too intrigued to even ask the price.

"Should I put it in the mail or are you actually going to visit me for a change? It's been months."

"Five weeks, if you're counting," I say.

"Who's counting?"

"I'll be by later today if I can catch a ride with someone."

"There are buses that come out this far," she says with a smile in her voice.

"If you don't mind walking the last couple of miles."

"That's right, I forgot. You're an artiste and need to be chauffeured. So is she cute?"

Sometimes Holly's abrupt changes of topic throw me. You'd think I'd get used to it, hanging around with Jilly who can be worse, but I never do. Conversations between her and Holly are bewildering for common folk to follow.

"What do you mean, cute?" I ask.

"Oh, come on. You're calling up, looking for books by someone whose last name you don't even know and then—and this is the real giveaway—you don't even ask how much the book is. She's got to be cute."

"Maybe I'm just stimulated by her, intellectually."

I can almost see her shake her head. "Uh-uh. It's a guy thing, Christy. I know I've called you an honorary woman in the past, but you're still a guy. A single guy, yet."

So I tell her about last night.

4

It starts with a heartbeat, rhythm laid down, *one*-two, *one*-two, deep in your chest. It's not the pulse of everyday life but something that runs more profound, a dreaming cadence, a secret drumming that you can't share at first, not with anyone and especially not with her. The melody and chordal patterns might come later, when you've first made contact, when you discover that you haven't made an utter fool of yourself and she might actually reciprocate what you feel, adding her own harmonies to the score tattooed across your heart.

For now, all you can do is repeat her name like a mantra.

Saskia Madding. Saskia Madding. Saskia . . .

For now, it's all unrequited. New Age washes of sound when you think of her, great swelling chords if you happen to catch her going about her business. There, across the street, walking briskly in a light rain, skin glistening, hair feathered with moisture. There, squeezing melons at a fruit vendor's stall, laughing at something the man's said, standing with one hip jutted out, leaning over the front of the stall. There, leafing through a magazine in a smoke shop, a brief glimpse of her on the other side of the glass before you force yourself to walk by.

The music thunders in your chest. Nothing with structure. Nothing that can be transcribed or scored. But it leaves you helpless before its tumultuous presence, desperate to breathe.

5

I've read *Mirrors* a half-dozen times since Sue drove me by Holly's to pick it up. I've got Holly doing book searches for the other two collections. I've been by Angel's walk-in on Grasso Street and gone through her back issues of *Street Times*. I've even got my own modem hooked up—the one the professor gave me that's been languishing unused in a drawer of my desk for the past few months—entering the Wordwood myself to see if I can find some trace of her that Holly might have missed. A bio. A review. Anything.

In short, I've become obsessed with Saskia Madding.

I couldn't meet her now if I wanted to because I've become too desperate and there's nothing quite so pathetic or off-putting as the scent of desperation. It clings to you like a second skin, a nimbus of melancholy and pathos that, contrary to the Romantics with their marble skin and pining eyes, adds nothing to your attractiveness. You might as well have "Avoid me, I'm so hopeless" stenciled on your brow.

"The problem," Holly tells me the next time we're talking on the phone, "is that you're treating her no better than Aaran or Jenny do. No, hear me out," she says when I try to protest. "They've got their misconceptions concerning her and you're blithely creating your own."

"Not so blithely," I say.

"But still."

"But still what?"

"Don't you think it's time you stopped acting like some half-assed teenager, tripping over his own tongue, and just talked to her?"

"And say what?" I ask. "The last time I saw her was at that launch for Wendy's new book, but before I could think of something to say to her, Aaran showed up at my elbow and might as well have been surgically implanted he stayed so close to me. She probably thinks we're friends and I told you how he feels about her. I don't doubt that she knows, too, so what's she going to think of me?"

"You don't have to put up with him," Holly says.

"I know. He was on about her half the night again until I finally told him to just shut up."

"Good for you."

"Yeah, Geordie'd be proud, too. Wait'll Aaran reviews my next book."

"Does that bother you?" Holly asked.

"Not really. What bothers me is that I can't get her out of my head, but I can't even find the few ounces of courage I need to go up to her. Instead I just keep seeing her everywhere I go. I feel like I'm being haunted, except I'm the one playing the stalker and I'm not even doing it on purpose. She's probably seen me as often as I've seen her and thinks I'm seriously twisted."

"A dozen pieces of advice come to mind," Holly says, "but they'd all sound trite."

"Try one on me anyway. I need all the help I can get."

Sitting there in my apartment, receiver cradled against my ear, I can picture Holly at her desk in the bookshop. The image is so clear I can almost see her shrug.

"Just go up to her," Holly tells me. "Ask her if she wants to go for a coffee or something. The worst she can do is say no."

6

I love the poems in *Mirrors*. They're as simple as haiku and just as resonant. No easy task, I know. Every so often I turn from prose to verse, but under my direction the words stumble and flail about on the page and never really sing. I sit there and stare at them and I can't fix them. Give me a pageful of the crappiest prose and some time and I can whip it into shape, no problem. But I don't know where to begin with poetry. I know when it doesn't work. I even know what makes it work in someone else's lines. But I'm hopeless when it comes to trying to write it myself.

Saskia's poems are filled with love and sadness, explorations of social consciousness, profound declarations and simple lyric delights. The same small verse can make me smile and weep, all at the same time. But the one that haunts me the most, the one I return to, again and again, is "Puppet."

> *The puppet thinks:*
> *It's not so much*
> *what they make me do*
> *as their hands inside me.*

In what shadows did those words grow? And why wasn't I there to help her? That makes me laugh. I can't even get up the nerve to approach her and I expect to protect her from the dangers of the world?

7

In the end it's my brother Geordie, of all people, who introduces her to me. We're sitting on the patio of The Rusty Lion on a Sunday afternoon, trying to do the familial thing that neither of us is much good at, but at least we try. Jilly always says the family we choose for ourselves is more important than the one we were born into; that people have to earn our respect and trust, not have it handed to them simply because of genetics. Well, blood ties aside, I'd still want Geordie as my brother, and I think he'd want me, but we've got so much weird history between us that our good intentions don't always play out the way we'd like them to. Every time we get together I tell myself I'm not going to rag him, I'm not going to be the know-it-all big brother, I'm not going to tell him how to live his life, or even suggest that I know better. Trouble is, we know each other too well, know exactly which buttons to push to get under each other's skin and we can't seem to stop doing so. Bad habits are the hardest to break.

We immediately start off on a bad foot when he orders a beer and I hear myself asking if he doesn't think a few minutes past noon is a little early for alcohol. So he orders a whiskey on the side, just to spite me, and says, "If you're going to have a cigarette, could you at least not blow the smoke in my face?" We're sitting there glowering at each other and that's when Saskia comes walking by, looking like she stepped out of an Alma-Tadema painting for all that she's wearing jeans and a baggy blue sweater that perfectly matches her eyes.

Geordie's face brightens. "Hey, Sass," he says. "How's it going?"

I've had this mantra going through my head for weeks now—*Saskia Madding, Saskia Madding*—and all of a sudden I have to readjust my thinking. Her friends call her "Sass"? And how'd Geordie become one of them?

She smiles back at my brother. "Taking the day off?" she asks.

I have to give Geordie this: He works hard. He may play in a half-dozen bands and meet his rent and utilities by busking on street corners, but lazy he's not. Suddenly I want to tell him how I blew Aaran off the other night and didn't care what it might mean about how I'd get reviewed in the *Journal* in the future. I want to know if he's ever talked to Saskia about me, and if he has, what he's said. I want to ask Saskia about "Puppet" and a half-dozen other poems from *Mirror*. Instead, I sit there like a lump with a foolish grin. Words are my stock and trade, but they've all been swallowed by the dust that fills my throat. I find myself wiping the back of my hand across my brow, trying to erase the "Avoid me" I know is written there. Meanwhile, Geordie's completely at his ease, joking with her, asking her if she wants to join us. I wonder what their relationship is and this insane feeling of jealousy rears up inside me. Then Saskia's on the patio, joining us. Geordie's introducing us. My throat's still full of dust and I wish I'd ordered a beer as well instead of my caffè latte.

"So that's who you are," Saskia says as she sits down in the chair between Geordie's and my own. "I keep seeing you around the neighborhood."

"He's the original bad penny," Geordie says.

A part of me feels as though I should be angry with him for saying that. I wonder does he really mean it, have we drifted that far apart? But another part of me feels this sudden absurd affection for him for being here to introduce Saskia and me to each other. Against the rhythm of my pulse, I hear the first strains of melody, and in that instant, everything is right with the world. The desperate feeling in my chest vanishes. My throat's still dry, but the dust is gone. My features feel a little stiff, but my smile is natural.

"I've seen you, too," I find myself saying. "I've been wanting to meet you ever since I read *Mirrors*."

Her eyebrows arch with curiosity. "You've actually read it?" she asks.

"A number of times. I've tried to find your other two collections, but so far I haven't had any luck."

Saskia laughs. "I don't believe this. Newford's own Jan Harold Brunvand not only knows my work, but likes it, too?"

It never occurred to me that she might have read any of my books.

"Okay," Geordie says. "Now that we've got the mutual admirations out of the way, let's just try to enjoy the afternoon without getting into a book-by-book rundown of everything the two of you have written."

He seems as relaxed as I am, but I'm not surprised. We always do better in other people's company. It's not that we feel as though we have to put on good behavior. For some reason we simply don't pick at each other when anybody else is around. He also reads voraciously and loves to talk about books—that's probably the one thing we really have in common beyond the accident of our birth—so I know he's kidding us. I wish we could always be this comfortable with each other.

We both love books, only I'm the one that writes them. We both love music, only he's the musician. That makes us something of a rarity in our family. It wasn't that our parents didn't care for culture; it's just that they didn't have time for it. Didn't have time for us, either. I'm not sure why they had children in the first place and I really don't know why they had three of us. You'd think they'd have realized that they weren't cut out to be parents after our older brother Paddy was born.

The only thing they asked of us was that we be invisible which was like an invitation to get in trouble because we soon learned it was the only way we'd get any attention. None of us did well in school. We all had "attitude problems" which expanded into more serious run-ins with authority outside of school. The police were forever bringing us home for everything from shoplifting (Geordie) and spray-painting obscenities on an underpass (me) to the more serious trouble that Paddy got in which eventually resulted in him pulling ten-to-fifteen in a federal pen.

None of us talked to each other, so I don't know for sure why it was that Paddy hung himself in his cell after serving a couple of years hard time. But I can guess. It's hard to be alone, but that's all we ever knew how to be. Walled off from each other and anybody else who might come into our lives. Geordie and I made a real effort to straighten ourselves out after what happened to Paddy and tried to find the kind of connection with other people that we couldn't get at home. Geordie does better than I. He makes friends pretty easily, but I don't know how deep most of those friendships go. Sometimes I think it's just another kind of wall. Not as old or tall as the one that stands between us, but it's there all the same.

8

Holly looks up in surprise when I walk into her shop the next day.

"What?" she asks. "Two visits in the same month? You sure you haven't gotten me mixed up with a certain blonde poet?"

"Who?" I reply innocently. "You mean Wendy?"

"You should be so lucky."

She accepts the coffee and poppyseed muffin I picked up for her on my walk from the bus stop and graciously makes room for me on her visitor's chair by the simple expediency of sweeping all the books piled up on it into her arms and stacking them in a tottery pile beside the chair. Naturally they fall over as soon as I sit down.

"You know the rules," she says. "If you can't treat the merchandise with respect—"

"I'm not buying them," I tell her. "I don't care how damaged they are."

Holly pops the lid from her coffee and takes an appreciative sip before starting in on the muffin. She no sooner unwraps it, than Snippet is on her lap, looking mournfully at every bite until I take a doggie bone out of my pocket and bribe her back onto the floor with it. I know enough to come prepared.

Holly doesn't ask what I'm doing here and for a long time I don't get into it. We finish our muffins, we drink our coffee. Snippet finishes her bone then returns to Holly's lap to look for muffin crumbs. Time goes by, a comfortable passage of minutes, silence that's filled with companionship, a quiet space of time untouched by a need to braid words into a conversation. We've done this before. There've been times we've spent the whole afternoon together and not needed to talk or even react to each other's presence. Sometimes just being with a friend is enough. I've never been able to tell Holly how much I appreciate her being a part of my life, but I think she knows all the same.

After a while I tell her about finally meeting Saskia yesterday, how Geordie introduced us, how I'm going to be seeing her tonight.

"So you're deliriously happy," Holly says, "and you've come by to rub it in on a poor woman who hasn't had a date in two months."

Holly smiles, but I don't need to be told she's teasing me.

"Something like that," I say.

She nods. "So what's the real reason you're here?"

"I logged onto the Wordwood last night and something really weird happened to me," I tell her. "I wasn't really thinking about what I was doing and started to type a question to myself—the way I do when I'm writing and I don't want to stop and check a fact—and the program answered me."

Holly makes an encouraging noise in the back of her throat to let me know she's paying attention, but that's it. I can't believe she's being this blasé and figure she hasn't really understood me.

"Holly," I say. "I didn't type something like 'Go Emily Carr' and wait for the program to take me to whatever references it has on her. I entered a question—misspelled a couple of words, too—and before I had a chance to go on, the answer appeared on my screen."

She shrugs. "That kind of thing happens all the time in the Wordwood."

"What? There's somebody sitting at their keyboard somewhere, scanning whoever else happens to be online and responding to their questions?"

Holly shakes her head. "The program wasn't set up for two-way dialogues between users. It's just a database."

"So who answered me?"

"I don't know." I hear a nervousness in the laugh she offers me. "It just happens."

"And you're not the least curious about it?"

"It's hard to explain," Holly says. "It's like the program's gone AI, kind of taken on a life of its own, and none of us quite knows how to deal with it, so we've sort of been ignoring it."

"But this has got to be a real technological breakthrough."

"I suppose."

I can't figure out why she's not as excited about it as I am. I don't keep up on all the scientific journals, but I've read enough to know that no one's managed to produce a real artificial intelligence program yet—something indistinguishable from a real person, except it hasn't got a body, it's just living out there in the Net somewhere.

"There's something you're not telling me," I say.

Holly gives me a reluctant nod. "None of us has been entering data into the program for months," she admits.

"What are you saying?"

"I'm saying it's getting the information on its own. The Wordwood's so comprehensive now that we couldn't have entered all the information it now holds even if each of us had spent all our time keying it in, twenty-four hours a day, seven days a week. And the really weird thing is, it's not on the hard drive of our server anymore. It's just . . . out there, somewhere."

I give her a blank look, still not understanding why she's not excited about this, why she hasn't trumpeted their accomplishment to the world.

"The Wordwood's everything we hoped it would be and more," she explains when I ask. "It's efficient beyond anything we could have hoped for."

"And?"

"And we're afraid of screwing around with it, or talking it up, for fear that it'll go away."

"It."

I suddenly find myself reduced to one-word responses and I don't know why.

"The program," Holly says. "The entity that's taken up residence in the Wordwood, whatever it is. It's like a piece of magic, our own guardian angel of books and literature. Nobody wants to take the chance of losing it—not now. It's become indispensable."

"Holly—"

"Did you recognize its voice?" she asks. I shake my head.

"Some of the others using the program recognize its speech patterns, the cadence of its language, as belonging to people they once knew—or still know, but rarely see anymore."

I finally manage a whole sentence. "You mean it's mimicking these people?"

"No. It's more like it really is these people—or at least it is them when you happen to be talking to it. When I'm online with the Wordwood, I hear my grandmother's voice in the way it responds to me. Sometimes . . ." She hesitates, then goes on. "Sometimes it's like I'm actually sitting in a forest somewhere with Gran, talking about books."

I love a good mystery and this has all the makings of the best kind of urban myth.

"How long has this been going on?" I ask.

"About two years."

It's not until much later that I realize this is around the same time Saskia first arrived in Newford.

9

Spirits and ghosts.

My last serious relationship was with a woman who wasn't so much flesh and blood as a spirit borrowing her cloak of humanity. Her name was Tally. Tallulah. The essence of the city, made manifest for the nights we stole from its darker corners, the hours in which we made light between us when everything else lay in shadows. She left because she had to be hard, she had to be tough to survive, the way the city is now. Loving me, she couldn't meet the spite and meanness with like intent. She couldn't survive.

She's out there still. Somewhere. I don't see her, but I can still feel her presence sometimes. On certain nights.

The last time Geordie got serious about a woman, she turned into a ghost.

My therapist would have a heyday with this material, but I've never come right out and told her about any of it. I couch the truths I give her with the same thin veneer of plausibility that I slip onto the facts of some of my stories. I know how weird that sounds, considering what I write, but I've seen things that are real—that I know are true—but they're so outrageous, the only way I can write about them is to start with "Once upon a time." Truth masquerading as lies, but then it's all artifice, isn't it? Language, conversation, stories. All of it. Since Babel fell, words can no longer convey our intent. Not the way that music can.

And the music I hear now . . .

I can't get enough of it. Long, slow chords that resonate deep in my chest for hours after Saskia and I have been together, tempered only by the fear that she's too deeply cloaked in mystery and that, like Tally, that mystery will one day take her away.

I don't mean the mystery that we are to each other, small islands of flesh and bone that are yet great with thought, lumbering like behemoths through dark waters, occasionally interacting with one another, but rarely understanding the encounter. No, I sense that Saskia is part of a deeper mystery, the kind that catwalks over the marrow of our spines, the kind that wakes awe deep in our chests and makes our ribs reverberate with their sacred tones. The kind that we may experience, but only briefly. The kind that resonates so deeply as much because of its brevity. Because our mortal frailty was not meant to hold such music for more than a whisper of time. A few days. A few weeks at most.

In short, I imagine Saskia as Geordie's ghost, as my Tallying spirit, a mystery that will hold me for a brief time, fill me with her inescapable music, then leave me holding only memories, chasing echoes.

I try to tell Geordie about it one day, but all he says is that I'm merely exaggerating what all new lovers feel, blowing my insecurities way out of proportion.

"Like you're suddenly an expert," I say, frustrated. "When was the last time you were even on a date?"

I regret the words as soon as they're out of my mouth—long before the hurt look comes into my brother's eyes. It was a cheap shot. Neither of us has to be reminded of his deficiencies, least of all by each other.

"I'm sorry," I tell him.

He knows it's true. He knows I mean it. But it doesn't change the fact that we're walking wounded, both of us, we've always been walking wounded, we've just learned how to hide it better than most. It's not simply the ghosts and spirits; it's the emotional baggage we've had to carry around with us ever since we were kids. Don't feel sorry for us. But don't pretend you understand, either.

"I know you miss Tally," Geordie says to me. "But—"

"Saskia's not Tally," I say.

Geordie nods.

"So what are you trying to tell me?" I have to ask.

"Just remember that," he says. "Take people as they are instead of always trying to second-guess them. Have some faith in her."

He smiles as he uses the word. We both know all about faith, how belief in something is a commodity that requires a coin that we usually find too dear to pay.

"What about music?" I ask suddenly, changing the subject as abruptly as Jilly or Holly might, but it doesn't faze Geordie. He and Jilly see so much of each other that he's obviously used to it by now.

"What about it?" he says.

"Where does it come from?"

Now he gives me a blank look.

"I mean, where does it originate for you?" I say. "When you write a tune, how do you hear it? Where does it come from?"

Geordie taps his ear. "I just hear them. Faintly at first. There's always music going on in my ear, but every once in a while a tune becomes insistent and won't go away until I work it out or write it down."

"So you have something like a soundtrack going on inside your head all the time?"

"No," he says. "It's not like that. I guess the tunes are always there, a kind of background to whatever else I'm doing, but I have to pay attention to them to bring one of them out from the rest. And it's not as though I can't ignore them. I can. But if I do ignore them for too long, they just go away. Like when I don't play my fiddle or whistle for awhile. The music kind of dries up inside me and all I know is that I'm missing something, but I don't always know what. That's why I can't do the regular nine-to-five—I'm away from the music too long and I end up carrying around this desert inside. I'd rather be broke but with a forest of tunes in my head."

I can't remember the last time Geordie talked to me like this, exposing such a private piece of himself at such length.

"For me it's like a soundtrack," I tell him. "I can't write a tune, but I hear this music all the time, especially when I'm with somebody."

Geordie smiles. "So what do you hear when you're with me?"

"Sad tunes," I tell him. "Adagios. A bittersweet music on bowed cellos and piano that seems to hold a great promise that never quite had the chance to break through."

Geordie's smile falters. He wants to think I'm kidding him, but he can tell I've given him an honest answer. One thing we've never been able to do is lie to each other. To ourselves, yes, but never to each other.

"I guess we should try harder," he says.

"We do try, Geordie. Look at us, we're here, talking to each other, aren't we? Have been for years. When was the last time you saw anybody else in our family? Our problem isn't a lack of trying, it's getting past all the crap we've let get in the way."

He doesn't say anything for a long time, but his gaze holds mine for longer than I can ever remember him doing.

"And Saskia?" he asks finally.

"I can't even begin to describe that music," I tell him.

10

Until I met Saskia, the most curious person I knew was Jilly. Everything interests Jilly—no object, no event, no person is exempt—but she's particularly taken by the unusual, the same as I. I know the reason I started chasing down urban legends and the like was because it was a way for me to escape from what was happening in my home life at the time, a chance for me to feel like I was a part of something. I don't know what her excuse is. She and Geordie have exchanged war stories, but conversations between Jilly and me invariably center around the latest curiosity we've happened to stumble across.

Saskia's inquisitiveness is more like Jilly's than mine—only multiplied a hundredfold. She wants to see and hear and taste everything. Whenever we eat out, it has to be at a different ethnic restaurant from the one before. I've seen her try every kind of coffee in a café, every kind of beer in a tavern, every kind of pastry in a bakery—not all in one day, of course. She simply keeps going back until she's had the chance to sample them all.

She's entranced with music and while she has very definite likes (opera, hip hop and flamenco) and dislikes (anything by Chopin—go figure), she approaches it in the same way she does food and drink: She wants to sample it all. Ditto live theater, films, TV, how and where we make love—everything except for books. The odd thing is that while she's incredibly knowledgeable with the background of just about everything she experiences, she savors each experience as though coming upon it for the first time. It can be disconcerting, this juxtaposing of familiarity and ignorance, but I like it. It's like being in the company of a friend with a particularly up-to-date edition of *Brewer's Phrase and Fable* in the back of her head.

What's less easy to accept is the negative reaction she garners from most people.

Even complete strangers seem to go out of their way to be rude or impolite to her. Needless to say, it infuriates me, though it doesn't seem to bother Saskia at all. Or at least not so she ever lets on. Who knows how she really feels about it? It's not exactly the kind of question I feel comfortable bringing up this early in our relationship. What if she's never noticed it?

I ask Holly about it when I drop by the store, almost a month to the day I made my last visit. This time I come bearing fresh slices of banana bread with the usual coffees and doggie bone for Snippet.

"So now you've met her," I say. Saskia and I ran into Holly at the opening for a new show by Sophie last night and went for drinks afterward. "What do you think?"

Holly takes a sip of coffee to wash down the last of her banana bread and smiles. "I think she's lovely."

"Me, too." I pause for a moment, then ask, "Did you notice anything unusual about her?"

Holly hesitates. "Well, she seems to know an awful lot about brandies for someone who says she's never had one before."

"Besides that."

Holly shakes her head.

"The way other people reacted to her in the bar?" I prompt.

Holly strokes the fur on Snippet's shoulders—the dog, having hopped up on Holly's lap when she finished her own treat, is now looking for possible holdouts in the folds of Holly's skirt. Holly glances at her computer screen. I recognize the Wordwood menu.

"A lot of people feel uncomfortable around magic," she says finally. "You must've noticed this by now. The way some people will review your work, going into it with a negative attitude simply because of its content. Or the way they start to fidget and look uneasy if the conversation turns to the inexplicable."

"Of course," I say. "But I'm not sure I'm getting your point."

"It's Saskia," Holly says. "She's magic."

"Magic." I'm back to one-word echoes again.

Holly nods. "Her being magic is what antagonizes them. They recognize it in her, but they don't want to believe it, they can't believe it, so they lash out at her in defense. Humanity's whole unfortunate history is one long account of how we attack what we don't understand, what's strange to us. And what's stranger than magic?"

"How is she magic?" I want to know.

"It's like . . . well, does she remind you of anyone? Not the way she looks, though that seems familiar, too, but the way she talks. The cadence of her voice."

I shake my head.

"Well, she reminds me of Gran."

I'm starting to get a bad feeling about this as I realize that after one brief meeting, Holly's picked up on something that I should have seen from the start.

"Your grandmother," I say.

"Mm-hmm."

This time I'm the one who glances at the Wordwood menu on her computer screen. I turn back to Holly, but she won't quite meet my gaze.

"What exactly are you saying?" I ask.

"Maybe you should ask her about the Wordwood," Holly says.

That's when I realize that Saskia does remind me of someone—not in what she's saying, but in how she says it. She reminds me of Tally.

11

I feel like the person in the folk tale who calls the cat by its true name which makes it leave. Like the shoemaker putting out clothes for the brownies. Like the seventh bride with Bluebeard's key in hand, approaching the forbidden door.

I can hear, in the joyful music that arcs between Saskia and myself, the first faint strains of sadness, a bittersweet whisper of strings, a foreshadowing of the lament to come. If this were a film, I'm at the point where I'd want to shout up at the screen, "Don't screw it up! Leave well enough alone." But I can't stop myself. I have to know. Even understanding the price one must pay when unmasking faerie, I have to know.

So, heart in throat, I ask Saskia that night, where did she live before she moved to Newford, where is she from, expecting I'm not sure what, but not that a merry laugh would start in her eyes and spread across her face. Not that she'd put her hand tenderly against my cheek, look long into my eyes and then lean forward to kiss my mouth. I can taste the good humor on her lips.

"I thought you knew," she says. "I lived in the forest."

"The Wordwood."

She nods. "A forest of words and names and stories. I love it there, but I had to know more. I had to experience firsthand what I could only read about in the forest. I knew what the sun was supposed to feel like. I knew about rain and how it must feel against your face. I could imagine what food tasted like and drink and music and love. But reading about something's not the same as doing it, is it?"

I shake my head.

"So I chose a shape from a magazine picture that I thought would be pleasing and came across to be here."

How? I want to ask, but I realize it's irrelevant. Mysteries are what they are. If they could be explained, they would lose their resonance.

"Do you miss it at all?" I end up asking.

Saskia shakes her head. "No. I . . ." She hesitates, looking for a way to explain herself clearly. "Part of me's still there," she settles on. "That's why I"—she laughs again—"seem to know so much. I just 'look' it up in the forest."

"When I put it all together," I tell her, "I didn't know what to think. I guess I still don't know."

"You think I'm going to leave you," she says. "You think I'm going back and when I do, I'll leave you behind."

I don't trust myself to speak. All I can do is nod. I can feel a deep chord welling up in my chest, building, building, to a crescendo. A tsunami of swelling, thrumming sound.

The merriment flees her eyes and she leans close to me again, so close I'm breathing her breathing. She looks so serious. The deep sea blue of her eyes starts to swallow me.

"The only way I'll leave you," she says, "is if you send me away."

The tsunami breaks over me as I hold her close.

12

Geordie doesn't usually come over to where I live unless it's to help me move, which I seem to do about once a year. So he gets to see the old place twice, the new place once, until I move again. The image he carries in his head of where I live must consist of empty apartments, bare walls and rugless floors, the furniture in odd arrangements, preparing to leave or having just arrived. And then there're all the boxes of books and papers and what-have-yous. Sometimes I think I just live out of boxes.

But we're in my study this evening and I'm not in the middle of a move, neither coming nor going, although there still are a half-dozen boxes of books in one corner, left over from the previous move. Geordie's standing by my desk, reading a poem called "Arabesque" that's taped to the wall beside my computer.

> *The artist closed her book,*
> *returning it to the shelf*
> *that stored the other*
> *stories of her life.*
> *When she looked up,*
> *there were no riddles*
> *in her gaze;*
> *only knowing.*
>
> *Don't make of us*
> *more than what we are,*
> *she said.*
> *We hold no great secret*
> *except this:*
> *We know that*
> *all endeavor is art*
> *when rendered*
> *with conviction.*
> *The simple beauty*
> *of the everyday*
> *strikes chords*
> *as stirring as*
> *oil on canvas,*
> *finger on string,*
> *the bourée in*
> *perfect demi-pointe.*

The difference is
we consider it art.

The difference is
we consider
art.

When it consumes us,
what consumes us,
is art:
an invisible city
we visit with our dreams

Returning,
we are laden down with
the baggage of
our journeys,
and somewhere,
in a steamer trunk
or a carry-on,
we carry souvenirs:
signposts,
guidebooks,
messages from beyond.

Some are merely
more opaque
than others.

Geordie stands there, whiskey in hand, and reads it through a couple of times, before coming back to join me on the other side of the room. I have two club chairs there with a reading lamp and a table set between them. Geordie places his whiskey glass on the table and sits down.

"Did you write that?" he asks.

I shake my head. "No, it's one of Saskia's. I couldn't write a piece of verse if my life depended on it."

I've got a roast in the oven, with potatoes baking in a circle around it. Saskia was making a salad, but she ran out to the market to get some lemons just before Geordie arrived.

"I like it," Geordie says. "Especially that bit about art being like an invisible city from which we bring things back. It reminds me of Sophie's serial dreams."

Saskia moved in a couple of months ago, setting up her own study in what was my spare bedroom. It's a bright, airy room, with a thick Oriental carpet on the floor, tons of pillows, a shelf filled with knickknacks running along one wall and all sorts of artwork on the others. She writes at a small mahogany desk by the window that stands so short it won't take a chair. She sits on one of the pillows when she writes at it. There aren't any books in the room, but then she doesn't need them. She's got her own reference library in her head, or wherever it is that she connects with the Wordwood.

Now that I know, about that forest of words, how she grew up in the shelter of its storied trees, she doesn't remind me of Tally anymore. I can't remember how she ever did, though Holly still hears her Gran, and I suppose other people hear who they expect to hear. I don't know how, exactly, she crossed over from the Wordwood in the first place, but the longer she stays here, in this world, the more she becomes a part of it and the less she rattles people. Which is a good thing since it means no more unwarranted frowns and catty remarks directed her way.

"You guys seem pretty happy," Geordie says.

I smile. "We are. Who'd have thought I'd ever settle down?"

Ever since Saskia moved in, we've had Geordie over for dinner at least once every couple of weeks. But this is the first time we've been alone in the apartment.

"You know," I say, "there are things we never talk about. About back when."

I don't have to explain "back when" to him. Back when we lived at home. Back when Paddy was still alive. Back when we hid from each other as much as from our parents. Back when we shut each other out because that was the only way we knew how to deal with people, the only way we knew to relate to anybody. Stand back. Give me room.

"You don't have to say anything," Geordie tells me.

"But I do," I say. "I want to explain something. You know how sometimes you want something so badly, all you can do is drive it away? You keep looking for the weak link so that you can point at it and say, there it is. I knew this couldn't work out. I knew this was too good to be true."

He looks a little confused. "You're talking about what you went through with Saskia now, aren't you?"

"I went through that with Saskia," I agree. "But she was patient and waited me out instead of walking away."

"What's that got to do with us?" Geordie wants to know.

"I just want you to know that I'm not simply going through the motions here. That it's not only Saskia who wants to see you. I want to see you, too. I should have been there for you when we were kids. I was your older brother. I shouldn't have let you grow up alone the way I did."

"But we *were* just kids."

I nod. "But you had to resent me for not being the big brother you needed. I know I sure as hell resented Paddy. It's taken me a long time to work through that, but now that I finally have, it's way too late to tell him. I don't want the same thing to lie there between us."

"I never hated you," Geordie says. "I just didn't understand why things had to be the way they were."

"I know. But we've had that lying between us for all these years, the knowing that we weren't there for each other then and maybe we won't be there for each other in the future, some time when it really matters. It's the same self-fulfilling prophecy. You don't trust something to be true, so you push it to the point when it isn't true."

"That'll never happen," Geordie says, but I can see it's something he wants to believe, not something he really believes.

"We can't let it happen," I say. "So that's why I'm telling you now what Saskia said to me: The only way I'll leave you, is if you send me away."

13

I don't envy the music others hear anymore; I'm too filled with my own now, the strains that connect me to Saskia and my brother and the other people I love in my life. I'm not saying my world's suddenly become perfect. I've still got my ups and downs. You should see the review that *The Daily Journal* gave my last book—Aaran Block at his vitriolic worst. But whenever things get bad, all I do is slow down. I stop and listen to the music and then I can't help but appreciate what I do have.

It's funny what a difference a positive attitude can have. When you go out of your way to be nice to people, or do something positive for those who can't always help themselves the way Saskia does with her editorial work on *Street Times*, it comes back to you. I don't mean you gain something personally. It's just that the world becomes a little bit of a better place, the music becomes a little more upbeat, and how can you not gain something from that?

See, when you get down to the basics of it, everything's just molecules vibrating. Which is what music is, what sound is—vibrations in the air. So we're all part of that music and the worthier it is, the more voices we can add to it, the better off we all are.

Sure beats the silence that's threatening to swallow us otherwise.

14

"Tell me a story," Saskia says that night after Geordie's gone home.

I turn my face toward her and she snuggles close so that my mouth is right beside her ear.

"Once upon a time," I say, "there was a boy who lost his ability to sing and the only person who could find it for him lived in a forest of words, but he didn't meet her until he was much, much older. . . ."

In This Soul
of a Woman

> *If I were a man, I can't imagine it would have*
> *turned out this way. I will say no more except*
> *what I have in my mind and that is that you*
> *will find the spirit of Caesar in this soul*
> *of a woman.*
> —from the letters of Artemisia Gentileschi
> (1593–c.1652)

1

"Eddie wants to see you."

"What's he want?" Nita asked. "Another blow job?"

"Probably. I think he's tired of the new girl."

"Well, fuck Eddie. And fuck you, too."

"Christ, Nita. You on the rag or what? I'm just passing along a message."

Nita didn't turn to look at Jennifer. She stared instead at her reflection in the mirror, trying to find even one familiar feature under the makeup. Even her eyes were wrong, surrounded by a thick crust of black eye shadow, the irises hidden behind tinted red contacts. From beyond the dressing room came the thumping bass line of whatever David Lee Roth song Candy used in her act. That meant she had ten minutes before she was up again. Lilith, Mistress of the Night. Black leather and lace over Gothic-pale skin, the only spots of color being the red of her eyes, her lips, and the lining of her cape. Nita's gaze dropped from her reflection to the nine-foot-long whip that lay coiled like a snake on the table in front of her.

"Fuck this," she said.

The dressing room smelled of cigarettes and beer and cheap perfume which just about summed up her life. She swept her arm across the top of the table and sent everything flying. Whip and makeup containers. A glass, half full of whiskey. Cigarettes, lighter, and the ashtray with butts spilling out of it. A small bottle filled with uppers. The crash of breaking glass was loud in the confined quarters of the dressing room.

Jennifer shook her head. "I'm not cleaning that shit up," she said.

Nita looked up from the mess she'd made. The rush of utter freedom she'd felt clearing the table top had vanished almost as quickly as it had come.

"So who asked you to?" she asked.

Jennifer pulled a chair over from one of the other tables and sat down beside her. "You want to talk about it?"

Nita bit back a sharp retort. Jennifer wasn't her friend—she didn't have any friends—but unlike ninety-nine-point-nine percent of the world, Jennifer had always treated her decently. Nita looked away, wishing she hadn't sent her shot of whiskey flying off the table with everything else.

"Last time I was up, my ex's old man was in the audience," she said.

"So?"

"So the only way I could keep my visitation rights with Amanda was by promising I'd get a straight job."

Jennifer nodded, understanding. "The old bad influence line."

"Like she's old enough to know or even care what her old lady does for a living." Nita was really missing that drink now. "It's so fucking unfair. I mean, it's okay for this freak to come into a strip joint with his buddies and have himself a good time, but my working here's the bad influence. Like we even want to be here."

"I don't mind that much," Jennifer said. "It beats hooking."

"You know what I mean. He's going to run straight to a judge and have them pull my visiting rights."

"That sucks," Jennifer agreed. She leaned forward and gave Nita a quick hug. "But you gotta hang in there, Nita. At least we've got jobs."

"I know."

"And you'd better go see Eddie or maybe you won't even have that."

Nita shook her head. "I can't do it. I can't even go out on the stage again tonight."

"But . . ." Jennifer began, then she sighed. "Never mind. We'll figure out a way to cover for you."

"And Eddie?"

Jennifer stood up and tugged down on the hem of her miniskirt. "That's one you're going to owe me, girl."

2

When Nita stepped out the back door of the Chic Cheeks in her street clothes all that remained of her stage persona was the shock of jet-black hair that fell halfway down her back in a cascade of natural curls. She was wearing faded blue jeans that were tucked into cowboy boots. The jeans had a hole in the left knee through which showed the black fabric of her body stocking. Overtop of it was a checked flannel shirt, but-toned halfway up, the tails hanging loose. Her purse was a small khaki knapsack that she'd picked up at the Army Surplus over on Yoors Street. Her stage makeup was washed off and all she wore now was a hint of eye shadow and a dab of lipstick.

She knew she looked about as different from Lilith in her leathers and lace as could be imagined, so Nita was surprised to be recognized when she stepped out into the alleyway behind the club.

"Lilith?"

Nita paused to light a cigarette, studying the woman through a wreath of blue-grey smoke. The stranger was dressed the way Nita knew the club's customers imagined the dancers dressed offstage: short, spike-heeled boots; black stockings and miniskirt; a jean vest open enough to show more than a hint of a black lace bra. She wore less makeup than Nita had on at the moment, but then her fine-boned features didn't need it. Her hair was so blonde it was almost white. It was cut punky and seemed to glow in the light cast from a nearby streetlamp.

"Who wants to know?" Nita finally asked.

"Does it matter?"

Nita shrugged and took another drag from her cigarette.

"I saw you dancing," the woman went on. "You're really something."

Now she got it.

"Look," Nita said. "I don't date customers and—no offense—but I don't swing your way. You should go back inside and ask for Candy. She's always looking to make a little something on the side and I don't think she much cares what you've got between your legs, just so long as you can pay."

"I'm not looking for a hooker."

"So what are you looking for?"

"Someone to talk to. I recognized a kindred soul in you."

The way she said it made Nita sigh. She'd heard this about a hundred times before.

"Everybody thinks we're dancing just for them," she said, "but you know, we're not even thinking about you sitting out there. We're just trying to get through the night."

"So you don't feel a thing?"

"Okay, so maybe I get a little buzz from the attention, but it doesn't mean I want to fuck you."

"I told you. That's not what I'm looking for."

"Yeah, yeah. I know." Nita ground her cigarette out under the heel of her boot. "You just want to talk. Well, you picked the wrong person. I'm not having a good night and to tell you the truth, I'm not all that interesting anyway. All the guys figure women with my job are going to be special—you know, real exotic or something—but as soon as we go out on a date with somebody they figure out pretty quick that we're just as boring and fucked up as anybody else."

"But when you're on the stage," the woman said, "it's different then, isn't it? You feed on what they give you."

Nita gave her an odd look. "What're you getting at?"

"Why don't we go for a drink somewhere and talk about it?" the woman said. She looked around the alleyway. "There's got to be better places than this to have a conversation."

Nita hesitated for a moment, then shrugged. "Sure. Why not? It's not like I've got anything else to do. Where'd you have in mind?"

"Why don't we simply walk until we happen upon a place that appeals to us?"

Nita lit another cigarette before she fell in step with the woman.

"My name's not Lilith," she said.

"I know." The woman stopped and turned to face her. "That's my grandmother's name."

Like people couldn't share the same name, Nita thought. Weird.

"She used to call me Imogen," the woman added.

She offered her hand, so Nita shook it and introduced herself. Imogen's grip was strong, her skin surprisingly cool and smooth to the touch. Shaking hands with her was like holding onto a hand made of porcelain. Imogen switched her grip on Nita's hand, shifting from her right to her left, and set off down the alleyway again. Nita started to pull free, but then decided she liked the feel of that smooth cool skin against her own and let it slide.

"What does 'Nita' mean?" Imogen asked.

"I don't know. Who says it's supposed to mean anything?"

"All names mean something."

"So what does your name mean?"

" 'Granddaughter.' "

Nita laughed.

"What do you find so humorous?"

Nita flicked her cigarette against the nearest wall which it struck in a shower of sparks. "Sounds to me like your grandmother just found a fancy way of not giving you a name."

"Perhaps she had to," Imogen said. "After all, names have power."

"Now what's that supposed to mean?" Nita asked.

Imogen didn't answer. She came to an abrupt halt and then Nita saw what had distracted her. They'd been walking toward the far entrance of the alley and were now only a half-dozen yards from its mouth. Just ahead lay the bright lights of Palm Street. Unfortunately, blocking their way were three men. Two Anglos and a Hispanic. Not yet falling-down drunk, but well on the way. Palm Street was as busy as ever but Nita knew that in this part of the city, at this time of night, she and Imogen might as well have been on the other side of the world for all the help they could expect to get from the steady stream of pedestrians by the mouth of the alley.

"Mmm-mmm. Looking good," one of the three men said.

"But the thing is," added one of his companions, "I've just got to know. When you're fucking each other, which one's pretending to be the guy?"

Drunken laughter erupted from all three of them.

Imogen let go of Nita's hand. She was probably scared, Nita thought. Nita didn't blame her. She'd be scared herself if it wasn't for the fact that she'd come to a point in her life where she just didn't give a shit anymore. Reaching into one of the front pockets of her jeans, she pulled out a switchblade. When she thumbed the button on the side of the handle, it opened with an evil-sounding *snick*.

"Oh, *conchita*," the Hispanic said, shaking his head in mock sorrow. "We were just going to have some fun with you, but now there's got to be some pain."

He stepped forward, the Anglos flanking him, one on either side. Before Nita could decide which of them was going to get the knife, Imogen moved to meet them. What happened next didn't seem to make any sense at all. It looked to Nita that Imogen picked up the first by his face, thumb on one temple, fingers on the other, and simply pitched him over her shoulder, back behind them, deeper into the alley. The second she took out with a blow to the throat that dropped him on the spot. The third tried to bolt, but she grabbed his arm and wrenched it up behind his back until Nita heard the bone snap. He was still screaming from the pain when Imogen grabbed his head and snapped his neck with a sudden twist.

Imogen held the dead man for a long moment, staring into his face as though she wanted to memorize his features, then she let him fall to the pavement. Nita stared at the body, at the way it lay so still on the ground in front of them. Her gaze went to the other two assailants. They lay just as unmoving. One moment there had been three half-drunk men about to assault them and in the next they were all dead.

"What—" Nita had to clear her throat. "What the fuck did you do to them?"

Imogen didn't even seem to be breathing hard. "It's a . . . a kind of judo," she said.

Nita looked at her companion, but it was hard to make out her features in the poor light. She seemed to be smiling, her teeth flashing as white as did her hair. Nita slowly closed up her knife and stowed it back in her jeans.

"Judo," Nita repeated slowly.

Imogen nodded. "Come on," she said, offering Nita her hand again.

Nita hesitated. She lit a cigarette with trembling fingers and took a long drag before she eased her way around the dead man at her feet to take Imogen's hand. The porcelain coolness calmed her, quieting the rapid drum of her pulse.

"Let's get that drink," Imogen said.

"Yeah," Nita said. "I think I could really use a shot right about now."

3

They ended up in Fajita Joe's, a Mexican bar on Palm Street with a terrace overlooking Fitzhenry Park. The place catered primarily to yuppies and normally Nita wouldn't have been caught dead in it, but by the time they were walking by its front door she would have gone in anywhere just to get a drink to steady her jangled nerves. They took a table on the terrace at Imogen's insistence—"I like to feel the night air," she explained. Nita gulped her first shot and immediately ordered a second whiskey, double, on the rocks. With another cigarette lit and the whiskey to sip, she finally started to relax.

"So tell me about yourself," Imogen said.

Nita shook her head. "There's nothing to tell. I'm just a loser—same as you've got to be if the only way you can find someone to have a drink with you is by hanging out around back of a strip club." Then she thought of the three men in the alley. " 'Course, the way you took out those freaks . . . those moves weren't the moves of any loser."

"Forget about them," Imogen said. "Tell me why you're so sad."

Nita shook her head. "I'm not sad," she said, lighting up another cigarette. "I'm just fucked up. The only thing I'm good at is running away. When the going gets tough, I'm gone. My whole life, that's the way I deal with the shit."

"And the dancing doesn't help?"

"Give me a break. That's not dancing—it's shaking your ass in a meat market. Maybe some of the girls've convinced themselves they're in show business, but I'm not that far out of touch with reality."

"But you still get something from it, don't you?"

Nita butted out her cigarette. "I'll tell you the truth, I always wanted to be up on a stage, but I can't sing and I can't play a guitar and the only way I can dance is doing a bump 'n' grind. When you've got no talent, your options get limited real fast."

"Everyone has a talent."

"Yeah, well, mine's for fucking up. I work with women who are dancing to put themselves through college, single mothers who're feeding their families, a writer who's supporting herself until she can sell her first book. The only reason I'm dancing is that I couldn't make that kind of money doing anything else except hooking and I'm not that hard up yet."

"Perhaps you've set your sights too high," Imogen said. "It's hard to attain goals when they seem utterly beyond your reach. You might consider concentrating on smaller successes and then work your way up from them."

"Yeah? Like what?"

Imogen shrugged. "Breathing's a talent."

"Oh, right. And so's waking up in the morning."

"Feel this," Imogen said.

She caught Nita's wrist and started to bring it toward her chest.

"Hey!" Nita said, embarrassed. "I told you I'm not like that."

She was sure everybody on the terrace was staring at them, but when she tried to pull free, she couldn't move her hand. She might as well have been trying to move the building under them. Imogen brought Nita's palm through the open front of her jean vest and laid it against the cool smooth skin between her breasts. In the light cast from the terrace lanterns, her eyes gleamed like a cat's caught in a car's headbeams.

"What do you feel?" Imogen asked.

"Look, why don't you . . ."

Just get out of my face, was what Nita was going to say, except as her palm remained on Imogen's skin, she suddenly realized—

"You . . . you're not breathing," she said.

Imogen released Nita's wrist. Nita rubbed at the welt that the grip of Imogen's fingers had left on her skin.

"I'm sorry," Imogen said. "I didn't mean to hurt you."

"How can you not breathe?"

Imogen smiled. "It's a talent I don't have," she said.

This was seriously strange, Nita thought. She was way, way out of her depth.

"So," she began. She had to stop to clear her throat. Her mouth felt as though it was coated with dry dust. She took a gulp of whiskey and fumbled another cigarette out of her package. "So what are you?" she finally managed.

Imogen shrugged. "Immortal. Undead."

That moment in the alley flashed in Nita's mind. The three men, dispatched so quickly and Imogen not even out of breath. The vise-like strength of her fingers. The weird gleam in her eyes. The cool touch of her skin. The fact that she really didn't breathe.

Nita tried to light her cigarette, but her hand shook too much. She flinched when Imogen reached out to steady it, but then accepted the help. She drew the smoke in deeply, held it, exhaled. Took another drag.

"Okay," she said. "So what do you want from me?"

"No more than I told you earlier: company."

"Company."

Imogen nodded. "When the sun rises this morning, I'm going to die. I just didn't want to die alone."

"You want me to die with you?"

"Not at all. I just want you to be there when I do. I've lived this hidden life of mine for too long. Nobody knows me. Nobody cares about me. I thought you'd understand."

"Understand what?"

"I just want to be remembered."

"This is too weird," Nita said. "I mean, you don't look sick or anything."

Like I'd know, Nita added to herself.

"I'm not sick. I'm tired." Imogen gave a small laugh that held no humor. "I'm always amazed at how humans strive so desperately to prolong their lives. If you only knew. . . ."

Nita thought about her own life and imagined it going on forever.

"I think I see where you're coming from," she said.

"It's not so bad at first—when you outlive your first set of friends and lovers. But it's harder the next time, and harder still each time after that, because you start anticipating the end, their deaths, from the first moment you meet them. So you stop having friends, you stop taking lovers, only to find it's no easier being alone."

"But aren't there . . . others like you around?" Nita asked.

"They're not exactly the sort of people I care to know. I'm not exactly the sort of person I care to know. We're monsters, Nita. We're not the romantic creatures of myth that your fictions perpetuate. We're parasites, surviving only by killing you."

She shook her head. "I look around and all I see is meat. All I smell is blood—some diseased, and not fit for consumption, it's true, but the rest . . ."

"So how do I smell?" Nita wanted to know.

Imogen smiled. "Very good—though not as good as you did when those men attacked us in the alley earlier. Adrenaline adds a spicy flavor to human scent, like a mix of jalapeños and chili."

The new turn their conversation had taken made Nita feel too much like a potential meal.

"If your life's so shitty," she asked, "why've you waited until now to put an end to it?"

"My existence is monstrous," Imogen told her. "But it's also seductive. We are so powerful. I hate what I am at the same time as I exult in my existence. Nothing can harm us but sunlight."

Nita shivered. "What about the rest of it?" she asked, thinking of the dozens of late-night movies she'd watched. "You know—the running water, the garlic, and the crosses?"

"Only sunlight."

"So tomorrow morning you're just going to sit in the sun?"

Imogen nodded. "And die. With you by my side to wish my spirit safe-journey and to remember me when I'm gone."

It was so odd. There was no question in Nita's mind but that Imogen was exactly what she said she was. The strange thing was how readily she accepted it. But accepting it and watching Imogen die were two different things. The endings of all those late-night movies went tumbling through her in all their grotesque glory.

"I don't know if I can do it," Nita said.

Imogen's eyebrows rose questioningly.

"I'm not real good with gross shit," Nita explained. "You know—what's going to happen to you when the sunlight touches you."

"Nothing will happen," Imogen assured her. "It's not like in the films. I'll simply stop living, that's all."

"Oh."

"Have you finished your drink?" Imogen asked. "I'd like to go for a last walk in the park."

4

Fitzhenry Park was probably the last place Nita would go for a walk at this time of night, but remembering how easily Imogen had dealt with their attackers in the alley behind the club, she felt safe enough doing so tonight. Walking hand in hand, they seemed to have the footpaths to themselves. As they got deeper inside the park, all sense of the city surrounding them vanished. They could have been a thousand miles away, a thousand years away from this time and place. The moon was still working its way up to its first quarter—a silvery sickle hanging up among the stars that came and went from view depending on the foliage of the trees lining the path.

Nita kept stealing glances at her companion whenever there was enough light. She looked so normal. But that was how it always was, wasn't it? The faces people put on when they went out into the world could hide anything. All you ever knew about somebody was what he or she cared to show you. Nita normally didn't have much interest in anyone, but she found herself wanting to know everything she could about Imogen.

"You told me you live a hidden life," she said, "but the way you look seems to me would turn more heads than let you keep a low profile."

"I dress like this to attract my prey. Since I must feed, I prefer to do so on those the world can do better without."

Makes sense, Nita thought. She wondered if she should introduce Imogen to Eddie back at the club.

"How often do you have to . . . feed?" she asked.

"Too often." Imogen glanced at her. "The least we can get by on is once a week."

"Oh."

"I've been fasting," Imogen went on. "Preparing for tonight. I wanted to be as weak as possible when the moment comes."

If Imogen was weak at the moment, Nita couldn't imagine what she'd be like at full strength. She wasn't sure if she was being more observant, or if her companion had lowered her guard now that they were more familiar with each other's company, but Imogen radiated a power and charisma unlike anyone Nita had ever met before.

"You don't seem weak to me," she said.

Imogen came to a stop and drew Nita over to a nearby bench. When they sat down, she put a hand on Nita's shoulder and looked her directly in the face.

"It doesn't matter how weak or hurt we feel," she said, "we have to be strong in here." Her free hand rose up to touch her chest. "We have to project that strength or those around us will simply take advantage of us. We can take no pride in being a victim—we belittle not only ourselves, but all women, if we allow that to happen to us without protest. You must stand up for yourself. You must always stand up for yourself and your sisters. I want you to remember that as you go on with your life. Never give in, never give up."

"But you're giving up."

Imogen shook her head. "Don't equate the two. What I am doing is taking the next step on a journey that I should have completed three hundred years ago. I am not surrendering. I am hoping to kill the monster that I let myself become and finally moving on."

Imogen looked away then. She shifted her position slightly, settling her back against the bench. After a few moments, she leaned her head against Nita's.

"What do you think it's like when you die?" Nita asked. "Do you think everything's just over, or do we, you know, go on somewhere?"

"I think we go on."

"What'll you miss the most?"

Imogen shrugged. "What would you miss if you were in my position?"

"Nothing."

"Not even your daughter?"

Nita didn't even bother to ask how Imogen knew about Amanda.

"You've got to understand," she said. "I love her. And it makes me feel good to know that something I was a part of making isn't fucked up. But it makes me feel even better knowing that she's going to be raised properly. That she'll be given all the chances I never had. I didn't want her to grow up to be like me."

"But you still visit her."

Nita nodded. "But once she's old enough to understand what I am, I'll stop."

If not sooner. If John's old man didn't get the judge to revoke her visitation rights because of what he'd seen her doing tonight.

"It's getting late," Imogen said. She stood up, drawing Nita to her feet.

"Where're we going?"

"To my apartment."

5

To call it an apartment was a bit of a misnomer. It turned out that Imogen owned the penthouse on top of the Brighton Hotel, overlooking the harbor. The only time Nita had ever seen a place this fancy was in the movies. While Imogen went to get her a drink, she walked slowly around the immense living room, trailing her hand along the polished wood tables and the back of a chesterfield that could seat five people comfortably. There was even a baby grand in one corner. She finally ended up at the glass doors leading out onto a balcony where she saw two images superimposed over each other: a view of the lake and Wolf Island in the distance, and one of herself standing at the window with the living room behind her, Imogen walking toward her with a brandy glass in each hand.

Nita turned to accept the brandy. Imogen touched her glass against Nita's and then they both drank.

"Why'd you pick me?" Nita asked.

"The name on the flyer outside the club first caught my eye," Imogen said. "Then, when I began to study your life, I realized that we are much the same. I was like you, before the change—deadened by the ennui of my life, feeding on the admiration of those who courted my favor much the same as you do with those who come to watch you dance. It's not such a great leap from using their base interest as a kind of sustenance to taking it from their flesh and blood."

Nita couldn't think of anything to say in response to that so she took another sip of her brandy.

"I want you to have this when I'm gone," Imogen went on.

"Have what?"

Imogen made a languid movement with her arm that encompassed the penthouse. "This place. Everything I have. I've already made the arrangements for everything to be transferred into your name—barring unforeseen difficulties, the transaction will be completed tomorrow at noon."

"But—"

"I have amassed a considerable fortune over the years, Nita. I want it to go to you. It will give you a chance to make a new start with your life."

Nita shook her head. "I don't think it'd work out."

She'd won a thousand dollars in a lotto once. She'd planned to do all sorts of sensible things with it, from taking some development courses to better herself to simply saving it. Instead, she'd partied so hearty over the space of one weekend she'd almost put herself in the hospital. The only reason she hadn't ended up in emergency was that everybody else that weekend had been too wasted to help her. She still didn't know how she'd managed to survive.

"It'd just make me fuck up big-time," she said.

Imogen nodded—not so much in acceptance of what she was saying, Nita realized, as to indicate that she was listening.

"I have to admit that I haven't been entirely honest with you," Imogen said. "What we're about to embark upon when the sun rises could be very dangerous to you."

"I . . . don't understand."

"I won't die the instant the sunlights strikes me," Imogen said. "It will take a few minutes—enough time for the beast inside me to rise. If it can feed immediately and get out of the sun, it will survive."

"You mean you'd . . . eat me?"

"It's not something I would do, given a choice. But the survival instinct is very strong."

Nita knew about that. She'd tried to kill herself three times to date—deliberately, that is. Twice with pills, once with a razor blade. It was astonishing how much she'd wanted to survive, once it seemed she had no choice but to die.

"I will fight that need," Imogen told her. "It's why I've been fasting. To make the beast weak. But I can't guarantee your safety."

Nita filled in the silence that followed by lighting a cigarette.

"Understand," Imogen said, "it's not what I want. I don't normally have conversations with my meals any more than you would with a hamburger you're about to eat. I truly believe that it's time for me to put the monster to rest and go on. Long past time. But the beast doesn't agree."

"You've tried this before, haven't you?" Nita asked.

Imogen nodded.

"What happened?"

"I'm still here," Imogen said.

Nita shivered. She silently finished her cigarette, then butted it out in an ornate silver ashtray.

"I'll understand if you feel you must leave," Imogen said,

"You'd let me go—even with everything I now know?"

Imogen gave her a sad smile. "Who'd believe you?"

Nita lit another cigarette. She was surprised to see that her hands weren't even shaking.

"No," she said. "I'll do it. But not for the money or this place."

"It will still be in your name," Imogen said.

Unspoken between them lay the words: if you survive the dawn.

Nita shrugged. "Whatever."

Imogen hesitated, then it seemed she had to ask. "Is it that you care so little about your life?"

"No," Nita said. "No matter how bad shit gets, whenever it comes down to the crunch, I always surprise myself at how much I want to live."

"Then why will you see this through?"

Nita smiled. "Because of you. Because of what you said about us having to be strong and stand up for each other. I won't say I'm not scared, 'cause I am, but . . ." She turned to the glass doors that led out onto the balcony. "I guess it's time, huh? We better get to it before I bail on you."

She put down the glass and butted out her cigarette after taking a last drag. Imogen stepped forward. She brushed Nita's cheek with her lips, then hand in hand they went out onto the balcony to meet the dawn.

The Big Sky

> *We need Death to be a friend. It is best to have*
> *a friend as a traveling companion when you*
> *have so far to go together.*
> —attributed to Jean Cocteau

1

She was sitting in John's living room when he got home from the recording studio that night, comfortably ensconced on the sofa, legs stretched out, ankles crossed, a book propped open on her lap which she was pretending to read. The fact that all the lights in the house had been off until he turned them on didn't seem to faze her in the least. She continued her pretense, as though she could see equally well in the light or dark and it made no difference to her whether the lights were on or off. At least she had the book turned right-side up, John noted.

"How did you get in?" he asked her.

She didn't seem to present any sort of a threat—beyond having gotten into his locked house, of course—so he was more concerned with how she'd been able to enter than for his own personal safety. At the sound of his voice, she looked up in surprise. She laid the book down on her lap, finger inserted between the pages to hold her place.

"You can see me?" she said.

"Jesus."

John shook his head. She certainly wasn't shy. He set his fiddlecase down by the door. Dropping his jacket down on top of it, he went into the living room and sat down in the chair across the coffee table from her.

"What do you think?" he went on. "Of course I can see you."

"But you're not supposed to be able to see me—unless it's time and that doesn't seem right. I mean, really. I'd know, if anybody, whether or not it was time."

She frowned, gaze fixed on him, but she didn't really appear to be studying him. It was more as though she was looking into some unimaginably far and unseen distance.

Her eyes focused suddenly and he shifted uncomfortably under the weight of her attention.

"Oh, I see what happened," she said. "I'm so sorry."

John leaned forward, resting his hands on his knees. "Let's try this again. Who are you?"

"I'm your watcher. Everybody has one."

"My watcher."

She nodded. "We watch over you until your time has come, then if you can't find your own way, we take you on. They call us the little deaths, but I've never much cared for the sound of that, do you?"

John sighed. He settled back in his chair to study his unwanted guest. She was no one he knew, though she could easily have fit in with his crowd. He put her at about twenty-something, a slender five-two, pixy features made more fey by the crop of short blonde hair that stuck up from her head with all the unruliness of a badly-mowed lawn. She wore black combat boots; khaki trousers, baggy, with two or three pockets running up either leg; a white T-shirt that hugged her thin chest like a second skin. She had little in the way of jewelry—a small silver ring in her left nostril and another in the lobe of her left ear—and no makeup.

"Do you have a name?" he tried.

"Everybody's got a name."

John waited a few heartbeats. "And yours is?" he asked when no reply was forthcoming.

"I don't think I should tell you."

"Why not?"

"Well, once you give someone your name, it's like opening the door to all sorts of possibilities, isn't it? Any sort of relationship could develop from that, and it's just not a good idea for us to have an intimate relationship with our charges."

"I can assure you," John told her. "We're in no danger of having a relationship—intimate or otherwise."

"Oh," she said. She didn't look disappointed so much as annoyed. "Dakota," she added.

"I'm sorry?"

"You wanted to know my name."

John nodded. "That's right. I—oh, I get it. Your name's Dakota?"

"Bingo."

"And you've been . . . watching me?"

"Well, not just you. Except for when we're starting out, we look out after any number of people."

"I see," John said. "And how many people do you watch?"

She shrugged. "Oh, dozens."

That figured, John thought. It was the story of his life. He couldn't even get the undivided attention of some loonie stalker.

She swung her boots to the floor and set the book she was holding on the coffee table between them.

"Well, I guess we should get going," she said.

She stood up and gave him an expectant look, but John remained where he was sitting.

"It's a long way to the gates," she told him.

He didn't have a clue as to what she was talking about, but he was sure of one thing.

"I'm not going anywhere with you," he said.

"But you have to."

"Says who?"

She frowned at him. "You just do. It's obvious that you won't be able to find your way by yourself and if you stay here you're just going to start feeling more and more alienated and confused."

"Let me worry about that," John said.

"Look," she said. "We've gotten off on the wrong foot—my fault, I'm sure. I had no idea it was time for you to go already. I'd just come by to check on you before heading off to another appointment."

"Somebody else that you're *watching*?"

"Exactly," she replied, missing, or more probably, ignoring the sarcastic tone of his voice. "There's no way around this, you know. You need my help to get to the gates."

"What gates?"

She sighed. "You're really in denial about all of this, aren't you?"

"You were right about one thing," John told her. "I am feeling confused—but it's only about what you're doing here and how you got in."

"I don't have time for this."

"Me neither. So maybe you should go."

That earned him another frown.

"Fine," she said. "But don't wait too long to call me. If you change too much, I won't be able to find you and nobody else can help you."

"Because you're my personal watcher."

"No wonder you don't have many friends," she said. "You're really not a very nice person, are you?"

"I'm only like this with people who break into my house."

"But I didn't—oh, never mind. Just remember my name and don't wait too long to call me."

"Not that I'd want to," John said, "but I don't even have your number."

"Just call my name and I'll come," she said. "If it's not too late. Like I said, I might not be able to recognize you if you wait too long."

Though he was trying to take this all in stride, John couldn't help but start to feel a little creeped out at the way she was going on. He'd never realized that crazy people could seem so normal—except for what they were saying, of course.

"Goodbye," he told her.

She bit back whatever it was that she was going to say and gave him a brusque nod. For one moment, he half expected her to walk through a wall—the evening had taken that strange a turn—but she merely crossed the living room and let herself out the front door. John waited for a few moments, then rose and set the deadbolt. He walked through the house, checking the windows and back door, before finally going upstairs to his bedroom.

He thought he might have trouble getting to sleep—the woman's presence had raised far more questions than it had answered—but he was so tired from twelve straight hours in the studio that it was more a question of, could he get all his clothes off and crawl under the blankets before he faded right out? He had one strange moment: when he turned off the light, he made the mistake of looking directly at the bulb. His uninvited guest's features hung in the darkness along with a hundred dancing spots of light before he was able to blink them away. But the moment didn't last long and he was soon asleep.

2

He didn't realize that he'd forgotten to set his alarm last night until he woke up and gave the clock a bleary look. Eleven-fifteen. Christ, he was late.

He got up, shaved and took a quick shower. You'd think someone would have called him from the studio, he thought as he started to get dressed. He was doing session work on Darlene Flatt's first album and the recording had turned into a race to get the album finished before her money ran out. He had two solos up first thing this morning and he couldn't understand why no one had called to see where he was.

There was no time for breakfast—he didn't have much of an appetite at the moment anyway. He'd grab a coffee and a bagel at the deli around the corner from the studio. Tugging on his jeans, he carried his boots out into the living room and phoned the studio while he put them on. All he got was ringing at the other end.

"Come on," he muttered. "Somebody pick it up."

How could there be nobody there to answer?

It was as he was cradling the receiver that he saw the book lying on the coffee table, reminding him of last night's strange encounter. He picked the book up and looked at it, turning it over in his hands. There was something different about it this morning. Something wrong. And then he realized what it was. The color dust wrapper had gone monochrome. The book and . . . His gaze settled on his hand and he dropped the book in shock. He stared at his hand, turning it front to back, then looked wildly around the living room.

Oh, Jesus. Everything was black and white.

He'd been so bleary when he woke up that he hadn't noticed that the world had gone monochrome on him overnight. He'd had a vague impression of gloominess when he got up, but he hadn't really thought about it. He'd simply put it down to it being a particularly overcast day. But this . . . this . . .

It was impossible.

His gaze was drawn to the window. The light coming in was devoid of color where it touched his furniture and walls, but outside . . . He walked slowly to the window and stared at his lawn, the street beyond it, the houses across the way. Everything was the way it was supposed to be. The day was cloudless, the colors so vivid, the sunlight so bright it hurt his eyes. The richness of all that colour and light burned his retinas.

He stood there until tears formed in his eyes and he had to turn away. He covered his eyes with his hands until the pain faded. When he took his palms away, his hands were still leached of color. The living room was a thousand monochrome shades of black and white. Numbly, he walked to his front door and flung it open. The blast of color overloaded the sensory membranes of his eyes. He knelt down where he'd tossed his jacket last night and scrabbled about in its pockets until he found a pair of shades.

The sunglasses helped when he turned back to the open door. It still hurt to look at all that color, but the pain was much less than it had been. He shuffled out onto his porch, down the steps. He looked at what he could see of himself. Hands and arms. His legs. All monochrome. He was like a black and white cutout that someone had stuck onto a colored background.

I'm dreaming, he thought.

He could feel the start of a panic attack. It was like the slight nervousness that sometimes came when he stepped onto stage—the kind that came when he was backing up someone he'd never played with before—only increased a hundredfold. Sweat beaded on his temples and under his arms. It made his shirt clammy and stick to his back. His hands began to shake so much that he had to hug himself to make them stop.

He was dreaming, or he'd gone insane.

Movement caught his eye down the street and he recognized one of his neighbors. He stumbled in the man's direction.

"Bob!" he called. "Bob, you've got to help me." The man never even looked in his direction. John stepped directly in front of him on the sidewalk and Bob walked right into him, knocking him down. But Bob hadn't felt a thing, John realized. Hadn't seen him, hadn't felt the impact, was just walking on down the street as if John had simply ceased to exist for him.

John fled back into the house. He slammed the door, locked it. He pulled the curtains in the living room and started to pace, from the fireplace to the hallway, back again, back and forth, back and forth. At one point he caught sight of the book he'd dropped earlier. Slowly, he walked over to where it lay and picked it up. He remembered last night's visitor again. Her voice returned to him.

If you change too much . . .

This was all her fault, he thought.

He threw the book down and shouted her name.

"Yes?"

Her voice came from directly behind him and he started violently.

"Jesus," he said. "You could've given me a heart attack."

"It's a little late for that."

She was wearing the same clothes she'd worn last night except today there was a leather bomber's jacket on over her T-shirt and she wore a hat that was something like a derby except the brim was wider. There was one other difference. Like himself, like the rest of his house, she'd been leached of all color.

"What did you do to me?" he demanded.

She reached out and took his hand to lead him over to the sofa. He tried to pull free from her grip, but she was stronger than she looked.

"Sit down," she said, "and I'll try to explain."

Her voice was soothing and calm, the way one would talk to an upset child—or a madman. John was feeling a little bit like both at the moment, helpless as a child and out of his mind. But the lulling quality of her voice and the gentle manner of her touch helped still the wild drumming of his pulse.

"Look," he said. "I don't know what you've done to me—I don't know how you've done this to me or why—but I just want to get back to normal, okay? If I made you mad last night, I'm sorry, but you've got to understand. It was pretty weird to find you in my house the way I did."

"I know," she said. "I didn't realize you could see me at first, or I would have handled it differently myself. But you took me by surprise."

"I took *you* by surprise?"

"What do you remember of last night?" she asked.

"I came home and found you in my living room."

"No, before that."

"I was at High Lonesome Sounds—working on Darlene's album."

She nodded. "And what happened between when you left the studio and came home?"

"I . . . I don't remember."

"You were hit by a car," she said. "A drunk driver."

"No way," John said, shaking his head. "I'd remember something like that."

She took his hand. "You died instantly, John Narraway."

"I . . . I . . ."

He didn't want to believe her, but her words settled inside him with a finality that could only be the truth.

"It's not something that anyone could have foreseen," she went on. "You were supposed to live a lot longer—that's why I was so surprised that you could see me. It's never happened to me like that before."

John had stopped listening to her after she'd said, "You were supposed to live a lot longer." He clung to that phrase, hope rushing through him.

"So it was a mistake," he said.

Dakota nodded.

"So what happens now?" he asked.

"I'll take you to the gates."

"No, wait a minute. You just said it was a mistake. Can't you go back to whoever's in charge and explain that?"

"If there's anyone in charge," she said, "I've never met or heard of them."

"But—"

"I understand your confusion and your fear. Really I do. It comes from the suddenness of your death and my not being there to help you adjust. That's the whole reason I exist—to help people like you who are unwilling or too confused to go on by themselves. I wasn't ready to go myself when my time came."

"Well, I'm not ready either."

Dakota shook her head. "It's not the same thing. I wasn't ready to go because when I saw how much some people need help to reach the gates, I knew I had to stay and help them. It was like a calling. You just aren't willing to accept what happened to you."

"Well, Christ. Who would?"

"Most people. I've seen how their faces light up when they step through the gates. You can't imagine the joy in their eyes."

"Have you been through yourself?" John asked.

"No. But I've had glimpses of what lies beyond. You know how sometimes the sky just seems to be so big it goes on forever?"

John nodded.

"You stand there and look up," she went on, "and the stars seem so close you feel as though you could just reach up and touch them, but at the same time the sky itself is enormous and has no end. It's like that, except that you can feel your heart swelling inside you, big enough to fill the whole of that sky."

"If what's waiting beyond these gates is so wonderful," John wanted to know, "why haven't you gone through?"

"One day I will. I think about it more and more all the time. But what I'm doing now is important and I'm needed. There are never enough of us."

"Maybe I'll become a watcher instead—like you."

"It's not something one takes on lightly," Dakota said. "You can't just stop when you get tired of doing it. You have to see through all of your responsibilities first, make sure that all of your charges have gone on, that none are left behind to fend for themselves. You share the joys of your charges, but you share their sorrows, too. And the whole time you know them, you're aware of their death. You watch them plan, you watch their lives and the tangle of their relationships grow more complex as they grow older, but the whole time you're aware of their end."

"I could do that," John said.

Dakota shook her head. "You have always been sparing with your kindnesses. It's why your circle of friends is so small. You're not a bad person, John Narraway, but I don't think you have the generosity of spirit it requires to be a watcher."

The calm certainty with which she delivered her judgment irritated John.

"How would you know?" he said.

She gave him a sad smile. "Because I've been watching you ever since you were born."

"What? Every second of my life?"

"No. That comes only at first. It takes time to read a soul, to unravel the tangle of possibilities and learn when the time of death is due. After that it's a matter of checking in from time to time to make sure that the assessment one made still holds true."

John thought about the minutiae that made up the greater portion of everyone's life and slowly shook his head. And what if you picked a person who was really dull? Everybody had slow periods in their lives, but some people's whole lives were one numbed shuffle from birth to death. And since you knew the whole time when the person was going to die . . . God, it'd be like spending your whole life in a doctor's waiting room. Boring and depressing.

"You don't get tired of it?" he asked.

"Not tired. A little sad, sometimes."

"Because everybody's got to die."

She shook her head. "No, because I see so much unhappiness and there's nothing I can do about it. Most of my charges never see me—they make their own way to the gates and beyond. I'm just there as a kind of insurance for those who can't do it by themselves and I'm only with them for such a little while. I miss talking to people on a regular basis. Sometimes I see some of the other watchers, but we're all so busy."

"It sounds horrible."

She shrugged. "I never think of it that way. I just think of those who need help and the looks on their faces when they step through the gates." She fell silent for a moment, then gave him a smile. "We should go now. I've got other commitments."

"What if I refuse to go? What happens then?"

"No one can force you, if that's what you mean."

John held up his hand. He looked around himself. Okay, it was weird, but he could live with it, couldn't he? Anything'd be better than to be dead—even a half-life.

"I know what you're thinking," she said. "And no, it's not because I'm reading your mind, because I can't."

"So what's going to happen to me?"

"I take it you're already experiencing some discomfort?"

John nodded. "I see everything in black and white—but only in the house. Outside, nothing's changed."

"That will grow more pronounced," she told him. "Eventually you won't be able to see color at all. You might lose the clarity of your vision as well so that everything will seem to be a blur. Your other senses will become less effective as well."

"But—"

"And you won't be able to interact with the world you've left behind. In time, the only people you'll be able to see are others like yourself—those too willful or disturbed to have gone on. They don't exactly make the best of companions, John Narraway, but then, by that point, you'll be so much like them, I don't suppose it will matter."

"But what about all the stories of ghosts and hauntings and the like?"

"Do you have a particularly strong bond with a certain place or person?" she asked. "Someone or something you couldn't possibly live without?"

John had to admit that he didn't, but he could tell that she already knew that.

"But I'll still be alive," he said, knowing even as he said the words that they made no real sense.

"If you want to call it that."

"Don't you miss life?"

Dakota shook her head. "I only miss happiness. Or maybe I should say, I miss the idea of happiness because I never had it when I was alive."

"What happened to you?" John wanted to know.

She gave him a long sad look. "I'm sorry, John Narraway, but I have to go. I will listen for you. Call me when you change your mind. Just don't wait too long—"

"Or you won't be able to recognize me. I know. You already told me that."

"Yes," she said. "I did."

This time she didn't use the door. One moment she was sitting with him on the sofa and the next she faded away like Carroll's Cheshire cat except with her it was her eyes that lingered the longest, those sad dark eyes that told him he was making a mistake, those eyes to which he refused to listen.

3

He didn't move from the sofa after Dakota left. While the sunlight drifted across the living room, turning his surroundings into a series of shifting chiaroscuro images, he simply sat there, his mind empty more often than it was chasing thoughts. He was sure he hadn't been immobile for more than a few hours, but when he finally stood up and walked to the window, it was early morning, the sun just rising. He'd lost a whole night and a day. Maybe more. He still had no appetite, but now he doubted that he ever would again. He didn't seem to need sleep, either. But it scared him that he could lose such a big chunk of time like that.

He turned back to the living room and switched on the television set to make sure that all he'd lost had been the one day. All he got on the screen was snow. White noise hissed from the speaker grill. Fine, he thought, remembering how he'd been unable to put a call through to the recording studio yesterday morning. So now the TV wouldn't work for him. So he couldn't interact with the everyday mechanics of the world anymore. Well, there were other ways to find out what he needed to know.

He picked up his fiddlecase out of habit, put on his jacket and left the house. He didn't need his shades once he got outside, but that was only because his whole street was now delineated in shades of black and white. He could see the color start up at the far ends of the block on either side. The sky was overcast above him, but it blued the further away from his house it got.

This sucked, he thought. But not so much that he was ready to call Dakota back.

He started downtown, putting on his sunglasses once he left the monochromic zone immediately surrounding his house. Walking proved to be more of a chore than he'd anticipated. He couldn't relax his attention for a moment or someone would walk into him. He always felt the impact while they continued on their way, as unaware of the encounter as his neighbor Bob had been.

He stopped at the first newsstand he came upon and found the day's date. Wednesday, he read on the masthead of *The Newford Star*. November tenth. He'd only lost a day. A day of what, though? He could remember nothing of the experience. Maybe that was what sleep would be like for him in this state—simply turning himself off the way fiction described vampires at their rest. He had to laugh at the thought. The undead. *He* was one of the undead now, though he certainly had no craving for blood.

He stopped laughing abruptly, suddenly aware of the hysterical quality that had crept into the sound. It wasn't that funny. He pressed up close against a building to keep out of the way of passing pedestrians and tried to quell the panic he could feel welling up inside his chest. Christ, it wasn't funny at all.

After a while he felt calm enough to go on. He had no particular destination in mind, but when he realized he was in the general vicinity of High Lonesome Sounds, he decided to stop by the studio. He kept waiting for some shock of recognition at every corner he came to, something that would whisper, this is where you died. This is where the one part of your life ended and the new part began. But the street corners all looked the same and he arrived at the recording studio without sensing that one had ever had more importance in his life than the next.

He had no difficulty gaining entrance to the studio. At least doors still worked for him. He wondered what his use of them looked like to others, doors opening and closing, seemingly of their own accord. He climbed the stairs to the second floor loft where the recording studio was situated and slipped into the control booth where he found Darlene and Tom Norton listening to a rough mix of one of the cuts from Darlene's album. Norton owned the studio and often served as both producer and sound engineer to the artists using his facilities. He turned as John quietly closed the door behind him but he looked right through John.

"It still needs a lead break," Norton said, returning his attention to Darlene.

"I know it does. But I don't want another fiddle. I want to leave John's backing tracks just as they are. It doesn't seem right to have somebody else play his break."

Thank you, Darlene, John thought.

He'd known Darlene Flatt for years, played backup with her on and off through the past decade and a half as she sang out her heart in far too many honky-tonks and bars. Her real name was Darlene Johnston, but by this point in her career everyone knew her by her stage name. Dolly Parton had always been her idol and when Darlene stepped on stage with her platinum wig and over-the-top rhinestone outfits, the resemblance between the two was uncanny. But Darlene had a deeper voice and now that she'd finally lost the wigs and stage gear, John thought she had a better shot at the big time. There was a long tradition of covering other people's material in country music, but nothing got tired more quickly than a tribute act so far as John was concerned.

She didn't look great today. There was a gaunt look about her features, hollows under her eyes. Someone mourned him, John realized.

"Why don't we have Greg play the break on his Dobro?" Darlene said. She sounded so tired, as though all she wanted to do was get through this.

"That could work," Norton said.

John stopped listening to them, his attention taken by the rough mix that was still playing in the control booth. It was terrible. All the instruments sounded tinny and flat, there was no bass to speak of, and Darlene's voice seemed to be mixed so far back you felt you had to lean forward to be able to hear it. He winced, listening to his own fiddle-playing.

"You've got a lot more problems here than what instrument to use on the break," he said.

But of course they couldn't hear him. So far as he could tell, they liked what they were hearing which seemed particularly odd, considering how long they'd both been in the business. What did they hear that he couldn't? But then he remembered what his mysterious visitor had told him. How his sight would continue to deteriorate. How . . .

Your other senses will become less effective as well.

John thought back to the walk from his house to the studio. He hadn't really been thinking of it at the time, but now that he did he realized that the normal sounds of the city had been muted. Everything. The traffic, the voices of passersby, the construction site he'd passed a couple of blocks away from the studio. When he concentrated on Darlene and Norton's conversation again, listening to the tonal quality of their voices rather than what they were saying, he heard a hollow echo that hadn't registered before.

He backed away from them and fumbled his way out into the sitting room on the other side of the door. There he took his fiddle out of its case. Tuning the instrument was horrible. Playing it was worse. There was nothing there anymore. No resonance. No depth. Only the same hollow echoing quality that he'd heard in Darlene and Norton's voices.

Slowly he laid his fiddle back into its case, loosened the frog on his bow and set it down on top of the instrument. When he finally made his way back down the stairs and out into the street, he left the fiddle behind. Outside, the street seemed overcast, its colors not yet leached away, but definitely faded. He looked up into a cloudless sky. He crossed the street and plucked a pretzel from the cart of a street vendor, took a bite even though he had no appetite. It tasted like sawdust and ashes. A bus pulled up at the curb where he was standing, let out a clutch of passengers, then pulled away again, leaving behind a cloud of noxious fumes. He could barely smell them.

It's just a phase, he told himself. He was simply adjusting to his new existence. All he had to do was get through it and things would get back to normal. They couldn't stay like this.

He kept telling himself that as he made his way back home, but he wasn't sure he believed it. He was dead, after all—that was the part of the equation that was impossible to ignore. Dakota had warned him that this was going to happen. But he wasn't ready to believe her either. He just couldn't accept that the way things were for him now would be permanent.

4

He was right. Things didn't stay the same. They got worse. His senses continued to deteriorate. The familiar world faded away from around him until he found himself in a grey-toned city that he didn't always recognize. He stepped out of his house one day and couldn't find his way back. The air was oppressive, the sky seemed to press down on him. And there were no people. No living people. Only the other undead. They huddled in doorways and alleys, drifted through the empty buildings. They wouldn't look at him and he found himself turning his face away as well. They had nothing they could share with each other, only their despair, and of that they each had enough of their own.

He took to wandering aimlessly through the deserted streets, the high points of his day coming when he recognized the corner of a building, a stretch of street, that gargoyle peering down from an utterly unfamiliar building. He wasn't sure if he was in a different city, or if he was losing his memory of the one he knew. After a while it didn't seem to matter.

The blank periods came more and more often. Like the other undead, he would suddenly open his eyes to find himself curled up in a nest of newspapers and trash in some doorway, or huddled in the rotting bulk of a sofa in an abandoned building. And finally he couldn't take it anymore.

He stood in the middle of an empty street and lifted his face to grey skies that only seemed to be kept aloft by the roofs of the buildings.

"Dakota!" he cried. "Dakota!"

But he was far too late and she didn't come.

Don't wait too long to call me, she'd told him. *If you change too much, I won't be able to find you and nobody else can help you.*

He had no one to blame but himself. It was like she'd said. He'd changed too much and now, even if she could hear him, she wouldn't recognize him. He wasn't sure he'd even recognize himself. Still, he called her name again, called for her until the hollow echo that was his voice grew raw and weak. Finally he slumped there in the middle of the road, shoulders sagged, chin on his chest, and stared at the pavement.

"The name you were calling," a voice said. "Did it belong to one of those watchers?"

John looked up at the man who'd approached him so silently. He was a nondescript individual, the kind of man he'd have passed by on the street when he was alive and never looked at twice. Medium height, medium build. His only really distinguishing feature was the fervent glitter in his eyes.

"A watcher," John repeated, nodding in response to the man's question. "That's what she called herself."

"Damn 'em all to hell, I say," the man told him. He spat on the pavement. " 'Cept that'd put 'em on these same streets and Franklin T. Clark don't ever want to look into one of their stinkin' faces again—not unless I've got my hands around one of their necks. I'd teach 'em what it's like to be dead."

"I think they're dead, too," John said.

"That's what they'd like you to believe. But tell me this: If they're dead, how come they're not here like us? How come they get to hold onto a piece of life like we can't?"

"Because . . . because they're helping people."

Clark spat again. "Interferin's more like it." The dark light in his eyes seemed to deepen as he fixed his gaze on John. "Why were you calling her name?"

"I can't take this anymore."

"An' you think it's gonna be better where they want to take us?"

"How can it be worse?"

"They can take away who you are," Clark said. "They can *try,* but they'll never get Franklin T. Clark, I'll tell you that. They can kill me, they can dump me in this stinkin' place, but I'd rather rot here in hell than let 'em change me."

"Change you how?" John wanted to know.

"You go through those gates of theirs an' you end up part of a stew. Everythin' that makes you who you are, it gets stole away, mixed up with everybody else. You become a kind of fuel—that's all. Just fuel."

"Fuel for what?"

"For 'em to make more of us. There's no goddamn sense to it. It's just what they do."

"How do you know this?" John asked.

Clark shook his head. "You got to ask, you're not worth the time I'm wastin' on you."

He gave John a withering look, as though John was something he'd stepped on that got stuck to the bottom of his shoe. And then he walked away.

John tracked the man's progress as he shuffled off down the street. When Clark was finally out of sight, he lifted his head again to stare up into the oppressive sky that hung so close to his face.

"Dakota," he whispered.

But she still didn't come.

5

The day he found the infant wailing in a heap of trash behind what had once been a restaurant made John wonder if there wasn't some merit in Clark's anger toward the watchers. The baby was a girl and she was no more than a few days old. She couldn't possibly have made the decision that had left her in this place—not by any stretch of the imagination. A swelling echo of Clark's rage rose up in him as he lifted the infant from the trash. He swaddled her in rags and cradled the tiny form in his arms.

"What am I going to do with you?" he asked.

The baby stopped crying, but she made no reply. How could she? She was so small, so helpless. Looking down at her, John knew what he had to do. Maybe Clark was right and the watchers were monsters, although he found that hard to reconcile with his memories of Dakota's empathy and sadness. But Clark was wrong about what lay beyond the gates. He had to be. It couldn't be worse than this place.

He set off then, still wandering aimlessly, but now he had a destination in mind, now he had something to look for. He wasn't doing it for himself, though he knew he'd step through the gates when they stood in front of him. He was doing it for the baby.

"I'm going to call you Dolly," he told the infant. "Darlene would've liked that. What do you think?"

He chucked the infant under her chin. Her only response was to stare up at him.

6

John figured he had it easier than most people who suddenly had an infant came into their lives. Dolly didn't need to eat and she didn't cry unless he set her down. She was only happy in his arms. She didn't soil the rags he'd wrapped her in. Sometimes she slept, but there was nothing restful about it. She'd be lying in his arms one minute, the next it was as though someone had thrown a switch and she'd been turned off.

He'd been frantic the first time it happened, panicking until he realized that she was only experiencing what passed for sleep in this place.

He didn't let himself enter that blank state. The idea had crept into his mind as he wandered the streets with Dolly that to do so, to let himself turn off the way he and all the other undead did, would make it all that much more difficult for him to complete his task. The longer he denied it of himself, the more seductive the lure of that strange sleep became, but he stuck to his resolve. After a time, he was rewarded for maintaining his purposefulness. His vision sharpened; the world still appeared monochromatic, but at least it was all back in focus. He grew more clearheaded. He began to recognize more and more parts of the city. But the gates remained as elusive as Dakota had proved to be since the last time he'd seen her.

One day he came upon Clark again. He wasn't sure how long it had been since the last time he'd seen the man—a few weeks? A few months? It was difficult to tell time in the city as it had become because the light never changed. There was no day, no night, no comforting progression from one into the other. There was only the city, held in eternal twilight.

Clark was furious when he saw the infant in John's arms. He ranted and swore at John, threatened to beat him for interfering in what he saw as the child's right of choice. John stood his ground, holding Dolly.

"What are you so afraid of?" he asked when Clark paused to take a breath.

Clark stared at him, a look of growing horror spreading across his features until he turned and fled without replying. He hadn't needed to rely. John knew what Clark was afraid of. It was the same fear that kept them all in this desolate city: Death. Dying. They were all afraid. They were all trapped here by that fear. Except for John. He was still trapped like the others; the difference was that he was no longer afraid.

But if a fear of death was no longer to be found in his personal lexicon, despair remained. Time passed. Weeks, months. But he was no closer to finding these fabled gates than he'd been when he first found Dolly and took up the search. He walked through a city that grew more and more familiar. He recognized his own borough, his own street, his own house. He walked slowly up his walk and looked in through the window, but he didn't go in. He was too afraid of succumbing to the growing need to sit somewhere and close his eyes. It would be so easy to go inside, to stretch out on the couch, to let himself fall into the welcoming dark.

Instead he turned away, his path now leading toward the building that housed High Lonesome Sounds. He found it without any trouble, walked up its eerily silent stairwell, boots echoing with a hollow sound, a sound full of dust and broken hopes. At the top of the stairs, he turned to his right and stepped into the recording studio's lounge. The room was empty, except for an open fiddlecase in the middle of the floor, an instrument lying in it, a bow lying across the fiddle, horsehairs loose.

He shifted Dolly from the one arm to the crook of the other. Kneeling down, he slipped the bow into its holder in the lid of the case and shut the lid. He stared at the closed case for a long moment. He had no words to describe how much he'd missed it, how incomplete he'd felt without it. Sitting more comfortably on the floor, he fashioned a sling out of his jacket so that he could carry Dolly snuggled up against his chest and leave his arms free.

When he left the studio, he carried the fiddlecase with him. He went down the stairs, out onto the street. There were no cars, no pedestrians. Nothing had changed. He was still trapped in that reflection of the city he'd known when he was alive, the deserted streets and abandoned buildings peopled only by the undead. But something felt different. It wasn't just that he seemed more himself, more the way he'd been when he was still alive, carrying his fiddle once more. It was as though retrieving the instrument had put a sense of expectation in the air. The grey dismal streets, overhung by a brooding sky, were suddenly pregnant with possibilities.

He heard the footsteps before he saw the man: a tall, rangy individual, arriving from a side street at a brisk walk. Faded blue jeans, black sweatshirt with matching baseball cap. Flat-heeled cowboy boots. What set him apart from the undead was the purposeful set to his features. His gaze was turned outward, rather than inward.

"Hello!" John called after the stranger as the man began to cross the street. "Have you got a minute?"

The stranger paused in mid-step. He regarded John with surprise, but waited for John to cross the street and join him. John introduced himself and put out his hand. The man hesitated for a moment, then took John's hand.

"Bernard Gair," the man said in response. "Pleased, I'm sure." His look of surprise had shifted into one of vague puzzlement. "Have we met before . . . ?"

John shook his head. "No, but I do know one of your colleagues. She calls herself Dakota."

"The name doesn't ring a bell. But then there are so many of us—though never enough to do the job."

"That's what she told me. Look, I know how busy you must be so I won't keep you any longer. I just wanted to ask you if you could direct me to . . ."

John's voice trailed off as he realized he wasn't being listened to. Gair peered more closely at him.

"You're one of the lost, aren't you?" Gair said. "I'm surprised I can even see you. You're usually so . . . insubstantial. But there's something different about you."

"I'm looking for the gates," John told him.

"The gates."

Something in the way he repeated the words made John afraid that Gair wouldn't help him.

"It's not for me," he said quickly. "It's for her."

He drew back a fold of the sling's cloth to show Gair the sleeping infant nestled against his chest.

"I see," Gair said. "But does she want to go on?"

"I think she's a little young to be making that kind of decision for herself."

Gair shook his head. "Age makes no difference to a spirit's ability to decide such a thing. Infants can cling as tenaciously to life as do the elderly—often more so, since they have had so little time to experience it."

"I'm not asking you to make a judgment," John said. "I'm just asking for some directions. Let the kid decide for herself once she's at the gates and can look through."

Gair needed time to consider that before he finally gave a slow nod.

"That could be arranged," he allowed.

"If you could just give me directions," John said.

Gair pulled up the left sleeve of his sweatshirt so that he could check the time on his wristwatch.

"Let me take you instead," he said.

7

Even with directions, John couldn't have found the gates on his own. "The journey," Gair explained, "doesn't exercise distance so much as a state of mind." That was as good a description as any, John realized as he fell in step with his new companion, for it took them no time at all to circumvent familiar territory and step out onto a long boulevard. John felt a tugging in that part of his chest where his heart had once beaten as he looked down to the far end of the avenue. An immense archway stood there. Between its pillars the air shimmered like a heat mirage and called to him.

When Gair paused, John came to a reluctant halt beside him. Gair looked at his watch again.

"I'm sorry," he said, "but I have to leave you now. I have another appointment."

John found it hard to look at the man. His gaze kept being drawn back to the shimmering air inside the arch.

"I think I can find my way from here," he said.

Gair smiled. "I should think you could." He shook John's hand. "Godspeed," he murmured, then he faded away just as Dakota had faded from his living room what seemed like a thousand lifetimes ago.

Dolly stirred against John's chest as he continued on toward the gates. He rearranged her in the sling so that she, too, could look at the approaching gates, but she turned her face away and for the first time his holding her wasn't enough. She began to wail at the sight of the gates, her distress growing in volume the closer they got.

John slowed his pace, uncertain now. He thought of Clark's cursing at him, of Gair telling him that Dolly, for all her infancy, was old enough to make this decision on her own. He realized that they were both right. He couldn't force her to go through, to travel on. But what would he do if she refused? He couldn't simply leave her behind either.

The archway of the gates loomed over him now. The heat shimmer had changed into a warm golden light that washed out from between the pillars, dispelling all the shadows that had ever taken root in John's soul. But the infant in his arms wept more pitifully, howled until he covered her head with part of the cloth and let her burrow her face against his chest. She whimpered softly there until John thought his heart would break. With each step he took, the sounds she made grew more piteous.

He stood directly before the archway, bathed in its golden light. Through the pulsing glow, he could see the big sky Dakota had described. It went on forever. He could feel his heart swell to fill it. All he wanted to do was step through, to be done with the lies of the flesh, the lies that had told him, this one life was all, the lies that had tricked him into being trapped in the city of the undead.

But there was the infant to consider and he couldn't abandon her. Couldn't abandon her, but he couldn't explain it to her, that there was nothing to fear, that it was only light and an enormous sky. And peace. There were no words to capture the wonder that pulsed through his veins, that blossomed in his heart, swelled until his chest was full and he knew the light must be pouring out of his eyes and mouth.

Now he understood Dakota's sorrow. It would be heartbreaking to know what waited for those who turned their backs on this glory. It had nothing to do with gods or religions.

There was no hierarchy of belief entailed. No one was denied admittance. It was simply the place one stepped through so that the journey could continue.

John cradled the sobbing infant, jigging her gently against his chest. He stared into the light. He stared into the endless sky.

"Dakota," he called softly.

"Hello, John Narraway."

He turned to find her standing beside him, her own solemn gaze drinking in the light that pulsed in the big sky between the gates and flowed over them. She smiled at him.

"I didn't think I'd see you again," she said. "And certainly not in this place. You did well to find it."

"I had help. One of your colleagues showed me the way."

"There's nothing wrong with accepting help sometimes."

"I know that now," John said. "I also understand how hard it is to offer help and have it refused."

Dakota stepped closer and drew the infant from the sling at John's chest.

"It is hard," she agreed, cradling Dolly. Her eyes still held the reflected light that came from between the gates, but they were sad once more as she studied the weeping infant. She sighed, adding, "But it's not something that can be forced."

John nodded. There was something about Dakota's voice, about the way she looked that distracted him, but he couldn't quite put his finger on it.

"I will take care of the little one," Dakota said. "There's no need for you to remain here."

"What will you do with her?"

"Whatever she wants."

"But she's so young."

The sadness deepened in Dakota's eyes. "I know."

There was so much empathy in her voice, in the way she held the infant, in her gaze. And then John realized what was different about her. Her voice wasn't hollow, it held resonance. She wasn't monochrome, but touched with color. There was only a hint, at first, like an old tinted photograph, but it was like looking at a rainbow for John. As it grew stronger he drank in the wonder of it. He wished she would speak again, just so that he could cherish the texture of her voice, but she remained silent, solemn gaze held by the infant in her arms.

"I find it hardest when they're so young," she finally said, looking up at him. "They don't communicate in words so it's impossible to ease their fears."

But words weren't the only way to communicate, John thought. He crouched down to lay his fiddlecase on the ground, took out his bow and tightened the hair. He ran his thumb across the fiddle strings to check the tuning, marveling anew at the richness of sound. He thought perhaps he'd missed that the most.

"What are you doing?" Dakota asked him.

John shook his head. It wasn't that he didn't want to explain it to her, but that he couldn't. Instead he slipped the fiddle under his chin, drew the bow across the strings, and used music to express what words couldn't. He turned to the gates, drank in the light and the immense wonder of the sky and distilled it into a simple melody, an air of grace and beauty. Warm generous notes spilled from the sound holes of his instrument, grew stronger and more resonant in the light of the gates, gained such presence that they could almost be seen, touched and held with more than the ear.

The infant in Dakota's arms fell silent and listened. She turned innocent eyes toward the gates and reached out for them. John slowly brought the melody to an end. He laid down his fiddle and bow and took the infant from Dakota, walked with her toward the light. When he was directly under the arch, the light seemed to flare and suddenly the weight was gone from his arms. He heard a joyous cry, but could see nothing for the light. His felt a beating in his chest as though he was alive once more, pulse drumming. He wanted to follow Dolly into the light more than he'd ever wanted anything before in his life, but he slowly turned his back on the light and stepped back onto the boulevard.

"John Narraway," Dakota said. "What are you doing?"

"I can't go through," he said. "Not yet. I have to help the others—like you do."

"But—"

"It's not because I don't want to go through anymore," John said. "It's . . ."

He didn't know how to explain it and not even fiddle music would help him now. All he could think of was the despair that had clung to him in the city of the undead, the same despair that possessed all those lost souls he'd left there, wandering forever through its deserted streets, huddling in its abandoned buildings, denying themselves the light. He knew that, like Dakota and Gair, he had to try to prevent others from making the same mistake. He knew it wouldn't be easy, he knew there would be times when it would be heartbreaking, but he could see no other course.

"I just want to help," he said. "I have to help. You told me before that there aren't enough of you and the fellow that brought me here said the same thing."

Dakota gave him a long considering look before she finally smiled. "You know," she said. "I think you do have the generosity of heart now."

John put away his fiddle. When he stood up, Dakota took his hand and they began to walk back down the boulevard, away from the gates.

"I'm going to miss that light," John said.

Dakota squeezed his hand. "Don't be silly," she said. "The light has always been inside us."

John glanced back. From this distance, the light was like a heat mirage again, shimmering between the pillars of the gates, but he could still feel its glow, see the flare of its wonder and the sky beyond it that went on forever. Something of it echoed in his chest and he knew Dakota was right.

"We carry it with us wherever we go," he said.

"Learn to play that on your fiddle, John Narraway," she said.

John returned her smile. "I will," he promised. "I surely will."

Birds

Isn't it wonderful? The world scans.
—Nancy Willard, from "Looking for Mr. Ames"

1

When her head is full of birds, anything is possible. She can understand the slow language of the trees, the song of running water, the whispering gossip of the wind. The conversation of the birds fills her until she doesn't even think to remember what it was like before she could understand them. But sooner or later, the birds go away, one by one, find new nests, new places to fly. It's not that they tire of her; it's simply not in their nature to tarry for too long.

But she misses them. Misses their company, the flutter of wings inside her head and their trilling conversations. Misses the possibilities. The magic.

To call them back she has to approach them as a bride. Dressed in white, with something old and something new, something borrowed and something blue. And a word. A new word, from another's dream. A word that has never been heard before.

2

Katja Faro was out later than she thought safe, at least for this part of town and at this time of night, the minute hand of her old-fashioned wristwatch steadily climbing up the last quarter of her watch face to count the hour. Three A.M. That late.

From early evening until the clubs close, Gracie Street is a jumbled clutter of people, looking for action, looking for gratification, or just out and about, hanging, gossiping with their friends. There's always something happening, from Lee Street all the way across to Williamson, but tag on a few more hours and clubland becomes a frontier. The lights advertising the various cafés, clubs, and bars begin to flicker and go out, their patrons and staff have all gone home, and the only people out on the streets are a few stragglers, such as Katja tonight, and the predators.

Purple combat boots scuffing on the pavement, Katja felt adrift on the empty street. It seemed like only moments ago she'd been secure in the middle of good conversation, laughter and espressos; then someone remarked on the time, the café was closing and suddenly she was out here, on the street, by herself, finding her own way home. She held her jean jacket closed at her throat—the buttons had come off, one by one, and she kept forgetting to replace them—and listened to the swish of her long flowered skirt, the sound of her boots on the pavement. Listened as well for other footsteps and prayed for a cab to come by.

She was paying so much attention to what might be lurking behind the shadowed mouths of the alleyways that she almost didn't notice the slight figure curled up in the doorway of the pawnshop on her right. The sight made her pause. She glanced up and down the street before crouching down in the doorway. The figure's features were in shadow, the small body outlined under what looked like a dirty white sheet, or a shawl. By its shape Katja could tell it wasn't a boy.

"Hey, are you okay?" she asked.

When there was no response, she touched the girl's shoulder and repeated her question. Large pale eyes flickered open, their gaze settling on Katja. The girl woke like a cat, immediately aware of everything around her. Her black hair hung about her face in a tangle. Unlike most street people, she had a sweet smell, like a field of clover, or a potpourri of dried rosehips and herbs, gathered in a glass bowl.

"What makes you think I'm not okay?" the girl asked.

Katja pushed the fall of her own dark hair back from her brow and settled back on her heels.

"Well, for one thing," she said, "you're lying here in a doorway, on a bed of what looks like old newspapers. It's not exactly the kind of place people pick to sleep in if they've got a choice."

She glanced up and down the street again as she spoke, still wary of her surroundings and their possible danger, still hoping to see a cab.

"I'm okay," the girl told her.

"Yeah, right."

"No, really."

Katja had to smile. She wasn't so old that she'd forgotten what it felt like to be in her late teens and immortal. Remembering, looking at this slight girl with her dark hair and strangely pale eyes, she got this odd urge to take in a stray the way that Angel and Jilly often did. She wasn't sure why. She liked to think that she had as much sympathy as the next person, but normally it was hard to muster much of it at this time of night. Normally she was thinking too much about what terrors the night might hold for her to consider playing the Good Samaritan. But this girl looked so young. . . .

"What's your name?" she asked.

"Teresa. Teresa Lewis."

Katja offered her hand as she introduced herself.

Teresa laughed. "Welcome to my home," she said and shook Katja's hand.

"This a regular squat?" Katja asked. Nervous as she was at being out so late, she couldn't imagine actually sleeping in a place like this on a regular basis.

"No," Teresa said. "I meant the street."

Katja sighed. Immortal. "Look. I don't have that big a place, but there's room on my couch if you want to crash."

Teresa gave her a considering look.

"Well, I know it's not the Harbor Ritz," Katja began.

"It's not that," Teresa told her. "It's just that you don't know me at all. I could be loco, for all you know. Get to your place and rob you. . . ."

"I've got a big family," Katja told her. "They'd track you down and take it out of your skin."

Teresa laughed again. It was like they were meeting at a party somewhere, Katja thought, drinks in hand, no worries, instead of on Gracie Street at three A.M.

"I'm serious," she said. "I've got the room."

Teresa's laughter trailed off. Her pale gaze settled on Katja's features.

"Do you believe in magic?" she asked.

"Say what?"

"Magic. Do you believe in it?"

Katja blinked. She waited for the punch line, but when it didn't come, she said, "Well, I'm not sure. My friend Jilly sure does—though maybe magic's not quite the right word. It's more like she believes there's more to this world than we can always see or understand. She sees things. . . ."

Katja caught herself. How did we get into this? she thought. She wanted to change the subject, she wanted to get off the street before some homeboys showed up with all the wrong ideas in mind, but the steady weight of Teresa's intense gaze wouldn't let her go.

"Anyway," Katja said, "I guess you could say Jilly does. Believes in magic, I mean. Sees things."

"But what about you? Have you seen things?"

Katja shook her head. "Only 'old, unhappy, far-off things, and battles long ago,' " she said. "Wordsworth," she added, placing the quote when Teresa raised her eyebrows in a question.

"Then I guess you couldn't understand," Teresa told her. "See, the reason I'm out here like this is that I'm looking for a word."

3

I can't sleep. I lie in bed for what feels like hours, staring up at the shadows cast on the ceiling from the streetlight outside my bedroom window. Finally I get up. I pull on a pair of leggings and a T-shirt and pad quietly across the room in my bare feet. I stand in the doorway and look at my guest. She's still sleeping, all curled up again, except her nest is made up of a spare set of my sheets and blankets now instead of old newspapers.

I wish it wasn't so early. I wish I could pick up the phone and talk to Jilly. I want to know if the strays she brings home tell stories as strange as mine told me on the way back to my apartment. I want to know if her strays can recognize the egret which is a deposed king. If they can understand the gossip of bees and what crows talk about when they gather in a murder. If they ever don the old-woman wisdom to be found in the rattle-and-cough cry of a lonesome gull and wear it like a cloak of story.

I want to know if Jilly's ever heard of bird-brides, because Teresa says that's what she is, what she usually is, until the birds fly away. To gather them back into her head takes a kind of a wedding ritual that's sealed with a dream-word. That's what she was doing out on Gracie Street when I found her: worn out from trying to get strangers to tell her a word that they'd only ever heard before in one of their dreams.

I don't have to tell you how helpful the people she met were. The ones that didn't ignore her or call her names just gave her spare change instead of the word she needs. But I can't say as I blame them. If she'd come up to me with her spiel I don't know how I'd have reacted. Not well, probably. Wouldn't have listened. Gets so you can't walk down a block some days without getting hit up for change, five or six times. I don't want to be cold; but when it comes down to it, I've only got so much myself.

I look away from my guest, my gaze resting on the phone for a moment, before I turn around and go back into my room. I don't bother undressing. I just lie there on my bed, looking up at the shadow play that's still being staged on my ceiling. I know what's keeping me awake: I can't decide if I've brought home some poor confused kid or a piece of magic. It's not the one or the other that's brought on my insomnia. It's that I'm seriously considering the fact that it might be one or the other.

4

"No, I have a place to live," Teresa said the next morning. They were sitting at the narrow table in Katja's kitchen that only barely seated the two of them comfortably, hands warming around mugs of freshly brewed coffee. "I live in a bachelor in an old house on Stanton Street."

Katja shook her head. "Then why were you sleeping in a doorway last night?"

"I don't know. I think because the people on Gracie Street in the evening seem to dream harder than people anywhere else."

"They're just more desperate to have a good time," Katja said.

"I suppose. Anyway, I was sure I'd find my word there and by the time I realized I wouldn't—at least last night—it was so late and I was just too tired to go home."

"But weren't you scared?"

Teresa regarded her with genuine surprise. "Of what?"

How to explain, Katja wondered. Obviously this girl sitting across from her in a borrowed T-shirt, with sleep still gathered in the corners of her eyes, was fearless, like Jilly. Where did you start enumerating the dangers for them? And why bother? Teresa probably wouldn't listen any more than Jilly ever did. Katja thought sometimes that people like them must have guardian angels watching out for them—and working overtime.

"I feel like I'm always scared," she said.

Teresa nodded. "I guess that's the way I feel, when the birds leave and all I have left in my head are empty nests and a few stray feathers. Kind of lonely, and scared that they'll never come back."

That wasn't the way Katja felt at all. Her fear lay in the headlines of newspapers and the sound-bites that helped fill newscasts. There was too much evil running loose—

random, petty evil, it was true, but evil all the same. Ever-present and all around her so that you didn't know who to trust anymore. Sometimes it seemed as though everyone in the world was so much bigger and more capable than her. Too often, confronted with their confidence, she could only feel helpless.

"Where did you hear about this . . . this thing with the birds?" she said instead. "The way you can bring them back?"

Teresa shrugged. "I just always knew it."

"But you have all these details. . . ."

Borrowed from bridal folklore, Katja added to herself—all except for the word she had to get from somebody else's dream. The question she'd really wanted to ask was, *why* those particular details? What made their borrowed possibilities true? Katja didn't want to sound judgmental. The truth, she had to admit if she was honest with herself, wasn't so much that she believed her houseguest as that she didn't disbelieve her. Hadn't she woken up this morning searching the fading remnants of her dreams, looking for a new word that only existed beyond the gates of her sleeping mind?

Teresa was smiling at her. The wattage behind the expression seemed to light the room, banishing shadows and uncertainties, and Katja basked in its glow.

"I know what you're thinking," Teresa said. "They don't even sound all that original except for the missing word, do they? But I believe any of us can make things happen— even magical, impossible things. It's a matter of having faith in the private rituals we make up for ourselves."

"Rituals you make up . . . ?"

"Uh-huh. The rituals themselves aren't all that important on their own—though once you've decided on them, you have to stick to them, just like the old alchemists did. You have to follow them through."

"But if the rituals aren't that important," Katja asked, "then what's the point of them?"

"How they help you focus your will—your intent. That's what magic is, you know. It's having a strong enough sense of self and what's around you to not only envision it being different but to *make* it different."

"You really believe this, don't you?"

"Of course," Teresa said. "Don't you?"

"I don't know. You make it sound so logical."

"That's because it's true. Or maybe—" That smile of Teresa's returned, warming the room again. "—because I'm *willing* it to be true."

"So would your ritual work for me?"

"If you believe in it. But you should probably find your own—a set of circumstances that feels right for you." She paused for a moment, then added, "And you have to know what you're asking for. My birds are what got me through a lot of bad times. Listening to their conversations and soliloquies let me forget what was happening to me."

Katja leaned forward. She could see the rush of memories rising in Teresa, could see the pain they brought with them. She wanted to reach out and hold her in a comforting embrace—the same kind of embrace she'd needed so often but rarely got.

"What happened?" she asked, her voice soft.

"I don't want to remember," Teresa said. She gave Katja an apologetic look. "It's not that I can't, it's that I don't want to."

"You don't have to talk about it if you don't want to," Katja assured her. "Just because I'm putting you up, doesn't mean you have to explain yourself to me."

There was no sunshine in the smile that touched Teresa's features now. It was more like moonlight playing on wild rosebushes, the cool light glinting on thorns. Memories could impale you just like thorns. Katja knew that all too well.

"But I can't not remember," Teresa said. "That's what so sad. For all the good things in my life, I can't stop thinking of how much I hurt before the birds came."

5

I know about pain. I know about loneliness. Talking with Teresa, I realize that these are the first real conversations I've had with someone else in years.

I don't want to make it sound as though I don't have any friends, that I never talk to anyone—but sometimes it feels like that all the same. I always seem to be standing on the outside of a friendship, of conversations, never really engaged. Even last night, before I found Teresa sleeping in the doorway. I was out with a bunch of people. I was in the middle of any number of conversations and camaraderie. But I still went home alone. I listened to what was going on around me. I smiled some, laughed some, added a sentence here, another there, but it wasn't really me that was partaking of the company. The real me was one step removed, watching it happen. Like it seems I always am. Everybody I know seems to inhabit one landscape that they all share while I'm the only person standing in the landscape that's inside of me.

But today it's different. We're talking about weird, unlikely things, but I'm *there* with Teresa. I don't even know her; there are all sorts of people I've known for years, known way better, but not one of them seems to have looked inside me as truly as she does. This alchemy, this magic she's offering me, is opening a door inside me. It's making me remember. It's making me want to fill my head with birds so that I can forget.

That's the saddest thing, isn't it? Wanting to forget. Desiring amnesia. I think that's the only reason some people kill themselves. I know it's the only reason I've ever seriously considered suicide.

Consider the statistics: One out of every five women will be sexually traumatized by the time they reach their twenties. They might be raped, they might be a child preyed upon by a stranger, they might be abused by the very people who are supposed to be looking out for them.

But the thing that statistic doesn't tell you is how often it can happen to that one woman out of five. How it can happen to her over and over and over again, but on the statistical sheet, she's still only listed as one woman in five. That makes it sound so random, the event an extraordinary moment of evil when set against the rest of her life, rather than something that she might have faced every day of her childhood.

I'd give anything for a head full of birds. I'd give anything for the noise and clamor of their conversation to drown out the memories when they rise up inside of me.

6

Long after noon came and went the two women still sat across from each other at the kitchen table. If their conversation could have been seen as well as heard, the spill of words that passed between them would have flooded off the table to eddy around their ankles in ever-deepening pools. It would have made for profound, dark water that was only bearable because each of them came to understand that the other truly understood what they had gone through, and sharing the stories of their battered childhoods at least reminded them that they weren't alone in what they had undergone, even if it didn't make the burden easier to bear.

The coffee had gone cold in their mugs, but the hands across the table they held to comfort each other were warm, palm to palm. When they finally ran out of words, that contact helped maintain the bond of empathy that had grown up between them.

"I didn't have birds," Katja said after a long silence. "All I had was poetry."

"You wrote poems?"

Katja shook her head. "I became poetry. I inhabited poems. I filled them until their words were all I could hear inside my head." She tilted her head back and quoted one:

> *Rough wind, that moanest loud*
> *Grief too sad for song;*
> *Wild wind, when sullen cloud*
> *Knells all the night long;*
> *Sad storm, whose tears are vain,*
> *Bare woods, whose branches strain,*
> *Deep caves and dreary main,—*
> *Wail, for the world's wrong!*

"That's so sad. What's it called?" Teresa asked.

" 'A dirge.' It's by Shelley. I always seemed to choose sad poems, but I only ever wanted them for how I'd get so full of words I wouldn't be able to remember anything else."

"Birds and words," Teresa said. Her smile came out again from behind the dark clouds of her memories. "We rhyme."

7

We wash Teresa's dress that afternoon. It wasn't very white anymore—not after her having grubbed about in it on Gracie Street all day and then worn it as a nightgown while she slept in a doorway—but it cleans up better than I think it will. I feel like we're in a detergent commercial when we take it out of the dryer. The dress seems to glow against my skin as I hand it over to her.

Her something old is a plastic Crackerjack ring that she's had since she was a kid. Her something new is her sneakers—a little scuffed and worse for the wear this afternoon, but still passably white. Her borrowed is a white leather clasp-purse that her landlady loaned her. Her blue is a small clutch of silk flowers: forget-me-nots tied up with a white ribbon that she plans to wear as a corsage.

All she needs is that missing word.

I don't have one for her, but I know someone who might. Jilly always likes to talk about things not quite of this world—things seen from the corner of the eye, or brought over from a dream. And whenever she talks about dreams, Sophie Etoile's name comes up because Jilly insists Sophie's part faerie and therefore a true dreamer. I don't know Sophie all that well, certainly not well enough to guess at her genealogy, improbable or not as the case may be. But she does have an otherworldly, Pre-Raphaelite air about her that makes Jilly's claims seem possible—at least they seem possible considering my present state of mind.

And there's no one else I can turn to, no one I can think of. I can't explain this desperation I feel toward Teresa, a kind of mothering/big sister complex. I just have to help her. And while I know that I may not be able to make myself forget, I think I can do it for her. Or at least I want to try.

So that's how we find ourselves knocking at the door of Sophie's studio later that afternoon. When Sophie answers the door, her curly brown hair tied back from her face and her painting smock as spotless as Jilly says it always is, I don't have to go into a long explanation as to what we're doing there or why we need this word. I just have to mention that Jilly's told me that she's a true dreamer and Sophie gets this smile on her face, like you do when you're thinking about a mischievous child who's too endearing to get angry at, and she thinks for a moment, then says a word that at least I've never heard before. I turn to Teresa to ask her if it's what she needs, but she's already got this beatific look on her face.

"Mmm," is all she can manage.

I thank Sophie, who's giving the pair of us a kind of puzzled smile, and lead Teresa back down the narrow stairs of Sophie's building and out onto the street. I wonder what I'm going to do with Teresa. She looks for all the world as though she's tripping. But just when I decide to take her home again, her eyes get a little more focused and she takes my hand.

"I have to . . . readjust to all of this," she says. "But I don't want to have us just walk out of each others' lives. Can I come and visit you tomorrow?"

"Sure," I tell her. I hesitate a moment, then have to ask, "Can you really hear them?"

"Listen," she says.

She draws my head close to hers until my ear is resting right up against her temple. I swear I hear a bird's chorus resonating inside her head, conducting through skin and bone, from her mind into my mind.

"I'll come by in the morning," she says, and then drifts off down the pavement.

All I can do is watch her go, that birdsong still echoing inside me.

8

Back in my own living room, I sit on the carpet. I can feel a foreign vibe in my apartment, a quivering in the air from Teresa having been there. Everything in the room carries the memory of her, the knowledge of her gaze, how she handled and examined them with her attention. My furniture, the posters and prints on my walls, my knickknacks, all seemed subtly changed, a little stiff from the awareness of her looking at them.

It takes a while for the room to settle down into its familiar habits. The fridge muttering to itself in the kitchen. The pictures in their frames letting out their stomachs and hanging slightly askew once more.

I take down a box of family photos from the hall closet and fan them out on the carpet in front of me. I look at the happy family they depict and try to see hints of the darkness that doesn't appear in the photos. There are too many smiles—mine, my mother's, my father's. I know real life was never the way these pictures pretend it was.

I sit there remembering my father's face—the last time I saw him. We were in the courtroom, waiting for him to be sentenced. He wouldn't look at me. My mother wouldn't look at me. I sat at the table with only a lawyer for support, only a stranger for family. That memory always makes me feel ashamed because even after all he'd done to me, I didn't feel any triumph. I felt only disloyalty. I felt only that I was the one who'd been bad, that what had happened to me had been my fault. I knew back then it was wrong to feel that way—just as I know now that it is—but I can't seem to help myself.

I squeeze my eyes shut, but the moment's locked in my brain, just like all those other memories from my childhood that put a lie to the photographs fanned out on the carpet around me. Words aren't going to blot them out for me today. There aren't enough poems in the world to do that. And even if I could gather birds into my head, I don't think they would work for me. But I remember what Teresa told me about rituals and magic.

It's having a strong enough sense of self and what's around you to not only envision it being different but to make *it different.*

I remember the echoing sound of the birds I heard gossiping in her head and I know that I can find peace, too. I just have to believe that I can. I just have to know what it is that I want and concentrate on having it, instead of what I've got. I have to find the ritual that'll make it work for me.

Instinctively, I realize it can't be too easy. Like Teresa's dream-word, the spell needs an element to complete it that requires some real effort on my part to attain it. But I know what the rest of the ritual will be—it comes into my head, full-blown, as if I've always known it but simply never stopped to access that knowledge before.

I pick up a picture of my father from the carpet and carefully tear his face into four pieces, sticking one piece in each of the front and back pockets of my jeans. I remember something I heard about salt, about it being used to cleanse, and add a handful of it to each pocket. I wrap the fingers of my left hand together with a black ribbon and tie the bow so that it lies across my knuckles. I lick my right forefinger and write my name on the bare skin of my stomach with saliva. Then I let my shirt fall back down to cover the invisible word and leave the apartment, looking for a person who, when asked to name a nineteenth-century poet, will mistakenly put together the given name of one with the surname of another.

From somewhere I hear a sound like Teresa's birds, singing their approval.

Passing

*Great God! I'd rather be
A pagan suckled in a creed outworn;
So might I, standing on this pleasant lea,
Have glimpses that would make me less forlorn.*
—William Wordsworth,
from "The World Is Too Much With Us"

1

The sword lies on the grass beside me, not so much a physical presence as an enchantment. I don't know how else to describe it. It's too big to be real. I can't imagine anyone being able to hold it comfortably, little say wield it. Looking at it is like looking through water, as though I'm lying at the bottom of a lake and everything's slightly in motion, edges blurring. I can see the dark metal of the sword's pommel and cross guard, the impossible length of the blade itself that seems to swallow the moonlight, the thong wrapped round and round the grip, its leather worn smooth and shiny in places.

I can almost believe it's alive.

Whenever I study it, time gets swallowed up. I lose snatches of the night, ten minutes, fifteen minutes, time I don't have to spare. I have to be finished before dawn. With an effort, I pull my gaze away and pick up the shovel once more. Hallowed ground. I don't know how deep the grave should be. Four feet? Six feet? I'm just going to keep digging until I feel I've got it right.

2

Lucy Grey was a columnist and features writer for *The Newford Sun*, which was how she first found herself involved with the city's gay community. Her editor, enamored with the most recent upsurge of interest in gay chic and all things androgynous, sent her down to the girl bars on Gracie Street to write an op-ed piece that grew into a Sunday feature. Steadfastly heterosexual in terms of who she'd actually sleep with, Lucy discovered she was gay in spirit, if not in practice. Sick of being harassed by guys, she could relax in the gay clubs, stepping it out and flirting with the other girls on the dance floor and never having to worry about how to go home alone at the end of the night.

Her new girlpals seemed to understand and she didn't think anybody considered her a tease until one night, sitting in a cubical of a washroom in Neon Sister, she overheard herself being discussed by two women who'd come in to touch up their makeup. They were unaware of her presence.

"I don't know," one of them said. "There's something about her that doesn't ring true. It's like after that piece she did in *The Sun*, now she's researching a book—looking at us from the inside, but not really one of us."

"Who, Lucy?" the other said.

Lucy recognized her friend Traci's voice. It was Traci who befriended her the first night she hit Gracie Street and guided her through the club scene.

"Of course Lucy. She's all look, but don't touch."

"Sounds more to me like you're miffed because she won't sleep with you."

"She doesn't sleep with anybody."

"So?"

"So she's like an emotional tourist, passing through. You know what happens when the straights start hanging out in one of our clubs."

It becomes a straight club, Lucy thought, having heard it all before. The difference, this time, was that the accusation was being directed at her and she wasn't so sure that it was unfair. She wasn't here just because she preferred the company of women, but to avoid men. It wasn't that she disliked men, but that her intimacy with them never seemed to go beyond the bedroom. She was neither bisexual nor experimenting. She was simply confused and taking refuge in a club scene where she could still have a social life.

"You're reading way too much into this," Traci said. "It's not like she's seriously coming on to anyone. It's just innocent flirting—everybody does it."

"So you don't want a piece of what she's got?"

Traci laughed. "I'd set up house with her in a minute." Sitting in the cubicle, Lucy found herself blushing furiously, especially when Traci added, "Long-term."

"What you're setting yourself up for is a broken heart."

"I don't think so," Traci said. "I try to keep everything in perspective. If she just wants to be friends, that's okay with me. And I kind of like her the way she is: social, but celibate."

That was a description Lucy embraced wholeheartedly after that night because it seemed to perfectly sum up who she was.

Until she met Nina.

3

It all starts out innocently enough. Nina shows up at the North Star one night, looking just as sweet and lost as Traci said I did the first time she saw me on Gracie Street, trying to work up the nerve to go into one of the clubs. She has her hair cut above her ears like Sadie Benning and she's wearing combat boots with her black jeans and white T-shirt, but she looks like a femme, and a shy one at that, so I take her under my wing.

Turns out she's married, but it's on the rocks. Maybe. There's no real intimacy in their relationship—tell me about it. Thinks her husband's getting some on the side, but she can't swear to it. She's not sure what she's doing here, she just wants a night out, but she doesn't want to play the usual games in the straight bars, so she comes here, but now that she's here, she's not sure what she's doing here.

I tell her to relax. We dance some. We have a few drinks. By the time she goes home she's flushing prettily and most of the shadows I saw haunting the backs of her eyes are gone.

We start to hang out together. In the clubs. Have lunch, dinner once. Not dates. We're just girlpals, except after a few weeks I find myself thinking about her all the time, fixating on her. Not jealous. Not wondering where she is, or who she's with. Just conversations we had running through my mind. Her face a familiar visitor to my mind's eye. Her trim body.

Is this how it starts? I wonder. There's no definition to what's growing inside me, no "I used to like men, now I'm infatuated with a woman." It's just this swelling desire to be with her. To touch her. To bask in her smile. To know she's thinking of me.

One night I'm driving her home and I don't know how it happens, but we pull up in front of her apartment building and I'm leaning toward her and then our heads come together, our lips, our tongues. It's like kissing a guy, only everything's softer. Sweeter, somehow. We're wrapped up against each other, hands fumbling, I'm caressing her hair, her neck, her shoulder—until suddenly she pulls away, breathless, like me, a surprised look of desire in her eyes, like me, but there's something else there, too. Not shame. No, it felt too good. But confusion, yes. And uncertainty, for sure.

"I'm sorry," I say. I know she's been passing, just like me. Gay in spirit. We've talked about it. Lots of times.

"Don't be," she says. "It felt nice."

I don't say anything. I'm on pins and needles, not understanding the intensity of these feelings I have for her, for another woman, not wanting to scare her off, but knowing I want more. Nice doesn't even begin to describe how it felt to me.

Nina sighs. "It's just . . . confusing."

This I understand.

"But it feels wrong?" I ask.

She nods. "Only not for the reason you're probably thinking. It's just . . . if I was sure Martin was cheating on me . . . that our marriage was over . . . I think it would be different. I wouldn't feel like *I* was betraying him. I could do whatever I wanted, couldn't I?"

"Do you still love him?"

"I don't know," Nina says. "If he's cheating on me again, the way I think he is . . ." She gives me a lost look that makes me want to just take her in my arms once more, but I stay on my own side of the front seat. "Maybe," she says in this small voice, her eyes so big and hopeful, "maybe you could find out for me . . . for us. . . ."

"What? Like follow him?"

Nina shakes her head. "No. I was thinking more like . . . you could try to seduce him. Then we'd *know*."

I don't like the way this is going at all, but there's a promise in Nina's eyes now, a promise that if I do this thing for her, she'll be mine. Not just for one night, but forever.

"You wouldn't actually have to *do* anything," she says. "You know, like sleep with him. We'd only have to take it far enough to see if he's cheating on me."

"I don't know," I tell her, doubt in my voice, but I can already feel myself giving in.

She nods slowly. "I guess it's a pretty stupid idea," she says. She looks away embarrassed. "God. I can't believe I even asked you to do something like that."

She leans forward and gives me a quick kiss, then draws back and starts to get out of the car.

"Wait a minute," I say, catching hold of her arm. She lets me tug her back in the car. "I didn't say I wouldn't do it. It's just . . . we'd need a good plan, wouldn't we? I mean, where would I even meet him in the first place?"

So we start to talk about it and before I know it, we've got the plan. She tells me where he goes after work for a drink on Fridays. We figure it'll be best if she goes away somewhere for the weekend. We work everything out, sitting there in the front seat of my car, arms around each other. We kiss again before she finally leaves, a long deep kiss that has my head swimming, my body aching to be naked against hers. I don't even consider second thoughts until I wake up alone in my own apartment the next morning and begin to realize what I've gotten myself into.

I remember the last thing she said before she got out of the car.

"If he *is* cheating on me . . . and he takes you to our apartment, could you do something for me before you leave?"

"What's that?"

"There's a sword hanging on the wall over the mantel. Could you take it with you back to your place?"

"A sword."

She nodded. "Because if it's over, I'm not ever going back to that place. I won't ever want to see him again. But . . ." She gave me a look that melted my heart. "The sword's the only thing I'd want to take away with me. It used to belong to my mother, you see. . . ."

I lie there in bed thinking about it until I have to get up to have a pee. When I'm washing my face at the basin, I study my reflection looking back at me, water dripping from her cheeks.

"Lucy," I say to her. "What have we gotten ourselves into this time?"

4

It was a quiet night at Neon Sister, but it was still early, going on to eleven. Lucy saw Traci sitting by herself in one of the booths beside the dance floor. She was easy to spot with her shoulder-length dreadlocks, her coffee-colored skin accentuated by the white of her T-shirt. Lucy waited a moment to make sure Traci was alone, then crossed the dance floor and slid into the booth beside her. She ordered a drink from the waitress, but wasn't in the mood to do more than sip from it after it arrived. There was always something about being in Traci's calm, dark-eyed presence that made Lucy want to open up to her. She didn't know what it was that usually stopped her, but tonight it wasn't there.

"I'm not really gay, you know," she said when the small talk between them died.

Traci smiled. "I know."

"You do?"

Traci nodded. "But you're not sure you're straight, either. You don't know who you are, do you?"

"I guess. Except now I'm starting to think maybe I am gay."

"Has this got something to do with Nina?"

"Is it that obvious?"

"We've all been there before, Lucy."

Lucy sighed. "So I think I'm ready to, you know, to find out who I really am, but I don't think Nina is."

"Welcome to that club as well."

Lucy took another sip of her drink and looked out at the dance floor. An hour had passed and the club was starting to fill up. She brought her gaze back to Traci.

"Were you ever in love with a guy?" she asked.

Traci hesitated for a moment, then gave a reluctant nod. "A long time ago."

"Does it feel any different—I mean, with a woman?"

"You mean inside?"

Lucy nodded.

"It doesn't feel different," Traci confirmed. She studied Lucy, her dark gaze more solemn than usual, before going on. "Straights always think it's hard for us to come out—to the world—but it's harder to come out to ourselves. Not because there's anything wrong with what we are, but because we're made to feel it's wrong. I used to think that with the strides in gay rights over the past few years, it wouldn't be like that anymore, but society still feeds us so much garbage that nothing much seems to have changed. You know what kept going around and around in my head when I was trying to figure myself out?"

Lucy shook her head.

"That old *The Children's Hour* with Shirley MacLaine from the sixties—the one where she finds out she's a lesbian and she kills herself. I was so ashamed of how I felt. Ashamed and confused."

"I don't feel ashamed," Lucy said.

"But you do feel confused."

Lucy nodded. "I don't know what to do."

"Well, here's my two cents: Don't be in a rush to work it out. Be honest—to yourself as well as to Nina—but take it slow."

"And if I lose her?"

"Then it was never meant to be." Traci gave her a wry smile. "Pretty lame, huh? But there's always a grain of truth—even in populist crap like that. You wanna dance?"

Lucy thought about the night she'd overheard Traci and another woman discussing her in the washroom, thought about what Traci had said about her, thought about what she herself was feeling for Nina. Didn't matter the combination of genders, she realized. Some things just didn't change. She gave Traci a smile.

"Sure," she said.

It was a slow dance. She and Traci had danced together many times before, but it felt different tonight. Tonight Lucy couldn't stop focusing on the fact that it was a woman's body moving so closely to hers, a woman's arms around her. But then ever since kissing Nina last night, everything had felt different.

"Gay or straight," Traci said, her voice soft in Lucy's ear, "the hurt feels the same."

Lucy nodded, then let her head rest against Traci's once more. They were comforting each other, Lucy realized, but while Traci was offering more, the dance was all that Lucy had to give.

5

So I go ahead and do it. I meet Martin in Huxley's, that yuppie bar across from Fitzhenry Park, and I flirt outrageously with him. Picking him up is so easy, I wish there was a prize for it. I'd collect big-time.

By the time we've had dinner, I've got enough on him to take back to Nina, but I'm curious now, about him, about where they live, and I can't seem to break it off. Next thing I know I'm in their apartment, the same one I sat outside of a few nights ago, necking with his wife in the front seat of my car. Now I'm here with him, sitting on their couch, watching him make us drinks at the wet bar in the corner of the living room.

He comes back with a drink in each hand and gives me one. We toast each other, take a sip. This is seriously good brandy. I like it. I like him, too—not a man-woman kind of thing, but he seems like a nice guy. Except he cheats on his wife—whom I'm trying to get into my own bed. It's time to go, I realize. Way past time to go. But then he floors me.

"So when did you meet Nina?" he asks.

I look at him, unable to hide my surprise. "How did you—" I break off before I get in too deep and take a steadying breath to try to regain my composure. It's not easy with that pale blue gaze of his wryly regarding me. Earlier, it reminded me of Traci, kind of solemn and funny, all at the same time, like hers, but now there's something unpleasant sitting in back of it—the same place the hurt sat in Nina's eyes the night I first met her.

"She's sent other people to get the sword, you know."

I've been trying to avoid looking at it all night but now I can't stop my gaze from going to it. I remember thinking how big it was when I first stepped into the living room and stole a glance at it. No way it was going to fit into my handbag. I'd given up the idea of walking out with it pretty quick.

"What story did she tell you?" Martin went on. "That it belonged to her grandmother and it's the only thing she's got left to remind her of the old bag?"

Not grandmother, I think. Mother. But I don't say anything. One of the things I've learned working on the paper: If you can keep quiet, nine out of ten times the person you're with will feel obliged to fill the silence. You'd be surprised the kinds of things they'll tell you.

"Or did she tell you about the family curse," he asks, "and how the sword has to be sheathed for it to end?"

I still say nothing.

"Or did she tell you the truth?"

This time he plays the waiting game until I finally ask, "So what is the truth?"

"Well, it's all subjective, isn't it?"

There's an undercurrent of weirdness happening here that tells me it's really time to go now. I take a good swig of the brandy to fortify myself, then pick up my jacket and slip it on.

"I don't mean to sound so vague," he says before I get up. "It's just that, no matter what she's told you, it's only a piece of the truth. That's what I mean about it all being subjective."

I find myself nodding. What he's saying is something I learned my first week at the paper: There's no one thing called truth; just one's individual take on it.

"We're not married," he says.

"Uh-huh. It's kind of late for that line, isn't it?"

"No, you don't get it. She's not even human. She's this . . . this *thing*."

His gaze shifts to the sword above the mantel, then returns to mine. I realize the unpleasant thing I see sitting in the back of his eyes is fear.

"What are you saying?" I ask.

"She really is under a curse, except it's nothing like what she probably told you."

"She didn't say anything about a curse—except for being married to you."

"The way things look," Martin says, "I deserve that. But we're really not married. I don't have a hold over her. It's the other way around. She scares the shit out of me."

I shake my head. Considering the size of him and the size of her, I find that hard to believe.

"I met her a few years ago," he explains. "At a party. I made her a promise, that I'd help her break the curse that's on her, but I didn't. I broke my promise and she's been haunting me ever since."

Curses. Haunting. It's like he's trying to tell me Nina's a ghost. I'm beginning to wish that I'd just let it play out in the restaurant and gone on to my own place. By myself. Too late for that now. He's still sitting there, looking at me all expectantly, and I have to admit that while I think it's all a load of crock, I can't seem to check my curiosity. It's a bad habit I bring home from the office. It's probably why I applied for the job in the first place.

"So what's this curse?" I ask.

"She's trapped in the shape of that sword," he says, pointing to the mantel.

"Oh, please."

Nina passing as gay I can buy—I've been doing it myself. But passing as human as well?

"Look. I know what it sounds like. But it's true. She promised me a year of companionship—good company, great sex, whatever I wanted—and at the end of that year I had to fulfill my part of the bargain, but I couldn't go through with it."

"Which was?"

The only thing I'm really interested in now is how far he'll take all of this.

"The sword once had a scabbard," Martin says. "When it was sheathed, she could stay in human form. But the scabbard got lost or stolen or something—there was something enchanted about it as well. It kept its bearer free from all hurt and harm. Anyway, the way things are now, she can only be human for short bits of time before she has to return into the sword."

I give him a noncommittal "Uh-huh."

"The bargain I made," he says, "was that I'd sheathe the sword for her at the end of the year, but I couldn't do it."

"Why not?"

"Because I have to sheathe it in myself."

I sit up straighter. "What? You mean impale yourself on it—a kind of *seppuku* like the samurai used to do in Japan?"

He doesn't answer me, but goes on instead. "See, for the curse to be broken, I have to believe that it'll work while I do it. And I have to want to do it—you know, be a willing sacrifice. I can't do either."

I look at him, I read his fear, and realize that he really believes all of this.

"So why don't you just get rid of the sword?" I ask, which seems reasonable enough to me.

"I'm scared to. I don't know what'll happen to me if I do."

I think of Nina. I think of this big guy being scared of her and I have to shake my head.

"So . . . has Nina threatened you?"

He shakes his head. "No, she just stands there by the mantel, or at the foot of my bed, and looks at me. Haunts me. She won't talk to me anymore, she doesn't do anything but stare at me. It's driving me crazy."

Well, something sure is, I want to say. Instead I consider the sword, hanging up there on the wall. I try to imagine Nina's—what? Spirit? Essence?—trapped in that long length of blade. I can't even work up the pretense of belief.

"So give it to me," I say.

He blinks in confusion, then shakes his head again. "No, I can't do that. Something horrible will happen to me if I do."

"I don't think so," I tell him. "Nina specifically asked me to take the sword with me when I left. You say she's sent other people to get it. Doesn't it seem obvious that all she wants is the sword? Give it to me and we'll all be out of your life. Nina. The sword. Me." Your sanity, I add to myself, though maybe a good shrink can help you get some of it back.

"I . . ."

He looks from me to the sword, torn. Then he comes to a decision. He gets up and fetches a blanket, wraps the sword in it and hands it to me.

"Look," I say, staggering a little under its weight. "What you really should do is—"

"Just go," he tells me.

He doesn't physically throw me out, but it's close. Truth is, he looks so freaked about what he's doing that I'm happy to put as much distance as I can between us. I end up hauling the sword down to the street to where I parked my car. It won't fit in the trunk, so I put it on the backseat. I look up at the window of the apartment above me. Martin's turned all the lights off.

It's weird, I think, sliding into the driver's seat. He seemed so normal when I first picked him up in Huxley's, but then he turned out to be loopier than anyone I've ever met on this side of the Zebrowski Institute's doors. It just goes to show you. No wonder Nina wanted to leave him.

I stop at that thought, the car still in neutral. Except that wasn't why she said she wanted to leave him. I look up at the darkened apartment again, this time through my windshield. Though now that I think about it, if I were in her position, I probably wouldn't want to tell the truth about why I was leaving my husband either.

I shake my head. What a mess. Putting the car into gear, I drive myself home. I have a column due for the Monday paper and I don't know what it's going to be about yet. Still, I know this much—it won't be about swords.

6

Nina really was out of town, so Lucy couldn't call her. "I don't want to lie to him," she'd told Lucy. "That'd make me just as bad as he is." What about Nina's lying to her? Lucy wondered, but she knew she was willing to give Nina the benefit of the doubt, seeing how nuts her husband was. Besides, even if Nina wasn't out of town, the only number Lucy had for her was the same as Martin's—she'd looked his up as she was making herself a coffee on Sunday morning.

She'd left the sword where she'd dropped it last night—wrapped in its blanket on the floor in her hallway, right beside the front door—and hadn't looked at it since. Didn't want to look at it. It wasn't that she believed any of Martin's very weird story about the sword and Nina, so much as that something about the weapon gave her the creeps. No, that wasn't quite right. It was more that thinking about it made her feel odd—as though the air had grown thicker, or the hardwood floor had gone slightly spongy underfoot. Better not to think of it.

Saturday, she did some grocery shopping, but she stayed in with a video on Saturday night. Sunday afternoon, she went in to the office and worked on Monday's column—deciding to do a piece on cheap sources for fashion accessories. She finished it quickly and then spent a couple of hours trying to straighten out the mess on her desk without making any real noticeable progress. It was the story of her life. Sunday night, Nina called.

As soon as she recognized Nina's voice, Lucy looked down the hall to where the sword still lay and thought of what Martin had told her.

"I've got the sword," she said without any preamble. "It's here at my place. Do you want to come by to pick it up?"

"And take it where?" Nina asked. "Back to Martin's and my apartment?"

"Oh. I never thought of that. I guess you need to find a place to live first."

She hesitated a moment, but before she could offer her own couch as a temporary measure, Nina was talking again.

"I can't believe he just gave it to you," she said. "Did he give you a hard time? Was . . . seducing him . . . was it horrible?"

"It didn't go that far."

"But still," Nina said. "It couldn't have been pleasant."

"More like strange."

"Strange how?"

Was there a new note in Nina's voice? Lucy wondered. A hint of—what? Tension?

"Well, he hit on me just like you said he would," she said. "He picked me up at Huxley's after work, took me out for dinner and then back to—" she almost said "his" "—your place."

"I guess I'm not surprised."

"Anyway, as soon as we got to the apartment, almost the first thing he asked me was when I'd met you. Nina, he told me you guys were never married. He told me all kinds of weird things."

There was a moment's silence on the line, then Nina asked, "Did you believe him?"

"The stuff he was telling me was so crazy that I don't know what to believe," Lucy said. "But I want to believe you."

"I'll tell you everything," Nina said. "But not now. I've just got a few things to do and then I'll come see you."

Lucy could tell that Nina was about to hang up.

"What sort of things?" she asked, just to keep Nina on the line.

Nina laughed. "Oh you know. I just have to straighten my affairs, say goodbye to Martin, that kind of thing."

Lucy found herself remembering Martin's fear. Crazy as he was, the fear had been real. Why he should be scared of Nina, Lucy couldn't begin to imagine, but he had been afraid.

"Listen," she said, "you're not going to—"

"I have to run," Nina broke in. "I'll call you soon."

"—do anything crazy," Lucy finished.

But she was talking to a dead line.

Lucy stared at the phone for a long moment before she finally cradled the receiver. A nervous prickle crept up her spine and the air seemed to thicken. She turned to look at the sword again. It was still where she'd left it, wrapped in Martin's blanket, lying on the floor.

There's no such thing as an enchanted sword, she told herself. She knew that. But ever since leaving Martin's place last night there'd been a niggling little doubt in the back of her mind, a kind of "What if?" that she hadn't been able to completely ignore or refute with logic. She couldn't shake the feeling that *something* was about to happen and whatever it was was connected to the sword and Martin. And to Nina.

She stood up quickly and fetched her car keys from the coffee table. Maybe it was stupid, worrying the way she was, but she had to know. Had to be sure that the boundaries of what could be and what could not still existed as they always had. She left so quickly, she was still buttoning up her jacket when she reached the street.

It took her fifteen minutes to get to the apartment where Nina and Martin lived. She parked at the curb across from the building and studied their place on the third floor. The windows were all dark. There was no one on the street except for a man at the far end of the block who was poking through a garbage can with a stick.

Lucy sat there for five minutes before she reluctantly pulled away. She cruised slowly through the neighborhood, looking for Nina's familiar trim figure. Eventually the only thing left to do was drive back to her own apartment and wait for Nina to call. She sat up in bed with the telephone on the quilt beside her leg, trying to read because she knew she wouldn't be able to sleep. After a while she phoned Traci, nervous the whole time that Nina was trying to get through while she was tying up the line. She told Traci everything, but it made no more sense to Traci than it did to her.

"Weird," Traci said at last.

"Am I blowing this way out of proportion?" Lucy wanted to know.

She could almost feel Traci's smile across the telephone line.

"Well, it is a bit much," Traci said. "All this business with the sword and Nina. But I've always been one to trust my intuition. If you feel there's something weird going on, then I'm willing to bet that there is—something on a more logical level than curses and hauntings, mind you."

"So what do I do?"

Traci sighed. "Just what you're doing: wait. What else can you do?"

"I know. It's just . . ."

"You want some company?" Traci asked.

What Lucy wanted was Nina. She wanted to know that Martin had nothing to fear from her, that Nina wasn't about to do something that was going to get her into serious trouble. But Traci couldn't help her with any of that.

"No," she told her friend. "I'll be okay."

"Call me tomorrow."

"I will."

Finally she drifted off with the lights on, sitting up against the headboard, the book still open on her lap. She dreamed that the sword lay on the other side of the bed, talking to her in a low murmuring voice that could have belonged to anybody. When she woke, she couldn't remember what it had told her.

7

By nine o'clock, Monday morning, I'm a mess. Punchy from the weird dreams and getting so little sleep. Sick with worry. Nina still hasn't called and I'm thinking the worst. It kind of surprises me that the worst I imagine isn't that she's done something to Martin, but that she doesn't want to see me anymore.

I'm already late for work. I consider phoning in sick, but I know I can't stay at home—I'm already bouncing off the walls—so I go in to the office. I know I can check my machine for messages from there and at least I'll be able to find something to keep me busy.

I have this habit of going over the police reports file when I first get in. It's kind of a gruesome practice, reading the list of break-ins, robberies, rapes, and the like that occurred the night before, but I can't seem to shake it. It's not even my beat; I usually get assigned the soft stories. I think maybe the reason I do it is that it's a way of validating that, okay, so the city's going down the tubes, but I'm still safe. I'm safe. The people I know and love are safe. This kind of horrible thing goes on, but it doesn't really touch me. It's fueled by the same impulse that makes us all slow down at accidents and follow the news. Sometimes I think we don't so much want to be informed as have our own security validated.

This morning there's a report of an apparent suicide on a street that sounds familiar. They don't give the victim's name, but the street's all I need. Shit. It's Martin. It says, Caucasian male did a jump from his third-story apartment window, but I know it's Martin. The coroner's still waiting for the autopsy report; the cops are pretty much ruling out foul play. But I know better, don't I? Martin himself told me what'd happen if he got rid of the sword and he looked so terrified when I left his place Friday night.

But I still can't believe it of Nina. I can't believe all this crap he told me about her and the sword.

I've only been away from home for thirty-five minutes, but I immediately close the file and phone my apartment to check for messages. Nothing. Same as ten minutes ago—I called when I first got here.

There's nothing all day.

I try to stick it out, but in the end I have to leave work early. I start for home, but wind up driving by the apartment—looking for Nina, I tell myself, but of course she wouldn't be there, hanging around on the pavement where Martin hit. I know why I'm really doing this. Morbid curiosity. I look up at the windows, third floor. One of them's been boarded up.

I go home. Shower. Change. Then I hit the bars on Gracie Street, looking for Nina. The North Star. Neon Sister. Girljock. Skirts. No sign of her. I start to check out the hardcore places, the jack-and-jill-off scenes and clubs where the rougher trade hangs out. Still nothing. The last place I go into this blonde leatherette in a black push-up bra and hot pants smiles at me. I start to smile back, but then she makes a V with her fingers and flicks her tongue through them. I escape back up the stairs that let me into the place. I'm not sure what I am anymore—gay, straight, what—but one thing I know is I'm still not into casual sex.

Once outside, I lean against the front of the building, feeling just as lost as I did the night Traci took me under her wing. I don't know what to do anymore, where to turn. I start to look for a pay phone—I figure I can at least check my answering machine again—when someone grabs me by the arm. I yelp and pull free, but when I turn around, it's Nina I find standing beside me—not the blonde from the club I just left.

"Sorry," she says. "I didn't mean to make you jump like that."

She's smiling, but I can see she really means it. She leans forward and gives me a kiss on the lips. I don't know what to do, what to think. I'm so glad to see her, but so scared she had something to do with Martin's death. Not magic mumbo-jumbo, nothing like that. Just plain she couldn't take the shit from him anymore and it all got out of hand.

"Martin's dead," I say.

"I know. I was there."

My breath catches in my throat. "You . . . you didn't . . . ?"

I can't get it out, but she knows what I'm asking. She shakes her head. Taking my arm, she leads me off down the street.

"I think we have to talk," she tells me.

She leads me to my car, but I don't feel like I'm in any condition to drive. I start to go to the passenger's side.

"I can't drive," Nina tells me.

Right. So we sit there in my car, parked just off Gracie Street, looking out the windshield, not saying anything, not touching each other, just sitting there.

"What did he tell you about me?" Nina asks finally.

I look at her. Her face isn't much more than a silhouette in the illumination thrown by the streetlights outside. After a few moments, I clear my throat and start to talk, finishing with, "Is it true?"

"Mostly."

I don't know what to say. I want to think she's crazy but there's nothing about her that I associate with craziness.

"Where did you go after you called me?" I ask instead.

Nina hesitates, then says, "To the lake. To talk to my sister."

"Your sister?"

I hadn't stopped to think of it before, but of course she'd have family. We all do. But then Nina pulls that piece of normal all out of shape as well.

"She's one of the Ladies of the Lake," she says. "Bound to her sword, just like me. Just like all of us."

It's my turn to hesitate. Do I really want to feed this fantasy? But then I ask, "How many are you?"

"Seven of us—for seven swords. My oldest sister is bound to the one you'd know best: Excalibur."

I really have to struggle with what I'm hearing. I'd laugh, except Nina's so damn serious.

"But," I say. "When you're talking about a Lady of the Lake . . . you mean like in Tennyson? King Arthur and all that stuff?"

Nina nods. "The stories are pretty close, but they miss a lot."

I take a deep breath. "Okay. But that's in England. What would your sister be doing here? What are you doing here?"

"All lakes are aspects of the First Lake," Nina says. "Just as all forests remember the First Forest."

I can only look blankly at her.

Nina sighs. "As all men and women remember First Man and First Woman. And the fall from grace."

"You mean in Eden?"

Nina shakes her head. "Grace is what gives this world its worth, but there are always those who would steal it away, for the simple act of doing so. Grace shames a graceless people, so they strike out at it. Remember Martin told you about the scabbards that once protected our swords?"

"I guess. . . ."

"They had healing properties and when men realized that, they took the scabbards and broke them up, eliminating a little more of their grace and healing properties with each piece they took. That's why I'm in my present predicament. Of the seven of us, only two still have their swords, kept safe in their scabbards. Three more still retain ownership of their swords. Ailine—my sister—and I don't have even that. With our swords unsheathed, we've lost most of our freedom. We're bound into the metal for longer and longer periods of time. A time will come, I suppose, when we'll be trapped in the metal forever."

She studies me for a long moment, then sighs again. "You don't believe any of this, do you?"

I'm honest with her. "It's hard."

"Of course. It's easy to forget marvels when your whole life you're taught to ignore them."

"It's just—"

"Lucy," Nina says. "I'll make the same bargain with you that I made with Martin. I'll stay with you for a year, but then you must hold up your side."

I shake my head. I don't even have to think about it.

"But you wanted to sleep with me," Nina says. "You wanted my love."

"But not like this. Not bargaining for it like it's some kind of commodity. That's not love."

Nina looks away. "I see," she says, her gaze locked on something I can't see.

"Tell me what you'd want me to do," I say.

Nina's attention returns to me. "There's no point. You don't believe."

"Tell me anyway."

"You must take the sword inside yourself. You must do it willingly. And you must believe that by doing so, you are freeing me."

"I just stick it into myself?"

"Something like that," Nina says. "It would be clearer if you believed."

"And what would happen to me?" I ask. "Would I die?"

"We all die, sooner or later."

"I know that," I say, impatiently. "But would I die from doing this?"

Nina shakes her head. "No. But you'd be changed."

"Changed how?"

"I don't know. It's—" She hesitates, then plunges quickly on. "I've never heard of it being done before."

"Oh."

We look some more out the windshield. The street we're on is pretty empty, cars parked, but not much traffic, vehicular or pedestrian. Over on Gracie we can see the nightlife's still going strong. I want to ask her, Why didn't you tell me the truth before? but I already know. I don't believe her now so what difference would having heard it a few days earlier have made?

"Did you love Martin?" I ask instead. "I mean, at first."

"I'm not sure what love is."

I guess nobody really does, I think. Is what I'm feeling for Nina love? This feeling that's still swelling inside me, under the confusion and jumpiness—is it love? People die for love. It happens. But surely they *know* when they make the sacrifice?

"I really didn't kill him," she tells me. "I went to the apartment—I'm not sure why or what I meant to do—and let myself in. When he saw me, he went crazy. He looked terrified. When I took a step closer, he threw himself out the window—straight through the glass and all. He didn't say anything and he didn't give me a chance to speak either."

"He told me he was scared."

Nina nods. "But I don't know why. He had no reason to be scared of me. If I hadn't harmed him in the two years since he failed to keep his side of our bargain, why should he think that I'd hurt him now?"

I have no answer to that. Only Martin could explain it, but he'd taken the secret with him on his three-story plunge to the pavement below his window.

"I should go," Nina says then, but she makes no move to open the door.

"What about the sword?" I ask.

She turns to me. My eyes are adjusted enough to the vagaries of the lighting to see the expression on her face, but I can't figure it out. Sadness? My own feelings returned? Fear? Maybe a mix of the three.

"Would you do this for me?" she asks. "Would you bury the sword—in hallowed ground?"

"You mean like in a churchyard?"

She shakes her head. "It will need an older hallowing than that. There is a place where the river meets the lake."

I know where she's talking about. The City Commission keeps the lawns perfectly groomed around there, but there's this one spot right on the lake shore where a stand of old pines has been left to make a little wild acre. The trees there haven't been touched since the city was first founded, back in the eighteenth century.

"Bury the sword there," she tells me. "Tonight. Before the sun rises."

I nod. "What'll happen to you?"

"Ailine says it would let me sleep. Forever." She smiles, but it doesn't touch her eyes. "Or at least until someone digs it up again, I suppose."

"I . . . I'd do this other thing," I say, "but I'm too scared."

She nods, understanding. "And you don't believe."

She says it without recrimination. And she doesn't say anything at all about love, about how, to make the sacrifice willingly, I'd have to really love her. And she's right. I don't believe. And if I love her, I don't love her enough.

She leans across the seat and gives me a kiss. I remember the last time she did this. There was so much promise. In her kiss. In her eyes. Now she's only saying goodbye. I want to talk to her. I want to explain it all over again. But I just let her go. Out of the car. Down the street. Out of my life.

There's a huge emptiness inside me after she's gone. Maybe what hurts the most is the knowledge I hold that I can't let go—that I love her, but I don't love her enough. She asked too much of me, I tell myself, but I'm not sure if it's something I really believe or if I'm trying to convince myself that it's true to try and make myself feel better. It doesn't work.

I drive home to get the sword. I unwrap it, there in my hall, and hold it in my hands, trying to get some sense of Nina from it. But it's just metal. Eventually I wrap it up again and take it down to my car. I get a shovel from the toolshed behind the building. It belongs to the guy who lives on the ground floor, but I don't think he'll miss it. I'll have it back before he even knows it's gone.

And that's how I get here, digging a grave for a sword in hallowed ground. I can hear the lake against the shore, the wind sighing in the pines above. I can't hear the city at all, though it's all around me. Hallowed ground—hallowed by something older than what I was taught about in Sunday school, I guess. Truth is, I turned into an agnostic since those long-ago innocent days. I was just a girl then, didn't even know about sapphic impulses, little say think I might be feeling them.

It's easier to dig in amongst the roots of these pines than I would have thought possible, but it still takes me a long time to get the grave dug. I keep stopping to listen to the wind and the sound of the lake, the waves lapping against the shore. I keep stopping to look at the sword and the minutes leak away in little fugue states. I don't know where my mind goes. I just suddenly find myself blinking beside the grave, gaze locked on the long length of the sword. Thinking of Nina. Wanting to find the necessary belief and love to let me fill the emptiness I feel inside.

Finally it's getting on to the dawn. The grave's about four feet deep. It's enough. I'm just putting things off now. It's all so crazy—I *know* it's crazy—but I can't help but feel that it really is Nina I'm getting ready to lay in the hole and cover over with dirt.

I consider wrapping the sword back up again, but the blanket was Martin's and somehow it doesn't feel right. I pick the sword up and cradle it for a moment, as though I'm holding a child, a cold and still child with only one long limb. I touch the blade with a fingertip. It's not particularly sharp. I study the tip of the blade in the moonlight. You'd have to really throw yourself on it for it to pierce the skin and impale you.

I think maybe Nina's craziness is contagious. I find myself wishing I loved Nina enough to have done this thing for her, to believe, to trust, to be brave—crazy as it all is. I find myself sitting up, with the sword tip lying on my knees. I open my blouse and prop the sword up, lay the tip against my skin, between my breasts, just to see how it feels. I find myself leaning forward, putting pressure on the tip, looking down at where the metal presses against my skin.

I feel as though I've slipped into an altered state of consciousness. I look down to where the sword meets my skin and the point's gone, it's inside me, an inch, two inches. I don't feel anything. There's no pain. There's no blood. There's only this impossible moment like a miracle where the sword's slipping inside me, more and more of its length, the harder I push against it. I'm bent almost double now and still it going inside me, inch after inch. It doesn't come out my back, it's just being swallowed by my body. Finally I reach out with my hands, close my fingers around each side of the hilt, and push it up inside me, all the rest of the way.

And pass out.

8

When I come to, the air's lighter. I can't see the sun yet, but I can feel its light seeping through the trees. I can still hear the lake and the wind in the pines above me, but I can hear the traffic from the city, too.

I sit up. I look at the grave and the shovel. I look at the blanket. I look for the sword, but it's gone. I lift my hands to my chest and feel the skin between my breasts. I remember the sword sliding into my chest last night, but the memory feels like a hallucinatory experience.

No, I tell myself. Believe. I hear Nina's voice in my mind, hear her telling me,

It's easy to forget marvels when your whole life you're taught to ignore them, and tell myself: Don't invalidate a miracle because you've been taught they're not real. Trust yourself. Trust the experience. And Nina. Trust Nina.

But she's not here. My body might have swallowed the sword, impossibly sheathing the long length of its metal in my flesh, but she's not here.

My fingers feel a bump on my skin and I look down to see I've got a new birthmark, equidistant from each of my breasts. It looks like a cross. Or a sword, standing on its point. . . .

I feel so calm. It seems as though I should be either freaking out completely or delirious with wonder and awe, but there's only the calm. I sit there for a long time, running my finger across the bump of my new birthmark, then finally I button up my blouse. I fill the grave—this goes a lot quicker than digging it did—and cover up the raw dirt with pine needles. I wrap the shovel in my blanket and walk back to where I parked my car on Battersfield Road.

9

Traci has to know the whole story, of course, so I tell her everything. I don't know how much she believes, but crazy as it all sounds, she believes that I believe, and that's enough for her. I'm afraid of getting involved with her at first—afraid that I'm turning to her on the rebound from what I never quite had with Nina but certainly felt for her. But it doesn't work that way. Or if I am rebounding, it's in the right direction.

I remember Nina telling me that I'd be changed if I—I guess absorbed the sword is the best way to put it—but that she didn't know how. I do now. It's not a big thing. My world hasn't changed—though I guess my view of it has to some degree. What's happened is that I'm more decisive. I've taken control of my life. I'm not drifting anymore—either in my personal life or on the job. I don't go for the safe, soft stories anymore. One person can't do a whole lot about all the injustice in the world, but I'm making damn sure that people hear about it. That we all do what we can about it. I'm not looking for a Pulitzer; I just want to make sure that I leave things a little better behind me when I go.

Six months or so after Traci and I start living together, she turns to me one night and asks me why it didn't disappoint me that Nina never came back to me after I did what she asked.

"It's because I remember what she told me in that dream I had the night Martin died," I explain. "You know, when I dreamed the sword was lying on the bed beside me and talking to me? I didn't remember when I woke, but it came back to me a few days after I got back from the pine grove."

Traci gives me a poke with her finger. "So aren't you going to tell me?" she says when I've fallen silent.

I smile. "She said that if she was freed, she might not be able to come back. That really being human, instead of passing for one, might mean that she'd be starting her life all over again as an infant and she wouldn't remember what had gone before."

Now it's Traci's turn to fall silent. "Is that why you want us to have a kid?" she asks finally.

With modern medicine, anything's possible, right? Or at least something as basic as artificial insemination.

"I like to think she's waiting for us to get it together," I say.

"So you're planning on a girl."

"Feels right to me."

Traci reaches over and tracks the contour of my sword birthmark with a finger. "Think she'll have one of these?"

"Does it matter?" I ask.

"Doesn't matter at all," Traci says. She rolls over to embrace me. "And I guess it means we don't have to worry about what to name her either."

I snuggle in close. I love finally knowing who I am; loving and being loved for who I am. I just hope that wherever and whenever Nina is reborn, she'll be as lucky as I feel I am.

Held Safe by Moonlight and Vines

1

Lillie's in the graveyard again, looking for ghosts. She just can't stay away.

"I'm paying my respects," she says, but it doesn't make sense.

These days All Souls Cemetery's about as forgotten as the people buried in it. The land belongs to some big company now and they're just waiting for the paperwork to go through at city hall. One day soon they'll be moving what's left of the bodies, tearing down all those old-fashioned mausoleums and crypts and putting up something shiny and new. Who's going to miss it? Nobody goes there now except for the dealers with their little packets of oblivion and junkies looking for a fix.

The only people who care about the place are from the Crowsea Heritage Society. And Lillie. Everybody else just wants to see it go. Everybody else likes the idea of making a place gone wild safe again, never mind they don't put it quite that way. But that's what they're thinking. You can see it in the back of their eyes when they talk about it.

See, there's something that scares most people about the night, something that rises out of old memories, out of the genetic soup we all carry around inside us. Monsters in closets when we were kids and further back still, a long way, all the way back to the things waiting out there where the fire's light can't reach. It's not something anybody talks about, but I know that's what they see in All Souls because I can see it, too.

It's got nothing to do with the drug deals going down. People know a piece of the night is biding in there, thinking about them, and they can't wait to see it go. Even the dealers. You see them hanging around by the gates, money moves from one hand to the other, packets of folded paper follow suit, everything smooth, moves like magic—they're fearless, these guys. But they don't go any further in than they have to. Nobody does except for Lillie.

"There's been nobody buried there in fifty years," I tell her, but that just gets her back up. "All the more reason to give those old souls some respect," she says.

But that's not it. I know she's looking for ghosts. Thing is, I don't know why.

2

Alex's problem is he wants an answer for everything. All he ever does is go around asking questions. Never lets a thing lie. Always has to know what's going on and why. Can't understand that some things don't have reasons. Or that some people don't feel like explaining themselves. They just do what feels right. Get an idea in their head and follow it through and don't worry about what someone else is going to think or if anybody else understands.

In Alex's world there's only right and wrong, black and white. Me, I fall through the cracks of that world. In my head, it's all grey. In my head, it's all like walking in the twilight, a thousand shades of moonglow and dusky skies and shadow.

He thinks of me sitting here in the dark, all those old stone mausoleums standing around me, old and battered like the tenements leaning against each other on the streets where we grew up, and it spooks him. But All Souls comforts me, I don't know why. Half the trees inside are dead, the rest are dying. Most of the grass is yellow and brown and the only flowers in this place these days grow on weeds, except in one corner where a scraggly old rose bush keeps on trying, tough old bugger doesn't know enough to give up. The stone walls are crumbling down, the cast-iron gates haven't worked in years. There's a bunch of losers crowded around those gates, cutting deals, more nervous of what's here, inside, than of the man showing up and busting them. I come in over the wall and go deep, where the shadows hide me, and they never even know I'm here. Nobody does, except for Alex and he just doesn't understand.

I know what Alex sees when he looks at this place. I see it, too, at first, each time I come. But after a while, when I'm over the wall and inside, walking the narrow lanes in between the stones and tombs, uneven cobbles underfoot, the shadows lying thick everywhere I look, it gets different. I go someplace else. I don't hear the dealers, I don't see the junkies. The cemetery's gone, the city's gone, and me, I'm gone, too.

The only thing still with me are the walls, but they're different in that other place. Not so worn down. The stones have been fit together without mortar, each one cunningly placed against the other and solid. Those walls go up ten feet and you'd have to ram them with a bulldozer before they'd come down.

Inside, it's a garden. Sort of. A wild place. A tangle of bushes and briars, trees I've got no name for and vines hanging everywhere. A riot of flowers haunts the ground cover, pale blossoms that catch the moonlight and hold it in their petals.

The moonlight. That moon is so big in this place it feels like it could swallow the world. When I stand there in the wild garden and look up at it, I feel small, like I'm no bigger than the space of time between one moment and the next, but not the same way I feel small anywhere else. Where I come from there are millions of people living everywhere and each one of them's got his or her own world. It's so easy to lose a part of yourself in those worlds, to just find yourself getting sucked away until there's next to nothing left of who you are. But I don't have to be careful about that here. There aren't any of those millions of people here and that moon, it doesn't swallow up who I am, its golden light fills me up, reveling in what it knows me to be. I'm small in its light, sure, but the kind of small that can hold everything there is to be held. The moon's just bigger, that's all. Not more important than me, just different.

Those junkies don't know what they're missing, never getting any further inside the gates than the first guy in a jean vest with the right price.

3

Trouble is, Lillie doesn't understand danger. She's never had to go through the hard times some of us did, never really seen what people can do to each other when they're feeling desperate or just plain mean. She grew up poor, like everybody else in our neighborhood, but her family loved her and she didn't get knocked around the way those of us who didn't have her kind of parents did. She was safe at home; out on the streets, I always looked after her, made sure the hard cases left her alone.

I'm working as a bouncer at Chic Cheeks the night I hear she's been going to All Souls, so I head down there after my shift to check things out. It's a good thing I do. Some of the guys hanging around by the gates have gotten bored and happened to spot her, all alone in there and looking so pretty. Guess they decided they were going to have themselves a little fun. Bad move. But then they didn't expect me to come along.

I remember a teacher I had in junior high telling me one time how wood and stone make poor conductors. Well, they conduct pain pretty good, as those boys find out. I introduce one of them face-first to a tombstone and kind of make a mess of his nose, knock out a couple of teeth. His pals aren't chickenshit, I'll give them that much. I hear the *snickt* of their blades snapping open, so I drop the first guy. He makes some kind of gurgling noises when he hits the ground and rolls onto my boot. I push him away and then ignore him. He's too busy feeling his pain to cause me any immediate grief. I turn to his buddies, a little pissed off now, but we don't get into it.

"Oh Christ," one of them says, recognizing me.

"We didn't mean nothing, Al," the other one says.

They're putting their knives away, backing up.

"We knew she was one of your people, we never would've touched her. I swear it, man."

Guess I've got a bit of a rep. Nothing serious. I'm not some big shot. What it's got to do with is my old man.

Crazy Eddie is what they used to call him on the streets. Started running numbers for the bosses back when he was a kid, then moved into collections, which is where he got his name. You don't want to think it of your own flesh and blood, but the old man was a psycho. He'd do any crazed thing came to mind if you couldn't pay up. You're in for a few yards, you better cough it up, don't matter what you've got to do to get the money, because he'd as soon as cut your throat as collect the bread.

After a while the bosses started using him for hits, the kind where they're making a statement. Messy, crazy hits. He did that for years until he got into a situation he couldn't cut his way out of. Cops took him away in a bunch of little bags.

Man, I'll never forget that day. I was doing a short stretch in the county when I found out and I near laughed myself sick. I'd hated that old bastard for the way he'd treated ma, for what he did to my sister Juney. He used to kick the shit out of me on a regular basis, but I could deal with that. It was the things he did to them. . . . I knew one day I'd take him down, didn't matter he was my old man. I just hadn't got around to it yet. Hadn't figured out a way to let the bosses know it was personal, not some kind of criticism of their business.

Anyway, I'm not mean like the old man was, I'll tell you that straight-off, but I purely don't take crap from anybody. I don't have to get into it too much anymore. People take a look at me now and think, blood is blood. They see my old man's crazy eyes when they look in mine, and they find some other place to be than where I'm standing.

So I make the point with these boys that they don't want to mess with Lillie, and all it takes is a tap against a tombstone for them to get the message. I let them get their pal and take off, then I go to see what Lillie's doing.

It's the strangest thing. She's just standing there by one of those old stone mausoleums, swaying back and forth, looking off into the space between a couple of those stone crypts. I scratch my head, and take a closer look myself. She's mesmerized by something, but damned if I know what. I can hear her humming to herself, still doing that swaying thing, mostly with her upper body, back and forth, smiling that pretty smile of hers, short black hair standing up at attention the way it always does. I'm forever trying to talk her into growing it long, but she laughs at me whenever I do.

I guess I watch her for about an hour that night. I remember thinking she'd been sampling some of the dealers' wares until she suddenly snaps out of it. I fade back into the shadows at that point. Don't want her to think I've been spying on her. I'm just looking out for her, but she doesn't see it that way. She gets seriously pissed at me and I hate having Lillie mad at me.

She walks right by me, still humming to herself. I can see she's not stoned, just Lillie-strange. I watch her climb up some vines where one of the walls is broken and low, and then she's gone. I go out the front way, just to remind the boys what's what, and catch up with Lillie a few blocks away, casual-like. Don't ask her where she's been. Just say how-do, make sure she's okay without letting on I'm worried, and head back to my own place.

I don't know exactly when it is I realize she's looking for ghosts in there. It just comes to me one day, slips in sideways when I'm thinking about something else. I try talking to her about it from time to time but all she does is smile, the way only she can.

"You wouldn't understand," she says.

"Try me."

She shakes her head. "It's not something *to* understand," she says. "It's just something you do. The less you worry at it, the more it makes sense."

She's right. I don't understand.

4

There's a boy living in the garden. He reminds me a little of Alex. It's not that they look the same. This kid's all skin and bones, held together with wiry muscles. Naked and scruffy, crazy tangled hair full of burrs and twigs and stuff, peach-fuzz vying with a few actual beard hairs, dink hanging loose when he's not holding onto it—I guess you've got to do something with your hands when you don't have pockets. Alex, he's like a fridge with arms and legs. Big, strong, and loyal as all get-out. Not school-smart, but bright. You couldn't pick a couple of guys that looked less alike.

The reason they remind me of each other is that they're both a little feral. Wild things. Dangerous if you don't approach them right.

I get to the garden one night and the trees are full of grackles. They're feeding on berries and making a racket like I've never heard before. I know it's an unkindness of ravens and a murder of crows, but what do you call that many grackles all together? I'm walking around, peering up at them in the branches, smiling at the noise, when I see the boy sitting up in one of the trees, looking back down at me.

Neither of us says anything for a long time. There's just the racket of the birds playing against the silence we hold between us.

"Hey there," I say finally. "Is this your garden?"

"It's my castle."

I smile. "Doesn't look much like a castle."

"Got walls," he tells me.

"I suppose."

He looks a little put out. "It's a start."

"So when are you going to start building the rest?" I ask.

He looks at me, the way a child looks at you when you've said something stupid.

"Go away," he says.

I decide I can be as much of an asshole as he's being and play the why game with him.

"Why?" I ask.

"Because I don't like you."

"Why?"

"Because you're stupid."

"Why?"

"I don't know. Guess you were born that way."

"Why?"

"Have to ask your parents that."

"Why?"

"Because I don't know."

"Why?"

He finally catches on. Pulling a twig free from the branch he's sitting on, he throws it at me. I duck and it misses. When I look back up, he's gone. The noise of the grackles sounds like laughter now.

"Guess I deserve that," I say.

I don't see the boy for a few visits after that, but the next time I do, he pops up out of the thick weeds underfoot and almost gives me a heart attack.

"I could've just snuck up on you and killed you," he tells me. "Just like that."

He leans against a tree, one hand hanging down in between his legs like he's got a piece of treasure there.

"Why would you want to do that?" I ask.

His eyes narrow. "I don't want to play the why game again."

"I'm not. I really want to know."

"It's not a thing I do or don't want to do," he tells me. "I'm just saying I could. It was a piece of information, that's all."

There's something incongruous about the way he says this—innocent and scary, all at the same time. It reminds me of when I was a little girl, how it took me the longest time to admit that I could ever like a boy, they were all such assholes. All except Alex. I wouldn't have minded so much if he'd pulled my hair or pushed me on the schoolyard, but he never did. He was always so sweet and polite to me and then after classes, he'd go out and beat up the guys that had been mean to me. I guess I was flattered, at first, but then I realized it wasn't a very nice thing to do. You have to understand, we're both still in grade school when this is going on. Things weren't the same back then the way they are for kids now. We sure never had to walk through metal detectors to get into the school.

Anyway, I asked him to stop and he did. At least so far as I know, he did. I wonder sometimes, though. Sometimes my boyfriends have the weirdest accidents—walking into doors and stuff like that.

5

This one time Lillie's going out with this college-type. Dave, his name is. Dave Taylor. Nice enough looking joe, I suppose, but he's not exactly the most faithful guy you'd ever meet. Happened to run into him getting a little on the side one night, so I walk up to his table and tell him I have to have a word with him, would his lady friend excuse us for a moment? He doesn't want to step outside, so I suggest to his lady friend that she go powder her nose, if she understands my meaning.

"So what the hell's this all about?" Dave asks when she's gone. He's blustering, trying to make up for the face he feels he lost in front of his girlfriend.

"I'm a friend of Lillie's," I tell him.

"Yeah? So?"

"So I don't like the idea of her getting hurt."

"Hey, what she doesn't know—"

"I'm not discussing this," I say. "I'm telling you."

The guy shakes his head. "Or what? I suppose you're going to go running to her and—"

I hit him once, a quick jab to the head that rocks him back in his seat. Doesn't even break the skin on my knuckles, but I can see he's hurting.

"I don't care who you go out with, or if you cheat on them," I say, keeping my voice conversational. "I just don't want you seeing Lillie any more."

He's holding a hand to his head where the skin's going all red. Looks a little scared like I'm going to hit him again, but I figure I've already made my point.

"Do we understand each other?" I ask him.

He gives me a quick nod. I start to leave, then pause for a moment. He gives me a worried look.

"And Dave," I say. "Let's not get stupid about this. No one's got to know we had this little talk, right?"

"What . . . whatever you say. . . ."

6

I wonder about Alex—worry about him, I guess you could say. He never seems to be happy or sad. He just is. It's not like he's cold, keeps it all bottled in or anything, and he's always got a smile for me, but there doesn't seem to be a whole lot of passion in his life. He doesn't talk much, and never about himself. That's another way he and the boy in the garden differ. The boy's always excited about something or other, always ready for any sort of mad escapade. And he loves to talk.

"Old castle rock," the boy tells me one time. His eyes are gleaming with excitement. "That's what these walls are made of. They were part of this castle on the other side and now they're here. There's going to be more of the castle coming, I just know there is. Towers and turrets and stables and stuff."

"When's the rest of it going to come?" I ask.

He shrugs his bony shoulders. "Dunno. Could be a long time. But I can wait."

"Where's it coming from?" I ask then.

"I told you. From the other side."

"The other side of what?"

He gives me that look again, the one that says don't you know *anything*?

"The other side of the walls," he says.

I've never looked over the walls—not from the garden. That's the first thing Alex would have done. He may not have passion in his life, but he's sure got purpose. He's always in the middle of something, always knows what's going on. Never finished high school, but he's smarter than most people I meet because he's never satisfied until he's got everything figured out. He's in the public library all the time, reading, studying stuff. Never does anything with what he knows, but he sure knows a lot.

I walk over to the nearest of those tall stone walls and the boy trails along behind me, joins me when I start to go up. It's an easier climb than you might think, plenty of finger- and toe-holds, and we scale it like a couple of monkeys, grinning at each other when we reach the top. It's flat up there, with lots of room on the rough stone to sit and look out, only there's nothing to see. Just fog, thick, the way it rolls into the city from the lake sometimes. It's like the world ends on the other side of these walls.

"It's always like this," the boy says.

I turn to look at him. My first impression was that he'd come in over the walls himself and I never learned anything different to contradict it, but now I'm not so sure anymore. I mean, I knew this garden was someplace else, someplace magical that you could only reach the way you get to Neverneverland—you have to really want to get there. You might stumble in the first time, but after that you have to be really determined to get back in. But I also thought the real world was still out there, on the other side of the garden's magic, held back only by the walls.

"Where did you come from?" I ask him.

He give me this look that manages to be fierce and sad, all at the same time.

"Same place as you," he says and touches a closed fist to his heart. "From the hurting world. This is the only place I can go where they can't get to me, where no one can hurt me."

I shake my head. "I didn't come here looking for sanctuary. I'm not running from anything."

"Then why are you here?"

I think of Alex and the way he's always talking about ghosts, but it's not that either. I never really think about it, I just come. Alex is the one with the need to have answers to every question. Not me. For me the experience has been enough of and by itself. But now that I think about it, now that I realize I want an answer, I find I don't have one.

"I don't know," I say.

"I thought you were like me," the boy says.

He sounded disappointed. Like I've disappointed him. He sounds angry, too. I want to say something to mollify him, but I can't find those words either. I reach out a hand, but he jerks away. He stands up, looks at me like I've turned into the enemy. I guess, in his eyes, I have. If I'm not with him, then I'm against him.

"I would never hurt you," I finally say. "I've never hurt anybody."

"That's what you think," he says.

Then he dives off the top of the wall, dives into the fog. I grab for him, but I'm not fast enough. I hold my breath, waiting to hear him hit the ground, but there's no sound. The fog swallows him and I'm alone on the top of the wall. I feel like I've missed something, something important. I feel like it was right there in front of me, all along, but now it's gone, dove off the wall with the boy and I've lost my chance to understand it.

The next time I come to the garden, everything's the same, but different. The boy's not here. I've come other times, lots of times, and he hasn't been here, but this time I feel he won't be back, won't ever be back, and I miss him. I don't know why. It's not like we had a whole lot in common. It's not like we had long, meaningful conversations, or were in love with each other or anything. I mean, he was just a kid, like a little brother, not a lover. But I miss him the way I've missed a lover when the relationship ends.

I feel guilty, too. Maybe this place isn't a sanctuary for me, but it was for him. A walled, wild garden, held safe by moonlight and vines. His castle. What if I've driven him away forever? Driven him back to what he called the hurting world.

I hate that idea the most, the idea that I've stolen the one good thing he had in a life that didn't have anything else. But I don't know what to do about it, how to call him back. I'd trade my coming here for his in a moment, only how can I tell him that? I don't even know his name.

7

Lillie doesn't leave the graveyard this night. I watch her sitting there on the step of one of those old mausoleums, sitting there all hunched up, sitting there all night. Finally, dawn breaks in the east, swallows the graveyard's spookiness. It's just an old forgotten place now, fallen in on itself and waiting for the wreckers' ball. The night's gone and taken the promise of danger away with it. I go over to where Lillie is and sit down beside her on the steps. I touch her arm.

"Lillie?" I say. "Are you okay?"

She turns to look at me. I'm expecting her to be mad at me for being here. She's got to know I've been following her around again. But all she does is give me a sad look.

"Did you ever lose something you never knew you had?" she asks.

"I only ever wanted one thing," I tell her, "but I never had it to lose."

"I don't even know what it is that I've lost," she says. "I just know something's gone. I had a chance to have it, to hold it and cherish it, but I let it go."

The early morning sunlight's warm on my skin, but a shiver runs through me all the same. I think maybe she's talking about ghosts. Maybe there really are ghosts here. I get the crazy idea that maybe we're ghosts, that we died and don't remember it. Or maybe only one of us did.

"What was the one thing you wanted that you never got?" she asks.

It's something I would never tell her. I promised myself a long time ago that I'd never tell her because I knew she deserved better. But that crazy idea won't let go, that we're dead, or one of us is, and it makes me tell her.

"It's you," I say.

8

Did you ever hear someone tell you something you always knew but it never really registered until they put it into words? That's what happens to me when Alex tells me he loves me, that he's always loved me.

His voice trails off and I look at him, really look at him. He almost flinches under my gaze. I can tell he doesn't want to be here, that he wishes he'd never spoken, that he feels a hurt swelling up inside him that he would never have to experience if he'd kept his feelings to himself. He reminds me of the boy, the way the boy looked before he dove off the wall into the fog, not the anger, but the sadness.

"Why did you never say anything before this?" I finally ask.

"I couldn't," he says. "And anyway. Look at us, you and me. We grew up in the same neighborhood, sure, but . . ." He shrugs. "You deserve better than me."

I have to smile. This is so Alex. "Oh, right. And who decided that?"

Alex chooses not to answer me. "You were always different," he says instead. "You were always the first on the block with a new sound or a new look, but you weren't following trends. It's like they followed you. And you never lost that. Anyone looks at you and they can tell there's nothing holding you back. You can do anything, go any-where. The future's wide open for you, always was, you know what I'm saying? The streets never took their toll on you."

Then why am I still living in Foxville? I want to ask him. How come my star didn't take me to some nice uptown digs? But I know what he's talking about. It's not really about where I can go as much as where I've been.

"I was lucky," I say. "My folks treated me decently."

"And you deserved it."

"Everybody deserves to be treated decently," I tell him.

"Well, sure."

We grew up in the same building before my parents could afford a larger apartment down the block. My mom used to feel sorry for Alex's mother and we'd go over to visit when Crazy Eddie wasn't home. I'd play with Alex and his little sister, our moms would pretend our lives were normal, that none of us were dirt poor, everybody dreaming of moving to the 'burbs. Some of our neighbors did, but most of us couldn't afford it and still can't. Of course the way things are going now, you're not any safer or happier in the 'burbs than you are in the inner city. And living here, at least we've got some history.

But we never thought about that kind of thing at the time because we were just kids. Older times, simpler times. I smile, remembering how Alex always treated me so nice, right from the first.

"And then, of course, I had you looking out for me, too," I say.

"You still do."

I hadn't really got around to thinking what he was doing here in All Souls at this time of the morning, but now it makes sense. I don't know how many times I've had to ask him not to follow me around. It gives some people the creeps, but I know Alex isn't some crazed stalker, fixated on me. He means well. He really is just looking out for me. But it's a weird feeling all the same. I honestly thought I'd got him to stop.

"You really don't have to be doing this," I tell him. "I mean, it was kind of sweet when we were kids and you kept me from being bullied in the playground, but it's not the same now."

"You know the reason the dealers leave you alone?" he asks.

I glance toward the iron gates at the other end of the graveyard, but there's no one there at the moment. The drug market's closed up for the morning.

"They never knew I was here," I say.

Alex shakes his head and that's enough. He doesn't have to explain. I know the reputation he has in the neighborhood. I feel a chill and I don't know if it's from the close call I had or the fact that I live in the kind of world where a woman can't go out by herself. Probably both.

"It's still not right," I say. "I appreciate your looking out for me, really I do, but it's not right, your following me around the way you do. You've got to get a life, Alex."

He hangs his head and I feel like I've just reprimanded a puppy dog for doing something it thought was really good.

"I know," he mumbles. He won't look at me. "I . . . I'm sorry, Lillie."

He gets up and starts to walk away. I look at his broad back and suddenly I'm thinking of the boy from the garden again. I'm seeing his sadness and anger, the way he dove off the wall into the fog and out of my life. I'm remembering what I said to him, that I would never hurt him, that I've never hurt anyone. And I remember what he said to me, just before he jumped.

That's what you think.

I'm not stupid. I know I'm not responsible for someone falling in love with me. I can't help if it they get hurt because maybe I don't love them back. But this isn't anyone. This is Alex. I've known him longer than maybe anyone I know. And if he's looked out for me, I've looked out for him, too. I stood up for him when people put him down. I visited him in the county jail when no one else did. I took him to the hospital that time the Creevy brothers left him for dead on the steps of his apartment building.

I know that for all his fierceness, he's a sweet guy. Dangerous, sure, but underneath that toughness there's no monster like his old man was. Given a different set of circumstances, a different neighborhood to grow up in, maybe, a different father, definitely, he could have made something of himself. But he didn't. And now I'm wondering if looking out for me was maybe part of what held him back. If I'd gotten myself out of the neighborhood, maybe he would have, too. Maybe we could both have been somebody.

But none of that's important right now. So maybe I'm not in love with Alex. So what? He's still my friend. He opened his heart to me and it's like I didn't even hear him.

"Alex!" I call after him.

He pauses and turns. There's nothing hopeful in the way he looks, there's not even curiosity. I get up from where I've been sitting and go to where he's standing.

"I've got to let this all sink in," I tell him. "You caught me off guard. I mean, I never even guessed you felt the way you do."

"I understand," he says.

"No, you don't. You're the best friend I ever had. I just never thought of us as a couple. Doesn't mean all of a sudden I hate you or something."

He shrugs. "I never should have said anything," he says.

I shake my head. "No. What you should have done is said something a lot sooner. The way I see it, your big problem is you keep everything all bottled up inside. You've got to let people know what you're thinking."

"That wouldn't change anything."

"How do you know? When I was a kid I had the hugest crush on you. And later, I kept expecting you to ask me out, but you never did. Got so's I just never thought of you in terms of boyfriend material."

"So what're you saying?"

I smile. "I don't know. You could ask me to go to a movie or something."

"Do you want to go to a movie?"

"Maybe. Let me buy you breakfast and we'll talk about it."

9

So I'm trying to do like Lillie says, talk about stuff that means something to me, or at least I do it with her. She asks me once what I'd like to do with my life, because she can't see much future in my being a bouncer for a strip joint for the rest of my life. I tell her I've always wanted to paint and instead of laughing, she goes out and buys me a little tin of watercolors and a pad of paper. I give it a go and she tells me I'm terrible, like I don't know it, but takes the first piece I do and hangs it on her fridge.

Another time I tell her about this castle I used to dream about when I was a kid, the most useless castle you could imagine, just these walls and a garden in them that's gone all wild, but when I was there, nobody could hurt me, nobody at all.

She gives me an odd look and says, "With old castle rock for the walls."

10

So I guess Alex was right. I must have been looking for ghosts in All Souls—or at least I found one. Except it wasn't the ghost of someone who'd died and been buried in there. It was the ghost of a kid, a kid that was still living somewhere in an enclosed wild garden, secreted deep in his grown-up mind, a kid fooling around in trees full of grackles, hidden from the hurting world, held safe by moonlight and vines.

But you know, hiding's not always the answer. Because the more Alex talks to me, the more he opens up, the more I see him the way I did when I was a little girl, when I'd daydream about how he and I were going to spend the rest of our lives together.

I guess we were both carrying around ghosts.

In the Pines

Life ain't all a dance.
—attributed to Dolly Parton

1

It's celebrity night at the Standish and we have us some line-up. There are two Elvises—a young one, with the swiveling hips and a perfect sneer, and a white-suited one, circa the Vegas years. A Buddy Holly who sounds right but could've lost fifty pounds if he really wanted to look the part. A Marilyn Monroe who has her boyfriend with her; he'll be wearing a JFK mask for her finale, when she sings "Happy Birthday" to him in a breathless voice. Lonesome George Clark has come out of semi-retirement to reprise his old Hank Williams show and then there's me, doing my Dolly Parton tribute for the first time in the three years since I gave it up and tried to make it on my own.

I don't really mind doing it. I've kind of missed Dolly, to tell you the truth, and it's all for a good cause—a benefit to raise money for the Crowsea Home for Battered Women—which is how they convinced me to do that old act of mine one more time.

I do a pretty good version of Dolly. I'm not as pretty as her, and I don't have her hair—hey, who does?—but I've got the figure while the wig, makeup and rhinestone dress take care of the rest. I can mimic her singing, though my natural voice is lower, and I sure as hell play the guitar better—I don't know who she's kidding with those fingernails of hers.

But in the end, the looks never mattered. It was always the songs. The first time I heard her sing them, I just plain fell in love. "Jolene." "Coat of Many Colors." "My Blue Tears." I planned to do a half hour of those old hits with a couple of mountain songs thrown in for good measure. The only one from my old act that I was dropping was "I Will Always Love You." Thanks to the success Whitney Houston had with it, people weren't going to be thinking Tennessee cabins and Dolly anymore when they heard it.

I'm slated to follow the fat Elvis—maybe they wanted to stick all the rhinestones together in one part of the show?—with Lonesome George finishing up after me. Since Lonesome George and I are sharing the same backup band, we're going to close the show with a duet on "Muleskinner Blues." The thought of it makes me smile and not just because I'll get to do a little bit of yodeling. With everything Dolly's done over the years, even she never got to sing with Hank Williams—senior, of course. Junior parties a little too hearty for my tastes.

So I'm standing there in the wings of the Standish, watching Marilyn slink and grind her way through a song—the girl is good—when I get this feeling that something is going to happen.

I'm kind of partial to premonitions. The last time I felt one this strong was the night John Narraway died. We were working late on my first album at Tommy Norton's High Lonesome Sounds and had finally called it quits sometime after midnight when the feeling hit me. It starts with a hum or a buzz, like I've got a fly or a bee caught in my ear, and then everything seems . . . oh, I don't know. Clearer somehow. Precise. Like I could look at Johnny's fiddle bow that night and see every one of those horse-hairs, separate and on its own.

The trouble with these feelings is that while I know something's going to happen, I don't know what. I get a big feeling or a little one, but after that I'm on my own. Truth is, I never figure out what it's all about until after the fact, which doesn't make it exactly the most useful talent a girl can have. I don't even know if it's something good or something bad that's coming, just that it's coming. Real helpful, right?

So I'm standing there and Marilyn's brought her boyfriend out for the big finish to her act and I know something's going to happen, but I don't know what. I get real twitchy all through the fat Elvis's act and then it's time for me to go up and the buzzing's just swelling up so big inside me that I feel like I'm fit to burst with anticipation.

We open with "My Tennessee Mountain Home." It goes over pretty well and we kick straight into "Jolene" before the applause dies off. The third song we do is the first song I ever learned, that old mountain song, "In the Pines." I don't play it the same as most people I've heard do—I learned it from my Aunt Hickory, with this lonesome barred F# minor chord coming right in after the D that opens every line. I remember cursing for weeks before I could finally get my fingers around that damn chord and make it sound like it was supposed to.

So we're into the chorus now—

> *In the pines, in the pines,*
> *Where the sun never shines*
> *And the shiverin' cold winds blow.*

—and I'm looking out into the crowd and I can't see much, what with the spotlights in my eyes and all, but damned if I don't see her sitting there in the third row, my Aunt Hickory, big as life, grinning right back up at me, except she's dead, she's been dead fifteen years now, and it's all I can do to get through the chorus and let the band take an instrumental break.

2

The Aunt—that's what everybody in those parts called her, 'cept me, I guess. I don't know if it was because they didn't know her name, or because she made them feel uneasy, but nobody used the name that had been scratched onto her rusty mailbox, down on Dirt Creek Road. That just said Hickory Jones.

I loved the sound of her name. It had a ring to it like it was pulled straight out of one of those old mountain songs. Like Shady Groves. Or Tom Dooley.

She lived by her own self in a one-room log cabin, up the hill behind the Piney Woods Trailer Park, a tall, big-boned woman with angular features and her chestnut hair cropped close to her head. Half the boys in the park had hair longer than hers, slicked back and shiny. She dressed like a man in blue jeans and a flannel shirt, barefoot in the summer, big old workboots on those callused feet when the weather turned mean and the snows came.

She really was my aunt. She and Mama shared the same mother except Hickory had Kickaha blood, you could see it in the deep coppery color of her skin. Mama's father was white trash, same as mine, though that's an opinion I never shared out loud with anyone, not even Hickory. My daddy never needed much of a reason to give us kids a licking. Lord knows what he'd have done if we'd given him a real excuse.

I never could figure out what it was about Hickory that made people feel so damn twitchy around her. Mama said it was because of the way Hickory dressed.

"I know she's my sister," Mama would say, "but she looks like some no account hobo, tramping the rail lines. It's just ain't right. Man looks at her, he can't even tell she's got herself a pair of titties under that shirt."

Breasts were a big topic of conversation in Piney Woods when I was growing up and I remember wishing I had a big old shirt like Hickory's when my own chest began to swell and it seemed like it was never gonna stop. Mama acted like it was a real blessing, but I hated them. "You can't have too much of a good thing," she told me when she heard me complaining. "You just pray they keep growing a while longer, Darlene, 'cause if they do, you mark my words. You're gonna have your pick of a man."

Yeah, but what kind of a man? I wanted to know. It wasn't just the boys looking at me, or what they'd say; it was the men, too. Everybody staring down at my chest when they were talking to me, 'stead of looking me in the face. I could see them just itching to grab themselves a handful.

"You just shut your mouth, girl," Mama would say if I didn't let it go.

Hickory never told me to shut my mouth. But then I guess she didn't have to put up with me twenty-four hours a day, neither. She just stayed up by her cabin, growing her greens and potatoes in a little plot out back, running trap lines or taking to the hills with her squirrel gun for meat. Maybe once a month she'd head into town to pick up some coffee or flour, whatever the land couldn't provide for her. She'd walk the five miles in, then walk the whole way back, didn't matter how heavy that pack of hers might be or what the weather was like.

I guess that's really what people didn't like about her—just living the way she did, she showed she didn't need nobody, she could do it all on her own, and back then that was frowned upon for a woman. They thought she was queer—and I don't just mean tetched in the head, though they thought that, too. No, they told stories about how she'd sleep with other women, how she could raise the dead and was friends with the devil, and just about any other kind of foolish idea they could come up with.

'Course I wasn't supposed to go up to her cabin—none of us kids were, especially the girls—but I went anyways. Hickory played the five-string banjo and I'd go up and listen to her sing those old lonesome songs that nobody wanted to hear anymore. There was no polish to Hickory's singing, not like they put on music today, but she could hold a note long and true and she could play that banjo so sweet that it made you want to cry or laugh, depending on the mood of the tune.

See, Hickory's where I got started in music. First I'd go up just to listen and maybe sing along a little, though back then I had less polish in my voice than Hickory did. After a time I got an itching to play an instrument too and that's when Hickory took down this little old 1919 Martin guitar from where it hung on the rafters and when I'd sneak up to her cabin after that I'd play that guitar until my fingers ached and I'd be crying from how much they hurt, but I never gave up. Didn't get me nowhere, but I can say this much: whatever else's happened to me in this life, I never gave up the music. Not for anything, not for anyone.

And the pain went away.

"That's the thing," Hickory told me. "Doesn't matter how bad it gets, the pain goes away. Sometimes you got to die to stop hurting, but the hurting stops."

I guess the real reason nobody bothered her is that they were scared of her, scared of the big dark-skinned cousins who'd come down from the rez to visit her sometimes, scared of the simples and charms she could make, scared of what they saw in her eyes when she gave them that hard look of hers. Because Hickory didn't back down, not never, not for nobody.

3

I fully expect Hickory to be no more than an apparition. I'd look away, then back, and she'd be gone. I mean, what else could happen? She was long dead and I might believe in a lot of things, but ghosts aren't one of them.

But by the time the boys finish their break and it's time for me to step back up to the mike for another verse, there she is, still sitting in the third row, still grinning up at me. I'll tell you, I near choke right about then, all the words I ever knew to any song just up and fly away. There's a couple of ragged bars in the music where I don't know if I'll be finishing the song or not and I can feel the concern of the boys playing there on stage behind me. But Hickory she just gives me a look with those dark brown eyes of hers, that look she used to give me all those years ago when I'd run up so hard against the wall of a new chord or a particularly tricky line of melody that I just wanted to throw the guitar down and give it all up.

That look had always shamed me into going on and it does the same for me tonight. I shoot the boys an apologetic look, and lean right into the last verse like it never went away on me.

> *The longest train that I ever saw*
> *Was nineteen coaches long,*
> *And the only girl I ever loved*
> *She's on that train and gone.*

I don't know what anyone else is thinking when I sing those words, but looking at Hickory I know that, just like me, she isn't thinking of trains or girlfriends. Those old songs have a way of connecting you to something deeper than what they seem to be talking about, and that's what's happening for the two of us here. We're thinking of old losses and regrets, of all the things that might have been, but never were. We're thinking of the night lying thick in the pines around her cabin, lying thick under those heavy boughs even in the middle of the day, because just like the night hides in the day's shadows, there's lots of things that never go away. Things you don't ever want to go away. Sometimes when that wind blows through the pines, you shiver, but it's not from the cold.

4

I was fifteen when I left home. I showed up on Hickory's doorstep with a cardboard suitcase in one hand and that guitar she'd given me in the other, not heading for Nashville like I always thought I would, but planning to take the bus to Newford instead. A man who'd heard me sing at the roadhouse just down a ways from Piney Woods had offered me a job in a honky-tonk he owned in the city. I'm pretty sure he knew I was lying about my age, but he didn't seem to care any more than I did.

Hickory was rolling herself a cigarette when I arrived. She finished the job and lit a match on her thumbnail, looking at me in that considering way of hers as she got the cigarette going.

"That time already," she said finally, blowing out a blue-grey wreath of smoke on the heel of her words.

I nodded.

"Didn't think it'd come so soon," she told me. "Thought we had us another couple of years together, easy."

"I can't wait, Aunt Hickory. I got me a singing job in the city—a real singing job, in a honky-tonk."

"Uh-huh."

Hickory wasn't agreeing or disagreeing with me, just letting me know that she was listening but that she hadn't heard anything worthwhile hearing yet.

"I'll be making forty dollars a week, plus room and board."

"Where you gonna live?" Hickory asked, taking a drag from her cigarette. "In your boss's house?"

I shook my head. "No, ma'am. I'm going to have my own room, right upstairs of the honky-tonk."

"He know how old you are?"

"Sure," I said with a grin. "Eighteen."

"Give or take a few years."

I shrugged. "He's got no trouble with it."

"Well, what about your schooling?" Hickory asked. "You've been doing so well. I always thought you'd be the first one in the family to finish high school. I was looking forward to that—you know, to bragging about you and all."

I had to smile. Who was she going to brag to?

"Were you going to come to the graduation ceremony?" I asked instead.

"Was thinking on it."

"I'm going to be a singer, Aunt Hickory. All the schooling I'm ever going to need I learned from you."

Hickory sighed. She took a final drag from her cigarette then stubbed it out on the edge of her stair, storing the butt in her pocket.

"Tell me something," she said. "Are you running from something or running to something?"

"What difference does it make?"

"A big difference. Running away's only a partial solution. Sooner or later, whatever you're running from is going to catch up to you again. Comes a time you're going to have to face it, so it might as well be now. But running to something . . . well."

"Well, what?" I wanted to know when she didn't go on right away.

She fixed that dark gaze of hers on me. "I guess all I wanted to tell you, Darlene, is if you believe in what you're doing, then go at it and be willing to pay the price you have to pay."

I knew what she was trying to tell me. Playing a honky-tonk in Newford was a big deal for a girl from the hills like me, but it wasn't what I was aiming for. It was just the first step and the rest of the road could be long and hard. I never knew just how long and hard. I was young and full of confidence, back then at the beginning of the sixties; invulnerable, like we all think we are when we're just on the other side of still being kids.

"But I want you to promise me one thing," Hickory added. "Don't you never do something that'll make you feel ashamed when you look back on it later."

"Why do you think I'm leaving now?" I asked her.

Hickory's eyes went hard. "I'm going to kill that daddy of yours."

"He's never tried to touch me again," I told her. "Not like he tried that one time, not like that. Just to give me a licking."

"Seems to me a man who likes to give out lickings so much ought to have the taste of one himself."

I don't know if Hickory was meaning to do it her own self, or if she was planning to put one of her cousins from the rez up to it, but I knew it'd cause her more trouble than it was worth.

"Leave 'im be," I told her. "I don't want Mama getting any more upset."

Hickory looked like she had words for Mama as well, but she bit them back. "You'll do better shut of the lot of them," was what she finally said. "But don't you forget your Aunt Hickory."

"I could never forget you."

"Yeah, that's what they all say. But then the time always comes when they get up and go and the next you know you never do hear from them again."

"I'll write."

"I'm gonna hold you to that, Darlene Johnston."

"I'm changing my name," I told her. "I'm gonna call myself Darlene Flatt."

I figured she'd like that, seeing how Flatt & Scruggs were pretty well her favorite pickers from the radio, but she just gave my chest a considering look and laughed.

"You hang onto that sense of humor," she told me. "Lord knows you're gonna need it in the city."

I hadn't thought about my new name like that, but I guess it shows you just how stubborn I can be, because I stuck with it.

5

I don't know how I make it through the rest of the set. Greg Timmins who's playing Dobro for me that night says except for that one glitch coming into the last verse of "In the Pines," he'd never heard me sing so well, but I don't remember it like that. I don't remember much about it at all except that I change my mind about not doing "I Will Always Love You" and use it to finish off the set. I sing the choruses to my Aunt Hickory, sitting there in the third row of the Standish, fifteen years after she up and died.

I can't leave, because I still have my duet with Lonesome George coming up, and besides, I can't very well go busting down into the theater itself, chasing after a ghost. So I slip into the washroom and soak some paper towels in cold water before holding them against the back of my neck. After a while I start to feel . . . if not better, at least more like myself. I go back to stand in the wings, watching Lonesome George and the boys play, checking the seats in the third row, one by one, but of course she's not there. There's some skinny old guy in a rumpled suit sitting where I saw her.

But the buzz is still there, humming away between my ears, sounding like a hundred flies chasing each other up and down a windowpane, and I wonder what's coming up next.

6

I never did get out of Newford, though it wasn't from want of trying. I just went from playing with housebands in the honky-tonks to other kinds of bands, sometimes fronting them with my Dolly show, sometimes being myself, playing guitar and singing backup. I didn't go back to Piney Woods to see my family, but I wrote Aunt Hickory faithfully, every two weeks, until the last letter came back marked, "Occupant deceased."

I went home then, but I was too late. The funeral was long over. I asked the pastor about it and he said there was just him and some folks from the rez at the service. I had a lot more I wanted to ask, but I soon figured out that the pastor didn't have the answers I was looking for, and they weren't to be found staring at the fresh-turned sod of the churchyard, so I thanked the pastor for his time and drove my rented car down Dirt Creek Road.

Nothing looked the same, but nothing seemed to have changed either. I guess the change was in me, at least that's how it felt until I got to the cabin. Hickory had been squatting on government land, so I suppose I shouldn't have been surprised to find the cabin in the state it was, the door kicked in, the windows all broke, anything that could be carried away long gone, everything else vandalized.

I stood in there on those old worn pine floorboards for a long time, looking for some trace of Hickory I could maybe take away with me, waiting for some sign, but nothing happened. There was nothing left of her, not even that long-necked old Gibson banjo of hers. Her ghost didn't come walking up to me out of the pine woods. I guess it was about then that it sunk in she was really gone and I was never going to see her again, never going to get another one of those cranky letters of hers, never going to hear her sing another one of those old mountain songs or listen to her pick "Cotton-Eyed Joe" on the banjo.

I went outside and sat down on the step and I cried, not caring if my makeup ran, not caring who could hear or see me. But nobody was there anyway and nobody came. I looked out at those lonesome pines after a while, then I got into my rented car again and drove back to the city, pulling off to the side of the road every once in a while because my eyes got blurry and it was hard to stay on my own side of the dividing line.

7

After I finish my duet with Lonesome George, I just grab my bag and my guitar and I leave the theater. I don't even bother to change out of my stage gear, so it's Dolly stepping out into the snowy alley behind the Standish, Dolly turning up the collar of her coat and feeling the sting of the wind-driven snow on her rouged cheeks, Dolly fighting that winter storm to get back to her little one-bedroom apartment that she shares with a cat named Earle and a goldfish named Maybelle.

I get to my building and unlock the front door. The warm air makes the chill I got walking home feel worse and a shiver goes right up my spine. All I'm thinking is to get upstairs, have myself a shot of Jack Daniel's, then crawl into my bed and hope that by the time I wake up the buzzing in my head'll be gone and things'll be back to normal.

I don't lead an exciting life, but I'm partial to a lack of excitement. Gets to a point where excitement's more trouble than it's worth and that includes men. Maybe especially men. I never had any luck with them. Oh, they come buzzing around, quick and fast as the bees I got humming in my head right now, but they just want a taste of the honey and then they're gone. I think it's better when they go. The ones that stay make for the kind of excitement that'll eventually have you wearing long sleeves and high collars and pants instead of skirts because you want to hide the bruises.

There's a light out on the stairs going up to my apartment but I can't even find the energy to curse the landlord about it. I just feel my way to the next landing and head on up the last flight of stairs and there's the door to my apartment. I set my guitar down long enough to work the three locks on this door, then shove the case in with my knee and close the door behind me. Home again.

I wait for Earle to come running up and complain that I left him alone all night— that's the nice thing about Maybelle; she just goes round and round in her bowl and doesn't make a sound, doesn't try to make me feel guilty. Only reason she comes to the side of the glass is to see if I'm going to drop some food into the water.

"Hey, Earle," I call. "You all playing hidey-cat on me?"

Oh that buzz in my head's rattling around something fierce now. I shuck my coat and let it fall on top of the guitar case and pull off my cowboy boots, one after the other, using my toes for a boot jack. I leave everything in the hall and walk into my living room, reaching behind me for the zipper of my rhinestone dress so that I can shuck it, too.

I guess I shouldn't be surprised to see Hickory sitting there on my sofa. What does surprise me is that she's got Earle up on her lap, lying there content as can be, purring up a storm as she scratches his ears. But Hickory always did have a way with animals; dying didn't seem to have changed that much. I let my hand fall back to my side, zipper still done up.

"That really you, Aunt Hickory?" I say after a long moment of only being able to stand there and stare at her.

"Pretty much," she says. "At least what's left of me." She gives me that considering look of hers, eyes as dark as ever. "You don't seem much surprised to see me."

"I think I wore out being surprised 'round about now," I say.

It's true. You could've blown me over with a sneeze, back there in the Standish when I first saw her, but I find I'm adjusting to it real well. And the buzz is finally upped and gone. I think I'm feeling more relieved about that than anything else.

"You're looking a bit strollopy," she says.

Strollops. That's what they used to call the trashy women back around Piney Woods, strumpets and trollops. I haven't heard that word in years.

"And you're looking pretty healthy for a woman dead fifteen years."

Maybe the surprise of seeing her is gone, but I find I still need to sit me down because my legs are trembling something fierce right about now.

"What're you doing here, Aunt Hickory?" I ask from the other end of the sofa where I've sat down.

Hickory, she shrugs. "Don't rightly know. I can't seem to move on. I guess I've been waiting for you to settle down first."

"I'm about as settled down as I'm ever going to be."

"Maybe so." She gives Earle some attention, buying time, I figure, because when she finally looks back at me it's to ask, "You remember what I told you back when you first left the hills—about never doing something you'd be ashamed to look back on?"

"Sure I do. And I haven't never done anything like that neither."

"Well, maybe I put it wrong," Hickory says. "Maybe what I should have said was, make sure you can be proud of what you've done when you look back."

I don't get it and I tell her so.

"Now don't you get me wrong, Darlene. I know you're doing the best you can. But there comes a point, I'm thinking, when you got to take stock of how far your dreams can take you. I'm not saying you made a mistake, doing what you do, but lord, girl, you've been at this singing for twenty years now and where's it got you?"

It was like she was my conscience, coming round and talking like this, because that's something I've had to ask myself a whole pile of times and way too often since I first got here to the city.

"Not too damn far," I say.

"There's nothing wrong with admitting you made a mistake and moving on."

"You think I made a mistake, Aunt Hickory?"

She hesitates. "Not at first. But now . . . well, I don't rightly know. Seems to me you've put so much into this dream of yours that if it's not payback time yet, then maybe it is time to move on."

"And do what?"

"I don't know. Something."

"I don't know anything else—'cept maybe waiting tables and the like."

"I see that could be a problem," Hickory says.

I look at her for a long time. Those dark eyes look back, but she can't hold my gaze for long and she finally turns away. I'm thinking to myself, this looks like my Aunt Hickory, and the voice sounds like my Aunt Hickory, but the words I'm hearing aren't what the Hickory I know would be saying. That Hickory, she'd never back down, not for nobody, never call it quits on somebody else's say-so, and she'd never expect anybody else to be any different.

"I guess the one thing I never asked you," I say, "is why did you live up in that old cabin all on your ownsome for so many years?"

"I loved those pine woods."

"I know you did. But you didn't always live in 'em. You went away a time, didn't you?"

She nods. "That was before you was born."

"Where'd you go?"

"Nowhere special. I was just traveling. I . . ." She looks up and there's something in those dark eyes of hers that I've never seen before. "I had the same dream you did, Darlene. I wanted to be a singer so bad. I wanted to hear my voice coming back at me from the radio. I wanted to be up on that big stage at the Opry and see the crowd looking back at me, calling my name and loving me. But it never happened. I never got no further than playing the jukejoints and the honky-tonks and the road bars where the people are more interested in getting drunk and sticking their hands up your dress than they are in listening to you sing."

She sighed. "I got all used up, Darlene. I got to where I'd be playing on those dinky little stages and *I* didn't even care what I was singing about anymore. So finally I just took myself home. I was only thirty years old, but I was all used up. I didn't tell nobody where I'd been or what I'd done or how I'd failed. I didn't want to talk to any of them about any of that, didn't want to talk to them at all because I'd look at those Piney Woods people and I'd see the same damn faces that looked up at me when I was playing my heart out in the honky-tonks and they didn't care any more now than they did then.

"So I moved me up into the hills. Built that cabin of mine. Listened to the wind in the pines until I could finally start to sing and play and love the music again."

"You never told me any of this," I say.

"No, I didn't. Why should I? Was it going to make any difference to your dreams?"

I shook my head. "I guess not."

"When you took to that old guitar of mine the way you did, my heart near broke. I was so happy for you, but I was scared—oh, I was scared bad. But then I thought, maybe it'll be different for her. Maybe when she leaves the hills and starts singing, people are gonna listen. I wanted to spare you the hurt, I'll tell you that, Darlene, but I didn't want to risk stealing your chance at joy neither. But now . . ."

Her voice trails off.

"But now," I say, finishing what she left unsaid, "here I am anyway and I don't even have those pines to keep me company."

Hickory nods. "It ain't fair. I hear the music they play on the radio now and they don't have half the heart of the old mountain songs you and me sing. Why don't people want to hear them anymore?"

"Well, you know what Dolly says: Life ain't all a dance."

"Isn't that the sorry truth."

"But there's still people who want to hear the old songs," I say. "There's just not so many of them. I get worn out some days, trying like I've done all these years, but then I'll play a gig somewhere and the people are really listening and I think maybe it's not so important to be really big and popular and all. Maybe there's something to be said for pleasing just a few folks, if it means you get to stay true to what you want to do. I don't mean a body should stop aiming high, but maybe we shouldn't feel so bad when things don't work out the way we want 'em to. Maybe we should be grateful for what we got, for what we had."

"Like all those afternoons we spent playing music with only the pines to hear us."

I smile. "Those were the best times I ever had. I wouldn't change 'em for anything."

"Me, neither."

"And you know," I say. "There's people with a whole lot less. I'd like to be doing better than I am, but hell, at least I'm still making a living. Got me an album and I'm working on another, even if I do have to pay for it all myself."

Hickory gives me a long look and then just shakes her head. "You're really something, aren't you just?"

"Nothing you didn't teach me to be."

"I been a damn fool," Hickory says. She sets Earle aside and stands up. "I can see that now."

"What're you doing?" I ask. But I know and I'm already standing myself.

"Come give your old aunt a hug," Hickory says.

There's a moment when I can feel her in my arms, solid as one of those pines growing up the hills where she first taught me to sing and play. I can smell woodsmoke and cigarette smoke on her, something like apple blossoms and the scent of those pines.

"You do me proud, girl," she whispers in my ear.

And then I'm holding only air. Standing there alone, all strolloped up in my wig and rhinestone dress, holding nothing but air.

8

I know I won't be able to sleep and there's no point in trying. I'm feeling so damn restless and sorry—not for myself, but for all the broken dreams that wear people down until there's nothing left of 'em but ashes and smoke. I'm not going to let that happen to me.

I end up sitting back on the sofa with my guitar on my lap—the same small-bodied Martin guitar my Aunt Hickory gave a dreamy-eyed girl all those years ago. I start to pick a few old tunes. "Over the Waterfall." "The Arkansas Traveler." Then the music drifts into something I never heard before and I realize I'm making up a melody. About as soon as I realize that, the words start slipping and sliding through my head and before I know it, I've got me a new song.

I look out the window of my little apartment. The wind's died down, but the snow's still coming, laying a soft blanket that takes the sharp edge off everything I can see. It's so quiet. Late night quiet. Drifting snow quiet. I get a pencil from the kitchen and I write out the words to that new song, write the chords in. I reread the last lines of the chorus:

> *But my Aunt Hickory loved me,*
> *and nothing else mattered*
> *nothing else mattered at all.*

There's room on the album for one more song. First thing in the morning I'm going to give Tommy Norton a call and book some time at High Lonesome Sounds. That's the nice thing about doing things your own way—you answer to yourself and no one else. If I want to hold off on pressing the CDs for my new album to add another song, I can. I can do any damn thing I want, so long as I keep true to myself and the music.

Maybe I'm never going to be the big star the little girl with the cardboard suitcase and guitar thought she'd be when she left the pine hills all those years ago and came looking for fame and fortune here in the big city. But maybe it doesn't matter. Maybe there's other rewards, smaller ones, but more lasting. Like knowing my Aunt Hickory loves me and she told me I do her proud.

Shining Nowhere but in the Dark

If we look at the path, we do not see the sky.
—Native American saying

Because I could not stop for Death—
He kindly stopped for me—
—Emily Dickinson

1

"Spare change?"

The crowd eddies by on either side of me as I pause. It seems pointless, doling out a quarter here, a quarter there, as if twenty-five cents can make that much of a difference in anyone's life, but I can't stop myself from doing it, because it does make a difference. It means we're at least paying attention to each other, acknowledging each other's presence.

Come lunch time, some people buy lottery tickets, others waste their money on junk food. Me, I usually brown-bag it. Then after I've eaten, I go out for a walk, making sure I have a handful of change in the pocket of my jacket.

So I turn to the girl, my hand already in my pocket, fingers sorting through the coins by feel. She has a raggedy Gothic look about her, from her pale skin and the unruly tangle of her short dark hair to the way her clothes hang from her skinny frame. I find myself wondering, is this all she has to wear or a fashion statement? These days it's hard to tell. Scuffed workboots, torn jeans, black T-shirt, black cotton jacket. She has so many earrings in one ear that I'm surprised her head doesn't tilt in that direction. Her other lobe has only one small silver stud of an owl's head. Except for her blood-red lipstick, she's entirely monochrome.

She smiles as I drop a pair of quarters in her palm. "If this were a fairy tale," she says, "you'd have just guaranteed yourself some unexpected help later on in the story."

It's such a charming and unexpected line, I have to return her smile. "But first I suppose I'd have to stand on one foot and call your name three times while hopping in a circle."

"Something like that."

"Except I don't know your name."

She grins. "It's not supposed to be easy, is it? But maybe a random act of kindness is magic enough, in its own small way. Maybe I owe you now and I'll have to come to you if ever you need my help."

"That's not why I gave you the money."

"I know." She touches my arm, her fingers weightless on my skin and soft as a feather. "Thanks."

She pockets her fifty cents and turns away. "Spare change?" I hear as I start walking again.

Just before I fall asleep that night, I find myself thinking about fairy tales. I try to imagine myself in stories of old women and spoons that go adventuring and talking cats that repay a small kindness with a great kindness until I remember that I'm not a thirdborn child the way the central characters usually are in a fairy tale. That brings me wide awake again. Once upon a time I was the middle child; now I'm an orphan, without siblings. Thinking about family takes me to a place I try to never go, but it's too late now.

I lie awake for hours, watching the slow shadow of the streetlight outside my window as it crawls across my ceiling. Finally I get up and go to the window. I mean to pull the shade, but then I see someone standing out there on the street, under the streetlight, looking up at me.

He's dark-eyed, dark-haired, that ravened thatch an unruly nest of untamed locks standing up at attention around his head; alabaster skin—brow, cheeks, throat, hands, even his lips. He has a face like a knife, all sharp angles, and there's a Gothic look about him that reminds me of the girl panhandling earlier today. With him it's reinforced by the old-fashioned cut of his clothes—Heathcliff come off the moor, not exactly the way Brontë described him, but the way I imagined him, a figure of shadow and pale skin that haunted my sleep for weeks. I used to live in delicious dread of his appearing at the foot of my bed and sweeping me up into his arms and away. Where, I was never exactly sure. Before I got the chance to figure out where I might like a man like that to take me, my life was irrevocably changed and I didn't think about that kind of thing again for a very long time.

But that was over twenty years ago, when I was barely into my teens, and still had dreams. Right now I'm thirty-six, suffering from a familiar insomnia, and not at all happy to have acquired my very own stalker, no matter how handsome he might be. Bunching the open V of my nightgown closer to my throat with one hand, I step back, out of his line of sight, and sit down on the bed again. Safe, I think, only something makes me turn my head and that's when I see the spare-change girl from earlier today, sitting on the other side of my bed like an invited guest.

"Don't worry about him," she says. "He won't hurt you."

My heartbeat goes into overdrive. I start to ask how she got in here, but the words stick in my throat and a half second later I realize that I have to be dreaming. My pulse is still drumming way too fast, but I don't feel quite so nervous now. It's funny. Maybe I don't dream—or at least I don't remember my dreams—and I certainly can't remember ever knowing that I was dreaming *while* I was dreaming, but here I am, doing both. I wonder if I'll retain any of this tomorrow morning.

"Do you know him?" I find myself asking.

"He's my sister."

"He?"

She laughs. "Oh, I guess that sounds pretty confusing, doesn't it?"

Even for a dream, I think.

"We're . . . wyrds," she says. "Or at least that's what they used to call us."

"Weirds?"

I don't realize until later that we're using two entirely different words.

She nods. "Exactly. As in the fates. Sometimes we were called muses, too, though I doubt anyone would do that today. There doesn't seem to be a whole lot of interest in muses anymore."

I give her a blank look. My hand goes to the night table and finds cigarettes, matches and ashtray. I have the usual twinge of regret as I light up, that familiar I-really-should-quit-one-of-these-days nag, but I ignore it. Dropping the cigarette package and matches on the bed between us, I take a long drag, then tip the grey end of my cigarette into the middle of the ashtray.

"These days," she explains, "people don't really care about using the muscles of their own imaginations. I mean, why bother when the media can provide every thought or idea you'll ever need?"

"That's a bit cynical."

"But no less true."

I shrug. "And it doesn't explain what he's doing down there—or why you're in my bedroom, for that matter."

Or, come to think of it, what she was doing out on the street at noon, cadging spare change.

"My sister being down there is my fault," she says. "He saw me talking to you earlier today and when he realized that you don't dream at all, he had to have a closer look."

"I'm dreaming now."

"Are you?"

I better be, I think, but decide to change the subject.

"So you're fates," I say.

She nods again. "There are three of us—like in the stories. They got that much right."

I finally start to twig. "You mean like in the Greek myths?"

"Something like that."

I'm thinking, there are three of them in the stories, one to spin the threads of our lives, one to weave them, and one to cut them when you've reached the end of your thread. Spin, weave, cut. Birth, life, death. I steal a glance out the window and Heathcliff's still standing out there, looking up. He hasn't got a hooded cloak or a scythe, but I'm pretty sure I know which one of the three he is now. Snip, snip.

My cigarette's already at the filter. I stub it out and light another one. Even sucking smoke into my lungs the way I am, I can't believe my time has come. I'm not ready, but then who is? I've always subscribed to Woody Allen's philosophy: "I'm not afraid of dying," he's supposed to have said. "I just don't want to be there when it happens." Or I guess I just pretended I did. I feel guilty about being alive, but fear's a bigger emotion. I'm afraid of dying. Not because it means my life's over—what I've got is no big deal—but because of who I might meet when I do die and what they'll say to me.

"And . . . your other sister?" I ask.

"She's spinning."

I nod because it makes sense. The spare-change girl sitting on the edge of my bed is too much a part of the here and now, too full of vitality not to be the weaver. Life. I take a drag from my cigarette and sneak another look at her older sister, waiting for me down there on the street.

"Why does she look like a man?" I ask, thinking maybe I can postpone the inevitable if I can just keep her talking.

The girl shrugs. "He got disbelieved into looking the way he does. That sort of thing happens to us when people stop dreaming their own dreams. And no dreams at all makes it even worse."

I'm finding this way too confusing, even for a dream.

"Okay," I tell her. "So your sister's down there because I don't dream." I find that I don't want to let on that I know why she's really here—maybe because if I ignore it, it won't be real. "Why are you here?"

"Because it's my fault that he's here right now and I didn't want you to be upset. A lot of people find him unsettling."

Maybe the strangest thing about all of this is the way she keeps referring to her sister as "he."

"But sooner or later . . ." I begin.

"He would have come around to see you," she says, finishing when I let my voice trail off. "It just takes time, getting to everyone. You probably wouldn't have even known he was nearby, if you hadn't seen me earlier today."

One of the curses of fairyland, I think. Once you've had a glimpse of it, you can always see it, just there on the periphery of your vision. Or at least that's the way it goes in some of the old stories. I played Good Samaritan with fifty cents, and the next thing I know I've got two of the Greek fates hanging around.

I've finished my second cigarette even quicker than the first. I stub it out and light yet another one. I don't want to hold on to what she's telling me, but I can't let it go. Death's down there on the street, his gaze meeting mine every time I look out the window. Eternity seems to linger in his eyes and I can't read him at all. Is he bored, sad, amused?

"If he's busy," I say, turning back to the girl. "I can wait. Really. I'm in no hurry."

"That's not the way it works," she tells me. "Everybody has to dream, just as one day, everybody has to die."

2

Jenny Wray woke in a cold sweat. She sat up and stared frantically at the side of her bed, but of course there was no one there. She leaned forward so that she could see out the window and there was no one standing under the streetlight either. She started to reach for the cigarettes on her night table, then remembered that she'd given them up over ten years ago.

God, it had seemed so real. Death below, his younger sister in the room with her. The taste of the cigarette.

She sat up against the headboard, arms wrapped around her knees, reliving memories that had no business hanging on for so long, no business still being so clear. It was a long time before she could even think of trying to get back to sleep. Her visitors had been wrong about one thing, she thought as she stretched out once more.

"See," she murmured into her pillow. "I do dream."

Because what else could it have been?

"When we visit, we come like a dream," she heard someone reply. "But it's not the same. It's not the same thing at all."

She recognized the voice. It was the spare-change girl. She could picture her face without having to open her eyes, could imagine Death having joined her, standing at the foot of the bed now in all his Gothic trappings.

The idea of dreaming about them still being in the room with her gave her the creeps. Maybe if she pretended they weren't there, they'd simply go away. The skin prickled up and down her spine at the thought of their presence until she stole a glance through her eyelashes and saw she really was alone. When she finally drifted off, she wasn't sure if she was falling asleep, or dreaming she was falling asleep. The difference seemed important, but she was too tired to try to make sense of it now.

3

The dream wouldn't go away.

It followed Jenny through the day, clinging to the wool of her thoughts like a persistent burr until she knew she had to talk to someone about it. The trouble was, who? She was temping these days, only her second day at this particular office, so she couldn't approach one of her coworkers, and it wasn't the sort of topic that normally came up in conversations among her own small circle of acquaintances; she didn't have any real friends. It wasn't until she was leaving the office that she thought of someone who wouldn't think she was weird or laugh her off. So instead of taking the bus home, she caught a subway downtown.

It took her a little while to find the shop she was looking for. When she finally did and went inside, she stood in the doorway, momentarily distracted. The air in the shop was several shades darker than outside and redolent with the scent of incense. There were packets of herbs for sale and bins of candles; crystals displayed on swatches of dark velvet along with ornately-designed daggers and goblets; ceremonial hooded cloaks hanging along one wall and books crammed on shelves, many with the word *magic* or *magick* in the title, as well as any number of items that Jenny couldn't identify, or if she recognized the item, didn't know the use to which it would be put, presented as it was in this context.

Ash Enys, the young woman behind the counter, was the niece of a woman Jenny had met while sitting a booth at a craft show a few years before. She reminded Jenny of last night's dream, of the middle fate with her pale skin and punky hair. They shared the same monochrome wardrobe: black jeans, jacket and combat boots, white T-shirt, smudges of dark kohl around the eyes. Ash's lips even had the slash of blood-red lipstick, except the shade of hers ran more toward the purple spectrum. The only real difference was that the spare-change girl hadn't had a nose ring.

"Never thought I'd see you in here," Ash said with a smile when she recognized Jenny.

Jenny returned her smile. "Why not?"

"I don't know. Doesn't seem to be your style."

"So what is my style?"

"Uptown," Ash said. "No offense."

Jenny liked to dress well, not voguing, but definitely stylish. Today she was wearing patterned stockings, heels, a form-hugging short skirt, silk blouse. She didn't use much makeup, but the little she did was artfully applied. Her dark hair was a short pageboy with long bangs. Minimal jewelry—a stud and a dangling earring in one ear, the latter's match in the other, a plain silver band on the ring finger of her right hand.

"No offense taken," she said. "But everybody's got secrets."

They were alone in the store. Feeling bold, she tugged her blouse free from her skirt and lifted it so that Ash could see the small silver ring that pierced her navel. She got it one day when she wanted to prove to herself that she was brave. That hadn't happened. Bravery, she realized, had nothing to do with what one chose to do to one's self. But she did like the secret of it, the knowledge of its existence, hidden there under her clothes where no one else could see it.

"Cool," Ash said.

Jenny tucked the tails of her blouse back into her skirt.

"So what are you looking for here?" Ash asked.

"You." As Ash's eyebrows rose questioningly, Jenny went on to explain. "I remember Gwen telling me you'd gotten a job here and I had a question about, you know—" She waved her hand vaguely in the direction of a shelf full of books on dreaming. "Stuff like this. Dreams."

"I'm not exactly an expert," Ash said.

"Well, you're the closest to an expert that I know."

Ash smiled. "Uptown girl."

"That's me."

"So what do you want to know?"

"What does it mean when you dream about Death?"

"Yours or somebody else's?"

"I mean the personification of Death," Jenny said. "You know, a pale-faced guy, all in black."

"Did he ask you to play chess?"

Jenny smiled at the film reference, but shook her head. "He just stood in the street outside my apartment last night, watching me."

"Well, some people think dreams can be like premonitions—"

Jenny shivered.

"—while other people think that's bullshit."

"What do you think?"

Ash shrugged. "If I had a dream like yours, I'd definitely lean toward it being bullshit."

"No, seriously."

Ash leaned on the counter to look more closely at her. "This has really got you spooked, hasn't it?"

"No. Of course not. It's just . . ." Jenny sighed. There was no point in lying. "Yeah. I found it really creepy. Especially because, normally, I don't dream—or at least I never remember my dreams. But this one won't go away. It keeps popping back into my mind when I'm least expecting it."

"Well," Ash said, "symbolically, meeting Death isn't necessarily such a bad thing. I mean, Shiva is the god of both Dance and Death, and in the Tarot, the Death card is more often considered to be a symbol of transformation and spiritual rebirth. Even in Western culture we didn't always depict Death as the hooded skeleton with a scythe. The Greeks envisaged Death as the daughter of night and the sister of sleep." She cocked an eye at Jenny. "Maybe that's why Keats described himself as 'half in love with easeful Death.' They used to call sleep the little death, you know, so maybe when we die we step into a dream that never ends because we never wake up again."

Jenny stared at Ash, not really seeing her. She was remembering what the middle fate had told her about dreams and dreaming. When she finally focused her gaze she saw Ash wearing an apologetic look.

"I guess I'm not being much help, am I?" she said.

"She said the reason he'd come to see me is because I don't dream," Jenny told her.

"She?"

"The middle fate. That's what she said they were—wyrds. The fates—or at least two of them. She was the one who was actually in my room—Death was sort of hanging around on the street outside."

"This sounds like it was quite the dream."

"It was," Jenny said. "She looked a little bit like you."

Ash laughed. "Generic Goth, right? I guess I deserve that for my uptown-girl comments."

Jenny shrugged that off.

"So where does the girl come in?" Ash wanted to know.

"I don't know exactly," Jenny said. "The first time I saw her I was awake—she was panhandling near my office and I gave her some money. But then later I dreamed about her and that feels more true now than what I know for sure happened. She kept going on about muses and dreams and . . ." She let her voice trail off. "God, would you listen to me? I'm talking about it as though it actually happened, as though she really was in my bedroom."

"I've had dreams like that," Ash said. "Everybody does. It's like you wake up and you can't believe it didn't really happen. I know this guy who had a dream about cats Morris dancing. He really, really believed it had happened. He was so excited when he woke up, he wanted to tell everybody. I just happened to be the first person he saw that morning, so I saved him the embarrassment of trying to convince anybody else that it had been real."

Jenny was only half listening. "She said it wasn't a dream," she told Ash. "She said that they came like a dream, but it wasn't the same thing as a real dream. She was pretty emphatic about it."

"So what did they want?"

"That's what I was hoping you could tell me."

Ash lifted her hands, palms up. "The Goth strikes out," she said, "because I don't have a clue. I guess you'll have to ask them yourself if you dream about them again."

"I hope the opportunity never comes up," Jenny said.

4

But of course it does. Not that night, nor the next, but Friday, I no sooner put my head on the pillow, than I find myself in this club I've never been in before—at least I don't recognize the place. Dark, smoky, loud. The DJ's spinning "Le Bien, Le Mal" by Guru and MC Solaar. I remember the first time I heard the piece, I thought it was so weird hearing somebody rapping in French, but it's got a definite groove and the dance floor is happening, so I don't think I'm the only person who likes it.

There's a guy standing close beside me and I don't know if I'm with him, or if the crowd's just pushed together, but he lights my cigarette for me. The music's turned up past conversation volume which makes it hard to talk. He's nice-looking and I think maybe I'd like to dance, but then I see a familiar figure going up the stairs on the far side of the club and out the door. I think: It's Ash, but I know it's not. It's not any other generic Goth either. I tell the guy I've got to go, using sign language because the music's still seriously loud, and he just gives me a shrug. I guess I wasn't with him after all.

It takes me a while to make it across the club and up the stairs myself. By the time the cool air outside hits my face, there's no sign of the girl. I have that hum in my head—you know, the one that follows you home after a concert or a night of clubbing—and I figure I must have had enough loud music for one night, even though all I can remember is the last few minutes or so. I hail a cab and settle down in the back seat. We go about a half-dozen blocks before I turn to look out the window on my left and realize the girl's sitting beside me. Was she there all along, or did she simply materialize on the seat beside me? It doesn't really matter because that's when I figure out that I'm dreaming again.

"See," I say to her, "I told you I dream," but she shakes her head.

"And I told you," she says, "that we only seem like a dream. It's easier for you to deal with us that way."

"Who do you mean by 'us'?"

She shrugs. "People like me. Or my sisters."

One of whom's been disbelieved into looking like a guy and just happens to be Death. It's so strange, when you think about it. Death's got sisters. They never told us that, but then nobody has the real scoop on death, do they? There are all the light at the end of the tunnel stories, but those people come back, so who knows if their near-death experience really connected them into the secret, or if they simply imagined the light and the tunnel?

"So . . ." I clear my throat. "Where is your sister? Out taking a few lives?"

I don't feel nearly as cocky as I'm trying to sound.

She gives me a strange look. "More like living them," she says.

I've no idea what she's talking about, but I figure as long as I've got the ear of one of the fates, I might as well ask her a few questions, find out for sure what everybody else has to guess at.

"Why do we have to die?" I ask.

She shrugs. "What you really want to know is, 'Why do I have to die?' "

"I guess."

She doesn't answer me right away. Instead she says, "It's such a beautiful night, why don't we walk?"

When I agree, she taps the cabbie on the shoulder and tells him we'll get out here. He pulls over to the curb. She doesn't offer to pay, so I dig out my wallet, but he just shakes his head. Says we didn't go far enough to make it worthwhile. I don't argue. I just thank him the way my companion does and join her on the pavement, but it's the first time I ever saw a Newford cabbie turn down money.

The spare-change girl slips her arm in mine and we head off down the street. For some reason I don't feel weird, walking arm in arm with another woman like this. Maybe it's because it's such a beautiful night, one of those rare times when the lights of the city just can't drown out the starlight that's pouring down from the sky above. Maybe it's because I know I'm only dreaming.

"Why do you have to die?" she says, returning to our earlier conversation. "You might as well ask, why were you born? It's all part of the same mystery."

"But it's not a mystery to you, is it? Or at least it's not to your sister."

"Which one?"

"You know. The one who was standing outside my apartment the other night. He'd know, wouldn't he?"

"Perhaps," she says. "He's always had access to a lot of very potent imaginations. It wouldn't surprise me at all if he's run across the answer in one lifetime or another."

I know she doesn't mean he's immortal—though of course he is. She means all the lives he's taken.

"But you don't know," I say.

She shakes her head. "I think it's all part of a journey and what you're thinking of as the start and the end are just convenient markers along the way. You don't get the whole picture right away. Maybe you never do. Maybe it's like *tao* and it's only the journey itself that's important, what you do on it, how you grow, not where you come from or where you finally end up."

"I can't buy that," I tell her. I have an old pain aching in my chest, but I don't speak about it. It's not something I can speak about—that I even know how to speak about. But while I can't deal in specifics, the general injustice that crowds my head whenever I think about death and how people die is easy to verbalize.

"What about little kids?" I ask. "What about infants who die at birth? What do they get a chance to learn? Or what about all the terrible suffering that some people have to undergo while others just drift peacefully away in their sleep? If this isn't random, then, I'm sorry, but Death's one spiteful bastard."

She gets this sad look. "Death can't pick when you die, or how you die, just as no one can decide what you dream."

"You make it sound like the people who suffer *choose* to suffer. That a baby *chooses* to die when it does."

"You have so much anger in you."

"Well, excuse me," I tell her, "but I'm not like you and your sisters. I have to die."

And probably sooner than I want to, considering how my companion's older sister has taken this sudden interest in me. But that's not why I'm really angry. I think maybe she knows, only she doesn't call me on it.

"But is dying so bad?" she asks. "How else can you move on to what comes next, if you don't leave the baggage of this life behind? What comes next might well be more wonderful than anything you can even begin to imagine in this world."

"You don't know that."

"No," she admits. "I don't. Just as I don't know why some die in pain and others in their sleep. Why some die young and others in their old age. Why good people can suffer and evil ones prosper."

"Well, what about your sister?"

"What about him?"

"Doesn't *he* know? I mean, if anyone should know, it'd be him."

"My sister has many good qualities," she says, "but omniscience isn't among them."

"I just think if he's going to show up standing outside my apartment that he should at least have the decency to tell me where I'm headed next."

She shakes her head. "All he's concerned with is why you don't dream."

"Why should that bother him?"

"I told you. People not dreaming changes us. Every one who doesn't dream is like a little black hole. If it isn't tended to, it'll draw other dreamers into its net and soon there'll be vast numbers of you, abed and dreamless."

"Well, what does that matter? I mean, who really cares if we dream or not?"

"We do. He does."

I try to digest this. "So dreaming is important to him."

"Very much so."

"I was talking to someone recently," I tell her, "and they mentioned something about how people once called sleep the little death."

She nods her head. "I remember."

Like she was there, but I let it pass because she probably was.

"So maybe," I say, "dying is like going into a dream that never ends because you never wake up again."

This seems to interest her. "I like the idea of that," she says.

I feel like I'm on a roll now. "And maybe that's another reason why it's so important that I dream. Because if I don't dream, then I won't die."

She doesn't reply. Instead she says, more to herself than to me, "I wonder if that's the real reason John's been around for all these years."

"Excuse me?"

"John Buttadeus. It's like he just doesn't quite scan."

"What are you talking about?" I ask.

She blinks out of her reverie and gives me this irresistible smile that I can't help but return.

"What were you saying?" she asks.

I start to repeat what I've just said, until I realize she's gone back to what we were talking about before she spaced out on me.

"Does this mean that so long as I don't dream, I don't die?" I ask.

"I don't think there's been an appointment made for you yet," she tells me. "At least, not that anyone's told me."

"And we're not dreaming right now?"

She shakes her head.

"Well, I can sure live with that," I say and then I have to laugh at the double meaning of what I've just said.

I pause to light a cigarette. Our reflection in a store window catches my eye. She looks Gothic, I'm uptown, but the poor light and dark glass blend the differences. We could almost be sisters.

"Those are going to kill you," she says as I put away my lighter.

I blow a wreath of blue-grey smoke into the air between us.

"Is that inside information?" I ask.

She shakes her head.

"Because I quit years ago," I tell her. "And besides, I don't dream, remember? I'm going to live forever. I could probably take them up again if I wanted to."

I have this giddy feeling that I can't shake. I feel immortal, the way I did when I was a kid, when my life was still normal. That makes me almost fall into the trap of reliving the past, but I manage to sidestep the memories. I've had to live with them for almost as long as I can remember. Right now, I just want to hold onto this good feeling and never let it go.

I'm still smiling when I wake up the next morning, never mind that what I experienced last night had to be a dream. Except it wasn't—at least not according to Death's sister, the middle fate, and if anybody should know, it'd be her, right? So I'm safe from him—safe from what I know will be waiting for me when I die. Until I have a real dream. So I guess the big question is, how do I stop myself from inadvertently doing just that?

5

Saturday found Jenny back at The Occult Shop, but Ash didn't appear to be working this morning. In her place behind the counter was a tall, green-eyed woman who presented a look that was the direct opposite of Ash's Goth image. She wore a high-necked black dress over tights the same color and a pair of combat boots. The dress was unadorned except for a bone ankh broach pinned above her right breast. Her long blonde hair was gathered into a loose ponytail that hung down to the small of her back in a golden waterfall. She looked like she should be in a fashion magazine instead of working the counter here.

"Ash doesn't work Saturdays," the woman told Jenny when she asked. "Maybe I can help you. My name's Miranda."

The store was much busier than it had been the last time Jenny was here—too busy, she thought, for the kind of conversation that would ensue when she explained why she was here. And where would she even begin? Ash at least had the background.

"It's sort of personal," she explained, trying not very successfully to hide her disappointment.

"Well, you can usually find her over in the park on weekends," Miranda said.

"The park?"

"Fitzhenry Park. She's generally hanging somewhere around the War Memorial with Cassie or Bones."

Jenny had no idea who Cassie or Bones might be, or what they would look like, but she fastened onto Ash's possible whereabouts with a single-mindedness that surprised her and was almost out of the store before she remembered to thank Miranda for her help.

"No problem," Miranda replied, but she was speaking to a closed door.

6

Jenny found Ash sitting on the steps of the War Memorial with a man she decided had to be Bones. He was a Native American—probably from the Kickaha reservation north of the city. His skin had a dark coppery cast and his features were broad—the chin square, eyes widely set, nose flat. His hair was as long as Miranda's back in The Occult Shop, except he wore his in a single tight braid, with feathers and beads interlaced in the braiding. He looked to be in his early thirties and so far as Jenny was concerned he could have stepped into modern Newford right out of some forgotten moment in history, if it hadn't been for his clothing: faded jeans, torn at the knees, scuffed leather work boots, a white T-shirt with DON T! BUY! THAI! written across the front.

"Hey, pretty lady," he called to her as she came near. "Medicine's right here— plenty powerful—if you got the wampum."

Before Jenny could answer, Ash elbowed him in the side.

"Enough with the talking Tonto already," Ash said. "She's a friend. Jenny, this is Bones; Bones, Jenny."

Bones gave Jenny a grin that made him look a little demented and she took an involuntary step back.

"He likes to act the fool," Ash explained, "but don't mind him. He's okay."

"I'm okay, you're okay," Bones said. "Pull up some stone, Jenny, and have yourself a seat."

Jenny gave him an uncertain smile. There was something about the way he looked at her—some dark light in his eyes—that reminded her of the eldest fate, standing outside her apartment the other night, except it didn't wake awe in her so much as nervousness. An uncomfortable feeling washed over her, a sense that in this man's presence, anything could happen. And probably would. She wasn't sure she was ready for another strange encounter—not when she still hadn't gotten over the one that had brought her here in the first place, looking for advice.

"What are those for?" she asked, pointing at a pile of tiny animal bones that lay on a square of beaded deerskin by Bones' feet. "Besides giving you your name, I mean."

She asked as much out of curiosity as to get him to stop regarding her so intently.

"It's the eyes, isn't it?" Ash said. "That and the grin."

Jenny looked up at her. "What?"

"She thinks you don't know what to make of me," Bones said.

"Well, I . . ."

"Bones always makes people feel a little strange when they first meet him," Ash said. "He says his real name translates into something like Crazy Dog. I say, whoever named him knew what they were doing."

Bones nodded, still grinning. "And these," he said, indicating the bones, "are my medicine wheel."

"Oh."

Ash laughed. "But you didn't come here to get your fortune read—did you?"

"No. I . . ." Jenny hesitated, feeling as intimidated with Bones's presence as she'd felt in The Occult Shop with all the people standing around. But she took a breath and plunged on. "Do you know a way to make sure that you don't dream?" she asked.

Ash shook her head. "No, that's a new one on me."

"It's just that I know you sell herbs and stuff to help people dream. . . ."

"Like a dream-catcher?"

"I guess. What's that?"

Ash described the spider-web like weaving of threads that went back and forth around a twig that had been bent into the rough shape of a circle, how the pattern, and the feathers, beads, shells, and the like woven into it, were supposed to draw good dreams to a sleeper.

Jenny nodded. "Yes, like that. Only something that'll do the opposite."

"You've got me."

"You don't like your dreams?" Bones asked.

"No, it's not that. I don't dream."

"So what's the problem?"

"I want to make sure it stays that way."

"Maybe you should go back to the beginning," Ash suggested, "so Bones knows what we're talking about."

"I . . ."

"Don't feel shy. He's a good listener and maybe he can help. He's gotten me out of a jam or two."

Jenny felt a flush coming on. "I don't know. I feel weird. . . ."

"Weird is good," Bones said. "Means you're not locked into what's here and now, but you're seeing a little further than most people do."

That was an understatement if Jenny had ever heard one. "Okay," she said with a sigh. "It started with a dream that wasn't a dream. . . ."

7

"So one of the fates is a guy," Bones said when Jenny finished relating her recent experiences.

"I think he's like Coyote," Ash said. "A shapeshifter—only the face he wears is the one you least expect."

Jenny looked from one to the other. "What are you talking about?"

"The guy in your dream," Ash said. "The eldest fate."

Bones shook his head. "No, what we're really talking about is you, Jenny. The visions you're experiencing and the people you're meeting in them are just something the spirits are doing to try to get your attention."

"I'm not sure I follow you," Jenny said.

"I don't know you," Bones said, "and you don't know me, so I don't know how much I should tell you. I don't know what you want to hear." He sounded regretful, but the crazy look in his eyes seemed to make a lie of that.

"What's that supposed to mean?" she asked.

"I don't want to piss you off. I mean, what's the percentage in it? What do either of us get out of me telling you something you don't want to hear?"

"I'm listening."

"But are you hearing? The spirits spoke to you and what did you do? You took their gift and instead of learning from it, you're trying to turn it to your own advantage." He shook his head. "Never works, you know."

Jenny could feel her face go stiff. "What the hell's that supposed to—"

"Anger's good," Bones told her, breaking in. "It's one of the ways the spirits tell you that you're alive."

"I'm not—" Jenny began, but she broke off.

Angry? No, she was furious at his cocky, know-it-all manner, but she heard an echo of what he'd said a few moments earlier—*I don't want to piss you off*—and that was enough to make her wonder just why she was so angry. She looked at Ash, but Ash didn't want to meet her gaze. She turned back to Bones. His face gave away nothing. Crazy eyes watched her back, solemn and laughing at the same time. She took a couple of steadying breaths and forced herself to calm down, to let the hostility go. It wasn't that she was suddenly into making nice. It was more that she realized that Bones seemed to understand the experiences she'd had—certainly better than she did—and he was right: he had nothing to gain in making her angry, or hurting her feelings. So maybe it was worth her while to hear him out.

"Okay," she said finally. "I am feeling angry. But I want to hear what you have to say."

"You sure?"

Ash elbowed him again before Jenny could reply.

"Okay," he said. "Let me put it this way. Does the sun rise and set just for you?"

Jenny shook her head.

"But it passes over you and makes you a part of its wheel, doesn't it?"

"I guess."

"Then perhaps you should learn to accept that you are a part of the world's wheel and not struggle so hard against what must be."

"So what are you telling me?" Jenny asked. "That I should just lie down and die?"

Bones grinned that crazy grin of his. "No, I'm saying you should get back on the wheel. Dream. Live. Don't look at the ground when you want to see the sky. What's the point of living forever if you don't experience life now?"

"Who says I'm not experiencing life?"

"You do. Your dreams-that-aren't dreams do. The spirits that have come across from the medicine lands to talk to you do."

The anger rose up in Jenny again, but this time she was quicker to deal with it. She looked away from them, bit at her lip. The dark place inside started to draw her down into its grasp and she couldn't seem to fight it.

"I'm sorry," Bones said, and she sensed that he meant it.

"You don't understand," she said finally. "That's the problem with living, nobody really understands. But we've got to carry on all the same. The trick isn't to save up our points for when we die so that maybe we can buy ourselves into a better life. The trick is to have that better life now. To make it for ourselves. To take it, if people are trying to keep it away from us."

Jenny still couldn't look at them. She picked at a loose thread on the seam near the knee of her jeans. The past was swallowing her again and this time she couldn't trick it into going away. It lay too thick inside her, that miasma of old hurts and griefs.

"Sometimes . . ." she began.

She had to stop and gather up her courage before she could go on. This wasn't something she talked about. It was too hard to talk about. She took a steadying breath and tried again.

"Sometimes," she said in a small voice, "I don't feel I have anything to live for. Sometimes I feel like I don't deserve to live, but I'm more scared of dying." Finally she looked up. "I'm scared of dying and seeing them and of what they'll say to me, because I know it wasn't fair, that they had to die while I went on."

"Who died?" Ash asked softly.

"Everybody. My parents. My little sister. My older brother. My cousin did it. I was only . . . I was only twelve when it happened. He killed everybody except for me. I hid under my bed and waited for him to come . . . to come get me too, but he never did."

"Your own cousin?" Ash said. "Jesus. That's horrible."

"What happened to him?" Bones asked.

"He killed himself. That's why he never came after me. He . . . he killed everybody else and then he shot himself. I was under my bed for the rest of the night and most of the next day, just . . . just waiting for him."

Ash shook her head. "You poor thing. You were just a little kid."

"And then . . . then I went to live with my grandparents, but they died too."

"But your cousin . . . ?" Ash began.

"He . . . he didn't kill them. They just . . . died. . . ." It was getting harder and harder for Jenny to get it out. Starting had seemed tough, but going on was worse. Her chest was so tight she could barely breathe. She couldn't see because she was blinded with tears. Her throat felt thick, making her choke on the words before she could get the words out.

"None . . . none of them died easy. Not my own family. Not my grandfather from cancer, a few . . . a few years after I came to live with them. Not my grandmother . . . she had Alzheimer's. By the time she finally died she didn't even know who I was anymore. . . ."

She finally turned her face toward them. "Why did they all have to go like that? Why not me? I should have died with them. Instead, I've just got this emptiness inside where family's supposed to be. I feel so . . . so lonely . . . so guilty. . . ."

Ash came and sat beside her and put an arm around her, drawing Jenny's head down to her shoulder. Bones took her hand. She looked at him. Even through her tears she could see that crazy light in his eyes, but it didn't seem so strange anymore. It felt almost comforting.

"You've got to talk to those spirits one more time," he said. "This time you've got to tell them what you're feeling. That you don't want to die—not till it's your time—but you do want to live until it's your time. You want to be alive. You want to dream. You've got to ask them to help you let it all go."

"But she said the reason they came to me was *because* I don't dream. What's the point of me telling them what you're saying I should? Wouldn't they already know it?"

"The thing with spirits," Bones told her, "is they want you to work it out on your own. Then, when you ask them for the right gift, they might help you out."

"And . . . and if they won't?"

"Girl," Bones told her, "you've got a lot of strong medicine tucked away inside you. Everybody does. Those spirits don't want to help you, you come back and talk to me again and I'll see what I can do about waking it up for you."

"Why can't you just help her now?" Ash asked.

"Because these are spirits we're talking about," Bones said. "You don't mess with spirits unless you've got no choice, Ash—especially not spirits that are working their medicine mojo on someone else. There's no way I'm getting in between them until they get off this wheel and I can climb on it. That's the way it is."

8

So here I am, waiting for Death to show.

I'm trying to feel brave—or at least project a little courage even though I have none—but I don't think it's working. I don't know which I'm more afraid of: that I won't dream, that I know I'll never die and have to go on like this forever, or that maybe he'll take me away with him right now. Except in the end, it's not Death that joins me in my bedroom, but the middle fate, the spare-change girl.

"Where is he?" I ask her.

"You've decided to dream once more," she says, "so he's gone on to deal with other matters."

Harvesting other lives you mean—but I don't say that aloud. I don't know whether to feel relieved that it's not me this time, or angry that he even exists in the first place.

"Why can't he just leave us alone?"

She shakes her head. "Without his gift, what would you have?"

I'm sick of this idea that without death, that without knowing we're all going to die one day, rich and poor, whatever our creed or color, we can't appreciate life. Even if it is true.

"I wanted to talk to him," I say.

She gives me a long considering look. "Did you want to talk to him, or to the eldest of us?"

And then I understand. It hits me like a thunderclap booming under my skin. It's been her all along. *He's* the middle fate, Life; she's the one that cuts the thread and ferries us on. My heartbeat gets too fast, drumming in my chest. All my resolutions about facing the past and my fears drain away and I want to tell her that I've changed my mind again. I don't want to dream. I don't want to be more alive if it means I have to die.

"Is this it?" I ask her. "Have you come for me?"

"Would that be so bad?" she says.

She projects such a strange aura of comfort and happiness that I want to shake my head and agree with her.

"I'm scared," I tell her.

"Fear lets you know you're alive," she says, "but that doesn't mean you should embrace it."

"You're starting to sound like Bones."

"Ah, Bones."

"Do you know him?"

She smiles. "I know everybody."

I want to keep her talking. I want to put off the moment for as long as I can, so every time she finishes speaking, I try to fill the silence with another question.

"How do you decide when it's someone's time?" I ask.

"I told you," she says. "I don't choose when or how you die. I'm only there to meet you when you do."

"Do people get mad at you, or are they mostly just scared like me?"

The eldest fate shook her head. "Neither. Mostly they're too concerned with those they left behind to be angry or frightened. That old homily is true, you know: it's always harder for those left behind."

"So . . . so my family wasn't mad at me because I didn't die with them? And my grandparents . . ."

"How could they be? They loved you as much as you loved them."

"So I don't have to be scared of meeting them in . . . wherever it is I'll be going?"

"I don't know where you'll go or who you'll meet when you're there," the eldest fate says. "And I don't know what they'll say to you. But I don't think you have to be scared."

I take a deep breath. "Okay," I tell her, wondering as I'm saying it where I've found the courage. "I'm guess I'm ready."

I wonder how it'll happen. Maybe I'll be lucky. Maybe I'll be one of the ones who just drifts away in her sleep.

"I'm not here to take you," the eldest fate tells me.

I don't even have time to feel relief, I'm so confused. "But . . . then why are you here?"

"I came as a friend—to finish our earlier conversation."

"As a friend?"

"You know, returning a kindness," she says.

"But . . ."

"I'm everybody's friend," the eldest fate explains. "Most people just don't know it."

I think of what Bones told me. I think about what I can't let go of, how I'm always so afraid, how I'm too scared to get close to someone because I know they're just going to die on me, how most of the time I feel so lost and alone. I think about how sick I am of the way I've lived my life, how I want to change it, but I can't seem to do it. Not on my own. I think about all of this. I look in the eldest fate's eyes and I see she understands.

I'm not going to live forever. I know that. I don't expect that. I don't even really want it. All I've ever wanted is the chance to be normal, to have a piece of what everybody else seems to have: a respite from the hurt and pain. I don't have to die to find that.

"I could use a friend," I tell her.

If I Close My
Eyes Forever

*Beauty exists whether a person has the eye
to behold it or not. That principle
also applies to ugliness.*
—William Arthur Herring,
from A *Horse of a Different Color*

1

There are only a pair of old-fashioned cemeteries left in the Crowsea-Foxville area. All Souls, over in Crowsea, hasn't been used in fifty years, but it's under the protection of the Crowsea Heritage Society. Unfortunately, that protection only means that bodies haven't been moved, mausoleums, crypts, statuary, and other stonework haven't been torn down to make room for condos. The place is seriously run-down and overgrown, and the only people hanging there are drug dealers.

Foxville Cemetery is still a working graveyard, as witness the fresh grave I've just laid flowers on. Neither's a fun place to be, but then being here isn't about fun. It's about closure.

I think the same architect designed both places—someone with a serious jones for New Orleans-style graveyards. Has to be that, because Newford's certainly not under sea level, so we don't need the crypts and mausoleums. The closest we get to New Orleans is the seriously watered-down Mardi Gras that's organized every year by the owners of the Good Serpent Club. The parade they put together never gets to be much more than a big block party, but you can't fault them for trying. It's not like we have a French Quarter here, primed and geared to be party central, or the tradition of Mardi Gras. The people who observe Lent in Newford aren't thinking along the lines of a carnival Fat Tuesday, and to everybody else, it's just another weekday.

I look down at the bouquet of six red roses lying on the freshly turned earth at my feet, then my gaze rises to the small stone and its incomplete inscription.

ELISE
Born, . . .–Died, July 23, 1994
R.I.P.

No one claimed the body and the police never did identify her beyond what little I had to tell them.

I was working late in my office the first time I met her. No, let's be honest. I was pushing papers around, killing time—trying to make myself so tired that by the time I did get home, I'd just fall into bed and sleep.

There was nothing left for me at home anymore. Peter took everything when he walked out on me.

What I missed the most was my confidence. My self-esteem.

2

Thursday night.

My business card says: FINDERS, LTD.—IF YOU NEED IT, WE CAN FIND IT. KIRA LEE, PROP., followed by my e-mail address, my phone and fax numbers, and finally my office address. The office is the least important part of the equation—at least insofar as dealing with clients. It's basically a tiny hole-in-the-wall of a room in the old Sovereign Building on Flood Street that barely manages to hold a desk, swivel chair, and file cabinet, with another chair parked across the desk for a visitor. A computer takes up most of the desktop—the tower sits on the floor beside the desk while my printer and fax machine are on a table over by the window. There's also a phone, stacks of papers and files, and, inevitably, a cup of coffee in some stage of depletion and usually cold.

I don't worry about clients coming by the office. With the kind of work I do, they don't have to. I get my contracts by phone or messenger; I get paid when I deliver the goods. It's a simple system and helps me keep my overhead low because usually by the time a client contacts me, all they're interested in is how fast can I get the job done, not how pretty my workspace is.

That night I'm sitting behind the desk, feet propped up on a corner while I flip through a fashion magazine. The window behind me's tuned to the usual dull channel: a nighttime view of an inner-city block, shops on the ground floor, apartments above them. The most predominant piece of color is a neon sign that just says BAR. Looking at all the models preening on the glossy pages propped up on my legs, I'm thinking that maybe what I need is a makeover. My idea of work clothing is comfort: jeans and hightops, a T-shirt with a lightweight shirt overtop, blonde hair tied back in a ponytail. About the only thing I have in common with these models is my height.

Of course a makeover means maintenance and I don't know if I have the patience for it. Shower, brush my hair, dab on some lipstick. Anything more and I'll be running even later than I usually am in the mornings. Then she comes walking in, drop-dead gorgeous like she stepped out of the magazine I'm holding, and I think, why even try?

Dark hair cut stylishly short, eyes darker still. The makeup's perfectly understated. The clothes, too. Custom fit, snug black dress and heels, clasp purse, and tailored silk jacket, also black. Her only jewelry is a short string of pearls.

"I need you to find someone for me," she says.

"That's not exactly my line of work, Ms . . . ?"

She lets my question hang there as she sits down across the desk from me, tugs her skirt down.

"It's extremely urgent," she says.

I have to smile. "It's always urgent, but I still can't help you. I don't do people—only things."

"I don't understand. Your card says . . ."

Well-manicured fingers take my business card from her purse and place it on the desk between us.

"I'm sorry if it's misled you," I tell her. "It just means that I find objects." She looks confused, so I go on to explain. "You know, like tickets to *Cats* for a visiting businessman. Props for a theater company or a film crew. Maybe some long out-of-print book. The kinds of things that people could find on their own if they had the time or the inclination. Instead they've got money and I do the legwork for them."

Now she takes a package of cigarettes from her purse.

"But it *is* an object I need you to find for me," she says.

It's my turn to look confused. "You started off saying you wanted me to find someone. . . ."

"I do. She stole my heart and I want it back."

The woman lights her cigarette and places the package and matches on the edge of the desk. I turn in my chair to look out the window. The same channel is still playing out there.

Well, this was a first. No one's ever contracted me to find a broken heart before. I want to send her right back out the door, except I start thinking about Peter, about how I felt when he walked out and took my heart away with him. So it was a woman who took hers instead of a man. Big deal. It had to hurt the same.

I turn back to look at her. "I have to level with you. I'm not really sure I can be of much help. What you really want is a private detective."

"I tried a few of them, but none of them would help me. The last one gave me your card."

I raise my eyebrows. "Can you remember his name?"

"A Peter Cross of the Vax Agency. He said it was just the odd sort of thing that would appeal to you."

Great. First he dumps me—"You're too intense, Kira,"—and now he's sending crumbs of work my way. Like I can't find work on my own. Though I'm not saying business has been good lately. . . .

I realize I'm frowning, but I can't seem to stop myself. Instead I reach for the woman's cigarette package.

"Do you mind?" I ask.

"Not at all."

"Thanks."

She gives me enough time to put a cigarette in my mouth.

"Will you help me?" she asks.

I pause with a lit match in my hand. "You know you can't ever get something like that back. When someone wants to walk out of your life, you can't force them to stay."

I'm thinking as I light the cigarette, trust me on this. I know. But I don't say it aloud.

She shakes her head. "Oh, no. You've misunderstood me. It's true we had a relationship, and it's true she left me, but I'm not looking to get her back. I just want my heart back. It's a pendant. She took it with her when she left."

"This is still a job for a private detective," I tell her. "Or maybe even the police, if you can prove ownership of the stolen property."

"It's not that simple."

It never is, is it?

I prop my elbow up on the desk, cup my chin with my hand. The cigarette smolders between the fingers of my free hand. It doesn't taste nearly as good as I was hoping it would.

"So tell me about it," I say.

"The heart was a gift to me from Faerie," she says.

This is getting kinkier by the minute. "So you're into gay, or I guess, bisexual guys, too?"

"Not at all."

"Hey, I don't have a problem with it," I tell her. "Live and let live, I say."

"When I say Faerie," she says, "I mean the Otherworld. I did a favor once for a prince of the realm and he gave me the pendant in gratitude. It allows one the gift of second sight. Of piercing the barriers between what we believe we see and what is actually there."

Scratch the kinky, I think. This woman belongs in a padded cell at the Zeb. Except she's so earnest. I can't help but lean forward as she talks, knowing it's all hogwash, but *wanting* it to be real. I mean, how many of us didn't go through a rainbow-and-unicorn phase when we were eleven or twelve?

So I let her ramble on about gifts from the faerie folk and how they don't work for everybody, but then what does? How her particular pendant not only gives its bearer this second sight, but also protects her from some of the, shall we say, less friendly denizens of the Otherworld. The friendlies pretty much ignore you, but the others . . .

See, the way she tells it, once you get their attention, once they know you can see them, you've got to have protection or your ass is grass. Sounds like life on the street to me, business as usual, except she's describing creatures with knives for fingers and worse.

I feel like I'm trapped in a video edition of *The Weekend Sun*, directed by Roger Corman—somewhere between "Nun Gives Birth to Pig Twins" and the Elvis Spotter page—so when I find myself agreeing to help her track down her friend and the pendant, I startle myself.

I mean, this really isn't my line of work. I'm strictly an over-the-phone girl. I do research, go electronic-tripping through the on-line services. Sometimes I have to leave the office to work the stacks at the Newford Library or something similar. I wouldn't know where to begin to find a missing person except from what I've seen in the movies.

My nameless client isn't stumped. She tells me to hit the girl bars on Gracie Street and gives me a photo of her friend. Tells me she'll be in touch with me tomorrow night. Leaves me sitting there in my office wondering, if she knows how to do it so well, why's she bothering to hire me? Leaves me wondering just how much Peter's leaving me has screwed me up that I'd agree to something like this.

I don't know my client's name. I don't know the name of the woman I'm looking for. My head's spinning with fairy tales. But at least she left her smokes. I give them up every couple of months. Right now I'm off them. Was.

So I stuff the pack in my pocket and hit the street. It's going on eleven, which means the action's just starting on Gracie Street. It's busy down here—not Times Square before Disney cleaned it up, but still big-city, inner-core, out-for-some-fun busy. The names of the bars range from the obvious to the less so: The North Star, Neon Sister, Girljock, Skirts. There's plenty of traffic on the pavement, cars cruising, cabs. Plenty of people on the sidewalk, too—street people, couples, single men and women. The couples I pass are all same sex: male and male, female and female. It's not too outrageous out on the street—you know, leather scenes and the like—but inside the clubs it's a whole different story.

Some of the women are femmes, some butch. Lots of sexy tops, short hair, body piercing, tattoos, dancing, smoking, drinking. I try not to do the tourist thing and gawk as I show around a photograph of two women standing on a street corner—one's my client. In the photo she's got her hair tied back. She's wearing a black T-shirt and jeans, black cowboy boots, and still looks like a million dollars. Around her neck, sparkling against the black shirt, is a small gold pendant in the shape of a heart. She has her arm around an attractive smaller woman who has short, spiky dark hair, angular features. The second woman is dressed in a short black dress and is barefoot. She's holding a pair of high heels by their straps with one hand and leaning against my client.

I show the photo around, but I seem to be generating more interest for who I am than the picture. I remember what I told my client earlier—live and let live—and I believe it. But I've never been hit on so many times in such a short period of time as I have in the past couple of hours. And not once by a guy.

It really isn't a problem for me. My best friend in high school, Sarah Jones, came out to me in our senior year and we're still good friends. But I'm being hit on so often right now that I find myself seriously wondering what it'd be like to go out with another woman.

I take a look at these cigarettes my client left behind and wonder what's in them, because first, she has me out here playing detective for her and now I'm actually considering . . .

There's an attractive woman with short red hair sitting at the other end of the bar, looking back at me, one eyebrow raised questioningly. She makes a victory sign with the first two fingers of her right hand and then flicks her tongue through them.

No, I don't think so.

I turn away quickly and bump into a tall black woman who's standing on the other side of my stool. She's wearing a white halter top, a short skirt and pumps, and has a ship captain's hat scrunching down her kinky black hair. There are three studs in her nose, half a dozen more in each ear, running up from the lobes.

"Easy now," she says, steadying me.

I jerk away from her. "Look, I'm not interested in—"

I break off when I realize the woman was just helping me keep my balance. She smiles at me, obviously non-aggressive, and I feel like a fool.

"I'm sorry," I tell her. "I'm just feeling a little . . ."

"Flustered?" she asks.

I nod.

"First time down here?"

"Yes, but it's not what you think."

When she cocks an eyebrow, I show her the photo and point to my client's companion.

"The other woman in the picture has got me looking for her," I say.

We're both leaning against the bar now, the photo lying on the bar between us. The music's still loud, making it hard to talk. All around us is the press of bodies, women dancing with each other, flirting with each other.

"I know them," the woman says. "Are you sure you're really into their scene?"

"What do you mean?"

"You know, the whole S&M thing. The girl you're looking for is your client's slave."

"Slave?"

The woman smiles. "You really are a virgin, aren't you? Your client's a top—you know, a leatherdyke."

I give her a blank look.

"The sexually dominant one of the pair. The other girl's a femme." She's still friendly, but maybe a little too friendly now. "Like you."

I shake my head. "No way."

And I mean it. Except even I can hear the trace of uncertainty in my voice.

My companion shrugs. "Then what're you doing with a recruiter?"

I'm getting more confused by the minute.

"I'm not sure I know what you mean," I tell her.

She gets a tired look on her face. "The leatherdykes are always looking for new blood, but the trouble is, you sweet young femmes don't always know you're looking for them, too."

She turns away, leaning against the bar with her elbows supporting her. She doesn't look at me anymore, her gaze on the crowd. I get the sense that this conversation is finished, thank you very much, but then she adds, "So people like your friend go out and recruit them."

"Oh."

What the hell have I gotten myself mixed up in?

The woman turns to look at me. "It's nothing heavy. Nobody's forced to do anything against her will. But sometimes people get talked into doing things that they regret later. The leather crowd can get a little rough."

"I'm really just trying to find this woman," I tell her. "After that, my job's over."

"Whatever."

She points to the photo then, finger resting on the chest of my client's ex-girlfriend.

"Somebody told me she's dancing at Chic Cheeks," she tells me. "That's a straight club over in the Combat Zone. I don't think her top knows about the gig. It's a big city. Easy to disappear in, especially if you go someplace where no one's going to look for you. At least no one in this crowd. We've got our own strip joints."

"Thanks," I say. "I really appreciate—"

"And considering the kind of clientele it caters to, you might want to go round the back like the girls who work there do."

"I will," I tell her.

"I'd say be careful, but you girls never listen, do you?"

I smile and leave with the photo in hand, pretending I didn't hear her.

Back out on Gracie Street, I find myself thinking about lesbian relationships again. Do women treat each other better than guys treat us, or is it the same-old same-old only with the gender changed? Call me naive, but I don't feel like that sailor girl would have treated me the way Peter did. But while I liked her, and I know she liked me, I still can't muster up a sexual interest in another woman.

I pause to light a cigarette.

I remember something another friend of mine said to me once. She told me she was attracted to lesbianism, but "It's not because I have the hots for another woman or anything," she confided. "What I'm attracted to is the kind of freedom the word implies. These women don't seem to worry so much about what everybody else is thinking; they just do what they think is right."

And that makes me think of what Sarah said about lesbian sex. "It's soft and slippery and it just never ends. There's no hard-on to worry about and one orgasm leads to the next. Who wants a guy, if that's what you get to do all day?"

As I light my cigarette, I see yet another woman watching me with interest from across the street. She looks as straight as I am, but I can tell she's getting ready to come over and chat. Before she crosses the street, I walk briskly on, trailing cigarette smoke.

No, I decide. I like guys. That's not going to change. I want my sexual partner to be tender, but I want him to have a hard-on, too. It's just the way Peter treated me that's got me all screwed up.

So . . . live and let live.

I catch a cab and have it drop me off in the Combat Zone. It's only a half block to Chic Cheeks from where the cab lets me out. When I get to the strip club, I stand in front of it for a long moment, frowning at the advertising posters and thinking about what I've been told.

What about my client? *Is* she a recruiter? I think of what the woman back at the club called her—a leatherdyke—and how she looked when she came into my office, and I don't know which is the mask. And how about all this talk about Faerie and magic and shit?

What was *that* all about?

I turn down the alleyway that runs alongside the club.

I'd pack it all in right now, except I've come this far and really, what else am I going to do? Go home and obsess about Peter? Or maybe go home and think too much about what I've seen tonight?

I don't have any trouble getting in through the side door—the bouncers are all out front. From the wings of the stage I watch a woman dressed like Alice in Wonderland go through her routine. She's got blonde hair—same cut as mine—but I recognize her, even with the blonde wig. She looks enough like me from a distance that I'd be amused, if I didn't feel a little sick. The Lovin' Spoonful's "Do You Believe in Magic?" is blasting from the sound system. She's playing the little girl, like she's twelve years old, and the freaks in the audience are lapping it up.

I find myself wishing I was back on Gracie Street. They're selling sex as blatantly there, but they're sure as hell not pandering to pedophiles.

I watch a little longer. The dancer's removed her blouse now. When she turns, I see the heartshaped pendant.

I go have a smoke while she finishes her act.

The dressing room's about what you'd expect in a dive like this. There's not even a door to allow the women some privacy. Anybody walking by backstage can stand in the doorway like I am and check things out. Some of the women are putting on costumes, or simply trying to relax. Some are smoking cigarettes, drinking. I can smell the joint that one of them's lit up.

My client's girlfriend has removed her blonde wig. She's dressed in street clothes now—jeans and a T-shirt—and is leaning close to a mirror adjusting her makeup.

I'd be wanting to take a shower after doing a "show" like that.

I wait until she's leaving the room. As she comes up to me, I step aside to let her go by, then touch her arm.

"Can I talk to you for a moment?" I ask.

"Sure. What's it about?"

I thought we could go for a coffee, but she's only got forty-five minutes until her next show so we sit on the steps of the alleyway entrance. We've both got cigarettes going. The alleyway's dark, but a slice of light from the door behind us cuts through the darkness, illuminating litter, the brick wall of the building on the other side of the alleyway, the photo that I've passed over to the dancer.

"You have to understand," she says. "I was never really into her scene. I mean, I swing both ways, but I'm not into pain. Or maybe I should say, my relationships are always painful, but it's not something I go looking for. It's not what I want. It just seems to happen. But with her . . ."

I nod encouragingly.

She shrugs. "The whips and the piercings and all that shit, it was just too much." She pauses for a beat, then adds, "Do you know anything about that kind of scene?"

"Not really."

"You really are their slave," she tells me. "You cook, you clean, you do the laundry—all for free. You don't get beaten as a punishment—that's how they reward you. You get to feeling that the worst thing that can happen is you'll be ignored. You start to crave the bondage and the fisting and the whips."

I watch her as she talks. Her expression is that of one both attracted and repulsed by what she's discussing.

"See," she goes on, "the thing is, pain brings on an endorphin high. You know it's just a biochemical thing, you're not *attracted* to being hurt, but after a while you can't stop craving it. You'll be a slave, if that's what it takes."

She jerks a thumb back toward the door of the club. "What did you think of the scene in there?"

"It made me feel a little sick," I tell her.

"Me, too. But at the same time it makes me feel strong. Because when I'm up there on the stage, I'm in control. I feel like they're my slaves and I could make them do anything I want."

I give her a sad look. "But it's not really true, is it?"

"No," she says with a humorless smile. "But it's what made me strong enough to get out of her grip. Don't get me wrong," she adds. "I'm not saying the women in the S&M scene shouldn't be doing what they want to do. It's just not for me."

I nod. "But you didn't know what you were getting into until it was too late. That's not right, either. Don't you think it should be consensual?"

Her expression when she replies is unreadable, distant. "The only thing I didn't know when I got into that scene was that I'd fall in love with her as hard as I did. But I should have known. I always do. I always fall in love with the ones that'll hurt me the most."

We sit there and smoke in silence for a few moments.

"So what does she want from me?" she asks finally. "Why did she send you out to look for me?"

"She just wants the pendant back."

The dancer reaches up and closes her hand around it.

"I figured as much," she says. "That's why I took it. It's like it was the only thing she really seemed to care about. If I couldn't get her to care for me, then at least I'd have something that she does care about."

She opens her hand and looks down at the pendant.

"If I give it back to her," she says, "I'll have nothing."

I nod. "Maybe it's better that way."

She closes her hand around the pendant again and gives it a sharp tug. The chain breaks. Standing up, she drops the pendant into my hand and goes back inside. She doesn't say anything. Not even goodbye.

I sit there for a while longer, looking down at the pendant with its broken chain where it lies in the palm of my hand.

I don't know what to say either.

3

Friday night.

I'm sitting in my office, looking out the window. It's raining, turning the streets slick with wet reflections. I'm waiting for my client, but she doesn't show. On my desk is the pack of cigarettes she left here last night. Beside it is the photo she gave me, the pendant lying on top of the photo with its broken chain.

I have no reason to worry about her, but I'm uneasy.

I keep going over what she told me about this business with the pendant. How it was given to her by this Faerie prince. How it doesn't work for everybody, but when it does it can give the person wearing it second sight. How it protects the person wearing it from the dark side of Faerie—the ghouls and the goblins and the things that go bump in the night.

Not that I believe any of it. Not for a moment.

My gaze leaves the pendant and goes back to the window. It's still raining.

But all day long, I haven't been able to shake the feeling that somebody's watching me. There's no one thing I can point to with certainty. It's just a prickling sensation that I feel on the nape of my neck. A sense of movement caught out of the corner of my eye. A kind of intuition . . .

I light one of the last two cigarettes.

Or second sight?

I stand up, picking up the pendant. I can't wait for her any longer. I'm getting the willies sitting in here on my own. There's no one in the building except me. And whatever might be watching me. . . .

I leave the office and cross the street to the bar, holding my trench coat closed with my hand. I've got to be around some people. I hate being alone. I think that's why my relationships always fall apart. I've got too much need. I *am* too intense—just like Peter said. But that's because when I'm alone, I think too much. My imagination gets carried away with itself. I imagine the worst. I start to believe there really is a burglar lurking about. Some crazed fanatic. A rapist. . . .

Nasty creatures from fairy tales is a new one for me.

It's pretty empty inside. A neighborhood bar with a few serious drinkers, a couple at a table near the back, oblivious to their surroundings, and me. I take a seat at a table by the window. The glass is fogged and streaked with rain, but I've cleared a portion of the pane with my hand so that I can look out. There are three beer bottles on my table, all empty. My glass is half full. The pack of cigarettes that I got from my client is beside it, also empty, plus a new fresh pack that has a couple of cigarettes missing. One of them's burning in the ashtray amidst the butts. My left hand is closed in a fist on the table.

I give the window another swipe to clear the fog again. I don't know what I'm looking for. My client? Or the things she's got me half-believing are out there, invisible to normal sight?

I open my hand to look at the pendant lying there in the middle of my palm.

Except maybe I don't have normal sight anymore. Maybe the pendant's working for me like it did for her.

I sigh and have another sip of beer.

I wish she'd just show up and take this stupid thing away with her.

All I see in the window is a reflection of my own face, raindrops streaking across the glass.

I wish I had someone to go home to.

4

A week later.

I'm sitting on the edge of my bed, reconsidering the idea of getting up and facing the day. I'm hung over and my bedroom feels claustrophobic. The room's small and the view's not exactly expansive. When I look past the fire escape, all I can see is the brick wall of the building next to mine—about the width of an alley away. My room's a mess. Clothes on the floor, the bedclothes rumpled, dresser covered with makeup, more clothes, magazines, and books. Ditto, my night table.

I'm a mess.

The cops found my business card in her purse, but no identification. That's why they had me come in to ID her. They didn't have anybody else and I didn't bother to mention my client's ex-girlfriend—not after viewing the body.

Ari—at least that's her stage name—took it hard when I went by the club to tell her the next night. I guess she was holding on to broken hopes, pretending that she and the woman she knew as Elise would get back together again—the same way I've been pretending Peter will come back.

I know that, for all our physical frailties, we humans are capable of inflicting incredible amounts of damage on each other, but there's no way Ari could have killed Elise, so why get her involved?

Nothing *human* killed her. The cops are saying she got torn apart by a dog, but I'm not so sure. I keep remembering the way she looked when she was telling me about how the pendant protected her from these creatures she described to me—the ones with knives for fingers and mouths full of barracuda teeth in the middle of their palms.

I finally get up, have a shower, get dressed. When I wander into my small kitchen it feels just as claustrophobic as my bedroom. I ignore the mess and put the kettle on, but coffee and a cigarette don't help my mouth taste any better. What I really want is another drink. I haven't been sober for a week now, because this way I can just put it all down to the booze. I use it as a crutch—the same way I've been using cigarettes since that night Elise first came into my office. The cigarettes for Peter, the booze for what happened to Elise.

I would've had nightmares all night, just thinking about what I saw there in the morgue, if I hadn't had so much to drink before I finally dragged myself home. If I'm drunk, I can pretend she didn't die the way I can so easily imagine she did, torn apart by some creatures from the dark side of the Brothers Grimm.

I can pretend they're not looking for me now.

I put my coffee mug down on the counter with all the other unwashed dishes and get my jacket from where I tossed it last night. I have to get out of here before my imagination runs too wild.

I mean, I know it's crazy. Nasty goblins didn't kill Elise. It *couldn't* have gone down that way. It's got to be like the cops said, she got attacked by some animal. A pack of feral dogs, ranging out of the Tombs, say.

When I step outside my apartment building, the sun hurts my eyes. But there's no one watching me except for the old guy down the street who stares at anybody who's got breasts, doesn't matter if they're no bigger than buttons, or old and sagging and hanging down to your waist.

But everything still feels different. There are undercurrents that I never sensed before the pendant came into my possession. I can't begin to explain it. I just know now that there *is* more to what's around us than what we can see. Things moving in our peripheral vision. Events. Possibilities. Omens and portents and the stuff of dreams. What I can't swear to is that they're necessarily malevolent.

I think what we call to ourselves is what we expect to see. We're still not seeing what's really *there*—only our perceptions of what we expect could be there. If you were haunted by inner demons and into S&M the way Elise was, then maybe you'd see a faerie world that was beautiful and dangerous. And you'd call the darkness to you, in the same way Elise's ex-girlfriend told me she was always attracted to those who would treat her the worst, allowing herself to keep falling into abusive relationships even when she knew better.

Which isn't to say that it's Ari's fault. If you're beat on all of your life, how can you be expected to gain a sudden change of attitude all by yourself? Confidence and strength accrue in direct proportion to the breaks you get—the help and support that only someone else can give you.

I guess I'm making it sound as though I've suddenly gained this huge boost of confidence myself, but in my own way, I'm just as bad as Ari. She's still shaking her ass on stage at Chic Cheeks, untouched by her contact with the pendant. She still thinks that stripping gives her some kind of power over the freaks. She's right on the edge of another bad relationship because she can't break the cycle.

And me? I still don't want to be alone. The focus of my life is still eddying around the fact that Peter left me, that there's something intrinsically wrong with me, or why would my relationships always fall apart?

It can't just be that I get too intense. Love's *supposed* to be intense . . . isn't it?

And then there's this business with the pendant.

I still think something's watching me. Or some*things*. I don't know if they're stalking me, or simply curious.

I end up on the subway, not aware of what I'm doing until it takes me downtown. I get off and head up to street level and the first thing I see is a flower cart. I buy a half-dozen roses from the old man who runs the cart and catch a bus that takes me to the Foxville Cemetery. The gates loom up above me when I go inside and make my way to Elise's grave. When I get there, I kneel down and lay the roses on the dirt in front of her marker. It's just a small gravestone and cost a small fortune that I couldn't really afford. I had to dig deep into my rainy-day account to pay for it, but I felt she needed something and there was no one else to pitch in. Ari wanted nothing to do with it. I don't think she's willing to accept the idea that Elise is even dead.

My fingers rise to touch the pendant that I've taken to wearing. I don't think it affected Ari at all, but I can't say the same for myself.

It's funny how your whole life can change because of the smallest thing. Like someone walking in through the door of your office. . . . Everything still *looks* the same, but now I feel like the most common object has a secret history that most people can't see. The difference between them and me is, they don't even think about it.

I'm certain this knowledge killed Elise, but somehow I can't believe it's dangerous, in and of itself. The real danger would be to ignore it. The real danger would be to see what your preconceptions have led you to expect, instead of striving to see what really is there.

I'm not going to make Elise's mistake.

I won't say I'm not nervous. The idea of all these . . . presences around me really creeps me out. But they don't have to be malevolent, do they? Are hopes always broken?

Maybe I'm being a Pollyanna. Maybe the world really is an ugly piece of work. But I don't want to believe that. I want to think I'm breaking a cycle. I think I can look into this unseen world of Faerie the way that friend of mine looked into the lesbian scene. She took from it the image of a strong ideal, someone in control of her own destiny, and it made her stronger. She took the idea of it—the knowledge that it can be done—and that was what let her do it for herself.

And that's what I want to do. I want to look into Faerie and know that everything can be different. I want to break the cycle of my old patterns. I want to throw away my crutches and addictions. I want to step into a world where anything is possible—where I can be anything or anybody.

I want to find strength in my solitude so that when I do interact with other people, I won't hold on so tightly when they're with me. So that I can let them go when we have to be apart.

I know the danger. All I have to do is remember what happened to Elise. If I close my eyes, I can see her ravaged body as clearly as though it were still lying stretched out in the morgue in front of me. . . .

By looking into Faerie, I might be calling the same savagery down upon myself. But there's no point in being afraid. The danger's all around anyway. I might have imagined all those psychotics and rapists that peopled my fears, but that doesn't mean they're not out there. All you have to do is pick up a paper or turn on the news.

The dangers of Faerie are out there, too.

I guess what I should be saying is that while I have to be careful, I can't let my fear overwhelm me the way I have in the past.

I reach into my pocket to take the package of cigarettes I'm currently working on and lay it down beside the roses.

Break the old patterns. The old cycles.

"It's funny how it works out, isn't it?" I say to my client's gravestone. "I failed you, but you—however inadvertently—you didn't fail me."

I stand up and brush the dirt from my knees.

"I can't pay you back, but maybe I can help other people the way you've helped me: trip them out of their old patterns and show them what they're doing to themselves. Jump-start their lives onto a new track and then try to be there for them when they begin to put their lives back together again."

I touch the stone, trace its smooth surface with my fingers.

"I don't know where you are," I tell Elise. "I don't know if you can hear me or if it'll make any difference if you can, but I promise I'll give it my best shot."

I turn away from the grave, continuing the one-sided conversation in my head.

I'm going to start with Ari and see if, together, we can't break the pattern of her pain. Her pain, and mine. That'd be a kind of magic, too, wouldn't it? Because we can't close our eyes to it. Not the magic, not the pain. If we do that, we might as well close them forever.

The gates of the graveyard loom over me again as I leave, but they don't feel as oppressive as they did when I first went in. In my mind's eye, I'm picturing little figures the size of mice, slipping out from behind Elise's gravestone. They look like they've been put together with twigs and leaves and other debris. Their heads are wide, eyes slightly oversized and slanted, noses small on some, prominent on others, mouths very wide. Their hair is matted like dreadlocks mixed up with leafy vines.

They climb over the roses. One of them pulls a cigarette from the pack I left there and is awkwardly holding it, nose quivering like a rabbit's as it sniffs the paper and tobacco. A few of them clamber up onto the lower base of the gravestone and are shading their eyes, looking in my direction.

I don't turn around and look back. So long as I don't turn around, they can really be there. The magic can be real. The pain can be put away.

Heartfires

1

Nobody tells you the really important stuff so in the end you have to imagine it for yourself. It's like how things connect. A thing is just a thing until you have the story that goes with it. Without the story, there's nothing to hold on to, nothing to relate this mysterious new thing to who you are—you know, to make it a part of your own history. So if you're like me, you make something up and the funny thing is, lots of times, once you tell the story, it comes true. Not *poof*, hocus-pocus, magic it comes true, but sure, why not, and after it gets repeated often enough, you and everybody else end up believing it.

It's like quarks. They're neither positive nor negative until the research scientists look at them. Right up until that moment of observation they hold the possibility of being one or the other. It's the *looking* that makes them what they are. Which is like making up a story for them, right?

The world's full of riddles like that.

The lady or the tiger.

Did she jump, or was she pushed?

The door standing by itself in the middle of the field—does it lead to somewhere, or from somewhere?

Or the locked room we found one night down in Old City, the part of it that runs under the Tombs. A ten-by-ten-foot room, stone walls, stone floor and ceiling, with a door in one wall that fits so snugly you wouldn't even know it was there except for the bolts—a set on either side of the door, big old iron fittings, rusted, but still solid. The air in that room is dry, touched with the taste of old spices and sagegrass. And the place is clean. No dust. No dirt. Only these scratches on that weird door, long gouges cut into the stone like something was clawing at it, both sides of the door, inside and out.

So what was it for? Before the quake dropped the building into the ground, that room was still below street level. Somebody from the long-ago built that room, hid it away in the cellar of what must have been a seriously tall building in those days—seven stories high. Except for the top floor, it's all underground now. We didn't even know the building was there until Bear fell through a hole in the roof, landing on his ass in a pile of rubble which, luckily for him, was only a few feet down. Most of that top floor was filled with broken stone and crap, like someone had bulldozed another tumbled-down building inside it and overtop of it, pretty much blocking any way in and turning that top floor into a small mountain covered with metal junk and weeds and every kind of trash you can imagine. It was a fluke we ever found our way in, it was that well hidden.

But why was it hidden? Because the building couldn't be salvaged, so cover it up, make it safe? Or because of that room?

That room. Was it to lock something in? Or keep something out?

Did our going into it make it be one or the other? Or was it the story we found in its stone confines?

We told that story to each other, taking turns like we usually do, and when we were done, we remembered what that room was. We'd never been in it before, not that room, in that place, but we remembered.

2

Devil's Night, October 30. It's not even nine o'clock and they've already got fires burning all over the Tombs: sparks flying, grass fires in the empty lots, trash fires in metal drums, the guts of derelict tenements and factory buildings going up like so much kindling. The sky overhead fills with an evil glow, like an aura gone bad, gone way bad. The smoke from the fires rises in streaming columns. It cuts through the orange glare hanging over that square mile or so of lost hopes and despair the way ink spreads in water.

The streets are choked with refuse and abandoned cars, but that doesn't stop the revelers from their fun, the flickering light of the fires playing across their features as they lift their heads and howl at the devil's glow. Does stop the fire department, though. This year they don't even bother to try to get their trucks in. You can almost hear the mayor telling the chiefs: "Let it burn."

Hell, it's only the Tombs. Nobody living here but squatters and hoboes, junkies and bikers. These are the inhabitants of the night side of the city—the side you only see out of the corner of your eye until the sun goes down and suddenly they're all over the streets, in your face, instead of back in the shadows where they belong. They're not citizens. They don't even vote.

And they're having some fun tonight. Not the kind of recreation you or I might look for, but a desperate fun, the kind that's born out of knowing you've got nowhere to go but down and you're already at the bottom. I'm not making excuses for them. I just understand them a little better than most citizens might.

See, I've run with them. I've slept in those abandoned buildings, scrabbled for food in Dumpsters over by Williamson Street, trying to get there before the rats and feral dogs. I've looked for oblivion in the bottom of a bottle or at the end of a needle.

No, don't go feeling sorry for me. I had me some hard times, sure, but everybody does. But I'll tell you, I never torched buildings. Even in the long-ago. When I'm looking to set a fire, I want it to burn in the heart.

3

I'm an old crow, but I still know a few tricks. I'm looking rough, maybe even used up, but I'm not yet so old I'm useless. You can't fool me, but I fool most everyone, wearing clothes, hiding my feathers, walking around on my hind legs like a man, upright, not hunched over, moving pretty fast, considering.

There were four of us in those days, ran together from time to time. Old spirits, wandering the world, stopped awhile in this place before we went on. We're always moving on, restless, looking for change so that things'll stay the same. There was me, Crazy Crow, looking sharp with my flat-brimmed hat and pointy-toed boots. Alberta the Dancer with those antlers poking up out of her red hair, you know how to look, you can see them. Bear, he was so big you felt like the sky had gone dark when he stood by you. And then there was Jolene.

She was just a kid that Devil's Night. She gets like that. One year she's about knee-high to a skinny moment and you can't stop her from tomfooling around, another year she's so fat even Bear feels small around her. We go way back, Jolene and me, knew each other pretty good, we met so often.

Me and Alberta were together that year. We took Jolene in like she was our daughter, Bear her uncle. Moving on the wheel like a family. We're dark-skinned—we're old spirits, got to be the way we are before the European look got so popular—but not so dark as fur and feathers. Crow, grizzly, deer. We lose some color when we wear clothes, walking on our hind legs all the time.

Sometimes we lose other things, too. Like who we really are and what we're doing here.

4

"Hey, 'bo."

I look up to see it's a brother calling to me. We're standing around an oil drum, warming our hands, and he comes walking out of the shadows like he's a piece of them, got free somehow, comes walking right up to me like he thinks I'm in charge. Alberta smiles. Bear lights a smoke, takes a couple of drags, then offers it to the brother.

"Bad night for fires," he says after he takes a drag. He gives the cigarette a funny look, tasting the sweetgrass mixed in with the tobacco. Not much, just enough.

"Devil's Night," Jolene says, grinning like it's a good thing. She's a little too fond of fires this year for my taste. Next thing you know she'll be wanting to tame metal, build herself a machine and wouldn't that be something?

"Nothing to smile about," the brother tells her. "Lot of people get hurt, Devil's

Night. Gets out of hand. Gets to where people think its funny, maybe set a few of us 'boes on fire, you hear what I'm saying?"

"Times are always hard," I say.

He shrugs, takes another drag of the cigarette, then hands it back to Bear.

"Good night for a walk," he says finally. "A body might walk clear out of the Tombs on a night like this, come back when things are a little more settled down."

We all just look at him.

"Got my boy waiting on me," he says. "Going for that walk. You all take care of yourselves now."

We never saw the boy, standing there in the shadows, waiting on his pa, except maybe Jolene. There's not much she misses. I wait until the shadows almost swallow the brother before I call after him.

"Appreciate the caution," I tell him.

He looks back, tips a finger to his brow, then he's gone, part of the shadows again.

"Are we looking for trouble?" Bear asks.

"Uh-huh," Jolene pipes up, but I shake my head.

"Like he said," I tell them, jerking a thumb to where the brother walked away.

Bear leads the way out, heading east, taking a direct route and avoiding the fires we can see springing up all around us now. The dark doesn't bother us, we can see pretty much the same, doesn't matter if it's night or day. We follow Bear up a hillside of rubble. He gets to the top before us and starts dancing around, stamping his feet, singing, "Wa-hey, look at me. I'm the king of the mountain."

And then he disappears between one stamp and the next, and that's how we find the room.

5

I don't know why we slide down to where Bear's standing instead of him climbing back up. Curious, I guess. Smelling spirit mischief and we just have to see where it leads us, down, down, till we're standing on a dark street, way underground.

"Old City," Alberta says.

"Walked right out of the Tombs we did," Jolene says, then she shoots Bear a look and giggles. "Or maybe slid right out of it on our asses'd be a better way to put it."

Bear gives her a friendly whack on the back of the head but it doesn't budge a hair. Jolene's not looking like much this year, standing about halfway to nothing, but she's always solidly built, doesn't much matter what skin she's wearing.

"Let's take that walk," I say, but Bear catches hold of my arm.

"I smell something old," he tells me.

"It's an old place," I tell him. "Fell down here a long time ago and stood above ground even longer."

Bear shakes his head. "No. I'm smelling something older than that. And lower down."

We're on an underground street, I'm thinking. Way down. Can't get much lower than this. But Bear's looking back at the building we just came out of and I know what's on his mind. Basements. They're too much like caves for him to pass one by, especially when it's got an old smell. I look at the others. Jolene's game, but then she's always game when she's wearing this skin. Alberta shrugs.

"When I want to dance," she says, "you all dance with me, so I'm going to say no when Bear wants to try out a new step?"

I can't remember the last time we all danced, but I can't find any argument with what she's saying.

"What about you, Crazy Crow?" Bear asks.

"You know me," I tell him. "I'm like Jolene, I'm always game."

So we go back inside, following Bear who's following his nose, and he leads us right up to the door of that empty stone room down in the cellar. He grabs hold of the iron bolt, shoves it to one side, hauls the door open, rubs his hand on his jeans to brush off the specks of rust that got caught up on his palm.

"Something tried hard to get out," Alberta says.

I'm thinking of the other side of the door. "And in," I add.

Jolene's spinning around in the middle of the room, arms spread wide.

"Old, old, old," she sings.

We can all smell it now. I get the feeling that the building grew out of this room, that it was built to hold it. Or hide it.

"No ghosts," Bear says. "No spirits here."

Jolene stops spinning. "Just us," she says.

"Just us," Bear agrees.

He sits down on the clean stone floor, cross-legged, rolls himself a smoke. We all join him, sitting in a circle, like we're dancing, except it's only our breathing that's making the steps. We each take a drag of the cigarette, then Bear sets the butt down in the middle of the circle. We watch the smoke curl up from it, tobacco with that pinch of sweetgrass. It makes a long curling journey up to the ceiling, thickens there like a small storm cloud, pregnant with grandfather thunders.

Somewhere up above us, where the moon can see it, there's smoke rising, too, Devil's Night fires filling the hollow of the sky with pillars of silent thunder.

Bear takes a shotgun cartridge out of his pocket, brass and red cardboard, twelve-gauge, and puts it down on the stone beside the smoldering butt, stands it on end, brass side down.

"Guess we need a story," he says. He looks at me. "So we can understand this place."

We all nod. We'll take turns, talking until one of us gets it right.

"Me first," Jolene says.

She picks up the cartridge and rolls it back and forth on that small dark palm of hers and we listen.

6

Jolene says:

It's like that pan-girl, always cooking something up, you know the one. You can smell the wild onion on her breath a mile away. She's got that box that she can't look in, tin box with a lock on it that rattles against the side of the box when she gives it a shake, trying to guess what's inside. There's all these scratches on the tin, inside and out, something trying to get out, something trying to get in.

That's this place, the pan-girl's box. You know she opened that box, let all that stuff out that makes the world more interesting. She can't get it back in, and I'm thinking why try?

Anyway, she throws that box away. It's a hollow now, a hollow place, can be any size you want it to be, any shape, any color, same box. Now we're sitting in it, stone version. Close that door and maybe we can't get out. Got to wait until another pan-girl comes along, takes a break from all that cooking, takes a peek at what's inside. That big eye of hers'll fill the door and ya-hey, here we'll be, looking right back at her, rushing past her, she's swatting her hands at us trying to keep us in, but we're already gone, gone running back out into the world to make everything a little more interesting again.

7

Bear says:

Stone. You can't get much older than stone. First house was stone. Not like this room, not perfectly square, not flat, but stone all the same. Found places, those caves, just like we found this place. Old smell in them. Sometimes bear. Sometimes lion. Sometimes snake. Sometimes the ones that went before.

All gone when we come. All that's left is their messages painted or scratched on the walls. Stories. Information. Things they know we have to figure out, things that they could have told us if they were still around. Only way to tell us now is to leave the messages.

This place is a hollow, like Jolene said, but not why she said it. It's hollow because there's no messages. This is the place we have to leave our messages so that when we go on we'll know that the ones to follow will be able to figure things out.

8

Alberta says:

Inside and out, same thing. The wheel doesn't change, only the way we see it. Door opens either way. Both sides in, both sides out. Trouble is, we're always on the wrong side, always want the thing we haven't got, makes no difference who we are. Restless spirits want life, living people look for something better to come. Nobody *here*. Nobody content with what they got. And the reason for that's to keep the wheel turning. That simple. Wheel stops turning, there's nothing left.

It's like the woman who feels the cage of her bones, those ribs they're a prison for her. She's clawing, clawing at those bone bars, making herself sick. Inside, where you can't see it, but outside, too.

So she goes to see the Lady of the White Deer—looks just like you, Jolene, the way you were last year. Big woman. Big as a tree. Got dark, dark eyes you could get lost in. But she's smiling, always smiling. Smiling as she listens, smiling when she speaks. Like a mother smiles, seen it all, heard it all, but still patient, still kind, still understanding.

"That's just living," she tells the caged woman. "Those aren't bars, they're the bones that hold you together. You keep clawing at them, you'll make yourself so sick you're going to die for sure."

"I can't breathe in here," the caged woman says.

"You're not paying attention," the Lady of the White Deer says. "All you're doing is breathing. Stop breathing and you'll be clawing at those same bones, trying to get back in."

"You don't understand," the caged woman tells her and she walks away.

So she goes to see the Old Man of the Mountains—looks just like you, Bear. Same face, same hair. A big old bear, sitting up there on the top of the mountain, looking out at everything below. Doesn't smile so much, but understands how everybody's got a secret dark place sits way deep down there inside, hidden but wanting to get out. Understands how you can be happy but not happy at the same time. Understands that sometimes you feel you got to go all the way out to get back in, but if you do, you can't. There's no way back in.

So not smiling so much, but maybe understanding a little more, he lets the woman talk and he listens.

"We all got a place inside us, feels like a prison," he tells her. "It's darker in some people than others, that's all. Thing is, you got to balance what's there with what's around you or you'll find yourself on a road that's got no end. Got no beginning and goes nowhere. It's just always this same thing, never grows, never changes, only gets darker and darker, like that candle blowing in the wind. Looks real nice till the wind blows it out—you hear what I'm saying?"

"I can't breathe in here," the woman tells him.

That Old Man of the Mountain he shakes his head. "You're breathing," he says. "You're just not paying attention to it. You're looking inside, looking inside, forgetting what's outside. You're making friends with that darkness inside you and that's not good. You better stop your scratching and clawing or you're going to let it out."

"You don't understand either," the caged woman says and she walks away.

So finally she goes to see the Old Man of the Desert—looks like you, Crazy Crow. Got the same sharp features, the same laughing eyes. Likes to collect things. Keeps a pocket full of shiny mementos that used to belong to other people, things they threw away. Holds onto them until they want them back and then makes a trade. He'd give them away, but he knows what everybody thinks: All you get for nothing is nothing. Got to put a price on a thing to give it any worth.

He doesn't smile at all when he sees her coming. He puts his hand in his pocket and plays with something while she talks. Doesn't say anything when she's done, just sits there, looking at her.

"Aren't you going to help me?" she asks.

"You don't want my help," the Old Man of the Desert says. "You just want me to agree with you. You just want me to say, aw, that's bad, really bad. You've got it bad. Everybody else in the world is doing fine, except for you, because you got it so hard and bad."

The caged woman looks at him. She's got tears starting in her eyes.

"Why are you being so mean to me?" she asks.

"The truth only sounds mean," he tells her. "You look at it from another side and maybe you see it as kindness. All depends where you're looking, what you want to see."

"But I can't breathe," she says.

"You're breathing just fine," he says right back at her. "The thing is, you're not thinking so good. Got clouds in your head. Makes it hard to see straight. Makes it hard to hear what you don't want to hear anyway. Makes it hard to accept that the rest of the world's not out of step on the wheel, only you are. Work on that and you'll start feeling a little better. Remember who you are instead of always crying after what you think you want to be."

"You don't understand either," she says.

But before she can walk away, the Old Man of the Desert takes that thing out of his pocket, that thing he's been playing with, and she sees it's her dancing. He's got it all rolled up in a ball of beads and cowrie shells and feathers and mud, wrapped around with a rope of braided sweetgrass. Her dancing. Been a long time since she's seen that dancing. She thought it was lost in the long-ago. Thought it disappeared with her breathing.

"Where'd you get that dancing?" she asks.

"Found it in the trash. You'd be amazed what people will throw out—every kind of piece of themselves."

She puts her hand out to take it, but the Old Man of the Desert shakes his head and holds it out of her reach.

"That's mine," she says. "I lost that in the long-ago."

"You never lost it," the Old Man of the Desert tells her. "You threw it away."

"But I want it back now."

"You got to trade for it," he says.

The caged woman lowers her head. "I got nothing to trade for it."

"Give me your prison," the Old Man of the Desert says.

She looks up at him. "Now you're making fun of me," she says. "I give you my prison, I'm going to die. Dancing's not much use to the dead."

"Depends," he says. "Dancing can honor the dead. Lets them breathe in the faraway. Puts a fire in their cold chests. Warms their bone prisons for a time."

"What are you saying?" the caged woman asks. "I give you my life and you'll dance for me?"

The Old Man of the Desert smiles and that smile scares her because it's not kind or understanding. It's sharp and cuts deep. It cuts like a knife, slips in through the skin, slips past the ribs of her bone prison.

"What you got caging you is the idea of a prison," he says. "That's what I want from you."

"You want some kind of . . . story?"

He shakes his head. "I'm not in a bartering mood—not about this kind of thing."

"I don't know how to give you my prison," she says. "I don't know if I can."

"All you got to do is say yes," he tells her.

She looks at that dancing in his hand and it's all she wants now. There's little sparks coming off it, the smell of smudge-sticks and licorice and gasoline. There's a warmth burning in it that she knows will drive the cold away. That cold. She's been holding that cold for so long she doesn't hardly remember what it feels like to be warm anymore.

She's looking, she's reaching. She says yes and the Old Man of the Desert gives her back her dancing. And it's warm and familiar, lying there in her hand, but she doesn't feel any different. She doesn't know what to do with it, now she's got it. She wants to ask him what to do, but he's not paying attention to her anymore.

What's he doing? He's picking up dirt and he's spitting on it, spitting and spitting and working the dirt until it's like clay. And he makes a box out of it and in one side of the box he puts a door. And he digs a hole in the dirt and he puts the box in it. And he covers it up again. And then he looks at her. "One day you're going to find yourself in that box again," he says, "but this time you'll remember and you won't get locked up again."

She doesn't understand what he's talking about, doesn't care. She's got other things on her mind. She holds up her dancing, holds it in the air between them.

"I don't know what to do with this," she says. "I don't know how to make it work."

The Old Man of the Desert stands up. He gives her a hand up. He takes the dancing from her and throws it on the ground, throws it hard, throws it so hard it breaks. He starts shuffling his feet, keeping time with a clicking sound in the back of his throat. The dust rises up from the ground and she breathes it in and then she remembers what it was like and who she was and why she danced.

It was to honor the bone prison that holds her breathing for this turn of the wheel. It was to honor the gift of the world underfoot. It was to celebrate what's always changing: the stories. The dance of our lives. The wheel of the world and the sky spinning above it and our place in it.

The bones of her prison weren't there to keep her from getting out. They were there to keep her together.

9

I'm holding the cartridge now, but there's no need for me to speak. The story's done. Somewhere up above us, the skies over the Tombs are still full of smoke, the Devil's Night fires are still burning. Here in the hollow of this stone room, we've got a fire of our own.

Alberta looks across the circle at me.

"I remember," she says.

"That was the first time we met," Jolene says. "I remember, too. Not the end, but the beginning. I was there at the beginning and then later, too. For the dancing."

Bear nods. He takes the cartridge from my fingers and puts it back into his pocket. Out of another pocket he takes packets of color, ground pigments. Red and yellow and blue. Black and white. He puts them on the floor, takes a pinch of color out of one of the packets and lays it in the palm of his hand. Spits into his palm. Dips a finger in. He gets up, that Old Man of the Mountain, and he crosses over to one of the walls. Starts to painting. Starts to leave a message for the ones to follow.

Those colors, they're like dancing. Once someone starts, you can't help but twitch and turn and fidget until you're doing it, too. Next thing you know, we're all spitting into our palms, we're all dancing the color across the walls.

Remembering.

Because that's what the stories are for.

Even for old spirits like us.

We lock ourselves up in bone prisons same as everybody else. Forget who we are, why we are, where we're going. Till one day we come across a story we left for ourselves and remember why we're wearing these skins. Remember why we're dancing.

The Invisibles

What is unseen is not necessarily unknown.
—Wendelessen

1

When I was twelve years old, it was a different world.

I suppose most people think that, turning their gazes inward to old times, the long trail of their memories leading them back into territory made unfamiliar with the dust of years. The dust lies so thick in places it changes the shape of what it covers, half-remembered people, places and events, all mixed together so that you get confused trying to sort them out, don't even recognize some, probably glad you can't make out others. But then there are places, the wind blows harder across their shapes, or maybe we visit them more often so the dust doesn't lie so thick, and the memories sit there waiting for us, no different now than the day they happened, good and bad, momentous occasions and those so trivial you can't figure out why you remember them.

But I know this is true: When I was twelve years old, kids my age didn't know as much as they do today. We believed things you couldn't get by most eight year olds now. We were ready to believe almost anything. All we required was that it be true— maybe not so much by the rules of the world around us, but at least by the rules of some intuitive inner logic. It wasn't ever anything that got talked out. We just believed. In luck. In wishes. In how a thing will happen, if you stick to the right parade of circumstances.

We were willing to believe in magic.

Here's what you do, Jerry says. You get one of those little pipe tobacco tins and you put stuff in it. Important stuff. A fingernail. Some hair. A scab. Some dirt from a special place. You spit on it and mix it up like a mud pie. Prick your finger and add a drop of blood. Then you wrap it all up in a picture of the thing you like the best.

What if you don't have a picture of the thing you like the best? I ask.

Doesn't have to be a real picture, he says. You can just make a drawing of it. Might be even better that way because then it really belongs to you.

So what do you do with it? Rebecca asks.

I can see her so clearly, the red hairs coming loose from her braids, picking at her knee where she scraped it falling off her bike.

You stick it in that tin, Jerry says, and close it up tight. Dig a hole under your porch and bury it deep.

He leans closer to us, eyes serious, has that look he always gets when he's telling us something we might not believe is true, but he wants us to know that it is.

This means something, he says. You do it right and you'll always have that thing you like the best. Nothing will ever take it away.

I don't know where he heard about it. Read it in a book, or maybe his grandmother told him. She always had the best stories. It doesn't matter. We knew it was a true magic and that night each of us snuck out of our house and did it. Buried those tins deep. Made a secret of it to make the magic stronger is how Jerry put it.

I didn't need the magic to be any stronger. I just needed it to be true. We were best friends, the three of us, and I didn't want that to ever change. I really believed in magic, and the idea of the tin seemed to be about the best magic kids like us could make.

Rebecca moved away when we were in ninth grade. Jerry died the last year of high school, hit by a drunk driver.

Years later, this all came back to me. I'd returned to have a look at the old neighborhood, but our houses were gone by then. Those acre lots we grew up on had been subdivided, the roads all turned around on themselves and changed until there was nothing left of the neighborhood's old patterns. They're identical, these new houses, poured out of the same mold, one after the other, row upon row, street after street.

I got out of the car that day and stood where I thought my house used to be, feeling lost, cut off, no longer connected to my own past. I thought of those tins then and wondered whatever had happened to them. I remembered the drawing I made to put in mine. It was so poorly drawn I'd had to write our names under our faces to make sure the magic knew who I meant.

The weird thing is I never felt betrayed by the magic when Rebecca moved away, or when Jerry died. I just . . . lost it. Forgot about it. It went away, or maybe I did. Even that day, standing there in a neighborhood now occupied by strangers, the memory of those tins was only bittersweet. I smiled, remembering what we'd done, sneaking out so late that night, how we'd believed. The tightness in my chest grew from good moments recalled, mixed up with the sadness of remembering friends I'd lost. Of course those tins couldn't have kept us together. Life goes on. People move, relationships alter, people die. That's how the world turns.

There isn't room for magic in it, though you'd never convince Ted of that.

2

Ted and I go back a long way. We met during my first year in college, almost twenty years ago, and we still see each other every second day or so. I don't know why we get along so well unless that old axiom's true and opposites do attract. Ted's about the most outgoing person you could meet; opinionated, I'll be the first to admit, but he also knows how to listen. He's the sort of person other people naturally gravitate to at a party, collecting odd facts and odder rumors the way a magpie does shiny baubles, then jump-starting conversations with them at a later date as though they were hors d'oeuvre.

I'm not nearly so social an animal. If you pressed me, I'd say I like to pick and choose my friends carefully; the truth is, I usually have no idea what to say to people—especially when I first meet them.

Tonight it's only the two of us, holding court in The Half Kaffe. I'm drinking espresso, Ted's got one of those decaf lattés made with skim milk that always has me wonder, what's the point? If you want to drink coffee that weak, you can find it down the street at Bruno's Diner for a quarter of the price. But Ted's gone health-conscious recently. It's all talk about decaf and jogging and macrobiotic this and holistic that, then he lights up a cigarette. Go figure.

"Who's that woman?" I ask when he runs out of things to say about this *T'ai Chi* course he's just started taking. "The one at the other end of the counter with the long straight hair and the sad eyes?"

I haven't been able to stop looking at her since we got here. I find her attractive, but not in a way I can easily explain. It's more the sum of the parts, because individually things are a little askew. She's tall and angular, eyes almost too wide-set, chin pointed like a cat's, a Picasso nose, very straight and angled down. She has the sort of features that look gorgeous one moment, then almost homely the next. Her posture's not great, but then, considering my own, I don't think I should be making that kind of judgment. Maybe she thinks like I do, that if you slouch a bit, people won't notice you. Doesn't usually work.

I suspect she's waiting for someone since all she's been doing is sitting there, looking out the window. Hasn't ordered anything yet. Or maybe it's because Jonathan's too caught up with the most recent issue of the *Utne Reader* to notice her.

I look away from her when I realize that Ted hasn't answered. I find him giving me a strange look.

"So what've you got in that cup besides coffee?" he asks.

"What's that supposed to mean?"

He laughs. "I'm not sure. All I know is I don't see anyone sitting at this counter, male or female. I see you and me and Jonathan."

I'm sure he's putting me on. "No, seriously. Who is she?"

And he, I realize, thinks I'm putting him on. He makes an exaggerated show of having a look, taking off non-existent glasses, cleaning them, putting them back on, looks some more, but his attention isn't even on the right stool.

"Okay," he says. "I see her now. I think . . . yes, she's a princess. Lost a shoe, or a half-dozen feet of hair, or a bag of beans or something. Or maybe turned the wrong key in the wrong lock and got turned out of her bearded husband's apartment and now she's here killing time between periods of sleep just like the rest of us."

"Enough," I tell him. "I get the picture."

He doesn't see her. And it's beginning to be obvious to me that Jonathan doesn't see her or he'd have taken her order by now. The group at the table behind us, all black jeans and intense conversation, they probably don't either.

"So what's this all about?" Ted asks.

He looks half amused, half intrigued, still unsure if it's a joke or something more intriguing, a piece of normal that's slid off to one side. He has a nose for that sort of thing, from Elvis sightings to nuns impregnated by aliens, and I can almost see it twitching. He doesn't read the tabloids in line at the supermarket, he buys them. Need I say more?

So when he asks me what it's all about, he seems the perfect candidate for me to tell because it's very confusing and way out of my line of experience. I've never been prone to hallucinations before and besides, I always thought they'd be more . . . well, surreal, I suppose. Dadaistic. Over the top. This is so ordinary. Just a woman, sitting in a coffee bar, that no one seems to be able to see. Except for me.

"Hello, Andrew," Ted says, holding the first syllable of my name and drawing it out. "You still with us?"

I nod and give him a smile.

"So are you going to fill me in or what?"

"It's nothing," I say. "I was just seeing if you were paying attention."

"Um-hmm."

He doesn't believe me for a moment. All I've managed to do is pique his curiosity more.

"No, really," I tell him.

The woman stands up from the counter, distracting me. I wonder why she came in here in the first place since she can't seem to place an order, but then I think maybe even invisible people need to get out, enjoy a little nightlife, if only vicariously.

Or maybe she's a ghost.

"Did anybody ever die in here?" I ask Ted.

Ted gives me yet another strange look. He leans across the table.

"You're getting seriously weird on me," he says. "What do you want to know that for?"

The woman's on her way to the door now. Portishead is playing on the café's sound system. "Sour Times." Lalo Schifrin and Smokey Brooks samples on a bed of scratchy vinyl sounds and a smoldering, low-key Eurobeat. Beth Gibbons singing about how nobody loves her. At one time we both worked at Gypsy Records and we're still serious music junkies. It's one of the reasons we like The Half Kaffe so much; Jonathan has impeccable taste.

I pull a ten from my pocket and drop it on the table.

"I'll tell you later," I say as I get up from my stool.

"Andrew," Ted says. "You can't just leave me hanging like this."

"Later."

She's out the door, turning left. Through the café's window, I watch her do a little shuffle to one side as a couple almost walk right into her. They can't see her either. "Sour Times" dissolves into an instrumental, mostly keyboards and a lonesome electric guitar. Ted calls after me. He's starting to get up, too, but I wave him back. Then I'm out the door, jogging after the woman. "Excuse me!" I call after her. "Excuse me, miss!"

I can't believe I'm doing this. I have no idea what I'll say to her if she stops. But she doesn't turn. Gives no indication she's heard me. I catch up to her and touch her lightly on the elbow. I know a moment of surprise when I can feel the fabric of her sleeve instead of some cool mist. I half expected my fingers to go right through her.

"Excuse me," I say again.

She stops then and looks at me. Up close, her face, those sad eyes . . . they make my pulse quicken until my heartbeat sounds like a deep bass drum playing a march at double-time in my chest.

"Yes?"

"I . . ."

There's no surprise in her features. She doesn't ask how come I can see her and nobody else can. What I do see is a hint of fear in her eyes which shouldn't surprise me. A woman alone on the streets always has to be on her guard. I take a step back to ease the fear, feeling guilty and depressed for having put it there.

"I . . ."

There are a hundred things I want to ask her. About how she did what she did in The Half Kaffe. How come I can see her when other people can't. Why she's not surprised that I can see her. I'd even ask her out for a drink if I had the nerve. But nothing seems appropriate to the moment. Nothing makes sense.

I clear my throat and settle on: "Can you tell me how to get to Battersfield Road?"

The fear recedes in her eyes, but a wariness remains.

"Take a left at the next light," she tells me, "and just go straight. You can't miss it."

"Thanks."

I watch her continue on her way. Two women approach her from the other direction, moving aside to give her room when she comes abreast. So does what appears to be a businessman, suit and tie, briefcase in hand, working late, hurrying home. But the couple behind him don't see her at all; she has to dart to one side, press up against a store window so that they don't collide.

She's invisible again.

I follow her progress all the way to the end of the block as she weaves in and out of near collisions with the other pedestrians. Then she's at the crosswalk, a tall, slouching figure waiting for the light to change. She takes a right where she told me to take a left, and a storefront cuts her from my view.

I almost return to The Half Kaffe, but I don't feel up to being grilled by Ted. I almost go home, but what am I going to do at home on a Friday night? Instead, I run to the corner where she turned, cross against the light and almost get hit by a cab. The driver salutes me with one stiff finger and shouts something unintelligible at me, but I'm already past him, on the far curb now. I see her ahead of me, almost at the end of the block, and I do something I've never done before in my life. I follow a woman I don't know home.

3

The building she finally enters is one of those Crowsea brownstones that hasn't been renovated into condos yet—five stories, arches of tapered bricks over the windows, multi-gabled roof. There'd be at least twenty apartments in the place, crammed up against the other, shoulder to shoulder like commuters jostling in the subway. She could be living in any one of them. She could just be visiting a friend. She uses a key on the front door, but it could belong to anybody.

I know this. Just as I know she's not about to come walking out again. As I know she'd be able to see me if her window's facing this way and she looks out. But I can't help myself. I stand there on the street, looking at the face of the building as if it's the most interesting thing I've ever seen.

"She'll never tell you," a voice says from behind me, a kid's voice.

Here's what it's like, living in the city. The kid can't be more than twelve or thirteen. He's half my size, a scruffy little fellow in baggy jeans, hooded sweatshirt, air-pumped basketball shoes that have seen way better days. His hair is black, short and greasy, face looks as if it hasn't been washed in weeks, half-moons of dark shadow under darker eyes. I look at him and what do I do? Make sure he's alone. Try to figure out if he's carrying a gun or a knife. He's just a kid, and I'm checking out what possible threat he could pose.

I decide he's harmless, or at least means me no harm. He looks amused at the way I've been eyeing him, cocks his head. I look a little closer. There's something familiar about him, but I can't place it. Just the features, not the dirty hair, the grubby skin, the raggedy clothes.

"Who won't tell me what?" I finally ask.

"The invisible. She won't be able to tell you how it works. Half of them don't even know they go invisible. They just figure people treat them that way because that's all they're worth. Seriously low self-esteem."

I shake my head and can't stop the smile that comes. "So what are you? A psychiatrist?"

He looks back at me with a steadiness and maturity far belying his years and his appearance. There's a bead of liquid glistening under one nostril. He's a slight, almost frail figure, swamped in clothes that make him seem even smaller. But he carries himself with an assurance that makes me feel inadequate.

"No," he says. "Just someone who's learned to stay visible."

I'd laugh, but there's nothing to laugh about. I saw the woman in the café. I followed her home. If there's a conspiracy at work here, the number of people involved has to be immense and that doesn't make sense. No one would go through so much trouble over me—what would be the point? It's easier to believe she was invisible.

"So how come I could see her?" I ask.

The boy shrugs. "Maybe you're closer to her than you think."

I don't have to ask him what he means. Self-esteem's never been one of my strong suits.

"Or maybe it's because you believe," he adds.

"Believe in what?"

"Magic."

He says the word and I can see three small tobacco tins, the children burying them in the dirt under their porches. But I shake my head.

"Maybe I did once," I say. "But I grew out of it. There's nothing magic here. There's simply a . . . a phenomenon that hasn't been explained."

The boy grins and I lose all sense of his age. It's as if I've strayed into folklore, a fairy tale, tapped an innocent on the shoulder and come face to face with fanged nightmare. I feel I should turn my coat inside out or I'll never find my way back to familiar ground.

"Then explain this," the boy says around that feral grin.

He doesn't turn invisible. That'd be too easy, I guess. Instead it's like a sudden wind comes up, a dust devil, spinning the debris up from the street, candy wrappers, newspapers, things I can't identify. That vague sense of familiarity that's been nagging at me vanishes. There's nothing familiar about this. He's silhouetted against the swirling litter, then his shape loses definition. For one moment I see his dark eyes and that grin in the middle of a shape that vaguely resembles his, then the dust devil moves, comes apart, and all that's left is a trail of debris leading up the sidewalk, away from me.

I stare down at the litter, my gaze slowly drifting toward the invisible woman's building. Explain this?

"I can't," I say aloud, but there's no one there to hear me.

4

I return to my studio, but I'm too restless to sleep, can't concentrate enough to work. I stand in front of the painting on my easel and try to make sense out of what I'm seeing. I can't make sense of the image it once depicted. The colors and values don't seem to relate to each other any more, the hard edges have all gone soft, there's no definition between the background and the foreground.

I work in watercolor, a highly detailed and realistic style that has me laboring on the same piece for weeks before I'm done. This painting started the same as they always do for me, with a buzz, a wild hum in my head that flares down my arms into my fingertips. My first washes go down fast, the bones of light and color building from abstract glazes until the forms appear and, as Sickert said, the painting begins to "talk back" to me. Everything slows down on me then because the orchestration of value and detail I demand of my medium takes time.

This one was almost completed, a cityscape, a south view of the Kickaha River as seen from the Kelly Street Bridge, derelict warehouses running down to the water on one side, the lawns of Butler U. on the other. Tonight I can't differentiate between the river and the lawn, the edge of the bridge's railing and the warehouses beyond it. The image that's supposed to be on the paper is like the woman I followed earlier. It's taken on a kind of invisibility of its own. I stare at it for a long time, know that if I stay here in front of it, I'll try to fix it. Know as well that tonight that's the last thing I should be doing.

So I close the door on it, walk down the stairs from my studio to the street. It's only a few blocks to The Half Kaffe and still early for a Friday night, but when I get there, Ted's already gone home. Jonathan's behind the counter, but then Jonathan is always behind the counter. The servers he has working for him come and go, changing their shifts, changing their jobs, but Jonathan's always in his place, viewing the world by what he can see from his limited vantage point and through an endless supply of magazines.

He's flipping through the glossy pages of a British pop magazine when I come in. Miles Davis is on the sound system, a cut from his classic *Kind of Blue*, Evans's piano sounding almost Debussian, Davis's trumpet and Coltrane's tenor contrasting sharply with each other. I order an espresso from Jonathan and take it to the counter by the front window. The night goes about its business on the other side of the pane. I study the passersby, wondering if any of them are invisibles, people only I can see, wonder if there are men and women walking by that I don't, that are invisible to me.

5

I find Ted at Bruno's Diner the next morning, having his usual breakfast of late. Granola with two-percent milk and freshly-squeezed orange juice. All around him are people digging into plates of eggs and bacon, eggs and sausages, western omelets, home fries on the side, toast slathered with butter. But he's happy. There's no esoteric music playing at Bruno's, just a golden oldies station issuing tinnily from a small portable radio behind the counter. The smell of toast and bacon makes my stomach rumble.

"So what happened to you last night?" Ted asks when I slide into his booth.

"Do you believe in magic?" I ask.

Ted pauses with a spoonful of granola halfway to his mouth. "What, like Houdini?" He puts down the spoon and smiles. "Man, I loved that stuff when I was a kid. I wanted to be a magician when I grew up more than just about anything."

He manages to distract me. Of all the things I can imagine Ted doing, stage magic isn't one of them.

"So what happened?" I ask.

"I found out how hard it is. And besides, you need dexterity and you know me, I'm the world's biggest klutz."

"But that stuff's all fake," I say. Time to get back on track. "I'm talking about real magic."

"Who says it's not real?"

"Come on. Everybody knows it's done with mirrors and smoke. They're illusions."

Ted's not ready to agree. "But that's a kind of magic on its own, wouldn't you say?"

I shake my head. "I'm talking about the real stuff."

"Give me a for instance."

I don't want to lose my momentum again—it's hard enough for me to talk about this in the first place. I just want an answer to the question.

"I know you read all those tabloids," I say, "and you always let on like you believe the things they print. I want to know if you really do. Believe in them."

"Maybe we should backtrack a bit here," he says.

So I explain. I don't know which is weirder—the story I tell him, or the fact that he takes me seriously when I tell it.

"Okay," he says. "To start with, all that stuff about Elvis and bigfoot and the like—it's not what I'd call magic. It's entertainment. It might be true and it might not. I don't know. It doesn't even matter. But magic . . ."

His voice trails off and he gets a kind of dreamy look on his face.

"There's a true sense of mystery with magic," he says. "Like you're having a meaningful dialogue with something bigger than you—bigger than anything you can imagine. The tabloids are more like gossip. Something like what's happened to you— that's the real thing. It reaches into what we've all agreed are the workings of the world and stirs them around a little, makes a person sit up and pay attention. Not simply to the experience itself, but to everything around them. That's why the great stage illusions—I don't care if it's a floating woman or someone walking through the Great Wall of China—when they're done properly, you come away questioning every- thing. Your eyes are opened to all sorts of possibilities."

He smiles then. "Of course, usually it doesn't last. Most people go right back to the reality we've all agreed on. Me, I think it's kind of sad. I *like* the idea that there's more to the world than I can see or understand and I don't want to ever forget it."

What he's saying reminds me of the feeling I got after I first started to do art. Up until then I'd been the perennial computer nerd, spending all my time in front of a screen because that way I didn't have to take part in any more than the minimum amount of social interaction to get by. Then one day, in my second year at Butler, I was short one course and for no reason that's made sense before or since, decided to take life drawing, realized I had an aptitude for it, realized I loved it more than anything I'd ever tried before.

After that, I never looked at anything the same again. I watched light, saw every- thing through an imaginary frame. Clouds didn't just mean a storm was coming; they were an ever-changing picture of the sky, a panorama of movement and light that affected everything around them—the landscape, the people in it. I learned to pay attention and realized that once you do, anything you look at is interesting. Everything has its own glow, its own place in the world that's related to everything else around it. I looked into the connectedness of it all and nothing was the same for me again. I got better at a lot of things. Meeting people. Art. General life skills. Not perfect, but better.

"Have you ever heard of these invisibles?" I ask Ted.

"That's what the practitioners of *voudoun* call their deities. *Les Invisibles*."

I shake my head. "This kid wasn't speaking French. It wasn't like he was talking about that kind of thing at all. He was referring to ordinary people that go invisible because they just aren't *here* enough anymore." I stop and look across the table at Ted. "Christ, what am I saying? None of this is possible."

Ted nods. "It's easier to pretend it didn't happen."

"What's that supposed to mean?"

But I know exactly what he's talking about. You can either trust your senses and accept that there's more to the world than what you can see, or you can play ostrich. I don't know what to do.

"You had anything to eat yet?" Ted asks.

"Not since last night."

I let him order me breakfast, don't even complain when it's the same as his own.

"See, the thing is," he tells me while we're waiting for my cereal to arrive, "is that you're at the epicenter where two worlds are colliding."

"So now it's an earthquake."

He smiles. "But it's taking place on an interior landscape."

"I saw that woman last night—other people couldn't. That kid turned into a heap of litter right in front of my eyes. It happened here, Ted. In what's supposed to be the real world. Not in my head."

"I know. The quake hit you here, but the aftershocks are running through your soul."

I'd argue with him, except that's exactly how it feels.

"Why do you think that kid talked to me?" I ask.

I don't expect Ted to know, but it's part of what's been bothering me. Why'd he pick me to approach?

"I don't know," Ted says. "Next time you see him you should ask him."

"I don't think I want there to be a next time."

"You might not get a choice."

6

Maybe I could pretend to Ted that I didn't want any further involvement with invisible people and kids that turn into litter, but I couldn't lie to myself. I went looking for the boy, for the invisible woman, for things and people out of the ordinary.

There was still a pretense involved. I didn't wander aimlessly, one more lost soul out on the streets, but took a sketchbook and a small painting box, spent my time working on value drawings and color studies, gathering material for future paintings. It's hard for me to work *en plein*. I keep wanting to fuss and fiddle too much, getting lost in detail until the light changes and then I have to come back another day to get the values right.

A lot of those sketching sessions were spent outside the invisible woman's building, looking for her, expecting the boy to show up. I'd set up my stool, sit there flooding color onto the pages of my sketchbook, work in the detail, too much detail. I don't see the woman. Wind blows the litter around on the street but it doesn't rise up in the shape of a boy and talk to me.

I find myself thinking of fairy tales—not as stories, but as guideposts. Ted and I share a love of them, but for different reasons. He sees them as early versions of the tabloids, records kept of strange encounters, some real, some imagined, all of them entertaining. I think of them more metaphorically. All those dark forests and trials and trouble. They're the same things we go through in life. Maybe if more of us had the good heart of a Donkeyskin or the youngest son of three, the world would be a better place.

I'm thinking of this in front of the invisible woman's building on a blustery day. I've got the pages of my sketchbook clipped down, but the wind keeps flapping them anyway, making the paint puddle and run. Happy accidents, I've heard them called. Well, they're only happy when you can do something with them, when you don't work tight, every stroke counting. I'm just starting to clean up the latest of these so-called happy accidents when a ponytailed guy carrying a guitar walks right into me, knocking the sketchbook from my lap. I almost lose the paintbox as well.

"Jesus," he says. "I'm sorry. I didn't see you sitting there." He picks up my sketchbook and hands it over. "I hope I haven't totally ruined this."

"It's okay," I tell him. It's not, but what would be the point of being unpleasant?

"I'm really sorry."

I look down at the page I was working on. Now there's dirt smeared into the happy accident. Fixable it's not. My gaze lifts to meet his.

"Don't worry about it," I tell him. "It happens."

He nods, his relief plain. "I must've been dreaming," he says, "because I just didn't see you at all." He hesitates. "If you're sure it's okay . . ."

"I'm sure."

I watch him leave, think about what he said.

I just didn't see you.

So now what? I've become invisible, too? Then I remember the kid, something he said when I asked why I could see the invisible woman and others couldn't.

Maybe you're closer to her than you think.

Invisible. It comes to me, then. The world's full of invisible people and our not seeing them's got nothing to do with magic. The homeless. Winos. Hookers. Junkies. And not only on the street. The housewife. The businessman's secretary. Visible only when they're needed for something. The man with AIDS. Famine victims. People displaced by wars or natural disasters. The list is endless, all these people we don't see because we don't want to see them. All these people we don't see because we're too busy paying attention to ourselves. I've felt it myself, my lack of selfconfidence and how it translates into my behavior can have people look right through me. Standing in a store, waiting to be served. Sitting in the corner of a couch at a party and I might as well be a pillow.

The kid's face comes back to mind. I look down at my sketchbook, exchange the page smeared with happy accidents for a new one, draw the kid's features as I remember them. Now I know why he looked so familiar.

7

Ted opens his door on the first knock. He's just got off work and seems surprised to see me. I can smell herb tea steeping, cigarette smoke. Something classical is playing at low volume on the stereo. Piano. Chopin, I think. The preludes.

"Were we doing a movie or something tonight?" Ted asks.

I shake my head. "I was wondering if I could see that old photo album of yours again."

He studies me for a moment, then steps aside so that I can come in. His apartment's as cluttered as ever. You can't turn for fear of knocking over a stack of books, magazines, CDs, cassettes. Right by the door there's a box of newspapers and tabloids ready to go out for recycling. The one on top has a headline that shouts in bold caps: TEENAGER GIVES BIRTH TO FISH BOY!!

"You don't have to look at the album," he tells me. "I'll 'fess up."

Something changes in me when he says those words. I thought I knew him, like I thought I knew the world, but now they've both become alien territory. I stand in the center of the room, the furniture crouched around me like junkyard dogs. I have a disorienting static in my ears. I feel as though I'm standing on dangerous ground, stepped into the fairy tale, but Stephen King wrote it.

"How did you do it?" I ask.

Ted gives me a sheepish look. "How first? Not even why?"

I give the sofa a nervous look, but it's just a sofa. The vertigo is receding. My ears pop, as though I've dropped altitude, and I can hear the piano music coming from the speakers on either side of the room. I'm grounded again, but nothing seems the same. I sit down on the sofa, set my stool and sketching equipment on the floor between my feet.

"I don't know if I can handle why just yet," I tell him. "I have to know how you did it, how you made a picture of yourself come to life."

"Magic."

"Magic," I repeat. "That's it?"

"It's not enough?" He takes a seat in the well-worn armchair across from me, leans forward, hands on his knees. "Remember this morning, when I told you about wanting to be an illusionist?"

I nod.

"I lied. Well, it was partly a lie. I didn't give up stage magic, I just never got the nerve to go up on a stage and do it."

"So the kid . . . he was an illusion?"

Ted smiles. "Let's say you saw what I wanted you to see."

"Smoke and mirrors."

"Something like that."

"But . . ." I shake my head. He was right earlier. There's no point in asking for details. Right now, how's not as important as . . . "So why?" I ask.

He leans back in the chair. "The invisibles need a spokesperson—someone to remind the rest of the world that they exist. People like that woman you saw in The Half Kaffe last night. If enough people don't see her, she's simply going to fade away. She can't speak up for herself. If she could, she wouldn't be an invisible. And she's at the high end of the scale. There are people living on the streets that—"

"I know," I say, breaking in. "I was just thinking about them this afternoon. But their invisibility is a matter of perception, of people ignoring them. They're not literally invisible like the woman last night. There's nothing *magic* about them."

"You're still missing the point," Ted says. "Magic's all about perception. Things are the way they are because we've agreed that's the way they are. An act of magic is when we're convinced we're experiencing something that doesn't fit into the conceptual reality we've all agreed on."

"So you're saying that magic is being tricked into thinking an illusion is real."

"Or seeing through the illusion, seeing something the way it really is for the first time."

I shake my head, not quite willing to concede the argument for all that it's making uncomfortable sense.

"Where does your being a spokesperson fit in?" I ask.

"Not me. You."

"Oh, come on."

But I can tell he's completely serious.

"People have to be reminded about the invisibles," he says, "or they'll vanish."

"Okay," I say. "For argument's sake, let's accept that as a given. I still don't see where I come into it."

"Who's going to listen to me?" Ted asks. "I try to talk about it, but I'm a booking agent. People'd rather just think I'm a little weird."

"And they're not going to think the same of me?"

"No," he says. "And I'll tell you why. It's the difference between art and argument. They're both used to get a point across but the artist sets up a situation and, if he's good enough, his audience understands his point on their own, through how they assimilate the information he's given them and the decisions they can then make based on that information. The argument is just someone telling you what you're supposed to think or feel."

"Show, don't tell," I say, repeating an old axiom appropriate to all the arts.

"Exactly. You've got the artistic chops and sensibility to show people, to let them see the invisibles through your art, which will make them see them out there." He waves a hand toward the window. "On the street. In their lives."

He's persuasive, I'll give him that.

"Last night in The Half Kaffe," I begin.

"I didn't see the woman you saw," Ted says. "I didn't see her until you stopped her down the street."

"And after? When she went invisible again?"

"I could still see her. You made me see her."

"That's something anybody could do," I tell him.

"But only if they can see the invisibles in the first place," he says. "And you can't be everywhere. Your paintings can. Reproductions of them can."

I give him a look that manages to be both tired and hold all my skepticism with what he's saying. "You want me to paint portraits of invisible people so that other people can see them."

"You're being deliberately obtuse now, aren't you? You know what I mean."

I nod. I do know exactly what he means.

"Why bring this all up now?" I ask him. "We've known each other for years."

"Because until you saw the invisible woman, you never would have believed me."

"How do I know she's not another illusion—like the boy made of litter that was wearing your twelve-year-old face?"

"You don't."

8

He's wrong about that. I do know. I know in that part of me that he was talking about this morning over breakfast, the part that had a meaningful dialogue with something bigger than me, the part that's willing to accept a momentary glimpse behind the curtain of reality as a valid experience. And I know why he sent the illusion of the boy after me, too. It's the same reason he didn't admit to any of this sooner, played the innocent when I came to him with my story of invisible people. It was to give me my own words to describe the experience. To make me think about the invisibles, to let me form my own opinions about what can be readily seen and what's hidden behind a veil of expectations. Showing, not telling. He's better than he thinks he is.

I stand in my studio, thinking about that. There's a board on my easel with a stretched full-sized piece of three-hundred-pound Arches hot-pressed paper on it. I squeeze pigments into the butcher's tray I use as a palette, pick up a brush. There's a light pencil sketch on the paper. It's a cityscape, a street scene. In one corner, there's a man, sleeping in a doorway, blanketed with newspapers. The buildings and street overwhelm him. He's a small figure, almost lost. But he's not invisible.

I hope to keep him that way.

I dip my brush into my water jar, build up a puddle in the middle of the tray. Yellow ochre and alizarin crimson. I'm starting with the features that can be seen between the knit woolen cap he's wearing and the edge of his newspaper blanket, the gnarled hand that grips the papers, holding them in place. I want him to glow before I add in the buildings, the street, the night that shrouds them.

As I work, I think of the tobacco tins that Rebecca, Jerry, and I buried under our porches all those years ago. Maybe magic doesn't always work. Maybe it's like life, things don't always come through for you. But being disappointed in something doesn't mean you should give up on it. It doesn't mean you should stop trying.

I think of the last thing Ted said to me before I left his apartment.

"It goes back to stage magicians," he told me. "What's so amazing about them isn't so much that they can make things disappear, as that they can bring them back."

I touch the first color to the paper and reach for a taste of that amazement.

Seven for a Secret

It's a mistake to have only one life.
—Dennis Miller Bunker, 1890

1

Later, he can't remember which came first, the music or the birds in the trees. He seems to become aware of them at the same time. They call up a piece of something he thinks he's forgotten; they dredge through his past, the tangle of memories growing as thick and riddling as a hedgerow, to remind him of an old story he heard once that began, "What follows is imagined, but it happened just so. . . ."

2

The trees are new growth, old before their time. Scrub, leaves more brown than green, half the limbs dead, the other half dying. They struggle for existence in what was once a parking lot, a straggling clot of vegetation fed for years by some runoff, now baking in the sun. Something diverted the water—another building fell down, supports torched by Devil's Night fires, or perhaps the city bulldozed a field of rubble, two or three blocks over, inadvertently creating a levee. It doesn't matter. The trees are dying now, the weeds and grass surrounding them already baked dry.

And they're full of birds. Crows, ravens . . . Jake can't tell the difference. Heavy-billed, black birds with wedge-shaped tails and shaggy ruffs at their throats. Their calls are hoarse, croaking *kraaacks*, interspersed with hollow, knocking sounds and a sweeter *klu-kluck*.

The fiddle plays a counterpoint to the uneven rhythm of their calls, an odd, not quite reasonable music that seems to lie somewhere between a slow dance tune and an air that manages to be at once mournful and jaunty. The fiddle, he sees later, is blue, not painted that color, rather the varnish lends the wood that hue so its grain appears to be viewed as though through water.

Black birds, blue fiddle.

He might consider them portents if he were given to looking for omens, but he lives in a world that is always exactly what it should be, no more and no less, and he has come here to forget, not foretell. He is a man who stands apart, always one step aside from the crowd, an island distanced from the archipelago, spirit individual as much as the flesh. But though we are all islands, separated from one another by indifferent seas that range as wide as we allow them to be, we still congregate. We are still social animals. And Jake is no different. He comes to where the fires burn in the oil drums, where the scent of cedar smudge sticks mingles with cigarette smoke and dust, the same as the rest of us.

The difference is, he watches. He watches, but rarely speaks. He rarely speaks, but he listens well.

"They say," the woman tells him, "that where ravens gather, a door to the Otherworld stands ajar."

He never heard her approach. He doesn't turn.

"You don't much like me, do you?" she says.

"I don't know you well enough to dislike you, but I don't like what you do."

"And what is it that you think I do?"

"Make-believe," he says. "Pretend."

"Is that what you call it?"

But he won't be drawn into an argument.

"Everybody sees things differently," she says. "That's the gift and curse of free will."

"So what do you hear?" he asks. His voice is a sarcastic drawl. "Fairy music?"

The city died here, in the Tombs. Not all at once, through some natural disaster, but piece by piece, block by block, falling into disrepair, buildings abandoned by citizens and then claimed by the squatters who've got no reason to take care of them. Some of them fall down, some burn.

It's the last place in the world to look for wonder.

"I hear a calling-on music," she says, "though whether it's calling us to cross over, or calling something to us, I can't tell."

He turns to look at her finally, with his hair the glossy black of the ravens, his eyes the blue of that fiddle neither of them has seen yet. He notes the horn that rises from the center of her brow, the equine features that make her face seem so long, the chestnut dreadlocks, the dark, wide-set eyes and the something in those eyes he can't read.

"Does it matter?" he asks.

"Everything matters on some level or other."

He smiles. "I think that depends on what story we happen to be in."

"Yours or mine," she says, her voice soft.

"I don't have a story," he tells her.

Now she smiles. "And mine has no end."

"Listen," he says.

Silence hangs in the air, a thick gauze dropped from the sky like a blanket, deep enough to cut. The black birds are silent. They sit motionless in the dying trees. The fiddler has taken the bow from the strings. The blue fiddle holds its breath.

"I don't hear anything," she says.

He nods. "This is what my story sounds like."

"Are you sure?"

He watches as she lifts her arm and makes a motion with it, a graceful wave of her hand, as though conducting an orchestra. The black birds lift from the trees like a dark cloud, the sound of their wings cutting through the gauze of silence. The fiddle begins to play again, the blue wood vibrating with a thin distant music, a sound that is almost transparent. He looks away from the departing birds to find her watching him with the same lack of curiosity he had for the birds.

"Maybe you're not listening hard enough," she says.

"I think I'd know if—"

"Remember what I said about the ravens," she tells him.

He returns his attention to the trees, the birds all gone. When he looks for her again, she's already halfway down the block, horn glinting, too far away for him to read the expression in her features even if she was looking at him. If he even cared.

"I'd know," he says, repeating the words for himself.

He puts her out of his mind, forgets the birds and the city lying just beyond these blocks of wasteland, and goes to find the fiddler.

3

I probably know her better than anyone else around here, but even I forget about the horn sometimes. You want to ask her, why are you hiding out in the Tombs, there's nothing for you here. It's not like she's an alkie or a squatter, got the need for speed or any other kind of jones. But then maybe the sunlight catches that short length of ivory rising up out of her brow, or you see something equally impossible stirring in her dark eyes, and you see that horn like it's the first time all over again, and you understand that it's her difference that puts her here, her strangeness.

Malicorne, is what Frenchy calls her, says it means unicorn. I go to the Crowsea Public Library one day and try to look the word up in a dictionary, but I can only find it in pieces. Now Frenchy got the *corne* right because she's sure enough got a horn. But the word can also mean hoof, while *mal* or *mali* . . . you get your pick of what it can mean. Cunning or sly, which aren't exactly compliments, but mostly it's things worse than that: wickedness, evil, hurt, harm. Maybe Frenchy knows more than he's saying, and maybe she does, too, because she never answers to that name. But she doesn't give us anything better to use instead so the name kind of sticks—at least when we're talking about her among ourselves.

I remember the first time I see her, I'm looking through the trash after the Spring Festival, see if maybe I can sift a little gold from the chaff, which is a nice way of saying I'm a bum and I'm trying to make do. I see her sitting on a bench, looking at me, and at first I don't notice the horn, I'm just wondering, who's this horsy-faced woman and why's she looking at me like she wants to know something about me. Not what I'm doing here, going through the trash, but what put me here.

We've all got stories, a history that sews one piece of who we were to another until you get the reason we're who we are now. But it's not something we offer each other, never mind a stranger. We're not proud of who we are, of what we've become. We don't talk much about it, we never ask each other about it. There's too much pain in where we've been to go back, even if it's just with words. We don't even want to think about it—why do you think we're looking for oblivion in the bottom of a bottle?

I want to turn my back on her, but even then, right from the start, Malicorne's got this pull in her eyes, draws you in, draws you to her, starts you talking. I've seen rheumy-eyed old alkies who can't even put together "Have you got some spare change?" with their heads leaning close to hers, talking, the slur gone from their voices, some kind of sense working its way back into what they're saying. And I'm not immune. I turn my back, but it's on that trash can, and I find myself shuffling, hands stuck deep into my pockets, over to the bench where she's sitting.

"You're so innocent," she says.

I have to laugh. I'm forty-five and I look sixty, and the last thing I am is innocent.

"I'm no virgin," I tell her.

"I didn't say you were. Innocence and virginity aren't necessarily synonymous."

Her voice wakes something in me that I don't want to think about.

"I suppose," I say.

I want to go and get on with my business. I want to stay.

She's got a way of stringing together words so that they all seem to mean more than what you think they're saying, like there's a riddle lying in between the lines, and the funny thing is, I can feel something in me responding. Curiosity. Not standing around and looking at something strange, but an intellectual curiosity—the kind that makes you think.

I study her, sitting there beside me on the bench, raggedy clothes and thick chestnut hair so matted it hangs like fat snakes from her head, like a Rasta's dreadlocks. Horsy features. Deep, dark eyes, like they're all pupil, wide-set. And then I see the horn. She smiles when she sees my eyes go wide.

"Jesus," I say. "You've got a—"

"Long road to travel and the company is scarce. Good company, I mean."

I don't much care for weird shit, but I don't tell her that. I tell her things I don't tell anybody, not even myself, how it all went wrong for me, how I miss my family, how I miss having something in my life that means anything. And she listens. She's good at the listening, everybody says so, except for Jake. Jake won't talk to her, says she's feeding on us, feeding on our stories.

"It's give and take," I try to tell him. "You feel better after you've talked to her."

"You feel better because there's nothing left inside to make you feel bad," he says. "Nothing good, nothing bad. She's taking all the stories that make you who you are and putting nothing back."

"Maybe we don't want to remember those things anyway," I say.

He shakes his head. "What you've done is who you are. Without it, you're really nothing." He taps his chest. "What's left inside that belongs to you now?"

"It's not like that," I try to explain. "I still remember what put me here. It doesn't hurt as much anymore, that's all."

"Think about that for a moment."

"She tells you stuff, if you're willing to listen."

"Everything she says is mumbo-jumbo," Jake says. "Nothing that makes sense. Nothing that's worth what she's taken from you. Don't you *see*?"

I don't see it and he won't be part of it. Doesn't want to know about spirits, things

that never were, things that can't be, made-up stories that are supposed to take the place
of history. Wants to hold on to his pain, I guess.

But then he meets Staley.

4

The fiddler's a woman, but she has no sense of age about her; she could be thirty, she
could be seventeen. Where Malicorne's tall and angular, horse-lanky, Staley's like a
pony, everything in miniature. There's nothing dark about her, nothing gloomy except
the music she sometimes wakes from that blue fiddle of hers. Hair the color of straw
and cut like a boy's, a slip of a figure, eyes the green of spring growth, face shaped
like a heart. She's barefoot, wears an old pair of overalls a couple of sizes too big,
some kind of white jersey, sleeves pushed up on her forearms. There's a knapsack on
the ground beside her, an open fiddle case. She's sitting on a chunk of stone—piece
of a wall, maybe, piece of a roof—playing that blue fiddle of hers, her whole body
playing it, leaning into the music, swaying, head crooked to one side holding the
instrument to her shoulder, a smile like the day's just begun stretching across her lips.

Jake stands there, watching her, listening. When the tune comes to an end, he sits
down beside her.

"You're good," he tells her.

She gives him a shy smile in return.

"So did you come over from the other side?" he asks.

"The other side of what?"

Jake's thinking of Malicorne, about black birds and doors to other places. He shrugs.

"Guess that answers my question," he says.

She hears the disappointment in his voice, but doesn't understand it.

"People call me Jake," he tells her.

"Staley Cross," she says as they shake hands.

"And are you?"

The look of a Michelle who's been called *ma belle* too often moves across her
features, but she doesn't lose her humor.

"Not often," she says.

"Where'd you learn to play like that?"

"I don't know. Here and there. I just picked it up. I'm a good listener, I guess. Once
I hear a tune, I don't forget it." The fiddle's lying on her lap. She plays with her bow,
loosening and tightening the frog. "Do you play?" she asks.

He shakes his head. "Never saw a blue fiddle before—not blue like that."

"I know. It's not painted on—the color's in the varnish. My grandma gave it to me
a couple of years ago. She says it's a spirit fiddle, been in the family forever."

"Play something else," he asks. "Unless you're too tired."

"I'm never too tired to play."

She sets the bow to the strings, wakes a note, wakes another, and then they're in
the middle of a tune, a slow reel. Jake leans back, puts his hands behind his head, looks
up into the bare branches of the trees. Just before he closes his eyes, he sees those birds
return, one after the other, leafing the branches with their black wings. He doesn't hear

a door open, all he hears is Staley's fiddle. He finishes closing his eyes and lets the music take him to a place where he doesn't have to think about the story of his life.

5

I'm lounging on a bench with Malicorne near a subway station in that no-man's-land between the city and the Tombs, where the buildings are falling down but there's people still living in them, paying rent. Frenchy's sitting on the curb with a piece of cardboard cut into the shape of a guitar, dark hair tied back with a piece of string, holes in his jeans, hole in his heart where his dreams all escaped. He strums the six drawn strings on that cardboard guitar, mouthing "Plonkety, plonkety" and people are actually tossing him quarters and dimes. On the other side of him Casey's telling fortunes. He looks like the burned-out surfer he is, too many miles from any ocean, still tanned, dirty blond hair falling into his face. He gives everybody the same piece of advice: "Do stuff."

Nobody's paying much attention to us when Jake comes walking down the street, long and lanky, hands deep in the pockets of his black jeans. He sits down beside me, says, "Hey, William," nods to Malicorne. Doesn't even look at her horn.

"Hey, Jake," I tell him.

He leans forward on the bench, talks across me. "You ever hear of a spirit fiddle?" he asks Malicorne.

She smiles. "Are you finally starting a story?"

"I'm not starting anything. I'm just wondering. Met that girl who was making the music and she's got herself a blue fiddle—says it's a spirit fiddle. Been in her family a long time."

"I heard her playing," I say. "She's good."

"Her name's Staley Cross."

"Don't know the name," Malicorne says. There's a hint of surprise in her voice, as though she thinks she should. I'm not the only one who hears it.

"Any reason you should?" Jake asks.

Malicorne smiles and looks away, not just across the street, it seems, but further than that, like she can see through the buildings, see something we can't. Jake's looking at that horn now but I can't tell what he's thinking.

"Where'd she go?" I ask him.

He gets a puzzled look, like he thinks I'm talking about Malicorne for a second, then he shrugs.

"Downtown," he says. "She wanted to busk for a couple of hours, see if she can't get herself a stake."

"Must be nice, having a talent," I say.

"Everybody's got a talent," Malicorne says. "Just like everybody's got a story."

"Unless they give it to you," Jake breaks in.

Malicorne acts like he hasn't interrupted. "Trouble is," she goes on, "some people don't pay much attention to either and they end up living with us here."

"You're living here," Jake says.

Malicorne shakes her head. "I'm just passing through."

I know what Jake's thinking. Everybody starts out thinking, this is only temporary. It doesn't take them long to learn different. But then none of them have a horn pushing out of the middle of their forehead. None of them have mystery sticking to them like they've wrapped themselves up in double-sided tape and whatever they touch sticks to them.

"Yeah, well, we'll all really miss you when you're gone," Jake tells her.

It's quiet then. Except for Frenchy's cardboard guitar. "Plonkety-plonk." None of us are talking. Casey takes a dime from some kid who wants to know the future. His pale blue eyes stand out against his surfer's tan as he gives the kid a serious look.

"Do stuff," he says.

The kid laughs, shakes his head and walks away. But I think about what Malicorne was saying, how everybody's got a story, everybody's got a talent, and I wonder if maybe Casey's got it right.

6

"Blue's the rarest color in nature," Staley says.

Jake smiles. "You ever look up at the sky?"

They're sharing sandwiches her music bought, coffee in cardboard cups, so hot you can't hold the container. If Jake's still worrying about magic and spirit fiddles, it doesn't show.

Staley returns his smile. "I don't mean it's hard to find. But it's funny you should mention the sky. Of all the hundreds of references to the sky and the heavens in a book like the bible, the color blue is never mentioned."

"You read the bible a lot?"

"Up in the hills where I come from, that's pretty much the only thing there is to read. That, and the tabloids. But when I was saying blue's the rarest color—"

"You meant it's the most beautiful."

She nods. "It fills the heart. Like the blue of twilight when anything's possible. Blue makes me feel safe, warm. People think of it as a cool color, but you know, the hottest fire has a blue-white flame. Like stars. The comparatively cooler stars have the reddish glow." She takes a sip of her coffee, looks at him over the brim. "I make up for all the reading I missed by spending a lot of time in libraries."

"Good place to visit," Jake says. "Safe, when you're in a strange town."

"I thought you'd understand. You can put aside all the unhappiness you've accumulated by opening a book. Listening to music."

"You think forgetting is a good thing?"

She shrugs. "For me, it's a necessary thing. It's what keeps me sane."

She looks at him and Jake sees himself through her eyes: a tall, gangly hobo of a man, seen better times, but seen worse ones, too. The worse ones are why he's where he is.

"You know what I mean," she says.

"I suppose. Don't know if I agree, though." She lifts her eyebrows, but he doesn't want to take that any further. "So tell me about the spirit in that fiddle of yours," he says instead.

"It hasn't got a spirit—not like you mean, anyway. It comes from a spirit place. That's why it's blue. It's the color of twilight and my grandma says it's always twilight there."

"In the Otherworld."

"If that's what you want to call it."

"And the black of a raven's wing," Jake says, "that's really a kind of blue, too, isn't it?"

She gives him a confused look.

"Don't mind me," he tells her. "I'm just thinking about what someone once told me."

"Where I come from," she says, "the raven's an unlucky bird."

"Depends on how many you see," Jake says. He starts to repeat the old rhyme for her then. "One for sorrow, two for mirth . . ."

She nods, remembering. "Three for a wedding, four for a birth."

"That's it. Five for silver, six for gold . . ."

". . . seven for a secret never to be told . . ."

". . . eight for heaven, nine for hell . . ."

". . . and ten for the devil's own sel'." She smiles. "But I thought that was for crows."

He shrugs. "I've heard it used for magpies, too. Guess it's for any kind of black bird." He looks up at the trees, empty now. "That music of yours," he goes on. "It called up an unkindness of ravens this afternoon."

"An unkindness of ravens," she repeats, smiling. "A murder of crows. Where do they come up with that kind of thing?"

He shrugs. "Who knows? Same place they found once in a blue moon, I guess."

"There was a blue moon the night my great-great-grandma got my fiddle," Staley tells him. "Least that's how the story goes."

"That's what I meant about forgetting," he says. "Maybe you forget some bad things, but work at it hard enough and you forget a story like that, too."

They're finished eating now, the last inch of coffee cooling in their cups.

"You up to playing a little more music?" Jake asks. "See what it calls up?"

"Sure."

She takes the instrument from its case, tightens the bow, runs her finger across the strings to check the tuning, adjusts a couple of them. Jake likes to watch her fingers move, even doing this, without the music having started yet, tells her that.

"You're a funny guy," she says as she brings the fiddle up under her chin.

Jake smiles. "Everybody says that," he tells her.

But he's thinking of something else, he's thinking of how the little pieces of her history that she's given him add to his own without taking anything away from her. He's thinking about Malicorne and the stories she takes, how she pulls the hurt out of them by listening. He's thinking—

But then Staley starts to play and the music takes him away again.

"I was working on a tune this afternoon," she says as the music moves into three-four time. "Maybe I'll call it 'Jake's Waltz.' "

Jake closes his eyes, listening, not just to her music, but for the sound of wings.

7

It's past sundown. The fires are burning in the oil drums and bottles are being passed around. Cider and apple juice in some, stronger drink in others. Malicorne's not drinking, never does, least not that I can ever remember seeing. She's sitting off by herself, leaning against a red brick wall, face a smudge of pale in the shadows, horn invisible. The wall was once the side of a factory, now it's standing by itself. There's an owl on top of the wall, three stories up, perched on the bricks, silhouetted by the moon. I saw it land and wonder what owls mean around her. Jake told me about the ravens.

After a while, I walk over to where she's sitting, offer her some apple juice. She shakes her head. I can see the horn now.

"What's it with you and Jake?" I ask.

"Old arguments never die," she says.

"You go back a long time?"

She shakes her head. "But the kind of man he is and I do. Live long enough, William, and you'll meet every kind of person, hear every kind of story, not once, but a hundred times."

"I don't get what you mean," I say.

"No. But Jake does."

We hear the music then, Staley's fiddle, one-two-three, one-two-three, waltz time, and I see them sitting together on the other side of the fires, shadow shapes, long tall Jake with his raven hair and the firefly glow of Staley's head bent over her instrument. I hear the sound of wings and think of the owl on the wall above us, but when I check, it's gone. These are black birds, ravens, a flock of them, an unkindness, and I feel something in the air, a prickling across my skin and at the nape of my neck, like a storm's coming, but the skies are clear. The stars seem so close we could be up in the mountains instead of here, in the middle of the city.

"What are you thinking about?" Malicorne asks.

I turn to her, see the horn catch the firelight. "Endings," I find myself saying. "Where things go when they don't fit where they are."

She smiles. "Are you reading my mind?"

"Never was much inclined for that sort of thing."

"Me, either."

That catches me by surprise. "But you . . ." You're magic, I was going to say, but my voice trails off.

"I've been here too long," she says. "Stopped to rest a day or so, and look at me now. Been here all spring and most of the summer."

"It's been a good summer."

She nods. "But Jake's right, you know. Your stories do nourish me. Not like he thinks, it's not me feeding on them and you losing something, it's that they connect me to a place." She taps a finger against the dirt we're sitting on. "They connect me to something real. But I also get you to talk because I know talking heals. I like to think I'm doing some good."

"Everybody likes you," I tell her. I don't add, except for Jake.

"But it's like Scheherazade," she says. "One day the stories are all told and it's time to move on."

I'm shaking my head. "You don't have to go. When you're standing at the bottom of the ladder like we are, nobody can tell you what to do anymore. It's not much, but at least we've got that."

"There's that innocence of yours again," she says.

"What the hell's that supposed to mean?"

She smiles. "Don't be angry."

"Then don't treat me like a kid."

"But isn't this like Neverneverland?" she asks. "You said it yourself. Nobody can tell you what to do anymore. Nothing has to ever change. You can be like this forever."

"You think any of us want to be here? You think we chose to live like this?"

"She's not talking about you, William," Jake says. "She's talking about me."

I never heard the music stop, never heard them approach, Jake and the fiddler, standing near us now. I don't know how long they've been there, how much they've heard. Staley lifts her hand to me, says hi. Jake, he's just looking at Malicorne. I can't tell what he's thinking.

"So I guess what you need is my story," he says, "and then you can go."

Malicorne shakes her head. "My coming or going has nothing to do with you."

Jake doesn't believe her. He sits down on the dirt in front of us, got that look in his eye I've seen before, not angry, just he won't be backing down. Staley sits down, too, takes out her fiddle, but doesn't play it. She holds the instrument on her lap, runs the pad of her thumb along the strings, toys with the wooden curlicues on the head, starts to finger a tune, pressing the strings against the fingerboard, soundlessly. I wish I had something to do with my hands.

"See," Jake's saying, "it's circumstances that put most of these people here, living on the street. They're not bad people, they're just weak, maybe, or had some bad luck, some hard times, that's all. Some of them'll die here, some of them'll make a second chance for themselves and your guess is as good as mine, which of them'll pull through."

"But you chose to live like this," Malicorne says.

"You know, don't you? You already know all about me."

She shakes her head. "All I know is you're hiding from something and nobody had to tell me that. I just had to look at you."

"I killed a man," Jake says.

"Did he deserve it?"

"I don't even know anymore. He was stealing from me, sent my business belly-up and just laughed at me when I confronted him with it. Asked me what I was going to do, the money was all spent and what the hell could I prove anyway? He'd fixed the books so it looked like it was all my fault."

"That's hard," I say.

I'm where I am because I drank too much, drank all the time and damned if I can tell you why. Got nobody to blame but myself. Don't drink anymore, but it's too late to go back. My old life went on without me. Wife remarried. Kids think I'm dead.

"It was the laughing I couldn't take," Jake says. "He was just standing there, looking so smug and laughing at me. So I hit him. Grabbed the little turd by the throat and started whacking the back of his head against the wall and when I stopped, he was dead. First time I ever saw a dead person. First time I ever hit anybody, except for goofing around with the guys in high school." He looks at me. "You know, the old push and shove, but it's nothing serious."

I give him a nod.

"But this was serious. The thing is, when I think about it now, what he did to me, the money he stole, none of it seems so important anymore."

"Are you sorry?" Malicorne asks.

"I'm not sorry he's dead, but I'm sorry I was the one that killed him."

"So you've been on the run ever since."

Jake nods. "Twelve years now and counting." He gives her a long, steady look. "So that's my story."

"Do you feel any better having told us about it?"

"No."

"I didn't think you would," she says.

"What's that supposed to mean?"

"You've got to want to heal before you can get out of this prison you've made for yourself."

I'm expecting this to set him off, but he looks at the ground instead, shoulders sagging. I've seen a lot of broken men on the skids—hell, all I've had to do for years is look in a mirror—but I've never imagined Jake as one of them. Never knew why he was down here with the rest of us, but always thought he was stronger than the rest of us.

"I don't know how," he says.

"Was he your brother?" Staley asks. "This man you killed."

I've been wondering how she was taking this, sitting there so still, listening, not even her fingers moving anymore. It's hard to see much of anything, here in the shadows. Our faces and hands are pale blurs. The light from the fires in the oil drums catches Malicorne's horn, Staley's hair, awakes a shine on her lap where the blue fiddle's lying.

Jake shakes his head. "He was my best friend. I would've given him anything, all he had to do was ask."

"I'm sorry for you," Malicorne says, standing up. "I'm sorry for you both, the one dead and the other a long time dying."

She's going then, nothing to pack, nothing to carry, leaving us the way she came with her hands empty and her heart full. Over by the oil drums, nobody notices. Frenchy is rolling himself a cigarette from the butts he collected during the day. Casey's sleeping, an empty bottle of wine lying in the dirt beside his hand. I can't see the black birds, but I can hear them, feathers rustling in the dark all around us. I guess if you want to believe in that kind of thing, there's a door standing open nearby.

"Let me come with you," Jake says.

Malicorne looks at him. "The road I'm traveling goes on forever," she says.

"I kind of guessed that, what with the horn and all."

"It's about remembering, not forgetting."

He nods. "I know that, too. Maybe I can learn to be good company."

"Nobody ever said you weren't," she tells him. "What you have to ask yourself is, are you trying to escape again or are you really ready to move on?"

"Talking about it—that's a start, isn't it?"

Malicorne smiles. "It's a very good start."

8

Staley and I, we're the only ones to see them go. I don't know if they just walked off into the night, swallowed by the shadows, or if they stepped through a door, but I never see either of them again. We sit there for a while, looking up at the stars. They still seem so big, so near, like they want to be close to whatever enchantment happened here tonight. After a while Staley starts to play her fiddle, that same tune she played earlier, the one in three-four time. I hear wings, in behind the music, but it's the black birds leaving, not gathering. Far off, I hear hoofbeats and I don't know what to make of that.

Frenchy gets himself a job a few weeks later, sweeping out a bar over on Grasso Street, near the Men's Mission. Casey goes back to the coast, says he's thinking of going back to school. Lots of the others, things start to look up a little for them, too. Not everybody, not all of us, but more than tried to take a chance before Malicorne came into our lives.

Me, I find myself a job as a custodian in a Kelly Street tenement. The job gives me a little room in the basement, but there's no money in it. I get by with tips from the tenants when I do some work for them, paint a room, fix a leaky faucet, that kind of thing. I'm looking for something better, but times are still hard.

Staley, she hangs around for a few days, then moves on.

I remember thinking there's a magic about her, too, but now I know it's in the music she calls up from that blue fiddle of hers, the same kind of magic any good musician can wake from an instrument. It takes you away. Calls something to you maybe, but it's not necessarily ravens or enchantment.

Before she goes, I ask her about that night, about what brought her down to the Tombs.

"I wanted to see the unicorn," she says. "I was playing in a pick-up band in a roadhouse up on Highway 14 and overheard somebody talking about her in the parking lot at the end of the night—a couple of 'boes, on their way out of the city. I just kind of got distracted with Jake. He seemed like a nice guy, you know, but he was so lonely."

"The unicorn . . . ?"

For a minute there I don't know what she's talking about, but then Malicorne's horsy features come to mind, the chestnut dreadlocks, the wide-set eyes. And finally I remember the horn and when I do, I can't figure out how I forgot.

"You know," Staley's saying. "White horse, big spiraling horn coming out of her forehead."

"But she was a woman," I begin.

Staley smiles. "And Jake was a man. But when they left I saw a white horse and a black one."

"I didn't. But I heard hoofbeats. . . ." I give her a puzzled look. "What happened that night?"

Staley shoulders her knapsack, picks up her fiddlecase. She stands on tip-toes and kisses me lightly on the cheek.

"Magic," she says. "And wasn't it something—just that little piece of it?"

I'm nodding when she gives me a little wave of her hand.

"See you, William," she says. "You take care now."

I wave back, stand there, watching her go. I hear a croaking cry from the top of the derelict building beside me, but it's a crow I see, beating its black wings, lifting high above the ragged roofline, not a raven.

Sometimes I find myself humming that waltz she wrote for Jake.

Sometimes I dream about two horses, one black and one white with a horn, the two of them running, running along the crest of these long hills that rise and fall like the waves of the sea, and I wake up smiling.

Crow Girls

> *I remember what somebody said about nostalgia,*
> *he said it's okay to look back, as long as you don't stare.*
> —Tom Paxton,
> from an interview with Ken Rockburn

People have a funny way of remembering where they've been, who they were. Facts fall by the wayside. Depending on their temperament they either remember a golden time when all was better than well, better than it can be again, better than it ever really was: a first love, the endless expanse of a summer vacation, youthful vigor, the sheer novelty of being alive that gets lost when the world starts wearing you down. Or they focus in on the bad, blow little incidents all out of proportion, hold grudges for years, or maybe they really did have some unlucky times, but now they're reliving them forever in their heads instead of moving on.

But the brain plays tricks on us all, doesn't it? We go by what it tells us, have to I suppose, because what else do we have to use as touchstones? Trouble is we don't ask for confirmation on what the brain tells us. Things don't have to be real, we just have to believe they're real, which pretty much explains politics and religion as much as it does what goes on inside our heads.

Don't get me wrong; I'm not pointing any fingers here. My people aren't guiltless either. The only difference is our memories go back a lot further than yours do.

"I don't get computers," Heather said.

Jilly laughed. "What's not to get?"

They were having cappuccinos in the Cyberbean Café, sitting at the long counter with computer terminals spaced along its length the way those little individual juke-boxes used to be in highway diners. Jilly looked as though she'd been using the tips of her dark ringlets as paintbrushes, then cleaned them on the thighs of her jeans—in other words, she'd come straight from the studio without changing first. But however haphazardly messy she might allow herself or her studio to get, Heather knew she'd either cleaned her brushes, or left them soaking in turps before coming down to the café. Jilly might seem terminally easygoing, but some things she didn't blow off. No matter how the work was going—good, bad or indifferent—she treated her tools with respect.

As usual, Jilly's casual scruffiness made Heather feel overdressed, for all that she was only wearing cotton pants and a blouse, nothing fancy. But she always felt a little like that around Jilly, ever since she'd first taken a class from her at the Newford School of Art a couple of winters ago. No matter how hard she tried, she hadn't been able to shake the feeling that she looked so typical: the suburban working mother, the happy wife. The differences since she and Jilly had first met weren't great. Her blonde hair had been long then while now it was cropped short. She was wearing glasses now instead of her contacts.

And two years ago she hadn't been carrying an empty wasteland around inside her chest.

"Besides," Jilly added. "You use a computer at work, don't you?"

"Sure, but that's work," Heather said. "Not games and computer-screen romances and stumbling around the Internet, looking for information you're never going to find a use for outside of Trivial Pursuit."

"I think it's bringing back a sense of community," Jilly said.

"Oh, right."

"No, think about it. All these people who might have been just vegging out in front of a TV are chatting with each other in cyberspace instead—hanging out, so to speak, with kindred spirits that they might never have otherwise met."

Heather sighed. "But it's not real human contact."

"No. But at least it's contact."

"I suppose."

Jilly regarded her over the brim of her glass coffee mug. It was a mild gaze, not in the least probing, but Heather couldn't help but feel as though Jilly was seeing right inside her head, all the way down to where desert winds blew through the empty space where her heart had been.

"So what's the real issue?" Jilly asked.

Heather shrugged. "There's no issue." She took a sip of her own coffee, then tried on a smile. "I'm thinking of moving downtown."

"Really?"

"Well, you know. I already work here. There's a good school for the kids. It just seems to make sense."

"How does Peter feel about it?"

Heather hesitated for a long moment, then sighed again. "Peter's not really got anything to say about it."

"Oh, no. You guys always seemed so . . ." Jilly's voice trailed off. "Well, I guess you weren't really happy, were you?"

"I don't know what we were anymore. I just know we're not together. There wasn't a big blow up or anything. He wasn't cheating on me and I certainly wasn't cheating on him. We're just . . . not together."

"It must be so weird."

Heather nodded. "Very weird. It's a real shock, suddenly discovering after all these years, that we really don't have much in common at all."

Jilly's eyes were warm with sympathy. "How are you holding up?"

"Okay, I suppose. But it's so confusing. I don't know what to think, who I am, what I thought I was doing with the last fifteen years of my life. I mean, I don't regret the girls—I'd have had more children if we could have had them—but everything else . . ."

She didn't know how to begin to explain.

"I married Peter when I was eighteen and I'm forty-one now. I've been a part of a couple for longer than I've been anything else, but except for the girls, I don't know what any of it meant anymore. I don't know who I am. I thought we'd be together forever, that we'd grow old together, you know? But now it's just me. Casey's fifteen and Janice is twelve. I've got another few years of being a mother, but after that, who am I? What am I going to do with myself?"

"You're still young," Jilly said. "And you look gorgeous."

"Right."

"Okay. A little pale today, but still."

Heather shook her head. "I don't know why I'm telling you this. I haven't told anybody."

"Not even your mom or your sister?"

"Nobody. It's . . ."

She could feel tears welling up, the vision blurring, but she made herself take a deep breath. It seemed to help. Not a lot, but some. Enough to carry on. How to explain why she wanted to keep it a secret? It wasn't as though it was something she could keep hidden forever.

"I think I feel like a failure," she said.

Her voice was so soft she almost couldn't hear herself, but Jilly reached over and took her hand.

"You're not a failure. Things didn't work out, but that doesn't mean it was your fault. It takes two people to make or break a relationship."

"I suppose. But to have put in all those years . . ."

Jilly smiled. "If nothing else, you've got two beautiful daughters to show for them."

Heather nodded. The girls did a lot to keep the emptiness at bay, but once they were in bed, asleep, and she was by herself, alone in the dark, sitting on the couch by the picture window, staring down the street at all those other houses just like her own, that desolate place inside her seemed to go on forever.

She took another sip of her coffee and looked past Jilly to where two young women were sitting at a corner table, heads bent together, whispering. It was hard to place their ages—anywhere from late teens to early twenties, sisters, perhaps, with their small builds and similar dark looks, their black clothing and short blue-black hair. For no reason she could explain, simply seeing them made her feel a little better.

"Remember what it was like to be so young?" she said.

Jilly turned, following her gaze, then looked back at Heather.

"You never think about stuff like this at that age," Heather went on.

"I don't know," Jilly said. "Maybe not. But you have a thousand other anxieties that probably feel way more catastrophic."

"You think?"

Jilly nodded. "I know. We all like to remember it as a perfect time, but most of us were such bundles of messed-up hormones and nerves I'm surprised we ever managed to reach twenty."

"I suppose. But still, looking at those girls . . ."

Jilly turned again, leaning her head on her arm. "I know what you mean. They're like a piece of summer on a cold winter's morning."

It was a perfect analogy, Heather thought, especially considering the winter they'd been having. Not even the middle of December and the snowbanks were already higher than her chest, the temperature a seriously cold minus-fifteen.

"I have to remember their faces," Jilly went on. "For when I get back to the studio. The way they're leaning so close to each other—like confidantes, sisters in their hearts, if not by blood. And look at the fine bones in their features . . . how dark their eyes are."

Heather nodded. "It'd make a great picture."

It would, but the thought of it depressed her. She found herself yearning desperately in that one moment to have had an entirely different life, it almost didn't matter what. Perhaps one that had no responsibility but to draw great art from the world around her the way Jilly did. If she hadn't had to support Peter while he was going through law school, maybe she would have stuck with her art. . . .

Jilly swiveled in her chair, the sparkle in her eyes deepening into concern once more.

"Anything you need, anytime," she said. "Don't be afraid to call me."

Heather tried another smile. "We could chat on the Internet."

"I think I agree with what you said earlier: I like this better."

"Me, too," Heather said. Looking out the window, she added, "It's snowing again."

Maida and Zia are forever friends. Crow girls with spiky blue-black hair and eyes so dark it's easy to lose your way in them. A little raggedy and never quiet, you can't miss this pair: small and wild and easy in their skins, living on Zen time. Sometimes they forget they're crows, left their feathers behind in the long-ago, and sometimes they forget they're girls. But they never forget that they're friends.

People stop and stare at them wherever they go, borrowing a taste of them, drawn by they don't know what, they just have to look, try to get close, but keeping their distance, too, because there's something scary/craving about seeing animal spirits so pure walking around on a city street. It's a shock, like plunging into cold water at dawn, waking up from the comfortable familiarity of warm dreams to find, if only for a moment, that everything's changed. And then, just before the way you know the world to be comes rolling back in on you, maybe you hear giddy laughter, or the slow flap of crows' wings. Maybe you see a couple of dark-haired girls sitting together in the corner of a café, heads bent together, pretending you can't see them, or could be they're perched on a tree branch, looking down at you looking up, working hard at putting on serious faces but they can't stop smiling.

It's like that rhyme, "two for mirth." They can't stop smiling and neither can you. But you've got to watch out for crow girls. Sometimes they wake a yearning you'll be hard pressed to put back to sleep. Sometimes only a glimpse of them can start up a familiar ache deep in your chest, an ache you can't name, but you've felt it before, early mornings, lying alone in your bed, trying to hold onto the fading tatters of a perfect dream. Sometimes they blow bright the coals of a longing that can't ever be eased.

* * *

Heather couldn't stop thinking of the two girls she'd seen in the café earlier in the evening. It was as though they'd lodged pieces of themselves inside her, feathery slivers winging dreamily across the wasteland. Long after she'd played a board game with Janice, then watched the end of a Barbara Walters special with Casey, she found herself sitting up by the big picture window in the living room when she should have been in bed herself. She regarded the street through a veil of falling snow, but this time she wasn't looking at the houses—so alike that, except for the varying heights of their snowbanks, they might as well all be the same one. Instead, she was looking for two small women with spiky black hair, dark shapes against the white snow.

There was no question but that they knew exactly who they were, she thought when she realized what she was doing. Maybe they could tell her who she was. Maybe they could come up with an exotic past for her so that she could reinvent herself, be someone like them, free, sure of herself. Maybe they could at least tell her where she was going.

But there were no thin, dark-haired girls out on the snowy street, and why should there be? It was too cold. Snow was falling thick with another severe winter storm warning in effect tonight. Those girls were safe at home. She knew that. But she kept looking for them all the same because in her chest she could feel the beat of dark wings—not the sudden panic that came out of nowhere when once again the truth of her situation reared without warning in her mind, but a strange, alien feeling. A sense that some otherness was calling to her.

The voice of that otherness scared her almost more than the grey landscape lodged in her chest.

She felt she needed a safety net, to be able to let herself go and not have to worry about where she fell. Somewhere where she didn't have to think, be responsible, to do anything. Not forever. Just for a time.

She knew Jilly was right about nostalgia. The memories she carried forward weren't necessarily the way things had really happened. But she yearned, if only for a moment, to be able to relive some of those simpler times, those years in high school before she'd met Peter, before they were married, before her emotions got so complicated.

And then what?

You couldn't live in the past. At some point you had to come up for air and then the present would be waiting for you, unchanged. The wasteland in her chest would still stretch on forever. She'd still be trying to understand what had happened. Had Peter changed? Had she changed? Had they both changed? And when did it happen? How much of their life together had been a lie?

It was enough to drive her mad.

It was enough to make her want to step into the otherness calling to her from out there in the storm and snow, step out and simply let it swallow her whole.

Jilly couldn't put the girls from the café out of her mind either, but for a different reason. As soon as she'd gotten back to the studio, she'd taken her current work-in-progress down from the easel and replaced it with a fresh canvas. For a long moment she stared at the texture of the pale ground, a mix of gesso and a light burnt-ochre acrylic wash, then she took up a stick of charcoal and began to sketch the faces of the two dark-haired girls before the memory of them left her mind.

She was working on their bodies, trying to capture the loose splay of their limbs and the curve of their backs as they'd slouched in toward each other over the café table, when there came a knock at her door.

"It's open," she called over her shoulder, too intent on what she was doing to look away.

"I could've been some mad, psychotic killer," Geordie said as he came in.

He stamped his feet on the mat, brushed the snow from his shoulders and hat. Setting his fiddlecase down by the door, he went over to the kitchen counter to see if Jilly had any coffee on.

"But instead," Jilly said, "it's only a mad, psychotic fiddler, so I'm entirely safe."

"There's no coffee."

"Sure there is. It's just waiting for you to make it."

Geordie put on the kettle, then rummaged around in the fridge, trying to find which tin Jilly was keeping her coffee beans in this week. He found them in one that claimed to hold Scottish shortbreads.

"You want some?" he asked.

Jilly shook her head. "How's Tanya?"

"Heading back to L.A. I just saw her off at the airport. The driving's horrendous. There were cars in the ditch every couple of hundred feet and I thought the bus would never make it back."

"And yet, it did," Jilly said.

Geordie smiled.

"And then," she went on, "because you were feeling bored and lonely, you decided to come visit me at two o'clock in the morning."

"Actually, I was out of coffee and I saw your light was on." He crossed the loft and came around behind the easel so that he could see what she was working on. "Hey, you're doing the crow girls."

"You know them?"

Geordie nodded. "Maida and Zia. You've caught a good likeness of them—especially Zia. I love that crinkly smile of hers."

"You can tell them apart?"

"You can't?"

"I never saw them before tonight. Heather and I were in the Cyberbean and there they were, just asking to be drawn." She added a bit of shading to the underside of a jaw, then turned to look at Geordie. "Why do you call them the crow girls?"

Geordie shrugged. "I don't. Or at least I didn't until I was talking to Jack Daw and that's what he called them when they came sauntering by. The next time I saw them I was busking in front of St. Paul's, so I started to play 'The Blackbird,' just to see what would happen, and sure enough, they came over to talk to me."

"Crow girls," Jilly repeated. The name certainly fit.

"They're some kind of relation to Jack," Geordie explained, "but I didn't quite get it. Cousins, maybe."

Jilly was suddenly struck with the memory of a long conversation she'd had with Jack one afternoon. She was working up sketches of the Crowsea Public Library for a commission when he came and sat beside her on the grass. With his long legs folded under him, black brimmed hat set at a jaunty angle, he'd regaled her with a long, rambling discourse on what he called the continent's real first nations.

"Animal people," she said softly.

Geordie smiled. "I see he fed you that line, too."

But Jilly wasn't really listening—not to Geordie. She was remembering another part of that old conversation, something else Jack had told her.

"The thing we really don't get," he'd said, leaning back in the grass, "is these contracted families you have. The mother, the father, the children, all living alone in some big house. Our families extend as far as our bloodlines and friendship can reach."

"I don't know much about bloodlines," Jilly said. "But I know about friends."

He'd nodded. "That's why I'm talking to you."

Jilly blinked and looked at Geordie. "It made sense what he said."

Geordie smiled. "Of course it did. Immortal animal people."

"That, too. But I was talking about the weird way we think about families and children. Most people don't even like kids—don't want to see, hear, or hear about them. But when you look at other cultures, even close to home . . . up on the rez, in Chinatown, Little Italy . . . it's these big rambling extended families, everybody taking care of everybody else."

Geordie cleared his throat. Jilly waited for him to speak but he went instead to unplug the kettle and finish making the coffee. He ground up some beans and the noise of the hand-cranked machine seemed to reach out and fill every corner of the loft. When he stopped, the sudden silence was profound, as though the city outside was holding its breath along with the inheld breath of the room. Jilly was still watching him when he looked over at her.

"We don't come from that kind of family," he said finally.

"I know. That's why we had to make our own."

It's late at night, snow whirling in dervishing gusts, and the crow girls are perched on the top of the wooden fence that's been erected around a work site on Williamson Street. Used to be a parking lot there, now it's a big hole in the ground on its way to being one more office complex that nobody except the contractors want. The top of the fence is barely an inch wide at the top and slippery with snow, but they have no trouble balancing there.

Zia has a ring with a small spinning disc on it. Painted on the disc is a psychedelic coil that goes spiraling down into infinity. She keeps spinning it and the two of them stare down into the faraway place at the center of the spiral until the disc slows down, almost stops. Then Zia gives it another flick with her fingernail, and the coil goes spiraling down again.

"Where'd you get this anyway?" Maida asks.

Zia shrugs. "Can't remember. Found it somewhere."

"In someone's pocket."

"And you never did?"

Maida grins. "Just wish I'd seen it first, that's all."

They watch the disc some more, content.

"What do you think it's like down there?" Zia says after a while. "On the other side of the spiral."

Maida has to think about that for a moment. "Same as here," she finally announces, then winks. "Only dizzier."

They giggle, leaning into each other, tottering back and forth on their perch, crow girls, can't be touched, can't hardly be seen, except someone's standing down there on the sidewalk, looking up through the falling snow, his worried expression so comical it sets them off on a new round of giggles.

"Careful now!" he calls up to them. He thinks they're on drugs—they can tell. "You don't want to—"

Before he can finish, they hold hands and let themselves fall backward, off the fence.

"Oh, Christ!"

He jumps, gets a handhold on the top of the fence and hauls himself up. But when he looks over, over and down, way down, there's nothing to be seen. No girls lying at the bottom of that big hole in the ground, nothing at all. Only the falling snow. It's like they were never there.

His arms start to ache and he lowers himself back down the fence, lets go, bending his knees slightly to absorb the impact of the last couple of feet. He slips, catches his balance. It seems very still for a moment, so still he can hear an odd rhythmical whispering sound. Like wings. He looks up, but there's too much snow coming down to see anything. A cab comes by, skidding on the slick street, and he blinks. The street's full of city sounds again, muffled, but present. He hears the murmuring conversation of a couple approaching him, their shoulders and hair white with snow. A snowplow a few streets over. A distant siren.

He continues along his way, but he's walking slowly now, trudging through the drifts, not thinking so much of two girls sitting on top of a fence as remembering how, when he was a boy, he used to dream that he could fly.

After fiddling a little more with her sketch, Jilly finally put her charcoal down. She made herself a cup of herbal tea with the leftover hot water in the kettle and joined Geordie where he was sitting on the sofa, watching the snow come down. It was warm in the loft, almost cozy compared to the storm on the other side of the windowpanes, or maybe because of the storm. Jilly leaned back on the sofa, enjoying the companionable silence for a while before she finally spoke.

"How do you feel after seeing the crow girls?" she asked.

Geordie turned to look at her. "What do you mean, how do I feel?"

"You know, good, bad . . . different . . ."

Geordie smiled. "Don't you mean 'indifferent'?"

"Maybe." She picked up her tea from the crate where she'd set it and took a sip. "Well?" she asked when he didn't continue.

"Okay. How do I feel? Good, I suppose. They're fun, they make me smile. In fact, just thinking of them now makes me feel good."

Jilly nodded thoughtfully as he spoke. "Me, too. And something else as well."

"The different," Geordie began. He didn't quite sigh. "You believe those stories of Jack's, don't you?"

"Of course. And you don't?"

"I'm not sure," he replied, surprising her.

"Well, I think these crow girls were in the Cyberbean for a purpose," Jilly said. "Like in that rhyme about crows."

Geordie got it right away. "Two for mirth."

Jilly nodded. "Heather needed some serious cheering up. Maybe even something more. You know how when you start feeling low, you can get on this descending spiral of depression . . . everything goes wrong, things get worse, because you expect them to?"

"Fight it with the power of positive thinking, I always say."

"Easier said than done when you're feeling that low. What you really need at a time like that is something completely unexpected to kick you out of it and remind you that there's more to life than the hopeless, grey expanse you think is stretching in every direction. What Colin Wilson calls absurd good news."

"You've been talking to my brother."

"It doesn't matter where I got it from—it's still true."

Geordie shook his head. "I don't buy the idea that Maida and Zia showed up just to put your friend in a better mood. Even bird people can get a craving for a cup of coffee, can't they?"

"Well, yes," Jilly said. "But that doesn't preclude their being there for Heather as well. Sometimes when a person needs something badly enough, it just comes to them. A personal kind of steam-engine time. You might not be able to articulate what it is you need, you might not even know you need something—at least, not at a conscious level—but the need's still there, calling out to whatever's willing to listen."

Geordie smiled. "Like animal spirits."

"Crow girls."

Geordie shook his head. "Drink your tea and go to bed," he told her. "I think you need a good night's sleep."

"But—"

"It was only a coincidence. Things don't always have a meaning. Sometimes they just happen. And besides, how do you even know they had any effect on Heather?"

"I could just tell. And don't change the subject."

"I'm not."

"Okay," Jilly said. "But don't you see? It doesn't matter if it was a coincidence or not. They still showed up when Heather needed them. It's more of that 'small world, spooky world' stuff Professor Dapple goes on about. Everything's connected. It doesn't matter if we can't see how, it's still all connected. You know, chaos theory and all that."

Geordie shook his head, but he was smiling. "Does it ever strike you as weird when something Bramley's talked up for years suddenly becomes an acceptable element of scientific study?"

"Nothing strikes me as truly weird," Jilly told him. "There's only stuff I haven't figured out yet."

Heather barely slept that night. For the longest time she simply couldn't sleep, and then when she finally did, she was awake by dawn. Wide awake, but heavy with an exhaustion that came more from heartache than lack of sleep.

Sitting up against the headboard, she tried to resist the sudden tightness in her chest, but that sad, cold wasteland swelled inside her. The bed seemed depressingly huge. She didn't so much miss Peter's presence as feel adrift in the bed's expanse of blankets and sheets. Adrift in her life. Why was it he seemed to have no trouble carrying on when the simple act of getting up in the morning felt as though it would require far more energy than she could ever hope to muster?

She stared at the snow swirling against her window, not at all relishing the drive into town on a morning like this. If anything, it was coming down harder than it had been last night. All it took was the suggestion of snow and everybody in the city seemed to forget how to drive, never mind common courtesy or traffic laws. A blizzard like this would snarl traffic and back it up as far as the mountains.

She sighed, supposing it was just as well she'd woken so early since it would take her at least an extra hour to get downtown today.

Up, she told herself, and forced herself to swing her feet to the floor and rise. A shower helped. It didn't really ease the heartache, but the hiss of the water made it easier to ignore her thoughts. Coffee, when she was dressed and had brewed a pot, helped more, though she still winced when Janice came bounding into the kitchen.

"It's a snow day!" she cried. "No school. They just announced it on the radio. The school's closed, closed, closed!"

She danced about in her flannel nightie, pirouetting in the small space between the counter and the table.

"Just yours," Heather asked, "or Casey's, too?"

"Mine, too," Casey replied, following her sister into the room.

Unlike Janice, she was maintaining her cool, but Heather could tell she was just as excited. Too old to allow herself to take part in Janice's spontaneous celebration, but young enough to be feeling giddy with the unexpected holiday.

"Good," Heather said. "You can look after your sister."

"Mom!" Janice protested. "I'm not a baby."

"I know. It's just good to have someone older in the house when—"

"You can't be thinking of going in to work today," Casey said.

"We could do all kinds of stuff," Janice added. "Finish decorating the house. Baking."

"Yeah," Casey said, "all the things we don't seem to have time for anymore."

Heather sighed. "The trouble is," she explained, "the real world doesn't work like school. We don't get snow days."

Casey shook her head. "That is *so* unfair."

The phone rang before Heather could agree.

"I'll bet it's your boss," Janice said as Heather picked up the phone. "Calling to tell you it's a snow day for you, too."

Don't I wish, Heather thought. But then what would she do at home all day? It was so hard being here, even with the girls and much as she loved them. Everywhere she turned, something reminded her of how the promises of a good life had turned into so much ash. At least work kept her from brooding.

She brought the receiver up to her ear and spoke into the mouthpiece. "Hello?"

"I've been thinking," the voice on the other end of the line said. "About last night."

Heather had to smile. Wasn't that so Jilly, calling up first thing in the morning as though they were still in the middle of last night's conversation.

"What about last night?" she said.

"Well, all sorts of stuff. Like remembering a perfect moment in the past and letting it carry you through a hard time now."

If only, Heather thought. "I don't have a moment that perfect," she said.

"I sort of got that feeling," Jilly told her. "That's why I think they were a message—a kind of perfect moment now that you can use the same way."

"What *are* you talking about?"

"The crow girls. In the café last night."

"The crow . . ." It took her a moment to realize what Jilly meant. Their complexions had been dark enough so she supposed they could have been Indians. "How do you know what tribe they belonged to?"

"Not Crow, Native American," Jilly said, "but crow, bird people."

Heather shook her head as she listened to what Jilly went on to say, for all that only her daughters were here to see the movement. Glum looks had replaced their earlier excitement when they realized the call wasn't from her boss.

"Do you have any idea how improbable all of this sounds?" she asked when Jilly finished. "Life's not like your paintings."

"Says who?"

"How about common sense?"

"Tell me," Jilly said. "Where did common sense ever get you?"

Heather sighed. "Things don't happen just because we want them to," she said.

"Sometimes that's *exactly* why they happen," Jilly replied. "They happen because we need them to."

"I don't live in that kind of a world."

"But you could."

Heather looked across the kitchen at her daughters once more. The girls were watching her, trying to make sense out of the one-sided conversation they were hearing. Heather wished them luck. She was hearing both sides and that didn't seem to help at all. You couldn't simply reinvent your world because you wanted to. Things just were how they were.

"Just think about it," Jilly added. "Will you do that much?"

"I . . ."

That bleak landscape inside Heather seemed to expand, growing so large there was no way she could contain it. She focused on the faces of her daughters. She remembered the crow girls in the café. There was so much innocence in them all, daughters and crow girls. She'd been just like them once and she knew it wasn't simply nostalgia coloring her memory. She knew there'd been a time when she lived inside each particular day, on its own and by itself, instead of trying to deal with all the days of her life at once, futilely attempting to reconcile the discrepancies and mistakes.

"I'll try," she said into the phone.

They said their goodbyes and Heather slowly cradled the receiver.

"Who was that, Mom?" Casey asked.

Heather looked out the window. The snow was still falling, muffling the world. Covering its complexities with a blanket as innocent as the hope she saw in her daughters' eyes.

"Jilly," she said. She took a deep breath, then smiled at them. "She was calling to tell me that today really is a snow day."

The happiness that flowered on their faces helped ease the tightness in her chest.

The grey landscape waiting for her there didn't go away, but for some reason, it felt less profound. She wasn't even worried about what her boss would say when she called in to tell him she wouldn't be in today.

Crow girls can move like ghosts. They'll slip into your house when you're not home, sometimes when you're only sleeping, go walking spirit-soft through your rooms and hallways, sit in your favorite chair, help themselves to cookies and beer, borrow a trinket or two which they'll mean to return and usually do. It's not breaking and entering so much as simple curiosity. They're worse than cats.

Privacy isn't in their nature. They don't seek it and barely understand the concept. Personal property is even more alien. The idea of ownership—that one can lay proprietary claim to a piece of land, an object, another person or creature—doesn't even register.

"Whatcha looking at?" Zia asks.

They don't know whose house they're in. Walking along on the street, trying to catch snowflakes on their tongues, one or the other of them suddenly got the urge to come inside. Upstairs, the family sleeps.

Maida shows her the photo album. "Look," she says. "It's the same people, but they keep changing. See, here she's a baby, then she's a little girl, then a teenager."

"Everything changes," Zia says. "Even we get old. Look at Crazy Crow."

"But it happens so fast with them."

Zia sits down beside her and they pore over the pictures, munching on apples they found earlier in a cold cellar in the basement.

Upstairs, a father wakes in his bed. He stares at the ceiling, wondering what woke him. Nervous energy crackles inside him like static electricity, a sudden spill of adrenaline, but he doesn't know why. He gets up and checks the children's rooms. They're both asleep. He listens for intruders, but the house is silent.

Stepping back into the hall, he walks to the head of the stairs and looks down. He thinks he sees something in the gloom, two dark-haired girls sitting on the sofa, looking through a photo album. Their gazes lift to meet his and hold it. The next thing he knows, he's on the sofa himself, holding the photo album in his hand. There are no strange girls sitting there with him. The house seems quieter than it's ever been, as though the fridge, the furnace, and every clock the family owns are holding their breath along with him.

He sets the album down on the coffee table, walks slowly back up the stairs and returns to his bed. He feels like a stranger, misplaced. He doesn't know this room, doesn't know the woman beside him. All he can think about is the first girl he ever loved and his heart swells with a bittersweet sorrow. An ache pushes against his ribs, makes it almost impossible to breathe.

What if, what if . . .

He turns on his side and looks at his wife. For one moment her face blurs, becomes a morphing image that encompasses both her features and those of his first true love. For one moment it seems as though anything is possible, that for all these years he could have been married to another woman, to that girl who first held, then unwittingly, broke his heart.

"No," he says.

His wife stirs, her features her own again. She blinks sleepily at him.

"What . . . ?" she mumbles.

He holds her close, heartbeat drumming, more in love with her for being who she is than he has ever been before.

Outside, the crow girls are lying on their backs, making snow angels on his lawn, scissoring their arms and legs, shaping skirts and wings. They break their apple cores in two and give their angels eyes, then run off down the street, holding hands. The snow drifts are undisturbed by their weight. It's as though they, too, like the angels they've just made, also have wings.

"This is so cool," Casey tells her mother. "It really feels like Christmas. I mean, not like Christmases we've had, but, you know, like really being part of Christmas."

Heather nods. She's glad she brought the girls down to the soup kitchen to help Jilly and her friends serve a Christmas dinner to those less fortunate than themselves. She's been worried about how her daughters would take the break from tradition, but then realized, with Peter gone, tradition was already broken. Better to begin all over again.

The girls had been dubious when she first broached the subject with them—"I don't want to spend Christmas with *losers*," had been Casey's first comment. Heather hadn't argued with her. All she'd said was, "I want you to think about what you just said."

Casey's response had been a sullen look—there were more and more of these lately—but Heather knew her own daughter well enough. Casey had stomped off to her room, but then come back half an hour later and helped her explain to Janice why it might not be the worst idea in the world.

She watches them now, Casey having rejoined her sister where they are playing with the homeless children, and knows a swell of pride. They're such good kids, she thinks as she takes another sip of her cider. After a couple of hours serving coffee, tea and hot cider, she'd really needed to get off her feet for a moment.

"Got something for you," Jilly says, sitting down on the bench beside her.

Heather accepts the small, brightly-wrapped parcel with reluctance. "I thought we said we weren't doing Christmas presents."

"It's not really a Christmas present. It's more an everyday sort of a present that I just happen to be giving you today."

"Right."

"So aren't you going to open it?"

Heather peels back the paper and opens the small box. Inside, nestled in a piece of folded Kleenex, are two small silver earrings cast in the shapes of crows. Heather lifts her gaze.

"They're beautiful."

"Got them at the craft show from a local jeweler. Rory Crowther. See, his name's on the card in the bottom of the box. They're to remind you—"

Heather smiles. "Of crow girls?"

"Partly. But more to remember that this—" Jilly waves a hand that could be taking in the basement of St. Vincent's, could be taking in the whole world. "It's not all we get. There's more. We can't always see it, but it's there."

For a moment, Heather thinks she sees two dark-haired slim figures standing on the far side of the basement, but when she looks more closely they're only a baglady and Geordie's friend Tanya, talking.

For a moment, she thinks she hears the sound of wings, but it's only the murmur of conversation. Probably.

What she knows for sure is that the grey landscape inside her chest is shrinking a little more, every day.

"Thank you," she says.

She isn't sure if she's speaking to Jilly or to crow girls she's only ever seen once, but whose presence keeps echoing through her life. Her new life. It isn't necessarily a better one. Not yet. But at least it's on the way up from wherever she'd been going, not down into a darker despair.

"Here," Jilly says. "Let me help you put them on."

Wild Horses

Chance is always powerful. Let your hook be always cast;
in the pool where you least expect it, there will be a fish.
—Ovid

1

The horses run the empty length of the lakeshore, strung out like a long ragged necklace, perfect in their beauty. They run wild. They run like whitecaps in choppy water, their unshod hooves kicking up sand and spray. The muffled sound of their galloping is a rough music, pure rhythm. Palominos. Six, seven . . . maybe a dozen of them. Their white manes and tails flash, golden coats catch the sunlight and hold it under the skin the way mine holds a drug.

The city is gone. Except for me, transfixed by the sight of them, gaze snared by the powerful motion of their muscles propelling them forward, the city is gone, skyline and dirty streets and dealers and the horse that comes in a needle instead of running free along a beach. All gone.

And for a moment, I'm free, too.

I run after them, but they're too fast for me, these wild horses, can't be tamed, can't be caught. I run until I'm out of breath and stumble and fall and when I come to, I'm lying under the overpass where the freeway cuts through Squatland, my works lying on my coat beside me, empty now. I look out across a landscape of sad tenements and long-abandoned factories and the only thing I can think is, I need another hit to take me back. Another hit, and this time I'll catch up to them.

I know I will. I have to.

There's nothing for me here.

But the drugs don't take me anywhere.

2

Cassie watched the young woman approach. She was something, sleek and pretty, newly shed of her baby fat. Nineteen, maybe; twenty-one, twenty-two, tops. Wearing an old sweater, raggedy jeans and sneakers—nothing fancy, but she looked like a million dollars. Bottle that up, Cassie thought, along with the long spill of her dark curly hair, the fresh-faced, perfect complexion, and you'd be on easy street. Only the eyes hinted at what must have brought her here, the lost, hopeful look in their dark depths. Something haunted her. You didn't need the cards to tell you that.

She was out of place—not a tourist, not part of the bohemian coterie of fortune-tellers, buskers, and craftspeople who were set up along this section of the Pier either. Cassie tracked her gaze as it went from one card table to the next, past the palmist, the other card readers, the Gypsy, the lovely Scottish boy with his Weirdin discs, watched until that gaze met her own and the woman started to walk across the boards, aimed straight for her.

Somebody was playing a harp, over by one of the weavers' tables. A sweet melody, like a lullaby, rose above the conversation around the tables and the sound of the water lapping against the wooden footings below. It made no obvious impression on the approaching woman, but Cassie took the music in, letting it swell inside her, a piece of beauty stolen from the heart of commerce. The open-air market and sideshow that sprawled along this section of the Pier might look alternative, but it was still about money. The harper was out to make a buck, and so was Cassie.

She had her small collapsible table set up with a stool for her on one side, its twin directly across the table for a customer. A tablecloth was spread over the table, hand-embroidered with ornate hermetic designs. On top of the cloth, a small brass change bowl and her cards, wrapped in silk and boxed in teak.

The woman stood behind the vacant stool, hesitating before she finally sat down. She pulled her knapsack from her back and held it on her lap, arms hugging it close to her chest. The smile she gave Cassie was uncertain.

Cassie gave her a friendly smile back. "No reason to be nervous, girl. We're all friends here. What's your name?"

"Laura."

"And I'm Cassandra. Now what sort of a reading were you looking for?"

Laura reached out her hand, not quite touching the box with its cards. "Are they real?" she asked.

"How do you mean, real?"

"Magic. Can you work magic with them?"

"Well, now . . ."

Cassie didn't like to lie, but there was magic and there was magic. One lay in the heart of the world and was as much a natural part of how things were as it was deep mystery. The other was the thing people were looking for to solve their problems with and it never quite worked the way they felt it should.

"Magic's all about perception," she said. "Do you know what I mean?"

Laura shook her head. She'd drawn her hand back from the cards and was hugging her knapsack again. Cassie picked up the wooden box and put it to one side. From the inside pocket of her matador's jacket, she pulled out another set of cards. These ones were tattered around the edges, held together by an elastic band. When she placed them on the tablecloth, the woman's gaze went to the top card and was immediately caught by the curious image on it. The card showed the same open-air market they were sitting in, the crowds of tourists and vendors, the Pier, the lake behind.

"Those . . . are those regular cards?" Laura asked.

"Do I look like a regular reader?"

The question was academic. Cassie didn't look like a regular anything, not even on the Pier. She was in her early thirties, a dark-eyed woman with coffee-colored skin and hair that hung in a hundred tiny beaded braids. Today she wore tight purple jeans and yellow combat boots; under her black matador's jacket was a white T-shirt with the words DON'T! BUY! THAI! emblazoned on it. Her ears were festooned with studs, dangling earrings, and simple hoops. On each wrist she had a dozen or so plastic bracelets in a rainbow palette of Day-Glo colors.

"I guess not," the woman said. She leaned a little closer. "What does your T-shirt mean? I've seen that slogan all over town, on T-shirts, spray-painted on walls, but I don't know what it means."

"It's a boycott to try to stop the child-sex industry in Thailand."

"Are you collecting signatures for a petition or something?"

Cassie shook her head. "You just do like the words say. Check out what you're buying and if it's made in Thailand, don't buy it and explain why."

"Do you really think it'll help?"

"Well, it's like magic," Cassie said, bringing the conversation back to what she knew Laura really wanted to talk about. "And like I said, magic's about perception, that's all. It means anything is possible. It means taking the way we usually look at a thing and making people see it differently. Or, depending on your viewpoint, making them see it properly for the first time."

"But—"

"For instance, I could be a crow, sitting on this stool talking to you, but I've convinced everybody here that I'm Cassandra Washington, card reader, so that's what you all see."

Laura gave her an uneasy look that Cassie had no trouble reading: Pretty sure she was being put on, but not entirely sure.

Cassie smiled. "The operative word here is *could*. But that's how magic works. It's all about how we perceive things to be. A good magician can make anything seem possible and pretty soon you've got seven-league boots and people turning invisible or changing into wolves or flying—all sorts of fun stuff."

"You're serious, aren't you?"

"Oh, yeah. Now fortune-telling—that's all about perception, too, except it's looking inside yourself. It works best with a ritual because that allows you to concentrate better—same reason religion and church works so well for some people. Makes them all pay attention and focus and the next thing you know they're either looking inside themselves and working out their problems, or making a piece of magic."

She picked up the cards and removed the elastic band. Shuffled them. "Think of these as a mirror. Pay enough attention to them and they'll lay out a pattern that'll take you deep inside yourself."

Laura appeared disappointed. But they always did, when it was put out in front of them like this. They thought you'd pulled back the curtain and shown the Wizard of Oz, working all the levers of his machine, not realizing that you'd let them into a deeper piece of magic than something they might buy for a few dollars in a place like the Pier.

"I . . . I thought it might be different," Laura said.

"You wanted it all laid out for you, simple, right? Do this, and this'll happen. Do this, and it'll go like this. Like reading the sun signs in the newspaper, except personal."

Laura shook her head. "It wasn't about me. It was about my brother."

"Your brother?"

"I was hoping you could, you know, use your cards to tell me where he is."

Cassie stopped shuffling her pack and laid it face down on the table.

"Your brother's missing?" she said.

Laura nodded. "It's been two years now."

Cassie was willing to give people a show, willing to give them more than what they were asking for, sometimes, or rather what they were really asking for but weren't articulating, but she wasn't in the business of selling false hopes or pretences. Some people could do it, but not her. Not and sleep at night.

"Laura," she said. "Girl. You've come to the wrong place. You want to talk to the police. They're the ones who deal with missing persons."

And you'll have wanted to talk to them a lot sooner than now, she thought, but she left that unsaid.

"I did," Laura told her.

Cassie waited. "And what?" she asked finally. "They told you to come here?"

"No. Of course not. They—a Sergeant Riley. He's been really nice, but I guess there's not much they can do. They say it's been so long and the city's so big and Dan could have moved away months ago. . . ."

Her eyes filled with tears and voice trailed off. She swallowed, tried again.

"I brought everything I could think of," she said, holding up her knapsack for a moment before clutching it tightly to her chest again. "Pictures. His dental records. The last couple of postcards I got from him. I . . ." She had to swallow again. "They have all these pictures of . . . of unidentified bodies and I . . . I had to look at them all. And they sent off copies of the stuff I brought—sent it off all over the country, but it's been over a month and I know Dan's not dead. . . ."

She looked up, her eyes still shiny with unshed tears. Cassie nodded sympathetically.

"Can I see one of the pictures?" she said.

A college-aged boy looked back at her from the small snapshot Laura took out of her knapsack. Not handsome, but there was a lot of character in his features. Short brown hair, high cheek bones, strong jawline. Something in his eyes reflected the same mix of loss and hopefulness that was now in his sister's. What had *he* been looking for?

"You say he's been missing for two years?" Cassie asked.

Laura nodded. Showing the picture seemed to have helped steady her.

"Your parents didn't try to find him?"

"They never really got along. It's—I don't know why. They were always fighting, arguing. He left the house when he was sixteen—as soon as he could get out. We live—we *lived* just outside of Boston. He moved into Cambridge, then maybe four years ago, he moved out here. When I was in college he'd call me sometimes and always send me postcards."

Cassie waited. "And then he stopped?" she said finally.

"Two years ago. That's when I got the last card. I saw him a couple of months before that."

"Do you get along with your parents?"

"They've always treated me just the opposite from how they treated him. Dan couldn't do anything right and I can't do anything wrong."

"Why did you wait so long?"

"I . . ." Her features fell. "I just kept expecting to hear from him. I was finishing up my master's and working part-time at a restaurant and . . . I don't know. I was just so busy and I didn't realize how long it had really been until all of a sudden two years have gone by since he wrote."

She kept looking at the table as she spoke, glancing up as though to make sure Cassie was still listening, then back down again. When she looked up now, she straightened her back.

"I guess it was pretty crazy of me to think you could help," she said.

No, Cassie thought. More like a little sad. But she understood need and how it could make you consider avenues you'd never normally take a walk down.

"Didn't say I wouldn't try," she told Laura. "What do you know about what he was doing here?"

"The last time I saw him, all he could talk about were these horses, wild horses running along the shore of the lake."

Cassie nodded encouragingly when Laura's voice trailed off once more.

"But there aren't any, are there?" Laura said. "It's all . . ." She waved her hand, encompassing the Pier, the big hotels, the Williamson Street Mall further up the beach. "It's all like this."

"Pretty much. A little further west there's the Beaches, but that's all private waterfront and pretty upscale. And even if someone would let him onto their land, I've never heard of any wild horses out there."

Laura nodded. "I showed his picture around at the racetrack and every riding stable I could find listed in the Yellow Pages, but no one recognized him."

"Anything else?" Cassie asked.

She hesitated for a long moment before replying. "I think he was getting into drugs again." Her gaze lifted from the card table to meet Cassie's. "He was pretty bad off for a few years, right after he got out of the house, but he'd cleaned up his act before he moved out here."

"What makes you think he got back into them?"

"I don't know. Just a feeling—the last time I saw him. The way he was all fidgety again, something in his eyes. . . ."

Maybe that was what she'd seen in his picture, Cassie thought. That need in his eyes.

"What kind of drugs?" she asked.

"Heroin."

"A different kind of horse."

Laura sighed. "That's what Sergeant Riley said."

Cassie tapped a fingernail, painted the same purple as her jeans, on the pack of cards that lay between them.

"Where are you staying?" she asked.

"The Y. It's all I can afford. I'm getting kind of low on money and I haven't had much luck getting a job."

Cassie nodded. "Leave me that picture," she said. "I'll ask around for you, see what I can find out."

"But . . ."

She was looking at the cards. Cassie laid her hand over them and shook her head.

"Let me do this my way," Cassie said. "You know the pay phone by the front desk? I'll give you a call there tomorrow, around three, say, and then we can talk some more."

She put out her hand and Laura looked confused.

"Um," she began. "How much do you want?"

Cassie smiled. "The picture, girl. I'll do the looking as a favor."

"But I'm putting you to so much trouble—"

"I've been where you are," Cassie said. "If you want to pay me back, do a good turn for someone else."

"Oh."

She didn't seem either confident or happy with the arrangement, but she left the picture and stood up. Cassie watched her make her way back through the other vendors, then slowly turned over three cards from the top of the deck. The first showed a set of works lying on worn blue denim. A jacket, Cassie decided. The second had a picture of an overpass in the Tombs. The last showed a long length of beach, empty except for a small herd of palominos cantering down the wet sand. In the background, out in the water, was the familiar shape of Wolf Island, outlined against the horizon.

Cassie lifted her head and turned to look at the lake. Beyond the end of the Pier she could see Wolf Island, the ferry on a return trip, halfway between the island and the mainland. The image on her card didn't show the city, didn't show docking facilities on the island, the museum and gift shop that used to be somebody's summer place. The image on her card was of another time, before the city got here. Or of another place that you could only reach with your imagination.

Or with magic.

3

Cassie and Joe had made arrangements to meet at The Rusty Lion that night. He'd been sitting outside on the patio waiting for her when she arrived, a handsome Native man in jeans and a plain white T-shirt, long black braid hanging down his back, a look in his dark eyes that was usually half solemn, half tomfool Trickster. Right now it was concerned.

"You don't look so good," he said as she sat down.

She tried to make a joke of it. "People ask me why I stay with you," she said, "and I always tell them, you just know how to make a girl feel special."

But Joe would have none of it.

"You've got trouble," he told her, "and that means we have trouble. Tell me about it."

So she did.

Joe knew why she was helping this woman she'd never seen before. That was one of the reasons it was so good between them: Lots of things didn't need to be explained, they were simply understood.

" 'Course you found Angie too late," he said.

He reached across the table and took her hand, wanting to ease the sting of his words. She nodded and took what comfort she could from the touch of his rough palm and fingers. There was never any comfort in thinking about Angie.

"It might be too late for Laura's brother, too," she said.

Joe shrugged. "Depends. The cops could be right. He could be long gone from here, headed off to some junkie heaven like Seattle. I hear they've got one of the best needle-exchange programs in the country and you know the dope's cheap. Twenty bucks'll buy you a 30 piece."

Cassie nodded. "Except the cards . . ."

"Oh, yeah. The cards."

The three cards lay on the table between them, still holding the images she'd found in them after Laura walked away. Joe had recognized the place where the horses were running the same as she had.

"Except I never heard of dope taking someone into the spiritworld before," he said.

"So what does it mean?" Cassie asked.

He put into words what she'd only been thinking. "Either he's clean, or he's dead."

She nodded. "And if he's clean, then why hasn't he called her, or sent another postcard? They were close."

"She says."

"You don't think so?"

Joe shrugged. "I wasn't the one who met her. But she waited two years."

"I waited longer to go looking for Angie."

There was nothing Joe could say to that.

4

It was a long time ago now.

Cassie shows them all, the white kids who wouldn't give her the time of day and the kids from the projects that she grew up with. She makes top of her graduating class, valedictorian, stands there at the commencement exercises, out in front of everybody, speech in hand. But when she looks out across the sea of mostly white faces, she realizes they still don't respect her and there's nobody she cares about sitting out there. The one person who ever meant something to her is noticeably absent.

Angie dropped out in grade nine and they really haven't seen each other since. Somewhere between Angie dropping out and Cassie resolving to prove herself, she and her childhood best friend have become more than strangers. They might as well never have known each other, they're so different.

So Cassie's looking out at the crowd. She wants to blow them off, but that's like giving in, so she follows through, reads her speech, pretends she's a part of the celebration, but she skips the bullshit parties that follow, doesn't listen to the phony praise for her speech, won't talk to her teachers who want to know what she plans to do next. She goes home and takes off that pretty new dress that cost her two months' working after school and weekends at McDonald's. Puts on sweats and hightops. Washes the makeup from her face and looks in the mirror. The face that looks back at her is soft, that of a little girl. The only steel is in the eyes.

Then she goes out looking for Angie, but Angie's not around any more. Word on the street is she went the junkie route, mixing crack and horse, selling herself to pay for her jones, long gone now or dead, and why would Cassie care anyway? It's like school, only in reverse. She's got no street smarts, no one takes her seriously, no one respects her.

She finds herself walking out of the projects, still looking for Angie, but keeping to herself now, walking all over the city, looking into faces but finding only strangers. Her need to find Angie is maybe as strong as Angie's was for the drugs, everything's focused on it, looking not only for Angie but for herself—the girl she was before she let other people's opinions become more important than her best friend. She's not ready to say that her turning her back on Angie pushed her toward the street life, but it couldn't have helped either. But she does know that Angie had a need that Cassie filled and the drugs took its place. Now Cassie has a need and she doesn't know what's going to fill it, but something has to or she feels like she's just going to dry up and blow away.

She keeps walking further and further until one day that jones of hers takes her to an old white clapboard house just north of the city, front yard's got a bottle tree growing in the weeds and dirt, an old juju woman sitting on the porch looking at her with dark eyes, skin so black Cassie feels white. Cassie doesn't know which is scarier, the old woman or her saying, " 'Bout time you showed up, girl. I'd just about given up on you."

All Cassie can do is stand there, can't walk away, snared by the old woman's gaze. A breeze comes up and those bottles hanging in the tree clink against each other. The old woman beckons to her with a crooked finger and the next thing Cassie knows she's walking up to the porch, climbing the rickety stairs, standing right in front of the woman.

"I've been keeping these for someone like you," she says and pulls a pack of tattered cards out of the pocket of her black dress.

Cassie doesn't want to take them, but she reaches for them all the same. They're held together with an elastic band. When the old woman puts them in her hand, something like a static charge jumps between them. She gets a dizzy feeling that makes her sway, almost lose her balance. She closes her hand, fingers tight around the cards and the feeling goes away.

The old woman's grinning. "You felt that, didn't you, girl?"

"I . . . I felt something."

"Aren't you a caution."

None of this feels real, none of it makes sense. The old woman, the house, the bottle tree. Cassie tries to remember how she got here, when the strip malls and fast-food outlets suddenly gave way to a dirt road and this place. Is this how it happened to Angie? All of a sudden she looks at herself one day and she's a junkie?

Cassie's gaze goes down to the cards the old woman gave her. She removes the elastic and fans a few of them out. They have a design on one side; the other side is blank. She lifts her head to find the old woman still grinning at her.

"What are these?" she asks.

"What do they look like, girl? They're cards. Older than Egypt, older than China, older than when the first mama woke up in Africa and got to making babies so that we could all be here."

"But . . ." It's hard to think straight. "What are they for?"

"Fortunes, girl. Help you find yourself. Let you help other people find themselves."

"But . . ."

She was valedictorian, she thinks. She has more of a vocabulary than her whole family put together and all she can say is "but."

"But there's nothing on them."

She doesn't know much about white people's magic, but she's heard of telling fortunes with cards—playing cards, Tarot cards. She doesn't know much about her own people's magic either.

The old juju woman laughs. "Oh, girl. 'Course there isn't. There won't be nothing on them until you need something to be there."

None of this is making sense. It's only making her dizzy again. There's a stool beside the woman's chair and she sits on it, closes her eyes, still holding the cards. She takes a few deep breaths, steadies herself. But when she opens her eyes again she's sitting on a concrete block in the middle of a traffic median. There's no house, no bottle tree. No old woman. Only the traffic going by on either side of her. A discount clothing store across the street. A factory outlet selling stereos and computers on the other side.

There's only the cards in her hands and at her feet, lying on the pavement of the median, an elastic band.

She's scared. But she bends down, picks up the elastic. She turns over the top card, looks at it. There's a picture now, where before it was blank. It shows an abandoned tenement in the Tombs, one of the places where the homeless people squat. She's never been in it, but she recognizes the building. She's passed it a hundred times on the bus, going from school to the McDonald's where she worked. She turns another card and now she's looking at a picture of the inside of a building—probably the same one. The windows are broken, there's garbage all over, a heap of rags in one corner. A third card takes her closer to the rags. Now she can see there's somebody lying under those rags, somebody so thin and wasted there's only bone covered with skin.

She doesn't turn a fourth card.

She returns the cards to the pack, puts the elastic around them, sticks the pack in her pocket. Her mouth feels baked and dry. She waits for a break in the traffic and goes across to the discount clothing store to ask for a drink of water, but they tell her the restroom is only for staff. She has to walk four blocks before a man at a service station gives a sympathetic look when she repeats her request, hands her the key to the woman's room.

She drinks long and deep, then feels sick and has to throw up. When she returns to the sink, she rinses her mouth, washes her face. The man's busy with a customer, so she hangs the key on the appropriate hook by the door in the office and thanks him as she goes by, walking back toward downtown.

Normal people don't walk through the Tombs, not even along well-trafficked streets like Williamson or Flood. It's too dangerous, a no-man's-land of deserted tenements and abandoned factories. But she doesn't see she has a choice. She walks until she sees the tenement that was on the card, swallows hard, then crosses an empty lot overgrown with weeds and refuse until she's standing in front of it. It takes her a while to work up her nerve, but finally she steps into its foyer.

It smells of urine and garbage. Something stirs in a corner, sits up. Her pulse jumps into overtime, even when she sees it's only a raggedy boy, skinny, hollow-eyed.

"Gimme something," he says. "I don't need to get high, man. I just need to feel well again."

"I . . . I don't have anything."

She's surprised she can find her voice. She's surprised that he only nods and lies back down in his nest of newspapers and rags.

It doesn't take her long to find the room she saw on the second card. Something pulls her down a long hall. The doors are all broken down. Things stir in some of the rooms. People. Rats. Roaches. She doesn't know and doesn't investigate. She just keeps walking until she's in the room, steps around the garbage littering the floor to the heap of rags in the corner.

A half hour later she's at a pay phone on Gracie Street, phoning the police, telling them about the dead body she found in the tenement.

"Her name's Angie," she says. "Angie Moore."

She hangs up and starts to walk again, not looking for anything now, hardly able to see because of the tears that swell in her eyes.

She doesn't go home again. She can't exactly explain why. Meeting the old woman, the cards she carries, finding Angie, it all gets mixed up in her head with how hard she tried to do well and still nobody really cared about her except for the friend she turned her back on. Her parents were happy to brag about her marks, but there was no warmth there. She is eighteen and can't remember ever being embraced. Her brothers and sisters were like the other kids in the projects, ragging on her for trying to do well. The white kids didn't care about anything except for the color of her skin.

It all came down to no one respecting her except for Angie, and she'd turned her back on Angie because Angie couldn't keep up.

But the cards mean something. She knows that.

She's still working at the McDonald's, only now she saves her money and lives in a squat in the Tombs. Nobody comes to find out why she hasn't returned home. Not her family, not her teachers. Some of the kids from school stop by, filling up on Big Macs and fries and soft drinks, and she can hear them snickering at their tables, studiously not looking at her.

She takes to going to the library and reading about cards and fortune telling, gets to be a bit of an expert. She buys a set of Tarot cards in The Occult Shop and sometimes talks to the people who work there, some of the customers. She never reads or hears anything about the kind of cards the old woman gave her.

Then one day she meets Joseph Crazy Dog in the Tombs, just down from the Kickaha rez, wild and reckless and a little scary, but kind, too, if you took the time to get to know him. Some people say he's not all there, supposed to be on medication, but won't take it. Others say he's got his feet in two worlds, this one and another place where people have animal faces and only spirits can stay for more than a few days, the kind of place you come back from either a poet or mad. First thing he tells her is he can't rhyme worth a damn.

Everybody calls him Bones because of how he tells fortunes with a handful of small-animal and bird bones, reads auguries in the way they fall upon the buckskin when he throws them. But she calls him Joe and something good happens between them because he respects her, right away he respects her. He's the first person she tells about the old juju woman and she knows she was right to wait because straightaway he can tell her where she went that day and what it means.

5

It was almost dark by the time Cassie and Joe reached the overpass in the Tombs that was pictured on the card. At one time it had been a hobo camp, but now it was one more junkie landmark, a place where you could score and shoot without being hassled. The cops didn't bother coming by much. They had bigger fish to fry.

"A lot of hard times bundled up in a place like this," Joe said.

Cassie nodded.

Some of the kids they walked by were so young. Most of them were already high.

Those that weren't, were looking to score. It wasn't the sort of place you could ask questions, but neither Cassie nor Joe were strangers to the Tombs. They still squatted themselves and most people knew of them, if they'd never actually met. They could get away with showing around a picture, asking questions.

"When did heroin get so popular again?" Cassie said.

Joe shrugged. "Never got unpopular—not when it's so easy to score. You know the drill. The only reason solvents and alcohol are so popular up on the rez is no one's bringing in this kind of shit. That's the way it works everywhere—supply and demand. Here the supply's good."

And nobody believed it could hurt them, Cassie thought. Because it wouldn't happen to them and sure people got addicted, but everybody knew somebody who'd used and hadn't got strung out on it. Nobody set out to become an addict. Like most bad things, it just snuck up on you when you weren't paying attention. But the biggest problem was that kids got lied to about so much, it was hard for them to accept this warning as a truth.

They made a slow pass of the three or four blocks where most of the users congregated, showing the photo of Laura's brother when it seemed appropriate, but without much luck. From there they headed back downtown, following Williamson Street down Gracie. It was on the gay bar strip on Gracie Street that they finally found someone who could help.

"I like the hair, Tommy," Cassie said.

It was like a close-cut Afro, the corkscrew curls so purple they had to come from a bottle. Tommy grinned, but his good humor vanished when Joe showed him the picture.

"Yeah, I know him," Tommy said. "Danny Packer, right? Though he sure doesn't look like that now. How come you're looking for him?"

"We're not. His sister is and we're just helping her out. Any idea where we could find him?"

"Ask at the clinic."

Cassie and Joe exchanged glances.

"He's working there?" Cassie asked.

Tommy shook his head.

6

"What is this place?" Laura asked.

They were standing in front of an old yellow brick house on McKennitt Street in Lower Crowsea. Cassie had picked her up outside the Y a little after four and Joe drove them across town in a cab he'd borrowed from a friend.

"It's a hospice," Cassie said. "It was founded by a writer who died of AIDS a few years ago—Ennis Thompson."

"I've read him. He was a wonderful writer."

Cassie nodded. "His royalties are what keeps it running."

The house was on a quiet stretch of McKennitt, shaded by a pair of the tall, stately oaks that flourished in Crowsea. There wasn't much lawn. Geraniums grew in terra cotta planters going up the steps to the front door, adding a splash of color and filling the air with their distinctive scent. They didn't seem to make much of an impression on Laura.

She was too busy studying the three-storied building, a small frown furrowing the skin between her eyebrows.

"Why did Dan want me to meet him here?" she asked.

Cassie hesitated. When they'd come to see him last night, Laura's brother had asked them to let him break the news to her. She understood, but it left her in the awkward position of having to be far too enigmatic in response to Laura's delight that her brother had been found. She'd been fending off Laura's questions ever since they'd spoken on the phone earlier and arranged to drive out here.

"Why don't we let him tell you himself," Cassie said.

Joe held the door for them. He nodded a greeting to the young woman stationed at a reception desk in what would once have been a front parlor.

"Go ahead," she told them. "He's expecting you."

"Thanks," Joe said.

He led the way down the hall to Dan's room. Rapping softly on the door, he opened it when a weak voice called out, "It's open."

Laura stopped and wouldn't go on.

"Come on," Cassie said, her voice gentle.

But Laura could only shake her head. "Oh god, how could I have been so stupid? He's a patient here, isn't he?"

Cassie put a hand on her arm and found it trembling. "He's still your brother."

"I know. It's not that. It's just—"

"Laura?"

The voice pulled her to the door and through it, into the room. Cassie had been planning to allow them some privacy for this meeting, but now she followed in after Laura to lend her moral support in case it was needed.

Dan was in bad shape. She only knew him from the picture that Laura had lent her yesterday, but he bore no resemblance to the young man in that photograph. Not anymore. No doubt he had already changed somewhat in the years since the picture had been taken, but now he was skeletal, the skin hanging from his bones, features hollow and sunken. Sores discolored his skin in great blotches and his hair was wispy and thin.

But Laura knew him.

Whatever had stopped her outside the room was gone. She crossed the room quickly now, sat down on the edge of the bed, carefully took his scrawny hands in her own, leaned forward and kissed his brow.

"Oh, Danny. What have you done to yourself?"

He gave her a weak smile. "Screwed things up as usual."

"But this . . ."

"I want you to know—it wasn't from a needle."

Laura threw a glance over her shoulder at Cassie, then returned her attention to her brother.

"I always knew," she said.

"You never said anything."

"I was waiting for you to tell me."

He shook his head slowly. "I could never put one past you."

"When were you going to tell me?" Laura asked.

"That's why I came back the last time. But I lost my nerve. And then when I got back to the city, I wasn't just HIV-positive anymore, but had full-blown AIDS and . . ."

His voice, already weak, trailed off.

"Oh, Danny, why? What did you think—that I wouldn't love you anymore?"

"I didn't know what to think. I just didn't want to be a bother."

"That's the last thing you are," Laura assured him. "I know . . ." She had to swallow and start again. "I know you won't be getting better, but you've got to at least have your family with you. Come home with me."

"No."

"Why not? Mom and Dad will want to—"

Dan cut her off, anger giving his voice some strength. "They won't want anything to do with me."

"But—"

"You never understood, did you? We lived in the same house, but it was two different worlds. I lived in one and the rest of you lived in the other. I don't know why things worked out that way, but you've got to accept that it's never going to change. That not even something like this could change it."

Laura didn't say anything for a long moment. She simply sat there, holding his hands, looking at him.

"It was so awful for you," she said finally. "Wasn't it?"

He nodded. "Everything, except for you."

That seemed to be too much for her, knowing that on top of his dying, how hard his life had been, right from when he was a child. She bowed down over him, holding him, shoulders shaking as she wept.

Cassie backed out of the room to join Joe where he was waiting in the hall.

"It's got to be tough," he said.

Cassie nodded, not trusting her voice. Her own gaze was blurry with tears.

7

"You never told her how you found me," Dan said later.

When Laura had gone to get tea, Cassie and Joe came back into the room, sitting on hardbacked chairs beside the bed. It was still hours until dusk but an overcast sky cast a gloomy light into the room.

"And you won't, will you?" he added.

Cassie shook her head.

"Why not?"

"It's hard to explain," she said. "I guess I just don't want her to get the wrong idea about the cards. You don't use them or any oracular device to find answers; you use them to ask questions. Some people don't get that."

He nodded slowly. "Laura wouldn't. She was always looking for miracles to solve everything. Like the way it was for me back home."

"Her heart was in the right place," Joe said.

Dan glanced at him. "Still is." He returned his attention to Cassie. "But those cards aren't normal Tarot cards."

Cassie had shown him the cards the night before, the three images that had taken her and Joe up into the Tombs and eventually to Dan's room here in the hospice.

"No," she said. "They're real magic."

"Where did you get them? I mean, can I ask you that?"

Cassie smiled. "Of course you can. They come from the same place where your wild horses are running."

"They . . . they're real?"

"Depends on how you translate real," Joe said.

Cassie gave him a light tap on his shoulder with a closed fist. "Don't start with that."

"What place are you talking about?" Dan asked.

For once, Joe was more forthcoming than he usually was with a stranger.

"The spiritworld," he said. "It's a lot closer than most people think. Open yourself up to it and it comes in close, so close it's like it's right at hand, no further away than what's out there on the other side of that window." He paused a moment, then added, "Dangerous place to visit, outside of a dream."

"It wasn't a dream that took me there," Dan said.

"Wasn't the drugs either," Joe told him.

"But—"

"Listen to me, what took you there is the same thing that called Cassie to the old juju woman who gave her those cards. You had a need. Doesn't happen often, but sometimes that's enough to take you across."

"I still have that need."

Joe nodded. "But first the drugs you kept taking got in the way. And now you're dying and your body knows better than to let your spirit go visiting. It wants to hang on and the only thing that's keeping you going is spirit."

"What about Laura's need when she was looking for me?" Dan asked. "Why didn't the spiritworld touch her?"

"It brought her to me, didn't it?" Cassie said.

"That's true."

Dan looked away, out the window. The view he had through it was filled with the boughs of one of those big oak trees. Cassie didn't think he was seeing them.

"You know," he said after a moment, not looking away from the window. "Before all of this, I wouldn't have believed you for a moment. Wouldn't have even listened to you. But you start thinking about spiritual things at a time like this. When you *know* you're going to die, it's hard not to." His gaze returned to them, moving slowly from one to the other. "I'd like to see them again . . . those horses."

Cassie glanced at Joe and he nodded.

"When you're ready to leave," he said, "give me a call."

"You mean that? You can do that?"

"Sure."

Dan started to reach for the pen and paper that was on the table beside his bed. "What's your number?"

"We don't have a phone," Joe said. "You just think about me and those horses hard enough and I'll come take you to them."

"But—"

"He can do it," Cassie said. "Even at the best of times, he's walking with one foot in either world. He'll know when you're ready and he'll take you there."

Dan studied Joe for a moment and Cassie knew what he was seeing, the dark Coyote eyes, the crow's head sitting just under his human skin. There was something solemn and laughing wild about him, all at once, as though he knew a joke no one else did that wrapped him in a feral kind of wisdom that could scare you silly. But Dan was past fear.

"That's something else you discover when you're this close to the edge," he said. "You get this ability to cut away the bullshit and look right into a person, see them for exactly as they are."

"So what are you seeing?" Joe asked.

Dan smiled. "Damned if I know. But I know I can trust you."

Cassie knew exactly what he meant.

8

Summer gave way to fall. On a cold October night, Cassie woke near dawn to find Joe sitting on the edge of the bed, pulling on his boots. He came over to the bed and kissed her cheek.

"Go back to sleep," he said. "I might be a while."

They'd been up late that night and she fell back asleep before she could think to ask where he was going.

9

Dan's funeral was two days later. It was a small service with few in attendance. Laura. Cassie. A few of the caregivers from the hospice. After the service, Cassie took Laura down to the lakefront. They sat on a bench at the end of the Pier where they'd first met, looking out at Wolf Island. A cold wind blew in off the lake and they sat close to each other for warmth.

"Where's Joe?" Laura asked.

"He had to go out of town."

Laura looked different to Cassie, more sure of herself, less haunted for all her sadness. She'd been working as a bartender for the past few months—"See, I knew that M.A. would be useful for something," she'd joked—spending her afternoons with Dan.

"It's been really hard," she said. "Especially the last couple of weeks."

Cassie put her arm around Laura's shoulders. "Probably the hardest thing you'll ever do."

"But I wouldn't give up any of it. What Dan had to go through, yes, but not my being with him."

"He was lucky you found him in time."

"It wasn't luck," Laura said.

Cassie raised her eyebrows.

"He told me about the cards." She shook her head before Cassie could say anything. "No, it's okay. I understand. I know it would be so tempting to use something like that to make all your decisions for you. I'm not asking for that." She hesitated a moment, then added, "But I was wondering . . . can they show me Dan one last time? Just so I can know if he finally caught up with those horses? Just so I can know he's okay?"

"I don't know," Cassie said. "I think the only way we ever find out where we go in the end, is when we make the journey ourselves."

Laura gave a slow nod, unable to hide her disappointment. "I . . . I guess I understand."

"But that doesn't mean we can't look."

She took her arm away from Laura's shoulders and brought out the set of cards the old juju woman had given her, sitting there on her porch with the bottle tree clinking on the lawn. Removing the elastic, she gave the cards a shuffle, then offered the pack to Laura.

"Pick one," she said.

"Don't you have to lay them out in some kind of pattern?"

"Ordinary Tarot cards, yes. But you're looking to see into someplace they can't take you now."

Laura placed her fingers on the top of the deck. She held off for a long moment, then finally took the card and turned it over. There were horses running along the lakeshore on it, golden horses with white manes and tails. The image was too small to make out details, but they could see a figure on the back of one of them, head thrown back. Laughing, perhaps. Finally free.

Smiling, Laura returned the card to the pack.

"Where he goes," she said, "I hope he'll always be that happy."

Cassie wound the elastic back around the cards and returned them to her pocket.

"Maybe if we believe it strongly enough it'll be true," she said.

Laura turned to look at her. Her eyes were shiny with tears but that lost, haunted look Cassie had seen in them that first time they met was gone.

"Then I'll believe it," Laura said.

They leaned back against the bench, looking out across the water. The sound of the ferry's horn echoed faintly across the water, signaling its return from the island.

In the Land of
the Unforgiven

*No people sing with such pure voices as those who live in deepest hell;
what we take for the song of angels is their song.*
—Franz Kafka

The little dead boy shows up in his dreams, the night after Cray hears how he died.
Stands there in a place that's only half-light and shadows. Stands there singing, part
of a chorus of children's voices, the other singers hidden in the darkness.

The pure, sweet sound of their voices wakes Cray and puts tears in his eyes. The
springs creak as he turns to lie on his back. He stares up at the cracks in the ceiling
and can't get the sound out of his head.

Cray waits in the shadows pooling at the mouth of the alley, his gaze on the lit window.
Third floor of a brownstone, middle apartment. A swollen moon is just setting, so big
and close it feels like it's going down only a few blocks over. He watches the last fat
sliver slip away, then returns his gaze to the apartment.

A silhouette moves across the window. Cray starts to take a step back, stops himself
when he realizes what he's doing. Like Erwin could see him.

The guys he came up with in the old neighborhood wouldn't have let it go so
long. Something like this, you moved in, hard, fast. You didn't take time to think. You
just popped him, end of story.

But Cray's a long way from the old neighborhood. Not so much where he is, but
who he is.

Earlier that afternoon, Danny Salmorin comes into the gym for a workout. He's stand-
up for a cop. Detective, Crowsea Precinct. There's nothing soft about him. He's in here
regular as clockwork, three days a week. Free weights, jogs on the machines.

"Hey, Joe," Danny says. "How's it hanging?"

Cray doesn't have time for small talk. This thing's been on his mind for a couple of days now.

"Sonny Erwin," he says. "You know him?"

"He's scum. What's to know?"

"He's selling babies, Danny. Selling them for sex, body parts—whatever people are buying."

Something flickers darkly in Danny's eyes. "You've got something solid on this?"

Cray tells him about Juanita's little boy.

"Let me talk to her," Danny says. "I'll set up a meeting with the D.A.'s office and—"

He breaks off when Cray shakes his head.

"She's illegal," Cray says. "No way she'll talk to the D.A."

"You're tying my hands."

"This guy's a freak—you know what I'm saying?"

Danny nods. "I don't need an excuse to look for some way to take him down, Joe. We've been on him for two years now and we can't touch him. He plays it too clean."

"These kids . . ."

Cray lets his voice trail off. He sees it in Danny's eyes. No forgiveness. Shame for how the system keeps a freak like Erwin on the street. The law's reactive these days—it can't protect anymore, it can barely avenge, and even then you need hard facts to grease the wheels of justice and get them moving. Danny's carrying the weight of all those lives taken, all those lives that will be taken, and he can't do a damn thing to stop it.

"Something was to happen to Erwin," Danny says, measuring the words out, careful, "and there was any kind of a problem, I'd be the one to call."

Cray doesn't get it, not then, but he nods to let Danny know he's listening.

Later he's sitting up in his office, can't concentrate on the paperwork. All he can think of is what Mona told him about Juanita and her little boy. He looks out through the window, down to where Danny's jogging on one of the machines. The darkness has settled deep in Danny's eyes. Sweat's dripping from his brow, soaking his T-shirt. He's been on the machine for forty minutes now and he hasn't begun to burn off his frustration and anger.

Cray remembers the last stretch he pulled. He's been clean a long time, but you never forget what it's like inside. He swore he'd never go back, and he's held good to that promise, but he's thinking now that maybe there are some things worth giving up your freedom for.

All he has to do is ask himself, what kind of freedom did Juanita's kid have?

Cray squares his shoulders and crosses the street. As he walks up to the entrance of the brownstone, he hears the sound of a steel door closing. The sound's in his head, only he can hear it. A piece of memory he's going to be reliving soon.

It takes him maybe six seconds to jimmy the door—the lock's crap. It's been ten years since he's creeped a joint, but he could've done this one in his sleep.

He cracks the door, steps inside. Starts up the stairs. Takes them two at a time. He's not even winded when he reaches the third floor landing.

The sound in his head now is that of a children's chorus.

* * *

"Let it go," Mona says before he leaves for the day.

She's standing in the door to his office, tall and rangy in purple and pink Spandex shorts, black halter top. Red hair pulled back into a tight ponytail. She's got an aerobics class in ten minutes. Anywhere from eight to fifteen out-of-shape, well-heeled yuppies who never come up against the kind of thing he can't get out of his head.

Guys like Erwin know the drill. They're hitting the poor and the illegals. The ones who can't complain, can't defend themselves.

The closest Mona's class is going to come to it is maybe a couple of lines in the morning papers—if one of the kids gets even that much coverage. Most of them simply disappear and nobody hears about it, nobody cares except for their families.

"Juanita's got to come forward," he says. "Without her, they can't do a thing."

"She's got three other kids. What's going to happen to them if she gets deported?"

"That's what I told Danny."

She waits a beat, then says, "We did what we could."

He can see it cost her to say that, but she's got to know he can't let it go now.

"And the next kid he snatches?" he asks.

She looks at him, knows where this is taking him.

"I should never have told you," she says.

He shrugs.

"You'll never get away with it."

"I don't plan to," he tells her. "If there's one thing I've learned, you've got to take responsibility for your actions."

"But Erwin—"

Cray knows how cold his voice is. "That's something Erwin still has to learn."

It goes easy. Three A.M. and Erwin doesn't even ask who's at the door. He just opens it up, smiles. He probably gets deliveries all the time—whenever opportunity presents itself to those who're snatching the kids and babies for him.

The thing that gets to Cray is, Sonny Erwin looks so normal. Just an average joe. The monster's hiding there in his eyes, but you have to know it's there to see it.

"You know why I'm here?" Cray asks.

Erwin's brows rise in a question. He's still smiling. Cocksure.

Cray straight-arms him and sends Erwin backpedaling for balance. He follows him into the apartment, kicks the door closed behind him with the heel of his boot. Erwin's finally lost the smile. The switchblade drops from Cray's sleeve, into his palm. The blade slides into place with a *snik* that seems loud in the confined space of the apartment.

"Somebody's got to stand up for those kids," he says.

He never gives Erwin time to reply.

Danny Salmorin shows up with his partner in tow. Cray doesn't know why he's here. All Cray did was call 911; he never mentioned Danny to the dispatcher. Never even mentioned his own name. Just said, "There's a dead man here," gave the address, then hung up. Sat down and waited for them to come.

Roland Johns is a tall black man, almost as broad-shouldered as Cray. He's from the neighborhood—like Danny, he's one of the few of them that made good. He looks at the body sprawled in the middle of the living room floor, takes in the cut throat, the blood that's soaking Erwin's thick plush.

"What are you doing here?" Cray asks. "Where's the uniforms?"

"I like him in red," Roland says around the toothpick he's chewing on. "It's really his color, don't you think? Someone should've done a makeover on him years ago."

Danny ignores his partner. "We were in the area and caught the call," he tells Cray.

Cray gets the sense that maybe they were waiting for the call. But that's okay. Dealing with people he knows'll make it easier to get through this.

"Was he carrying?" Danny asks.

Cray shakes his head. He watches Danny reach behind his back and pull a .38 from the waistband of his pants. Danny wipes the piece clean with a cloth he takes from the pocket of his jacket, then kneels down. He puts the .38 in Erwin's hand, presses the fingers around the grip, then lays the gun on the carpet, like it fell there.

For a moment Cray doesn't understand what Danny's doing. Then he gets it. The .38's Danny's throwdown, serial numbers eaten away with acid. A clean weapon he's been hanging on to for an occasion like this. No history. Can't be traced. Lots of cops carry them.

"This is the way it went down," Danny says. "Sonny sets up a meet. When he tells you he wants access to the youth programs in the gym, you argue. He pulls his piece. You struggle, next thing you know he's dead. You call us like a good citizen and here we are."

Cray shakes his head. "I can't do it. That's playing the game his way."

"You already played it his way," Danny says. "He's dead, isn't he?"

"That's right. And I'll take the fall for it."

"Bullshit. You want to do time for getting rid of a piece of crap like that, makes his living selling kids to short-eyes and worse?"

"Maybe we should start arresting people for killing rats and roaches, too?" Roland adds.

"It's not right," Cray says. "I did what I had to do, but now I've got to stand up for it."

"Let me tell you what's not right," Danny says. "You going back inside, the gym closing up—that's not right. You think we don't know what you do in there? The women's self-defense courses. The youth programs. The sliding scale on memberships so nobody gets turned away. You're bringing some sense of community back into the neighborhood, Joe. You think losing that's worth this dipshit's life? Play this my way and you're not even going to court."

"I crossed a line—"

"Yeah, and now you're crossing right back over it again. Sonny Erwin *lived* on the other side of the line, Joe, and we couldn't touch him. You did us all a favor."

Beside him, Roland nods. "You broke a big link in the chain," he says. "This is going to put a serious cramp in a lot of freaks' lifestyles."

"I still broke the law," Cray says. "Where are we going to be if everybody settles their problems this way?"

"You making a career of this?" Danny asks. "You gonna be some kind of superhero vigilante now?"

"You know it wasn't like that," Cray says.

Danny nods. He looks tired.

"Yeah, I know," he says. "Thing I need to know is, do you?"

The next day Danny catches up with Cray outside the cemetery, after the service. He offers his condolences to Juanita, treats her respectfully. Holds the door of the cab for her so that she and her kids can get in. Mona's sitting in the front with the driver. She nods to Danny.

Cray and Danny watch as the cab pulls away from the curb, drives away under skies as dirty grey as the pavement under its tires.

"You clear on last night?" Danny asks.

Cray shakes his head. "Not really."

"You think Roland and me, we're on the pad or something? Running our own businesses on the side?"

"I've got no reason to think that."

Danny nods. "We're living in a war zone now, Joe. The old neighborhood's turned into a no-man's-land where a freak like Sonny Erwin can market kids and we can't touch him. When we were growing up we could leave our doors unlocked—remember that? Sure, we had to deal with the wiseguys and their crap, but things still made sense. Now nothing seems to anymore. Now there's no justice, no forgiveness—it's like we're not even human anymore. Nobody's looking out for anybody but themselves. Christ, half the department's on the pad."

"What're you trying to say?" Cray asks.

"I'm saying it's not right. We've lost something and I don't know that we can ever get it back. All of us who live down here, who don't have the money or the moneymen in our pocket, we get tarnished with the same brand, like there's no right, no wrong. Just us. The unforgiven."

"What I did last night wasn't right," Cray says. "I'm pretty clear on this."

Danny shakes his head. "It was against the law, but it was right, Joe. It was something that had to be done only nobody else had the balls to do it. Who wanted to do the time?"

"I could've done it."

"You're already doing time," Danny says. "That's what I'm trying to tell you. The way we're living now . . . we're all doing time. That's what it's come to." He shakes his head. "You tell me. Where's the difference?"

"You ever been inside?" Cray asks.

"No, but you have. Why do you think I'm asking you?"

Cray nods slowly. He looks down the street, but he's not seeing it. He's thinking about being kept four to a cell that was built to hold two. How you couldn't scratch your ass without a screw watching you. How you had to walk the line between the sides, the blacks and the Aryans, and if you couldn't fit in, you did your time in the hole. How you fought back with whatever it took so you didn't end up somebody's girlfriend.

"We have choices out here," he says. "We can make a difference."

"You make a difference," Danny says. "With the gym and with what you did last night."

"Last night I deliberately set out to kill a man. I never knew I had that in me.

Never knew that I could plan it and do it, like I was ordering a new piece of equipment for the gym."

Cray frowns as he's speaking. The words seem inadequate to express the bleakness that has lodged inside him.

"There's a big difference," he adds, "between what I did and killing someone who's in my face, somebody jumps me in an alley, tries to hurt my family. I got through this by knowing I'd have to pay for it. You understand? But now . . ."

"Now you have to live with it."

Cray nods.

"You see what I'm trying to tell you?" Danny says. "You *are* paying for it. You're doing your time, only you're doing it on the outside where you can still make a difference. Same as me."

"Same as you?"

"Accessory after the fact." Danny gives him a long, serious look. "You think I don't respect this badge I'm carrying . . . what it stands for? You think what went down with Erwin didn't keep me up all night? I'm asking myself the same questions you are and I figure we handed ourselves life sentences. We're doing time like everybody else, except we know it. And we know why."

Cray nods again.

There's a long moment of silence.

"So if you could roll back time," Danny finally asks. "Would you do it the same?"

Cray wonders if Danny hears the children's voices, the sweet angel chorus that echoes faintly in the back of his head and makes his heart break to hear. He wonders if it ever goes away.

"I don't know," he says. "I'd have to stop him." Their gazes meet. "I'd have to do whatever it took."

"Yeah," Danny tells him. "Me, too."

There's nothing more either of them has to say.

My Life as a Bird

From the August, 1996 issue of the Spar Distributions catalogue:

The Girl Zone, No. 10. Written & illustrated by Mona Morgan. Latest issue features new chapters of The True Life Adventures of Rockit Grrl, Jupiter Jewel & My Life As A Bird. Includes a one-page jam with Charles Vess. My Own Comix Co., $2.75 Back issues available.

"MY LIFE AS A BIRD"
MONA'S MONOLOGUE FROM CHAPTER THREE:

The thing is, we spend too much time looking outside ourselves for what we should really be trying to find inside. But we can't seem to trust what we find in ourselves—maybe because that's where we find it. I suppose it's all a part of how we ignore who we really are. We're so quick to cut away pieces of ourselves to suit a particular relationship, a job, a circle of friends, incessantly editing who we are until we fit in. Or we do it to someone else. We try to edit the people around us.

I don't know which is worse.

Most people would say it's when we do it to someone else, but I don't think either one's a very healthy option.

Why do we love ourselves so little? Why are we suspect for trying to love ourselves, for being true to who and what we are rather than what someone else thinks we should be? We're so ready to betray ourselves, but we never call it that. We have all these other terms to describe it: Fitting in. Doing the right thing. Getting along.

I'm not proposing a world solely ruled by rank self-interest; I know that there have to be some limits of politeness and compromise or all we'll have left is anarchy. And anyone who expects the entire world to adjust to them is obviously a little too full of their own self-importance.

But how can we expect others to respect or care for us, if we don't respect and care for ourselves? And how come no one asks, "If you're so ready to betray yourself, why should I believe that you won't betray me as well?"

"And then he dumped you—just like that?"

Mona nodded. "I suppose I should've seen it coming. All it seems we've been doing lately is arguing. But I've been so busy trying to get the new issue out and dealing with the people at Spar who are still being such pricks. . . ."

She let her voice trail off. Tonight the plan had been to get away from her problems, not focus on them. She often thought that too many people used Jilly as a combination den mother/emotional junkyard, and she'd promised herself a long time ago that she wouldn't be one of them. But here she was anyway, dumping her problems all over the table between them.

The trouble was, Jilly drew confidences from you as easily as she did a smile. You couldn't not open up to her.

"I guess what it boils down to," she said, "is I wish I was more like Rockit Grrl than Mona."

Jilly smiled. "Which Mona?"

"Good point."

The real-life Mona wrote and drew three ongoing strips for her own bi-monthly comic book, *The Girl Zone*. Rockit Grrl was featured in "The True Life Adventures of Rockit Grrl," the pen-and-ink-Mona in a semi-autobiographical strip called "My Life as a Bird." Rounding out each issue was "Jupiter Jewel."

Rockit Grrl, aka "The Menace from Venice"—Venice Avenue, Crowsea, that is, not the Italian city or the California beach—was an in-your-face punkette with an athletic body and excellent fashion sense, strong and unafraid; a little too opinionated for her own good, perhaps, but that only allowed the plots to pretty much write themselves. She spent her time righting wrongs and combating heinous villains like Didn't-Phone-When-He-Said-He-Would Man and Honest-My-Wife-and-I-Are-as-Good-as-Separated Man.

The Mona in "My Life as a Bird" had spiky blonde hair and jean overalls just as her creator did, though the real life Mona wore a T-shirt under her overalls and she usually had an inch or so of dark roots showing. They both had a quirky sense of humor and tended to expound at length on what they considered the mainstays of interesting conversation—love and death, sex and art—though the strip's monologues were far more coherent. The stories invariably took place in the character's apartment or the local English-styled pub down the street from it, which was based on the same pub where she and Jilly were currently sharing a pitcher of draught.

Jupiter Jewel had yet to make an appearance in her own strip, but the readers all felt as though they already knew her since her friends—who did appear—were always talking about her.

"The Mona in the strip, I guess," Mona said. "Maybe life's not a smooth ride for her either, but at least she's usually got some snappy come-back line."

"That's only because you have the time to think them out for her."

"This is true."

"But then," Jilly added, "that must be half the fun. Everybody thinks of what they should have said after the fact, but you actually get to use those lines."

"Even more true."

Jilly refilled their glasses. When she set the pitcher back down on the table there was only froth left in the bottom.

"So did you come back with a good line?" she asked.

Mona shook her head. "What could I say? I was so stunned to find out that he'd never taken what I do seriously that all I could do was look at him and try to figure out how I ever thought we really knew each other."

She'd tried to put it out of her mind, but the phrase "that pathetic little comic book of yours" still stung in her memory.

"He used to like the fact that I was so different from the people where he works," she said, "but I guess he just got tired of parading his cute little Bohemian girlfriend around to office parties and the like."

Jilly gave a vigorous nod which made her curls fall down into her eyes. She pushed them back from her face with a hand that still had the inevitable paint lodged under the nails. Ultramarine blue. A vibrant coral.

"See," she said. "That's what infuriates me about the corporate world. The whole idea that if you're doing something creative that doesn't earn big bucks, you should consider it a hobby and put your real time and effort into something serious. Like your art isn't serious enough."

Mona took a swallow of beer. "Don't get me started on that."

Spar Distributions had recently decided to cut back on the nonsuperhero titles they carried and *The Girl Zone* had been one of the casualties. That was bad enough, but then they also wouldn't cough up her back issues or the money they owed her from what they had sold.

"You got a lousy break," Jilly told her. "They've got no right to let things drag on the way they have."

Mona shrugged. "You'd think I'd have had some clue before this," she said, more willing to talk about Pete. At least she could deal with him. "But he always seemed to like the strips. He'd laugh in all the right places and he even cried when Jamaica almost died."

"Well, who didn't?"

"I guess. There sure was enough mail on that story."

Jamaica was the pet cat in "My Life as a Bird"—Mona's one concession to fantasy in the strip since Pete was allergic to cats. She'd thought that she was only in between cats when Crumb ran away and she first met Pete, but once their relationship began to get serious she gave up on the idea of getting another one.

"Maybe he didn't like being in the strip," she said.

"What wasn't to like?" Jilly asked. "I loved the time you put me in it, even though you made me look like I was having the bad hair day from hell."

Mona smiled. "See, that's what happens when you drop out of art school."

"You have bad hair days?"

"No, I mean—"

"Besides, I didn't drop out. You did."

"My point exactly," Mona said. "I can't draw hair for the life of me. It always looks all raggedy."

"Or like a helmet, when you were drawing Pete."

Mona couldn't suppress a giggle. "It wasn't very flattering, was it?"

"But you made up for it by giving him a much better butt," Jilly said.

That seemed uproariously funny to Mona. The beer, she decided, was making her giddy. At least she hoped it was the beer. She wondered if Jilly could hear the same hysterical edge in her laugh that she did. That made the momentary good humor she'd been feeling scurry off as quickly as Pete had left their apartment earlier in the day.

"I wonder when I stopped loving him," Mona said. "Because I did, you know, before we finally had it out today. Stop loving him, I mean."

Jilly leaned forward. "Are you going to be okay? You can stay with me tonight if you like. You know, just so you don't have to be alone your first night."

Mona shook her head. "Thanks, but I'll be fine. I'm actually a little relieved, if you want to know the truth. The past few months I've been wandering through a bit of a fog, but I couldn't quite figure out what it was. Now I know."

Jilly raised her eyebrows.

"Knowing's better," Mona said.

"Well, if you change your mind . . ."

"I'll be scratching at your window the way those stray cats you keep feeding do."

When they called it a night, an hour and another half pitcher of draught later, Mona took a longer route home than she normally would. She wanted to clear her head of the decided buzz that was making her stride less than steady, though considering the empty apartment she was going home to, maybe that wasn't the best idea, never mind her brave words to Jilly. Maybe, instead, she should go back to the pub and down a couple of whiskeys so that she'd really be too tipsy to mope.

"Oh, damn him anyway," she muttered and kicked at a tangle of crumpled newspapers that were spilling out of the mouth of an alleyway she was passing.

"Hey, watch it!"

Mona stopped at the sound of the odd gruff voice, then backed away as the smallest man she'd ever seen crawled out of the nest of papers to glare at her. He couldn't have stood more than two feet high, a disagreeable and ugly little troll of a man with a face that seemed roughly carved and then left unfinished. His clothes were ragged and shabby, his face bristly with stubble. What hair she could see coming out from under his cloth cap was tangled and greasy.

Oh my, she thought. She was drunker than she'd realized.

She stood there swaying for a long moment, staring down at him and half expecting him to simply drift apart like smoke, or vanish. But he did neither and she finally managed to find her voice.

"I'm sorry," she said. "I just didn't see you down . . . there." This was coming out all wrong. "I mean . . ."

His glare deepened. "I suppose you think I'm too small to be noticed?"

"No. It's not that. I . . ."

She knew that his size was only some quirk of genetics, an unusual enough trait to find in someone out and about on a Crowsea street at midnight, but at the same time her imagination or, more likely, all the beer she'd had, was telling her that the little man scowling up at her had a more exotic origin.

"Are you a leprechaun?" she found herself asking.

"If I had a pot of gold, do you think I'd be sleeping on the street?"

She shrugged. "No, of course not. It's just . . ."

He put a finger to the side of his nose and blew a stream of snot onto the pavement. Mona's stomach did a flip and a sour taste rose up in her throat. Trust her that, when she finally did have some curious encounter like the kind Jilly had so often, it had to be with a grotty little dwarf such as this.

The little man wiped his nose on the sleeve of his jacket and grinned at her.

"What's the matter, princess?" he asked. "If I can't afford a bed for the night, what makes you think I'd go out and buy a handkerchief just to avoid offending your sensibilities?"

It took her a moment to digest that. Then digging in the bib pocket of her overalls, she found a couple of crumpled dollar bills and offered them to him. He regarded the money with suspicion and made no move to take it from her.

"What's this?" he said.

"I just . . . I thought maybe you could use a couple of dollars."

"Freely given?" he asked. "No strings, no ties?"

"Well, it's not a loan," she told him. Like she was ever going to see him again.

He took the money with obvious reluctance and a muttered "Damn."

Mona couldn't help herself. "Most people would say thank you," she said.

"Most people wouldn't be beholden to you because of it," he replied.

"I'm sorry?"

"What for?"

Mona blinked. "I meant, I don't understand why you're indebted to me now. It was just a couple of dollars."

"Then why apologize?"

"I didn't. Or I suppose I did, but—" This was getting far too confusing. "What I'm trying to say is that I don't want anything in return."

"Too late for that." He stuffed the money in his pocket. "Because your gift was freely given, it means I owe you now." He offered her his hand. "Nacky Wilde, at your service."

Seeing it was the same one he'd used to blow his nose, Mona decided to forgo the social amenities. She stuck her own hands in the side pockets of her overalls.

"Mona Morgan," she told him.

"Alliterative parents?"

"What?"

"You really should see a doctor about your hearing problem."

"I don't have a hearing problem," she said.

"It's nothing to be ashamed of. Well, lead on. Where are we going?"

"*We're* not going anywhere. I'm going home and you can go back to doing whatever it was you were doing before we started this conversation."

He shook his head. "Doesn't work that way. I have to stick with you until I can repay my debt."

"I don't think so."

"Oh, it's very much so. What's the matter? Ashamed to be seen in my company? I'm too short for you? Too grubby? I can be invisible, if you like, but I get the feeling that'd only upset you more."

She had to be way more drunk than she thought she was. This wasn't even remotely a normal conversation.

"Invisible," she repeated.

He gave her an irritated look. "As in, not perceivable by the human eye. You do understand the concept, don't you?"

"You can't be serious."

"No, of course not. I'm making it up just to appear more interesting to you. Great big, semi-deaf women like you feature prominently in my daydreams, so naturally I'll say anything to try to win you over."

Working all day at her drawing desk didn't give Mona as much chance to exercise as she'd like, so she was a bit touchy about the few extra pounds she was carrying.

"I'm not big."

He craned his neck. "Depends on the perspective, sweetheart."

"And I'm not deaf."

"I was being polite. I thought it was kinder than saying you were mentally disadvantaged."

"And you're *certainly* not coming home with me."

"Whatever you say," he said.

And then he vanished.

One moment he was there, two feet of unsavory rudeness, and the next she was alone on the street. The abruptness of his disappearance, the very weirdness of it, made her legs go all watery and she had to put a hand against the wall until the weak feeling went away.

I am *way* too drunk, she thought as she pushed off from the wall.

She peered into the alleyway, then looked up and down the street. Nothing. Gave the nest of newspapers a poke with her foot. Still nothing. Finally she started walking again, but nervously now, listening for footsteps, unable to shake the feeling that someone was watching her. She was almost back at her apartment when she remembered what he'd said about how he could be invisible.

Impossible.

But what if . . . ?

In the end she found a phonebooth and gave Jilly a call.

"Is it too late to change my mind?" she asked.

"Not at all. Come on over."

Mona leaned against the glass of the booth and watched the street all around her. Occasional cabs went by. She saw a couple at the far end of the block and followed them with her gaze until they turned a corner. So far as she could tell, there was no little man, grotty or otherwise, anywhere in view.

"Is it okay if I bring my invisible friend?" she said.

Jilly laughed. "Sure. I'll put the kettle on. Does your invisible friend drink coffee?"

"I haven't asked him."

"Well," Jilly said, "if either of you is feeling as woozy as I am, I'm sure you could use a mug."

"I could use something," Mona said after she'd hung up.

"MY LIFE AS A BIRD"
MONA'S MONOLOGUE FROM CHAPTER EIGHT:
Sometimes I think of God as this little man sitting on a café patio somewhere, bewildered at how it's all gotten so out of his control. He had such good intentions,

but everything he made had a mind of its own and, right from the first, he found himself unable to contain their conflicting impulses. He tried to create paradise, but he soon discovered that free will and paradise were incompatible because everybody has a different idea as to what paradise should be like.

But usually when I think of him, I think of a cat: a little mysterious, a little aloof, never coming when he's called. And in my mind, God's always a he. The bible makes it pretty clear that men are the doers; women can only be virgins or whores. In God's eyes, we can only exist somewhere in between the two Marys, the mother of Jesus and the Magdalene.

What kind of a religion is that? What kind of religion ignores the rights of half the world's population just because they're supposed to have envy instead of a penis? One run by men. The strong, the brave, the true. The old boys' club that wrote the book and made the laws.

I'd like to find him and ask him, 'Is that it, God? Did we really get cloned from a rib and because we're hand-me-downs, you don't think we've got what it takes to be strong and brave and true?"

But that's only part of what's wrong with the world. You also have to ask, what's the rationale behind wars and sickness and suffering?

Or is there no point? Is God just as bewildered as the rest of us? Has he finally given up, spending his days now on that café patio, sipping strong espresso, and watching the world go by, none of it his concern anymore? Has he washed his hands of it all?

I've got a thousand questions for God, but he never answers any of them. Maybe he's still trying to figure out where I fit on the scale between the two Marys and he can't reply until he does. Maybe he doesn't hear me, doesn't see me, doesn't think of me at all. Maybe in his version of what the world is, I don't even exist.

Or if he's a cat, then I'm a bird, and he's just waiting to pounce.

"You actually believe me, don't you?" Mona said.

The two of them were sitting in the windowseat of Jilly's studio loft, sipping coffee from fat china mugs, piano music playing softly in the background, courtesy of a recording by Mitsuko Uchida. The studio was tidier than Mona had ever seen it. All the canvases that weren't hanging up had been neatly stacked against one wall. Books were in their shelves, paintbrushes cleaned and lying out in rows on the worktable, tubes of paint organized by color in wooden and cardboard boxes. The drop cloth under the easel even looked as though it had recently gone through a wash.

"Spring clean-up and tidying," Jilly had said by way of explanation.

"Hello? It's September."

"So I'm late."

The coffee had been waiting for Mona when she arrived, as had been a willing ear as she related her curious encounter after leaving the pub. Jilly, of course, was enchanted with the story. Mona didn't know why she was surprised.

"Let's say I don't disbelieve you," Jilly said.

"I don't know if I believe me. It's easier to put it down to those two pitchers of beer we had."

Jilly touched a hand to her head. "Don't remind me."

"Besides," Mona went on. "Why doesn't he show himself now?" She looked around Jilly's disconcertingly tidy studio. "Well?" she said, aiming her question at the room in general. "What's the big secret, Mr. Nacky Wilde?"

"Well, it stands to reason," Jilly said. "He knows that I could just give him something as well, and then he'd be indebted to me, too."

"I don't *want* him indebted to me."

"It's kind of late for that."

"That's what he said."

"He'd probably know."

"Okay. I'll just get him to do my dishes for me or something."

Jilly shook her head. "I doubt it works that way. It probably has to be something that no one else can do for you except him."

"This is ridiculous. All I did was give him a couple of dollars. I didn't mean anything by it."

"Money doesn't mean anything to you?"

"Jilly. It was only two dollars."

"It doesn't matter. It's still money and no matter how much we'd like things to be different, the world revolves around our being able to pay the rent and buy art supplies and the like, so money's important in our lives. You freely gave him something that means something to you and now he has to return that in kind."

"But anybody could have given him the money."

Jilly nodded. "Anybody could have, but they didn't. You did."

"How do I get myself into these things?"

"More to the point, how do you get yourself out?"

"You're the expert. You tell me."

"Let me think about it."

Nacky Wilde didn't show himself again until Mona got back to her own apartment the next morning. She had just enough time to realize that Pete had been back to collect his things—there were gaps in the bookshelves and the stack of CDs on top of the stereo was only half the size it had been the previous night—when the little man reappeared. He was slouched on her sofa, even more disreputable looking in the daylight, his glower softened by what could only be the pleasure he took from her gasp at his sudden appearance.

She sat down on the stuffed chair across the table from him. There used to be two, but Pete had obviously taken one.

"So," she said. "I'm sober and you're here, so I guess you must be real."

"Does it always take you this long to accept the obvious?"

"Grubby little men who can appear out of thin air and then disappear back into it again aren't exactly a part of my everyday life."

"Ever been to Japan?" he asked.

"No. What's that got to—"

"But you believe it exists, don't you?"

"Oh, please. It's not at all the same thing. Next thing you'll be wanting me to believe in alien abductions and little green men from Mars."

He gave her a wicked grin. "They're not green and they don't come from—"

"I don't want to hear it," she told him, blocking her ears. When she saw he wasn't going to continue, she went on, "So was Jilly right? I'm stuck with you?"

"It doesn't make me any happier than it does you."

"Okay. Then we have to have some ground rules."

"You're taking this rather well," he said.

"I'm a practical person. Now listen up. No bothering me when I'm working. No sneaking around being invisible when I'm in the bathroom or having a shower. No watching me sleep—or getting into bed with me."

He looked disgusted at the idea. Yeah, me too, Mona thought.

"And you clean up after yourself," she finished. "Come to think of it, you could clean up yourself, too."

He glared at her. "Fine. Now for my rules. First—"

Mona shook her head. "Uh-uh. This is my place. The only rules that get made here are by me."

"That hardly seems fair."

"None of this is fair," she shot back. "Remember, nobody asked you to tag along after me."

"Nobody asked you to give me that money," he said and promptly disappeared.

"I *hate* it when you do that."

"Good," a disembodied voice replied.

Mona stared thoughtfully at the now-empty sofa cushions and found herself wondering what it would be like to be invisible, which got her thinking about all the ways one could be nonintrusive and still observe the world. After a while, she got up and took down one of her old sketchbooks, flipping through it until she came to the notes she'd made when she'd first started planning her semi-autobiographical strip for *The Girl Zone*.

"My Life as a Bird"
Notes for Chapter One:
(Mona and Hazel are sitting at the kitchen table in Mona's apartment having tea and muffins. Mona is watching Jamaica, asleep on the windowsill, only the tip of her tail twitching.)

MONA: Being invisible would be the coolest, but the next best thing would be, like, if you could be a bird or a cat—something that no one pays any attention to.

HAZEL: What kind of bird?

MONA: I don't know. A crow, all blue-black wings and shadowy. Or, no. Maybe something even less noticeable, like a pigeon or a sparrow.

(She gets a happy look on her face.)

MONA: Because you can tell. They pay attention to everything, but no one pays attention to them.

HAZEL: And the cat would be black, too, I suppose?

MONA: Mmm. Lean and slinky like Jamaica. Very Egyptian. But a bird would be better—more mobility—though I guess it wouldn't matter, really. The important thing is how you'd just be there, another piece of the landscape, but you'd be watching everything. You wouldn't miss a thing.

HAZEL: Bit of a voyeur, are we?

MONA: No, nothing like that. I'm not even interested in high drama, just the things that go on every day in our lives—the stuff most people don't pay attention to. That's the real magic.

HAZEL: Sounds boring.

MONA: No, it would be very Zen. Almost like meditating.

HAZEL: You've been drawing that comic of yours for too long.

The phone rang that evening while Mona was inking a new page for "Jupiter Jewel." The sudden sound startled her and a blob of ink fell from the end of her nib pen, right beside Cecil's head. At least it hadn't landed on his face.

I'll make that a shadow, she decided as she answered the phone.

"So do you still have an invisible friend?" Jilly asked.

Mona looked down the hall from the kitchen table where she was working. What she could see of the apartment appeared empty, but she didn't trust her eyesight when it came to her uninvited houseguest.

"I can't see him," she said, "but I have to assume he hasn't left."

"Well, I don't have any useful news. I've checked with all the usual sources and no one quite knows what to make of him."

"The usual sources being?"

"Christy. The professor. An old copy of *The Newford Examiner* with a special section on the fairy folk of Newford."

"You're kidding."

"I am," Jilly admitted. "But I did go to the library and had a wonderful time looking through all sorts of interesting books, from K. M. Briggs to *When the Desert Dreams* by Anne Bourke, neither of whom writes about Newford, but I've always loved those fairy lore books Briggs compiled and Anne Bourke lived here, as I'm sure you knew, and I really liked the picture on the cover of her book. I know," she added, before Mona could break in. "Get to the point already."

"I'm serenely patient and would never have said such a thing," Mona told her.

"Humble, too. Anyway, apparently there are all sorts of tricksy fairy folk, from hobs to brownies. Some relatively nice, some decidedly nasty, but none of them quite fit the Nacky Wilde profile."

"You mean sarcastic, grubby and bad mannered, but potentially helpful?"

"In a nutshell."

Mona sighed. "So I'm stuck with him."

She realized that she'd been absently doodling on her art and set her pen aside before she completely ruined the page.

"It doesn't seem fair, does it?" she added. "I finally get the apartment to myself, but then some elfin squatter moves in."

"How *are* you doing?" Jilly asked. "I mean, aside from your invisible squatter?"

"I don't feel closure," Mona said. "I know how weird that sounds, considering what I told you yesterday. After all, Pete stomped out and then snuck back while I was with you last night to get his stuff—so I *know* it's over. And the more I think of it, I realize this had to work out the way it did. But I'm still stuck with this emotional baggage, like trying to figure out why things ended up the way they did, and how come I never noticed."

"Would you take him back?"

"No."

"But you miss him?"

"I do," Mona said. "Weird, isn't it?"

"Perfectly normal, I'd say. Do you want someone to commiserate with?"

"No, I need to get some work done. But thanks."

After she hung up, Mona stared down at the mess she'd made of the page she'd been working on. She supposed she could try to incorporate all the squiggles into the background, but it didn't seem worth the bother. Instead she picked up a bottle of white acrylic ink, gave it a shake and opened it. With a clean brush she began to paint over the doodles and the blob of ink she'd dropped by Cecil's head. It was obvious now that it wouldn't work as shadow, seeing how the light source was on the same side.

Waiting for the ink to dry, she wandered into the living room and looked around.

"Trouble with your love life?" a familiar, but still disembodied voice asked.

"If you're going to talk to me," she said, "at least show your face."

"Is this a new rule?"

Mona shook her head. "It's just disorienting to be talking into thin air—especially when the air answers back."

"Well, since you asked so politely . . ."

Nacky Wilde reappeared, slouching in the stuffed chair this time, a copy of one of Mona's comic books open on his lap.

"You're not actually reading that?" Mona said.

He looked down at the comic. "No, of course not. Dwarves can't read—their brains are much too small to learn such an obviously complex task."

"I didn't mean it that way."

"I know you didn't, but I can't help myself. I have a reputation to maintain."

"As a dwarf?" Mona asked. "Is that what you are?"

He shrugged and changed the subject. "I'm not surprised you and your boyfriend broke up."

"What's that supposed to mean?"

He stabbed the comic book with a short stubby finger. "The tension's so apparent—if this bird story holds any truth. One never gets the sense that any of the characters really likes Pete."

Mona sat down on the sofa and swung her feet up onto the cushions. This was just what she needed—an uninvited, usually invisible squatter of a houseguest who was also a self-appointed analyst. Except, when she thought about it, he was right. "My Life as a Bird" was emotionally true, if not always a faithful account of actual events, and the Pete character in it had never been one of her favorites. Like the real Pete, there was an underlying tightness in his character; it was more noticeable in the strip because the rest of the cast was so Bohemian.

"He wasn't a bad person," she found herself saying.

"Of course not. Why would you let yourself be attracted to a bad person?"

Mona couldn't decide if he was being nice or sarcastic.

"They just wore him down," she said. "In the office. Won him over to their way of thinking, and there was no room for me in his life anymore."

"Or for him in yours," Nacky said.

Mona nodded. "It's weird, isn't it? Generosity of spirit seems to be so old-fashioned nowadays. We'd rather watch somebody trip on the sidewalk than help them climb the stairs to whatever it is they're reaching for."

"What is it you're reaching for?" Nacky asked.

"Oh, god." Mona laughed. "Who knows? Happiness, contentment. Some days all I want is for the lines to come together on the page and look like whatever it is that I'm trying to draw." She leaned back on the arm of the sofa and regarded the ceiling. "You know, that trick you do with invisibility is pretty cool." She turned her head to look at him. "Is it something that can be taught or do you have to be born magic?"

"Born to it, I'm afraid."

"I figured as much. But it's always been a fantasy of mine. That, or being able to change into something else."

"So I've gathered from reading this," Nacky said, giving the comic another tap with his finger. "Maybe you should try to be happy just being yourself. Look inside yourself for what you need—the way your character recommends in one of the earlier issues."

"You really have been reading it."

"That is why you write it, isn't it—to be read?"

She gave him a suspicious look. "Why are you being so nice all of a sudden?"

"Just setting you up for the big fall."

"Uh-huh."

"Thought of what I can do for you yet?" he asked.

She shook her head. "But I'm working on it."

"MY LIFE AS A BIRD"
NOTES FOR CHAPTER SEVEN:

(So after Mona meets Gregory, they go walking in Fitzhenry Park and sit on a bench from which they can see Wendy's Tree of Tales growing. Do I need to explain this, or can it just be something people who know will understand?)

GREGORY: Did you ever notice how we don't tell family stories anymore?

MONA: What do you mean?

GREGORY: Families used to be made up of stories—their history—and those stories were told down through the generations. It's where a family got its identity, the same way a neighborhood or even a country did. Now the stories we share we get from television and the only thing we talk about is ourselves.

(Mona realizes this is true—maybe not for everybody, but it's true for her. Argh. How do I draw this???)

MONA: Maybe the family stories don't work anymore. Maybe they've lost their relevance.

GREGORY: They've lost nothing.

(He looks away from her, out across the park.)

GREGORY: But we have.

In the days that followed, Nacky Wilde alternated between the sarcastic grump Mona had first met and the surprisingly good company he could prove to be when he didn't, as she told him one night, "have a bee up his butt." Unfortunately, the good of the one didn't outweigh the frustration of having to put up with the other and there was no getting rid of him. When he was in one of his moods, she didn't know which was worse: having to look at his scowl and listen to his bad-tempered remarks, or telling him to vanish but knowing that he was still sulking around the apartment, invisible and watching her.

A week after Pete had moved out, Mona met up with Jilly at the Cyberbean Café. They were planning to attend the opening of Sophie's latest show at The Green Man Gallery and Mona had once again promised herself not to dump her problems on Jilly, but there was no one else she could talk to.

"It's so typical," she found herself saying. "Out of all the hundreds of magical beings that populate folk tales and legends, I had to get stuck with the one that has a multiple personality disorder. He's driving me crazy."

"Is he with us now?" Jilly asked.

"Who knows? Who cares?" Then Mona had to laugh. "God, listen to me. It's like I'm complaining about a bad relationship."

"Well, it is a bad relationship."

"I know. And isn't it pathetic?" Mona shook her head. "If this is what I rebounded to from Pete, I don't want to know what I'll end up with when I finally get this nasty little man out of my life. At least the sex was good with Pete."

Jilly's eyes went wide. "You're not . . . ?"

"Oh, please. That'd be like sleeping with the eighth dwarf, Snotty—the one Disney kept out of his movie and with good reason."

Jilly had to laugh. "I'm sorry, but it's just so—"

Mona wagged a finger at her. "Don't say it. You wouldn't be laughing if it was happening to you." She looked at her watch. "We should get going."

Jilly took a last sip of her coffee. Wrapping what she hadn't finished of her cookie in a napkin, she stuck it in her pocket.

"What are you going to do?" she asked as they left the café.

"Well, I looked in the Yellow Pages, but none of the exterminators have cranky dwarves listed among the household pests they'll get rid of, so I guess I'm stuck with him for now. Though I haven't looked under exorcists yet."

"Is he Catholic?" Jilly asked.

"I didn't think it mattered. They just get rid of evil spirits, don't they?"

"Why not just ask him to leave? That's something no one else but he can do for you."

"I already thought of that," Mona told her.

"And?"

"Apparently it doesn't work that way."

"Maybe you should ask him what he can do for you."

Mona nodded thoughtfully. "You know, I never thought of that. I just assumed this whole business was one of those Rumpelstiltskin kind of things—that I had to come up with it on my own.

"What?" Nacky said later that night when Mona returned from the gallery and asked him to show himself. "You want me to list my services like on a menu? I'm not a restaurant."

"Or computer software," Mona agreed, "though it might be easier if you were either, because then at least I'd know what you can do without having to go through a song and dance to get the information out of you."

"No one's ever asked this kind of thing before."

"So what?" she asked. "Is it against the rules?"

Nacky scowled. "What makes you think there are rules?"

"There are always rules. So come on. Give."

"Fine," Nacky said. "We'll start with the most popular items." He began to count the items off on his fingers. "Potions, charms, spells, incantations—"

Mona held up a hand. "Hold on there. Let's back up a bit. What are these potions and charms and stuff?"

"Well, take your ex-boyfriend," Nacky said.

Please do, Mona thought.

"I could put a spell on him so that every time he looked at a woman that he was attracted to, he'd break out in hives."

"You could do that?"

Nacky nodded. "Or it could just be a minor irritation—an itch that will never go away."

"How long would it last?"

"Your choice. For the rest of his life, if you want."

Wouldn't that serve Pete right, Mona thought. Talk about a serious payback for all those mean things he'd said about her and *The Girl Zone*.

"This is so tempting," she said.

"So what will it be?" Nacky asked, briskly rubbing his hands together. "Hives? An itch? Perhaps a nervous tic under his eye so that people will always think he's winking at them. Seems harmless, but it's good for any number of face slaps and more serious altercations."

"Hang on," Mona told him. "What's the big hurry?"

"I'm in no hurry. I thought you were. I thought the sooner you got rid of Snotty, the eighth dwarf, the happier you'd be."

So he had been in the café.

"Okay," Mona said. "But first I have to ask you. These charms and things of yours—do they only do negative stuff?"

Nacky shook his head. "No. They can teach you the language of birds, choose your dreams before you go to sleep, make you appear to not be somewhere when you really are—"

"Wait a sec. You told me I had to be born magic to do that."

"No. You asked about, and I quote, 'the trick *you* do with invisibility,' the emphasis being mine. How I do it, you have to be born magic. An invisibility charm is something else."

"But it does the same thing?"

"For all intents and purposes."

God, but he could be infuriating.

"So why didn't you tell me that?"

Nacky smirked. "You didn't ask."

I will not get angry, she told herself. I am calmness incarnate.

"Okay," she said. "What else?"

He went back to counting the items on his fingers, starting again with a tap of his right index finger onto his left. "Potions to fall in love, to fall out of love. To make hair longer, or thicker. To make one taller, or shorter, or—" he gave her a wicked grin "—slimmer. To speak with the recent dead, to heal a person who's sick—"

"Heal them of what?" Mona wanted to know.

"Whatever ails them," he said, then went on in a bored voice. "To turn kettles into foxes, and vice versa. To—"

Mona was beginning to suffer overload.

"Enough already," she said. "I get the point."

"But you—"

"Shh. Let me think."

She laid her head back in her chair and closed her eyes. Basically, what it boiled down to was that she could have whatever she wanted. She could have revenge on Pete—not for leaving her, but for being so mean-spirited about it. She could be invisible, or understand the language of bird and animals. And though he'd claimed not to have a pot of gold when they first met, she could probably have fame and fortune, too.

But she didn't really want revenge on Pete. And being invisible probably wasn't such a good idea since she already spent far too much time on her own as it was. What she should really do is get out more, meet more people, make more friends of her own, instead of all the people she knew through Pete. As for fame and fortune . . . corny as it might sound, she really did believe that the process was what was important, the journey her art and stories took her on, not the place where they all ended up.

She opened her eyes and looked at Nacky.

"Well?" he said.

She stood up and picked up her coat from where she'd dropped it on the end of the sofa.

"Come on," she said as she put it on.

"Where are we going?"

"To hail a cab."

She had a taxi take them to the children's hospital. After paying the fare, she got out and stood on the lawn. Nacky, invisible in the vehicle, popped back into view. Leaves crackled underfoot as he joined her.

"There," Mona said, pointing at the long square block of a building. "I want you to heal all the kids in there."

There was a long moment of silence. When Mona turned to look at her companion, it was to find him regarding her with a thoughtful expression.

"I can't do that," he said.

Mona shook her head. "Like you couldn't make me invisible?"

"No, semantics this time," he said. "I can't heal them all."

"But that's what I want."

Nacky sighed. "It's like asking for world peace. It's too big a task. But I could heal one of them."

"Just one?"

Nacky nodded.

Mona turned to look at the building again. "Then heal the sickest one."

She watched him cross the lawn. When he reached the front doors, his figure shimmered and he seemed to flow through the glass rather than step through the actual doors.

He was gone a long time. When he finally returned, his pace was much slower and there was a haunted look in his eyes.

"There was a little girl with cancer," he said. "She would have died later tonight. Her name—"

"I don't want to know her name," Mona told him. "I just want to know, will she be all right?"

He nodded.

I could have had anything, she found herself thinking.

"Do you regret giving the gift away," Nacky asked her.

She shook her head. "No. I only wish I had more of them." She eyed him for a long moment. "I don't suppose I could freely give you another couple of dollars . . . ?"

"No. It doesn't—"

"Work that way," she finished. "I kind of figured as much." She knelt down so that she wasn't towering over him. "So now what? Where will you go?"

"I have a question for you," he said.

"Shoot."

"If I asked, would you let me stay on with you?"

Mona laughed.

"I'm serious," he told her.

"And what? Things would be different now, or would you still be snarly more often than not?"

He shook his head. "No different."

"You know I can't afford to keep that apartment," she said. "I'm probably going to have to get a bachelor somewhere."

"I wouldn't mind."

Mona knew she'd be insane to agree. All she'd been doing for the past week was trying to get him out of her life. But then she thought of the look in his eyes when he'd come back from the hospital and knew that he wasn't all bad. Maybe he was a little magic man, but he was still stuck living on the street and how happy could that make a person? Could be, all he needed was what everybody needed—a fair break. Could be, if he was treated fairly, he wouldn't glower so much, or be so bad-tempered.

But could she put up with it?

"I can't believe I'm saying this," she told him, "but, yeah. You can come back with me."

She'd never seen him smile before, she realized. It transformed his features.

"You've broken the curse," he said.

"Say what?"

"You don't know how long I've had to wait to find someone both selfless and willing to take me in as I was."

"I don't know about the selfless—"

He leaned forward and kissed her.

"Thank you," he said.

And then he went whirling off across the lawn, spinning like a dervishing top. His squatness melted from him and he grew tall and lean, fluid as a willow sapling, dancing in the wind. From the far side of the lawn he waved at her. For a long moment, all she could do was stare, open-mouthed. When she finally lifted her hand to wave back, he winked out of existence, like a spark leaping from a fire, glowing brightly before it vanished into the darkness.

This time she knew he was gone for good.

"MY LIFE AS A BIRD"
MONA'S CLOSING MONOLOGUE FROM CHAPTER ELEVEN:

The weird thing is I actually miss him. Oh, not his crankiness, or his serious lack of personal hygiene. What I miss is the kindness that occasionally slipped through—the piece of him that survived the curse.

Jilly says that was why he was so bad-tempered and gross. He had to make himself unlikeable, or it wouldn't have been so hard to find someone who would accept him for who he seemed to be. She says I stumbled into a fairy tale, which is pretty cool when you think about it, because how many people can say that?

Though I suppose if this really were a fairy tale, there'd be some kind of "happily ever after" wrap up, or I'd at least have come away with a fairy gift of one sort or another. That invisibility charm, say, or the ability to change into a bird or a cat.

But I don't really need anything like that.

I've got *The Girl Zone*. I can be anything I want in its pages. Rockit Grrl, saving the day. Jupiter, who can't seem to physically show up in her own life. Or just me.

I've got my dreams. I had a fun one last night. I was walking downtown and I was a birdwoman, spindly legs, beak where my nose should be, long wings hanging down from my shoulders like a ragged cloak. Or maybe I was just wearing a bird costume. Nobody recognized me, but they knew me all the same and thought it was way cool.

And I've touched a piece of real magic. Now, no matter how grey and bland and pointless the world might seem sometimes, I just have to remember that there really is more to everything than what we can see. Everything has a spirit that's so much bigger and brighter than you think it could hold.

Everything has one.

Me, too.

China Doll

*In theory there is free will, in practice
everything is predetermined.*
—Ramakrishna,
nineteenth-century Bengali saint

The crows won't shut up. It's late, close on midnight. The junkyard's more shadow than substance and the city's asleep. The crows should be sleeping, too—roosting somewhere, doing whatever it is that crows do at night. Because you don't normally see them like this, cawing at each other, hoarse voices tearing raggedly across the yard, the birds shifting, restless on their perches, flecks of rust falling in small red clouds every time they move.

They can't sleep and they won't shut up.

Coe can't sleep either, but at least he's got an excuse.

The dead don't sleep.

He's sitting there on the hood of a junked car, three nights dead. Watching the flames lick up above the rim of an old steel barrel where he's got a trash fire burning. Waiting for China to show up. China with her weird tribal tags: the white mud dried on her face, eyes darkened with rings of soot, lips blackened with charcoal, cheeks marked with black hieroglyphic lines. He looks about the same. The two of them are like matched bookends in a chiaroscuro still life. Like they just stepped out of some old black and white movie, except for that red dress of hers.

He's not exactly looking forward to seeing her. First thing you know, she'll start in again on who they're supposed to kill and why, and he's no more interested in listening to her tonight than he was the day he came back.

He thinks of standing by the barrel, holding his hands up to the flames for warmth, but that's a comfort he's never going to know again. The cold's lodged too deep inside him and it's never going away, doesn't matter what China says.

Killing's not the answer. But neither's this.

"Just shut up," he tells the birds.

They don't listen to him any more than they ever do, but China comes walking out of the shadows like his voice summoned her.

"Hey, Leon," she says.

She jumps lightly up onto the hood of the car, stretches out her legs, leans back against the windshield. Her dress rides up her legs, but the sight of it doesn't do anything for him. She's too young. Hell, she could be his daughter.

Coe gives her a nod, waits for her to start in on him. She surprises him. She just sits there, quiet for a change, checking out the birds.

"What do you think they're talking about?" she asks after a while.

"You don't know?"

Ever since they came back, it's like she knows everything. Maybe she was like that before they died. He doesn't know. First time he saw her she was in that tight red dress, running down a narrow alleyway, black combat boots clumping on the pavement. Came bursting out of the alley and ran right into him where he was just walking along, minding his own business. They fall in a tumble, and before they can get themselves untangled, there's a couple of Oriental guys there, standing over them. One's got a shotgun, the other an Uzi. For a moment, Coe thinks he's back in the jungle.

He doesn't get a chance to say a word.

The last thing he sees are the muzzles of their guns, flashing white. Last thing he hears is the sound of the shots. Last thing he feels are the bullets tearing into him. When he comes back, he's lying in a junkyard—this junkyard—and China's bending over him, wiping wet clay on his face. He starts to push her away, but she shakes her head.

"This is the way it's got to be," she says.

He doesn't know what she's talking about then. Now that he does, he wishes he didn't. He looks at her, lounging on the car, and wonders, was she always so blood-thirsty, or did dying bring it out in her? Dying didn't bring it out in him and it wouldn't have had to dig far to find the capacity for violence in his soul.

She sits up, pulls her knees to her chin, gazes over them to where he's sitting on the hood.

"Look," she tells him, her voice almost apologetic. "I didn't choose for things to work out the way they did."

He doesn't reply. There's nothing to say.

"You never asked why those guys were chasing me," she says.

Coe shrugs.

"Don't you want to know why you died?"

"I know why I died," he says. "I was in the wrong place at the wrong time, end of story."

China shakes her head. "It's way more complicated than that."

It usually is, Coe thinks.

"You know anything about how the Tongs run their prostitution rings?" she goes on.

Coe nods. It's an old story. The recruiters find their victims in Southeast Asia, "loaning" the girls the money they need to buy passage to North America, then make them work off the debt in brothels over here. The fact that none of their victims ever pays off that debt doesn't seem to stop the new girls from buying into it. There's always fresh blood. Some of those girls are so young they've barely hit puberty. The older ones—late teens, early twenties—make out like they're preteens, because that's where the big money is.

He gives China a considering look. Her name accentuates the Chinese cast to her features. Dark eyes the shape of almonds, black hair worn in a classic pageboy, bangs in front, the rest a sleek shoulder-length curve. He'd thought she was sixteen, seventeen. Now he's not so sure anymore.

"That what happened to you?" he asks.

She shakes her head. "I never knew a thing about it until I ran into one of their girls. According to a card she was carrying, she was the property of the Blue Circle Boys Triad—at least the card had their chop on it. She was on the run and I took her in."

"And the Tong found out."

She shakes her head again. "She could barely speak a word of English, but a woman in the Thai grocery under my apartment was able to translate for us. That's how I heard about what they're doing to these girls."

There's a look in her eyes that Coe hasn't seen there before, but he recognizes it. It's like an old pain that won't go away. He knows all about old pain.

"So what put the Tong onto you?" he asks, curious in spite of himself.

"I turned them in."

Coe thinks he didn't hear her right. "You what?"

"I turned them in. The cops raided their brothel and busted a couple of dozen of them. Don't you read the papers?"

Coe shook his head. "I don't—didn't—need more bad news in my life."

"Yeah, well. I've been there."

Coe's still working his head around what she did. Blowing the whistle on the Blue Circle Boys. She had to have known there'd be cops in their pocket, happy to let them know who was responsible. It was probably only dumb luck that the cop she'd taken her story to was a family man, walking the straight and narrow.

"And you didn't think the Tong'd find out?" he asks.

"I didn't care," she says. She's quiet for a long moment, then adds, "I didn't think I cared. Dying kind of changes your perspective on this kind of thing."

Coe nods. "Yeah. Dying brings all kinds of changes."

"So I was out clubbing—the night they were chasing me. Feeling righteous about what I'd done. Celebrating, I guess. I was heading for home, trying to flag down a cab, when they showed up. I didn't know what to do, so I just took off and ran."

"And we know how well that turned out," Coe says.

"It wasn't like I was trying to get you killed. I liked being alive myself."

Coe shrugs. "I'm not blaming you. It's like I said. I was just in the wrong place."

"But our dying still means something. Doesn't matter if there's crooked cops, or that they rolled me over to the Tong. The brothel still got shut down and the Blue Circle Boys are hurting bad. And now those girls have a chance at a better life."

"Sure. They're going to do really well once they're deported back to Thailand or Singapore or wherever they originally came from."

Anger flares in her eyes. "What are you saying?"

"That nothing's changed. The Tong's had a bit of a setback, but give it a month or two and everything'll be back to business as usual. That's the way it works."

"No," she says. "This means something. Just like what we've got to do now means something."

Coe shakes his head again. "Some things you can't change. It's like the government. The most you can do is vote in another set of monkeys, but it doesn't change anything. It's always business as usual."

"Have you always been such a chickenshit?"

"I'm a pacifist. I don't believe violence solves anything."

"Same difference."

Coe looks at her. He's guessing now that she's maybe twenty, twenty-two. At least half his age. When he was younger than she is now, the government gave him a gun and taught him how to kill. He was good at it, too. Did two tours, in country, came back all in one piece and with no other skills. So they hired him on. Same work, different jungle. There was always work for a guy like him who was good at what he did, good at doing what he was told. Good at keeping his mouth shut.

Until the day an op went bad and a little girl got caught in the crossfire. After that he couldn't do it anymore. He looked at that dead kid and all he could do was put the gun down and disappear. Stopped living like a king, the best hotels, the best restaurants, limos when he wanted them, working only nine, ten times a year. He retired from it all, just like that. Vanished into the underground world of the homeless where he was just one more skell, nobody a citizen'd give a second look.

It had to be that way. The people he worked for didn't exactly have a retirement plan for their employees. At least, not one that included your staying alive.

"You don't know what I am," he tells her.

He slides down from the hood of the car and starts walking.

"Leon!" she calls after him.

The crows lift up around the junkyard, filling the air with their raucous cries. It's like they think he's going to follow them, that he's going to let them lead him back to where an eye for an eye makes sense again. But it isn't going to happen. Dying hasn't changed that. They want to take down the shooters who killed China and him, they can do it themselves.

"Leon!" China calls again.

He doesn't turn, and she doesn't follow.

He walks until he finds himself standing in front of a familiar building. Looks like any of the hundreds of other office buildings downtown, nothing special, except the people he'd worked for had a branch in it. There are lights up on the twelfth floor where they have their offices.

His gaze is drawn to the glass doors of the foyer, to the reflection he casts on their dark surfaces. He looks like he's got himself made up for Halloween, like he's wearing warpaint. Back when he was a grunt, there'd been an Indian in his platoon. Joey Keams, a Black Hills Lakota. Keams used to talk about his grandfather, how the same government they were fighting for had outlawed the Ghostdance and the Sun Dances, butchered his people by the thousands, but here he was anyway, fighting for them all the same.

Keams was a marvel. It was like he had a sixth sense, the way he could spot a sniper, a mine, an ambush. Handy guy to have around. Eight months into his tour, they were out on patrol and he stepped on a mine that his sixth sense hadn't bothered to warn him about. There wasn't enough left of him to ship home.

Coe glances around, but the birds are all gone. All that's left is one dark shape sitting on a lamppost, watching him.

Funny the things you forget, he thinks. Because now he remembers that Keams talked about crows, too. How some people believed they carried the souls of the dead on to wherever we go when we die. How sometimes they carried them back when they had unfinished business. He'd have got along real well with China.

"I don't have any unfinished business," he tells the bird.

It cocks its head, stares right back at him like it's listening.

Coe hasn't had anything for a long time. Once he stopped killing, he went passive. Eating at soup kitchens, sleeping under overpasses, cadging spare change that he gave away to those who needed it more than he did. He didn't drink, didn't smoke, didn't do drugs. Didn't need anything that you couldn't get as a handout.

He gives the building a last look, gaze locked on his reflection in the glass door. He looks like what he is: a bum, pushing fifty. Wearing raggedy clothes. No use to anyone. No danger to anyone. Not anymore.

The only thing that doesn't fit is the face-painting job that China did on him. Pulling out his shirttails, he tries to wipe off the war paint, but all he does is smear the clay, make it worse. Screw it, he thinks. He turns away, heading up the street.

It's close to dawn and except for the odd cab that wouldn't stop for him anyway, he's pretty much got the streets to himself. Even the whores are finally asleep.

The crow leaves its perch, flies overhead, lands on the next lamppost.

"So what are you?" he asks it. "My personal guide?"

The bird caws once. Coe pauses under the lamppost, puts his head back to look at it.

"Okay," he says. "Show me what you've got."

The crow flies off again and this time he follows. He's still not bought into any of it, but he can't help being curious, now that he's heard China's story. And sure enough the bird leads him into Chinatown, up where it meets the no-man's-land of the Tombs. As far as Coe can see, there's nothing but abandoned tenements and broken-down factories and warehouses. He follows the crow across an empty lot, gravel and dirt crunching underfoot.

Used to be he could walk without a sound, like a ghost. Now that he is one, you can hear him a mile away.

He stops in the shadows of one of the factories. There are no streetlights down here. But dawn's pinking the horizon and in its vague light he can make out the graffiti chops on the walls of the building across the street that mark it as Blue Circle Boys' turf.

He hears footsteps coming up behind him, but he doesn't look. His crow is perched on the roof of an abandoned car. A moment later, it's joined by a second bird. Finally he turns around.

"You were in the trade, right?" he says to China.

She nods. "I guess you could say that. I was an exotic dancer."

"China . . . ?"

"Was my stage name. China Doll. Cute, huh? My real name's Susie Wong, but I can't remember the last time I answered to it."

"Why'd the cops listen to a stripper?"

"Dumb luck. Got a real family man, hungry for a righteous bust."

"And now?" Coe asks.

"We have to take them out. The ones the cops didn't pick up."

Coe doesn't say anything.

"The ones that killed us."

"The crows tell you all that?" he asks. He lifted a hand to his cheek. "Like they told you about this war paint?"

She nods.

He shakes his head. "They don't say anything to me. All I hear is their damned cawing."

"But you'll help me?" China asks. "We died together, so we have to take them out together."

More crow mumbo-jumbo, Coe supposes.

"I told you," he says. "I won't buy into this Old Testament crap."

"I don't want to argue with you."

"No, you just want me to kill a few people so that we can have a happy ending and float off to our just reward."

She cocks her head and looks at him, reminding him of one of the crows.

"Is that what you're scared of?" she asks. "Of what might be waiting for you when we cross over to the other side?"

Coe hasn't even been thinking of himself, of other vengeful spirits that might be waiting for him somewhere. But now that China's brought it up, he has to wonder. Why haven't the crows brought back any of the people he's killed? And then there was the part he'd played in the death of at least one little girl who really hadn't deserved to die. . . .

"It's not fear," he tells her. "It's principle."

She gives him a blank look.

Coe sighs. "We play out this eye-for-an-eye business, then we're no better than them."

"So what are you doing here?" she asks. She points at the Tong's building with her chin.

He doesn't have an answer for her.

"We'd be saving lives," she says.

"By taking lives."

It's an old argument. It's how he got started in the business he fell into after his two tours in 'Nam.

China nods. "If that's what it takes. If we stop them, they won't kill anybody else."

Except it never stops. There's always one more that needs killing, just to keep things tidy. And the next thing you know, the body count keeps rising. One justification feeding the next like endless dominos knocking against each other. It never stops anything, and it never changes anything, because evil's like kudzu. It can grow anywhere, so thick and fast that you're choking on it before you know it. The only way to eradicate it is to refuse to play its game. Play the game and you're letting it grow inside of you.

But there's no way to explain that so that she'll really understand. She'd have to see through his eyes. See how that dead little girl haunts him. How she reminds him, every day, of how she'd still be alive if he hadn't been playing the game.

The thing to aim for is to clear the playing board. If there's nothing left for evil to feed on, it'll feed on itself.

It makes sense. Believing it is what's kept him sane since that little girl died in the firefight.

"So why are you here?" China asks again.

"I'm just checking them out. That's all."

He leaves her again, crosses the street. Along the side of the building he spots a fire escape. He follows its metal rungs with his gaze, sees they'll take him right to the roof, four stories up. The two crows are already on their way.

Just checking things out, he thinks as he starts up the fire escape.

He hears China climbing up after him, but he doesn't look down. When he gets to the end of the ladder he hauls himself up and swings onto the roof. Gravel crunches underfoot. He thinks he's alone until the crows give a warning caw. He sees the shadow of a man pull away from a brick, box-like structure with a door in it. The roof access, he figures. The man's dark-haired, wearing a long, black raincoat, motorcycle boots that come up to his knees. He's carrying an Uzi, the muzzle rising to center on Coe as he approaches.

He and Coe recognize each other at the same time.

Coe's had three days to get used to this, this business of coming back from the dead. The shooter's had no time at all, but he doesn't waste time asking questions. His eyes go wide. You can see he's shaken. So he does what men always do when they're scared of something—he takes the offense.

The first bullet hits Coe square in the chest. He feels the impact. He staggers. But he doesn't go down. Coe doesn't know which of them's more surprised—him or the shooter.

"You don't want to do this," Coe tells him.

He starts to walk forward and the shooter starts backing away. His finger takes up the slack on the Uzi's trigger and he opens it up. Round after round tears through Coe's shirt, into his chest. He feels each hit, but he's over his surprise, got his balance now, and just keeps walking forward.

And the shooter keeps backing up, keeps firing.

Coe wants to take the gun away. The sound of it, the fact that it even exists, offends him. He wants to talk to the shooter. He doesn't know what he's going to say, but he knows the man needs to get past this business of trying to kill what you don't understand.

The trouble is, the shooter sees Coe's approach through his own eyes, takes Coe's steady closing of the distance between them for a threat. He turns suddenly, misjudges where he is. Coe cries out a warning, but it's too late. The shooter hits his knees against the low wall at the edge of the roof and goes over.

Coe runs to the wall, but the shooter's already gone.

There's an awful, wet sound when the man hits the pavement four stories down. Coe's heard it before; it's not a sound you forget. The shooter's gun goes off, clatters across the asphalt. The crows are out there, riding air currents down toward the body, gliding, not even moving their wings.

"That's one down," China says.

She steps up to the wall beside him to have a look. Coe hadn't even heard her footsteps on the gravel behind him. He frowns at her, but before he can speak, they hear the roof access door bang open behind them. They turn to see a half-dozen men coming out onto the gravel. They fan out into a half circle, weapons centered on the two of them. Shotguns with pistol grips, automatics. A couple more Uzis.

Coe makes the second shooter from the alleyway. The man's eyes go as wide as his partner's had, whites showing. He says something, but Coe doesn't understand the language. Chinese, maybe. Or Thai.

"Party time," China says.

"Can it," Coe tells her.

But all she does is laugh and give the men the finger.

"Hey, assholes," she yells. *"Ni deh!"*

Coe doesn't understand her either, but the meaning's clear. He figures the men are going to open fire, but then they give way to a new figure coming out from the doorway behind them. From the deference the men give him, he's obviously their leader. The newcomer's a tall, Chinese man. Coe's age, late forties. Handsome, black hair cut short, eyes dark.

Now it's Coe's turn to register shock. He doesn't see a ghost of the dead, like the shooters from the alleyway did, but it's a ghost all the same.

A ghost from Coe's past.

"Jimmy," Coe says softly. "Jimmy Chen."

Jimmy doesn't even seem surprised. "I knew I'd be seeing you again," he says. "Sooner or later, I knew you'd surface."

"This an agency op?" Coe asks.

"What do you think?"

"I think you're flying solo."

"Wait a minute," China breaks in. "You guys *know* each other?"

Coe nods. "We have history."

Sometimes the office sent in a team, which was how Coe ended up on a rooftop with this psychopath Jimmy Chen. The target was part of a RICO investigation, star witness kept in a safehouse that was crawling with feds. In a week's time he'd be up on the witness stand, rolling over on a half-dozen crime bosses. Trouble was, he'd also be taking down a few congressmen and industry CEOs. The office wanted to keep the status quo so far as the politicos and moneymen were concerned.

That was where he and Jimmy Chen came in. If the witness couldn't make it into court, the attorney general'd lose his one solid connection between the various defendants and his RICO case would fall apart. The office didn't want to take any chances on this hit, so they sent in a team to make sure the job got done.

Coe wasn't one to argue, but he knew Jimmy by reputation and nothing he'd heard was good. He set up a meet with the woman who'd handed out the assignment.

"Look," he said. "I can do this on my own. Jimmy Chen's a psycho freak. You turn him loose in a downtown core like this and we're going to have a bloodbath on our hands."

"We don't have a problem with messy," the woman told him. "Not in this case. It'll make it look like a mob hit."

He should have backed out then, but he was too used to taking orders. To doing what he was told. So he found himself staking out the safehouse with Jimmy. He forced himself to concentrate on the hit, and a safe route out once the target was down, to ignore the freak as best he could.

The feds played their witness close to the vest. They never took him out. No one went in unless they were part of the op. In the end, Coe and Jimmy realized they'd have to do it on the day of the trial.

They took up their positions as the feds' sedan pulled up in front of the safehouse to pick up the witness. The feds had two more vehicles on the street—one parked two cars back, one halfway up the block. Coe counted six men, all told. And then there were the men inside the house with the witness. But when they brought him out, he was accompanied by a woman and a child. The witness held the child as they came down the steps—a little girl, no more than six with blonde curly hair. It was impossible to get a clear shot at him.

Now what? Coe thought.

But Jimmy didn't have any problem with the situation.

"How d'you like that?" he said. "They're using the kid as a shield. Like that's going to make a difference."

Before Coe could stop him, Jimmy fired. His first bullet tore through the girl and the man holding her. His second took the woman—probably the man's wife. All Coe could do was stare at the little girl as she hit the pavement. He was barely aware of Jimmy dropping the feds as they scattered for cover. Jimmy picked off four of them before Coe's paralysis broke.

He hit Jimmy on the side of his head with the stock of his rifle. For a moment he stood over the fallen man, ready to shoot the damned freak. Then he simply dropped the weapon onto Jimmy's chest and made his retreat.

"Oh, yeah," Jimmy says. "We have history."

He laughs and Coe decides he liked the sound of the crows better. Jimmy's men give way as he moves forward.

"That's one way to put it, Leon," Jimmy goes on. "Hell, if it wasn't for you, I wouldn't even be here."

"What's that supposed to mean?" Coe asks.

But he already knows. He and Jimmy worked for the same people—men so paranoid they put conspiracy buffs to shame. When it came to that, they'd probably been on that grassy knoll in '63. Or if not them, then one of their proxies.

When Coe went underground, Jimmy must have taken the heat for it, sent him running till he ended up with the Blue Circle Boys. The fact that he's still alive says more for Jimmy's ability to survive than it does for the competence of the feds or any kindness in the hearts of their former employers. Unless Jimmy's new business *is* part of an op run by their old employers. Coe wouldn't put it past them. The Blue Circle Boys' war chest had to look good in these days of diminishing budgets, especially for an agency that didn't officially exist.

"How do you know this guy?" China asks.

"That's Leon," Jimmy says, smiling. "He always was a close-mouthed bastard. Best damn wet-boy assassin to come out of 'Nam and he doesn't even confide in his girlfriend."

"She's not my girlfriend," Coe tells him. "She's got nothing to do with this."

Because now he knows why he's here. Why the crows brought him back from the dead and to this place.

Jimmy's giving China a contemplative look.

"Oh, I don't know," he says. "Can you say 'stoolie,' Leon?"

"I'm telling you—"

"But it's a funny thing," Jimmy goes on, like he was never interrupted. "She's supposed to be dead, and here she shows up with you. You did kill her, didn't you, Gary?"

He doesn't turn around, but the surviving shooter from the alleyway is starting to sweat.

"We shot them both, Mr. Chen," he says. "I swear we did. When we dumped them in the junkyard, they were both dead."

"But here they are anyway," Jimmy says softly. "Walking tall." He looks thoughtful, his gaze never leaves Coe's face. "Why now, Leon?" he asks. "After all these years, why're you sticking your nose in my business now?"

Coe shrugs. "Just bad luck, I guess."

"And it's all yours," Jimmy says, smiling again.

"Screw this," China tells them.

As she lunges forward, Coe grabs her around the waist and hauls her back.

"Not like this," he says.

She struggles in his grip, but she can't break free.

"Kill them," Jimmy tells his men. "And this time do it right." He pauses for a heartbeat, then adds, "And aim for their heads. That Indian war paint's not going to be Kevlar like the flak vests they've got to be wearing."

That what you want to believe? Coe has time to think. China couldn't fit a dime under that dress of hers.

But then the men open up. The dawn fills with the rattle of gunfire. Coe's braced for it, but the impact of the bullets knocks China hard against him and like the shooter did earlier, he loses his balance. The backs of his legs hit the wall and the two of them go tumbling off the roof.

For a long moment, Jimmy watches the crows that are wheeling in the dawn air, right alongside the edge of the building where Coe and his little china doll took their fall. There have to be a couple of dozen of them, though they're making enough noise for twice that number.

Jimmy's never liked crows. It's the Japanese that think they're such good luck. Crows, any kind of black bird. They just give him the creeps.

"Somebody go clean up down there," he tells his men. "The last thing we need is for a patrol car to come by and find them."

But when his men get down to the street, there's only the body of the dead shooter lying on the pavement.

Coe and China watch them from the window of an abandoned factory nearby. The men. The crows. China runs her finger along the edge of a shard of broken glass that's still stuck in the windowframe. It doesn't even break the skin. She turns from the window.

"Why'd you drag us in here?" she asks. "We could've taken them."

Coe shakes his head. "That wasn't the way."

"What are you so scared of? You saw for yourself—we can't die. Not from their guns, not from the fall."

"Maybe we only have so many lives we can use up," Coe tells her.

"But—"

"And I've got some other business to take care of first."

China gives him a long considering look.

"Was it true?" she asks. "What the guy you called Jimmy said, about you being an assassin?"

"It was a long time ago. A different life."

"No wonder the crows wanted you for this gig."

Coe sighs. "If our being here's about retribution," he says, "it's got nothing to do with us. What does the universe care about some old bum and a stripper?"

"According to your friend, you're not just some—"

"That freak's not anybody's friend," Coe tells her, his voice hard.

"Okay. But—"

"This is about something else."

He tells her about the hit that went sour, the little girl that died. Tells her how Jimmy Chen shot right through her to get the job done.

China shivers. "But . . . *you* didn't kill her."

"No," Coe says. "But I might as well have. It's because of who I was, because of people like me, that she died."

China doesn't say anything for a long moment. Finally she asks, "You said something about some kind of business?"

"We're going to a bank," he tells her.

"A bank."

She lets the words sit there.

Coe nods. "So let's wash this crap off our faces or we'll give my financial advisor the willies. It'll be bad enough as it is."

"Why's that?"

"You'll see."

Coe can see the questions build up in China's eyes as he takes her into an office building that's set up snug against Cray's Gym over in Crowsea, but she keeps them to herself. The "bank" is up on the second floor, in back. A single-room office with a glass door. Inside there's a desk with a laptop computer on it, a secretary's chair, a file cabinet, and a couple of straight-backs for visitors. The man sitting at the desk is overweight and balding. He's wearing a cheap suit, white shirt, tie. He's got a take-out coffee sitting on his desk. Nothing about him or the office reflects the penthouse he goes home to with the security in the lobby and a view of the lake that upped the price of the place by another hundred grand.

The man looks up as they come in, his already pale skin going white with shock.

"Jesus," he says.

The hint of a smile touches Coe's lips. "Yeah, it's been a while. China, this is Henry, my bank manager. Henry, China."

Henry gives her a nod, then returns his gaze to Coe.

"I heard you were dead," he says.

"I am."

Henry laughs, like it's a joke. Whatever works, Coe thinks.

"So how're my investments doing?" he asks.

Henry calls up the figures on the laptop that always travels with him between the office and home. After a while he starts to talk. When the figures start to add up into the seven digits, Coe knows that Henry's been playing fair. In Coe's business, people disappear, sometimes for years, then they show up again out of the blue. It's the kind of situation that a regular financial institution can't cope with all that well. Which keeps men like Henry in business.

"I want to set up a trust fund," he tells Henry. "Something to help kids."

"Help them how?"

Coe shrugs. "Get them off the streets, or give them scholarships. Maybe set it up like one of those wish foundations for dying kids or something. Whatever works. Can you do it?"

"Sure."

"You'll get your usual cut," Coe tells him.

Henry doesn't bother to answer. That'd go without saying.

"And I want it named in memory of Angelica Ciccone."

Henry's eyebrows go up. "You mean Bruno's kid? The one that died with him the day he was going to testify?"

"You've got a long memory," Coe tells him.

Henry shrugs. "It's the kind of thing that sticks in your mind."

Tell me about it, Coe thinks.

"So you can do this?" he says.

"No problem."

"And we're square?"

Henry smiles. "We're square. I like this idea, Leon. Hell, I might even throw in a few thou' myself to help sweeten the pot."

"Where'd you get that kind of money?" China asks when they're back out on the street again.

Coe just looks at her. "Where do you think?"

"Oh. Right." But then she shakes her head. "You had all that money and you lived like a bum. . . ."

"Blood money."

"But still . . ."

"Maybe now it can do some good. I should've thought of this sooner."

"To make up for all the people you killed?" China asks.

Coe looks down the street to where a pair of crows are playing tag around a lamppost.

"You don't make up for that kind of thing," he says. "The foundation's just to give a little hope to some kids who might not get to see it otherwise. So that they don't grow up all screwed up like me."

China's quiet for a long moment.

"Or like me," she says after a while.

Coe doesn't say anything. There's nothing he can say.

"So now what?" China asks after they've been walking for a few blocks.

Coe spies a phone booth across the street and leads her to it.

"Now we make a call," he says. "You got a watch?"

She lifts her wrist to show him the slim, knock-off Rolex she's wearing.

"Time me," he says as he drops a quarter into the slot, punches in a number. "And tell me when three minutes are up. Exactly three minutes. Starting . . ." He waits until the connection's made. "Now."

While China dutifully times the call, Coe starts talking about Jimmy Chen, the hit on Bruno Ciccone, what Jimmy's up to these days, where he can be found, how many men he's got.

"Two-fifty-eight," China says. "Two-fifty-nine."

At the three-minute mark, Coe drops the phone receiver, lets it bang against the glass wall of the booth. He grabs China's hand and runs with her, back across the street, down the block and onto the next, ducks into an alley.

"Okay," he says. "Watch."

He barely gets the words out before the first cruiser comes squealing around a corner, blocks the intersection the pair of them just crossed, cherry lights flashing. Moments later, another one pulls across the intersection at the other end of the block. They're joined by two more cruisers, an unmarked car, and then a couple of dark sedans. The feds step out of those, four of them in their dark suits, looking up and down the street.

China turns to Coe. "Jesus. That was seriously fast."

Coe's smiling. "A guy who kills as many feds as Jimmy did is going to give them a hard-on that won't go away. C'mon," he adds as the police start to fan out, heading up and down the sidewalks, checking doorways, alleys. "We're done here."

China keeps her questions in check again. She lets Coe take the lead and he slips them out of the net the police are setting up like he doesn't even have to think about it. Some skills you just don't lose.

He takes her back to the junkyard. They ease in through the gates when the old man running the place isn't looking and make their way back to the rear. The dogs the old man keeps won't even come near them. But the crows follow, a thickening flock of them that settle on the junked cars and trash around them.

"That business with the phone call and the cops," China wants to know. "What was all that about?"

"We just dealt with Jimmy."

She shakes her head. "His lawyers'll have him back on the streets before the end of the day."

"Unless he resists," Coe says. "What do you think, China? Think Jimmy's the kind of guy who'll go quietly and stand trial on murder one charges for killing a half-dozen cops?"

"No. I guess not. But if he gets away . . ."

"What do the crows tell you?" Coe asks.

She sits quietly for a moment, looking at them, head cocked, like she's listening. Coe doesn't hear anything except for their damned cawing. Finally she turns back to look at him.

"It's over," she says. "We're done."

Coe raps a knuckle against the fender he's sitting on. It's solid. So's he.

"How come we're still here?" he asks.

"I guess we'll cross over tonight."

Coe nods. There's a kind of symmetry to that.

"I like you better without the war paint," he says.

"Yeah? I think on you it was an improvement."

She smiles, but then she gets a serious look.

"I'm glad we did it your way, Leon," she says. "I feel better for it. Cleaner."

Coe doesn't say anything. His own soul's stained with too much killing for him to ever feel clean again. He didn't do this for himself, or because of the pacifism he's embraced since Angelica Ciccone was killed. He did it for China. He did it so she wouldn't have to carry what he does when the crows take them over to wherever it is they're going next. Into some kind of afterworld, he guesses, if there really is such a place.

He's been thinking. Maybe there is, considering the crows and how they brought the two of them back. And the thing is, if there *is* someplace else to go, he figures she deserves a shot at it with a clean slate.

Him, he'll settle for simple oblivion.

It's late at night now, close on to the anniversary hour of their dying. The crows are leading them back to where Jimmy Chen's boys shot them down. When they reach the mouth of the alley, Coe hesitates. The skin at the nape of his neck goes tight and a prickle of something walks down his spine.

"It's okay," China tells him.

The air above them's thick with crows, wheeling and cawing. Coe still can't make any kind of sense out of them.

China takes his hand.

"If you can't trust them," she says, "then trust me."

Coe nods. He doesn't know where they're going, but he knows for sure that there's nothing left for him here. So he lets her lead him out of the world, the crows flying on ahead of them, into a tunnel of light.

In the Quiet After Midnight

> *It's a winter's night, the stars are bright*
> *And the world keeps spinning around. . . .*
> —Kiya Heartwood, from "Robert's Waltz"

1

I'm fifteen when I realize that I don't remember my mother anymore. I mean, I still recognize her in pictures and everything, but I can't call her face up just before I fall asleep the way I once did. I used to tell her about my day, the little things that happened to me, all the things I was thinking about, and it made the loneliness seem less profound—having her listening, I mean. Now I can't remember her. It's like she isn't inside me anymore and I don't even know when she went away.

I still remember I had a mother. I'm not stupid. But the immediacy of the connection is gone. Now it's like something I read in a history book in school, not something that was ever part of my life and it scares me because it was never supposed to go away. She was always supposed to be with me.

It's a seriously hot day in the middle of June and I'm walking home from school when it hits me, when it stops me dead in my tracks right there in the middle of the sidewalk, near the corner of Williamson and Kelly. I can't tell you what makes it come to me the way it does, so true and hard, bang, right out of nowhere. But all of a sudden it's like I can't breathe, like the hot air's pressing way too close around me.

I look around—I don't know what I'm looking for, I just know I have to get off the street, away from all the people and their ordinary lives—and that's when I see this little Catholic church tucked away on a side street. Kelly Street was a main thoroughfare years ago, back when the church was really impressive, too, I guess. Now they're both looking long neglected.

I don't know why I go in. I'm not even Catholic. But it's cool inside, dark after the sunlight I just left behind, and quiet. I sit down in a pew near the back and look up toward the front. I've heard of the Stations of the Cross, but I don't know what they are, if they're even something you can see. But I see Jesus hanging there, front and center, a statue of his mother off to one side, pictures of the saints. I wonder which one is the patron of memory.

I bring my gaze back to the front of the church. This time I look at the candles. There must be thirty, forty of them, encased in short red glasses. Only five or six are lit. They're prayers, I'm guessing, or votive offerings. Whoever lit them doesn't seem to be around.

I slouch in the pew and stare up at the vaulted ceiling. It's easier to breathe in here, the world doesn't seem to press down on me the way it did outside, but the sick, lost feeling doesn't go away.

I don't know how long I've been sitting there when there's a rustle of cloth behind me. I turn to see a hooded man kneeling, two pews back, head bent in prayer. He's all in black, cloak and hood, shadows swallowing his features. A priest, I think, except they don't dress like that, do they? At least none of the ones I've ever seen—on the street or in the movies.

Maybe he's not even a man, I find myself thinking. Maybe he's a she, a nun, except they don't dress like that either. I guess I'm thinking about him so hard that my thoughts pull his head up. I still can't see anything but the hint of features in the spill of shadows under the hood, but the voice is definitely male.

"A curious sanctuary, is it not?" he says, sitting back on the pew behind him.

I have no idea what he means, but I nod my head.

"Here we sit, neither of us parishioners, yet we have the place to ourselves."

"The priest must be around here someplace," I say, hoping it's true.

It's suddenly occurred to me that this guy could easily be some kind of pervert, following young girls into an out-of-the-way place like this and hitting on them. I'm very aware of how quiet it is in here, how secluded.

He shakes his head. "They are all long gone," he says. "Priest and parishioners all."

Now I'm really getting the creeps. I don't want to turn my back on him so I gesture with my chin toward the front of the church. I clear my throat.

"Somebody lit those candles," I say.

"At one time," he agrees. "But now we see only the memory of their light, the way starlight is but a memory of what burns in the heavens, crossing an unthinkable distance from where they flared to where we stand when we regard them."

"My, um, dad's expecting me," I tell him. "He knows where I am."

As if, but it seems like a good thing to say. I might be alone in here, but I don't want him thinking I'm an easy mark. I sit up a little straighter and try to look bigger than I am. Tougher. If worse comes to worst, I'll go down kicking and screaming. I may be small, but I can be fierce, only ferocity doesn't seem to be the issue since all he's doing is sitting there looking at me from under the shadows of his hood. A footnoted script would be good, though, since nothing he's saying really makes much sense.

"What is it you have lost?" he asks.

The confused look I give him isn't put on like my bravado. "What do you mean, lost?"

"We've all lost something precious," he says. "Why else would we find ourselves in this place?"

Maybe I'm not a Catholic, but I know this conversation has nothing to do with their doctrines. I should get up and see if I can make it back out the door. Instead I ask, "What have you lost?"

"My life."

Okay. Way too creepy. But I can't seem to get up. It's like it's really late at night and I know I have to get up for school the next day, but I still have to finish the book first. I can't go to sleep, not knowing how it ends.

"You don't look dead," I say.

"I don't believe in death," he tells me.

There's a glint of white in the shadows under his hood. Teeth, I realize. He just smiled. I don't feel at all comforted.

I clear my throat again. "But . . ."

I can't see his eyes, but I can feel the weight of his gaze.

"I have lost my life," he says, "but I cannot die."

He shrugs and I realize there's something wrong under that hood of his, the way the folds of the cloth fall. He's bumpy, but in the wrong places.

"And you?" he asks.

"My mother," I find myself saying. I remember what he said about the candles and starlight. "The memory of my mother."

I don't even know why I'm telling him this. It's not the kind of thing I'd tell my dad, or my best friend Ellie, but here I am, sharing this horrible lost feeling with a perfect stranger who doesn't exactly make me feel like he's got my best interests at heart.

"Some would embrace the loss of memory," he says, "rather than lament its absence."

I shake my head. "I don't understand."

"Remembering can keep the pain too fresh," he explains. "It is so much easier to forget—or at least it is more comfortable. But you and I, we are not seeking comfort, are we? We know that to forget is to give in to the darkness, so we walk in the light, that we hold fast to our joys and our pains."

At first I thought he had a real formal way of speaking, but now I'm starting to get the idea that maybe English isn't his first language, that he's translating in his head as he talks and that's what makes everything sound so stiff and proper.

"There was a glade in my homeland," he says. He settles further back against his pew and I catch a glimpse of a russet beard, a pointed chin, high cheekbones before the hood shadows them again. "It had about it a similar air as does this church. It was a place for remembering, a sanctuary hidden in a grove where the lost could gather the fraying tatters of their memories and weave them strong once more."

"The lost . . ."

Again that flash of a smile. There's no humor in it.

"Such as we."

"I just came in here to get out of the heat," I tell him.

"Mmm."

"I was feeling a little dizzy."

"And why here, do you suppose?" he asks. "I will tell you," he goes on before I can answer. "Because like us, this place also seeks to hold on to what it has lost. We help each other. You. I. The church."

"I'm not . . ."

Remembering anything, I'm about to say, but my voice trails off because suddenly it's not true. I am remembering. If I close my eyes, I know I can call my mother's face up again—not stiff, like in a photo, but the way it was when she was still alive, mobile and fluid. And not only her face. I can smell the faint rose blush of her perfume. I can almost feel her hand on my head, tousling the curls that are pulled back in a French braid right now.

I look at him. "How . . . ?"

He smiles again and stands. He's not as tall as I was expecting from his broad shoulders.

"You see?" he says. "And I, too, am remembering. Reeds by a river and a woman hidden in them. I should never have cut a pipe from those reeds. Her voice was far sweeter."

He's lost me again.

"I can pretend it was preordained," he says. "That the story needed to play out the way it did. But you and I, we know better, don't we? The story can't be told until the deed is done. Only the Fates can look into the future and I have known them to be wrong."

"I'm not sure I know what you're talking about," I say.

He nods. "Of course. Why should you? They are my memories and it is an old story, forgotten now. But remember this: There is always a choice. Perhaps destiny will quicken the plot, but what we do with the threads we are given is our choice."

I've taken this in school.

"You mean free will."

He has to think about that.

"Perhaps I do," he says finally. "But it comes without instruction and the price of it can be dear."

"What do you mean?"

He shrugs. "I can only speak of what is pertinent to my own experience, but if there were any advice I would wish I had been given, it would be to believe in death."

"How can you not believe in it?" I say. "It's all around us."

There's a tightness in my chest again, but this time it's because I can remember. It's because my memories are immediate and clear, the good and the bad, the joy of my mother's love and the way she was taken away from me.

"It was not always so," he says.

"Then it was a better time."

"You think so?" he asks. "Consider the alternative. Imagine being alive when all consider you dead. You walk through the changing world as a ghost. You can touch no one. No one can see you."

I could really use those footnotes now.

"But—"

"Be careful with your choices," he says and turns away.

I hear the rustling of cloth as he moves, the faint click of his heels on the stone floor, except they don't sound like leather-soled shoes. There's a hollow ring to them, like a horse's hoof on pavement. He turns to face me again when he reaches the door, pushes back his hood. He has strong, handsome features, with a foreign cast. Dark, olive skin, but his hair is as red as his beard, and standing up among the curls are two small horns, curled like a goat's.

"You . . . you're the devil," I say.

I can't believe he's here in a church. I want to look up above the altar, to see if the statue of Jesus is turning away in horror at this unholy invasion, but I can't move, can't pull my gaze from the horned man. I feel sick to my stomach.

"Where one might see a devil," he says, "another might see a friend."

I'm shaking my head. I may not be much of a churchgoer, but even I've heard about what happens to people who make deals with the devil.

"Remember what I said about choices," he tells me.

And then he's gone.

It's forever before I can get up the nerve to walk back out through that door myself and go home.

2

They'd all gotten together at The Harp to share a pitcher of beer after finishing the evening classes they taught at the Newford School of Art. After the quiet of the school, the noisy pub with its Irish session in full swing in one corner was exactly what they needed to wind down. They commandeered a table far enough away from the music so that they could talk and hold forth, but close enough so that they could still hear the music.

They made a motley group. Jilly and Sophie, alike enough in the pub's low light that they could be sisters, except Jilly was thinner, with the scruffier clothes and the longer, curlier hair; Sophie was tidier, more buxom. Hannah, all in black as usual, blonde hair cropped short, blue eyes sparkling with the buzz her second glass of beer was giving her. Desmond, dreadlocked and smiling, dressed as though he was still living on the Islands, wearing only a thin cotton jacket, despite the below-zero temperatures outside. Angela, the intensity of her dark eyes softened by her pixy features and a fall of silky Pre-Raphaelite hair.

It was Hannah who'd come up with the question—"What's the strangest thing that ever happened to you?"—and then looked around the table. She'd expected something from Jilly because Jilly could always be counted on for some outlandish story or other. Hannah was never quite sure if they were true or not, but that didn't really matter. The stories were always entertaining, everything from affirmation that Bigfoot had indeed been seen wandering around the Tombs to a description of the strange goblin kingdom that Jilly would insist existed in Old Town, that part of the city that had dropped underground during the Big Quake and then been built over during the reconstruction.

And, of course, she told them so well.

But the first story had come from Angela and instead of giving them a fit of the giggles, it made them all fall quiet. Her calm recitation created a pool of stillness in the middle of the general hubbub of the tavern as they regarded her with varying degrees of belief and wonder: Jilly completely accepting the story at face value, Desmond firmly in the rational camp, Sophie somewhere in between the two. Hannah supposed she was closest to Sophie—she'd like to believe, but she wasn't sure she could.

Angela smiled. "Not exactly what you were expecting, was it?"

"Well, no," Hannah said.

"I think it's lovely," Jilly put in. "And it feels so absolutely true."

"Well, you would," Sophie told her. She looked around the table. "Maybe we should order another pitcher so that we can all work at seeing the world the way Jilly does."

"We'll be needing a lot more than beer for that," Desmond put in.

Jilly stuck out her tongue at him.

"So?" Angela asked. "Was he the devil?"

Desmond shook his head. "As if."

"What do you think?" Hannah asked.

"I have no idea," Angela replied. "I was young and impressionable and certainly upset at the time. Maybe I saw what I thought I saw, or maybe I imagined it. Or maybe he was suffering from one of those deforming diseases like elephantiasis and those weren't horns I saw coming up out of his hair, but some sort of unfortunate growth."

"I'll side with Desmond on this one," Jilly said.

Everyone looked at her in surprise. Jilly and Desmond never agreed on anything except that their students needed a firm grounding in the basics of classical art—figure studies, anatomy, color theory, and the like—before they could properly go on to create more experimental works.

Jilly rolled her eyes at the way they were all looking at her. "I mean that Angela didn't meet the devil," she said. "Or at least not the devil according to Christian doctrine. What she met was something far older—what the Christians used as a template for their fallen angel."

"I definitely need that beer," Desmond said and got up to order another pitcher.

"But in a church?" Hannah found herself saying.

Jilly turned to her. "Why not?"

"Who exactly are we talking about here?" Sophie asked.

"Well, think about it," Jilly replied. "You've got him talking about chasing a nymph into the reeds and making music that can't compare to her singing. He had goat's horns and probably goat's feet—Angela says his footsteps sounded like hooves on the floor."

Angela nodded in agreement.

"And then," Jilly went on, "there's this business of being dead but living forever." She sat back, obviously pleased with herself.

Hannah shook her head. "I still don't see what you're getting at."

"Old gods," Jilly said. "She met Pan. Like it says in the stories, 'Great Pan is dead. Long live Pan!' "

"Not to be picayune," Sophie put in with a smile, "but I think you're quoting the Waterboys."

Jilly shrugged. "Whatever. It doesn't change anything."

"I thought about that, too," Angela said, "but it makes no sense. What would Pan be doing here, thousands of miles from Arcadia, even if he ever did exist and was still alive?"

"I think he travels the world," Jilly told her. "Like the Wandering Jew. And besides,

Newford's a cool city. We all live here, don't we? Why *shouldn't* Pan show up here as well?"

"Because," Desmond said, having returned with a brimming pitcher in time to hear the last part of the conversation, "Roman gods aren't real. Aren't now, never were, end of story."

"He was Greek, actually," Sophie said.

"Whose side are you on?" Desmond asked.

He poured them all fresh glasses, then set the empty pitcher down in the middle of the table.

Sophie clinked her glass against his. "The side of truth, justice, and equality for all—including obstinate, if talented, sculptors."

"Flatterer," he said.

"Hussy."

"Men can't be hussies."

"Can too!" all four women cried at once.

3

The talk went on for hours along with another couple of pitchers of The Harp's draught lager. By the time Sophie said they should probably call it a night—"It's a night!" Jilly pronounced to a round of giggles—Hannah was feeling dizzy from both.

She and Angela had the same bus stop, so after a chorus of goodbyes, they left together, slightly unsteady on their feet, breath clouding in the cold air. Happily the bus stop wasn't far and there was a bench where they could sit while they waited. Hannah settled back in her seat, not really feeling the cold yet. She looked up at the sky, wishing she was out in the country somewhere so that she could fully appreciate the stars that were cloaked by the city's light pollution. That was one of the things she missed the most about having moved to the city—deep night skies and country quiet.

"Did that really happen?" she asked after a moment.

Angela didn't need to ask what.

"I don't know," she said. "I can joke about it, but the truth is, that was a pivotal moment for me—one of those crossroads they talk about where your life could have gone one way or the other. It doesn't matter to me whether it was real or not—or rather, if I had some extraordinary experience or not. I still came away from it with the realization that I always have to think my choices through carefully, and then, when I make a decision, take full responsibility for it."

Like moving to the city, Hannah thought. It was no use bemoaning the things she missed, though of course that didn't stop her from worrying a half-dozen times a week over whether she'd made the right decision. She wanted to be a painter, and the community and contacts she'd come here to find were what she needed to be able to do it—not to mention the fact that back home she could never make her living with the odd sorts of jobs she held here: art instructor, sometime artist's model, waitress, messenger, the occasional commission for an ad or a poster. Maybe when she was somewhat better established she could afford to move back to the country, but not now. Not and feel that her career was actually moving forward.

But that didn't stop her from missing everything she'd left behind.

"Think it through first," Hannah said, "but then don't look back."

Angela nodded. "Exactly. If you embrace the decision you've made, everything seems that much clearer because you're not fighting self-doubt."

"You got all that when you were fifteen?"

"Not the way you're thinking. It wasn't this amazing epiphany and my whole life changed. But I couldn't get him—whoever or whatever he was—out of mind. Nor what he'd told me. And whatever else happened, I had my mom back." Angela touched a mittened hand to her chest. "In here." She got a far-away look in her eyes. "Jilly's always saying that magic's never what you expect it to be, but it's often what you need. I think she's right. And it doesn't really matter if the experience comes from outside or inside. *Where* it comes from isn't important at all. What's important is that it *does* come—and that we're receptive enough to recognize and accept it."

"I could use a piece of magic to change my life," Hannah said. "I seem to be in this serious rut—always scrambling to make ends meet, which also means that I never have the time to do enough of my own work to do more than participate in group shows."

"Well, you know what they say: Visualize it. If you see yourself as having more time, being more successful, whatever, you can make it happen."

"I think if I'm going to visualize magic, I'd rather it was dancing on a hilltop with your horned man."

Angela's eyebrows rose.

Hannah smiled. "Well, that's what I think magic should be. Not this." She waved a hand to take in the city around them. "Not being successful or whatever, but just having a piece of something impossible to hold on to, if only for a moment."

"So visualize that."

"As if."

They fell silent for a time, watching the occasional car go by.

"Did you ever see him again?" Hannah asked.

Angela smiled and shook her head. "I think it was pretty much a once-in-a-lifetime sort of experience. That piece of something impossible you were talking about that I only got to hold on to for a moment."

Her bus arrived then.

"Can you get home okay?" she asked.

"I'm not *that* tipsy," Hannah told her.

"But almost."

"Oh, yes."

Her own bus took another five minutes to arrive.

4

Later that night, Hannah lay in bed, studying the splotchy plaster on her ceiling, and let her mind drift. Visualize, she thought. How would she visualize Angela's mysterious visitor? Like that painting in *The Wandering Wood*, she decided. The watercolor by Ellen Wentworth that depicted the spirit of the forest as some kind of hybrid Greek/Native American being—goat legs and horns, but with beads and feathers and cowrie shells braided into the red hair and beard, even into the goaty leg hair.

She smiled, remembering how she'd copied the painting from out of the book when she was twelve or thirteen and had kept it hanging up in her room for ages—right up until her last year of high school when the sheer naiveté of its rendering finally made her put it away. She was doing such better work by that time. Her grasp of anatomy alone made it difficult to look at the piece anymore. What had become of it? she wondered.

She got up out of bed, but not to go searching through stacks of old art—most of that early juvenile stuff was still stored in boxes on the farm anyway. No, she'd had a cup of herbal tea when she got home and now she had to pay the price with a trip to the bathroom. She got as far as putting a thick flannel housecoat on top of the oversized T-shirt she slept in before being distracted by the scene that lay outside her bedroom window.

There was nothing particularly untoward to catch her eye. Back yards and fences, half of the latter in desperate need of repair that they'd probably never get. Narrow lanes made more narrow by garbage cans, Dumpsters and snowbanks. Above them, fire escapes and brick walls, windows—mostly dark, but a few lit from within by the blue flicker of television screens—rooflines, telephone poles and drooping wires criss-crossing back and forth across the alleys and lanes.

The snow covering softened some of the usual harshness of the scene, and yes, it could be almost magical during a snowfall, the kind when big sleepy flakes came drifting down, but it was still hard to imagine the city holding anything even remotely as enchanting as Jilly's stories of gemmin, which were a kind of earth spirit that lived in abandoned cars, or Angela's mysterious goatman—even if such things were possible in the first place. If she were a magical being, she wouldn't live here, not when there were deep forests and mountains an hour or so's drive north of the city, or the lake right smack at the southern end of the urban sprawl. She'd run through the woods like one of Ellen Wentworth's elfish tree people, or sail off across the lake in a wooden shoe.

She smiled. Leaving the window, she went and had her pee, but instead of getting back into bed, she pulled on a pair of jeans under her housecoat, stuck her feet into her boots and left her apartment. She took the stairs up to the roof. The door was stuck so she had to give it a good shove before she could get it open and step outside into the chilly air.

She wasn't sure what time it was. After four, at any rate. Late enough that you could almost tune out the occasional siren and the vague bits of traffic that drifted from the busier streets a few blocks over. The wide expanse of the rooftop was covered with a thin layer of snow, granulated and hard, clinging to the surface of the roof like carbuncles. Her flowerboxes were up here, a half-dozen of them in which she grew all sorts of vegetables and flowers—a piece of the farm transplanted here so that she didn't feel quite so cut off from the land. The dirt in the boxes was all frozen now and snow covered them. She'd pulled most of the dead growth out in the autumn, but there were still a few browned stalks pushing hardily out of the snow that she hadn't gotten to. Cosmos and purple coneflowers. Some kale, which was better after a frost anyway, only it was finished now.

She shivered, but didn't go back inside right away. She looked out across the rooftops, a checkerboard of white squares and black streets and yards. There was a sort of magic, she supposed, about the city this late at night. The stillness, the dark, the sensation that time seemed to have stopped. The knowing that she was one of a select few who were awake and outside at this hour. If you were going to discover a secret, if you were going to get the chance to peer under the skin of the world, if only for a moment, this was the time for it.

Are you out there? she wondered, addressing the mysterious man Angela had met in a church long before Hannah had even thought of moving to the city herself. Will you show yourself to me? Because I could use a piece of magic right about now, a piece of something impossible that shouldn't exist, but does, if only for this moment.

Her straits weren't as desperate as Angela's had been. And compared to how so many people had to live—out of work, on the streets, cadging spare change just to get a bowl of soup or a cup of coffee—what she had was luxury. But she still had a deficit, a kind of hollow in her heart from which bits and pieces of her spirit trickled away, like coins will from a hole in your pocket. Nothing she couldn't live without, but she missed them all the same.

She wasn't sure that magic could change that. She wasn't sure anything could, because what she really needed to find was a sense of peace. Within herself. With the choices she'd made that had brought her here. Magic would probably confuse the issue. She imagined it would be like an instant addiction—having tasted it once, you'd never be satisfied not tasting it again. She didn't know how Angela did it.

Except, not having tasted it created just as much yearning. This wanting to believe it was real. This asking for the smallest, slightest tangible proof.

She remembered what Angela had said. Visualize it.

Okay. She'd pretend she was thinking up a painting—a made-up landscape. She closed her eyes and tried to ignore the cold air. It wasn't winter, but a summer's night, somewhere near the Mediterranean. This wasn't a tenement rooftop, but a hilltop with olive trees and grape vines and . . . the details got a little vague after that.

Oh, just try, she told herself.

Some white buildings with terra-cotta roofs in the distance, like stairs going down to the sea. Maybe some goats, or sheep. A stone wall. It's night. The sky's like velvet and the stars feel as though they're no more than an elbow-length away.

Where would he be?

Under one of the olive trees, she decided. Right at the top of the hill. Starlight caught on the curve of his goat horns. And he'd be playing those reed pipes of his. A low breathy sound like . . . like . . . She had to use her father's old Zamfir records for a reference, stripping away the sappy accompaniment and imagining the melody to be more mysterious. Older. No, timeless.

For a moment there, she could almost believe it. Could almost smell the sea, could feel the day's heat still trapped in the dirt under her feet. But then a cold gust of wind made her shiver and took it away. The warm night, olive trees and all.

Except . . . except . . .

She blinked in confusion. She *was* on a hilltop, only it was in the middle of the city. The familiar roofs of the tenements surrounding her apartment were all still there, but her own building was gone, replaced by a snowy hilltop, cleared near the top where she stood, skirted with pine and cedar as it fell away to the street.

She shook her head slowly. This couldn't . . .

The sound she heard was nothing like the one she'd been trying to imagine. It still originated from a wind instrument, was still breathy and low, but it held an undefinable quality that she couldn't have begun to imagine. It was like a heartbeat, the hoot of an owl, the taste of red wine and olives, all braided together and drawn out into long, resonating notes. In counterpoint she heard footsteps, the crunch of snow and the soft sound of shells clacking together.

"Dance with me," a voice said from behind her.

When she turned, he was there. Ellen Wentworth's forest spirit, horns and goat legs, the hair entwined with feathers, beads and shells. She seemed to fall into his eyes, tumbling down into the deep mystery of them and unable to look away. He was a northern spirit, as much a part of the winter and the hills north of the city as a wolf or a jack pine, but the Mediterranean goatman was there, too, the sense of him growing sharper and clearer, the further she was drawn into his gaze.

"You . . . I . . ."

Her throat couldn't shape the words. Truth was, she had no idea what she was trying to say. Perhaps his name—the name Jilly had given him.

She let him take her in his warm arms and felt ridiculous in her tatty housecoat, cowboy boots, and jeans. He smelled of pine sap and cedar boughs, and then of something else, a compelling musky scent she couldn't place, old and dark and secret. His biceps were corded and hard under her hands, but his touch was light, gentle as she remembered the brush of wildflowers to be against her legs when she crossed a summer meadow.

The music had acquired a rhythm, a slow waltz time. His music. He was dancing with her, but somehow he was still making that music.

"How . . . ?" she began.

His smile made her voice falter. The question grew tattered in her head and came apart, drifted away. Magic, she decided. Pure and simple. Visualized. Made real. A piece of impossible, a couldn't-be, but here it was all the same and what did it matter where it came from, or how it worked?

He led beautifully, and she was content to let everything else fall away and simply dance with him.

5

She woke to find that she'd spent the night sleeping on the landing outside the door that led out onto the roof of her building. She was stiff from having slept on the hard floor, cold from the draft coming in from under the door. But none of that seemed to matter. Deep in her chest she could still feel the rhythm of that mysterious music she'd heard last night, heard while she danced on a hilltop that didn't exist, danced with a creature that couldn't possibly exist.

She remembered one of the things that Angela had said last night.

Jilly's always saying that magic's never what you expect it to be, but it's often what you need.

Lord knows she had needed this.

"Hey, *chica*. You drink a little too much last night?"

Mercedes Muñoz, her upstairs neighbor, was standing on the stairs leading up to where Hannah lay. Hand on her hip, Mercedes wore her usual smile, but worry had taken up residence in her dark eyes.

"You okay?" she added when Hannah didn't respond.

Hannah slowly sat up and drew her housecoat close around her throat.

"I've never felt better in my life," she assured Mercedes. It was true. She didn't even have a hangover. "For the first time since I've moved to this city, I finally feel like I belong."

It made no sense. How could it make her feel this way? A dream of dancing with some North American version of a small Greek god, on a hilltop that resembled the hills that rose up behind the farm where she'd grown up. But it had all the same. Maybe it was simply the idea of the experience—wonderful, impossible, exhilarating.

But she preferred to believe it hadn't been a dream. That like Angela, she'd met a piece of old-world magic, however improbable it might seem. That the music she was still carrying around inside her had been his. That the experience had been real. Because if something like that could happen, then other dreams could come true as well. She could make it here, on her own, away from the farm. It hadn't been a mistake to come.

Mercedes offered her a hand up.

"And now what?" Mercedes asked. "You going to try sleeping in a cardboard house in some alley next?"

Hannah smiled. "If that's what it takes, maybe I will."

The Pennymen

*. . . and then there are the pennymen, linked to
the trembling aspens, or penny trees, so called
because their leaves, when moving in a breeze,
seem like so many twinkling coins.*
—Christy Riddell,
from *Fairy Myths of North America*

1

It's a Sunday morning in January and there's a tree outside my window, full of birds.
I'm not exactly sure what kind. They look like starlings with their winter-dark feathers
and speckled breasts and heads, but I could be wrong. I've never been much good at
identifying birds. Pigeon, crow, robin, seagull, sparrow . . . after that, I'm pretty much
guessing. But the tree's a rowan, a mountain ash. I know that because Jilly named it
for me when she helped the boy and me first move into this apartment.

Jilly says they're also called wicken, or quicken trees, an old name that seems
both quaint and evocative to me. She claims they're a magic tree—real magic, she
insists, like faeries dancing on hilltops, Rhine maidens rising up from the river bottom,
little hobgoblins scurrying down the street that you might glimpse from the corner of
your eye. As if. All I can do when she starts in on that sort of thing is smile and nod
and try not to roll my eyes. Jilly's sweet, but she does take some things way too
seriously. I mean, you can have all the romantic notions in the world, but just because
you think you feel a tickle of enchantment, like you're peeking through a loose board
in the fence that divides what we know from what could be, doesn't mean it's real.

Magic belongs in stories, it's that simple. Real life and that kind of story don't mix.

Except lying here in bed this morning, pillows propped up on the headboard and
looking out the window, for some reason I feel as though I'm in a story. Nothing
overly dramatic, mind you. It's not like I expect spies to come crashing in through the
front door, or to find a body in the bathtub when I get up to have a pee. It's more like

an establishing shot in a movie, something glimpsed in passing, a scene to set the mood of what's to come.

So if this is a movie, here's what the audience would see: It's a blustery day, the sky thick with fat snow that blurs the world outside the glass panes. Against a backdrop of a Crowsea street, there are the birds and the tree, or more properly the stand of trees, since the rowans are growing in a bunch, trunks no thicker than my forearms. The berries are orange, not the bright orange of autumn. They're a deeper color this time of year, but they still stand out against the white snow, the dark lines of the branches, and those birds. Tiny splashes of color. The ground under the tree is littered with them, though the snow's covering them up now.

I can't hear the starlings through the glass. They're probably not making any noise. Too busy chowing down on the berries and keeping their perches as the wind makes the branches sway wildly in sudden snowy gusts. I should get up, but I don't want to lose this moment. I want to lie here and let it stretch out as far as it can go.

I wish the boy were home. I'd ask her to bring me some tea, only she's off working at the gallery this morning. Commerce stops for no one, not even on Sunday anymore.

Have I confused you? Sorry. I started calling Eliza "the boy" after she got her hair cut. The longest she lets it grow anymore is about the length of my pinky finger. It used to fall to the middle of her back like mine still does and then we really looked like the sisters some people think we are.

The boy and I aren't really a couple, like we don't sleep together or anything, but we're closer than friends and don't date, which tends to confuse people when they first meet us and try to fit us into an appropriate mental pigeonhole. Sorry, I don't have one that really works any better myself. You could call us soul mates, I guess, though that's not much clearer, is it?

We met when we were both going through a particularly rough time. Neither of us had friends or family or any kind of support system to fall back on. We were solitary sadnesses until we literally bumped into each other at a La-La-La Human Steps performance and acquired each other. I can't explain it, but things just clicked between us, right there in the foyer of the Standish, and we've been pretty much inseparable ever since.

The boy's the creative one. Long before we met, she was always drawing and painting and making something out of nothing—an amazing ability if you ask me. Forget fairy-tale stuff; that's the only real magic we're going to find in this world. The creative impulse, and the way that people can connect—you know, we might be separate islands of muscle, bone, and flesh, but something in our souls is still able to bridge that impossible gap.

Okay, that's two magics. So sue me.

It's through the boy that we got involved with the Crowsea arts crowd and met Jilly, Sophie, and the others. Me? Well, when I was younger, the only thing I was any good at was being a troublemaker. These days my claim to fame is that I've cleaned up my act and don't cause problems for people anymore.

The boy and I opened the gallery about a year and a half ago, now. The Bone Circus Gallery—don't ask where we got the name. It was just there waiting for us when we decided this was what we wanted to do. We have a different artist showcased every month as well as a general selection of miscellaneous artists' work, postcards, posters, and prints. We carry art supplies, too, and the boy has a studio in back. The art supplies really pay the rent some months, plus it's a way for the boy to get a deep discount on the stuff she needs for her own work.

So life's been treating us well. Maybe we're not rich, and the boy's not famous—yet—but we pay the bills. Better still, she gets to work at what she loves and I've discovered that not only do I like running this little shop and gallery of ours, but I'm good at it, too. It's the first time I've ever been good at anything.

Of course the way the world works is, you don't ever get too comfortable with what you've got, because if you do, something'll come along to pull the rug out from under you. In our case, it's how the boy got co-opted into this fairyland of Jilly's.

It starts while I'm lying in bed, watching the starlings gorge on rowan berries.

2

Eliza Casey loved a winter's day such as this. Clouds of fat, lazy snow drifting down, the sounds of the city muffled by the ever-deepening white blanket—footsteps, traffic, sirens, all. She didn't mind being bundled up like a roly-poly teddy bear as she trundled down the snowy streets, nor that it was her turn to open the gallery this Sunday morning. Not when it entailed her getting up early and out into this weather.

Too much of winter in the city involved dirty slush and bitter cold, frayed tempers and complaints about the wind chill, the icy pavement, the perceived interminable length of the season. A snowfall like this, early in the morning when she pretty much had the streets to herself, was like a gift, a whisper of quiet magic. A piece of enchanted time stolen from the regular whirl and spin of the world in which it felt as though anything could happen.

She was humming happily to herself by the time she reached the gallery. A gust of wind rocked the store sign as she went up the steps, dropping a clump of snow on her head and making her laugh even as some of it went sliding down the back of her neck. She swept the porch and steps, then went inside and stomped the snow from her boots in the hall. By the time she'd put the cash float in the register and made a cup of tea, another inch or so of snow had already accumulated on the porch. Since she wasn't opening for another twenty minutes, she decided to wait until then before sweeping again. First she'd have her tea.

Her studio at the back of the store tempted her, but she resolutely ignored its lure. Carrying her tea mug around the gallery with her, she busied herself with dusting, straightening the prints and postcards in their racks, tidying and restocking the art supplies that provided the gallery with its main bread and butter. By the time she was done, it was a few minutes before opening.

She put her parka back on and went out into the hall. It was as she was reaching for the broom where it was leaning up in the corner by the door that she noticed the coppery glint of a penny lying on the floor. The old rhyme went through her mind:

Find a penny, pick it up, and all the day you'll have good luck.

She bent down, fingers stretched out to pluck it up from the hardwood floor, then jumped back as the penny made a turtle-like transformation from coin into a tiny man. Legs, arms, and a head popped out from a suddenly plump little body and he scurried off, quick as a cockroach. Hardly able to believe what her own two eyes were showing her, she watched as he sped toward a crack between the baseboard and the floor, squeezed in through the narrow opening, and was gone.

Slowly she sat down on the floor, gaze locked on where he'd disappeared.

"Oh my," she said, unaware that she was speaking aloud.

She looked up and down the length of the hall, wishing there was someone with her to confirm what she'd just seen. It was like something out of Mary Norton's *The Borrowers*, or one of William Dunthorn's Smalls come to life. But she was alone with the impossibility of the experience and already the rational part of her mind was reshuffling the memory of what she'd seen, explaining it away.

It hadn't been a penny in the first place, so of course it hadn't turned into a little man. It was only a bug that she'd startled. A beetle, though it wasn't summer. A cockroach, though they'd never had them in the building before.

Except . . . except . . .

She could so clearly call up the round swell of the little man's tummy and his spindly limbs. The tiny startled gaze that had met her own before he had scooted away.

"Oh, my," she said again.

3

It's not that I don't want to believe; it's that I can't.

I'm as romantically inclined as the next person and can fully appreciate the notion of faeries dancing in some moonlit glade, or dwarves laboring over their silver and gold jewelry in some hidden kingdom, deep underground. Really, I can. But I also believe it's important to differentiate between fact and fiction—to keep one's day-dreams separate from the realities of day-to-day life. It's when you mix the two that the trouble starts. Trust me. Living the first seventeen years of my life with a seriously schizophrenic mother, I know all about this.

So I subscribe to the scientific contention that nothing is proven until it can be shown to be repeatable. It makes perfect sense to me that anything that only happens once should be considered anecdotal, and therefore worthless from a scientific point of view. If faeries live at the bottom of the garden, they should always be observable. Even if you have to stand on one foot during the second night of the full moon, with a pomegranate in your pocket and your head cocked a certain way. Every time you complete the specifications, you should see them.

"The problem with that," Jilly said when we were talking about it a while ago, "is that *everything* happens only once."

"You're being too literal," I told her.

"Maybe you're not being literal enough."

I shook my head. "No. I just think it's important to be grounded, that's all. To know that if I drop something, gravity will do its thing. That if I open the door to my room, I won't find some forgotten ruin of Atlantis there instead of my bed and dresser. I couldn't live in a world where anything can happen."

"That's not what it's about. It's about staying open to the possibility that there's more to the world than what most of us have agreed is there to be seen. Just because something can't be measured and weighed in a laboratory doesn't mean it doesn't exist."

"I don't know," I said. "Sounds like a pretty good guideline to me."

But Jilly shook her head. "If you're going to be like that, what makes it any less of a leap in faith to believe in something that you need a microscope or other special equipment to see? Who's to say how much your observations are being manipulated by electronics and doodads?"

"Now you're just being silly."

Jilly smiled. "Depends on your point of view. Lots of people would say I was only being practical."

"Right. The same people who didn't believe in elephants at the turn of the century because they'd never seen one themselves."

"It's the same difference with an otherworldly being," Jilly said. "Just because you've never seen one, doesn't mean they don't exist."

I refuse to accept that. Accepting that would only lead to craziness and I've had enough of that to last me a lifetime. My mother spent more time with her imaginary companions, arguing and fighting and crying, than she did with us kids. There's no way I'm even cracking the door on the possibility of that happening to me.

4

It was a long moment before Eliza finally stood up again. Mechanically, she took the broom, went outside and swept the porch and steps once more, then returned to the gallery. She hung her parka in the closet and sat down behind the cash counter, started to reach for the phone, then thought better of it. What would she say? Sarah would think she'd gone mad. But she felt she had to tell someone.

Picking up a pencil, she turned over one of the flyers advertising a Zeffy Lacerda concert at the YoMan next weekend and made a sketch of what she'd seen. Thought she'd seen. The tiny man with his round moon of a body and twig-thin arms and the little startled eyes. She drew him changing from penny to little man. Another of him looking up at her. Another of him squeezing in through the crack between the baseboard and floor, fat little rear end sticking out and legs wiggling furiously.

No, she thought, looking at her drawings. Sarah definitely wouldn't believe that she'd seen this little man. No one would. She hardly believed it herself. Truth was, the whole experience had left her feeling vaguely nervous and unsettled. It was as though the floor had suddenly gone spongy underfoot, as though the whole world had become malleable, capable of stretching in ways it shouldn't be able to. It was hard to trust that anything was the way it seemed to be. She found herself looking around the shop, constantly imagining movement in the corner of her eye. She grew increasingly more tense with the pressure of feeling that at any moment the unknown and previously unseen was about to manifest again.

But at the same time she was filled with a giddy exhilaration, a kind of heady, senseless good humor that stretched a grin on her lips and made her feel that everything she looked at she was seeing for the first time. The art hanging from the walls was vibrant, the colors almost pulsing. The spiraling grain in the room's wooden trim, window frames, and wainscotting pulled at her gaze, drawing it down into its twists and turns. The smell of the turps and solvents from her studio behind her had never had such a presence and bite before. It wasn't so much unpleasant as so very immediate.

This, she realized suddenly, was what Jilly meant when she talked about the epiphany of experiencing magic, howsoever small a piece of the mystery you stumbled upon. It redefined everything. It wasn't a scary thing, in and of itself; it only felt scary at first because it was so surprising.

She smiled. That's who she could call, she thought. She laid her pencil down and reached for the phone, but before she could dial, she heard the front door open and someone stamping their feet in the hall. When she looked up, it was to find Jilly standing in the doorway. Jilly gave her a wave, then shook the snow from her tangled hair, brushed it from her parka.

"Oh, good," she said, removing her mittens. "You are open. I wasn't sure when I saw the closed sign in the window, but I could see that the steps had been swept so I thought I'd give it a try anyway."

Eliza blinked in surprise. "I can't believe you're here."

"Oh, come on. The weather's not that bad. In fact, I rather like this kind of a snowfall. Pooh on the winter grinches, I say."

"No, I mean I was just about to call you."

"With the most tremendous good news, I hope."

"Well, I . . ."

But by that point Jilly was standing by the counter and looking down at Eliza's sketches. Her eyes, already a startling blue, sparkled even brighter with merriment.

"Pennymen!" she said. "Oh, aren't they just the best?"

"You know what he is?"

Jilly gave her a puzzled look. "You don't? But they're your drawings."

"No. I mean, they are, but I've never heard of a pennyman before. I just thought . . . I just saw one a few moments ago . . . out in the hall . . . and . . ."

Her voice trailed off.

Jilly smiled. "And now you don't know what to make of it at all."

You didn't have to spend much time with Jilly for the conversation to turn to things not quite of this world. She claimed an intimate knowledge with the curious magical beings that populated many of her paintings, a point of view that frustrated die-hard realists such as Sarah at the same time as it enchanted those like Eliza who would love to believe, couldn't quite, but definitely leaned in that direction under the spell of Jilly's stories and firm belief. Or at least Eliza did so for the duration of the story.

"I guess that's pretty much it," Eliza admitted.

Jilly took off her parka and dropped it on the floor, then settled down in the extra chair that they kept behind the counter for visitors.

"Well," she said, "pennymen are very lucky. Christy wrote about them in one of his books."

She cocked an eyebrow, but Eliza had to shake her head. Christy Riddell was a friend of Jilly's, a local author considered to be quite the expert on urban folklore and myths. Eliza had lost count of how many books he'd written.

"I guess I haven't read that one," she said.

Jilly nodded. "Who can keep up with the man?" She scrunched her brow for a moment, thinking, then went on. "Anyway, the pennymen are all tied up with penny folklore. They start their lives in the branches of the penny trees."

Eliza gave her a blank look.

"Which is another name for trembling aspens," Jilly told her.

"Their leaves *do* look like coins," Eliza said. "The way they move in a breeze."

"Exactly. Except the pennymen are a coppery color—skin, hair, clothes, and all—and sort of turtlelike, since they can draw in their limbs and head and lie flat on the ground, looking exactly like a coin. Seeing one is like picking up the penny for luck. When they live in your house, they project a . . . I suppose you could call it an aura that promotes thriftiness and honesty."

Eliza smiled. "As in pennywise?"

"You've got it. And then there's that business with 'a penny for your thoughts.' Supposedly, every time that's offered, the pennymen acquire those thoughts and add them to what Christy calls 'the long memory'—the history of a people, or a family, or a city, or a social circle; a kind of connective stream of thoughts and memories that define the collective. A non-monetary wealth of song and poetry, stories and gossip, that we can access through dreams."

"Really?"

Jilly shrugged. "That's what Christy says—though they have to take a liking to you first. The problem is, they can also be mischievous little buggers if they decide you need to be taken down a notch or two. Not malicious, but definitely . . ." She looked for the word she wanted. "Vexing."

"But they're so small—what could they do?"

"Being small doesn't necessarily mean they can't be a bother. They can be very good at hiding your keys, or the pen you were sure you put down, right there, just a moment ago. Maybe they'll switch all the auto-dial numbers on your phone. Or wet your postage stamps so they're all stuck together when you go to use them. Little things."

Jilly looked down at Eliza's sketches again.

"I've never seen one myself," she said, "but you've drawn them exactly the way I imagined they'd look from Christy's descriptions."

"So what does it mean—my seeing one the way I did?"

Jilly laughed. "Mostly, it doesn't mean anything. It just is. It's like seeing a murder of crows, or a particularly wonderful sunset—you just appreciate the experience for what it is. The beauty of it. And the wonder. And how it can make you smile."

"But everything feels so different now," Eliza said. "It's like . . . I don't know. It's like I feel as though anything can happen now."

"And somewhere, it probably does."

"You know what I mean."

Jilly nodded. "Let me see if I can remember how Christy first explained it to me. What's happened is that you've now cracked open a door in the wall set up by the rational part of your brain—the part that makes it easier for us to function in what everybody perceives as the regular, logical world—and your own logic is struggling to shut it while the part of you that leans toward whimsy and wonder wants to push it as wide open as it can go. You have to learn to balance the two, though most people end up simply shutting the door again and not even remembering that it's there. They're not even aware that they're doing it; it's simple self-preservation because living with the door open, or simply ajar, can be very confusing."

"I'll say."

"But not necessarily a bad thing."

Eliza sighed. "Unless you're Sarah."

"There's that," Jilly agreed sympathetically.

5

There's something different about the boy when she comes home that night, but I can't quite put my finger on it. She's wearing a glow, but that could just be the weather. She loves the kind of snowfall we've had today. Some people get grumpy during a Newford winter; the boy only gets more cheerful. It's in the summer that she wilts.

I've finally gotten out of bed and made up for my earlier laziness by tidying the apartment and putting together dinner—a chicken curry, with nan and a yogurt-cucumber salad on the side. We have dinner and later we watch a video, a remake of *Sabrina* that I decide was much better in the original with Hepburn and Bogey, but the boy likes it.

Later, when I stop by the door of her bedroom to say goodnight, I find her looking at sketches of little round cartoon men that it turns out she did at the gallery earlier today. I'm surprised to see them because she usually works in a much more realistic mode, like the project she's been working on for the past few months, a series of landscapes, the connective thread being that each has a ladder in it. You don't always spot it right away, but it's there. The nice thing about the paintings is that the inclusion of the ladder is never forced. Odd, sometimes. Even a little startling. But never forced. These drawings . . . they're more along the lines of what Jilly does. Fat-bellied mini-ature men—I know they're tiny because of the size references she's included in a couple of the drawings. A running shoe in one. Tubes of oil paint in another. They're fun—whimsical—and I find myself wondering if she's taken on a commission for a poster or something. Or maybe she's decided to develop a comic strip. There're worse things than having your work syndicated in hundreds of morning papers.

"What are these?" I ask.

"Pennymen," she tells me. "Coins that turn into little people when they think we're not looking."

I see the connection now. Lose the little heads and skinny limbs and they'd look just like pennies. In fact, there are coins in a couple of the sketches, which must be the pennymen at rest.

"Cute," I say.

She shrugs and bundles the sketches together, tosses them onto her desk. I wonder again why she's drawing them, but she doesn't say, and I don't ask. I get that funny feeling again—like I did when she first came home—that there's something different, something changed, only then she smiles and says goodnight, and I stop worrying about it.

But in the days that follow, I find myself thinking about it again because the boy seems to have developed a few odd mannerisms. Sometimes I see her sitting with her head cocked, listening, when there's nothing to hear. Or she'll turn quickly, as though she caught movement from the corner of her eye, but there're only the two of us in the room.

There's something familiar about all of this, but I don't place the familiarity immedi-ately. Then one day it hits me.

She reminds me of my mother—my mother and her invisible companions—and my heart sinks.

6

It was two weeks before Eliza caught another glimpse of a pennyman. She was sitting in her studio, working on a canvas, when from the corner of her eye, she saw the slow, careful movement along the baseboard. As soon as she turned toward him, the little man dropped to the ground and there was only what appeared to be a penny lying there on the floor.

Eliza put her brush down and stepped around her easel. The pennyman remained motionless as she approached it. She knelt down for a closer look and cleared her throat. Feeling a little self-conscious, she addressed the coin.

"You don't have to be afraid," she said. "I would never hurt you. Honestly."

Not surprisingly, the copper penny made no reply. She didn't even get a small head poking its way turtlelike out of the body to look back at her. What response she did get came from the doorway to the gallery where Sarah was now standing, a puzzled look on her face.

"Eliza," she said. "*Who* are you talking to?"

"The pennyman," Eliza said, without thinking.

She'd looked over at Sarah, then back at where the pennyman had turned into a coin, but neither penny nor little man were there now.

"The pennyman," Sarah repeated.

Slowly Eliza returned her attention to her roommate.

"It's not like what you think," she told Sarah.

"How's that?"

You don't have to be afraid, Eliza wanted to say. I'm not going crazy like your mother did.

But of course she couldn't.

"They're real," Eliza said instead. "I didn't make them up."

Sarah nodded and Eliza watched her roommate's features close up, could feel the distance grow between them.

"Of course you didn't," Sarah said.

She turned away and went back into the gallery. Eliza gave the empty stretch of wooden floor a last scrutinizing look, then rose from where she'd been kneeling.

"Sarah!" she called.

Sarah reappeared in the doorway.

"Don't," she said, before Eliza could speak. "Don't make it worse."

"But there really are pennymen. I've seen them. It's true."

Sarah shook her head. "No, it's only true for you."

7

I know I'm being a lousy friend. I should be more sympathetic, but the boy should know that this is the last thing in the world I can deal with. I can't *ever* go through this again. It's not like she doesn't know. It's not like we haven't talked it out a hundred times before—the separate sorrows that we each had to carry and deal with on our own until that day we met. My mother and the boy's fiancé.

She got left at the altar, which is weird enough, except he was the one who wanted to get married so badly, he wanted the huge wedding, he's the one who blew it all up way out of proportion so that when he abandoned her in the church, the embarrassment and lack of self-worth she felt was exaggerated all out of proportion as well. And somehow the whole sorry mess became her fault. Her family blamed her. His family blamed her. She became the pariah in their circle of friends, none of whom would stand by her when she needed them, not even those who'd been her friends before she'd met him.

We helped each other. We made each other. Being an artist was something she'd only ever dreamed of before; I'm the one who stood by her and convinced her to make it a reality. I don't say this to make it seem like I should be getting some kind of a medal for perseverance and support above and beyond the call of duty, because she went through just as much for me. She's the one who finally made me believe I could be a normal functioning human being myself, that my mother's genes weren't going to tune me into broadcasts from loopyville and everything that would subsequently entail.

Except now she's the one who's gone all *X-Files* on me. The truth isn't out there; it's on TV and it's not truth at all, it's just tabloid stories brought to life by writers trying to make a buck. The truth is we can't buy into the paranormal because it undermines everything that grounds us, that lets us function in the real world. And never forget, whatever little fairy-tale encounters we think we've had, whatever mysterious voices we hear whispering in our ears, or lights we see in the sky that can't be explained, at some point, we all have to return to the real world.

I guess the worst thing is that now there's a part of the boy that I don't recognize anymore. Now there's a whole side to her that's stopped making sense and that scares me. Because if part of her can become a stranger, what's to stop the rest of her from doing the same?

She could become anyone. She could have been anyone all along and I was just kidding myself that we knew each other. I find myself needing to ask, is this how we spend our lives—imagining each other? Because you can never really *know* what another person's thinking or feeling, can you? And just because they're thinking or feeling one thing at one time, what's to stop them from changing their minds about it?

Someone once told me never to fall in love with a place or a person because they're only on loan. What kind of a way is that to live? I thought when I first heard that. But now I understand a little better. It's because what you fall in love with doesn't last. Everything changes. Sometimes you can grow with it, but sometimes you just grow apart instead.

Earlier I said that magic belongs in stories and that the real world isn't a story. Not that kind, anyway.

I still believe that. Only now I wish I didn't.

8

Jilly found Eliza sitting in the window booth of The Dear Mouse Diner on Lee Street, nursing a cup of coffee that had long since gone cold. Outside, the snow had turned to freezing rain, making the footing more than a little slippery. Jilly was on her way home from an evening course she was teaching at the Newford School of Art and had almost taken a fall more than once before spying Eliza in the window and deciding to come in to join her.

"Hey, you," she said, sliding into the booth across from Eliza.

Eliza looked up and nodded hello. "Hey, yourself."

Jilly leaned over the table and peered into Eliza's cup. Her cold coffee looked about as appealing as old bathwater, complete with a dark ring at surface level crusted on the white china.

"You want a refill?" she asked.

Eliza shrugged, which Jilly took to mean yes. She brought the cup over to the counter and returned with a fresh one for each of them. They were busy for a moment, opening creamers and sugar packets, stirring the contents into their cups. Then Eliza sighed and looked out the window again.

"I feel this is all my fault," Jilly said.

Eliza looked back at her. "Don't. I'm the one who saw what Sarah can't handle as being real."

"But if I hadn't talked them up to you . . ."

Eliza shook her head. "It still wouldn't change my having seen the pennymen. I didn't mean to ever say that I believed they were real. Not to her. I mean, of all people, I *know* how she feels about that kind of thing. But she caught me off guard and it kind of slipped out and then, well, I wasn't about to start lying to her. That's just not something we'd do to each other."

"Of course not."

"Lying by omission was bad enough."

Jilly nodded. "So what's she doing now?"

"I'm not sure. I know she's staying at the Y, but she hasn't been back to the gallery in a week and she won't talk to me at all."

"I don't understand. Was it that bad with her mother?"

"Probably worse. I think she's scared of two things, actually. The first is that the pennymen aren't real, and that means I'm going to go the same route her mother did."

"And the second?"

"That the pennymen are real and so maybe her mother wasn't crazy."

"But she was diagnosed—"

"By the same terms of reference that say pennymen can't exist."

Jilly gave a slow nod. "I get it."

"The guilt would kill Sarah. You know, what if the voices and the invisible people were real?"

"Except there's a big difference between mental illness and an encounter with magic," Jilly said.

"But you can see how some people wouldn't see it that way. For them it has to be one or the other with no grey areas in between."

"Too true," Jilly said. "Unfortunately."

"And it was so hard for Sarah," Eliza went on. "I mean, by all accounts, her mother was way out there. Violent, if she stopped taking her medication. Imagine growing up in an environment like that. Screaming and flailing at things no one else could see. And maybe the worst thing was that her father wouldn't accept that it was an actual illness they were dealing with, so he wouldn't let her be hospitalized during the worst of it. He'd go off to work during the day, hang out with his buds in the evening, and there'd be Sarah and her little brother, left at home, trying to deal with all of this."

Eliza looked away, out the window again. The freezing rain was still coming down.

"Anyway," she said without looking away. "You can see why she wouldn't want to go through it again."

"So what are you going to do?"

"I don't know," Eliza said. "All I know is I miss her terribly."

"Would it help if I tried to talk to her?"

That woke the first smile Jilly had gotten from her so far this evening.

"What do *you* think?" Eliza said.

"This is true," Jilly admitted. "I'm not exactly renowned for my objective point of view when it comes to this sort of thing."

"But thanks awfully for offering."

Jilly nodded. "I guess we'll just have to hope that when she really thinks about it, when she weighs your friendship against how she has to deal with what you've experienced, the friendship will win out. That she'll realize that you're not her mother."

"I suppose," Eliza said. "But I'm not holding my breath waiting for it to happen."

"But you can hope."

"Of course," Eliza said. "There's always hope."

She didn't sound convinced. Jilly reached across the table and took her hand.

"The one thing I refuse to do," she said, "is give up on anyone. We're all carrying around devils inside us, but the thing to remember is, we're carrying angels, too. Sometimes we just have to wait a little longer for the angels to show up, that's all."

"Thanks," Eliza said. "I needed to hear something like that."

9

I've taken to riding the subways this past week—like I used to before I met the boy. Somehow I don't feel quite so lost and all alone sitting in one of these rattling cars, watching the dark tunnels go by. I don't know what I'm trying to find—or maybe hide from. I'm not really thinking at all. Except that's a lie, because at the same time as my head feels like a numbed bruise that can't hold one clear thought, I'm thinking about everything, all at once. The boy and my mother and coins that can turn into little men. Or is it vice versa?

I went to the Crowsea Public Library, to the Newford Room, and took down the faerie-myth book of Christy's. There's a whole section on the boy's pennymen in it and I read it through a few times. Doesn't make it any more real. I mean, where's the proof? Where's some straightforward empirical evidence? Surely if they actually existed we'd be reading about them in the real newspapers. They'd have pennymen in labs somewhere, running experiments on them, scientists would be publishing their findings. But there's nada. Just a few inches of type in an admittedly entertaining, but hardly textbook-factual collection of folk tales and myths.

The train pulls into the Williamson Street Station. The three people sharing my car get off. Nobody gets on. I stare down at my feet as the train pulls away again, heading for the next station. My clunky shoes don't hold a lot of interest, so I keep going, looking at the floor in the middle of the aisle, attention traveling across the car, under the opposite seat. Then I stop, gaze locked on the shiny copper penny lying there beside a candy wrapper.

I smile mirthlessly.

Penny? Or pennyman?

If I reach over to pick it up, will it scurry away? Or will it hold to its shape? Would I pick up a coin, or something soft and fleshy, squirming in between my fingers as it tries to escape?

We hit a rough patch of track and I grab for the nearest pole to keep my balance. When I look back under the opposite seat, the coin is gone. Did it simply roll away, or did it sprout limbs and walk away?

I realize it doesn't matter. Somewhere between seeing the coin and its disappearance, I remember how much the boy means to me. Her friendship is more important than the question of whether or not pennymen exist. Where does it say that we both have to agree on everything to be friends? Where does it say that just because she's convinced her pennymen are real, she's going to slide away from me the way my mother did?

I get off at the next station and find a pay phone. I'm calling home, but the boy doesn't answer. That's okay. I'd rather talk to her in person, anyway.

I decide to walk back to the apartment. Maybe she'll be back by the time I get there. If not, I can wait.

I don't know what I'll say to her when I see her. I won't say I believe—I can't do that because it wouldn't be true. I guess I'll just start with I'm sorry and see where that takes us.

Twa Corbies

*As I was walkin' all alane
I heard twa corbies makin' mane . . .*
—from "Twa Corbies," Scots traditional

1

Gerda couldn't sleep again. She stood by the upright piano, wedding picture in hand, marveling at how impossibly young she and Jan had been. Why, they were little more than children. Imagine making so serious a commitment at such an age, raising a family and all.

Her insomnia had become a regular visitor over the past few years—often her only one. The older she got, the less sleep she seemed to need. She went to bed late, got up early, and the only weariness she carried through her waking hours was in her heart. A loneliness that was stronger some nights than others. But on those nights, the old four-poster double bed felt too big for her. All that extra room spread over the map of the quilt like unknown territories, encroaching on her ability to relax, even with the cats lolling across the hills and vales of the bed's expanse.

It hadn't always been that way. When Jan was still alive—before the children were born, and after they'd moved out to accept the responsibility of their own lives—she and Jan could spend the whole day in bed, passing the time with long conversations and silly little jokes, sharing tea and biscuits while they read the paper, making slow and sweet love. . . .

She sighed. But Jan was long gone and she was an old woman with only her cats and piano to keep her company now. This late at night, the piano could offer her no comfort—it wouldn't be fair to her neighbors. The building was like her, old and worn. The sound of the piano would carry no matter how softly she played. But the cats . . .

One of them was twining in and out against her legs now—Swarte Meg, the youngest of the three. She was just a year old, black as the night sky, as gangly and unruly as a pumpkin vine. Unlike the other two, she still craved regular attention and loved to be carried around in Gerda's arms. It made even the simplest of tasks difficult to attend to, but there was nothing in Gerda's life that required haste anymore.

Replacing the wedding picture on the top of the piano, she picked Swarte Meg up and moved over to the window that provided her with a view of the small, cobblestoned square outside.

By day there was always someone to watch. Mothers and nannies with their children, sitting on the bench and chatting with each other while their charges slept in prams. Old men smoking cigarettes, pouring coffee for each other out of a thermos, playing checkers and dominoes. Neighborhood gossips standing by the river wall, exaggerating their news to give it the desired impact. Tourists wandering into the square and looking confused, having wandered too far from the more commercial streets.

By this time of night, all that changed. Now the small square was left to fend for itself. It seemed diminished, shadows pooling deep against the buildings, held back only by the solitary street lamp that rose up behind the wrought-iron bench at its base.

Except . . .

Gerda leaned closer to the windowpane.

What was this . . . ?

2

Sophie's always telling me to pace myself. The trouble is, when I get absorbed in a piece, I can spend whole days in front of the canvas, barely stopping to eat or rest until the day's work is done. My best times, though, are early in the morning and late at night—morning for the light, the late hours for the silence. The phone doesn't ring, no one knocks on your door. I usually seem to finish a piece at night. I know I have to see it again in the morning light, so to stop myself from fiddling with it, I go out walking—anywhere, really.

When the work's gone well, I can feel a deep thrumming build up inside me and I wouldn't be able to sleep if I wanted to, doesn't matter how tired I might be. What I need then is for the quiet streets of the city and the swell of the dark night above them to pull me out of myself and my painting. To render calm to my quickened pulse. Walking puts a peace in my soul that I desperately need after having had my nose up close to a canvas for far too long.

Any part of the city will do, but Old Market's the best. I love it here, especially at this time of night. There's a stillness in the air and even the houses and shops seem to be holding their breath. All I can hear is the sound of my boots on the cobblestones. One day I'm going to move into one of the old brick buildings that line these streets—it doesn't matter which one, I love them all. As much for where they are, I suppose, as for what they are.

Because Old Market's a funny place. It's right downtown, but when you step into its narrow, cobblestoned streets, it's like you've stepped back in time, to an older, other place. The rhythms are different here. The sound of traffic seems to disappear far more quickly than should be physically possible. The air tastes cleaner and it still carries hints of baking bread, Indonesian spices, cabbage soups, fish, and sausages long after midnight.

On a night like this I don't even bother to change. I just go out in my paint-stained clothes, the scent of my turps and linseed trailing along behind me. I don't worry about how I look because there's no one to see me. By now, all the cafés are closed up and except for the odd cat, everybody's in bed, or checking out the nightlife downtown. Or almost everybody.

I hear the sound of their wings first—loud in the stillness. Then I see them, a pair of large crows that swoop down out of the sky to dart down a street no wider than an alleyway, just ahead of me.

I didn't think crows were nocturnal, but then they're a confusing sort of animal at the best of times. Just consider all the superstitions associated with them. Good luck, bad luck—it's hard to work them all out.

Some say that seeing a crow heralds a death.

Some say a death brings crows so that they can ferry us on from this world to the next.

Some say it just means there's a change coming.

And then there's that old rhyme. One for sorrow, two for mirth . . .

It gets so you don't know what to think when you see one. But I do know it's definitely oh so odd to see them at this time of night. I can't help but follow in their wake. I don't even have to consider it, I just go, the quickened scuff of my boots not quite loud enough to envelop the sound of their wings.

The crows lead me through the winding streets, past the closed shops and cafés, past the houses with their hidden gardens and occasional walkways overhead that join separate buildings, one to the other, until we're deep in Old Market, following a steadily narrowing lane that finally opens out onto a small town square.

I know this place. Christy used to come here and write sometimes, though I don't think he's done it for a while. And he's certainly not here tonight.

The square is surrounded on three sides by tall brick buildings leaning against each other, cobblestones underfoot. There's an old-fashioned streetlight in the center of the square with a wrought-iron bench underneath, facing the river. On the far side of the river I can barely see Butler Common, the wooded hills beyond its lawns, and on the tops of the hills, a constellation of twinkling house lights.

By the bench is an overturned shopping cart with all sorts of junk spilling out of it. I can make out bundles of clothes, bottles and cans, plastic shopping bags filled with who knows what, but what holds my gaze is the man lying beside the cart. I've seen him before, cadging spare change, pushing that cart of his. He looks bigger than he probably is because of the layers of baggy clothes, though I remember him as being portly anyway. He's got a toque on his head and he's wearing fingerless gloves and mismatched shoes. His hairline is receding, but he still has plenty of long, dirty blonde hair. His stubble is just this side of an actual beard, greyer than his hair. He's lying face-up, staring at the sky.

At first I think he's sleeping, then I think he's collapsed there. It's when I see the ghost that I realize he's dead.

The ghost is sitting on the edge of the cart—an insubstantial version of the prone figure, but this one is wearing a rough sort of armor instead of those layers of raggedy clothes. A boiled leather breastplate over a rough sort of tunic, leggings and leather boots. From his belt hangs an empty scabbard. Not big enough for a broadsword, but not small either.

I start forward, only I've forgotten the crows. The flap of their descending wings draws my gaze up and then I can't hold onto the idea of the dead man and his ghost anymore, because somewhere between the moment of their final descent and landing, the pair change from crows into girls.

They're not quite children, but they don't have adult physiques either. I'm just over five feet, but they're shorter and even slighter of build. Their skin is the color of coffee with a dash of milk, their hair an unruly lawn of blue-black spikes, their faces triangular in shape with large green eyes and sharp features. I can't tell them apart and decide they must be twins, even dressing the same in black combat boots, black leggings, and black oversized raggedy sweaters that seem to be made of feathers. They look, for all the world, like a pair of . . .

"Crow girls," I hear myself say in a voice that's barely a whisper.

I lower myself down onto the cobblestones and sit with my back against the brick wall of the house behind me. This is a piece of magic, one of those moments when the lines between what is and what might be blur like smudged charcoal. Pentimento. You can still see the shapes of the preliminary sketch, but now there are all sorts of other things hovering and crowding at the edges of what you initially drew.

I remember how I started thinking about superstitions when I first saw these two girls as crows. How there are so many odd tales and folk beliefs surrounding crows and other black birds, what seeing one, or two, or three might mean. I can't think of one that says anything about seeing them flying at night. Or what to do when you stumble upon a pair of them that can take human form and hold a conversation with a dead man. . . .

One of the girls perches by the head of the corpse and begins to play with its hair, braiding it. The other sits cross-legged on the ground beside her twin and gives her attention to the ghost.

"I was a knight once," the ghost says.

"We remember," one of the girls tells him.

"I'm going to be a knight again."

The girl braiding the corpse's hair looks up at the ghost. "They might not have knights where you're going."

"Do you know that?"

"We don't know anything," the first girl says. She makes a steeple with her hands and looks at him above it. "We just are."

"Tell us about the King's Court again," her twin says.

The ghost gives a slow nod of his head. "It was the greatest court in all the land. . . ."

I close my eyes and lean my head back against the wall of the building I'm sitting against, the bricks pulling at the tangles of my hair. The ghost's voice holds me spellbound and takes me back, in my mind's eye, to an older time.

"It was such a tall building, the tallest in all the land, and the King's chambers were at the very top. When you looked out the window, all creation lay before you."

I start out visualizing one of the office buildings downtown, but the more I listen, the less my mind's eye can hold the image. What starts out as a tall, modern office skyscraper slowly drifts apart into mist, reforms into a classic castle on top of a steep hill with a town spread out along the slopes at its base. At first I see it only from the outside, but then I begin to imagine a large room inside and I fill it with details. I see a hooded hawk on a perch by one window. Tapestries hang from the walls. A king sits on his throne at the head of a long table around which are numerous knights, dressed the same as the ghost. The ghost is there, too. He's younger, taller, his back is straighter. Hounds lounge on the floor.

In Old Market, the dead man talks of tourneys and fairs, of border skirmishes and hunting for boar and pheasant in woods so old and deep we can't imagine their like anymore. And as he speaks, I can see those tourneys and country fairs, the knights and their ladies, small groups of armed men skirmishing in a moorland, the ghost saying farewell to his lady and riding into a forest with his hawk on his arm and his hound trotting beside his horse.

Still, I can't help but hear under the one story he tells, another story. One of cocktail parties and high-rise offices, stocks and mergers, of drops in the market and job losses, alcohol and divorce. He's managed to recast the tragedy of his life into a story from an old picture book. King Arthur. Prince Valiant. The man who lost his job, his wife, and his family, who ended up dying, homeless and alone on the streets where he lived, is an errant knight in the story he tells.

I know this, but I can't see it. Like the crow girls, I'm swallowed by the fairy tale.

The dead man tells now of that day's hunting in the forests near the castle. How his horse is startled by an owl and rears back, throwing him into a steep crevice where he cracks his head on a stone outcrop. The hawk flies from his wrist as he falls, the laces of its hood catching on a branch and tugging off its hood. The hound comes down to investigate, licks his face, then lies down beside him.

When night falls, the horse and hound emerge from the forest. Alone. They approach the King's castle, the hawk flying overhead. And there, the ghost tells us, while his own corpse lies at the bottom of the crevice, his lady stands with another man's arm around her shoulders.

"And then," the ghost says, "the corbies came for their dinner and what baubles they could find."

I open my eyes and blink, startled for a moment to find myself still in Old Market. The scene before me hasn't changed. One of the crow girls has cut off the corpse's braid and now she's rummaging through the items spilled from the shopping cart.

"That's us," the other girl says. "We were the corbies. Did we eat you?"

"What sort of baubles?" her companion wants to know. She holds up a Crackerjack ring that she's found among the litter of the ghost's belongings. "You mean like this?"

The ghost doesn't reply. He stands up and the crow girls scramble to their feet as well.

"It's time for me to go," he says.

"Can I have this?" the crow girl holding the Crackerjack ring asks.

The other girl looks at the ring that's now on her twin's finger. "Can I have one, too?"

The first girl hands her twin the braid of hair that she's cut from the corpse.

After his first decisive statement, the ghost now stands there looking lost.

"But I don't know where to go," he says.

The crow girls return their attention to him.

"We can show you," the one holding the braid tells him.

Her twin nods. "We've been there before."

I watch them as they each take one of his hands and walk with him toward the river. When they reach the low wall, the girls become crows again, flying on either side of the dead man's ghostly figure as he steps through the wall and continues to walk, up into the sky. For one long moment the impossible image holds, then they all disappear. Ghost, crow girls, all.

I sit there for a while longer before I finally manage to stand up and walk over to the shopping cart. I bend down and touch the corpse's throat, two fingers against the carotid artery, searching for a pulse. There isn't any.

I look around and see a face peering down at me from a second-floor window. It's an old woman and I realize I saw her earlier, that she's been there all along. I walk toward her house and knock on the door.

It seems to take forever for anyone to answer, but finally a light comes on in the hall and the door opens. The old woman I saw upstairs is standing there, looking at me.

"Do you have a phone?" I ask. "I need to call 911."

3

What a night it had been, Gerda thought.

She stood on her front steps with the rather self-contained young woman who'd introduced herself as Jilly, not quite certain what to do, what was expected at a time such as this. At least the police had finally gone away, taking that poor homeless man's body with them, though they had left behind his shopping cart and the scatter of his belongings that had been strewn about it.

"I saw you watching from the window," Jilly said. "You saw it all, but you didn't say anything about the crow girls."

Gerda smiled. "Crow girls. I like that. It suits them."

"Why didn't you say anything?"

"I didn't think they'd believe me." She paused for a moment, then added, "Why don't you come in and have a cup of tea?"

"I'd like that."

Gerda knew that her kitchen was clean, but terribly old-fashioned. She didn't know what her guest would think of it. The wooden kitchen table and chairs were the same ones she and Jan had bought when they'd first moved in, more years past than she cared to remember. A drip had put a rusty stain on the porcelain of her sink that simply couldn't be cleaned. The stove and fridge were both circa 1950—bulky, with rounded corners. There was a long wooden counter along one wall with lots of cupboards and shelves above and below it, all loaded with various kitchen accoutrements and knickknacks. The window over the sink was hung with lacy curtains, the sill a jungle of potted plants.

But Jilly seemed delighted by her surroundings. While Gerda started the makings for tea, putting the kettle on the stove, teacups on the table, she got milk from the fridge and brought the sugar bowl to the table.

"Did you know him?" Gerda asked.

She took her Brown Betty teapot down from the shelf. It was rarely used anymore. With so few visitors, she usually made her tea in the cup now.

"The man who died," she added.

"Not personally. But I've seen him around—on the streets. I think his name was Hamish. Or at least that's what people called him."

"The poor man."

Jilly nodded. "It's funny. You forget that everyone's got their own movie running through their heads. He'd pretty much hit rock bottom here, in the world we all share, but the whole time, in his own mind, he was living the life of a questing knight. Who's to say which was more real?"

When the water began to boil, Gerda poured some into the pot to warm it up. Emptying the pot into the sink, she dropped in a pair of teabags and filled the pot, bringing it to the table to steep. She sat down across from her guest, smoothing down her skirt. The cats finally came in to have a look at the company, Swarte Meg first, slipping under the table and up onto Gerda's lap. The other two watched from the doorway.

"Did . . . we really see what I think we saw?" Gerda asked after a moment's hesitation.

Jilly smiled. "Crow girls and a ghost?"

"Yes. Were they real, or did we imagine them?"

"I'm not sure it's important to ask if they were real or not."

"Whyever not?" Gerda said. "It would be such a comfort to know for certain that some part of us goes on."

To know there was a chance one could be joined once more with those who had gone on before. But she left that unsaid.

Jilly leaned her elbow on the table, chin on her hand, and looked toward the window, but was obviously seeing beyond the plants and the view on the far side of the glass panes, her gaze drawn to something that lay in an unseen distance.

"I think we already know that," she finally said.

"I suppose."

Jilly returned her attention to Gerda.

"You know," she said. "I've seen those crow girls before, too—just as girls, not as crows—but I keep forgetting about them, the way the world forgets about people like Hamish." She sat up straighter. "Think how dull we'd believe the world to be without them to remind us. . . ."

Gerda waited a moment, watching her guest's gaze take on that dreamy distant look once more.

"Remind us of what?" she asked after a moment.

Jilly smiled again. "That anything is possible."

Gerda thought about that. Her own gaze went to the window. Outside she caught a glimpse of two crows, flying across the city skyline. She stroked Swarte Meg's soft black fur and gave a slow nod. After what she had seen tonight she could believe it, that anything was possible.

She remembered her husband Jan—not as he'd been in those last years before the illness had taken him, but before that. When they were still young. When they had just married and all the world and life lay ahead of them. That was how she wanted it to be when she finally joined him again.

If anything was possible, then that was how she would have it be.

The Fields Beyond the Fields

I just see my life better in ink.
—Jewel Kilcher, from an interview on MuchMusic, 1997

Saskia is sleeping, but I can't. I sit up at my rolltop desk, writing. It's late, closer to dawn than midnight, but I'm not tired. Writing can be good for keeping sleep at bay. It also helps me make sense of things where simply thinking about them can't. It's too easy to get distracted by a wayward digression when the ink's not holding the thoughts to paper. By focusing on the page, I can step outside myself and look at the puzzle with a clearer eye.

Earlier this evening Saskia and I were talking about magic and wonder, about how it can come and go in your life, or more particularly, how it comes and goes in my life. That's the side of me that people don't get to see when all they can access is the published page. I'm as often a skeptic as a believer. I'm not the one who experiences those oddities that appear in the stories; I'm the one who chronicles the mystery of them, trying to make sense out of what they can impart about us, our world, our preconceptions of how things should be.

The trouble is, mostly life seems to be exactly what it is. I can't find the hidden card waiting to be played because it seems too apparent that the whole hand is already laid out on the table. What you see is what you get, thanks, and do come again.

I want there to be more.

Even my friends assume I'm the knowledgeable expert who writes the books. None of them knows how much of a hypocrite I really am. I listen well and I know exactly what to say to keep the narrative flowing. I can accept everything that's happened to them—the oddest and most absurd stories they tell me don't make me blink an eye—but all the while there's a small voice chanting in the back of my head.

As if, as if, as if. . . .

I wasn't always like this, but I'm good at hiding how I've changed, from those around me, as well as from myself.

But Saskia knows me too well.

"You used to live with a simple acceptance of the hidden world," she said when the conversation finally turned into a circle and there was nothing new to add. "You used to live with magic and mystery, but now you only write about it."

I didn't know how to reply.

I wanted to tell her that it's easy to believe in magic when you're young. Anything you couldn't explain was magic then. It didn't matter if it was science or a fairy tale. Electricity and elves were both infinitely mysterious and equally possible—elves probably more so. It didn't seem particularly odd to believe that actors lived inside your TV set. That there was a repertory company inside the radio, producing its chorus of voices and music. That a fat, bearded man lived at the North Pole and kept tabs on your behavior.

I wanted to tell her that I used to believe she was born in a forest that only exists inside the nexus of a connection of computers, entangled with one another where they meet on the World Wide Web. A Wordwood that appears in pixels on the screen, but has another, deeper existence somewhere out there in the mystery that exists concurrent to the Internet, the way religion exists in the gathering of like minds.

But not believing in any of it now, I wasn't sure that I ever had.

The problem is that even when you have firsthand experience with a piece of magic, it immediately begins to slip away. Whether it's a part of the enchantment, or some inexplicable defense mechanism that's been wired into us either by society or genetics, it doesn't make any difference. The magic still slips away, sliding like a melted icicle along the slick surface of our memories.

That's why some people need to talk about it—the ones who want to hold on to the marvel of what they've seen or heard or felt. And that's why I'm willing to listen, to validate their experience and help them keep it alive. But there's no one around to validate mine. They think my surname Riddell is a happy coincidence, that it means I've solved the riddles of the world instead of being as puzzled by them as they are. Everybody assumes that I'm already in that state of grace where enchantment lies thick in every waking moment, and one's dreams—by way of recompense, perhaps?— are mundane.

As if, as if, as if. . . .

The sigh that escapes me seems self-indulgent in the quiet that holds the apartment. I pick up my pen, put it down when I hear a rustle of fabric, the creak of a spring as the sofa takes someone's weight. The voice of my shadow speaks then, a disembodied voice coming to me from the darkness beyond the spill of the desk's lamplight, but tonight I don't listen to her. Instead I take down volumes of my old journals from where they're lined up on top of my desk. I page through the entries, trying to see if I've really changed. And if so, when.

I don't know what makes sense anymore; I just seem to know what doesn't.

When I was young, I liked to walk in the hills behind our house, looking at animals. Whether they were big or small, it made no difference to me. Everything they did was absorbing. The crow's lazy flight. A red squirrel scolding me from the safety of a hemlock branch, high overhead. The motionless spider in a corner of its patient web.

A quick russet glimpse of a fox before it vanished in the high weeds. The water rat making its daily journeys across Jackson's Pond and back. A tree full of cedar wax-wings, gorging on berries. The constantly shifting pattern of a gnat ballet.

I've never been able to learn what I want about animals from books or nature specials on television. I have to walk in their territories, see the world as they might see it. Walk along the edges of the stories they know.

The stories are the key, because for them, for the animals, everything that clutters our lives, they keep in their heads. History, names, culture, gossip, art. Even their winter and summer coats are only ideas, genetic imprints memorized by their DNA, coming into existence only when the seasons change.

I think their stories are what got me writing. First in journals, accounts as truthful as I could make them, then as stories where actuality is stretched and manipulated, because the lies in fiction are such an effective way to tell emotional truths. I took great comfort in how the lines of words marched from left to right and down the page, building up into a meaningful structure like rows of knitting. Sweater stories. Mitten poems. Long, rambling journal entries like the scarves we used to have when we were kids, scarves that seemed to go on forever.

I never could hold the stories in my head, though in those days I could absorb them for hours, stretched out in a field, my gaze lost in the expanse of forever sky above. I existed in a timeless place then, probably as close to Zen as I'll ever get again. Every sense alert, all existence focused on the present moment. The closest I can come to recapturing that feeling now is when I set pen to paper. For those brief moments when the words flow unimpeded, everything I am is simultaneously focused into one perfect detail and expanded to encompass everything that is. I own the stories in those moments, I am the stories, though, of course, none of them really belongs to me. I only get to borrow them. I hold them for a while, set them down on paper, and then let them go.

I can own them again, when I reread them, but then so can anyone.

According to Jung, at around the age of six or seven we separate and then hide away the parts of ourselves that don't seem acceptable, that don't fit in the world around us. Those unacceptable parts that we secret away become our shadow.

I remember reading somewhere that it can be a useful exercise to visualize the person our shadow would be if it could step out into the light. So I tried it. It didn't work immediately. For a long time, I was simply talking to myself. Then, when I did get a response, it was only a spirit voice I heard in my head. It could just as easily have been my own. But over time, my shadow took on more physical attributes, in the way that a story grows clearer and more pertinent as you add and take away words, molding its final shape.

Not surprisingly, my shadow proved to be the opposite of who I am in so many ways. Bolder, wiser, with a better memory and a penchant for dressing up with costumes, masks, or simply formal wear. A cocktail dress in a raspberry patch. A green man mask in a winter field. She's short, where I'm tall. Dark-skinned, where I'm light. Red-haired, where mine's dark. A girl to my boy, and now a woman as I'm a man.

If she has a name, she's never told me it. If she has an existence outside the times we're together, she has yet to divulge it either. Naturally I'm curious about where she goes, but she doesn't like being asked questions and I've learned not to press her because when I do, she simply goes away.

Sometimes I worry about her existence. I get anxieties about schizophrenia and carefully study myself for other symptoms. But if she's a delusion, it's singular, and otherwise I seem to be as normal as anyone else, which is to say, confused by the barrage of input and stimuli with which the modern world besets us, and trying to make do. Who was it that said she's always trying to understand the big picture, but the trouble is, the picture just keeps getting bigger? Ani DiFranco, I think.

Mostly I don't get too analytical about it—something I picked up from her, I suppose, since left to my own devices, I can worry the smallest detail to death.

We have long conversations, usually late at night, when the badgering clouds swallow the stars and the darkness is most profound. Most of the time I can't see her, but I can hear her voice. I like to think we're friends; even if we don't agree about details, we can usually find common ground on how we'd like things to be.

There are animals in the city, but I can't read their stories the same as I did the ones that lived in the wild. In the forested hills of my childhood.

I don't know when exactly it was that I got so interested in the supernatural, you know, fairy tales and all. I mean, I was always interested in them, the way kids are, but I didn't let them go. I collected unusual and odd facts, read the Brothers Grimm, Lady Gregory, Katharine Briggs, but *Famous Monsters* and ghost stories, too. They gave me something the animals couldn't—or didn't—but I needed it all the same.

Animal stories connected me to the landscape we inhabited—to their world, to my world, to all the wonder that can exist around us. They grounded me, but were no relief from unhappiness and strife. But fairy tales let me escape. Not away from something, but *to* something. To hope. To a world beyond this world where other ways of seeing were possible. Where other ways of treating each other were possible.

An Irish writer, Lord Dunsany, coined the phrase "Beyond the Fields We Know" to describe fairyland, and that's always appealed to me. First there's the comfort of the fields we do know, the idea that it's familiar and friendly. Home. Then there's the otherness of what lies beyond them that so aptly describes what I imagine the alien topography of fairyland to be. The grass is always greener in the next field over, the old saying goes. More appealing, more vibrant. But perhaps it's more dangerous as well. No reason not to explore it, but it's worthwhile to keep in mind that one should perhaps take care.

If I'd thought that I had any aptitude as an artist, I don't think I'd ever have become a writer. All I ever wanted to capture was moments. The trouble is, most people want narrative, so I tuck those moments away in the pages of a story. If I could draw or paint the way I see those moments in my head, I wouldn't have to write about them.

It's scarcely an original thought, but a good painting really can hold all the narrative and emotional impact of a novel—the viewer simply has to work a little harder than a reader does with a book. There are fewer clues. Less taking the viewer by the hand and leading him or her through all the possible events that had to occur to create this visualized moment before them.

I remember something Jilly once said about how everyone should learn to draw competently at an early age, because drawing, she maintains, is one of the first intuitive gestures we make to satisfy our appetites for beauty and communication. If we could acknowledge those hungers, and do so from an early age, our culture would be very different from the way it is today. We would understand how images are used to compel us, in the same way that most of us understand the subtleties of language.

Because, think of it. As children, we come into the world with a natural desire to both speak and draw. Society makes sure that we learn language properly, right from the beginning, but art is treated as a gift of innate genius, something we either have or don't. Most children are given far too much praise for their early drawings, so much so that they rarely learn the ability to refine their first crude efforts the way their early attempts at language are corrected.

How hard would it be to ask children what they see in their heads? How big should the house be in comparison to the family standing in front of it? What is it about the anatomy of the people that doesn't look right? Then let them try it again. Teach them to learn how to see and ask questions. You don't have to be Michelangelo to teach basic art, just as you don't have to be Shakespeare to be able to teach the correct use of language.

Not to be dogmatic about it, because you wouldn't want any creative process to lose its sense of fun and adventure. But that doesn't mean you can't take it seriously as well.

Because children know when they're being patronized. I remember, so clearly I can remember, having the picture in my head and it didn't look at all like what I managed to scribble down on paper. When I was given no direction, in the same way that my grammar and sentence structure and the like were corrected, I lost interest and gave up. Now it seems too late.

I had a desk I made as a teenager—a wide board laid across a couple of wooden fruit crates. I'd set out my pens and ink, my paper, sit cross-legged on a pillow in front of it and write for hours. I carried that board around with me for years, from rooming house to apartments. I still have it, only now it serves as a shelf that holds plants underneath a window in the dining room. Saskia finds it odd, that I remain so attached to it, but I can't let it go. It's too big a piece of my past—one of the tools that helped free me from a reality that had no room for the magic I needed the world to hold, but could only make real with words.

I didn't just like to look at animals. I'd pretend to be them, too. I'd scrabble around all day on my hands and knees through the bush to get an understanding of that alternative viewpoint. Or I'd run for miles, the horse in me effortlessly carrying me through fields, over fences, across streams. Remember when you'd never walk, when you could run? It never made any *sense* to go so slow.

And even at home, or at school, or when we'd go into town, the animals would stay with me. I'd carry them secreted in my chest. That horse, a mole, an owl, a wolf. Nobody knew they were there, but I did. Their secret presence both comforted and thrilled me.

* * *

I write differently depending on the pen I use. Ballpoints are only good for business scribbles, or for making shopping lists, and even then, I'll often use a fountain pen. When I first wrote, I did so with a dip pen and ink. Colored inks, sometimes—sepia, gold, and a forest green were the most popular choices—but usually India ink. I used a mapping nib, writing on cream-colored paper with deckled edges and more tooth than might be recommended for that sort of nib. The dip pen made me take my time, think about every word before I committed to it.

But fountain pens grew to be my writing implement of choice. A fat, thick-nibbed, deep green Cross from which the ink flowed as though sliding across ice, or a black Waterman with a fine point that made tiny, bird-track-like marks across the page.

When I began marketing my work, I typed it up—now I use a computer—but the life of my first drafts depends on the smooth flow of a fountain pen. I can, and did, and do, write anywhere with them. All I need is the pen and my notebook. I've written standing up, leaning my notebook on the cast-iron balustrade of the Kelly Street Bridge, watching the dark water flow beneath me, my page lit by the light cast from a street-lamp. I've written in moonlight and in cafés. In the corner of a pub and sitting at a bus stop.

I can use other implements, but those pens are best. Pencil smears, pen and ink gets too complicated to carry about, Rapidographs and rollerballs don't have enough character, and ballpoints have no soul. My fountain pens have plenty of both. Their nibs are worn down to the style of my hand, the shafts fit into my fingers with the comfort of the voice of a long-time friend, met unexpectedly on a street corner, but no less happily for the surprise of the meeting.

Time passes oddly. Though I know the actual contrast is vast, I don't feel much different now from when I was fifteen. I still feel as clumsy and awkward and insecure about interacting with others, about how the world sees me, though intellectually, I understand that others don't perceive me in the same way at all. I'm middle-aged, not a boy. I'm at that age when the boy I was thought that life would pretty much be over, yet now I insist it's only begun. I have to. To think otherwise is to give up, to actually *be* old.

That's disconcerting enough. But when a year seems to pass in what was only a season for the boy, a dreamy summer that would never end, the long cold days of winter when simply stepping outside made you feel completely alive, you begin to fear the ever-increasing momentum of time's passage. Does it simply accelerate forever, or is there a point when it begins to slow down once again? Is that the real meaning of "over the hill"? You start up slow, then speed up to make the incline. Reach the top and gravity has you speeding once more. But eventually your momentum decreases, as even a rolling stone eventually runs out of steam.

I don't know. What I do know is that the antidote for me is to immerse myself in something like my writing, though simply puttering around the apartment can be as effective. There's something about familiar tasks that keeps at bay the unsettling sense of everything being out of my control. Engaging in the mundane, whether it be watching the light change in the sky at dusk, playing with my neighbor's cat, or enjoying the smell of freshly brewed coffee, serves to alter time. It doesn't so much stop the express, as allow you to forget it for a while. To recoup, catch your breath.

But writing is best, especially the kind that pulls you out of yourself, off the page, and takes you into a moment of clarity, an instant of happy wonder, so perfect that words, stumbling through the human mind, are inadequate to express.

The writer's impossible task is to illuminate such moments, yes, but also the routines, the things we do or feel or simply appreciate, that happen so regularly that they fade away into the background the way street noise and traffic become inaudible when you've lived in the city long enough. It's the writer's job to illuminate such moments as well, to bring them back into awareness, to acknowledge the gift of their existence and share that acknowledgment with others.

By doing this, we are showing deference to the small joys of our lives, giving them meaning. Not simply for ourselves, but for others as well, to remind them of the significance to be found in their lives. And what we all discover, is that nothing is really ordinary or familiar after all. Our small worlds are more surprising and interesting than we perceive them to be.

But we still need enchantment in our lives. We still need mystery. Something to connect us to what lies beyond the obvious, to what, perhaps, *is* the obvious, only seen from another, or better-informed, perspective.

Mystery.

I love that word. I love how, phonetically, it seems to hold both "myth" and "history." The Kickaha use it to refer to God, the Great Mystery. But they also ascribe to animism, paying respect to small, mischievous spirits that didn't create the world, but rather, are *of* the world. They call them mysteries, too. *Manitou.* The little mysteries.

We call them faerie.

We don't believe in them.

Our loss.

Saskia is still sleeping. I look in on her, then slowly close the bedroom door. I put on my boots and jacket and go downstairs, out onto the pre-dawn streets. It's my favorite time of day. It's so quiet, but everything seems filled with potential. The whole world appears to hold its breath, waiting for the first streak of light to lift out of the waking eastern skies.

After a few blocks, I hear footsteps and my shadow falls in beside me.

"Still soul searching?" she asks.

I nod, expecting a lecture on how worrying about "what if" only makes you miss out on "what is," but she doesn't say anything. We walk up Lee Street to Kelly, past the pub and up onto the bridge. Halfway across, I lean my forearms on the balustrade and look out across the water. She puts her back to the rail. I can feel her gaze on me. There's no traffic. Give it another few hours and the bridge will be choked with commuters.

"Why can't I believe in magic?" I finally say.

When there's no immediate response, I look over to find her smiling.

"What do you think I am?" she asks.

"I don't know," I tell her honestly. "A piece of me. Pieces of me. But you must be more than that now, because you've had experiences I haven't shared since you . . . left."

"As have you."

"I suppose." I turn my attention back to the water flowing under us. "Unless I'm delusional."

She laughs. "Yes, there's always the risk of that, isn't there?"

"So which is it?"

She shrugs.

"At least tell me your name," I say.

Her only response is another one of those enigmatic smiles of hers that would have done Leonardo proud. I sigh, and try one more time.

"Then tell me this," I say. "Where do you go when you're not with me?"

She surprises me with an answer.

"To the fields beyond the fields," she says.

"Can you take me with you some time?" I ask, keeping my voice casual. I feel like Wendy, waiting at the windowsill for Peter Pan.

"But you already know the way."

I give her a blank look.

"It's all around you," she says. "It's here." She touches her eyes, her ears. "And here." She moves her hand to her temple. "And here." She lays a hand upon her breast.

I look away. The sun's rising now and all the skyscrapers of midtown have a haloing glow, an aura of morning promise. A pair of crows lift from the roof of the pub and their blue-black wings have more color in them than I ever imagined would be possible. I watch them glide over the river, dip down, out of the sunlight, and become shadow shapes once more.

I feel something shift inside me. A lifting of . . . I'm not sure what. An unaccountable easing of tension—not in my neck, or shoulders, but in my spirit. As though I've just received what Colin Wilson calls "absurd good news."

When I turn back, my companion is gone. But I understand. The place where mystery lives doesn't necessarily have to make sense. It's not that it's nonsense, so much, as beyond sense.

My shadow is the parts of me I'd hidden away—some because they didn't fit who I thought I was supposed to be, some that I just didn't understand.

Her name is Mystery.

St. John of the Cross wrote, "If a man wants to be sure of his road he must close his eyes and walk in the dark."

Into his shadow.

Into mystery.

I think I can do that.

Or at least I can try.

I pause there a moment longer, breathing deep the morning air, drawing the sun's light down into my skin, then I turn, and head for home and Saskia. I think I have an answer for her now. She'll still be sleeping, but even asleep, I know she's waiting for me. Waiting for who I was to catch up with who I'll be. Waiting for me to remember who I am and all I've seen.

I think I'll take the plants off that board in the dining room and reclaim the desk it was.

I think I'll buy a sketchbook when the stores open and take one of those courses that Jilly teaches at the Newford School of Art. Maybe it's not too late.

I think I'll reacquaint myself with the animals that used to live in my chest.

I think I'll stop listening to that voice whispering "as if," and hold onto what I experience, no matter how far it strays from what's supposed to be.

I'm going to live here, in the Fields We Know, fully, but I'm not going to let myself forget how to visit the fields beyond these fields. I'll go there with words on the page, but without them, too. Because it's long past time to stop letting pen and ink be the experience, instead of merely recording it.

About the Author

Charles de Lint and his wife, the artist MaryAnn Harris, live in Ottawa, Ontario, Canada.

Copyright Acknowledgments

"Saskia" first appeared in *Space Opera,* edited by Anne McCaffrey and Elizabeth Ann Scarborough; DAW Books, 1996. Copyright © 1996 by Charles de Lint.

"In This Soul of a Woman" first appeared in *Love in Vein,* edited by Poppy Z. Brite; HarperPrism, 1994. Copyright © 1994 by Charles de Lint.

"The Big Sky" first appeared in *Heaven Sent,* edited by Peter Crowther; DAW Books, 1995. Copyright © 1995 by Charles de Lint.

"Birds" first appeared in *The Shimmering Door,* edited by Katharine Kerr; Harper-Prism, 1996. Copyright © 1996 by Charles de Lint.

"Passing" was first published in *Excalibur,* edited by Richard Gilliam, Martin H. Greenberg and Edward E. Kramer; Warner Books, 1995. Copyright © 1995 by Charles de Lint.

"Held Safe by Moonlight and Vines" first appeared in *Castle Perilous,* edited by John DeChancie and Martin H. Greenberg; DAW Books, 1996. Copyright © 1996 by Charles de Lint.

"In the Pines" first appeared in *Destination Unknown,* edited by Peter Crowther; White Wolf Publishing, 1997. Copyright © 1997 by Charles de Lint.

"Shining Nowhere but in the Dark" first appeared in *Realms of Fantasy,* Vol. 3, No. 1, October, 1996. Copyright © 1996 by Charles de Lint.

"If I Close My Eyes Forever" is original to this collection.

"Heartfires" first appeared as a limited edition chapbook published by Triskell Press, 1994. Copyright © 1994 by Charles de Lint.

"The Invisibles" first appeared in *David Copperfield's Beyond Imagination,* edited by David Copperfield and Janet Berliner; HarperPrism, 1997. Copyright © 1997 by Charles de Lint.

"Seven for a Secret" first appeared in *Immortal Unicorn,* edited by Peter S. Beagle and Janet Berliner, New York: HarperPrism, 1995. Copyright © 1995 by Charles de Lint.

"Crow Girls" first appeared as a limited edition chapbook published by Triskell Press, 1995. Copyright © 1995 by Charles de Lint.

"Wild Horses" first appeared in *Tarot Fantastic,* edited by Martin H. Greenberg and Lawrence Schimel; DAW Books, 1997. Copyright © 1997 by Charles de Lint.

"In the Land of the Unforgiven" is original to this collection.

"My Life as a Bird" first appeared as a limited edition chapbook published by Triskell Press, 1996. Copyright © 1996 by Charles de Lint.

"China Doll" first appeared in *The Crow: Shattered Lives and Broken Dreams,* edited by James O'Barr and Edward E. Kramer; Del Rey, 1998. Copyright © 1998 by Charles de Lint.

"In the Quiet After Midnight" first appeared in *Olympus,* edited by Bruce D. Arthurs and Martin H. Greenberg; DAW Books, 1998. Copyright © 1998 by Charles de Lint.

"The Pennymen" first appeared in *Black Cats and Broken Mirrors,* edited by John Helfers and Martin H. Greenberg; DAW Books, 1998. Copyright © 1998 by Charles de Lint.

"Twa Corbies" first appeared in *Twenty 3: A Miscellany,* edited by Anna Hepworth,